STAR TREK
DAY OF HONOR

For orders other than by individual consumers, Pocket Books grants a discount on the purchase of **10 or more** copies of single titles for special markets or premium use. For further details, please write to the Vice-President of Special Markets, Pocket Books, 1633 Broadway, New York, NY 10019-6785, 8th Floor.

For information on how individual consumers can place orders, please write to Mail Order Department, Simon & Schuster Inc., 200 Old Tappan Road, Old Tappan, NJ 07675.

STAR TREK®

DAY OF HONOR

ANCIENT BLOOD

Diane Carey

ARMAGEDDON SKY

L.A. Graf

HER KLINGON SOUL

Michael Jan Friedman

TREATY'S LAW

Dean Wesley Smith & Kristine Kathryn Rusch

THE TELEVISION EPISODE

Michael Jan Friedman

Based on *Day of Honor* • Written by Jeri Taylor

HONOR BOUND

Diana G. Gallagher

Day of Honor concept by John J. Ordover and Paula M. Block

POCKET BOOKS

New York London Toronto Sydney Tokyo Singapore

POCKET BOOKS, a division of Simon & Schuster Inc.
1230 Avenue of the Americas, New York, NY 10020

ISBN: 0-671-02813-8

First Pocket Books trade paperback printing March 1999

10 9 8 7 6 5 4 3 2 1

Printed in the U.S.A.

These titles were previously published individually by Pocket Books.

CONTENTS

DAY OF HONOR

ANCIENT BLOOD

Diane Carey

Dedicated to our great-aunt Katie Simon, who, by not retiring until the age of 89, taught us and our kids all about hard work and its wonderful rewards.

CHAPTER 1

"CAPTAIN PICARD, MY MISSION IS URGENT. IF IT FAILS, SIX STAR SYSTEMS AND ten Federation colonies are going to fall under the influence of the most nefarious planet in this sector. I can't give you any more details than I have already. All I can say is we're picking up two key witnesses on whom our entire plan depends."

Interesting words.

Strange.

Evasive, yet somehow revealing.

"Commissioner…you're asking me to use my starship to delay a legal transport in authorized spacelanes."

"That's right, Captain."

"So you can arrest two of the passengers?"

"Arrest is a little harsh. Take them into protective custody is how I'd put it."

"Very well. If it's so vital, let's go get it done."

Jean-Luc Picard hadn't bothered to sit down in his ready room just off the ship's bridge. The commissioner followed him out, and Picard felt the other man's eyes all the way.

His first officer and security chief were waiting on the bridge. They were the only bridge crew who looked at him. The others—ops, helm, science station, tactical, engineering—were all fixed on their duties. Lieutenant Commander Data, in his elementally android manner, concentrated on his console and on the dominating main viewscreen at the fore of the bridge, which showed a docile vision of an oncoming ship.

"Transport on the screen, Captain," William Riker reported. "Roughly ten kilotons, carrying cargo and thirty-two life-forms."

"Pull them over, Number One." Picard turned then to the security officer. "Mr. Worf, prepare to go aboard and take two persons into custody. We'll be remanding them to Commissioner Toledano."

The Klingon officer nodded once. "Aye, sir."

At Picard's side, the commissioner leaned close and murmured, "Must've been hard for you, getting used to having a Klingon on the bridge of a Federation starship."

Will Riker—a bit taller than the Klingon though not as brawny—came down the port ramp, his eyes fixed on the transport as they drew nearer. "Hail them, Mr. Worf."

"Aye, sir," Worf responded, and played the glossy console before him to open hailing frequencies. Then he spoke into the com receptors. "This is the U.S.S. *Enterprise.* Stop your engines and prepare to be boarded."

"Do our—passengers—know we're coming?" Picard asked.

"No," Toledano replied. "It was too risky to tell anyone. There are two people on that ship who have to be isolated and protected. There's no place safer than a starship. Then, we'll rendezvous with another starship, which will take them to an unspecified starbase. Even I don't know the ship or base. Not yet anyway."

"We're in the vicinity of the Vaughn-Creighton system, aren't we?"

"Uh, yes."

"Does this have anything to do with the planet Sindikash?"

"I can't talk to you about that yet."

"Yes, you said that."

"Sir, they are not reducing speed." Commander Data's android face remained typically expressionless.

"No answer to our hail, sir," Worf added from the upper aft bridge, his bass voice like low thunder.

Picard deliberately said nothing. There was a certain art to captaincy, and that involved not doing his crewmen's jobs for them.

"Tractor beams," Riker decided.

Data looked at his board and worked it. "Tractor beams engaging, sir. Sir . . . their engines are still not reducing power. There is no response at all. They have not raised shields."

"Prepare to beam aboard immediately," Picard injected. "We'll shut those engines off ourselves, or they'll overload."

"Why wouldn't they respond?" Toledano asked as he, Picard, and Worf headed for the turbolift. "Aren't they required to answer you?"

"Could be any number of problems," Picard said as Worf stepped aside to let him board the lift first.

Despite not wanting to talk to him "yet," Toledano had already told him a great deal. Two witnesses were involved in a tentacled network of espionage and were willing to speak to the Federation in exchange for sanctuary. Their information probably had something to do with Sindikash, the only habitable planet in the Vaughn-Creighton system, a colony of the Federation inhabited by Earth people from . . . Asia? No . . . Bulgaria? Something like that.

He felt Riker's questioning eyes follow them into the lift. The first officer should know what was going on, and there was a subtle chastisement in that trailing gaze.

A twinge of resentment boiled up in Picard as the lift doors closed. Not at Riker, but at Toledano. If the Federation had briefed him, told him what was going on, had followed procedure for covert missions, he'd have known whether he was dealing with Romulans or Orions or lizards or insects by now. He'd have reviewed the situation and informed his officers. Certainly no information could funnel off the ship without their knowing about it, and those witnesses would've been just as safe. Might it be asking so much for the Federation to trust its captains as much as the captains trusted their officers?

Instantly in his head he heard the arguments both ways, and pressed his lips rather than voice the thought to Commissioner Toledano, who would eagerly detail the Federation's side. Picard would be obliged to counter with the captains' side, and since he was already hearing it all in his mind, why hear it again in the lift?

"Mr. Worf, have you notified your security team?" he asked, determined to change his mind's subject.

"Four guards will meet us in the transporter room, sir," the big Klingon rumbled. "Also, one engineering technician, who will shut down the transport's engines, if they are not shut down already."

"Very good. Commissioner, I would appreciate some idea of exactly why I'm sending guards to my transporter room."

Toledano, a middle-aged man who had once been handsome and was now a somewhat silver-haired echo of that, sighed. "Captain, I can't talk to you about this yet."

"Regardless, I have to be able to give my team some idea of what they're looking for, or they won't be able to do their jobs. They won't be able to protect anybody if they don't know what they're protecting against."

The commissioner frowned, tried to add that up, and sighed a second time.

"These two people are witnesses to an event that could tie an interstellar espionage network to a person we haven't been able to implicate," he said. "No one on that transport knows who those two people are. When we get on board, the witnesses will disclose their identities to us, and we'll take them into custody. That's all there is to it, really."

"Mmm," Picard responded, and thought very little else. He fixed his eyes on the lift doors before them.

"No one on board this transport knows who the witnesses are?"

"Except the witnesses themselves," the commissioner said.

"Of course."

"They did all this themselves. They contacted us, they arranged transport, they didn't purchase tickets or book passage until the last possible second—we don't even know what they look like."

Worf's comm badge beeped then, and he tapped it. "Lieutenant Worf."

"Security, sir. Transporter Room One is under repair. The molecular stabilizers are off-line."

"Very well. Divert to Transporter Room Three. Worf out." The Klingon touched the controls. "Diverting to Room Three, sir."

"Very well," Picard said. Another forty-five seconds in the lift.

"Hopefully, by the time we reach the transporter room, Mr. Riker will have pulled that transport over and be holding it. We should be able to beam directly on board and isolate your two witnesses straightaway."

"I'll breathe a sigh of relief then, Captain," the commissioner told him.

In the transporter room they came upon Worf's four security guards and Ensign Jensen, a new transferee barely out of Starfleet Academy but one who Worf had high hopes for. Since the *Enterprise* was so far away from central Federation space, the young man had been on two starships, two transports, and four Starfleet supply ships just to get out to the *Enter-*

prise. He was twitching with anticipation to actually beam out in the captain's company.

Picard could tell—he'd seen the look. And Jensen's eyes never once left him. As if the commissioner's jolly attention weren't altogether plenty.

"Ready, sir," the transporter officer said as they walked in. "The transport is stabilized. Mr. Data linked into their computer and managed to reduce their engine power by about forty-eight percent so far. He'll keep trying, but the rest'll most likely have to be done on board."

"I'm ready, sir!" Jensen piped.

Picard nodded. "Very good, gentlemen. Still no response from the crew?"

"No response, sir," the transporter officer answered. "But there are some scrambled emissions coming from over there, and Mr. Data thinks it might be an on-board mechanical malfunction. They might be trying to answer. They may be trying to shut down their engines, too."

"Understood." He turned to Toledano as he accepted a standard issue handphaser from Worf. "Let's take care not to startle them. Mr. Warren, energize as soon as we're in position."

He motioned the boarding party to the raised transporter platform, where each took a place on one of the clear disks as the transporter officer replied, "Aye, sir."

"Energizing, sir," Warren informed, and the familiar faint buzzing began.

In an unnoticeable minute, Picard's surroundings had changed to the chalky walls of the transport's docking bay. That moment of mental fog when the surroundings changed was shunted quickly aside. This place smelled like a slaughterhouse.

This place was also crushingly silent. Not even the throb of engines anymore. Data must have succeeded in shutting them down by remote.

But that smell—

"All hands, stand by . . . security alert." The sound of his own voice startled him.

Jensen moved into the captain's periphery. "Sir, permission to confirm engine shutdown?"

"Negative. Stand by."

"Ah . . . aye, sir."

Picard stepped across the small loading bay toward the passenger entrance, which was recessed downward about three inches and carpeted. A few paces beyond the step was the door to the seating coach. Worf stepped behind him, without requesting permission. Evidently he wasn't going to allow Picard to open that door without guard cover, and Picard did him the courtesy of not pointing out his defying the stand by order.

Together they descended the single step onto the carpet. Picard looked down, suddenly feeling as if he'd stepped into a soaked sponge and gone down to the ankle.

Behind him, someone gasped.

His foot and Worf's were down into the nap of the carpet, which was indeed soaked through. A ring of glossy liquid cuffed his boot and Worf's. Only now did he realize that the burgundy color had nothing to do with the carpet itself. He had no idea what color it once had been.

Now it was the color of blood.

"Oh . . . God . . ." Commissioner Toledano's voice quavered with subdued violence. He drew a breath, but couldn't choke out another word.

His jagged face severe, Worf stepped past Picard to the door. He put his hand on the controls, then turned and motioned his four guards forward onto the gore-soaked carpet. He glanced at Picard. "Captain, if you would please step aside."

Though he summoned his voice, Picard also found it in the same state as Toledano's, and cut it back before some choked squawk came out. He nodded and stepped to one side, instantly nauseated by the pull of sticky suction on his boot.

How many life-forms had someone said were here?

Thirty?

He had started adding that up in gallons when the door sloshed open.

Worf went in first. Another security man flanked him, and together they aimed their phasers sharply in two directions. Then the three other guards splashed in, crouched, and took over the aim.

Leading the way into the coach, Worf's stiff posture wavered in a way that could only be described as shock. The other guards each reacted subtly, but they reacted. A shiver. A drooping phaser. A stumble down to one knee on the soaked carpet. Picard's alarm doubled as he followed them inside.

The coach was engulfed in the syrupy odor of corruption, blood, slaughter. To his left was the forward part of the cabin, to his right the aft. The rows of seats were all occupied, but with corpses.

All human or humanoid, he noticed first off, one head, two arms, two legs—except that the first ten or so rows of seats were occupied by people whose torsos were drenched from the necks down with bodily fluids. Their faces stretched upward, sideward, mouths aghast, eyes tight or wide, all staring in that last moment's frozen horror.

Under the astounded eyes of his captain, the stunned security men, the frozen commissioner, and poor Engineer Jensen, who still hadn't quite made it through the doorway, Worf took one confirming step toward the nearest couple of rows, then squished his way back to Picard.

"Sir," he rasped, "their arms . . . are missing."

"How many . . . like that?"

"Twenty-one, sir. Arms forcibly avulsed at the shoulder. Two of those have had their eyes gouged out. The remaining passengers' throats have been cut."

Standing near the entry, unable to move, Commissioner Toledano gulped, "What's 'avulsed'?"

Worf glanced at the commissioner, then at Picard, then the Commissioner again. "Torn off, sir."

Not cut. Not phasered. Torn.

Sheer force.

"The blood splatters on the bulkheads," Worf went on, "suggest the torture was done in this area. Then the victims were dumped back into their seats."

The lieutenant of the security squad, pale with revulsion, came back from his reconnaissance of the rest of the ship and the cockpit. He swallowed a couple of times. "Sir . . . captain and copilot are both . . . the arms are the same. The steward's over there, behind that serving cart. Guess he tried to hide. Didn't help, though. Engine room's pretty bad, too. Both engineers had their throats cut."

"Some with throats cut," Picard murmured, "some with arms pulled off."

He squinted at the rows of seats, a hideous procession of gore from fore to aft, and he walked along the rows, now desensitized to the squish of his boots on the blood-soaked carpet. The first two people's facial expressions were relaxed, almost as if they could look up and say, "Hello." Only the indelible stare of their eyes and the paper whiteness of their drained faces gave away their true condition, give or take the tunic of blood each wore. The second, third, fourth row . . . muscles frozen in perpetual astonishment, brows drawn, teeth bared, eyes wide. And it went that way, all the way to midships.

"These," Worf said, "saw those in front being killed. Their faces are mottled, as if flushed with panic before being drained by hemorrhage. The murderers started up there and worked their way aft, forcing these people to watch. Then . . . here," he said, stepping aft past several bodies who still possessed their arms; he paused at two corpses who were missing arms.

Picard noticed what he was getting at—those in front had their arms ripped off, then some didn't, then two did.

"Then these two spoke up," Worf suggested, as if relating the details of an ancient battle. "The attackers found what they wanted and came back here. And these two paid by having their living eyes gouged out before their arms were taken off."

The two pathetic corpses, a man and a woman, slumped in their ghastly final throes. The woman's head rested upon what was left of the man's shoulder, her hair matted with his blood and muscle tissues.

"Commissioner," Picard said, turning, "let me introduce you to your two witnesses."

Poor Toledano picked his way through faint impressions of the other men's footprints in a vain attempt to avoid the unavoidable blood soaking the carpet. "Do you really think so?"

"Our medical and forensic departments will confirm all these people's identities in comparison with the ship's manifest and the departure records. Assuming that *someone* knows who your witnesses were, I'll bet these two are the ones."

"Because their eyes are . . . "

"Yes, partly. They were obviously punished more than the others, with the intent that the message of this should get back to someone. Perhaps a lot of someones."

"How?"

"I don't know. Word does tend to escape in these kinds of events. A memo here, a whisper there, a security officer's spouse—it gets out. Whoever did this was counting on that, or they wouldn't have resorted to such theatrics. They didn't know who the two witnesses were, so they tortured everyone until the witnesses spoke up. They were brave people, hoping to save others by giving themselves up. Unfortunately, it failed. After the attackers found and tortured the witnesses, they took care of these others with some dispatch."

He looked sadly at the remaining passengers, whose throats had been cut.

"Those were the lucky ones," he added as his heart twisted in empathy. Innocent passengers, on a safe, well-traveled spacelane.

Worf splashed toward them, his legs bloody to the knees now. "Forensics will be making a complete investigation, but so far tricorders have failed to pick up any physical clues. There may be some dusty residue of skin tissue, but it will take some time to sort those out and do DNA identification." The Klingon stepped a little closer, and spoke more intimately than Picard had ever remembered him doing. "Sir, whoever did this . . . we are dealing with people who have no honor at all."

The weight of that was evident in the tenor of his voice, which seemed somehow deeper than Picard had ever heard it. Worf was deeply disturbed, and there was enough of his upbringing among humans left in him to let his feelings show.

Toledano turned a shade greener and sidled closer to Picard. "I'm sorry to say, I have a pretty good idea who did this."

Picard glanced at Worf, then frowned at Toledano. "Well, speak up, Commissioner, now's the time."

The nauseated Federation official steeled himself visibly. "We're pretty sure . . . it was a band of Klingons."

Worf stiffened. "Impossible!"

"I'm sorry," Toledano said again, but he seemed certain.

Suddenly furious, Worf confronted both Picard and the commissioner so powerfully that even Picard felt the threat in that posture. "Klingons do not arbitrarily torture anyone! Klingons will kill—but not like this!"

Toledano gathered his voice. "You know more about Klingons than I do, obviously, but . . . I'm sorry, but that's what I think we've got here."

"We'll discuss it back on the *Enterprise,*" Picard interrupted, seeing where this was going.

"Klingons do *not* behave this way!" Worf continued.

Picard shot him a warning look. "I said *later,* Mister Worf."

Clamping his mouth shut, Worf blew his fury out his nostrils.

"At the moment," Picard said, "we have a few more troubling questions. For instance," he went on tightly, "where are the arms?"

His crew and the commissioner glanced about, as if expecting to see a pile of ripped-off limbs in some corner. Such a presence would be dreadful. Its absence was somehow more so.

As the stink of the slaughter suffused the air around them, and Engineer Jensen shuddered in the doorway, driven mute by the horror of his first boarding-party mission, Commissioner Toledano managed the two steps to bring him to Picard's side. Pale as the thirty-plus victims, visibly holding down his supper, he lowered his gaze briefly to the bloody carpet, then raised it to Picard.

"Captain . . . I think we'd better talk."

The true danger is when liberty is nibbled away, for expediency, and by parts.

Edmund Burke

CHAPTER 2

"NOW YOU UNDERSTAND THE KIND OF PEOPLE WE'RE DEALING WITH. WE have the specter of Sindikash, an entire planet, becoming a planet of criminals, a haven for the worst the galaxy has to offer. They'll take the whole sector down. We're right on the edge."

Federation Commissioner Perry Toledano crushed his hands into each other over and over, as if to wipe off the blood with which they had all been so thoroughly saturated. How surreal it had been, to board the *Enterprise* again and hurry off to separate quarters, to change clothing before many of the crew had to be exposed to the stink of uniforms saturated to the knees with blood. What a strange thing for a captain to have to consider.

"Why did you say that the Klingon Empire was involved in this?" Picard asked.

"I didn't say the Empire was involved," Toledano explained. "I said there were Klingons involved."

Worf smoldered so hotly it seemed his chair could have melted out from under him. "And *I* told you Klingons do not behave in that way."

"These Klingons do." Toledano offered a sympathetic but unforgiving shrug. "They're not working for the Empire. They're working for the ringleader of this crime network. I'm telling you, it's true."

"Commissioner," Picard interrupted, trying to pacify both men, "what Mr. Worf means is that Klingons are hardwired to react emotionally and violently. Because of that, they could never have survived as a culture unless they developed certain restraints."

"Restraints? Like what?"

"Like shame," Worf boiled over. "Klingons do not slaughter innocent people who have no weapons with which to fight back."

"It's a matter of honor," Picard added. "They even celebrate it. The Day of Honor is coming up next week, isn't it, Mr. Worf?"

Worf glared at Toledano. "Thursday. It could *not* have been Klingons."

"Okay," Toledano attempted, "but it was."

"Wait a minute," Riker interrupted. "I don't understand something. The criminal organization on this planet is no secret. Are you telling me that the ringleader is a secret?"

"No," Toledano said. "We know who it is. But we can't find any witnesses. You saw what happened to those who dared try to speak out. According to the laws of Sindikash, two witnesses are required to speak against a capital crime. Two, not just one. Two."

"This situation has been going on for nearly fifty years," Riker continued, "on a planet that was colonized well over a hundred years ago. What's the rush?"

Toledano bobbed his brows as if to indicate the validity of the question. "The rush is that they're about to hold a referendum—a special election. We've only got ten days. The election will do two things—one, it will select the new governor. The current governor is lying in a sickbed, in a coma, with an assassin's wound to his brain."

"Assassin? What kind of wound?"

"A projectile weapon."

"You mean like a bullet?"

"Something like that. When the colony was set up, they outlawed energy weapons for everyone except law enforcement officials. But there's a loophole—a lot of people started carrying propellant weapons and old style pistols, mostly for protecting their herds from predators. They found out they liked having those weapons, and a lot of people there even collect antique weapons. One of those struck the governor in the side of his head. Local doctors took the projectile out, but he's in a coma. Federation physicians were refused. We're not sure who refused them, but we have a pretty good idea."

"I can understand that," Riker commented. "A planet tends to trust its own, after all."

"We *are* 'its own,' Commander," Toledano told him. "These people are humans, settlers from Earth. They're directly descended from Earth people, and some of them are right from Earth. It's not like we were offering human physicians to work on Cardassians."

Worf shifted his legs impatiently. "What is the second thing the election will do, other than decide who the governor is?"

The commissioner met his eyes. "The second referendum is to decide whether the planet should secede from the Federation. Both candidates are promising to support withdrawal if that's what the people want. Sindikash will be just outside Federation jurisdiction, but *inside* the sphere of Starfleet patrol space. That'll throw all our jurisdictional laws into a gray area. What can we stop and what can't we?"

Riker nodded. "It's only happened five times in the whole of Federation history, and four of those were disasters. Surely the Sindikashians know that. Or Sindians. Or Kashites—what do they call themselves?"

"Seniards, Commander," Toledano corrected. "They call themselves Seniards."

"Why?" Worf asked.

The commissioner shrugged weakly. "I don't know—why are people from France called 'French' instead of 'Francians'?"

Riker shifted his long legs self-consciously. "Beats me," he mumbled, and glanced at Picard as if they had an inside joke.

Toledano looked ten years older than he had ten hours ago. His Federation agency suit was gone now, the crisp, gray, blood-stained suit now replaced by a more casual shirt and pants that didn't match. His face was creased with the memory of what he had seen aboard that ravaged transport. "That's why we chose the *Enterprise* for this mission. We need a Klingon." The commissioner looked nervously at Worf.

"There's a group of Klingon expatriates on Sindikash," the commissioner continued. "We can trace several instances of this kind of action—well, maybe not *this* bad, but bad—right back to them. They're not giving the orders, though. We need to get the person who is. So, Mr. Worf, this is a voluntary mission. You don't have to take it. Once you take it, though, you'll have to consider yourself committed, because we can't do it twice. And you can be sure that any lingering suspicions about whether your loyalties are to the Federation or the Klingon Empire will certainly disappear."

Worf felt all his body hairs go suddenly prickly and his eyes widen. He looked at the audaciously affable man, then at Picard, then back at the commissioner.

"Sir," he said sharply, "I will do this because it is my mission and my duty to do so. I will do it *because* I am a Klingon. If Klingons are doing these things, then I am the one to go."

Toledano seemed completely shocked at Worf's tone of voice. As his lips fell open, he glanced at Picard for explanation.

"You're insulting him, Mr. Toledano," Picard said. "You're lucky it's Worf you said that to, or *you* might be missing an arm."

"I'm . . . I didn't mean anything—"

"You implied," Worf said, "that I would have to be bribed to do my duty, sir."

Only willing to be apologetic to a degree, the commissioner nodded. "I don't think I exactly meant that. But it *will* look good on your record. It's not like Starfleet has a lot of Klingons. Accept the apology and call me names after I leave. I don't really care. This problem is in my lap, and I've got to handle it the best way I know how. Right now, you're the best way."

To his credit, the commissioner stopped talking and let his words sink in. He was at once a troubled man, friendly, both certain and uncertain of himself, but he seemed to believe in what he was doing.

Worf allowed him that. "I understand."

"Thanks," Toledano replied gracefully. "If we can get two witnesses against the person we've targeted, we can make an arrest. The lieutenant governor's been acting as leader, but he's under constant attack by the other person on the ballot. That other person is the one we believe is the undisclosed kingpin of this network of crime webbing out into the sector. No—we don't *believe* it. We *know* it. We just can't secure evidence. You saw what happens when they feel threatened—"

"And that's why we're so interested in this election, isn't it?" Picard noted. A queasy feeling rose in his stomach. "If we can make an arrest, there can't be an election at all."

"That's right. Colonial law. You need both candidates, or no election."

"So your main objective is not to dissolve a criminal organization, but subvert an election process."

Toledano frowned. "You're making it sound bad. When the evidence is gathered, we want official Starfleet personnel to make the arrest. That way the trial can be held off-world, and be completely objective. That's not what

I'd call subversive. Since there happens to be no *in absentia* clause in Seniard law, it'll be at least a year before another election can be organized. We have to arrest this candidate before the election, and have witnesses who'll testify that the organization leads right back to its source."

"And who is this candidate, Commissioner?"

"Her name is Odette Khanty. Captain, she's the injured governor's wife."

"The lieutenant governor and I have legitimate disagreements, and I'll address those, but not these tawdry allegations contrived for political gain. There's simply no evidence to support any of these frivolous accusations against me."

Mrs. Khanty was quoted two days ago in the Ozero Square in Burkal City, where she spoke to Early News's Dushan Smith about the possible indictments against her and her staff.

"There will always be bad people. I can't know what's in the hearts of others. I only want what my husband wanted. I want what's best for the working people of Sindikash. Yes, I know there are risks. An assassin's attack has cost my husband a normal life. I know they'll get me eventually. All I can hope for is to live long enough to help the colony achieve independence from the United Federation of Planets. If that costs me my life . . . so be it. My husband has nearly given his life. I can do the same."

In the background, the gathered crowd launched into applause and cheers, and some chanted, "O-DETTE! O-DETTE!"

"Mind-boggling."

The captain's unhappy comment settled over the disturbing images of politics at work.

Nearby, William Riker leaned forward and manually clicked off the viewscreen. "It's as if she's speaking to six-year-olds."

From a chair set off to one side, as if in its own universe, Lieutenant Worf watched the captain, but said nothing. The idea that Klingons had done the torture on that transport still burned deep in him. He had not been able to eat or rest since Commissioner Toledano had first made that claim.

If he could jump out of the starship and descend to that planet on the power of his outrage, he would do it.

He knew his own thoughts, but wanted to know Picard's. The captain would be Worf's barometer of action, for he could no longer trust himself.

The captain leaned back in the chair behind his desk. Picard's quiet presence always dominated any room.

As Worf watched Jean-Luc Picard now, he saw the captain as he often did—more scholar than warrior. Yet Worf knew Picard as a strong man who would fight fiercely when he felt the time was right. It was clear that Odette Khanty's pseudo-philosophy troubled Picard. He seemed disturbed that the intellect of deceit was gaining an upper hand, and a Federation planet was slipping away in the grease of artful deception.

"You'll notice the media didn't challenge Mrs. Khanty at all," Commissioner Toledano pointed out, sitting on the other side of Riker. "She controls most of them, but there are still some who speak up against her. They just get shouted down. How can the people of Sindikash make an educated choice if they only see one side of anything?"

Riker, sitting near Worf in front of the captain's desk, added, "After the governor got shot, Odette Khanty's approval rating was higher than the lieutenant governor's, but now that's starting to wear off. They're about fifty-fifty."

Toledano nodded. "She's risen to popularity not on her own ability, but on sympathy for her husband. Any criticism is met with portrayals of her as a devoted wife being harassed by her husband's enemies. The people know Sindikash is degenerating into the local center of criminal action, but Mrs. Khanty has been claiming the Federation refuses to do anything about it. What gall! It's *her* criminal action!"

Despite the challenges of the mission, Worf's attitude was flagging. He could not muster much concern for a planet full of people who would swallow such tripe. His hands clenched and unclenched so hard that his fingernails cut into his palms with every grip. Anchoring himself on the pain, he burned to get going on this mission, to sweep up the filthy rumors of Klingons indulging in frivolous torture.

There had to be some other explanation, some key fact that had gone undiscovered.

He wanted to go there, turn Sindikash inside out until the molten core of the planet froze solid in the cold of space, and uncover those cursed facts.

Then he wanted to cram them in Commissioner Toledano's nostrils until his eardrums popped.

"This is a bizarre situation," Riker admitted, "but I've got to tell you, I'm uneasy about intruding into a free election, even on a Federation colony."

Toledano shrugged impolitely. "What's your solution, then? Walk away from Federation citizens and let them be terrorized by criminals because you're 'uncomfortable' about interfering? Do we sit by and allow a group of thugs to spread to other planets? You're a pretty cold man if you can forget the blood we walked through just a little while ago."

The captain gazed in new admiration at the commissioner, and noted the annoyed glares of Worf and Riker. Toledano had more guts than he had first seemed to possess.

"Sindikash is still a Federation establishment," Picard told them. "The colony's been enriched, the standard of living has shot up, mortality rate's dropped, and the market for their goods is now quadrant-wide. It's always difficult to know how tightly to hang on when a colony wants independence. These things occur so rarely. Dozens of planets are petitioning to become part of the United Federation of Planets; it's suspicious when a planet tries to break off—especially when they'll still be within our sphere of protection."

"And they darn well know that," Toledano rushed in.

"Won't be easy," Riker pointed out. "Local power can be a monster to push aside. If she can manipulate the next judicial appointments alone, she'll be shielded from all kinds of charges. I hate when this sort of thing happens. The guidelines are always so vague."

"It *is* vague," Picard agreed.

Riker turned to him. "Sir, don't you think the people of Sindikash should choose their own leaders?"

Picard nodded forthrightly. "Yes, I do. However, we certainly should assure they have legitimate, honest leaders to choose from. If I were a citizen of Sindikash, I'd look to the Federation to help assure that."

"Mrs. Khanty is far from honest, sir," Worf said with undisguised contempt. "There are bogus trials and frequent executions, maimings in the name of justice, nighttime kidnappings, and mysterious deaths of key persons."

"Mmm," Picard intoned, obviously troubled. "She's only in position to take over the governorship because her husband's in a coma."

"That's right. If he were dead," Toledano said, "the election would already have taken place. If he were conscious, there wouldn't have to be an election. With him in a coma, Odette Khanty's merrily sculpting public opinion in her favor. She'd never even be a candidate if this hadn't happened to him. She was running this illegal network, but she wasn't anywhere near planetary power. Now she's one election away from it. If we can find a way to arrest her, we can postpone the election. Then we'll have time to convince the colony not to secede."

Riker raised a brow. "You mean, time to pressure them."

The commissioner looked at the captain with grudging respect. "You're very blunt, Mr. Riker."

"His job is to be blunt," Picard spoke up. "And he's right. The Federation wants time to cut the favored-trade status, let the Seniards know what it's like to be out there alone, threaten to withdraw protection—"

"Look, we're not the brutes here!" Toledano said sharply, offended. "We're not going in with battleships like the Cardassians do!"

"No," Riker agreed, "but you'll cut trade, hit their goods with tariffs, withdraw patrols, frighten them, and you know very well that Starfleet won't stop patrolling this space."

Toledano waved his arms. "If this were the Klingons, you think they'd let any of their colonies go? Or the Romulans? Or the Cardassians? If Sindikash votes to secede, we won't go in with force."

Picard nodded. "But we certainly have a right to convince them otherwise, after the huge investment we've made. Let's face it—Odette Khanty knows the Federation'll still stick its neck out for Sindikash."

"And *you'll* be the ones doing it, Captain," the commissioner added. "You and the rest of Starfleet. Your job is to find a reason to arrest Mrs. Khanty. Not to frame her, but a legitimate charge—from her own records, a crime with witnesses, or a recorded confession. She's not forthright enough to ever admit having done anything wrong, so that leaves us the other two options. It took years for her to create this criminal structure, and it'll take time to bring it down, but with this secession vote we're running out of time. We're in a race to make Odette Khanty a criminal before she becomes a governor."

Riker settled back in his chair, still troubled. "The people of Sindikash have the right to make a bad decision, Commissioner."

"You've made that point," Picard told him. "But don't forget—almost fifty percent of the population still wants to be part of the Federation. They've got rights to protection, too. If delaying this election process is the only way to ensure those rights, then we're willing to chance it."

Toledano pointed at Picard, but looked at Riker. "We don't want to *affect* the election. We just want to *postpone* it."

Now that all the conflicting points had butted antlers, the ready room fell suddenly quiet.

Picard sat in the midst of that silence for several seconds, running over in his mind all that had been said. He knew the decision was essentially his, even though this sounded like orders for a mission. He knew he could object if he believed he should when it came to something that was internal to a planetary government.

After a time, he sighed. "This is like opening a diplomatic pouch, gentlemen. We *can* do it, but we had better find illicit goods inside."

"So you'll do it?" Toledano pushed.

As he felt the eyes of Riker and Worf, each pulling in his own direction, Picard stood up. "We'll do it."

CHAPTER 3

"IS HE HERE YET?" ALEXANDER ASKED IMPATIENTLY.

"Not yet. I asked you to wait in our quarters, Alexander."

"I couldn't wait. I never thought Uncle Ross would come onto the ship! I'm going to show him everything! Can I take him into main engineering?"

"Probably." Looking down at his son as they both waited in the transporter room, Worf realized that he had rarely seen such joy of anticipation in Alexander's face. A visit from a close family friend, almost a relative—no, such events did not occur often in starship life. Ross Grant had been very close to Alexander when he was living with K'Ehleyr, his now-deceased mother. How friendly Ross had been with K'Ehleyr was something Worf had no desire to learn, especially since Ross Grant had many times provided Worf with information that aided one investigation or another, and Worf had learned that Ross was excellent at his job, a reliable friend and, for a human, surprisingly driven by honor.

Alexander had not seen Grant in years. What else was Worf depriving his son of experiencing? Life on the starship had once seemed a good option. There were a few other children on board, though as tensions increased on the Romulan and Cardassian borders, such practice had become less and less popular with ship's crewmen.

Should I find another way? Would he be happier with relatives, on a planet, on Earth with his grandparents, rather than on a starship with his father? How much is a father worth? Should I ask him?

He turned to Alexander, opened his mouth to speak, and was driven silent by the boy's anxious twitching. Alexander looked at the transporter pad as if he could will the machine to start buzzing, then glanced at the console and the young transporter trainee adjusting the controls.

How much is a father worth who can barely summon the will to ask a simple question?

Worf cursed himself, and faced the pad again.

This business of being a parent . . . he had not planned for anything like that in his life, never anticipated these critical minutes. He had been shut out of Alexander's early childhood, but suddenly found himself responsible for the boy's youth. An important time for any boy, but especially a Klingon boy.

Now what?

He was rescued by the first signal beep of the transporter console, signalling that the person to be transported was ready on the other end. The other end was a Starfleet supply ship bringing necessaries to the starship, as well as serving as a transport for any persons who might be shifting assignments. Or visitors.

But Ross Grant was not a visitor today—he was on assignment from the United Federation of Planets Intelligence Agency, assigned to Worf's mission.

"Here he comes!" Alexander yelped, and rushed toward the transporter pads, to be stopped by his father's quick grab.

"Wait until he materializes," Worf admonished.

The transporter whined happily, singing the song of its job, and a pillar of lights appeared at the center right of the platform. A fog-faint sizzle of electrical action touched Worf's face and told him the transport process was finishing up. That surge of power was a long-familiar clue.

"Uncle Ross!" Alexander called, unable to control himself until the process finished.

The lights swirled around a solidifying form, then washed the form in one last sparkle and dissolved, leaving a human of average height and build standing in the chamber, wearing a bright yellow plastic hat with a conical top and a wide brim in the back and a flat plate on the front.

"Uncle Ross!" Alexander charged the platform.

"Lex! Look at the size of this boy!" Ross Grant dropped his duffel bag and jumped down from the platform, where he met Alexander with an encompassing hug. The boy's lanky frame came right off the deck. The yellow plastic hat tumbled off Grant's head and fell on its conical top on the deck. "Yike! Dropped your present."

"A present?" The boy broke the embrace and dove for the hat.

"It's a helmet," Grant said. "Firefighter's helmet. It's over almost 180 years old. Belonged to my great-great-great uncle. He was a fireman in Seattle. See? Engine Company 9. I come from a whole long line of firemen and rescue workers. 'Course, then there's me, the computer wimp."

"You're not a wimp." Alexander swept the yellow helmet off the deck and turned it over and over in his hands. "It's for me? You mean it? Your family helmet?"

"Sure, I mean it. After all, you're the closest thing to a son I've got." Grant folded an arm around the boy. "That makes us family. So who's better to have it than you? It's your Day of Honor present. Your grandparents told me all about the whole deal, and I couldn't just let a commemoration go sliding by, could I? Kinda like Christmas. Now, don't forget to leave me milk and cookies tonight!"

"I won't!" Alexander beamed at him and slipped on the helmet. "How does it look?"

"Like it was made for you, buck. Now, clear out of the way and let me say hi to this mutant gorilla over here. Hey, Wuff! We're finally going to work together on a mission! Is this great?"

Worf reached out and caught the hand offered by their old friend. "Very great," he offered. "It gives me reassurance to have you along."

"Liar," Grant laughed. "You're nervous as hell. You shouldn't have recommended me for this if you didn't want an old pal along."

"Grant," Worf moaned, knowing this would come up, "I did not recommend you."

Grant's smile didn't fade. "You didn't? Come on! What're the odds!"

"Evidently better than we expected." Worf stepped past him and picked up the duffel bag. "This is a complete coincidence. As impossible as it is to believe, you actually possess the skills this mission needs."

"Whoa—zing! Right in the heart. Don't play games now—you need me this time as much as during the Preficon II incident." Grant coiled his arm around Alexander again and struck a heroic pose. "I'm still putting out fires, just like all the Seattle Grants before me, except I put 'em out with brains instead of retardants."

"I'll carry that," Alexander announced, and took the duffel bag from his father.

"Oh—just a critical-mass second, buck," Grant said, and made him put down the bag. He opened it and pulled out a package. "Here you go, Lex. It's your Day of Honor present."

"But you gave me the helmet."

"The helmet's from me. This one's from your grandparents. It's a holodeck program. Journals from one of your Earth ancestors. They thought that since you're having a Klingon rite of passage, you ought to have something from your human side, too. I thought it was a nice idea. They're always thinking of you, punk."

"Thanks . . . " Alexander looked up at Worf. "Can I go see what's in it?"

Worf nodded. "You may scan the content, but do not use the holodeck without supervision. Understand?"

"Can you do it with me, then?"

The innocent question sent a lance of regret through Worf as he felt the answer tighten his throat. "I have a mission on a planet."

"On Sindikash?" Alexander anticipated.

"How do you know about that?"

"News gets around. The whole crew's talking about what happened on that transport."

"So much for security," Grant chuckled. He smiled and jabbed Worf in the chest. "Isn't that your job, big guy? Got no poker face at all, do you?"

"I had nothing to do with it."

"Yeah, yeah."

"Can I go scan the tape?" Alexander asked.

"Sure," Grant pushed in. "I'll get my gear squared away, and we'll go get some chow. It'll be like old times at your grandma's table. Big slabs of homemade bread, baklava, lamb chops—"

"We have replicator food on board the starship, Grant," Worf pointed out.

"Well, we can pretend, can't we? I'll see you later, Lex. Dibs on the biggest slice of ultra-super-replicator double-dollop slow death by melted caramel, deal?"

"Deal!"

With one last warm hug, Grant gave Alexander a little shove and sent the delighted boy dodging out of the transporter room.

Worf watched his son leave and fought to control a terrible grumble of regret. He could never remember hugging Alexander. Did the boy want to be hugged? Worf's foster parents on Earth were warm and friendly people, but they had held back in their demonstrations, wisely knowing that some day he would have to survive as a Klingon, and heavy emotions would have to be masked. He had assumed they were right, and taken the same course with Alexander.

But he and the boy lived on a ship full of humans. Did that mean Worf was the only person holding back in the boy's presence? Did his son see him as a cold island in a sea of warmth? Grant's free-flowing affection blanketed Worf with sudden self-reproach, and he didn't know what to do about that.

And Grant complicated matters when he turned to Worf and slung an arm around him—as best he could, given that he was a head shorter than Worf and half as wide.

"I can't believe I'm here!" he bubbled, and waved to the transporter trainee. "Hey, hi there."

"Afternoon, sir," the young officer responded, a little ill at ease with the chief of security right here.

"Like the job?" Grant asked.

"Yes, sir, I do. I've just started here."

"You married?"

"Grant," Worf snapped, pulling his old friend toward the door panels. "Back to work, Ensign Escobar."

"Yes, sir." The young officer averted his gaze instantly.

Worf scooped up the duffel bag that Alexander had frivolously forgotten now that its secrets were out, and steered Grant out into the corridor.

"What a great ship!" Grant gushed. "I couldn't keep my eyes off it as we were coming around to the docking port. Man, it's big. Ship's big, you're big . . . everything but me is big!"

As some of the tension of the past few days flowed away, Worf sighed. "You can stay in our quarters. After your gear is stowed, I can brief you on the mission."

"I know most of it," Grant said. "I heard about the . . . y'know . . . the . . ." He pointed at his shoulder and made a ripping motion.

"The arms." Worf sighed again, and more of that tension let go of him. He was no longer alone in this task before him. There was someone here who had a common background, if not common heritage, someone who knew him better than anyone else on board, and who was not intimidated or ill at ease around him.

Ross Grant wasn't ill at ease around anyone, and somehow that helped.

Grant lowered his voice. "Do you really think it was Klingons? Torture like that? People without any way of defending themselves? I mean, flash-and-burn is one thing, but torture . . . that's something else."

"The Federation suspects a band of Klingons on Sindikash. I intend to find out. Klingons would not consider those kinds of actions honorable. If the rumor is true, I want to know what kind of Klingon could do those things."

"Oooh, hot button," Grant cooed. "Not taking this personally or anything, are we? Even if it's Klingons doing this stuff, how is it your fault?"

"Not my fault," Worf told him. "Somehow my responsibility."

"You're nuts. If humans are doing it, it sure isn't my fault. You always screwed yourself to the wall with that kind of thinking, and you're still doing it. This is a mission. You've got a job to do. That's all it is. We'll go down there, I'll work my magic, you'll break some heads, we'll crack the crime network, and leave a silver bullet behind as we ride into the sunset. You, me, a couple of white horses—you know the drill."

"I know."

Leading the way into the turbolift, Worf gripped the duffel bag as if it were some kind of lifeline, and he met Grant's easy expression and friendly eyes.

"For Alexander's sake," Worf said quietly, "your presence is a good comfort. He needs to see some elements of family from time to time."

"Well, he's got you, doesn't he? You're his dad. What else does any kid need?"

"More," Worf told him candidly. "Especially now, as he gets older."

Grant laughed. "You're so hardwired! Don't worry. I can see right through you, just like I always could. You just get a nice steel rod to chew on, tell me all about this graft on Sindikash, we'll go down and clear the field, then we'll come back to this crate and have a family reunion that'll shake the bulkheads."

As the lift doors opened on the deck where Worf lived with his son, he stepped out into the corridor, then paused. He tried to feel better about what was ahead of them, and in some ways he did, yet nagging anticipation kept him from being pleased that he and Ross Grant would now get the chance to blend their dissimilar abilities.

"Such an event," he said, "will be much more pleasant after this mission is over. I hope it ends soon."

With a nod, Grant chuckled again. "And you'll break its legs if it doesn't, right?"

"And that guy over there . . . a ferret." Grant was speaking quickly, clearly nervous.

"What?" Worf felt nervous as well. It was not fear of battle or conflict that was bothering him. It was the fear that Toledano had been right, that Klingons were involved in these dishonorable acts.

"You know. An Earth ferret."

"That is a human, not a . . . ferret."

"Oh, come on. Get involved, will you?"

Sitting in a public square watching passersby and trying to decide which animal they were in a previous life did not strike Worf as a pleasant way to pass the time. Grant's insistence on this activity was on a par with other eccentricities Grant had shown over the years, all of which amounted to speaking when there was nothing to say, or when speech was a detriment to their plans. But his flawless record had shown Worf that his sometimes strange behaviour was worth the price of his involvement.

"Oh, look at that guy over there. Elephant. No doubt about it. Ouch—and he's walking with a peacock!"

Worf grunted.

"An earth peacock, I mean. Oh—right there. Guy with the hat. Some kind of lizard, for sure. You can tell by the way he walks that he's got that kind of personality. And look at that mouth!"

"He is not a lizard. I have fought lizards."

"You always did have a concrete imagination. You shipboarders ought to unclench once in a while . . . chihuahua . . . panther . . . slime devil . . . hey, you're not eating. Aren't you hungry?"

"No."

"You didn't eat much when we had dinner with Alexander, either. It's the honor thing, right? Klingons shouldn't act like that. Y'know, I sure hated to say good-bye to Alexander so soon. I hope we can wrap this up fast. Will you relax? Why are you so nervous? You checked the schedule, didn't you? She's coming eventually, right?"

"Yes, she is coming."

"Vulture . . . mugatu . . . tribble . . . you can get me inside, can't you?"

"We shall see very soon."

"Because if you can, then I can find the trail. I've cracked criminal organizations on fifteen planets so far. You know how?"

"You talk too much, Grant. You always talk too much."

"Because I understand how technology helps criminals, that's why. They *have* to keep records. Any organization bigger than three people nowadays has to keep records."

"You have explained this before."

Grant continued without a break. ". . . They steal huge amounts of wealth and they have to keep track of it. And that track leaves prints. The riches flow back and point. And that's how you bring 'em down. You just get me to a computer inside the governor's private square. I can sniff out—hey! Hey! Look—there she is! She's coming!"

"Grant! Do not turn that way! Pretend you do not see her."

"Don't see her? How can anybody miss her? She's surrounded by guards."

"I *see* that."

"Man, they're ugly. They're coming this way! We're gonna be face to face with Odette Khanty! Do you think her husband's really in a coma?"

"Quiet! Get up very casually and walk to the side of the square. Move into the crowd. Leave me to deal with them."

"Forget it. This is my mission, too. I'm not leaving you here all by yourself. Even a gorilla like you needs a little backup."

"Then sit still. Sit very still. Whatever happens, do not be moved."

He felt the eyes of Odette Khanty and her guards. The Cafe D'Atraq was in the middle of the city square, and he knew she would not notice him as long as he and Grant did not get up. All the natives were clearing a path, tightening into the sides of the square to allow her and her elite team of Klingon guards to pass through.

This place, this planet and its townships, was a tapestry woven of the Oriental Express and the American Old West. With a transplanted populace of Greeks, Turks, Lebanese, Armenians, Assyrians, Tuscans, and Moors, Sindikash bore a decidedly Gothic atmosphere. The planet's buildings were frontierish, its prevailing spirit exotic, and Worf and Grant were two outworlders in a place that knew its identity.

Watching Mrs. Khanty and her hooded guards move toward them under the tiled arches of the mosquelike square, Worf and Grant were now alone in a deserted cafe, while dozens of people eyed them from the sides of the square. All others had moved politely aside.

The woman touched the front of her pink suit to make sure it was perfectly presentable, then fingered the silk Paisley scarf neatly pinned at her neck. Her dark blond hair had been put perfectly in place, though it appeared to be casual; straight but thick, curved under slightly at the bottom, just above her shoulders. Just right. Feminine, yet efficient. Worf knew about her—she was not born to the place with which she had become so unbreakably associated. She saw herself as having earned her position.

Anger bled into Worf's heart as the eyes of the guards, the Rogues, fixed upon him and he felt their animosity.

Klingons. They really were Klingons! Every one of them was a *Klingon!*

Khanty nodded to her vanguard to keep moving forward in spite of Worf blocking their path.

Klingons. Klingons in service to a human. A human woman. A woman criminal.

What kind of Klingons . . .

He knew Commissioner Toledano wasn't lying, and Worf had expected Klingons, yet until this moment he had been hoping that the perpetrators of such atrocities were not *just* Klingons. Perhaps dregs had been dug up from all sorts of cultures across space, and Starfleet Intelligence had mentioned only the Klingons because Klingons were so visibly different from most humanoids. Perhaps that.

But now, as he looked at Mrs. Khanty's Rogues, as they were known on Sindikash, he saw that this was a pack of Klingons and only Klingons, a pack who had simply rejected anything Klingons are supposed to think about right and wrong, not here because of any sense of honorable conquest, duty, family loyalty, or anything else Klingons might be motivated by. These had just thrown all that away, cast off centuries of attachment to the things that held a culture together. These Klingons were destructively pursuing personal power, rather than acting in some way that would hold society, even Klingon society, together. Profit and gain could be pursued in a way that strengthened culture, but these Klingons wanted to go around those rules and achieve through the basest acts of brutality and opportunism.

Scum. Nothing. He was looking at empty hoods. Empty!

"Ugulan." Mrs. Khanty's voice sounded in the quiet square as she spoke quietly to the sergeant of her guard. "The Klingon."

"Yes, Mrs. Khanty." As if he didn't notice that he himself was Klingon and so were all his men, Ugulan motioned for his men to halt, but they remained in formation around her.

Then Ugulan himself stepped forward, his face deeply shaded by the purple hood. He moved through the empty tables to the one where Worf sat defiantly. With his purple hood and the dagger at his belt, he was effectively threatening.

"You will stand aside for Mrs. Odette Khanty to pass through," he said.

Grant looked at Worf, but said nothing.

Worf sipped his drink, took a long, considered swallow, then said, "I will not be moved."

"All citizens must stand aside when a public official comes through," Ugulan insisted. His tone implied this would be the last polite suggestion.

Worf looked up at him. "I am not a Seniard. Therefore I do not move."

"Therefore," Ugulan responded, pulling his dagger, "your friend is arrested."

Springing to his feet, Grant gasped, "What? Hey! I'm just visiting!"

The dagger swung upward as if to be its own exclamation point, and was on the downward arc when Worf came to life. Ah! At last! His move was extremely simple and not particularly inspired, a basic block of Ugulan's arm, but Worf imagined he had Ugulan nearly figured out already and could afford to not be creative.

He was right. Ugulan was thrown off, and clattered into a stand of empty iron chairs. The chairs went over, clanging like gongs against the brickwork street, and Ugulan went down among them. By the time he had scrambled to one knee, Worf was squared off between Ugulan and Grant, standing ground like a living portcullis.

One of the other Rogues clasped Mrs. Khanty's arm to draw her away from the developing trouble, but she resisted.

Worf didn't wait for Ugulan to get entirely to his feet, but freely charged the guard and drove him into a parqueted wall, knocking a stenciled sign from its hook. Ugulan's hood fell from his head, revealing his spinelike brow ridge and showing clearly that he, too, was a Klingon, as if there had been a bit of doubt.

Worf had clung to that silly doubt, but now his rage drove down his illogic.

Angry now, Ugulan reached into his jacket and drew his government phaser.

Worf didn't back off. "So," he said, "the Rogue Force of Sindikash uses women's weapons."

Evidently one of the universe's classic simpletons, Ugulan allowed himself to be goaded. He thrust himself to his feet and accommodated his opponent by holstering the phaser and bringing the dagger forward again.

Guarding Mrs. Khanty, the other Rogues were furious, too. Any guard who had his phaser out now put it away.

"You're so predictable, boys," the woman commented.

"Let us!" one demanded.

Would they make no move without her permission? Were Klingons not Klingons?

"Go, Genzsha," she said.

Two of the Rogues stayed with her, but the forward four rushed to Ugulan's side, and all squared off against Worf.

The big contenders circled slowly against the square's buildings. By appearance, Klingons fit well among the medieval dye colors of Sindikash—earthy, moody, deep and stirring colors that gave an impression of permanent autumn, flickering with gilded designs crafted from the planet's micalike ores. Even the brickwork imitated the woven texture of the Persian-style carpets the colony was famous for.

It also made a mean surface to knock against. Hitting a wall on Sindikash was entirely different from hitting a wall anywhere else. The walls here had exposed dentils of brick to smash against, and the newcomer made good use of that. Careful not to let Ugulan get a grip on him, Worf shoved Ugulan and two other Rogues into the same wall so hard that the impact set a stained glass window rattling. They all came up again, but came up bruised and gashed from the ragged brickwork. If only all planets cooperated so well.

Holographers who had been following Mrs. Khanty and the Rogues sprang forward now and began recording the moment. Some even dared skirt the onlookers or dodge through the grappling Klingons so they could get images of Mrs. Khanty standing there, watching calmly.

A silk wall covering shivered as Worf blew past, with two Rogues in his grip. The cafe became a blur of kicks, spins, elbows, and grunts. Stacks of etched clay urns dissolved and skittered across the brick, matched instantly by the audible crack of a limb. Worf almost stopped to make sure the limb wasn't his—then decided a broken arm would only make him angrier and that might help.

An instant later, though, one of the Rogues went down groaning. Genzsha moved forward to drag his fallen comrade from the arena, but did not join the fight himself.

Worf decided he would have to do without a broken arm, and therefore crammed his elbow into the face of a second Rogue and knocked him silly. Two down.

He knew he might be giving himself away—certainly, if they paid any attention they would see the Starfleet training involved in his movements. Not just the systematic moves of a schooled Klingon, but uneven elements of surprise, attack, feint, never letting his timing or style be mapped. Just when he was expected to block a punch, he would let it through, but dodge it, ripping every tendon in his attacker's arm. The two remaining Rogues were still fighting, but they were also dizzy and grunting.

Driven by the personal insult these men were to him, Worf took on both at once, not allowing them to divide the attack as they attempted. He took a vicious blow from one, but, instead of swinging back, he reached out to the other and dragged them together before him.

Then, with physical control that surprised even himself, Worf lowered his arms and stood very still. His shoulders went slack. His stance changed. He stopped fighting.

Since he had stopped, the two remaining Rogues could no longer be justified in attacking him again. Like wolves twitching around a stag who refused to run, they blinked, gaped, shifted, and glanced back at Mrs. Khanty, but they didn't know what to do. Boiling with frustration, Ugulan burped a command in Klingon, and then the Rogues grappled the newcomer.

Their eyes rolled with contempt, for he had humiliated them by stopping. Clearly, they knew, Worf hadn't had to let himself be arrested.

His plan was a success. Odette Khanty was intrigued.

She moved between her battered guards and stood before the only Klingon in the square who didn't work for her.

"Why did you let yourself be taken?" she asked.

Worf controlled his breathing enough to imply that he wasn't even winded. He could breathe later.

"Because you have to maintain order," he said, too quietly for the people watching to hear. "If your men are not feared, you will not have order."

"Then why did you fight in the first place?"

"To demonstrate that I did not have to be moved if I did not want to be."

"If you had just let yourself be stunned, you'd have just woken up later on the street. Now they're going to have to beat you."

"Fine."

"And after making your point, you'll let yourself be beaten?"

"That's right."

"You'd have done very well during the Middle Ages. On Earth, I mean. Where did you learn to fight?"

He felt his dark face flush bronze. "I tried to join Starfleet."

"Why?"

"Some Klingons claimed that Starfleet is the place to be. That they were trying to get in. I spit on them all."

"On Starfleet?"

"Daily."

"Why do you spit on a force you tried to join?"

"I spit on their insistence that lessers should be able to tell me what to do. That I should be subservient to people I knew were not my equals. They do not allow men who disagree to settle it like men."

"So what happened? They kicked you out? Why?"

"I disciplined my commanding officer."

Odette Khanty grinned. She seemed to find that idea appealing, considering Starfleet's buttoned-up manners.

"Well, you're going to be taken into custody for a while for disturbing the peace. What's your name?"

Worf said nothing.

The woman continued to gaze at him, refusing to ask again.

Finally he shifted and answered, "My name is Worf."

"All right, Worf. I'll probably speak to you later."

Odette Khanty looked through the groaning guards to Ugulan, who was glaring through his own wounded ego at Worf.

"Detain him in the capitol prison. Hold his friend, too."

"On what charge?" Ugulan asked.

"The same. And check out his story about Starfleet."

"Yes, Mrs. Khanty."

"Well, here we are. In jail."

Grant seemed untroubled by their predicament, Worf thought.

"Obviously." Stating the obvious was another of Grant's habits that Worf found hard to bear. Then again, what was obvious to Grant might not be obvious to others. An observation Grant had made on Garlath IV had saved ten people's lives.

"Not bad, as jails go. I mean, they got carpets, y'know?"

As vital as Grant's obsevations might be, Worf could not force himself to listen. Grant's voice faded into the background as he reflected on what his oath to Starfleet and his own honor had forced him into: He had lost a battle on purpose, which was difficult enough. But to lose it to warriors who had forsaken their code of honor!

But by his action, Worf had gotten this powerful woman's personal attention. For good or otherwise? Worf refused to judge yet but clung to the statement the woman had made about talking to him later. He knew he had managed to tickle her interest in him, and that she preferred using Klingons as her personal security team. She had shown definite curiosity about him when he'd proven that he was more clever, if not stronger, than any of her current Rogues.

How the other Rogues would feel if he joined them—he would deal with that when the time came.

"Somebody's coming!" Grant said suddenly.

Worf sat up, listened to the faint thud of several footsteps on the stone outside this dugout holding area, then carefully eased back and tried to look as if he didn't care about much.

Under the soft lights of the cellblock corridor, Ugulan and two of his guards strode in, with Odette Khanty in their midst. She was a poised woman who struck Worf as efficient but cold, colder in person than her carefully crafted public image. She approached the cell bars as if they weren't even there.

She looked directly at Worf, ignoring Grant entirely. "It's even worse than you said. You broke your commanding officer's jaw and three ribs."

Worf offered only a limited shrug. "It is not my fault if he had weak bones."

"Why did you come to Sindikash?"

"I like the architecture."

Mrs. Khanty's mouth pursed a bit, rounding her cheeks. "You came because Starfleet has so little authority here at the moment. You came because we're in a state of flux between Federation membership and autonomy. You weren't kicked out of Starfleet. You're absent without leave. There's a pending assault charge."

"How interesting."

"Why didn't you go back to Q'onos?"

Sudden silence fell between them. They looked at each other, dueling.

"Same problems there, hm?" Mrs. Khanty eventually said.

Worf scowled. "Many Klingons no longer understand the need for authority. They made a treaty with the Federation."

"I understand that sort of feeling."

"It is not a feeling. It is fact."

"Yes, of course." She watched him for a moment. "You beat my Rogues. How did you do that?"

Worf clenched his fists to keep from spitting on her. Here was a woman who had found a way to make Klingons turn from their honor. They were nothing but low-life murderers, souring the reputation of Klingons all around. Could he pretend to be a Klingon with no honor?

"Klingons are ethnocentric," he said. "They have a tendency, more than most, to think they are superior in every way. They do not see the strength in others. That is why we could not, for so long, beat back the Federation. But I have grown beyond such constraints. I see the strength of rigorous rationality in Vulcans. I see the stubbornness of humans. There is strength in patience. There is strength in calmness. I remained calm and stubborn in the face of your Rogues, and I beat them."

"By understanding those who would be your enemies, yes," she said. "I see that. Very good. I like that. You beat Klingons by understanding the weakness of Klingons."

Stung by this woman's approval, Worf forced a nod of thanks. He saw in her eyes an incredible coldness that seemed to compensate for her inability to wield a weapon. Oh—it burned to be admired by such a person! He was embarrassed for himself because he had to gain her approval at all, but embarrassed also for the Rogues, who were for some reason ruled by this person.

"I have an offer for you. As you noticed, I have a special security team of Klingons. They call themselves the Rogues. That's their own name for themselves. I need them, because I can't trust anyone else. Not until my husband recovers and can take his governorship again. My husband wants us to establish our independence. I stand by that."

"Sindikash is a Federation colony."

"Was. Was a colony. We stand on our own now. We're frontiersmen, we Seniards. We're all expatriates from Earth, mostly from middle and eastern Europe. We're very tough people; we want our own identity. The lieutenant governor doesn't want us to have that chance. With the governor ill, I have to stand alone against those who would destroy my husband's dream."

"You think the lieutenant governor arranged the assassination attempt on your husband?"

The woman paused. "You're very blunt, aren't you?"

"Yes."

"I appreciate that. Within the next two hours, you should decide whether you might like to be part of the Rogue Force. If so, I can offer you protection from Starfleet."

"Can I have this human as my assistant?"

"Why would you want a human assistant?"

"He saved my life once. I owe him."

Khanty seemed to appreciate that on some level or other. "I guess you can have whatever you want. The Rogues are very independent. We appreciate independence here. But be clear on this: I need loyalty. Things happen to those who betray me or don't keep their agreements. The rewards of loyalty are equally bountiful."

Worf eyed her. "And what if you fail to keep your part of the agreement?"

The woman looked at him, and she was suddenly as cool as the wall.

"Then you may kill me," she said. "That's the deal."

The ship took it up as she tugged at her
tether,
Brace, footrope, and halyard all singin'
together;
So did the seagulls which round us did call,
But, O, my heart sang it the strongest of all!

CHAPTER 4

BEFORE WORF LEFT FOR SINDIKASH, THERE WAS A FAVOR HE HAD HAD TO ASK of his captain.

"Captain . . ."

"Mr. Worf? Something else?"

Worf stepped inside the captain's ready room through a haze of uncertainty, feeling as if he were stepping into a tunnel.

When the captain's muted voice bid him enter, he did. The cloying glances of his shipmates on the bridge gave way to the steady gaze of Captain Picard, and now Worf once again stood before the glossy black desk.

"I have . . . "

"Yes?"

"A request, sir."

The captain put down the padd he was working on, some ship's business or other, and asked, "Something about your mission you don't understand or approve of?"

"No, sir, nothing like that."

"Is everything all right with Ross Grant? Have you explained the mission to him?"

"He already understood much of it, sir," Worf said. "He enjoys this kind of thing."

"Oh, I don't blame him. He's had noted success on several planets. He's quite innovative with computer trails." The captain paused, and his voice turned mellow. "And I'm glad you're able to spend time with a family friend. I hope you'll be an effective team."

Feeling oddly small on the smooth, utilitarian carpet of the captain's office, Worf shifted his feet and nodded in silent agreement to that, then forced himself to move forward on why he was really here.

"Sir, I have a personal request."

Picard tilted his head. "Yes?"

"Next week is the Klingon Day of Honor."

"Oh, yes. Thursday."

Clearing a roughening throat, Worf nodded again. "The actual observation period is roughly four days."

The captain leaned forward and pressed an elbow to his desktop, instantly understanding. "And, of course, you won't be here."

Relieved, Worf let his shoulders sag a bit, and even shrugged. "This is Alexander's first real exposure to the Day of Honor as more than a time set aside to tell stories. He is now twelve years old. That means he must begin to study the history of the Day of Honor, and to understand the full meaning of honor and respect for an enemy's honor."

"The Klingon meaning of honor, or the human meaning of honor, Worf?"

"I beg your pardon, sir?" Worf paused, bandied a few things about in his mind, then decided to take a stab at his own answer. "There is only one honor."

Picard offered a somewhat rare smile. "Oh, no. No, not at all. How often have you heard the term 'Klingon honor'?"

"But I was not raised Klingon. My foster parents did their best to keep me close to my natural culture, but I've found many discrepancies in the actual practice of . . . being Klingon. Alexander has not really been raised Klingon, either, though I have tried. I would like him to at least be familiar with the rites of passage."

The captain leaned back again. "That doesn't really answer my question, but what is your request?"

Worf hesitated, and shuddered down a plaguing doubt. Was this a mistake? Was he overstepping his privileges as much as he thought?

Could it be that having Ross Grant on board had made him assume his other crewmates, even his captain, could be put upon as friends at any moment of inconvenience?

Blood flushed hot in his cheeks and behind his eyes.

"Perhaps this was ill-considered," he struggled. "If you will excuse me—"

"No, I will not excuse you," Picard objected. "State your request."

Curse me for a weakling. He knows me too well.

Knowing he was caught, Worf knotted his fists, battled with himself—and lost. All right, there was no way out.

He drew a breath.

"Since you know more about Klingon culture than most others aboard, since you have been so associated with the structure of Klingon government and know something of our history, I . . . "

"Yes?"

"I would like . . . "

Picard offered a reserved smile, and Worf nearly melted with embarrassment.

The captain pocketed the smile. "You'd like me to usher Alexander through the Day of Honor."

Feeling a wince cross his spine, Worf managed to smother his inner storm long enough to grind out, "Yes, sir."

Jean-Luc Picard pushed to his feet. Striding before the panorama of open space as it showed through the tall viewports behind his desk, he gazed out for a moment, looking in the direction of Sindikash. The planet shone on the star horizon as only a shimmering dot. Even its sun was barely visible from this far away, obscured by several nebulae and a belt of asteroid pebbles.

"You're quite right about me, Mr. Worf," he said many seconds later. "I *am* uneasy around children. They seem as alien a life-form to me as any I've met. A child's first Day of Honor celebration is akin to a bar mitzvah or some other such rite of passage. It's really your place as the boy's father to give him the proper exercise, to make sure he's truly a changed person when it's over."

Feeling the muscles in his legs tighten, Worf worked past the pressure of his choice. "I know that, sir. I would prefer to be here with him, but not at the cost of honest government for Sindikash. If these atrocities are being carried out by Klingons, I have a primary responsibility. I made a commitment, and I must follow it through."

"Yes, you must. Mr. Worf, this is one of those times when we realize how clumsy a situation we've made for ourselves by having families aboard starships. It divides the attention of personnel who need very much to concentrate. It also seems to enhance our awareness of our own mortality, and the cost if we risk our lives. We *must* risk our lives. It's endemic to our duty here."

"And I will, sir," Worf croaked, "willingly."

The captain nodded, seeming to understand the layers of the situation.

"And I'll do all I can for Alexander," he promised. "But keep in mind that you're quite right—I'm not the best person to handle a child's pivotal moments. Yes, I have a few intimacies with Klingon culture, but I'm not sure it'll help as much as you hope."

Worf's whole life had been a series of choices, each chased by doubt. Both he and his captain were uneasy now, and things had not begun that way. "Do your best with your mission, Mr. Worf," the captain finished, "and be assured, I shall do my best with mine."

"Alexander, this is entirely unacceptable!"

"But you said I could pick!"

"I assumed you would pick Klingon history! Not human history!"

"You said I could pick from any historical period in my ancestry. And I'm one-quarter human!"

"But the American Revolutionary War?"

"That's when my ancestor was alive! You said I had to pick one of my own ancestors."

"Yes, I know what I said . . ."

"My grandparents sent me this program for my first Day of Honor. It was my mother's, they got it from her human relatives on Earth."

"But why a human experience?" Picard had to shout over the cannonfire. "It's a Klingon holiday!"

"I know that," the boy shouted back. "Since it was Captain James T. Kirk and Dahar Master Kor working together who founded the Day of Honor, and I've got both human and Klingon blood in me, I think I should be able to choose either one."

Picard ducked a lashing line. "Yes, well—"

The boy grasped his arm. "You're not going to freeze it, are you? Just because of some ship attacking?"

"Not the attack, per se . . . but this particular holoprogram is very old and doesn't comply with the safety controls as well as the more up-to-date programs."

"It's not my fault. My Mother's great-aunt had this journal made into a holoprogram over fifty years ago. She got it from her great-grandmother. The journal's been in the family since—"

"Yes, I know. Since 1777!"

"You said I could choose! You *said!"*

"I said."

Jean-Luc Picard found himself grappling an old style ship's pin rail, his hands entangled in coiled sisal ropes hanging from belaying pins, wondering how children survived at all with so concrete a sense of right and wrong, and what had been once said that could never later be altered.

He *had* said. He had told Alexander to select an ancestor's struggle with honor, and prepare to study that. He had expected the boy to select a Klingon ancestor, something relatively recent, with which Picard had some familiarity.

An officer in a blue jacket charged past him and hurried along the amidships deck, calling, "Reload and run 'em out! Try a ranging shot, please, Mr. Nightingale! Ready on the heads'l sheets! Ready on the braces! MacCrimmon, cross on the weather side, you idiot! Wollard, that main brace is fouled, lee side! Up the shrouds with you!"

"Aye, sir!"

"All hands, wear ship!"

Picard looked up as three men scrambled up the supporting cables of the middle mast—the main. He'd played at this part of history, sailing ships and all, but the holoprograms made up for people of his age had built-in foolproofs. He could give an order to wear the ship then pull the wrong line, and the pretend ship would somehow compensate.

This wasn't one of those foolproof programs. This was a journal of the real thing, and he found it even smelled different from a made-for-entertainment holoprogram.

Smoke spun like Spanish dancers through the infernal din of cannonfire. The boy at his side had proved more clever than Picard expected.

Instead of examining his Klingon heritage for a Klingon holiday, he had chosen a relative from his deeply buried human heritage and provided Picard with these holotapes, long ago dramatized from the diaries of that ancestor.

Now here they were, huddled on the bow of a ship of war, with canvas rattling above and the boom of battle drumming at close range.

He didn't even know which battle this was. The year—1777. The American Revolutionary War.

"Not my best period," he muttered. His voice was snatched away by a tail of cannon smoke. "Couldn't you have had a Napoleonic relative?"

"What?" Alexander huddled at his side, wincing at the sound of heavy artillery. The Klingon boy was incongruous here among the scrambling human crew. But this was a computer program, and the crew would see him as a human youth.

"Why did you choose this program?" Picard asked again. "The Day of Honor is a Klingon exercise."

"I've been hearing about Klingon honor all my life," Alexander said. "Stand your ground, choose strong enemies, fight forward, and die in battle. There has to be more to it. I wanted to see what's in my human background. Maybe we can find something."

"Maybe." Picard grasped the lines nearest his head and pulled himself to his feet, then leaned over the ship's varnished rail and peered downward. The letters on the nameplate were carved and painted—*Justina.*

He looked up then, into the rigging, to seek the skittering ensigns flying at the mastheads. There, whipping eccentrically with the staggered motions of the ship, was the unmistakable arrangement of white lines, blue background, and red bands. The H.M.S. *Justina.*

He scanned the deck. Seemed to be a ship of about a hundred fifty feet, at least two decks above the waterline—not particularly large, even for this era. And there were three masts. Not a brig. Some kind of frigate, perhaps.

Which battle was this? A critical encounter? The battle of Long Island, perhaps?

He cursed himself for not knowing enough about naval battles of the Revolutionary War, and almost called a pause to the program so he could go off and study.

Then again, this wasn't grade school, nor was it a lesson even meant for him.

Only the lowermost sails, the biggest ones, were flying, and at the front of the ship there were three triangular sails reaching out to the bowsprit. He thought there could be more, but wasn't certain.

Soot-stained and glazed with sweat, crewmen scrambled like insects all over the ship, each tending to a particular job, mostly involving the row of cannons on the port side, facing that enemy ship. On the stepped-up aft deck—that would be the quarterdeck—at least two officers surveyed the battle and siphoned orders to the gun crews and the helm. Lined up on the quarterdeck and the main deck were a whole other set of men who weren't working any part of the ship. These wore red jackets and worked with long-muzzled rifles. They were firing independently, taking aim in almost leisurely fashion, picking off men on the other ship, then going through the many steps of the reloading process.

"Marines," Picard murmured. "Sharpshooters . . . how interesting. I've rarely seen that."

Often he'd just had members of his own crew stand in as the "crew" of the holoship, for the fun of it. He'd had the holodeck provide the ship and the sea, and taken it from there.

This program, however, had its own crew, its own weapons, its own grit of reality. Whoever had designed the program had done an excellent job, and had clearly fleshed the journal entries out with historical sources and references. To the extent possible, this was what really happened on this date centuries ago.

Alexander peeked over the port rail at the other ship and gasped. "That ship's shooting at us with noise!"

Picard looked, not understanding.

The other ship was smaller than the vessel they were on, but seemed to have more maneuverability, twisting in the bright gray-blue water as if turning on a corkscrew. It charged toward them, swinging about to put its fresh guns abeam, and it was very close now, hardly more than fifteen yards or so. Dangerously close.

POK BOOM—a puff of smoke appeared near the forward quarter.

"That isn't just noise," he said. "Those are cannons. They're shooting—"

Puff. The rectangular sail over their heads imploded, wagged, then struggled to take the shape of the breeze again, but now there was a shivering two-foot rip in it.

"Cannonballs," Picard finished. How to explain? "Heavy iron balls fired from . . . from heavy iron tubes."

"What would those do?" Alexander screwed up his face. "Just hit the ship? Put a hole in those blankets up there?"

"A great deal, if I recall correctly." Picard glanced around. "They can smash the wood, tear the lines, or crush the men. And those blankets are sails."

He felt movement of the ship beneath him, and crouched closer to the pin rail as crewmen dashed back and forth across the forward deck. Some were shouting, others concentrating on the process that would reload the run-out cannons. Some had to climb overboard to do that. The stench of the last discharge rolled over Picard and the boy, setting them both hacking until their chests ached.

A gust of fresh breeze relieved their stinging lungs and eyes somewhat, and Picard opened his eyes in time to see what he thought was the swinging boom—a heavy wooden shaft to which one of the headsails was attached. Then, as if the giant shaft had stabbed his very chest, he realized he was really seeing the bowsprit of the attacking colonial ship swinging inboard over the *Justina*'s port rail

"Good God!" he choked.

His own voice barely sounded over the devilish scratch of the other ship's dolphin striker and chains knocking against the rail and bulwarks. They'd collided!

For Picard, a starship captain, "near" was hundreds of thousands of kilometers. Not here, though. "Near" now translated into mere inches as the two battling ships jutted hard against each other, heaving sickeningly, then jockeyed for position. Without engines, there was no way to reverse the course of the attacking ship and back out of the *Justina*'s shrouds.

A terrible series of popping noises sounded from the other ship, and several of the marines on Picard's ship suddenly fell dead or dying. The other ship had sharpshooters, too!

"Stay down, Alexander!" he called.

"But they can't hurt us," the boy protested. "It's just a holoprogram."

"I'm not certain of that. Do as I say."

The sea beneath them heaved unevenly, putting the *Justina* down into a trough and raising the other ship up on a swell. The other ship's bow was magnified a thousand times in Picard's eyes as it rose, as if it meant to climb over the rail and crawl onto *Justina*'s foredeck. The hull was narrow-beamed and shallow, the bow sharp, masts raked at an angle that made the ship look as if it were going ten knots standing still. It was rigged differently from this vessel—the sails were not square and set perpendicular to the body of the ship, but were fewer, larger in proportion to the body of the ship, and flew, streamlined with the hull, from fore to aft.

Picard recognized it—the early rig of the American schooner. It would someday become famous for its simplicity and speed. At this point, the word "schooner" didn't even exist.

The enemy's nameplate crawled upward and tipped high behind *Justina*'s mast supports—what were those called?—and Picard suddenly had an identity on the attackers. *Chincoteague.*

An American ship. In 1777, those would be colonists who had declared themselves independent and were now fighting a war for the final decision.

The *Chincoteague*'s fifteen-foot bowsprit bashed fitfully into one of *Justina*'s masts and both ships staggered. The colony ship's bow grated against *Justina*'s side, gouging off layers of paint and wood. The paralyzingly loud cannonfire fell momentarily silent, other than one or two pops from the stern of the British ship. The American ship couldn't fire because none of its cannon could aim at its enemy now, with its bow pressing against the side of the *Justina,* and evidently it had no bow guns. That would've been acceptable—except that they would grind each other into sawdust if this colliding was allowed to continue.

"Well, this can't go on, can it?" Picard shoved himself upward, climbing first onto the rail, then farther up into the vertical cables and horizontal footropes and wrapped one leg well into them. Then he grasped the other ship's chains with both hands and hauled for all he was worth.

He found himself attempting to push over a mountain with his bare hands. The bodies of the two ships grated against each other with unimaginable power. The other ship's bowsprit grated hard against the mast again, turned as if nauseated, as if it meant to disengage itself from its own bow, and rolled away down the deck of the *Justina.* Picard kept hauling.

"What are you doing, Captain?" Alexander cried from the deck.

"Better not call me 'captain,' " Picard told him. "We're not sure what rank I am."

"Oh . . . " The boy glanced around, trying to decide just how real a holoprogram could be.

Picard knew from experience—bad ones—that the quirky holograms as old as this one were much less manageable and more subject to participation than current technology, and that things could go wrong.

He rearranged his leg and kept hauling on the chains. Suddenly the *Chincoteague* surged back a good two meters. He grabbed a different part of the chain and hauled again.

"Hands off, redcoat!"

Startled, Picard glanced over his shoulder. On the bow of the colonial ship, a rough-looking sailor aimed a flintlock pistol at his face. Rough, yes, but under the layer of dare and contempt, he was only about twenty years old.

Picard kept pulling. "We have to get these ships apart, or we'll maul each other into the sea! Is that what you want?" Without waiting for an answer, he reached down, snatched a coil of line from one of the pins, and tossed it at the colonist. "Now, haul away, boy! We have to change the angle of this ship!"

The line was made fast to its pin, and stayed fast as the sailor paled a shade, belted his pistol, and did as he was told. He braced both feet on the bow rail of that ship and hauled back.

"When this is over," the sailor called, "I'll be shooting you, sir!"

"Better than drowning," Picard drawled back.

Sir. Well, he was *some* kind of officer. He hadn't even bothered to look at what kind of jacket he was wearing.

"Captain?" Alexander's knobby head appeared below.

"Stay down. And don't call me 'captain.' " Picard kept the pressure on the bowsprit chains, though his arms were shuddering now. But the ship—the *Chincoteague* was moving!

Or perhaps the *Justina* was moving beneath him, under the combined force of his actions and the pulling of the other ship's sailor on the line. The *Justina* began sluggishly swinging around, putting the ships more side by side than bow to beam. That allowed the bowsprit of *Chincoteague* to release its dance with the *Justina*'s foremast and bob freely in the rigging.

With the cooperation of the swells and a slacking breeze, the colonial ship's bowsprit moved outboard another yard. It stalled, then began moving again, and this time floated completely out. In a surreal motion, the other ship continued moving away. Its hull turned abeam and the cannons began roaring once again.

True to his promise, the colonial sailor dumped the line joining the ships, fumbled off the rail, jumped down to the deck, and drew his pistol again. He aimed it as squarely at Picard as the bobbing of *Chincoteague* would allow, but *Chincoteague* drifted backward and was swallowed by a dense shroud of cannon smoke just as the sailor tried to take aim. He made a wild shot, but it was far off.

"Shrouds! That's it!" Picard shouted victoriously and grasped the cables that supported the masts from side to side. Then he grasped the horizontally tied footropes. "And ratlines! Yes, of course. Ah, these were the days! Sometimes I wish we had things like this aboard the *Enterprise!"*

Ridiculous. What a thought.

"Why don't we have them?" Alexander asked, appearing at his side.

"Because we don't have masts to support. If you look up at these, you can see what they do."

Alexander craned his neck to look up at the maze of lines and pullies. "This boat has too many things on it. Do you know what all this does?"

"No, not all of it," Picard admitted. "I've played at the era, but I've never actually *worked* at it. I've paid more attention to tactics of these types of battles than the details of sail handling. Perhaps this is a good time to—"

His words were blasted apart by a half dozen cannonshots at stunningly close range. The *Chincoteague*'s brief dance with *Justina* had allowed both ships time to reload and run out their guns again. Now both ships had opened fire again.

Instinctively, Picard ducked and pushed Alexander down as the ship beneath them shuddered from hits on her hull. The sound of cracking wood was as disgusting as bones breaking, and was punctuated by the screams of dying men on the gundeck below.

Alexander pushed out from under Picard's arm and looked along the deck, then suddenly drew a sharp breath and trembled. Not five steps away, a crewman lay shuddering and gasping, dying. He raised his head pathetically and looked at his own body, now a field of jagged splinters from the broken bulwark. A cannonball had come through the body of the ship between the deck and rail, skewered this poor man with dozens of sharp stakes, then plunged across the deck and out another passage it had carved for itself in the opposite bulwark. Picard still heard the water hissing where the hot ball struck, and there was a column of steam out there in the water.

Alexander struggled to breathe as he watched the poor man die like that, full of splinters. This was a boy who came from an age of cauterizing weapons and distance fighting. Yes, he was born of a culture that prized hand-to-hand fighting, but Klingon stories and Klingon day-to-day life were two different things. There really wasn't that much blood drawn anymore.

There was blood drawn today, plenty of it. The dying man turned his eyes to Alexander in a ghastly, final plea that Picard felt bolting through the boy.

"Barbaric . . . " Picard waved at the sulfurous smoke rising from the *Justina*'s own cannons, and peered through the gray clouds at the other ship.

The hull was cracked in several places above the waterline. The top half of the foremast was broken like a twig, bent over to one side, caught in the rigging. But with that fore-and-aft rig, the colonial ship didn't have as many lines tangling the space above her decks, and the broken mast was being cleared quickly away by men smeared with soot and blood.

This was all very close and immediate—very personal. Not like a battle aboard a starship, where the enemy was half a solar system off. Hologram or not, this program was based on detailed diaries of someone who had been here and seen this, on this day, in 1777, who could still taste the gore and sweat as he wrote his journal.

Where was that person? Where was Alexander's ancestor?

One of the gun crew? An officer? One of that line of redcoated marines who were now taking aim with rifles?

At his side, Alexander flinched hard as the marines fired their volley, all at once, with cold organization. Withering fire rained across the other ship. Screams rose from the deck, and the *Chincoteague* fell off her attack stance. Even from here, Picard could see the wheel spinning. The helmsman had been mown down, and so had anyone near enough to take his place.

Letting out a moan of empathy, Picard stuffed down a ridiculous urge to jump over there and help steer the other ship.

Suddenly a commotion on the main deck caught his eye—three men in officers' dark blue coats were joining the gun crew in a supreme task—one of the huge ship's cannons had tipped over on its side, guntruck and all, and the fabulous weight of the iron monster would take several men to heave up.

Those must be the command officers. Yet Picard saw in their effort the long years they had spent on board ship. They didn't look at all as he had when he had played at historical programs before. Their uniforms were tattered and smutty with gunpowder and splinter dust, and the wool strained around their muscles as they threw their weight onto the cannon with force matching the effort of the deckhands. Slowly the big gun began to shift.

The cannon was enormous—what did that thing weigh? A thousand pounds? Beneath the deadweight maw of iron, a jagged scream erupted. Some poor crushed soul was still alive under there!

The deckhands and officers got the cannon up a foot or so, but the effort took all the men in that area of the ship. There was no one who dared let go long enough to pull the injured man out. For a moment, the team floundered as the unfortunate sailor screamed and tried to claw his way out of the man-made trap.

"I can pull him out!" Alexander piped, and slipped past Picard.

But a man from another gun crew waved a copper knife with one hand and grasped Alexander's arm with the other.

"Y'ain't headin' for the main deck, is you, swab?" the man barked, spinning Alexander around and giving him a sturdy shove. "Y'know the rules. Niver go within a boathook's length of d'captain. Got that, boy?"

Alexander managed a nod, then looked at Picard. Pretty clear message—should he stay a boathook's length from Picard? And what the devil was a boathook?

"Sergeant!" one of the uniformed men at the cannon gasped, straining horribly to keep the cannon's bulk up.

Instantly a tall young soldier appeared from behind the mast—he wore a red jacket over his sailor's shirt, and he took a moment to put down a black-muzzled rifle. A marine sharpshooter. A sergeant.

The marine sergeant dropped to the deck and crawled under the cannon. Unthinkable!

"Oh, my," Picard murmured with admiration.

"He's going to get crushed!" Alexander said. "He just went right under that thing!"

"And it would've been you being crushed if you hadn't been stopped."

"I'm not afraid!"

"That's commendable, but you're also not strong enough to pull that injured man out of there. You have to use common sense. Sometimes you're of more help staying out the way."

"Doesn't sound very good," the boy complained. He fell silent and watched as the marine sergeant squirmed under the massive cannon, then reappeared with his arms around the half-crushed sailor. Blood drained from the sailor's mouth.

Picard winced. He knew a lost cause when he saw one.

A slice of empathy rushed through his chest. Holoprogram or not, this incident had really happened, and those men had really died, or lay moaning in agony until they finally died. Medical science in colonial times couldn't hope to snatch many back from the maw of death in battle.

"He did it!" Alexander jumped in victory as the Marine shimmied the sailor out from under the cannon.

An instant later, the officers and deckhands gratefully let the cannon dump to the deck. The *boom* of its weight on the planks sent a shudder up and down the entire ship.

The officers instantly dispersed to other parts of the ship, undistracted by the good deed they had just done.

Alexander, Picard noticed, continued watching the marine sergeant.

The marine was crouched on the bloody deck, holding the crushed sailor as if cradling a child, and he continued to do so, speaking softly and inaudibly over the din of gunfire, until the sailor's grasping hands fell limp and his frightened eyes glazed over.

Alexander continued to watch, deeply moved by what he saw.

"Starboard gun crews ready?" someone called.

"Ready!" the answer came.

"Hands to the fore course braces!" The shout came from the main deck, somewhere amidships, not far from the discarded cannon. At first Picard didn't pay attention, but then the same voice shouted, "Mr. Picard, fore braces! Aren't you paying attention?"

Well, so much for a simple lesson.

He shot a stare in that direction, and saw one of the officers waving at him.

For a terrible instant he glanced around at all the lines, in a panic that he couldn't remember what a fore brace was and how to work it; then he forced himself to think. The officer had said "Mister" Picard.

And Picard was wearing a blue jacket of the same type as that man. The deckhands were wearing striped shirts, or no shirts at all, dark bell-bottom trousers, and most had bare feet. Picard's breeches were white, not bell-bottom, and he had shoes on.

Inhaling sharply, he looked toward the nearest bunch of sailors, who were scrambling to ditch some wreckage overboard and secure a cannon truck, and he shouted, "Hands to the fore braces, gentlemen!"

Two of those men jumped forward to the area where Picard and Alexander were standing. "Aye, sir!" one of them responded, then they separated.

They snatched at two lines made fast to belaying pins on opposite sides of the ship. Picard followed those lines up into the sky, into the rigging, and discovered that they were attached to the ends of the long yard from which the biggest forward sail hung.

"The fore . . . main," he muttered. "No . . . the fore tops'l—topgal lant . . ."

No use. He didn't remember what that sail was called. It had a specific name, but he couldn't scrape it up. He could tell that those lines would turn the sail, and could probably turn it almost perpendicular to the body of the ship if necessary. The yard, a long spoke of wood that looked very heavy, wasn't attached to the mast, but moved freely on its own lines.

The men unmade the lines from the pins, took hold of them, then turned to Picard for orders.

He looked aft. Nobody was paying any attention. Was he supposed to do something?

"Uh . . . stand by," he said to the men.

"Standing by, sir," one responded.

"Prepare to come about!" somebody called—that same officer from amidships.

Picard looked at the men. Oh, well. "Prepare to come about," he repeated.

"Ready, sir," the port side sailor acknowledged, and he and his crewmate looked up, then tugged or released the brace lines until the sail lay across the body of the ship without favoring either side.

As the wind changed, Picard heard a new voice carried to him, a slightly deeper voice, but quieter. "Wear ship," the voice said.

Amidships, the officer called, "Helm alee!"

From the wheel, a third voice called back, "Helm's alee!"

Lee . . . lee side . . . windward was where the wind was coming from, so lee was where it was going. Wear ship—turn so the breeze was at their stern. He knew that.

Sure enough, the ship bobbled on the surging water and began swinging about into the direction the breeze was blowing. The ship set into a troubled roll, not up, not down, not side to side, not fore and aft, but somehow all of those at the same time. Up, side, pitch, aft, roll, side, down, down more—ghastly! Why was there so much romance about this way of life?

The sails sagged, fluttered, whipped as if confused, then—*whap, whap,* SNAP—the air socked into them and the ship sluggishly moved toward the other vessel.

Only now did Picard notice they were just a kilometer or two from land! A vast stretch of green hills flickered under the warm sun. He wondered where they were. Coastal United States, likely, but where? Off Florida? Maine?

The brand-new United States, declared so by its defiant founders only a year before this. Now there was a war, a great test of resolve, because it was surely not one of resource.

He knew how the Revolutionary War would come out, but he still shivered with excitement at seeing this. The brilliant technology of his own time was allowing him and Alexander to see the technologies upon which it was built. And even more, the attitudes that built it.

"Adjust that sail to the new heading, gentlemen," he said, trying to sound as if he knew what in hell he was talking about.

But they did it. One of them let out his line, and the other drew his line in. They watched the sail the whole time, and soon it matched the angle of the sail in the middle of the ship and the one on the third mast. Mizzen. Mizzenmast.

"Simple enough," he said aloud. "Well, I'm recalling a few things at least."

"That's well!" the officer amidships called. "Make fast, all hands. Starboard gun crews, stand by! Mr. Picard, the bedamned heads'ls, if you please! Captain Sobel wants the ship brought about some time today!"

"Oh—" Picard swung around and looked at the triangular sails running from the bowsprit, but hadn't any idea what to do with them. Then, as he forced himself to think, he realized that the headsails were filled from the wind coming from the port side, but were still tied to pins on the starboard side of the ship. "Gentlemen, take care of these immediately."

He tried to be noncommittal, because he wanted to see whether or not he had guessed right.

Sure enough, the men bounced to the lines holding the free corners of the sails, unfastened them from the pins, then ran to the same lines on the other side and drew them tight. So the headsails had to be shifted from one side to the other, depending upon where the wind came from.

Now the *Justina* had come all the way around and had her bow to the land. The *Chincoteague* now lay off the British ship's starboard side, the side with the loaded and ready guns. Those marines who were still standing now picked their way across the wreckage-littered deck, through the blood and over the bodies of fallen men, and took up position on the starboard side.

All seemed to relax some and watch as the sailors and ship's officers struggled to clear the decks of wreckage and bodies, and to find the wounded.

Picard looked at Alexander, but the boy was fascinated by the actions of the one marine sergeant who had impressed him before, by not letting that poor crushed gunner die alone.

"Are those men in red going to shoot those weapons again?" Alexander asked.

"I think they're out of range," Picard told him. "I don't believe they had rifled muskets yet . . . but I'm not sure about that. It means the inside of the barrel has a kind of twisted ridge that makes the bullet—ah, the ball—spin as it comes shooting out."

"What would that do?"

"Improves range and accuracy. But I don't believe they have that—well, they might."

"Mmm," Alexander uttered. "Phasers are better."

"Yes, but with every invention comes a countermeasure. With bullets came kevlar vests. With phasers, we came up with shields. Every age has its challenges."

"Fire as you bear starboard, Mr. Pennington," the deep voice from aft filtered on the wind, and with a sudden flicker of awareness Picard realized he was hearing the captain's voice. Captain Sobel was his name, wasn't it?

Pennington, the officer at amidships, ordered, "Starboard guns as you bear . . . fire!"

The ship was still moving, coming slowly around until most of her guns could focus on the *Chincoteague,* but, given the curved shape of the ship's side, not all the guns could aim at the same time. There were four . . . yes, four cannons on each side of the main deck. How many were below, on the gun deck? Ten? That would make this ship an eighteen-gunner.

"Formidable," Picard muttered. He looked across the glinting water at the other ship. *Chincoteague,* as he now counted her gunports, seemed to have about half that, with only guns on the main deck. But she was more maneuverable and quicker, turning brilliantly out there on hardly a puffing breeze.

If her gunners were more skilled, or just more determined, or more desperate—

FFFFOOOM! The deck beneath him shuddered bodily with the paralyzing report of bow and midship cannons. A few seconds later, as *Justina* jolted on a swell, the midship to aft cannons pounded the sea's surface. Guntrucks thundered on the deck planks as the cannons jolted backward with the power of their own percussion, to be yanked to awkward halts by strong retaining ropes. Amazing—the cannons probably weighed fifteen hundred or two thousand pounds each.

Any standard-issue hand phaser was a million times more deadly, but somehow at this moment Picard couldn't muster any more respect for that delicate weapon than for these monoliths, which took such cooperation to make, board, and use.

Puffs of smoke and fire appeared on *Chincoteague*'s black side. Impact tremors disturbed the swells. Screams of wounded men pierced the clear day, even more disturbing than the thunder of cannons.

The *Chincoteague*'s sails fluttered and the ship briefly staggered, then the bow swung out of sight in a pall of cannon smoke and Picard couldn't judge what was happening out there.

But there was fire on the other ship.

He was sure of that.

"She's bearing off!" someone shouted, and the crew—those still standing—broke into cheers.

"Shameful," Picard commented, "to cheer the defeat of an enemy."

Alexander looked up at him. "Why is it shameful?"

"Could just as easily have been us. It's not polite."

"But we beat them. Why shouldn't we celebrate?"

"It's not my taste to do so."

The boy looked at the retreating colonial ship. "It's mine," he admitted, and he stood up and started cheering with the rest of the crew.

Picard stared at the boy, caught by the child's disrespect for the opinion of his mentor, but also by his defiant sense of self. Hadn't quite expected that . . .

"Alexander," he began, "Alexander, pay attention. We have to be somewhat careful. This holoprogram is over seventy-five years old, and was written by historians, not technicians. Things can happen."

The boy divided his attention between Picard and the retreating *Chincoteague.* "Bad things?"

"Yes. This program is only barely compatible with the ship's modern systems. The safeties may not work properly. I have no way to know whether or not that sailor's pistol would actually have hurt me."

"We're not quitting, are we?"

"No, no."

"We're going to stay and look for my ancestor, aren't we?"

"Yes, I'm sure he's here somewhere."

"Then what should we do about the safeties?"

"Until we know," Picard said, "I suggest we duck."

CHAPTER 5

"ATTENTION, CARGO SINDIKASH FOUR-ZERO-FIVE, THIS IS COMMANDER William Riker aboard the Starfleet scout Jackson Taylor. Shut your engines down immediately and prepare to be boarded."

The words sounded familiar. Similar words had triggered the entire mission Worf was on, and he couldn't shake the sensation of having been through this before.

The odor of blood by the gallon still wafted in Worf's nostrils. Such a visceral reaction boiled inside him that he could barely keep from challenging every last Rogue here and now. Bitter embarrassment electrified him—he had defended the indefensible. Commissioner Toledano had been right about the grim murders on that transport.

He was among Klingons, and he should feel at ease, yet he did not. He must pretend to be their comrade, yet he could barely make himself do it.

Yet I must.

The vision of the thirty-some dead innocents, the mutilated witnesses who were not even spared their own eyes, and the sorrowful disillusionment in Captain Picard's face haunted him more with every minute.

And all the arms were still missing.

"Starfleet!" Ugulan choked out from the pilot's seat at Worf's side. "I *told* you someone was spying on us!"

"They patrol this space," Worf fiercely shot back, despising himself for even speaking to such a being. "We took our chances. Chance went against us."

"It was probably you!"

"You never had a mission fail before I came?"

"Curse your skull! Put the automatic defenses on! We have to try to outrun them!"

"Ridiculous. We have to fight them."

"That is Starfleet!"

"So it is. And you are a frightened woman in man's armor."

Nettled by shame and broiling inner fury, Worf poured all his frustration into goading Ugulan. He had to control himself—restrain himself from driving his knuckles into Ugulan's mouth and out the back of his neck. Not yet . . . not yet . . .

He concentrated on the screen.

The air in the cockpit was hot. He was sweating under his Rogue uniform. He hated the uniform. He hated the screen. He hated everything.

What had made these Klingons become what they were? What had driven them from their loyalty and honor to the strengths that made the Empire survive? He had managed to fight them and win in the square in Burkal City, and that gave him a clue. Were they simply inadequate? Had battle training been too rigid for them? How had someone like Ugulan ended up doing the bidding of a human woman?

The answer might be here, now. Ugulan wanted to escape at the sight of one Starfleet shuttle. Where were his parents? Who was his family, and were they ashamed? Was their name ever spoken in their own land anymore?

He thought back to the names of the dishonored families whose power in Klingon society had been lost, and wondered—was he flying with their sons? With the fathers of disgraced Klingon boys who would pay all their lives for the dishonor here?

His hands played on the controls with a hunger so deep that his fingers hurt. The shame of pretending to be one of them boiled beneath his skin. Mission or not, he could not banish the nausea of humiliation.

On the cargo ship's forward screen—the only screen that could pull up a view of outside—the Starfleet scout angled toward them, its small, tight body gleaming in the light of the nearby sun.

Piloted by Ugulan and the other Rogues, the freighter was old and underteched, the perfect kind of ship to be completely ignored by Starfleet or anybody else. Odette Khanty had counted on that. Worf knew this shipment was organized by the governor's wife, and that it was a shipment of something illegal according to Federation interstellar trade regulations, but Grant had been able to find no shred of recorded evidence that led back to her.

Odette Khanty was ahead in the polls, but only slightly, and she wanted an edge. Her husband's injury had pushed her ahead for a while, but now sympathy was beginning to wear off. She needed to boost public opinion in her favor again, and Worf was riding in her way of doing that.

This freighter was Odette Khanty's latest plan. It was loaded with illegal goods and headed for Cardassian space, but it was never intended to arrive there. It was supposed to be "captured" by Sindikash patrols. By then, the Rogues would have abandoned the freighter, and left in it only the name and the identity codes, not of Odette Khanty, but of the lieutenant governor. This was a giant warp-powered frame-up.

And here I am, volunteering for this delivery, without even knowing what I am delivering. I wish I could deliver a foot into the throat of each Klingon here.

Forcing himself to stop dreaming, he shook himself back to the action of the moment. Now a Starfleet scout had spotted them and veered in at high warp, and Ugulan was panicking. The other six Rogues on board were agitated, but waiting for Ugulan to make a decision.

Pathetic invertebrate cowards . . .

The freighter belonged to the lieutenant governor's brother, and this morning the Rogues had stolen it and loaded it with unmarked crates. Worf, as the new Rogue, had been careful not to ask questions, for surely that would be a signal. Once the cargo of illicit goods was discovered, Odette Khanty's plan was for the freighter's ownership to be revealed, and the lieutenant governor implicated—at least in enough people's suspicions to tilt the election handily.

Begrudgingly, Worf admired the craft of the plan, but still his hands grew cold in spite of the heat in the cockpit. This was not his kind of mission. He was the wrong man for espionage.

"Betrayed! Betrayed . . . " Ugulan frantically worked the controls as the ten-man Starfleet scout closed in on them. He barked at his men, who negotiated the ship around a dust belt and between two asteroids, but there was no universe in which a loaded freighter could outmaneuver or certainly outrun a Starfleet pack.

"Attention Cargo Sindikash," Riker's voice came again, more forceful this time, angry. *"Heave to or we will fire on you. Do you copy? This is your last warning. Stop forward propulsion immediately."*

"We have to do it," the Rogue named Goric said. "They'll cut us to shreds."

"Do it, Ugulan!" another Rogue demanded.

Ugulan snarled, "We are supposed to destroy ourselves before ever giving up."

"For her?" Goric charged. "I have no wish to die for that woman!"

Worf turned and sneered at him, and for a moment he could be himself. "What *will* you die for?"

Goric gaped back at him, caught briefly in the magnetism of underlying meaning.

A strained silence, bizarre stillness, folded over the cockpit.

What are you and how did you come to this?

"That was the oath we made to her," Ugulan reminded them, but not with enthusiasm. "We swore on our honor we would never allow ourselves to be captured as evidence against her. She has not violated her agreement with us."

"You are all cowards," Worf snarled. "You swear an oath that swallows your honor, then you betray even that."

On that, Goric spun again to Ugulan. "It does me no good if she wins and we are all dead!"

Ugulan growled, looked at the other Rogues, deciphering their agreement with Goric, and decided whether or not he wanted to self-destruct for Odette Khanty's purity of position. "If we fail her, we'll be hunted down."

"Better dead tomorrow than today," Goric declared.

The other Rogues grumbled their agreement.

Worf held his breath, prepared to circumvent disaster if he had to, for he indeed did not intend to die for Khanty, but that turned out not to be necessary. Ugulan pounded the helm console, slowed the ship down, and prepared to comply.

All around Worf, the Rogues' faces were pasted with bloody-minded anger as they realized their acrimony would get them nowhere. Worf scrutinized them as if their pasts would rise in print on their foreheads if he looked hard enough. Were their plans for power and influence eroding before their eyes? Were they angry that all they could do now was be angry?

His stomach twisting with disgust, Worf found a certain sorrow in watching the wreckage of Klingons thinking there was nothing to do but give up.

Give up! Curse you all into the dirt!

Worf plunged in between Ugulan and the helm and slammed the thrusters back on again, and doubled the freighter's speed under them.

"What are you doing!" Ugulan demanded. "We can never outrun them!"

"Then we should do something else!" Worf bellowed back.

Ugulan came halfway out of his chair. "We are not stupid! That is Starfleet!"

Worf cast him a glare. "Frightened children!"

Mortash, the nearest Klingon behind Ugulan, shouted, "A penal institution is better than dead!"

"How would *you* know?" Worf tossed over his shoulder. He shoved Ugulan away from the helm and took it himself. "Filth!"

Instantly Ugulan came to his feet again, and his phaser pressed into Worf's cheek. "I command this ship," he said.

On the same breath, the Starfleet patrol vessel blew a direct phaser shot in what might have been a crippling attack had Worf not tilted the freighter and caused the blow to glance. The Klingons shuddered, but everyone stayed upright.

"Under your command, the ship is dead and so are we." Worf went on piloting as if Ugulan's weapon were nothing but a stick pressing his face. "I can force that ship's shields to flutter."

Ugulan changed his stance to accommodate the slight tilt of the deck. "How can you?"

"I know the Starfleet prefix codes."

"How can you know that?"

Worf piloted the freighter in a clumsy elliptical course back toward the underbelly of the Starfleet patroller. "I stole them before I left."

Ugulan stared at him and growled, "You can make the shields drop?"

"Not drop. But I can make them shift. Long enough to drive one shot in. Sit down here and fly directly at it."

His mind obviously boggled, Ugulan glanced at Goric, Mortash, Gern and the other slime. Worf saw a bizarre anxiety crawl through their expressions, as though only now realizing they might not be forced to the wall after all. Hair-raising excitement charged them all suddenly.

Ugulan's phaser fell away. "You had better leave no traces, lunatic! I will not pay your price for you!"

The head Rogue made a quick motion, and Worf gave him the helm, then shifted to the weapons and tactical board to do what he said he could do.

"They are firing!" Mortash shouted, and his words were eaten in a pounding uproar from outside.

Malignant electricity bolted through the freighter, its plates shrieking, funnels of lubricants and gases spitting from a dozen places in the inner frame. Suddenly the whole cabin was twenty degrees hotter. Worf felt his uniform become an oven as he furiously played the controls, tapping in the complex codes. On the screen, the Starfleet patroller no longer looked small. They were on collision course, and the freighter was making no return shots.

Mortash clutched his console and shouted, "Veer off!"

He plunged forward and swiped Worf's head with his armored cuff.

Worf's brain wobbled, and for a few moments his eyesight blurred. He felt blood drain down the back of his neck, but before he could lash out, Ugulan did it for him.

"Down, maniac! A chance is a chance!" the Rogue leader smashed Mortash back, and Worf was free to clear his head and continue feeding the codes.

"Stay on course," he ordered, and Ugulan resentfully complied, maintaining the collision heading. "Ready . . . ready . . . "

From the sensor grid console, Goric shouted, "Their shields are shifting! Now! Now!"

With his left fist, Worf hammered the firing controls. Half-power defense-only phasers bolted from the body of the freighter—nothing near the power of Starfleet phasers, but formidable enough if they could be fired on a ship without shields.

"This is Commander Riker! Cease fire immediately or we will target your engines!"

"Did it get through?" Ugulan gasped, staring at the screen. "We are still on collision! They did not explode! Did the shot get through?"

"They are not dead, are they?" Mortash roared from behind Worf. "Do you see them dying?" He pointed at Worf. "This one has killed us! We are damaged! Veer off!"

"Shields are stabilizing," Gern called over the crackle of their own damage. "Starfleet's, not ours."

Ugulan shot a piercing glare at Worf. "I will cut your throat myself just to hear the sound!"

"Do it while you steer!" Worf spat back. *Animals, pathetic animals!*

Ugulan leaned hard to one side, and the ship moved with him, heeling up onto its starboard warp package, leaving barely enough passing space under the hull for the Starfleet vessel to shoot by, so close that the hullplates rattled with the force of the other ship's engine wash.

"You have seconds before they come about," Mortash mourned. "We should both cut his throat before they slaughter us!"

Casting a fearless glower, Worf bit his tongue. *Why not just pull out their arms?*

Luckily, he kept it to himself.

"They are coming about!" one of the Rogues shouted from the aft panels.

On the main screen, sensors were following the Starfleet ship as it arched around, its top hullplates gleaming and showing off the rectangular body shape of the vessel and the glowing red phaser ports. It was coming around to finish them.

"What is it doing?" Mortash shuddered then. "It is—slowing down!"

"Why would it?" Ugulan struggled with the half-frozen helm, trying to bring the bulky freighter around so they could pretend to go down fighting.

One by one the Rogues moved through the noxious stink of damage and gathered around the main screen, crowding up behind Worf and Ugulan. Together they watched the small Starfleet scout come around to kill them. It was slowing down to draw out its own victory and to shame them, so they thought.

Worf watched it, barely breathing. His quaking hands on the console nearly gave away his bitter delight.

The patroller was indeed slowing.

Then, in a shocking change, it pitched to one side and spun half a turn.

"Look!" Ugulan pointed at the screen.

The patroller's back was broken by a sudden explosion from inside its aft topdeck, blowing the impulse engine across space. The sparks washed back and engulfed the Starfleet scout.

Mortash grabbed for the sensor grid readouts. "It is hulled! It is hulled! Our shot got through! We hulled it!"

He stumbled back to the main screen, just in time to see the Starfleet ship spark, crackle, then turn itself inside out, its skin peeling back an instant before the warp engines blew themselves into solar balls.

Worf clamped his mouth shut, determined to hold back his grunt of victory. If they showed no restraint, then he would show all of his.

The ignoble crowd erupted into a cheer, and less than a full second later the freighter rocked upward violently on an impact wave and half of them were thrown to the deck. They clawed back to their feet, staring at the screen.

A puff of blue residue twisted where moments ago a Starfleet ship had hovered.

Gone.

"Commander Riker!" Ugulan bolted. "Hah!"

Then he spat on the deck, hitting Worf's boot with his comment.

CHAPTER 6

"THAT'S DONE. DAMNED REBELS."

The officer from midships, Mr. Pennington, was probably the first officer, Picard now figured. There were other men in blue jackets, too, who would be other lieutenants of various tenure, and midshipmen. They each seemed to have a particular assignment. One tended the main deck gun crews. Another monitored sail handling. There must be more of those men below decks, taking care of other aspects of the ship's business now that the fight with *Chincoteague* was over.

"Not so different from the way a starship is run," he murmured, mostly to himself.

"Is this an important battle?" Alexander asked quietly.

"I don't know yet," Picard told him as they enjoyed a moment of fresh breeze pressing through the lingering gunsmoke. "There were thousands of skirmishes between 1776 and 1787. It was a long war."

"Why don't you take over the ship and find out?"

"Well, this isn't like a holonovel, you know. This is real history. I've been on pretend ships, but this one was real."

"What difference does that make?"

A little embarrassed, Picard hesitated, then plunged ahead. "There's a difference between a passive interest and a way of life. It's one thing to enjoy naval history, and quite another to actually be on board an historic ship and make it go. No one likes to admit he hasn't the faintest idea of what he's doing, but here I am. Let's just listen and see what we can learn."

The boy stared at him for a moment of awakening, then simply nodded.

Picard and Alexander kept their mouths shut and listened as the crew muttered about whether or not the captain would decide to pursue the colonial ship or to go on with their mission, whatever that mission was. Where had they been heading when the attack came under the clear afternoon sun?

Why had the colonist attacked in broad daylight, when the larger ship had a decided advantage? What had they been trying to protect?

Picard took a moment to look at the land. Was something there worth protecting—with a valuable ship, costly guns and ammunition, and the lives of men, at great risk under a noon sun, with the wind on the enemy's other side?

"Mr. Picard!"

Pennington. This was a bulky man, but quick at picking his way through the dead and wounded and all the splinters and chunks of smashed wood. He came through the maze of clutter as if he'd spent his life doing it. Probably had.

"What are you going to do?" Alexander asked.

Picard glanced down. "Answer him." He looked up at the officer and called, "Yes?"

Instantly he realized he should've said "sir." Fact was, he wasn't used to saying that to anyone on board his own ship. He was used to having it said to him.

"Mr. Picard, are you injured?"

"Oh . . . no, sir, I'm not injured."

"Perhaps you should see to your duties then."

"Yes, of course. I will."

Pennington immediately about-faced and headed aft again, barking at the crew and surveying the damage.

"Well, there's something," Picard said. "Apparently I'm in charge of the foredeck."

"What's your rank?"

"Lieutenant, I'd say. A second or third officer. Or fourth. Let's see if they'll do what I say, shall we?"

He moved toward the nearest clutch of men, a gun crew and sail handlers, who were standing at the starboard rail, watching the retreat of the colonial ship, its sides still boiling smoke. That was a busy crew over there.

His crew should be busy, too. Picard glanced about, assessed what he saw, and simply said, "Gentlemen, let's clear away this wreckage and secure the guns. And coil those . . . those . . . "

"Aye, sir!" two of the men chimed, and others muttered the same. They were all sweat-drenched, blackened with cannon soot and shot grease, and their horny hands were bloody, but they seemed to know exactly what he meant.

Good thing, because he didn't. He wouldn't have known himself how to secure the guns, or which part of this wreckage had to be salvaged and which cast overboard.

"Salvage what you can," he said pointlessly, just as a test.

"Yes, sir," one of the Englishmen said.

"Take the wounded below," Picard threw in after glancing again at the litter of wounded men, and particularly the man who had been slaughtered by splinters. "And see to the dead."

One of the sailors stood up and stepped to him. "Sir, the wounded on the orlop deck?"

"Uh, yes," Picard agreed, "the orlop deck."

"And the dead?"

Alexander was looking at him.

Picard hesitated. "The hold."

"Very good, sir." The sailor turned to his mates and told them what to do.

"Well," Picard sighed to Alexander, "that seems to be some of my job."

"Can we help them?" Alexander said.

Clapping the boy on the shoulder, Picard smiled. "Exactly what I had in mind. You help those men shove off the wreckage. I'll triage the wounded."

"But you're not a doctor!" the boy protested.

"I'll just do my best. Promise me you'll do yours."

"I will."

"And don't throw anything overboard without asking."

"I won't."

Picard drew a breath to steel himself, and was instantly assaulted by the overpowering odor of blood and sweat, but mostly blood. It had a hot, salty, cloying presence as he moved into the litter of wreckage and wounded. He knelt immediately beside a groaning sailor whose leg had been shattered at the thigh by hurling wood. A blown-apart piece of line served well enough as a tourniquet, but the leg was clearly destroyed. This man would probably die, given this technology, and it would be a long, tortuous passing. Giving the delirious man a sorry pat on the shoulder, Picard moved on.

He knew, of course, that this was a vision of something that had happened in the distant past, and he couldn't really save a life, but there was a certain stinging reality in the fact that this *had* happened. As he had told the boy, this was not a holonovel. It was true history. These men had fallen on this ship, they had bled into its planks, they had driven back the desperate colonial ship, and men had died there, too. This suffering beneath his hands was very real, a taste of a witnessed event without need of imaginary embellishment, and it was his responsibility, as the posterity this program had been created for, to appreciate what he was seeing for the truths it displayed.

But it was time for him to get some rest, and then command his starship again. Picard found himself oddly disappointed to return to the twenty-fourth century. It was a transition he would have to make several times in the next few days, and it never ceased to be disconcerting.

The next evening, Picard and Alexander returned to the ship, the program waiting patiently for their return to the 1700s.

Until the sun sank into the milky sky, they cleaned the ship and sorted the dead from the dying from the might-live. Picard and Alexander both engaged in a crash course of squaring away a ship after a battle. The cannons had to be lashed down and cleaned. The wounded had to be tended with the eighteenth-century version of voodoo they called medicine, and, though appalling, it involved more common sense than Picard would've expected. He knew he had been guilty of disparaging the past as primitive, but they weren't really primitive. They simply hadn't the advantage of several more centuries of brilliant shoulders upon which to prop themselves. They were far more on their own than he had ever been, and he gained respect for them as this battered ship and crew saw to themselves without the advantage of retreating to a starbase for repairs and treatment. Whatever happened to them, they *had* to handle it.

He and Alexander became intimately part of that, and were learning very fast. Inevitably, the moment came when Picard, officer or not, helped carry a wounded man below.

What a heart-punching experience—he grimaced as his fingers sank into the blood-drenched flesh of the agonized sailor. The deck beneath his feet was gritty with a stew of powder grains, splinters, and blood. He fought to keep from retching.

Every "old" sailing vessel or museum ship he had ever visited had been clean as newspun cotton and had no particular odor. The cotton, oakum, and pitch once used to caulk decks had ages ago been replaced by epoxy and some kind of synthetic that looked the same, but wasn't as messy.

This ship was different. It wasn't a replica, or even a museum preservation. It was the real thing, in full function.

The moment his head went under the deck supports of the companionway hatch, his innards heaved under the assault of fumes of sulfur, tar, pitch, coal, bilge water, blood, oil-soaked sisal ropes, and the slimy excuse for drinking water. Eternal dampness pervaded the stenchy darkness, and for several minutes he could barely stay conscious. Every breath brought a wash of nausea. He was glad Alexander was up on the deck. Some things a boy should not have to endure. No lesson was worth this.

Even as he entertained that revelation, two boys younger than Alexander dashed past with lanterns, heading down the gloomy, stinking orlop deck, crunching on the sand-coated deck. Powder monkeys.

Children aboard a fighting ship . . .

If he had cherished any fantasies about living this way, they now faded fast.

Four hours later, the main deck was cleared of wreckage and wounded, the cannons were cooling, the ship's carpenters were shoring up the holes blown in *Justina* by iron balls, crew were scrubbing the blood from the decks—and so, by the way, was Alexander—and there was talk of rowing ashore to pick out a tree that could replace part of a topmast that had been shattered.

Order was slowly and deliberately returning, with a remarkably steady sobriety. No one complained. Even the wounded resisted their moans. It was a sight to behold.

Picard was indulging in a moment of admiration when a young man in a uniform jacket approached him, a fellow who at second glance couldn't have been more than sixteen years old. But wearing an officer's uniform. A yeoman?

"Mr. Picard, sir," the young man began, "Mr. Pennington's regards, and would you please assign two men to assist the afterdeck brace splicing."

"Regards to Mr. Pennington, and you may select any two men who are not right in the middle of something else."

"Very good, sir."

"Oh, and Mister—I'm sorry, my boy, what's your name again?"

The young, dark-haired fellow's brow furrowed, as if he thought Picard must have got a knock on the head. "Nightingale, sir. Midshipman Edward Nightingale."

"Oh, yes—I'm sorry. Must be the smoke."

"Aye, sir."

"When you've discharged your current duty, report back to me, please."

"I will, sir."

The young man was skinny and long-legged, as tall as Picard but half the weight. He hadn't gained his late-teenage meat yet, though there were signs of that coming.

"And, Mr. Nightingale, bring that boy over there with you when you come back."

"The swab? Oh, aye, sir."

He watched Nightingale hurry back across the scrubbed deck, and once again scanned the working crew. Which of these men was Alexander's ancestor? Was he lying wounded below, perhaps? How many days of this program would they have to endure before singling him out?

Alexander's relatives, who had saved this diary program and passed it along to him, had never specified the ancestor's name. They thought part of the exercise was for Alexander to find the man.

But Picard had a ship to run, and a tinderbox situation on the planet of Sindikash to handle. Riker would interrupt the holodeck experience if necessary, however, and the ship was hovering just outside Sindikash's sensor range, waiting for Worf's reports.

Beyond that, the ship would run itself. Like the captain of this frigate, he also had lieutenants whose job it was to mind specific decks and departments. No point hovering about, micromanaging. He wasn't actually inclined to do so, though he felt the tug of other responsibilities. He had learned better many years ago, when he himself was officer of the watch.

Standing here on this old-fashioned deck, with the sunset of the past glowing on his face and neck, he felt as custodial about this British frigate as he did about his own ship, for in many ways this small vessel needed him more.

At least, today it did.

Today, the H.M.S. *Justina* was in hostile waters, thousands of miles from a friendly port, defending what her captain, officers, crew, and king believed was right.

And he had a boy's idea of honor to tend. He mustn't forget that.

A week ago, he might've huffed off the concept that a twelve-year-old child's view of the universe would be important to him. Something was different, now that Worf had made this request of him. The universe had gotten a little smaller.

Ah, here came the boys.

Alexander's white shirt was drenched from the chest down with blood-streaked water. Behind him came Mr. Nightingale, expectantly looking at Picard.

"Mr. Nightingale," Picard began, "I'd like to have you give this lad a quick lesson in the structure of this ship and its rigging."

The midshipman blinked, confused. "Sir?"

"You heard me," Picard said, clasping his hands behind him. "It's an exercise for you both. Please begin."

"Oh . . . " Nightingale paled somewhat, as if afraid he were being tested, as Picard had carefully implied. "Yes, sir. Here, swab, pay attention."

Alexander frowned at the nickname, and Picard wondered if there were indeed some powder monkey on this ship who had been given that nickname. Just as he himself had been given the position of a lieutenant who probably did exist, Alexander seemed to be taking the place of a boy who had really been here.

"That's the bow and bowsprit," Nightingale began, quite obviously uneasy with this simplistic, even weird, assignment. "The rigging from there to the masts are called stays. The sails running on the forestays are heads'ls. The supports athwartships are the shrouds, which come down to deadeyes and lanyards, and are affixed to the chainwales on the outer hull. We have three masts, fore, main, and mizzen, and raise five sails on the fore and main, which would be the course, the lower and upper tops'ls, then the t'gallants and royals. The mizzen is rigged with a fore-and-aft spanker and a tops'l . . . "

Leaning toward Alexander, Picard muttered, "Sounds like Mr. Data and Engineer LaForge having a technical debate in the engine room, doesn't it?"

Alexander grinned conspiratorially and nodded.

Midshipman Nightingale paused, glanced at Picard to judge whether or not this lesson were too entirely idiotic to believe, but since he got no disapproval from his senior, the young man struggled on.

"We carry twenty-four guns and a squadron of marines. Uh . . . the fore and mains'ls are squares, and they're suspended from yards, and the painted part on the ends are the yardarms. The sails are lowered and hoisted by halyards, swung about with brace lines, furled with clews and bunts, adjusted by sheets, um, which are all called running rigging, on account of they're moving about—"

"All right, enough," Picard interrupted, letting him off the hook. "Well done, Mr. Nightingale. Alexander, you will be quizzed later."

Both boys stared at him as if he'd grown—well, hair.

Satisfied, he nodded and glanced up at the rigging, hoping it wasn't obvious that he was, in fact, stapling all those cursory details into his mind. Running rigging, standing rigging, clew bunt somethings, main, fore, so on. All right, so he'd missed a bit. Some of the tangle of lines and cables was beginning to make sense enough that he needn't embarrass himself. There was a certain amount of cooperation any holoprogram required of its user. If he failed to do his part to understand and fit in, the computer program would twist itself into knots, and Alexander's lesson would go wanting.

Or take weeks.

As the sun set, the heat went out of the day. Now the breeze was almost chilly. Picard decided they must be somewhere north of the mid-United States. No farther south than Chesapeake Bay—

"Chesapeake Bay!" he uttered. "The *Chincoteague!* Of course. I should've realized."

"Pardon, sir?" Midshipman Nightingale asked.

Picard parted his lips to fumble out an explanation but was drowned out when a cannon was fired off their stern.

Nightingale spun around, scanned the water, and shouted, "Spider catchers! My God! Spider catchers!"

He lunged for the ship's bell and rang it viciously.

"Spider catchers!" he shouted again.

Pulling Alexander away from the ship's rail, Picard peeked over and scanned the water. Against the darkness he made out the forms of three small boats, about the size of whaleboats, perhaps twenty or twenty-five feet long, approaching the stern. Just as he looked, one of the boats flashed with a cannon shot directly on its bow. He saw the gun move independently of the body of the boat, and realized that at least one of these small attackers was armed with a swivel gun. Something that small could be reloaded much faster than the ship's cannons.

"All hands!" he called out. "All hands on deck!"

What the hell—somebody had to.

By now much of the crew had heard the bell, and with his shout they began pouring out of the hatches and companionways. The captain appeared on the afterdeck, with Pennington and two other officers. The captain of the marines appeared, only half-dressed, and peered over the side, then rushed below again to muster his sharpshooters.

In the raiding boats, the colonists were faster. About ten to a boat, they maneuvered their craft along the sides of *Justina* and opened fire with hand pistols and rifles.

On the ship's deck, several men stumbled and fell even as they scrambled to run out a gun or two. At least two cried out in pain.

The captain stooped to his left, and for a bad instant Picard thought he'd been struck, but, in fact, he was reaching to help Mr. Pennington, who had staggered to one knee. The first officer—hit!

The spider catcher flotilla skulled about in the ship's own shadow, almost invisible against the dark water. Picard peered over at them, trying to gauge their movements, but the complete lack of light was dumbfounding. The sun was a memory now and there was no moon, no stars through a descending cloud cover. Briefly he thought about lighting lanterns on deck, but wouldn't that provide excellent target practice for the assaulting flotilla?

Mr. Nightingale appeared beside him again. "They must be desperate, sir!"

"Desperate for what, Mr. Nightingale? What are they defending?"

"The Delaware Station Boatyard, wouldn't it be, sir?"

"Oh . . . yes, quite likely."

He was about to say, "Is that all?" but remembered that installations like boat-building operations, docks, supply stores, and anything else that mobilized the enemy was always a target in wartime. Military installations were few in colonial America, for there was little formal military, no navy to speak of. A few shabby fortifications here and there, and a loose militia of untrained colonists, but that was all.

The captain came to midships, where he could see what was happening, assessed the problem, and turned to one of the other officers. Then that officer turned to the foredeck and said, "Raise heads'ls, Mr. Picard."

"Aye, sir," Picard responded, and turned to the nearest bunch of crewmen. "Hands to the heads'ls, please."

Five . . . seven . . . nine, ten crewmen came rushing to the bow of the ship, and he met them there. They busily unmade eight coils, and three men unfurled the headsails, though that meant climbing out onto the bowsprit and possibly becoming targets. They were single-minded despite the booming of pistol shots and the response from Marine Captain Newton's sharpshooters, who had rushed out onto the deck. There were cries from wounded men every few moments as shots hit home on the spider catchers, and also from them to the deck of the British ship.

"Ready on the jib halyards, sir," one of the foredeck crew gulped.

"Acknowledged," Picard responded numbly. "Haul away."

They did, and the triangular jibs ran up the stays, popped full of the offshore breeze and tightened to life, giving the ship some steerage way. The bow began swinging inward toward the land, turning the broadside of the ship toward the spider catchers who had been hiding in the ship's aft quarter shadow. He felt the connection between the hull and the water, the sails and the wind, and even through his boots felt the rudder bite deep. By golly, there *was* some fun to this.

And he saw the logic to it. The spider catchers were on the port side, using their swivel gun to blow damage into the ship's sides every few minutes, and trying to pick off the sailors with hand weapons. Now that the ship was turning on the breeze from offshore, she was putting her stern to the small attacking boats and slowly bringing her starboard side around—her starboard side, where men had been quickly loading the main deck midships guns.

"Fire, Mr. Simon."

Foom! The first gun went off at the captain's steady direction, and its response was a clap of water only inches from the stern of the nearest spider catcher.

"Next gun, please. Fire."

The second gun went off.

Instantly, the spider catchers' boat broke in half, spilling its men into the sea. Those still alive swam frantically toward another boat, whose oarsmen were quickly drawing away from *Justina.*

"Are they giving up?" Alexander asked.

Their oars dashing the water white, the spider catchers coordinated their efforts and stroked hard to put distance between themselves and the deadly bite of the marines' rifles, not to mention the starboard cannons.

Still . . . something was odd about this. Why would they come all the way out here, only to quit so soon? That wasn't the nature of rebels. If the British won this war, the colonists would remain colonists, and the price of their audacity would be high and brutal.

Just as the last few marines fired off considered shots into the dark night, Picard felt a sickening lurch come up through his feet and legs, and he was thrown sideways into Nightingale, and both drove into the ship's rail.

Right through the deck he felt the consistency of the sandy bottom—soft, mushy, gritty, but plenty hard enough to stall the ship.

He realized instantly what had happened. The *Justina* had been duped by these men who knew these waters, teased into turning inward toward shore. Although there appeared to be water for another quarter mile, indeed it was shallow water. They were aground.

Aground, and under attack!

CHAPTER 7

"OH, BEAUTIFUL! COME HERE, PRECIOUS, RIGHT UP HERE ON MY LAP. YOU, too, honey. There we go. Isn't this nice?"

Holographers, cameras, video equipment, sensor broadcasters, and every manner of recording device available on Sindikash hummed merrily as the governor's wife gathered several handicapped children against her, drawing two of them up onto her lap.

The governor's mansion was decorated for the holiday of the founding of Sindikash, which would come in three weeks. Traditional colors were gold, purple, and black, so banners and ribbons of those danced about the halls, and wreaths of grape vines with fake plastic grapes were hung on every window and over the mansion's massive stone hearths, which were virtually symbols of Sindikash themselves. Most homes had these chunky hearths, or at least a mock version, and they were traditional in the lobbies of most public buildings. Sindikash liked its traditions.

Worf was getting tired of tradition. He wanted to be on the ship, with his son, celebrating his own tradition, but instead he was here, standing beside the entrance, standing guard over somebody else's.

Back in the quarters he and Grant shared now that they were Rogues, Grant was pecking away at an old style computer terminal, trying to find the track he spoke of, the trail that would tie Odette Khanty to her seedy network.

Worf, Ugulan, and the other Rogues had just come back from space, limping back on the freighter they had failed to "deliver" to Sindikash authorities on the Cardassian border. Worf hoped his message would get through to Picard that the trick had come off as planned. The heavily coded message had been sent along very thin civilian lines, through several trading packets and one drunken lightship keeper. Might take four or five days.

Could he keep Grant safe for five days? The election was ticking closer with each day. They barely had a week left.

He and Grant were completely isolated on Sindikash. Communication with the ship was rare, costly, slow, and dangerous. Any quicker method would attract attention or trip signals. The two were on their own, and that meant Grant's life was in Worf's hands.

He started to wonder if teaming up with a close friend might not be a ghastly mistake.

With some effort, he managed to stuff down those thoughts. Again.

One room beyond the executive office, the comatose governor lay in his sickbed, hooked up to several machines that were monitored by doctors in a small in-house clinic one floor below this. The door to the governor's room was open, and the end of the bed visible, with the unconscious man's feet creating an uneven bulge in the red blanket.

Worf watched Odette Khanty with the children, hugging and smiling, letting them tug at her hair, as the image of her with them was teleported all over the planet, into the perception of the Sindikash public.

"So wonderful," she murmured, then laughed. "All right! Let's just send all of you down to the mezzanine to have ice cream and mints!"

The children cheered and clapped, and she clapped with them. Then a gaggle of aides and parents helped the children out of the room and down the wide carpeted hall, leaving only the media with their recording equipment and lights.

Mrs. Khanty stood up, still aglow with the adoration of the children, and held her hands out graciously to the reporters. "Anything else I can do for you today, anyone?"

From the back of the small crowd, a reporter asked, "Mrs. Khanty, what about allegations tying you to the explosion at the Lowelli Granary in the Great Eastern Territory? And about the Sindikash One-Four Transport? Rumors say there were two witnesses about your involvement with that explosion aboard Sindikash One-Four. Is that true?"

Mrs. Khanty controlled her expression masterfully, putting forth a beaming face of sympathy for the reporter. "I understand your feeling obligated to ask those kinds of questions, and all I can say is that there's no evidence linking me or anyone around me with any such event. There's simply no evidence. And I can't help it if some people are so consumed by greed and hate that they say evil things about us. We simply have to rise above all that."

"Thank you, ladies and gentlemen," Paul Stefan, Mrs. Khanty's assistant said, interrupting gracefully. The boyish-faced young man motioned them toward the door. "Mrs. Khanty has had a very busy morning. Don't forget tomorrow morning at ten—we're going to allow several of you to film Mrs. Khanty as she tends the governor. Those will be the first public viewings of the governor since the assassination attempt."

The reporters and cameramen murmured their thanks, but no one threw any more questions back.

"If you'll excuse us now," Stefan continued, "see you in the morning, Nick . . . thank you, Max, nice to see you . . . Celia, thank you for coming . . . Louisa, you lost weight!"

Mrs. Khanty nodded and chatted with a few reporters who cooed with the thrill of being so close to her. Their obsequiousness gave Worf a twisting stomach.

Finally, Stefan managed to herd them all out, and he went with them to make sure none "strayed."

He closed the office door behind him.

"Scan," Mrs. Khanty said instantly to Ugulan.

While Ugulan took out his old style tricorder and scanned the room for any devices that may have been left behind, Mrs. Khanty went to the sink in the kitchenette and ostentatiously washed her hands, making sure to scrub between the fingers and halfway up her arms.

"Dirty urchins," she grumbled out loud with a visible shudder. "Their fingers are always sticky. Why can't their parents keep them clean? Filthy, smelly embryos. Why do people have children? Ugulan!"

She came back into the outer reception room, her face flushed now, her expression thoroughly different than that which had met the cameras.

"Ugulan, get your pack of swine in here, you beetle-headed cur!"

"Yes, Mrs. Khanty." Ugulan put down his tricorder and whipped out a communicator, quickly signaling the Rogues without a word. Since they were just outside, guarding the hallway, they arrived in seconds and came crowding through the marquetry doorway.

By then, Mrs. Khanty had finished drying her hands and was standing with her face to a wall, her shoulders tense and her head slightly bowed.

Worf sharpened to some kind of attention. Disgust rolled through his stomach as the Rogues filed in, silent as statues, and one by one took positions along the wall, and even behind furniture, if possible.

How he hated to be in their company! To be dressed as they were, to be counted as one of them, to walk through the streets, assumed to be a Rogue! He watched the procession with uneasy curiosity and roiling animosity, and the moment slowly became surreal.

Seven Klingon warriors, fully armored, fully armed, holding the only energy handweapons allowed on the planet, other than law enforcement officers. They stood with their shoulders pinned to the walls and their eyes unfixed. Some of the toughest warriors in the quadrant now steeled themselves to face a single human female.

I am not one of them, yet I drown in their shame. When can I finish this?

The antique clock on the mantel ticked passively, its pendulum ushering in a creeping dread. The single window, with its leaded glass panels and stone frame, made Worf long to be anywhere but here.

"Luck."

Odette Khanty's first word was as soft as dripping rain. Worf had to strain to hear it.

She was still facing the desk. Across from Worf, against the far wall, Ugulan's face was forward but his eyes were on the woman. His fists clenched and unclenched repeatedly.

"Nothing but luck. Certainly brains weren't involved."

Mrs. Khanty seemed to be speaking to herself, as if reading something on the desk before her.

"Or loyalty."

Slowly she turned now, eyes down to the woven carpet's bundled flowers and Paisley scrolls. Her arms remained at her sides, her hands fanned out somewhat, as if she meant somehow to steady herself.

"Endangered my plans for this planet . . . a mission worth more than all your lives and all your mothers' lives. A chance to slander our opposition and get everything we want in one sweeping blow. And you couldn't follow through. Couldn't do one thing right. Wouldn't follow through on the promises you made. How can I ever trust any of you again? What am I going to do *now?*"

The word "now" came out like a slap. She suddenly raised her head so sharply that her hair bounced in punctuation.

Her face had changed. This one—Worf had never seen this face before. Her dark-smudge brows were flat, tight, the grooves around her lips suddenly defined, and her eyes were severe as dry ice. In them were both contempt and pure rage, as if she were dressing down a demure protégée who had unexpectedly said a bad word.

Worf's face turned hot from bitterness and embarrassment for the whole Klingon race. He had tried all his life to be an individual, to resist taking the course of this group or that faction, or even this or that culture, but today he was a clutching mass of Klingon, both aggravated that a human woman was dressing down those who should be warriors, and yet pleased that Ugulan and these low-lifes had to endure being chastised like children.

They deserved it!

Step by step, Odette Khanty strode slowly down the middle of the office area, not looking any Rogue in the face, her eyes instead fixed on the carpet. None looked at her.

"Do you have any idea . . . what I could arrange to have done to you?"

She passed the last Rogue, turned around, and slowly strode back. She looked at none of them. Her eyes fixed upon the wall at the opposite side of the room.

"Do you comprehend how far," she went on, "you would have to run?"

The clock clicked, then bonged. *One, two, three . . .*

"The sewers you would have to hide in?"

Five, six.

"There's only one real man among you. If not for him," she said with a sharp gesture at Worf, "where would I be?"

Worf stiffened and held his breath. *Marvelous! To be a superior weed among a field of chaff! What am I now?*

As its heavy knob clacked, the office entrance door brushed open against the thick carpet. One of the teenaged pages stepped in, carrying a bundle of wood for the fireplace's evening fire. Fire was completely symbolic on Sindikash, a custom to have most nights. A warmth of spirit and connection with the difficult past.

But not tonight.

The page stopped, stared, realized what was happening, found himself skewered on Odette Khanty's glare, and ducked out without even turning around. The heavy door clunked shut, and two of the Rogues winced at the sound.

Mrs. Khanty glared at the door, frozen in her fury.

Then she turned to the Rogues, and started looking them in the eyes, one by one.

In the next minutes, hell itself found voice.

CHAPTER 8

"MRS. KHANTY . . . YOU SENT FOR ME."

"Worf. Yes, I sent for you. One moment, please . . . all right, now . . . you were the one who kept the freighter from being captured by Starfleet."

"How do you know?"

"I know. Why did you do that?"

"Because . . . I would rather not specify."

The private office smelled of the wood fire burning at the other end of the room. Wood fires were popular on Sindikash, though unnecessary as of fifty or so years ago. Worf stood before Odette Khanty, who sat passively behind her carved 18th century barrister's desk. He felt strangely small. Somehow the comforting smells and old-fashioned decor made him aware of how out of place he was. Every fiber of the carpet was another twist in the tightrope he walked.

She was wearing a thick velvet robe of some kind with brocade sleeves and a satin collar, posing Worf with an image of casual royalty. The robe must have possessed some kind of sentimental value, for the end of one sleeve was a bit frayed and no one had repaired it.

Worf was in privileged quarters here, for he was upstairs from the governor's recovery suite, and no one—no one—came up here without personal and confirmed request by Mrs. Khanty and without jumping four or five hoops of security clearance. The fact that he was here, without any other guards, came as a message to him, direct from her.

"Then I'll specify for you," the woman said steadily, unintimidated by his presence or his size. "Because Ugulan and the other Rogues were going to let themselves be captured instead of destroying themselves as they swore to me they would. You didn't want to be captured. But you also didn't want to die. Isn't that right?"

"True." Straightening his back, Worf looked over Mrs. Khanty's head at the sculpture of a hawk on a wall shelf and allowed himself to be honest for one flashing second. "I am not a man who will die easily."

The governor's wife leaned back in her chair, which with its drape of embroidered fabric looked more like a throne—and she knew that. Her neatly done hair fingered her shoulders. Her cheekbones caught the pale light.

"But you didn't let yourself be captured either," she said.

At her candid tone, Worf relaxed his stance and looked her in the eyes. For the first time, he felt as if he could speak as something of an equal.

"That would have been bad for both of us, Mrs. Khanty," he said. "I am absent without leave from Starfleet, and you . . . "

He deliberately paused, but continued sparring with that firm gaze. He told her with that gaze that he knew what she was.

"Yes," she murmured. "This was my chance to suck twenty percentage points away from the lieutenant governor. I could've handily won the election. Now, it'll be close. I don't like 'close.' I'm down to three days now. What can I do in three days? Do you know what will happen to you and all the Rogues if I lose?"

Several possible answers of varied degrees of intensity ran through his mind. Finally he plucked one. "The lieutenant governor will take action against us."

Mrs. Khanty did not smile, nor did she in any way offer tacit approval.

"No," she said. "I will."

He stood before her in the amber aura of the imitation gaslights that pervaded the compound, and said nothing.

"I have an assignment for you," she went on, "which is going to put you over the line into my complete trust. The Rogues have to pay for their cowardice."

Worf frowned in protest, abruptly defensive about Klingons and cowardice fielding the same sentence. Right through his sudden distaste at defending the Rogues, he said, "It was not their fault that the Starfleet scout picked up the freighter."

"Not that part," Mrs. Khanty agreed. "It's this other part. We had a pact. They swear allegiance to me, stay on my planet, enjoy expatriate status here, be my elite guard, gain influence and power, and in return they swore they would self-immolate before letting themselves be caught, which would cast me under suspicion. They didn't hold up to that pact. They understand there's a price. They will have to pay it. I want you to be the collector."

The heat from a burning log snapping in the fireplace pressed against the back of Worf's neck. Mrs. Khanty was completely unreadable. There was no inflection in her words, no evil gleam in her eye, no conniving enjoyment, no sultry threat. She might as well have been speaking to a chef while arranging a banquet menu.

"Choose any one of them. Make sure you don't leave any flotsam," she added, without waiting for him to accept the assignment. "I can't have this kind of thing happening again."

She paused then, and folded her hands on her lap, and crossed her legs. And waited.

He stood before her and simply could not think of a single thing to say. How did one accept a job to kill someone else just to make a point?

Since he first heard Commissioner Toledano's claim that Klingons had inflicted torture and callous murder, he had wanted to kill. His gut had churned since that moment until this moment, and now he felt as if his innards had been pulled out. He was being handed a chance to kill a dishonorable Klingon. He could do it in the line of duty. He *could* do it . . .

"One question," Worf said. "You have not asked me for my oath of allegiance. May I ask why?"

"Because I wouldn't get it, would I?"

"No."

Mrs. Khanty was evidently not interested in his oath or too used to no one's ever defying her. She seemed perfectly comfortable with the situation.

She nodded, once.

"With or without an oath, don't betray me, Worf," she said. "It's not a good idea."

• • •

"You should've whipped out your badge and arrested her! This is great! We've got her! She just asked a Starfleet officer to go out and assassinate somebody so she could get her revenge and keep her hoods in line!"

Ross Grant spread his arms in victory, not taking it personally that he hadn't been the one to "crack" Odette Khanty's pretty cover. He spun about the room like wind, amazed at the audacity of their opponent.

Inwardly grateful for his friend's generosity, Worf sadly shook his head. "She said it was an 'assignment.' Someone had to 'pay the price.' She told me to be 'the collector.' She was very careful. She said nothing that might not be taken in some innocent way, given some other context. And you know how skillful she is at twisting facts."

"Do I!"

"Also, she made sure we were alone. There were no other witnesses. Sindikash law requires two, not one."

Grant started to say something, paused, then shook his head. "Yeah, right, well . . . yeah, I know that, I know . . . damn."

Glad not to have to make that point again, Worf sat down to adjust his boot. As he watched his fingers work down there, all he saw was those two knarled hands, strong and trained, closing around a Klingon throat.

"The larger problem still remains. She wants me to kill one of the Rogues as an example. If I do it, then she will trust me."

"Oh, you bet," Grant uttered. "She wants to kill two birds with—well, you know what I mean."

"Yes," Worf sighed, "and if I fail to do it, we could lose our chance to get you 'inside.' "

"Hell, don't do that! Whatever happens, we can't let that happen. I'm the only thing she can't be careful against."

Worf buckled his boot again and sat straight. His eyes ached from all these hard thoughts. "Yes . . . and in order to keep her trust, I must earn it by completely incriminating myself. She and I will be obligated to each other."

Grant shrugged. "Standard mob procedure. Make your henchmen do something they definitely don't want to get caught doing, make sure all the right people know it was done, so you're not the only one committing crimes. Then they gotta stick with you. Oldest story in the book. Seen it a dozen times."

Frustrated, Worf only nodded.

"Y'know," Grant added, "this is a big step you've taken here. From what I've been finding out, she used to give these special jobs to Ugly-an. Now he's out and you're in. You watch out for that guy, bud. I don't want you coming back without arms."

"I intend to keep my arms," Worf assured, and stood up. He drew a choppy breath, held it briefly, let it out, then headed for the doorway. "Be sure to lock yourself in."

"Hey!" Grant called. "Where're you going? You shouldn't be going out alone. You want me to go with you?"

"Not this time." Worf yanked the door open, squared his shoulders, and forced himself not to look back. "I have a Klingon to kill."

The midnight sky lay upon the domes of the city complex. Gothic spires toyed with low-lying clouds. The scent of wet grass and steamy wool rode an inbound breeze from the herd of American bison grazing passively in the valley just outside of town.

Cafes and clubs murmured with laughter and music, from the twang of mandolins to the whistle of clarinets. Sindikash was a comfortable place with a great deal to lose.

Mud. Rain had come lately, but briefly. The cobblestones were greased, hard to walk upon. His boots slipped as he moved, and each slip injected him with a tremble of insecurity. This was not a good place to be.

In the darkness of the alley between a church and a post office, he could see nothing.

Not even his own hands.

He should not have come alone. No one alone was safe on Sindikash.

Since he was a child he had a sense of when there was someone else around. His father had been the same way. Suspicious.

Everything made him suspicious. The shivering wind. The click and whistle of music. The pale flickering lights from the street beyond, which caused a bizarre doorway of silver fog in the distance. That was the end of the alley. He wished to be there, so his spine would cease its quaking. This was a bad time to go alone.

As his hunger for the angled light at the end of the alley grew, he realized he was already halfway through. Now he could not turn back safely. He would have to go all the way through. How many steps had brought him to this point? How many were left? Usually he counted his steps. Tonight he had forgotten.

A buffalo mooed in the deep night. He longed to be among them, where the jab of a blade or the lance of a phaser might be blocked by a quick dive behind a furry body. Protection, protection . . .

The mouth of the alley glowed like battle before him. He wanted to be there. His own heartbeat pounded from his hips to his head with a drum that blinded him to all but the far light and its tinsel curtain of mist.

Step, step, mud, slip, feel absurd, balance, step again—

Suddenly his left knee buckled and shot out from beneath him. His spine screamed as it slammed to the mud-slicked cobblestones. One of them struck the back of his skull, dazing him abruptly and blurring the vision overhead of the tops of the buildings and the gauzy sky.

Then hands—fists—at his throat, dragging him to his feet—he struggled to react, but his hands were tingling from the fall and for a critical instant he couldn't even find them.

Dizziness spun through his skull and his equilibrium snagged as someone hauled him to his feet—and no one could do that but another Klingon.

In an instant of panic, he clamped his numb arms to his chest, clumsily hoping to protect his vital organs from the blade bite he knew was coming—

But none came.

"Walking alone in the city," a voice rumbled before his blurred eyes. "Not very wise, Genzha."

"Worf! You!"

Genzha pressed back against the brick church, wildly thinking that he might be able to use the wall as a brace, but before he could raise hand or knee, or find his own dagger with these numb fingers, his arms were pinioned behind him and clasped with some kind of strap.

Unbidden fear dashed through him as he realized that he was being held down by a professional, trained soldier—a Starfleet-trained soldier.

Surprised that he wasn't dead yet, Genzha gasped, "But Ugulan is the one! I was watching out for Ugulan! She chose you to do this instead of him?"

"She chose me. A strange universe we live in, where nothing is certain for long."

"What do you want? I sicken of your gloating!"

"I want you to remain very quiet." Worf's breath was hot against Genzha's ear. "Walk before me, and we'll talk about who lives until morning, and who dies."

"Transporter room to Riker."

"Riker here. Data, what are you doing in the transporter room?"

"The trainee requested that I come here to handle a situation. I am, in turn, requesting your advice."

"What've you got?"

"We accepted a parcel from Mr. Worf, sir, transported from an asteroid breaker, which picked it up from a Torkezzi fuel ship, which evidently received it from a container vessel out of Sindikash."

"Okay, what's in the parcel?"

"A very angry Klingon, sir."

"A Klingon!"

"Yes, sir. Evidently he was drugged until seven hours ago, when he awakened on board the breaker and let his dissatisfaction be known."

"Did he hurt anybody?"

"Negative, sir, his wrists and ankles were manacled. However he is very loud and no one could get close enough to gag him."

"Have you got him under control?"

"I succeeded in gagging him, sir."

"I guess there are advantages to being an android. Why would Worf send us a hogtied Klingon?"

"No idea, sir. We have only a request from Worf that the Klingon be detained in secrecy for an as yet undetermined period of time."

"Hmmm . . . all right, we'll do that, if he wants."

"Where would you like me to detain the Klingon, sir?"

"The brig. He'll be fine. Our brig is nicer than most."

"But the charges, sir? He can be detained only twenty-four hours without logging charges."

"I'll think about that. Just lock him up for now. Make him comfortable."

"Yes, sir."

"Data?"

"Yes, sir?"

"Not too comfortable."

"Understood, sir."

"Riker out."

"He's late. What has he got to do that makes him late for a meal? He has no assignment, he has no duty, he has no reason to be absent from a Rogue supper."

Worf listened to Ugulan's trumpeting with a touch of amusement and said nothing. He sat at the far end of a long table laid out nightly with Klingon food for the Rogues. They were expected to eat together. It was the only way they could interact. Or keep an eye on each other.

But Genzha was breaking the pact. He was not here in time for supper.

According to the agreement between themselves, they could not begin eating until all were accounted for.

And Worf was hungry. Hungry and satisfied. He'd had a chance to kill, and he had found his reserve. He wished Alexander had been there to see it. He wished Picard had been. He wanted somebody to know.

And why not? What good was control unless he could gloat over it a little?

He glanced around at his ready-made audience. In a minute, they would all be afraid of him. He liked that.

"Genzha," he said, "will not be joining us."

Ugulan's eyes widened and he rounded on Worf. "What do you know? Where is he?"

Worf leaned a casual elbow upon the table and picked up a stick of rolled meat. "He will no longer be with us. That is what I know."

The other Rogues—Mortash, Tyro, all—suddenly turned stiff with realization, stared at Worf, then glanced at each other. None seemed to know what to say.

Also staring at Worf, Ugulan seemed the most shocked of all—Worf had just stolen his job.

Worf punctuated his point by taking a bite of the rolled meat stick.

Then, quite unexpectedly, Mortash broke out in a barroom laugh that rolled along the carpet-hung walls. He scooped up his tankard, raised his glass to Worf, and indulged in a deep swig. Tyro and Kev laughed then too, and soon Tyro and the other Rogues nodded in satisfaction and plunged into their food.

Momentary confusion gripped Worf as he tried to figure out what was happening. Why were they laughing?

These were not just guards—they were Klingon guards. Expatriates or not, Klingons needed structure. That was the reason for the supper together ever day, for their pact with Odette Khanty, and their agreements between themselves. Evidently, it was no mystery to them that one of their own had disappeared. Worf expected them to take revenge upon him for his actions against another Klingon, and his legs were tense for the fight he thought had been coming.

Yet they weren't reacting that way at all.

Suddenly he understood what was going on. What he saw around him, this bizarre cheerfulness—except for Ugulan—was pure relief! They knew one of them was destined to "pay" for the freighter incident, and now that debt had been fulfilled. And each Klingon was glad it wasn't paid with his blood. He realized with some loss that these were not only not particularly good Klingons, but not particularly good people.

They were cowards! Shameful!

His appetite withered. He put down the meat stick. All he did now was watch the others wolfing down their dinner.

They ate their meal with the joviality of water purging over a dam, gushing merrily past a blockade that had minutes ago seemed insurmountable. They talked and gulped, back-slapped, chewed and laughed in some kind of purging, and even seemed to be enjoying each other's company.

All but Worf, and Ugulan. The two rivals sat in silence.

And they watched each other.

CHAPTER 9

IF WORF HAD NOT BELIEVED IN WITCHCRAFT, HE DID NOW. SHE HAD SPUN A spell of underlying fear that could not be lightly banished.

Worf felt the lingering heat of that spell. He was sustained only by the thought of the starship backing him up and the fact that he did not have to stay here much longer.

Amazing! She had made Klingons afraid!

There must be something more to her than meets the eye, he thought, cherishing his shoulder sockets and appreciating possession of his elbows. He quickened his pace as he crossed the brightly tiled Burkal City Central Courtyard to the onion-domed Rogue apartments. Sindikash posed a stirring Orient-express sensation, and Worf found the escape from Mrs. Khanty's domination to be a relief.

So much shame, he thought. *To want refuge from an enemy I could lift with one arm. I must be getting old.*

He hurried into his quarters, glancing around as he ducked behind the curtain of wooden beads and through the heavy oak arched doorway.

In the small chamber, utilitarian in spite of the warm carpets on the walls and the stenciled ceilings, Grant hunched over a portable computer terminal whose screen cast a shifting glow upon his tired face.

"How are you doing?" Worf asked.

Ross Grant shook his head in strange admiration. "Captain Picard's plan worked great. You're in tight with her. She's dismissing two of Ugulan's choices from being her husband's private guard and installing you. Must've been some dilly of a cargo on that freighter."

"We are not even certain what the cargo was," Worf rumbled. "Can you find out?"

"I tried. Couldn't find it. Could be chemical poison for agricultural sabotage," Grant said. "She could strangle a whole planet by holding their crops hostage. She's into that lately."

"With her name involved?" Worf asked hopefully.

Grant shook his head and tapped at his computer. "Hell, no such luck! She's good. Damn, is she good. I never saw anybody with this much strata of coverage. We could only prosecute about halfway up to her. But look at this—one by one, everybody associated with her is being arrested. Her organization could crumble in ten minutes if we could find the one link tying her to all the stuff she's doing. It's weird, Worf—she's doing so *much* illegally that it's hard to get everything in your head that she's doing, but somehow that creates a tapestry that she just hides behind. She just shrugs and acts like she can't understand why anybody would be mean to her. But she's got this ruthless inner person—"

"I know," Worf commented. "She bolted the Rogues to the wall with words alone. She inflicted mortal fear into fully grown Klingon warriors. There is something more to her. They seemed in terror for their souls."

"They did? Wish I'd seen it! Bet it was a party."

Relaxing for the first time in hours, Worf sighed. "They were actually afraid of her."

"Why not? I sure am."

Grant leaned back, grimaced, stretched his arms and winced at the stiffness in his back and shoulders. Then he tapped his computer readout screen with one finger.

"I've got her whole organization in here. The Fed's right—she's jockeying to take over the planet and break off from the Federation so she doesn't have to follow anybody's rules but her own. Sindikash'll be a fortress of crime, and its people will be trapped inside. I got it all. Mountains of it. But there's nothing to tie *her* to it. Without that one shred of evidence linking her to a major crime, something that can be prosecuted, something simple enough for the people to understand, the planetary authorities won't have dink to go on." He looked up at Worf, his eyes drawn and tired. "I don't know what else to do."

"Continue working," Worf said. "Be a Rogue. Do your job. Then . . . we'll be here when she makes a mistake."

Grant looked up at him. "She doesn't make any, ever!"

"Everyone does." Putting his hand on the precious computer console with its raft of criminal charges aching to be made, Worf fixed his gaze on Grant. "You and I are inside now. We will be here when she makes her mistake. Or we will arrange one."

Jean-Luc Picard watched the spider catchers from a deck tilted fifteen degrees, expecting them to turn back, now that *Justina* was aground, and make some different sort of assault.

But they didn't. They kept hauling on their oars, scooping their comrades from the water, and rowing out of range.

"Captain! Captain!"

It was the helmsman calling. Picard almost answered. Instead, he turned to his foredeck crew and said, "Gentlemen, let those heads'ls go loose. They're only serving to push us over onto the shoal."

"Aye, sir," several of the men responded. They seemed ready to do exactly that, so he'd apparently thought right.

Without taking the moment to pat himself on the back, he noticed that quite a bit of this sailing-ship business simply involved common sense and simple observation. Rationally, of course, he knew he could commonsense around for a year and still not know everything. Still, the crash course was operative.

"Officers midships, please."

Picard looked at Nightingale and Alexander. "Come with me, boys."

They thunked across the deck planks sixty feet or so to midships, and joined the captain, the captain of the marines, and the other lieutenants. Picard moved next to Mr. Pennington, who was clutching a bloody right arm.

"You all right, Mr. Pennington?" he asked sociably.

"Well enough," the first officer rasped, obviously grappling with considerable pain. "The ball missed the bone."

"Let me bind it up for you."

The bulky man leaned back on the ship's rail. "Thank you . . . thank you very much. Very kind."

Picard glanced around and was gratified to receive Nightingale's instant donation of a black neckerchief.

The captain appeared around the mainmast after observing the retreat of the spider catchers. "We're aground, gentlemen," he said simply. "We have to get off immediately. There's also damage to the rudder from that swivel gun. Mr. Simon and the carpenter's crew are about to go offboard to attempt repairs. We must be able to steer the ship, or we are lost. Clearly, the insurgents will be coming back now that we're foundering. We must act quickly. We'll have to warp her out."

Tying a sturdy bandage around Pennington's wound, Picard smiled and shook his head.

"Is something funny?" Pennington asked.

"Oh, no, no, sir," Picard demurred. "Just thought of something else. Sorry."

Alexander pulled on his sleeve and whispered, "He said warp! Do they have warp speed?"

"No, no . . . this is where the phrase came from. It's rather comforting how little some things change."

"Mr. Picard?" the captain said sharply, annoyed by the murmuring. "You have something to suggest?"

Picard faced him. "Well, yes, sir. I'd like to volunteer to lead the away team—the landing party."

"Very well. Take Mr. Nightingale and one other fellow, and go ashore with a hawser. Make fast to a tree, and we'll use the capstan to reel the ship off the bar. Once we've done that, you shall unmake the line, travel north on the shore, make fast to another tree, and we'll warp the ship up the coast until we find better bottom. Mr. Chappell, run all but four of the guns inboard and secure them until we get off the bar."

A young lieutenant nodded. "Very good, sir."

"Let's station Captain Newton's marines on deck as security until we can run the guns out again."

"Aye, sir."

"And make certain the hold is secure also. I thought I felt some shifting."

"Aye, aye, sir."

"Oh, and Mr. Picard—"

"Sir?"

"Take along a marine with you as your armed guard."

Picard nodded. "Thank you, sir."

He pressed back a smile. This business of taking orders was downright nostalgic, and easier than he'd remembered. Been a long time. He found some comfort in it, letting somebody else decide.

"Take that marine," Alexander suggested excitedly, pointing at the tall blond fellow who had caught their eye before.

The captain had started to walk away, but now turned back. "Yes, fine, take the sergeant with you. Mr. Pennington, where do you believe we're aground?"

"Where, sir?"

"Where on the hull."

"Oh—midships, sir. Midships to the stern, sir."

"I'd say that as well. Better run six of the guns on each aft deck up forward of midships. Shift the weight off the aft keel. Pay out a heavy warping line . . . "

He paused, looked down at the tilted deck, and seemed troubled.

"Perhaps a spring line, sir?" Pennington suggested.

The captain nodded. "I was thinking that, but as I consider it now, I believe we'd rather swing the bow about. Run the line out the forward cathead."

"Aye, aye, sir."

"Oh, and while we're at this, best we station a boat midway between ourselves and Mr. Picard on the shore, to relay communication."

"Very good, sir."

Pennington summoned his resolve, mastered his pain, and hustled away, carrying all that on his shoulders, as the captain peered briefly at the shore, then also went aft.

Picard at once felt sympathy and admiration for these people, who had to come up with clever ways to do the simplest things, even communicating over short distance. In his time, he had only to push a button, and unthinkable technology allowed him to communicate through billions of kilometers of spatial vacuum. As he watched these officers try to work out their problems, he realized he was standing upon their accomplishments. Things were easier for him because things had been so hard for them.

On the other hand, they knew their enemy. The last man standing would be the winner. Picard never knew ahead of time whether the strange alien he encountered would befriend him, kill him, marry him, or eat him. In his universe, a person could step into a faulty transporter, and come out in the shape of a turnip.

Well, every generation had its burdens.

Short minutes later, he was in a row boat with Alexander, Nightingale, two deckhands who were acting as oarsmen, and the sergeant of the marine grenadiers, with his loaded rifle.

The sergeant wore a formal scarlet coat with white facings and brass buttons, but beneath that he wore a sailor's checked shirt and rather loose trousers, probably because he had been living aboard ship and the typical tight breeches and waistcoats were taxing in that environment. Picard had noticed that the grenadiers were usually indistinguishable from the sailors, except when engaged in battle. Then they put on their red coats and stiff-fronted yellow headgear with the embroidered letters GR—*George Rex.*

Of course. King George the Third.

The sergeant was a tall young man in his mid-twenties, perhaps a little over six feet, his hair as blond as Mr. Nightingale's was dark, and he possessed enviable cheekbones and a set of very Aryan blue eyes. He seemed a bit nervous, glancing at the dark shoreline, probably worried about snipers or a trap. He was not sitting, as the others all were. Instead he rested a knee on one of the slat seats, and balanced as well as possible there, with his rifle at the ready.

For a few precious minutes, while rowing toward the broccoli-bunch trees of the shoreline, there seemed to be peace in the bay. Behind them, a faint moon glowed through the haze, casting little light, but enough to make out the ghostly image of the ship against the gauzy night.

Picard paused for several minutes and just watched the ship, taking in the shape of the hull, the high transom, the heads'ls slapping loose, and the phantomish movement of dark, small men along her deck.

"It's so pretty . . . " Alexander was watching the frigate, too. As a child of space travel, he wasn't used to seeing the ships he lived upon except from the inside, and this was a whole different perception.

"There's the repair party," Picard said quietly, noticing a small boat with four men who appeared at the stern of the *Justina.*

"They're getting ready to fight again, aren't they?" the boy asked.

"Yes, repairing the damage to the rudder. The ship has to be able to maneuver or she's lost. The captain thinks another wave of attacks is coming."

"He thinks this is . . . a trap?"

"A wave of targeted attacks, yes. The colonists know they can't win against an armed frigate of Royal Navy seamen and soldiers with a direct attack. They have to weaken the enemy first."

Alexander scowled. "Doesn't seem honorable to me. They should come out in the open and fight."

"How would you fight against an enemy far larger, better trained, better armed, and well-financed? Come out and stand before him?"

"Isn't that better?" The boy turned to him. "Isn't that more honorable?"

So at least he hadn't forgotten why they were doing this.

Picard seized the moment. "Let's start with this—what do you think honor is, Alexander?"

At the bow, the grenadier sergeant snapped to look at him suddenly, and seemed about to say something, but Alexander spoke up without noticing that the sergeant's blue eyes were fixed on the two of them now.

"Honor," the boy began, "is winning."

Picard nodded, and gave him the courtesy of a pause. "But many win through dishonoring themselves. So there must be more to it."

The boy frowned, trying to visualize what he was talking about, and seemed to accept that things like that happened. He searched for another answer and finally decided to try one.

"Honor is . . . *how* you win, then."

"Mmm," Picard uttered, and glanced one more time at the ship. "I see I'll have to be more creative about this."

The Grenadier turned partly around, readjusting his stance in the shifting boat. "I'm sorry, sir, I do not know you. What is your name?"

"Picard."

"French?"

"Yes, as a matter of fact. Jean-Luc."

"But you sound quite British. And you serve the Royal Navy."

"Yes. I was educated at Oxford."

The marine puffed up a little, smiled with mischievous collegiate rivalry, and said, "Cambridge."

"You speak exceptional English," Picard observed, "but you're not English either, are you?"

The sergeant smiled. "My name is Alexander Leonfeld. I am Austrian. My father is the Fifth Duke of Leonfeld and my mother was born to the family of Gosch-Embourg."

Picard nodded as if he understood the significance. "Very nice."

And not really surprising. If Picard remembered his military history, marine sharpshooters were usually of high standing, even royal or peered birth. They were the most intelligent, the most educated, and were favored as choices if they came from respected, established families.

Mindful of his duty, Sergeant Leonfeld turned back toward the land and continued scanning for movement. He fitfully caressed his loaded rifle.

Alexander stared and stared at the sergeant, and finally he scooted closer to Picard in the stern of the boat.

"It's him!" the boy whispered.

"Pardon?"

"That's my ancestor!"

"How do you know?"

"Because his name is Alexander! I was named after him!"

CHAPTER 10

WITH HER KEEL BALLASTED BY NEW REVELATIONS, THE SMALL ROWBOAT surged toward the land, heaved up on a new tide every few seconds by the oarsmens' pull.

Picard drew Alexander very close and put his lips to the boy's ear. "Any other clues?"

The boy nodded vigorously. "He wasn't American or English," he whispered back.

"Mmm," Picard murmured. "Good clue."

"Alexander" was not an uncommon name in these times, and the *Justina* was tightly packed with crew and soldiers. Still, the holoprogram would likely shove Picard and Alexander together with the person they were supposed to be meeting, in a kind of cyber-destiny.

How clever that Alexander's relatives hadn't told him the name of the ancestor, but made him hunt for the man. Rather than striking straight for their quarry, Picard and Alexander had spent considerable hours, and a notable adventure, learning to understand the lifestyle, rather than just sitting and listening. Far better.

And now, here the man knelt, in this little boat. Alexander was watching the other Alexander with new eyes, the eyes of a boy gazing upon legend embodied.

Picard grimaced as the boat's keel rasped against the stony bottom, and they were ashore. Embarrassed by the flinch, he noted how very real all this had become for him in the past few hours, and hoped Alexander—the boy—felt the same. Of course, he realized again, this *had* happened. It wasn't a story. In moments, he and Alexander would step out onto a shore with young men who had been here, in these very woods at this very moment, for this was Alexander Leonfeld's journal of his American experience.

That night these woods had held this cloying chill, left over from the day's humidity, still tacky beneath their wool uniforms. These were times far before the sweat-wicking fabrics of Picard's age. That night, the moon up there had hovered in its shroud of haze and looked down with unhelpful dimness upon the H.M.S. *Justina,* and it was the same moon Picard now looked up to see. The moon of Chesapeake Bay, sometime in the summer of 1777.

He waited until the two oarsmen jumped out and dragged the boat farther up onto the gravelly shoreline. Then he, Alexander, and the other Alexander climbed out and together they all dragged the rowboat to a stable position, then came around to its stern to haul up the four-inch-diameter braided hawser that had come along with them, strung all the way from the ship. In fact, it was a modified dockline—really three docklines fixed to each other with two carrick bends, making it long enough to reach the shore.

Picard assisted in hauling the line ashore and directed his men to walk it several yards north of the ship's bow; then he himself selected a tree. With a certain small vestige of pride, he threw the bitter end of the meaty line into a clove hitch around the trunk. As he surveyed his handiwork with some satisfaction, he regretted being one of several upperclassmen at Starfleet Academy who had petitioned to have the marlinspike seamanship course dropped from the requisites. After all, what good was knot-tying and simple line repair to a Starfleet serviceman?

What good, indeed?

Luckily, the petition had been denied and he had grimly taken the course.

"Not bad," he muttered. "Thank you, Commander Graves. And I do apologize." Then he turned to the rocky shoreline and looked out at a second rowboat that was holding position midway between the shore and *Justina.* He cupped his hands around his mouth and shouted, "Haul away!"

From the small boat, the order was relayed to the ship: "Haul away, all!"

A moment or two passed as the efforts of the crew were coordinated on the ship's capstan bars. The capstan was essentially a large winch, pushed around by men holding baseball-bat-sized spokes. Ordinarily such a contraption was used to raise the anchor, but as today witnessed, there were other uses.

Hovering just under the surface of the water, the hawser danced tenderly with the tides, disappeared below, then came up again and into the carved cathead at the ship's bow. As movement on deck became steadier, the line began bouncing on the surface, then lapping the top as it grew shorter and tighter, drawn inboard by the turning capstan.

This was slow business. Picard couldn't quell a twitch of impatience.

He took a moment to glance at Alexander, and true enough to Picard's suspicions, the "swab" was staring unremittingly at his human ancestor. Alexander Leonfeld was oblivious to the attention, but stood, looking rather majestic, on the shoreline, his youth and stature adding to that scarlet uniform jacket with its white facings and gold buttons, still somehow bright in spite of weeks at sea, and his white leggings, and his long musket . . . yes, quite a figure, compared with a midshipman, a couple of deckhands, and a rather dour uncle-type whom the boy perceived only vaguely as a real ship's captain. Sergeant Leonfeld cut a statuesque form against the shimmering evening sea as he stood guard, his rifle ready, his eyes scanning the curving shoreline.

"It's up!" Nightingale rejoiced. Picard looked, and saw that the line had finally cleared the water and was now wagging like a giant jump rope, barely over the surface. Glittering droplets of water poured from its soaked braids. Gradually, the line lost its drape and became straighter and straighter.

Finally, at the tree, the line began to strain and groan. The tree spat bark and squawked as the tourniquet tightened. Picard and his landing party watched the ship. The line grew straighter, and stiffer.

Mired on the shoal, *Justina*'s great bulk began to heel over, her keel biting into the shoal as her weight shifted. If she didn't come off, she'd either be stranded, or she'd turn on her side altogether. The captain was letting her go over very far, until Picard could see the deck almost as a wall, tilted at forty or more degrees. Each degree attested to the captain's determination to deny the enemy this prize if he could. What was the code of honor here? Would the captain destroy his own ship before letting her be taken? Picard didn't remember the habits of the British Royal Navy at this time, but he also knew that several colonial fighting ships, and other ships during other wars, were often refitted enemy ships that had been captured. A captain could conceivably survive a battle, lose a ship, gain a new command, and find himself firing on the very vessel he had once commanded.

"Stand back, gentlemen," Picard said as the line grew tight and hard as stone. If the line parted, or one of the knots came free, it would whip back and shear someone's head off. Given the tenuous nature of this old-tech program, he couldn't take a chance of that being himself or Alexander.

"Mr. Picard!" Edward Nightingale gulped as if holding down his dinner, and pointed frantically out onto the water beyond the ship. "Look! Sir, look!"

Two more ships were swinging out of an inlet! One was a single-masted ship with a fore-aft sail, large enough to deck perhaps a half dozen cannon, but the other was a two-masted ship of about eighty feet. Both that ship's masts were square-rigged.

"More spider catchers are with them!" one of the two oarsmen said. "We gotta get on back!"

He struck off toward the rowboat, but Alexander Leonfeld plunged from his guard stance, caught the frantic sailor, and roughly held him back. "Bennett! We'll be ambushed on the water!"

The brawny sailor swung around and wrenched his arm back. "You can't order me! You're not a Navy officer!"

"But I am," Picard said, stepping between them. "Stand down, Mr. Bennett."

Sergeant Leonfeld still didn't let go of the panicked sailor, and that mastery of the moment reflected itself almost comically in Alexander's face as Picard glanced at the boy. Leonfeld was ankle-deep in shore water, but seemed uncaring of that. He was determined that this man not be sacrificed to an impossible situation.

Helpless, the men and the boy watched in soul-sick frustration as two attacking ships and the spider catcher boats opened fire on the stranded *Justina.* The cannon blasts wakened the settling night with bright orange flashes and bits of flaming material. Red-hot bits rocketed through the darkness and sliced into *Justina*'s heads'ls, ripping them to shreds and leaving the shreds burning.

"Canister!" Nightingale choked. "Dear God, that brig's using hot shrapnel against us! Oh, how impolite!"

Now, *that* Picard knew about. Bits of metal, nails, broken glass, heated up and poured into canisters, then fired out of a cannon, to blast apart in midair, scatter, and rip up anything it struck. It would set fire to sails and wood, and shred flesh on contact. Not nice.

Then again, neither was an armed phaser bank.

The *Justina*'s headsails were on fire now, causing the crew to scramble to put out the flames, thereby keeping them from efficiently returning cannonfire. Picard wished he could see what was happening on the deck as it tilted more and more.

The line—should they cut the line joining the frigate to the land? Or were the capstan men still pushing the bars? Still trying to warp the ship off the shoal?

No one had called from the relay boat. So far there was no order. And if the captain wanted the line cut, he could just as easily sever it from the deck.

The quiet bay at once became a hornet's nest. Cannonfire was met with vicious and sporadic response from the *Justina* as the British ship's crew struggled to run out her guns quickly. Rifle fire, though, cracked every few seconds from *Justina*'s deck. The grenadiers.

Beside Picard, Alexander Leonfeld's whole body quaked with the same helplessness Bennett had expressed. Shuddering, the grenadier sergeant suddenly raised his own rifle and took a quickly considered shot at one of the spider catchers. *Snap-flash-CRACK.*

And an eddy of acrid gunsmoke. Now his flintlock was empty. He rushed to reload it, while Alexander the swab gazed in mute adoration from a few steps away.

"Hold your fire, Mr. Leonfeld," Picard said quietly.

The sergeant looked up sharply and demanded, "Why should I?"

"Because you could hit our own men in the other rowboat. Look—they're trying to get back to the ship. And you'll also draw attention to us. That'll serve no good."

Leonfeld quaked with hopelessness, continued to load his flintlock—which took quite a few steps—but did not fire again.

Alexander said, "Captain . . . "

Picard looked, and noticed the boy speaking to him but still staring not at the ship, not at the water or the battle, but at Sergeant Leonfeld. Picard instantly understood. Alexander wanted him to let this strapping young man, whom now the boy "possessed" as a relative, take action. Any action; but that would not be appropriate. Picard could only guess about his own participation in this scenario, but surmised what the officer whose place he was taking might have done. If the boy's hero worship fit poorly into that scheme, so be it.

The screams of their shipmates and their enemies alike splintered the night. *Justina*'s crew kept up a valiant fight, but the ship was lost. Surrounded. Either she would burn, or her captain would strike his flag, put out the fire, and surrender.

"Why are those boats so determined?" Alexander asked. "Why are they attacking us again and again!"

"They're defending the boatyard," Midshipman Nightingale told the boy. "They want to be sure the British assault fails. They must've known we were coming somehow."

"How would they know?"

"Spies, likely. Traitors."

Alexander shook his head, confused. "Why do the British want to attack a boatyard?"

Edward Nightingale peered with his youthful eyes through the trees at the battling ships, wincing each time a puff of cannon smoke burst into the moonlit haze, then pausing until seconds later, the accompanying *poom* would reach them. His soft English accent added a certain lilt to his sentences. "Delaware Station Boatyard specializes in converting working ships to fighting ships in mere weeks. American vessels are built low and narrow, without much room for provisions. After all, they rarely have to cross the ocean. They're built—"

Suddenly hell's gates opened before them as *Justina*'s port broadside cannons lit off all at once, instantly shattering one of the spider catcher boats, but completely missing the single-masted ship that quickly dodged around her stern and fired a raking shot.

Nightingale winced and swallowed hard, then spoke with a terrible struggle. "American ships are built primarily . . . primarily for coastal trade or fishing. As such, they're considerably faster and more maneuverable than . . . ours."

Alexander prodded, "What does it take to make one into a fighting ship? What's the difference?"

Picard almost spoke up to say the differences were essentially the same as in their time, but Nightingale was still clinging to the conversation, even as his hands trembled on the branches he clutched. "The bulwarks must be pierced with gun ports, certainly, and the decks reinforced for the weight of cannon. Shot lockers and an antifire magazine must be built, and the crew quarters enlarged, because a fighting crew is so many more men than a cargo crew. Such alterations convert a beast of burden into a fighting rig . . . "

The midshipman's voice trickled off as he paused, deeply disturbed by what he saw out on the water.

"Interrupt holoprogram, code Riker Zero One."

Around Picard and Alexander, the old-style holoprogram slowed to a crawl, but this time, due to its partial incompatibility with the modern holosystem, didn't entirely freeze. A cannon puff from out on the water groaned toward the *Justina,* its flash of fire and violence slowed to a long bright yellow slash, and there it seemed to stay.

To their right, the door to the holodeck appeared, opened, and William Riker strode through.

"Sorry to interrupt, Captain."

"Mr. Riker," Picard sighed heavily, shaking himself back to his other world. "Are you dead yet?"

"Yes, sir, I'm dead. Everything went as you planned. The patroller trick was a good one, sir."

"Thank you. Alexander, why don't you go get lunch while I speak to Mr. Riker."

Alexander glanced furtively out at the ship and the battle, clicking along very, very slowly, then shrugged and nodded. He started to leave, but hesitated one last moment to gaze fondly at the paused form of Alexander Leonfeld, the man whose name he carried. The boy seemed unwilling to leave his new hero in such a state. Only the silent eyes of Picard and Riker eventually drove him off the holodeck and on toward lunch.

After he was gone, Riker looked around at the nearly still men from the past and said, "Heck of a lesson plan, sir."

"Yes, I'm rather enjoying myself, more than I expected to. But you can see this technology isn't completely compatible with ours. It's still moving along. The computer can't completely stop it unless I authorize a complete shutdown. Interesting."

"Yes, it is." Riker peered out over the slowly flickering waters at the stranded frigate. "Lose your ship?"

"Not mine," Picard said peevishly. "Well? What's going on?"

"Oh, sorry. Worf destroyed the drone ship with his usual panache."

Riker offered a canny grin. "The freighter had to turn back to Sindikash, so I assume that happened because Worf successfully sabotaged it and kept that shipment from reaching Romulan space. The Rogues didn't make a very good showing for themselves. They're supposed to throw themselves on their swords for Odette Khanty, and they didn't. I guess she wasn't worth dying for."

"So she failed to frame the lieutenant governor."

"Right. And Worf made it look as if they almost got caught, so now she's not very happy with her Rogue force. That can work in our favor."

"Yes. It'll make her desperate," Picard observed. He looked out at the *Justina,* a template for desperation.

Riker nodded. "And now Worf's a hero in Khanty's eyes, because he kept the freighter and the Rogues from being arrested. If she had any doubts about him, she won't anymore."

"Perfect. Very good—*very* good. What was in that shipment, Mr. Riker?"

Riker retired an itch on one ear and said, "We aren't sure, sir. Tainted seed, bogus pharmaceuticals, chemical adulterants—Odette Khanty's done 'em all. Things would've looked bad for the lieutenant governor, to be attached to a cargo like that. Even Worf couldn't find out what was in that ship, but whatever it was, I'll bet we're glad it didn't get through."

Picard nodded and peered out over the barely frozen bay and said, "Poor luck often forces men to fail at their missions. I'm glad to hear Mr. Worf is having better fortunes. Has Mr. Worf been able to maneuver Mr. Grant into an inside position?"

"I don't think so. Worf's last communication came through several relays, but he indicated that he is gaining the trust of Mrs. Khanty. He'll find a way to get Grant inside. Even if the Rogues don't particularly like him, they certainly trust him now. He's slowly wheedling his way to the upper levels of security at the governor's mansion, and he's taking Grant right along with him—"

The door section, hanging independently in the middle of the forest, parted again. Commander Data strode in, his pale golden face shining in the moonlight of Chesapeake Bay. His catlike android eyes flickered a bit as he spotted them in the trees and picked his way through to the bay shore.

"Sir," he said cordially to Riker, then looked at Picard. "Captain."

"Yes, Mr. Data?" Picard acknowledged.

"I have scanned and reviewed all available information about arms shipments, distributions, contraband, or disposals in the sector, and found no caches of weapons numbering between ten and forty. I am sorry, sir."

Picard felt his brow draw, and saw that Riker had the same expression. "Weapons, Mr. Data? I don't recall a need to check records of weapons shipments or disposals—"

"The weapons belonging to the passengers of the transport who were killed, sir," Data said, with his innocent manner of reporting facts as he saw them.

His amber eyes flicked to Riker, then back to Picard. When neither seemed to know what he was talking about, he pointedly added, "The arms, sir."

Riker's eyes got big and his lips pressed flat.

"Oh . . . the *arms* . . . " Picard rubbed a hand over his own mouth to wipe down the gallows grin.

Data nodded. "Yes, sir. You said they were missing."

Will Riker developed a cough, folded his arms around his chest, and nurtured a sudden fascination with Sergeant Leonfeld's scarlet tunic and white breeches.

"Nice uniform," he muttered.

Data's childlike face tilted. "Is there some problem, sir? Did I misunderstand? The murdered passengers were disarmed, correct?"

Picard looked at Riker and found no help from a man whose knuckles were pressed to his tightening lips.

"Eh, yes," Picard began, "they . . . were disarmed. Em . . . Mr. Data, cancel that search for now. I'll give you more specific orders later regarding that . . . Mr. Riker, do you concur?"

"Mmmhmm." Riker's back was to them, his arms still folded, one hip cocked. The moonlight silhouetted his head and shoulders. Picard raised his chin. "Carry on, Mr. Data."

"Very well, sir." The android turned and strode back through the freestanding doorway.

Picard cleared his throat and squeezed his eyes shut for a moment, contemplating the vagaries of linguistic communication.

Still hugging his rib cage, Riker sidled toward him, eyes a little wide and one brow a little up.

"Maybe you'd . . . like some lunch now, sir?" he suggested.

"Lunch?" Picard tossed back. "Lunch, Mr. Riker? While my ship is out there being captured? I'm surprised at you, man. Such ideas. I've a mind to disarm you."

Riker smiled and nodded. "Have a nice stranding, sir."

"See? Right here. The governor was leaning toward independence, but he wanted strong ties to the Federation and eventual readmittance as a full-fledged member planet. Mrs. Khanty wanted no more ties at all. She was careful about it, though. I can only find one time when she slipped and mentioned it while she was talking to a women's club. Let me change this—there."

"Play it."

Worf peered over Grant's shoulder in the privacy of their Rogue quarters, where they had set up their computer access terminal. Grant had spent every off-duty hour, including some he should've spent sleeping, digging into the government computer links, trying to find his way to Odette Khanty's private holdings, that "track" he spoke of.

On the tiny screen, Odette Khanty came to life, speaking to a group of women.

"*—valiant type, aren't we? We're frontier stock. Seniards don't like being told what to do from way over there somewhere. The Federation wants to levy controls on us about how we ship our ores. We* know *how to ship ore!*"

"Frontier stock! She's never been within transporter distance of a real frontier in her whole—"

"Be silent, Grant."

"My husband is a great statesman who only wants the best for Sindikash. No one outside of Sindikash should say what the best is. Our families, our children are more important to us than to anyone else. I mourn the fact that my husband and I never had the chance to have our own children. Perhaps when he recovers from his terrible injuries, and I have great hopes for this, we will be able to begin that spirited enterprise of raising a baby."

"Incredible!" Grant reached forward and used the keyboard to pause the computer playout of Mrs. Khanty addressing the women's club.

Worf leaned back and fixed his eyes on the frozen image of the woman. "Which part?"

"The way she gets away with this chopped fodder! You know how she feels about kids. And I think she likes her husband a whole lot better now that he's unconscious. Now that the governor's in a coma, Mrs. Khanty's maneuvering her little pink self into power on the planet. But she's doing it in this innocent, sweet-me way. Makes me gag."

"This mission is getting under our skin," Worf said with worry. "It makes me burn, pretending to be one of these people. I still feel saddled with the actions of the Rogues, no matter how I try to remember that I am *nothing* like them. I hear the captain's voice in my head, telling me not to take all this so personally, but it *is* personal! It *is.*"

Shrugging with an endearing sense of himself, Grant nodded and muttered, "Eh, it's our flaw. That's what makes us such a great team. We take things personally. Now look at her face. See how she keeps her eyebrows just a little bit up? That's a body language thing. And her chin only goes up when she's talking about Sindikash as a whole unit. When she talks about herself, she tucks her chin and gives her head a little tilt, like a shy person does. And she nods real slow in agreement with herself. I'll bet she practices in front of a mirror. Hitler used to do that, y'know. The Seniards like to think they're ferociously independent, but they follow her like sheep if she appeals to them as a group. She uses their independent spirit to steer them to her course. She's a marketing genius. Especially when you consider she's selling an empty pot."

"The pot has a great deal in it," Worf corrected, more loudly than he intended. "All corrupt!"

"I know. There are dozens of incidents where hundreds of people die—mishandling of ore during shipments that cause load-shifting . . . extortion . . . bribery . . . jury tampering . . . cutting corners that shouldn't be cut . . . she's setting this planet up to be the platform for her organization, and the people are swallowing it."

Troubled by the caginess of their adversary, Worf glowered until his eyes hurt. Was there some way to just handle this clever woman with a phaser or *bat'telh* or a club? Challenge her to a warp equation?

"Public perception can be steered," Worf commented, trying to keep distance. "If the election can be postponed, there might be a chance to clean things up."

"Yeah, but wow!" Grant leaned back and stretched his aching arms. He slumped again and waved his hand at the computer. "The trail of bodies and indictments and convictions behind her goes back as far as the eye can see. Her former associates are all dead or in jail! And she gets up and rails about independence and how they need to make their planet pure from dirty outside influence. It's like Al Capone complaining that there's too much crime! How does she keep anybody's loyalty?"

"Fear," Worf told him. "Desperation for some, and for others, greed. Like the Rogues. They hope to have influence all the way back to the Empire. Most powerful enticement for expatriate Klingons."

Grant looked up and smiled. "Like you, huh, toughy?"

"In another life." Worf took the seat next to his partner and concentrated now more on Grant than on the screen.

"Can't help it." Grant scratched at the Rogue uniform as if to communicate its inappropriateness for him. "This is a woman who pulls people's arms out, and I can't find the trail! Can you imagine what it must be like to have your arms pulled out?"

Worf did his best to calm his friend, although he felt little calm himself. "You will find the trail. As you did on Pasha IX." Worf almost smiled. "In your way, you are a warrior. The hand of Kahless will guide you."

Grant smiled briefly, then turned back to his work.

His guts curling in frustration, Worf wished Captain Picard were here to deal with this wily woman. He felt patently not clever enough for such an adversary.

"Play the rest of it," he said, feeling his throat go raw.

Grant grimaced, and started the computer again.

"We must protect the identity of our planet, the integrity of our economy, and the individuality of our people. We do that by circling our wagons against those who would have a say in our way of life. We need independence to stretch our wings—"

Huffing once again, Grant pounded the keyboard until the image stopped again. Worf almost stopped him, but couldn't find it in his soul to disturb the wave of emotion surging in Grant's eyes.

"By the time they realize what's happened, she'll have chains on those wings," Grant said. "What she doesn't tell them about is the den of thieves the planet will attract without any Federation presence. She can turn the place into a clearing house for any lowlife who wants to work outside the law. And she'll get a cut of everything, from non-replicables to slavery. All I can think of is all the little Alexanders running around this planet who'll have a crummy life because I can't find one simple link."

Grant shook his head, overwhelmed by the frozen image of Mrs. Khanty speaking at a time when she didn't think she was being recorded. After several long seconds, Grant's silence betrayed to Worf just how deeply his partner had been moved by what had begun as a simple computer search.

"I've got it all here," Grant mourned. "Just nothing to tie *her* to all this illegal stuff. The bees swarm around this dragon lady, and none of them ever stings her. She's just never *quite* close enough to anything bad that happens. She has these things done by the Rogues or by her gardener's wife's jester's grandmother." He slumped further and crushed his hand over his weary face. "Ooooh, I just gotta get something . . . folks are dying."

Worf pushed up from the chair. "You need rest."

"Mmm, can't. Gotta keep picking. And you gotta go, too. You're on duty in the governor's corridor in fifteen minutes. If you don't show up, you could end up on her bad side. And believe me, pal, we don't want to get on this dame's bad side. Don't worry. I'm okay. I'm just . . . "

"Frustrated," Worf filled in. "As am I. This is not my kind of enemy."

"Heck, I know," Grant chuckled. "No live grenades for you to fall on, then try not to grunt when they go off. Nah, she's more in my line of work, anyway, Wuff. After all, they sent you here for a whole other reason than they sent me. You're here to get attention and beat people up and growl and make Ugulan look like a U-gu-rangutan." Pointing at the computer, Grant said. *"This* is me. I just gotta get *inside* somehow, to some source of private records. A terminal inside the shielded area."

"There must be a way," Worf said. "I will contact you. Be ready."

Standing over his old friend, Worf saw a man who often seemed a clownish, uninteresting computer technician with a rather simple assignment. Indeed, Worf often found him quite annoying. Yet he was a man in whose heart beat a code of honor as strong as any Klingon's. Much stronger than the *P'taks* who served with Khanty, and feared her for reasons Worf could not understand.

If Worf had found this mission unsatisfying, it suddenly bored itself deeply into his mind and heart. If he had been shamed by the actions of the Rogues, he now took those shames personally. He wanted a good end to this, not for the people of Sindikash or the integrity of the Federation, but to redeem Klingon honor, to wipe the stain of the Rogue Klingons actions from the galaxy, to make certain that Alexander, just now learning the meaning of honor, would have no reason to feel ashamed of his Klingon heritage.

He ran over and over again in his mind things he should say to Grant. Mission partners should be able to offer each other sustenance. Old friends, even more.

As inadequacy plagued him, Worf found his thoughts straying to Alexander. Was he nurturing his son, or only raising him? Hadn't he seen the same expression in Alexander's face as he just saw in Grant's? A search for elusive peace of the soul?

"I will get you inside, Grant," he said. "I promise you that."

The corridor provided sanctuary and distraction. The colors were like the streets and buildings of Sindikash. Earthy, moody. The walls were hung with carpet-woven tapestries rich with deep colors—beet, plum, copper, wedding cake white, mustard, otter brown. Mosquelike doorways to other offices and tiled moldings offered a prevailing spirit of the exotic. Elaborately colored stencils mapped the walls. The bushy brown skins of bison served as rugs and chair coverings.

In Worf's time here, he had found the Seniards to be generally enthusiastic and decent, charitable and honest. Unfortunately, a significant percentage of them failed to see that others were not so noble, and that they were being led around by their noses. Soon they would suffocate.

The offices were deserted. The mansion was in nighttime repose. The aides and pages had gone home or retired to their quarters. Mrs. Khanty was down the corridor, in her own private chambers.

Worf was here, guarding the executive suite, where Odette Khanty had chewed the heads off the Rogues, and where the governor lay, as he had for many weeks now, in the silence of his coma, monitored from the clinic upstairs.

The quiet was enraging.

Still, Worf forced himself not to be lulled into complacency. He stood guard until almost midnight before pressing the private signal in his subcutaneous transponder.

Across the courtyard, the other transponder, embedded in Grant's forearm, would be vibrating softly. *Come now.*

Those minutes waiting for Grant to arrive were far worse than Worf expected. Was he losing control of himself? Was he becoming too personally involved in this mission? Was he rushing things in order to hurry back to the ship and take over as Alexander's mentor?

"Hey! I'm here." Grant appeared at the end of the corridor, speaking in a quick whisper. "Can I . . . " He pointed to the suite door.

Worf nodded, keeping his gaze on the corridor beyond Grant as his partner hurried toward him. Quickly he unlocked the door and let Grant inside. "The computer terminal is in the kitchenette. Work quietly. There may be listening devices inside."

"Right," Grant murmured, his eyes wide. He was tense as a cable. "This is our big chance. No more picking up bits by hacking from outside. Everything's got to be on her private—"

"Go, Grant, go." Worf shoved him in and pulled the door shut again.

Now the fire was lit. If anyone came, there would be no getting Grant out in time.

He scanned and scanned the corridor, his head constantly swiveling. Imitation candles in sconces cast a softening glow upon the corridor, offering the eerie sensation of a castle in twilight, and casting shadows that seemed sometimes to move. He wished he could be like Data, divorcing himself from his emotional core and his imagination.

What was that?

Had he heard something? Had the outside door just creaked?

He took a step to his right, toward the lobby.

Before his second step he swung around and froze, listening. Voices? Was someone coming from the stairway? Or the elevator? Mrs. Khanty?

His spine felt as if it were twisting. There seemed to be nothing to fear from this single, small woman—how was she so effective? How did she control Klingon warriors? What kind of enemy was this?

His hands were cold, his fingers aching. He flexed them fitfully, and thought of those who no longer had fingers. Or lives.

He listened, watched, turned, listened again, but no one came. The corridors were still as rocks. He hoped Grant could make good use of the time on the private terminal. Something, anything, to end this mission.

Worf chided himself for such feelings. This mission could not be rushed. Then he angrily reminded himself that Klingons were not Vulcans, and his feelings were valuable possessions that could drive his resolve. He was a Klingon, raised as a Klingon, but by humans, and he had found his adoptive parents' interpretation of being Klingon to be sketchy and not always serviceable. Sometimes he was too Klingon, sometimes too human, and sometimes, other things.

Troubled, Worf tried to shake off his worries, to tell himself that he was isolated, and this was why he felt so troubled. Things were much clearer on board a starship, his duties delineated, and his role as Alexander's father somewhat easier. Somehow, that job got harder whenever he was separated from Alexander. What kind of man would his son become, living with a foot in two cultures so unlike each other?

The corridor whispered back at him, its lemony sconces passively imitating gaslights, though without the sense of warmth. Worf found himself chilled, but from within. He was trying not to focus on problems insurmountable from the hallway, when the silence was abruptly ruptured by the thunderous howl of an alarm. The red emergency lights were flashing!

Bolting away from the doorway, he stared for that first uncontrolled instant at a looping red light above the door to the governor's chamber. The alarm was deafening, furious, like the exaggerated barking of a terrorized seal.

Before Worf could so much as flex a leg, two distant doors flew open and the entrance to a stairway thundered with pounding feet; suddenly, the corridor was filled with medical personnel. And four Rogues! Ugulan, Mortash, Goric, Tyro—

The alarm was from the governor's life-support system.

As the doctors and police plunged into the private doorway, Worf plunged for the office entrance and yanked the door open.

The inner rooms were chaotic. Alarms all over the medical equipment squealed and flashed. Grant backed slowly out of the recovery room as the medical staff flooded in. All Worf saw was the back of Grant, his tensed shoulders, his clenched fists.

The governor's legs twitched convulsively beneath the linen cover, and just as Worf entered the room the legs stiffened and went still. The swarming doctors, nurses, and technicians went into clinical emergency treatment, but as Worf slowly moved to stand beside Grant, a sense of desperation shivered across their actions.

The other Rogues pressed back from the action as the medical personnel swarmed over the bed. One doctor crawled up onto the bed and pounded the governor's chest.

"It was poison!" Grant belted out, gasping. "You've got to find out what she put in there!"

"What who put in where?" the doctor on the bed demanded.

"Mrs. Khanty!" Grant pointed desperately at a tube leading into the governor's left arm. "She came in through that door over there and she put something into that tube! Then everything went crazy! She poisoned him! You've got to find out what she gave him!"

Stunned, the doctor plucked at the tube. More medics rushed to the bedside with intubation devices and syringes. As Grant stared at the doctors, Worf at Grant, and the Rogues at both of them, the doctors and technicians worked to decipher what had happened. They took a quick blood sample and slipped it into a portable analyzer. Sure enough, the doctor confirmed Grant: "He's right. Neurotoxin. Get a neutralizer in here!"

"It's too late," another doctor said cryptically. He stood back, and all the others paused ever so slightly as, with a final twitch of one important knee, Governor Khanty slipped beyond reach.

Then they tried to keep working, but there was no more hope on their faces.

One of the medical technicians backed away from the bed with the same horrified expression as Grant's. A nurse pushed him farther back, and checked a machine. Then she paused, sighed, and her shoulders went slack as the inevitable set in. She turned, and watched.

"Grant," Worf pressed. He took Grant's arm. "What happened?"

Breathing only in the most uneven huffs, Grant stared into the chamber at the event he had been unable to stop.

"She did it," he choked, shivering. "Mrs. Khanty did it. She came in here. She didn't see me . . . she didn't know I was here."

Ugulan, Goric, and three medics turned sharply and looked at Grant and Worf.

"The governor was alive," Grant said. "He was stable. She came in . . . and now he's dead. And I let her be in there with him."

He looked at Worf, and suddenly it was as if the two were alone on an island.

"She did something to make him die," Grant struggled. "And it's my fault."

All despotism is bad, but the worst is that which works with the machinery of freedom.

Junius

CHAPTER 11

"LIAR!" UGULAN SHOVED A FINGER AT GRANT'S CHEST. "YOU'RE COVERING the fact that you murdered the governor!"

"Keep your dishonorable mouth shut, Ugulan!" Worf had managed to hold himself in check until he heard that. He crashed forward past Grant and landed the heel of his hand on Ugulan's chin, driving the Rogue back a step. "I will brand your face with your own words!"

The Rogues couldn't have stopped him, but when two of the medics got between him and Ugulan, Worf stopped his forward surge. What good would it do to peel Ugulan's skin off?

"If I poisoned him," Grant shouted at Ugulan, "why would I tell them what was wrong so they'd have a chance to save him?"

"Quiet, human!" Ugulan turned sharply to Goric and said, "Contact Paul Stefan."

"Begin an investigation," the doctor said, looking at his own staff. "Time of death is 12:41 a.m. Coastal Standard Time. Get a statement from Mrs. Khanty about her whereabouts in the last fifteen minutes." He turned again to Grant. "I don't want you to speak to anyone until the investigation can be officially started. Is that clear?"

Grant tried to say something, then only nodded.

"You, too," the doctor told Worf. "You were on duty here, too, weren't you?"

"Yes!" Worf blurted. He stepped back to Grant's side, hoping everyone here would take that as a vote of support. What a smell this situation put off!

"Don't say anything more, any of you." The doctor turned to Ugulan and said, "Seal off these rooms. Put these two men in isolation until we figure out what happened here."

"Yes, Doctor," Ugulan said, and his gray eyes gleamed with the idea of setting Worf away from the other Rogues.

Worf bristled instantly. What would happen if Ugulan managed to isolate him and Grant?

"No!" he challenged quickly. "I will confine both of us to our quarters. Until there are charges made, if any, you have no precedent for jailing us!"

Another Rogue, a comparatively short-statured Klingon whose name was Tyro, rose unexpectedly to Worf's defense. "Confine them to quarters, Ugulan. There are no charges yet."

"Do not defend me, coward!" Worf shouted, raising a fist to Tyro. He knew in a cold flash that Tyro's help came not from his status as a fellow Klingon, a fellow Rogue, or any other kind of fellow. Tyro only wanted to avoid setting a more threatening precedent—that the Rogues could imprison each other at all without charges.

Ugulan drew his dagger—because phasers weren't allowed in the mansion—and swung on Tyro. "I will decide!" Instantly, he swung back to Worf and gestured toward the hall door. "Out!"

The hunger of that dagger pricked at Worf's angry mind as he led the way out of the executive suite, with Grant right behind him. The twists of this mission were maddening! If only he could just roar out all the truths!

After them, the Rogues filed out, too, leaving behind a corpse and its doctors. Through the doorway and down the corridor which barely accommodated their wide shoulders, the ghastly queue walked. Two Klingons—even if there *were* two real Klingons here—could not easily walk abreast in this corridor, and Worf felt as if his clothing were crawling around on his skin. Why did this corridor need to be so cursed long? Who had built this stupid, foolish, ugly building!

The tiled lobby approached slowly, as if detached, and in his mind Worf saw the stone veranda outside, the long, curving flagstone stairways leading to the tiled courtyard and the expanse of ground they would have to cover in order to survive.

Grant let out a startled grunt behind him.

Like a trigger snapping, Worf swung around, yanked Grant past him, then raised a foot and slammed it into Ugulan's chest.

"Back away!" he snarled, jamming his fist into Ugulan's throat. Ugulan's arms flared, and sure enough, that dagger had been forward, toward Grant's spine. Another few seconds—

No one was carrying a phaser today—a sour bit of luck having something to do with regulations during certain hours. It didn't matter—it gave Worf an advantage. He held Grant protectively away, positioning himself between his partner and the other Rogues, most of whom were still corralled in the hallway.

"Stay away from him!" he snarled.

"Protecting a human?" Ugulan accused. "And a liar?"

Worf gritted his teeth. "He is not lying."

"Did you see what he saw?" Goric blistered from behind Ugulan, and pushed his way forward.

"I will not speak to any of you sniveling weaklings!" Worf spat. "I will make my statements to the City Police."

Ugulan surged forward, unintimidated by Worf's dagger. Clearly, the Rogues believed Grant about what Mrs. Khanty had done, and they meant to silence him or anyone else who could endanger the ruthless woman they had come to fear, their last line to power and influence.

Worf shoved Grant back and deflected Ugulan's blade with his own, making a ghastly *scratch* that echoed under the domed ceiling fresco and made the crystal chandelier tinkle with sympathetic vibration. It felt good, finally, to kick and shove!

"Run, Grant!" he shouted as the Rogues crowded toward him. Battle honor went to the wind—he knew they would gladly gang up on him, but Ugulan was blocking their way.

"I don't want to leave you!" Grant protested as he scrambled for maneuvering room.

Worf feinted backward toward the main door and swung around long enough to blast it open with his boot. Then he twisted back in time to rake his blade across Ugulan's chest, driving the head Rogue back a step.

"Out!" he shouted to Grant. "Run! Get to the police!"

"Oh, damn—" Grant looked around frantically, glanced upward and saw something, then clasped a heavy brass vase from a cloisonné table.

Using both hands and every excuse for a muscle he owned, he heaved the vase into the air toward the ceiling. It sailed in an arc, its own weight soon compromising the flight, and tumbled end-first as if Grant had cast a bowling pin. At the apex of its flight it slashed through the giant crystal chandelier. The thousand bangles of cut glass barely affected the vase, but the glass was blasted to bits. With a harplike chime, the chandelier dissolved. Needles of glass rained down upon the startled Rogues, who never even had time to raise their arms to cover their faces. Glass scalpels rocketed downward, slicing their cheeks, scalps, and eyes, embedding in their hands, popping through the fabric of their Rogue uniforms to impale their arms and shoulders.

Worf made a maniacal leap toward Grant and the open main door. In midair he felt a dozen glass shards drive into his left hip and leg, but his head was clear.

And Grant was clear!

The two of them skidded to the brick deck of the veranda and crashed into an iron table and chair set. The chairs clanged on the veranda's circular brick rail and tumbled over, but the table stayed up and Grant landed under it.

Worf's pelvis and leg were gripped by pain, and he felt blood drain down his leggings. He shoved himself to his good foot and hauled Grant out from under the table.

"See? You are a true warrior," he complimented as he hauled Grant down the curved stairs toward the courtyard. A blotchy trail of amethyst-colored blood smeared the steps behind him.

He glanced back at the veranda. Goric staggered out, clawing at his right eye. Blood covered his face and he was completely disoriented, gasping with pain and fear. After him came Gern, then Tyro, both picking at blades of glass embedded in their heads and arms. Ugulan staggered out, staring viciously, with the central tine of the chandelier protruding from his shoulder. He balled his fists around a dagger in one hand and a large spear of glass in the other, and roared with fury.

"Uh-oh," Grant gulped. "Think we made him mad?"

"I hope we made him insane! Come!" Worf urged and pulled Grant into the tiled expanse of the courtyard.

Each step sent blistering pain up and down his left side as the shards of glass continued to drill into skin and muscle. Grant dodged under Worf's arm and gave him some support, but on the veranda Ugulan, Mortash, and the other Rogues were overcoming their own injuries, or at least becoming insensitive in the blur of their fury and insult. Their future was shuffling away across the courtyard, and they meant to throw a rope on it.

If that meant dying on the tile, so be it!

"They're coming," Grant gasped. "They're halfway down the stairs . . . they're making it onto the tiles . . . oh, man, we're gonna be butchered—"

"You go," Worf choked. "Run for the police."

Struggling with Worf's considerable weight, Grant glanced behind them again. "No chance, bub. We go, we go together."

"You cannot fight Klingons!" Worf spat out his contempt. "Not even *those* Klingons!"

"Wish I had a flare gun or something—"

"Grant, they will not kill me. Klingons do not attack fallen Klingons."

Now who was lying?

But Grant, unfortunately, was not fooled. "Oh, not *those* Klingons! What's with you? Competing with Mrs. Khanty for Flimflam of the Month? They'll kill you and eat you!"

"Too gristly," Worf grunted as he slipped to one knee.

Hauling Worf to his feet, Grant heaved. "Don't try to snow me anymore, will ya? We just gotta make the outer gatehouse." He cast another nervous glance at the staggering Rogues, who were closing the distance between them, slowly becoming numb to their own pain, blinded by the trouble they were in if Worf and Grant made it out.

Worf leaned heavily on Grant and forced his throbbing leg to move. There were more lives at stake than their own—all those doctors and medics and nurses who had heard Grant's claim about Mrs. Khanty. Those people were all dead if Worf and Grant were brought down here. The bodies would disappear, the courtyard would be scrubbed of the blood, and Odette Khanty would implicate the "missing" conspirators in the murder.

Aggravated that he and Grant might just have handed Mrs. Khanty her alibi, Worf drove furiously for the ornate stone gatehouse. His chest pounded. His pulse roared in his ears. Through the iron gates he saw people milling about in the public square. If they could reach the square—

His leg folded under him again. The dozen glass shards were impaling more and more muscle with every flex, working their way deeper through his clothing. The pain was crippling, searing his body as he struggled forward, scraping across the tiles, clinging to Grant, who didn't have the power to carry a man the size of Worf.

They scraped across the tiles, driven by the clack of Ugulan's boots and those of the other Rogues who were still able to see and move. The main gate began to swirl before Worf's eyes. He was losing blood. Shock was setting in, blurring his vision. Desperation began to take over, just as rage was driving the Rogues in spite of their injuries. He had to reach the gate, he had to get Grant to the City Police. They could not be caught here!

Suddenly, Grant choked and grimaced hard, arching his spine as he staggered. He dropped Worf and dropped to one knee. As he fell, Worf shivered at the sight of Ugulan's dagger embedded in the fleshy part of Grant's back, just under the shoulder blade.

"Aw!" Gasping in pain, Grant coiled his convulsing arm against his body and braced himself on the tiled floor with his other hand. His eyes crimped tight. "Crap! Aw, crap, we're all done now! Iced by gorillas!"

"Get up!" Worf snapped. "Up! Use your legs!"

He shoved himself upright, damning agony down his leg and halfway up his side, and scooped Grant up with his good arm.

"Move! Move!"

He could hear Ugulan's footsteps and those of the other Rogues, getting closer and closer, clapping on the tiles unevenly. The Rogues were all hurt and staggering, but the distance between them was shrinking. Worf harbored no doubts that if that space closed, Ugulan and the others would find the strength for one more slaughter.

"Oh, God . . . " Grant sank against him.

"Move!" Worf demanded again.

"She won . . . "

"She did not win!"

"We're beat, Worf, she beat us—"

"Not yet! Move!"

"You never listen to me."

"Walk!"

Yard by yard they slogged toward the gate, but Ugulan's very breath was chasing them now. Mere inches separated them from the bloody hands of the head Rogue and the bite of Mortash's extended dagger.

Worf willed the blurring iron gates open before them, and the gates began to shudder with movement. The might of his determination caused the gates to part and swing inward toward them—magic! The gates were opening!

As effort drained him and once again dragged Grant to one knee at his side, Worf grieved at the steps between them and the opening gates. Just steps—

"Hold it! Stop!"

He raised his sagging head at the shout that came from the gate.

"City Police!"

A dozen officers of the law surged into the courtyard, weapons drawn on the stunned Rogues and on Worf and Grant, though it was plain who was chasing and who was being chased.

"Hold it, all of you! City Police!"

A stocky police officer, with thick hair that was silvering prematurely, got between Worf and Ugulan. The Rogues had no choice but to back off, faced down by the police weapons that would have cut their daggers out of their hands. The policemen surrounded the Rogues and divested them of their blades.

The lead officer, the one who had barked the desist order, approached Worf and Grant.

"I'm Lieutenant Stoner. You're the two who witnessed the governor's death?"

"Yes!" Grant gasped, spittle flying from the corner of his mouth.

Trying not to lean on Grant, Worf squinted through the blur. "How do you know?"

"The doctors notified us."

Grant pointed back at the Rogues. "They're gonna kill us to cover it up!"

Ugulan shot out an accusing finger. "They're spies, infiltrating the governor's mansion! You cannot keep us from our rightful revenge! We are Klingons!"

Worf took a faltering step toward him. "How would *you* know what it is to be Klingon!" he shouted in Klingon. He could no longer hold back. "What is it," he shouted at Ugulan, "that makes you cower like a beaten slave before that woman? That you obey her orders no matter how much shame you bring to yourself, to the Empire, to all Klingons?"

Ugulan stepped close, so only Worf could hear him. "She has our oath," he said quietly, sadness replacing his fury. "She has our Oath of Sto–vo–kor. It was the only way she would grant us sanctuary on this world."

Worf had been prepared for any answer except that. Sto–vo–kor was the Klingon Valhalla, the place all warriors went when they died. The Oath of Sto–vo–kor was no mere oath of allegiance. It gave a commander the power to decide a warrior's fate after death. These Rogue Klingons feared for their very souls, which, at a word from Khanty, would have been sent to oblivion.

Worf's anger flowed out of him. He faced Ugulan proudly. "I pity you," Worf said.

As he spoke, three policemen held him back. And it took all three of them.

"Quiet, quiet," Stoner said. "Everybody just hold your lunch," he said evenly. "We'll sort it all out. You're all under arrest until we do. Your 'rightful revenge' will have to wait."

"You can't hold us!" Grant protested. "They'll get to us if you do!"

Stoner looked at him, then looked at Ugulan. "Mmm, yeah," he uttered.

Incredible—he understood! A flicker of hope shot up through Worf's pain as he watched the police lieutenant's amicable face. The shock that he wasn't alone anymore struck him with the power of a phaser stun.

"They cannot circumvent the law!" Ugulan protested. "They have to be held!"

"I said, quiet, and I asked nicely, didn't I?" Stoner told him. "You Rogues think you run the whole planet. Nobody's going to get to anybody. We'll put all of you in custody until we know what's going on. Okay, boys, take the Rogues away. Medium security till we figure out who to charge."

"This is criminal!" Mortash argued.

"We'll see," Stoner said, unimpressed. "Bye. Those Rogues, they're just so noble, you know?"

"Oh, man . . . " Grant sagged against the police officer who was holding him up.

Stoner watched the Rogues until they disappeared, flanked by other officers, through the gate and down the street toward the City Police Central Station.

"Okay, gentlemen," Stoner said with a sigh. "What's your story?"

"He's a Starfleet officer," Grant said. "I'm a Federation agent, and we're investigating certain shipments of contraband through open spacelanes."

"Hmm . . . well, I'm sorry your welcome to Sindikash couldn't be any better, but I don't have any more reason to believe you than to believe them. Do I? Are you carrying any I.D.?"

"Obviously not," Worf grumbled.

"But . . ." Stoner pushed back his maroon police hat. "But the doctors did contact me and tell me you were in trouble, so somebody believes you, so . . . I'll confine you to quarters under guard until I can sort out your identity. Can you give me a contact code or something I can use to verify who you are?"

"Yes," Worf snarled. "You can contact my ship."

"What's your ship?"

"The *Enterprise*."

"Wow . . ." Stoner's blue eyes widened. "Wait'll I tell my kids. My son built models of the first two *Enterprises* for a school project, with individual hull plates."

"I shall arrange a tour of the real thing," Worf offered, "assuming we survive."

"Yeah," Stoner uttered sympathetically. He kept his voice down from the curious crowd that had gathered near the gates. "I know what you mean. Let's get you guys some treatment. Then I have to confine you till I clear this up. We'll see what happens."

"Sit down, Grant," Worf instructed. "You'll have no feet left if you continue to pace. It hardly serves you to be walking around on stumps."

"I can't sit," Grant shuddered, his whole body shaking as he twisted like a wind sock. His shoulder was bandaged and he rubbed his arm fitfully. "She killed him. She killed her own husband! I told you she didn't like him! That's what always happens to people who get in her way. It was all because that freighter didn't go the way she wanted it to. She couldn't frame the lieutenant governor, and she needed public opinion to go her way. This was the one thing she *had* to do herself. She's trying to get that public sympathy back."

"I know."

Grant paused. "Then you believe me?"

Shifting his injured leg, Worf offered a nod and wished the two of them had taken a day off to reminisce before embarking on this mission.

"Yes, of course I believe you. However, I did not see her enter the governor's suite."

He settled back into the big overstuffed buffalo-hide chair and tried to get Grant to relax by example.

Oblivious to Worf's effort, Grant hugged his own body tightly and swung about, pacing in front of the flagstone fireplace. "I should've stopped her the second I knew she was in there. I just froze. She didn't see me, and I just couldn't make myself move. I let her kill him."

"Nonsense," Worf told him evenly. His voice was like a deep drum beneath the frantic tight-throated choke of Grant's panic, and he clung to the sound of his own words. "The governor might've died anyway."

"But he didn't just die. He was stable! The blood is on her hands this time. Her own, personal hands. Grant, please try to avoid obsessing."

"I can't believe this fell into our laps!" Grant blustered on. "We're turning ourselves inside out to get proof of her activities, and she does this right in front of me! But if it's just me saying it . . . "

Suddenly his entire expression changed. He swung around, his legs braced.

"Worf! You believe me, right?"

"Yes, of course I do."

"You know she killed the governor to make sure the independence referendum takes place on schedule, right? She must know the Federation's got a stake in postponing it, right?"

Uneasily, Worf nodded. "Yes, both also right."

Grant rushed to Worf's chair and knelt beside it, gripping the thick buffalo fur on the chair's arm with both hands.

"According to Sindikash law, they need two witnesses for a capital crime! You haven't made your statement yet!" He pounded the buffalo hide and leveled a finger at Worf. "You gotta back me up! You gotta say you were in there, too! You gotta say you saw her in there at the same time I did!"

Worf sat up straight, his legs and arms suddenly tight. Had he heard right?

"You want me to lie under oath?"

"Oh, what lie? You know she did it!"

"Yes . . . I know she did it."

"If there aren't two witnesses, then she can't even be charged or held in custody pending an investigation. She'll be free to do—" Grant stopped, his throat knotting again, and made a gesture with one hand toward the other arm—a ripping gesture.

Shoving to his feet, Worf put a few steps between them, as if to stride away from the whole idea of what Grant was asking of him. A sudden jolt of hope—one stretch of the truth. That was all, to free Grant and bring down this corrupt organization before it became interstellar.

"We can get you off the planet," he attempted. "The captain will make sure—"

"No!" Grant stood up and braced his legs. "Forget it. I'm not leaving. This is our chance to stop this woman from all these things she's been doing. And it's a chance to save a lot of lives she's got in her sights. The whole planet'll go down the sink if we don't hold our ground." He put his hands on his chest and grimaced. "I can't be the one to let that happen. I couldn't live with myself, y'know?"

After a moment Grant held out a beseeching hand as the small fire crackled behind him.

A friend . . . a fellow warrior despite his oddities . . . and as close to a godfather as his son possessed. . . .

Grant's voice was a crackle of strain. "You've got to say you were inside, Worf, in the room. You know what the truth is. All you have to do is *say* that it is!"

His whole body suddenly numb, Worf wanted from the pit of his being to give the answer Grant so desperately needed—and deserved.

Yes, deserved!

Why could he find no voice?

Though his response was bogged down in hesitation, he knew his face told clearly what he was deliberately not saying.

He knew, because of the way Grant was staring at him.

"You're . . . " Grant's jaw slackened in astonishment and his face went painfully white. "You're not gonna back me up, are you? Oh, my God . . . you're not going to back me up!"

Feeling his face crumple, Worf forced himself to speak. "I cannot perjure myself for you. I have my honor to consider."

Grant looked as if his chest were collapsing. "Honor? You've got to be kidding! We've got a whole planet and a fifth of the sector to think about here! You talk about law? There have to be two witnesses—that's the excuse for law on this godforsaken rock! She made sure of that! You think she wasn't setting that up for just this kind of incident? She pushed that law through to protect herself, not to protect the people of the planet! And it's working! And you're gonna let it?"

The last few words stuck in Grant's throat, yet his meaning came across as clearly as subspace beacons.

The sudden silence nearly broke Worf's legs beneath him. Ten thousand answers surged and receded in his mind before he mouthed the only one he could push out.

"I am sorry . . . "

Instantly, Grant gasped. "Sorry? We're partners!"

"Partners in *law,*" Worf said on a raw breath. "Not in dishonor."

How hollow the words sounded. How fleeting, weightless.

Grant shook his head, his eyes narrowing to pain-ridden slits. He shuddered and turned cold as a blade in winter. Sweat broke out on his face, and his whole body seemed to steam. He leaned forward over a rug-covered table and clutched at the rug until it bunched in his hands.

Quaking as if old age had rushed up on him, he shivered and gagged. "She'll turn my skin inside out . . . "

Gripped with empathy, Worf moved to Grant's side, hoping to provide some physical support. "We can get you off the planet, Grant. Mrs. Khanty—"

"I told you, I'm not leaving." Grant shook his head emphatically. "I'm gonna stick up for what I know."

Fraught with his burden, he turned, pressing his legs up against the table, and gripped Worf's Rogue uniform collar with gnarled fingers.

Worf gritted his teeth, suddenly light-headed and possessing no more substance than a useless bit of paper. He felt as if he were fading away where he stood. Fading to nothing. He was nothing—he could do nothing . . .

"You've got to stick up for it, too," Grant rasped. "It's the truth, and you know it. You can make the truth happen if you just say what you know! You've gotta do it!"

His fingers twisted tighter, his brows knitted, and Grant took one breath and held it until finally it came bursting out.

"For God's sake . . . *lie!"*

• • •

"We'll get you off the planet. And all this will be sorted out according to the law."

The ghastly decision had been made, and now lay in stone at the bottom of Worf's stomach. A half hour had crept by.

Grant no longer argued about getting off Sindikash and into the protective shell of the *Enterprise,* where Odette Khanty's tentacles could not reach.

Instead, Grant sat on a kilim ottoman, staring at the carpet, not looking up.

"Lie," he croaked.

Worf struggled to his feet and forced his swollen leg and hip to move. He dared not let his body stiffen up, so he paced behind Grant, as Grant had before him. "Another team can come here from Starfleet and continue the work. Mrs. Khanty is beginning to make errors."

"We've got her *now,*" Grant pleaded. "Lie. Do it."

"Killing her husband herself was a major step toward distrust of everyone around her. She can enshroud herself only so long, taking things into her own hands this way."

"I'd do it for you."

Worf looked at the back of Grant's head, haloed by imitation candlelight from a stained glass sconce. Grant did not turn to meet his eyes.

The rejection sizzled on his skin.

Could he blame Grant, who could see no other course? A chance was a chance. Their last.

A knock at the heavy oak door broke his thoughts, but not his concerns. He limped across the carpet, nearly tripping on the fringe, and opened the door only two inches to see who was there.

"Hi, sir, it's Ted Stoner."

"Lieutenant," Worf said with notable relief. "Come in."

The police officer stepped inside with another officer, then nodded to three other police guards to stay out in the entryway, then removed his hat and unbuttoned his thick maroon jacket.

"This is Officer Zared," Stoner said.

Worf nodded. "Officer."

"Sir," the policeman responded, and clasped his hands as he stood by the door as formally as a Starfleet yeoman.

"Well," Stoner began, "we checked out your story and everything clicked. You're a Starfleet officer from the *Enterprise.* We've got confirmation from a Jean-Luc Picard."

"*Captain* Picard," Worf corrected, more amused than he would have expected to be.

"Oh . . . sorry."

"Forgiven."

Stoner offered an easy shrug. "Anyway, I can't hold you. You're being remanded to Starfleet custody. They've agreed not to remove you from the sector until the preliminary investigation is wrapped up. But Mr. Grant," he said, turning, "has to stay here. He's a Federation operative, but he's also a civilian, and Sindikash law requires we hold him on the planet for further review of his case."

"No!" Worf protested. "He will be killed!"

"What d'you care?" Grant moaned.

As his chest tightened, Worf swung to face him. "Never say that again!"

With a sigh and a nod, Stoner said, "I don't blame you for worrying about that. I know how things are here. I'll hold him in protective custody under my own recognizance until there are charges filed. By then, I think I can get Starfleet fully involved, and you guys can protect him yourself."

"You expect me to leave him on this planet?" Worf challenged, stinging with Grant's loss of faith in him.

The lieutenant's round face tilted in understanding. "You don't have a choice. There's been an injunction issued to evict you from the planet, and, unfortunately, I can't let Mr. Grant go yet. I think the judge is afraid that if we let you both go, we'll never see Starfleet again, and some of us really want to see Starfleet again, if you get what I mean. And I've got some . . . well, let's just say I've got some other people to protect. Everything's a trade-off around here, I'm sorry to say."

"We were hoping to change that," Worf commented bitterly, suddenly caught up in the officer's candidness.

"I got that idea," Stoner said, careful not to commit. "Officer Zared is here to escort you to the City Spaceport and see that you're put on a transport out of Sindikash space. I've arranged a security passage, so you'll be safe till you reach your ship, but I can't authorize any weapons. Meantime, I'll take care of Mr. Grant. You can count on that."

As Worf gazed into Ted Stoner's eyes, he saw the problems of the planet suddenly borne by a young law officer whose burden should not have been so overwhelming. He saw an honest man in the middle of a corrupt web, and he empathized deeply. After all, sooner or later, Worf and Grant would leave this place. Ted Stoner and his other honest comrades would still be here.

Perhaps Worf could arrange for Sindikash to be a better place, if he held the course. Yet his sense of loss was growing heavier by the moment, especially as he looked at the crushed shell of a being who had been his partner and friend.

In every fiber of his posture, Grant communicated a sad slippage of trust between them.

Worf looked at Stoner, desperate for some glimmer of hope, but there was no other course. Not now.

Finally, Worf limped around in front of Grant, but no power on the planet could make Grant look up at him and see the friend he had seen just a day ago.

"Grant," Worf began, "Lieutenant Stoner will see to your safety. He will protect you. And I'll be back. Grant? Do you hear me? I *will* be back."

CHAPTER 12

"I NEVER IMAGINED THEY COULD TAKE A ROYAL NAVY FRIGATE . . . NEVER, never . . ."

Midshipman Edward Nightingale stared out onto the open water of Chesapeake Bay. Picard watched him, deeply sympathizing with the shocked young sailor.

Here they were, huddled in landed exile as their ship was attacked from all quarters. The cannonfire on *Justina* had ceased now. The captain was surrendering rather than lose the ship and crew in a futile battle.

"We have to get out of here," Picard said sharply. "They've seen the warp line and they know there was a landing party. They'll come ashore to find us."

Nightingale turned to him. "But the ship—"

"The ship is captured," Picard snapped, making sure to destroy any thoughts of heroic insanity. "Its crew will be prisoners of war. We must see to ourselves, or we'll be the same."

"Yes, sir . . . but where should we go?" Nightingale asked. "Where can Royal Navy men find safe haven in the colonies?"

"I know," Grenadier Leonfeld said. "I have family here. In Delaware Station."

Worry creased his brow. He was embarrassed to have relatives in the colonies.

"Who are they?" Picard asked.

"My cousin and his family, sir. He was born in England and came here a few years ago. He is a Tory, loyal to the Crown. By trade he's a master weaver. I wrote to him and told him I was coming to the colonies."

"What was his response?"

"I received no response before the ship set sail." His voice grew soft as he added, "I hope he is still . . . alive."

"Alive? Why wouldn't he be?" Picard asked, then instantly regretted that. People died of the lowest, commonest germs in these times, of simple wounds and infections, of childhood diseases that no one in Picard's time even knew about anymore.

"There was a fever, sir," Leonfeld said. "He wrote to tell me his mother had died of it. That was the last time I heard from him."

For the first time in a while, Alexander actually spoke up—and, indeed, Picard noticed this was *the* first time the boy had spoken to his ancestor. "Were you very close, Sergeant?" he asked.

Leonfeld sighed, but it was more of a shudder. His eyes tightened again. "We were more brothers than cousins. We lived in the same house for all our childhood summers. When I came of university age, I went to England and lived with him while attending Cambridge. He wanted me to go into business with him. In point of fact, he wanted me to come here with him. But I wanted a military future. Thus I became a grenadier, and he became an American."

Anticipation blended with fear as Leonfeld gazed down the bay beyond the movement of those ships, and unconcealed emotion clutched his eyes. "If Jeremiah is still here, he will shield us for a while."

Picard clarified. "You say he's loyal?"

"Oh, yes," Leonfeld said sharply. "A proud servant of the Crown. Jeremiah knows well his own blood."

"Is his name Leonfeld also?"

The sergeant looked at him, as if somehow this cast more doubt on their situation, then he peered again through the trees.

"Coverman," he said. "Jeremiah Coverman."

A faint breeze floated down from the night sky and embraced the name of the man they needed to find. Just as Picard braced to rise and step forward, the men around him went suddenly glassy-eyed and began to slow down.

"Oh—" Picard glanced at Alexander and stood up. As they turned, looking for the holodeck entrance, it appeared and opened right in front of a magnificent four-foot diameter oak tree.

"Captain?" Riker came through the entry, but didn't see them right away in the darkness.

"Here, Mr. Riker." Picard pushed his way through the bushes.

"Sir," Riker began, and strode toward them over the mossy roots. "Worf just contacted us from an approaching Sindikash trader. He'll be here in about four hours. They released him when you confirmed his identity. And we have another problem.

"Which is?"

"Evidently, Ross Grant witnessed Odette Khanty's presence in her husband's hospital room seconds before the man unexpectedly died of some kind of aneurysm caused by toxin."

"He was poisoned? Is that confirmed?"

"Yes, it's confirmed. His condition was improving, and he did have a large quantity of two toxic substances in his system, and he sure didn't give them to himself. Grant says he saw Mrs. Khanty put something into the IV tube."

"And Mr. Grant's the only witness?"

"Yes, sir. Sindikash planetary law requires—"

"At least two witnesses for capital crime conviction. I know."

"But Worf hasn't made a statement yet," Riker explained. "His cover's blown, by the way. That's the only way he got off the planet. Grant's in protective custody with the City Police as a material witness."

Picard frowned, irritated at this turn of events. "Well, this is very troublesome, Mr. Riker."

"It's worse than that, sir. Worf knows Grant isn't lying. We know the kind of crimes this woman's engineered, and there's no doubt in my mind or Worf's—"

"Or mine, very definitely. I would certainly find it satisfying to discover some way to convict this individual for the things she's done."

A voice out of the trees behind him caused a tug between Picard's two current realities.

"Is my father in trouble, Captain?"

The captain turned. "Oh—Alexander. No, not in the way you mean. He'll be here shortly. It's Mr. Grant who's in trouble."

"Uncle Ross?" Alexander came forward out of the trees. "He's in trouble? He's practically family." The boy looked at Picard, then at Riker. "I really care about him."

Riker put a hand on Alexander's shoulder. "We'll all do our best to make sure that nothing happens to him."

"You won't let anything happen to him, will you?"

"No, son, no."

"My father won't let anything happen to Uncle Ross, will he?" Suddenly the boy picked up on a bit of expression that Riker allowed to slip through, and Alexander swung back to Picard. "You should at least tell me what's happening. I deserve that. I'm a member of the crew, you know!"

Up to that moment, Picard would have happily deceived the boy into the candy-land of partial realities that children certainly deserved, but something about that declaration stopped him. Where Alexander got this perception of membership in the crew he had no idea, but that was perhaps part of the ballast of living on board a ship—there was no dividing of social structure here. There were no sailors and civilians, no adults and children. They all lived together on this dangerous island. Somehow the ship's sense of inclusion had infected the boy, and now he wielded it with an altogether proper embrace. Alexander saw himself as eligible for the truth.

And when had Picard heard anything so utterly pure and enheartening as that?

Picard looked at Riker. "He's right. He deserves to know."

Dubious, Riker shifted from one foot to the other, and his blue eyes carried a spike of doubt. "There's been a murder, Alexander. The governor of the planet has been assassinated, and your father believes the man's wife did it.

"Mrs. Khanty?" the boy filled in instantly.

"How do you know?" Picard asked sharply.

"I checked. When my father and Uncle Ross headed for that planet, I had Mr. Data show me the files. I read all the headlines and letters. A lot of people don't like her, but a lot of other people think she's practically an angel."

Frowning away his disapproval, Picard said, "Mmm . . . angels are always fodder for street brawls."

"She's no angel," Riker said.

"I know," the boy answered. "Uncle Ross is too nice to go up against somebody like her. He's not a Klingon, like me or my father."

Mouths of babes again, Picard thought with a sigh. True enough. He gazed into the boy's clear and decisive eyes, and could not bring himself to mollify that courage and concern.

"He's a witness to Mrs. Khanty's presence in the room just moments before the governor suddenly died, and apparently she assisted the dying somewhat."

Riker nodded. "Mr. Grant needs corroboration for what he saw, according to Sindikash law, and even though Worf absolutely believes what happened, he can't truthfully *say* he witnessed it."

"Has Worf made his official deposition yet?" Picard asked.

"No, sir, not yet. Worf thinks Grant could be in danger if Mrs. Khanty isn't charged. She'll be able to consolidate her power almost instantly if public opinion goes her way."

"What?" Alexander pulled on Picard's arm. "You mean, if my father doesn't back Uncle Ross up, he could get hurt?"

Both men looked down at the boy, weighing need to know against the right to know.

"You've got to tell me!" Alexander insisted. "I've heard things!"

Picard paused, but realized he'd already crossed that bridge and, like the fleeting of youth, there was no turning back.

"Your father didn't see the woman hurt her husband, Alexander. He can't say he did."

Alexander backed away a step and squared off in a position where he could look at both officers. "Why can't he?"

The simplicity of youth was still effecting a cost despite all the rites of passage. Picard gazed into the boy's determined eyes, but there was little assurance to be given.

"If he knows the truth happened," Alexander persisted, "why can't he *say* it happened?"

Picard drew his brows tight. "It's a matter of honor, Alexander. For your father, it is."

The boy looked at him, struggling. "But honor and truth are supposed to be the same, aren't they? They go together, don't they?"

"Number One, I've faced some of the most challenging adversaries in the galaxy. I've come up against the Borg, the Q, the Cardassians, Romulans, Orions, the Klingons, and even my own holodeck gone hog-wild, yet never have I been so paralyzed as I was five minutes ago, staring down at a boy with one damnably simple question."

As the two men strode down the ship's corridor toward the captain's office, Commander Riker replied, "Sometimes facing the simple logic of a kid's mind can be pretty daunting, sir."

"It's not the child. It's the question."

A work crew doing repairs on the bridge jumped out of Picard's way as he and Riker headed for the Ready Room. Picard chuckled inwardly at himself, thinking in terms of the *Justina* and not crowding the captain on the command deck. He stared briefly at the working ensigns, then his own knees, seeing beyond the Starfleet uniform to the 1777 Royal Navy breeches and jacket that now felt somehow as natural. He wished he were still wearing them. He felt as if he'd abandoned something, and ached to go back.

"Why didn't I have an answer for Alexander?" he mourned. "Poor boy, he certainly deserved one."

"Yes," Riker said, settling down in the chair at one end of the couch. He smiled and his eyes sparkled devilishly. "After all, he's a member of the crew."

"Well, yes, he is," Picard said, brushing away Riker's attempt at a joke. "Everyone subject to the fate of any vessel over any stretch of time is a member of its crew. Alexander has a sense of self. He doesn't just feel he's part of the crew because of his father. He thinks that because of himself and his loyalties. He's quite a young man."

Riker smiled again. "Learning more than history, are we, sir?"

"On two fronts, I'm afraid," the captain admitted as he watched two ensigns attempt to dislodge a heavy climate-control unit from the ceiling panels. "When I first began the program I never imagined either would take on this much substance. And this Odette Khanty is a poisonous creature." Picard leaned back thoughtfully. "If Worf doesn't back Grant up, Khanty can put her organization in place and the planet'll never be rid of her. She'll be the single most powerful person in the quadrant."

"And you'll never hear the end of it from Mr. Toledano."

"Oh, I don't care about—Good God!"

Picard nearly jumped out of his skin when a reddish-gold life-form vaulted from behind the couch and landed on his shoulder. Then the alien announced, "MMrrrrrewwwww!" in his ear and put a paw on his nose.

"What—what is Mr. Data's *cat* doing in my ready room!"

Riker reached over and scratched the cat's neck. The amenable tabby arched in gratifying response and leaned into Picard's ear. "Don't you like cats, sir?"

"I can't imagine what an android needs with a cat, Mr. Riker!" He shouldered the liquid creature down onto his elbow, and somehow the cat melted onto his lap from there.

"What does anybody 'need' with cats, sir?" Riker tortured.

"Well, I *need* this one out of my Ready Room. Please return it to Mister Data." Handing the cat away to Riker, Picard grumbled, "I'd rather face Odette Khanty and all her Rogues."

"Mmm." Riker stroked the cat's ball-shaped head. "Worf says he's never seen a person whose private personality is so diametrically opposed to the public one. Ordinarily, there's *some* flicker of resemblance. She's like an old Earth union boss—self-insulating."

"Worf's never been a hypocrite," Picard told him evenly. "That's why he's sometimes been confused in his personal searches. It's why the Day of Honor bothers him. He doesn't always define honor the way other Klingons do. He tries very hard to fit into the Klingon mold, but every time he's come to a fork in the road, he's chosen the Federation path."

"I don't like this kind of enemy," Picard went on, his mind still on Odette Khanty. "I imagine it's even worse for Worf. He's used to someone he can challenge openly, honestly. With a bat'leth."

Riker nodded as he led the way into the nearest turbolift. "This is a lot more Mr. Toledano's kind of thing, all this espionage, subterfuge, spying, assassinations, all this local business—"

"It's just politics, Mr. Riker. So there's some politics going on. So what? Bringing down a criminal of this sort, with tentacles out to the Romulans and Cardassians . . . it's a good thing to do. What difference does it make how we're doing it? Certainly, being convinced to stay in the Federation isn't the worst thing that can happen to those people."

"No, sir," Riker agreed, "but it's tricky, this independence business. Do we or don't we? Should they or shouldn't they? Federation membership has its obligations, one being a long secession process."

"But Sindikash isn't a member that came in from outside," Picard pointed out. "There's a whole different set of procedures for colonial independence. Much harder ones."

"I don't know much about that," Riker admitted. "A planet we invested in and built decides, 'Well, we don't like this or that, so we're checking out.' Doesn't make sense."

"Like the Colonial United States," Picard said. "That didn't seem to make sense either, yet its successful independence helped sculpt the model for the galaxy as we now know it, and build the thriving civilization we now enjoy. I'm finding it difficult not to afford Sindikash the same chance."

As the lift opened and deposited them on Deck 10, Riker tilted his head. "That doesn't sound like you, sir."

"Doesn't it? What Sindikash wants to do is just what the Colonies did. Seize someone else's investment."

"But, sir, the Colonies weren't being represented. Britain was a caste system. What level you were born to was everything. And what about the people on Sindikash who want to remain in the Federation? They're our citizens, and their rights can't be abrogated simply by a planet's threat to secede."

"They can always leave the planet. That's what Mrs. Khanty would say. That's what the patriots of the Colonies said. Now, what's the problem with it?"

Riker smiled. "Quizzing me, sir?"

"Why not?"

"Well, given Mrs. Khanty's type of action, I'd say she would pass a one-hundred-percent departure tax."

The doors to Ten Forward opened. Picard scanned the empty room.

"And where is Mr. Toledano, anyway?" he asked, irritated.

"He's taking a shuttle ride, sir," Riker said.

"I beg your pardon?"

"He wanted to see the ship from the outside. So as soon as the Ferengi freighter passed along Worf's message, I sent Mr. Toledano on a nice, *long* tour."

"Oh, he's all right," Picard acceded, leading the way back to the holodeck. "He's quite correct when it comes to the planet's effects on the sector if Mrs. Khanty entrenches herself." Riker frowned. "I can't help thinking that the people on that planet deserve the right to make a free and *uninfluenced* choice."

"They can't have one," Picard pointed out sternly. "They either get influenced by Mrs. Khanty or by us. Unless she leaves them alone, *we* don't dare."

The captain booted up Alexander's program, which materialized in its semifrozen state, with Grenadier Leonfeld, Midshipman Nightingale, and the *Justina*'s two deckhands moving at the pace of sick snails. Since he'd left, they hadn't moved an entire step, and yet there seemed to somehow be life in them, as though once called into being, like spirits in a seance, they couldn't be exorcised until their own mission was complete.

He gazed at them, troubled. "Odette Khanty is manipulating the people of Sindikash. The Federation has a right to countermanipulate."

"Aren't we using subterfuge to maneuver an outcome that should be a free choice?" Riker gestured toward the holodeck door. "So the British used cannons to do the same—what's the difference? I wonder . . . are we playing the part of the British?"

Picard tucked his chin. "Will, we're going after a criminal organization. That's the difference. A very big one." He looked at Grenadier Leonfeld, and his mind divided between worlds. "Find Alexander and have him come back here. I'd like to get on with this. We've got several hours before Worf arrives. I'd like to distract the boy."

"Right away, sir," Riker responded, and there was a clarity of purpose in his tone now, too. One final time he gazed at the pretty picture of the ship on Chesapeake Bay. "Was it a decisive battle, sir?"

"I think not," Picard said. "Sadly, it seems to be one of the hundreds of unnoticed skirmishes that took many men's lives and eventually contributed to a larger end. Odd, isn't it, how many footnotes it takes to make up a past . . . " He shook his head and balled his fists, and felt himself bristling. "It's a big galaxy, Mr. Riker. How do our problems get so finely concentrated?"

Riker glanced sidelong at the old-world crew of the old-world ship, with all their old-world problems, and seemed, like Picard, to see a reflection of something much closer.

"Talent, sir," he said.

CHAPTER 13

"DO YOU KNOW WHERE THIS JEREMIAH COVERMAN LIVES?"

"A house beside a factory. He has a linen factory. He risked everything. His family rejected him when he came here. He was penniless. I sent him some silver to start his business."

"Then he should be happy to see you," Picard said as he crouched beside Sergeant Alexander Leonfeld. "Let's go down there."

"How shall we find the linen factory?" Midshipman Nightingale asked. "We're in uniform. We can hardly ask about."

"The town's scarcely two kilometers in diameter. We'll find it."

Bennett and the other oarsman, an impressed cobbler named Wollard, shuffled forward in the trees. "Sir," Bennett began, "me and Wollard 'ere, we ought to volunteer to go an' 'ave a look before you an' the young sirs go in there."

Picard rewarded him with a thready smile. "That's very gentlemanly, Mr. Bennett, but we'll all go. Better we stay together for now."

They'd walked half the night. More than that. And now they stood on a heavily treed ridge, looking down at a coastal village, where only a few candles glowed at this late hour. Just beyond the town, the small boatyard and the port could be identified by several masts sticking up into the moonlight.

"They must be asleep, sir," Wollard guessed.

"No, they're not asleep. Look," Picard pointed out. "There are lanterns lit at the boatyard. There's activity. I see people moving about."

"Fortifying," Leonfeld suggested. "In case we got through. Preparing to defend the yard."

"Then they don't know yet," Nightingale added.

"That could work in our favor," Picard said hopefully. "They'll be distracted, and they don't know anyone made it ashore. Let's hurry. And, Sergeant, you should leave that headgear behind. It'll be cumbersome and a little obvious."

Leonfeld nodded, ditched his tall yellow headpiece, and they moved out. They hustled together through the trees, making use of the darkness, and found their way to the narrow dirt streets. Picard was gratified to be quite right about the size of the town. There were only a handful of streets to be checked, a few of which were cobbled with rounded stones from the size of melons to the size of eggs. He recalled that many streets in the old eastern United States were paved with stones carried as ballast aboard ships. He warmed to the little town instantly.

Systematic reconnaissance paid off within a half hour. Three streets from the riverfront, they discovered a building with the right sign over the door.

"That's a factory?" Alexander ridiculed. "It's so small!"

Indeed, the word implied a massive complex to people of the 24th century, but here in 1777 a factory was something entirely different. The linen factory was a narrow three-story clapboard building, painted blue but weathered to gray, with a nicely carved business sign: COVERMAN TEXTILES.

Sergeant Leonfeld gazed at the sign with his cousin's name upon it and murmured, "Jeremiah . . . "

Alexander smiled in empathy for his relative, glad that the sergeant had found what he needed to see.

Picard, though, realized that the fact that Leonfeld's cousin's business was still here said precious little about whether or not the cousin was still alive. This could be the man's family running the business, or an entirely new owner who had kept the name.

"When last I heard from Jeremiah, he had employed four people," Leonfeld said. "I know it seems insignificant . . . "

"Perhaps to the landed aristocracy of Europe," Picard commented, annoyed.

Leonfeld cast him a crabby glare, but said nothing. Of course, the sergeant still believed he was speaking to a lieutenant of the Royal Navy.

What would he have thought if he knew he was speaking to a captain of Starfleet?

They were hiding behind a wooden slat fence, watching men dash back and forth, carrying tools and boxes. The boxes probably held precious ammunition with which the fort would be defended. They thought there was a British ship coming in, but of course that wouldn't be happening now. These colonists had been victorious with their frontal assault, but didn't even know it yet. They were still afraid. Picard saw it in their faces. Afraid, defiant, dreading a battle while anxious to get it started.

"Perhaps we should go around back, sir," Nightingale offered. "After all . . . " He touched the facing of his blue uniform jacket.

Picard nodded. "Mr. Leonfeld, your recommendation?"

Leonfeld studied the cobbled street, the front of the linenworks, the house on the other side that they needed to get to, and the sporadic activity in the street. "The back. Yes. My cousin wrote that he lived in a house beside the factory . . . " He pointed to a house made of split logs, rather small, with two stories and square windows with painted shutters.

"Alexander," Picard murmured, taking the boy by the arm, "you stay close to me."

The boy looked at him, then turned longingly to the sergeant, who was obviously the person he really wanted to keep close to. However he made no protests, and the landing party moved out on Picard's signal.

Staying under cover of darkness and any structure that would hide them, they picked their way clumsily around the back of the factory, stumbling several times in the darkness over packing barrels and mechanical parts, until they found the aft end of the log house.

There, they crouched and surveyed the house.

A small back window beside a clay chimney glowed with the light of two candles on tin sconces. So someone was awake.

But there was no noise of movement, talking.

"Mr. Leonfeld," Picard murmured, "look in that window. See if there is anything or anyone you recognize."

Leonfeld nodded, but couldn't find his voice. He handed his rifle to Nightingale, and picked his way to the window. Even at his height of nearly six feet, he had to stand on tiptoe to see into that small window. He pressed his fingers against the painted wooden sill and looked straight in, then left, then right.

"No one," he said. "No one at all . . . but candles burn within . . . and there is a pitcher and some papers on a table."

"Inside," Picard said. He made straight for a very narrow back door and gripped the latch.

The door opened hospitably before him, and the scent of a wood fire drew him inward, where he stood beneath a claustrophobic ceiling, scarcely tall enough to admit Sergeant Leonfeld. Until this moment, when the warmth of the crackling cobblestone fireplace and the sooty scent of burning logs coiled around him, Picard hadn't realized how chilled he'd become. Now his hands began to flex again and his arms and knees to ease their aches, and for a moment he was almost dizzy with the charming sensation.

The cabin was a single keeping room, with a narrow stairway to their left, leading most likely to sleeping quarters. An oval rag rug in the middle of the room was the only covering upon a worn wooden slat floor that had a few visible sags. The two candles stood in tin sconces with rubbed backings that reflected their glow forward from the exposed-log walls, casting a dim light upon the side of the room farthest from the fireplace.

The fireplace was also made of those ballast stones, soot-darkened from the cooking hearth, and laden with iron utensils hanging from hooks. Iron pots, molded muffin tins, and a rolling pin hung from one of the four ceiling beams. Near one of the two front windows was a trestle table, flanked by two simple benches made of half-logs and standing upon stumpy wooden legs. On the table near the pitcher were several pamphlets and papers. Over the nearest bench was spread a dull-colored quilt with star patterns. Picard smiled when he saw that.

Near the fire was a simple Welsh-type lambing chair and a small crooked tavern table, and on the other side of the room, the cool side, was a collection of grass baskets, a chopping block, and a barrel that might be a grain bin—

"Stand very still or die turning!"

Despite the sharp order, all five swung about toward the voice and found themselves staring down the barrel of a wide-muzzled pistol.

The pistol barrel protruded from the narrow stairway, in which there was only a blurred shadow of a man.

"What are you doing in this town?" the voice demanded. "Are you advance scouts?"

At the sound of the voice, with its decidedly English accent, Picard held his hands up cautiously. "We're survivors. Our ship ran aground. We only want safe haven until we can sort things out."

"There's no safe haven for you here. In this town, you'll be turned over to the Continental Army as prisoners of war."

"We're not here to participate in the war," Picard persisted. "We're looking for the owner of the linen factory. Jeremiah Coverman."

At the sound of the name, the gunman stepped out of the stairway shadow. He was a young man, perhaps twenty-five, medium height and muscular, and he possessed the same blue eyes as Alexander Leonfeld. The family resemblance was instantly recognizable, despite this man's much darker brown hair, more weathered complexion, and stockier build.

"What is it you want here?" Coverman asked, still leveling the pistol on Picard, as if understanding quite well that he was the officer of rank here. Evidently he knew something about the British military. He came into the room, and there was some movement in the stairwell behind him, but Picard couldn't yet see who else was there.

Without answering, Picard glanced around at Sergeant Leonfeld, who until now had been standing off to one side, near the wide cooking hearth.

Leonfeld was only staring, with a peculiar nostalgia gripping his features. As Picard looked at him, he choked up a voice. "Jeremiah?"

Coverman squinted into the candlelit dimness at the tall grenadier in the bright scarlet uniform coat with its white facings and brass buttons, and for the first time he saw something other than the clothing.

The pistol wavered, then finally came down.

Jeremiah Coverman narrowed his eyes again, crossed the line over to believing what he saw, and rasped, "Sa—"

Leonfeld dropped his rifle onto a bench, Coverman shoved his pistol onto the table, and the cousins came together in a long-overdue embrace. They seemed truly shocked to see each other, as if each had thought the other dead or forever lost.

"Sandy!" Coverman finally choked out the rest of the name.

After a moment Sergeant Leonfeld was laughing as he hugged his cousin, and Jeremiah Coverman simply gasped, "My God! My God! Oh, God, dear God!"

His enthusiasm was so heartrending that Picard half expected the roof to part and an answer to be delivered from on high.

Grinning happily, Alexander sidled to Picard's side during this distraction, and uttered, "Is this another relative of mine?"

Glancing down at the boy with a wistful grin of his own, Picard simply said, "Seems so."

Evidently, the two cousins were not the only ones in the room just discovering long-lost relations. The boy seemed overwhelmed by these human relations suddenly popping up in a life in which human things had seemed the more elusive and Klingon things the most important.

"My God . . . Sandy, Sandy . . . Sandy!" Jeremiah finally allowed his cousin to pull him back so they could get a good look at each other. "When—did you get taller? Look at you! My heaven, look at your hair! It's so light! And you actually fill out that jacket! You never filled out a piece of clothing in all our lives!"

"You always filled yours out mightily well," the rechristened Sandy chuckled, thumping his cousin's middle, "and now you've worked it off!"

"Starved it off, more like. My God . . . this is unthinkable! What are you doing here? Why didn't you write that you were coming?"

"I attempted to do so, but the ship upon which my letter traveled evidently was attacked and sunk. Your little war."

"Yes, yes . . . " Coverman pulled away another step, though he kept one hand clasped tightly on Sandy's elbow, and leaned toward the narrow stairway. "Amy!" he called on a laugh. "Amy, come down! It's all right! This is our Sandy! Can you believe it?"

A teenaged girl came peeking from the stairwell, her brown hair twisted up under a lace cap, and she was dressed in a day dress even though this was the middle of the night. Apparently the town had indeed been expecting trouble on the water tonight. Jeremiah, Picard noticed now, was also dressed, despite the hour, in a simple linen shirt with long full sleeves, a brown vest, and gray breeches.

Coverman caught the teenaged girl's hand and pulled her into the room. "This is Amy," he said, beaming. "My wife."

Picard almost bolted a protest—the girl could hardly be fifteen years old.

"Sandy . . . not really?" Amy Coverman's voice was very soft, far more demure than any female Picard had ever known. She offered her hand to her husband's cousin. "Mr. Leonfeld, I'm deeply glad you've come here!"

"Madam." Sandy took her hand and bowed at the waist, morphing instantly into that elegant aristocrat who was never far beneath the surface. "My dear cousin," he added as he looked at her pale young face. "I see, Jeremiah, you've transgressed into child-stealing."

Jeremiah smiled at his very young wife. "Our marriage was arranged by the pastor of our chapel. We were married when Amy turned fourteen. And so lucky a man as I never walked in less than Heaven."

The girl smiled back, blushing in the candlelight, and Picard could hardly deny the adoration that had evidently survived the wearing away of girlish infatuation.

At the stairs another person appeared, a second woman of thirty or more, pulling behind her a child who seemed, by Picard's faulty reckoning, to be about four years old. The woman cautiously kept the child, a boy, behind her aproned skirts, but he peeked out at the strangers.

"Pardon me," Amy Coverman said. "Aunt Mercy, it's all right to come down. Gentlemen, may I present my mother's second sister, Mercy Starrett, and her son, Seth Starrett."

"Madam," Picard offered.

"Sir," the other woman said. She was very plump and nervous, wide-eyed at the sight of the strange men, and hid her child behind her skirts even as she entered the room.

"Have you eaten?" Jeremiah Coverman suddenly asked, pumping Sandy Leonfeld's arm. "How did you get here? Where is your regiment? I can hardly get over that uniform! Cursed if you don't look like a proper British tyrant in it! And who are these other men?"

"Oh—I beg your pardon." Leonfeld stepped back and motioned to Picard and the others. "This is Lieutenant Picard of Her Majesty's Fighting Ship *Justina,* Midshipman Nightingale, Seamen Bennett and Wollard, and Ship's Swab Alexander."

Scowling, Alexander didn't seem to care much for that particular title, and glanced at Picard in something like self-consciousness. Picard wasn't sure if the name had insulted the boy, or if the boy was bothered by having Sandy Leonfeld be the one to call him that. Nothing to be done about it.

Coverman scanned them, but something else was on his mind. "Where is the ship?" he asked.

Leonfeld started to answer, then thought better and turned to Picard, allowing an officer of the Royal Navy ship's command to speak for it.

Picard responded with an inward shrug. "I'm afraid our frigate is aground in the Bay and has fallen to colonials."

"Has it, now! Think of that!" Coverman turned to his wife. "Amy, think of it!" He swung around again. "How on earth did you escape?"

"We were on the land when the final attack came," Picard said.

"What exceptional luck!" Jeremiah gasped with a nervous, overwhelmed shudder.

Sandy Leonfeld patted his cousin warmly on the shoulder, and turned to look at Picard and the other displaced crew of the lost British ship. "You see? I told you we would find a Loyalist haven in this nest of rebellion!"

At once Jeremiah Coverman's smile fell away and a pasty fear took over his rosy expression. "Well, yes, you may have haven here."

He ducked under his cousin's arm, hurried first to one front window and drew shut the calico curtains, then crossed the closed front door and also drew together the curtains on the other front window.

"Yes—you could be safe here for a time, but . . . Delaware Station is a stronghold of patriots. Not like New York or Philadelphia, where there are forty or more percent of those still loyal to King George. You would be safer there, if you must stay. Loyalists are poorly tolerated here, especially among those who work at the boatyard, which are many. Have a care what you say and to whom you say it. How we can get you back upon a British vessel, I'm sure I've no idea . . . certainly, we must find that way, or all is lost." He ran a finger through the air to illustrate the clothes they were wearing. "Better you not be seen in your uniforms—I shall give you other livery. Oh, and you must be hungry! Amy, Mercy . . . please."

He motioned to the two women. Amy Coverman turned and hurried back upstairs, and Mercy put her child by the fire and hurried to a wooden cabinet with cut metal doors, from which she extracted loaves of bread, a deep tin with a pie-crust topping, and a round whey-colored mound that might be cheese. She took those to the trestle table and set them beside the salt-glazed pitcher that was already there. Then she went after several pewter tankards on a shelf.

"Please," Jeremiah said, and Picard noted that the cousin was suddenly nervous.

Picard empathized with the poor man, a Crown Loyalist living in a rebel port, now with a houseful of escaped British sailors, and even two officers, whom he felt a familial obligation to hide. This surely put Jeremiah Coverman in tricky straits.

"Please, sit down," Jeremiah repeated, taking Sandy by the elbow and gazing briefly at him with a sad warmth. "Let me give you a few moments of comfort before the difficulties ensue."

"Difficulties?" Sandy eyed his cousin, but stepped to the table and lowered himself onto the bench. He was tentatively joined by the two sailors, by Mr. Nightingale, and finally by Alexander and Picard.

Picard found himself watching the two cousins, especially Coverman. For a man caught in a strange country in which he was an enemy, Sandy Leonfeld was strangely relaxed. On the other hand, Jeremiah Covernman drew his brows, pressed a hand to his lips, tried to think, and each decision seemed to come at a price, even as simple as pouring ale from that pitcher into Sandy's tankard. And strong-smelling stuff it was, too—

What was this? A poke at his thigh. Picard looked automatically to his side. Alexander was knuckling him in the leg. The boy's eyes were wide, and he seemed aware of something Picard had missed.

"Something?" he asked, figuring matters were as well handled with honesty, but he asked it low, as the clatter of pewter plates and the murmuring of the women overrode his utterance.

Alexander didn't answer, but nodded twice, vigorously, and looked at Jeremiah.

The cousin's eyes were tight with concern as he oversaw their spare meal. What did Alexander see there, and what was Picard missing? A man frightened for his cousin's well-being? Even survival, probably. These were hot times. Of those in this cabin, only Picard and the boy knew that Sandy would indeed survive the war to pass his chronicles along to future generations, or that his legacy would indeed reach so far, or that there would someday be such a telescope as this with which to gaze back.

Jeremiah was just now moving the stack of pamphlets aside to make room for Sandy's plate, and seemed to feel awkward about doing so, so much that Sandy noticed the pamphlets and plucked one off the top of the stack just before his cousin had a chance to turn away.

"What's this?" the sergeant asked. "Do they indeed possess literature in the Colonies? I hadn't thought so." He smiled, and looked at the pamphlet, not noticing his cousin's suddenly blanched face.

Then Sandy laughed spontaneously.

"Common Sense'! I've heard of this. Thomas Paine, yes—I recall when that slackard left England. And good riddance as well. A failure and a scoundrel and troublemaker, that one. I've heard of his rantings since he came here. He's bent upon success here which he could not legitimately achieve in England. He wants it by wresting away the possessions by rebellion that he could not acquire by merit. He's worse than a rebel. He's an Englishman turned traitor."

And Sandy laughed again, this time looking up at Jeremiah and smiling. He gave the pamphlet a little shake.

"Why do you have this?" he asked.

CHAPTER 14

"OH, NO . . ."

The small cabin turned suddenly chilly.

"You cannot be one of these creatures," Sandy Leonfeld declared to his cousin.

Flinty resentment surged through Jeremiah Coverman's contriteness. "Can't I?"

Caught fast by curiosity, Picard watched both men very carefully, and noted that Alexander was rapt as a hawk on prey.

Sandy Leonfeld looked like a man with the stuffing kicked out of him. His shoulders sagged, his proud chest caved in, his chin sank. His whole uniform seemed suddenly soggy.

He moaned upward from a sickened heart. Over and over he warbled, "No . . . no . . . no . . ."

He shook his head and blinked repeatedly at the pamphlet in his hands, then looked up.

"You're a British citizen," he uttered on a breath. "The Crown, Jeremiah . . . the Crown is everything!"

"The Crown is *nothing,*" Jeremiah countered with sudden abrasion, as if he had just taken the disagreement as an insult.

The two cousins, so lately reunited in great joy, stared at each other astringently.

Pity gripped Picard as he saw that Sandy Leonfeld was a man watching a precious thing die. Great loss shone upon his young face, in lines as purely etched as ancient rivers gouging the surface of a planet. His eyes disappeared in a shadow beneath his thick blond hair as he lowered his head and mourned.

That pain was mirrored fully in Jeremiah Coverman, and now threatened to be the only thing left the two had in common. Perhaps shame and certainly sorrow limned his face as well, but unlike his cousin he did not lower his eyes. He evidently had no intention of making excuses. Now Picard understood why the communication between the cousins had eventually ceased—Jeremiah hadn't wanted to tell Sandy what was happening in this household, in his mind and heart.

No—not shame. Picard looked again for it, expected it, but found none in Jeremiah's demeanor. Resentment, yes, but no embarrassment for this turn he had taken.

Sandy Leonfeld battled his very physical reaction to this news, and found the strength to square his shoulders. "The divine right of kings is beyond refute," he simmered. "A person *can* be born better than others. All blood is not alike. These Colonial ideas of equality are awkward, and their declarations are truant."

Though bread and cheese stood guard on the trestle, no one touched it. The two deckhands and the "ship's boy" waited for their superiors to begin, and the superiors were busy.

"Jeremiah, you deceive yourself," Sandy blazed. "You are not one of these rabblers. The Crown and the European system has given you everything. It set these Colonies into business. Gave you land, and the tools to work it. Provided you trade and market, protected you, sent you food and tea—we have *built* you. If this shabby, backward place were to somehow become a country, it would only be by the grace of your country and your King. And now you, an aristocrat, will spit in his face?"

Jeremiah's face turned rosy with emotion and he shifted as if aware of all the eyes, all the judgments, upon him. "I cannot be Tory any longer," he said simply. "The class system does not work in the New World."

"Because malcontents cannot work it!" Sandy shot back. And he stood very straight.

Picard deliberately said nothing. He was watching the two men, but also watching Alexander, who had stepped forward in rapt attention to what was happening between his ancestors. The complexities of human history, so often simplistic in the minds of spacefaring races, was coming to light for the boy.

And for his captain, guilty sometimes of the same charge.

Before Jeremiah could respond, someone knocked on the front door.

"Please, stand away." Jeremiah became suddenly nervous, and his wife crowded him as they both went to the door.

He opened it, and luckily its method of opening prevented anyone standing outside from seeing the trestle table and those who sat or stood around it. Picard motioned for the men to remain quiet and still.

"Thank you, Angus," Jeremiah said, and immediately closed the door again. Whoever had been there had said nothing at all.

As Jeremiah closed and latched the door again, he now held a piece of cloth, rolled and folded. He turned to his wife, and together they opened the tiny package. Inside, Picard could see a message scrawled on the cloth, and a large hand-forged square-headed nail.

Jeremiah glanced at Picard. "It's from Elder Nethers. He owns the nailery."

"Ah!" Sandy impugned. "Communicating with the elite, are we? Let us by all means sup with the nailer, the chandler, the cooper, the cobbler, and let us not snub the butcher, else we starve."

Jeremiah looked up sharply. "Have a care, Sandy."

"Cousin," Amy Coverman chided softly. "You insult us."

Glowering at her, Sandy responded, "You insult yourselves, madam."

"What does the note say?" Picard asked, hoping to scope out a plan of action that didn't end in these two men having a duel under some crooked tree.

Jeremiah almost answered, then suddenly looked at Sandy. Picard noticed with regret Jeremiah's abrupt realization that he might not be able to trust one of the dearest people to his heart in the world.

In that terrible instant, he crossed the line into distrust. He and Sandy became enemies.

And a sad thing it was to witness.

Jeremiah shielded his sorrow in the act of folding the note and stuffing it into his waistcoat; then he stepped to the mantel over the fireplace and placed the forged nail into a tin box with several others of its kind. Clearly, there had been messages before from the nailery.

Anxiety crawled through despair in Jeremiah's eyes as he turned with resolve to Sandy once again.

"I am a patriot," he quietly proclaimed. "We are decent people who want charge of our possessions."

"Decent?" Sandy shook his head. "Are your Committees of Safety decent when they arrest loyal British citizens? Tar and feather them? Seize their property because they fail to embrace your selfish rebel causes? Send them to prison? For people who speak of rights and freedoms, you suspend those for any who disagree with your politics. Have a care yourselves, Jeremiah, for frivolity is devil's play. Beware burning too many candles. The whim of the day is a dangerous tool with which to govern."

"Whim?" Jeremiah's tone turned abrasive for the first time. "Who exactly are you to come here with your powdered wigs and tell us what to do with the fruits of our pursuits?"

Sandy Leonfeld had been standing with one shoulder toward his cousin, as if attempting to mentally stalk away from the proceedings, but now he turned fully to face Jeremiah Coverman, and his shoulders drew slightly back.

His eyes burned as he made his cold announcement.

"We are your betters."

Tension reached critical mass in the small cabin, braced passively by the fire snapping crisply in the hearth.

The sailors remained silent, riveted by the friction between the cousins, so clearly defining the little, sparking war that now embraced two continents.

"Everyone is better than someone," Jeremiah allowed. "I cannot deny others the chance to acquire betterment."

"One cannot 'acquire' the status of a gentleman," the sergeant clarified. "One must be born to that status. Officers and gentlemen have run the British government and military since ancient times, and that is why Britain has survived. Tradition must be respected, else we are no longer civilized. Look at France! Where would that cesspool of peasants be if not for the aristocracy? Should the elite crumble, Europe would go to pot. The class system in the military is the only reason the lowest soldier can eat. So it is in all of society. The system is run on our honor. While we are out here, thousands of miles from our king, we still owe loyalty to him. We owe loyalty to the system that feeds us. If it falls, we fall."

"You're living an illusion," Jeremiah told him quietly. "You've simply never seen any other way."

"Oh?" Sandy's eyebrow went up like a rising barometer. "Do you know you're insulting me now?"

"I'm insulting myself, then," Jeremiah said, "for mine is high birth as well."

Sandy Leonfeld's eyes narrowed, and his shoulders squared once again upon that narrow figure.

With great luster he said, "Not as high as *mine.* I am a peer of the realm. My descendants will be dukes and princes, lords, barons, and kings."

Picard leaned toward Alexander. "And Klingons," he murmured.

"Jeremiah, be reasonable!" the sergeant pleaded. "Do you honestly believe this clatter of colonies is a nation? Do you think you can survive without selling yourself to another foreign power? There is a king in your future, America, for that is where the power lives, and you need power to survive against power. Soon or late, the colonies will make deals with kings. If you're successful in breaking from Britain, I hope you enjoy being a Spaniard or a Dutchman. Or, God forbid, French! Independence! What a lie!"

He stalked away from Jeremiah, putting what precious little distance between them this cabin's keeping room allowed. As he paused near the fireplace, glaring into the fire with menacing eyes, he cast a single glance at Picard, noted what had just been said, but decided not to apologize. The sergeant seemed as baneful as he was appalled, and the level of his conviction was clearly met by the conviction in Jeremiah Coverman's face, and those of the two women.

He placed his hands on his hips and glared around at the cabin and its humble accoutrements; certainly, he was measuring it up with the splendor of his life, and Jeremiah's former life, as the aristocracy of Britain and Austria. Surely this place was humbled by the past of both these young men, and all that was reflected, down to the sconces, in Sandy Leonfeld's contemptuous survey.

"Freeze program." Picard waited for the computer to slow the holoprogram, but it didn't happen. Instead, all the people in the room turned to look at him and try to figure out what he was talking about.

"I beg your pardon, lieutenant?" Jeremiah asked.

Aunt Mercy craned about as if expecting spirits to come out of the walls.

"Computer, I *said,* freeze the program," Picard repeated.

Finally the holoprogram slowed to a stop.

He turned to the boy.

"Why did you stop it?" Alexander asked, his adolescent fists balling with attempted manliness. "It was just getting good!"

"Alexander, how did you know?" Picard wondered. "Before Jeremiah said anything, you realized he was no longer loyal to the Crown, didn't you?"

"Yes." The boy looked at him, his face crumpled with dissatisfaction and disappointment. He thought back, and said, "Jeremiah was acting like a kid who was afraid to say what he'd done. He just acted sort of . . . ungood."

As the corner of his mouth came up involuntarily, Picard smiled ruefully and repeated, "Ungood. Shakespeare couldn't have said it better. And what do you think was 'ungood' about his new beliefs?"

"He wanted to keep them a secret. He knew Sandy wouldn't like it that Jeremiah has turned against everything they both used to stand for. They had loyalties. They made promises. Sandy's oath was made for life. Jeremiah went back on his oath. I don't think I like Jeremiah very much. And I think he knows he's wrong, or he would be prouder of himself. He wouldn't be trying to keep secrets."

"Mmm," Picard uttered again. "May have something there. With which of these men do you find yourself agreeing?"

Alexander speared him with a glare. "With the sergeant, of course!"

"Why, Alexander?"

The boy balked at the question, not because of its difficulty, but that there should be any question at all. "Jeremiah made a promise to the king! That has to mean something. Sandy's sticking with his promise. *That*'s honor."

"What about Jeremiah's honor? Remember, the Day of Honor holiday is meant to appreciate your enemy's hon—"

"He doesn't have any!" the boy said scornfully. "Or else, how could he turn his back on his whole family? His family raised him to be something, and they worked to give him things, and he swore an oath, and he's dumping all that so he can be a rebellion person." The boy leaned toward Picard and lowered his voice. "I think he changed so he could get that pretty wife. *She*'s American, you know."

Trying not to grin, Picard nodded.

Alexander's eyes widened in a parody of suggestiveness, and he nodded in agreement with himself.

"Mmm-hmm," Picard muttered. "I do know that, yes . . . "

"These colonists," Alexander went on, "none of them have any honor! How am I supposed to understand celebrating your enemy's honor when he doesn't have any to celebrate? This holiday doesn't make any sense."

He dumped himself down like a sack on the bench, next to the slowly turning form of Midshipman Nightingale.

"What makes you say they have none at all?" Picard persisted.

Alexander fanned his arms. "Why else would they attack a ship that's stranded? That's not honorable at all! It's what cowards do!"

Picard tipped his head. "Actually, I thought it wasn't a bad tactic at all."

The boy hurled him a glowering look. "You'd do that?"

"If I had to, yes."

Astounded by the lack of shame in Picard's voice and his studied casualness at such an idea, Alexander pushed off the bench and stalked the room, patently avoiding the semistill figure of Jeremiah Coverman.

At the pie cabinet, he placed his hands on his hips and shook his head. "I never thought we were that kind of people!"

The purity of the boy's heart rang and rang, and Picard began to realize that somehow, despite Alexander's jostled upbringing and his life on board the starship—questionable at best for any growing child—he was turning out to be a young man of principle.

Feeling something shine in his chest from this revelation, Picard moved toward the boy.

"Alexander," he asked, "what's really wrong with you?"

The boy didn't look at him this time, but other things about his demeanor changed. His posture declared that this had gone beyond a history lesson, beyond a tradition, and, in fact, beyond a rite of passage. A certain fundamentality had taken hold.

"Oh, I see . . . " Picard circled around in front of him without crowding him. "It's your father and Mr. Grant, isn't it?"

Alexander kicked the leg of a spinning wheel that had been tucked into a corner. "Don't talk to me about my father! I don't want to talk about him."

"Why not?"

"Because I don't. And it's none of your business if I don't."

"Now, really," Picard said. "Who's being dishonorable now?"

Fuming, the boy toed the spinning wheel, but didn't kick it this time. He gnashed and grieved, spun around as if to challenge, then recoiled, and finally chafed out his thoughts.

"He's letting Uncle Ross down. And his life is in danger! You can't pretend it's not, because I know what's been happening on Sindikash."

"Are you worried that your father has lost his honor?" Picard asked. "It's his sense of honor that prevents him from lying, you know."

"What honor? If he knows Mrs. Khanty did bad things, why would he throw away a chance to lock her up? If he knows she's guilty, why can't he use what he knows to keep her from hurting more people? Maybe the person she hurts next will be Grant!"

Picard drew a troubled breath, balking at the boy's relentless logic. "Things are complex," he attempted. "Adult things."

Like a prosecutor in court, Alexander shot back, "If he saw her do these things, he'd use his phaser, wouldn't he?"

Taken by surprise, Picard admitted, "Well . . . I would hope so, yes."

Alexander fanned his arms. "Then I don't understand this! He won't lie, but he wouldn't *really* be lying, because he'd be making the truth happen. Instead, he's making Uncle Ross look like a liar. It's not fair."

"Unfortunately," Picard sighed, "'fairness' isn't all it's cracked up to be."

"He should come up with a way to support Grant," Alexander went on. "He should *make* it work. It's not honorable to just *say* you're honorable. I don't like my father very much right now."

The boy half-turned away from Picard, and fell starkly silent. That mouths-of-babes thing rose again as Alexander made perfect sense. What good was it to stand on thin honor while the platform of justice collapses beneath? None at all.

But how could he explain to Alexander the dishonor of perjury, even to bring in a criminal? He already knew that simply explaining rarely did the trick for a child.

As Picard watched, Worf's image as a parent, a warrior, and a starship officer tarnished in his son's eyes.

Picard frowned. Perhaps he should have better minded the boy's sensitivities, protected him from what was happening on the planet. Alexander shouldn't have to bear the fallout of Worf's mission and its personal repercussions.

This was one of the difficulties of shipboard life. Alexander's friendship with Grant could compromise events. Yet, throughout history—from the first rowed boats, to sails, to starships—no one had found a way for a crew, however dapper, to keep from becoming a family. Nor had any but the stiffest Blighs expected otherwise.

These lessons were getting awfully big for one young boy to absorb. Even more troubling was his own rising doubt. He'd always found it easy to look down his nose at the simpler past, but he was finding that these times were not so simple at all. These were the times in which the laws he took for granted had been forged by fire, and he luxuriated in his loft built of others' great trials. They had stood the test, and he reaped the rewards.

Now Worf was going through the same thing—looking down from the platform of his honor, for which Ross Grant would pay the price.

Picard started wondering just who was getting the biggest lesson out of all this.

"You know what the colonies eventually became, don't you?" Picard asked, framing his question carefully.

"The United States of America," Alexander grumbled back, refusing to look up. "I know, I know. And later they brought the whole world together and started exploring and the Vulcans met 'em and they became the Federation." Now he did look up. "So what? How does that change the fact that *he* went back on his promise?"

He pointed fiercely at Jeremiah Coverman, which seemed somehow cruel, since Jeremiah was down to slow motion and couldn't speak for himself. Fostering a clear case of hero worship, Alexander went to stand beside his *favorite* relative—Sandy Leonfeld.

Together, spanning centuries, the two Alexanders made quite a figure as Picard gazed at them. Somehow the boy was less a boy now.

"I'm sorry about this," the captain said slowly. "I've failed to help you understand that honor is not so simple a thing. That was *my* mission."

"I'm tired of missions," Alexander rebuffed him, folding his arms. He stepped elbow to elbow with the sergeant, even though his elbow wasn't quite high enough yet. "Sandy didn't go against his family and government. He's an officer. He's a born gentleman. Klingons have the same thing. You can be born into a powerful family. *I* was! We're the same, him and me. Me and him. Him and I."

"Yes, but—"

"He didn't go into the British Grenadiers because it was that or starve!" the boy went on. "A lot of soldiers joined because of that, you know. I checked."

"When did you check?"

"When Mr. Riker came in. I didn't eat lunch. I went and looked in the historical banks about this time period."

Hmm—one step in the right direction, at least. Looking for his own answers.

"Your father was born into a powerful family, yes," Picard said, "but there are limitations of all kinds. Your father is trying to choose between his honor, Mr. Grant's safety, and the influence of Mrs. Khanty on the planet. It's not easy, and not as simple as you may think."

"It's simple," Alexander countered. "He's chickening out. And I don't know why. If that's Klingon honor, then I don't want it. I think I'd rather stay here and be a grenadier."

Picard smiled. "You can't stay here. It's a holoprogram."

"Well, there must be some planet somewhere with a Royal Marine unit I can join!"

In a moment of complete insanity, Picard almost turned to Mr. Nightingale and the seamen and told them they could resume eating. These people around them, still alive with minimal movement, were not the same cold, flat figures conjured up by the holodeck's amusement programs, like characters in some story. These were real people who had lived and died, who had real passions and grieved real losses, no less than he and the boy. They had simply done all that in a different blink of time. On the cosmic scale, he felt very close to them.

Obviously, tragically, Alexander did, too.

"Well," Picard began, "why don't we play all this out, and make our judgments later? After all, there are a few sides we have yet to hear. Shall we?"

Alexander hung his head, but his eyes still peered up at his captain. "I guess."

"Computer," Picard snatched at the moment, "resume program."

"I can no longer bear this!" Sandy Leonfeld's voice filled the cabin. He chopped a hand between himself and his cousin and made for the front door, clearly of no mind to remain in this den any longer.

"Sandy!" Frightened, Jeremiah rushed forward and caught the sergeant before Sandy's hand touched the iron latch. He took Sandy by the arms with the same urgent familiarity they had shown to one another moments ago, when things were so different, though little of that was returned from the grenadier. "Please . . . you must not go out."

"And why not?" Sandy gnashed. "Am I not in a clutch of my enemies? What safety does this place afford loyal Britons? Why should I not take my leave of you?"

Jeremiah pulled him away from the door. "Because you'll be hanged."

Sandy twitched, ready to shoot him an angry response, but what could he say?

Imploring with his eyes, Jeremiah waited until Sandy stopped pushing against his grip. "The message from the nailery . . . your ship is being towed upriver to the boatyard, where it will be converted for use by the patriots. Those officers and seamen still alive are imprisoned in the public stable. If you're caught, it'll be assumed you're attempting escape. You'll be executed as spies. Please—now, please. We disagree, yes . . . but I couldn't bear it if you were killed."

A crushing emotion rose between them. Despite his attempt at indignation, Sandy Leonfeld was clearly very upset. This was a terrible inner blow, not just a rift in philosophy. These things were deeply ingrained in his heart, and his heart was breaking.

"Sergeant," Picard interrupted, taking Sandy's elbow, "why don't we sit down and have something to eat?"

"I would retch," Sandy muttered.

"Please," Amy Coverman came to life, fluttering around and pouring cider into the tankards. "I shall have no one hungering in my home."

"Thank you," Picard said as he took a seat, surmising from their hesitation that the midshipman and deckhands would probably not eat until he did. He looked up as his tankard was filled, and spoke to Sandy. "Sergeant?"

Responding only with the barest attention he must give to a superior officer, Sandy Leonfeld lowered himself as noncommittally as possible to the edge of the bench nearest him. He did not face the table fully, but sat on the end of the bench. Nor did he eat.

"Go ahead, gentlemen," Picard ordered. "We must keep our strength up. Alexander, eat something."

"I don't want anything."

Picard tucked his chin and gave the boy that look all children understand. "Regardless."

Pouting at full warp, Alexander flung himself onto the bench and ripped off a chunk of cheese, then smelled it and grimaced, determined not to have a good time.

The cheese was moldy, the cider was stale, the bread was crusty, and Picard began to regret the damned accuracy of the holodeck as he realized he wasn't hungry, but had just committed himself to setting an example. He tentatively bit into the bread, expecting to get the juicy end of a weevil, when abruptly the holodeck entryway opened again.

He looked up. "Freeze program," he said, but the computer didn't respond. Once again everyone around him blinked in confusion, and then all Klingon broke loose.

Worf walked through the entryway into the keeping room of the cabin, with First Officer Riker close behind.

"Computer, freeze the program," Picard repeated more firmly, but not soon enough.

Striding freely under a ceiling so low that his brow ridge almost scratched it, Worf presented a vision so monstrous that Amy Coverman screamed at the sight. Jeremiah jumped to protect his wife as the holodeck program twisted itself into knots, trying to compute the psychology of 1777 American colonists reacting to a Klingon.

"Demon!" Amy's aunt flew around the table, passed the fireplace, and scooped up the kettle of soup from the hook—luckily not directly over the fire—wheeled back, and creamed Worf directly in the face with the pot.

Barley soup splashed across Worf's entire head and cascaded down his shoulders to drench the front of his Rogue uniform. His mouth had been open, about to speak, and now came down upon a sprig of greenery lingering on a lip. Riker sidestepped just in time to avoid the splash.

"Great God above!" Jeremiah intoned.

Sandy Leonfeld vaulted toward his rifle and drew it to his shoulder, aimed and—

"No, no!" Picard plunged across the table like some kind of wild athlete, just gracefully enough to slam the rifle off its aim with the palm of his hand.

Then the grace played out, and he landed on top of the plate of bread, with his face in the cheese.

He lifted his head enough to shout out, "I said, freeze program, blast it all!"

The people in the cabin froze in position at last.

"Blast!" Picard rolled over and squeezed between Wollard and Alexander. "Hang this archaic technology!"

Someone caught his elbow and kept him from tripping over the bench, and he looked up to see that it was Riker.

Worf stood in the middle of the room, dripping, his arms slightly fanned outward, his uniform drenched; he smelled of barley. He looked around at the setting. "What is *this?* This is Earth! The Day of Honor is a Klingon experience! And why did this relic strike me with a tub of stink!"

Stifling a grin, Picard stepped toward him, wiping cheese off his face. "I believe you've been promoted to the supernatural, Mr. Worf. This is an old style program. You have to be listed as a participant at the beginning or the computer doesn't know what to do with you. If we had any doubts that the safeties aren't functioning, we know it for certain now."

"I was wondering why you deflected that rifle," Riker mentioned. "Are you sure you want to keep this up?"

"Captain!" Worf interrupted. "What is all this!"

Riker smiled, and his eyes twinkled with mischief. "It's the American Revolutionary War. The captain lost a ship. Didn't you, sir?"

"This was my idea," Alexander said, stepping forward into his father's sphere of disgust.

Worf slapped his wet hands at the slowed figure of Mercy. "But this is supposed to be a lesson in Klingon culture! Not an excursion into witchcraft!"

"It's supposed to be a lesson in honor," Picard pointed out, "Strange how it's working out, though—"

"It was *my* idea!" Alexander repeated. "I got to pick the way the Day of Honor was taught to me, and I picked my ancestor's journal from Earth.

I'm part-human, too, you know." He cocked a hip, folded his arms, and raised his chin. "And I'm figuring out a few things about honor that I don't think *you* know."

Worf dripped and stared. He looked over Alexander's head to Picard. "Captain! What are you teaching him?"

"I'm not *teaching* him," Picard said. "I'm guiding him. These people you see around us are doing the teaching. He's coming to his own conclusions. Isn't that the idea? Of course, we're not finished—"

"And we're going to finish." Alexander came up on his toes, to be noticed between the two men. He ignored Picard, and spoke directly to his father. "I'm going to stay here with Sandy until I hear everything he's got to say. You don't have any business telling me how to learn about honor."

Not liking the sudden discord that he felt was his fault, Picard stepped to the boy's side. "Alexander, that's enough."

"What are you talking about?" Worf demanded, glowering down at his son.

Alexander tightened his folded arms. "You say you have honor, but you won't face up to Mrs. Khanty. You're throwing away a chance to win. You won't stick up for Uncle Ross."

Stunned, Worf wiped the soup from his face and glared at Picard again. "Sir! How did he find out about that?"

"Because I'm old enough to know," Alexander said, insisting that the conversation remain focused on him instead of going over his head between the two adults. "You won't say that you saw what Ross saw, even if it saves his life and catches that Mrs. Khanty."

Facing his son's disdain, Worf was kicked in the heart as no challenge from any bruising enemy ever could.

Picard's own chest tightened with empathy and the wish that he could spare Worf this torture. What could he say—what could any parent say—that would not sound shallow, empty? He was endangering a real, living, precious person so an ethereal concept could retain its integrity.

"Alexander," he began with effort, "I will not lie."

"You mean you won't embarrass yourself," the boy kicked back. "You know she's wrong, don't you? And you won't do one thing to save a whole planet."

"I told you," Worf steamed, watching his son's respect for him dissolve before his very eyes. How could he snatch it back? "I refuse to lie."

"You're already lying!" the boy countered, unfolding his arms as if preparing to wrestle. "Your whole mission was a lie! You were never just hiding out on Sindikash like you told them! Isn't that a lie? You're not a Rogue! Isn't *that* a lie? Your whole existence there was lie after lie. Do you think you have to say words to be lying?"

Riker leaned past the captain and plucked at the holo-cheese. "He's right about that, Worf. Can't deny it."

"Mr. Riker," Picard muttered. "You're not helping . . ."

"Sorry, sir."

Worf ignored them, smoldering in the confusion of what to do. Here he was, this huge warrior, nearly pathetic and sad with this fundamental loss, which no battle or angry demonstration could mend. He could not simply order his son to respect him. What did parents do in these moments?

"Alexander," he attempted, hoping to reinstate something, "you should not be speaking to me this way."

Picard held up a quieting hand. "The boy has a good point, Mr. Worf. Any covert mission is by nature a lie. We all lie at some time or another, to protect or spare others. Anyone who says he never lies is lying as he says it."

"That's not the point!" Alexander spoke up again. He squared off before his father. "If you can protect Grant by telling something you know is true, even if you didn't see it, why won't you do that? How is it honorable to do one right thing and let a bigger wrong thing happen? You think it's honor to let people die because you won't say one thing? How important can it be? Grant's gonna die because you won't tell a fib. Will your tongue snap off if you keep up the masquerade a little longer? That's pretty simpleminded honor, I think. Either you can press yourself to the limit or you can't! There's more to being a warrior than war!"

Worf stared in raw astonishment at his son, who had been only a boy, in the truest sense, when he left. Now there was something else here.

Picard found himself staring, too. Was this Alexander? Was this a *child?*

He flinched involuntarily when Worf swung toward him. "Is this how you teach him? By not explaining the difference between a covert mission and perjury? Captain, I must protest—"

"Don't talk to the captain! Talk to *me.*" Alexander gave his father a little push on the belt to get his attention again. "You'd shoot Mrs. Khanty if you saw her doing something bad, wouldn't you? So what's the difference? Are you going to stick up for Ross or aren't you?"

"All right, all right, belay this!" Picard pushed between them. "Mr. Riker, I want Worf, Dr. Crusher, Mr. Data, and yourself in the briefing room in fifteen minutes. Alexander, go somewhere and gain control over yourself until I call for you. We'll continue the Revolutionary War shortly. All hands, dismissed. Computer, store the program at this stage and end it until further notice. Don't look at me that way, Mr. Worf. I said you were dismissed. Go wipe off."

"All right, Mr. Worf, say what you have to say."

"I am deeply disturbed that Alexander yelled at me, sir."

"I mean about Sindikash, Lieutenant."

"Oh . . . yes." Worf fought inwardly to bury his frustration with his son and the captain, and forced himself to concentrate on his mission.

He sat stiffly in the briefing room, directly opposite the captain, who was at the far end of the long table. At Worf's right, Will Riker sat quietly. To Worf's left sat Dr. Beverly Crusher; standing near the large viewport, Commissioner Toledano twisted and twitched, his arms in constant movement and his hands repeatedly clenching.

Worf twitched uneasily. Strange how out of place he felt among these people and on this ship. Like coming from the mountains to the flatlands and feeling as if he were about to fall off.

He drew a breath and plunged into his summary.

"The freighter, piloted by myself and the other Rogues, was supposed to be 'caught' on the border of Romulan space, in order to frame the lieutenant governor. When we circumvented Mrs. Khanty's plan, she no longer trusted the Rogues to sacrifice themselves for her, and was forced to take events into her own hands. The only one she trusted was me, after I 'saved' the freighter from Starfleet capture with her Rogues aboard, which would have compromised her. So she put me on guard outside the suite, but evidently still did not trust me quite enough to ask me to assassinate the governor."

"Good thing she didn't," Dr. Crusher's fluid voice broke in. "You'd have blown your cover by refusing."

"Very likely," Worf agreed. "She needed public opinion to swing back to her, and to make that happen, she assassinated her husband. However, Grant witnessed her action, and he informed the doctors that there was some sort of toxin involved, which was confirmed. Now Mrs. Khanty is accusing Grant of being the assassin. However, he could easily have kept quiet and not claimed he was in the suite at all. The doctors and Lieutenant Stoner of the City Police all quietly agree that Grant needn't have spoken up about the toxin if he had been the assassin. However, he sacrificed himself on the slim chance of saving the governor's life."

"Yes, I see the line of logic," the captain agreed. "He could easily have protected himself. What's happened since then?"

"I told you, sir," Worf said abrasively, "Mrs. Khanty has claimed that Grant's presence in the suite and my exposure as a Starfleet officer amounts to a confession. Federation personnel were in the room when they weren't supposed to be there, and the governor was poisoned. She says any reasonable person would conclude the obvious."

Picard frowned and rubbed his eyes. "That's not what we had in mind, is it?"

"I'll say it's not!" Commissioner Toledano spoke up suddenly, spreading his hands in frustration. "None of you have taken this mission seriously enough from the very beginning!"

Was the room fogging up? Worf squinted to see through his anger. He planted his hands on the slick black table and leaned forward. "We have risked our lives!"

Toledano pressed his legs against the table on his side. *"That* is expected of you!"

The blood of shame rose and made Worf's face hot. He gritted his teeth and responded with a blistering silence.

"That big mouth on Grant's face is going to work in Khanty's favor," Toledano stormed on, giving no quarter to the official decorum of the starship's briefing room or the presence of most of her senior officers. "If we continue our efforts, she'll say we killed her husband and now we're trying to frame her. She'll say Grant didn't get out in time and now he's trying to cast blame on her. She'll say she wanted no animosity with the Federation, but we insisted on interfering. Damn it! She's been spoon-feeding that corpse for weeks now, stoking public sympathy and waiting for an opportunity, and we handed it to her! Attempts to keep Sindikash in the Federation have completely backfired now. She might've lost the election before; now she certainly won't. You've handed everything to her."

"Commissioner," the captain began, "the decision to interfere was made by you and the Federation Council, not by Worf or Grant. Sindikash was a Federation colony with nearly fifty percent of its people still considering themselves citizens. The whole situation could've been handled more diplomatically, without extreme action. Much like the British who decided to flex their muscle and thereby pushed the American colonies away by power of resentment, this attempt at influence may well have cost us Sindikash."

"We're not the ones who made the mistake," Toledano said. He swung back to Worf. "That whole planet will have to suffer because you and Grant botched this mission!"

"Botched?" Worf erupted. The sides of his chair were getting tight. His boots didn't fit any more. His hair was boiling—

Straightening in his chair, Will Riker spoke very sharply. "Mr. Toledano, you're addressing a senior officer of a starship, and I'd advise you to do it with some respect."

Toledano twisted toward him, unintimidated, and pointed at Worf. "When he deserves it, I'll give it."

"Missions do sometimes fail, gentlemen," Captain Picard commented. "Ships are lost, people die, civilizations collapse . . . some turnings of the cogs can't be stopped, Commissioner. We can't always stem a tide the size of a planet. The people of Sindikash will pay for their gullibility. After a great deal of suffering and loss, they'll have to recover for themselves. Mr. Worf, I assume you haven't changed your mind about your official statement."

"I cannot say I saw something that I did not see," Worf repeated. The words scratched his throat. He thought of Alexander again.

"That's fine, you keep your Klingon integrity." Toledano's whole body tightened in anguish. "And Odette Khanty's criminal organization gets control of the planet and a fifth of the sector. You'll be an honest man, and millions of lives will be destroyed. Good decision."

"Mrs. Khanty will act freely now," Data spoke up. "Certainly she knows there will be no act of direct force from the Federation."

Picard seemed annoyed at the confirmation of what they all knew, and he looked at Worf again. "What do you think is happening now to Mr. Grant?"

"No amount of protective custody will protect him on that planet," Worf said with contempt. "She'll find a way to put him on trial, or have him murdered and blame it on me. His only hope is Lieutenant Stoner, whom I believe is not corrupt. I can only hope Stoner will buy me time."

"Time for what?" Toledano interrupted.

"To go back and rescue my partner, Commissioner." Hadn't it been perfectly clear?

"You can forget about that. Just forget it. Forget you ever said it. I'm going to contact Starfleet Command and have a professional recon team sent in for Mr. Grant. You just stay out of this from now on. They'll get him out and that'll be that."

"That could take days."

"So what? You said he's in the hands of a noncorrupt policeman, didn't you? Do you believe it or not? After all, you *said* it, didn't you? So you sure must *believe* it!"

"That's enough, Commissioner," Picard steamed.

"No, it's not anywhere near enough. Mr. Worf, Captain Picard has command over you on this starship and on any mission sanctioned by Starfleet Command or the Federation Council, but as of this second, any further actions by you on or about Sindikash are not, and I mean *not,* sanctioned. Stay away from that planet. It's out of your hands. Got it?"

Toledano didn't have the bulk, the might, or the prowess to challenge a trained mountain like Worf, but he certainly did wield the biggest weapon of all—authority. Any other Klingon would have peeled the commissioner's face and eaten the leavings, but Worf was indeed a Starfleet officer, which canceled all bets.

The commissioner pushed himself away from the table. "Just stay out of it," he concluded. "All of you, just stay out of it."

With that, the man who had at first been so affable and well-intended now left the briefing room with the lowest perceptions of persons he had once respected. Worf felt the loss keenly, and especially for the captain, who would bear the brunt of this.

First Grant, and now the captain would pay for Worf's honor. He wasn't used to that. Hadn't expected it.

"Well . . . " Captain Picard gazed at the door panels as they softly closed behind the commissioner, leaving the command crew uneasy with each other. "That could've gone better."

"You were right, Jean-Luc," Beverly Crusher reassured him. "Missions do fail now and then."

"I don't have to like it, Doctor. Well, Mr. Worf, now that you're back aboard, do you want me to stop being Alexander's mentor?"

Sweating like a jungle rain, Worf struggled between his responsibility as a father and the request he had made of his captain. There was some honor involved here, too, and a respect for his captain which he would be troubled to compromise.

"No, sir," he ultimately said, and nearly choked. "I gave you the right. I will not rescind it."

Because of his honor, as he saw it, Worf had to go back to the planet, therefore he had to leave Alexander's rite of passage into honor where he had put it in the first place. With Captain Picard.

The captain was watching him.

"I'll try to find some way to make him understand," Picard reassured him. "You're sure about this, Mr. Worf?"

"Yes, sir, very sure." Worf stood up. "I will not be here to take over with Alexander."

"Why not?"

"Because I must ask you to allow me to return to Sindikash to rescue Grant."

Picard looked at him and folded his hands in mock-passivity. "*Allow* you? I'm afraid not, Mister Worf. I can't give you *permission* to go on a rescue mission for someone who is in legal custody and not a Starfleet crewman. There is no way I can *authorize* such an expedition . . . "

"I understand, sir," Worf said tightly.

Was he reading the captain's tone correctly, with its oddly emphasized words? He would soon know.

Tenatively, he added, "Then I will not *ask* you, of course, sir."

"Good," the captain said, his eyes twinkling. "And don't ask Mr. Riker to go with you. I would not grant *him* permission either."

At Worf's side, Riker smiled.

Hope sprung high inside Worf's chest.

"Yes, sir," he said. "I would like to avoid asking Mr. Data as well."

Slowly Picard stood up and gestured at their resident android.

"Agreed. Too much trouble. In any event, his appearance would be too difficult to explain. You'd have to put some kind of makeup on him so he would appear human."

Worf nodded somberly.

"And, of course, if you asked Dr. Crusher, that would be unacceptable as well."

"Well, I don't know about any of them," Riker said. "But I have no intention of going on any rescue missions. I'm going to lie down in my cabin for the next twenty hours or so, and leave orders that nobody disturb me. Mr. Data's going to do the same. He's having his first headache."

Data stood up, tipped his head in confusion, and said, "I beg your pardon, sir?"

Riker took Data's arm. "It's terrible. I can see the pain in your eyes. You'll need lots of rest. Right, Dr. Crusher?"

"Oh, lots," Crusher said, taking Data's other elbow. "At least twenty hours. I'll stay with him the whole time and press a cool cloth to his brow. Come on, Data."

"Are we going somewhere?" the android asked innocently.

"Oh, yes," Riker told him, and grinned at Worf. "You have an appointment at the beauty shop."

CHAPTER 15

"COMPUTER, REVERSE PROGRAM THIRTY SECONDS AND RESUME."

Jean-Luc Picard nudged Alexander back into his place at the trestle table in Jeremiah Coverman's keeping room. Around them, the characters reversed like an old newsreel to a point before Worf had entered, and Picard sat down just as the scenario started moving again and the characters groaned to life.

"Alexander, don't pout," he murmured just as the characters took a reanimating breath.

"I've got a right," the boy shot back.

"Not on my time, you don't."

"Lieutenant Picard?" Nightingale asked. "Is something wrong, sir?"

"Nothing at all, Midshipman," Picard said, and turned. "Mr. Coverman, what affected you most in your new way of thinking?"

All eyes struck Picard like whips. He had dared to keep the flames of dissent burning. But he wanted to know, and turning away from a problem did nothing but cause it to fester.

To ease the dare, he handed the sergeant a chunk of bread and some cheese, causing Sandy to begin eating whether he liked it or not, because he couldn't disobey an order.

Sometimes rank could be an advantage.

Jeremiah sighed, but there was no vice left in him. He had plainly thought all this through for months, possibly years, and done his emotional wrestling long since. He seemed also to have anticipated this confrontation with his family, though Picard suspected he hadn't wanted to have it with Sandy.

He took the pitcher from Amy and poured Mr. Nightingale's drink.

"The class system doesn't work here. There is unthinkable mobility. The poor can become wealthy in mere months. The wealthy can lose fortunes even faster. Many live on the frontier. We are *months* away from Britain. Our remoteness reduces the edicts of the king to the baying of hounds in the distance. We scarcely hear it. No one cares to listen. The elite of Europe—Sandy, I'm sorry. For the elite, who have never set foot here and think of this place as a manure-filled backwater to be telling us what to do . . . it becomes untenable after a short time. British tariffs choke us, we are required to use their currency and none other, we are patently tried and convicted, treason is undefined—we may not even speak out against the Crown's policies, lest we risk our very lives. Is that freedom?"

No one made any response, but Picard suspected there were a half dozen different responses running under the table, each riding on some condition or other. No, yes, maybe, only if—

Jeremiah put the pitcher down on the table and sat opposite his cousin. He laid out a hand and implored, "Sandy, please try to understand. Even you must have trouble defending the abuses of the monarchy. You defend the Magna Carta, do you not? This is the next step of granting rights to everyone. This rebellion asks, 'Why do we need a king at all? Why does the gentry need the aristocracy?' "

Sandy swallowed the whole lump of bread that was in his mouth and buried his response in a slug of cider. His eyes never left his cousin's.

"What's that?" Alexander asked, and his voice broke Picard's thoughts. "Magna something."

Stepping back into an element he found more comfortable, Picard answered, "In the early 1500's, King John I was forced to sign the Magna Carta because he was a bad king. It lessened the power of the Crown and shared it with the nobility. The power of the king was no longer absolute."

"And he was a bad king," Jeremiah picked up, "because he was king by blood and not by merit." He looked again at his cousin, evidently finding his stride with his convictions. "Why should anyone be born into power over another? If the government should have say over a man's life, that man should have say over the government. Government is a necessity, but we should accept that it is always excessive and inefficient by its very nature, and should be strictly limited, else we lose control."

Amy Coverman nodded as she placed a bowl of fruit on the table, but she said nothing. Picard looked at her, expecting her to speak up, as the women did in his own time, but obviously this was a discussion for the men. Yet, she didn't seem to disagree with a single one of her husband's words, for she nodded and beamed proudly.

"We pay taxes here," Jeremiah continued, and looked at Picard suddenly, "but no one speaks for us in the British Parliament. Since the Magna Carta, the Crown has shared power with the Houses of Lords and Commons, but no one represents us in the colonies. We are less than commoners here. Men born to their titles are running our lives. We understand the need for taxation, but who goes with our portion to speak for us in Parliament? No one. Our voice is mute. We have no lords here, because no one is 'born higher' than anyone else. Some colonists have been here for centuries. Amy's family, for instance, since Plymouth!" He motioned to his shy wife. "She is an American, not an Englishwoman at all. Yet England would have rule over her. Yet England tells her, 'Lowborn you are and lowborn you will remain, for you have no birthright. You will have a meager existence and then die, because that is what God wants, because the king's right is divine. Accept your place and harbor no ambition.' "

Picard glanced up as Mercy came down the stairs with a pile of folded clothing in her arms. He hadn't even noticed that she'd gone up there, but apparently these were the disguises he and the sailors would wear to keep from being hanged as "spies."

"For the first time," Jeremiah went on, "average men are demanding that no one have arbitrary power. All government power should be answerable to those whom it governs. How can such a thought be forever so foreign to humanity?"

"Only a thousand years or so, Mr. Coverman," Picard pointed out. "A very brief period, once you have a more cosmic perspective."

"But troubling, Lieutenant, troubling. Power should flow from the people on up, not from God to the king and on down."

"God ordains who should rule," Sandy rasped, putting down the bread for which he had no appetite. "There *is* divine right of kings. God blesses the highborn with their place in society."

"Then God has a jester's humor," Jeremiah challenged, "given the shabby judgment of those who call themselves the 'blessed.' "

Sandy looked sharply at him and for a moment seemed about to explode again. Instead, he spoke rather quietly, like a storm rumbling on the horizon.

"This is a waste of breath," he told his cousin. "You can't possibly win a war against the might of Britain. The Colonial militia will be slaughtered. You have no navy . . . what will you do, my dear cousin, when this is over and you are still British? Will you travel into the western wilderness where you cannot be found? Drag these women and this child even farther from civilization until you all die where there are no roads?"

Jeremiah looked with deep regret at his young wife, then drew a long breath. "No," he said. "Win or lose, I shall not leave Delaware."

"Then do you realize," Sandy asked, his voice finally softening, "that you *will* be executed for treason?"

As Amy Coverman came around the table and took her husband's hand to steady him, Jeremiah beamed at her, then nodded at Sandy. "Yes. I know."

Picard looked at Alexander. The boy had stopped eating too, and was staring at Jeremiah with new realizations. Jeremiah was no scoundrel. All he wanted was possession of his own life.

Beset with confusion, Alexander looked hard at his other cousin, and the hero worship for Sandy Leonfeld got sudden competition.

"Someone will remember," Amy Coverman finished on her husband's behalf.

With those three words, the young wife told her whole story. She believed in her husband, and she was ready to sacrifice him and herself for their beliefs and the future of others yet unknown.

Picard knew he was living with the fruits of their courage. He looked to his side.

Alexander gaped at her, absorbing the depths of her convictions. He glanced at Picard, and tucked his shoulders with shame for what he had said earlier.

"If you persist with these loyalties," Sandy said poignantly to Jeremiah, "then one of us will have to kill the other eventually. I am an officer and a gentleman. I've sworn an oath. I will not betray it."

Jeremiah gazed at him. "You would turn me in?"

"I would have to," Sandy said. "It is my sworn duty."

Not as surprised as Picard would have expected him to be, Jeremiah offered only a shrug. "So be it. I have a duty as well, yet I will compromise mine to make sure you survive. I know how you think, and I hold no malice toward you for it. You have sanctuary here, all of you, until we can find a way to return you to England."

The words caused a great deal of trouble in Sandy Leonfeld's face, washing away the defiance to some degree. Clearly, he was disturbed that his cousin would protect him, when he had just declared refusal to do the same for Jeremiah.

"What if we can't go back, sir?" Seaman Wollard asked, his food still in his mouth. "If there's no ship—"

Picard looked up, noting the "sir" and knowing that meant him.

"Then we'll find safety in one of the larger cities, Seaman," Picard told him. "Philadelphia or New York."

"We should steal *Justina* back!" Seaman Bennett declared. "We can free the captain and the others!"

"You'll be killed instantly," Jeremiah said. "They're under guard of the Colonial militia. Men who hunt squirrels and foxes. They can kill two of you with one shot."

Picard wondered what Jeremiah really thought—whether the former Briton would allow such action to occur, now that he was loyal to independence. A man's devotion could be stretched only so far.

He thought suddenly of Worf, torn between devotion to his honor and to Grant, devotion to a principle and to a better end to a problem that could affect millions of lives. Odette Khanty seemed like small potatoes on the scale of galactic politics, just part of the muscle-stretching that had gone on in governments for thousands of years, but for most of those thousands of years, there generally weren't lives and lifestyles at stake on the kind of scale as nowadays faced the Federation.

But was that true? He wondered, as he looked at Jeremiah and his wife. These people's struggle seemed almost silly, insignificant, even annoying if Sandy Leonfeld were consulted. Sandy was right—no one thought the colonies could win. In fact, they probably couldn't have, if Britain's willpower hadn't been slackened by preoccupation with France and by selective British blunders at running a war so far and so much time away from their center of command.

Yet, despite its humility, this upstart militia attempt had become the foundation for the most encompassing law and justice in the galaxy. His mind reeled with the breadth of scope of these words, spoken in these small houses, during these long-faded days, and he charged himself never again to forget.

"I must go for a little," Jeremiah said, standing up. "Mercy has your clothing. Your uniforms will be hidden here. With common clothing, you shall be able to walk among the villagers, but be wary, all of you. This is a close community, and strangers can be easily noticed. Stay quiet, go out with greatest caution, and I beg you, do not approach the stable. If you care to go off to Philadelphia or New York, I have no power to stop you. That is for the lieutenant to decide, as your commanding officer."

The men stripped out of their uniform jackets and handed them to Amy Coverman and Aunt Mercy. Picard noted with some concern that Sandy Leonfeld resisted the longest, and it took Amy's plaintive gaze to get his scarlet coat off his shoulders. His being a gentleman came in handy, as he broke down under Amy's comely insistence.

Jeremiah watched the change of officers and soldiers to common townsmen, then reluctantly went to his front door and left. Amy latched the door behind him, then she and Mercy carried the men's uniforms up the narrow stairs.

Except for the little child drowsing at the hearth, Picard and the men were alone for the first time since coming here.

"This is unacceptable!" Midshipman Nightingale seethed. "We're in an enemy camp!" He appealed first to the seamen, who only stared at him, then turned to Picard. "Sir!"

"We'll look around," Picard said evenly. "There will be absolutely no action until and unless I order it. Is that clear?"

The two sailors instantly responded, "Aye, aye, sir."

But the two officers had said nothing, and Picard wasn't opening that door without confirmation of his authority, despite the conditions.

"Mr. Leonfeld?" he prodded. "Mr. Nightingale? Is it clear?"

All eyes shifted to the grenadier. Sandy's golden hair twinkled like stars in the firelight. "Clear, sir," he moped finally.

On that cue, young Edward Nightingale echoed, "Aye, sir."

Picard stood up and indulged in a surge of reckless excitement.

"I'll hold you to it. Because we're going to recapture our ship."

If I were an American, as I am an Englishman, while a foreign troop was landed in my country, I never would lay down my arms—never—never—never!

William Pitt, Earl of Chatham

CHAPTER 16

"MAKE FAST TWO!"

"Make fast two, aye!"

"Take up three! Make fast one!"

"Aye, sir! One's fast!"

"Let out four!"

"Four, out!"

"Line three, wake up, man! Take up that line!"

A grind of wood against a dock . . . the slap of water somewhere below . . . the creak of broken yards.

Itchy.

The wool breeches felt as if they had chunks of wood floating in the weave. The cotton shirt lay stiff against Picard's neck and shoulders, beneath a rather loosely fitted linen waistcoat.

He wanted to scratch, but in an impolite place. And he was hurrying along a public street. And there were women.

In fact, it seemed the whole town had turned out at the docks to rejoice at the tying-up of His Majesty's Ship *Justina.*

And a pathetic sight it was. Now, in the dimness of predawn, Picard could see just how much damage had been sustained by the frigate, such as he had not been able to see at night from a distance. The ship and crew had evidently put up more of a fight than he had been able to measure from the shoreline, for she was brought in with canister-shredded sails hanging torn from smashed yards broken in two or three places, and part of the bow stove in from a cannonball. Luckily, above the waterline.

Justina was by far the largest ship in this demure marina, including the boats being worked on or converted in the boatyard. All around were craft the size of the spider catchers, as well as utilitarian fishing craft and loading barges. This was a small port, but a working and busy one.

At his right side, Alexander pressed close to Sandy Leonfeld. To his left, Mr. Nightingale and the two deckhands crowded the wooden fence that funneled down to the two narrow docks. No one said anything as they watched their ship nudge up to the dock, crewed by colonists in common clothing and a half dozen blue-jacketed Delaware Light Infantry militiamen. And their long-barreled rifles. And flintlock pistols. And the cannons on board the ship.

Those uniformed men, and the ones waiting on the shore, Picard guessed, must be of the battalion authorized by the Delaware Committee of Safety, which Sandy had mentioned. Picard had harbored disparagements about them, about how he was of an advanced era and could have vaporized them without a thought if he had a single phaser, but now he looked at them, saw the familiarity with which they handled those long guns, and the strapping, survival build of their bodies. These were neither the coddled aristocracy who lived above the streets of Europe nor the emaciated masses who starved below. These were strong, hardened, frontier-taming Americans, who had taken this wild young seacoast and whipped it into a burgeoning civilization, and who, Picard knew, would do much more in the decades to come.

Take back the ship. It had seemed a bold and simple statement when he'd said it quickly, but now, as he looked down at the forbidding size and complications of the frigate, and the damage they would have to deal with, and the men guarding it, the concept took on afflictions.

And he was curious that the computer hadn't made somebody stop him. This was a holoprogram, of course, not just a book or a play, There were interactive elements. Yet this particular program was also history—real events that had to happen a certain way. He could go back and win Trafalgar for the French if he wanted to, but that couldn't happen in this kind of program. Certain things had to happen. The *Justina* had to be overtaken. Jeremiah and Sandy had to be reunited. Jeremiah had to have changed his loyalties. The program would naturally steer Picard and

Alexander in certain directions, or keep them from doing something that absolutely did not occur, like killing Jeremiah or burning the town.

But how far could he push it?

Retaking the ship . . . had it really happened? Was he taking the place of an officer who had orchestrated it? Would they succeed?

Or did the computer even know? Sandy Leonfeld's journals hadn't been this detailed, of course. The essence of conversations had been noted, but not the actual lines. Yet the computer, with its vast billions of bits of data, had reached into history and reconstructed all this. And eyewitness tests with contemporary events had proven time and again that the holodeck computers did their jobs remarkably well. There was good reason to believe just as excellent a job would be done with the past.

So, could he save the ship? Or would he be thwarted? And would this clumsy old program accidentally slice his head off with a slashing headsail sheet?

Whatever the chances, he suspected this program would give him the chance to manipulate events. So be it. He would deal with the risk. Right now he felt like saving something.

"They got their own crew on board," Wollard commented with bald disgust from Picard's side. "On *our* ship!"

"Bloody rebel colonists on a British ship!" Bennett echoed with the same invective, his teeth pressed together.

"Keep quiet, both of you," Picard said. He glanced at the militia soldiers who stood barely paces down the dock from them. "If we're found out, we'll be shot."

"Sir, look!" Wollard gasped, and pointed.

Picard—and all—looked down the fence, beyond three women in Quakerlike dress.

"It's Mr. Pennington!" Nightingale uttered, remembering to hold his voice down, and he stepped away from the fence.

Reaching out quickly, Picard snatched the young officer's arm, then crossed by him. "Wait! I'll speak to him. All of you stay here."

"I'll go with you!" Alexander spoke up, and hurried forward.

Picard almost stopped him, then remembered the reason he was here at all. "Yes, all right."

He stepped away from the small fence and felt the eyes of the men follow him down the wharf. Pennington stood grimly watching the ship being tied to the dock. He was still in uniform and his injured right arm was in a crude sling.

Just before Picard would have reached Pennington's side, Pennington noticed his approach and blinked in shock.

"Mr. Picard!" he choked out. Then he suddenly noticed that Picard was out of uniform, and glanced about almost frantically.

"Mr. Pennington," Picard responded, "are you well, sir?"

"Yes, I'm reasonably well, but how is it that you're here? Have you been captured?" Pennington's voice barely went over a whisper, and he was supremely aware of the people victoriously crowding the dock to watch the big ship being brought in, and of the armed guards.

"We came in under cover of night," Picard explained. "Sergeant Leonfeld has a relative living in the town. We took refuge there. Are you under guard, sir?"

"No, I'm paroled. The crew has been imprisoned, but the officers are on our own recognizance, allowed to walk about if we swear on our honor not to leave the town or take any aggressive actions."

"How many officers are here?"

"Myself, Fourth Lieutenant Frost, Engineer Rollins, and Midshipman Parks."

A chill ran down Picard's arm. "Captain Sobel?"

Pushing up behind him, Alexander peeked around at Pennington. "What about the captain?"

Sympathy crossed Mr. Pennington's face, such as Picard had never witnessed from this man aboard the ship. The first officer looked down at Alexander, then back up. "I'm sorry to report that the captain died as we were rowed in. Rather slowly and grotesquely, I'm pained to say . . . . We lost many men, including the second lieutenant. Nearly a third of the crew, and seven marines, including Marine Captain Newton, who took a ball through the eye. They fought so valiantly, too . . . "

"I know, sir," Picard said gently. "We saw it all."

"Of course, that makes you the ranking nonparoled officer, Picard," Pennington told him. "Any decisions and actions on land or on the ship will be yours to make now."

"I see . . . yes, of course."

Together they watched as the last lines were belayed securely to the dock and the bulky British prize became a spoil of war, her masts dominating the dockscape, her cracked yards draping rags of sail that fluttered fitfully in the Delaware River breeze.

"Do you have the entire landing party with you?" Pennington asked, taking Picard's arm urgently.

"Yes, all accounted for, sir."

Pennington glanced down the dock, saw Nightingale and the two deckhands and Sandy. "Six of you . . . not enough."

"To do what, sir?"

"To take the ship back, of course."

Alexander bolted forward. "There are only six of us, but with all the officers walking around in the open, we could break the crew out of jail! Let's do it!" He pulled at Picard's sleeve. "You said we could *do* it! Mr. Pennington could lead us!"

Pennington's sympathy extended once again as he gazed down upon the face of hope and defiance. "I couldn't possibly participate, swab."

Instantly shot down, Alexander frowned. "Why not?"

The naval officer dropped a hand on the boy's shoulder. "Because, my boy, I've given my word of honor. I promised not to fight. To break that trust would be second only to treason."

Alexander looked up into the first officer's eyes and tried to speak, but couldn't.

Pennington, who had until now seemed so hardened a seafarer and so stiff an officer, softened into an uncle figure. He saw the trouble in the boy's face, and took time to assuage it.

"The reason we hold to our honor," he said, "is what war would become if we didn't. If I could not be trusted to be paroled, they would no longer parole anyone, and all soldiers captured would be shot, or die in some stinking camp. I give my word to my enemy, and sometime in the future, when he gives his word to me, I will have reason to expect him to keep it."

The boy gazed up at this man whom he clearly admired, and his confusion deepened, just as it was deepening toward Sandy Leonfeld, and Jeremiah Coverman, and his own father.

"But . . . it's war," he protested. "Shouldn't you do anything you can, anything you have to . . . to win?"

Pennington smiled through his pain. "I would sacrifice my life, or any officer's—indeed, the entire crew—rather than break my parole. The cost to everyone of breaking my word is too great to live with. Rules of civility give us our society. There are some things we shall never do, no matter the circumstance. Where there are no rules, in warfare or peace, life becomes chaos. You say it's war . . . yes, of course it is. Exactly my point. Warfare without rules becomes barbarism."

Gazing at Pennington in a comradelike admiration, Picard was glad to see the doubts and troubles in Alexander's eyes. No answer was crystal clear in times like these, and the boy was looking for clarity where he would never find it. The confusion was a good thing.

Pennington patted Alexander once more on the shoulder, and turned. "Picard," he said, "listen to me now—"

"Sir?"

"In case this arm proves fatal, you must report your activities to Mr. Frost. He won't be able to participate, since he's on his honor as well, but he should be informed. He'll be the ranking officer among the prisoners. He's now third lieutenant, and you are now second lieutenant."

"Begging pardon, sir," Picard pointed out, "but if the captain is dead, you're now the captain. I'm now first officer, and Mr. Frost is second."

Pennington eyed him sadly. He evidently knew all that, but had been unable to actually vocalize it.

"Yes," he said reluctantly. "It's very hard for me . . . the captain and all. I've been his first lieutenant since . . . "

He lowered his eyes, pressed his lips tight, rubbed his sore arm, and worked to regain control. A few moments later he summoned the will to continue.

"In any case, Picard, we are the Royal Navy, and we must maintain discipline or we're lost. If I should die, be sure you look after the men. They've done their duty, and they deserve to be treated accordingly."

Picard paused for a moment of admiration for this wounded officer. The injury seemed minor for a man of the twenty-fourth century, but in 1777, not so. These people had no anesthetics, no antibiotics, and they didn't know how wounds got infected, how fever came, or why people died. Families would have six, eight, ten children, some eighteen or twenty children, in hopes that three or four would survive to adulthood and care for each other and their aging parents.

And Mr. Pennington was displaying officer thinking, not worrying about himself, though he might yet face a slow, unpleasant death. He was concerned about how his crew would fare without him.

"You shouldn't be out in the open," Pennington advised. "Go back to your sanctuary and make your plans. Whatever you do, keep control of Seaman Wollard and Gunner Bennett. You know how independent-minded sailing men can be."

"Mmm . . . yes, I do. Take care of yourself, sir."

"Thank you, Picard. Be extremely careful. This circumstance is not good."

"Agreed, sir. Come on, Alexander, quickly."

"Thank God! Where've you been?"

Jeremiah Coverman rushed to them as the gaggle of *Justina*'s crew piled in his narrow front door.

"We wanted to see the ship," Picard explained.

"It's right there at the dock!" Alexander piped in. "It looks a lot bigger than it did from the deck!"

Picard dropped a quieting hand on the boy's shoulder. Alexander glanced at him, and shut up.

"Please, all of you come back in immediately." Jeremiah fanned them into the warm room, glanced out the door, then closed it.

Amy and Mercy were both here, and Mercy's child was now asleep on a blanket near the fire, completely oblivious to the shufflings of the adults. The cabin possessed a bucolic peace that was entirely false.

"My heavens, I thought the worst," Jeremiah gasped, actually out of breath with worry as he turned and reached for Sandy, then abruptly drew back at Sandy's hard expression.

Empathy creased Picard's brow, for Jeremiah was hurt by that hardness. Hurt, yet not ashamed. Somehow that came across in spite of everything.

Picard turned to Nightingale, Wollard and Bennett. "Sit down, gentlemen. Stay quiet."

"Yes, sir," Nightingale responded, and herded the seamen to the table.

Before Picard could even turn back to Jeremiah and Sandy, the door crashed open suddenly, knocking Sandy back a step. A red-haired colonist tumbled in and caught himself on the back of the lambing chair, gasping and clearly in pain. If he'd been standing straight, Picard would figure his height to be just between Sandy and Jeremiah, and he was a lean fellow in his thirties, though at the moment he seemed to feel a hundred years old.

"Patrick!" Jeremiah plunged in to support the newcomer before he fell over. "Amy, bring water! Good Lord, what happened?"

As Mercy rushed to close the door, Jeremiah and Picard helped the man to the bench beside Edward Nightingale, and Jeremiah stood beside the fellow in such a manner that allowed the exhausted, injured man to lean against him.

"Patrick, what happened to you?" Jeremiah asked again.

"My horse . . . shot out from under me . . . took a ghastly fall."

The man bent forward briefly and shuddered for breath.

"Who is this person?" Sandy asked, somewhat snappishly, as if he had some right to demand anything in another man's home.

Jeremiah shot him a reproving look. "This is Patrick O'Heyne. The man who changed my life." He looked down now at the exhausted visitor. "He's also my dearest friend. Patrick, who shot your horse?"

"Royal Marines!" Patrick O'Heyne grasped Jeremiah by the arm, his words clipped by a clear American accent, without a trace of Jeremiah's lingering British. "There's been a landing! Another Royal Navy ship . . . the bayside sh—"

He coughed suddenly and crumpled against the edge of the table. Amy Coverman supplied a tin cup of water, which O'Heyne gulped down. Then the gentle young girl pressed a moist cloth to a patch of blood on the side of O'Heyne's head.

"Patrick, you're hurt," Jeremiah said solicitously. "You should lie down."

"No time. The ship must've been waiting to rendezvous with the *Justina*. When the frigate failed to appear, they landed a company of redcoats five miles south of our shore. Grenadiers. I was barely ahead of them the whole way! They'll be here any time—we must get word to Colonel Fox to bring the militia. He's billeted three miles northeast of the mill tributary—"

A sudden grip of pain cut him off again, but there was already a flurry of movement in the room.

"I'll go!" Mercy snatched a wool shawl from a hook and flung it around herself.

"Mercy!" Jeremiah snapped. "Nonsense! I would be no gentleman to let you go!"

"You stay and defend our town!" the woman insisted. Don't you worry about me. I've got my guardian angel, and I'm out this door after the Dover Light Infantry!"

And she was gone, the clap of the door as her send-off. Picard got the idea she'd have happily cracked the elbow of anyone who tried to stop her.

Jeremiah helped Patrick O'Heyne get a more controlled drink of water, and looked at his wife. "Amy, take the baby upstairs. Stay in the back of the house, in case balls fly."

"I will, Jeremiah," the girl said, and moved to comply.

As the hem of her skirt licked the stairway corner and she was gone, leaving only men in the keeping room, her husband's friend looked around with clearing eyes at Picard and Sandy, and at the sailors sitting near him, who all wore nondescript clothing of ordinary colonists.

He didn't seem to buy that entirely.

"I don't know these gentlemen," he said, suddenly cautious.

Picard found O'Heyne's instincts impressive, especially since he was seeing these strangers in the home of his best friend and should have trusted that. Yet, he knew better. Interesting.

Perhaps these were suspicious times.

Jeremiah locked eyes briefly with Sandy, and luckily Sandy decided on forbearance.

"This is Sandy Leonfeld, my cousin from Austria," Jeremiah said tensely. "And his traveling companions, Mr. Picard, Mr. Nightingale, Mr. Wollard, Mr. Bennett, and . . . Mr. Picard's son."

"Alexander," the boy spoke up, demanding to have a name if everybody else was going to.

A strained glance passed between Picard and the boy, then nothing more was made of it, especially since they were interrupted by Amy's reappearance; she, too, was now wearing a heavy wool knitted shawl that drowned her shoulders and went almost to her knees.

"What's this?" Jeremiah asked.

"I shall ring the bell for the minutemen. They must man the picket line."

Her husband protested. "But I'm just going."

"You stay with Patrick and make your plans," the brave teenager insisted. "I can certainly ring a chapel bell, can't I? After all, it's my town, too."

And she dashed out the front door, allowing for no protests.

"Wonderful family," Patrick O'Heyne said. Then he suddenly shivered and pressed a hand to his forehead.

"Are you all right, Patrick?" Jeremiah asked.

O'Heyne offered him a smile. "Recovering. I've bruised my hip notably . . . a knee, my shoulder, and I wisely stopped my fall by striking a tree with my ribs."

"And your head is bleeding, Mr. O'Heyne," Picard pointed out.

The redheaded man looked up with something like gratitude. "Is it? Well, it's only my head. If the redcoats take the Station, I won't have long need of it."

Evidently, Picard's British accent was common enough among patriots, for O'Heyne took no particular note.

Picard said passively, "Then you'd better learn to think from your knee, because the British are fiercely organized warriors."

He truly meant nothing but to voice his admiration for the action he saw on board the *Justina,* but Patrick O'Heyne noted something else about those words, and about all these strangers in the room.

O'Heyne blinked around at the disguised seamen, then finally back around to Sandy, then back to Picard. "Sir . . . how come you to be here? And how do you know Jeremiah?"

"Patrick," Jeremiah uttered. "Please . . . things are somewhat complicated this morning."

Brushing his tousled red hair out of his eyes, O'Heyne scanned Picard and Sandy, evidently taking them for being the ones in charge, since they were standing and the others seated. He gestured at Sandy, but looked at Jeremiah. "Your cousin?"

"Yes," Jeremiah confirmed. "Yes, he's my cousin. We grew up together."

"Well, then." O'Heyne looked at Picard and Sandy. "I'm glad these are your relatives, Jeremiah, else we would have some tension here, I think, wouldn't we?"

He coughed briefly, winced, then surveyed Wollard, Bennett, Nightingale, and Alexander with a keen and experienced eye. After a moment of sheepish, tense glances from those men back to him, O'Heyne looked once again at Sandy and Picard.

"The *Justina?"* he asked.

"Yes," Picard flatly answered.

"The warping party?"

"Yes."

"And you are an officer?"

"Yes. Mr. Leonfeld is sergeant of the grenadiers."

He didn't mention that the captain of the marines was dead now, giving Sandy that rank. He just didn't want to get into it, or offer Sandy a rank technically higher than his own. Not yet, anyway.

"Mmm . . . " O'Heyne stood up, pondering the problem. After a moment he said, "Jeremiah, you're not thinking. Don't you know what you've done to these men by taking them out of their uniforms? If they're discovered out of uniform by the Dover Infantry and found to be British, they won't simply be impounded as prisoners of war. They'll be hanged as spies. Like criminals. That's certainly no way for a soldier to die, is it? In the enemy's clothing?"

Jeremiah stared at him, then looked at the simple breeches, shirts, and jackets he had supplied his guests.

"Oh, my . . . I didn't think of that," he said, his face suddenly flushed.

"Gentlemen," O'Heyne addressed, "if you know what's good for you, you'll put your uniforms back on and go out and get killed. Otherwise, you'll go out there and pretend to be colonists until a chance comes to turn yourselves over to the King's men. I put you on your honor not to shoot anyone in the back, or without identifying yourselves."

Sandy Leonfeld puffed up with noble insult. "No man here will shoot anyone in the back, sir. We are not brutes, you know."

"I know," O'Heyne said. "I've been to England." He paused, surveyed all the men, and added, "We're not that different."

Quite unexpectedly, he reached out a welcoming hand to the sergeant, whom he now knew to be his sworn enemy.

Sandy did not comply right away, but took several strained seconds before he accepted the gesture. Beside O'Heyne, Jeremiah quaked with relief.

Picard tucked back a smile as he appreciated the sight of the two powerful young adversaries, each well-armed with conviction, standing only a pace from each other, neither really knowing what to do next to keep the situation from exploding.

At once, Sandy stepped back and narrowed his eyes as if something had struck him. He pointed with discovery at Jeremiah's friend. "Patrick O'Heyne . . . "

"Yes?"

"Patrick Harper O'Heyne? Of the Liverpool-New York Convoy Company?"

"Yes, thank you. My brother and myself."

"Sir, we—" Sandy said on a gasp, "we have met before!"

Alexander stepped up to Picard's side, overcome by his surprise. "You two know each other?"

"Evidently," O'Heyne said. "Where might that meeting have happened, Mr. Leonfeld?"

The color rose in Sandy's face. "At . . . the court of King George, sir."

"Oh—you must mean the Royal birthday banquet."

"I'm . . . I must mean that, sir."

O'Heyne smiled. "Well, in that case, it's mighty pleasant to meet again, Mr. Leonfeld. I'm sorry for the circumstances—"

He swayed with the dizziness brought on by his head wound, caught himself on the edge of the table, and Jeremiah reached out and clasped his arm to steady him, and Picard caught the other one.

"Patrick, you really ought to rest."

"We'll have eternity to rest soon enough, Jeremiah." O'Heyne regained control through some effort, gave his friend a not-very-convincing pat of comfort. Then, favoring his injured knee and hip, he stepped to a cabinet on the wall and opened it with the familiarity of one who indeed nearly lived here.

From the cabinet he drew four American muzzle-loading rifles, powder horns, bullet pouches and ramrods, and relayed two of the rifles to Jeremiah.

Then he turned to Sandy and Picard. "Do I have your word of honor that, until the redcoats breach our picket line, you'll take no action against any patriot who is honorably fighting for his cause?"

Sandy visibly shuddered, and Midshipman Nightingale's eyes were wide as eggs. The two seamen stood up, and turmoil showed clearly in their faces, but, being seamen, they would follow the word of their commanding officer—who was now First Lieutenant Picard.

Suddenly everyone was looking at him.

For the sake of gamesmanship, he said, "Agreed."

He signed the other men up with a stern glance, and noted that they didn't like his compliance.

"However, Mr. O'Heyne," he said, "we are still men of the Royal Navy. There will come a moment when that will play itself out. Until then, we will not take any dishonorable action against anyone who does not know our identity. Fair enough?"

"Does that include us?" O'Heyne said with a canny smile, and handed Picard an American musket. "In that case, unless you mean to slaughter us here and now, Jeremiah and I have a town to defend. In all fairness, it's no less than you would do. I invite you to come with us and see what we're all about."

Limping toward the door, he opened it for Jeremiah, whose lingering gaze on Sandy was simply heartwrenching. O'Heyne gave him time, but finally, torn and tortured, Jeremiah hurried out the door.

O'Heyne made good on his belief of Picard's promise, and dared turn his back to the Royal Navy men as he, too, went out of the cabin.

Picard looked down at the American rifle in his hands and luxuriated in the balance and weight of the classic weapon. Beautiful! Imagine actually firing it!

He turned a glinting eye to his crew.

"Well, men?" he prodded.

"I'm uneasy with our duty, sir," Sandy said, "being in the company of colonists and even protected by them . . . trusted by them . . . "

"Nonsense!" Midshipman Nightingale said. "There's a skirmish coming! We can't stand by, sir!"

"We can do terrible damage from this side of the line," Bennett spoke up. "I'm a gunner!"

"Not without orders, you won't," Picard pointed out. "We made an agreement."

"*You* made it," Bennett shot back.

Picard reached out with all the piled-up frustration of both his man-of-war and his starship, and grasped Bennett by the black neckerchief the sailor wore.

"I *am* you, seaman," he clarified. "Don't forget it."

Bennett leaned back, sneered, but did not dare react physically to his senior officer.

Sandy put out a hand. "And I refuse to fire at any man's blind side, even my enemy's. Nor will I fire at any man of King George's military under any condition."

Throwing Bennett off and gripping the American rifle in both hands, Picard looked at him. "Where does that put you, Sergeant?"

Sandy Leonfeld paused, a dozen emotions passing through his eyes. For the first time Picard saw flaming doubt rise, and the shield of aristocratic superiority grow thinner.

Picard didn't wait for an answer. He stepped to a corner and scooped up Sandy's British-issue rifle and handed it to him, then turned to grasp Alexander by one arm.

"Oh, what the devil," he said. "Let's go out and see what happens. After all, we've been invited."

CHAPTER 17

"DATA, YOU ALMOST READY?"

"Yes, sir. The shuttlecraft is hidden in the emission blind of an orbital processing station, and the helm is on automatic hover outside of orbit range. All broadcast systems are heavy-duty to avoid overload, and satellite connections are tied in and operating."

"Good. Doctor? Ready?"

"Ready. Listening devices sewn into my cuffs—right here in the lace—"

"Perfect. I can barely see them."

"And here's the camera."

"That's huge."

"It's the width of two human hairs."

"But it's visible, is what I mean."

Worf listened to the conversation between Riker, Data, and Beverly Crusher, and had to shudder down a distasteful fit of nerves about this whole mission. He was determined to get Grant, but the captain's idea of taking shipmates along did not sit well. Four persons could not hide as well as one, could not effect stealth, and quadrupled the risks for great loss. These people's lives were in his hands, and their deaths would be on his conscience.

Still, he was also deeply moved by their willingness to go after a Federation operative whom they didn't even know and whose cover had been blown. Many would consider that too much risk for very little gain, and they would be right. All talk of operatives, partners, missions, and official business was thinning out. They were now doing all this just to get his friend back.

He wanted to thank them, to turn warmly and display his gratitude for their devotion. Somehow that desire kept turning inward each time it began to surface. How much could one man bottle up?

"Sir," he turned to Riker, disturbed by what he had heard the first officer say to the doctor. "You also have audio and video devices on—you must both have them on your persons. I know how Ugulan thinks."

Riker smiled reassuringly. "I've got mine. Right here." He plucked at a button on his Sindikash city-style buffalo-hide jacket. "And here's the audio." He pointed at a fingernail, which had a thin layer of gloss upon it. Virtually invisible.

Beverly Crusher palmed her red hair back and tied it out of the way. "I hope this goes the way you plan, Worf. Khanty had enough spies everywhere that she knew where two unidentified witnesses were. What are the chances she'll know we're coming?"

"Pretty darned good," Riker filled in.

Worf sighed. "This is too dangerous."

Riker gripped his arm. "Don't worry. It'll just distract you."

"The situation is deadly. We can die."

"Decision's been made."

Feeling his bones rumble, Worf knew Riker was forcing him to shift back into obey-the-order mode just long enough to get him to stop hesitating.

"Aye, sir," he complied, irritated.

"Data?" Riker strode away from Worf, somehow moving casually despite the cramped quarters of the shuttlecraft cockpit.

"Ready to beam down anytime you wish, sir," the android said, and looked up. "Coordinates are set for the central government compound, outside the holding cell area."

"Did you try to beam us directly into the cell?"

"I found those coordinates, sir, but we have no way of knowing which specific cell Mr. Grant is in. Also, the cells have scrambler shields around them. We might materialize, but without most of our extremities."

"Well, I'd like to keep my extremities. So we'll just break in. Let me have a look at you, Data."

Data came to his feet and turned to face them. He wore a dark gray double-breasted vest that was made of corduroy, a drover's yellow embroidered bandana, like the kind Sindikash wives and sweethearts made for their men before the annual bison drive, and a simple brown shirt and trousers. The most remarkable change, however, was to his skin and eyes. A prosthetic covering had been fitted to his face and hands, so hair-thin and sensitive that it was completely indistinguishable from real human skin. He even looked a little tan. His amber eyes were now blue. His lips had some color for a change, and he had eyebrows.

"You look like my little brother," Riker said with a grin of satisfaction.

"I rather enjoy the appearance," Data mentioned. "Except that the prosthetic loses its integrity with time and begins to shrink."

"Not a bad way to lose weight. Worf, you ready to do this?"

"No, sir."

"Good. Let's beam down."

"Oh, my God . . ."

Beverly Crusher was a physician, and not easy to shock.

Worf knew she was being shocked not by the sight of a mutilated human form, but by the thoughts of what had mutilated that form and who could have done it.

Before them, in the cell surrounded by stone walls and with crisscrossed metal grids in front, Ross Grant's body hung from a mattress cord tied to a light fixture. He was as still as drying meat. His head was tilted slightly to one side, his scorched hands splayed in the final muscle spasm and frozen that way.

Crusher pushed past Worf, who could no longer make himself move, though adrenaline still ran hot in him from their breaking into the jail. Fortunately, jails were arranged to keep people from breaking out, not the other way around.

Behind Worf, Riker scanned quickly for recording devices. "Nothing here," he said. His voice cracked. "We can talk."

The doctor was already running her medical scanner along Grant's body, and somehow the sight of that jarred Worf into movement. He wrapped his arms around Grant and took the weight off the cord around the neck until Crusher untied the cord.

Worf lowered Grant's body to the cool floor, then stood back to absorb what he saw before him. What could he say to Alexander? How could he tell his son that he had let this happen?

Grant had been stripped down to his undershirt and trousers. The trousers were slashed to the knees, exposing his legs. His arms had been slashed, too, as if the skin were fabric.

The slash wounds had been allowed to bleed freely until the blood caked on his body and clothing, then later cauterized. There were burns. Deep burns that still smoldered. Some of the wounds were coagulated. Others were still moist. This had gone on for hours upon hours.

Of the freshest wounds were the two that had gouged out Grant's gentle eyes.

The pain in Crusher's face as she examined the body was enough to smash the strongest constitution. She wasn't telling Worf anything, but she knew.

And from her expression and the condition of the body, Worf knew, too. Grant had not died of the wounds. Not even the eyes. From the swollen smear that ringed his neck, they had finished him slowly, drawing him gradually upward instead of putting him high and kicking something out from under him. There had been no quick snap of the neck. There had been no hint of mercy.

"Time of death," Crusher struggled, "about two hours ago. Maybe a little longer. Some of these cut wounds have been cauterized, as if they didn't want him to bleed to death or lose consciousness too soon. Both feet are broken . . . his clavicle is cracked. There's no brain damage. His groin is badly burned. So are his fingers and toes. Cause of death . . . asphyxiation."

She glanced up at Worf's narrowed eyes.

He felt her gaze, her pity. His arms and legs were suddenly double their normal weight. A thousand bitter emotions piled upon him, coupled with the burden he now put upon his shipmates, for they wanted to give him comfort, and he would have none. Of all the challenges he had ever faced and stemmed in his life of struggle for identity and cause, never before had he been so completely afraid as he was of this—facing his twelve-year-old son.

He stared at the swollen body of Ross Grant. What had the last hour been like? Had Grant waited for him to come? Had he found sustaining courage in the faith that Worf would show up in time?

"They had to kill him," Worf ground out. His voice was rough as sandpaper. "He would not die from their torture. He made them kill him. He was more courageous than I ever . . . imagined."

"Worf, I'm so very sorry," Crusher murmured. Her medical distance suffered as she accepted that horrible punishment of not being able to do anything for her patient.

Worf shook himself to movement. His cold fingers dug into the hem of Grant's T-shirt. In a fit of anger, he tore the hem open, fished through the fabric, and drew out a single thread with a tiny bead tied to one end. It looked like all the other threads in Grant's clothing, except that on close examination there was a faint satin sheen.

"Grant organized all his findings and committed them to this metallic thread. He coordinated dates and facts, statements, shipping orders and times, signatures on bills of lading and manifests, locations of various Rogues at key moments before, during, and after suspicious incidents, and a thousand bits of circumstantial evidence against Mrs. Khanty."

They all looked at the single foot-long thread as if it were about to sing.

"He was no fighter," Worf went on tightly. "He was no soldier. He had never trained to resist torture. Yet here this is in my hands. He never gave it up. He knew I would retrieve it. He expected . . . me . . . to come back."

Riker stepped to him. "Worf, don't do this. This isn't your fault. It's Odette Khanty's fault. Don't get that mixed up."

His innards shriveling, Worf bottled up a need to spit in Riker's face and drive those words back. Not his fault?

"He died because of me. I kept my honor, but he paid the price."

Shuddering, Worf gazed down at the body of his brave, dead friend, and his heart snagged.

He stuffed the critical thread into Beverly Crusher's hands, and noted peripherally that she quickly fed it into her tied-back hair. Once that was done, Worf plowed between Riker and Crusher and out of the cell.

"Worf!" Riker called after him, but the warning had no effect.

Five seconds later Worf was back, with a terrorized Burkal City police lieutenant in his claws. He drove the policeman before him into the cell and bent the man over Grant's body.

"Dead!" Worf roared.

"I know . . . I know he's dead," the policeman quivered.

"Why was he still hanging there so long after he died?"

"There's—there's an investigation underway—"

"You mean there's a cover-up being developed! Who did this to him!"

Barely able to move his head because of Worf's unkind grip on the base of his neck, the policeman glanced at Riker and Crusher. "He did it to himself."

"He inflicted these burns on himself?" Crusher shot back. "He gouged out his own eyes? You've got to be kidding!"

"I—I—he did it to himself. That's what's on the report. He hanged himself."

"You tell the *truth!"* Worf shrieked in the policeman's ear, reaching his breaking-somebody's-neck point.

"It's—look—" The policeman raised his hands and winced. "Look, it's suicide. It's in the report."

"What about all these wounds!"

"They're . . . " The policeman grimaced. ". . . self-inflicted."

"Curse you!" Worf shook the man violently.

"Worf, let go of him." Riker stepped forward and took the rattled policeman away from Worf.

He must have seen something that Worf, through his rage, could not see. As the policeman looked at the body, then up again, Worf found it in himself to notice that there were tears in the man's eyes.

The officer's voice was thin and miserable. "I can only tell you . . . what's in the report. Sorry."

"Where is Lieutenant Stoner?" Worf demanded.

The policeman sighed hard. "They say he didn't show up for work this morning."

Then the man shrugged.

"When the truth comes out," Worf threatened, "I will see you again."

Obviously more afraid of something else than he was of Worf, the policeman looked at him firmly now and with great sympathy. "If I were you, I'd worry about seeing morning."

He reached into his pocket and pulled out a plum-sized device that was flashing a blue and red pattern of lights. Worf recognized it—the policeman had notified the Rogues. Understanding boiled through the anger. The policeman had no choice.

"Sorry," the man said again. "I got four kids."

"Get out!" Worf thundered.

"Going." The policeman veered for the cell door, hurried down the narrow stone corridor, and disappeared.

"Poor guy," Riker uttered.

Though there was no charity in Worf's heart, he felt for the first time Grant's intense passion to cure this planet for the sake of its people, and not just for the integrity of the Federation as a whole. His knees and elbows trembled with the strain of containing his rage.

Contain it? Why!

He swung about and rammed his fist into the wall.

The wall cracked. Plaster clattered to the cold floor.

Riker eyed him sympathetically. "Don't do that again. You'll hurt yourself."

"I will hurt *someone!"*

From the corridor outside the cell, a voice was there to answer.

"Hurt *me."*

The Starfleet team swung full about and found themselves staring down the phasers of Ugulan, Goric, Tyro, Mortash, and four other Rogues whose names Worf had never bothered to learn.

Ugulan stood in the forefront, with an expression of bizarre pleasure on his harsh face. He was getting revenge on Worf, and he liked that. Simple pleasures.

"Search them," he snarled, drawing each word out twice as long as it needed to be.

Mortified at the arrival of dishonorable Klingons in the presence of his Starfleet crewmates, Worf shuddered and bottled up a surge of insane rage. He hadn't anticipated this reaction—his stomach heaved as Riker, Crusher, and Data were forced to look into the faces of these bottom feeders. It was one thing to face them alone, but this—

Not yet . . . not yet . . .

Tyro, Mortash, Goric, and one other came forward, dividing among the four Starfleeters. They each pulled out a scanning device, far more advanced than most technology on Sindikash, and within seconds they had possession of Crusher's recording devices—both of them—and Riker's audio fingernail. Another few seconds' searching gave up Riker's video button.

At the same time, Mortash began locating and scooping up their hidden palm phasers. "Starfleet issue," he said.

"Naturally," Ugulan agreed. He stepped to Riker and surveyed him up and down. "Who are you?"

Riker lifted his chin and met Ugulan's glower with an aloof courage. "Kirk. James Kirk."

Ugulan sneered. "Starfleet?"

"Iowa Regional Militia."

Confused, Ugulan was interrupted as the recording equipment Riker and Crusher had carried was gathered by the Rogues and handed over to him. He immediately rumbled up to Data and surveyed his face disapprovingly.

"What about this one?"

"Nothing on that one," Tyro said, clearly perplexed. "Why would those two have something and this one have nothing?"

"Is he stupid?" Ugulan suggested, pushing his face close to Data's. "Or is he here for something else? Well, skinny?"

Data glanced at Worf and tried to lean away from Ugulan, but said nothing.

"Where are you going?" Ugulan's hand flashed to Data's throat and dragged him closer. "You can go exactly nowhere. To make sure you go nowhere, I think you need a leash."

He backed Data up against the wall. At the same instant, Tyro and two other Rogues shoved their phasers into Riker's ribs and crammed both him and Crusher against the cell's forward grid.

Worf raised both his arms at the same time, in two directions. He drove his elbow into Mortash's chin and his other fist into another Klingon's teeth.

They both went down, but three more Rogues were on him, then suddenly a fourth. A fifth.

And he was held. They wasted no time with him, but instantly pressed him to the cell grid and tied his hands far out at his sides. He strained and yanked, but they had him.

And they had Riker and Crusher pinned on the other side of the front grid. He knew what was happening—they were being positioned as an audience.

Ugulan humphed in satisfaction and turned again to Data, then made a sharp gesture that brought Mortash and Goric to his sides, with a cord.

This cord was braided, and evidently this time they didn't care whether appearances implied that the rope had come from somewhere inside the cell. Their confidence was peaking. They believed they couldn't be caught, for their only real threats were now at their phaserpoints.

Ugulan tugged at Data's neckerchief until it came off. He stuffed it into his belt. Mortash and Goric clasped Data's arms while Ugulan slipped a noose around Data's neck, then tossed the other end through the metal ceiling grid.

"No!" Crusher shouted. She tried to bolt forward, and endured a fierce throttling until she fell back. Riker tried to protect her, and fielded a vicious slug.

Worf quaked and wanted to roar, but he knew that would only encourage Ugulan. He could only watch, as he was meant to, as the noose tightened around Data's throat. Data slipped backward, tripped over the cot, and fell. The force of his fall constricted his throat and he clawed at the cord, his mouth going wide on a gasp. He tried to get his legs back under him, but tripped again, and now Ugulan himself enjoyed heaving back on the tied end of the rope.

"Not again!" Riker shouted. "Isn't Grant enough for you in one day? You can't do that to him!"

"No?" Ugulan shook his head. "Are you sure? Is it 'inhuman'?"

He heaved harder. Data's feet toed at the floor as he was hoisted beyond reach. He kicked frantically, trying to knock Ugulan away from the rope, but there was no doing it.

His kicking made his body jerk back and forth in a corkscrew motion. His fingers dug at the cord around his neck. He expelled breath after breath, but could suck none in.

"See what happens to someone who fails to gain our trust?" Ugulan said. "All of you will follow Skinny, and we will have more entertainment with each of you until we get to the traitor."

Worf gritted his teeth and felt his lips peel back at Ugulan's glance.

Halfway to the ceiling now, Data kicked more frantically, forcing Mortash and Goric to step away from the flailing boots. Data's throat gurgled and gagged, and the terrible sounds washed through the cell, torturing his shipmates and delighting the Rogues.

Disgusted, Worf took in a shiver of shame that they were so completely enjoying themselves, and understood that this was part of the reason they stayed with Odette Khanty. Not just the power or the promise of influence, but the bloodlust.

Hideous. Inexcusable. His sudden distaste surprised him, for it extended not just to these particular bandits, but to all Klingons, for it was giving in to their Klingon nature that made them so sadistic. Suddenly he wanted nothing to do with them. He wanted nothing in common with them. He did not want even to look like them.

And he wanted to rush back to the ship and yank Alexander out of that Day of Honor ritual. His shame itched all over his body.

He realized his eyes were fixed on Data again—just in the last second. Just in time to hear Data gag out one whimpering gasp and see him finally fall limp. His eyes lost focus, and glazed over.

"Oh, no . . . oh, no," Beverly Crusher moaned, and sank to her knees.

Riker drove his shoulder into Tyro's chest, but was hammered back by Mortash's enormous fists. When Riker recovered and looked slowly up again, his lip was bleeding, and his cheekbone bore a purpling bruise.

Worf lashed out a foot at Ugulan, but the Rogue easily sidestepped. Ugulan teased him with a laugh, and pointed at Data's sagging body.

"The other one took longer," he crowed, swinging his gesture around to where Grant's sorry corpse lay on the floor. "This one is even more of a child, to go so fast. This one's not drooling. I like it when they drool."

"Pig!" Worf snarled. "Coward!"

"Yes," Ugulan said. He turned to Riker and Crusher, as if trying to choose who would be next.

Breath came and went in heaves from Worf's chest. Had he timed things wrong? Had he miscalculated? A few minutes would be critical.

Seconds began to tick by as Ugulan measured Riker and Crusher on his enjoyment meter. Would a woman be more fun to torture? Or would it be more fun to watch a woman's reaction as a handsome man like Riker was tortured?

Worf knew he was meant to see the deaths of all his friends before he, too, would have his skin peeled off.

Before Ugulan could make his choice, a commotion at the end of the dark corridor drew the attention of all, and in strode Odette Khanty with two more Rogues in attendance.

That made . . . ten.

Mrs. Khanty strode into the cell as easily as a woman entering church. She wore a salmon-colored business suit with a Sindikash embroidered silk scarf at her collar, and she looked entirely out of place among the rampart of Rogues around her. On her arm was a black armband with a noticeable purple orchid—a real one—affixed to it, and she wore a polite black velvet hat with a lace swirl of some kind. Mourning garb. Just enough to remind everyone who saw her.

Without saying a word, she opened a hand, palm up. Ugulan delivered the tiny listening and video devices to her and she looked at them with a skilled eye. "This is the best Starfleet could do?" She looked up at Worf. "These are the people you're loyal to, and they couldn't do better than this? I've seen this kind of thing on Cardassian smugglers."

She handed the tiny pile over to one of the Rogues, then snapped her fingers. Another Rogue handed her a metal stick, about a meter long with a bulbous handle, and she pressed a switch with her thumb. She didn't look at Worf, but she moved toward him.

"All of you, pay attention," she said. "so nobody will ever do this to me again. I want—"

She paused, noticing Data's pathetic body hanging from the cord.

"That's not the same one," she said.

"No," Ugulan told her. "Grant is behind you."

She looked around, saw Grant's body on the floor, and seemed satisfied just that easily.

Once again she looked at the metallic stick.

"This is a *T'kalla* prod," she said. "It's stronger than a cattle prod. From Alak IV. We use it on our bison because buffalo fur is so thick. Almost as thick as your hide, Worf."

Abruptly, she swung the stick around and thrust it into Worf's rib cage.

Electrical shock ripped through his body, choking out a grunt and crackling through the metal grid behind him.

And his brain began to fry.

CHAPTER 18

EVEN WHEN MRS. KHANTY TOOK THE STICK AWAY, THE ELECTRICITY SNAPPED and sizzled through Worf another two or three eternities.

He coughed and fought, but only when he shuddered down the last surge and his gasping steadied did Mrs. Khanty speak again.

"Now pay attention" she said, glancing around at the ten Rogues. "The parts of his body will never be found. You think you have imagination? Think you're scary? Wait until you see what I do with this man."

Now she turned to Worf again.

"The election is tomorrow, you know. Your plan backfired. People on this pissant planet are believing that it was a Starfleet plot to kill my husband. Before this, I stood a chance of losing the election. If that happened, my empire would collapse. But, thanks to you and your dead friend over there, I'm going to sweep it. My polls are higher than ever. Everything you wanted to stop is going to happen. All because you betrayed me."

"I never betrayed you," Worf choked. "You never deserved my loyalty. You never had it. You showed no loyalty to anyone. Not the people, not the children, not even your husband."

She twisted the handle of the buffalo prod, and the instrument began a faint hum. She had powered it up.

She reached out and poked him again with the prod. *Dzzzzt—*

Electricity bolted through Worf even more jarringly than before, and sent him crashing against the grid. Mrs. Khanty watched and waited for the snapping and sizzling to die down, until Worf was groaning and gasping.

As he gasped, she said, "My husband was a patsy. He couldn't make a decision. He was a wind sock. Whatever the day demanded. His goals were a mile wide and an inch deep. I was the only one who had a vision."

"You . . . had . . . ambition," Worf coughed, "not vision."

She clicked the buffalo prod up another grade until the rod hummed angrily, then zapped him again, this time in the hollow of his shoulder.

Dzzzzzzaaat—

The surge was blinding. He stiffened in agony, and his entire side went numb. When she drew the prod back, Worf sagged and began twitching uncontrollably. In his periphery he saw Riker and Crusher gazing at him with tortured eyes, and he hoped they would keep quiet. He knew what he was absorbing, and knew their human frames would be blown to rags with very little of this.

Looking at the Rogues again, she said, "There's got to be buffalo pee in the water on this colony. I dress like Bo-Peep and tell them there's no evidence, and they think it's the same as saying I didn't do anything. And thanks to Worf, no matter how much I control, no matter who I kill for the next ten years, I'll be able to blame it on Starfleet. Not everybody's as hard to kill as my husband. It took two tries to finally get rid of him."

Beverly Crusher peered around Mortash's considerable shoulder. "You mean you're the one who attempted to kill your husband the first time?"

"With my own lily-white hands," Khanty said. "Only he didn't have the common courtesy to die. I finally had to finish him, and Worf and Grant were very polite to take the blame. And these colonial yokels will swallow it. I don't know what to do to thank you, Worf. So I'll kill you."

"Betrayer," Worf rasped. "Conscience does not confuse you. You are a public hack. Any lie that advances you is fair play. Simple justice never impedes you. How long can you keep control that way? You can not even control me. Remember, you do not have *my* Oath of Sto'vo-kor.

"These people . . . " Worf continued, "trusted you . . . you could have helped build a . . . fine community . . . here."

"Here? You think I'm spending the rest of my life with manure on my shoes? This dump is a stepping-stone."

Mrs. Khanty clicked the buffalo prod up another setting. Then another, until it hummed and actually sparked. Another click or two and it would easily become a shuttlecraft prod.

"I've ordered thousands of deaths, but I've only done two with my own hands. My husband, and now you."

She turned to Worf and moved closer, as if sizing him up. Even the Rogues were tight with nervousness and empathy. Ugulan had stepped away—well away.

Interesting way to die. Prodded to death. What would that look like on his service record?

She surveyed him as if trying to decide which part of his body would be more fun to poke with that heartless device, and he knew she was giving him time to think about what was coming. Him, and the Rogues.

She raised the prod, and stepped back to give herself room to use it—

"Wait!" Riker called.

Mrs. Khanty looked at him. "Wait for what?"

The first officer made a motion at the wall-mounted observation screen just outside the cell. "You might want to turn that on."

"That will do you no good!" Ugulan shouted. "That one is a security display monitor, not a recording monitor, fool."

"Why don't you see if there's anything to display?" Riker suggested.

Crusher gave Khanty a thick woman-to-woman look and added, "I think there is."

Khanty's expression lost its smugness. She gestured to Goric. "Turn it on."

Ugulan swung to her. "That monitor cannot possibly record anything you've said. It has no way of doing that!"

"Turn it on!" Khanty roared.

Goric plowed out of the cell. Every body in the place was tense now, sensing complication. Goric pounded the monitor control until it came on.

A fritzing picture jumped to life, fielding some interference, and struggled to clarify itself. The sound crackled, then settled into a voice.

"There's got to be buffalo pee in the water on this colony. I dress like Bo-Peep and tell them there's no evidence, and they think it's the same as saying I didn't do anything. And thanks to Worf, no matter how much I control, no matter who I kill for the next ten years, I'll be able to blame it on Starfleet. Not everybody's as hard to kill as my husband. It took two tries to finally get rid of him."

"You mean you're the one who attempted to kill your husband the first time?"

"With my own lily-white hands. Only he didn't have the common courtesy to die. I finally had to finish him, and Worf and Grant were very polite to take the blame. And these colonial yokels will swallow it. I don't know what to do to thank you, Worf. So I'll kill you."

The picture fritzed again, shifted, and settled again, this time on a close-up of Mrs. Khanty as she turned to Worf.

"I've ordered thousands of deaths, but I've only done two with my own hands. My husband, and now you."

The Rogues stared and stared, utterly stunned and no doubt running over in their minds how this could possibly be happening.

"It is being broadcast colonywide," Worf shuddered out. "All the airwaves have been pirated. The whole planet has been watching you."

"How!" Khanty shrieked. "It's a trick! This is a trick! How could this happen!"

Abruptly, a hand clamped on her wrist and held her in place. She automatically tried to wrench away, but she was held as tightly as Worf was to the grid. She looked up, and sucked in a hard breath. She was staring up into Data's bright, living eyes and his pain-free face.

"You are being most discourteous, madam," Data said blandly. "Perhaps a pause to regain composure would serve us all."

The Rogues gawked in shock, unable even to swing their phasers around before Mrs. Khanty reacted.

She howled and twisted the buffalo prod upward toward Data's face.

Though he was still hanging and without leverage, he managed to crank his face away from her just as the prod veered toward his eyes. The prod struck his vest lapel, zapped brightly, and set the vest instantly on fire in a hail of sparks. The fabric enjoyed burning, and flames quickly swept the front of Data's clothing. Still, he did not let go of Odette Khanty's wrist.

Terrorized, the woman transferred the rod to her other hand and swung it wildly, striking Tyro with a numbing jolt of electricity and setting him on fire, too. He slammed backward, numb and convulsing. He tumbled into two other Rogues, who also rolled into flames and scrambled away, trying to put out their clothing.

Riker blew into action, pulling from his belt a simple shielded stunner, unscannable, and driving it into Mortash's sternum. The big Klingon stared at his body, looked at Riker, and clawed at the air. Riker instantly took possession of Mortash's phaser and started dropping Rogues when he could get a clear shot.

Unfortunately, that wasn't easy. The small cell burst into a flurry of movement. Under cover of that movement, Crusher pulled out a medical injection device—smaller than the usual sickbay version—and lanced another Rogue in the throat. He knocked her to the ground, then dropped like a sandbag, unconscious. As another Rogue sprung after Riker, Crusher got that one, too, with an injection directly in the face.

How many was that? Worf tried to clear his head. How many Rogues were left standing?

Data raised his other hand and tried to pat out the flames on his clothing. The heat was becoming intense enough for Worf to feel it several steps away, and Data wouldn't be able to see through the fire, which might also damage the delicate camera mechanisms in his eyes.

The prosthetic sheath on his face was now melting, his human disguise curling like parchment, revealing the golden android skin beneath. His special contact lenses were fading, spreading wide and losing their integrity, revealing his catlike amber eyes. Those eyes stared down at Odette Khanty.

Mrs. Khanty struggled insanely, but now looked up at the creature holding her wrist in his iron clamp and saw the corpse becoming a wraith. She pulled back and screamed out her horror.

At the metal grid, Worf yanked and strained, but could not break the cords that bound his wrists. "Data!" he shouted.

Data slapped at his clothing, and decided to sacrifice his grip on Odette Khanty long enough to reach up and rip the noose off his neck. He dropped to the ground, distracted for a fraction of a second.

During that instant, Odette Khanty swung her buffalo prod in a great arc, snapping and setting fire to another Rogue, and Crusher's lace sleeve, then bolting for the corridor. She slammed into the opposite wall, just under the monitor.

"Here? You think I'm spending the rest of my life with manure on my shoes? This dump is a stepping-stone."

She swung the prod upward and smashed the viewscreen. Sparks erupted in a violent display that blanketed half the corridor, and in that fog of fireworks, she disappeared.

"Data!" Worf howled again, this time over the whine of Riker's careful phaser shot.

"Coming," Data said evenly. Plowing over the fallen Rogues, he snapped Worf's braided bonds as if they were shoelaces.

As Worf struggled to regain control over his numb legs, Data whirled on the remaining Rogues and drove two of them into the back wall, one with each hand, hard enough that they both collapsed with head injuries. Data's violence could be very precise.

Then he turned to the last Rogue standing—Ugulan. Ugulan's notable obstinancy ran out as he gaped into the shredded face of a powerful wraith whose clothing still smoldered, embroiling Data in a monstrous shroud. Every move he made threw off a tendril of smoke, as if he were a wizard casting spells.

Ugulan didn't even try. He spun around and headed for the cell entrance.

In his panic he forgot that Worf was standing there.

Worf reached out as Ugulan tried to pass him by. For an instant they simply stared at each other, until Worf's fury peaked.

He skewered Ugulan with a long, cold glare, gritted his teeth, and roared, "It is a good day to die!"

His right fist drew back and flew forward in a short, hard punch to Ugulan's rib cage. Never had Worf thrown such a punch in his entire life. Never had he felt such rage driving his actions. His fist struck Ugulan's sternum, cracking the bone, then his other fist drove into the other Klingon's chest. Before Worf's eyes, Ugulan's body collapsed. Living or dead, Worf did not know. Either way, his soul was doomed.

Dizzy and wheezing, Worf spun twice to make sure all the Rogues were down or gone, then looked around to where Riker was snuffing out the flames on Crusher's sleeve. "All of you stay here!" he shouted.

Data smoldered forward. "I will go with you—"

"No! This is for me alone!"

"You'd better run," Riker said. "She's getting away."

"She will not get away," Worf snarled back. "And I refuse to run."

CHAPTER 19

DARKNESS STILL COMMANDED THE PORT OF DELAWARE STATION, ALTHOUGH the first pale periwinkle of coming day now showed itself above the black cutouts of trees, houses, and the boatyard. The details of *Justina*'s rigging jumped out against the velvety purple predawn sheen.

Amazing. All this in one night.

Behind them, the chapel bell rang and rang, and around them armed men poured out of cottages, inns, cabins, and rooming houses. Old, young—every manner of man came out with a rifle or flintlock pistol. Some seemed confused, then joined others who were following behind Picard, Alexander, Patrick O'Heyne, Jeremiah Coverman, and their men. The patriots seemed pathetically disorganized, but determined and of a single mind as they flocked to face the incoming redcoats.

"Cavalry? Artillery?" Jeremiah asked O'Heyne as they ran toward the south side of the town.

"No," O'Heyne said, struggling with his wounds. "They landed no artillery or horses that I saw. They have, by my estimate, about two hundred men on foot. And they do have sharpshooters, I'm sorry to recall for the sake of my poor Whistler. I loved that horse . . . "

Caught in a moment of sorrow, O'Heyne didn't mind his wounds and tripped on a small wooden plank, skidding to one knee on the dirt road. Jeremiah, understandably, rushed to help him up, but so did Sandy, and that was enheartening. Picard helped O'Heyne over the discarded plank that had tripped him. "Perhaps go a little slower."

"Not tonight," O'Heyne said, bothering to knock back the ponytail loosely tied at the nape of his neck. "I'm all right. There's the barricade."

At the end of a stand of houses and shops, likely the edge of town as well, minutemen with rifles and townsfolk, including women, were building up a line of scrimmage made of sea barrels, crates, and a horse trough that had been spilled and moved into place. The barricade looked all too fragile, and would stop no one from rushing through, but Picard noted that it would provide fair cover for those shooting over it, which the flanking trees wouldn't.

"Hear them?" Jeremiah said abruptly, looking down the dark road. "Drums! They're nearly here!"

"Yes, marching snares," O'Heyne agreed. "Remarkable sound. Keeps the soldiers marching for hours and somehow their backs don't hurt when they're done. There's nothing like marching drums. You should hear the sound when they've got pipers along. They can go for days, and I find myself wanting to go with them."

Enjoying himself more than he should have been, Picard glanced at him. "Mr. O'Heyne, I think you're a bit crazy."

"I'd have to be, wouldn't I?"

That sound *was* stirring! The *clap-trrrrap-ap* of snares coming through the trees like approaching rattlesnakes, and the sounds of footsteps as the march drew close enough to be heard. Picard crouched behind the barrels with all the other men, with Alexander and Sandy to his left, and beyond Sandy were O'Heyne and Jeremiah. To Picard's right were Nightingale, Bennett, and Wollard. Nightingale and Bennett had two of Jeremiah's rifles, and Wollard seemed perfectly happy holding the ball pouches and powder horns. He seemed less warrior than just a clumsy, landed sailor at the moment. Bennett, on the other hand, seethed with frustration at Picard's agreement to take no action.

Alexander twisted around suddenly and looked back at the town's main business area. "I can't believe all those people came out because the bell rang! They came out in a minute, just like my teacher told me! And with their rifles and pistols! Look at them! I think it was *less* than a minute! They should be called half-a-minutemen!"

Picard gave him a conciliatory glance, then looked back at the town, where indeed people were scooting out of doorways, but then made a quieting motion. "Relax, Alexander. We're British, remember?"

"I know, I know." And the boy cast him a mischievous grin that made Picard think of Will Riker.

"Load your guns, gentlemen," Patrick O'Heyne said, and smiled. "And how's that for taking my life in my hands?"

How could he smile at a time like this?

"You must fight," Jeremiah added, leaning so Picard and Sandy could see him. "At least pretend. Shoot at the trees if you like. For all our sakes, while you wear these clothes you must behave as Yankees, or you'll be shot as traitors."

"Feel like one," Bennett grumbled, but Picard and Nightingale were the only ones to hear him.

"This rifle is different from the sergeant's," Alexander said, pointing at the musket Picard held.

"You've not seen an American musket before, swab?" Sandy asked, pressing an elbow into the crate in front of him.

Alexander shook his head. "It's longer than yours."

"Explain the difference to the boy, Sergeant," Picard said, seizing on the opportunity.

Sandy glanced at the woods nervously, measuring the nearness of the snares. "Mine is a British sea-service musket. It's shorter so I may more easily maneuver it among the ship's rigging. The butt is flat on the bottom, not crescent-shaped like this American gun. This way I can easily load it while the butt rests flat on the ship's deck. The barrel of mine is blackened and its ramrod is made of wood, to fend away corrosion from the salt sea and air."

"Never thought of that," Picard murmured, and smiled at Alexander. He handed his musket to Sandy. "Here, Sergeant. Show the boy how it's loaded."

Sandy blinked, dismayed, clearly wondering why Picard didn't just show the boy himself. Picard hoped Sandy wouldn't notice how closely a lieutenant of the Royal Navy was paying attention to the process.

"This is my powder horn," the sergeant began, pulling his equipment around. "This little thing is my powder measurer, this is my bullet pouch, with about fifty rounds remaining . . . the ramrod comes out so . . . the powder is measured . . . poured in the barrel, and keep a pinch to use for priming. Drop the ball inside . . . the ramrod goes down, a firm push, and out again. Gun up, pull back the cock, put the priming pinch on the pan, take aim, and fire. And hope your flint doesn't crack. Then do it all again, and fire into the center of the smoke from your last shot, because you now cannot see. In the smoke of a dozen muskets, the enemy is but a ghost. Try it, boy."

"Oh—" Suddenly parental, Picard spoke up as Alexander took the musket. "I don't think that's wise."

"He's old enough," Sandy said defensively. "I began at the age of seven, sir."

"Great!" Alexander shouldered the long rifle and tested the weight. "I can do this."

A sad moment, perhaps, but it had to come sometime. It had come for Picard, and would for every young man who decided to serve.

Sandy leaned on the barrel before him and peered into the dimness. "Decisions come for us all."

"Is something wrong?" Alexander asked.

Glancing at his other side—at Patrick O'Heyne, as the Yankee businessman spoke quietly to Jeremiah—Sandy lowered his voice and spoke to Picard and Alexander.

"He left a thriving business in England and New York. How could a man do that? His schedules and methods of correspondence relay revolutionized Atlantic shipping. He was received at the British court! Why would he forsake all that to crawl in the dirt and risk his life?"

Picard prodded, "Must be a compelling reason."

"I cannot imagine," Sandy murmured.

Alexander made a face. "Neither can I."

"Why don't you ask him?" Picard suggested.

"Really?" The boy looked at him.

"That's what we're here for."

"Right!" The boy shimmied closer to Sandy. "Yes, ask him!"

"Very well!" Sandy twisted around to his other side. "Mr. O'Heyne—"

O'Heyne turned. "Mr. Leonfeld?"

"Yes, we have a question."

"I'm at your service."

"You're an educated, successful man of high standing, yet here you are holding a musket. Why would you fight with these common people when you could be safe and comfortable elsewhere?"

"Thank you for that, but I'm not of high birth at all," O'Heyne admitted openly. "My father was a Dublin pauper. He came to the colonies as a criminal."

"Criminal?" Alexander asked. "What kind?"

O'Heyne looked at the boy. "A murderer. Killed a landowner with a shovel to the side of the head. I don't know the situation, but the dead man's wife took pity on my father. Rather than go to prison, he was sent here. He began as a collier and gradually gained security. He made certain my brother and I were educated in the concerns of finance."

"And you built a business?" the boy pursued.

"My brother and I built it together, but the British impounded our business, both in Liverpool and New York, when I spoke up against the monarchy. We sacrificed it all. My brother is now a captain in the Fourth Continental Light Dragoons."

"You could have lived in riches in England, or even here," Sandy protested, "if you had simply run your business and not become involved in this dispute. Why on this earth would you give up everything, sir?"

O'Heyne's green eyes flickered. "For freedom, sir. Not to worry. If I live, I'll build my fortune again. Wealth cannot be kept out of the hands of the industrious."

He paused briefly, leaned over the crates, and looked down the dim tree-lined road.

"In England, I've been treated with respect, but in a bastard-son manner. They'll have me for tea, but they don't *prefer* to have me. You gentlemen should walk among the English dressed as you are now and see what it's like. As colonists, you have no right to speak your mind. You'll be lower than the lowest East Ender. You'll be required to quarter soldiers of the British military, no matter what your loyalties are. Your goods are required to be sold through Britain, and you have no say in how these revenues are spent or—"

"But that," Picard said, "is how the protection of the colonies is paid for, Mr. O'Heyne. Your movement is wresting away a large and legitimate British investment."

"The investment of those living and working here isn't considered at all. The British have some legitimate claims, but not enough. This is a philosophical disagreement, not just two bullies striking at each other. It's an argument over the worth of a human being. How long should the class system last? How long does God want me to keep my station of birth? If I'd kept to my father's station, I'd be hitting you with a shovel. Now that I've achieved 'betterment,' even in your eyes, should my sons have to go back to the shovel? Or can we continue the pattern until all are 'better'?"

"I love to hear you talk, Patrick," Jeremiah said with a grateful smile. He seemed glad not to be holding up the platform by himself anymore.

"Thanks, Jeremiah," O'Heyne said with another grin. "You hear those drums, Mr. Leonfeld? Those soldiers are coming here to shoot me for wanting sway over my own destiny. Should I be shot for that? Who is it I've stolen from by making myself successful? What is it I've done? What should I be hanged for? What have I taken from my king or countrymen? We desire to determine our own fate. We'll rise or fall, right now. This country is so open, everyone is so busy surviving and building and being productive that no one has time to worry about who's born to what and who shall marry whom. I want to make sure it stays that way. I owe this little nation a great debt. Live or die, I think our message will survive us. Freedom has to start somewhere. That's why I'm here with a musket."

He seemed to know the speech by heart—or perhaps it *was* his heart speaking. He turned toward Sandy and Picard, relaxing as if those drums weren't rattling in the closing distance.

"If you're going to come here and shoot me, you'd better be *damned* sure you're right. You'd better be able to look me in the eye and tell me why you're doing it, and still be able to sleep at night. Can you?"

Both Sandy Leonfeld and Alexander seemed suddenly nauseated with their own self-doubt. Even Picard felt a niggling wonderment at his own convictions. How sure had he been, all those times in the past?

"If your beliefs are so strong," O'Heyne said, "you have your gun. Shoot us now."

Pale, Sandy Leonfeld looked as if the invitation had physically slapped him across the face and knocked him back.

Alexander stared at his worshiped cousin, baffled by the doubts he saw in Sandy's elegant young face.

"They're here," O'Heyne said then, peering through the night. "There they are."

Picard looked out through the dark road, expecting to catch a glimpse of ghostly figures hiding among the trees.

Instead, he was confronted by—

"They're all in rows!" Alexander burst out. "They're coming right at us in long lines! Why would they do something that stupid?"

"Because battle by ranks has won them war upon war for centuries," Picard recalled. "It hearkens back to the days of hand weapons. It doesn't take guns and artillery into consideration. Apparently something about it still works."

"It works," Wollard muttered, his voice dripping with contempt.

Still, there certainly was some shock in seeing rank after rank of redcoats blend out of the darkness on the road, each holding a rifle with the muzzle at a tilt slightly in front of his white crossbelt. Their scarlet jackets and white facings were cast nearly gray in the darkness, but a forgiving moon lanced the trees and frequently gave a strike of red in the picture, as if hinting of what was to come. As the Royal troops drew closer with each step, the moonlight began to catch the savage flicker of bayonets, which would do their work if the two masses, redcoat and rebel, came hand-to-hand.

Abruptly, a shot popped from the British ranks. None of the redcoats seemed startled, but the colonists all flinched.

The musketball whined in and buzzed away, well over their heads, and tore through an oak tree overhanging a house.

"Ranging shot," Picard uttered automatically.

"And they're within range," Alexander replied.

A voice shouted something unintelligible in the woods, and the marching ranks stopped abruptly, barely within sight.

"Heads down," Patrick O'Heyne warned.

Around them, on all sides, Yankee riflemen tucked themselves deeply behind trees and around corners of the cabins, and behind steps and in doorways. The fear was palpable. Of course, most of these were not regular soldiers. They were people defending their homes.

"Grenadiers, ready! First rank, kneel!" The voice in the darkness was muffled. "Present arms!"

Dark muzzles of British guns were eerily invisible in the night, making it appear as if the soldiers were pantomiming the aiming of guns, as boys might playact a battle.

A thunderous rocking volley erupted, and musketballs slammed into every barrel and crate, every building, and many human bodies, who now suffered the onslaught of the famous and formidable British military. Smoke from fifty muskets rolled into a single murderous fog, and the phantom guns took on a slamming reality. Picard crushed Alexander down, beginning to see in his mind all the wars that the British had waged and won, and how many in the coming years they would win with their dogged discipline and raw courage. As the terrible sound pounded in his head, he couldn't tell past from future at all.

Not quite a headlong fight yet. They were just shooting, as if to scrape off the icing of cowardice or weakness before the real men got at it.

But no one here ran away.

"First rank, reload! Second rank! Fire!"

Another roar, more musketballs splattered the barricade and pocked into human flesh. Injured and dying Yankees screamed and moaned. Two men beyond Jeremiah skidded hard into the dirt and lay slaughtered. Astonishing!

And the intimacy of it—phasers had eased all that, and before that the distance weapons of higher technology. With these gunpowder weapons, one had to get close enough to watch one's target die. As O'Heyne had said, better be sure.

Jeremiah checked the dead man nearest him, then scooped up the man's rifle and passed it to Picard.

"In case you must defend yourself," he said. "After all, they won't know who you are. Shoot if you must, for they surely will."

"Fire!" O'Heyne suddenly shouted, knowing something about timing this that eluded Picard.

SNAP—BOOM!

Musketfire from mere steps away nearly deafened him. The first and second ranks of the red mass now dissolved, every other man crumpling. Behind them was another wall of red. Behind that, another.

"Quick, maaaaarch!"

The drums started again, and the darkened menace surged forward with a stinking white cloud of gunsmoke rolling before them.

Not too far from the back of Picard's mind were the words *freeze program.* He primed himself to say them at an instant's notice, in case he or Alexander were immediately threatened. The holodeck could reverse itself or dissolve a holo-musketball, but it couldn't pull back the damage done. He toyed with the idea of stopping everything now, but this was what he and the boy had come for. If he stopped in the middle of this blistering attack, what would Alexander learn about honor? That these patriots stood up for each other's lives, and his father wouldn't?

Beside him a musket *crack-boomed* loudly. Alexander had just let fly his first deadly element. Had he aimed high? Or had the target of oncoming soldiers been too much for him to deny?

"Ow!" The boy bellowed. "Ow, that hurt! My shoulder! And it's burning my face!"

Picard saw the hot grains of powder stuck to the boy's cheeks, but made no move to brush them off. Alexander might as well learn here and now.

Around them, the Yankees took careful aim and fired. Musket volleys pocked the nightscape, creating a surreal dance of smoke, darkness, musket flashes, and patches of moonlight. River breeze made the musket smoke twist fitfully and seem to entangle, obscuring Picard's vision, and he possessed neither the training nor the experience for this.

He brought up his own rifle and tucked it into the hollow of his shoulder, aimed high, and pulled the trigger. The cock snapped down—*crack-boom!—hissss—*

His musket gasped fire like a dragon in the dark. The blast of priming powder in the pan stung his face. Acrid smoke and bits of powder grains burned his eyes. Nasty.

Among the British ranks, a man holding a sword high came strutting forward, waving the sword. "Forward! Forward!" he cried.

An officer. Captain, or colonel.

A Yankee stood up on the other side of Jeremiah, ignoring the danger of exposing himself, shouldered his long rifle, and took his time aiming. *Boom!* The rifle went off, and on the road the officer spun to his death. His sword clattered into the rifles of his own grenadiers.

"Rebel bastard!" Seaman Wollard roared. He swung around, aimed over Picard's head, and fired at the Yankee who had just shot the British officer.

The Yankee spun, stunned, and gaped at Wollard, then looked down at the sprawling gore that was now his rib cage, blinked up one more time, then slid to his knees. He was dead before he struck the ground. Picard knew the look.

"Sergeant!" he snapped.

But Sandy's rifle was already swinging about, and Wollard was blown into a disgusting mass. The concussion slammed the dying seaman a good ten feet back, and he lay twitching in the shadow of a porch.

"Thank you, sir," Sandy said. "I would've shot him anyway, but I cherish your approval. After all, he was your crew."

"We made an agreement," Picard confirmed, and fumbled to reload his rifle.

Above the heads of the oncoming British floated the King's colors, the flag of Great Britain emblazoned with the badge of that particular grenadier unit out there. The red-jacketed wraiths' faces were blackened with powder burns now, but they kept coming, unaffected by the sight of Yankee minutemen being mowed down in the town road as one might mow grass. Some grenadiers marching, and others were pausing to fire, then moving on forward. They were doing that by ranks, in disciplined shifts, and Picard found it stunning that such efficient destruction could be so messy.

Behind him, daring patriots were hurled backward and lay moaning in the thickening musket smoke that crippled aim from both sides. Musket-balls plucked at the dirt street and snapped bark off trees.

Terror for Alexander knitted Picard's spine. If one of those hit him, there would be no time to hold the program. "Keep firing!" O'Heyne shouted over the tangled howl of musketfire from the British.

Picard tipped his musket down in an effort to see what was happening, then brought it up quickly and fired, though he couldn't see a damned thing, not enough to avoid hitting those who were ironically his allies. The explosion came again, but this time there was no "kick."

Had he forgotten to put the ball in?

He glared at the pigheaded musket as if it was about to grow lips and answer him. Had it misfired?

Sandy Leonfeld leaned down in front of Picard and came up with a lead ball in his hand. "You tipped the barrel down, Lieutenant. The ball rolled out."

"Oh . . . thank you, Sergeant."

"Your servant, sir."

Picard fielded a perplexed glower from Sandy, intimating that the sergeant didn't understand why a naval officer wouldn't know to hold his gun up.

Jeremiah grasped O'Heyne's arm. "Patrick, we'll hold this line if we can. You hurry and meet Colonel Fox and tell him what's happening."

"I don't like that much," O'Heyne said.

"Like it or not, you'd better go. I can't explain the military approach those men are using, and I think it would be patently beyond the call of our agreement to ask any of these other gentlemen to do our reporting for us."

O'Heyne glanced through the pale trees at the fleeting phantoms of British soldiers, and reluctantly nodded. He threw an arm around Jeremiah and added, "Fall back if you must. Promise me, now. You have a wife to live for. I'll have to marry her if you die, and she's too young for me. Besides, you're not that good a soldier."

Jeremiah smiled, but before he could answer, a huge jarring boom burst out behind them!

Picard twisted to see what had happened. Out of the maddened night came a flock of soldiers armed with bayoneted rifles and wearing green jackets faced with red. The colonial militia—the Dover Light Infantry!

"Oh, how nice," Picard murmured. "Look at that."

"Can I stay now?" O'Heyne laughed.

Strangely romantic and compelling, the Dover Lights braced in the middle of the street, took aim, and fired as a unit without anyone shouting an order to them, unleashing a hideous punishment over the heads of Picard and the others. The British column hunched forward against the blistering attack, but did not break.

Now there was smoke on both sides of the barricade and it crippled the aim of both units. That didn't stop or even slow the crack of gunfire or the whine of musketballs. Picard looked up and saw bloody nothing. There was noise, though, lots of it—the boom of rifles, the sounds of gasping, screaming, vomiting, and the rattle of snare drums. Everything was muted, though. He was half deafened.

Jeremiah shouted cryptically, "We can't hold against them!"

"Maybe they'll let you be prisoners," Alexander coughed. "If you give up, they won't kill you. That's right, isn't it?"

"I've been supplying the Colonial militia," O'Heyne told him. "If Delaware Station is taken, I'll be hanged. If there's one thing the British hate, it's an uppity American who made some money in England. They'll take it out of my throat, I think."

On O'Heyne's last two words, a Dover infantryman rushed up and tried to go over the barricade between Picard and Alexander, and was met by a musketblast that twisted his head full about, though his body remained facing forward.

Alexander blinked right up into that terrible sight, the laid-open face, the stare of a remaining eye, until finally the man stumbled backward—was he still alive?—and dropped to his knees. The mass of gore wobbled, and fell forward on top of Alexander.

The boy yelled out his fear and kicked fiercely. Picard shoved the heavy body off the boy and thought about holding the program.

But he didn't say it.

"Sir!" On Picard's other side, Nightingale came to life and pointed at the British lines.

Picard, O'Heyne, Jeremiah, and the others all peeked through the barricade. The British, rather than being driven back by the appearance of the Dover Light Infantry, were rising from the bloodied dirt.

Another officer, or someone who had taken that role, waved a sword and screamed, "Chaaaaarge!"

And the invasion became a stampede. Hell cracked open. British soldiers plowed over the barricade to meet the Dover Infantry. Men from both sides fell in heaps, entangled enemy with enemy, and died in each other's embrace.

"Fall back!" Picard shouted.

He grabbed Alexander and rushed to his right, shoving Nightingale before him, hoping the others would follow. They were just in the way now.

Suddenly he tripped over something and slammed to his knees. Before him, Edward Nightingale's neck had been torn open. Picard had tripped on the midshipman's paralyzed legs.

"Aw!" Alexander choked as if it had been his neck instead of the midshipman's.

Half of Nightingale's left shoulder was gone, too. The young man's eyes pleaded and his hand dug into Alexander's sleeve.

"He's still alive!" Alexander gasped. "We've got to save him!"

Picard put the muzzle of his long rifle to the midshipman's chest, careful to angle it so the ball wouldn't roll out. He pulled the trigger. The gun discharged, blew a hole in Nightingale's heart, and the young officer's beseeching eyes glazed over mercifully.

"I can't believe you did that!" Alexander choked.

"You came here to learn," Picard said coldly. "Now you're learning. Let's go."

With Seaman Bennett stumbling before them and Sandy and Jeremiah after—there was no sign of O'Heyne now—they dodged into the protection of a building. On the street behind them, a mass of uniformed men tangled. More and more redcoats surged out of the woods, though. The Dover Lights were being overwhelmed by sheer numbers.

Jeremiah scrambled out into the street and yanked the red jackets off two dead grenadiers. Somehow he made it back alive and shoved the bloodied jackets into Picard and Sandy's hands.

"Put these on," he said. "The agreement is satisfied. Do what you must. Thank you for being honorable men." He gripped Sandy's arm. "Thank you most sincerely."

And without waiting for a family farewell, Jeremiah plunged back out onto the street and into the fight. He disappeared in the pall of white smoke.

Sandy gazed after him sorrowfully.

"What'll we do now, sir?" Bennett choked out.

Picard paused, then raked on the jacket. It was too big, but would serve to keep him from being shot by *both* sides. At least now only one side would shoot him.

"Defend the ship," he said. "The colonists will burn it before allowing it to be repossessed and used against them."

"How do you know?" Alexander asked.

"Because that's what I would do. The shipyard! Follow me!"

CHAPTER 20

THEY MADE IT TO THE DOCK ALIVE.

Behind them, patriots plunged through the streets, along with panicked residents, mostly women. Some of the women weren't panicking at all, but were busily reloading muskets and relaying them to nearby men.

Picard led his little band to the top of the wharf, leading out to where the *Justina* rested at the point of deepest water, for her draft was a good ten feet deeper than any other vessel here.

"What's holding us back, sir?" Bennett wanted to know when Picard paused.

"Looking for Committee of Safety guards," Picard answered. "Seems they've all gone to defend the town. All right, let's board and load."

There were only the four of them now, their shoes throbbing on the dock as they ran out to the gangplank and charged onto the ship. The *Justina* was eerily quiet, without another living soul on board. And yet there seemed to still be a pulse of life here, as if the beast were just in repose, waiting for its master to return.

So it was true . . . no ship was entirely inert. The life pulse of the shipwrights, the sailors, the officers remained on board somehow. She was alive.

"Is this your first action on this continent, Mr. Leonfeld?" Picard asked as they reached the main deck.

"Yes . . ."

"What do you think so far?"

Sandy tightened visibly. He sighed twice. "I cannot believe it can work for the mob to decide . . . yet how can I tell a man like Patrick O'Heyne to go and be a collier because he was born to a collier? To go back to his 'station' in life? And my dear, decent Jeremiah, whose heart I know as my own . . . . How can the right of kings be less than divine and still be sacred?"

"Perhaps power flows the other way in a better world, Sergeant," Picard said. "From the people to the government, instead of the other way round."

Sandy shook his head. "You are a confusing man, sir! And I am confused."

Picard nodded. "Congratulations."

In the town, shouts pierced the night, the voices of commanders barking instructions spared them from pressing the issue.

"Close up!"

"Wheel right!"

"Forward!"

"Fix bayonets!"

"Uh-oh," Picard uttered. "Mr. Bennett, arm phasers. Eh—instead of that, prepare a cannon to fire. We're going to make the dock impassable."

"Aye, sir!" Bennett sprang for a midships gun. "I'll use the foredeck gun, sir, beggin' your pardon. We'll get a good punch taking the dock at a bit of an angle."

"Very well. Help him, Sergeant."

"Yes, sir." Sandy put down his sea-issue rifle and hurried to assist.

As the skirmish escalated on the visible street beyond the wharf, Picard and Alexander crouched at the ship's rail, weapons aimed. Dim outlines of redcoats and patriots picked through bloodsoaked bodies cluttering the ground.

It took time to load and run out a cannon, and before Wollard and Sandy were finished, several armed townsmen appeared on the wharf, running toward the extended dock that would bring them out to the ship's T-shaped dock.

Picard raised his rifle and fired, but the unfamiliar weapon damned his aim, and shot downward and a foot to the left of the colonist he had sighted down. Fortunately, it did take out the dock plank the man was standing on, and the colonist fumbled and spun into the water. With a soaked rifle and heavy clothing, the floundering man was now paddling about uselessly, trying to find a way out of the water.

Alexander looked at the other colonists pounding down the dock. "Should I shoot?"

Picard glanced at the boy. "Do what you think is right."

The boy stared at him, then looked down at the long rifle in his hands. Unexpectedly, he lowered the gun, and looked up again. "They're only defending their say over their own lives. They just want to keep what they earn."

At first he seemed to be waiting for approval for his words, but when none was forthcoming, Alexander glowered fiercely as if making up his mind a second time, put his rifle down, and turned his back.

In that silent moment, the halyards flapped against the mast, the water patted the ship's planks, and the pop of riflefire pressed into the night, each percussion ticking off a second. A full minute went by, and still the boy did not turn.

"Mmm," Picard mumbled. "Progress." He gripped the nearest shroud and called, "How's that cannon, Wollard?"

"Ready, sir!"

Bennett's voice cracked on a grunt as he and Sandy put their shoulders to the lines. The loaded gun groaned out on its heavy truck. It took considerable strain, and all the leverage the blocks could offer for only two men to move that twelve-hundred-pound gun outboard through the gunport. Luckily, the gun carriage was weighted well, and the whole system of ropes and blocks were brilliantly arranged to do this, and the gun went out. Picard began to see why these ocean-going fighting ships, so much smaller than his starship, needed a crew almost as large.

He looked out at the approaching patriots. "Take aim on the dock and fire! Quickly!"

Bennett aimed the gun by shoving down a heavy stick that changed the elevation of the cannon's back end, then Sandy shoved in a wooden wedge to hold the cannon in place. Sandy already had a spark reddening on a linstock—some kind of fuse—and Bennett snatched the linstock and touched it to the base ring. He avoided the actual touchhole itself, Picard noticed.

The explosion was instantaneous, thrumming the whole side of the ship with its concussion. Below, the dock dissolved into splinters, dispensing a half dozen patriots into the water. Four of them came up sputtering. Two never came up at all.

The ship's two middle docklines now hung limp, tied to pilings that no longer had a dock. The two outer ones, however, bow and stern, were made off to other docks for stability, and held the ship to the boatyard. However, there was no longer a dock leading up to the side of the ship.

They were defensible now.

Scarcely had the thought of his success sunk in when a fleshy mass dropped before his eyes and clamped over his mouth, leaving only one nostril free so that he could barely breath. It was a human forearm, and he was caught! He pressed out one fitful "Mmmmmph!" as he was pulled backward off balance, and two more figures charged past him.

As he gripped the arm around his mouth and twisted around the other piece of meat that had coiled around his chest to keep him off balance, he watched the two invaders plunge up the maindeck toward the bow and attack Sandy and Bennett, and—horribly—he also saw Alexander charge the armed patriots!

The patriots had stripped off their jackets and shirts in order to swim effectively and climb the chains, and now their wet backs glistened in the first spark of morning light. Their shoulders flexed as they raised swords and brought them slashing down upon Bennett and Sandy. Sandy fell back and tumbled behind the foremast, then rolled to his feet and squared off to parry his opponent.

Bennett was less fortunate. The seaman took a shattering blow to the left cheekbone from the second patriot. Bennett bellowed his gutwrenching agony and dropped like a stone. As he lay on the deck, clawing at the destruction of his face, blood flowed freely from the wound, which continued to open as his skull lost its structural integrity.

And Alexander now reached the foredeck, snatched up the red-hot linstock, and took a mighty swing at the back of the man who had killed Bennett.

Picard dug his heels into the deck and heaved backward on the man holding him, squeezing part of his mouth out from behind the mighty forearm. "Hulllfff—"

Freeze program! Freeze program!

The arm tightened against his mouth. He tried to shove the words right out through his nostrils, but the computer evidently didn't understand the command.

Engulfed in the horror of his own lack of foresight, Picard watched as the linstock in Alexander's hands whipped down on the patriot's bare back and dealt the man a searing burn, which the man repaid instantly by a swirl of flesh and steel. The man's sword swiped toward Alexander. The boy ducked back and to one side, but the sword's point laid open the tip of one shoulder and slashed diagonally across his chest as the patriot bent his elbow at the wrong instant.

Picard roared against the strap of human forearm that clamped his mouth. He forced his jaws open, and sank his teeth into the nearest muscle.

A howl of pain blew against his ear and the arm came loose. He rammed an elbow back and drove it into the man's diaphragm, then clamped his hands into a rock and swung around, driving his makeshift club into the patriot's ear. Dizzied and breathless, the patriot staggered back and fell on top of the maindeck hatch.

"Freeze—oh, to hell with it!" Picard rushed to the foredeck and drove a shoulder into the patriot, who was about to finish Alexander with another sword swipe. Together, Picard and the patriot went sprawling.

The man was half his age, but Picard was twice as mad. He grasped the armed man by the neck, raised him up a bit, then slammed his head into the deck. The sword clattered from the man's numbed hand.

"Alexander!" Picard spun off his knees and scrambled to the boy, who was trying to sit up.

"I'm getting up!" Alexander insisted valiantly. "Don't stop the program! It's just a cut! That's all!"

Damn, the boy was quick! Before Picard could hold him down he cranked his legs under him, grasped the ship's rail, and hoisted himself up. The front of his shirt was soggy with plum-colored blood, and the same for the cut shoulder. One arm hung numb, but other than that he was looking out at the wharf.

"Look!"

British soldiers were swarming from the street onto the wharf, lined up just beautifully, and took stern aim at all the patriots on the docks.

"Cease fire!" a voice called from the docks. "Colonials, cease fire! Cease fire!"

Picard looked . . . it was Patrick O'Heyne, standing at about the middle of the main wharf, holding both hands up. His rifle lay on the wharf at his feet.

He was giving up, to spare the lives of the cornered patriots—people who had been led out here by the need to possess this ship.

The patriot sparring with Sandy backed off, and Sandy cautiously came around to Picard's side. "The boy is wounded, sir," he said.

"I know! What kind of swine attacks a child!"

"But, sir, it's *war,*" Sandy explained simply, and of course he was right.

The patriot who was still standing on the deck stepped well away from them and waved to O'Heyne, then put his sword down reluctantly. He was giving up.

Like so much of the Revolutionary War, this skirmish had been for nothing but the philosophical point struggling to have its meager voice heard. The frigate *Justina* was once again a Royal Navy ship.

The night was blessedly cool against his hot skin and the hairs on his neck that were still standing from the electrical jolts.

On his way to the main doors of the jail complex, Worf had stepped through a half dozen fires set by Odette Khanty as she tried to block him from following her. She had kicked her awkward business shoes off and set fire to them, too. She was probably running now.

Worf refused to run. He balled his fists and stalked, step upon step, as regulated as a parade. His boots made an authoritative *chunk* on the brick with stride. He began to concentrate on the sound, for it brought his mind slowly back from the effects of the buffalo prod.

Behind him, the jail building burned more and more excitedly as the fires began to spread to floor cloths and fabric-covered chairs, and anything else. Even in a jail, fire would find something to consume, even if only the paint on the walls.

He felt like the fire. Ready to burn and determined to avenge his friend's death.

He approached the balcony of the governor's mansion, as he saw the guards there and the dozen or more police vehicles rolling or hovering into the courtyard behind him, drowning the courtyard in scene lights. They were all coming to arrest Odette Khanty. He ignored them. He saw his target.

A good day to die.

The police officers flooded from their vehicles and hurried across the courtyard toward the balcony. Worf felt them closing behind him, but he refused to break into a run. It was as if he had a deflector shield around his body. None of them approached him or tried to stop him. Whether they recognized him from the broadcast or simply wanted to concentrate on the woman, he did not know or care.

Each bootstep drove into his aching head like a nail. He wished he had treated Grant with more respect. How impressive—the data thread had still been there. Grant never gave it up. He might've bought himself a more merciful death if he had, but the thread was still there. Hours upon hours of circumstantial evidence that, when combined with Data's recordings of Odette Khanty's own words, would damn the woman to where she belonged. Anything Data recorded was admissible in court. They had her.

Yet the loss . . . it nearly took him down with every step. The vision of Grant's body hanging there, ravaged, would not leave him alone.

Honor was not always being tough, he now knew. Bravery did not always define itself in raw strength. When strength—real strength—was required, Ross Grant had summoned it. Certainly, those hours must have been wretched persecution. Worf felt every minute of every hour now as he stalked his prey.

Anguish squeezed him hard. Action charged the courtyard as the police surrounded the mansion.

Worf climbed the brick stairs to the balcony and turned immediately to his right. He could still see her.

She was running along the wide balcony. Worf could not imagine where she thought she was going, but certainly a woman as clever as this one might have an escape plan or two worked out.

He didn't care. He would walk—not run—after her if he had to walk into black space on the stairway of his own rage.

Sirens and flashing lights from far off before him cast the mansion's balcony, and the form of Odette Khanty, in silhouette, as she pulled the iron chairs over into Worf's path. The police were blocking her way. She would not get off this balcony.

He saw her glancing back at him and fancied that she was terrified of him as she ran and he walked. He hoped she was.

She disappeared unexpectedly. Worf heard the slam of a door. When Worf reached that place, he realized he was looking at a utility closet of some kind.

He kicked the door in.

She slammed another one in front of him. He kicked that in, too. When the door smashed before him, he noticed the T'kalla prod lying on the floor, its LOW BATT sign blinking.

There was no one in this room.

He looked up. A wall-mounted ladder led through some kind of conduit.

He climbed it.

"You can't do this to me!" Her voice came down with a slight echo.

"Yes, I can," he said, climbing steadily into the dimness.

"I'll recover from this!"

"No, you will not."

"I've got influence in places you never heard of!"

"Not any more."

He had no idea where she was heading, but he would meet her there.

He continued to climb. The metal rungs were cold on his hands, and he realized his fingers were twitching with pain.

The sky opened up before him. Mrs. Khanty had apparently climbed out of the conduit, and now there was sky. Night sky. In his mind Worf saw the shuttlecraft hovering out in space, dutifully broadcasting over and over the self-immolating words of Odette Khanty in the cell.

The whole population would know, if they didn't already.

And the profit was interesting. He hadn't realized she had shot her husband in the first place.

There she was. As he climbed out of the conduit, he saw Odette Khanty at the edge of the roof. They were four stories high, all the way to the top of the mansion.

All around, the courtyard glowed with police lights and buzzed with activity. Below, people flocked to see what was happening.

All eyes were fixed on the edge wall of the roof, where Odette Khanty was trapped against the open air.

"Stay back," she said as Worf walked across the roof toward her.

There was a short wall framing the roof. She climbed up onto it, having some difficulty with her narrow skirt.

Worf stopped.

She crawled a few feet along the brick riser, then paused. She had nowhere to go.

"I'll throw myself off," she called on the wind that swept down.

"No," Worf countered. "You will not."

"You can't win here," she insisted. "I'll go down as a trapped heroine. The people here will think it was all a plot. A frame. They love me!"

Worf felt the wind tug at his hair and cool his face. "The time has passed for that. You have done ten thousand heinous things in your life, and Ross Grant cared about every one of them. I care only about two."

He stepped closer to her, close enough that he could easily have yanked her off the edge of the roof.

"One thing you should never have done," he said, "was kill my friend."

Baffled, Odette Khanty drew her brows together and peered at him as she remained there on her hands and knees, her black hat now missing and her stockings shredded by the brick.

"You came back for *that?"* she wondered. "For *him?"*

"Yes, for him." Worf raised his hand.

One push. Barely enough to feel against his skin, and she would be gone. Gone, quickly and abruptly, with only a few moments of terror, a free-fall, and a quick death.

"And the other?"

"Your death will release the Rogues from their Oath of Sto–vok–or. They would be able to recover what honor is left to them, and perhaps gain more."

"Wait," she cried, "I release them, they are freed of their oath!"

"Thank you. Will you now restore my friend to life?"

"Don't!" Khanty shouted as Worf reached for her.

He clasped her elbow as easily as plucking a flower, and dragged her away from the ledge.

Behind him, the conduit began burping policemen. One after another, they surged out onto the roof and formed a jagged half-circle around him and the woman. He knew they were there, but he did not look at them.

He looked only at her.

"Odette Khanty," he said, "by authority of Starfleet and the United Federation of Planets, I place you under arrest for murder, attempted murder, extortion, espionage, and treason. Be glad you are in my custody, and not the custody of those who 'love' you."

CHAPTER 21

THE DIRT OF THE TOWN WAS LITTERED WITH SPENT BALLS, SPILLED POWDER, bits of torn fabric, smears of blood, lost ramrods, and severed limbs. Most of the dead had been removed to a clearing area at the churchyard, and the wounded had been taken somewhere to be treated or to complete their dying.

With trembling hands, Picard patched Alexander's shoulder and chest enough to let the bleeding clot, and thought more than once about stopping all this, but something in himself, and in the boy's eyes, kept him from uttering those words. There were times when safety wasn't all it was cracked up to be.

He, Alexander, and Sandy Leonfeld were removed from the *Justina* and a dockside crew of grenadiers had been put on board to secure the ship and then guard it. Now Picard and his remaining crew were being escorted to the British field headquarters.

It was Jeremiah Coverman's house.

The keeping room had been transformed into a military outpost. Amy Coverman was being forced to serve dinner to British officers, and at the trestle table sat an infantry captain with a heavy brown mustache and a thatch of graying hair. Picard stood before the man, with Sandy on one side of him and Alexander on the other.

The captain looked up at them and eyed the inappropriate, ill-fitting red coat on Picard. "Are you a lieutenant of the *Justina?*"

"Yes, sir. Picard, sir."

"I'm Captain Holmes."

"How do you do, sir."

"Well. Mr. Picard, I have new orders for you. The captain has authorized me to reestablish Mr. Pennington's status as senior officer of the *Justina* and confer upon him a field rank of captain. He and his crew are being released as we speak. Because the first and second lieutenants have been killed, you're now his first lieutenant. It will be his and your responsibility to return the ship to fighting condition and take a blockading position in Delaware Bay. You'll have the boatyard to use at your convenience."

"Yes, sir."

"Mr. Pennington has indicated that you've been conducting some espionage among the colonists, and are more familiar with the situation than he is."

"Yes, sir."

"Very well. Then confirm something for me. Corporal." Holmes looked at a guard who stood at the back entrance.

"Sir!" The guard opened the back door and waved.

Another guard came in, leading Jeremiah Coverman and Patrick O'Heyne. Behind them were two more guards.

"I believe these are the men who have been leading the colonialists, the minutemen, in Delaware Station. Can you confirm their role?"

Picard felt Sandy tense at his side. As British officers, they were expected to eagerly condemn the civilian rebel leaders, who were seen not as military equals, but as insurrectionists. Traitors.

They would be hanged.

"Captain, I am Patrick O'Heyne," Jeremiah's friend interrupted before Picard had to commit himself. "I've been organizing the minutemen in this area. You have no need to confirm beyond my word. No one else is responsible."

Jeremiah nudged forward, but Sandy reached out and pushed him back before he could speak up for part of the blame. Captain Holmes noticed the gesture, but didn't seem to know what to make of it.

"Captain," Sandy spoke up, bringing attention back to himself. "I am Sergeant Alexander Leonfeld, His Majesty's Grenadiers, H.M.S. *Justina.*"

"Sergeant?"

"Begging your pardon, sir," Picard interrupted, "but the sergeant is now captain of the marine unit. Both Captain Newton and his lieutenant were killed when the ship was taken."

Holmes looked at Sandy with new respect, even though that made no sense at all. That's the way it was, though. "Understood. You have some observations, Captain Leonfeld?"

"I do, sir. This has been a forthright battle. The colonists have lost in good military style and have behaved like soldiers. I suggest they be treated as such, whether infantrymen or civilians. That is how they see themselves and I've come to see them that way also."

"Really . . . "

"Yes, sir," Picard agreed. "The colonists here have treated our crew with utmost respect and properness. I find it my charge to see that the same decency is afforded to them. We are at war, but we are not savages."

"These are commoners, Picard," Holmes snapped. "If we choose to hang these two men, to slap the women in stocks, to ship out the children for a proper upbringing as the servants they are, then that will be my decision. Not yours, or Captain Leonfeld's."

Picard lowered his chin. "No, sir. These two men will not be hanged. They will be treated as officers. We do not hang officers who have done their duty, even if it is not duty to King George. We owe a certain respect to our enemy's gallantry or we lose our own, palling of victory."

"Sir, Britain made an investment," Sandy Leonfeld pushed in, "but that investment was a gift. These people did not serve themselves up as chattel."

Holmes bolted to his feet. "You dare to speak to me that way! I've never been spoken to that way!"

"And while you're here," Picard surged on, "your men will respect the women, you will respect property, and you will treat these two gentlemen as you yourself would wish to be treated should you fall into enemy custody. I don't think that's asking too much, to keep our platform of decorum from crumbling beneath us. Any misconduct toward these people by uniformed men of the King would be irremediable. The world is dangerous, and we may someday find the obligations reversed."

Holmes' face turned red. "Who are you to dictate conduct to an officer of the King's Grenadiers!"

Picard's arms flexed at his sides. But before he could speak, Sandy Leonfeld spoke up "I am, sir, an officer of the King's Royal Navy who helped make it possible for you to successfully regain control of a British frigate, which was the goal of this entire maneuver. Your assignment is to protect and defend His Majesty's ships. Therefore, the entire maneuver is under the authority of the Royal Navy. And that, sir, is Mr. Pennington, and it is *me*."

The two stared at each other and Holmes' face got nearly purple, but he finally leaned back a bit and lowered his brows.

"God's hair, that's a lot of gall," he commented. "Quite a hell of a lot of gall. Almost as much as these upstarts here." He waved his quill pen at Jeremiah and O'Heyne. "Hmmm . . . are you a barrister in civilian life, Mr. Leonfeld, by chance?"

He put down the quill and came out from behind the table, stalking Jeremiah and O'Heyne. When they didn't look away from his glare, he seemed to be noting something in their eyes that Picard and Sandy insisted was there.

"Hmm," he uttered again. "Can't have a dirty reputation for the King's uniform . . . tell you what, I'll confer with Mr. Pennington and his bidding will win the day. I'll leave it to him to decide whether or not these two are hanged in the morning."

"Thank you, sir!" Sandy heaved out, shuddering with relief.

"Don't thank me yet," Holmes said. "He may decide they should be *shot* in the morning instead. All right, my men are billeted in the linen factory next door. You men, round up your crew and restore them to the ship and get them working. We'll supply any further crewmen if you need muscle. Get moving before insult sets in and I become surly. And clean up this powder monkey. He's bleeding on my floor."

Without offering the captain the respect of a "Yes, sir," Picard put his hand on Alexander and ushered the boy out. Sandy followed them, and when the door closed behind them he sagged against the doorframe.

"Thank you for your help, Mr. Picard," he huffed. "Perhaps Jeremiah's life will be spared."

"If so, it was your doing," Picard said.

The next moment, the door opened again and two guards led Jeremiah and O'Heyne out onto the plank porch. Jeremiah instantly rushed to Sandy and the two clasped hands warmly.

"You're everything I knew you were," Jeremiah lauded. "Someday this will end and we'll be family again."

"I'll always be your family," Sandy told him warmly. "I swore an oath to the king and I'll honor it, but I know now that I'm not your better at all."

Jeremiah patted his hand. "Oh, in a few ways!"

"Don't worry," O'Heyne said, clapping Jeremiah on a shoulder. "England and the continent will be friends one way or the other, because we simply can't have this for long." He reached out to shake Picard's hand. "Thank you deeply."

"Quite welcome," Picard responded drably. "Fair weather, Mr. O'Heyne."

The guards took the two men away, and Sandy Leonfeld stared emotionally after them.

"You'd better go and inform Mr. Pennington," Picard told him. "The ship is ours. And the fate of your cousin and O'Heyne are in his hands."

"Yes," Sandy said. "Yes—thank you." He clasped Picard's hand, then Alexander's. "Thank you both!"

As he jogged off through the British military men now common in the brightening street, Alexander swung around to Picard.

"Wow!" the boy gushed. "I wonder if that really happened! I hope it did!"

"Well, the holodeck computer didn't stop me," Picard said on a sigh, "or contradict me either. So perhaps something like that *did* happen."

"Sandy really stood up to that captain! He actually defended Britain's enemies right to his face!"

"So he did. I liked what he said very much."

"Do you think Mr. Pennington'll let Jeremiah and Mr. O'Heyne live?"

"Mr. Pennington's a compassionate and decent man. He doesn't strike me as vindictive. And if war dictates otherwise . . . well, there are worse ways for a patriot to die."

"Do you really think that? That there are good and bad ways to die?"

"Yes, and things very much worth dying for. You've heard these men, these colonists saying what they're about, and you've seen dauntless behavior from the British as well. Higher civilization is emerging here. It's bringing a higher morality with it. The old system of monarchy saw humanity through primitive times with great success, but with progress is coming the morality of individualism. It's given us all we possess in our time, and we'd better nurture it, or we'll lose everything."

Alexander looked around at the morning scene—the early American town, masts stemming over the rooftops, the quaintly costumed people trying to get through this difficult day after a difficult night, and redcoat guards leading groups of Dover Infantrymen to the guardhouse.

"I think I get it now," he said.

Picard couldn't manage a smile. "I think I do, too."

"What do you mean?"

"I mean that people have the right to make a decision, good or bad. How closely should anyone else hold the lens? And at what cost? Now, let's get you to the sickbay. The real one. And I'd better make a will, because when your father finds you've been wounded, he's going to relieve me of some important cerebral matter, I think."

He paused, and gazed over the houses at the masts of the *Justina.* He let the Delaware River breeze brush his face as he memorized the masts and rigging, so he also would never forget.

"Computer," he said, "end program."

CHAPTER 22

"AND NEVER COME WITHIN A BOATHOOK'S LENGTH OF THE CAPTAIN UNLESS you have a good reason. Remember that, Number One."

"Oh, I will, sir. How long a boathook?"

Picard led Will Riker into the ready room off the bridge and headed for his desk, but never got a chance to sit down.

The door slid open without the courtesy of an entry request, and a gargantuan fit of fury plowed in.

"My son has been wounded in the Revolutionary War!"

The walls rattled. The desk buzzed. Riker backed off a good four feet.

"Yes," Picard responded, and continued getting behind his desk. He didn't sit down. No sense dying in a chair. "Yes, Mr. Worf, I know. I'm very sorry about that. I understand I was supposed to protect him, and you left him on the *Enterprise* for safety—"

Worf's brow came down. "I am proud of his wound!"

With a blink, Picard asked, "You are? Oh—of course you are."

Stepping closer, Worf demanded, "Captain, I must know if the scar will be an honorable one."

"Oh, yes," Picard assured him. "He fought valiantly to protect our ship. I was hard-pressed to tell him from the actual soldiers."

Worf fell silent for a moment, absorbing all this, all the parental worries about a wounded child crashing up against the Klingon sensibilities about where this fit on the honor scale of injuries.

Yet there were other things playing in those nut-dark eyes, things more complicated, more tortuous.

Before either spoke again, the door opened a second time without a chime for permission, and Alexander charged in at full tilt, almost slamming into the captain's desk.

"Father!" the boy blurted.

Worf worked to control himself, and did about as well as any overheating steam engine. "The Captain has informed me that your wound was an honorable one."

"Mr. Worf," Picard broke in, "I'm glad you came. I'm logging a commendation for you—or, rather, I would be, if your 'mission' had been authorized. On a more pratical note, I have blocked the reprimand that will no doubt be forthcoming from Commissioner Toledano—"

"Captain," Worf interrupted, "I cannot accept any commendations, or any other consideration, for this particular mission.

Picard eyed him. "Because of . . . "

"Yes, sir." Worf lowered his voice a little. "I do not suffer about my decision, Captain, but I must not gain from it. To honor me in any way would be an insult . . . to Grant's memory."

Startled, Alexander looked up at his father. "What does that mean? What are you talking about?"

A chilly tension blanketed the ready room as both Picard and Riker realized just then that Alexander hadn't been told what had happened on the planet. Worf did not shirk the moment. He looked at his son and said, "Alexander . . . I was not strong enough or fast enough to rescue Grant."

Father and son stood barely beyond arms' length from each other. Between them the terrible meaning of Worf's words festered and cried.

"He's dead?" Alexander's voice was thin, tiny.

Picard buried a shuddering desire to interfere. His custodial feelings toward the boy were supposed to be released now, yet he couldn't retire them. He wanted somehow to soothe Alexander, and hold the program long enough to explain how such things could happen.

But life was no holoprogram, and there would be no pauses to think things out. There would be no scrolling back to save Grant's life.

"He died," Worf said slowly, "before I could get to him. I failed him, Alexander . . . I failed you."

Grief twisted Alexander's face. He averted his eyes from everyone for a long minute, working valiantly to keep control. Alexander kept staring at the carpet, nodded at some thought or other with which he grappled, then finally looked up. He couldn't look in his father's eyes, but stared instead at his father's uniform.

"Some things are worth dying for," he rasped.

At the boy's generous words, Worf twitched, squinted, and fixed a perplexed look on his son. His lips parted, but nothing came out. What his son said was something all Klingons knew, but until now Worf had never known if his child believed it in his heart.

Tight-lipped, Alexander stepped back a pace or two, so he could face his father without seeming to look up so sharply. His voice was thready, full of effort.

"The Day of Honor is meant to help us understand that our enemy might have honor, right?"

Worf forced his voice up. "Yes . . . "

"Mrs. Khanty didn't understand that. She didn't think her enemy had any honor, but she was the one who didn't have any. So she underestimated you. I don't know if what you did was right, but I know honor isn't simple. Sometimes it means both sides might be partly right, and you've got to figure that out before you go killing people."

The room fell silent. All three men were riveted by the echo of a child's words. And the same pride.

Alexander's gaze rose to his father's face, never flinched, never wavered.

"I still don't know what honor is," the boy said, "but I know it's *why* you fight, not *how* you fight."

Speechless, Worf stared down at his son. Then he looked up at Picard, and his expression changed. Anger still lingered, but there was something more—as if he thought that perhaps Picard did far more than had been expected.

"If it's all right," Alexander said, "I have to talk to the captain for a minute."

Perplexed by his son's command of the moment, Worf squeezed the tension out of his hands, nodded, and said, "Very well. Captain . . . thank you."

Satisfied, Picard nodded back. "My pleasure, Mr. Worf." Given the price paid, Worf guarded his reaction and left the ready room.

After the door panels closed and Worf was gone, Riker asked, "Do you want me to leave, too, Alexander?"

"No, you don't have to." Alexander came forward to the desk and looked at Picard. "I checked on some things."

"Oh? Things like what?"

"Like whether or not Mr. Nightingale died that night. He did. And the name of the British colonel. And Patrick O'Heyne really did have a business in London and New York. And Mr. Pennington wrote some articles and letters that were published, so the computer was probably using his own words when he was talking to me. A lot of what we saw really did happen."

"That's good work," Picard told him. "Did you also check as to the fates of Jeremiah and Sandy?"

"No . . . I thought about it, but I decided not to."

"Why not? You have the rest of the journals, don't you?"

"My relatives have them. I can get them."

Picard leaned forward suddenly. "Just a minute—you're not thinking about using a holoprogram again, are you?"

The boy nodded. "Yes, I want to go back. But . . . I think I'll wait until next year's Day of Honor to see the rest. And if it's all right with you," he added, steeling himself, "I think I'll go with my father next time."

Behind the boy, Riker's blue eyes gleamed and he smiled.

"It's quite all right with me," Picard said. "A most honorable decision. Dismissed, swab."

"Thank you, sir."

Like a proper sailing man, Alexander came to attention, turned on a heel, and strode out of the ready room.

Picard leaned back and grinned at Riker. "Hmm . . . what do you know about that? Perhaps I wouldn't do such a bad job of raising a child after all."

Riker chuckled. "Well, sir, I have to admit—"

The door flashed open again. Wasn't anybody using the damned door chimes anymore?

"Captain Picard!"

"Ah, Mr. Toledano . . . good evening."

"You are going to be the captain of a mule train when the Federation Council gets done with you! You handed Odette Khanty over to the planetary law enforcement!"

"Yes, I did. And she's been charged with assassinating her husband, along with a long trail of other corruptions. Mr. Data's recordings are admissible as evidence and—"

"With her present on the planet, the election could still be held! It was held today!"

"And the lieutenant governor won," Riker supplied. "He's now planetary governor."

Toledano rounded on him. "And they also voted to secede from the Federation!" He whirled back to Picard. "We've lost the planet because of your damned defiance!"

Picard kept his voice controlled and relaxed. "Think what you will, Commissioner, but I refused to put myself in the position of the British."

"The *what?"*

"Sindikash has the right to set its own course. Independence was once a concept to be warred over, but I see it as the right of any colony that can prove itself self-reliant and stable. There'll be a muscle-stretching period, a generation or two of struggle, hunger, weakness, and, if they survive, they'll probably join forces with us again someday."

"Assuming they don't self-immolate! The whole area will be unstable for decades! How many colonies flare briefly, only to be snuffed out in power struggles? The toll is always high—"

"And the story disastrous and the songs very sad," Picard filled in, "but that is part of political autonomy. It's up to them, Commissioner, not us. In all conscience, I can't deny the people of Sindikash the same advantage of hindsight with which I look upon the early United States."

Toledano put a pointed finger on the edge of Picard's desk, tried to think of something more to say, then decided he'd be better off saying it to the Federation Council. He stalked out.

Riker let out a long breath, and sat down. "What a week, sir."

"On two fronts," Picard agreed. He leaned back and crossed his legs. "I've got a peculiar taste for a rum toddy tonight. Isn't that odd? Care to join me?"

Riker tipped his head. "Are you worried, sir?"

Picard raised and dropped one shoulder. "It'll be a black mark on my record. There'll be people who want my head on a pike. Sindikash voted for independence, but its new governor wants a relationship with the Federation. The Council can work with that, don't you think?"

"Yes, sir, I do think that."

"As for me . . . if I lose the ship, well, nothing lasts forever. Maybe I'll never get an admiralty, but I'll be able to sleep at night. So we made a value judgment—if not us, then who? And don't forget, if you look at history, it's simply not believable that the United States actually won the Revolutionary War. So keep up hope, Mr. Riker. Save the galaxy a couple of times, you get some friends in key circles."

Picard puffed up and raised his chin.

"After all," he declared, "we're not brutes, you know."

DAY OF HONOR

ARMAGEDDON SKY

L.A. Graf

To all you bonobos,
wherever you are.

CHAPTER 1

KIRA ARCHED PERILOUSLY BACKWARD TO DODGE HER OPPONENT'S *BAT'LETH,* scraping her heel on the edge of one carved bone step. She stumbled and felt her way up the irregular steps with one hand thrust out behind her. From both above and below, the ancient Klingon courtyard echoed with the sounds of fierce and bloody combat: metallic crashes, ground-shaking thuds, and occasional curses spat out in the dozen languages Dax spoke fluently. At least one of those had been Bajoran, and from its breathless invocation of Prophetic aid, Kira gathered the battle on the courtyard's floor wasn't going well at all. Neither was the battle on the shivering balcony above her—the thunder of booted footsteps across it exploded abruptly into shattered bone balustrade and splintered crystal floor tiles. The cascade of debris startled Kira so much that she almost missed the spectacle of Odo whirling to the courtyard floor in a splash of effluvium.

In retrospect, she realized she should have expected it. The constable had been all but forced into joining Dax's holographic "defense of honor"; during the preliminary arming ceremonies he'd grumbled nonstop that the Trill's insistence on authentic medieval Klingon armor was going to exhaust his shape-changing abilities before his duty shift even began that night. Odo might not have been able to withstand Dax's wheedling any more than Kira, but since he'd only agreed to participate if he wasn't forced to use a *bat'leth,* he was too pragmatic not to avail himself of the first opportunity to remove himself from the combat.

Unfortunately, flinging herself into glorious, bloody death was not exactly an option for Kira. Tearing her eyes away from the still-rippling evidence of Odo's demise, she refocused her attention on the battle just in time to catch an armored elbow in the face. The holographic Klingon warrior who had backed her up the stairs might have been carefully programmed by Worf to match her fighting skills, but it hadn't been given her ability to be distracted—or her underlying impatience with this ridiculous ritual challenge.

It wasn't a full-force blow—Kira could have avoided it if she'd been paying attention—but it was enough to stagger her off the stairs and back down into the courtyard. She chased her balance with two backward steps, then felt her heel come down in something slick and rubbery. She realized what—*who*—it was an instant before her foot whisked out from under her.

Odo's gelatinous flinch had to have been more from sympathy than any need on his part. Kira pinwheeled to land without use of her hands, worried for one absurd moment that she might crush him. The jolt of discomfort that thumped up her spine was enough to inspire a curse of her own, this time so vile that even the Klingon looming over her blinked in surprise.

"That's it." She heaved her *bat'leth* toward the open courtyard and called out, "Program: delete 'Kira,' " just to watch the weapon evaporate before it could hit the ground. "I quit."

Dax, chestnut hair loose and wild about her armor-plated shoulders, threw Kira an irritated scowl as she whirled to avoid a downward lunge from Odo's former opponent, nimbly kicking him in the teeth as she did so. "You can't quit!" she complained, to both Kira and her own former adversary, now leaning down to help Kira to her feet. "What about the insult to my honor?"

Odo rippled with what might have been a snort if he'd had the nose and lungs to produce it. He extruded a rudimentary head big enough to remark, "Either it doesn't require as much defense as you thought, or you've picked the wrong warriors to help defend it." The platter of gel under Kira's hand twitched testily. "Major, if you don't mind . . ."

"Oh...sorry." Kira shifted her weight as best she could, ignoring the clench of indignant muscles across the small of her back. Odo oozed out from under one hand, then the other. The bulge at the top of the gelatin pool glided smoothly into a humanoid outline, then sketched in its own details of color, texture, and form.

"Come on, you guys." Dax's *bat'leth* struck holographic sparks off holographic armor as she swung around to confront Kira's former attacker. Deprived by the holo-suite computer of their programmed targets, both of Worf's seconds were now closing in on the Trill. She seemed more exasperated than intimidated by this development. "You can't just walk away from our *Suv'batlh!"*

Worf fastened a huge hand around Kira's elbow. "It is not *our Suv'batlh,"* he rumbled. His expression, always somewhat grim by Bajoran standards, all but smoldered beneath the shadows of his lacquered face-mask. Kira fitted her hand between a seam in his armor's vambrace, and tried to take at least some of her own weight as the big Klingon heaved her to her feet. "This is not any *Suv'batlh* at all."

If Dax appreciated the thunder on Worf's dark face, Kira saw no sign of it. "Speak for yourself," she countered, knocking the second holographic Klingon onto his back with a fierce swing of her *bat'leth,* then thumping Worf in the small of his back with the rounded edge of her weapon. "I'm not going to stand by while you tell me where I can and can't go, like I was one of your courtesans."

Worf spun on her, growling with all the fury of a *ghar*-wolf as he seized her *bat'leth* in both hands. In that instant, Kira appreciated how much of his Klingon nature he hid from them every moment of every day. "Computer: End program!"

A polite, nonintrusive chime wafted through the burning air of the DuHoH desert, rippling the edges of *meO* trees and Klingon-hewn stone until it seemed the whole world was melting in the heat. By the time the computer informed them, "Program ended," their slice of ancient Klingon history had dissolved down to four black walls and a gridwork of intersecting lines. Kira felt the same startling press of claustrophobia that always swarmed over her when the holo-suite's illusion of openness was over.

"You make a mockery of an honorable tradition." His words were accusatory, but Worf's tone sounded more disappointed than angry. He released Dax's weapon with a snarl. "I should not have accepted your challenge."

Dax shook her hair back from her face, exposing the very unKlingon-like spattering of freckles at each temple. "I'm not trying to mock anything." She looked tall and lanky in her exoskeleton of Klingon armor; the intricate structure of both *rantou* lacquer and *bat'leth* stood out in even greater relief now that the holo-suite's walls were all that surrounded them. "You knew that going with the *Victoria Adams* was important to me." Kira had heard this argument in every permutation ever since the Terran science vessel left the station two days ago, but the indignation in Dax's voice still sounded freshly minted. "Do you have any idea how many thousands of years it's going to be until I get another chance to witness a cometary deluge like this one?"

"The rarity of an astronomical event does not make it imperative that every science officer in Starfleet view it," Worf informed her bluntly. "As station tactical officer, I determined that your primary duty is here. On DS9."

Sighing, Kira wearily popped the straps at the knee joints of her armor and settled to the floor to wait out the debate.

Dax grounded her *bat'leth* with a thump that rang painful echoes off the bare holo-suite walls. "On DS9, Commander Worf, my *duty* is to document all scientific phenomena in and around this region of space."

"Not when a Starfleet research vessel has already been dispatched expressly for the purpose of observing that phenomenon," Worf snarled back. "In that case, your duty consists of—"

"I know, I know." The Trill's voice sizzled with a level of annoyance that didn't quite match the wry glint in her grey eyes. "Making sure the station is prepared for all the possible scientific emergencies that might arise. Emergencies that *you* felt the need to enumerate in a four-page report that convinced Benjamin he couldn't afford to let me go!"

"It is important for a commanding officer to know all the strategic considerations that might influence his decision. And the current situation with the Klingons—"

"No matter how many Klingons may or may not be violating the Neutral Zone, the *Victoria Adams* is no less likely to be attacked just because *I'm* not on board." A hint of youthful petulance crept into Dax's voice. "And I *wanted* to watch the comets fall."

Worf scowled, not yielding. "The danger to the *Victoria Adams* is beside the point. As a senior science officer, you are too valuable to this station to risk yourself on frivolous scientific tourist excursions."

"How about frivolous Honor Combats?" Dax retorted, giving her *bat'leth* a twirl.

The tactical officer grunted, and Kira almost thought she saw him flush. "Precisely why I should not have accepted your challenge."

That gruff admission was apparently retreat enough for Dax. Her resilient, puckish humor returned with a fierce smile. "Admit it," she cajoled, dancing forward a step to chuck his arm with the side of her *bat'leth.* "With the Day of Honor coming up, you thought a little *Suv'batlh* might be a fun way to celebrate the holiday."

Worf stiffened, but didn't pull away. "Honor is not meant to be fun. And the *Batlh Jaj* is not a *holiday.* It is the occasion on which true Klingons re-affirm their own sense of honor and commemorate the honor of their most esteemed enemies."

"Like Captain James T. Kirk of the first *Enterprise,"* Dax said, with a mischievous smile. "My old friend Kor used to demonstrate the esteem he felt for Kirk by drinking an extra keg of blood wine on every *Batlh Jaj."*

"That," said Worf repressively, "is *not* the correct way to celebrate the Day of Honor."

"Neither is increasing the number of provocative intrusions into the Klingon-Cardassian Neutral Zone, if you ask me." Odo folded his hands atop updrawn knees in unconscious mimicry of Kira. "It makes me wonder if your people still believe in celebrating the honor of their enemies, Commander."

"Not all enemies *have* honor," Worf growled. "To those that do not, the Klingons owe no commemoration of *Batlh Jaj."*

Odo snorted. "From the response we've been getting to this holiday of yours, I'd say the Humans feel exactly the same way about the Klingons."

Kira found herself forced to agree with that. While she thought the observance of *any* Klingon holiday within the Federation a dubious practice, considering the recent tensions that had flared between the two former enemies, she certainly hadn't expected the violent antipathy that had ignited throughout the Alpha Quadrant as preparations for the Day of Honor drew near. On DS9—which had acknowledged the holiday for as long as the Federation had kept a presence there—there'd been a distinct increase in racist grumbling. As the grumbling increased, they'd gradually phased out plans for a display of locally owned Klingon art, then the Klingon food festival, and finally even the re-enactment of the Klingons' traditional Honor Combat—*Suv'batlh*—for fear of how station personnel would respond to the Klingon costumes and weapons.

Worf shoved off his lacquered battle-mask to reveal a grim face streaked with rivulets of sweat. Dax might not have been winning their face-to-face combat, but she'd certainly managed to press the Klingon warrior to his limits. "I advised Captain Sisko that to commemorate the Day of Honor so soon after the invasion of Cardassia might be unwise."

"I don't think it's the Cardassians who are the problem," Kira said soberly.

"No," Dax agreed. "The problem is that the Day of Honor is supposed to celebrate a time when Humans and Klingons united against a common enemy, even while they were fighting each other. And now, when we're facing a common enemy greater than any we've encountered before—"

"*My* people," Odo interjected, with the bitter resignation that always soured his voice when he spoke those words.

"—the Klingons have endangered the entire Alpha Quadrant by dividing it rather than uniting it. It makes the Day of Honor—"

She broke off again, this time slanting Worf a wary look. However, the Klingon tactical officer finished the thought for her with the ruthless lack of self-pity Kira found so characteristic of his race.

"—a mockery of what it is supposed to represent." His dark eyes slitted down to angry lines of frustration. "Which is why I cannot even challenge those who spit upon *my* honor with their signs and their curses!"

Kira winced at the snarling tone of repressed fury, and wondered if, all along, this holographic combat hadn't just been Dax's Trill-clever way to give Worf's bottled rage a safe place to erupt. The fact that this possibility had just occurred to her now, she thought wryly, was a testimony to her own naiveté about the conflict brewing between the Klingons and the Federation.

Kira hadn't known any Humans until after the Cardassian Occupation ended, didn't even really know what a Klingon was except for having heard their name and practices invoked in Cardassian threats. When she'd first been forced to work with Humans in the rebuilding years after the Occupation, she'd found them incomprehensibly diplomatic, infuriatingly even-tempered, and maddeningly dense. The first Klingons she encountered—staunch allies of the Federation for what had seemed, at the time, an eternity—had struck her as being even less understandable, despite their refreshingly straightforward lack of Human manners. They'd comprised different facets of her indoctrination into galactic culture. And, after four years' immersion on board Deep Space Nine, she'd learned to appreciate—even like—Humans, if still not completely understand them. The Klingons, however, still completely eluded her.

They were a hard people, in many ways more complicated than the simplicity of their behavior suggested. Their separation from the Federation and all its friendship meant had seemed irrational to Kira. She saw their sudden, aggressive expansion into every border star system that couldn't drive them off as being no more forgivable than anything the Cardassians had ever done. In the months that followed, she heard the Humans around her speak in ways she'd never expected. Of populations battered to extinction, starbases brutalized, grandparents or uncles or even older siblings tortured to death by an enemy too different, too barbaric to ever trust or understand. They'd sounded like they were talking about demonic creatures of such supernatural evil that they threatened the very existence of the universe. Instead, they were talking about the Klingons. That was how Kira found out about the world before the Khitomer Accords.

Venerable Human politeness had prevented the Federation from lingering over the fact that they'd been mortal enemies with the Klingons for generations longer than they'd ever been friends. They'd graciously granted the Klingons their cultural differences, learned not to take offense at the aggressiveness Klingons tended to fling around them like spittle, prided themselves on their respect for Klingon history and tradition. In return, the Klingons endeavored to be less obvious in their disdain for Federation bureaucracy, and stopped bullying Starfleet officers. Apparently, everyone had thought this great progress at the time.

But from Kira's point of view it had seemed to be progress built more on tolerance than respect, and doomed to fail because of that. For a comparatively short period of time, it had looked like the Klingons and the Federation needed each other—two vast giants coming to grips with the fact that even the greatest behemoth needed someone to guard its farthest edges. Maybe if their peace had lasted longer they would have eased into a more lasting symbiosis. As it was, their fledgling romance hadn't lasted past the first cultural spat. Borders slammed, families remembered all the atrocities and fears passed down from beloved grandfolk and historical texts, and the comfortable shackles of hatred slipped back into place, as though no one had ever loosened them.

"It's not you." She hadn't really meant to say anything—if there was one thing she'd come to understand about Worf since he joined the crew, it was that he was proud, and intensely private. But the words popped out as though tumbling directly off her thoughts. She knew when he turned his frown on her that she'd trapped herself into completing her observation, whether Worf would appreciate it or not. "The people here—they're not even seeing *you.* They're seeing political battles that are keeping them from getting letters to their loved ones, or spare parts for the atmospheric propagators." She lifted one shoulder in a somewhat apologetic shrug, even though she wasn't sure what she herself had to apologize for. "Don't take it personally."

Worf gave her a sharp frown, as if her words had translated into a threat rather than the friendly advice she'd intended. More proof that Kira still didn't understand Klingons. "Hatred is always personal," he told her bleakly. "It is only the face of your enemy that changes."

There didn't seem to be anything she could say in response to that; Kira was glad when her comm badge chirped and gave her an excuse to look away. "Sisko to Kira."

She fumbled with latches on her armor with one hand as she answered, anticipating. "Kira here."

"Major—" Sisko's deep voice was hard to read, colored over by the busy sounds of Ops in his background. "I believe you're with Commander Dax and the Constable."

Kira glanced reflexively at the officers surrounding her. "And Commander Worf," she said, rolling carefully to her knees. Then, in response to the tension in his tone, "Is there a problem?"

"Why don't we discuss that here in Ops?" The captain had an unnerving way of sounding his most calm when things were approaching their most perilous. "Right now, we're facing either a delicate rescue operation or a full-scale Klingon war. I thought I'd collect a few second opinions before I decide."

Benjamin Sisko could still remember precisely what he'd felt three months ago, in the moment he'd heard about the breaking of the Khitomer Accords. A single icy spike of disbelief, then an explosion of frustrated anger at the success of the Dominion's divide-and-conquer tactics. Despite all the later emotions that had knitted themselves into the tangled tapestry of his feelings toward the Klingons—betrayal, annoyance, even unexpected sympathy for Worf's impossible position in Starfleet—the sharp memory of that initial reaction had never faded. Great moments in history did that to the people who lived through them—crystallized a single day's events inside the shifting smoke of memory the way a supernova hammered a permanent singularity through the fabric of space and time. Sisko sometimes wondered if those shock-carved memories weren't the truest imprint of history, more real and indelible than any datachip's video record.

Unfortunately, not enough time had passed since that day for his deep-seated rage to be relegated entirely to memory. The embers of it still smoldered, banked beneath the accumulated worries and stress of the hundred intervening days. And the disrupted emergency transmission he had just watched flicker across the main screen of Ops hadn't done a thing to quench it.

The turbolift platform hissed into sight, rising far too slowly, as it always seemed to do in tense situations like these. When it finally arrived, what looked like a medieval Klingon melee poured out into Ops, making one of the junior officers gasp and another stifle a laugh. Sisko lifted an eyebrow as he recognized the senior officers who made up the core of his tactical analysis team beneath the sweat and jangle of lacquered armor. Kira shot him a rueful glance of apology, while Worf just looked stoic. Dax went to her science console as if reporting for duty in ancient Klingon fighting garb were something she'd done a dozen times before. Knowing Curzon, that might even be true.

"We got a report in from the *Victoria Adams* already?" she asked, reading the signature frequency of the transmission on her display before Sisko could even open his mouth to brief them. "But they can't have had time to gather much data on the cometary event. They were only scheduled to arrive in the KDZ-E25F system a few hours ago."

"It's not a scientific report." Sisko crossed Ops to join her in front of the panel, frowning at the digital gibberish that scrolled across her screen. "Unfortunately, right now that's all I'm sure of. The message was so badly disrupted that all we could make out was that Captain Marsters encountered Klingons and an emergency situation had developed. Can you sift through the interference and clean the signal up, old man?"

"I can try." Dax handed him her *bat'leth* and pulled back her unruly mane of hair, then focused on her data display with the kind of instant intensity that only a joined Trill symbiont and host could summon. Sisko took a step back and reined his simmering impatience in with an effort. Badgering Dax for results right now would only slow her down.

Instead, he wrapped his fingers tight around the traditional Klingon weapon he'd been given, feeling the deep warmth of the metal blade radiating through its sweaty leather grip. Whatever archaic Klingon ritual his senior officers had been re-creating down in Quark's holo-suite, their battle gear hadn't just been donned for authenticity. Only a long and hard-fought battle could have soaked so much of Dax's body heat into her weapon. Sisko raised an eyebrow at Kira, and saw his first officer drop her hand almost guiltily from the sore shoulder she'd been massaging.

"Could you reconstruct the *Victoria Adams*'s coordinates at the time of transmission?" the major asked, clearly determined to ward off any questions about her fitness for duty. "If they veered off course toward one of the areas the Klingons have claimed as theirs—"

Sisko shook his head. "The signal tracked right back to the E25F system. That's nowhere near any of the disputed territory."

Worf frowned over his armored shoulder. "Still, there has been a significant increase in Klingon incursions throughout the entire demilitarized zone in the last few months," he reminded Sisko. "If you recall my warnings on the possible dangers of this scientific observation mission—"

Sisko winced. It had been easy at the time the *Victoria Adams* had departed to dismiss Worf's warnings as Klingon paranoia. No incidents, other than a few distant sightings of warships and smugglers, had disturbed the uneasy peace of that part of the Klingon-Cardassian demilitarized zone. And there had been nothing special about the KDZ-E25F system—aside from its unfortunate ownership of a disintegrating giant comet—to attract the attention of either the Cardassian or Klingon empires. "Limited landmass, no significant resources, and utterly impassable vegetation" was how the ancient Starfleet survey charts had summarized the system's single Class-M planet. It had seemed a safe enough place for a small shipload of planetary scientists and retired Starfleet officers to go to view a cosmic fireworks show.

"This isn't deliberate signal-jamming," Dax said abruptly, saving Sisko from having to answer his tactical officer. "The interference cuts randomly across the entire subspace spectrum."

"Couldn't the noise be coming from all those comet impacts the *Victoria Adams* went to observe?" O'Brien inquired.

Dax shook her head. "Not unless the comet fragments in that shower are made of dilithium instead of ice. The electromagnetic noise generated by bolide impacts on a Class-M planet might very well contaminate the radio and visible bands, but it shouldn't touch subspace frequencies. Not even to mask—"

Her voice broke off without warning, and her fingers began to fly across the computer panel. Sisko shot a frowning glance at her data output screen, but saw nothing he could recognize as a significant change in the random display of noise.

"What is it, old man?"

Dax looked up, her eyes crackling with sudden realization. "This interference we're seeing—it's not a generated signal at all, natural or artificial. It never adds to any wavelength of the *Victoria Adams*'s subspace signal, it only decreases it to a greater or lesser extent. In the places where the transmission's nearly wiped out, there's no static in its place. Just *nothing.*"

"What does that mean?" Kira asked.

"It means the *Victoria Adams*'s subspace signal has been filtered through a massive depolarizing field."

A rumble too fierce for a groan and too wordless for a curse emerged from somewhere deep in Worf's chest. Sisko shot a questioning look at him, and saw the bared-teeth grimace that said his chief tactical officer didn't like what he was going to have to say.

"There is only one way to create that kind of field in open space." Worf's voice deepened in a bleak mixture of vindication and regret. "Massive Klingon disruptor fire."

"Yes," Dax agreed. "The *Victoria Adams* must have been under Klingon attack when she sent this message."

For a moment, the only sound in Ops was the beep and hum of computers handling the routine business of the space station. The machines were the only ones oblivious to the military and political crisis crashing down upon them. Then Sisko grunted and allowed three months of stifled anger to escape in a cascade of orders.

"Dax, get me the best resolution you can on that transmission. I want to know as much as we can about what happened out there." He swung to face the rest of his crew. "Major Kira, put in a high-priority call to Starfleet and brief Admiral Nechayev about the attack on the *Victoria Adams.* Commander Worf, I want an updated report from Intelligence on all known and suspected Klingon forces in the demilitarized zone. O'Brien, get the *Defiant* ready for immediate departure and notify Dr. Bashir to assemble an emergency medical team."

"Yes, sir." The cadet-sharp response from the whole crew told Sisko he was probably letting a little too much of his temper spill into his voice. He took a deep breath, but it didn't do much to ease his tension. Bad enough that the Klingons had decided to spit in the face of the Federation by attacking a civilian ship. But to have that ship be the defenseless research vessel *Victoria Adams* with its load of vacationing Starfleet retirees—it made Sisko's gut burn with a rage fierce enough to scorch any remnant of hesitation from his mind.

The familiar, gravelly sound of a throat being cleared brought his narrowed gaze around to the one senior officer to whom he had issued no orders. Odo gazed back with a quizzical expression in his not-quite-human eyes, his eyebrows arched in wordless inquiry.

"Is there a problem, Constable?"

"I don't know. *You* certainly seem to think so."

Kira snorted without looking up from her communications panel. "The Klingons just declared war on the Federation, Odo. You don't call that a problem?"

"Did they?" the Changeling asked dryly. "It's not as if the *Victoria Adams* was in Federation space when she was attacked. Maquis and Cardassian ships have been getting fired on and chased out of the Klingon demilitarized zone for the past three months. We knew there was a risk the same thing would happen to the *Victoria Adams.* Wasn't that why Commander Worf recommended our science officer not join the expedition?"

"True," Sisko agreed. "But that doesn't mean the Federation can turn a blind eye to the destruction of an unarmed research vessel on a scientific mission."

"Or that we can ignore a Federation vessel's distress call, and leave its survivors to die, just because we are afraid of Klingon retaliation," Worf added grimly.

"Ah." Odo tilted his head, an ironic glitter in his pale eyes. "No doubt you all learned that lesson at the Academy, from that Starfleet training exercise—the *Kobayashi Maru.*"

Sisko exchanged frowning looks with his chief tactical officer. "This is *not* a no-win situation, Constable," he said at last. "If we can get to the

E25F system in time to rescue the crew of the *Victoria Adams,* we might be able to avert a diplomatic crisis—"

"—over a misunderstanding that could be resolved just as easily by negotiation between the Federation and the Klingon Empire," Odo pointed out, with the same unerring logic that made him such an impartial arbiter of merchant disputes on the Promenade. "The loss of a small research vessel—"

"—might be smoothed over," Sisko agreed. "But the loss of the last two surviving officers from the long-range explorer *Glimmerglass,* the only captain to take her ship successfully through the Chienozen passage, the science officer who established contact with the first inhabited neutron star, the diplomatic liaison who—"

Odo held up a hand, giving Sisko the stiff nod he used to acknowledge his mistakes. "You're saying we have to interfere because the Starfleet veterans who went along for the comet show were unusually important—"

"No, they weren't," Sisko said bluntly. "Except for one or two, they were just the normal run of Starfleet retirees. What I'm saying, Constable, is that the loss of *anyone* who served in uniform as long and as honorably as those people did is going to poison Starfleet's relations with the Klingons for years to come. No matter what the Federation diplomats may say or do."

"Enhanced transmission coming up on the main screen." Dax broke into the argument without ceremony. "I managed to extrapolate an additional seventy percent of the signal from the fragments that got through. Be prepared—we're still going to lose the end."

The main screen of Ops blanked, then exploded into a signal so brilliantly over-enhanced that Sisko had to squint to make out the burned-in shadows of the *Victoria Adams'*s bridge. Dax frowned and adjusted some control on her screen, muting the stilled image down to more bearable levels of brightness. The colors of deck and uniforms and bridge stations remained artificially monotone, however, a computer's extrapolation rather than the varied tints and shadings of real life. A single rawboned figure occupied the captain's chair. Dax's enhancements hadn't changed the tense set of his lantern jaw or erased his scowl, but they had brought into finer focus the sweat that beaded his face. He looked out across time and space with intent eyes, making Sisko once again feel that the man was making eye contact directly with him.

"This is Captain Charles Marsters of the Federation research vessel *Victoria Adams,*" said a clipped, precise voice. Sisko barely recognized it as the same static-fuzzed drawl he'd managed to decipher only a few words from fifteen minutes ago. "Request urgent assistance from Deep Space Nine. We've encountered an armed Klingon blockade around the planet KDZ-E25F." A blast rocked the science vessel, staggering the captain and momentarily knocking the image back to glittering white nothingness.

"Blockade?" Kira demanded incredulously.

Sisko grunted. "I thought that was what he said before, but I couldn't be sure. This was where we lost the audio feed."

Dax adjusted something on her panel, and the *Victoria Adams*'s bridge did a slow fade back into existence on the screen. "—attacked us for not leaving fast enough," Marsters said, still sounding calm despite the crackle of on-board fire beneath his words. "Hull and warp core integrity are holding, but we lost all life support systems in the initial attack. We're running on limited emergency backup now. All passengers and nonessential crew have—" The transmission shattered into nothingness again, presumably due to another close-range disruptor blast. This time, when the visual feed coalesced back into existence, it looked more ghostly and snowed over than before. And although Marsters's lips were still moving, no sound emerged.

Sisko cursed in fierce disappointment. "That's the best you can do, old man? We still don't know exactly what happened."

"The subtractive effects of the disruptor fire were worst in the audio portion of the signal. I can't extrapolate something from nothing, Benjamin."

"They evacuated the rest of the crew and passengers in a large planetary sampling shuttle," Odo said unexpectedly. "The *Victoria Adams* is going to cover their departure by leading the Klingons as far out of the system as possible."

Sisko swung around, startled. His chief security officer stared so intently at the screen that he didn't even blink at the final, blinding explosion of white nothingness. It was at times like this that Sisko remembered Odo's humanoid shape was merely assumed, and not hampered by any biological limitations.

"Constable, how do you know that?"

"I can read lips." Odo's pale eyes swung over to him, irony washing through them like a chill of frost across a windowpane. "It's a valuable skill to have when you're watching Ferengi make illegal bargains across a noisy bar."

Sisko lifted an eyebrow, but it was with respect, not skepticism. His years of experience had taught him that the Constable never claimed to have skills he didn't possess. "Did Captain Marsters say where the shuttle went after it left the ship?"

"Down to the planet," Odo said promptly. "I believe he said something about deliberately taking a depowered entry path, to make it look to Klingon sensors as though they were a falling comet fragment."

Dax frowned. "But in a thick Class-M atmosphere like that, a steep entry path could destabilize the shuttle and force them into a crash landing. It seems like such a risk—"

"Not as much of a risk as staying on the *Victoria Adams,* with the Klingons in pursuit and life support failing." Sisko felt his jaw tighten around the next question he had to ask. "Was that final explosion the ship blowing up, Dax?"

She surprised him with a shake of her head. "I don't think so. The signal strength was actually fading compared to the disruptor depolarization toward the end. I'd say the *Victoria Adams* was actually pulling away from her pursuers."

"I just hope they pulled all the Klingons away with them," O'Brien said. "That would leave the system clear for us to go in."

"Yes." Sisko turned to pin Kira with a frowning glance. "Any reply yet from Starfleet Command?"

Kira grimaced. "Regional headquarters acknowledged our hail, but says Admiral Nechayev is in a crucial meeting with representatives from the Vorta. She left orders that all emergency situations be handled under the protocol of sector commander recognizance."

Sisko's breath hissed through his teeth, but it was in satisfaction, not annoyance. "That means that, for now, the decision is up to us. Recommendations?"

"Go," said O'Brien curtly.

"Go," Dax agreed.

"Go now!" growled Worf.

That was the Starfleet side of his mixed command crew, reacting exactly as Sisko had expected. Their majority vote essentially settled the question, but Sisko forced himself to look over at his Bajoran second-in-command, trying to make sure he wasn't allowing service loyalties to overrule his better judgment. He got back a look of crackling impatience.

"Of course, we *have* to go," Kira said. "Give the Klingons a research ship in the demilitarized zone, and they'll take a starship in the Alpha Quadrant. If we don't stop them now, we'll just have to deal with them later."

"Constable, do you agree?"

Odo snorted. "I think we're going to start exactly the war we're trying to prevent. But since I appear to be the only one who feels that way, I'll save my energy for saying 'I told you so' a few days from now."

"I appreciate that," Sisko said dryly. "In the meantime, could you assemble a skeleton security squad for the *Defiant?* I want to take minimal crew, so we'll have enough room to evacuate all survivors." He glanced over at Dax. "Do you remember how many passengers and crew the *Victoria Adams* carried?"

"Fifteen scientists, ten ship's crew, and twelve passengers," Worf said before the science officer could reply.

"If they were on emergency life support, the captain couldn't have taken more than four of the crew with him when he tried leading the Klingons away," O'Brien added.

"Then we'll need to have room to evacuate at least thirty-two." Sisko scrubbed a hand across his face, mentally counting out the crew he could spare. "Dr. Bashir will still have to take a full medical team, which means we cut down ship's crew to fifteen. Agreed?"

Dax gave him a somber look. "I don't think we need to be that conservative. You're assuming all the survivors we rescue are going to be healthy. If the medical bay is filled, we'll end up with five empty bunks that could have held ship's crew."

"All right, twenty. Staff all sectors accordingly and assemble in docking bay five in fifteen minutes." Sisko vaulted out of the central hub of Ops and headed for the turbolift that would take him to his ship, reining in his impatience just long enough to let his five senior officers board the lift with him. "Promenade," he told the computer, confident he would find Bashir and his team already waiting to join them. "O'Brien, will you brief the doctor on what injuries he can expect to find in the crash survivors?"

His chief engineer shot him a startled look across the crowded turbo-lift platform. "Why me?"

Sisko lifted an eyebrow at him. "I assumed you'd know what kind of space-drive the planetary sampling shuttle had, so Dr. Bashir could know whether he needs to deal with radiation damage or plasma burns."

O'Brien grunted. "Crash damage is probably the least of the survivors' worries, Captain."

"What do you mean?"

"Well, nobody told that giant comet out there to stop disintegrating just because the Klingons fired on our research vessel. The survivors from the *Victoria Adams* are taking shelter on a planet where fire is raining out of the sky and the days are as dark as the nights—"

"And tsunami shock waves are coming in from any impacts that happen to hit the ocean." Dax sounded more wistful than worried. "It must be like—"

"Hell," Worf suggested.

"Not hell, *sylshessa.*" Kira saw their questioning looks and shook her head until her earring tinkled, obviously at a loss to translate the Bajoran word into English. "It's an old legend from Tal Province, about a future time when the sky burns and the earth explodes and the waters of the sea crash together—"

"Armageddon," Sisko said softly. "That's the Human version of the prophesy."

Odo grunted. "And in your version, is Armageddon the utter end of everything?"

"No," Sisko said grimly. "It's the beginning of war."

CHAPTER 2

At first glance, it didn't look much different from any other planetary system. A saffron yellow star spit out a normal amount of heat, light, and solar wind; three gas giants circled in far-flung orbits. But where the inner rocky planets should have spun in the star's golden glow, an ominous parabola of dust and ice enshrouded half the system. Dax's long-range scanners detected two small, airless planets orbiting outside that haze, one swung out beyond its perigee and the other caught between the curving arms of debris. Magnification of their sun-baked surfaces revealed a crazy quilt of craters and impact scars from past orbital swings through the comet track.

Dax stored the surface images for later analysis, then ran a quick check on the extrapolated orbital parameters for both inner and outer planets. As she'd suspected, all of them showed perturbations from a third, rocky inner planet, whose orbital diameter should have put it midway between the other two. It must be somewhere inside the remnants of the disintegrated giant comet. She turned her attention to the difficult task of filtering interference out of the sensor beams as they refracted through the debris.

"Major Kira, any sign of Klingon ship activity?" Sisko watched the main screen with a frown. Devoid of sensor enhancements, all that could be seen of their destination was the central twinkle of its star and a frosty trail of debris. That crescent of scattered gauze didn't look anywhere near as threatening in real life as it did on her sensor scans. Unfortunately, Dax knew her computer-enhanced version was closer to the truth.

The Bajoran shook her head without looking away from her output screens. "I've jacked up the sensitivity of our ion detectors as high as they can go, but they're showing no trace of any cloaked vessels in the vicinity." She pursed her lips as though considering, then added, "No sign of uncloaked activity, either." Meaning the *Victoria Adams.*

"That's a good sign. It means Captain Marsters got away and took the Klingons with him." Sisko frowned at the *Defiant*'s main viewscreen. "I'd like to know what's on the surface of those planets. There's a chance the planetary shuttle might have landed there. Dax, can you enhance the display?"

"I can, but sensor scans show no sign of a recent landing on either planet." She transferred her two stored images up to the main screen, assigning them to their proper locations around Armageddon's golden sun. "Computer analysis of their orbital parameters, however, indicates there's a third inner system planet inside the cometary debris cloud. I haven't been able to image it yet." She glanced across at Sisko, reading his impatience in his drumming fingers. "But it's the most likely location for the shuttle to land, since it's the planet the *Victoria Adams* went to study. Unfortunately, it's also the one that's being most heavily bombarded by cometary impacts—at least once every two or three days."

O'Brien frowned over his shoulder at her. "Just what is going on in this system, Commander? Why did the *Victoria Adams* come here to begin with?"

"Because it's one of the few planetary systems in this quadrant whose Oort cloud agglomerated into a single body, too fluffy to be a planet but much too big to be a comet. It got kicked into an inner-system orbit fifteen thousand years or so ago when another star grazed past this one. The stresses of that new orbit kept tearing it apart, scattering debris along its path, until it finally disintegrated completely on its last solar swing, just last year. What you're seeing are its final remains." She shot a vexed look across the bridge at Worf. "It's a perfect re-creation of the kind of event that we think caused a mass extinction on the Trill homeworld. Observing it would have been a once-in-a-lifetime opportunity, even for a Trill."

"Had you gone with the *Victoria Adams,* you might have found it the last-in-a-lifetime opportunity," the Klingon tactical officer reminded her. He looked up from the pilot's console he'd taken over while Dax concentrated on her sensor scans. "Can you obtain a rough fix on the planet's position using the curvature of its gravity well? I need to plot a course."

"And I'd like a visual image," Sisko added.

"I can fix the third planet's position, but I can't image it through all the interference. This is the best I can do." Dax sent the blotched gray image she had captured to the main viewscreen. It looked even worse when it was magnified, so vaguely outlined that it could have been the veiled halo of a comet as easily as a planet. "Chief, can you give me any more resolution on my sensor beam?"

O'Brien tapped a scan into his control panel and grunted. "I can give you a sixty-five percent increase in beam confinement, Commander, but only for a few minutes. On your mark."

Dax carefully delimited her scanning range to the exact coordinates of the planet to avoid wasting sensor power. "Mark."

The image on the screen slowly swam into focus as the tightened beam scanned across it. Its blurred outer edge became the hazy smudge of an atmospheric layer, as oxide-browned as a heavily industrialized planet's. But its nightside showed no signs of urban lights, and the isolated sprawl of island archipelagos dotting its blue-green oceans seemed too small to support any kind of machine-based civilization. There was only one larger landmass in view, half-hidden by the planet's terminus. Dax thought she saw the hint of a massive impact crater in that shadowed twilight edge, but the resolution faded back to fuzzy gray before she could confirm it. She hoped it had been a comet that made that scar.

"Sorry, Commander," O'Brien sighed. "That was all the power I could jack in without burning out the sensor array."

"That's all right. I can't confirm impact structures, but that brown color means there's been a lot of dust and ash kicked into the stratosphere recently. We'll have to get a lot closer before I can tell you if there's a crash site."

Worf glanced back across his shoulder at Sisko. "Shall I lay in an orbit, Captain?"

Sisko rubbed his chin. "Can we navigate safely through all that cometary debris?"

"Our shields should take care of the smaller debris," Kira pointed out. "And we can program short-range sensors to alert us to any imminent collisions with larger fragments."

Worf frowned at her. "Given the political situation, I strongly recommend that we remain under cloak at all times on this mission. If we were to fire at an oncoming comet fragment, we would give away our presence to the Klingons."

"Assuming there are any Klingons here to give it away to," Kira retorted. "I'm still getting no trace of ion trails anywhere in the system."

"But that doesn't mean we can assume they aren't here. The Klingons might have already come back from chasing the *Victoria Adams,* and dropped into a Lagrangian orbit around the planet to conserve power." Sisko drummed his fingers on the arm of his command chair, looking intensely thoughtful. "O'Brien, can we recalibrate our shields to an angle that will deflect any oncoming debris fragments without disturbing our cloaking effect?"

"We can try." The chief engineer hunched over his panel as he ran the calculations. "But we're not going to have full power as long as we're under cloak. It looks like we should be able to deflect about ninety percent of the debris we encounter without any significant change in vector. The rest will hit at such a direct angle that we'll feel the impact, even through shields. It shouldn't cause any real damage, but if someone was watching us closely, they might notice the fragment bouncing off." He glanced up unhappily. "It also means I can't promise we'll maintain shield integrity under a disruptor hit."

"That's a chance we'll have to take." Sisko turned back to the pilot's console. "Mr. Worf, as soon as the shields are recalibrated, take us into a circumpolar orbit at minimum impulse power. That should give us an opportunity to scan the whole planet without having our signals or our ion trail picked up by anyone who might be watching."

"Aye-aye, sir."

Sisko swung his command chair back in the other direction. "Major Kira, as we come in, I want you to concentrate your ion detection scans on the planet's Lagrange points. If there *are* Klingon vessels present, we may be able to pick up some minor leakage from their warp cores. Dax, I want full scans of the planet's surface, calibrated for humanoid life signs, as soon as we hit orbit."

"It may take longer than usual with all that atmospheric pollution," she warned. It didn't seem worth adding that the racial diversity of *Victoria Adams*'s crew would also add unique convolutions to the readings.

"Understood." Sisko stood and paced down to the front of the *Defiant*'s bridge, as if physical proximity to the fuzzy planet displayed there would show him something he hadn't already seen. "I wonder why the Klingons would risk attacking a civilian ship all the way out here? What's in this system that they don't want us interfering with?"

"Besides generic Klingon aggression?" Kira asked. "You don't think that's reason enough for them to sweep their borders clean?"

Sisko made an impatient gesture with his hands. "Maybe. But I can't see any tactical advantage to this. Something about it just doesn't feel right."

"That is because it is not honorable to wage war on a weakened enemy," Worf said stiffly. "And all Klingons know that scientists are the weakest warriors of all."

"Oh, are they?" O'Brien raised his eyebrows toward Dax, and she rewarded him with an amused smile.

"That's a prejudice that's cost them a lot of battles in the past," she assured him.

The bridge doors hissed apart before Worf could do more than glower at her joke. Bashir and Odo came through them together, the doctor glancing curiously up at the viewscreen while the security officer went to join Kira at the weapons station. "Any sign of Klingons yet?" Odo asked.

"Not an ion's worth." Kira yielded the panel to him, stretching as she turned to look up at the main screen.

"What about survivors?" Bashir followed Kira's gaze, drifting almost unconsciously toward Dax. The gauzy veil of debris had resolved into hazy streaks and glowing gas streamers while they approached it, a tangled braid of cometary fragments trapped and melting in the heat of Armageddon's saffron sun.

"We're still working on that," Dax assured the doctor. "Worf's taking us in for a closer look."

A worried frown settled over his lean face, but Sisko silenced any protest he might have voiced with a single raised finger and a calmly spoken, "Patience, doctor." He nodded down at Dax in a clear gesture of redirection. "Dax, how can this much ice exist in such close proximity to the star?"

"It can't," Dax admitted. "That's why the whole debris belt looks so fuzzy with vapor. But there's enough debris from the ice giant to last for quite a while."

"So comet fragments will continue to bombard the inner planets for years." Kira shook her head, looking somber. "I wouldn't wish that fate on *any* inhabited world."

"At least they don't have to suffer it all year round," O'Brien pointed out. "They have an 'impact season' while they're inside the debris field, but then they can recover during the time they spend outside it."

"That doesn't seem to have helped the two smallest planets in the system," Dax said. "They've suffered such intense bombardment in the past that they don't have an atmosphere or hydrosphere left. It's all been blasted into space."

"Let's hope the escape shuttle actually made it to the Class-M, then." Bashir folded his arms as though to hide the nervous clenching and unclenching of his hands. "What was it called again? KPZ-E20-something?"

"KDZ-E25F," Odo said precisely. "Not exactly a memorable designation."

"No," Dax agreed. "In my science notes, I've started calling it Armageddon."

"You would," Bashir said, more in resignation than disgust.

"Why not *sylshessa?"* Kira demanded.

"Because there already is a planet called Sylshessa. It's a Tellarite colony near Vulcan." Dax threw a cautious look at the captain, knowing her odd Trill sense of humor didn't always sit well with him at times of tension. The glint in his dark eyes encouraged her to add, "At least Armageddon is a better name than Splat. That's what the crew of the *Victoria Adams* was calling the Class-M planet."

"Let's hope neither of those names becomes a self-fulfilling prophecy, old man," Sisko retorted. "For us or for the survivors."

"We are entering the cometary debris field now, Captain." The deep tone of Worf's voice never varied under pressure, but Dax knew him well enough now to read the strain in his carefully clipped syllables. She felt the *Defiant* lurch a little as a large ice fragment impacted its newly angled shields. "Our shields appear to be deflecting most of the debris, but we are losing some directional control to friction

"Lower speed to warp one and compensate for course deviations." Sisko resumed his command seat, staring up at the viewscreen with the fierce attention he usually reserved for opponents in battle. The image of the Class-M planet slowly resolved as they drew closer, condensing back into the dust-stained, blue-green sphere they'd caught a glimpse of before. The terminator had crept slightly westward, exposing more of the long, oblong gouge scarring the one large landmass.

"Is that the crash site?" Bashir asked.

"No." The increased magnification of her science panel showed Dax the scatter of smaller craters trailing away from the main one, each surrounded by a starburst of exploded rock and soil. "It's a cometary strike—looks like a large bolide shattered just before impact. There's almost no erosion on the debris fans. I'm guessing it happened within the last few weeks."

"We are entering circumpolar orbit now, Captain."

"Very good. Dax, begin scanning for life-signs."

"Yes, sir." She punched in extra sensitivity filters for humanoid vital signs, then paused to read the flickering output from her sensors. "I'm showing a standard oxygen-nitrogen atmosphere, with traces of methane, carbon dioxide, and argon."

"Also methyl iodide at a level indicative of marine-dominant photosynthesis." Bashir leaned over her shoulder to point at the telltale spike on her spectrographic display. "The ocean's still full of life, despite getting blasted by rocks from outer space. Are you picking up any life-signs on land?"

"Yes. A surprising amount, actually." Dax read through her scanner output again, to make sure she hadn't misinterpreted the unusual readings it gave her. "According to this, the main continent is pretty much desolate in the interior, but swarming with native life around its edges. Thick vegetative cover of some kind is showing up on IR, both on the coast and on the islands. I suspect there are several types of higher vertebrates still inhabiting the surface, many of them exhibiting herding or pack behavior."

Sisko waved a hand, impatient as always with the dry basics of biology and planetology. "What about the escape shuttle? Any sign of it?"

"Not so far." The *Defiant* cruised slowly over the planet's unglaciated polar region, then down across its other hemisphere. Here, night was falling across a second enormous blue-green sea, this one even more thickly laced with surf-fringed tropical islands. "Life-sign scans are still showing only native vertebrates and marine life—no, wait . . . We've got a hit!"

"The crew?" Kira demanded.

"I don't know . . . " Dax flicked her eyes back and forth across her panel, trying to absorb every reading at once. "I'm showing about twenty life-signs on one of the small islands in that central archipelago. They're masked by some kind of phased energy field—I think it might be the shield generator from the shuttle."

"What about the shuttle itself?" Sisko asked.

Dax shook her head at her display. "I'm not picking up any kind of equipment or power-source reading at all. Just the field interference and the—" A flutter in the readings distracted her. "Julian, come take a look at this." She leaned to one side to let the doctor bend over her shoulder. "Is this a problem with my scanning filters, or are almost all of these life-forms injured?"

Bashir tapped a query on her computer, cursing softly at the response he saw. "There's nothing wrong with your filters. These are humanoid readings, and at least thirteen of them are injured, seven critically. Three of them are nearly dead."

A grim silence fell over the *Defiant* while everyone stared at Armageddon's unrevealing freckled oceans as if they could somehow answer all their questions. "That must be the *Victoria Adams*'s crew," O'Brien said at last, voicing the conclusion that none of them wanted to reach.

"But there were thirty-two passengers and crew on the *Victoria Adams,*" Kira protested. "You're saying half of them are dead or dying?"

"I'm saying they're in urgent need of medical help, whoever they are." Bashir glanced across at O'Brien. "Chief, can we transport them straight to the medical bay?"

"Not as long as that shield generator is going. And I doubt they're going to drop it—they're probably using it to try and ward off comet impacts."

"Very well." Bashir straightened and turned toward Sisko, suddenly wearing the innate dignity that his strong sense of medical ethics could bestow on him despite his youth and *joie de vivre.* "Captain, request permission to take an emergency medical team to the planet's surface."

"Granted," Sisko said without hesitation. "Major Kira, go with him. And Dax"—he fixed her with a not-entirely humorous glower—"this had better be the end of your complaining about not going on the *Victoria*

Adams, old man." Dax winced, but the acidic comment couldn't entirely quench the scientific enthusiasm bubbling through her.

Worf glanced over his shoulder, furrowed brow drawn into tighter lines than usual. "Captain, I am the obvious choice to accompany Dr. Bashir as protection. As chief tactical officer—"

"I'm going to need you here in case the Klingons show up and challenge us," Sisko returned. "Don't worry, Mr. Worf. I'm sure Dax and the major can take care of themselves."

The Klingon grunted and threw Dax the severely reproving look she was never quite sure how to interpret. "Under normal circumstances, I would agree," he said grimly.

"How reassuring." Dax set her sensors on autoscan until her replacement could arrive on the bridge. Kira was already accompanying Bashir to the turbolift, leaving Odo in sole command of her console. As she turned to follow them, Dax paused only long enough to blow Worf a facetious kiss. It made him wince and look away, just as she'd expected. "You be careful, too. You're going to be getting bombarded by as many comet fragments as I am."

The chief tactical officer growled up at the viewscreen, although Dax didn't think it was the view that had enraged him. "Somehow," he said between his teeth, "I think the comets are going to be the least of our problems."

Bashir's first impression of Armageddon was that it stank like a butchery.

The stench slapped over them with a force completely overriding any images of dust-shrouded sun, crystal blue ocean, or pearlescent sand. Bashir brought his arm up to shield his nose and mouth. He knew it was pointless, a blind make-work instinct, even as his left hand scrambled to open his medical kit and dig out the tube of olfacan by feel.

He'd carried olfacan in every medkit, and stored some in half a dozen sick bay drawers, ever since his first medical school autopsy. Logic understood that illness could be ugly. Sight could be trained to see the person beyond radiation burns, to understand the pathology of trauma and disease. But smell spoke directly to those most primitive places of one's brain; it simply refused to be reasoned with. Still, after half a lifetime of downplaying his own assets for the sake of peer acceptance, it had taken him by surprise to discover a weakness he hadn't suspected. Later, he would try to convince himself that it was his supernaturally acute sense of smell that had betrayed him. At the time, his stomach gave in to a fight-or-flight reflex that no amount of intellectual resistance could override, and he'd fled the autopsy theatre in an effort to minimize his humiliation. It was afterward that an older resident introduced him to the joys of an anesthetized olfactory nerve—a fingerful of colorless ointment across the upper lip, and even Bashir's keen sense of smell faded into blissful nonexistence for a good two to three hours. Years later, he still greeted the cessation of smell with a kind of guilty relief; the animal mind at work again, convincing him that no one with a half-million credits worth of biological enhancements should need something so trivial as protection from unpleasant odors. But the guilt didn't stop him from using it.

Warded against his baser instincts, he extended the tube to his physician's assistant, Heiser. The young lieutenant took a grateful smear with one index finger and passed half along to nurse LeDonne. Bashir twisted to include Dax and Kira in his offer, explaining, "It's a nasal anesthetic. It'll help block out the smell."

Kira gave a wry little snort. It was one of many sounds Bashir had learned to associate with the major's private conviction that he had the intestinal fortitude of a sand flea. "No, thanks. I learned to ignore worse than this a long time ago."

Of course. There was little Starfleet could expose her to that was as bad as Cardassian prison camps. Bashir wondered if she'd ever considered that the ability to tolerate something unpleasant didn't obligate you to do so. Or maybe that was more of what she labeled sand flea thinking, and not even worth mentioning.

He slipped the olfacan back into its protective sleeve and worked loose his tricorder instead. "My God . . . " He may not have been able to smell, but his eyes still stung; he felt like he was going to sneeze. "How many crew members did *Victoria Adams* carry?"

"Smells like thousands." Heiser scrubbed at his sparse blond mustache as though trying to help the olfacan work. "Should we do a reconnoiter?"

"No." Dax glanced up from her own singing tricorder in response to Bashir's startled glance. "Those aren't dead bodies," she clarified, dipping a nod toward her scan results. "Not humanoid dead bodies, at least. If the

Victoria Adams crashed here, she did it too recently to allow for this level of putrefaction. Besides, we aren't close enough to the source of that shield generator to be smelling any corpses from that site." She snapped shut her tricorder and repositioned it on her belt, pinching at her nose again despite the olfacan. "Let's get going before this smell makes me vomit."

But the stench got worse instead of better as they made their way down the long curve of beach. Smooth, white sand—so fine that it packed almost as solidly as soil where the waves shushed up to dampen it—made a level shelf more than thirty meters wide for as far as Bashir could see. To his right, tropical blue water undulated like a platter of softened glass, bending itself into mountains, valleys, and gently stroking tongues of wave. On his left, what looked to be a wall of woven sticks and vines rose to more than twice his height, its seaward side decorated by draperies of mummified kelp and tangles of long-dead detritus. Some sort of weather wall to protect against ocean storms? Erected by—who? The crash survivors? The natives? No, there was too much greenery beyond it, just as high and twisted as the wall fronting the shore, and stretching as far to that direction as the ocean stretched in the other. And Armageddon's volatile local environment made the possibility of sentient natives more than just highly unlikely. It was some sort of natural vegetative feature, then—the planet's attempt to defend itself against itself.

At first, Bashir thought perhaps the rotten odor originated with this littered hedge. He and his assistants were sufficiently shielded by the olfacan to no longer notice what smells surrounded them. But Trills apparently didn't respond as well to the anesthetic, and Kira had refused it from the outset. Bashir rather easily tracked the strength of the stench through the simple expedient of watching the women's faces. Dax squinted to protect her eyes from the fumes, and Kira's already wrinkled nose wrinkled even further in disgust. It wasn't until they stepped in front of a gaping rent in the wall of brush that whatever they'd been smelling must have rolled out in force: Dax grunted a little sound of disgust, and Kira jerked away from the opening as though she'd been slapped. Even Bashir imagined he detected a pungent belch of stench too strong for the olfacan to fully counter. Still, it was the tacky blaze of clotted blood darkening broken foliage that jolted his heart up into his throat. It was already too old and rotten to tell if it had come from any familiar species. Touching a hand to his tricorder as though it were a talisman, he stepped gingerly into the crushed-down path and forced himself to keep a measured pace until he reached the end.

"Julian!"

The passage widened abruptly into a lidless natural amphitheater, its sides as smashed and shattered as the corridor. He meant to call back a reassurance to Dax. Instead, he looked up at the mountain of gore in front of him and coughed abruptly into one hand. There was a horrible moment in which he thought he'd be sick even with his immunity to the fetor, but he managed to swallow his stomach under control just as Kira trotted up from behind. He heard something that might have been a stunted sneeze, then the major croaked softly, "Maybe I'll take a noseful of that stuff after all."

In all his life, Bashir could not remember imagining something so wretchedly horrific. Carcasses—each easily three tons even with skins and half their internal organs removed—lay piled within a veil of buzzing flies and decomposition gases. They'd been stacked higher than Bashir's own head, but the combined weight of the upper layers had crushed the bodies on the bottom until only shattered bone ends and the occasional rotting hock jutted up from the bloody mud into which they'd been pressed. Some clinically detached segment of his brain noted the internal structures that said they were probably mammalian, and the flat, cylindrical teeth which suggested they were herbivorous. Some more emotional part of him struggled to pin a number on how many bodies one needed to build a pile of carnage five meters high and perhaps another twenty meters long.

He felt the warmth of someone close on his left elbow several moments before noticing a science tricorder's distinctive warble. "In case it matters," Dax said quietly, "I was right—these carcasses are definitely too old to have anything to do with the *Victoria Adams*."

It was no consolation at all, and Bashir bitterly envied Dax the lifetimes of experience that let her face something like this without losing composure. "If not the survivors, then what?" Relief throbbed in his stomach when he finally dragged his eyes from the slaughter. "The comet impacts?"

Dax shook her head. "Even the nearest comet damage is too recent."

"What else could have killed so many animals at one time?"

"Spears."

He didn't want to look at Kira—he'd have to glimpse the mutilated pile as he turned, and everything inside him wanted to avoid that more than he was comfortable admitting. Dax rescued him by tossing a silent question at the major over Bashir's shoulder, then looking where Kira apparently gestured. "And somebody field-dressed them, too," the major went on. "I don't think they normally come with exposed organs and no hair."

Dax nodded slowly, thoughtfully. "You're right . . . "

"Do you think it was natives?" Bashir asked. Partly because the question of intelligent life brought to mind his original thoughts about the weather wall, and partly because he didn't want to seem so completely weak-kneed that he wasn't even following their conversation.

Dax glanced at him with a scholarly frown, as though prepared to debate all aspects of that question in the interests of science. Then something in his face softened her expression. Bashir suspected it was his waxen pallor, or perhaps the first hint of nauseated tears in his eyes. Whatever the cause, she slipped her arm across his shoulders and turned him back toward the beach with its virginal stretch of bright white sand.

"I don't know enough about the planet yet to even take a guess," she said, voice smooth with equal parts consideration and sympathy. "We'll ask the survivors about it when we find them."

By the time they reached the survivors' settlement, natives were the last thing on Bashir's mind.

"Cholegh'a' chIm ghobDu'wI'!"

Dax's voice—raised and roughened to bark the words with what Bashir assumed was either authority or challenge—fell flat amongst wreckage no longer tall enough to encourage echoes. From inside the shimmer of force field, swarthy, chiseled faces lifted, turned to them with no particular malice or interest. They'd apparently finished salvaging hours ago; by now, adult and sub-adult males clustered with adult females in the meager shade of the weather wall, well away from the shield's humming margins yet well protected by its umbrella. Their bodies were lowered into deep squats, their hands balanced on their knees as though prepared to spring into action despite the weariness etched into all their faces. Klingon faces. Bruised and weary and creased with despair, but still undeniably *Klingon klingon sapiens.* Bashir counted less than ten scattered about the tumbles of debris, standing or sitting. Judging from the bright blossoms of Klingon blood splashed across every survivor's clothing, there were at least that many again wounded or already dead. He saw no sign of Humans.

"NgliS Hol Sajatlh'a'?"

It hadn't been a big village even before its devastation. A row of strongly woven huts, opposing ends open to the air, seemed to have been extruded directly from the weather wall. They were little more than a scatter of twisted sticks now. The shield's irridescent bubble covered only the centermost sections of the camp, leaving exposed blankets and racks that had no doubt filled the tiny hovels only a few days before. The blurry touch of Armageddon's sun warmed hoops of braided vine and their circles of stretched hide, while hammocks of dessicating organ meat slowly dried beside what looked like racks of some frothy yellow gland. It was an impressive collection of foodstuffs, obviously the bounty from the hunting 'scraps' the landing party had already found. This was certainly no temporary castaways' camp, and couldn't have been erected in the short time since *Victoria Adams* had reported Klingons in the area.

Dax halted with her toes just brushing the terminal margin of the shield. *"Devwi'ra 'Iv?"* Tiny sparks skittered in the sand between her boots.

Bashir wasn't sure if it was the Trill's words that ignited the flutter of interest among the silent Klingons, or the distinctly Klingon bravura of her approach. Whichever it was, something passed from Klingon to Klingon on a chain of turning heads until one of them rose to his feet from amidst a ring of other adult males. Bashir thought he recognized the arrogance of a Klingon commander despite the warrior's limping stride.

He didn't even stand as tall as Dax, but the broadness of his chest and limbs betrayed a strength easily a match for the entire landing party. Shoulder-length hair, still curling and black with Klingon vigor, went well with an equally vigorous beard but not so well with the bruise-deep shadows of exhaustion beneath his eyes. Despite that, and despite the swollen foot that he favored when he walked, Bashir saw none of the gauntness of long-term starvation in the warrior. The absence of traditional Klingon armor only accentuated the ripple and bunch of his muscles, the smoothly filled planes of his broad face. It was clear why his crew felt secure enough to waste so much of the animals they'd hunted and killed, rather than utilizing the whole.

Bashir made an effort to push that last bitter thought away. For all he knew, the meat was inedible and the skin and glands were the only parts the Klingons could use. Besides, the entire planet would probably be blasted clear of life in just another few days. It hardly seemed reasonable to hold ecological grudges.

The bandy-legged commander looked as though he might split the seams of his dusty civilian tunic when he halted just opposite the shield from Dax and flexed his shoulders. "I never believed I would someday be happy to stand unarmed among Starfleet officers." His Standard was clear, though heavily accented. If he'd meant his greeting as a joke, it didn't sound like a happy one. Thumping one fist against his chest, he rumbled, "I am Gordek, of the House of Gordek."

Dax lifted one eyebrow in what Bashir took to be surprise, but said nothing to expound on her gesture. "Lieutenant Commander Dax, from space station Deep Space Nine." She apparently felt no need to reciprocate Gordek's theatrical physicality. Bashir was just as glad. "This is Major Kira. And Dr. Bashir, Lieutenant Heiser, and Ensign LeDonne."

The Klingon's onyx-chip gaze leapt instantly to Bashir, but skidded away again before allowing interpretation. "You are here because of the Federation shuttle that crashed yesterday, out in the *tuq'mor*." His deep voice made it a statement rather than a question.

"Yes." Dax never broke her own gaze away from Gordek's. "Did you find any survivors at the wreckage site?"

"None," said the Klingon curtly. Bashir's rush of bitter disappointment was sliced off unexpectedly by Gordek's next words. "We found no bodies, either. We had to hike several miles of *tuq'mor* to reach that ship. Whoever rode in it left long before we got there."

Kira frowned at him. "Are you the ones who made it crash?"

A throaty rumble of what might have been Klingon threat or Klingon laughter. Bashir always found it hard to tell the difference. "Yes, of course. We attacked a Federation ship and destroyed it, then immediately beamed ourselves down and built this village, threw away all our technology, armed ourselves with spears, and then waited for a comet to destroy us." The points of his teeth gnashed when he grinned, but Bashir still wasn't sure if he was amused or angered. "Is that what you wanted to hear?"

"What she wants to hear," Dax said clearly, "is whether you are the reason that the ship was attacked, not whether you are the ones who attacked it."

"Ah." Gordek's gaze swung back to the Trill, his oddly angry amusement fading to a more recognizable emotion. Surprise. "You know what we are, then?"

"I think so," she said calmly. "Will you tell me, or are you going to make me guess?"

"Guess." The Klingon spat over one shoulder as casually as a Human might gesture with one hand.

Dax said something long and intricate in Klingon, something that made a muscle jerk in Gordek's cheek, as though something had stung him. "Vrag," he said reluctantly, and the Trill nodded as though that single word had brought enlightenment. She took a step back from the glittering shield, looking for all the world as if she expected it to drop now. Bashir and Kira followed her back to where Heiser and LeDonne had waited for them, wearing matching looks of concern and bafflement.

"What did you just say?" Bashir demanded. "Are they going to let us in to treat the wounded, or are they sending us away?"

"They'll let us in." Dax sounded more somber than usual. "They may not be happy about it, but they don't have anywhere else to turn for help. They're *ada'ven*—political exiles from the Klingon Empire, sent here to live out the rest of their lives in isolation from their society."

There was a long silence, filled only with the muffled groans and stirrings from the wounded. Gordek was limping over to the central firepit, beyond which Bashir could just see the actual shield generator. Its glittering duranium husk was roughly cobbled to an equally out-of-place portable power supply. Both looked like standard Federation issue to Bashir.

"How did you know?" Kira asked at last, while Gordek fiddled with the field controls. The wall of force that separated them from the Klingons began to waver and ripple, as if an unfelt wind was blowing through it.

Dax sighed again. "I didn't recognize the House of Gordek as any traditional Klingon clan. Starfleet intelligence has noticed that for the past year any small Klingon house that comes into conflict with Chancellor Gowron quickly disappears from view. I think Gowron's decided to put his past experience with the House of Mogh to use by duplicating it on other politically inconvenient families. All I did was name those houses, until I came to one that made him blink."

"Vrag," Kira repeated.

"Yes. Unfortunately, of all the exiled houses, that's the one I know the least about. They could have been thrown out for being pacifists or for wanting to start an outright attack on the Federation. We should be—"

The shield rippled one last time, then vanished. Bashir promptly crossed into the center of the Klingon encampment, drawn by the universal sounds of suffering that he could now hear clearly.

"—careful," Dax finished behind him, ruefully. He could hear her and Kira following along, but his attention now was locked to his medical tricorder and the flickering vital signs it guided him toward.

The little alcove trampled into the brush wall was more just a place to dump the wounded than any real attempt at an infirmary. Bashir covered the last meter with a few quick strides and knelt beside the first in what seemed an impossibly long line of patients. Heiser had already headed for the other end of the line, tricorder and medkit in hand, while LeDonne positioned herself near the middle. Bashir would suddenly have given an arm for another dozen medics, all of them only half as good as these two.

The female now laid out before him was still young by Klingon standards. Her brow ridges were fully carved, but twelfth-year incisors only showed perhaps five or six years' worth of wear. A depressed skull fracture had been bandaged with only a single strip of fine-weave cloth, and not even so much as a half-cured hide had been spread over her to keep out the chill. Of course not—Klingons should be strong enough not to require coddling. Even when they were more than half dead. Grey matter in the tangle of her hair, and no reflexive response from either pupil. Bashir closed her eyes with a gentleness he suspected she wouldn't appreciate, and moved on to the next body in line.

Gordek circled behind the doctor, limping to a stop just outside Bashir's range of vision. Bashir could feel the Klingon's stare on him as he compiled tricorder readings on the patient, a burning itch on the back of his skull. "What happened here?" he asked, more to tell the Klingon he knew he was being watched than because he really needed to know.

That gained him only another streak of spittle, this one landing distressingly close to his tricorder. "What do you think? You must have seen the sky as you came here."

"Comet impact," Kira translated. It sounded as if she spoke through clenched teeth, and Bashir was oddly glad to know he wasn't the only one reacting badly to Gordek's blend of anger, aggression, and reserve. "When did it happen?"

"Three days ago, just at sunset. We saw a streak across the sky, but we have seen many such streaks in the last few months. This one was different. This light came down further into the sky, then exploded around us, like a photon torpedo."

"Lower atmosphere burst," Dax said. "The most damaging kind of impact."

Gordek grunted. "Several of my house were killed outright. Others have died since. But there are still enough of us left to survive." The statement was almost defiant, as if he thought they might have some reason to question. "After we found the wrecked Federation ship, I knew we would be fine. The shield will keep us safe from any more explosions in the sky."

Straightening carefully, Bashir took a moment to sterilize his hands before he moved on to the next critical patient. Dax watched in silence while he knitted ribs and sutured the punctures they had made in the skin. Klingon physiology was remarkable in many respects, not the least of which was their ability to stoically endure damage that would have killed a human or a Trill within hours.

It was Kira who resumed the interrogation. "When you were stripping the wreckage, did you see any evidence of where the crash survivors might have gone?"

Gordek spat again, this time in her direction. It was apparently an all-purpose expression of scorn rather than a personal comment. "Following tracks in the *tuq'mor* is a fool's errand. There was a trail close to where your ship crashed, one that I followed northwest from here. It continues another half-day's walk to the main settlement."

"Main settlement?" Dax inquired, while Bashir reached the last patient in his third of the row. He had added an open pelvic fracture and lateral pneumothorax to his list of casualties, and reached to tip first Heiser's, then LeDonne's tricorder screen to a readable angle so he could add their lists to his before Gordek answered the Trill's question.

"It is where the *epetai* keeps those loyal to her, a warren of burrows in the middle of the *tuq'mor.*" He spat again, more fiercely this time and in a direction away from them. "All underground, the better to rot and die where they stand!"

Bashir exchanged enlightened glances with Dax. "No wonder you got so few humanoid readings on this planet," he said softly. She dipped a single thoughtful nod in agreement.

Kira pushed in front of Gordek, either oblivious to or determined to ignore his growing belligerence. "Could the survivors from the crashed Federation vessel be at this main settlement?"

"They might." Gordek stepped back, his broad face emotionless but his onyx-cold eyes skipping from one to another of them with a look of unexpected calculation. "If I tell you how to find it," he said, "will you send down phasers and a permanent power generator for our new shield?"

"You want to stay here?" Bashir tried not to sound too appalled by this loyalty to any planet that had doled out such ruthless punishment for crimes that were none of its affair. He couldn't help noticing Dax's matching frown of surprise. "You've got at least six critical injuries so far, plus another four who might not die but who need bones regrown or limbs regenerated." He glanced behind him, and was only half-startled to find both Dax and Gordek so close that he bumped them with his shoulder when he turned. "I'd like to beam them up to the ship right away."

"You have doctors on your ship who can tend to Klingon warriors?"

Bashir made himself scowl back into Gordek's accusing glower. "No. But we have stasis facilities that can keep them alive until we get to a better equipped sick bay." Although he found it hard to believe this Klingon cared overmuch how many of his people did or didn't survive the journey. Thinking of the first young woman with her brain in her hair, he offered more gently, "We also have a morgue, if you'd—"

Gordek waved off the suggestion with a whuff of disgust. "The dead are dead." He looked as though the sight of his dead people annoyed him. "Leave them."

"There will be more dead," Dax warned him. "Even with the shield, you can't survive a direct comet strike."

The Klingon leader's glossy black head lifted in a faint echo of Worf's towering pride in his heritage. "I prefer to die under a killing sky than to accept mercy from my enemy. You may transport my people to your ship for treatment," he added to Bashir arrogantly. "But you will beam them down again along with the power generator I have asked for. Is it a bargain?"

"Yes." Kira overrode Dax's more tentative response with the crisp confidence of someone who'd been a field commander for longer than she'd been an adult. "You have my word of honor as a Bajoran."

The thick muscle of Gordek's cheek spasmed again, but whatever had startled him apparently wasn't worth commenting on. "I accept that," he said promptly. "And you have the word of honor of one who will be *epetai* someday."

CHAPTER 3

KIRA FELT THE DIFFERENCE IN THIS NEW KLINGON ENCAMPMENT EVEN before the transporter had fully released her. Sunlight—harder and hotter, with no ocean breeze to mitigate its strength—cut patchwork patterns through shadow too woven and deep to come from trees; peaty-smelling mud leveled the ground with flaccid puddles; and the volume and snarl of the voices crowding about her reminded her abruptly that, even on the best of days, Federation personnel had no reason to expect a warm reception from Klingons.

Unfortunately, it was a little late to voice that kind of pithy observation. Solidity raced through her limbs with an almost electric shock. With it came the full return of sight and sound and movement. She had barely jerked away from the first Klingon who lunged to grab her arm when Dax's shout took over where the transporter had left off. "Kira, don't! Julian, don't fight them!"

Not that they had much choice—one thick, stone-hard arm snaked around Kira's middle while someone else seized her wrist and pinioned it between two hands. She couldn't even see Bashir, only hear his thin hiss of pain somewhere behind her. Her teeth gnashed so hard they hurt, but she didn't use her free hand to gouge anybody's eyeballs. She thought Dax should at least appreciate the heroic proportions of that restraint, considering how incomprehensible Kira found the whole concept of passivity.

She estimated more than four dozen Klingons just within the sweep of her eyes, most of them drifting in menacing orbit around her, Dax, and Bashir. Another unseen handful held them all immobile. Bandages, rough splints, even a pair of crutches lashed together from twists of local wood. Nothing in sight like the massive injuries they'd left LeDonne and Heiser to tend at Gordek's camp, but also hardly representative of this encampment's entire populace. Although surrounded by the same tangled brush growth that had bordered the shoreline, this campsite was many times larger and obviously more permanent. What might have been trees, except that they'd been planted upside down, punctuated the huge clearing, dotting the edges and even marching a way into the brush. Klingons sat comfortably atop arching roots-that-should-have-been branches, emerged curiously from the cavernous hollows dug under the enormous barrel trunks, looked up from where they etched intricate symbols into the still-growing wood to expand on patterns already months—if not years—old.

A tall, white-haired female climbed with unhurried dignity from the depths of the largest tree-cavern. Her head plates braided into an elegant arch from the bridge of her nose to the peak of her skull, and hair that must have been longer than she stood tall had been coiled and woven into a regal coronet. Kira didn't think she'd ever seen a Klingon so obviously old, or so impressive.

Striding through the corridor that suddenly appeared before her in the press of bodies, the matriarch halted less than an arm's length from the prisoners to fold her hands in front of her polished bronze belt. She regarded them with aristocratic reproach. *"TlhIngan Hol Dajatlh'a'?"*

"Yes." Dax spoke up without waiting for either of the others to ask for a translation. "But my friends speak only Standard."

The Klingon measured Kira and Bashir together with a single flick of her eyes, the way a hunter casts off unnecessary tissue with a single sweep of his knife. "There is no honor in exploiting your enemy's confusion." She managed to convey a wealth of disdain, even in her graciousness. "I am Rekan, *epetai* of the House of Vrag."

Not the House of Gordek, Kira noticed, and was not too surprised by that.

Rekan *epetai* Vrag listened to Dax's introductions with an almost Vulcan stoicism, only tipping her head once with interest when the lieutenant commander said her own name. "You are a Trill."

Even Kira could tell that wasn't a question. Dax nodded.

"Were you once called by the host-name Curzon?"

The Trill seemed to weigh her answer carefully, studying Rekan's face as though looking for her words in that queenly sculpting of planes and angles. "I'm sorry," she said at last. "I'm sure Curzon would have remembered such a striking female."

If Rekan found the remark as condescendingly masculine as Kira did, she didn't show it. "I never had the honor of meeting Curzon Dax while he was among us. But he was said to be an extraordinary man." She delivered a short, glancing blow to whoever stood behind Kira, the way a *ghar*-wolf cuffs at its offspring. Just that quickly, the grip on Kira's throat and arm was released. Rekan *epetai* Vrag stepped back, but only far enough to prevent physical contact between herself and the outsiders, not far enough to suggest a retreat. "You have come to retrieve your soldier."

Kira glanced sideways at Dax, and was relieved to see the Trill more concerned with the health of her tricorder than her own rough handling. Bashir rubbed gingerly at one biceps, but seemed none the worse for wear. Neither of them seemed to have noticed the odd nature of that statement. Kira frowned and turned back toward the older Klingon female. "Soldier?"

"From your crashed ship," Rekan said calmly. "We have been waiting for you to come retrieve him."

"There's only one?" Bashir's dismay roughened his normally smooth voice. "There should have been over thirty, most of them scientists and older people."

The Klingon leader shook her majestically silvered head. "We have seen none of those. We have only one young male Human, wounded." Her mouth compressed in a smile that showed none of Gordek's aggressive baring of teeth. "And all he will tell us is his name, rank, and identification number. He says he is a communications officer. We assumed he was from a downed warship."

Kira frowned back at her. "He's from a Federation research vessel, sent here to observe the comet fall," she informed the exiled Klingon leader. "Your people shot it down."

"My people?" The Klingon matriarch lifted her chin in either interest or amusement, Kira wasn't sure which. "Look around you. We have no ability to shoot anyone down."

"But if it wasn't for you—"

Bashir interrupted with the sidelong scowl that Kira knew meant he'd had enough of unproductive truculence. "Can we have this discussion later, please? I'd like to see my patient."

"Ah." Rekan nodded as if something had been vaguely puzzling her but was now resolved. "You are a doctor. I understand now. Follow me."

Bashir did so without pause, leaving Kira hesitating in the center of the main exile colony. Dax gave her a wordless nod, but that didn't do much to reassure her. After all, this was the same Trill who thought coming down to this comet-battered planet was a once-in-a-lifetime treat. Still, when Dax swung past her to catch up to Rekan's long, purposeful strides, the barrage of hostile glances Kira could feel pouring out of the myriad hollows and caves was enough to speed her steps as she followed

Rekan Vrag had threaded her hands into her sleeves, a gesture that must have dated from a time when she wore the more elegantly draped robes of the Klingon military aristocracy. Somehow, even dressed in drab utilitarian brown, the gesture did not demean or humble her. "Enter," she said simply, pausing at the threshold of one small overhang. Kira's warning instincts rose to full clamor when she saw the featureless, dim interior. But when Dax snapped on a belt-lamp and used it to pick out the single slim figure huddled against the far wall, Kira was the next one in after Bashir. At least these Klingons had spared him the luxury of a blanket.

The survivor stirred when Bashir started his examination, his hands rising in a move Kira recognized as a standard defense technique taught at Starfleet Academy. She caught his hands back easily from Bashir's oblivious throat, feeling them shake with frustrated weakness between her own.

"It's all right," she said, hearing her voice drop to the crooning hush she'd used to soothe younger children in the camps during attacks. "You're safe."

"Safe." The young man licked dry lips, barely able to say the words past them. He peered up at her puzzledly, then his gaze moved to Bashir's familiar uniform and eased. "Starfleet . . . ?"

"That's right." It didn't seem worth pointing out that Kira was with the Bajoran military, not Starfleet. She suspected that just not being Klingon would have been enough to reassure him. "I'm Major Kira. This is Lieutenant Commander Dax and Dr. Bashir."

"I'm . . . my name's Alex, Alex Boughamer. How did you know I was here?"

Kira tossed a warning glance at Dax, inclining her head toward the tall and rail-thin shadow that still slanted across the mouth of this deep overhang. Dax nodded back at her soundlessly, then answered. "We picked up the *Victoria Adams*'s distress call at Deep Space Nine yesterday." She paused, carefully eying the pale face below them. "Alex, did anyone else survive?"

Boughamer startled Kira with a breathless chuckle. "Hell, *all* of us survived, Lieutenant. In fact, I'm the worst off. Captain Marsters packed us three deep in the sampling shuttle—you should have heard the geologists bitch about that—and one of the . . . " His drifting words sliced off abruptly, as if he'd just recollected that he was still among Klingons. " . . . um, an older guy among the passengers who used to be a pilot or something—he piloted us down. He was amazing. We took some bumps in the comet field—that's when the spectrometer fell on me—but otherwise we made it down pretty much in one piece. I couldn't believe it." His blue eyes sharpened to a more crystalline alertness as Bashir's bone regenerator skated across his ribs. "What about the *Vicky A,* Major? You said you got a distress call. Did she make it out okay?"

"We don't know," Dax said, in the gentle voice she usually reserved for hopeless causes and untimely deaths. "So far, there's no word."

Boughamer's face seemed to crumple in on itself for a moment, then firmed up again. "That's okay. We knew—Captain Marsters knew she might not make it. He just wanted to make sure we got away, and we did. He'd be glad about that."

They were silent for a moment, listening to the hum of the deep-tissue regenerator that Bashir scanned across Boughamer's abdomen. The daylight slanting in from outside seemed too bright, now that Kira's eyes had adjusted to the darkness. She restrained an urge to ask Rekan to step closer to the mouth of the overhang to provide more shade.

Dax touched Boughamer's shoulder to get back his drifting attention. "You said all the other survivors were alive. Where are they?"

"With the Klingons," he said simply.

Kira glanced out at Rekan's silhouetted figure and frowned. "*Which* Klingons? There's no one here but you."

Boughamer shook his head, then groaned and dropped his head back to the ground. "Not here. They caught us at the crash site and took us someplace far away. It was dark . . . we were in a cave, I think. Deeper and colder than this—more wind blowing through. But I don't know—" He started to shake his head again, but desisted when Bashir laid a gently restraining hand across his forehead. "They had me blindfolded part of the time, and I was passed out the other half. All I remember is waking up and being in some kind of vehicle—something that lurched a lot, like a big landhopper or all-terrain crawler. I was there for what seemed like forever, then I was here. That's all I know."

Kira fell silent again, this time in sizzling frustration over the lack of clues she could follow to the missing survivors. She lifted an eyebrow at Dax to see if the Trill had any other questions.

"Alex," Dax said, "the Klingons who found you after you crashed—what did they look like?"

"Was one of them a heavy guy, long black beard and hair?" Kira put in.

"No." Boughamer's eyes closed, but his voice sounded so much clearer now that Kira guessed he was doing it to better remember. "They were too young to be a ship's crew, no armor, nobody in charge. And they've lived there, wherever we were, for a while. I could smell that—the smoke smell and the food smells and the Klingon smells."

"Why did they take the rest of the crew and passengers back to the caves with them? Why didn't they bring them all here?" Bashir asked.

Boughamer's eyes flashed open, looking startled and oddly angry. "Didn't I tell you already?" He cursed when he saw their heads shake. "I'm sorry, I thought I had—I've been repeating it over and over in my head until I wasn't sure what I'd said and what I'd just thought. It's what they sent me here to tell you, it's *why* they sent me. They knew someone would come to look for us, and this is what they want you to do."

He took a deep breath, then launched himself into a message so singsong and practiced that its original Klingon cadences could scarcely be heard anymore. "You are from Starfleet who listen to this, and you have come to rescue your people from the comets. But there are people on this planet that you haven't come to rescue, and to us their lives are more valuable than these are to you. So we say to you, we who live on this planet and for this planet and with this planet, that we will not release these people of yours from the threat of the comets until you have released our people from it, too, forever. If you do not, then the comets will release us all." Boughamer's breath whistled out of him in near-exhaustion, but his eyes were already anxiously turning from Kira to Dax to Bashir. "I really said it that time, didn't I? I didn't just imagine that I did?"

"You really said it." It was a good thing at least one of the Trill's brains could still form words, because judging from the arrested expression on his face, Bashir had been thumped as speechless as Kira. "The rest of the survivors from the *Victoria Adams* are being held hostage by a group of Klingons. They'll be released only when we've managed to protect the entire planet from the comets. Otherwise—"

"—otherwise they hang on to the hostages until *sylshessa,"* Kira said grimly. "Until Armageddon, when everybody dies."

It was the mark of a mission going bad, Sisko thought ruefully, when your first instinct upon being hailed by your sector commander was to have your communications officer tell her you'd beamed down with your away team. Had it only been a few hours ago that he'd felt utterly confident that he could swoop into the Armageddon system, elude the Klingon blockade, beam up the survivors from the *Victoria Adams,* and be back at the station before Admiral Nechayev had finished conferring with her Vorta equivalents? Now that he was orbiting high above this comet-scorched planet, his sensors blinded by impact debris, his ship in imminent danger of detection by a returning Klingon blockade, and his away team stymied by Klingon ecological activists—of all the unlikely antagonists!—he wasn't sure Nechayev was even going to believe his progress report, much less endorse his continuing mission. And he could tell from the surreptitiously sympathetic glances he was getting from O'Brien and Worf that they shared all of his doubts.

With a resigned sigh, Sisko nodded at the young ensign who'd taken Dax's place on the bridge. "Put the admiral through."

"Captain Sisko." Interference from the comet field fuzzed the high-security channel, making Nechayev's image waver. As usual, though, the admiral's polished steel voice cut through the background hum with ease. "Do you know what's going on right now?"

"We're still trying to locate the survivors from the *Victoria Adams,"* he said. "We've gotten proof that most of them are alive, but—"

Nechayev waved his explanation to an unexpected stop, her carved face tightening with an emotion too cold to be anger and too tense to be irritation. "Let me update you on the larger situation. Twenty minutes ago, the *Victoria Adams*—and the Klingon ship she appeared to be traveling with—were destroyed by a Cardassian military outpost at KDZ-A17J. The Cardassians claim it was an act of self-defense."

"What?" The shout resounded so loudly around the *Defiant*'s bridge that Sisko knew it hadn't just been his voice raised in unconscious protest. "How could Captain Marsters attack a Cardassian outpost? The *Victoria Adams* wasn't armed!"

Nechayev frowned. "According to the Cardassians, Marsters came into the system at high speed and made a suicide run straight at their outpost. When they destroyed the *Victoria Adams* to prevent the impact, a cloaked Klingon vessel that was shadowing her—or pursuing her—returned their fire. The ensuing battle took down two Cardassian warships and half the station's defense system before the Klingons were destroyed."

Sisko whistled softly. He'd only met Marsters once, and although he'd been impressed with the research captain's intelligence and good judgement, he would never have expected a Vulcan Science Academy graduate to display such reckless courage in defense of his passengers and crew. "He deliberately incited that battle to keep the Klingons from returning here," he told Necheyev without hesitation. "He must have known it was the only way he could stop them."

Worf let out a rumble of Klingon respect. "That was the act of a great warrior."

"You know that, and I know that," Nechayev snapped back. "But all the Cardassians know is that they've been attacked by what looked like a joint Federation-Klingon force. It's taking all the diplomatic pressure we can muster to keep open war from breaking out all along the border."

"Look at the bright side," O'Brien offered. "At least we won't have to worry about the Klingon blockade for a while. They'll be so busy shoring up their border patrols—"

"I disagree," Worf interrupted. "If the Klingons blockading this system were willing to fire on an unarmed Starfleet vessel and pursue her into the teeth of a Cardassian outpost, there is something of immense importance to them in this system. I do not believe they will abandon it."

Nechayev's image fractured into hissing rainbow prisms as a chunk of cometary ice rebounded against the *Defiant*'s angled shields, then reformed into an ironic frown. "For once, our diplomatic corps agrees with you, Commander Worf. They tried to make some subtle inquiries about this KDZ-E25F planet of yours, but couldn't get their usual Klingon informants to spill so much as a word. The best guess our tactical analysts can make is that it was the site of some heroic Klingon military action in the Cardassian invasion."

"Unlikely," said Worf. "The only battlefields sacred to Klingons are those where a single warrior or ship held off an overwhelmingly superior force. The Cardassians were never that."

Nechayev's frown deepened. "Then what's *your* explanation, Commander? Do you really believe the Klingons are shooting down Federation science vessels just to keep the cometary fireworks show to themselves?"

"No." If he felt discomfited at having drawn the needling attention of their sector commander, Worf didn't show it in either voice or expression. "What we are seeing is most likely an internal Klingon dispute of some kind, with the *Victoria Adams* inadvertently caught in the middle. The presence of only a single house among the Klingons stranded on the planet—"

"*What* Klingons stranded on the planet?" Nechayev blinked in surprise.

Sisko cleared his throat to draw the transmitter's autofocus back to him. "I started to tell you that our crash survivors are being held hostage by one of three groups of Klingons who say they have been stranded on this planet."

Nechayev's eyes narrowed. "And the fact that all these stranded Klingons come from a single house makes you think they might be political exiles? Imprisoned in the neutral zone because of some power struggle in the Klingon High Command?"

"Yes." The glint of Worf's dark eyes now held surprise and discomfiture in equal quantities. Sisko could have told him not to underestimate Nechayev's intelligence. He might not always like her strategic decisions, but he had to admit that the admiral had a raptor-swift grasp of salient facts. "However, since we do not yet know why or how these Klingons came to be marooned here, I cannot speculate as to the exact nature of the dispute."

Nechayev's thin, pale brows arched. "It could be anything. With all the recent unrest and turmoil he just quelled in the Klingon High Council, Chancellor Gowron could be unwilling to let *any* hint of internal dissension get out."

"Agreed," said Worf. "It will thus be a point of great honor to the

Klingons to keep the blockade manned, to prevent the dishonored ones from escaping their sentence of exile."

"Which is now," Sisko pointed out, "a sentence of death."

"Because of the comet disintegration." Nechayev followed his logic as easily as she had followed Worf's. "Are the Klingons demanding evacuation to safe haven in return for releasing the crash survivors?"

"No." Sisko tried to mask the exasperation in his voice, but suspected he didn't do a very good job. "Most want us to just leave them alone to die. A few want us to give them enough technology to let them survive the bombardment. But the ones who actually have custody of the survivors from the *Victoria Adams* want us to save the entire planetary ecosystem by sweeping the comet debris out of the system."

Sisko had rarely seen Admiral Nechayev taken by surprise, and never seen her speechless. Until now. The arctic blue of her eyes glittered at him for a long moment, but only the background sizzle and thrum of small ice particles vaporizing off their shields filled the stunned silence.

"The Klingons want you to protect the planet they were stranded on against their will?" Her words were so filled with disbelief that they sizzled almost as much as the melting ice. *"Why?"*

Sisko took a deep breath. "We don't know. We haven't even made direct contact with them yet. So far, my away team has gotten all of its information from the *Victoria Adams*'s communications officer. He was sent to the main exile camp to deliver the ultimatum, but he was wounded too badly to identify where he was brought from. Major Kira and Commander Dax are interrogating the other Klingon exiles now in an attempt to locate where this splinter group might be hiding."

"Do they really think the other Klingons will betray them?"

"They might, if Dax can convince them it's the honorable thing to do. Even if she can't, we can always divert a few of the oncoming fragments, to convince them of our good intentions for long enough to evacuate the crash survivors. After that—"

"After that, it's not our problem," Nechayev said bluntly. "Are we absolutely sure the rest of the *Victoria Adams* crew and passengers are still alive?"

"Yes." He wasn't, but had a feeling it wouldn't be wise to admit that to Nechayev.

"Then your orders, Captain, are to negotiate their release as soon as possible. If you don't succeed before the Klingons reestablish their blockade, I suggest you clear the area at that time."

"You *suggest?"* Sisko cocked a startled look at his commander. "You're not making that an order?"

Nechayev grimaced. "God knows, I'd like to. I'd rather not lose the best ship in my sector—not to mention the entire staff of a space station that isn't exactly the most requested post in Starfleet—over a few damned chunks of comet." She fell silent and her lips tightened, as if it was difficult for her to decide how to phrase the next part of her transmission. "There is a retired officer among the tourist party who under no circumstances must fall into the hands of the Klingon High Council. *Under—no—circumstances."* She repeated it with enough emphasis to make Sisko's eyebrows lift.

"Can you tell me—"

"No," said Nechayev flatly. "Even the knowledge of his whereabouts is classified information. If the Federation Diplomatic Service ever found out that he risked his life just to see some comets crash into KDZ-E26—I mean E25—"

"We've been calling it Armageddon," Odo informed her.

"Appropriate," said Nechayev dryly. "Considering the hell there's going to be to pay if we lose the *Defiant* as well as the *Victoria Adams* there. Not to mention starting a three-way war between the Federation, the Cardassian Empire, and the Klingons."

"But if we manage to evade the Klingon blockade long enough to rescue our crash survivors—" Sisko let the sentence trail off, eyeing his commander closely for signs of disapproval.

The admiral regarded him with cold eyes, but allowed an ironic slice of smile to appear. "In that case, Captain, I might just be willing to overlook your blatant disregard for my opinion."

Sisko nodded. "Understood."

Nechayev reached forward to cut the contact, then paused to give him a last icy look. "One more thing. If you get a confirmed report from your away team that the *Victoria Adams*'s survivors have been killed, either by comet impact or by your Klingon activists, I want you out of that death trap immediately. And *that*'s an order."

Sisko scowled up at the viewscreen for a long moment after the admiral's image snapped out of existence, but it wasn't the dusty skies of Armageddon that were aggravating him. He now had breathing space in which to find a solution to his unexpected hostage crisis, but it was breathing space with an enormous price tag attached. What he needed was a way to protect the scorched planet below him from further cometary damage, and he needed it soon enough to get his crash survivors freed before the *Defiant* started an interplanetary war.

"Commander Worf," Sisko said abruptly. "If we angle and disperse our shields to sweep up as many comets as possible, how many trips across the debris tail will we have to make to protect the planet from impact for the next few days?"

The Klingon officer tapped a query into Dax's piloting console and scowled at the results. "Approximately two hundred and seventeen," he said unhappily. "The maneuver will take almost two days to complete."

"Too slow," O'Brien warned. "And too risky. There's bound to be a couple of comets that sneak past us while we're sweeping up the rest."

"And if a Klingon ship arrives to resume the blockade, there's too much chance they'll catch us only partially shielded. That's not good enough." Sisko strode up and down the length of the bridge, ignoring the wary look he got from his replacement science officer. No doubt the young man was wondering if his commanding officer's legendary temper was about to erupt. "We need another strategy, gentlemen, and we need it fast. We have to convince those Klingons down there that we're making good on our promise—"

"—without actually making good on it?" Odo lifted a caustic eyebrow.

Sisko favored his security officer with an impatient look. "Constable, if you have a better way to get rid of all those comets out there—"

"Why don't we just shoot them?"

It could have been a mocking question, but the steady intensity of Odo's gaze told Sisko he was serious. He paused with his mouth half-open to snap a dismissive reply, then slanted a glance at his chief tactical officer. "Is that feasible?"

This time, Worf didn't have to consult the computer to answer. "There is a limit to how wide a spread we can achieve without losing the ability to vaporize, but cometary ice has such low density that it does not present a significant constraint. However, when any kind of debris is clustered this closely in space, phaser beams tend to be diffracted by the leading edge and leave the interior of the debris cloud untouched."

"So we can't do broad-beam destruction," Sisko concluded. "What about point and shoot?"

"Selecting just the largest and most threatening fragments?" Worf nodded as if to answer his own question. "If we keep the phaser beam narrowly focused, it will not diffract. We can target almost any fragment in the tail for destruction."

Sisko grunted. "Then all we need to know is which fragments have the highest probability of impacting with the planet's surface." He paused, glancing over at the young ensign manning the science station. "Ensign Farabaugh?" he prodded, when he got no response.

"Sir?" The young man glanced back at him worriedly, alert but obviously unsure of exactly what was needed.

Sisko tried not to let too much impatience show in his voice. It wasn't Farabaugh's fault that Dax would have already realized what he wanted and programmed her scan accordingly. "Have the computer mark and track all fragments with an eighty-five percent probability of impact over the next five days. Concentrate on the most dangerous fragments—the large ones within a ten thousand kilometer range."

"Aye, sir." Looking relieved to be assigned a specific task, Farabaugh bent over his console, punching in the scanning parameters. "Um—I'll probably need to run a probabilistic vector model to account for fragment interactions. First results might take about seven minutes."

"Very well." Sisko swung back to eye the remainder of his bridge crew, smiling for the first time in what seemed like a long while. He always felt better when he had some immediate goal to pursue. "I think we could all stand to brush up on our manual track-and-fire skills, don't you, Commander? Who wants to go first?"

"Not me," Odo assured him. "I don't find blowing up inanimate objects as pleasurable an activity as you humanoids appear to."

"That's all right, Constable. I need you to keep an eye on the entire system, watching for ion trails." Sisko glanced over his shoulder. "Ready with tracking coordinates, Mr. Farabaugh?"

"Almost, sir. I still need to plot—" The young science officer broke off, staring down at something on his screen. "Captain Sisko, we've just been hailed by a Cardassian battle cruiser! I'm putting it on-screen now."

The dust-stained oceans of Armageddon vanished, replaced by a deeply furrowed Cardassian face. "Captain Sisko of the U.S.S. *Defiant,* this is *Gul* Hidret of the Cardassian war-cruiser *Olxinder.*" It was unusual to see such an elderly soldier still serving as a *gul,* but the shrewd glitter in Hidret's eyes told Sisko he wasn't dealing with some political appointee or recalled reserve officer. "If you wish to avoid a conflict, please acknowledge this hail at once."

Sisko flexed his fingers on the arms of his command chair, hard enough to feel the duranium core beneath the padding. "Whatever you do, Mr. Farabaugh," he said through his teeth, "do *not* acknowledge that hail." He swung to scowl at Odo. "Constable, why the hell didn't you detect the Cardassians' arrival in the system?"

"For the very good reason that they haven't arrived yet," the Changeling shot back, unintimidated. "There are no uncloaked vessels present within the entire scanning range of my sensors."

"The communicator signal's red-shift indicates the Cardassians are hailing us from at least eighteen light-years out," Farabaugh volunteered. "It's so distant, I can't even tell for sure if they're heading our way or not."

Sisko's scowl swung back to the image of *Gul* Hidret, now waiting in confident silence for a reply. "Then how in God's name did they detect our presence?"

"They didn't," O'Brien said. "They're beaming a directed wide-cast over the entire Armageddon system. They just suspect we're here." The engineer looked up from his console, baffled. "What I want to know is how they learned our travel plans. That information sure didn't come from Starfleet."

"No doubt Cardassian High Command has its sources." Sisko tapped a reflective finger across his chin, debating pros and cons. Although it was tempting to remain silent and shatter *Gul* Hidret's smug sureness about the *Defiant*'s presence here, this wasn't a decision he could entrust to gut feelings. "Gentlemen, give me your opinions," he said abruptly. "Do we respond or not?"

Odo turned to give him a quizzical look. "Our orders from Admiral Nechayev were to refrain from starting a war. I assume that means she'd prefer that no one know we're here. Am I missing something?"

"The fact that the Cardassians already *know* we're here," O'Brien retorted. "If we don't warn them away, they might tangle with the Klingon blockade and start the war that way."

"True," agreed Worf. "But I do not advise we reply. The Cardassian battle cruiser is at least eighteen hours away, but there may be other Cardassian ships in the area who can backtrack our communications signal."

Sisko let out a frustrated breath. "And I want to know what *Gul* Hidret is up to. Deadlock."

Ensign Farabaugh cleared his throat, looking tentatively back and forth between them. "Would it help if we could respond to the Cardassians with a ricochet signal?"

Sisko swung to face his youngest bridge officer. "A signal that can't be traced back to the *Defiant?* Can you do that?"

He got a shy grin in response. "With all the comets around here, Captain? No problem. The signal quality will degrade a lot when it bounces, but it should still get through."

"Do it." Sisko turned back to face the waiting image of *Gul* Hidret, summoning up all his self-control for the next few minutes. "Notify me when we're on-line."

"Hang on, sir, I'm working out a three-way bounce . . . scanning for target . . . All right, we're connected. Go ahead, Captain."

"Gul Hidret of the *Olxinder,* this is Captain Benjamin Sisko of the *Defiant.* Can you read me?"

"Barely." Judging from the squeal of feedback and the way Hidret squinted at his viewscreen, the Cardassian wasn't lying. "Are you engaged in battle with the Klingons?"

Sisko lifted one eyebrow, knowing the gesture probably couldn't be detected by his counterpart. Had there been a slightly hopeful tone in that question? "We're just experiencing some cometary interference, *Gul* Hidret. What do you want?"

"To save Cardassia," Hidret snapped back, brusquely enough to make Sisko's gut tighten with apprehension. When a *gul* dispensed with sly innuendo and circumspect hints, you knew you were in trouble. "We know the system you are in is under Klingon control. If you aren't fighting them, I'll have to assume you're in league with them and proceed accordingly."

Sisko grimaced. "*Gul* Hidret, there *are* no Klingons in this system right now." Sisko ignored Worf's frown and Odo's disapproving look. He knew a Federation diplomat would probably have fainted to hear him dish out that information so generously, but there was a method to his madness. "And our own presence here is only temporary. As soon as we locate some Federation crash survivors—"

"—you'll abandon the system?" *Gul* Hidret snorted in deep suspicion, the lines in his face deepening. "Forgive me if I doubt you. The Federation *cannot* be ignorant of the reason the Klingons have set up a blockade around such a worthless old scar of a planet."

"You mean the political exiles they stranded here?"

That innocent question turned the engraved lines in the old Cardassian's face from crevasses to ravines. "So they say! If you ask me, it's just an convenient excuse to claim they control the system."

Sisko exchanged baffled looks with his bridge crew. None of them, not even Odo, looked as if the *gul*'s comment made any more sense to them than it did to Sisko. But the shrewd glint of dark eyes on the screen assured him that, no matter how preposterous his story sounded, this old officer wasn't senile yet.

"*Gul* Hidret, you just finished telling us how worthless this planet is. Why would the Klingons need an excuse to claim it?"

That got him the bared teeth of a more normally unctuous Cardassian smile. "I expect because it's the source of all Cardassia's *geset.*" Even through the bounced and fuzzy signal, he must have seen Sisko's incomprehension. "It is the only known cure for *ptarvo* fever, a disease that decimates our young," he elaborated. "And it's only available in quantity from that dead and blasted planet you now orbit."

That comment, so apparently reasonable on the surface, sparked a snort of pure derision from Odo. Sisko shot him a quick glance, and the Changeling emphasized his skepticism by smacking a palm down to cut the audio channel on his communications board before he spoke.

"*Gul* Hidret is either a remarkably incompetent liar, or doesn't have much respect for our intelligence," he told the captain bluntly.

"What makes you say that, Constable?"

"*Ptarvo* fever is a colloquial term for the first stirrings of *paltegen* hormones in young Cardassian males. What Humans might call 'spring fever.' " Odo inclined his head at the *gul,* now mouthing unheard words at the viewscreen. "He's hiding something."

Sisko grunted, and motioned him to open the audio channel again. He didn't waste any time responding to the *gul*'s indignant accusations. "If *ptarvo* fever is such an emergency, why aren't you bringing a scientific and medical ship to study the *geset* and learn how to synthesize it? Why send in a military vessel?"

Hidret heaved a patently exaggerated sigh. "Precisely what we were planning to do, Captain, before the Klingons arrived and set up their illegal blockade. Since then, the Empire has been biding its time, hoping the Klingons would leave—but finding out that the Federation is now on the side of our old enemies was too much. The High Command decreed that it was time to intervene, before the vital secret of *geset* was lost to us forever."

"We're not on the side of the Klingons," Sisko said impatiently. "In fact, we couldn't be further from it."

"Then why have they allowed you to stay in a system that they have chased all of our scouts and warships away from?"

Sisko groaned. That was exactly the kind of flawed reasoning that could lead to military confrontation. But how could he correct Hidret's assumptions without opening up awkward questions about his own foolhardy presence in this system? Somehow, he didn't think Nechayev would approve of telling the Cardassian High Command about the strategically important Starfleet veteran who had crashed with the other survivors.

Fortunately, Worf took that decision out of his hands. "Why do you think the Klingons on the planet are not truly exiles?"

"Because when we first detected their presence, we offered to evacuate them," *Gul* Hidret retorted. "And they flatly refused. If they had been sent to that comet-blasted planet against their will, why would they not want to leave?"

Worf's low rumble echoed across the squealing feedback from the bounced signal. "It is a matter of honor. That is why you cannot possibly understand it."

"Ah, the excuse Klingons always use to disguise their covert activities!" Hidret snapped back. "I feel confident that whatever those so-called exiles are doing on that planet, it is far from honorable—and it is probably aimed at destroying the Cardassian Empire!"

"And I feel confident that you are lying through your teeth," muttered Worf, before Sisko waved him into silence.

Fortunately, the squeals of feedback must have distorted the tactical officer's words enough to mask them. *Gul* Hidret screwed his face into a squint again. "What did you say?"

Sisko took a deep breath. A reckless plan, kindled from equal parts desperation and cynicism, had assembled itself in his brain while Worf and the *gul* had been talking. He saw no reason to delay putting it into action. "I said you can easily discover whether those exiles are working against your government. Why don't you ask them to let you harvest *geset* in return for protecting them against the comets that are hitting the planet? Your battle cruiser's big enough to sweep the debris away just by recalibrating and diffusing your shields. That way, even if the exiles refused your terms, you would at least protect your source of *geset* from destruction."

"*What?*" He couldn't tell if it was anger, loathing, or just sheer surprise that bleached out Hidret's face to the color of old wax, but the reaction was even more vehement than he'd expected. "You expect me to de-power my shields and risk the safety of my ship just to save the lives of some *Klingons?*"

"No," Sisko said silkily. "I expect you to risk your ship to save the lives of your children."

The old Cardassian's face tightened, showing stubborn bones beneath his sagging wrinkles, but he gave no other sign of having had his bluff called. "A valiant try, Captain. Unlike Klingons, you Humans do occasionally manage to create battle strategies almost devious enough to be interesting. But your attempt to render me helpless is a little on the transparent side. If I agreed to play janitor to your cometary debris, no doubt I'd soon find myself under attack from you and your Klingon allies."

Sisko didn't bother to deny that, since he was sure his Klingon "allies" would have been only too happy to fulfill Hidret's prophecy. "Then I strongly suggest you keep away from this system, *Gul* Hidret."

"And tell your children with *ptarvo* fever to try a cold shower instead of *geset,*" Odo added, in an even more sardonic voice than usual.

"So much for Federation mercy and fairness!" All pretense of affability vaporized under a boiling rage that turned Hidret's wrinkled face copper brown. "We will see who ends up in control of this system in the end, after the Klingons return and find you in it!"

Sisko smiled, buoyed up by the grim satisfaction of having forced a Cardassian to admit to something resembling the truth. "Ah, but don't forget," he said pleasantly. "The Klingons are now our allies."

With one last howl that could have been retransmitted static or pure Cardassian rage, the connection between them went black. Sisko took a deep breath, then glanced across at Odo. "Well, Constable? Does *Gul* Hidret really think we're allied with the Klingons?"

Odo's face might not have been very expressive, but he made up for that by the depth of disgust he could express in a single snort. "What *Gul* Hidret thinks is that we're going to get massacred by the Klingon blockade. Right now, he's just positioning himself to come in after the battle's over."

"Then let us hope he miscalculates and arrives early," Worf said fiercely. "Because if there is a choice between us and the Cardassians when the Klingon blockade reforms, I know which of us will be the first target."

CHAPTER 4

In his long years of Starfleet Service, Benjamin Sisko had seen sulfur ice moons torn apart and neutron stars lashed into turmoil by passing cosmic strings. As a young ensign, he'd once watched a red giant star go nova; as a much older and wiser commander, he'd not only discovered the Bajoran wormhole, but had been the first Human to travel through it. In all his years and parsecs of passage through the galaxy, however, he'd never seen the effects of a comet impact on a Class-M planet.

Until now.

There had not even been a flare of comet tail across the field of the *Defiant*'s vision to alert them. Five minutes after *Gul* Hidret's apoplectic face had cut to black and Ensign Farabaugh had hurriedly transferred Armageddon's rusty image back up on the viewscreen, a brilliant white explosion spasmed over the planet's sea-covered northern pole. Sisko jerked back from the glare, even though he knew they were orbiting far above the planet's stratosphere. He swung instinctively toward the weapons console. "Report!"

"Sensors have detected a seventeen gigajoule explosion at planetary coordinates seventy-three point five by one-twenty-four point nine," his security officer said. "The radiation signal shows only natural thermal decay, no evidence of ionized plasma or radioactivity."

"That's a comet impact." O'Brien sent Sisko a grim look from engineering. "And it's only a few hundred kilometers from our away team at the main Klingon outpost."

"Four-hundred-and-ninety-seven kilometers, to be precise," Worf clarified in a stiffly proper voice. "However, vital signs on all away team members appear stable."

Sisko didn't bother asking why the Klingon had programmed that information—ordinarily the responsibility of the *Defiant*'s science officer—to route through his piloting console. Instead, he turned his frown on Dax's young replacement. "Ensign Farabaugh, I asked you to locate the most threatening fragments in the cometary field. What happened?"

"Nothing, sir."

Worf slewed around at his pilot's station to bestow an even fiercer scowl on the young man. "Seventeen gigajoules is equivalent to the force of nine photon torpedoes! Would you call that nothing if *you* were down on that planet?"

Farabaugh's eyes widened slightly, but his sincere look never wavered. "The explosion was thirty-seven kilometers up in the atmosphere, Commander Worf. I doubt our away team even heard a rumble of thunder from it."

"Lucky for them," O'Brien commented. "And for us. What are the odds the one comet we miss intercepting is the one that explodes prematurely?"

"We didn't miss that comet, sir," Farabaugh said in mild surprise. "The computer noted its trajectory ten minutes ago, while the captain was talking to *Gul* Hidret. It just didn't trigger an alarm."

Sisko lifted an eyebrow at his young science officer. "You knew that fragment was going to disintegrate too high to cause any damage? How?"

"Relative velocity, sir." Farabaugh punched a series of commands into his science console, and the fading afterglow of the comet impact on Armageddon disappeared. The starless black screen that replaced it told Sisko this was a computer simulation, rather than a real sensor view. Multicolored streaks swam and spiraled across the black background like minnows in a chaotic school, leaving faint, glowing trails behind them. "After I scanned the comet field to find the ones most likely to collide with Armageddon, I ran impact simulations for each of them. You can see from the white and blue streaks that most of the ice fragments are moving at extremely or moderately high velocity relative to the orbital motion of Armageddon."

"And those are the most threatening ones?" O'Brien guessed.

"Actually, no, sir. Any comets that hit the planet's atmosphere fast are subjected to enormous crushing forces. Given the low density of cometary ice, almost all the fast-moving fragments detonate high in the stratosphere. Only the ones over seventy kilometers in diameter will survive long enough to affect the surface." Farabaugh tapped another command into his panel, and a few dozen comet fragments lit up in reds and yellows. "These are the dangerous fragments—the ones that are either big enough or slow enough to survive their passage through the atmosphere. They're the ones we have to worry about."

"Will they also crash into the planet with no warning?" Worf demanded.

Odo sent him a sardonic glance. "Comets are not Klingon warriors, Commander. You can hardly expect them to issue a proper challenge before they attack."

"No." Despite his agreement, however, Sisko noticed the Klingon sat scowling up at the screen, as if he could somehow intimidate the comets into more honorable behavior.

"How much leeway do we have before an impact event, Mr. Farabaugh?" Sisko asked.

"I've programmed the computer to issue a priority-one alarm half an hour before each projected impact." The young science officer glanced back at him uncertainly. "Will that be long enough?"

"That depends on what preventive action we're going to take." Odo glanced across at Sisko. "Which was what I believe we were discussing before we were so rudely interrupted by the Cardassians."

"I don't think there's much left to discuss." Sisko sat back in his command chair and steepled his fingers. "Phasers are ready and the coast is clear. Which of these comets do you want us to shoot first, Mr. Farabaugh?"

"Um—actually, Captain, there's something I wanted to tell you about that." The young officer cleared his throat diffidently. "I'd rather we didn't shoot any of them, if you don't mind."

Sisko saw Worf turn to scowl again at the beleaguered ensign, and waved the Klingon into fuming silence. "All right, Mr. Farabaugh. Explain."

"Actually, sir, I think I know what he means," O'Brien said before Farabaugh could gather himself together. "We learned about this in planetary engineering. If you explode a comet that's threatening to strike a planet, all you do is increase the area of devastation by turning it from one big impactor into a whole bunch of medium-sized ones."

"Exactly," Farabaugh said, looking relieved. "The destruction quotient goes up anywhere from four to ten times, depending on the number of fragments and their trajectories. And since a phaser blast would tend to selectively refract through cracks and fissures in the comet, it would be almost impossible not to break it into fragments."

Worf's scowl faded into a more thoughtful frown. "What if we increased dispersion and decreased intensity on the phasers? That should vaporize the whole comet even if it breaks apart."

"Except it will also create a radiating impulse wave that will disturb other comets in the cloud into new orbits," O'Brien said. "Which means we might add one or two more major threats for every one we remove."

"And there's no way to know that without running the tracking program all over again every time we vaporize," added Farabaugh.

"Too risky. We might bunt a comet at the planet before we even knew we did it." Sisko tapped his steepled fingers against his chin, considering his rapidly dwindling alternatives. "Well, the one thing we agree on is that we can't just sit here and let Armageddon happen. So we'll have to find something we *can* do." He shot an inquiring glance at his chief engineer. "You must remember something else from that planetary engineering class of yours, Chief. What were the recommended ways of dealing with an imminent comet impact?"

"Deflection by modulated photon torpedo blast," O'Brien said promptly. "The idea was not to break it up, just alter its trajectory enough to turn the hit into a miss."

"And the photon blast probably stripped off just enough of the dust mantle to vaporize a layer of interior ice," Farabaugh guessed. "Then the gas spurt would push the comet in the opposite direction."

"Right." O'Brien waved a hand at the multitude of colored streaks on the main viewscreen. "The problem is, there's a lot more red and yellow blobs up there than we have torpedoes. And even quantum torpedoes aren't strong enough to reach more than one or two comets at a time."

"Can we achieve the same effect by modulating our phaser array?" Worf demanded.

The chief engineer shook his sandy head. "We'd have to remodulate it for each blast, and you know how many hours that would take."

"Not to mention the fact that it would make the phasers inoperable for defensive purposes," Odo commented. "And considering that I've just detected the ion trail of a cloaked vessel entering the system—"

"Location, velocity, estimated size?" Sisko demanded. For all the implicit trust he felt in Odo and Kira, there were times when the captain would have given anything for them to have had Starfleet training. "Extrapolated destination?"

Odo scanned his panel. "Cloaked vessel is currently two-hundred-and-fifty thousand kilometers out from system center, traveling at seventy-five percent impulse speed and slowing rapidly. It appeared to be a *Jfolokh*-class vessel, but with the ion trail dissipating as it slows, the computer can't be sure. Extrapolated destination is an equatorial orbit around Armageddon." He looked up at Sisko. "If I had to guess, Captain, I'd say the Klingon blockade was back in town."

Sisko grunted. "Mr. Worf, notify the away team that from now on, all communications are on secure channels only. And tell them they either beam up soon or not for a while." He turned toward his chief engineer. "I don't care how you do it, Chief, but I want the *Defiant*'s emissions down as close to zero as you can manage for the next few hours. I don't want those Klingons to get even a sniff of our presence here until we've located the survivors and are ready to beam them out."

O'Brien grimaced. "I don't know about zero, sir. I can recirculate the ship's thermal output and put a magnetic bottle around our warp exhaust, but there's not too much I can do about the diffuse ionization off the shields. And with all the comets bumbling through our current orbit—"

"—we can't turn shields off," Sisko finished for him. "But we may be able to lower the transfer charge without compromising our deflection capacity. Do the best you can, Chief."

"Aye, sir." O'Brien scrambled out of his chair, pausing only long enough to tap open his direct channel down to the Engineering deck. "Frantz, cap the warp exhaust, *now.* Ornsdorf and Frisinger, start recycling our waste heat through the impulse baffles to equalize it with ambient."

"Aye, sir." The competent calmness of that reply was so obviously modeled after O'Brien's own legendary composure that Sisko had to smile. "Desired delta on the heat output?"

"As close to planetary infrared output as possible," O'Brien said. "And

I'm coming down to recalibrate the power circuits for the shields, so get all those lines stripped and ready for modulation."

"Aye, sir."

Satisfied that his ship was going to be as invisible as any able-bodied vessel could be, Sisko turned his attention back to Worf. "Any response from the away team, Commander?"

The Klingon's glum look told him the answer before he even began to speak. "Dr. Bashir says he is not finished evaluating casualties among the new Klingon encampment, Captain. They appear to have experienced at least three impact events, although none were as direct and damaging as the one that affected the first settlement. He has asked me to beam Ensign LeDonne into the new camp to aid him."

"Is the Klingon ship still out of short-range sensor detection limit?" Sisko asked his security officer. When Odo assented with a grunt, he nodded his approval back to Worf. "Tell the doctor this will be his last chance to reassign his team, or to beam any Klingons aboard for medical treatment. What progress have the others made in locating the hostages?"

"Commander Dax has sent a full report on the interrogations she and Major Kira have conducted so far, but says they have been unable to convince any among this group of exiles to cooperate with them as Gordek did. She is no closer to identifying who the hostage-takers are, much less what their location might be. She has also transmitted the data she has collected on the planet's environmental conditions, to be attached to your logs."

"Hmm." Rather than reassuring him, that news made Sisko's skin crawl with apprehension. The only time Dax went out of her way to keep him informed of her scientific discoveries was when she thought she might not be coming back to explain them in glorious detail herself. "Keep a high-security communications channel available for the away team to use at all times, Mr. Worf. And keep a close eye on their vital signs. We still don't know if the exiles they're dealing with are any more trustworthy than the ones who found the *Victoria Adams.*"

Worf grunted curt approval of that policy. "I have already programmed an automated linkage between the shields and the main transporter controls. We can have the away team aboard with only a moment's loss in defensive capability."

"Good work, Commander." Sisko saw the irritated look Ensign

Farabaugh threw Worf, and shook his head warningly at the younger man. It was true that Worf's preemptive action had usurped some of the science officer's traditional responsibilities, but the end result was all that mattered right now, not how it was achieved. He distracted Farabaugh with a wave of his hand at the viewscreen. "As long as we've got a computer simulation running up there, can we add the Klingons' estimated course-heading to it?"

"Yes, sir. All I need is the tracking data from Mr. Odo's station."

"I'm transferring it to you now. And for your information, young man, I am not *Mister* Odo."

"Yes, sir. Sorry, sir." Farabaugh ducked his head over his panel, and, a moment later, a bright green disk appeared at the far edge of the viewscreen. Even if he hadn't known it was the ion-trace of the cloaked Klingon vessel, Sisko's space-trained eyes would have been caught by its unusual rate of deceleration and its erratic slalom swings through the comet field. "The Klingon vessel isn't deflecting the comet debris, Captain," Farabaugh said unnecessarily. "It's taking evasive action."

"I can see that." Sisko could admire the fierce jerks and swoops of the unknown vessel, even while he pitied any Klingons aboard with weak stomachs. No inertial dampener in the galaxy could cope with shifts that rapid. "Interpretation, Mr. Worf?"

"I am not sure, Captain." Worf squinted up at the screen as if he could visualize the Klingon ship better that way. "Perhaps they are practicing battle maneuvers. If so, they are not standard ones."

"If I didn't know any better," Odo said drily, "I would say they were out glee-riding."

"Glee-riding?" Worf repeated.

"It's what Bajoran adolescents call careening as close as they can to the rocks when they're out ice-sailing. Personally, I call it trying to kill themselves just for the fun of it."

Watching the green disk swing wildly out of its way to needle between two closely orbiting comet fragments, Sisko had to admit that Odo's description did seem apt. "If that really is a *Jfolokh*-class vessel, it's running damn close to its operating tolerances. The pilot's either very good or very foolish."

"Or both," Worf said grimly. "I find it difficult to believe that this ship has been sent to resume the official Klingon embargo."

"They don't know that we're here," Sisko reminded him. "And they've probably sent all their better ships to man the Cardassian border. No matter how it's getting here, it's certainly headed for the orbit I'd expect a blockading ship to take up."

"True." Worf glanced back over his shoulder. "In that case, sir, I suggest continuous passive scanning to be sure the Klingon vessel does not attempt to beam anyone to or from the planet surface."

Sisko nodded at Farabaugh. "Do it. And monitor their communications, too. I doubt they'll be saying much on open channels, but it never hurts to listen."

"Aye, sir."

The green disk that was the cloaked Klingon vessel made one last swashbuckling swoop around a spiraling comet fragment, then settled reluctantly on station around the glowing amber sphere representing Armageddon in the computer simulation. Sisko lifted an eyebrow, noticing that the skimmed comet fragment had been blasted into a different direction by the encounter with the Klingon's warp exhaust.

"Looks like you'd better rerun your impact prediction model, too, Mr. Farabaugh," he said. "After all those close encounters with the Klingons—" He broke off, sitting straighter in his command chair. *"That's* what we can do!"

Odo gave him a caustic look. "Have a close encounter with the Klingons?"

"No—with any comet that looks like it's going to hit the planet." Sisko leaped out of his chair and began pacing, trying to gather together his whirling thoughts. "We'll have to uncap our warp core exhaust, at least long enough to alter the orbit of the fragment we want to intercept. It's either that or vent some of the thermal waste stored in the impulse engines."

"Either way, we would leave a clear trail for the Klingons to see," Worf pointed out. The tactical officer did not sound negative, just thoughtful. "If we plotted our course carefully, however, we could use the planet's gravitational field to loop us toward the comet with just a one- or two-second impulse thrust. Then we would only need to graze the comet with our angled shields in order to deflect it."

Farabaugh looked up from his science console. "Can we plot a course that won't affect the other comets in the field, Commander? That way, our collision models won't need to be rerun every time we interfere."

"We can if we wait until the comet is just about to enter Armageddon's gravity well." Sisko came to a halt in front of the viewscreen and pointed at the halo of clear space around the planet. "All we'll need to do is adjust the velocity of our circumpolar orbit to be sure we're close to the comet's projected entry point."

Odo snorted. "And you don't think the Klingons will notice when a comet suddenly bounces off of empty space?"

"Not if they are on the opposite side of the planet at the time," Worf said simply.

"But that means solving some intricate orbital mechanics equations—" Sisko came to a halt in the center of his bridge, stymied once again by the absence of Dax at the science station. There was no way he could expect a single-brained human to do all the monitoring, modeling, and scanning his Trill science officer could have handled with ease. "Mr. Farabaugh, who else on the *Defiant*'s crew has had science officer training?"

"Um—well, I went to the Academy with Ensign Osgood down in the main weapons bay, sir. I know she aced all her celestial mechanics courses. And I think there's an engineering tech named Thornton who did a stint on a science research vessel. He's also an expert on sensor systems."

"Good. Contact Thornton and tell him to come up and man your station. His job will be to scan the Klingons and report back to you on any changes in their orbit. You and Osgood commandeer one of the science labs and a sector of the main computer, and set up a full-scale model of the comet belt. I don't just want to know when every comet's going to hit this planet, I want to know far enough in advance to adjust our orbit, so we can intersect and deflect it while it's still on the Klingon's blind side. Is that clear?"

"Aye, sir!"

"I want your first report by—" Sisko glanced at the shipboard clock to estimate a reasonable deadline, and only then realized why his eyes felt like he was squinting past sand. From the time they'd left Deep Space Nine yesterday until now, he'd put in seventeen straight hours on duty. And so had the rest of his original bridge crew, with the exception of Odo, who had been forced to return to his cabin and regenerate several hours ago. "—oh-three-hundred hours. Odo, you have the conn. Commander Worf, call up replacements for your station and Chief O'Brien's."

He got the scowl he'd expected from the Klingon. "Captain—"

"No buts, Mr. Worf," Sisko said crisply. "I refuse to take the *Defiant* slow-dancing with comets unless my pilot is fit and rested. Report back to the bridge by oh-four-hundred. I assume we won't be looking to deflect any impacts before then, Mr. Farabaugh?"

"No, sir."

"Unless the Klingons start up some target practice of their own." Odo's ability to find a cloud in every silver lining would have amused Sisko if his chief of security wasn't right so depressingly often.

"Let's hope that doesn't happen, Constable." Sisko cast a sardonic look at the viewscreen. "Although if our glee-riding friends over there do decide to start shooting, with any luck they'll either be too drunk or too motion-sick to aim straight."

The first dull crash jerked Kira's head around so fast she nearly tumbled off the tall root she'd been straddling. A puff of dust—or dislodged vapor?—belched skyward like volcanic ejecta above the impenetrable tract of plant life before her. A tree just like the one on which she sat shuddered dully where it poked up through the brush a dozen meters away. Another unhurried tremor; she felt this one vibrate through her bones, and clenched at the roots underneath her as a flock of silent, grey-green primates scattered away from the rumble like startled pigeons.

For just an instant, she thought about calling out in alarm. She'd never heard anything like this, couldn't scramble up any kind of mental image to scare away more dire thoughts. The closest thing memory could offer was the Cardassians' giant mining drones, crunching their way through everything that wasn't the ores they sought. But there were no ores here, and presumably no Cardassians, either, so her mind leapt to the only other thing this alien environment had to offer: a comet.

The very ridiculousness of that mental leap blew the rest of her fears into silence. Back toward the main expanse of clearing, dark Klingon figures slunk moodily from place to place. Quiet yet surly, biding the time leading up to their destruction with what no doubt constituted a Klingon display of good grace. While their lack of alarm helped solidify her suspicion that no murderous rain of ice was imminent, it also made her scowl in private disgust.

In the years since Bajor had won its independence from Cardassia,

Kira had spent a great deal of effort trying to free herself of what seemed unavoidable racism. In her youth, fierce pride in her Bajoran heritage had been the only thing that let her justify the anger and bloodshed saturating her life as an antiCardassian terrorist. It wasn't until she worked side by side with Humans and Trills and Ferengi and Vulcans every day that she became aware of how much her hatred of Cardassians had slipped over into hatred of anything not Bajoran.

The realization had proved unexpectedly painful. Disgust and loathing for the race who tortured your people to near extinction had always seemed fair and right. To forgive was the first step in forgetting, and forgetting was a dishonor to the millions of Bajorans who had died under Cardassian rule. She'd taken a private satisfaction in flaunting the Prophets' warning, "Hatred poisons the soil so that nothing but more hatred can grow there." Her hatred was different. Her hatred was just.

And her impatience with the Humans? Her distrust of the Ferengi? Her disbelief in the Vulcans' sincerity? Her secret suspicion that Trills did something immoral by sharing themselves with a symbiont? It took her many months to accept that all her fears, dislikes, suspicions, and disdain were simply fruits of the soil she'd let her just hatred poison. After that, she'd begun the long task of redemption. She'd even allowed herself the vanity of believing she'd made brilliant progress in learning to embrace the values offered by other worlds and cultures.

Until today.

She'd spent the better part of the last two hours trying to wrap her mind around the concept that being thumped, spat on, and snarled at by scowling Klingons was little more than exchanging social pleasantries. Not that she was any sort of expert in their cultural ways. Still, her gut instincts just didn't seem able to align themselves with what amounted to a cultural habit of aggression.

And I thought I *was a barbarian,* she admitted with a sigh. Picking her way carefully up the tree's rough bark, she found a handhold above the tallest knee of root and used that to hike herself almost a full meter higher in an effort to improve her view. *My problem is, I just can't pretend I don't feel what I feel.* Dax's careful, rational explanations aside, Kira found it hard to silence those old instincts just for the sake of pretending she respected any society that functioned more on intimidation and posturing than on any kind of true merit. Sympathy kept running aground on the basic reality that every interview she and Dax conducted had someone shouting and growling as though eager to encourage a fight. If Dax hadn't suggested that Kira spend some time off on her own—to "cool off"—the major might just have precipitated a political situation of her own.

A slow, chuffing grumble crack-crashed its way closer through the stand of brush to her left. Kira craned up on tiptoes to steal a glimpse of the topmost surface of the foliage, and instead caught only a methane-tangy belch of breath in the face when the creature making its way toward her finally smashed its languorous way out of the undergrowth.

By the time her brain released some of its processing capabilities from the act of bolting straight up the tree, she was perhaps another two meters farther from the clearing floor. She peered down—at least slightly down—at the peaceful behemoth now stripping bark from the woody growth it had just muscled through.

Not a Cardassian mining drone, but easily a hefty second in both mass and size. It towered a good four meters at the shoulder, with a huge, blunt head that sloped down and forward to give it the look of a crashball guardsman. A flare of bony plate ridged the back of its skull like a tiara, angling to fit almost seamlessly with the armorlike skin encasing the rest of its bulk; necessary, no doubt, to protect against whips and thorns and brambles as it plowed its way through the hostile overgrowth that Dax and Kira had reluctantly deemed impossible to move through. The eyes it turned up toward Kira were gentle, if stupid, and it paid her no more attention than it took to fondle her toe with the tip of its mobile upper lip before seeking out more edible fare among the tree's scrubby leaves.

"Don't worry—she's harmless."

Kira twisted a look toward the voice, trying to look more annoyed than embarrassed. "I was just climbing up for a better view." Then she realized how awkwardly she'd wrapped herself around a limb too narrow to truly hold her weight, and couldn't hold back her blush. "I guess I wasn't expecting company," she finally managed.

The Klingon girl smiled—a smile remarkably free of Klingon disdain, for all that it came and went like a shooting star. Tossing a coil of woven plant fiber onto one shoulder, the girl picked her way across the top of the undisturbed brush-forest with an ease almost rivaling that of the silent primates who still danced back and forth across the large pachyderm's trail.

Even the bloody bandage cinched around her thigh didn't seem to slow her much. She was easily the youngest Klingon Kira had seen here at the Vrag main camp, maybe a year or two past puberty, the equivalent of a Bajoran fourteen-year-old. She'd braided her glossy black hair into a queue more severe even than Worf habitually wore, but managed to offset that austerity with simple formfitting clothes and not so much as a suggestion of the armor and metalwork normally incorporated into even the most casual Klingon attire. She trailed one hand lightly down the huge animal's side as she passed. The gesture reminded Kira of nothing so much as the Bajoran farmers of her youth, dropping unconscious touches here and there as they walked among their herds, lest the clumsy creatures forget a fragile humanoid moved among them.

"It's not like you couldn't have heard her coming," the girl remarked as she stepped from brush-tops to tree and offered Kira her hand. *"Banchory* aren't very good at sneaking up on anyone."

Kira was surprised to recognize the Klingon word for *war wagon.* She cast another nervous look at the beast now languidly splintering a branch the size of her thigh, and it occurred to her that "war wagon" wasn't a bad description for these animals.

Gingerly lowering one foot toward the brace the girl created with her fist against the tree, Kira did her best to unwind herself from her perch in something resembling a dignified manner. "So did you bring these . . ." She tried to remember exactly how the girl had pronounced the word. ". . . these *banchory* from Qo'noS with you?"

The girl shook her head, caught Kira's other foot against her shoulder before the major could lose her balance, and guided her to the relative safety of the roots with a strength that would have been disproportionate in a Bajoran girl her age. "No, the *banchory* are native to Cha'Xirrac. There used to be thousands of them." She watched the *banchory* near them strip a long peel of bark from one of the other trees, turning it over, around, and inside out using nothing but the delicate manipulations of its lips and tongue. A flash of what might have been anger darkened the young girl's face. "They once used this clearing in the *tuq'mor* as an overnight spot, but they pretty much avoid us now."

By now, Kira had come to understand that *"tuq'mor"* meant the impossibly thick snarl of vines, bushes, trees, and ferns that seemed to cover every inch of Armageddon's surface. It occurred to Kira that she should have known that even Klingons couldn't beat out a clearing the size of this one without some kind of assistance.

Kira forced herself to sit without flinching when the *banchory* turned to examine the other side of its newly made clearing, all but brushing Kira with its stubby tail as it lumbered past. "So why do they stay away now?" she asked, as much to distract herself as because she really cared for an answer. She remembered the pile of mammoth carcasses by the sea. "Is it because you hunt them?"

"Because Gordek and the other men hunt them." The bitterness in her young voice startled Kira. She clutched the rope over her shoulder as though it were a precious *bat'leth,* defiantly meeting Kira's gaze. "Grandmother thinks we can do whatever we want because everyone on Cha'Xirrac will soon be dead. Gordek thinks we can do whatever we want just because we can." A peculiarly childlike frustration pursed the girl's lips. "I thought honor was about more than just how long your conduct was remembered, or what you could force others to do."

Kira's comm badge chirped before she could think of how best to respond to such a comment. "Dax to Kira." The Trill's voice sounded stiff with frustration. "Could you join me and *epetai* Vrag?"

"I'll be right there." She tapped off her badge, then managed a smile for the girl with less effort than she'd expected. "It was a pleasure to meet you—"

"K'Taran." She thrust out her hand with charmingly Human exuberance, but performed the actual handshake with a certain clumsiness that told Kira she'd never actually performed the social ritual before. "Any pleasure belongs to me," she said with deep sincerity. "The adults say that you are the one who brought a doctor, to help relieve our suffering while we wait for the end."

"Yes, we did." Kira felt abruptly stupid. Here she was chatting about local wildlife when it seemed almost everyone and everything in the House of Vrag could benefit from medical attention. "He was over in the children's billet earlier, but probably has time to look at your leg." She pointed out the trio of dugouts where she'd last seen Bashir, as though K'Taran might not know which ones they were. "He's slim and dark, with dark hair." Then she remembered the awkward Human handshake, and realized the girl might have mistaken her for Human despite her distinctly

Bajoran features. If recognizing more subtle racial differences was challenging for Klingons, she didn't want to think about how hard it might be for the girl to tell Human male from Human female. Especially when the female was as tall and strong-boned as Dax. "He's the one with short hair, and no freckles."

"Thank you." For a moment, she looked like she might try the handshake again, but instead defaulted to one fist against her chest in the Klingon equivalent. "The concern you show for my people is honorable."

Kira watched her clamber off across the *tuq'mor,* marveling again at the complexity of any word that so many people could use to mean so many different things. That there could be so many different forms of Klingon pleasantry seemed only slightly more remarkable.

The dugout tree-cave currently hosting the Vrag Household conference didn't look appreciably different than when Kira had fled it more than an hour ago. Still too dark, still too humid, still crammed with snarling, snapping Klingons battling over yet another gradation in the definition of "honor." Roots snaked and intertwined so tightly through the walls that it was impossible to tell what had been naturally eroded into hollows by dripping water and what the Klingons had excavated themselves. All their attempts to personalize the dank, formless space—all their tapestries and sculptures and crudely fashioned furniture—only accentuated what a dark, dirty, pitiful hovel the dugout really was.

"Kira . . ."

Dax seemed to appear out of nowhere, her soft summons coalescing her figure from the shadows just inside the dugout's low door. She stood beside a rickety table, toying with the handle of a simple water jug and watching the Klingons as they argued. "We've got a problem."

Kira nodded. "You mean besides a shipload of missing Starfleet retirees and rocks the size of space stations falling on our heads?"

The humor seemed to break through Dax's pensiveness, and she turned away from the discussion with a crooked smile. "In addition to that." She dropped her voice to a more conspiratorial tone. "The Klingon blockade is back. Captain Sisko's going to cloak the *Defiant* and try to avoid detection."

Kira felt a little clench in her stomach. "What about the away team? Can we beam out?"

"Only if we leave now. No guarantees if the *Defiant* is discovered."

Because then the ship would have to raise shields, and there'd be no telling when they could lower them again. Kira paced in a slow circle, rubbing at her eyes. "That would mean leaving without the *Victoria Adams*'s crew." Prophets, what time was it back on board the *Defiant?* She felt as though she hadn't slept in weeks. "And we'll have to drag Bashir out by the hair. He won't leave as long as there are casualties."

"But if we don't leave now," Dax pointed out, ruthlessly nonpartisan, "we might not leave at all."

"Then you will simply be equal to the rest of us."

Kira tossed a glance over her shoulder, surprised to find what had seemed a truly apocalyptic argument now lulled enough for Rekan to eavesdrop. The others arrayed beyond her, waiting; Kira couldn't tell how much of their sour expressions were aimed at their *epetai* and how much at her. "We're not completely equal." Kira turned to face them squarely. She'd be damned if she'd let anyone claim the moral high ground, least of all a band of defeatist Klingon exiles. "We intend to survive."

Epetai Vrag lifted her lip in a civilized snarl. "Fighting a pointless battle does not add to your honor. The comets grow more thick daily. The longer you are here, the greater the likelihood you will be involved in a large-scale strike." She reached out with almost prim disapproval and flicked Dax's hand away from the water jug. "You would better serve yourselves by accepting the inevitable and preparing your spirits for their passage, or taking the one soldier you have found and leaving now."

Kira forced herself not to slap the jug to the floor. "I'm not ready to ignore all our options just yet." She turned pointedly to Dax. "Now that the blockade is back, we can't count on the *Defiant* deflecting any comets away from the planet."

"But the Klingons holding the hostages—"

"Can't get any help from us if we've broken cloak and been attacked by Klingons. We'll have to assume that the comets are going to keep coming. As it gets darker, we might be able to see them hit the atmosphere, maybe get a better feel for the volume and frequency."

"Unfortunately," the science officer sighed, "that won't help us pinpoint the impact zones." Dax lifted her eyes only a fraction, but Kira knew she'd made eye contact with the Klingon matriarch still hovering behind

Kira's right shoulder. "We'd be safer if we moved farther inland. Right now, a major impact in the ocean could flood this camp."

Kira couldn't help blurting a disbelieving laugh. "We're fifty kilometers from the ocean!"

"Someday, when we have time," Dax said sweetly, "I'll tell you all about how tsunamis on twelfth century Caladaan created coast-to-coast flood plains on most of their lesser continents."

Kira didn't really care to hear the whole explanation—the fact that the example existed was point enough. "What about initiating a physical search for the survivors? Have we found out *anything* of use in your interviews?"

Dax shook her head, sighing. "Even if we knew exactly where to look, we can't get through the undergrowth unless we use phasers. And that would take longer than we have."

"What about using the *banchory?"*

Kira had meant the question to stimulate discussion, not to slap shock through the gathering like a hand across the face. The Klingons fell into knife-sharp silence, every one, and Dax asked, "The 'war wagons?' Kira, what are you talking about?"

"They're a native animal, four or five meters tall and built like a runabout. I saw one outside." She pointed behind her, out the door and vaguely in the direction of her encounter. "Dax, you've never seen something plow through brush the way these things can. We could cover literally kilometers every hour."

Dax turned a questioning look on the matriarch. "*Epetai* Vrag . . . ?" she prompted.

Rekan spoke without looking up from her hands, apparently fascinated with their cords of muscle and patterns of veins. "Was anyone with this beast you saw?"

"A girl." Kira tried to decipher the strange flux of emotion across the old Klingon's face, only to find herself wondering if every deep Klingon emotion looked to a Bajoran like anger. "She said her name was K'Taran."

A Klingon so old that his brow ridge had begun to gnarl huffed with sour laughter. "Another intractable daughter of Vrag."

Rekan snarled what might have been a Klingon threat, or perhaps just an animal noise of anger. It came overlaid with a memory of a young girl's voice saying, *Grandmother thinks we can do whatever we want,* and a sudden awareness of how similar two individual faces could be. "*Epetai* Vrag," Kira heard herself saying, almost gently, "is K'Taran your granddaughter?"

Rekan answered almost before the question was finished. "I do not have a granddaughter."

"They do not cease to exist simply because you might wish it so." The older male Klingon who'd spoken before shook off one elder's grasping hand, and aimed a backhanded swing at another.

The *epetai* composed her face into a haughty mask that might almost have been convincing if not for the anguish in her eyes. "The young ones who have left us live and die by their own choosings now. They have chosen a path that holds no honor and are no longer a concern to this House."

"They're a concern to *us,* if they are the ones who found our comrades." For about the fiftieth time since beaming down to Armageddon, Kira wondered how Dax could maintain such a show of nonjudgmental courtesy when all Kira wanted to do was tear stubborn Klingon heads off. "If you know where they are, tell us, so we can talk to them and perhaps help them all survive."

Rekan met Dax's gaze with a glare of challenge, but otherwise gave no sign that she'd heard much less intended to answer. "Honor dictated that this House be destroyed," she said instead. "That could not be avoided, but it was never *my* decision. We stand where we are because honor gave us no choice."

"And because you've agreed to die, everyone else has to die here with you?" Even Dax's voice had begun to sharpen with annoyance.

"She does not know where they are." The older male sniffed at the air as though displeased with the smell. "None of us knows. They have made themselves native. They wander the *tuq'mor* like animals. Except for the trails from their *banchory,* we see nothing of them."

Dax glanced at Kira. "But you said K'Taran was just here?"

Kira nodded. "She thanked us for bringing in a doctor and said—" The words were barely out of her mouth before their implication kicked her in the stomach. Turning slightly away from Dax, away from the others, she slapped at her comm badge so hard she was sure it would bruise her palm. "Kira to Bashir."

Furious at her own stupidity, more furious still at her embarrassment when nothing but silence echoed back across subspace.

"Kira to Bashir!"

Nothing. No doctor, no wayward Klingon, not even an open channel to hint that Bashir's communicator still existed. The doctor was gone.

Rekan Vrag was the first to break the silence, and although there was triumph in her voice, its icy chill told Kira it wasn't a triumph she was proud of. "You have given up another hostage," she said accusingly. "Now do you begin to see what an abomination is a Klingon without honor?"

CHAPTER 5

BASHIR WASN'T SURE WHICH IRRITATED HIM MORE—BEING BOUND AND blindfolded like some sort of political prisoner, or knocking his head against the floor of his captors' lumbering vehicle every time it jolted over uneven terrain or crashed its way through a new stand of underbrush. He *did* know that the coil of fear gaining strength at the pit of his belly only exacerbated the more facile emotions that lurched to the surface. Fear for the *Victoria Adams*'s still-missing crew; fear for his two assistants, who shouldn't be abandoned to deal with so many Klingon casualties on their own; and, yes, fear for himself at the thought of being separated from his landing party with a star system full of potential disaster hanging over all their heads. Being all alone in an alien scrub forest when a comet sterilized the ecosystem was not one of his more romantic visions of a heroic death.

He felt the little flutter of his comm badge's chirp from where his body weight pinned it against the rocking floor. Above him, the Klingon whose knee had been in contact with his back since the beginning of their trip stirred uneasily, grunting.

"Look, this is ridiculous." Bashir paused, waiting with muscles tensed for a blow or a shove or a wad of gag in his mouth to silence him. When none came, he swallowed hard and disciplined his voice into something resembling composure. "That's my away team. If you don't let me talk to them, they'll just trace my badge signal and find me."

A strong hand snaked beneath him, prying him away from the floor less roughly than Bashir expected and plucking the badge from his uniform breast with the same casual dexterity an entomologist might use to capture a roving beetle. He thought he felt his captor shift and spin the way a person did when flinging a small object, but couldn't very well listen for the whisper of the badge's flight over the crash and rumble of their transportation. Fear finally cut its moorings in his stomach and diffused throughout his system.

"All right. The badge is gone. Fine." Pushing up with one knee and one elbow, he managed to roll himself clumsily. If hopelessness had one good trait, it was that it wasted little time converting fear into the anger more useful for survival. "Can you please untie me now?"

A grab at the front of his uniform caught him when he struggled to his knees. "Sit!"

It was the first time anyone had spoken to him since the girl who'd served as bait lured him into the underbrush in search of casualties. This voice sounded suspiciously the same. "Just tell me where—"

"Sit!"

She didn't wait for his compliance this time. Tugging firmly downward on the front of his tunic, she clearly meant to muscle him back to the floor, where he'd spent the first part of this liaison. He didn't consciously resist—rearing back away from her grip was no more than an instinctive reaction against being forcibly placed anywhere when he couldn't see the world around him. But he knew it was a mistake the moment his center of gravity slipped past thirty degrees. Hands clutched first at his shoulders, then at his waistband as he tumbled backward, then disappeared entirely when he hit free-fall.

The ground he landed on was softer than he'd thought, not to mention much closer to the start of his fall than it had seemed when he'd first been hauled up several meters and dumped into the transport's open bed. It poked and prodded him like a bundle of sticks, but gave just enough not to puncture anything. Springy vibrations sketched frantic movement all around him, but it was the young girl's voice—"Get aside! Humans are fragile—let him breathe!"—that surprised him the most. Perhaps he wasn't such an insignificant prisoner after all.

Thin, rough fingers picked at the bindings on his wrists, the knot at the base of his skull cinching his blindfold into place. He squinted hard against the light—

Oh, God, it's only barely morning back home!

—and blinked focus into the ring of faces crouched around him.

For one instant, the term "going native" meant a little more to him than it ever had before.

Then he realized that none of the muzzled, grayish faces bending over him were Klingons, and it relieved his confusion at least a little. Their eyes seemed big only in comparison to the smallness of their other features, muddy green and curious above a button rodent-nose and a mouth so tiny that it announced "insectivore" even before the first of them rolled out a long, prehensile tongue to swipe at its corneas. Bashir thought he might be able to scoop one up under either arm—they couldn't have massed more than fifteen kilos apiece—but they probably didn't need his help to move about their native environment. They ran on all fours like lemurs, their slim question-mark tails lifted playfully over their backs. The grace with which they navigated the upper stories of dense foliage put a zero-g dancer to shame.

They didn't even scatter or squawk when the young female Klingon jumped down into their midst. "Are you damaged?" she demanded of Bashir, somewhat testily.

"I . . . uh . . . " He managed to tear his eyes away from the plushly furred primates, only to fixate all over again on the huge, armor-plated monster calmly picking at whatever brush and limbs it could reach. It had smashed an impressive trail through the knotted undergrowth without even breaking a sweat; Bashir was suddenly glad he'd been caught by the foliage canopy and hadn't toppled all the way to the ground, another two or three meters down. "Uh . . . no . . . " he finally stammered. A Klingon—that's right, there was a Klingon, and he should probably look at her when he answered instead of staring at her strange menagerie. "No, I'm fine, thank you . . . "

"Good." She clapped both hands to the front of his uniform, then hauled him very carefully to his feet, as though afraid he might break if she dropped him again. "Then will you behave?"

Bashir hazarded a glance to left and right. Except for the winding trail torn like a scar through the brush cover, there was nothing to see except kilometer upon kilometer of undulating, scrubby plain. As though the plants had clawed their way a half-dozen meters above the ground and re-created their own surface beyond the touch of mud and burrowing creatures. Even though a loose, light foliage above them shielded most of the humid undergrowth from the sun, Bashir couldn't glimpse so much as a hint of the massive trees that had marked the perimeter of the Klingon's camp.

"Will you behave?" the girl asked again, more loudly.

How many days would it take people on foot to cross the same terrain this creature had traveled in an hour? "Yes," he admitted faintly. "Yes . . . I guess I will."

The big herbivore was more comfortable to ride than Bashir expected. More comfortable than when he'd thought its broad back was the floor of a land-going truck, at least, and he'd been forced to endure every bump and thump and rattle. He knelt just aft of the great beast's shoulders the way the girl showed him, tucking his heels beneath him and being careful to keep all body parts clear of where its bony skull ridge scissored against the plates on its back when it moved its head. The rocking of its big, slow steps proved almost soothing now that he could see where he was going and move his body to compensate.

It pushed through the snarl of plant life with such unhurried power that Bashir smiled slightly in awe. One ponderous step at a time, chin lifted above the froth of greenery, casually splintering thickets and trampling bracken like a ship smashing through Arctic ice. It didn't even seem to notice the schools of primates capering alongside it, dolphins in the wake of a great whale.

Bashir twisted to look at the silent girl behind him. "This . . . animal—"

"They're called *banchory*."

This was the first word she'd spoken that wasn't in Standard. The unconscious data collector at the back of his brain noted this as an interesting detail, even though nothing about it really seemed to mean anything. "These *banchory*, then. I saw some of their carcasses when we first beamed down, back on the beach near Gordek's camp." Feeling the life and majesty in the animal under him only made that memory all the more horrific. "They're clearly not Klingon in origin. I hadn't realized you'd had time to domesticate anything on Armageddon."

The girl still didn't look at him, her eyes trained forward as though guiding the *banchory* with her own sight. "The Klingons have domesticated nothing here. The *banchory* belong to the *xirri*."

"The . . . ?" He broke off the question when she swept a gesture toward the rear of their mount. No point trying to turn any further without standing—he'd only tip himself off the *banchory* again. Besides, he had a feeling he knew what she'd meant to indicate. They surrounded the *banchory* like monkey-tailed butterflies.

The slender, silent primates snatched handfuls and tonguefuls of bugs from the air as the *banchory* shook the undergrowth with its passage. Once or twice, a bevy of what appeared to be adolescents bounced eagerly up from below with forelimbs full of broken nuts and shattered seed pods. Bashir couldn't tell if it was insects their agile tongues probed for among those broken pieces, or pulverized bits of plant meat to complement the rest of their diet. Whichever it was, they hardly looked the role of master *banchory* trainers as they chased after swarms of disturbed lizards and jumped for escaping flies. More like ramoras, taking advantage of some greater creature's impact on the world.

It didn't seem an observation worth sharing, considering his situation.

Looking behind him, he offered his hand over his left shoulder and tried on one of his more charming smiles. "By the way, I'm Dr. Julian Bashir. I thought you might like to know who you were kidnaping."

"I know." But, to his surprise, she still took his hand and shook it with solemn gusto. "K'Taran."

"Of the House of Vrag?

A flush of warm magenta darkened her face, and she gnashed her teeth quietly. "Of the House of me."

"I see . . . " That seemed as good an end to that round of discussion as any. Shifting himself to look forward again, Bashir watched the world dip and sway in time with the *banchory*'s ground-eating strides. "Might I ask where we're going?"

"You're a doctor," K'Taran said bluntly in his ear. "We have wounded."

His first thought was to question who exactly "we" might be. Then he caught a flash of velvet khaki out of the corner of his eye, as three playful *xirri* raced past in some kind of game, and he thought perhaps he already knew. "K'Taran . . . " He glanced away from the bobbing horizon, wanting to look back at her but unsure if she'd appreciate his scrutiny. "You realize there's a very good chance everything on this planet—*xirri* and *banchory* included—will be dead in just another few days?"

He almost thought he felt the chill of her denial sweep its way up his spine. But perhaps it was just the threat of imminent rain that seemed to hang on every dew-damp leaf they passed. "Klingons don't cease to fight just because the odds are hopeless."

"I'm sure that's true. But the crash victims you've been holding hostage aren't a part of your fight. If you let us evacuate them, I'm sure we can make arrangements to take anyone else who—"

"My grandmother will never let anyone go." For just that moment, she sounded like a little girl—petulant, angry, despairing for something she'd hoped for from her adults but never gotten. "Besides," she continued in a more defiant tone, "my shield-mates and I would never leave without the *xirri.* They're our friends. Like your scientists, they took no honor promise to die."

Neither did I, Bashir wanted to tell her. But a roll of distant thunder distracted him, and a vision of tragedy swirled up from the forest floor to swallow his thinking before he could recapture his train of thought.

Despite the unchanging nature of the planet's overgrown surface, the site of the devastation somehow snuck up on them when Bashir wasn't ready to see it. Naked, burn-scarred limbs jutted out over a wasteland of mud, charcoal, and blackened bone The brush was singed well beyond this terminal edge; it hadn't been easy to see amid the normal mix of woody scrub and needlelike leaves, but now Bashir recognized the sere of heat so intense it had razed a vast patch of forest down to stubble. The local plants had already begun to fight their way back—faster-growing and more tenacious even than Britain's notorious heather. A furry blush of green laid an inch-high carpet over stubble, stones, and half-dead brush. Rather than renewing the desolation, though, it served instead to highlight the great emptiness. As though someone had thrown a hasty blanket over the corpses in the hopes no one would recognize the outlined forms.

The *banchory* brought them some distance into the wasteland. Its heavy steps hushed to a negligible crunching over the baby growth, but it filled the void with a low groaning that sounded almost like sobs. Anthropomorphizing, Bashir realized. It only greeted the pod of other *banchory* milling near a confusion of upthrust stones; they answered in equally loquacious murmurs, waggling their flexible upper lips and swishing the stubs of their hairless tails. It was a hard image to shake, though, when he glimpsed what looked like a half-filled inland sea another kilometer or two toward the horizon. Peaty brown water gushed into it from all sides, waterfalls of runoff from the mud underlying a continent of canopy. Bashir doubted there could ever be enough to fill the void.

"Have you been living here?" he asked K'Taran as she climbed past him to slide down the *banchory*'s nose.

"No." She waved him down, holding out her arms the way a parent might when preparing to catch a child at the end of a slide. "But we came when they needed us."

The *banchory*'s nose was as solid as the rest of it, and it hardly seemed to notice his weight as he shuffled down it. Mud, slick and swimming with ash, belched up around his ankles when he landed, and he added another couple of days to a search party's travel time. Assuming, of course, anyone had a chance to come looking for him at all.

They slogged toward a long row of shelters at the edges of the destruction. Long, stiff fans of greenery had been stacked across what remained of the undergrowth's canopy, pitiful protection from both sun and rain. The cadre of Klingons milling among the injured *xirri* tested and reinforced the structure almost unconsciously as they went about their duties. A deeper mat of branches had been piled directly on top of the mud to form a crude bedding for the wounded. Bashir reassured himself that they'd at least tried to keep their patients above the mire, if not strictly out of the elements. This was a great show of consideration for Klingons, if what he'd seen at Gordek's camp was any indication.

"How did you know they needed you?" He dropped to his knees on the edge of the branch carpet, not wanting to actually walk on the mat and spread muck among the wounded. "Did the *xirri* send for you?"

A pair of Klingon men—neither much older than K'Taran—glanced up from a few feet away, but it was K'Taran who finally answered. "We knew they had a home near here. Once Kreveth realized what had happened, we knew the *xirri* would be needing help. So we came." She remained standing behind him, out of both his light and way. Even so, Bashir could feel defiance rolling off her like heat. "I told you before—they're our friends."

Indeed she had. He decided not to press the question further.

A *xirri* appeared with his medkit, dropping out of the brush's fringes like a bird hopping off a branch. Bashir thanked the little primate absently, and didn't even think about blushing until after he'd cracked the case and dug out his tricorder and one of the smaller tissue regenerators. It wasn't as though

K'Taran would laugh at him for such a display of automatic courtesy. In fact, she was probably delighted to see him apparently taking her pronouncements so seriously. Still, he didn't want to lie to her, not even by implication. What he saw in front of him was a thin, sick lemur with no more evidence of sentience in its expressionless face than there was in its prehensile tail. It didn't change his willingness to help it in any way he could, but it also didn't distract him from the awareness that there were perfectly sapient creatures hidden somewhere in this jungle who also desperately needed saving.

He was almost halfway through the medical tricorder's primary scan when he realized that nothing about the readings made any sense. Frowning, he reinitialized the sequence and passed it over the *xirri*'s unmoving body again. K'Taran waited until he aborted that scan altogether before demanding, "What's wrong?"

Something about being so close to an impact site, probably. Interference on a level Dax could no doubt explain, but which left him only with a kit full of half-useless equipment and not even a suspicion of how to fix it. All the same, he punched up the tricorder's recalibration command. "Something's the matter with my equipment," he explained, not looking up from the growing scroll of gibberish on the small device's screen. "I'm not getting intelligible readings."

"Fine." She suddenly bent close over one shoulder and plucked the tricorder from his hand. "Then you can stop playing with your toys and start helping them."

Bashir stopped himself from attempting to snatch back the device, scowling up at her instead. "It's not that simple. I don't know anything about *xirri* physiology. Unless I can collect data on how their bodies function, I can't determine what drugs they can tolerate, or what treatments they might require. I don't even know how to calibrate a tissue regenerator!"

"The *xirri* will tell you if what you're doing is right."

Frustration throbbed dully at the back of his forehead. He hunched over and rubbed at his eyes, suddenly wanting to be home and safe and sleeping in his own Cardassian bed with no Klingons or alien lemurs to worry about. "K'Taran," he sighed. "Can the *xirri* even speak?" He hadn't heard a sound from them. Not even so much as a grunt.

K'Taran verified this observation with a simple, "They make no noise at all."

Of course they didn't—speech, language, true communication . . . It would all make things too easy, too straightforward for this mission. "They're monkeys," Bashir heard himself saying. The sound of his voice wrapped around those words almost shocked him. "However close you've grown to them, whatever feelings they might have for you, it's not the same as language. You can't run on your own instincts and call it communication." He looked up, expecting to see fury on her face, and added sincerely, "I'm sorry."

She stared back at him, a surprising amount of weary frustration in her own young features. Waving brusquely at the *xirri* who'd first approached with the medkit, she fished into her pocket without saying so much as a word. The skinny primate flashed over to her, green eyes intent, and K'Taran flipped a small polygonal token toward it with a flick of her thumb. The *xirri* caught it with its tongue, then spat the chip into one naked palm. It looked like something broken off a seal of pressed wax, or chipped from a larger stone. Popping the token back into its mouth, the *xirri* leapt into the burned-out brush and disappeared.

Curiosity burned sleepily in his eyes, but Bashir had learned better than to ask for what K'Taran hadn't volunteered. He sat with the remnants of his medkit, and waited.

By the time the *xirri* returned, sitting still had combined with the abysmal lateness of the hour shipboard to sink Bashir almost over the brink into dozing. He thought at first that he'd imagined the *xirri*'s multicolored companion, a nonsense dream caricature brought to life. But when it approached to within touching distance, he could smell the musky plant life odor of the pollen scrubbed into its fur, and see the sheen of drying wetness among the crust of colored muds striped over its skull and face and shoulders. The painted *xirri* squatted into a tall sit that placed it almost on a height with Bashir, and peered intently first at the doctor's hands, then the insensate patient on the grassy mat before them.

K'Taran slapped a tissue regenerator into Bashir's lap. "Go on, healer. Heal."

It was pointless. Bashir knew it was pointless—he was too tired, the *xirri* was too badly injured, and he just didn't have time to learn everything he needed to know to be an adequate physician to these animals. But even if he could find it in his heart to deny treatment while there was some small chance he could give relief, he had a feeling K'Taran and the other Klingons now gathering around her wouldn't have much patience with his ethical standards. Hadn't he said everything on the planet would be dead in a matter of days, no matter what they did here? So what real difference did it make if even his best efforts couldn't save a single *xirri?* His best efforts couldn't save any of them. He had to depend on Dax and the captain for that.

He examined the little *xirri* in front of him as best he could by touch and sight, making assumptions about its body chemistry based on such slight evidence as the condition of its mucal membranes, the color of its blood. Where muscle showed beneath folds of torn dermal layer, he probed the elasticity with gentle fingers, pretended its ropes and striations told him anything really useful. Then he set the regenerator with a few tentative taps at the controls.

He'd barely turned the head of the device toward his patient before the painted *xirri* next to him reached out and wound cool fingers about his wrist. Bashir hesitated, switched off the regenerator by reflex, and blinked down at the little primate.

Licking its eyes in what might have been agitation, the painted *xirri* abruptly ducked one long finger into the pucker of its mouth and brought it out smeared with the same colored pollen that tinted its hair. It drew slowly, lightly around the edges of the wound. Brilliant red on the innermost edges, followed by rings of saffron and umber shot through with smears of green. Apparently happy with whatever it had meant to convey, it settled back on its haunches with a final flick of its long tongue, and cocked an unreadable look up at Bashir.

He didn't know what else to do—the pounding of his heart against his breastbone seemed to drown out rational thought, leaving him to flounder in emotion. He reset the device almost at random, moved toward the patient again.

This time when the *xirri* stopped him, it was already busy accentuating the ugly green, blotting out the saner colors with bold, hectic strokes. Bashir adjusted the regenerator in the other direction; the *xirri* didn't interfere again.

As he watched bundles of muscle gradually repair, and skin begin its slow crawl across the open wound, it occurred to Bashir that it was probably best that his main diagnostic equipment had failed him for the moment, limiting what treatment he could supply. The way his hands were shaking, he wouldn't have been safe doing surgery, anyway. And even the most newly recognized sentient species—no matter how silent and unassuming—deserved better than the jitterings of a shell-shocked Human doctor.

Sisko's luck held for four of the five hours he'd allotted himself for sleep. His dreams roiled uneasily with cloaked Klingon vessels that turned out to be Cardassian warships hurling comets at the *Defiant.* When Odo's gravelly voice condensed out of one thunderous collision, Sisko at first burrowed deeper into his pillow and tried to ignore it.

"Captain Sisko, report to the bridge," Odo repeated impatiently. "There's a Cardassian vessel entering this system."

"Damn!" Sisko rolled out of his bunk, still feeling trapped in the remnants of his nightmare. He yanked on his uniform and boots. "Have the Klingons done anything to it yet?"

"No, but they may just be biding their time. The Cardassian ship is still out of weapons range."

"I'm on my way." He headed for the door without waiting for an acknowledgment. Worf met him in the narrow corridor bisecting the crew's quarters, looking much more alert than Sisko felt. They strode into the turbolift and told it, "Bridge!" in curt unison. The lift hummed upward.

"Any news from the away team?" he asked his tactical officer.

Worf slanted him a curious glance. "You were aware that I had the away team's secure channel routed to my cabin?"

"Just a lucky guess. What have you heard?"

"Little of promise," the Klingon said somberly. "Dr. Bashir was discovered missing after Commander Dax last spoke with us. They have a fix on his comm badge and are looking for him now, but Dax estimates it could take several hours to reach his presumed location."

"How did he get lost?"

"Unclear, sir. Major Kira believes he might have been kidnapped by the same group holding the *Victoria Adams*'s crew."

"Lovely." Sisko scrubbed a hand across his face, wondering what else could possibly go wrong on this mission. The turbolift doors hissed open before he could ask further questions.

Odo turned to face them from his watchful stance beside the command chair. As far as Sisko knew, the Changeling never did sit there, even when he was left in command of the *Defiant*'s bridge.

"The Cardassian ship is preparing to enter the far end of the cometary belt," Odo said, passing information along with Starfleet succinctness. Sisko glanced up at the viewscreen, but Farabaugh's computer model had been replaced by a real-time image of Armageddon against a comet-hazed starfield. A blinking red cursor now marked the position of the cloaked Klingon vessel, in what looked like a geostationary orbit above the comet-scarred main continent. "Mr. Thornton is constructing an approximate sensor image of the Cardassian vessel, using preliminary data from our long-range scans."

"Good." Sisko sat and gave an approving nod to the dark-haired engineering tech who'd replaced Farabaugh at the science console. "Put it on screen when ready."

"Aye, sir. Convergent resolution coming up now."

The viewscreen abruptly distorted, shrinking Armageddon to a distant dust-stained globe in the upper corner, while a steady twinkle in the background enlarged into a massive battle-armored ship, many times larger than the *Defiant.* Sisko whistled when he saw its familiar military markings. "Looks like we have some very official Cardassian visitors," he remarked.

"My data banks identify this ship as the Cardassian battle cruiser *Olxinder,"* Odo said from his console. "Commanded by our friend *Gul* Hidret."

"Why am I not surprised?" Sisko leaned back in his chair, frowning as he watched the Cardassian ship enter the comet field. Unlike the Klingons, they took no evasive action, nor did they appear to slow and angle their shields to deflect the comets they encountered. Sisko wondered if Hidret understood the danger he was in—unlike the small *Defiant* and equally small *Jfolokh*-class Klingon vessel, the *Olxinder* was practically guaranteed to get itself slammed with comets at the speed it was traveling. A moment later, the blue-white flare of phasers across the viewscreen answered his question. *Gul* Hidret was dealing with the comets with characteristic Cardassian arrogance, by summarily shattering to pieces every large fragment in his battle cruiser's path. Sisko supposed the ship's heavy armor could take care of the rest.

"For someone who was worried about Klingon aggression, he's not exactly trying to sneak in, is he?" Odo commented.

"No," Worf agreed. "I thought *Gul* Hidret did not believe us when we said there were no Klingons here."

Sisko shook his head. "Commander, I've found that what Cardassians say they believe and what they truly believe have about as much in common as Ferengi prices do with the true value of an object." He watched the *Olxinder* execute a gracelessly efficient turn, its corona of phaser fire leaving an afterglow of superheated gases in its wake.

"But then why come? He must know he cannot locate either of us while we are cloaked," Worf pointed out. "Why would Hidret make himself such a tempting target for attack?"

"Perhaps to provoke us into it," Sisko said.

Odo snorted. "More likely to provoke the Klingons into it."

"Thus giving the Cardassians all the excuse they need to start a war," Sisko finished grimly.

"The Klingons have just opened a hailing frequency to the Cardassian battleship, Captain," Thornton said, glancing over his shoulder. "It's on an open channel."

Sisko exchanged puzzled looks with Worf and Odo. The last thing he'd expected the Klingons to do was talk first and shoot later. "Put it on the main screen, split channel."

"Aye, sir." The phaser-wreathed glow of the *Olxinder* vanished, turning instead into *Gul* Hidret's furrowed visage on one side and an even more familiar Klingon face on the other. It wasn't the magnificent mane of gray hair or the broad brow that jogged Sisko's memory so much as the surprising glint of humor in those crinkled eyes. He snapped his teeth closed on a surprised curse. What in God's name was Curzon Dax's old drinking buddy doing out in the middle of the Cardassian demilitarized zone?

"Ah, Hidret," Kor purred in the same tone of pleasant reminiscence he might have used to greet an old lover. "What a joy it is to see your face and recall once more the delightful memory of how I demolished your last battle cruiser. How nice of the Cardassian High Command to give you another."

"It pleases me, too, Dahar Master Kor, to see that your legendary drunken stupors have not cost you *all* of your titles and privileges in the Klingon Empire," Hidret shot back with equally venomous politeness. The old *gul*'s lined face was rigid with some fierce emotion, but Sisko couldn't tell whether it was fury or satisfaction. "Although they have obviously condemned you to manning an obscure post in an unimportant system."

"How unimportant can it be, when a Cardassian ship as magnificent as yours drops by to pay a visit?" Kor retorted. "Although it is a Klingon tradition to welcome visitors, I'm afraid you might not like my particular brand of hospitality."

Hidret raised his brows in mock incredulity. "Are you telling me I have to leave? And here I thought you would welcome my help in evacuating the planet."

"What?" All traces of humor evaporated from Kor's eyes, giving Sisko a glimpse of the formidable warrior Jadzia Dax had once been willing to risk her life for. "What are you talking about?"

A little more satisfaction leaked out around the edges of Hidret's inscrutable expression. "Aren't there Klingons stranded down on that planet, being bombarded by comets? I came to help you rescue them."

Sisko exchanged startled glances with O'Brien and Worf. "I thought Hidret suspected those exiles of being planted, to give the Klingons an excuse to claim the planet."

Worf snorted. "More Cardassian lies."

"More Cardassian lies!" Kor echoed, his voice a bubbling growl. "I don't know where you got that information, but it's wrong. No one here needs to be rescued."

"You're telling me there are no Klingons on that planet?"

The Dahar Master bared his stained and shattered teeth. "I'm telling you that *no one needs to be rescued.* The Klingons on this planet have chosen their fate, and it is my duty as a Dahar Master to make sure that no one interferes with it. It is a matter of honor."

Hidret pointed an accusing finger at the viewscreen. "And you can make no allowances for the Cardassians who are dying of *ptarvo* fever, and need the drug that only this planet can provide?"

Kor snorted. "Bring me a Cardassian dying of *ptarvo* fever, and I'll be glad to let him beam down to Cha'Xirrac to be cured. In the meantime, old enemy, the only allowance I will make is to let you turn tail and run before I start firing."

"But—"

"But *nothing!"* The Klingon's sudden eruption into a roar made even Sisko start. "And if you ask one more question, your answer is going to be a photon torpedo!"

Gul Hidret snorted in apparent disgust, but the triumphant glint in his eyes made Sisko's stomach roil in apprehension. He was starting to suspect why the old Cardassian had engineered this unlikely confrontation. "From you or from your ally?"

"Ally?" Kor demanded.

"The cloaked Starfleet vessel we spoke to several hours ago. Her transmission originated from within this system."

"You spoke to a cloaked Starfleet vessel?" Kor's eyes narrowed. "That means the *Defiant* is here."

"And they didn't even bother to inform you?" *Gul* Hidret showed his own teeth in a maliciously triumphant smile. "How rude of them—" A photon torpedo explosion slammed across the open channel, and the Cardassian's smile vanished. "All right, I'm leaving, damn you! Stop shooting!"

Hidret's side of the connection sizzled and went black, but Kor's scowling face didn't vanish with it. "I know you're listening in on this, Benjamin Sisko. If not, then Dax probably is. Take my advice, both of you, and follow that old Cardassian fool out of this system. If you don't, I'm afraid I will be honor-bound to hunt you down and kill you."

CHAPTER 6

"NOW I KNOW WHY THEY CALL THIS STUFF *TUQ'MOR*."

From several feet above Dax's head—which was currently at the same elevation as her feet, although none of her was actually on the ground—Kira peered down through the tangled vegetation at her. Even higher up, an eerily silent troop of lemur-like primates leaped and skittered through the swaying twigs of the scrub forest, spattering them with dislodged rain drops and pollen.

"What does *tuq'mor* mean, anyway?" Kira asked, her tone so carefully measured that Dax knew she was trying hard not to laugh.

"It's the name of an ancient Klingon goddess. Also known as the mother of curses." Her rump-first fall into a pocket of weaker branches had left Dax suspended in a position too jackknifed to scramble out of. Even though she was surrounded by thickly grown shrubs and intertwining ivy, their rain-slick branches gave her nothing to grab onto. She wriggled a hand down beneath her to see if she was close enough to the ground to push off. Cool muck promptly closed around her fingers, soft and clinging as liquid silk. She cursed in Klingon and wiped her hand across her damp trousers. "See what I mean?"

"I'm starting to." Kira reached a hand down to her through the greenery. "You better let me help you up."

"Brace yourself," Dax warned as they locked hands. "My skeleton alone probably weighs more than you do."

"Never fear. I won't drop you." Kira dug her boot heels into the braided mat of branches on which she stood, making it bounce a little beneath her. She used her smaller weight to advantage, Dax noticed, leaning back to leverage it into her motion without overbalancing. With one smooth pull, she hauled Dax out of her jackknifed spill up to stand beside her, then lifted a smug eyebrow. "Easy as a zero-g somersault."

"Don't rub it in." Dax snagged an overhead vine to steady herself, feeling the branches creak and sag beneath her weight. Now that she was upright and free, she had time to notice the welt of smarting skin on her cheek where a branch had slapped her during her fall. "I'm already jealous that you can walk across branches I break."

"Sorry." Kira took a backward step to ease the load on the swaying *tuq'mor.* "Maybe you better go first from now on, to make sure the branches can hold you."

"I probably should." Ever since they had entered the maze of vegetation, they had been forced to walk anywhere from one to three meters above the densely forested ground level, with another meter or two of shrubbery making an interlaced canopy overhead. The air inside the *tuq'-mor* was shadowed and cool, mist-filled in places, and always soundless. No vagrant breeze could stir the densely knotted branches of this ecosystem. It reminded Dax of a coral reef, braced to withstand the crashing of unseen waves. "Although that means we'll be going even slower."

Kira glanced up at the place where the leaves glowed brightest, backlit by unseen sunlight. "We're only making about half a kilometer an hour through this stuff as it is. Another hour or two shouldn't matter. At this rate, we're not going to catch up with Dr. Bashir until sometime next week."

Dax tapped a familiar command into her tricorder, then frowned as she compared the response it gave her with previous readouts. "No, we're getting much closer. According to Julian's comm badge, he's located just a few hundred meters northeast of us."

Kira must have heard the worry beneath her words. "His readings haven't changed at all?"

"No." Dax pushed onward through the tangled branches, trying not to think of all the ominous reasons for that consistency. More to herself than to Kira, she said, "If these Klingon children really are trying to protect the whole planet, they have no reason to hurt Julian. They could have taken him to tend to some wounded survivors—"

"But Boughamer said he was the only one badly hurt," Kira reminded her.

More rain drops dappled down from the forest canopy, stirring up shreds of mist from the swamp below. Tiny, silent lizards leaped through the leaves to escape Dax's progress, jeweled flashes in the shadowy light. "Didn't you say, though, that K'Taran herself was hurt?"

"No, I said she *looked* hurt," Kira said, gloomily. "She had a bloody bandage wrapped around one leg. But that might have been as much a lie as the rest of what she said."

Dax slanted a curious look back through the greenery at her. "Did she really lie to you, Nerys? I thought you said she admitted to being *epetai* Vrag's granddaughter."

"She did," the Bajoran admitted with grudging fairness. "And mostly what she talked about was how she didn't think there was any honor in killing the *banchory.* Or in waiting around for the comets to hit. I suppose she was telling the truth about that, too." Kira snorted. "She's at least fighting to survive *sylshessa,* instead of just folding her hands and getting sanctimonious about it. I might not like how she's doing it, but I have to give her credit for trying."

Dax shook her head at her friend's exasperated comment. She should have known that Kira, former freedom fighter and military officer, would find more to admire in K'Taran's active resistance to death than in Rekan Vrag's honorable acquiescence to it. "There are as many codes of honor among the Klingons as there are interpretations of Prophecies among the *vedeks,*" she informed the Bajoran. "By not lying to you when she kidnaped Bashir, K'Taran may have been obeying her own code. But, in a larger sense, by struggling to evade the justice meted out by the High Council, in her *epetai*'s eyes she has dishonored their house."

"And was Chancellor Gowron being honorable when he exiled the House of Varg to certain death on this planet?" Kira demanded.

"Possibly." Dax felt the branches below her thin out over a more watery stretch of swamp, and angled to the left to find more secure footing. Another troop of primates skittered out of a flowering hedge as she skirted it, their velvet-plush shoulders freckled with colorful blossoms and pollen dust in an unconscious imitation of Trill freckling. "What a Klingon considers honorable depends as much on context as on precedent. Depending on what infraction the House of Vrag committed, this sentence of exile might have been vindictive, or it might have been an act of mercy."

Kira heaved a sigh. "I'll never understand Klingons."

"And they'll never understand us," Dax smiled. "They find our Vulcan and Human and Trill codes of law almost totally incomprehensible, because they're meant to apply no matter what the motive or result." She paused to map a path across an almost-open stretch of running water before she trusted her weight to the arching branches. "I can understand *epetai* Vrag and I can even understand her granddaughter. The only Klingon here I find hard to decipher is Gordek."

"Really?" Kira leaped through the screen of delicate branches to land on the other side, if her wildly swaying perch on a flexing limb could really have been called a landing. Her athletic ease was all the more enviable because it was totally unconscious. "What's so hard to figure out about him? He's a petty tyrant who wants to start his own little empire, even if it's only going to last until the next tsunami levels the coast."

"True." Dax ventured out at last on the largest bridging limb. "But the fact that he was willing to bargain with us to get the equipment he wanted—"

The wood cracked ominously beneath her weight as she reached the end. Dax cursed and took a long, not entirely directed step across the cooler breeze of the stream chasm with its murmur of hovering insects, then found herself sinking through bracken like a turbolift descending. A small hand reached out and caught her, this time by the indestructible nape of her Starfleet tunic, and hauled her back to safe footing for a second time.

"Thanks," she said, regaining her breath. "Damn *tuq'mor.*"

"Mother of curses," Kira reminded her. "Maybe we should have made a sacrifice to her before we started chasing after Bashir."

"Or maybe we should have followed that *banchory* trail, even though it didn't seem to lead in the right—"

Dax broke off abruptly. She'd found an open crevice through the hedge wall and thrust her head and shoulders through it, only to emerge into an unexpected chasm in the *tuq'mor.* It looked as if someone had taken a phaser and carved a canyon through the dense vegetation: one meter wide, four meters high and stretching out of sight along its sinuous length. Coppery gold sunlight slanted down into it, warm and inviting. She cursed again, long and hard this time.

"What is it?" Kira demanded, wriggling through the dense hedge to pop out just to Dax's left. "Blood of the Prophets!"

"Mother of curses," Dax said again, wryly, then hauled herself free of the hedge and clambered down to the open path. It was floored by the same silk-soft mud as the rest of the *tuq'mor,* but her boots sank only a few centimeters in before they hit firmer soil. The *banchory* had compacted this forest highway as well as blazed it. She cocked her head, listening to the distant, deep hooting that echoed up the path. "If we follow this now, we might have to make a real quick exit."

Kira landed beside her with a squishy thump, oblivious to the spatters of mud that threw across both her and Dax. "Will it take us to Bashir's comm signal?"

Dax consulted her tricorder and nodded. "Yes, it's the perfect heading from here. Almost too perfect . . ."

Kira glanced over her shoulder, squinting against the sun. "You think it's a trap?"

"I don't know." Dax kept her tricorder on as they walked, watching their mapped coordinates get closer and closer to the ones she was receiving from Bashir's comm badge. "But it's definitely not a coincidence." She skirted a large pile of olive brown *banchory* droppings. Their half-sweet, half-fetid alien smell was so strong in the still air that she knew they had to be recent. "Wait." She grabbed at Kira's shoulder to stop her, then swung around with the tricorder chirping a proximity alert at her, louder and louder. "According to this, Julian should be within a meter of us. It looks like the signal's coming from the wall of *tuq'mor* over there."

Kira scowled and began yanking apart the thick stems of succulents, ivy, and shrubs, trying to find a place wide enough to step through. The *tuq'mor* seemed thicker along the edges of the *banchory* trail, almost as if it was defending itself against further inroads by the massive animals. When the Bajoran finally found a gap wide enough to squeeze through, however, the shadowy interior looked just as pristine as the rest of the scrub forest. There was absolutely no sign of Bashir, alive or dead.

Dax fought her way into the dense vegetation, then glanced down at her tricorder and frowned. The two sets of map coordinates were now dead-on, but her proximity display still insisted she was a meter away from where the comm signal was originating.

"I'm reading a vertical discrepancy," she said, puzzled. "Julian's comm badge must be at least a meter up from here."

"Or down." Kira slanted a grim look at the wet muck of the *tuq'mor,* now only a few centimeters beneath their feet. The interwoven mat of shrubbery above it looked undisturbed. "Although it doesn't look like anything's been buried here."

"No." Dax tilted her head back, peering up at the maze of branches above their heads. "Here, you hold the tricorder."

Kira took it reluctantly. "I can climb up there more easily than you can—"

"I'm not climbing." Dax flexed her knees, then leaped upward, catching hold of the two largest branches within reach and shaking them with all her considerable weight. The entire forest canopy creaked and flexed under her assault, sending a scurry of tiny gleaming lizards out in all directions. One of the jeweled glitters didn't leap, however. It fell straight down from the branches, half a meter too far away for Dax to catch.

Fortunately, quick Bajoran reflexes sent Kira diving after it before Dax could even open her mouth to shout. A mat of intertwined ivy strands bounced beneath the major's impact, trampolining her back again just as Dax dropped from her precarious overhead hold. They collided hard enough to elicit mutual grunts, but Kira's fingers never unclenched from around her catch.

"Is it—?" Dax demanded, steadying her companion.

"Yes." Kira rebalanced herself in the tangled *tuq'mor,* then uncurled her fingers to show Dax the gleam of gold and silver from the Starfleet communicator pin. The frantic chirping of the tricorder confirmed that it was Bashir's. "And it looks like it was at just the right height to have been tossed off a *banchory.*"

From the first moment he'd seen the *Defiant,* Sisko had loved it for its surprising combination of cheetah speed and leonine power, purebred sleekness and alley cat durability. However, the one thing he had to admit his ship didn't have was space. Where a larger starship like the *Saratoga* boasted a wardroom for conferences and planning sessions, he had to make do with a bridge where veteran command officers mixed with untested young ensigns and technicians. And when a renowned Klingon warrior has just announced his intention to hunt you down and kill you, the last thing a commander needed was panic among his crew.

"Mr. Thornton," he said, more by way of test than because he really needed to know, "do we still have a fix on the cloaked Klingon ship's position?"

"Aye, sir." The junior engineer glanced over his shoulder, not looking particularly panicked. "I have the long-range sensors cranked to maximum sensitivity. Even though the Klingon ship has reduced its ion emissions to zero and is modulating its waste heat to match the planetary infrared spectrum, just like us, we're still picking up a minute gravitational anomaly along its extrapolated orbit."

"Enough of an anomaly to link to our weapons targeting systems, so we can track and fire on the Klingons?" Odo inquired.

"Yes, sir." Thornton tapped a command sequence into his science panel. "I can also export my tracking data to the viewscreen display, if you want."

"Do it." Sisko watched a fuzzy, computer-generated halo bloom on the distant curve of Armageddon's oxide-stained atmosphere, then glanced over his shoulder as the turbolift doors hissed open to admit his chief engineer. "We've got a Klingon Dahar Master on the lookout for us, Chief. How invisible are we?"

"We've battened every electromagnetic hatch we've got, from ions to infrared." O'Brien detoured long enough to cast a critical look at Thornton's sensor settings, then gave his young technician an approving clap on the shoulder before continuing to his own seat at the empty engineering console. "Providing you don't want to leap into warp any time soon, the Klingons shouldn't even be able to prove we're here."

"How close can we get to their ship without getting caught?"

"Seventy kilometers, give or take a few." O'Brien grinned at Sisko's surprised look. "I did a little retuning on the shield voltage controls. We're still putting out some magnetic discharge, but now the polarity is tuned to look just like the planet's magnetosphere."

"What about our gravitational field?" Odo asked. "Can't the Klingons track us the same way we're tracking them?"

"No," Worf said, before the chief engineer could reply. "Not unless they already know where we are. A cloaked vessel cannot be detected by gravitational signature alone."

"Especially in a system as orbitally complicated as this one," Thornton added. "The gravity well's way too bumpy to resolve individual events unless you already know roughly where you're looking."

"Good." Sisko leaned back in his command console, as pleased with the coordinated response of his bridge team as with the information they'd given him. He thumbed the communicator controls. "Ensign Farabaugh, how soon do you have us scheduled to intercept an incoming comet?"

"In a little over ten minutes, sir. I was just about to alert you." The junior science officer sounded as tired as O'Brien looked, his voice scratchy but confident. "Sorry for the short notice, but we had to redo half our calculations after that Cardassian battleship banged its way through the debris field."

"Understood. Are we still scheduled to nudge that comet off course on the opposite side of the planet from the Klingons?"

"Aye, sir." Farabaugh hesitated, and Sisko heard the murmur of a second voice in the computer room. "But to get to our intercept point, we're going to have to pass pretty close to the Klingon ship on at least one orbit."

"How close?"

"About one hundred kilometers."

Sisko winced. "My old piloting instructor at the Academy used to call that kissing distance." He looked over at O'Brien again. "You're *sure* the Klingons won't be able to pick us up?"

"Not unless they have their scanners focused directly on our position when we pulse the impulse engines," O'Brien assured him. "Otherwise, we'll be running on gravitational forces and momentum. We should slip by like a Ferengi going through a customs check."

"Then let's do it." Sisko sat back in his command chair, listening to the distant whisper of cometary dust vaporizing off the shields. It occurred to him that the sound couldn't actually be coming from the ice itself as it smoked and vanished into empty space. It must be the internal echo of the shield compensators, constantly readjusting to keep the voltage gap steady and the external forces balanced across the ship's hull.

"Course plotted and laid in for minimum impulse thrust," Worf announced, his deep voice anomalously loud in the thrumming silence. Sisko wasn't sure if that was the result of his tactical officer's tension or his own. "Ten seconds to engine pulse."

"Mark." O'Brien sounded much calmer, but, then, he was the only one who really knew how well their waste-heat output blended with the ambient infrared. "Five, four, three, two . . . pulse detected."

Sisko could have told him that. Despite the parsimonious engine firing, designed to put the cloaked *Defiant* into the correct orbit with minimal expenditure of energy, his years as her commander had attuned him to the little warship's slightest movements. He felt the shiver of redirected momentum, subtle as the shifting weight of a baby asleep in its mother's arms. "New heading?"

"Orbital plane forty-three degrees to spin axis, rotation thirty degrees from planetary prime," Worf said with satisfaction. "We are on the correct heading for comet intercept at the lip of the gravity well."

Sisko glanced over at Thornton, whose gaze never seemed to waver from his sensor output. "What about our Klingon intercept?"

"Still one hundred kilometers, assuming the Klingons maintain their orbit. Estimated time of closest passage: two-point-five minutes."

"Commander Worf, please lay in potential course changes to prepare for possible Klingon detection. Straight attack, evasive attack, evasive retreat."

"Aye, sir."

Sisko swung his chair back toward O'Brien. "How's the magnetic signature of our shields holding out?"

"Still matched to planetary polarity, plus or minus ten percent. I'm slowly modulating as we cross the magnetosphere."

"Good." Sisko brushed his gaze across the viewscreen, eyeing the familiar face of Armageddon with its halo of cometary debris only long enough to be sure that nothing had changed. He tapped his communications control panel. "Farabaugh, any changes in comet trajectories caused by our new orbit?"

"No, sir. We're traveling far enough inside the gravity well to be out of range."

"Good," Sisko said again, but he was frowning as he lifted his hand. That unexceptional answer had left him with nothing left to do, no occupation to soak up his surging tension for the final minute of countdown. He contented himself with drumming his fingers softly on the arm of his command chair and running through all the possible battle-plans, should the Klingons somehow detect their presence. It wasn't that he didn't trust his chief engineer's camouflage or his chief tactical officer's piloting skills.

But to a Starfleet officer who'd had ingrained a thousand kilometers as the minimum undetectability limit throughout most of his career, the idea of sliding invisibly past a Klingon bird-of-prey at one hundred klicks or less fell just short of requiring divine intervention.

"Klingons off the aft side," said Thornton. His voice was so quiet and emotionless that it took Sisko a moment to realize the announcement meant they'd slipped past. "No sign of ship activity detected from passive scanning."

The *Defiant*'s bridge murmured with the exhaled breath of her five vastly relieved officers. No, make that four, Sisko thought wryly. Odo looked just as relieved as the rest of them, but the Changeling didn't have the lungs needed to produce a thankful sigh.

"Estimated time of encounter with comet?" he asked briskly. After a tense encounter like that, a good commander knew how to focus his crew's attention on the next challenge. Otherwise, relief had a way of turning to distraction.

"I am not sure," Worf said unexpectedly. "I have the orbital course, but I do not have the exact coordinates of the comet copied to my piloting console."

Sisko frowned. "Thornton?"

The dark-haired engineering tech shook his head. "Sorry, sir. I can get sensor readings on all the comets, but I'm not sure which one Farabaugh's aiming us at."

A frustrated breath trickled out between Sisko's teeth. Trying to deflect a comet without getting caught by the Klingons was like trying to leave Quark's bar without leaving a tip . . . it seemed easy to do at first, until you kept getting tangled in one layer of obstacles after another. Unfortunately, in this case you couldn't flip a coin to a Ferengi barman and have the obstacles magically vanish. "Odo, open an on-line channel to Farabaugh so he can hear us down in that science lab. O'Brien, I want you and Osgood to start working on transferring the comet impact model up to a spare station on the bridge. And someone find out where that damned comet is!"

The words had no sooner left his mouth than the *Defiant* shuddered under a scraping impact. A moment later, a massive, smoking, black hulk of cometary ice floated into the main screen's view. One whole side was sheared freshly white from its contact with the *Defiant*'s angled shields.

"I hope," said Sisko ominously, "that was the comet we were supposed to be deflecting. Because if not . . ."

"Comet deflection one hundred percent successful, sir!" The excitement in Farabaugh's voice echoed brightly across the open communications channel. "With the momentum added from sublimation, its new trajectory will take it out of the debris field entirely."

"Well, there you go." O'Brien looked up from his shield modulator controls with a mischievous smile. "All we need is to do that another hundred-thousand times, and Armageddon will be safe."

Even Sisko felt his lips stretch into a smile at that image. "By then, most of the Klingons should have died of old age," he agreed. "Allowing us to leave the system just in time to collect our pensions." The stifled spurt of laughter that trickled out of his communicator panel told him Odo had added a permanent channel between the bridge and the science lab. He didn't bother reaching for his panel controls. "When's our next deflection scheduled for, Ensign?"

"Not for another forty-five minutes, sir." There was a pause while two young voices conferred in a murmur at the other end of the channel. "With your permission, sir, Osgood and I would like to grab some breakfast before then."

"Breakfast?" O'Brien said blankly. "Don't you mean lunch?"

Worf rumbled disagreement from his piloting station. "According to the ship's chronometer, it is currently fifteen-twenty hours. Any meal served now would be classified as supper."

Sisko felt his own stomach growl uncomfortably. "I don't care what you call it, anyone who wants some can get it. Just be sure to be back on station by sixteen-hundred." He sat back in his chair and steepled his fingers. "We have an appointment with a comet, and it won't wait for us if we're late."

By the time they met up with their fourth comet, Sisko's bridge crew had subversive interception down to a fine art.

"Critical point coming up at coordinates two-sixty and four-forty-three mark twenty-nine." Farabaugh looked up from the makeshift tracking console O'Brien had rigged from one of the life-support stations at the back of the *Defiant*'s bridge. They'd spent the slow hours between comet deadlines moving both junior science officers back onto the bridge, streamlining their data transfer procedures, and perfecting their deflection maneuvers. Osgood had settled in at the main computer access panel, where she could concentrate on the constant adjustments they needed to make in their cometary impact model, while the *Defiant* jockeyed back and forth through the cloud of cometary debris. Thornton and Odo had adjusted the main viewscreen's detection parameters, autoprogramming it to focus on their cometary targets both before and after impact.

So far, their peripatetic path and jarring encounters with comets hadn't drawn any unwelcome attention from the Klingons, although with Kor's ship settled in a stable equatorial orbit, Sisko feared it was only a matter of time until one of their intercept points fell recklessly close to their enemies. In the meantime, the constant short-range passes they had to endure on their unpowered gravitational orbits made the muscles between Sisko's shoulders harden with accumulated tension. Worf claimed the additional challenge of evading detection while deflecting comets made them better warriors, and even O'Brien admitted that the adrenaline rush of those close passes kept him awake and gave him new motivation as the hours dragged on. Personally, Sisko thought he could have limped along on the old motivation—saving Armageddon and all its inhabitants from mass destruction—for quite a while yet.

"Time to gravity-well intercept?" he asked, knowing the routine now by heart.

"Twelve minutes and counting." Osgood swung around at her computer station, blue eyes somber in her fine-boned face. "Captain, this comet fragment masses three kilotons, four times as big as the others we've intercepted. We're going to have to give it a much stronger nudge with the shields to deflect it."

"It's also heading straight-line into the gravity well," Farabaugh warned. "There's no curve-back capture loop at all. We're not going to get a second chance to bump it if we miss."

"Understood." Worf punched the new data into his navigational computer, then transferred the resulting course changes onto the orbital model of Armageddon Thornton had inserted in a corner of the main viewscreen. The new loops added additional frills to the fading lacework of their past orbits. Sisko narrowed his eyes, watching the golden target spot that beaded their path on the third orbit.

"Mr. Farabaugh, correct me if I'm wrong, but it looks like we're deflecting this comet on the same side of the planet the Klingons are orbiting."

"We are, sir," the young man admitted. "Due to this comet's straight trajectory, it was the only intercept point we could find. But at least we'll be in the terminus when we do it. The dusk might help disguise the comet's change in direction."

"Let's hope so." Sisko glanced across at Worf. "What will our closest pass to the Klingons be this time?"

"One-hundred-and-twenty-five kilometers," the tactical officer replied.

"Piece of cake," said O'Brien.

Sisko grunted. "Begin preparation for course change—"

The blinding shock of a phaser blast across the viewscreen sliced across his words like a *bat'leth.* Sisko cursed and leaped to lean over Odo's shoulder, scanning the *Defiant*'s shield and systems outputs for damage. All the indicators were bafflingly normal. "What the hell did Kor just shoot at?" he demanded.

"As far as I can tell, absolutely nothing." Odo swept an impatient hand across his displays. "It looks like the shot went wide of us by several hundred kilometers. There's no evidence of impact with any comet fragments, either."

"Don't tell me they're just shooting in the dark, hoping to hit us?" O'Brien demanded incredulously.

Worf let out a scornful snort. "The odds against that are far too high to justify the waste of power. I would have expected better from a Dahar Master. Unless he was very, very drunk."

"The odds will get a lot better at a hundred-and-twenty-five kilometers distance," Sisko said grimly. More phaser fire shattered across the screen. "And Kor only needs one hit to extrapolate our location and zero in." He stood and began pacing, even though he knew the motion couldn't ease the frustrated ache of inactivity between his shoulders. He needed to be out doing something, going somewhere—not trapped in this clandestine, cloaked orbit, unable to move a muscle for fear of Klingon detection. "All right, gentlemen, time for a quick command conference. Do we try for deflection and risk getting shot at by Kor?"

Odo gave him a somber look. "What other options do we have? That comet isn't going to wait for us to find a safer orbit."

"We could allow the impact to occur." Worf's scowl looked as if it had embedded itself permanently in his massive forehead, but his voice remained carefully neutral. "That would allow us to remain at maximum distance from the Klingon ship."

O'Brien threw the Klingon an astounded look. "But it would break the deal the hostage-takers offered us—who knows what they would do to the *Victoria Adams* crew then? Not to mention that Julian and Dax and Major Kira will be left at the mercy of that comet!"

Worf's face darkened. "True. But if we chase this comet to our death, many others will fall on Armageddon after it. Should we sacrifice our ability to deflect them all just to deflect this one?"

Odo cleared his throat, a humanoid habit he'd learned in his years among solids. "You're assuming the first one we deflect will be our last? Why? Is Kor so invincible in battle?"

"The last time I saw Dahar Master Kor," said Worf succinctly, "he was a drunken, reckless, nonsense-spouting old fool. But he was at one time one of the mightiest warriors of the Empire. I would not underrate him, even now."

A last flicker of phaser fire stabbed across the nightside of Armageddon, then the Klingon ship slid around the planet's curvature, still firing randomly into space. Farabaugh glanced over his shoulder. "Captain, if we're going to deflect that comet, we've got to move soon. Otherwise, we won't be able to maneuver into an intercept orbit at all."

Sisko rubbed a hand across his slim beard, giving in to the frustrated longing for action that had been building in him since they'd first arrived. "Commander Worf, lay in course change for comet intercept. Chief, get our warp engines on-line and our shields back as close to battle-ready as you can without losing all magnetic polarization. Odo, punch a high-security contact through to the away team. We need to let them know what's going on."

"Aye, sir," said O'Brien and Worf in unison. Odo merely punched the order into his screen, moving so rapidly that Sisko suspected he'd been practicing the sequence in advance. "I've got Major Kira now, sir."

"Major," Sisko said without preliminaries. "Any luck locating Dr. Bashir?"

"No, sir." Sisko could hear the heavy rattle of rain on leaves all around her, with a background thrum from some nocturnal creature chirping despite the downpour. "We followed the trail of whoever took him as far as we could, but we never even caught sight of them. If they really are using the native pachyderms for transport, they can probably cover nine times the distance we can in a day."

"Understood." Sisko drummed his fingers on the arms of his console, wrestling with the decision he had to make. "Major, I want you to return to the main Klingon camp," he said at last. "If the hostage-takers decide to contact you or to release any of the survivors, that's where they'll expect you to be."

He heard the breath Kira drew in, even through the sound of distant thunder. "You're expecting a comet to fall?" she guessed. "But the hostage-takers—"

"—can't keep Kor from finding us sooner or later, so long as we keep bouncing comets away right under his nose," Sisko finished.

For a moment, all he heard in response was rain and chirping. "What about the survivors from the *Victoria Adams?*" Kira asked at last. "And Dr. Bashir?"

Sisko grimaced. "We'll have to gamble that the comets won't hit near them. Once the battle's over—with luck—we'll be able to resume the search for them. And to resume warding off Armageddon."

"Sylshessa." He could hear the wry smile in Kira's voice. "I suspect Kor's not going to give you enough time to drop your shields and transport us now. So I guess I'll see you after you've won."

Sisko allowed himself a smile in return. "And good luck to you, too, Major. Sisko out."

"Captain." Odo turned to catch his glance as soon as the transmission was cut. Sisko turned to face him, barely noticing Armageddon's terminator spinning massively toward them as they crossed the planet's rusty dayside. "We're being hailed on all wide-beam channels by the Klingons. Should we acknowledge?"

"Under no circumstances." Sisko slapped a hand down on his communications console. "All hands to battle stations," he snapped over the ship's intercom, trying not to think of how few souls were actually aboard the *Defiant* to hear him. "I want all phasers charged and all photon torpedoes armed and ready."

"Captain." That was Odo again, glowering down at his panel as if it had betrayed him. "The Klingons didn't wait for our acknowledgment. Kor is broadcasting some kind of message to us on all channels."

"Put it on screen," Sisko said curtly.

Armageddon's rusty image vanished, replaced by a broad Klingon face tipped back in a roar of gusty laughter. Kor looked very cheerful and very drunk, but not a whit less threatening for that.

"Sisko!" he roared, sloshing what looked like blood wine toward the viewscreen. A spray of ink red droplets momentarily blotted the display, then trickled into a few out-of-focus runnels dripping down it. "I know you're out there, Sisko! Come out of hiding and *fight!"*

"Not if I can help it," Sisko said between his teeth. "Odo, get him off the main screen, but monitor his transmission, just in case he says something useful."

"Yes, sir." The ancient Klingon warrior's brazen face and disheveled gray hair vanished, but the image that replaced them wasn't the planet below. It was a crusted, black bulk of ice, fractured in places and on the verge of breaking into multiple, smaller fragments.

O'Brien whistled. "We'll have to be careful how we hit that."

"Yes," Osgood agreed. "Too strong a blow will fragment it and send some pieces falling onto the planet. Too weak a nudge, and we won't deflect it at all. What we should probably try for is—"

An explosion splashed through the cometary haze before she could finish speaking, the familiar searing glare of phaser fire. Sisko cursed and swung toward Thornton. "Where's that coming from?"

"The Klingons." The sensor tech sounded shaken by the data now scrolling across his output screen. "They must have changed orbit while they were rounding the planet—they're coming up fast, heading fourteen-forty mark three—"

More phaser fire, this time near enough to send a ripple of magnetic interference humming through the *Defiant*'s shield controls. "Still firing randomly?" Sisko demanded.

"Yes." That answer was Odo's, confident and calm at his panel. "They should pass us in approximately—"

A closer phaser blast interrupted him, spasming the entire viewscreen to white in a way that only a close-range blast could do. "Damage report!" Sisko ordered over the automatic shrilling of proximity alarms.

"Shields at ninety-eight percent, no direct hit on any sector," O'Brien said promptly. Sisko opened his mouth to acknowledge, but the image condensing into view on the main screen stopped the words in his throat.

The cometary fragment they had intended to hit was glowing like an incendiary had hit it, all of its fractures and breaks standing out like shards of jagged lightning against the black-crusted surface. The light inside grew brighter instead of dimming as phaser fire refracted and reflected its way through the weakest points—until, with an explosion of smoking icy debris, the comet shattered into a spray of high-velocity fragments. Each chunk spun off in a different direction, almost too fast to see except for the plume of white vapor left behind it like a contrail. With a cold ache in his stomach, Sisko abruptly understood why Farabaugh had advised them against trying to destroy the comets with phaser fire.

He spun toward the science officer, holding his voice steady with an effort. "Do we need to stop any of those fragments?"

"Working on that now, sir." Farabaugh's words were clipped, his voice tense enough to make the skin on Sisko's back crawl with foreboding. "Osgood, check intercept on fragment nine, that's the fastest one—"

"Too late." Even muffled across the hum of the computer, Sisko could hear the frustration in the other ensign's voice. "It's already gone atmospheric."

"Can we hit it again with our phasers?" O'Brien demanded. "Maybe blast it smaller, into more harmless pieces."

"I don't have any targeting data," Odo warned. "I need specific coordinates transferred in from the computer, *now!*"

Sisko opened his mouth to confirm that order, but a brilliant explosion across the viewscreen stopped him. That hadn't been the fierce, probing flare of Kor's phasers—it had been the raging red-tinged fireball of a comet, exploding up from Armageddon's dense lower atmosphere. Fragment nine hadn't waited for them to intercept it.

"Damage report," he said grimly. "On the planet."

"Long-range sensors show that fragment nine exploded over the open ocean, Captain," Thornton said. "There'll probably be some damage from shock waves and tsunamis along the coast, but the away team shouldn't be affected."

Jaw muscles he hadn't even realized he'd locked unclenched with Sisko's sigh of relief. Before he had even exhaled the last of it, however, Osgood had spun to give him an urgent look.

"Computer models show three more large fragments and a mass of smaller bodies on impact courses, Captain," she warned. "They appear to be headed for the main continent, near the away team." She saw Odo's scowl and swung back to her station. "Transferring data to weapons control—"

"It's too late for us to run an intercept course on them, Captain," Farabaugh added unnecessarily. "We'll have to use photon torpedoes for deflection."

"And we can fire only two at a time," Worf pointed out. "In the meantime, the Klingons will have pinpointed our location."

Sisko grunted, rapidly weighing up his options and finding them all unpleasant. "Farabaugh, mark the two largest fragments for Worf to aim at," he snapped. "Commander, fire when ready." He took a deep breath, seeing the distant flare of phasers that told him Kor's ship had passed them and was rolling merrily along their course, oblivious to their cloaked presence. That wouldn't last much longer. "Odo, prepare for evasive course maneuvers on my mark. Prepare to engage upon firing, at my mark."

"Firing torpedos, *now.*" Worf tapped at his controls with fierce restraint, making the distant hiss of torpedo launch echo through the ship. An instant later, two blossoms of rose-stained light sprouted within the dust brown curve of Armageddon's upper atmosphere.

"Both comet fragments were deflected into high-angle trajectories, and are on course to exit the atmosphere without exploding," Farabaugh reported without being asked.

Sisko grunted acknowledgment. "As soon as torpedoes are rearmed, I want to target the third large fragment—"

"Klingons approaching, seventeen-ninety mark six," Thornton said abruptly. The rusty curve of Armageddon vanished from the screen, replaced by a thousand smeared-out streaks of gauzy light as the cloaked Klingon ship flashed through the comet debris field at close range. "Firing phasers—"

Sisko opened his mouth to order return fire, but the shattering impact of a direct phaser rocked him sideways before he could speak. Instinct more than thought spat the next words out of his mouth. "Red alert! Evasive maneuver alpha!" Worf threw the ship into a skidding turn, hard enough to slam half the bridge crew into their consoles and tear the other half away. "Damage reports."

Odo answered first, as calmly as if they hadn't just been attacked without provocation. "Shields are holding at seventy-eight percent. No structural damage."

"All ship's systems on line and functioning," O'Brien reported. "But it looks like we might have lost one of our comet-trackers."

Sisko spared a quick glance over his shoulder in time to see Osgood prop Farabaugh up from where he'd been flung by the shock of impact. Blood trickled down the young science officer's forehead, but his eyes were already fluttering open. He groaned a protest as Osgood used her own weight to wedge him into the corner between his console and hers, but she sensibly ignored him.

"Klingons are firing again," Odo warned. A moment later, the *Defiant* shuddered under a second direct impact, this time knocking Thornton away from his science station. "Shields holding at sixty-three percent."

"Evasive maneuver delta!" Sisko snapped, then braced himself as the *Defiant*'s spinning course reversal again tugged at them harder than the inertial dampeners could compensate for. "Increase speed to warp five. Where are the Klingons?"

Thornton had to scramble to regain his seat, but his response was still fast and confident. "Klingon ship is four-hundred-and fifty-kilometers away and dropping fast. We'll be out of phaser range in fifteen seconds."

"Maintain evasive maneuvers until then." Sisko turned to check on the status of his comet-tracking team and found Farabaugh on his feet again, squinting painfully at his display screen. "Mr. Thornton, please call someone up from the medical bay to treat Mr. Farabaugh."

"I have, sir. Medic Walroth's on her way."

"It's too late, Captain," Farabaugh murmured.

Sisko frowned, but the young science officer looked so unaware of his own bloodstained condition that he couldn't mean himself. "Too late to stop the last comet fragment, Ensign?"

"Too late to warn the away team, sir." Farabaugh gave him an anguished look. "I can't be a hundred percent sure, but it looks like that fragment is headed for the area of the Klingon's main encampment. It will hit in just a few seconds."

Sisko's gut clenched in dismay. "Notify them anyway," he snapped at Thornton, then vaulted up to scowl at the latest computer model results. "How large an impact are we looking at?"

The sidelong glance Osgood gave Sisko held a wealth of regret. "The fragment was the smallest of the three, but it was still larger than a shuttlecraft. And its velocity was low enough to allow it to penetrate deep into the troposphere. The best estimate is that it will probably be about as powerful as a hundred quantum torpedoes. And there are a dozen smaller fragments right behind it."

A somber echo of silence filled the bridge, until the first bloom of light burst through the blue-black shadow of planetary night. "God help the away team," O'Brien said, watching the light spread like a stain across the atmosphere. His voice was so fervent it was hard to tell if the words were a curse or a prayer. "God help Armageddon."

CHAPTER 7

SHALLOW, RESTLESS SLEEP. HOURS AFTER BASHIR'S BODY HAD COLLAPSED IN exhaustion, his mind remained feverishly kinetic—aware that he slept, yet frustratingly unable to order his thoughts beyond a miasma of dreams. The bark and cough of Klingon voices melded with the skritch of *xirri* feet on *tuq'mor,* an eerie symphony of worry and unidentifiable sounds.

Even the sharp, here-again-gone-again thunder that had preceded each spastic downpour throughout the long evening had soaked into his unconscious until it twisted into a rolling, swollen snake, filling the world, licking the edges of the sky. It coiled into a knot that filled his empty stomach; his sleeping body rearranged on its stiff bower of limbs, hands clenching into fists in front of his eyes to block the actinic glare of the thunder's menace. *I can't even run from you,* he admitted wearily. *There are wounded here I can't leave, and I'm too tired to be afraid anymore. Whatever you're going to do, you might as well get it over with.*

The serpent struck with explosive speed, and Bashir jerked violently awake.

What could only have been thunder's contrail still echoed off toward infinity. Its deep, almost physical waves pounded hotly inside Bashir's skull. The warm, plush bodies that had nestled on all sides of him during sleep popped up with equal alarm, all of them slapped from dreams by a giant's hand. He reached instinctively to smooth the fur on the closest *xirri*'s skull. Light stung his eyes—daylight, except . . . not daylight.

Bashir rose slowly, his breath squeezed into a fist in his chest, and raised his eyes to a roaring, flame-colored sky.

Overlapping shadows swung in wild arcs across the ground, across the faces and bodies of Klingons and *xirri.* Burning ribbons crisscrossed the night sky like flares. Beyond the farthest stretch of horizon, a fat cylinder of fire rocketed straight downward, dragging a brilliant scar of light behind it. Gas and dust and fire mushroomed suddenly skyward, exploding light across the *tuq'mor* canopy, bathing the world in a scarlet-and-gold brilliance that somehow leached all life from it. Bashir stared into the roiling inferno in an agony of silence. It seemed hours later that the coarse cannonade of thunder finally cracked through their tiny camp.

"Is that the direction we came from?" For some reason, he expected someone other than the painted *xirri* doctor when he looked down at whoever clenched his hand. Panic, struggling awake through his confusion, lifted his voice to a near shout. "Was that anywhere near the main camp?" he asked, looking all around him for someone who could understand the question.

Xirri scampered past, some of them already carrying wounded on their backs, others randomly snatching up blankets, foodstuffs, tools in their flight. The crash and rumble of *banchory* plowing their way into the *tuq'mor*'s leading edge almost drowned the Klingons' alarmed shouting, but not the brave battle-chants some of the young men had begun as they swept up gear and passed it off to others. Bashir wondered if they intended to stay and fight. Against what? He spun about, searching the swarm of bodies for a familiar face, and found K'Taran herding her own small flock of *xirri* into step with the rest of the exodus. He ran to her, grabbing at her arm. "Where did that come down?"

"Over the ocean." She took hold of his hand, gripping it possessively instead of pushing it away as he expected. "There's nothing that direction but the poacher's camp."

The poacher's camp . . . and Heiser. Bashir watched the blackening cloud slowly turn itself inside out. It was a terrible thought, but he found himself hoping dismally that the comet's destruction had been horrifying—that a lone Human physician's assistant would have barely had time to notice the approach of the light. That no one had felt any pain.

The rank stink of burning wood feathered into their clearing like fleeing ghosts.

"Come." K'Taran pulled insistently at his hand. "We can't stay out here."

Bashir tried to tug himself free, resorting to peeling her fingers loose one at a time. "I've got to get back to my friends."

"You'll never make it."

"Then take me on a *banchory!*"

"No."

He pried his hand from hers with a last angry yank. "If there's another comet strike—"

"Then you will all die together." She made an abortive swipe to catch him again, but took the hint and clenched her fists at her side when he jerked back out of her reach. "It will serve no purpose!"

What purpose did it have to serve? Die apart or die together, they would still all die in the end. And Bashir had no honor issues to prevent him from being with his friends when that happened. Whirling away from her, he pushed through the jostling crowd, squeezing his way against the flow of bodies until he reached the makeshift bed he'd shared with his *xirri* helpers.

He didn't need any extra light to riffle through his small clutter of belongings—the sky was still bright as dawn, crisscrossed with contrails and filled with a rumbling like a million launching shuttles. His tricorder lay where it had fallen when he passed into sleep, open and on its side atop the pile of branches. The regenerator he found a few layers farther down, where it had slipped between gaps in the foliage. Its power cell still glowed reassuringly, charged and ready to work.

Only his main medkit was gone.

He dragged aside handfuls of branch, searching with both sight and feel for the metal satchel. Mud, bits of broken *tuq'mor,* the remnants of what might have once been some thick-skinned fruit, but no medkit. Twisting in place, he caught a glimpse of movement through the dancing shadows, and watched three *xirri* heft one of the unconscious patients between them by each grabbing an outflung limb. A fourth *xirri* trailed them, its arms filled with supplies and the strap of a square metal container slung over one narrow shoulder. The medkit bounced noisily along the burned ground behind it as it ran.

"Hey!" Bashir scrambled to his feet. A growing layer of smoke met him when he stood, catching at his breath and making him cough. "Hey, wait! You have my gear!"

As though the *xirri* might understand. They disappeared into the confusion and smoke, scaling the charred edges of *tuq'mor* and joining the general mass of activity between the fires in the underbrush and the fires in the sky. When K'Taran appeared at his side again—this time minus any *xirri*—he asked breathlessly, "Where are they going?" as he fitted his tricorder back into its pouch.

She moved him a few steps to one side, out of the path of a *banchory* half-loaded with supplies. "I don't know."

Bashir watched two *xirri* pet a fidgeting *banchory* into stillness so four waiting Klingons could clamber aboard. "But you're going with them," he said, more to indicate that he realized it than because he expected any sort of explanation.

"Wherever it is"—she stepped up close behind him to avoid another approaching *banchory*—"it has to be safer than here."

And then her arms were around him, iron-hard and tight. Bashir barely had the chance to gasp a protest before she yanked him off balance with enough force to shock the wind out of him.

His feet skittered in the mud; a clink of boot-on-metal kicked his dropped regenerator out of sight beneath a skirt of branches and burned leaves. K'Taran dragged him backward as inexorably as a tractor beam. When the pungent smell of wet *banchory* wrapped around them like a wool blanket, panic swelled in Bashir's stomach. He surged against her hold, tried to tangle his feet in the burned detritus all around, kicked back against K'Taran in a desperate attempt to wrench himself free. New hands—bigger, stronger—pinned his arms, lifting him against an armor-plated side.

"Let me go!"

Then he was flat atop a *banchory*'s wide shoulders, pushed face downward by the weight of two Klingons, his tricorder grinding into his hip. "Stop it!" he pleaded. "You can't do this!" He managed to work one arm under himself, but couldn't gain the leverage to lift himself before the force of the *banchory* lurching up from its kneel knocked him flat. *"Let me go!"*

He felt K'Taran's hand flex slightly between his shoulders, but she said nothing.

The trail they used stretched wider than their *banchory,* smashed open by everyone who had fled ahead of them, then gnawed at by the streamers of flame that still trailed randomly from the sky. Smoke curdled at *ban-*

chory-height, snaking through the *tuq'mor* canopy; Bashir heard the shattering crash of a tree cleaving its own path toward the ground disturbingly nearby. Coughing, he struggled upright, away from the worst of the heat pouring off the burning *tuq'mor.* This time K'Taran let him.

I hate you, he wanted to growl at her. Except he didn't, not really. He hated this grief, and the leaden, aching despair, but K'Taran hadn't been the one to bring the comets raining. She'd just forced him into what a Klingon no doubt considered honorable inaction. And he hated that. Hated having no way to save himself, and no one else to save.

Xirri raced along the crumbling canopy, some slower than the laboring *banchory,* some faster. Everything scorched by the impact that had first exploded the clearing—everything two kilometers on all sides—crackled and puffed into flame in uneven spurts. The burn front seemed barely moving, just irregular platters of fire scattered throughout a nightmare landscape. When he first glimpsed shadow figures jerking and turning behind the tongues of light, he unconsciously identified them as refugees like themselves, heading into whatever insanity waited at the end of this pointless flight. Then something in the parallax between *banchory* and *tuq'mor* penetrated his stunned numbness, and he realized that the trio of *xirri* were simply struggling behind the path of the flame, not actually moving; K'Taran and her *banchory* were passing them by.

He didn't consciously decide to rescue them. One moment, he knelt on all fours on the back of a running *banchory;* the next, he was grabbing at ash-blackened *tuq'mor* limbs and hauling himself off his mount and into the inferno.

"Human, *no!*"

But he was free of her, still moving, outrunning her in truth even as his thoughts raced precious seconds into the future.

He gained the weave of charred canopy easily enough. It gave gently under his weight, springy and firm, like a trampoline. But the narrow fingers of vine and wood felt more like a tightrope beneath his feet as he picked his way across the surface. Thank God and his parents' vanity for the coordination needed to navigate the deadly course. Little worms of fire twice darted unexpectedly upward from below. The understories were burning, he realized. Suddenly, the image of creeping along a tightrope was replaced with a burning mine field, and Bashir felt a sting of sweat trickle into his eyes.

The painted *xirri* looked up when Bashir bent over it. A tiny, blood-stained figure that could only be a child clung to the older native's back, and the adult *xirri* dragged imploringly at the arm of another, unconscious, adult. Bashir recognized her from his earlier round of triage on the *xirri* wounded—a young female suffering from what had seemed like smoke inhalation and dehydration. Lucky, compared to the others. He'd assigned a geriatric male to keep her upright and feed her water, but hadn't had the ability to do much more for her at the time. Now, only the faint twitching of her eyelids betrayed that she was still alive. Too much smoke, too much excitement. Tug as it might, the painted *xirri* wouldn't get her even five steps closer to wherever they headed.

"Go." Stooping, Bashir set his feet as widely as he dared and scooped the panting female up with one arm. "Go!" he shouted again, pushing at the painted *xirri.* "I've got her."

For a terrible instant, he thought the message wouldn't pass between them. Then the painted *xirri* touched his hand, light as a butterfly's kiss, and bounded away with startling speed, the youngster still clinging to its back.

Cradling the unconscious female against his shoulder to shield her from the smoke, Bashir straightened and turned back for the trail. He could hear K'Taran shouting, even though he couldn't make out the words, and thought he glimpsed her a ridiculous distance away. Flames cracked and snapped in a wandering line between them; she'd moved farther down the trail, away from the unburned path he'd clambered across to reach here. The thought of circling around turned his stomach to lead. All he would do was lose himself and never find his way back to the others before the fires overran him. Taking a deep, smoke-tainted breath, he hugged his patient protectively and ran at the line of fire before his common sense could suggest otherwise.

Heat washed across him like a blast of desert air. A brief, searing sting across the exposed backs of his hands, then he was clear of it. Not even burned, he realized as the trampoline canopy caught him and staggered him with its chaotic gives and bounces. Then his foot crashed through to nothingness, and he fell to one knee so heavily that his jaw cracked against the top of the little *xirri*'s head.

"K'Taran!"

Instinct, that was all—he'd shouted because some foolish primate instinct said that any other ape close enough to hear you might be recruited to help. He could see her already leaping onto the *tuq'mor,* so very far away, too very far away to do anything about the predatory fire or the unravelling footing beneath him. Still, when the next layer caved in with a roar, and K'Taran abruptly slipped above his line of sight, she was the one who called out. Bashir was too busy jamming his foot into a knot of *tuq'-mor* vines to answer.

He had to lift the little *xirri* over his head to roll her onto the top of the canopy. He couldn't take her with him—*refused* to let her fall and burn simply because he'd been too stupid to find a path through the *tuq'mor* that would hold his Human weight. When K'Taran's ash-stained face appeared above the lip of the ever-growing hole, Bashir thrust the *xirri* toward her. "Take her! Take her!"

But he couldn't tell if K'Taran understood. Before her hands even found a grip in the little creature's fur, the world fell out from under him, and he went plunging into the abyss.

The sky ignited two seconds after Kira's hoarse shout of warning echoed down the *banchory* trail. Dax knew what it was immediately—her third Trill host, Emony, had seen an asteroid impact in her youth from the outskirts of Ymoc City. The memory had burned indelibly into her symbiont's neural circuits: the explosion of light in the sky and the long rumbling roar that followed, the iron-scented wind smashing down from fire-colored clouds, the thunder of flames in the distance as the central city burned. And, for hours afterward, the slow downward drift of silent, black flakes of ash.

The light this time was different—bright and sharp as a photon torpedo blast, consuming the entire sky with its flare. "Get under cover!" Dax shouted back at Kira, then turned and dove for the most open spot she could see in the wall of *tuq'mor* rimming the trail. The thick tangle of leaves and branches resisted her entry, snagging in her hair and gouging deep scratches across the exposed skin of face and hands. Dax cursed and dragged herself deeper, worming her way down through the underbrush to the muddy wetlands below. The drenching rains had covered the mud with a running glitter of water, making all of it look exactly the same.

Dax paused, unsure where to burrow in. With the clumsy noise of her passage through the *tuq'mor* silenced, she could hear the ominous stillness that had enveloped the scrub forest, as if every living creature held its breath in fear. Jadzia's blood jolted with a distracting surge of adrenaline, but the symbiont's shielded inner brain was less subject to such animal instincts. It calmly sent her eyes sweeping across the wet glimmer, seeking out the place where the *tuq'mor* sent the least roots snaking into the mud. That was where the water would be deepest—

Dax took a deep breath and dove headfirst for the hidden pool, feeling water and mud splash up around her even as her ears cracked with a sound so loud it registered as pain, not noise. An enormous boulder smashed down on her from above, slamming her breath out of her lungs and hammering her so deep into the muddy bottom that she felt the silken hug of sediment close over her entire body. Panic spiked through symbiont and host alike, and Dax struggled to stop her downward momentum, thrashing her arms and legs through the thickening sediment in a vain attempt to escape the rock pushing her down.

An instant later, the enormous weight was unaccountably gone. Dax twisted and speared her arms upward, fireworks exploding across her vision from lack of breath. She felt a last, sick surge of energy kick through her muscles—the release of her symbiont's inner reserves of oxygen and glucose in a desperate attempt to save its host's life and its own. With an effort that strained every muscle in her body, Dax hauled herself upward, swimming and climbing simultaneously through the mud to unseen light and air.

Two convulsive jerks broke her head free of mud—and slapped her face with scalding hot water instead. Instinctive panic launched Dax further upward, her face lifting with a gasp to meet the hot, dry kiss of air. There wasn't time to worry if the comet's fiery breath would burn her lungs—air rushed into her starved chest without her even willing it, oxygen and smoke and heat all mixed together in treacherous blessing.

Dax gasped twice, then smoke burned her throat like acid and she lost all her breath again in helpless coughing. She sank back down into hot water and cooler mud, submerging up to her chin before her frantically outstretched fingers caught hold of an exposed root and steadied her. Her next breath, however, was surprisingly free of smoke. She opened mud-crusted eyes and saw a swirl of steam and exhaled gases rising from the wetland's scalded surface, creating a layer of clear, warm mist that buoyed up the sinking smoke from above.

For a long time, Dax did nothing but lie there, gasping like a beached fish and allowing her symbiont's internal reserves to build up to tolerable levels again. The blinding light of the comet's first impact was gone, but Armageddon's night sky still glowed with the pale radiance of explosive afterglow. The top of the *tuq'mor* glowed, too, sullen charcoal red where the topmost branches and leaves had withstood the worst of the fireball's passage. A flaming brand fell into the water beside her, its ruby embers turning cold and black after it hit. Something about that wasn't right. It took a minute of muzzy thought for Dax to realize she hadn't heard the sizzle the burning wood must have made as it quenched. In fact, now that she had time to think about it, she realized she couldn't hear anything at all—no crackling of fire from the forest canopy burning overhead, not even a splash of water when she moved. The only noise her brain registered was a sort of soundless shrilling that she guessed came from her own deafened ears.

Another burnt branch dropped into the water from above, this time close enough to splash Dax with *raktajino*-hot water. She cursed—silently—and scrambled to free herself from her muddy sanctuary. The burning canopy wouldn't stay alight much longer, she guessed; the smoke was already starting to clear as the fires were extinguished by water-sodden wood. But deaf as she was, she had no way to find Kira if she stayed inside the tangled scrub forest. She would have to return to the *banchory* trail—and hope her companion was ambulatory enough to do the same.

With a scientist's unquenchable curiosity, Dax noticed that the lower levels of the *tuq'mor* had survived the comet explosion amazingly intact, protected from the fireball by their own dense, damp foliage. Many of the softer ivy leaves had curled and crisped from the heat, but the thicker succulents looked undamaged. Even some of the ivy-brambles had survived where they dipped long tendrils into the wetlands. This odd ecosystem may have been damaged by the comet's blow, Dax thought, but it had by no means been destroyed.

The same thing couldn't be said of the *banchory* trail, however. Huge swathes of its *tuq'mor* rim had been smashed across the once-clear path and now lay smoldering on the seared ground. The lack of interlaced support at the scrub forest's edge must have allowed the comet's shock wave to penetrate more deeply there, while the open air of the slashed trail had let the fireball blacken the vegetation all the way down to the ground. Dax's hopes of locating Kira sank as she realized her line of sight wasn't much better here than it had been back in the forest interior. For a long moment, she hesitated on the edge of the destruction, watching the silent flakes of black ash drift slowly downward. Uneasy memory stirred inside her, sparking the same morbid fear in Jadzia that Emony had felt at Ymoc City . . . were any of those ashes the remains of someone she had known?

Under her drying crust of mud, something fluttered against her shoulder. Dax cursed again and slapped at her uniform tunic, convinced she must have inadvertently hauled some inhabitant of the wetland out with her when she emerged. All she felt beneath her fingers, however, was the cool lump of her Starfleet communicator, clinging stubbornly to her despite her head to toe immersion in mud. It wasn't until the small metal pin quivered again that she realized she was being hailed by someone, and just couldn't hear the chirp.

She tapped down the communicator's response button and held it to override whoever was hailing. "Dax here," she said, feeling the vibration of her words in her mouth and jaw even though she couldn't hear them. "If this is the *Defiant* calling, I can't hear you. You'll have to buzz the communicator off and on in universal signal code."

She got a reply as soon as she lifted her fingers, but it wasn't the staccato coded message she'd expected. Instead, it was a long, chirping pulse, almost exactly the same length as hers had been.

Eyes narrowing in suspicion, Dax held down the communicator response button again, but didn't speak into it. This time, she was careful to keep her transmission much shorter. She was rewarded with an equally short quiver in response, despite the silence that was all anyone on the other end of that connection would have heard. Assuming they could hear at all.

"Kira!" It was joyful instinct that made Dax say it into the communicator, even though she knew her companion had to be just as deaf as she was. Then she slowly buzzed the same message through the pin in short on-off bursts, spelling out each letter of the Bajoran major's name in universal signal code.

There was a long pause after she finished, during which Dax began to worry that Kira's lack of Starfleet training meant she might not know how to translate that coded message. Then her own pin began to vibrate, long and short bursts beneath her cupping fingers. "Dax," it spelled out first. Then, more slowly, "Tricorder position."

Dax cursed and yanked her mud-covered tricorder up from her belt, praying it worked. It wasn't the immersion in mud she was worried about—the legendary durability Starfleet built into its equipment could withstand much worse conditions. But air-burst explosions like the one they'd just endured had a tendency to emit an invisible wave of electromagnetic radiation in addition to its atmospheric shock wave. Depending on how strong that EM pulse had been, there was a good chance the tricorder's delicate quantum circuits had been fused by stray electrons.

The instrument's display lit up correctly, but the babble of machine code that streaked across it when she punched in the request for Kira's communicator pin coordinates confirmed Dax's fears. It looked like all the higher-level programming circuits had been scrambled. She scowled down at the display's final result. *Alett gerivok*—Vulcan computer code for the number twenty-seven. But twenty-seven of what units? In what direction? Could she even be sure the tricorder had understood her request to begin with, and wasn't just spitting out random nonsense?

Well, there was only one way to find out. Dax took three experimental steps down the cluttered banchory trail toward the place she'd last seen Kira, then paused to reinput the request for her coordinates. This time the racing lines of codes steadied out on *prern gerivok te prern*—the code for twenty-five-point-five. She glanced back at her initial position, gauging the distance she had traveled. A meter and a half seemed just about right.

Encouraged, she continued walking in that direction, pausing to recheck the tricorder's output every time she had to clamber through another tangle of downed trees. At her sixth checkpoint, the Vulcan number on the tricorder was higher than before. Painstakingly, Dax retraced her steps and checked both sides of the trail until the readout would go no lower, then shoved herself into the charred embrace of the *tuq'mor.* According to the tricorder, Kira was only six meters away from her now, and the sky still held enough luminous violet light to see through the tangled vegetation. Dax rechecked the readout once more to make sure she was heading in the right direction, then clipped the tricorder back on her belt and started searching through the smoky shadows.

After a moment, her communicator pin quivered again. Dax paused, translating the vibrating dashes and dots in mounting impatience. "Turn right under," they spelled out enigmatically. Dax turned right as ordered but saw nothing to go under, just more tangled *tuq'mor* wetland. "Log," added her communicator pin in slow, tired quivers. "In water."

Dax cursed, loud enough this time for her recovering ears to give her a faint, tinny backwash of the sound, and knelt down to scan the water line, looking for a charred log big enough to trap a Bajoran female. She found it not half a meter away, protruding from a wetland pond like a tilted obelisk. Its burnt wood was still ruby-warm on the upper surface where it hadn't been quenched. The dying firelight sparked glowing reflections in two dark eyes, peering up at her caustically from beneath the log's heavy shadow. Kira tilted her chin up just enough to lift her mouth above the waterline and, faint as a cricket's chirp, Dax heard her say, "About time."

Dax didn't bother replying, instead plunging down into the still-warm muck beside her friend, fearful that her position meant crushed limbs or battered organs. To her relief, she found the log split into a twisted fork half a meter below the water line, trapping Kira's half-turned torso in a vise of chokingly thick thorned branches. At least half a dozen of them had snagged on the tough fabric of her Bajoran uniform.

Kira said something else, too faint for Dax's shrilling ears to hear, then demonstrated by reaching both hands up over her head and wrapping them around the still-smoldering log. Her wet uniform sleeves began to steam before she could even lock her hands for one good tug against the tangled thorns. She pulled them away a moment later just as smoke began to rise. Dax winced, seeing the places where the cloth had seared through on the major's more stubborn attempts to extricate herself.

Lifting a finger at Kira to make her wait, Dax pulled out her phaser and set it to its narrowest, knife-thin firing spray. Taking a deep breath, she let herself sink down into the muddy water. She couldn't see much through the murk, but by patting her way along the edge of Kira's torso with one hand, she managed to sweep a careful line of phaser fire at a ten-centimeter distance, severing thorny twigs from their parent branch without trying to disentangle Kira from them. She bobbed up to take a second deep breath, then submerged again and sliced through the tangled vegetation on the other side of the fork. By the time she'd surfaced again and swiped the muddy water out of her eyes, Kira was already reaching up to grasp the smoldering log again.

"Wait." Dax tugged her friend's arms apart, then began scooping water onto the glowing wood with both cupped hands. It sizzled and steamed and exploded in little hissing pops, making the log slowly darken. Dax kept splashing until most of the surface was completely sodden, then stepped back and came around the log to stand behind Kira, holding a thumb up where the major could see it. She nodded and lifted her arms to clench tightly around the dampened wood.

"Now!" Kira's voice said faintly, and she hauled herself half out of the water with one strong upward jerk. Dax caught and steadied her when her momentum faded, giving Kira a chance to shake one booted foot free of the thorny tangle. With the flexibility that came with her size, the Bajoran then planted her heel on the log at the same height as her chest and kicked herself clear of the thorns, so powerfully that she staggered both of them back a step in the mud.

Dax caught her balance first, grabbing hold of the nearest unburnt branch to steady them both. "Are you all right?" she shouted at her companion.

Kira grinned at her through a mask of ashen dribbles. Despite the burns on her sleeves and the thorn cuts that had already started dappling her legs with drops of blood, the Bajoran major looked surprisingly unaffected by her ordeal. "I've been through worse tortures in low-security Cardassian prisons!" she shouted back. What little Dax could hear of her voice sounded cheerful. "At least here the water's nice and warm."

Dax shook her head, remembering the instant of scalding heat just after the fireball's passage. Her face still felt tender from that momentary immersion. "Too warm for me!" she shouted back, then paused to listen. A distant rumble echoed through the fading shrill of her blasted ears. "That sounds like another comet strike, either smaller or further away. This must have been a major debris cluster."

Kira winced. "Don't say that like it's a good thing. Another one could hit right here."

"That's statistically unlikely," Dax informed her.

"So is a stable wormhole." Kira hauled herself out of the muck, swinging up to balance with enviable ease on the low-hanging branch. Dax groaned and forced her aching muscles to scrabble their way to the same perch, feeling weighted down by her wet and mud-sodden uniform. "Our first priority right now is to get back to the Klingon exile camp and see if anyone's still alive there. After that, we'll contact the *Defiant* and see if they're still—I mean, see if the battle with Kor is over."

Dax lifted an eyebrow at her. "Are we going to beam up if it is?"

"No. We're going to stay here and locate Bashir, even if we have to throw away our communicator pins to do it." Kira took a deep, decisive breath. "I never left behind a member of the Shakaar who could have been rescued. And no matter what Captain Sisko says, I'm not going to start now."

"Sounds good to me." Dax led the way back through the charred *tuq'-mor* to the smoke-filled chasm of the *banchory* trail. The late night sky was even more radiant with afterglow than before, spiked near the horizon with a sunrise-bright flame and banded above that with rust-tinged sky and coppery clouds. If she hadn't known better, Dax would have thought it was dawn. "Of course, by the time we make it back to *epetai* Vrag's settlement, Julian may already have been there for hours, waiting for us."

Kira opened her mouth to reply, then caught sight of the destruction wrought in the *banchory* trail by the comet strike and broke into a fit of startled coughing instead. "Not hours," she said sourly, when she finally regained her voice. "Weeks. Because that's how long it's going to take us to get back."

CHAPTER 8

ALL HE KNEW WAS THAT HE WAS COUGHING. SO HARD AND SO BREATHLESSLY that he thought he'd tear his body apart. No up. No down. He didn't know who he was talking to when he croaked, "Stop! Stop! Put me down!" But they listened to him. And even though the pain followed him and rode up through him in waves so thick he thought he'd vomit, Bashir realized it was true darkness pressing in all around him, not just his own unconsciousness. Strong Klingon hands lowered him into a sitting position against a cool, uneven wall.

Distant thunder—or perhaps the explosions of primitive mortars—trembled through the hard floor, shivered through his stomach. *Shock.* Undoubtedly. Whatever had happened, the pain alone was enough to bottom out his blood pressure, and he harbored a morbid suspicion that the cold wetness he felt collected in his boot was something other than water.

A vague sixth sense of other bodies in the same enclosed space. Bashir stirred only enough to rocket pain up his leg and into his stomach, but felt someone move touchably close in response to his gasp. He wound his fingers in that someone else's sleeve. "Where are we?" he whispered.

Another bone-deep rumble shuddered through the world, just below the level of hearing. Then K'Taran's voice, aberrantly loud, "Underground."

It told him nothing. But told him enough: all the rules had changed. "The *xirri* . . . the one I gave you . . ."

"She's fine. She's with the others."

Better than could be said for him. He closed his eyes and leaned his head back against the wall.

A warm blur of light bloomed against the outside of his eyelids. He blinked, forcing himself alert, watching a handful of Klingon youngsters appear behind the spread of light as though chasing it ahead of them. Singed and filthy, they each brandished some form of fire, most of them carrying burning handfuls of *tuq'mor* in the slings of their wet tunics. The huge cave came alive with firefly motes of light as they scattered to distribute fire all over the chamber. Voices—some Klingon, some not—bloomed in the warming darkness alongside the light.

"The fire outside is dying." One of the boys drew closer, a tree limb almost as thick as his arm wrapped in cloth and sputtering erratically. "But more fire is coming from the sky. We will be here for some time." He knelt beside K'Taran. The flames strengthened somewhat now that he'd stopped moving, and the sudden flare of their intensity hurt Bashir's eyes. "Will he die?"

K'Taran reached to take the torch from the boy, her own eyes stark and gray in the unreliable light. "He is the Human doctor. He will tell us." And she held the light across his outstretched legs. As though doing him some favor.

Years of practice with trauma patients prevented him from vocalizing any sounds of horror, but Bashir couldn't stop the panicky whirl of his thoughts any more than he could stop his heart from thundering. His uniform was soaked and muddy, tunic and trousers all reduced to the same ash-riddled iron gray. Rents in the fabric exposed minute flashes of scarlet, but none of them accounted for the glossy overlay of blood down the inside of his right leg. He followed the stain upward to a knee already misshapen with swelling. Then realized that it wasn't edema pushing the fabric of his trousers medially out of alignment. It was bone.

His hands trembled as he pried his tricorder out of its pouch. Its normally reassuring warble rang piercingly off the flowstone walls, and at least the scroll of readings made a modicum of sense. BP was better than he expected, although he didn't like his heart rate or the shallowness of his breathing. Just reading the figure on how much blood he'd lost made him dizzy. Still, there was no arterial damage, and at least the hemorrhaging was slowing. Folding the tricorder closed in his lap, he rubbed shakily at his eyes.

"So . . . " K'Taran glanced down at his leg, then up at his face again with painfully adolescent bravery. "Will you die?"

Leave it to Klingons to stick with the most basic of questions. "Not immediately." And for some reason, that struck him as funny. He decided not to laugh, for fear he'd frighten them. "Where's the rest of my equipment?"

Even as he asked, the bump and scrape of a dragging container hurried up on one side. Bashir turned his head and smiled at the painted *xirri* doctor. "Thank you," he said, taking the strap of the medkit when it was offered. As though some signal passed between them, the Klingon boy left abruptly, and the little *xirri* sidled over into his place.

Only two at a time with any given dead man, Bashir found himself thinking as he fumbled with the latches on the kit. It unfolded clumsily, the front panel clattering onto the floor. *Just another of many quaint Klingon traditions.* He found a vial of stimulant and fitted it carefully onto his hypospray. "I'm sorry about this," he said as he calibrated the dosage.

A brittle, unreadable expression flitted across K'Taran's face. "It is not your fault."

"I should have stayed to the trail. The first rule of emergency medicine is to avoid making new victims."

This time she caught his hand, halting him just before he delivered the injection. "It is not your fault!" she declared when he blinked up at her. Then, in a tone of choked embarrassment, "It is my fault. You were caught in the *tuq'mor,* and the fire was coming . . . " She released him and clenched her hands miserably in front of her. "I did not realize you would break so easily."

He wondered what she would think if she knew he was far less fragile than most.

Arguing the finer points of blame was ultimately useless, though. Die from a comet strike, die from starvation, die from an open leg fracture. What difference did it really make? Digging a container of sterile water out of the open medkit, Bashir held the almost-empty bottle out toward the painted *xirri.* He remembered using most of his supply irrigating *xirri* wounds, and remembered his native counterpart following him from patient to patient with keen interest as he performed the procedure. Now, Bashir only had to shake the bottle once before the *xirri* ducked forward to take it from him and scampered away—hopefully in search of water.

K'Taran watched in silence as Bashir sorted through the rest of his limited pharmacy in search of something that might tackle the pain of a comminuted fracture. Nothing powerful that wouldn't also render him useless for both himself and any other wounded. Choosing a more lightweight analgesic, he was still counting vertebrae upward from his sacrum when K'Taran asked quietly, "Is it true?"

Bashir finished counting, then carefully injected as large a dose as he dared into his spine. "Is what true?"

She swallowed hard, but didn't drop her gaze. "That you will die."

Ah—that eternal Klingon pragmatism again. Moving slowly to give the spinal time to do its work, Bashir twisted apart the hypospray and tossed the empty vial back into his kit. "I don't know," he admitted wearily. "I've lost a lot of blood, and with no other Humans around, I can't replace it. And whenever fractured bone is exposed to air . . . " Just mentioning it made his leg shriek with remembered pain, but the spinal already smothered some of the reality. He managed to push the phantom anguish aside. "Well, that's not good even when you've got a whole sickbay to work with. If we're really stuck down here, and this is all the treatment I'll receive . . . " He met her gaze frankly, not wanting her to see just how badly he was afraid. "Yes," he said at last. "I'll very likely die."

The *xirri* returned with the water; Bashir was just as glad to distract himself from K'Taran's disturbing fixation with his impending demise. He flash-sterlized the entire container, then screwed on the irrigation lid with more dexterity than he expected. Bending forward flexed the spur of protruding bone, so he only sliced away the fabric at the point of the actual break, instead of opening his pantleg to the ankle the way he would have with another patient. Blessed numbness let him approach the procedure at a professional distance. A patient's fracture, a patient's blood. It didn't matter who the patient was. He showed the *xirri* how to hold the bottle overhead so gravity could work its magic on the water, and used both his own hands to explore the fracture as he irrigated. Only once did he find himself wishing he had gloves or even sterile drapes. No sense wishing for things that couldn't be had in an emergency, though; he banned the thought from his mind and went back to concentrating on his patient.

They were almost through the third bottle of sterilized water when a reassuring hand closed on his shoulder and a warm voice remarked, "You know, I'm getting less enamored with the native botany by the hour."

It was the humanness of the voice that jerked Bashir's head up; the swiftness of his movement scattered sparks across his vision. He clapped one hand abruptly to the floor, steadying himself, and blinked furiously to keep from losing sight of consciousness. The slim, elderly Asian man squatting beside him rolled smoothly to his knees and closed both hands protectively around the doctor's upper arm. "It's all right—I've got you."

And the Klingons have us both. Still, it eased his dizziness to relax his weight onto someone else's strength. Leaving the *xirri* to finish with the water, Bashir let the older Human ease him back against the stone wall. He almost felt a rush of blood back into his brain as his sense of his surroundings realigned and sharpened. *Well, thank God,* he thought wearily, turning to really look at the man kneeling beside him. *At least we've found the* Victoria Adams*'s crew.*

He was fit, trim, and flexible in a way completely at odds with the ancient wisdom in his dark eyes. At least one hundred, Bashir decided, for all that he looked not a day over seventy. He wasn't one of the scientists—the cheerfully commercial jumpsuit on his slim frame was a familiar staple of the Interplanetary Space Foundation, a nonprofit organization that supplied volunteers to research projects in need of enthusiastic, unskilled help. Although their advertisements promised nonspecific "adventure and opportunity," Bashir had a feeling being shot down by Klingons wasn't the type of adventure the Foundation had intended. Still, there was something about his friendly, high-cheeked face and the cut of his iron gray hair that said "Starfleet Brass," and Bashir found himself wishing he could sit up straighter to convey his respect. "Captain . . . " He wasn't even sure why he said it. It just seemed the proper title for the easy competence surrounding this man.

A little glimmer of something bordering on panic chased itself through the old man's eyes. "Not here, son," he said gently. Just that quickly, his contagious smile resurfaced. "Here, we're just two Humans stuck in the same problem." He shifted position to offer one hand. "Why don't you call me George?"

Something in the keen way the old man watched him after this pronouncement said that this was both a lie and an order. Bashir nodded to show he understood, and lifted his own hand for shaking. "I—" Blood coated him like a torn glove. He pulled back before their palms could make contact. "My name's Julian, Julian Bashir."

"Dr. Bashir." He flicked his eyes across Bashir's medical uniform and dipped an acknowledging nod. "Our hostess tells me you could use a few willing donors."

The blood. On his hand, his pantleg, the floor. Everywhere but where it should be. "B negative," he admitted, "at least two units." Which would buy him time, clear his head a little, but hardly solve his problem. Necrosis was necrosis, no matter how much blood your heart pumped through it.

"Well, I'm A positive," George told him. "But we've got at least seventeen other Humans I think we can count on." He braced one hand on his knee in preparation to stand, and Bashir reached out to catch his wrist. George halted, eyes alert.

"No wounded," Bashir said firmly. He held the other officer's gaze to make sure his commitment to this was clear. "If they aren't completely healthy and uninjured, I won't take their blood." First rule of emergency medicine: avoid creating new victims.

George nodded solemnly. "Understood. You hang tight until I get back." Then he trotted briskly into the deeper cave, leaving Bashir feeling cold and unaccountably alone.

"Honor grants you the right of restitution." K'Taran waited until the doctor flicked a glance at her, then continued formally, "Traditionally, your family would inherit the right should you . . . no longer be able to exercise it yourself. But as you have no family here . . . I will take whatever action you require of me. By my own hand."

Taking the empty water bottle from the *xirri,* Bashir shook his head to stop the little native from running off for another refill. "What are you talking about?" he asked K'Taran.

"If you ask me, I will kill myself." She lifted the bottle from his shaking hands and carefully wrapped it with its own bloody irrigation tubing. "A life for a life."

Bashir snugged the bottle and its tubing back into the kit, shaking again and feeling a little sick. "Don't be ridiculous. I don't want you to kill yourself."

"Then what? Should I maim myself in equal measure?"

"Stop it," he said firmly. There was only one hypo of system stimulant left, and he wasn't sure he wanted to use it just yet.

K'Taran surprised him by slamming the kit shut almost on his fingers. "No!"

Bashir jerked away from her slightly, pushing himself back against the wall. Some distant awareness knew he'd moved the bones in his leg again, but what the spinal didn't fully quench surprise had already washed away.

"Do not leave me with this dishonor on my name!" K'Taran bent over him fiercely, her breath hot against his face and her eyes bright with a pain rivalling his own. "I have done you a terrible wrong. I know from your face that even Human blood will not erase it. Please . . . allow me to balance the debt."

He tried to imagine offering up his life for anything when he was only fourteen. Then he thought about Dax and Kira, trapped God only knew where as the sky fell down around them, and he wondered if it was really worth raising such impassioned children when they only grew up to be inflexible, impassioned adults.

"There's only one thing I want." He made himself relax, but stopped just short of touching her hand. "Go find my friends. There's room enough for everyone down here, your grandmother's people included. But I can't go to them now. Do that for me."

At first he thought she might refuse him. The mention of her grandmother darkened her brow ridges with anger, and her jaw muscles bunched in frustration. Then her eyes strayed for only an instant to his twisted, bloody leg, and all her adult determination returned with leonine grace. "I will take the duty," she solemnly announced. "Will you accept this as honorable restitution for my crime?"

The last painful knot of fear loosened its grip on Bashir's heart. "I will."

She nodded once, grimly, and sprang to her feet with all the vigor of a warrior marching into honorable combat even though she'd almost certainly lose. Perhaps that was all that was really facing her now. Still, Bashir put out one hand to stop her before she could launch herself toward the outside. "I have one more favor to ask of you."

K'Taran hesitated, eyes dark and flinty with suspicion. "Our honor is in balance," she told him.

The doctor shook his head, suddenly strangely embarrassed at having been misunderstood, as though caught in a grave imposition. "Not an honor debt," he assured her hastily. "A favor." Then, swallowing hard, Bashir sat as straight as he could, and clenched his hands behind his back. "I was wondering if I might impose on you to set a fractured bone. . . ."

• • •

According to Dax's autistic tricorder, they were halfway back to the main Klingon encampment when their communicators chirped again. This time, Dax could actually hear as well as feel the signal, although there was still an odd metallic flatness to the high-pitched sound. She waited a moment for Kira to tap her pin and answer, frowning at her when she didn't.

"Aren't you even going to acknowledge the captain's hail?" It was one thing to contemplate disobeying orders when it came to evacuating without Julian, Dax discovered, and quite another to simply ignore the chain of command.

"That's not the *Defiant* hailing us," Kira answered. "It's the wrong frequency."

Dax took a breath, realizing that for once her aching ears hadn't lied to her about a sound. "Why would someone else be hailing us?" she asked, then answered in the same breath. "The Klingons."

"From Kor's ship?" Kira shook her head. "If they knew we were here, they'd either beam us out or phaser us. No, this has to be someone who wants something from us . . . "

Their communicators chirped again, strangely high and urgent. "Should we just ignore them?"

"Probably," Kira said. Her dark eyes met Dax's in a mutually thoughtful look. "But what if it's the group who took Bashir?"

In response, Dax tapped her communicator on. "Jadzia Dax here," she said calmly. "Identify yourself."

"I am sending coordinates." The shock of hearing Gordek's gruff, graceless voice on the other end of that connection was only exceeded by the shock of his next words. "Come and help us, or I will have the Cardassians destroy your ship and all aboard it."

Dax lifted her hand to break the connection. "Cardassians?" she asked Kira in astonishment. "How could a member of *epetai* Vrag's exiles have any control over the Cardassians?"

"The same way he could have a subspace communicator," Kira shot back, her face hardening to reveal the ruthless guerrilla leader she'd once been. "Because he's been dealing with the Cardassians all along."

Dax blinked at her for a long, disbelieving minute. "Dealing in what? Armageddon isn't exactly brimming with galactic treasures."

"That's what we're going to find out." The Bajoran tapped her communicator pin on. "Send your coordinates, Gordek," she said shortly. "We'll be there."

The Klingon grunted and rattled off a string of planetary coordinates, then cut the connection as rudely as he'd opened it, giving Dax no chance to tell him that those numbers meant nothing to her. "He must be using Cardassian plotting data," she told Kira in frustration. "I have no idea where this location is."

"Could we focus in on his communicator signal, if we could get him to turn it on again?"

Dax gave her tricorder a jaundiced look. "Not unless O'Brien beams down and fixes this first."

"I don't think the captain will let me do that," said a totally unexpected Irish voice from her communicator. "But if you really want to have a heart-to-heart chat with your friend Gordek, I may be able to get you there."

"Chief?" Dax demanded. "Were you listening in on that transmission from the Klingons?"

"We've been scanning every frequency for your signal, old man, ever since the EM surge of the comet impacts cleared." That was Benjamin Sisko's familiar coffee-dark voice, sounding more impatient than relieved. "What took you so long to report in? Didn't you think we'd be worried about you?"

Kira and Dax exchanged slightly guilty looks. "We wanted to ascertain the condition of the Klingon refugees at the main encampment first, sir," Kira said at last.

"And give Dr. Bashir a little more time to show up before you abandoned him?" It was never easy to fool Sisko, Dax thought wryly, especially when what you were trying to do would have been his first instinct as well. "Are you two all right?"

Kira's answer to that was more confident, if no more accurate. "Just a few bumps and bruises, sir. Request permission to stay on planet and investigate the nature of Gordek's dealings with the Cardassians."

"Granted with pleasure, Major," Sisko said grimly. "We're currently out of Kor's firing range, so we can drop shields long enough to beam you and Dax straight to the origination point of Gordek's signal."

"Any idea how many Klingons are with him, Captain?" Dax asked.

She heard the mutter of an unfamiliar voice on the bridge, then Sisko said, "Long-range sensors indicate at least a dozen life-signs there, although not all of them are strong. Watch yourself, old man."

"Yes, sir." Dax dropped her hand from her pin and braced her aching muscles for the jerk of transport. An instant later, the smoke and downed trees of the *tuq'mor* vanished, replaced by a crackling red-gold inferno. Dax barely had time to squint her eyes shut against the glare before a pair of fierce hands seized her shoulders and dragged her closer to the fire.

"This is *your* fault!" Gordek's dark mane of hair was half-seared on one side, but his blistered face held more fury than pain. "Your shield generator didn't protect us when the comet came! Look what came of it!"

"Look what came of not telling us the truth!" Kira might have been half the Klingon's size, but her determined shove and angry scowl still backed him a step away from Dax. With her vision tempered to the glare, Dax could now see the charcoal ghosts of three pole buildings engulfed in the flames. The sprawled bodies of several dead Klingons rimmed the edge of fire, as if they'd been dragged out only far enough to be checked for life-signs before their rescuers dropped them and went back for more. The injured had been moved to the shelter of the one building left standing, built where the damp wall of *tuq'mor* around this forest clearing had deflected the cometary blast. A handful of Klingon hunters looked up from that sanctuary, then came to ring Gordek, Kira, and Dax in a deadly circle.

Dax took a slow, steadying breath and turned to watch their backs, making sure the phaser on her hip faced Kira rather than the exiles. "Why is this our fault?" she demanded, aiming the question at the hostile watchers rather than Gordek. "We never claimed that shield would save you from a direct impact. And we offered you evacuation to our ship—*you're* the one who insisted on staying here!"

That sparked a mutter of unease around the ring of fierce, furrowed Klingon faces. Dax pressed the advantage, pointing a finger at the Cardassian communicator Gordek still carried in one meaty fist. "If you would rather wait for the Cardassians to evacuate you than have the Federation do it, that's fine. But where are they now that you need them? Are they braving the Klingon blockade? Have they responded to your calls for help?"

It was a shot in the dark, but it went home. Two of the hunters turned scowling faces toward Gordek. "Why aren't the Cardassians here?" one demanded. "We told them we had the last *geset* for them days ago. Didn't they promise to evacuate us?"

"That was before the Starfleet ship was here!" Gordek snapped back at them.

"So? If our homeworld was dying, as they claim theirs is, would we not invade Hell for the cure?" growled an older, battle-scarred Klingon. He pulled out a vial of golden brown fluid from one tattered pocket and held it up to catch the firelight. Its high-tech polytex surface glittered anomalously bright in this primitive setting. "What is the character of their honor, these Cardassians you have bound us to, Gordek? They will not brave a single Klingon ship for the drug they say saves their children's lives! I say we let their children die!"

He dropped the vial contemptuously to the ground, then wrung a shout of protest out of Gordek by smashing it with one heavy, booted foot. "That is our passage out of here!" the Klingon house leader growled as the frothy yellow liquid ran and puddled underfoot. An unpleasantly caustic smell rose up from it—not familiar, but evocative of something else Dax knew. She frowned and juggled out her mud-encrusted tricorder, then ran a discreet analysis of the fluid running between her boots. The display panel flickered, then coughed up a response in enigmatic Vulcan machine-code.

The older hunter spat into the spilled *geset,* making his opinion of it offensively clear. "I see no Cardassian ships here to rescue us," he said brusquely. "All I see here is an outcast from a once-noble Klingon House—a small creature who cannot salute the sky."

Gordek snarled in wordless anger at that insult, his shoulders rolling for a roundhouse punch that Kira's lifted phaser stopped in midswing. The big Klingon took a step back, glaring down at her and breathing hard between bared teeth. "Our wounded die while we dither here! You should be transporting them up to stasis on your ship, as your doctor did before."

"No." Dax's harsh voice jerked the Klingon's furious glare over to her instead. "I may not know the character of the Cardassians' honor, Gordek, but I know the character of Benjamin Sisko's. He'll defy the blockade to evacuate innocent Klingon refugees, but he won't give shelter to a single Klingon traitor."

Her accusation ignited the roar of response she'd expected from all the hunters. "Who calls us traitors?" demanded a younger, dark-skinned male. "We have done nothing to betray the Empire!"

"Except sell this to the Cardassians." Dax lifted her tricorder to show the frowning Klingons the Vulcan chemical symbols it displayed. "According to my instrument, this is the active ingredient in that *geset* you just spilled on the ground. And if any of us were Human, we would be dead now."

Kira scowled down at the yellow rivulets trickling toward her boots, stepping back to make sure none of them came into contact. "What is it?"

"Drevlocet," Dax said simply.

Even the Klingons hissed in response to that statement. "The neurotoxin that the *Jem'Hadar* used to murder hundreds of Humans at the Hjaraur colony?" Kira growled.

"Yes. One of the native animals—I'm guessing the *banchory,* considering the number of them you've killed—must synthesize it naturally, as a defense against the biting insects here. It's been outlawed in every military convention signed in the Alpha Quadrant since Hjaraur." Dax fixed Gordek with her coldest look. "But you've been purifying it and stocking it up for the Cardassians. What did they promise you to get you to make this drug for them? It must have been something worth turning down our offer of evacuation."

"A return to the Klingon homeworld?" Kira asked shrewdly.

Gordek snarled and spit toward their feet. "As if I would gratify that fool Gowron by giving him a chance to exile me again. No, they said they would give us our own ship and escort us through the wormhole, so we could disappear into the Gamma Quadrant. It was a high price, but they said they were desperate to cure their home planet of *ptarvo* fever."

"*Ptarvo* fever?" That made Kira snort. "That's about as lethal as a foot cramp!"

Another wash of discontent rumbled through the surviving Klingon hunters. "Then why would they pay so much for this drug?" a younger one demanded, brow ridges clenched with suspicion.

"Because it can be chemically modified to attack almost any humanoid race—Romulans, Vulcans, Trill, and Klingons as well as Humans," Dax said flatly. "In fact, the only species whose neural matter we know it can't affect are the Cardassians." She aimed another ice-cold gaze at Gordek. "Did you know, when you agreed to purify this drug for them, that it could be turned against your own people?"

"No!" The exile's roar was loud, but the undertone of guilt in it rang clear to Dax's ears. "How could I? We didn't have the equipment to know they were lying!"

"No," said the older, scarred hunter. "But we knew they insulted our honor by the way they forced us to bargain our lives for this drug. We should have refused to deal with them from the beginning." He turned toward Dax, dark eyes narrowed in suspicion. "We have been in exile many months. Are the Cardassians at war with the Humans now?"

"Not yet," Dax said. "But they are certainly at war with the Klingons."

"Then they will use this drug against the Klingon Empire?"

"Quite possibly," Kira agreed, her voice caustic. "When it comes to war, Cardassians don't pay much attention to ethical conventions."

The older Klingon took a deep breath, eyes closing for a long, bitter moment. "*Epetai* Vrag was right. We should have resigned ourselves to this new life, and relinquished any hope of honorable redemption. Now we have endangered our entire race through our dishonorable striving."

"And what if we have?" Gordek snarled savagely. "Did the Klingon High Council care that they had endangered us when they abandoned us on this death-trap planet? Our crime was misplaced loyalty, nothing more! Should that condemn us to bear the brunt of heaven's wrath and die beneath this Armageddon sky, just for the sake of our honor?"

Silence followed his words, a silence filled with the sullen crackle of dying flames. Then the scarred older hunter spat again, this time aiming his contempt directly at the leader of his house. "*Batlh potlh law' yIn potlh puS.*" Then he raised his long hunter's knife and stabbed it deep into his own throat.

Kira gasped and stepped back from the sudden rush of bright Klingon blood, but Dax had been steeled for it. She knew this proud warrior race almost as well as she knew her own. From the moment she had discovered what *geset* really was, she had known no honorable Klingon could survive learning he had doomed his own people with it.

The ring of hunters watched their eldest fall to his knees in indomitable silence, then slowly collapse face down in the frothy yellow toxin. Then, with a wordless glance of agreement, all beside Gordek drew their own knives. "Before I die, I will hold the knife for those wounded who are still conscious," said the dark-skinned youngest, and the others nodded. He turned slitted obsidian eyes toward Dax. "You can transport the others up to your ship to heal, but you must promise afterwards to give them the truth. And a knife."

"I promise," she said in somber Klingon. "And I promise also to sing the honor of your actions in every great house in the Empire."

"Then it is a good day to die." The young man nodded a silent farewell to his companions, then turned on his heel and headed for the survivors in the unburnt hut. Kira frowned after him, then turned an urgent gaze on Dax.

"Do we have to—"

"Yes." Without flinching or protest, Dax watched the last two hunters of Gordek's house end their lives in equally dignified silence. Hers was now the task of *cha'DIch,* the honor witness, even if the battle here was only one of internal principles. She let her cold gaze settle afterwards on Gordek, still standing with clenched fists and scowling down at his fallen hunters as if their deaths had been an insult he could fight them over. "Gordek," she said softly. "You also have a knife."

His fire-lit gaze lifted to meet hers, swirling with resentment and frustrated fury. "Yes," he said thickly. "And I will use it on you!"

Dax took a quick step back when he launched himself, reaching desperately for her phaser even as her eyes judged the distance and her heartbeat drummed out *too late, too late, too late!* She heard the familiar shrill sound, but it wasn't until the big Klingon actually thudded down across the seared ground, sprawling limply over his own dead warriors, that she realized Kira had pulled her own weapon even earlier.

"Is he dead?" Dax demanded.

"Of course not." Kira rolled her victim off to one side, careful not to let any of his clothing come in contact with the *geset.* "He's coming back to the *Defiant* with us."

Dax frowned, her stomach roiling with the injustice of four honorable Klingons dead and this self-centered traitor saved. "You're really going to evacuate him from Armageddon?"

"That's right." Kira gave her a hard-edged Bajoran smile. "I'm going to wake him up just long enough for Odo to extract a confession that names the Cardassians as his buyers. Then we're going to extradite him—straight to Dahar Master Kor's ship."

CHAPTER 9

"GET ME KOR. NOW."

Sisko never particularly noticed how his voice sounded, especially in the middle of a tense situation. The only reason he suspected something about it changed was the way his bridge officers and ensigns dove into their work at times like these, as if Furies stood behind them breathing fire down their necks. Even Worf wasn't immune to the effect, although his stiff posture made it clear he could have resisted that aura of command if his officer's instincts ever told him to. Sisko suspected he himself had looked much the same way when he'd been on the receiving end of Admiral Nechayev's steely voice only a few hours before.

"Excellent work, Captain," the admiral had said, her ice-pale eyes gleaming despite the cometary interference that danced through her high-security transmission. "The loss of the *Victoria Adams*—perhaps even the loss of her passengers—may very well be worth finding out that the Cardassians planned to smuggle drevlocet off this Armageddon planet of yours. You may have just saved millions of lives."

"Thank you, Admiral," Sisko said shortly. "But don't start filing any obituaries. I haven't given up on the crash survivors yet, or on my away team."

Nechayev arched her eyebrows. "But I thought you said you had to drop back into a depowered and cloaked orbit to evade the Klingon blockade. How are you going to protect the planet from comet impacts now?"

Sisko grimaced. "I don't know." Dropping abruptly out of warp with his exhaust camouflaged and his shields repolarized to blend in with the magnetosphere had seemed like the best way to evade Kor's drunken, wild chase. It wasn't until after the fact that he'd realized he'd once again trapped himself into doing nothing. "I'll think of something."

"Perhaps," Nechayev suggested, "you could negotiate with Dahar Master Kor."

Sisko eyed his sector commander in deep suspicion. He'd never known the admiral to make a joke, especially not in a situation as tense as this one, but surely she couldn't be serious now. "What makes you think the Klingons are going to be any more amenable to negotiation now than when they fired on the *Victoria Adams?"*

"Because now," she pointed out gently, "you can inform them that this planet is a natural source of drevlocet."

That brought Worf's head up from his intent scrutiny of his piloting screens. "The Klingon High Council swore to uphold the military convention banning drevlocet!" he growled. "On the Honor of the Emperor Kahless! They would never use it."

"I am aware of that, Commander," the admiral retorted. "In fact, it's all that's keeping me from ordering five starships to take control of that system immediately. I trust the Klingons will protect Armageddon adequately, once they know how dangerous the planet really is."

"That's why you want me to talk to Kor," Sisko realized. "So he knows the real reason why the Cardassians have been trying to goad us into a fight."

"Precisely." The admiral transferred her steely gaze back to Sisko. "The stakes in this game are now very high, Captain. Whatever you and Kor decide to do, make sure it doesn't leave the system open to Cardassian intervention again. And that," she added, tapping her Starfleet Academy ring on the table in front of her for emphasis, "is an *order."*

Sisko gritted his teeth and agreed, recognizing the unwritten code that meant Nechayev really meant it this time. And as soon as her transmission had flickered out, he'd ordered the confessed traitor Gordek transferred over to Kor's ship. It had been his best stab at getting the Dahar Master to turn a sympathetic eye on Armageddon's evacuation. If Kor didn't respond to a warning that could save millions of Klingons from dying in a Cardassian chemical attack, he wasn't going to respond to anything.

Unfortunately, after an hour of silence, that looked to be exactly the case.

"Kor refuses to acknowledge our hail, Captain." Thornton looked frustrated, as if the Klingon's stubborn silence were his own personal failure. "I've coded it as a priority request, but the Klingons still won't answer."

"Are they jamming our transmission?"

"No, sir. Just refusing to reply."

"Maybe Kor's still interrogating Gordek," O'Brien said doubtfully. "Just because he told Odo all the gory details of his dealings with the Cardassians doesn't mean he's going to be as cooperative with Kor."

"Unlikely," Worf said. "We transported the exile collaborator over three hours ago. By now, Kor has either debriefed him or killed him."

"Or both," Odo said dryly.

Sisko rubbed a hand across his beard, his gaze never leaving the dangerous haze of cometary debris haloing Armageddon's horizon. "Ensign Osgood, how much time do we have before the next fragment is scheduled to impact the planet?"

The science officer glanced up from her computer model, looking worried. "Almost forty-five minutes, sir—but the next impact isn't a single fragment, it's a cluster that stretches over two degrees of arc. Unless we start soon, I'm not sure we'll have time to deflect them all."

"Then we can't afford to wait on Kor's convenience." Sisko launched himself out of his chair, a flare of anger burning off the stiffness that came from too long a period of inactivity. "After seeing us fire on the comet fragments that he blew apart, he must know what we've been doing to protect the planet. He might even know what maneuvers we've been using to do it. The only thing he doesn't know right now is exactly which comet fragments we need to deflect."

"I wouldn't be too sure of that, Captain," Thornton said. "I've been seeing a lot of diffuse scanner activity from the Klingon ship in the past three hours. It looks like they're tracking the whole cometary debris cloud now, just like we are."

"Kor is making sure he knows our next move in advance." Sisko smacked a hand against his useless weapons panel as he passed it, making both Thornton and Osgood start. Odo merely gave him an inquiring, upward look. "So when we go to deflect those comets—"

"—Kor will obliterate us," Worf finished grimly.

Sisko scowled and paced off another circuit of his bridge. "What we need is a way to distract the Klingon blockade long enough for us to deflect that cluster of comets. The trouble is, if I were Kor, I wouldn't be taking my eyes off those comets for a second. What could possibly distract me and my whole crew?"

"An act of God?" asked O'Brien. "Like an ion storm or a solar flare?"

Sisko shook his head. "Hard to duplicate in under an hour, Chief. What else?"

"A summons from the Emperor, or from Chancellor Gowron?" Odo suggested.

"Constable, if a summons came in from Starfleet calling us away from Armageddon right now, would you believe it?"

"No," Odo admitted.

"Me, either. What else?"

A long silence followed his question this time. It was broken at last not by words, but by one of the rarest sounds Sisko had ever heard on the bridge of the *Defiant.*

Worf was laughing.

It was a full-throated roar of Klingon amusement, barely distinguishable from a warrior's fighting bellow. It made Odo jump and O'Brien curse, while Sisko swung around to stare at his tactical officer in disbelief and dawning hope. *"What?"* he demanded. "What have you thought of?"

"The *Batlh Jaj!"* Worf's eyes gleamed with the dancing red sparks that either danger or delight could ignite. He saw Sisko's baffled look and shook his head, so hard his braid whipped against his shoulders. "The *Batlh Jaj,* Captain. The Klingon Day of Honor. It is today!"

"What?" Two long strides took Sisko over to the nearest panel, which happened to be Osgood's. She gave him a quizzical look when he leaned over her shoulder, but it wasn't the arcane model of cometary orbits he was interested in—it was the standard date-time readout in the corner of her display screen. "Stardate 3692 is the Day of Honor?"

"It varies from year to year, since the Klingon calendar does not correspond to Federation standard," Worf informed him. "But the day we left Deep Space Nine was *wa'ChorghDIch*—first day of the ninth month. The Day of Honor falls three days after that."

"I don't know about the *wa'ChorghDIch,"* said O'Brien. "But it has been almost exactly three Standard days since we left the station."

Adrenaline began to fizz through Sisko's blood, born of both excitement and foreboding. "Let me see if I can remember my Klingon history," he said slowly. " 'On the Day of Honor, the Klingons treat even their fiercest enemies as blooded Klingon warriors, with all the privileges and rights and ceremonial duties that entails.' " He threw a challenging look at his tactical officer. "Are you thinking what I'm thinking?"

Worf's savage, glinting smile told him the answer without any need for words.

"Oh, no." Odo's deep voice was heavy with foreboding. "Commander, you're not going to make us fight one of those hand-to-hand ritual battles again, are you?"

"In reality, the *Suv'batlh* is not a ritual," Worf replied. "It is a battle to the death to resolve a challenge to one's honor."

"And on the Day of Honor, the combatants don't need to be blooded Klingon warriors. They can even," Sisko said in deep satisfaction, "be Starfleet officers."

"Correct," said Worf.

Sisko swung to face Thornton again. "I want you to ram a connection through to the Klingons—don't wait for them to acknowledge it, just patch it straight into their display. Can you do that?"

The young sensor tech grinned back at him, as if his reckless energy were contagious. "I can feed it right through their viewing sensor circuits, sir, so it replaces their external scan. The only problem is, they can probably jam it within a few minutes if they want to."

"They won't want to. Just give me a minute's warning before we're on-line." Sisko turned back toward Worf. "We'll need to hold the *Suv'-batlh* on the Klingons' ship, to distract them while the *Defiant* deflects comets."

"Agreed. But allow me to point out, sir, that if we win, we will not only have defended our honor." Red battle sparks were dancing in Worf's eyes again. "We will also have forced Kor to grant any request we ask on that day."

"*Any* request?" Sisko demanded. "Even cooperating with us to keep the Cardassians away from Armageddon?"

"Yes, sir."

Sisko's breath hissed between clenched teeth as he weighed the odds and juggled probabilities. "It's a gamble," he said at last. "But I think we have a chance of success. And if we fail, we'll still have managed to distract the Klingons without making any overt acts of war against them."

"Somehow, that wasn't what I had in mind for my official Starfleet obituary," O'Brien commented.

"Don't worry, Chief," Sisko told him. "You're not going. You've got a family at home to worry about—"

"—and you'd like a chance to actually win this fight," O'Brien finished, sounding resigned. "Thank you, sir. So who are you taking?"

"Worf," Sisko said, then glanced over his shoulder inquiringly. He got a reluctant Changeling nod in return, but the metal-hard gleam in his constable's eyes told him his instincts were correct. "And Odo. That way—"

"I've punched into the Klingon sensors, Captain," Thornton interrupted, voice calm despite the frantic way his fingers flew across his controls. "Communications signal will be on their viewscreen in ten seconds. Nine . . . eight . . . seven . . ."

Sisko took a deep breath and prepared himself to glare straight at the unoffending curve of Armageddon's rusty atmosphere. He'd get no return signal from this unauthorized transmission, at least at first.

" . . . three . . . two . . . on-line."

"Kor, this day is *Batlh Jaj,"* Sisko said, cutting straight to the heart of the matter with Klingon-like brusqueness. "You cannot refuse a challenge, even from a Starfleet officer who has interfered in your blockade. I challenge you on behalf of my insulted honor to engage in *Suv'batlh,* three on three." He saw Worf nod at him approvingly, although he wasn't sure if it was his phrasing or his Klingon pronunciation that was being evaluated. "Right here, Kor. Right now. *Suv'batlh."*

There was an agonizingly long pause, during which the distant spiked bloom of an upper-atmosphere comet impact flared at him from the curve of Armageddon's smoke-clouded sky, a foretaste of the disaster looming just outside the gravity well. Then the screen rippled and became Kor's broad-shouldered form, seated in his own stark command chair. The older Klingon's furrowed face was alight with surprise, respect, and laughter.

"A noble effort, Sisko!" Kor applauded in the Klingon style, fist thumping on chest, while the warriors around him watched and rumbled with amusement. "Ironic, but still noble!"

Sisko narrowed his eyes, ignoring the queasy ripple of unease that twisted in his gut. "What do you mean, 'ironic'?"

"Ironic because your request comes just a little too late." Kor's grin showed stained and straggling teeth, but its honesty couldn't be doubted. "You may have matched the Klingon calendar to your Federation days correctly, but you forgot about the length of the Klingon day. The day of *Batlh Jaj*—what you call our Day of Honor—ended ten minutes ago."

The devastation to Armageddon's surface seemed endless. Kira had given up hoping to find any sign of life among the burned and buried wreckage. Ash carpeted what remained of the *tuq'mor* like a silky gray shroud, and the mud no longer steamed or simmered. A featureless black cloud of ejecta had crept inland from over the ocean, dimming the sky to dull amber. Only the hiss and creak of cooling embers accompanied them as they trudged along the dark tunnel that used to be a *banchory* trail. That, and the distant, hollow *boom* of comet fragments bursting not nearly far enough away.

Kira couldn't remember the last time her body had hurt so much. Her ankles ached from supporting her full weight on toes and arches while climbing the jungle-gym roadblocks of *tuq'mor* thrown down in their way; every other muscle all the way up to her ass burned with a fatigue so deep she almost couldn't imagine it fading. Dax had made her last humorous comment uncounted hours ago. Now, all Kira heard from the Trill was the squelch and slap of her feet in the sticking mud, and hoarse panting that sounded suspiciously like Kira's own.

If I ever get home, Kira thought, *I will never walk anywhere without pavement again.*

Dax's grab at her sleeve stung the burns on her arm and made her gasp. "Do you hear that?" the Trill whispered, hauling her to a stop.

Hissing through her teeth, Kira pried the Trill's fingers from around her scorched forearm. *No,* she wanted to grumble. *I don't hear anything but us hiking into oblivion!* But something in the dark wasteland silenced her—something about the metronomic quality of the thunder she'd first taken for exploding bolides. Something about the way it shivered in her stomach and made the *tuq'mor* rattle.

She pushed Dax toward one singed-but-still-living hedge. "Come on!"

Finding cover within the blackened *tuq'mor* was probably the easiest thing Kira had done in the last seven hours. Wriggling between knotted limbs like a fish darting among river reeds, she hauled herself into what now served as the topmost story. What parts of her weren't already blackened by ash, burns, and mud readily picked up a grimy coating of soot from the limbs and brush that had taken the brunt of the last big air strike. She crouched as low to the burned-out canopy as exhausted muscles would allow, then hoped she looked like any other clump of burned foliage as she peered back down the trail.

The *banchory*'s huge shadow preceded it. Dark as the bordered path seemed to Kira's night-adjusted eyes, it washed darker still, smothering even the vestiges of detail. A figure, slim and wild-haired, perched astride the moving mountain; Kira doubted the rider would have stood out more clearly on the brightest day. She didn't even have to worry about missing the *banchory*'s back when she leapt from the *tuq'mor.*

Her phaser jabbed the startled Klingon in the spine before he could do more than jerk a startled look over his shoulder. Kira used the flat of her hand to push his chin forward, then looped her arm around his throat for good measure. "Yes," she announced, very close to his ear, "this is a real weapon. No, I have no reservations about using it. You'd better hope you can tell me something I want to hear."

The Klingon spread both hands with fingers splayed—the age-old symbol of unarmed threat. It was a youthful female's voice that told her, "A Human doctor named Bashir has sent me to find his companions so they can wait out the comets in a place of safety." K'Taran tipped just the slightest glance back at Kira's startled face. "Will that do?"

Nighttime cloaked the worst of the destruction, but a few Klingon-tended fires and a renewed blast of light in the southern sky let Kira pick out enough details to know that honor hadn't spared Rekan Vrag's encampment from Armageddon's wrath. She clung uneasily to K'Taran's middle as the *banchory* minced with surprising delicacy around lumps in the carpet of ash. Kira only recognized them as charred corpses with considerable use of her imagination. It wasn't worth the effort. As the beast finally slowed to a shuffling standstill in what might have once been the camp's center, Kira realized she didn't even know for sure which part of the camp they were facing. Nothing about the place looked the same; only the bottom-most rootballs of the trees were left standing.

Oh, Prophets, I want to go home!

"Major! Commander!"

LeDonne's slim, dark figure peeled away from one of the still smoldering tree hovels. Kira saw the eager relief in the young Human's movements, knew what the nurse must be thinking when she slowed abruptly and looked carefully from front to rear on the *banchory* again.

Still, it was Dax who announced, almost cheerfully, "We found him," as the *banchory* labored meticulously to its knees.

"Sort of." Kira slid to the ground, suppressing a grimace at the packed-dirt fullness in her knees and the overall anguish in the soles of her feet. "K'Taran says Dr. Bashir sent her to get us." She caught at the *banchory*'s small, conical ear for support in the hopes none of the approaching Klingons would sense her weakness. "There are caves several kilometers west of here. They'll be protected from the explosions—safe from anything but a direct ground strike. There's room enough there for everyone." Everyone who was left, at least. Kira could count the gathered faces on both hands. She looked around for *epetai* Vrag, and found her standing stiffly near the middle of the tiny crowd.

"She's lying." Rekan didn't even move her eyes toward Kira.

K'Taran, proudly matching her grandmother's glare, hopped to the ground beside Kira and lifted her chin. "An honorable Klingon does not lie."

"And I say again"—Rekan bared teeth still sharp despite her age—"you are lying."

Kira felt K'Taran flash with anger hot enough to reignite the foliage. Stepping quickly away from the *banchory,* Kira threw up one elbow to halt the girl's forward surge, and thanked the Prophets when K'Taran stopped without a protest. Kira was in no shape to reinforce the suggestion. "What possible motive does she have to lie to us?" she asked Rekan.

The old matriarch looked as though she wanted to spit. "Dishonor needs no motive."

"You have no right to question my honor!" This time, K'Taran shrugged off Kira's restraining arm and lunged forward to shove aside the two adults standing between her and Rekan. "I stand here, do I not?" she snarled. "I have tied my life to this cursed planet. I held my head proudly while our ancestors' keep was burned and our family name shattered and thrown to the dust. What more would you have of me?"

"Honor does not abandon its House!" Rekan's eyes gleamed with a passion brighter than all the stars Armageddon had thrown down on them. "Honor does not bend law to whatever meaning suits it."

"Law said only that we should remain exiled on this planet," K'Taran reminded her. "Law never stated that we must necessarily die."

"The intent of a command is as important as the words."

Kira blurted a disbelieving laugh without having meant to. "That's what this is all about?" she asked, limping away from the *banchory* to stand shoulder-to-shoulder with K'Taran. "Because Gowron expected you to be killed here, you're not allowed to take action to prevent it?"

Rekan lifted her eyes to a place just above Kira's head, not even deigning to meet her gaze. "I will not have this House judged as being without honor," she stated grimly. "I will not have this family go to Sto'vo-Kor and recite to Kahless how we tried to trick honor—how we held hostages unrelated to our battle and tried to run from our duty like Ferengi picking holes in a contract of their own making."

K'Taran moved in front of her grandmother's stare. The electricity when their eyes met made Kira's stomach twist. "You do not believe I am lying." The girl's voice sounded only hurt, and not as angry as Kira had expected. "You fear I'm telling the truth—that there actually *is* some chance for life."

For the first time, Kira glimpsed what might have been the love fueling this angry war between them. "I fear that you are *wrong,*" Rekan almost whispered. "I fear we will die while fleeing, irrevocably disgraced."

"Shouldn't everyone be allowed to choose their own path?" That was a question that had gnawed at Kira since Rekan's first refusal to evacuate her clan. "Is it honorable to force your own fears on the rest of them?"

Rekan hissed at her through the darkness. "Swallow your bile. You know nothing of honor."

"I know that my people can feel right and wrong inside their own hearts," Kira shot back. Fear, anger, and fatigue stripped her of all social graces. It was all she could do not to shake the older Klingon. "We don't need a High Chancellor or anyone else to tell us how to be honorable. Are Klingons so simple that they can't decide that for themselves?"

Rekan's backhanded blow didn't surprise Kira so much as the raw force in the old woman's swing. She was on the ground, stunned and blinded with pain, before her conscious mind even identified what had smashed her down. "Be glad you are not a Klingon," the *epetai*'s scorn rained like comet-fire from above her. "I would feed your own heart to you where I stand."

And Kira heard her own voice say groggily, "I accept."

Her vision cleared with painful slowness, seeming somehow brighter and less focused than it ought to be. But the shock and suspicion on Rekan Vrag's face was unmistakable, even through a haze of pain and rattled thinking. "Your challenge to combat," Kira continued, more carefully. "I accept."

The *epetai* frowned. "I did not challenge you!"

"You struck me." It was one of those moments Odo would have scoffed at as being more creative than was good for her. Some disconnected part of her kept spinning out the words, with no particular concern for the battered body still splayed out on the ground. "When one Klingon strikes another, it means you want to do combat."

"You are not a Klingon!" Rekan countered.

And at last Kira's instincts let the rest of her in on what they were doing. *"Batlh Jaj."*

The silence that crashed down among them was almost hard enough to hurt. Certainly heavy enough to crush most of the breath from Rekan's lungs; her voice was thin when she said, "You cannot conduct *Suv'batlh.* There are only two of you."

"Three."

Even Kira felt the hurt that must have throbbed in Rekan when K'Taran stepped forward. The older Klingon growled and swiped at the air; Kira forced herself to crawl to all fours, then slowly to her feet.

"If we win," Kira said, moving to form a bridge between K'Taran in front of her grandmother and Dax still waiting by their *banchory,* "then that will mean our honor is more true. We can lead anyone who wants to follow us to K'Taran's refuge, and you won't do anything to stop us."

Rekan didn't nod. "And if I win?"

"Then we all die." It was the answer that had been true since before the challenge was even leveled. Kira pulled herself as tall as her aching muscles would let her. "I believe the choice of battlefield is mine."

CHAPTER 10

"TEN MINUTES!"

It was a simultaneous exclamation from at least three of the *Defiant*'s officers. Odo said the words in frustration, O'Brien in disgust, but their voices were almost completely overridden by Worf's furious roar of indignation. Sisko was the only one who remained silent, keeping his gaze locked on Kor's until the uproar on both ships subsided into uneasy silence.

"I never thought to see a day when *Klingons* hid like cowards behind the letter of the law," he said at last, and had the satisfaction of seeing Kor's laughter wiped abruptly from his eyes. "What does the Day of Honor really mean? That it is the only day on which Klingons will behave honorably?"

A snarl whistled between Kor's clenched teeth. "Take care what you say, Benjamin Sisko. If you were a Klingon, that would be an insult worthy of *Suv'batlh* on any day."

"Would it?" Worf growled, before Sisko could reply. "Then allow me to say that I, Worf, son of Mogh, never thought to see a day when Klingons hid like cowards behind the law, acting as if *Batlh Jaj* were the only day on which they needed to behave honorably!"

Kor crashed the mug he was holding against the arm of his chair, splashing dusky blood wine out in a violent spray. Anger had darkened his broad face to almost the same shade. "You insult my honor, Worf son of Mogh!"

"Good," said the Klingon tactical officer between his teeth. "That was my intention."

Kor fell abruptly silent, staring at them with a flicker of wariness breaking through the wine-soaked fury in his face. After a moment's pause, however, he acknowledged Worf's challenge with a stiff, ceremonial nod. "As the one whose honor has been challenged, we hold the *Suv'batlh* on my territory. Your party will beam over in fifteen minutes, Worf, son of Mogh, armed and ready to fight. *Qapla'!*"

The connection sliced off, leaving the bridge of the *Defiant* suspended in disbelieving silence. "You did it, Worf," O'Brien said at last, sounding dumbfounded. "You actually got Kor to accept the challenge."

Sisko let his breath trickle out, feeling his jaw muscles quiver with the release of accumulated tension. "Now all we need to do is win it. Or at least entertain Kor long enough for the *Defiant* to finish sweeping up that comet cluster." He vaulted out of his command chair, fiercely eager to be off the bridge and accomplishing something. "Worf, Odo, you're with me. Osgood, Thornton, plot the fastest deflection course you can through that cluster, and don't worry about keeping out of sight of the Klingons. Just try not to use photon torpedoes unless you have to. O'Brien, you've got the conn. Call Clark and Nensi up to man navigations and weapons while we're gone."

His chief engineer winced, uncomfortable as always with the assumption of command, even though he was technically the highest-ranking member left of Sisko's decimated crew. He swung around at his station to watch as they headed for the turbolift. "Captain, don't you want a subcutaneous transmitter? How else will you know when we're done chasing comets?"

"It will not matter," Worf said sternly. *"Suv'batlh* cannot be conceded. It can only be fought to the finish."

"Oh." O'Brien looked as glum as if he'd just been condemned to a long prison sentence, Sisko noted in amusement. "Well, in that case, good luck and—er—*Qapla.'* "

Odo snorted his scorn at that send-off, but followed Sisko and Worf into the turbolift with no visible reluctance. The doors hissed shut, locking the three of them in tense, prebattle silence. Odo broke it at last, his voice gruff.

"I assume that, since this is a ritual combat, I won't be permitted to use my shape-shifting abilities to win it."

"No." Worf's voice was equally brusque and businesslike. "A Klingon warrior does not attack by subterfuge. Any change in shape would be considered a deceit and would disqualify you from the *Suv'batlh.*"

"Too bad," Odo said. "I might be able to look just like a Klingon warrior, but that doesn't mean I can fight like one." Especially true, Sisko knew, because the Constable would refuse to wield any weapons.

Worf frowned across at the Changeling, but it was a thoughtful rather than an angry look. "Klingons measure their worth as warriors by the strength and valor of their enemies. The honor that accrues in ritual combat increases as the task becomes more difficult. I think it would be acceptable to ignore any blows that do not actually decapitate or dismember you."

"Good. Then I won't have to actually wear armor." Odo followed the others onto C Deck, heading not for the main transporter room but for the equipment bay next to it where they had a closet-sized clothing replicator capable of creating authentic Klingon outfits. As he went, his dun-colored Bajoran uniform swelled and shifted, turning to polished lacquer plates in gleaming shades of ebony and maroon.

Fortunately, Klingon weapons and armor were stock items in the replicator's data banks, along with most clothing items from known space. Worf was humming as he waited for his weapons to be made, a song so deep and tuneless that it had to be a Klingon battle-chant.

"Klingon armor and *bat'leth,* suitable for ritual combat," Sisko told the replicator when it was his turn. A moment later he was settling chest-armor over his shoulders, making sure all the side-latches were snugged tight. He'd lost count of how many times he'd done this over the last few years, sparring Dax in various holo-suite recreations. This time was different, however. This time his life really would depend upon what he was wearing.

He became acutely aware, as he hefted the shallow helmet whose curving cheek-plates had been designed more for intimidation than protection, that this was armor meant for warriors whose arteries ran deep under leather-tough ligaments and whose skeletons already made bony protective plates around their vital organs. The warm pulse of blood beneath the skin of his throat, a mammalian evolutionary quirk he'd never had cause to regret before, suddenly seemed like an invitation to disaster.

"Second thoughts, Captain?" Odo asked, when he stepped out.

Sisko glanced up at his security chief, startled, then realized he'd put on and taken off his spiked gauntlet three times, searching for a comfortable fit that just didn't exist. Worf paused on the threshold of the clothing replicator, looking dismayed.

"Only about the armor." Sisko motioned Worf into the machine, managing an almost-real smile. It was ironic that the two warriors in their party with the least mortal weaknesses were depending on him for their morale. He rubbed a hand across his exposed abdomen and sighed. "I'll just have to hope Kor went to school before the Klingons were teaching Human anatomy."

"I shall endeavor," Worf said from inside the replicator, "to make sure you do not have to face the Dahar Master personally, Captain. You are as good with a *bat'leth* as any Human I've seen, but Kor would have you disarmed and at his mercy within . . . minutes."

Sisko raised an eyebrow at him as he stepped out. "Why do I get the feeling you were about to say 'seconds,' Mr. Worf?"

The Klingon's chagrined look told him he was right. "It is not that I doubt your skill, Captain. But to become a Dahar Master, you must have fought a hundred battles, survived a hundred *Suv'batlh,* and trained a hundred blooded warriors. No amount of blood wine can dull the fighting instincts of such a warrior."

"Are you sure *you* can survive for more than a few minutes in a fight with him, Commander?" Odo demanded, never shy about asking embarrassing questions.

"No," Worf said frankly. "But in *Suv'batlh,* it is the overall outcome that counts, not the individual winners and losers. If you and the captain can surprise your opponents and win your matches, then it does not matter that Kor defeats me."

"Unfortunately," Sisko said, "that is a rather big 'if.' " He slid on his helmet, then hardened his face to the expressionless mask that served him so well during space battles. "Gentlemen, let's go defend our honor."

He'd stopped being physically conscious of the pain what seemed a whole lifetime ago. K'Taran, following his instructions with stern determination, reduced the fracture with an ease Bashir almost envied; the advantages of physical strength. Then, after she left with one of the sluggish *banchory* trailing behind, Bashir had taken further advantage of Klingon prowess by coaxing one of the boys to carry him around the massive caverns to check on the *Victoria Adams*'s crew and his *xirri* patients. Bad enough that he didn't have the proper equipment to do any of them any good—the traumatic relocation to this damp, cool chamber wasn't helping the wounded, either. He almost felt guilty accepting blood from two hale and youthful volunteers, considering he had no such panacea to offer the *xirri.*

He didn't specifically remember returning to his own little blood-stained corner, and hoped fervently he hadn't lost consciousness before tending the last of the patients. It all seemed so unfair. If he was going to break a leg during a planetary mission, why the hell couldn't he have done it when no one else needed his services? Or, at the very least, have done it so that he didn't hemorrhage a liter of blood in the process?

He wrestled his thoughts back to the moment, and concentrated instead on the small, neat movements of the painted *xirri* near his feet.

The little native doctor—a male, Bashir had finally determined when he'd been able to catch a glimpse of hemipenile bulges while they made their rounds—had found a piece of what looked like broken chert, and now used it to nick carefully, gently at the fabric of Bashir's trouser leg. He'd already extended the doctor's original cut clear to the groin, and was almost finished in the other direction, slicing patiently down toward the ankle and the terminal hem. *I've had nurses who weren't so thoughtful.* He certainly couldn't argue with the *xirri*'s diagnosis—even with the fracture reduced, his knee had swollen dramatically. Another few centimeters, and the clothing would have compromised his circulation.

"Thank you."

The *xirri* blinked huge eyes at him, with no expression Bashir could readily discern. Then it bent again to its work, tongue flicking rhythmically.

Small, unglazed dishes filled with a foul-smelling mash littered the cave floor around them, the contents burning with an almost invisible flame. Bashir patted around him in the thin, watery light, wondering what trick of nature made all the illumination seem to pool in his lap and run no further. By the time his hand thumped against the open medkit, his thoughts had already staggered so far in search of that explanation that he couldn't quite remember what he'd been looking for.

A cool, gray-green hand slipped past his own, pulling his attention toward the instruments laid out in their tray. The scalpels. Of course—he'd wanted something a bit better suited to cutting. But when he tried to lever himself away from the wall to lean forward toward his ankle, a great spasm of pain ripped up his leg and knocked him back again. God, this was so embarrassing. He was supposed to know enough to foresee what kind of movements would send him crawling out of his skin. Opening his eyes, he found the *xirri* watching him with its tongue coiled curiously just outside its tiny mouth. It turned the piece of chert over and over in nimble fingers, then scooted slightly closer to taste the laser scalpel with its tongue.

It tugged at the scalpel very gently. The piece of chert ended up in Bashir's lap almost as an afterthought.

"Here . . ." He tightened his grip just enough to make the native pause and look up at him. "You activate it like this." He turned the instrument until the power switch faced the *xirri* doctor, then turned the scalpel carefully away from them both and depressed the switch with his thumb. A thin, glowing blade of light hissed into being from the end. "Use it like a normal knife, but for God's sake be careful—it'll cut through bone and fingers just as easily as it will my pants!"

Deactivating the scalpel with almost ritualistic care, the *xirri* held it at a respectful arm's length as it repositioned itself beside Bashir's leg.

"It's a shame they can't talk."

Bashir's thoughts seemed to be ringing, his head full of broken glass as he looked meticulously left and right in search of the voice he only half-remembered. He found George just inside the touch of the tiny lights, his head resting back against the same wall that supported Bashir, his hands neatly folded atop his knees. "The Federation may be lenient when it comes to determining sentience, but I have a feeling K'Taran's elders are going to want some more quantifiable evidence than kindness and a good bedside manner."

For some reason, it didn't even seem odd to be sitting in the blood-smelling dark debating sentience ethics with a Starfleet demigod while he felt beside him for the tricorder he couldn't remember last using. "So you believe they're sentient?" he asked George. But quietly, as though their discussion might embarrass the *xirri*.

George turned a wry look toward Bashir across the darkness. "Don't you?"

He finally found the tricorder close against his left hip. He wondered if he'd snugged it there for safekeeping, or simply dropped it the last time he'd slipped away from consciousness. Not that it mattered. The device had reverted to whatever dementia had addled its brain hours ago. A frightfully low blood pressure played hide-and-seek behind a skirl of signal so strong it almost washed his screen to white. By the time the *xirri* tapped the tricorder's casing to gain his attention, Bashir could barely tell he was a Human through the confusion of contradictory readings. Dropping the useless tricorder into his lap, he forced a wan smile when the *xirri* politely offered the butt end of the deactivated scalpel.

"Thank you again." His fingers felt cold when he reached for the instrument, and his thoughts ricocheted briefly off the idea that all his heat had collected into a burning coil by his knee. But whatever rationality he'd half-seen in that thought evaporated as he watched the *xirri* pick up the empty water bottle and toddle off toward the cavern's water supply.

Even the exertion necessary to follow the *xirri*'s movement with his eyes proved too much to sustain. Leaning his head back against the wall again, he listened to the shiver of his bones as the planet rumbled with distant damage.

"When I was young," George offered, his voice warm and soothing, "I served under a man who had a very flexible view of the Prime Directive." He laughed softly. "He didn't have much patience for politics and rhetoric. If he knew that innocent lives were being threatened, he'd move heaven and earth to save them, and the Prime Directive be damned."

Behind the darkness of his closed eyes, Bashir half-remembered, half-dreamed an image of Starfleet as it must have been on the frontier. "He sounds like a great man."

"He was. The best." George was quiet again, and when he finally spoke, his deep voice smiled. "He would have had a field day with Armageddon."

Bashir would have gladly given it to him. The planet, the comets, the killing, impenetrable foliage, the spiraling, threatening slash of fiery rain. Ice as hard as boulders, boulders the size of houses, shattering the mantle and spewing megatons of ash and rock and gas back into an atmosphere growing wintery cold for lack of sun. Feverish dozing offered a nightmarish flash of Kira and Dax swept up in a vortex of fire. He jerked himself awake, leaping away from that image, and his hand seized convulsively on the tricorder still open in his lap.

It chirped politely, scrolling out a neat queue of test results.

Bashir stared at the device for nearly thirty seconds, trying to remember why seeing the tricorder hum through its paces surprised him. It certainly wasn't the dismal readings and predictions it produced—his white-cell count was no higher than he'd already suspected, and it wasn't like he'd expected any better from his serum O_2. Cupping the tricorder between both hands, he lifted it and passed it across his torso. "Why am I not getting interference?" he asked aloud.

"What?"

"My tricorder . . . " He tipped it to face George as the older man scooted closer. "It hasn't worked since I left the Vrag main encampment. But now . . . " As though the tricorder heard him, a long scrawl of pointless code sketched itself through the middle of the readings, swelling like an amplified virus until it had taken over the small device's brain.

Cool water splashed across his exposed leg, startling him. Bashir looked up, catching the painted *xirri*'s indifferent gaze, and the tricorder hissed with renewed interference.

George's thoughtful, "I wonder what's happened now," barely penetrated the pulselike hammer of Bashir's thoughts.

It had been the *xirri* patients the tricorder first refused to scan. And when he'd first been carried into this cavern, before any *xirri* had come close to him down here—hadn't the tricorder produced perfectly coherent scans in those first few minutes? He made himself really *look* at the bands of distortion while the *xirri* neatly irrigated his leg precisely as he'd done himself a few hours before. What did this look like? What could this be that assumption simply hadn't let him see?

Medical school. A long, painfully boring lecture on reducing tricorder interference patterns that might crop up during extravehicular triage missions. Oh, God, he'd barely listened because he'd been so worried about an upcoming xenosurgery rotation, and this had struck him as something better left to the engineers. But now his memory—which misplaced so little, even when it was only half-overheard behind a bout of narcissistic fretting seven years ago—exploded the answer across the front of his brain like a supernova.

"Radio waves . . . "

High frequency radio waves, intersecting the tricorder's fragile sensory circuits.

George dutifully held the small device while Bashir popped open the casing over the brains of his tricorder. "A doctor and an engineer," the older officer commented playfully after watching Bashir work for several minutes. "You're a man of many talents."

"You have no idea." By the time he mated the interference signal through the tricorder's translator and back, the result through the tricorder's speaker was no more than squeaky, scratchy nonsense. The *xirri* recoiled slightly, as if from fingernails on a blackboard.

Bashir reached out to catch its hand before it could scurry away. "I know this is just a matter of sampling," he said, keeping his eyes and smile on the *xirri* in the hopes it might realize he was speaking to it. It licked once, twice at its huge corneas, but didn't move away. "Once enough language goes into the translator, something I can understand comes out. So I hope it works the same way for you. Is there something I can do to keep you talking? To make you feed enough data—"

"—wish <wistfully, regretfully> for more true communication—"

The voice seemed almost too small to be real. No emotion, no inflection, just words spelled out as mechanically as type on a bare computer screen. But *words!* Bashir's heart raced against his breastbone. George hissed a little sound of surprise.

"—Noises <loudly, vocally> made become a language? Such kindness comes—"

George couldn't hold himself silent any longer. "Hello?"

The voice snapped silent. The tricorder blinked, but said nothing.

"Can you hear us?" Bashir fought the urge to say the words too loudly, but found it a hard impulse to ignore. "Can you understand what I'm saying?"

The *xirri* licked its eyes again, rapidly, in nervous stutters. "Can you <plainly, clearly> hear me?"

Bashir exchanged a triumphant glance with George, smiling so wide it hurt his cheeks. "Yes."

"These <inanimate, unliving> things—" The *xirri* whisked its tail around in front to hover the tip above the tricorder arrangement. "These give you my words?"

"Yes. I . . . " For the briefest instant, he thought of explaining the differences between sound waves and electromagnetism, and instead said only, "I can't hear your words with my ears without the help of these things."

The *xirri* nodded as though that only made sense. "Before this, I was only aware of <vocal, random> noises from your kind. We did not know this was <intelligent, rational> speaking."

No more than the Klingons—or Bashir—had expected to discover *xirri* radio language in their silences. "You led us to these caves," he said, gesturing around them. "Do you understand what's happening outside?"

"We have not <personally, recently> seen fire falling from the sky." Its tail swept into a neat bracelet around its ankles as it settled back on its haunches. "But we have <old, remembered> stories of such fires from the past. These caves are where the *xirri* are told to go."

"Then why didn't you? When the first comets fell, there were *xirri* outside who were injured." He thought about the smoke-poisoned female, and the child this very *xirri* had carried all the way from the blast crater. "Why didn't you all come to the caves then?"

"Many <elderly, young> did. Others went in search of our <alien, childlike> friends. They have no <old, remembered> stories to protect them. Some were not among us, and we feared they would burn."

He remembered K'Taran's voice saying, *We knew the* xirri *would be needing help. So we came.* But it was George who finally said, very gently, "The *xirri* have been good friends to the Klingons."

The painted *xirri* cocked its head, reminding Bashir of nothing so much as a serious child considering the weightiness of its reply. "The sky has welcomed them with <fierce, renewing> fire," it said after a very long time. "If that does not forge them into oneness with the *xirri,* what will?"

Bat'leths met and locked with a clash of steel that thundered through the cold, dry air of the Klingon ship. "You fight well," said the stocky warrior scowling across that expanse of blood-splattered metal at Sisko. The thick tendons of his neck had made Sisko's slashing cut a minor annoyance rather than a telling blow, but it had still wiped the smug arrogance from his face. "For a Human."

"Thanks." Blood dripped down Sisko's face and seeped its salt taste between his gritted teeth, but it didn't impair his vision. The spiraling cheek-plate he'd thought was ornamental had stopped a wicked thrust of the pronged *bat'leth* point just short of his eye. His shoulder muscles burned with exhaustion and trembled with the effort of holding off his attacker, but his grin was still exultant. Five minutes into the *Suv'batlh* was longer than he'd ever expected to last.

Much of the credit for his survival had to go to the space in which they fought. He'd known that *Jfolokh*-class Klingon ships were small, but he'd never seen the inside of one before. It was a single cramped and cluttered deck, inhabited by a minimal crew of five in addition to its captain. As a result, Sisko and his opponent—a middle-aged Klingon engineer even more beer-bellied than Kor himself—had ducked and chopped their way through the various ship's stations in a chaos of swinging *bat'leths* and ducking Klingon ensigns.

With the steely clash of their weapons silenced, Sisko could hear the disrupted sounds of Odo's hand-to-hand battle with the young Klingon tactical officer and Worf's more titanic clash with Kor. The Dahar Master had refused to pursue his challenger, forcing Worf to come forward and attack him or risk forfeiting the *Suv'batlh* for cowardice. Despite Kor's stolid stance, however, there was nothing indolent or inebriated about his flying *bat'leth.* The constant, shattering crash of his blade against Worf's at times blended into continuous metallic thunder.

"Captain!" The young Klingon manning the sensor desk swung around, dark braids flying in alarm. "The Starfleet vessel is moving away at full impulse speed!"

Kor grunted, dropping to one knee to avoid a desperation roundhouse swing by Worf, then lunged up from below with the point of his blade. Worf flung himself backward, tripping over the empty chair of the weapon's console. He brought his *bat'leth* up just in time to avoid a wicked downward stab at his supine body, deflecting Kor's blade just enough to skate off his ribcage. Another bloody slash was added to the magenta lacework he already wore.

"Ignore the ship." Kor took a step back, catching his breath and incidentally giving Worf a chance to scramble back to his feet. "If we win, they leave no matter where they are. If we lose, they go wherever they like. Watch them for signs of attack, that is all."

They'd played this same scenario out several times now, the gasping old Dahar Master and the less accomplished but far more fit Starfleet officer. Each break in their furious fencing grew longer and each interval of blade-work shorter, giving Sisko a shred of hope that Worf might yet win, if he could just wear Kor down. Odo, on the other hand, was already teetering on the verge of failure. His long-armed and lithe young opponent had settled on a strategy of lunging and striking, oblivious to Odo's apparently ineffectual attempts to block him. Odo had reformed the rents in his mock-armor so many times that it had lost all its detail now, blurring into a generic solid surface, randomly swirled with black and red. The constant platinum flashes of protoplasmic matter beneath it, revealed every time a blow sliced through him, seemed to egg his Klingon opponent on to wilder and wilder swings. Sisko doubted the constable could hold his shape much longer.

Not that he was in much better condition, with his straining lungs and the dry rasp in his throat that came from trying to breathe the Klingons' harsher atmosphere. With a painful squeal of gouged metal, Sisko's *bat'leth* slipped across the engineer's blood-wet blade and slid violently off to one side. He cursed and swung toward the Klingon's knees, praying that his opponent's defensive instincts would yank him back rather than aiming his descending blade at Sisko's undefended torso.

He was half-successful—his opponent did jerk away, but not fast enough to keep the flat of his blade from unintentionally slamming into Sisko's solar plexus. All the breath from his lungs exploded out, making his vision darken abruptly. Choking, Sisko tried to stagger backward, away from wherever his opponent now was. Fortunately, the small Klingon ship chose that moment to stagger, too, its hull thundering with a barely shielded explosion.

"What was *that?"* Kor bellowed, giving the sprawled and even bloodier Worf another respite to climb to his feet. Seeing that his own opponent had swung around to scowl at his readouts with single-minded engineering focus, Sisko clung, gasping, to the back of an empty console. The black edges faded from his vision just in time to let him see the violent spray of glittering white fragments that erupted across the sensor's field of view. It looked like a firework made of ice.

"Comet impact," the engineer said unnecessarily.

"OI'yaH! Ghuy'cha' gu'valth!" Kor's curses were as magnificently extravagant as his flowing silver-streaked mane. With absentminded ease, he warded off a slashing attack from Worf, then smacked his *bat'leth* against the back of his pilot's chair to express his displeasure. "You're supposed to be flying us through these things, D'jia, not watching the fight!"

She curled her lip without ever breaking her gaze away from the main viewscreen. "*What* fight? All I've seen is a *bat'leth* practice, and not a very good one at that."

"Answer my question!" Kor snarled, seemingly oblivious to Worf's cat-silent approach right up to the second when he turned and struck at the Starfleet officer, hurling him halfway across the deck with the power of his *bat'leth* blow. Blood trickled from Worf's nostrils. "Why are we suddenly hitting comets?"

"We're not." Another shuddering impact hit the Klingon ship, making the female pilot curse pretty magnificently herself. "They're hitting us. All of a sudden, none of them are where they're supposed to be!"

"Well, take evasive action!"

"I'm trying!" The Klingon ship looped and danced through the thickening platinum haze of debris that seemed to be closing around them. Sisko's stomach lurched, feeling the drag and kick of uncompensated inertial fields. "But something keeps disturbing them, and it's throwing them right at us!"

"What a coincidence." In one fluid motion, Kor tore his engrossed engineer away from his damage reports and threw him back toward Sisko, then met Worf's next *bat'leth* thrust with a blade-locking twist and jerk. "I don't suppose your ship had anything to do with that, Worf, son of Mogh?" he growled into the younger man's blood-streaked face.

"No," Worf said with exhausted honesty. "They are far from here by now, deflecting other comets away from Cha'Xirrac."

Kor's furious roar drowned out the wet, hollow sound of a *bat'leth* sinking deep into flesh, but it couldn't drown the involuntary scream of pain that followed. Sisko didn't have time to see who was hit—he was too busy bracing himself against the ship's drunken swoops to meet the engineer's next blow. Rather than try to parry this one, he used the same maneuver he'd seen Kor try on Worf—dropping to one knee so that his opponent's blade whistled over his head, then lunging up with the wicked tip of the *bat'leth.*

The blade hit the Klingon engineer's rib cage at what seemed like an awkwardly obtuse angle, but to Sisko's immense surprise, it slid over one rib and under another to bite deep within his burly chest. The engineer staggered back, looking more dazed than hurt, and peered down at the *bat'leth* still protruding from his chest. "Good aim," he croaked, then collapsed unconscious at Sisko's feet, a bright trickle of blood oozing from the wound. Grabbing at the nearest bulkhead to steady himself, Sisko stared down at him, still not quite believing he had won.

The female pilot glanced over her shoulder. "Beginner's luck," she said in disgust. "You bruised his *gla'chiH*—the shielded nerve plexus in his chest. He's out for a day at least." She jerked her chin at Sisko, scowling. "Go ahead, pull the *bat'leth* out. Nothing will hurt him now."

Sisko did as she said, watching the trickle of blood slow as the wound closed. Then he jerked his head up, suddenly becoming aware of the silence around him. Not a single clash of *bat'leths,* not a thud of falling bodies disturbed the ragged sound of exhausted and pain-racked breathing.

He looked for Worf first, anxiously, and found him in exactly the position he'd most feared. His tall tactical officer lay sprawled across the empty weapons panel, one arm dangling brokenly and the other locked above his head in Kor's massive fist. The Dahar Master had leaned all his considerable weight on his opponent, keeping him trapped despite weakening struggles. When the point of Kor's *bat'leth* dug into his throat, deep enough to spring a bright pulse of blood out with each beat of his strong heart, Worf stopped struggling and just scowled up at him.

"Qapla'." Despite his swollen and blood-wet face, Worf sounded as stubbornly indomitable as ever. It was hard to believe he had really lost. "The *Suv'batlh* belongs to you, Dahar Master. Now kill me."

CHAPTER 11

"IS THE *SUV'BATLH* MINE? ON ALL COUNTS?" KOR GLANCED OVER HIS SHOULDER, frowning when he saw his engineer recumbent at Sisko's feet. It wasn't until his gaze skated past them toward the third pair of fighters, though, that his face darkened to the consistency of a thundercloud. "Kitold! How in the name of the dead Klingon gods did that happen?"

His weapons officer stepped forward, swaying as another comet thundered off the aft shield. One hand was locked around his battle-gloved forearm to hold his dislocated arm in place. The greenish pallor of his face told Sisko he wouldn't stay on his feet much longer.

"It was subterfuge," he said hoarsely. "The Changeling pretended to be more weary than he actually was, in order to lure me into position for his strike."

Sisko's gaze went past the wounded Klingon to Odo, whose mock-Klingon armor flowed back into the constable's usual pristine uniform even as he watched. "Is that true?" he demanded.

Odo gave him a stiff nod of acknowledgment. "It seemed like a legitimate maneuver. I admit, I did alter my appearance to a certain extent to achieve the deception, but it is not as if I *can* turn pale or sweat with fear. Nothing about my shape-shifting ever endangered my opponent."

"It was trickery!" insisted the young Klingon.

"More like strategy." Kor yanked his *bat'leth* abruptly from Worf's throat, releasing him to stagger back and clutch at his own wounded arm. "You were taken in by the oldest warrior's trick in the book, Kitold! You deserve to lose that arm, but I don't want to smell your corpse all the way back to the homeworld. Go put yourself into a medical stasis chamber—*now!*"

The wounded Klingon growled in ungrateful acknowledgment before he pushed past Sisko, heading toward the bank of stasis lockers at the back of the main deck. Worf watched him go, then turned a puzzled gaze on Kor. *"Wej Heghehugh vay', SuvtaH SuvwI'?* If someone has not yet died, how can a Klingon warrior stop fighting?"

Kor snorted, richly scornful. "Only a fool takes a death that means nothing. I didn't get to be a Dahar Master by being a fool." He reached out to steady Worf as the younger male staggered, either thrown off-balance by the ship's evasive swerves or perhaps just noticing the pain of his many wounds. The only thing splashed on Kor's robe, Sisko noticed wryly, was blood wine. *"Dujeychugh jagh nIv yItuHOo'.* There is nothing shameful in falling before a superior enemy. Through the luck of your captain and the wiles of your Changeling, you have won the *Suv'batlh* you challenged me to, Worf, son of Mogh. What is your will of me?"

Worf opened his mouth, but before he could say a word, the female pilot swung around at her console, pale eyes blazing. "Captain! Security alert! Those comets that keep hitting us—I think they're being deflected by a vessel entering the system!"

"What?" Kor cursed and shoved Worf aside, diving for his command chair. "Identity of vessel?"

"I can't tell!" The young Klingon sensor technician pounded on his unresponsive panels. "My instruments can't even penetrate the mass of comets gathered in front of it! The debris is a hundred times more dense than it should be. Whoever it is, they must have followed the ice-giant's orbital track all the way into the system, collecting debris with their tractor beams the whole way."

"Cardassians!" Kor said with disgusted certainty. "Who else would apply themselves so diligently to such a coward's strategy?" He threw an ironic look at Sisko. *"Gul* Hidret is probably scanning the system as we speak, hoping to find the charred remains of *both* our ships."

"Possibly." Sisko took a step closer to the viewscreen, as if that could somehow make the unknown vessel appear out of the icy haze. It didn't, but the silent, dusty curve of Armageddon's horizon swung into view as the female pilot looped around a particularly thick comet cluster. He felt his gut twist with foreboding. "How many comets is that unknown ship pushing in front of them?"

"Ten thousand, maybe more," the sensor technician said grimly. "All gathered into a space of only nineteen cubic kilometers and accelerated to a quarter impulse speed."

That made Kor's breath whistle out in shock. "In what direction?" he demanded. "Toward us?"

"No." The female pilot glanced up at the blood-colored image of Armageddon on the viewscreen, pity flickering in her cold Klingon eyes. "Toward the planet."

Sisko and Odo exchanged appalled looks. "The away team," Worf said hoarsely. "We must notify them."

"To let them prepare for their deaths with honor." Kor nodded gravely. "It is a reasonable request. Boost their comm badge signals through our transmitter, Bhirq."

Sisko slapped a hand to his chest without even waiting for the Klingon technician to reply. "Sisko to Kira, Sisko to Dax."

"Dax here." Her calm Trill voice brought a reminiscent smile to Kor's face, one that faded into regret an instant later. "Go ahead, Benjamin."

"A Cardassian battleship has just swept up ten thousand comet fragments and launched them toward Armageddon," Sisko said, with brutal curtness. "You've got to beam out, *now!*"

"Understood." The advantage of having a subordinate with three hundred cumulative years of experience was that she knew when to ask for details and explanations, and when not to. "Time to impact?"

"Forty minutes," said the Klingon pilot. "Max."

"Then we might have a shot at getting everyone on the planet into shelter. Julian and the crash survivors have taken refuge in a deep cave system. If we can get there, we should be immune even to the impact of ten thousand comets." Dax's voice had taken on the steely determination that meant she wasn't going to take "no" for an answer. "Permission to stay on planet, Captain?"

"Granted," Sisko said, scowling. "Just be damned sure you're inside that cave in thirty minutes, old man, not out gathering up some last DNA samples from an endangered plant."

The Trill science officer made a wordless noise of amusement. "Don't worry, Benjamin. The plants down here can take care of their own DNA without any help from me. Dax out."

Kor glanced at Worf, who was quietly dripping blood across the empty weapons panel that propped him up. "You could make your *Suv'batlh* request the phasering of these Cardassian comets," the Dahar Master said suggestively. "Every one we shoot—"

"—becomes a cluster of smaller ones and spreads the destruction even further," Sisko said flatly. "And there are far too many to deflect with our shields, even using both our ships."

Odo gave the older Klingon an ironic look. "In any case, wouldn't those actions violate the honorable exile of your countrymen?"

Kor spat toward the comet-clouded viewscreen. "The Cardassians have already done that, Changeling."

The viewscreen flared with wild static for a moment, then resolved into a forced transmission from the *Defiant.* O'Brien's bleak gaze scanned across them, unable to focus on Sisko since the Klingons weren't transmitting back. "Captain, sensors have picked up the arrival of the *Olxinder* on your side of the planet, pushing a forced impact wave of twelve thousand comet fragments in front of them. The away team says you know about it. I'll wait ten minutes for your orders, then start flying through the field, trying to target the largest and most destructive fragments. O'Brien out."

Worf groaned, not entirely in pain. "The *Defiant*'s shields cannot survive the onslaught of twelve thousand comets!"

"Ten thousand," the Klingon sensor tech interrupted peevishly.

"So what is your *Suv'batlh* request, Worf, son of Mogh?" Kor repeated impatiently. "To save your shipmates by making us sacrifice our own ship to the comets?"

"No," Sisko said, before his wounded tactical officer could reply. "Our request is to consider this system from now on as a joint Klingon-Federation protectorate. Correct, Mr. Worf?"

His tactical officer nodded, with the utter trust in his commander that had won Sisko's appreciation from the first. "And to cede to Captain Sisko any rights won by me in the *Suv'batlh* combat." Worf fell to his knees with a massive thud that Sisko felt across the deck. "I fear I will not remain conscious long enough to exercise them."

Kor scowled. "The second of those requests is reasonable and I agree to it. But what sense does the first make?"

"It gives us the joint ability to defend this system from the Cardassians," Sisko retorted. "And prove to the entire galaxy that they are not only smuggling banned neurochemical weapons, they are also destroying an ecosystem they don't own to obtain it."

Kor's scowl grew more thoughtful. "You think they didn't just bring those comets in to hide behind? You think they actually planned to wipe out everything alive on that planet, just to get their hands on the last dregs of drevlocet?"

"That sounds like a rhetorical question to me," Odo said caustically.

Sisko took a step forward, ignoring the angry ache of strained shoulder muscles. "Your ship is cloaked, just like the *Defiant,* and we know the Cardassians aren't very good at detecting ion trails. They won't know we're here until we fire our weapons, either at the comets or at them. If we let them think what they want to think—that we destroyed each other battling over this planet, and left the coast clear for them to move in, I have a hunch they'll incriminate themselves exactly forty minutes from now."

"So we play dead, while the planet beneath us dies?"

Sisko grimaced. "I don't like that either—but all our people should be safe and I trust my science officer when she says the planet will recover. What we do have time to save is the rest of the Alpha Quadrant. Now, are you going to cooperate with us, or does our *Suv'batlh* request have to be the self-destruction of this ship?"

Kor gave that ultimatum the fierce snort of disdain it deserved, since Sisko never had any intention of enforcing it. "What about the House of Vrag? If any live after the comet deluge, are they going to be rescued against their will?"

"Federation policy only allows us to evacuate planet residents who wish to leave." Sisko never thought he would live to be grateful for diplomatic equivocation. "The House of Vrag will get to decide their own fate, and preserve their own honor."

The Dahar Master mulled that over, then jerked his head in a satisfied Klingon nod. "That will satisfy the High Council, provided there are no more traitors like that *garg*-carcass you sent here for disposal. When we get back to the homeworld, I'm going to have to decontaminate my stasis chambers just to get the stink of him out of them."

At that moment, Worf slumped into unconsciousness with a violent crash of armor. Sisko cursed and sprang to catch him before he rolled across the deck.

"We need to beam him back to the *Defiant* for medical attention," he said to Kor. "And I need to tell O'Brien not to fly into that comet storm. Have you accepted our *Suv'batlh* conditions? Is Armageddon now a joint Klingon-Federation protectorate?"

"No." Kor grinned wickedly at Odo's startled frown. "But Cha'Xirrac is."

Sisko threw the elderly Klingon an exasperated glare. He was starting to see why Kor and Curzon Dax had gotten along so well. "Then my first request as coprotector of Cha'Xirrac is for you to beam me back aboard the *Defiant.* We'll patrol opposite sides of the planet—whoever first detects the Cardassians beaming down to the planet after the comet impacts gets to confront them, but it has to be on a wide-open channel. Agreed?"

"Agreed." Kor glanced up at the viewscreen, no longer hazed with icy glitter now that they had escaped the Cardassian-gathered swarm. Distant light bloomed in the planet's dust-stained atmosphere, the harmless high-level explosion of a natural comet collision. Sisko's gut still jerked with dismay, anticipating the inferno to come. "Provided there is a planet left for them to beam down to."

"I can't believe you thought this was a good idea."

Kira bent as low as she dared, ignoring the twinge in her lower back, pretending her thighs and knees and ankles weren't screaming complaints loud enough to wake all of Armageddon's past extinctions. "You've got to admit," she grunted, grabbing Dax's arms and hauling back with all her might, "it does give us some advantages."

They toppled to the burn-scarred *tuq'mor* canopy one on top the other. Eyebrow arched, Dax tossed a look at the Klingons still struggling to climb the tangled brush as she extricated herself from Kira and rolled clumsily onto her back. "Let's hope it's advantage enough."

If it wasn't, then they were no worse off than they'd been on the ground. *Give or take a few fall-related injuries.* At least she and Dax weren't pinwheeling their arms or lurching about with one hand always in contact with the *tuq'mor.* She watched Rekan's two honor companions crack the scorched surface of the canopy more than once as they stumbled into the formal *Suv'batlh* wedge. If Dax and K'Taran could lead their opponents over some of the more fire-weakened surfaces, they might be able to keep their footing even when the heftier Klingons broke through. Kira, on the other hand, had a feeling *epetai* Vrag would be harder to displace than her less-dedicated counterparts. She would hang onto Kira's throat with her teeth before she fell.

For some reason, the Klingon matriarch looked taller on top the *tuq'-mor,* standing proudly—if not comfortably—with her chin held high. She'd dragged loose the rhodium comb pinning her hair in place the moment the challenge was official. The mass of silver white hair that cascaded down her back gleamed unexpectedly bright in their ash-faded surroundings. A wild mane of icy fire. When she fitted the comb back into her hair, Kira thought it looked like a thin, silver tiara framing the back of her skull, an appropriate addendum to her cool alien beauty.

Kira positioned herself the required three paces in front of the *epetai,* resolutely squaring her tired shoulders. "The *tuq'mor* is the battleground," she announced, loudly enough that the Klingons now crowding the ground level could hear. "Falling from the *tuq'mor* constitutes leaving the combat, and that warrior is forfeit. Agreed?"

Rekan nodded once, fiercely. "Agreed. *Qapla'!"*

Kira had imagined a slightly more ritualized beginning to the combat, although it struck her upon reflection that this was naive. Klingons were nothing if not straightforward. Rekan launched herself at Kira like a leaping rock-cat, slamming the smaller Bajoran with the full weight of her body and driving them both to the *tuq'mor.* Limbs cracked and jabbed at Kira's back like broken ribs, then gave way and dropped her a good foot into the dry underbrush. Rekan pressed down on her from above, her hand clamped under Kira's jaw.

"If this were a true *Suv'batlh,"* she growled, "you would be dead and I would already be the victor. Yield!"

Kira sucked a painful breath and locked her arms in the *tuq'mor* beyond her head. "Warriors do not yield!" And she kicked downward with both feet before Rekan could respond.

Limbs splintered in an irregular mass, reclosing around Kira's slim body with springy resilience all out of proportion to their brittleness.

Rekan tangled in the upper story, her torso suddenly angled abruptly downward, and Kira willfully snatched double handfuls of white hair to twist among the brambles before dragging herself laterally out of the older Klingon's reach.

It felt like wriggling on her back through a shattered maintenance duct; cables of vine fouled her passage so that spindly fingers of shrubbery could tear at her uniform, prick at her eyes. By the time she found an opening to haul herself back to the upper surface, she bolted into the open like an ice-swimmer reclaiming the surface. The *tuq'mor* canopy no longer seemed such a sturdy playing field. Adrenaline spiked her bloodstream with every placement of her feet, every shift and crackle of failing timber. She floated her arms out to either side in search of a constantly wandering balance, and insisted to her fear that running along the jouncing bushtops was no different than walking scaffolding or climbing trees. The dry sourness at the back of her throat suggested she didn't find herself very convincing.

Kira half-hopped, half-stumbled in a circle to try and place herself in the combat. Rekan had vanished, leaving only snarls of torn silver hair fluttering in the hot breeze. Growls and labored breathing far to her right rear helped Kira locate K'Taran, where the young girl wrestled a tall male almost three times her age near the remnants of one great hut-tree. *She's going to lose,* Kira realized abruptly. It was a wonder she'd held out as long as she had. Wrenching free of the older male's hold, K'Taran jumped nearly as high as his shoulder and scrabbled up the charred stump to leap from its top. Her landing was awkward, but it put distance between her and the big male; he lurched across the canopy like a drunken *mugatu,* huffing and cursing. *That's the way,* Kira thought. *If you can't beat him, wear him out.*

Taking the hint, she trotted a few more long steps away from where she'd left Rekan, scanning the dark battleground for the rest of the *Suv'batlh.* She faced a distressing lack of silhouettes against the flaming sky. "Dax?"

"Down here!" The Trill's voice floated up from below. She sounded distinctly irritated and impossibly far away. "I'm fine! K'Daq fell down with me, so we're both out."

Kira crouched as low as she dared, and peered between her feet for a closer look at shadow movement within the shadows. "You sure you're all right?"

"Nothing hurt but my pride. Look after yourself!"

Sound advice. If only it had come a moment sooner.

A dark hand shot upward out of the *tuq'mor,* as fast and fierce as a spider. Kira backpedaled, lifting her knees high to take her feet out of grabbing range, but not quickly enough. Rekan clamped strong fingers around one ankle, and Kira knew even before the Klingon hauled back on her leg that she'd run out of options. There was nowhere left to run.

Kira hit the *tuq'mor* canopy full length, her shoulders taking the brunt of the impact, just ahead of the back of her skull. She felt the *tuq'mor* creak and shiver, like a stand of marsh grass under the thrashing of a great wind, and her mind reeled wildly, *I didn't fall that hard? Did I really fall that hard?* Then she heard the thunder, and realized that these stomach-wrenching tremors came from farther away than her own collision with the *tuq'mor.* She struggled to climb to all fours.

At first, Rekan's torso blocked her view of the clearing and the Klingons standing witness on the ground. The *epetai* had dragged herself halfway out of the understory, the scratches on her cheeks and the brilliant blood in her hair only accentuating her fearful wildness. Now, her eyes met Kira's with a flash of purest hatred, and Kira knew in that instant that this battle wasn't between *epetai* Vrag and Kira Nerys—it was a battle between what used to be and what could never be again.

Kira said only, "Listen."

Tremors shook the brush in angry fists. Ash the color of powdered bone drifted up from the *tuq'mor* like smoke, and Kira had to grab at whatever whipping limbs she could reach to keep from being shaken down between the branches. Rekan only knelt where she'd stopped, head lifted, face hollow. She reminded Kira of one of the Klingons' dead goddesses. Even perched and bleeding on the edges of *sylshessa,* her dignity and grace were breathtaking.

Below them, the Klingons did not panic. It occurred to Kira that perhaps they were a people incapable of panic, those genes having been shriven from their species ages ago by warriors unwilling to tolerate such weakness. When K'Taran's *banchory* groaned a long, low bellow of distress, even the youngest of the children merely scurried clear of its thrashing. Then the first of the mounted *banchory* crashed into the open, and the bawling of these lumbering newcomers nearly drowned out the cries of surprise.

Ash-stained primates—the little green-gray lemurs Kira had seen haunting the edges of the camp from the beginning—crowded the backs of the great pachyderms. One of them scampered forward, down its *banchory's* plated rill to crouch on the wide nose-bridge between the mammoth's eyes. The "come hither" curling of its hands and wrists seemed unmistakable to Kira. And, apparently, to one of the children clustered at the base of the *tuq'mor.* The boy took only a single step forward before one of the older women reached out to stop him, stating simply, "*Epetai* says we must stay."

Kira shivered at the helplessly loyal chill that passed through the family. A few—most of them very young, although some might have been the parents of K'Taran and her rebel adolescents—turned their eyes upward toward Rekan. No recrimination in those stark gazes, no pleas. As though they all stated fact to one another, and their *epetai* simply represented what they already knew to be true.

Duty, Kira realized. *Honor.* It mattered so much to them, they would willingly forsake all else, even survival.

Sinking slowly to her heels, Rekan stared down at her children, and their children, and all the pasts and futures every Klingon House created. "Must honor always be cruel?" she asked softly. Not really to Kira, the major knew, even though there was no one else close enough to hear. "I know in my heart what honor demands of us . . . yet now that we face the final moments . . . I would not see my children die. . . . "

Kira looked down at her hands, not knowing what to say, and sensing the question was rhetorical anyway.

"I would not have love and honor always run in separate ways." The *epetai* straightened, and her voice rang purely, clearly over the roar of exploding comets and the rumble of fidgeting *banchory.* "Go. Take the children—they are this House's future. Put yourselves in safety until the sky no longer burns." When no one moved, she announced, more gently, "Honor commanded only that we remain on Cha'Xirrac forever. Not that we must die."

She turned to Kira as the first of the elders lifted a youngster into one of the primates' waiting arms. "The *Suv'batlh* is ended," she told Kira, very, very quietly. "Go."

Kira touched the *epetai's* arm when Rekan moved to turn away. "You should come with us."

Rekan stared toward the burning horizon, immobile.

"You can't abandon them now," Kira said. "Your House is going to need you when the comet strikes are over."

The Klingon shook her head, and a ghostly smile brushed her eyes without appearing on her features. "This House is of Cha'Xirrac now. It will need an *epetai* who is of Cha'Xirrac as well." She was silent for a moment, watching K'Taran and her *Suv'batlh* opponent work as allies in herding children onto the *banchory.* Then she caught sight of Kira from the corner of her eye, and smiled with what seemed genuine warmth. "Such a look! There is no shame in admitting that one's service is finished." She gave the major one last nod toward the others as she rose slowly to full height. "I go to Sto'vo-Kor at peace with the state of my honor," she assured her. "Save your pity for the survivors."

CHAPTER 12

Armageddon had, horribly, lived up to its name.

The comet storm had started violently enough, with the enormous smoke-shrouded flares of near-surface explosions. Within ten minutes, the planet's atmosphere had congealed and darkened everywhere, giving it an oddly opaque look in the oblivious saffron sunlight. Watching from his command chair on the bridge of the *Defiant,* Sisko realized he was watching the fall of cometary night, a dust-driven darkness whose dawn might not arrive for days or even weeks. But that was just the start.

"The first really big fragment is going in now." Ensign Farabaugh turned at the comet-tracking station, his eyes sober beneath a tidy bandage. "Impact in two minutes."

"Will it explode in the atmosphere?" Odo inquired. "Like the others, only bigger?"

"I don't think so," the young science officer said. "It looks like this one is actually big enough and solid enough to hit the surface. If it does, it could excavate a crater one or two kilometers deep."

"So much for being protected in a cave." O'Brien saw the irritated look Sisko sent him and shrugged. "Optimism is for command officers, Captain. Engineers prefer pessimism, because it saves lives instead of risking them. Are you sure we can't just beam up the away team? We've had a lock on their comms for the last ten minutes, and they've barely moved."

"Not while the Cardassians are on our side of the planet," Sisko said.

"Chief, if you want to be pessimistic, why don't you send those comm coordinates to Farabaugh? That way, he can alert us if it looks like a surface impact is going to come too close."

"Good idea." The chief engineer bent over his panel, just in time to miss the enormous steel-colored light that exploded across the upper half of Armageddon's huge eastern ocean. A slowly towering column of fire rose above it, its crenulated ash-black clouds rising so high into the planet's stratosphere that the topmost debris drifted out of the gravity well completely and was lost to space. A collective gasp of horror hit the bridge, bringing O'Brien's sandy head around toward the viewscreen so fast he almost slammed into his console. "God Almighty! Is that anywhere near the away team?"

"The impact wasn't," Farabaugh assured him. "And I don't *think* the tsunami will run quite that far inland—"

"The tsunami?" That was Ensign Frisinger, Worf's substitute pilot, whose fascinated gaze hadn't wavered from the viewscreen once since the comet storm had begun. Sisko hoped he knew his panel controls by touch. "What's that?"

"The shock wave in the ocean that the impact creates," Osgood explained. "High-level explosions don't usually make them, since they displace air instead of water."

Farabaugh was punching a quick calculation into his station. "Looks like the main wave should hit shore starting about three hours from now. The backwash and secondary waves will probably last through tomorrow evening."

"Let's hope the Cardassians don't know that," Sisko said, grimacing. "I don't feel like waiting that long to confront them."

The barrage of high-level airbursts rose to an almost continuous glare of explosions after that, as if the ocean impact had been some kind of floodgate, opening to let all the rest of the swarm pour through. The increasingly ash-choked sky turned each bloom of light a deeper crimson-tinted black, like roses charring in a celestial flame. It was hard, watching from the distant bridge of the *Defiant,* to remember that these silent fireworks represented destruction on a planetary scale.

"Still getting signal back from the away team, Chief?" Sisko couldn't repress the question any longer. A second surface impact had geysered up, this time from the shadowy darkness that he thought represented the main continent. This mushroom-shaped debris cloud rose even higher than the first, high enough that the debris sparked a firefly glitter of auroral light when it burst through the planet's magnetic torus.

"Off and on, between the EM pulses. At least, it doesn't seem to be getting any weaker." O'Brien glanced back over his shoulder. "There aren't any big fragments aiming for those caves, are there, ensign?"

"No, sir." Farabaugh glanced over at Sisko, the pale damp sheen of his face belying his claim of being completely healed. "In fact, there aren't any more big pieces left. The whole storm is tapering off. In another ten minutes, Armageddon should be back to business as usual."

Sisko sat up, his pulse sharpening to battle-ready alertness. "Scan for the Cardassian ship, maximum resolution."

"Got it." Thornton's hand flew across the science station, fine-tuning the resolution on his sensors. There was something to be said for assigning an engineering specialist to use his own instruments, Sisko thought. "Image coming through now, sir. It's the *Olxinder,* for sure."

"I can see that." The Cardassian battleship's sharp-edged silhouette was just rounding the planet's smoky horizon, leaving Kor's patrol and entering their own. Sisko would have bet all the antique baseballs in his collection that the Klingon Dahar Master followed them, and probably at a none-too-discreet distance. "I want to know the instant you get the hint of a shuttle launch, a transporter beam, or—"

"—a scan of the planet?" Thornton glanced over his shoulder, his quiet face lit with an unexpected smile. "They're doing it now, sir. Sensors seem to be set for native life-signs."

"Can their instruments penetrate into the caves?" Odo demanded. "The Cardassians might cut and run if they find evidence of any surviving Klingons, not to mention Humans, Trills, and Bajorans."

The young engineering tech shook his head. "I don't think they've even got the resolution to cut through the leftover EM furze. They're going to have to go down."

"In a shuttle, too, at least if they know what's good for them." O'Brien saw Odo's questioning look. "You wouldn't catch me trying to transport through that electromagnetic mess."

Sisko grunted. "Then get a tractor beam ready, Chief. Frisinger, make sure we're never out of tractor range—but don't bump into Kor while you do it."

"Aye, sir."

"—to *Defiant.*" The crackle of static coming from his chair's communicator couldn't disguise the vibrancy of Dax's voice—or the scientific excitement that ran through it. "Dax to *Defiant.* Can you—?"

"I'm working on it," O'Brien said, forestalling Sisko's unspoken command. "Signal resolution coming up now."

"Link a secure channel to Kor," Sisko said quietly. "He'll want to know that Dax is alive."

"Dax to Sisko. Can you read us yet, Benjamin?"

"Sisko here. What's your situation?"

"Completely secured, Captain." That was his second-in-command, sounding exhausted but just as competent as ever. "All the Klingon refugees are in stable health, and so are the survivors from *Victoria Adams*'s crew—all thirty-one of them. We've managed to save a surprising number of the natives, too, even the big pachyderms. They seemed to have an instinct—"

"It's more than an instinct for some of them." Sisko lifted an eyebrow, knowing Dax was never that rude unless a major scientific breakthrough was bubbling to the surface. "Benjamin, some of the natives are *sentient!*"

"Not just sentient." That was a voice Sisko hadn't heard in too long. Its weary British accent and carefully precise language dissolved a knot of tension he hadn't even realized he was feeling. "The *xirri* are a full-fledged Class-two civilization, Captain: oral history, medicine, long-distance radio communication—"

"The natives have *technology?*" Sisko exchanged startled looks with O'Brien and Odo. If the Klingons had knowingly violated the Prime Directive when they'd chosen this planet for their honorable exile, it was going to be a lot harder to convince the Federation that they now owned half of it.

"The *xirri*'s ability to communicate in radio wavelengths isn't technological, Benjamin." Dax sounded both dazed and delighted by that fact. "It's a biological adaptation, bred into them by reproductive isolation and the stress of cometary impact. As far as we can tell, all the native vertebrates have the same capacity, but—"

Sisko saw the urgent look Thornton cast him and cut ruthlessly across his science officer's explanation. "You can explain all the gory details to me later, old man. I've got a Cardassian *gul* getting ready to tip his hand, and I want to be ready to slap it."

"Understood." There was a muffled grunt behind Kira's voice, as if someone's toe had been stepped on. "Away team out."

"I'm reading a power surge in the circuits around the Cardassians' main shuttle door," Thornton told him, before the crackle of static had even faded from the bridge. "I think they're getting ready to launch an expedition to the planet."

"Shields at full power, cloak controls set for imminent drop," Sisko said. "Set tractor beam coordinates for a kilometer away from the launch door."

"Coordinates laid in," O'Brien confirmed. "Tractor beam fully charged and ready."

"Launch doors opening," Thornton said. The *Olxinder* slowly rotated as she orbited the ash-dark planet, bringing her belly-slit shuttle bay into gloriously clear resolution. "Shuttle deploying inside launch bay."

"Red alert. Quantum torpedoes armed and ready for launch." Sisko didn't really expect Hidret to put up a fight, but you could never tell what a weasel would do when cornered. It would be stupid to be unprepared. "Shuttle position, Mr. Thornton?"

"Four hundred meters and accelerating. Six hundred, eight hundred—"

"Drop cloak and engage tractor beam," Sisko snapped, anticipating the thousand meter mark. O'Brien must have been equally primed for action—the tractor beam flashed out before he'd even finished calling for it, its gold-dust glitter smacking through the silver cometary haze to seize on the Cardassian shuttlecraft. Sisko felt the *Defiant* rock with an unexpected jolt of backwash inertia, and threw a frown at O'Brien. The chief engineer was growling at his controls.

"If you're going to stay locked even though we were first, the least you could do is match your beam intensity . . . damn arrogant Klingons!"

Sisko's gaze rose to the viewscreen, startled. He could see, now that O'Brien had pointed it out, the mirror glimmer of a second tractor beam, refracting back across the planet's horizon. An instant later, the uncloaked silhouette of a *Jfolokh*-class ship rose above the ashen atmosphere, tracking back along its beam toward the mammoth Cardassian battleship like a fish reeling itself toward the fisherman.

"Hail the Cardassians on an open channel." The corner of Sisko's mouth kicked upward wryly. "And prepare for a three-way conference, Mr. Thornton."

"Aye, sir."

Armageddon's seared image vanished, replaced by a duplicate image of scowling, furrowed faces. Kor's expression, however, was one of pure military ferocity, while *Gul* Hidret's had clearly been plastered over shock and indecision.

"Is this an act of war, Captain Sisko?" he demanded, in what was probably meant to be a preemptive strike. "Are you actually working in league with these Klingon ruffians after all?"

"Yes, I am." Sisko allowed a cold slice of smile to show. "I'm legally required to, *Gul* Hidret, since this is now a joint Klingon-Federation protectorate."

"What?" The Cardassian's scowl lost a little more of its assurance. "When was that treaty signed?"

"An hour ago, in Klingon and Human blood," Kor retorted. "All it needs now is some Cardassian blood to be complete."

"Nonsense!" Hidret sounded as though he might choke on his own disbelief. "You think to fool me by making such wild, unreasonable claims."

"I admit, you were the one who first suggested this alliance," Sisko said wickedly. "The more I thought about it, the better an idea it seemed."

Hidret shook his head. "I don't believe it. You're going to let this Starfleet officer interfere with your dishonored exiles, Kor?"

"No," said the Dahar Master grimly. "We're going to make sure that my dishonored exiles haven't interfered with the sentient natives whose civilization we just discovered. Of course," he added maliciously, "any little ecological problems they may have caused will pale in comparison with the devastation we just saw you create."

"What?" Gul Hidret looked like a man whose worst fevered nightmares had just erupted into waking life. "You're lying! There are no sentients on that planet—"

"And how would you know that, *Gul,* if you've never set foot on Cha'Xirrac?" Sisko asked silkily.

"It—it was surveyed by the medical teams scouring this region for the cure to *ptarvo* fever."

Kor snorted. "If you ever needed a cure for the randiness of youth—which I very much doubt—your searches here found no cure for it."

"All you found here," Sisko continued, "was a cheap and easy source of drevlocet. Isn't that right, *Gul* Hidret?"

"Drevlocet that the Cardassian High Command would like to modify to use on Klingons," Kor finished. "Isn't *that* right, *Gul* Hidret?"

The elderly Cardassian grimaced, the wrinkled canyons of his face growing deep and darkly shadowed. "I refuse to answer such accusations in this—this inappropriate setting! I came here in response to a willful attack against the Cardassian people, only to find it was a trap!"

Sisko permitted himself a scowl. "Our diplomats can settle who set the traps in this system, *Gul* Hidret. But the fact remains that this planet beneath us is now its own sovereign state, subject to no external interference in its ecology or its affairs."

"Exactly what I'd be the first to tell you," the elderly Cardassian insisted. "And just as soon as you release my shuttle full of emergency medical personnel, I'll be on my way."

"Good," Kor said. "I hate to break it to you, old enemy, but your ship seems to have a most unfortunate attraction to comets. It would be a shame if one actually penetrated your shields and caused a hull breach." Snaggleteeth bared in a grin that would have done credit to a crocodile. "And the longer you stay in this area, the more likely that is to happen. Don't you agree, Captain Sisko?"

"Definitely."

Gul Hidret slapped at his communicator controls, breaking the connection without another word. Kor promptly broke into a massive roar of laughter.

"That old *targ*'s going to be swerving around every speck of dust between here and Cardassia Prime, thinking each one's got a photon torpedo buried in it," he decided. "I think I'll follow him halfway back and plant one, just to put him out of his misery."

"Be my guest." Sisko nodded at Thornton and O'Brien to disengage. The *Defiant*'s viewscreen shimmered back to a view of comet-haloed ships, just in time to show their tractor beam vanishing. The Klingons' paler beam twinkled out a moment later, and the Cardassian shuttle darted back into its launch pad like a reef fish diving for cover. A moment later, the battleship's warp nacelles glowed to life and it was gone, shaking them with the nearness of its jump to lightspeed. Kor's ship rippled into cloaked invisibility in that same instant, and Sisko felt a second wash of ion discharge tremble through his ship.

"Alone at last," said O'Brien, sighing.

"Not quite." Sisko lifted his gaze to the sliver of Armageddon's—no, *Cha'Xirrac*'s—darkened skies, seeing the charred but living planet beneath that ashen veil. "We have some new friends to meet, Chief. Let's hope they're a little easier to get along with."

"Than the Klingons and the Cardassians?" Odo snorted. "Captain, I believe that's what Quark would call an ears-on certainty."

Kira had climbed out of the cave system feeling worn, ancient, as battered as the surface of Cha'Xirrac. She'd kept her eyes downcast, preparing for the onslaught of bright light after hours in the womblike dark. Instead, a soft grayness enveloped the world, and the muted features of the terrain sent her memory tumbling backward a dozen years.

Before the Federation came to safeguard Bajor—before the Cardassians declared the planet raped to a shell and no longer worth the expense to maintain—Kira had walked through this same armageddon landscape under a different name. Rota Province had been battered for forty days and forty nights by every surface-launchable warhead the Cardassians bothered to keep on Bajor. Not atomics—the Cardassians were far too frugal to waste expensive destruction on Bajoran sheep who had no way to fight back or run. They'd shattered Rota with slow-moving conventional weaponry, all because of rumors that the Salbhai resistance cell had taken up hiding among the homesteads and villages of that wealthy province.

Well, they'd gotten Salbhai and her fighters, along with eleven thousand farmers, timbermen, and *peng* herders. The resultant desolation looked exactly like Cha'Xirrac did now—soil blasted down to the bedrock, trees blown down like a children's stick game, the rivers and marshes choked with carcasses, mudslides, and debris. It had been hard to imagine that anything would ever be able to live in Rota ever again. And it was hard to imagine Cha'Xirrac coming back to life after such apocalyptic devastation.

The view had not improved much from the roof of a shuttle. Kira sat, knees hugged to her chest, and watched a distant curtain of smoke ripple against a sky only just now dimming down to the color of natural dawn. No more trees poked their heads above the *tuq'mor* canopy. No more *banchory* crashed their slow, gentle ways through the foliage. Only ash pattered like sand through the brush still standing, tainted with the bitter scent of distant fires.

"Looking for someone?"

She glanced down, startled by Sisko's sudden presence. "Not really." The smile she forced on his behalf didn't feel very convincing, and his own amused expression suggested she could have done better. Sighing, she scooted toward the front of the small craft to slide down its nose. "How're negotiations coming?"

"Very well." The captain stepped judiciously aside as she jumped to the ground, neither helping nor hindering her descent. "Actually, there doesn't seem much to negotiate. The *xirri* are still more than happy to share Cha'Xirrac with their Klingon friends, and the Klingons still have nowhere else to go." He gave a little shrug that Kira thought indicated acceptance of the situation, although she wasn't completely sure. "I think the House of Vrag is relieved to have some purpose here. Something to call themselves other than 'exiles.' "

Kira nodded, warding off a thought about how a certain caliber of Klingon would have worn that label proudly, and looked out into the wounded *tuq'mor* again. If she looked very carefully, she could find a few spots of defiant green amid the wreckage.

"It looks like we'll be making several trips with the *Victoria Adams*'s crew," Sisko went on. "I'd rather not stack them in three deep this time, but I also don't want to make any more shuttle runs than absolutely necessary. Our friend George is busy sorting the survivors into shiploads while the Klingons work out the terms of an ongoing scientific study with Dax."

Kira nodded, a bit absently. "He's your secret dignitary—the one Starfleet didn't want the Klingons to get their hands on." When Sisko didn't say anything to refute that, she angled a weary grin up at him. "His name isn't really George, is it?"

Her captain changed the subject as smoothly as if she'd never brought it up at all. "So how is Dr. Bashir holding up?"

"LeDonne says he'll be fine. She's given him something that'll keep him out until we get back to the station." She glanced reflexively back toward the shuttle, even though she couldn't see inside. "She was doing patient triage with him when he was kidnapped. I think she's feeling guilty for not realizing what was happening and doing something to stop it."

Sisko followed her gaze briefly, then somehow ended up scrutinizing Kira with his head tipped slightly toward his shoulder. "And what are you feeling guilty about?"

The question caught her without a ready answer. "I don't know. Nothing." Everything. She started to pace away from him, aborted it, and ended up making a frustrated circle that only put her back where she'd started. "I guess I just don't understand what Klingon honor is supposed to be good for," she finally blurted. "What purpose does it serve to take the best, most noble members of their society and . . . sacrifice them! Why can't there be some middle ground between perfect compliance to honor and death?"

"Because sometimes perfect compliance *is* death." Sisko met her angry glare with a placidity that said he hadn't been making light of her dilemma. "Curzon once told me that he didn't think he would ever fully understand what the Klingons call honor, even if he had a dozen lifetimes to study it. In many ways, I think the Klingons are still learning and refining their own concepts every day. It's part of what makes a culture vibrant and adaptive. But it is a hard thing," he said with resonant seriousness. "A hard taskmaster. It's not our place to say whether or not the rewards are worth it."

Federation rhetoric—noninterference, respect for another culture's ways. Worse yet, it was rhetoric Kira's head believed in, even when her heart ached for want of a better, less tragic way.

"I've often thought honor among Klingons is more religion than social," Sisko continued, leaning back against the shuttle's nose and crossing his arms. "Like fate among Humans, *av'adeh'dna* among Vulcans, and *pagh* among your own people. Honor isn't just a list of rules that Klingons adhere to the way you might a recipe. It shapes them, leads them, determines the character of their souls." He motioned back toward the huddle of Klingons and *xirri* inside the mouth of the caves, and Kira was abruptly struck with the incongruity of that sight. Of the wondrous potential represented by a handful of battered warriors and the small gray-green primates who had adopted them. "Honor led them here to be protectors of Cha'Xirrac—better protectors than any combination of starships or comets could be. They've been reborn, through fire and ice." He smiled a little at the drama of his words. "No rebirth ever comes without loss. *Epetai* Vrag knew that." He caught Kira's gaze up in his own. "Maybe honor required a sacrifice to balance the scales—life for life. You can't hold it against her if she willingly made that choice."

Perhaps not. But Kira couldn't help wishing for a solution that didn't require bloodshed to water the seeds of new life.

"Dax says the planet will recover," she said suddenly. It was something to hang on to. A memory of Rota Province as it had been just a few months ago, soft and green and scattered with delicate prairie flowers that couldn't have existed in the shadows of Rota's forests. New life, celebrating with a song of colors. Someday, this planet would look like that, too.

"So not just a new life for the Klingons," Sisko commented. "A whole new existence. A whole new world."

"Yes." Kira stood up with sudden decision. "And maybe, if they're lucky, a whole new meaning of honor. One that involves cooperation rather than fighting, and survival rather than sacrifice."

Sisko made a somber noise. "I'm not sure that they'll still be Klingons then," he said. "And, somehow, I think there will always be a Day of Honor celebration on Cha'Xirrac."

"That's all right." Kira glanced back at those glints of water-shielded vegetation, as stubbornly tough as Klingons and as quietly surprising as the *xirri.* "Just as long as it is followed by a Day of Rebirth."

HER KLINGON SOUL

Michael Jan Friedman

To Estelle Mass, for her wit and generosity

AUTHOR'S NOTES

It was September 8, 1966. Thirty years ago, though it's pretty hard to believe.

This is how I remember it. I was eleven years old, sort of a bean pole with a Beatle haircut. I was also about as big a science fiction fan as you could find, which was why I'd been so intrigued by the promos I'd seen all week.

Something about a new show. A science fiction show. Like *Lost in Space,* but different. More serious. More adventurous. More like the novels and the comic books I'd always enjoyed.

Anyway, that was the promise. Even at that age, I knew the chances of it being fulfilled were pretty negligible. Still, at a couple of minutes before the hour, I turned the television to Channel Four, leaned back into my pillows, and waited for the commercials to end.

And then I saw it. "The Man Trap," it was called. A story about love and illusion and loyalty and courage. Looking back, I can't say it was the best episode of the original series. But at the time, it was the *only* episode, and it was much better than anything I'd seen on television before.

My god, I thought. This is so cool. It's so amazingly *cool.*

I didn't know that, thirty years later, I'd be toiling in the vineyards Gene Roddenberry planted with such care and vision. And after eighteen novels and more than a hundred comic books and a *Voyager* story credit, I'm still eager to toil some more.

If you ask me why *Star Trek* has been around so long, you won't get any special wisdom. I'll mention the same things everyone else does—the spirit of optimism, the sense of inclusion. But it's more than that. It's something I can't express, some resonance with my psyche I can't put into words. Except to say . . .

This is so cool. It's so amazingly *cool.*

Michael Jan Friedman
Long Island, New York
October, 1996

CHAPTER 1

HER SHIFT OVER BY A GOOD TWENTY MINUTES, CHIEF ENGINEER B'ELANNA Torres exited engineering and headed for the ship's mess hall. As she had hoped, the predictable change-of-shift traffic was over. There was no one in the corridor but her.

So far, so good. If she kept to herself, she imagined, she would get through the day with a minimum amount of agony.

"Lieutenant?" said a voice from behind her.

Oh, no, she thought. Reluctantly, she turned to look back over her shoulder.

It was Paisner from stellar cartography. He was smiling in his beard at her, smiling as warmly as she'd ever seen him smile.

"Happy—"

"Yeah," she said, "thanks."

And before he could finish his greeting, B'Elanna ducked down an intersecting corridor. Nor did she turn around until she was sure she'd left Paisner behind.

Unfortunately, as she approached a turbolift on her left, its doors opened and a couple of her fellow officers came out. One was Trexis, a stocky Bajoran who'd been with her in the Maquis. The other was Morganstern, an attractive redhead who ran the bio lab.

"Lieutenant," said Trexis. "A brave—"

"Right," B'Elanna interjected. "Uh-huh. See you later."

And she accelerated her pace, passing the two of them before they could say anything else. Again, the engineer found another corridor and took it.

She cursed inwardly. This was harder than she'd believed it would be.

Coming to another turbolift, B'Elanna ducked inside it. "Mess hall," she said, slumping against the side panel. But just as the doors were about to close, someone slipped inside with her.

It was Wu, who worked with her in engineering. He was obviously pleased to see her.

"Lieutenant," he said as the doors closed.

"Mister Wu," she responded, looking at the ceiling and not her colleague. She could feel the slight vibration that meant the lift compartment was moving.

"I didn't think I was going to see you today," he told her. "But since I have, allow me to wish you—"

"Hang on," she interrupted. Turning to him, she asked, "Why aren't you in engineering?"

Wu looked at her, surprised. "It's my day off."

B'Elanna eyed him. "Are you sure about that? I could've sworn I saw your name on the duty roster."

He thought about it for a moment. "I don't see how that could be. I distinctly recall—"

Suddenly, the doors opened. "Now that you mention it," the lieutenant remarked, "it *is* your day off. My mistake." And she exited the lift before Wu could say another word.

Turning left, she set her sights on the double doors of the mess hall. She was almost home free, she told herself. If she sat by herself and grimaced enough, she could eat and get out without meeting any more well-wishers.

Then, just as she was about to enter, the doors opened and a half-dozen of her crewmates spilled out. She sought a way around them, but there wasn't any—not unless she wanted to bowl them over.

"Lieutenant Torres," said one of them.

"Just the woman I wanted to see," said another.

"After all," said a third one, "it *is* your day, isn't it?"

B'Elanna wanted to crawl into an EPS conduit and die.

• • •

As First Officer Chakotay entered *Voyager*'s brightly lit mess hall, he wasn't looking for B'Elanna Torres.

Chakotay had no reason to be looking for her at that particular moment. After all, everything was running smoothly in the ship's engineering section, and there weren't any emergencies elsewhere on *Voyager* that required B'Elanna's special expertise.

Still, it was difficult not to pick out the lieutenant in the midst of all the other uniformed personnel in the room. After all, she was half-human, half-Klingon. That made her rather noticeable—the only one of her kind on the entire starship. Indeed, the only one of her kind in the entire Delta Quadrant.

But what made her even more noticeable was the fact she was sitting all by herself. The ship's engineer had sequestered herself in a corner of the mess hall, facing one of the observation ports, her back to the entrance and therefore to him as well.

Alone.

Though the first officer couldn't see her face, he couldn't imagine she was very happy right now. People usually didn't seclude themselves when their hearts were bursting with joy.

As her commanding officer in their days with the Maquis, Chakotay had known B'Elanna to be moody on occasion, even volatile. She had never resented his company, however, not even when she was at her worst. In fact, she had always welcomed it.

He hoped she would welcome it now. And beyond that, that she would let him help her with whatever was on her mind. It was tough enough to be a lifetime's journey away from home, but to make that journey by oneself was too great a burden for anyone.

Crossing the lounge, he headed for B'Elanna's table. But before he could get halfway there, someone else beat him to it.

It was Neelix, the ship's Talaxian chef and semi-official "morale officer," carrying a large metal pot with a flat bottom. No doubt it held another of his strange and exotic concoctions, thrown together from whatever planetary flora *Voyager*'s foraging parties could supply him with.

But something was different here, Chakotay told himself. Usually, Neelix served up his creations with undiluted eagerness. Right now, that eagerness was tempered with a certain . . .

Revulsion.

"Here you go," said the Talaxian, forcing a smile.

B'Elanna looked up at him, then at his pot. Clearly, she had no idea what Neelix was talking about.

"Here I go with *what?*" she asked.

"A mélange of traditional Klingon dishes," said the Talaxian, failing to suppress a shudder as he placed the pot on the table. "Serpent worms, heart of targ, and rokeg blood pie. All fresh from the replicator, no less. I'll just leave it here on the table, and you can..." He grimaced. "...pick it over at your leisure."

The lieutenant seemed surprised as she surveyed the contents of the pot. As he approached, Chakotay could see them as well.

Not being a connoisseur of Klingon cuisine, he had only a vague idea of what Neelix had come up with. One part of the pot held what looked like a mess of snakes, another some kind of internal organ.

None of it was cooked. Even Chakotay knew that Klingon delicacies were generally served raw—and whenever possible, still alive. Not up my alley, he thought. Even sushi made him a little queasy.

B'Elanna gazed at Neelix, perplexed. "You used your replicator rations to make these?" she asked.

He nodded proudly. "I sure did. But I felt it was something I had to do. After all, I've made plomeek soup for Mister Tuvok and pineapple pizza for the Devlin twins, but I've never attempted anything Klingon before. Then I got wind of this wonderful holiday of yours and..." He shrugged. "I couldn't resist. Bon appetit, Lieutenant." He leaned a little closer to her. "That means knock your socks off in French."

B'Elanna shook her head. "I can't eat this," she said. She pushed the pot away from her.

The Talaxian was mortified. "I...I don't understand," he replied after a moment. "I did extensive research on your cultural background. I could have *sworn* this was the way I was supposed to present these dishes."

The engineer got to her feet. "It's not the presentation," she said, her tone cold and blunt. "I don't eat Klingon food. In case you haven't noticed, I'm not your run-of-the-mill Klingon."

And with that, she stalked off, leaving Neelix and the pot behind. The Talaxian looked to Chakotay, who was the nearest person around.

"I didn't mean to offend her," Neelix explained, clearly at a loss. He watched B'Elanna's departure with genuine disappointment. "I knew she hadn't eaten these things before, but I thought it was because they weren't available. I didn't have any idea she would—"

The first officer put a hand on the Talaxian's shoulder. "It's all right," he said. "Your heart was in the right place."

Neelix glanced at the writhing, pulsating contents of the pot and sighed. "So was the targ's. But it didn't seem to make a difference."

Chakotay frowned. He didn't approve of B'Elanna's behavior. No matter what was bothering her, she had no right to take it out on the cook.

As the engineer exited the mess hall, Chakotay made his decision. "Excuse me," he said, and went after her.

Ensign Harry Kim glanced at his shuttle's instrument panel. On the monitor to his right, he could see the asteroid belt as his sensors saw it—a series of green blips, each a different size and configuration.

There was a path through the blip field, but not an easy one. In fact, it was kind of torturous. And at warp seven, it looked virtually impossible to maneuver through.

"You can do it," said his copilot.

Kim glanced at Tom Paris, who was sitting beside him. As always, Paris was the picture of casual confidence. "What makes you think this time is going to be different from the others?" the ensign asked.

"I've got a feeling," said Paris as he consulted his own monitors. "Pay attention now, Harry. Those asteroids are coming up fast."

They were, too. In a few moments, they'd be right on top of them. The ensign took a breath and let it out. At this speed, their shields would be of no use to them. One collision and they'd be space debris—if there was anything left of them at all.

"Ten seconds," Paris told him. "Nine. Eight. Seven..."

"I get the idea," Harry said.

Then he was operating on pure instinct. The first asteroid loomed on his port side; he cut it as closely as he could. That put him in position to cut even more sharply to port when the second asteroid appeared.

The third one required a quick dip, the fourth a sharp rise. The fifth and sixth required only minor adjustments. And the ensign handled them all without an error.

Then again, it wasn't that first sequence that had scared the daylights out of him. It was the next one. Harry gritted his teeth.

Hard to starboard to avoid a large asteroid, the largest he'd seen yet. Hard again, this time to port, to miss another one. To starboard; starboard again. And then a backbreaking ascent.

The shuttle shivered mightily with the force of each turn, but it managed to hold together. More importantly, there were no collisions, not even a particularly close call.

And there were only two asteroids ahead of him, virtually side by side, only a few meters apart. Two asteroids to beat and he was home free. The ensign bore down, concentrating harder than ever, rotating his craft ninety degrees in an attempt to slip between them.

You can do it, he told himself.

"You can do it," Paris echoed. "You can—"

Before the lieutenant could finish his sentence, Harry's shuttle wavered ever so slightly from the vertical—and clipped one of the asteroids. The impact sent it bouncing into the other one.

The ensign heard his copilot utter a curse. Then, before he could take another breath, his craft exploded in a cataclysm of light and sound.

Harry closed his eyes and scowled as he embraced oblivion. Then he felt Paris tapping his shoulder, and he opened his eyes again. The holodeck grid was all around them, a mocking reminder of the ensign's failure. Or at least, that's how it seemed to him.

"You did it again," said his friend. "Too much starboard thruster."

Normally, Harry didn't like to let his frustration show. He made an exception this time.

"I tried to keep her from heeling," he said. "I *thought* I had it."

Paris grunted. "If you'd had it, you and I would still be safely ensconced in the shuttlecraft, popping open some champagne—not standing here in the middle of the holodeck doing a postmortem."

The ensign pressed his lips together and turned away from his friend. If he'd cracked up just once or twice, it wouldn't have been such a big thing. But this was the *seventh* time he'd tried the very same maneuver—and each time, he'd run into the same crushing results.

"You know what?" he said at last.

"What?" Paris responded.

"I think I've had it with this program," Harry told him, shrugging. "I mean, what's the big deal? I'll probably never run into a situation like that one anyway. How many asteroid belts have we seen since we got ourselves stuck here in the Delta Quadrant? Two or three altogether?"

The lieutenant eyed him soberly. "I see. When in doubt, retreat. Or better yet, just run away."

Something in the ensign stiffened. "I'm *not* running away," he answered. "I'm just conceding my limitations. It's not as if everyone can be the kind of pilot *you* are."

Paris smiled. "Harry, I'm not asking you to be the kind of pilot I am. I'm just trying to prepare you as best I can. Don't forget, we're in terra incognita. We don't know what to expect here. And that's all the more reason to be prepared."

Truthfully, the ensign *wanted* to be able to execute the maneuver, and not just to get his friend off his back. It irked him that any move—no matter how difficult—could make such a monkey out of him.

"Tell you what," said Paris after a moment or two. "I'm going to let you in on a little secret. No, scratch that. It's actually a pretty big secret."

Harry regarded him. "I'm listening."

"The starboard thrusters aren't the problem," said the lieutenant. "Not really. The problem is you're afraid to go for broke."

"Go for broke?" the ensign repeated. "What does that mean? I'm not completing the maneuver because I haven't got the guts?"

Paris winced. "I didn't want to put it quite that way, but—"

"That's what you're saying?" Harry pressed. "I'm screwing up because I don't have the backbone for it? The nerve?"

"What I'm saying," his friend explained, "is you care too much about the outcome. The secret of piloting, whether it's in a holodeck or out in the real world, is to loosen up, to not give a damn—to not even entertain the *possibility* of failure. And then, if you lose—hey, it happens to the best of us. At least you gave it your best shot."

The ensign was beginning to get angry now. "I *am* giving it my best shot—for what it's worth."

Paris shook his head. "You only think that's your best shot. Stop worrying, stop thinking altogether—and maybe *then* we'll see Harry Kim's best shot." He clapped his friend on the shoulder. "Be a risk-taker, Harry."

The ensign threw his hands up in exasperation. "All right, all right.

We'll try it again. And this time, I'll try not to think." He sighed deeply. "Whatever that means."

Paris winked at him. "That's the spirit." He looked up at the ceiling. "Computer, program Paris beta—"

Abruptly, the empty holodeck rang out with the voice of authority. "This is Captain Janeway. All senior staff officers are to meet me in the observation lounge immediately. Janeway out."

Kim felt relief more than anything else. What's more, his friend seemed to sense that.

"I'm not done with you," Paris assured him. "Not by a long shot."

"Hey," said the ensign, "I'm just as disappointed as you are. I really wanted to tackle that program again."

"Yeah, right," his friend muttered, rolling his eyes. "Just like Tuvok wants to learn how to dance."

As the corridor curved, obscuring his view of the lieutenant, Chakotay lengthened his strides. He called after her.

"B'Elanna!"

After a moment or two, he caught up to her. She had stopped at the sound of her name. Or was it the fact that it was *he* who had called her?

"What is it?" she asked.

Chakotay could tell by her attitude that she didn't want to have this conversation. Tough. She would have it anyway.

"What is it, *sir,*" he corrected.

The engineer scowled. "What is it, sir," she echoed.

The first officer looked around to make sure no one else was present in the corridor. What he had to say wasn't necessarily for public consumption.

"You were rude to Neelix back there," he told her. "All he wanted to do was please you, and you shot him down. I want to know why."

"Isn't that between me and Neelix?" she asked. "Or am I under orders to eat whatever he puts in front of me?"

Chakotay sighed. "All right, forget I'm your superior. I'll speak to you as your friend—who was embarrassed by what he saw."

B'Elanna's lips pulled back, as if she were about to lash out at him. But in the end, she seemed to think better of it.

"Fine," she said, looking away from him as her anger ebbed. "Maybe my reaction was inappropriate. But you know how I feel about Klingons. And that includes the things they eat."

Chakotay knew, all right. He had served with B'Elanna long enough to hear the whole story. How her Klingon mother and her human father had separated when she was very young, so she had never really known her father.

How she and her mother had lived in a mostly human colony, where she was self-conscious about her Klingon characteristics. And how she had always emphasized her human characteristics, in an attempt to belong.

That desire for acceptance had gotten her all the way to Starfleet Academy, where she had excelled in the sciences. However, her Klingon side had surfaced there as well—manifesting itself in the way she argued with her teachers. Finally, it had forced her to quit the place.

But several months ago, B'Elanna had obtained a new perspective on her Klingon heritage. Abducted by the Vidiians, she had been split into separate Klingon and human personas, each with its own positive and negative attributes—and each incomplete without the other.

In order to escape her captors, B'Elanna's two halves had been forced to work together—to, in effect, form a whole. In the process, her human self had come to appreciate how much of her courage and determination came from the Klingon within her.

The first officer considered his protégé. "I don't buy it," he replied. "When you were sitting in sick bay, after the doctor had announced he would have to merge you again with your Klingon DNA—"

"I said I was incomplete without it," the lieutenant recalled. "I said I had come to admire my Klingon self. For her strength, her bravery."

"Exactly," said Chakotay. "And even though you'd never be at peace with her savagery, it seemed you'd at least come to terms with it."

B'Elanna shrugged. "So?"

"So, why did you abuse Neelix that way in the mess hall? His intentions were good—as always. And you treated him as if he'd insulted you."

The lieutenant sighed. "All right. Maybe there's more to it." She paused. "Maybe it's this damned holiday."

At first he didn't know what she meant. Then he recalled the Talaxian's reference a few moments earlier. "Holiday?" he prodded.

She frowned. "Yes. The Day of Honor. It grew out of an incident a hundred years ago. A Starfleet captain named Kirk risked his life to save some Klingons, and now the day is celebrated throughout the Klingon Empire."

Chakotay grunted. He had heard of Kirk, of course. The man's exploits were required reading at the Academy. And now that he thought about it, he remembered something about Kirk rescuing some Klingons early in his career.

"But why does that bother you?" he asked.

B'Elanna looked at him. "It would bother you, too, if you'd spent your life denying a part of yourself. The Day of Honor has always been a reminder that I'm different from everyone else. That no matter what I say or do, people will always look at me as an outsider."

Chakotay regarded her. He was starting to understand.

"To make matters worse," she went on, "my mother always wanted me to spend the day contemplating its meaning. And of course, I would run away when she wasn't looking and have some kind of bad luck. No—make that *horrible* luck. When I was six, I went exploring outside the colony and fell into a big hole. They had to send a search party out for me. And I didn't get found until well after dark, when the temperature had dropped below freezing."

Chakotay grimaced at the thought of it. "Not one of your fonder childhood memories, I imagine."

"It got worse," she told him. "When I was eight, I was fiddling with the controls to a sensor array when no one was looking. All I did was change the angle on a single data collector—no big deal, right? How was I to know a damaged ship was sending out a distress call, and that we would miss it because the collector was off?"

The first officer winced. "Was the crew rescued?"

B'Elanna nodded. "Eventually—after someone noticed that the collector was off and corrected it. But I caught hell for my fiddling—from my mother, especially."

He got the point. However, the engineer wasn't finished yet.

"When I was nine," she said, "I accidentally locked myself in a storage room. When I was eleven, I nearly lost my leg to a falling cargo container. When I was thirteen, the boy I liked—"

Suddenly she stopped. Her face was a bright shade of crimson.

"What?" he asked.

"Nothing," she muttered. "But you see what I mean? This holiday has been nothing but trouble for me. And yet, people always seem to want to thrust the Day of Honor on me, as if it were a badge of pride. If I—"

Suddenly, an intercom voice interrupted the conversation. Chakotay recognized it instantly, even before it identified itself.

"This is Captain Janeway. All senior staff officers are to meet me in the observation lounge immediately. Janeway out."

He looked at B'Elanna. She seemed relieved to have been provided with a distraction.

"I guess we'll have to continue this another time," Chakotay told her.

"Another time," she echoed as they headed for the turbolift.

B'Elanna and Chakotay were the last to arrive at the ship's observation lounge. As they took their seats around the table, the engineer saw the others look up at them.

Tuvok, the security officer, was as stone-faced as ever. But then, he was a Vulcan, and Vulcans had mastered their emotions hundreds of years earlier. Whatever he was feeling at the moment, he kept it well-hidden—even from himself, the engineer suspected.

Tom Paris, the helmsman, smiled a perfunctory smile at B'Elanna. In some ways he was the opposite of Tuvok, reveling in his human foibles and faults. But right now, he seemed pretty businesslike.

Harry Kim, the young ensign who'd been making his maiden voyage when *Voyager* was whisked into the Delta Quadrant, had taken a chair to one side of Paris. As always, he seemed eager to apply his intellect to the problem at hand—no matter what it might be.

Neelix was in attendance as well—not just cook and morale officer, but also their resident authority on people and places in the sector. As a being who had scavenged and traded his way from star to star, he was an invaluable guide in what often proved to be hostile territory.

The Talaxian didn't mention B'Elanna's behavior in the mess hall. But then, he didn't look at her either, so it was hard to tell if he harbored any resentment over it.

Finally, there was Janeway, their captain. She sat at the head of the table, her usual place. As always, she seemed calm and unruffled, hopeful without being demanding.

But then, she was the commanding officer of this vessel, the only real Starfleet presence in the entire Delta Quadrant. If she didn't maintain an even keel, who *would?*

B'Elanna was glad Janeway had summoned her staff when she did. More than likely, the engineer would soon have something to occupy her mind. If she was *really* lucky, this damned Day of Honor would be over before she had a chance to think about it again.

Janeway looked around the table, from one to the other of them. "Thank you for being prompt," she said. "This shouldn't take long." The captain leaned back in her chair. "Long-range sensors have identified a Class M planet not far from here. There's a good chance it'll have the kind of plant life we've discovered elsewhere—and put to good use."

"Excellent," said Neelix. "We're running low. As always." He had muttered the last part under his breath, but there wasn't anyone at the table who failed to hear it—or to understand what he meant.

As a ship on its own, with limited energy and raw material, *Voyager* couldn't produce large quantities of food through its replicators. The crew had to depend on natural flora for much of its diet. Some of it could be produced in the aeroponics bay, but the majority had to be foraged from the surfaces of alien planets.

"We'll send down three teams of two people apiece," Janeway announced. "Each team will take a different area, examine the local plant life firsthand—and coordinate its transport, if it fills our needs."

Janeway leaned forward in her chair. "Any questions?"

B'Elanna tried to think of one that wouldn't be a complete waste of time. But she couldn't. And no one else had a question either, apparently.

The captain nodded. "Dismissed." Then she turned to the engineer. "And, by the way, B'Elanna—I want to wish you a brave Day of Honor."

The lieutenant could feel herself blanch. Somehow, she managed to say, "Thank you, ma'am."

Then, with a glance at Chakotay, she made a quick exit—before someone decided to echo the sentiment.

CHAPTER 2

JANEWAY EMERGED ONTO THE BRIDGE WITH CHAKOTAY ALONGSIDE HER. "She doesn't *like* people saying that?" the captain asked.

"Apparently not," said the first officer.

Janeway frowned. "I'll have to remember that in the future." She thought for a moment. "You think I ought to—?"

"Apologize?" Chakotay ventured. He shook his head. "No, I think that would only make it worse."

The captain sighed and headed for her center seat, her thoughts reverting to a more immediate concern.

Neelix's remark at the briefing earlier had been an absolute understatement. Their provisions weren't just low—they were lower than they'd been at any time she could remember.

That made their foraging mission more than just necessary. It was nothing short of essential. And where was that planet anyway? By now, she estimated, it should have been well within—

"Visual range," said Tuvok. He was standing at his customary post, as poker-faced as ever.

The captain chuckled softly to herself. Vulcans were supposed to be able to read one's thoughts only during a mind-meld. However, Tuvok often seemed to read hers without one.

"Let's see it," Janeway replied.

In accordance with her orders, the flowing star field on the forward viewscreen gave way to the image of a Class M planet. She could tell by the degree of magnification that it was somewhat smaller than Earth, but not by much—though its continents were considerably larger.

The captain turned to Paris, who was manning the helm. "Estimated time to orbit?" she asked.

"One hour and forty minutes," he told her.

Janeway nodded. "Thank you, Lieutenant."

It was an hour and forty minutes longer than she cared to wait, but even warp drive could propel them only so fast. Taking her seat, she settled in and prepared herself for the vigil.

Fortunately for her, as well as everyone else, Janeway didn't enforce a rigid silence on her bridge the way some captains did. She felt comfortable with a certain amount of chatter, as long as it didn't distract anyone's attention from his or her duties.

Tuvok never took part in these conversations. But then, no one expected him to. By contrast, Paris liked to needle everyone a bit, the Vulcan included—though the helmsman's favorite target was Ensign Kim.

After all, they'd become close friends over the last several months. Whenever Paris made a remark, Kim would always frown good-naturedly and let it roll off his back.

But today seemed to be an exception. Paris didn't send a single barb in the ensign's direction. And that made the captain wonder. Had the helmsman jabbed his friend once too often?

No doubt, she told herself, she would find out in due time. Very little went on between the bulkheads of this ship that Kathryn Janeway didn't get a whiff of eventually.

B'Elanna had purposely waited until mealtime was over and the mess hall was likely to be deserted. As it turned out, there wasn't a soul around—except for the one who was cleaning up behind the serving counter.

Not wishing to take him by surprise, the lieutenant cleared her throat. A moment later, Neelix poked his head up. When he saw who it was, he paused a moment—then went back to his cleaning.

B'Elanna folded her arms across her chest and sighed. Apparently, the Talaxian wasn't going to make this easy for her.

"Listen," she said, "I'm ashamed of the way I acted earlier. It was uncalled-for. And I hope you'll accept my apology."

There. She'd said it. But there wasn't any reaction. Somewhere below the level of the counter, Neelix continued his chores rather noisily. But he didn't give her a response.

The lieutenant bit her lip. She'd tried, hadn't she? She'd done the right thing. If the Talaxian didn't think it was enough, there wasn't much she could do about that.

Except apologize one more time. "All right. Maybe I deserve the silent treatment. I just wanted you to know I'm sorry. Really."

Still no answer. Just more of Neelix's puttering. If anything, it was even louder than before.

B'Elanna looked at the floor and steeled herself. Then she forged ahead, despite the difficulty she had in saying such things.

"Look," she told the Talaxian, "I know you went to a lot of trouble for me. I know I acted like a spoiled child. And I know you're under no obligation whatsoever to speak to me, now or ever again. But I really wish you would. Not only because I would miss your company, but because every time you gave me the cold shoulder I'd be reminded of what an absolute jerk I was."

The puttering continued unabated. But no reply. Not even a hint of one. Obviously, she thought, she wasn't going to get anywhere with Neelix, no matter what she did or said.

The lieutenant was just about to leave the mess hall, her mission unfulfilled, when Neelix appeared above the level of the counter again. And this time, he had a plate in his hands.

"You turn *this* down," he said, "and I'll really be upset."

B'Elanna looked at it. "Cheese quesadillas? With salsa verde?"

The Talaxian nodded, obviously pleased with himself. "A traditional meal from the *human* side of your family tree. It's my way of saying I understand your being mad at me. Now come on. Dig in before it gets cold and the cheese starts to congeal."

The engineer couldn't help smiling at him as she accepted the plate. "Well...what can I say? Thanks, Neelix. Um...care to join me?"

"I've already eaten," he told her, "but I'll be glad to keep you company. I get a kick out of watching people enjoy their food."

As B'Elanna led the way to the nearest table, she took another look at the quesadillas and suppressed a grimace. Truth be told, she didn't like Mexican food either. But under the circumstances, she knew she'd better eat it—or lose Neelix's friendship forever.

Brave Day of Honor, she remarked inwardly. This holiday was nothing but torture for her.

Thanks in part to her curiosity about Paris and Kim, time passed quickly on the bridge for Janeway. Almost before the captain knew it, *Voyager* had reached the system that housed their target world.

"Reduce to impulse speed," she told her helmsman.

"Taking her down to impulse," Paris confirmed.

Janeway stood, as if to get a better look at the Class M planet, and glanced at Tuvok. At this range, the sensors could pick up a good deal more data than before.

"Sentient life forms?" she asked.

The Vulcan examined his instruments for a moment, then shook his head. "None, apparently. The little fauna that exists shows only rudimentary signs of intelligence."

The captain nodded. "I see. In your estimation, will any of it present a significant danger to us?"

Again, Tuvok consulted his instruments. "There are predators, of course, but nothing out of the ordinary."

"What about surface conditions?" she inquired. "Radiation? Unusual gases? Geothermal activity?"

"Nothing significant," the Vulcan told her. "At least not from the point of view of safety."

Janeway absorbed the information as she joined the Vulcan at his console. "And what would you say are the most promising beam-down sites?"

Tuvok didn't answer right away. But then, the security chief was a Vulcan through and through. He seldom made recommendations without carefully considering all his options.

"Here," he said finally. His monitor showed the two hemispheres that made up the planet. Tuvok pointed to a spot that displayed a concentration of foliage—or, to be more accurate, a particular sort of foliage.

It wasn't the kind of plant they needed to supplement their food supplies; that stuff often grew in amounts too sparse to identify with ship's sensors. Still, as the captain had learned from experience, the plant Tuvok had found was an indication that what they needed was probably nearby.

The Vulcan pointed again. "And here." He pointed to a second spot on his monitor, this time in the other hemisphere. "And lastly, here." He showed the captain a third location.

Janeway nodded. "I agree—although it appears there are some sensor blind spots in the vicinity of the third site." She took a closer look. "Probably mineral deposits. That could hamper communications."

Communications were important, considering how little they knew about most of the worlds they visited. But on the whole, she was willing to take the chance, given the lack of other hazards.

On other planets, the captain had been forced to overlook a promising source of supplies in the interest of keeping her people from harm. Fortunately, she mused, that wouldn't be the case here.

"Put together some landing parties," she told Tuvok. "I'll want them to beam down as soon as we establish orbit."

The Vulcan nodded. "Aye, Captain."

As he left the bridge, another officer moved over to take his place. Smooth and efficient, thought Janeway. She liked that. With a little luck, this entire mission would go that way.

As B'Elanna ascended the transporter platform, Kim was right beside her. Adjusting his shoulder strap and the tricorder that dangled from it, he winked in her direction.

"Ready, Maquis?" he asked.

She nodded, smiling a little. "Ready, Starfleet."

It was a private joke born of their experiences on the Caretaker's planet, shortly after their arrival in the Delta Quadrant. They had woken side by side in a stark, colorless laboratory, having never met each other before—but cognizant of the fact that they were the only two familiar elements in an otherwise alien picture.

At the time, she was hostile—mistrusting him. Since then, they had learned not only to get along, but to depend on each other—to watch each other's back. These days, B'Elanna wouldn't have thought twice about entrusting Harry Kim with her life.

Of course, this was slated to be a routine mission. And since the other survey teams had all beamed down already without incident, there was no reason to believe she would have to entrust Kim with anything—except maybe collecting his share of the data.

Best of all, he hadn't mentioned the Day of Honor to her. Not once.

The transporter operator, a petite, blonde-haired woman named Burleson, smiled at their banter as she made some small adjustments in her controls. "Stand by," she told them.

"Standing by," Kim assured her.

Finished with her ministrations, Burleson looked up at them. "Energizing."

When she was younger, B'Elanna had always wondered what it would be like to be transported. What it would *feel* like. Now, as an adult who had transported to and from space-going vessels hundreds of times, she knew the answer.

Nothing. It felt like *nothing.*

One moment, one was in a transporter room, with its muted lighting and hard echoes. The next moment, one was somewhere else.

In this case, it was a gently rolling hillside under a big, yellow-orange sun. As the sensors had indicated, there was plenty of vegetation around. The dominant form of flora was a plant with wispy blue tendrils, each the thickness of her pinky finger.

Kim took out his tricorder and started analyzing the stuff. After a moment, he grunted. "Poisonous. And even if it weren't, it's all but devoid of nutrients. At least, the kind *we* need."

B'Elanna tried another kind of plant. It wasn't poisonous to them, but it also didn't suit their needs. Nor did the next specimen she tried. Or the one after that.

She was beginning to get frustrated. So was the ensign, if his tight-lipped expression was any indication. "Let's expand the scan," she suggested.

Kim nodded. As B'Elanna adjusted her tricorder to analyze everything within one kilometer, he did the same.

"Still nothing," he told her. "Wait—maybe I spoke too soon."

She saw it, too. "In that direction." She pointed west. "Some kind of vegetation. And it seems to be more the kind of thing we're looking for. Of course, it's hard to tell for certain from this distance."

Kim shrugged. "So let's close the gap."

Putting away their tricorders, they headed in the direction B'Elanna had indicated. It wasn't an unpleasant walk, with the sun on their faces and a gentle breeze stirring the blue tendrils all about them.

And as she had predicted, her friend didn't mention the Day of Honor. They talked about the soil, the atmosphere, the temperature, and the ways in which they missed the Alpha Quadrant.

But they didn't refer to the Day of Honor.

There was something else they didn't talk about—something that was bothering Kim, though he tried not to let on. Out of respect for his wishes, B'Elanna didn't press the issue.

Before long, they arrived at the spot where they had detected the patch of edible vegetation. It turned out to be the mouth of a cave set into a particularly steep hillside.

The vegetation itself—something that looked like cabbage, except it was orange with white streaks running through it—was in sparse supply. But a glance deeper inside the cave revealed more of it, as well as evidence of some other useful-looking plants.

Unfortunately, neither B'Elanna nor Kim could tell just how deep the caves went. According to their tricorders, the signal-blocking minerals Tuvok had warned them about seemed to be in vast abundance here.

"We should take a look inside," B'Elanna said.

Her companion nodded. "But first, we'll let the captain know what we're up to." He tapped his comm badge. "Kim to Janeway."

The communication was plagued with static, but the captain's voice was recognizable nonetheless. "Janeway here. What can I do for you, Ensign?"

"We've located what appears to be edible vegetation," he said. "But it seems to prefer the dark. More specifically, a cave we've discovered."

"And you'd like to explore it," the captain deduced. "Taking all possible precautions, of course."

"Of course," B'Elanna chimed in.

There was a chuckle on Janeway's end of the communication. "Very well," she told them. "But don't stay down there long. I want a report in, say, fifteen minutes—no later."

"Acknowledged," said the ensign. "Kim out."

He turned to B'Elanna and indicated the cave mouth with a gesture. "Shall we?" he asked.

Snapping the palmlight off her uniform, B'Elanna shone it into the darkness. Then she hunkered down and took the lead. As it turned out, the cave was bigger than it looked—not just taller and wider once they got inside, but deeper as well. And if anything, it was more profuse with usable flora than they had imagined.

"This place is one big larder," Kim laughed. "Neelix is going to have a field day with this stuff."

"No doubt," she agreed. "I'll take the wall on the left, you take the one on the right."

"Sounds good to me," he told her.

Little by little, they worked their way deeper and deeper into the cavern, following its twists and turns. The orange-and-white stuff gave way to something big and fluffy and scarlet, then something that looked like a bunch of tiny purple tubers.

And all of it was edible, with a good variety of vitamins and minerals. The way it tasted was another matter—but, as always, B'Elanna would leave that to Neelix. Maybe her discovery would make up for the way she'd growled at him that morning.

The lieutenant was so busy cataloguing the cave vegetation, she didn't see her friend turn his head to look at her. That is, until he cleared his throat and drew her attention.

"Something on your mind, Starfleet?"

"Well," Kim said, "now that you mention it..."

Oh no, she thought. I can't escape it even *here.*

"...I understand you were a pretty fair pilot," the ensign finished. "You know, when you were with the Maquis."

B'Elanna smiled with relief. "I suppose. But then, we were all good pilots. We *had* to be." She tilted her head. "Why do you ask?"

Kim sighed. "There's a holodeck program Tom keeps running me through. We're in a shuttlecraft, and there's this asteroid belt..."

He went on to describe it for her—and how it was that one last obstacle that gave him the most trouble. "I can't seem to get the hang of it," he confessed. "I was wondering if you might have any..." He shrugged. "I don't know, any hints."

She went back to cataloguing the vegetation. "Well," she said, "you might want to try applying your thrusters sooner, then reversing them when you rotate too far. That's worked for me."

Kim shook his head ruefully. "I tried that. It didn't—"

Suddenly, they heard a *crunch.* It seemed to have come from the direction of the cave mouth.

Stopping in mid-remark, the ensign looked at her. B'Elanna swallowed and deactivated her palmlight, throwing her half of the cave into darkness. Then, as Kim extinguished his own light, she put her tricorder away and took out her phaser.

Of course, she was probably being overly cautious. There were animals on this world, after all. One of them had probably disturbed a rock. But it could also have been something more. And as she had heard often enough growing up, it was better to be safe than sorry.

Kim pulled his phaser out as well. But try as they might, they couldn't hear anything more. B'Elanna began to relax a little.

Then a bright blue beam sliced the air mere inches from her face, blinding her for a moment. She heard a shuffling, as of many pairs of feet. Pressing her back against the hard, sloping wall of the cavern, she blinked away her blindness and fired back.

The Kazon used directed-energy beams of that color. She cursed silently.

Kim looked at her from across the cave, little more than a shadow. He had likely come to the same conclusion she had. And if it *was* the Kazon, they could expect no mercy—only hostility and savagery and death.

Another directed-energy beam pierced the darkness, throwing the cavern into stark relief. Then a third beam, and a fourth. All of them missed—but by their light B'Elanna could see several large, poorly clad forms poking their bizarrely coifed heads around the bend.

Kazon, all right. She tapped her communicator. "Torres to Janeway. We've got a problem down here, Captain."

A moment passed. Then another.

"Torres to Janeway," she repeated.

Again, nothing. Was it the fault of the signal-blocking minerals in the ground? Or were the Kazon interfering with their communications?

At this point, it hardly mattered. Either way, they couldn't expect any help from the ship. For all intents and purposes, they were on their own.

Gritting her teeth, B'Elanna pushed away from the cave wall and fired in the direction of their adversaries. As her ruby red beam lanced out, she heard a grunt and saw one of the Kazon slump to the ground.

A lucky shot. At least, it seemed so at first.

Then a whole bunch of Kazon came roaring into the cave, scalding the air with a wild barrage of seething blue energy. Suddenly, the shot didn't seem so lucky anymore.

B'Elanna felt something hit her in the midsection—so hard it knocked the breath out of her. She staggered, fell. And as she lay gasping, she felt a second hammer-blow—this time, to her shoulder. And a third.

She fought hard to stay conscious, to hold on to the phaser in her hand. But it was no use. Against her will, darkness claimed her.

CHAPTER 3

"CAPTAIN?"

Janeway turned to look at DuChamps, the dark, stocky former Maquis who had replaced Tuvok at the tactical console.

"What is it?" she asked.

DuChamps frowned and shook his head as he consulted his instruments. "Some kind of unidentified vessel," he reported. "Heading our way at full impulse—three million kilometers and closing."

The captain sighed. Tuvok would have detected an approaching ship at twice that distance, maybe more. And by now, he almost certainly would have found a way to identify it.

But Tuvok wasn't here right now, was he? He was with Tom Paris at one of the beam-down sites.

"I've identified it," DuChamps said at last.

Janeway grunted. "Is it in visual range?"

"Aye, ma'am," the lieutenant responded.

A moment later, the main viewscreen filled with an all-too-familiar sight—that of a Kazon battleship under impulse power. The captain didn't have to know any more than that to realize there was trouble in the offing.

"Transporter room," she intoned, keeping her eyes on the screen. "Bring back the away teams—and I mean *immediately.*"

Janeway then turned back to DuChamps. "Lower shields." Otherwise, the transporter wouldn't work worth a damn. Of course, in the case of Torres and Kim, it might not work anyway.

The lieutenant nodded. "Lowering shields, Captain."

The captain gritted her teeth, watching the Kazon vessel on the viewscreen. At any second it could fire a devastating barrage, and *Voyager* was—at least for now—completely unprotected.

"Raise shields again," Janeway ordered, unable to wait any longer.

DuChamps did as he was told. "Shields up," he informed her.

As the captain watched, the Kazon ship slowed and assumed a parking orbit. It gave no outward sign of hostile intentions, but one never knew when it came to these people.

"What's the status of the Kazon vessel?" she asked DuChamps.

"Quiet," the lieutenant told her. "For the time being, anyway. Their shields are up, too, but they're not charging any weapons."

And the Kazon couldn't beam down to threaten the away teams, if there was anyone left on the surface. Thanks to Janeway's caution, *Voyager* still had the only transporter technology in the Delta Quadrant—and as far as she was concerned, it was going to stay that way.

"Hail them," she told DuChamps. Then she returned her attention to the away team personnel. "Janeway to transporter room. What's going on?"

"We retrieved two of the three teams," came Burleson's reply. "But I couldn't seem to get a lock on Torres and Kim."

Of course you can't, the captain remarked silently. They're in that damned cavern.

"Janeway to Torres," she said out loud.

No answer. Apparently, the mineral deposits were keeping Torres and Kim from hearing the summons.

Then again, there was another possibility—that something more intrusive was keeping Torres and Kim from responding. A cave-in, perhaps? Or—

"The Kazon aren't answering our hails," DuChamps informed her.

The captain bit her lip. "Keep trying."

On the viewscreen, the Kazon vessel was maintaining its position. But surely it was here for a reason. It hadn't made the trip just to admire *Voyager*'s lines.

She didn't like this. She didn't like it at *all.*

As she was pondering what to do, she heard the soft swoosh of the turbolift doors. A moment later, Tuvok and Paris emerged onto the bridge. Smoothly and efficiently, their replacements gave way to them.

The captain nodded to both her senior officers, glad to see them safe and sound—and pleased to have them at her side again. She hated the idea of facing the Kazon with anything less than her best people on hand.

Encouraged, she returned her attention to the viewscreen. The Kazon vessel showed no signs of changing its position.

"What is our situation?" asked the Vulcan, taking in the information on his tactical monitors at a glance.

"Torres and Kim are still down there," Janeway told him. "We can't seem to raise them. And while the Kazon aren't making any threatening moves, they're not speaking to us either."

Paris looked at her. "If you're thinking about a search party, I volunteer to go back down."

The captain frowned. "Don't anticipate me, Lieutenant."

Still, a search party might be their only option. The question was whether or not Torres and Kim had stumbled into a trap—and if so, whether she'd accomplish anything by throwing additional lives at the problem.

She was still considering the option when Tuvok called out her name. Janeway whirled, energized by the urgency in his voice.

"What is it?" she asked.

"There's a vehicle rising from the planet's surface," he told her. "It is Kazon in design, but smaller than any Kazon ship we have seen to date."

"On screen," she commanded.

As the Vulcan complied, the image on the viewscreen changed. Instead of a full-blown Kazon cruiser, the captain found herself looking at a shuttle-sized vessel. And it was indeed rising from the planet's surface, where it had been hidden until just a few seconds ago.

But why hide there—unless it was part of a trap to snare a *Voyager* away team? And why leave its hiding place now, unless it was trying to rejoin its Kazon mothership?

"Get a tractor beam on the smaller vehicle," Janeway snapped. "I want it intercepted immediately."

But before Tuvok could carry out her order, the larger Kazon vessel left its position. And it was all too clear what its commander had in mind.

"They're maneuvering to shield their shuttle from us," she observed out loud. "Compensate, Mr. Paris."

"Aye, Captain," said the helmsman, sending *Voyager* in the direction of the ascending shuttle.

But it was too late. Janeway saw that even before Paris made his move. And even if it weren't, the Kazon ship had begun firing at them for all it was worth, lighting up the heavens with its deadly barrage.

The bridge shivered with the impact. "Shields down twenty-two percent," Tuvok barked in the wake of it.

"What about that tractor beam?" the captain barked in return.

"I am finding it exceedingly difficult to establish a lock," the Vulcan reported as he wrestled with his controls.

And then it became downright impossible, as the smaller vehicle slipped behind the larger one. There was no way the tractors could snare the shuttle with the mothership blocking their line of sight.

"Come around her," the captain instructed. "Quickly, before we lose the shuttle."

Paris did his best. But by the time they reached the far side of the Kazon ship, the smaller vessel was already inside its cargo bay.

Janeway cursed beneath her breath. She wasn't going to give up Torres and Kim without a fight.

"Target phasers and torpedoes," she cried out. "Fire!"

Phaser beams sliced through the void, finding their objectives. Photon torpedoes exploded on impact. But the Kazon's shields held up.

And a moment later, it took off at warp speed, leaving a momentary trail of photon spill. The captain was just as quick.

"Stay with her," she told Paris.

"Aye, ma'am," came his response.

Before she knew it, they were proceeding at top speed. Unfortunately, that was only good enough to keep pace with the Kazon, not overtake them.

Janeway moved to her helmsman's side. "Can we wring any more speed out of the engines?" she asked.

Paris shook his head. "Not without risking a shutdown."

For a moment, the captain was tempted to try it anyway. Then she backed off from the idea. For now, she would go with the conservative approach. At least this way, they could stay in the game.

"Steady as she goes," she told Paris. "Steady as she goes."

Teeg'l, third Maj of the reknowned and feared Kazon-Ogla sect, stood over his helmsman and inspected his craft's monitors. Unfortunately, surrounded as they were with sensor-foiling energy fields, the monitors were all but useless.

Of course, it was those same energy fields that had allowed Teeg'l's vessel to go undetected until this time—without question, a great convenience. But now they were keeping the third Maj from ascertaining when it was safe to leave.

His helmsman, whose name was Shan'ak, looked up at him. "I await your orders, third Maj."

Teeg'l frowned and remembered his instructions. This was an important mission with which he had been entrusted—the first one since his promotion to third Maj. He didn't want to make any mistakes.

"How long has it been since we left the cave?" he asked.

The helmsman consulted his chronometer. "Twenty-seven small cycles."

Teeg'l's frown deepened. "Not enough. Our ship may still be in orbit, awaiting the other shuttlecraft—the one that will serve as a decoy. And if that is so, *Voyager* will be in orbit as well."

The third Maj glanced at the door behind him. Beyond it, the rest of his men were maintaining an armed guard over their *Voyager* captives. All had gone according to plan so far—at least from *his* point of view. It wouldn't hurt to remain here a little longer.

"We continue to wait," Teeg'l decided at last.

Shan'ak nodded. "As you wish, third Maj."

As soon as B'Elanna woke, she sat bolt upright and scanned her surroundings. She was in some kind of cargo hold, small and dark and pentagon-shaped, one of its five walls a yellow energy barrier that prevented her from seeing anything beyond it.

And she had the feeling the place was moving. She imagined she could hear wind on the outside of the walls.

Kim was lying a meter or so away, moaning as he began to regain his senses. There was a large purple bruise on his chin.

Neither one of them had their comm badges. More than likely, they'd been destroyed.

"Harry," she said, crawling over to him and gripping his shoulder. "Wake up."

His eyes opened instantly at the sound of her voice. Then they looked past her, trying to match a location to what they saw.

The ensign sat up. "Where are we?" he asked.

B'Elanna shook her head. "I don't know. But I'm guessing we're in the hands of the Kazon. The last thing I remember is the cavern flooding with them."

He nodded. "I saw them hit you with a couple of those energy beams." His face took on a more serious expression. "I thought they'd killed you—and that I wasn't too far behind. That's when I rushed them, figuring they wouldn't fire at close quarters. You know, for fear of hitting each other?"

"And?" she asked.

Kim winced and touched his black-and-blue mark. "I was right about them not firing. But one of them found another use for his weapon."

"He belted you with it," B'Elanna concluded.

"Knocked me right on my back," the ensign admitted. "*Then* he fired at me, for good measure."

The lieutenant sighed heavily. "And here we are. Neither one of us dead." She looked around again. "I shudder to think why."

"Very simple," said a voice. It seemed to have come from the other side of the energy barrier.

A moment later, the barrier crackled and disappeared—revealing three tall, burly Kazon warriors in the corridor beyond. B'Elanna stood to get a better look at them.

It had been hard to tell in the cavern, but now she recognized the garb of the Kazon-Ogla sect—the first one *Voyager* had encountered in the Delta Quadrant. Not that it mattered much. Janeway and her crew were despised by every Kazon they had run into.

Two of their captors were armed with handweapons. The third, by far the stockiest of the three, entered the cargo hold and smiled savagely.

"Very simple indeed," he said. "You see, you have something and we want it. Give it to us, and we will let you go."

"Just like that," Kim commented.

"Just like that," the Kazon echoed. "As entertaining as it might be to torture and kill you, we will forgo the pleasure if you cooperate. You have the word of Teeg'l, third Maj of the Ogla."

"And how do we know you'll keep your word?" asked B'Elanna.

The Kazon shrugged. "I don't see you have much of a choice."

The lieutenant scowled. "What is it you want?"

"I think you know the answer to that," their captor told them. "After all, we have asked for your transporter technology before. And you have declined to share it with us—though it would benefit our sect immensely."

"Enabling you to dominate the other sects," Kim suggested.

The Kazon nodded. "And others of our enemies as well."

B'Elanna looked the warrior in the eye. "You must know we can't give you what you're after."

"On the contrary," he growled, his smile fading suddenly. "I know you *can.* That is, you have the expertise. But for now, you have decided against it. We are not fools, you know. We have anticipated such a reaction."

"You have to understand," she explained, "we're sworn not to give such technology to anyone, friend or otherwise. It's our most sacred rule."

The Kazon's eyes narrowed. "Do not play games with me, Lieutenant. You are alone in this part of space. You are afraid to share your technology because it would take away your military edge—and therefore impair your chances of survival." He smiled again, but it was a thin-lipped smile. "You may have other reasons—but this is the most important one."

Not true, thought B'Elanna. But there was nothing to be gained by arguing the point.

"Maybe you think your friends will find you," Teeg'l went on. "Maybe you think all you have to do is hold out for a while, and they will free you. But I am here to tell you it is not so. In kidnapping you, we did not merely see an opportunity and take advantage of it. You are the result of a trap we have been planning for some time."

"A trap?" the lieutenant echoed.

She wanted to keep the Kazon talking. The more she knew, the better equipped she would be to find an escape route.

"Indeed," said Teeg'l. "The Ogla tracked your progress through the quadrant for months, seeing what kinds of planets attracted your attention and why. Once we realized what you were after and where you were headed, we determined the location of the next attractive planet in your path."

"And that's where you caught us," Kim deduced.

The Kazon frowned. "No, not right away. Twice before we set a trap and you went off in some other direction. It was only this third time that everything went according to plan."

"Which was?" B'Elanna prodded, perhaps a little too hard.

"A matter of misdirection," Teeg'l explained, unperturbed by her aggressiveness. "While you and your comrades were still foraging on the planet's surface, a Kazon cruiser appeared. No doubt wondering what this might mean, your captain retrieved your fellow crewmen. But, to her regret, she could not retrieve you."

"Because of the minerals in the crust," the ensign noted.

The Kazon laughed. "That's how it must have seemed. The truth is, we projected a field around the cave—one which simulated the effects of certain sensor-foiling minerals. The field also served to conceal this vessel—which was located on the surface all the time. And not just this vessel, but another as well."

B'Elanna was beginning to get the picture. But she let Teeg'l finish, still hoping he'd reveal something she could use to good advantage.

"Shortly after our cruiser arrived," the Kazon boasted, "that other vessel rose from its concealment—and eventually found safety in the cruiser's cargo bay. But not before it gave your captain the idea she had been duped. As far as she could tell, you had been captured by the Kazon and were being spirited away. It was then that our cruiser took off.

"Predictably, your captain chose to give pursuit. As far as we know, she is pursuing still—and will continue to do so until she realizes the *true* extent of our deceit." Teeg'l chuckled. "By that time, *this* vessel will have rendezvoused with a *second* Ogla cruiser, in an entirely different sector of space. And before long, we will have obtained the secret of your transporters—one way or another."

B'Elanna had no illusions as to how far the Kazon would go to get what they wanted. After all, they had two captives. If one died in the course of their tortures, it would only serve to loosen the lips of the other one.

Or so they believed. But it wouldn't work. Certainly not with B'Elanna herself, and probably not with Kim either. Starfleet officers took their vows pretty seriously—and the promise to observe the Prime Directive was the biggest vow of all.

"So, you see," said Teeg'l, "you have no choice but to cooperate. And as long as you must do that anyway, why wait until the rendezvous? Why not cooperate with *me?*"

Kim smiled humorlessly. "So you can get credit for it?"

"Credit I *deserve,*" the third Maj insisted. "Believe me, it will go better for you if you speak to me. I am, let us say, a good deal more generous than the other Kazon-Ogla you will encounter."

"Is that so?" asked the ensign. "Well, you and the other Kazon-Ogla can go straight to—"

"That's enough," B'Elanna snapped.

Kim was clearly surprised by the interruption. But, recognizing it as an order, he kept his mouth shut.

The lieutenant turned to Teeg'l. "Thanks for the advice," she told him. "We'll consider it."

The third Maj's eyes narrowed as he looked from one captive to the other. "See that you do," he replied.

Then he turned and led the other Kazon out of the room. As they departed, one of them reactivated the yellow energy barrier.

Only when she was sure their captors were out of earshot did B'Elanna turn to her companion. "Listen," she said, "I don't have any intention of giving them our secrets either. But if Teeg'l's not the one ultimately in charge here, why not keep him on the line? He'll be more inclined to treat us better for a while."

"But not forever," Kim reminded her. "Ultimately, we'll be turned over to someone who won't take maybe for an answer."

"With any luck," the lieutenant rejoined, "we'll have escaped by then."

The ensign smiled despite the bruise on his face. "The way you say it, I'm almost tempted to believe it."

"Believe it," she said defiantly.

Had he been a member of a species other than Vulcan, Tuvok would have been expressing considerable frustration. As it was, he was only mildly perturbed.

Since *Voyager* took off in pursuit of the Kazon vessel nearly fifteen minutes earlier, Tuvok had been probing for information they could use to their advantage. He had looked for anything and everything.

Weaknesses in the Kazon's shields, for instance. Blind spots in their sensor array. Gaps in their weapon spread, their structural integrity field—anything that might prove valuable in the recovery of Lieutenant Torres and Ensign Kim.

He hadn't found a thing. The vessel was remarkably sound, considering the Kazons' apparent lack of discipline.

The Vulcan didn't like to admit defeat. However, in this case, it seemed unavoidable.

Then another possibility occurred to him. If he could pinpoint the locations of their missing crewmates on the Kazon vessel, they might be able to beam them off—even with the Kazon's shields up.

It would mean finding the necessary frequency—no easy task in itself. And it would be a difficult maneuver, full of danger for those being transported. But it was less obtrusive and less likely to provoke retaliation than any attack they could mount.

At the very least, it was an option. And right now, the captain needed all the options she could get.

Cocking an eyebrow, Tuvok set to work. He couldn't detect any comm badge signals; no doubt the Kazons had destroyed the badges. Undaunted, he programmed the sensors to look for human and Klingon life signs and began a search—a time-consuming procedure, since Kazon biology didn't differ greatly from that of those other species.

But it wasn't the amount of time involved that took the Vulcan by surprise. It was the result.

"Captain Janeway," he said, looking up.

Janeway turned in response. "Yes, Lieutenant?"

Tuvok frowned. "Captain, I detect neither human nor Klingon life signs aboard the Kazon vessel."

Janeway's eyes opened wide as she started toward tactical. "Are you certain about that, Mister Tuvok?"

The Vulcan nodded. "As certain as I can be," he told her.

Joining him at his console, the captain inspected Tuvok's monitors for herself. What's more, he took no offense at this. It was, as he had learned years ago, simply human behavior.

"Damn," Janeway grated, looking up at him. Her face was ruddy with anger and embarrassment. "They conned us, didn't they?"

A rhetorical question, he thought. Once, he would have supplied an answer. But over the course of his Starfleet career, he had become conversant with human foibles—the captain's in particular.

Janeway set her jaw and glared at the viewscreen. "Mister Paris," she said, her voice low and determined, "bring us about. Set a course for the world where we lost Torres and Kim."

The helmsman didn't say anything. He just followed orders. No doubt he shared in the captain's embarrassment.

As they all did, Tuvok mused. He wished he had thought earlier to confirm their crewmates' presence on the Kazon vessel. However, as humans were fond of saying, that was water under the bridge. The important thing now was to find out what had really happened to the ensign and the chief engineer, so they could devise a new rescue strategy.

And hope they were not too late.

CHAPTER 4

JANEWAY PACED THE BRIDGE OF *VOYAGER* AS IT ORBITED THE CLASS M planet where they'd lost Torres and Kim. Not for the first time, she wondered how she could possibly have been so gullible. How she could have jumped to a conclusion so eagerly, without giving thought to the possible alternatives.

Dumb, she told herself. *Very* dumb.

In her own defense, she'd had to respond to the Kazon's departure in a heartbeat. If she'd let even a minute go by, the cruiser would have left them in the dust.

At the same time, she could have been more skeptical. She could have concentrated more of their resources on achieving a positive identification of her officers. She could have made *sure* they were aboard before she traversed half the sector trying to recover them.

Now she had lost precious time. Worse, she was compelled to start from the beginning, checking and rechecking her facts, before she decided on a course of action. Nor would she cut any corners this time around. She would sacrifice speed for accuracy, because—unfortunately—there was no other way.

An intercom voice cut through her internal dialogue. "Captain?" called her first officer.

"What have you got for me?" she asked Chakotay.

"Lots," he told her. "Evidence of a firefight, for starters. The walls of this cave have been scarred with directed-energy beams. And the ground's full of footprints that aren't B'Elanna's or Kim's."

Janeway nodded to herself. "So they were abducted—just not by the Kazon we took off after."

"That's the way it looks," Chakotay agreed.

"What else?"

"We found a field projector. One set to baffle our sensors, apparently. But get this—the field reads like a mineral deposit to our tricorders."

Janeway bit back her anger.

"Acknowledged," she said. "Bring your team back up, Commander. I think we've learned enough."

"Aye, Captain," came the reply.

Janeway felt her hands clench into fists at her sides. With a conscious effort, she unclenched them. Bad enough she'd let herself be fooled once. Letting her emotions distract her would only invite other mistakes.

"Captain?" said Tuvok, who was standing at his customary place on the bridge.

She turned to him. "Something?" she suggested hopefully.

The Vulcan nodded. "I have discerned an ion-trail."

"Good work," she told him, joining him at his post.

She could feel her hopes rising. This could be the breakthrough they needed to find their comrades.

"Judging by its density and spatial parameters," Tuvok went on, "I believe the trail was produced by a Kazon vessel—though one considerably smaller than the cruiser we were pursuing. Also, the trail leads in the opposite direction from our previous heading."

"Which would make sense," said the captain, "if they were trying to throw us off."

"Indeed," the Vulcan agreed.

Janeway regarded him for a moment. "Make this information available to the conn, Mister Tuvok."

He nodded. "Aye, Captain."

"Transporter room," called Janeway. "Has the away team returned yet?"

"They're back," Burleson reported. "All present and accounted for."

Unlike the last time, the captain thought. She turned to her helmsman. "Mister Paris, you'll be receiving data on a Kazon ion-trail. Plot a course and follow at best speed."

"Understood," Paris confirmed, already making the necessary adjustments on his control panel.

Janeway was glad to be taking action finally. It was only a beginning, she realized, and there were no guarantees they'd be successful—but at least they were *doing* something.

On the viewscreen, the planet waned as Paris brought the ship about and applied thrust from the impulse engines. It would be a little while before *Voyager* escaped the system's gravity well and the helmsman was able to engage the more powerful warp drive.

At this point, the captain was all but superfluous. She could have left the bridge and found something to do in her ready room. But she didn't want to give the impression she was hiding from what she'd done. She wanted—needed—to be out in the open with her crew.

Taking her seat, she leaned back and closed her eyes for a moment. Just for a moment. But as soon as she did, there it was. The embarrassment. The pain of loss…the litany came to mind again. Unasked for, it echoed in her brain.

Dumb, she told herself. *Very* dumb.

Teeg'l was disappointed as he hovered over his helmsman, awaiting the rendezvous with the *Barach'ma.* At first, he had believed he'd made a dent in the *Voyager* officers' resolve. Apparently, he'd been wrong about that.

They had no intention of telling him about their transporter technology. He saw that now. When the female had said she would consider his offer of leniency, she'd obviously been lying.

Under normal circumstances, he would have killed her for such audacity—or come close enough to it to make her *wish* she was dead. Unfortunately, that wasn't an option in this case.

Maj B'naia would want to see the prisoners in good condition when Teeg'l delivered them to the *Barach'ma.* If they were damaged unnecessarily, B'naia would know Teeg'l had risked the success of their mission to further his own ambitions—and that would go hard on him.

So the third Maj had swallowed his pride and left the *Voyager* officers alone. As it was, he told himself, he would see more than his share of honors for his part in their capture. He tried to picture the possessions that would be bestowed on him—the glory that would be his.

And he would deserve it, would he not? After all, the *Voyager* scum held the key to preeminence in the quadrant. The plan to obtain them, of course, had been Maj B'naia's from the beginning. But Teeg'l was the one who had executed it to perfection.

"Third Maj," said the helmsman. Shan'ak was leaning a little closer to his monitors, as if to see better.

Roused from his inner dialogue, Teeg'l grunted. "What is it, Shan'ak? Have you found the *Barach'ma* yet?"

The helmsman turned to look at him. Something in his eyes made the third Maj's stomach muscles tighten.

"The *Barach'ma* is not here," Shan'ak told him. His voice was tight with anxiety, his brow creased with concern.

"Then it is not here," Teeg'l allowed. "We will wait for it to appear."

The helmsman shook his head. "You do not understand," he said. "It is not going to meet us. Not *ever.*"

Is'rag, the Kazon at tactical, turned around to look at them. Obviously concerned, he searched his own monitors for an answer.

The third Maj grew angry. Grabbing the front of Shan'ak's leather tunic, he twisted the helmsman around in his seat and brought Shan'ak's face close to his own.

"What do you mean, it is not going to meet us?" he demanded. "Aren't these the coordinates we agreed on? Don't we have the prisoners second Maj B'naia coveted so much?" He rapped Shan'ak sharply on the nose with his forehead. "Speak, damn you!"

The helmsman recoiled in pain, blood spilling from his nostrils. "Look!" he cried, clutching his damaged nose. "See for yourself!" And he pointed to one of his monitors.

Teeg'l glowered at it. "What?" he spat. "I don't see anything."

"Look closer!" Shan'ak told him.

The third Maj looked closer. And at last he saw what his helmsman was talking about.

"Debris," he muttered.

For that's what it was. Tiny fragments of metal, scattered throughout the void. And, according to their sensors, it was the same metal used in the manufacture of the Kazon-Ogla's vessels.

"No," he whispered. "It can't be."

"It *is,*" the helmsman insisted. "Those are the remains of the

Barach'ma. Someone got here before us and destroyed it. *Voyager,* perhaps."

Teeg'l reeled as he considered where that left him and his little ship. He would have to seek out the Ogla's main fleet. But they were far away, and there were hostile races in between.

A vessel like the *Barach'ma* could have eluded them with its speed or intimidated them with its armaments. But a craft like Teeg'l's could do neither of those things. For all intents, it would be defenseless.

Swallowing hard, the third Maj grabbed Shan'ak again. But this time, he was too scared to be angry. "We've got to get out of here," he said. "Whoever did this might still be in the sector."

His words proved prophetic. They were barely out of his mouth when a proximity alarm went off on the helm console. Peering at the monitors, Teeg'l saw the cause of it.

It was a ship, even bigger than the *Barach'ma,* and more heavily armed. A Nograkh ship. And though it was nearly a million kilometers away, it was closing fast.

The third Maj cursed at the top of his lungs. It had been a Nograkh ambush all along. And he had fallen for it—just as the *Voyager* captain had fallen for the Kazon trap.

Still, Teeg'l told himself, he was Ogla. He would likely die this day, but he would die bravely.

"Is'rag," he said, still intent on Shan'ak's controls, "activate the cursed weapons banks."

There was no answer. Turning to the tactical station, Teeg'l saw that Is'rag had frozen, his eyes fixed on the monitor that showed him the approaching ship. Snarling, the third Maj lumbered across the bridge and shoved Is'rag aside. Then he took charge of the station himself.

As Is'rag looked on sullenly, Teeg'l activated the intercom system and called for N'taron and Skeg'g, whom he'd sent to check on the prisoners in the cargo hold.

"What is it, third Maj?" asked N'taron.

Teeg'l told him. "Forget the prisoners. I want you up on the bridge. *Now.*"

"As you wish," came the response.

The third Maj didn't really believe the presence of N'taron and Skeg'g would make any difference in the long run. But if Shan'ak was killed, at least one of them could fly the ship.

Teeg'l himself needed his hands free to work the weapons controls. Powering up the appropriate energy sources, he consulted his monitors.

And waited for the enemy to appear.

At first, when B'Elanna saw Teeg'l's henchmen enter the cargo hold, she imagined the worst—that the third Maj had lost his patience and was going to execute them, against all reason. After all, he was a Kazon. One never knew what passions ruled them from moment to moment. In that respect, they were a lot like some Klingons of her acquaintance.

Then she realized the pair was just checking to make sure their prisoners were secure. B'Elanna breathed a sigh of relief. So did Kim.

That's when Teeg'l contacted his men over the intercom, to tell them about the mysterious ship that was bearing down on them. As soon as he was done, they started out the door.

"Wait!" cried B'Elanna. "We can help!"

But the Kazon ignored them. Suddenly, the lieutenant's mouth went dry. In a matter of seconds, they had gone from the proverbial frying pan into an all-too-real fire.

Happy Day of Honor, she told herself.

Kim looked at her, the muscles working in his temples. "We've got to get out of here," he told her.

Her instincts agreed with him. In the event they were boarded, this cell would put them at a distinct disadvantage. Of course, if the Kazon vessel was blown out of space, it wouldn't matter if they were free or not—but B'Elanna tried not to think about that.

Teeg'l's jaw clenched as the enemy ship loomed. He rolled to starboard just as it fired, its weapons ports illuminating the void with a yellow-white directed-energy display.

Obviously, he thought, his adversary had underestimated the Kazon's maneuverability—and the skill of its pilot. The third Maj brought his vessel about and targeted the larger ship's weapons banks. Then he unleashed some directed energy of his own.

What's more, he hit his targets dead-on. But the enemy's shields held as they wheeled for a second pass. Teeg'l watched intently, trying to decide which way he'd move to avoid the next barrage.

Unfortunately for him, he never got a chance. Too late, he realized his adversary had been playing with him—testing him. And now that the test was over, the next stage had begun.

The larger ship spat stream after stream of yellow-white fire, each of them with unerring accuracy, battering Teeg'l's shields until there was nothing left of them. But the barrage didn't stop there. It went on, jolting the Kazon with hit after devastating hit.

The section of bulkhead beside Is'rag exploded, killing him instantly and showering the rest of the crew with flaming fragments. The deck shifted and bucked beneath their feet, throwing them this way and that.

Shan'ak struggled to regain mastery of their vessel, tapping his controls desperately in the lurid light of the emergency back-up system—until his helm console erupted in a geyser of sparks. Burned badly, he toppled from his seat to the deck below him.

"Skeg'g!" cried the third Maj, jerking his head in the direction of the empty helm station.

Immediately, Skeg'g lurched across the bridge to take Shan'ak's place. But no sooner had he taken a position behind the sparking helm console than the forward viewscreen went white with fury.

As Teeg'l flinched, blinded by the spectacle, he braced himself for the impact that would certainly follow. And follow it did.

B'Elanna could hear the pounding of enemy fire on the hull and feel the pitching of the deck beneath them. It only spurred her to greater efforts as she and Kim tried to pry away a plate from the bulkhead behind them.

"Damn," said Kim. "If we had a tool of some kind—"

"But we don't," she rasped, clawing at the plate for all she was worth. Her fingers were already scraped and bloodied, but she ignored the pain and focused on her objective.

If she could get to the circuitry that was almost certainly in the bulkhead, she could disable the barrier and give them a fighting chance. And really, that's all she'd ever asked for—a *chance.*

Suddenly, the deck rose up on one end of the cargo bay and made an impossible incline of the floor beneath her feet. With nothing to hold on to, she felt herself sliding toward the barrier.

The impact would stun her, make her woozy. She couldn't afford that right now. And neither could Kim, who was sliding along beside her, pressing his cheek and hands against the deck in an attempt to slow himself down.

It wasn't working—not for either of them. B'Elanna closed her eyes, dreading the jolt that was sure to follow. Somehow, it never came. The next thing she felt was the smooth, hard surface of the bulkhead next to the exit.

She looked at Harry, who pointed to the emitter grid that had produced the barrier. There were thin plumes of white smoke coming from some of the emitters, but no energy field.

The barrier was gone.

"Some kind of short circuit," he noted.

"From all the pounding," she agreed.

Just then, the ship staggered again, leveling the deck. B'Elanna and Kim got to their feet and tapped the padd by the side of the door at virtually the same time. A moment later, the metal surface slid aside, giving them a vision of the freedom they'd earned.

It wasn't pretty. The corridor was filled with white smoke and a sharp, sickening stench. Every few feet ahead of them there was a crackle and a pulse of naked energy.

"Let's go," she told Kim.

"Right behind you," he assured her.

It wasn't difficult to find their way. The corridor was short and it led to only one set of doors. Again, she placed her hand on the padd beside them, ready to fight if necessary.

It wasn't necessary at all. Control consoles were burning everywhere she looked. And the five Kazon who'd been their captors were strewn across the bridge, at least one of them dead of a broken neck.

Clearly, the priority was to try to save the ship. If they succeeded in that, they could take care of the surviving Kazons later.

But before either B'Elanna or Kim could move toward the controls, the ship jerked and sent them hurtling across the open space. Though she tried to protect herself with her arms, the lieutenant took a nasty blow to the head on one of the consoles.

She felt herself losing consciousness, but fought it off. Come on, she told herself. You've got to get up, dammit. You've got to get this Kazon bucket moving again.

Rolling over onto her side, she opened her eyes—and found herself staring into the eyes of a dead Kazon, half of his face a bloody ruin. Biting back her revulsion, B'Elanna took hold of the lip of the console above her and dragged herself to her feet.

Then she heard something—the creak of metal on metal. The turning of a hatch, she thought, somewhere in the rear of the ship. Whoever had attacked them was doing their best to force their way aboard.

Beside the door they'd used to come out onto the bridge, there were two others. One of them must have led to a hatchway. That's where the attack would come from.

"B'Elanna..." moaned a familiar voice.

She saw Kim roll out from under another section of console. There was a bloody gash just above his brow to go with the purple spot on his chin. He was grimacing in pain.

"Are you all right?" she asked, negotiating the body of the staring Kazon to get to him.

He nodded as he grabbed her for support. "I think so."

"Can you use a weapon?" she asked, helping him get to his feet.

He nodded a second time. "Are they here yet?"

Clearly, he'd heard the creak of the hatch just as she had. "Just about," she told him.

Leaving him to stand on his own—by no means a certain proposition—she turned to the corpse behind her and hunkered down beside it. As she'd hoped, there was a handweapon stuck in the Kazon's belt. Slipping it free, she stood and handed it to Kim. He leaned back against a control panel and peered at it, as if he'd never seen anything like it.

"Can't tell which one is the stun setting," he muttered.

"That's the least of our problems," she hissed at him, as another bulkhead plate blew out with a crackle of rampant blue energy.

True, they ran the risk of punching a hole in one of the bulkheads. But there was no time to study their hosts' weapons technology. Not with a boarding party knocking on the door.

Crossing to the next-nearest Kazon, she rolled him onto his back and wrested his weapon from him. In the process, he murmured something and even moved his hand to try to stop her—but he was too badly stunned.

Suddenly, B'Elanna heard the tramping of heavy boots. She turned to face the door to the left of the one she'd come through. Then there was more tramping—this time, from beyond the door to her right.

"Damn," said Kim. "They're coming at us from both sides."

He was right, of course. Raising her weapon, the lieutenant trained it on one door, then the other, uncertain as to where to use it first.

Then the choice was taken out of her hands. Both doors slid aside at once, revealing huge, hulking figures in stiff, dark bodyarmor. She caught a glimpse of angry red skin, heavy brow ridges, and wide, cruel mouths. Seeing her, one of them barked a guttural command.

She didn't try to figure out what he'd said. She simply began firing at the invaders on her left. As if by silent agreement, Kim sent a beam at the aliens on her right.

The first of B'Elanna's targets went down. Then another. But before she could lay into a third, the invaders erected some kind of invisible shield. Her beam just bounced off it.

Glancing at the other door to the bridge, the one Kim was firing at, she saw the same thing happen. The ensign's barrage splashed off the deflective surface, wreaking havoc on a bulkhead instead.

That's when the invaders started retaliating. A series of yellow-white bursts stabbed at the lieutenant. The first one punched her hard in the left shoulder, numbing her arm as it spun her halfway around and sent her stumbling into a console. The second one blasted the weapon out of her hand.

A moment later, Kim was disarmed as well. He looked to her across the width of the Kazon bridge, blood streaming down the side of his face. After all, she was the ranking officer here. It was up to her what they would do next.

What they would do, she decided bitterly, was surrender. As much as it went against her grain, she couldn't ignore the fact they were outnumbered and outgunned. And even if they somehow regained control of the ship, it wasn't going anywhere as long as the enemy was standing guard over it.

Slowly, so there would be no mistake, she raised her hands above her head. Seeing her move, Kim did the same.

The invaders looked about to make sure there was no one else worth worrying about. Then they came out onto the bridge, weapons at the ready. One of them inspected the fallen Kazon, while another walked up to B'Elanna.

He didn't say anything. He just stood there, peering at her from beneath his protuberant brow. His eyes, which seemed small compared to the rest of him, were silver grey with a vertical slash of black pupil.

"My name is B'Elanna Torres," she began, though she had her doubts the brute in front of her would care. "I serve as a lieutenant on the starship *Voyager,* a vessel from another quadrant. The Kazon took me and my companion captive against our will. If you could arrange to see us back to our ship, we would be—"

Suddenly, before she could defend herself, the invader backhanded her across the face. The next thing B'Elanna knew she was lying flat on her back, her mouth tasting of blood. It took her a moment to gather her senses and look up at her assailant.

"You will not speak," he told her, his voice as harsh as two stones grinding together. His mouth twisted. "Get up."

Kim started toward her, either to defend her or to help her up. Either way, she wanted no part of it—not when it meant he'd get the same kind of treatment she'd gotten. Or *worse.*

"No," she snapped.

Kim stopped in his tracks. But he still looked as if he didn't like the idea of leaving her to her own devices.

B'Elanna leveled a glare at him for emphasis. Then, though her head was swimming with the force of the blow she'd endured, she managed to stand herself up.

The invader's eyes narrowed. He seemed to approve of her obedience. Still looking at her, he jerked his head toward the door he'd come through and barked an order to his comrades.

Three of the other invaders bent and picked up the Kazon who weren't obviously dead already. Then they stood them up against the bulkhead and struck them smartly across the face.

After a while, the Kazon woke. Two of them, anyway, Teeg'l included. The third must have had a concussion or something worse.

He wouldn't live long enough for anyone to find out. Seeing that he was incapable of moving on his own, the invader who'd lifted him held his hands to the Kazon's temples.

By the time B'Elanna realized what was about to happen, it was too late. There was a cracking sound, and the Kazon crumpled to the deck, limp and lifeless. If his fellow Kazon cared at all, they didn't show it. And as far as the heavy-browed invaders were concerned, the corpse might have been an insect they'd squashed underfoot.

Without ceremony, the other two Kazon were rousted from the bridge. Then the invader in front of B'Elanna jerked his head again—this time for her benefit. It was clear he meant for her to leave the bridge as well.

Which she did. A moment later, Kim followed.

True, she thought, the two of them were still prisoners. Their fates were still in the hands of others, and those others didn't seem particularly inclined toward benevolence.

But if one wanted to look on the bright side, one might say they were no worse off than before. And more important, unlike some of the Kazon who'd abducted them, they were still alive.

CHAPTER 5

JANEWAY WAS SITTING IN HER CENTER SEAT, ONCE AGAIN GOING OVER THE events that had led to her officers' abduction.

She couldn't stop thinking about it, couldn't stop turning it over in her mind. Couldn't stop wondering if she might have prevented it.

She was so intent on her mental playback, she didn't notice when Tuvok came to stand beside her. Then he said, "Captain?"

She turned to look up at him. "Yes, Lieutenant?"

"I would like a word with you," the Vulcan told her. "In private."

Janeway nodded. "Very well. Let's go."

She led the way to her ready room. The door slid aside automatically, admitting them, then closed when they were both inside. In silence, they took seats on either side of her desk.

"All right," she said, "I'm listening. What did you want to talk about?"

Tuvok frowned. "You seem distracted. If I may be allowed to speculate, it has something to do with Lieutenant Torres and Ensign Kim."

The captain had to smile. "And the way we were duped by the Kazons."

The Vulcan tilted his head slightly. "Yes. It occurs to me you may be engaged in a process of self-recrimination. Of course, under the circumstances, that would be illogical."

Janeway sat back in her chair. "Oh? And why is that?"

"Because any experienced officer would have done the same thing—myself included. You made a rational choice based on the facts and probabilities at hand. Nor did you have a great deal of time to make that choice, considering the Kazon were attempting to escape."

"Or appearing to," the captain remarked.

"As it turns out," Tuvok conceded. "Though you had no way of knowing that at the time."

Janeway shrugged. "The bottom line is I took a guess. In this case, I guessed wrong."

"One cannot control the outcomes of one's decisions," Tuvok reminded her. "One can only make the best decisions possible."

"In other words," she said, "I shouldn't beat myself up over it."

The Vulcan cocked an eyebrow. "Not the precise words I would have chosen, but I agree with the sentiment."

Janeway was touched by his concern. She said so. "And don't worry," she added. "I'm not going to whip myself over what happened. But by the same token, I'm not going to forget about it. I want to make absolutely sure it never happens again."

Tuvok seemed satisfied. He stood. "That is all I wished to say."

The captain smiled, this time a little more freely. "I'm glad you did, Lieutenant. It seems I never fail to benefit from your logic." She paused. "You may resume your duties."

With a slight inclination of his head, he turned and left the room. Janeway watched him go.

He was right, of course. She couldn't allow herself to get distracted by what had happened. Otherwise, she might miss a chance to get her people back.

And one thing was for certain: she *was* going to get them back.

Up ahead of B'Elanna and the other prisoners, there was a hatchway that seemed to provide egress from the Kazon vessel. It seemed that was how the invaders had gotten aboard.

Apparently, she mused, they didn't have any more access to transporter technology than the Kazon did. More than likely, they hadn't even *heard* of such a technology. And unless Teeg'l and the others opened their mouths, they might *never* hear of it.

At the moment, neither of the surviving Kazon-Ogla was in much of a position to talk. Only now starting to regain consciousness, they were being herded along on legs that could barely support them, both of them nursing a host of cuts and bruises. Still, all in all, they'd been lucky—none of their injuries looked permanently debilitating.

One by one, the Starfleet officers and the Kazon were thrust through the open hatchway. One by one, they were grabbed on the other side and shoved down another corridor.

At one point, B'Elanna stumbled into Teeg'l. The third Maj turned and snarled at her with his bruised and swollen mouth, but didn't go so far as to retaliate. Obviously, he had no more desire to incur their captors' wrath than she did.

Finally, they reached their destination—a heavy door set into an inner bulkhead. One of the heavy-brows opened it, hefted his weapon meaningfully, then gestured for the prisoners to go inside.

B'Elanna was the last in line. Apparently, she didn't move fast enough, because she felt a meaty hand on her back. The next thing she knew, she was sprawling on the far side of the entrance. Then the door swung closed and shut with a resounding clang.

The lieutenant got to her feet and looked around. Clearly, she and Kim and their Kazon friends weren't the only ones that had been taken captive. The circular hold was full of prisoners—perhaps twenty in all.

Surprisingly, more than a few were of the same brutish race as their captors. But the majority were aliens whose ilk the lieutenant had never seen before. As if with one mind, they turned to get a gander at the new prisoners on the block.

B'Elanna had no reason to expect a hearty welcome from these people. Hell, they'd probably never even heard of *Voyager* or the Federation, so a certain wariness was probably the best she could have hoped for.

But the other prisoners were acting more than wary. The way they were glaring at the newcomers, one would have thought they were already guilty of some serious offense.

Kim looked at her. "What's going on? We haven't been here more than a couple of seconds and already we're not very popular."

"I wish I knew," she replied.

Their fellow captives were murmuring among themselves and looking angrier by the minute—angry enough to jump them, perhaps. If that was so, the lieutenant told herself, they wouldn't find her an easy adversary—though she already felt as if she'd been rolled through Neelix's pasta-maker.

"They don't hate *you,"* Teeg'l remarked unexpectedly. He sneered, despite the pain it must have cost him. "They hate *us."*

Only then did B'Elanna realize what was going on. Apparently, the Kazon-Ogla had made a few enemies in this part of space—not a difficult thing to imagine, given the coarseness of their personalities and the itchiness of their trigger fingers.

She and Kim had only been thrown into the hold with Teeg'l and the other Kazon. They weren't allies by any stretch of the imagination; only moments ago, they'd been bitter enemies. But in the eyes of the other prisoners, the two of them were already guilty by association.

She eyed the third Maj of the Ogla. "What's going on, Teeg'l? What are we doing in this place?"

The Kazon grunted. "We're prisoners of the Nograkh, one of the races that dominates this part of space. They're miners for the most part, traders when it suits them."

"What do they want with *us?"* asked Kim.

"There's a Nograkh station not far from here," said Teeg'l. "It was built by the race that ruled this sector before them. The Nograkh use it to mine precious minerals from an asteroid belt."

"And?" B'Elanna prodded.

The Kazon's eyes narrowed as he regarded her. Clearly, he didn't like to be rushed. "The minerals in question are radioactive. As a result, the workers don't survive very long—which is why the Nograkh need to replace them so often."

The lieutenant understood now. "We're here to supplement the work force on their station?"

Teeg'l nodded. "That's my guess."

"Slave labor," Kim remarked.

Judging by his expression, the prospect didn't sit well with him. But then, it didn't sit very well with B'Elanna either.

"Lovely," she said. But then, it *was* the Day of Honor. She jerked her head in the direction of the heavy-browed prisoners on the other side of their cell. "And these Nograkh down here with us?"

The Kazon's mouth twisted with disdain. "Who knows? Maybe they're criminals—the dregs of Nograkh society." He laughed. "But knowing the way the Nograkh treat each other, it's hard to imagine what sort of behavior would qualify as a crime."

B'Elanna looked at their fellow prisoners in a new light. Quite a character reference, she thought—to be called uncivilized by someone as low and vicious as a Kazon-Ogla.

"Thanks for the warning," she said.

Teeg'l shot a glance at her. "For all the good it'll do. To my knowledge, no one has ever escaped from the Nograkh."

"There's always a first time," Kim noted.

The Kazon eyed him. "Surely you're joking. Look around you at your fellow prisoners, human. Many of them are powerful warriors—the Nograkh even more so than the others. If they cannot escape, how will you?"

The ensign smiled mysteriously, despite the gash above his eye. It was more to taunt the third Maj than anything else.

Clearly, thought B'Elanna, if this conversation progressed much further, Teeg'l would go for Kim's throat. And she didn't want to draw any attention from their captors.

"Come on," she told her comrade. "Let's take a load off our feet."

Kim hesitated for just a second. Then he allowed her to guide him to a curved bulkhead, where they sat down side by side and placed their backs against the unyielding metal.

"All this for a bunch of vegetables," the ensign sighed. "There's got to be an easier way to put food on the table."

B'Elanna couldn't help but smile. "When we get back, you can come up with one, all right?"

"It's a deal," he told her.

But privately, she knew, he was wondering the same thing she was. Asking the same questions.

Where in blazes was *Voyager?* And how were they ever going to get out of this without her?

Leaning back in her center seat, Janeway used her thumb and forefinger to massage the bridge of her nose, where stress and weariness had conspired to form a growing ache.

A small price to pay, she remarked inwardly, if their efforts produced the desired effect and their friends were returned to them. Not that she knew for certain they would be, but she had to nurture the hope.

After all, she was the ranking officer around here. If she didn't maintain an air of confidence, who would?

"Captain?" said Tuvok.

She turned to look back at him. "Yes, Lieutenant?"

The Vulcan was intent on his instruments. "Sensors have detected a small object point nine million miles off the starboard bow. It appears to be a ship—of unknown origin."

Janeway looked surprised. "On screen," she ordered.

A moment later, the viewscreen showed her what Tuvok was talking about. It was a small vessel, little bigger than one of *Voyager*'s shuttlecraft. But that was where the resemblance ended.

This ship was slender and dark and elegant, with two bubblelike features—one near its bow and a second at its midpoint. Three slender, almost flat nacelles protruded from it, like the fins of a Terran fish.

She turned to the Vulcan. "Hail them, Mister Tuvok."

The Vulcan complied. But a moment later, he shook his head. "No response. In fact, I believe they may be incapable of responding. There seems to have been a plasma leak in their engine compartment."

He paused, his brow wrinkling. "The radiation appears to have killed everyone on board—except one individual in the aft compartment. And she will likely die as well if left to her own devices."

Janeway frowned. "Mister Paris, fix on the craft's coordinates and bring us within ten thousand kilometers."

"Aye, Captain," came the accommodating response.

It would only be a matter of seconds before that was accomplished. Knowing that, Janeway turned back to Tuvok. "Have the survivor beamed directly to sick bay," she told the Vulcan. "Then establish a link with her ship's computer and download its data base."

Tuvok nodded and went about his task. At the same time, the captain looked up at the intercom grid and summoned the ship's holodoctor into existence.

"Computer, initiate emergency medical holographic program."

In a heartbeat, the Doctor's balding, sardonic image appeared on her personal monitor. "Please state the nature of the medical emergency," he said, in a voice just this side of annoyance.

Of course, the Doctor would be far from annoyed to learn he had work to do. He had been created to heal the sick and infirm. However, his programmers had created him with several—unfortunately—disingenuous qualities, his tone of voice being only one of them.

"We're beaming over a patient from a derelict ship," Janeway advised him. "She'll be suffering from radiation exposure and perhaps other problems as well, but we'll probably have some medical data for you to go on."

"I see," the Doctor said simply.

"Is Kes down there?" the captain asked.

"She is," the Doctor confirmed. "I've had her working on a research project the last several hours."

Janeway nodded. "Then you'll have help if you need it."

The Doctor scowled. "I doubt I will require assistance if we're only talking about a single patient, no matter how alien she may be. But it'll be good for Kes to lend a hand. A learning experience, if you will."

"Whatever you say," the captain replied. "Janeway out."

She glanced at Tuvok. He seemed troubled. Rising from her seat, she joined him at his console.

"Problem?" she asked.

He nodded. "The radiation spilling from the vessel's power source is making it difficult to effect transport. However, I believe I can overcome the difficulty by boosting the annular confinement beam."

Leaving the Vulcan to his work, the captain turned again to the viewscreen, where the alien craft gave no indication of the turmoil and death inside it. It simply hung in the void, silent as the tomb it had become.

But not for its last surviving passenger, Janeway thought, lifting her chin as if facing down an adversary. With any luck, the data they would take from the vessel's computer files would give the Doctor a head start in treating her—and sometimes that made all the difference.

Of course, she wished they hadn't had to deviate from their course. Every moment they spent here was another setback in their pursuit of Torres and Kim, another nail in their proverbial coffins. But when Janeway had signed on as captain of *Voyager,* she had sworn to lend assistance to those in trouble—even when it meant jeopardizing her own crew in the process.

Suddenly, the vessel on the viewscreen exploded in a flare of blazing white light. The energy output was immediately dampened by the sensor mechanisms that fed the screen, but it made the sight no less horrifying.

The captain whirled to face Tuvok, fearing the worst. "The survivor . . . ?" she asked.

The Vulcan's countenance was as unreadable as ever. As the seconds passed, he checked his instruments carefully, so there would be no mistake. Then he looked up again.

"She is in sick bay," Tuvok reported at last. "Much of the vessel's computer data was salvaged as well—though, regrettably, not all of it."

Janeway breathed a sigh of relief. "Don't give it a second thought," she said. "You did your best." And after all, the survivor had been the priority. "Resume course," she instructed.

"Aye, Captain," said Paris. He looked relieved as well as he made the necessary adjustments on his control console.

"I'll be in sick bay if you need me," Janeway announced, naturally curious about the being they'd taken on.

Without another word, she made her way to the turbolift.

CHAPTER 6

VOYAGER'S DOCTOR WAS AS WELL-EQUIPPED TO HANDLE AN EMERGENCY AS any physician in the history of the Federation. After all, his program encompassed not only all the Federation's medical research and clinical experience, but a great deal of its distilled genius.

He could apply the diagnostic approaches of hundreds of doctors on dozens of worlds, and he could do it all in the blink of an eye. It was a good thing he could. With all *Voyager* and her crew had encountered here in the Delta Quadrant, it was unlikely any single physician could have pulled them through as effectively as he had.

So when he saw the alien female materialize on a biobed, writhing in agony, her scaly, purplish flesh ravaged with third-degree burns, the Doctor didn't even raise an eyebrow. He made a quick and necessarily superficial scan of the medical data downloaded from her vessel's computer and went to work.

Of course, Kes was by his side the whole time. For her sake, he described his strategy step by step.

"According to our instruments, the patient's biochemistry is similar to that of several Alpha Quadrant races. That means we can rely on familiar medications."

First, he checked her status on the bed's readout. She appeared to be in stable condition, at least for the time being. It would make treating her a lot easier.

However, that wasn't all he saw in the readout. There were indications of something else in her system as well—something that had nothing at all to do with radiation exposure.

"What is it?" Kes asked, obviously picking up on his surprise.

The Doctor shook his head. "We can talk about it later," he told her.

Concentrating on the task at hand, he introduced a drug to reinforce her vital signs and another to deaden the pain. In a matter of seconds, the woman seemed to relax.

"So far, so good," he remarked offhandedly. But he was still bothered by what he'd seen in the readout.

Next, the Doctor gave the woman a dose of hyronalyn to mitigate the effects of the radiation on her system. That, too, produced a favorable reaction. Encouraged, he went on to give her a healing agent for her burns and yet another agent to prevent infection.

Finally, he erected an electromagnetic field around her to keep her safe from germs in her new environment. Of course, there was no indication that she would have a particular vulnerability to them, but it was always better to err on the side of caution.

All in all, a smooth operation. Especially when one considered what he had found in the woman's bloodstream.

"Doctor?" said Kes.

He turned to her. "I know," he replied. "You're wondering what it was I saw in her readout."

"And what *did* you see?"

The Doctor sighed and considered his patient anew. She was sleeping soundly now, all her vital signs deceptively normal.

"This woman has a disease I've never seen before," he announced. "A disease that is communicable only by intimate contact, fortunately. But if left untreated, it will kill her in less than a week."

Kes swallowed. "But surely there's something you can do for her."

Just then, the door to sick bay slid aside and the captain entered. "How is she doing?"

The Doctor frowned and brought Janeway up to speed. "But before I can give you a prognosis," he explained, "I need to take a look at the data we salvaged from her ship. There may be something there that will help."

The captain eyed him. "Doctor, if there was a course of treatment contained in the data bank, wouldn't her own physicians have applied it already?"

He shrugged. "Certainly, that's a possibility. But I prefer not to jump to conclusions. Now, if you'll excuse me, I've got work to do."

Janeway smiled understandingly. "Of course. Just keep me posted on her condition, will you?"

"As you wish," he assured her.

Then, without waiting for the captain to leave, he deposited himself in his office and accessed the requisite data from the ship's computer. As he was himself little more than a computer program, it wouldn't take long to assimilate everything they'd downloaded.

Then he would put the Federation's best medical minds to work. With luck, they would do the trick.

One hour, maybe even a little less. That's all it took for bedlam to break out in the hold where Harry and his companion were being held.

The ensign had been resting his head against the bulkhead and looking up at the ceiling, trying to guess from the shape and size of the crisscrossing energy conduits what kind of power supply the Nograkh ship ran on. He'd have said it was microwave-based, along the lines of a Cardassian system, except there was no evidence of the rhodinium sheeting that usually went with the microwave approach.

Suddenly, there was a flurry of activity on the other side of the cargo hold. And a string of angry, guttural shouts. And before Kim knew it, a fight had started.

It was between two of the most powerful-looking Nograkh. None of the other Nograkh tried to break it up, either. In fact, they grew more excited by the moment, cheering the combatants on.

The ensign's first reaction was to look for B'Elanna, to make sure she was safe. As it turned out, she was standing by a stretch of bulkhead nowhere near the melee. But as it progressed, she joined Kim anyway.

He watched, fascinated despite himself, as hammerlike fists pounded at flesh and bone, each blow eliciting a resounding thud. But no matter how many times they were hit, neither of the Nograkh seemed daunted in the least. If anything, the punishment spurred them on to inflict some of their own.

B'Elanna sat down beside him. "Nice roommates," she said.

The ensign winced as one of the Nograkh drove his fist into the other's face, snapping his adversary's head back. "You think they might get tired of pummeling each other and come after us next?"

"A distinct possibility," said a voice to one side of them.

Following it to its source, they saw Teeg'l standing there, his fellow Kazon at his side. The third Maj smiled savagely at them.

"Didn't I tell you they were animals?" he asked. "A barbed remark, a misplaced elbow, and before you know it they're bludgeoning each other."

Still smiling, he turned to observe the Nograkh. There was no letup in the intensity of their combat, no abatement in the ferocity with which they went at one another.

"And no one makes a move to stop it," Teeg'l pointed out. "Not even the guards. And why should they? They're Nograkh, too."

Kim was so wrapped up in the violence of the spectacle, he had forgotten about the guards. But now that the Kazon mentioned it, he cast a glance in their direction.

Sure enough, the watchmen had taken note of what was going on. They would have to have been blind not to. And deaf as well. But the brawl didn't seem to faze them in the least. Hell, thought the ensign, they looked like they were enjoying it.

"Their only regret," Teeg'l remarked, "is that they can't jump in themselves. That they can't get in there and pound each other to pulp, the way their brethren are doing it."

Kim took a closer look at the guards and decided the third Maj was right. What had he called them?

"Animals," the ensign said out loud, answering his own question.

B'Elanna looked at him. "What did you say?"

The ensign shook his head. "Nothing."

The jabbing and the smashing and the clubbing went on for another minute or so. Then one of the combatants fell to his knees, unable to continue.

It was over, Kim thought.

He thought wrong. Hauling back, the other Nograkh—a strapping specimen with a scar along his jaw—drove his fist into the center of his opponent's face. There was a loud crack, audible to everyone in the hold.

Then, as a horrified Kim bore witness, the loser's head lolled back and his body fell sideways to the deck. A trickle of blood ran from the corner of the victim's mouth.

He was dead. Just like that.

What's more, it was no accident. It was murder, plain and simple.

But none of the Nograkh seemed to care. Oh, the guards intervened finally, but they didn't pay any special attention to the murderer. They just took hold of the dead man by his ankles and pulled him out of the hold.

"My god," Kim heard himself saying.

Beside him, B'Elanna grunted. "Quite a show." Her voice was hollow with dismay.

That's when the lights dimmed. It didn't take a genius to figure out their captors wanted them to sleep. And more than likely, there would be punishment for those who opposed that wish.

What's more, the Nograkh seemed to accept the situation. If they grumbled, they did so quietly. A couple of moments later, the other prisoners settled down as well.

It was almost peaceful in the cargo hold. But that didn't mean it would stay that way.

"Tell you what," B'Elanna suggested. "We'll sleep in shifts. I don't want to wake up in the middle of their next disagreement."

"Amen," said Kim.

It was bad enough he'd become a slave. He didn't want to become a *dead* slave into the bargain.

It was Kes's job to stand watch over the scaly-skinned female on the biobed and make sure her vital signs followed the expected course. As always, she took her job very seriously.

At the moment, their patient was sleeping soundly, still feeling the effects of the sedation the Doctor had prescribed for her. More important, she was healing. Nearly half her burns were already gone and the rest would likely disappear over the next couple of hours.

From all outward signs, she was well on her way to recovery. But then, those signs didn't take into account the disease that was festering in her, threatening her life.

Kes turned to look at the Doctor. He was hunkered over his computer terminal on the other side of his transparent office wall, brow furrowed, mulling over the data downloaded from the patient's vessel in significantly greater depth than before.

At first glance, one might have thought he was scanning the monitor screen, like a flesh-and-blood organism. But a closer look would have shown there was nothing on the screen. He was just standing there, his eyes intent on a point no one else could see.

That was because the data had been dumped directly into his program. It was faster that way, or so the Doctor said. Of course, he still had to sift through the information. He still had to test hypotheses and establish connections, and that could take a considerable amount of time.

In the meantime, their patient inched closer to death. The Doctor didn't seem to notice; he was too engrossed in his work. But his assistant noticed. She noticed all too well.

Kes regarded the woman and sighed. Not much longer now, she assured herself. Just a matter of time.

Funny, she thought. Growing up, she had always thought of herself as the patient sort. She had never pestered her elders as often as the other children, always willing to wait a while if it meant getting what she wanted in the end.

Then circumstances had landed her a berth on *Voyager,* where she was the only one of her kind. It didn't take long before she realized how short her life span was—at least, in comparison with the other races on board.

Tuvok could expect to live for a couple of centuries—perhaps more. The captain might live more than half that length of years. But Kes, an Ocampa, would be fortunate to see her ninth birthday.

Nine years had seemed like a lot, at one time. Now, it didn't seem like much at all. She felt compelled to try new things, to take on responsibilities no Ocampa her age would have dreamed of. To pack as much into her brief existence as she could.

With that came a certain eagerness. A certain impatience. As much as she had attempted to tone it down, knowing how irritating it could be, she wasn't always successful.

Now was a good case in point.

The Doctor didn't seem to be any closer to a cure than when he'd begun his think-session a couple of hours earlier. Yet he didn't seem ruffled or concerned. Obviously, he believed there was plenty of time in which to accomplish his task.

Kes, on the other hand, couldn't help but worry. She couldn't help but feel time was running out.

And the worst part, the part that made it almost intolerable for her, was that the Doctor's labor was a one-man operation. Talented as she was as a physician, she didn't have the empirical knowledge to expedite the process. She couldn't be of any assistance whatsoever.

All she could do was stand here. And watch the patient's biosigns. And fret. And wait.

Suddenly, out of the corner of her eye, she saw movement in the Doctor's office. Glancing in his direction, she saw him turn to her. And *smile.*

A cure, she thought excitedly. He's found a cure.

Janeway tossed and turned in her bed, caught in a limbo between waking and sleeping, troubled by an awareness of something dark and terrible prowling the starless night.

At first, she thought the dark thing was after *her.* Then she realized it wasn't interested in her at all. It was after Torres and Kim. But it was she who'd let it out. She who'd released it to prey on her officers—her friends. And she was the only one who could send it back the way it came.

Or *could* she? Wasn't it already too late for her to do anything? Hadn't she had her opportunity and failed? She wanted to believe otherwise, but—

Suddenly, Janeway sat up in bed. Her skin was clammy and her mouth was dry and her heart was slamming against her ribs.

A nightmare, she concluded. Just a damned nightmare. She took a breath, let it out. Another. And another. Gradually, her heart rate slowed to something approaching normal.

And she had the distinct feeling that someone was waiting for her to do something. Not Torres and Kim, as in her dream, but *someone.* She looked around her quarters, at the vague, shadowy contours of her furnishings. There was no one there, of course. Still . . .

She ventured a response: "Janeway here."

"Captain," said a familiar voice over the intercom. "Sorry to wake you, but sensors show the approach of a Kazon cruiser. Its weapons are powered up and it seems to be on an intercept course."

Doing her best to shrug off her cobwebs, Janeway tossed aside the covers and padded across the room on bare feet. "Acknowledged, Chakotay. I'll join you on the bridge in a minute or so. In the meantime, go to red alert. Then hail the Kazon and see what happens."

"Aye, Captain," came the commander's reply.

Opening her closet, Janeway took out a hanging uniform. Then, tossing it on her bed, she removed her nightgown and slipped into it. Finally, with practiced dexterity, she pulled her hair back and clipped it up.

By then, she could hear the whooping voice of the klaxons signaling the red alert. It reminded her that there were worse ways to wake up than getting a call in the middle of the night.

In a matter of seconds, the captain was emerging into the corridor, her destination the nearest turbolift. The klaxons were louder out here and the lighting was a bloody shade of red. Crewmen were hurrying up and down the hallway, heading for their posts—just as she was.

Janeway still felt a little groggy, but that couldn't be helped. She had a job to do—and no dark and terrible pursuer was going to prevent her from doing it.

CHAPTER 7

JANEWAY EMERGED ONTO *VOYAGER'S* BRIDGE, SECURE IN THE KNOWLEDGE that the ship's shields had been raised and her weapons powered up. What's more, she was surrounded by Chakotay, Tuvok, and Paris, the officers she trusted most. If the commander of the approaching Kazon cruiser was going to try something, he would find her prepared for anything.

Turning to Tuvok, she asked, "Any response to our hails?"

The Vulcan shook his head. "None, Captain. It would seem—" He stopped in mid-sentence, then inspected his monitors and arched an eyebrow.

"What is it?" Chakotay inquired.

"The Kazon have chosen to respond," Tuvok noted simply—though it was difficult to conceal his surprise.

"Well," said the captain, "open a channel, Lieutenant. We wouldn't want to keep our Kazon friends waiting."

At his helm station, Paris chuckled at the ironic nature of the remark. Ignoring the human's response, Tuvok worked his controls. A moment later, the image of a tall, bony-faced Kazon filled the viewscreen.

The captain lifted her chin. "This is Captain Kathryn Janeway of the Federation starship *Voyager.*"

"We know who you are," the Kazon blurted. "I am called Lorca, second Maj of the Kazon-Ogla."

"Why are you here?" she asked.

The Kazon laughed. "To destroy you as you destroyed our sister ship, the *Barach'ma.* Did you think we would let our comrades go unavenged? Or their slayers unpunished?"

Janeway frowned. Signaling to Tuvok, she had him cut out the audio portion of her transmission.

"Any idea what he's talking about?" she asked Chakotay.

The first officer frowned back at her. "Judging from the Kazon's course, he's already been to the place we're headed for. I guess he didn't like what he found there."

"A ship," she said. "Probably another cruiser, if Lorca's calling it his sister ship. And according to him, it was destroyed."

"Could it be," asked Tuvok, "that this *Barach'ma* was waiting for the smaller vessel we've been pursuing? Could the Kazon have been planning a rendezvous between the two?"

"Makes sense," Chakotay replied. "But then . . ."

He didn't have to finish his question. They all knew what the first officer was wondering. If the *Barach'ma* was supposed to take custody of Torres and Kim, and it had been destroyed . . . did that mean Torres and Kim had been destroyed as well?

The captain thought for a moment, then signaled for the audio portion to be restored. Her eyes narrowed as she faced second Maj Lorca.

"We haven't destroyed anything or anyone," she said sternly. "Though we might have been justified in doing so, considering the way you and your people stole my officers."

Janeway let the implied threat hang in the air, hoping she wouldn't have to back it up. It seemed to work. Lorca didn't flinch—but he didn't say anything hostile either.

"But," the captain added, softening her voice, "I would much rather join forces with you, in an effort to determine who *did* destroy your vessel—and if they took my officers off first. After all, there might have been Kazon who survived and were taken prisoner as well."

The second Maj considered Janeway for what seemed like a long time. Then he nodded. "For the time being, I choose to believe you, Captain. But we of the Ogla will continue to monitor your movements. If you are lying, we will be back in force."

"And what about the possibility of survivors?" Janeway asked.

Lorca made a gesture of dismissal. "I have no interest in risking my ship for a handful of failures," he told her.

"Failures?" she echoed.

"If they were *true* Kazon," he explained, "they died in battle defending their vessel. And if they were *not* true Kazon, they are no longer worth saving."

The captain sighed. Lorca's logic was impeccable—at least from the Kazon point of view. She wasn't going to get anywhere arguing with it.

"Then we will continue our investigation alone," she announced stubbornly. "Janeway out."

Taking his cue, Tuvok severed the communication. Once more, the viewscreen displayed an image of the Kazon ship.

For a second or two, it hung in space, still a threat. Then it described a tight loop and retreated. When it had put sufficient space between itself and *Voyager,* the vessel went to warp speed and vanished.

The captain breathed a sigh of relief. It appeared they were free to pursue the search for their missing crewmen—though when it came to the Kazon, one never knew.

Even when it was Kim's turn to keep an eye out for them, B'Elanna didn't sleep very well. It wasn't that she didn't trust her colleague. It was just the Klingon in her.

Thanks to her mother's bloodlines, her instincts and senses were still tuned to the world of predator and prey. The lieutenant was cued in to sounds and smells at a level Kim could only dream about.

Every so often, she bolted upright with her heart pounding and her lips pulled back over her teeth—primitive, ready for anything. But each time, her readiness was wasted. There was no threat—or at least none she could discern in the darkness of the cargo hold.

B'Elanna was actually relieved when it was time for her watch. That way, she could do away with the pretense, with the wearisome drifting in and out. In a funny way, she could *relax.*

Unlike her, Kim slept like a baby. But then, he was human—*completely* human—far enough removed from his barbaric forebears to pretend he was somewhere safe.

Of course, the lieutenant could only guess where that might be. Home, maybe, back on Earth? Or perhaps his quarters on *Voyager?* But in any case, a place where people weren't thinking about killing him.

By contrast, their neighbors in the cargo hold were almost as wakeful as the lieutenant had been. Some of them, it seemed to her, only pretended to sleep to keep their guards happy. Others drifted in and out as she had.

One thing B'Elanna noticed was that the Nograkh never cast wary glances at each other—only at those of other races. Despite their violent natures, despite the fact that a murder had been committed among them, the brutes seemed to trust one another when it came to their slumber time. To cease hostilities.

Just as well, B'Elanna thought. She'd seen enough hostilities to last her for a while.

She had barely completed her thought when a squad of Nograkh guards opened the door to their prison and barged in with their blasters at the ready. B'Elanna's instincts told her their ship had arrived at its destination. The mining station, if Teeg'l had guessed right about that.

Kim raised his head, trying to blink away the cobwebs. "We're there," he said, echoing her thoughts.

"Looks that way," she agreed.

With a series of harsh, guttural commands, the guards rousted everyone out of the hold and ushered them into the corridor beyond. There were rustlings of discontent, but not many. Also, furtive glances among the prisoners—but not many of those either.

Whoever didn't move quickly enough was poked mercilessly with the narrow barrel of a guard's weapon. Perhaps needless to say, none of them needed to be poked twice.

B'Elanna tried to stay close to Kim and vice versa. For a while, it worked. Then the corridor twisted, and their fellow captives were shuffled along by the guards, and before she knew it the lieutenant was lucky to catch a glimpse of her companion.

In a matter of minutes, they came to a pentagon-shaped air lock, bigger than the others they'd seen. It was open already, with more armed Nograkh on the other side. The prisoners were rushed through unceremoniously. Then the air lock door was closed behind them with a clash of metal on metal.

The sound had a finality to it, B'Elanna mused, a sense that, for her and all her fellow prisoners, that door would never open again. Teeg'l had certainly led her to believe that.

But no matter how grim things looked, she wasn't about to throw in the towel. Nor was Kim, judging from his earlier comments. Maybe that's why they'd become friends so easily. They were both optimistic by nature—inclined to hold out some hope, no matter how slim it might be.

The corridor on this side of the air lock was a lot like the corridor on the other side—except for a humming sound that seemed to come from everywhere at once. B'Elanna guessed it had something to do with the ore refinement process—again, based on what the Kazon had told her.

But she wasn't going to find out right away, it seemed. After the corridor jogged right and then left, they came to a large chamber with a narrow opening for an entranceway. Then, though it wasn't even remotely necessary, the guards began shoving them inside.

That's when Teeg'l appeared to lose his mind. After being stun-blasted and robbed of his ship, after being bumped and tossed about the Nograkh vessel, B'Elanna would have thought the Kazon had learned to endure rough treatment. She would have imagined his skin had thickened a bit.

Obviously, she hadn't known Teeg'l as well as she'd thought. As the third Maj was sent sprawling into the prisoners ahead of him, something seemed to snap inside him. His expression went from one of tolerance to blind, unreasoning fury.

Giving in to his instincts, he lashed out—and tore a blaster rifle out of the hands of the nearest guard. Then he turned it on the Nograkh who had humiliated him and pressed the trigger.

The blue-white blast caught the guard square in the chest, sending him pinwheeling through the air. Slamming into a bulkhead, he slumped to the deck in a tangle of heavy limbs. Even before she saw the angle of the Nograkh's broken neck, B'Elanna knew how dead he was.

For the space of a heartbeat, there was silence. Then, like air rushing in to fill a vacuum, time seemed to accelerate—first to its normal rate and finally well beyond it.

There were shouts of anger and cries of defiance and bodies flying every which way. More blue energy blasts, more fallen guards. And fallen prisoners as well, because neither Teeg'l nor his brutish captors seemed to give a damn about bystanders.

B'Elanna flung herself to the floor to avoid the beams, trying at the same time to catch a glimpse of Kim. Instead, she caught a glimpse of the other Kazon—the one whose name she had never learned.

As she watched, he wrestled a guard for his rifle. It seemed he was winning, too. Gaining the upper hand.

Then the weapon went off and the Kazon was flung high in the air. When he came down and hit the deck, it was with the loose-jointed posture of a rag doll. And he didn't move again.

Other prisoners fell as well—those who had tried to put up a fight of their own, or who had been unlucky enough to find themselves too near a panicky guard. In a matter of moments, the nature of the melee changed. The tide of battle ebbed and died.

Instead of several struggles going on all at once, there was just one. Instead of a scattering of insurgents, there was a single figure, left naked and alone. And that figure was Teeg'l.

As he roared at his captors, spraying them with burst after burst of blue-white energy, he had to know he was doomed—had to know they were drawing a bead on him. But it didn't seem to daunt him. He was too caught up in his outrage and his anger to stop himself.

So the Nograkh did it for him.

What seemed like a dozen azure beams hit him all at once. He spun in one direction, then the other, his weapon flying out of his hands. Then another stream of energy hit him sharply in the temple—and toppled him.

After that, he lay still. As still as death, B'Elanna thought.

And she'd thought *she* was having a bad Day of Honor.

One of the guards collected Teeg'l's borrowed rifle and tossed the third Maj of the Kazon-Ogla over his shoulder. Then, without even looking at the other prisoners, the Nograkh jerked his head.

"Against the wall," he growled.

The survivors did as they were told, gathering by the bulkhead the guard had indicated. While they watched, the other guards roused their colleagues—except for the one Teeg'l had killed when it all started. That one they just dragged out the door.

The guard carrying Teeg'l departed as well. That left the rest of the prisoners—both those who were standing and those who were unconscious. And no one bothered to wake the latter variety.

No longer required to stand by the bulkhead, B'Elanna picked an empty corner of the chamber and beckoned for Kim to follow her. Warily, he complied. Corners, after all, were easier to defend. She had learned that as a member of the Maquis.

"Some welcome wagon," she said as she and her companion hunkered down together.

"A barbecue would have worked just as well," he commented drily.

There was silence for a moment. "Hard to believe Teeg'l cracked so easily," the lieutenant added.

Kim glanced at her. "Maybe not."

"What do you mean?" she asked.

"He knew what we had to look forward to. Maybe he figured it was better to get it over with."

B'Elanna wished she had an answer for that. Unfortunately, that wasn't the case.

Kes looked at the Doctor. "Now?" she asked.

"Now," he confirmed.

They were standing on either side of the biobed, where their patient still lay sleeping. There was no evidence of her injuries, no sign of the burns that had covered a good part of her body.

Pressing the control padds on the bed, the Ocampa eliminated the electromagnetic field that had protected the woman since her arrival in sick bay. Then she cut off the flow of sedatives into the patient's blood and introduced a mild stimulant, no more powerful than smelling salts, to bring her out of her medicated sleep.

A moment later, the woman opened her eyes. Kes saw they were a startling shade of blue. For several seconds, they drifted in and out of focus. Then they seemed to lock onto the Doctor's face.

"Who . . . who are you?" she asked.

"I have no name," the Doctor explained, "unusual as that may seem. However, I do have a description. I am the emergency medical program for the starship *Voyager.* This physical manifestation you see is only a hologram, which allows me to interact with sentient organisms—much as I am doing now."

Their patient's brow creased down the middle. "I . . . see," she said tentatively. She turned to Kes. "And are you a hologram as well?"

The Ocampa smiled and shook her head. "No, I'm a flesh-and-blood organism, just as you are."

Kes resisted using the word "real" to distinguish between herself and the Doctor, since she considered him every bit as real as she was. After all, he was capable of independent thought, even feelings. The only significant difference was his lack of biological functions.

"How are you feeling?" she asked the woman.

Their patient seemed to take stock of herself for a moment. "Well," she concluded. "Very well." The crease in her brow deepened. "But on the ship, I was exposed—"

"To a significant amount of radiation from your damaged engine core," the Doctor noted. "Fortunately, we were able to counteract the effects of the exposure. As you can see, there will be no permanent scarring."

The woman nodded. "I'm grateful." Tentatively, she sat up. Examining her arms and legs, she began to smile. "You've performed a miracle."

The Doctor shrugged. "All in a day's work," he told her. Then, without another word, he retreated to his office.

Their patient watched him go for a second, then turned to Kes. "My name is Pacria," she said. "Pacria Ertinia."

"Kes," the Ocampa replied. "Good to meet you. Though, of course, I wish it were under better circumstances." She frowned. "We weren't able to save the others on your ship."

Pacria's expression became one of regret. "We ran into a subspace anomaly. Never knew what hit us."

Abruptly, the Doctor emerged from his office with a hypospray in his hands and held it against the woman's arm. "This won't hurt," he said reassuringly. "And more importantly, it'll save your life."

Pacria pulled her arm away. "What do you mean?" she asked.

"I'm introducing a vaccine to cure you of your disease." The Doctor explained where he had gotten it. "If you'll hold still, it'll take just a moment."

"I cannot allow that," Pacria told him.

The Doctor looked at her. "I beg your pardon?"

The muscles in the woman's temples worked furiously. "I said I cannot allow that," she told him.

Kes shook her head. "I don't understand. The Doctor has developed a vaccine that can save you from a fatal ailment—and you're refusing it?"

"That's right," Pacria insisted.

"But why?" asked the Ocampa, as gently as she could. "Why would you want to die when you can live?"

The patient turned away from her. "Please," she said, the protuberances on her jaw swelling and turning red. "I have my reasons."

Kes couldn't accept that. "If you shared your reasons with us, there might be something we could do to change your mind."

Pacria glared at her with unexpected anger. "I don't want my mind changed. I just want to be left alone."

The Ocampa swallowed. She wasn't used to being the object of such fury. "All right," she conceded. "Whatever you say."

"Indeed," said the Doctor. He scowled—first at Kes, then at Pacria. "Though I, too, would like to hear your reasons," he told Pacria, "your decision is yours and yours alone. For me to intrude on it would be a violation of my oath as a physician."

"Thank you," their patient replied. "Now if I can make arrangements for my passage home . . . "

"I'll speak to our captain about it," the Doctor promised. "However, a couple of our crewmen have been abducted and we are currently in the process of attempting to recover them. I expect it'll be a while before we can turn our attention to getting you home."

Pacria nodded, even though she had to know she probably wouldn't last that long. Kes bit her lip. What had the Doctor given the woman? A week?

"That's reasonable," the patient said.

But it wasn't reasonable, the Ocampa told herself. None of this was. And though she respected the Doctor's principles, she couldn't see the wisdom in them this time.

After all, life was so precious. So fleeting. It was a crime to throw it away when it could be preserved.

The Doctor held his hand out to Pacria. "Since it appears your treatment here is over, there's no reason for you to remain in sick bay. I'll see to it you're given appropriate quarters."

"Thank you," the woman told him. "Again."

Taking his hand, she swung her legs around and eased herself off the biobed. Then she followed him into his office.

Kes sighed. Was this why she'd maintained her lonely vigil over Pacria? Was this why the Doctor had worked so hard to find a cure? So she could spurn the gifts they'd given her?

And the worst part was she wouldn't even say *why.*

CHAPTER 8

Kes stood by the door to the Holodoctor's office and watched him circle sick bay, hands clasped behind his back. No doubt, he felt as if they were tied there.

"Clearly," he said, "Pacria has her reasons for refusing the treatment. And of course, it's her right to refuse it." He frowned. "It's also her right not to tell us those reasons, if she doesn't want to."

"I suppose so," the Ocampa replied. "But I can't help wishing it were otherwise."

"Neither can I," the Doctor admitted. He heaved a sigh. "This is the first time a patient has ever thanked me for not saving her life. And you know what? I don't like it—not one little bit."

Kes understood. He had been programmed to save lives, not watch them dwindle away without doing a thing about it.

"We've got to find out why Pacria's made this decision," she decided.

The Doctor's eyes narrowed. "Not if she doesn't want us to. As physicians, we must respect her right to privacy."

Kes thought for a moment. "Look," she said at last, "would it violate her right if I just asked her again? Nicely? Maybe now that she's had a while to get used to her surroundings . . ."

He regarded her. "You'll have to be *very* nice. I won't have anyone harassing my patient. Not even you."

"I promise," she told him. "I'll be discreet."

Then she left sick bay and headed for Pacria's quarters, already playing out the scene in her mind.

Tom Paris stared at the main viewscreen from his helm position. It was just as bad as he'd feared. Just as bad, in fact, as second Maj Lorca had led them to believe.

There was debris spread across space as far as the eye could see. Pieces of metal, mostly, according to the sensor report on his monitor. And whatever else was out there, he didn't want to know about it.

In any case, they knew two things for certain. First, that there had been a Kazon vessel here, if the alloys they'd detected were any indication. And second, that it had been destroyed.

What they didn't know was who had done it and why. Apparently Lorca hadn't known that either, or he wouldn't have accused *Voyager* of it. Most importantly, they didn't know if Harry and B'Elanna had been on the *Barach'ma* when its adversary blew it up.

Maybe they had gotten here after the encounter, and seen what *Voyager* was seeing. Maybe, Paris told himself, they had altered their course and found another ship to rendezvous with. Maybe this, maybe that.

Funny, he thought. Not so long ago, he'd considered his comrades' captivity a terrible thing. Their situation had seemed about as grim as it could get.

Now, it seemed a lot grimmer. He would've given his right arm to know they were in one piece—on a Kazon vessel or anywhere else.

Abruptly, Tuvok spoke up. "I have isolated another ion trail," he told the captain. "However, it is different from the trail we followed here. Clearly, it did not originate from a Kazon form of propulsion technology."

"That rules out another Kazon sect," Chakotay observed. "But it leaves the door open for a host of other possibilities."

Janeway looked at the Vulcan. "We can follow it, can't we? Just as we followed the other trail?"

Tuvok shrugged. "It will entail a recalibration of our instruments, but that should not take long."

The captain nodded. "Good. See to it, Lieutenant."

Tuvok assured her he would do that and set to work. Unlike the rest of the crew, unlike even Janeway herself, he never seemed to tire. It was a good thing, too, considering the Vulcan could do things no one else could—and in half the time.

Turning back to the viewscreen, Paris regarded the field of debris again. It could well be that his colleagues had bought the farm here. But clearly, the captain wasn't accepting that possibility. She was doing everything she could to find them and get them back.

He liked that. Because if it were he out there, lost and alone, he would want to know his friends hadn't given up on him.

B'Elanna was up and alert with the first sharp sound of footsteps inside the rest chamber. Glancing at the entrance, she saw several armed guards enter the room—and her heart leaped into her throat.

A reprisal for Teeg'l's outburst the day before? An object lesson, just in case his death and that of the other Kazon weren't enough?

Those were the possibilities that came to mind first. And wouldn't they have been right in line with her Day-of-Honor luck? Before long, however, the lieutenant realized her fears were groundless. The guards weren't just rounding up a *couple* of prisoners—they were rousting *all* of them, jerking their heads in the direction of the exit.

And, she asked herself, what would be the sense of killing the whole bunch of them? Especially since it would leave no one to benefit from the Nograkh's object lesson.

Of course, the guards might simply be taking them somewhere else, where they could conduct a little seminar on the value of rebellion. But B'Elanna didn't think so. The Nograkh seemed to her a particularly brutal and expedient people. If they intended to kill someone, to make an example of him, they would have done it then and there.

As she got to her feet, she looked at Kim. He looked wary of the guards' intentions as well.

"Where do you think we're going?" he asked as he stood.

"Nowhere we want to be," she assured him.

But they both knew the answer to his question—at least, the one Teeg'l had supplied them with. And if he was wrong, the lieutenant mused, they would find that out soon enough as well.

A hurried walk down a long corridor later, they found themselves in another chamber, maybe three times as big as the other one. Except this one wasn't so sparsely furnished.

An entire bulkhead was lined with a series of small, open hatches, through which chunks of rock were emptying into two-handled metal containers via heavy-duty conveyor belts. Apparently, the station was receiving a new load of raw material at that very moment.

On the other side of the room, there were massive, dark machines with monitors and control consoles, and more of the same kind of conveyor belts running in and out of them. Also, several more of the metal containers, waiting to transport the processed ore.

"Seems Teeg'l was right," she commented.

Kim grunted. "But he didn't do the place justice. It's much more oppressive-looking than I imagined."

A guard approached them and pointed to one of the hatches, where a container was almost full of debris. "Bring it to the processing unit," he told them. "And see you don't spill any."

They did as they were instructed. The other prisoners were given their orders at the same time—either to transport the incoming rocks alongside B'Elanna and Kim or to familiarize themselves with the processing controls. Either way, the lieutenant observed, it would be difficult to avoid exposure to the radioactive ore.

B'Elanna had never seen anyone who'd been a victim of radiation poisoning, but she'd heard about it. Apparently, there were quicker and less painful ways to die.

But the lieutenant wasn't going to think about dying just yet. She was going to think about *Voyager* tracking them down and getting them out of here. And she was going to do whatever it took to make that possible.

Before long, the prisoners settled into a routine under the watchful eyes of their guards. B'Elanna, Kim, and a handful of others dragged the containers full of rocks. Others worked the processing units, which separated the valuable ore from other debris. And still others dragged the containers full of ore out of the room for storage elsewhere in the station.

The debris was dumped in containers as well. But these were allowed to pile up until they took up too much room, then dragged off in another direction. More than likely, to be shoved out an air lock, the lieutenant thought.

This went on for hours. It wasn't long before B'Elanna experienced the first effects of the radiation. Her head felt light and her skin felt dry and raw. Judging by Kim's expression, he was enjoying the working conditions even less than she was. And still their captors kept them at it, until the last of the ore had been processed and put in storage.

Then they were herded back into the first chamber, where they slumped against the walls. The lieutenant felt a growling in her stomach, but somehow she didn't feel hungry.

Radiation will do that to you, she remarked inwardly. That and a whole lot more.

But she would have to eat sometime. Otherwise she'd become useless to her captors and get herself tossed out an air lock with the rest of the debris.

And wouldn't *that* make it a Day of Honor to remember?

The Nograkh prisoners sat on the other side of the rest chamber. Tired as they were, it didn't stop two of them from trading remarks—or getting into a pushing match. Almost as quickly as that other fight B'Elanna had seen—the one that had ended in the death of one of the combatants—this one escalated, too.

In a heartbeat, the pushing had turned into bone-jarring blows. No one, not even a healthy Nograkh, could have held up long under that kind of pounding. Nor did the lieutenant have to guess which Nograkh would buckle first.

After all, one of the brutes was considerably bigger than the other—and his superior strength was already staggering his opponent. Before long, she told herself, another Nograkh would be lying on the floor, his skull crushed or his neck broken.

B'Elanna couldn't let that happen. It didn't matter if this was someone else's fight, someone else's culture. She had to act.

A look from Kim told her he felt the same way. He was leery of what they'd be getting themselves into, but not so leery he wasn't willing to try.

They started for the combatants. But before they could get very far, a chorus went up from the other Nograkh. And it had a very distinct tone of disapproval about it.

Immediately, the two engaged in the fight stopped and looked around. They seemed to be searching the faces of the other Nograkh. Whatever they found there didn't seem to please them. Then the one with the scar on his face spoke to them.

B'Elanna wouldn't have expected him to play peacekeeper, considering how he'd murdered his fellow Nograkh in the last melee. Nonetheless, his comments sealed the deal.

With a last, hostile glance at one another, the combatants backed off and melted into the ring of spectators. For a little while, they spat and gesticulated and complained volubly—the bigger one in particular. Then even that subsided.

B'Elanna looked at Kim. He shrugged.

"Looks like our services aren't needed anymore, Maquis."

"No objections from me, Starfleet."

By then, a couple of the guards had poked their heads in to see what was going on. They seemed disappointed that the fight hadn't gone further. Still, they appeared to find some humor in the situation, and grinned with their wide, cruel mouths.

That was one sight she wouldn't miss when they were reunited with *Voyager,* the lieutenant decided. And they *would* get back—somehow.

She wouldn't accept any other outcome.

As the door to Pacria's quarters slid aside, Kes peered inside. The woman was seated at a computer terminal, its glare illuminating her alien visage and her impossibly blue eyes.

"Kes," she said.

It wasn't a greeting—not really. There was no warmth in it, certainly. Only suspicion.

Wonderful, thought the Ocampa. I haven't even opened my mouth and I already feel like I'm prying. Still, she had come here for a reason, so she went ahead with it.

"How are you feeling?" she asked.

Pacria leaned back from the terminal and shrugged. "Fine. Except for the virus, of course. But that's to be expected." She indicated a chair on the other side of the room. "Won't you have a seat?"

Kes nodded. "Thank you."

Taking the chair, she saw Pacria swivel to face her. She was about to broach the subject of the woman's reasons for turning down the vaccine—until Pacria herself broached it.

"You want to know why I'm doing this," she said.

The Ocampa leaned forward. "If you don't want to tell me, you don't have to. The Doctor takes that part of his programming very seriously."

"And you?" asked Pacria, her eyes narrowing. "Don't you take it seriously as well?"

"I'm not a doctor," Kes explained. "But I've been taught to respect people's rights. If you want to keep your reasons a secret, that's your prerogative." She paused. "Only . . . "

"Yes?" the woman prodded.

"Only I wish you would share them with me. You see, the average lifetime for one of my people is only eight or nine years. We see life as something to be treasured. And it's difficult for me to see why anyone would—"

"Waste it," Pacria suggested.

"I didn't say that," Kes pointed out.

The woman considered her. "No," she conceded at last. "You didn't. And maybe I'm being a little harsh on you. After all, you *did* save my life—you and your friend the Doctor. And, contrary to what you might think, I cherish the extra days you've given me—painful though they will be."

The Ocampa smiled sympathetically. "You're obviously a courageous person. I admire you for that."

Pacria grunted. "You won't gain anything by flattery." Her features softened. "But maybe I do owe you an explanation."

"I don't believe you *owe* me anything," Kes clarified. "But I'd still be glad to hear it."

"All right," said the woman. "I'll tell you, then. But to understand why I'm doing what I'm doing, you must first understand the history of my people. We call ourselves the Emmonac."

Pacria described the Emmonac—their devotion to learning, to the arts, to wisdom in general. And their invasion by the Zendak'aa, a haughty race of conquerors from a neighboring star system.

The woman's voice took on a husky tone. "The Zendak'aa enslaved the Emmonac—and worse. Entire clans were selected at random and herded into camps, where they became the subjects of all kinds of experiments. Terrible experiments, involving mutilation and misery—but all in the name of science." She swallowed. "One of those experiments concerned a disease."

"The one you're carrying around inside you?" Kes asked.

"Not exactly," Pacria replied. "It was a disease restricted to the Zendak'aa. But what I have is very much like it. So similar, in fact, that what the Zendak'aa developed to fight their own virus would be an effective vaccine against it.

"The problem," said the Emmonac, "is it was bought with the blood of my people. That makes it monstrous to me. It makes it evil. To use it would be to honor the Zendak'aa who developed it—and that is too hideous an idea for me to even contemplate."

Kes looked at her. "I see."

There was silence for a moment. Then Pacria said she was tired, and wondered if she might not have some privacy.

And Kes had little choice but to grant it to her.

CHAPTER 9

JANEWAY PUSHED BACK FROM THE COMPUTER TERMINAL IN HER READY ROOM and rubbed her eyes. She'd been at it for hours now, on and off—though it felt even longer.

With Tuvok in charge of tracking the ion trail of the Kazon battleship's mysterious destroyer, and her other officers busy with their own details, the captain had taken it on herself to more thoroughly analyze the sensor data on the debris field. What's more, it had yielded some interesting results.

First, she'd found there was more mass in the field than could be attributed to a battleship alone, but nothing with a Starfleet signature—nothing to indicate that the Kazon scout ship had definitely been destroyed at those coordinates as well.

Second, she'd been able to identify the sort of energy beam employed by the destroyer. Unfortunately, it hadn't come from any kind of weapon with which she was familiar. And when she'd asked Neelix about it, the Talaxian couldn't shed any light on the question either.

However, to this point, Janeway hadn't discovered what she was *really* looking for—some indication of where the destroyer had gone, some sense of its destination. Because if they knew that, they would be a big step closer to learning the fate of their missing crewmates.

The captain stretched her arms, feeling resistance from the cramps in her neck and shoulders. Somewhere in that mass of data, she told herself, was a clue. And she was determined to find it, with or without Neelix's—

Abruptly, she stopped herself. Neelix wasn't the only local guide they had aboard—not anymore. Their guest . . . what was her name? Pacria, wasn't it?

She came from this part of the Delta Quadrant. Odds were she knew it better than Neelix did.

And from what she'd heard, Pacria had recuperated enough to leave sick bay and occupy an empty suite. And, at her own request, the woman had been granted limited access to the ship's computer, so she had to be pretty alert.

Alert enough to entertain a visitor, the captain hoped.

By the time the guards brought them some food, B'Elanna's appetite had improved considerably. But it went downhill again when she saw what they were serving for dinner.

The *plat du jour* was a thin, yellowish gruel with lumps of something vaguely meatlike in it. The guards maneuvered it into the room in a huge pot, not unlike the containers they used in the ore-processing chamber—except the pot had wheels to make the going easier.

The prisoners were told to line up. Then each one was given a plateful of the stuff. After B'Elanna and Kim got their fair shares, they returned to their place in the corner.

The ensign swallowed as he inspected his meal. "You know," he said, "I'm starting to appreciate Neelix more than ever."

"So am I," she agreed. "At least when he was serving something inedible, he knew how to disguise it."

Her companion looked at her. "I thought Klingons could eat *anything.*"

The lieutenant shook her head. "I'm only *half*-Klingon, remember? And the other half is pretty discriminating."

She smiled wanly, remembering how the Talaxian had tried to please her a few short days ago. She was glad she'd had a chance to apologize to him. If that was the last she and Neelix saw of each other, at least he'd have something good to say at her funeral.

No, she reminded herself. No funeral—not for a good long while. She'd be tasting Neelix's food again before she knew it.

In the meantime, she noticed, the other prisoners didn't seem to appreciate the gruel they were being served either. Not even the Nograkh, whose needs it was no doubt designed to fulfill.

There was considerable grumbling. Sounds of discontent. Nothing new in this place, of course. B'Elanna herself had been tempted to grumble a little now and then.

One alien seemed to be complaining a little more loudly than the others. He had a single eye in the middle of his brow, right where the bridge of his nose would have been if he'd been human. He was dark—very dark, actually—and hairless as far as she could tell, and he had pale blue striations running down either side of his neck.

What's more, he towered over the prisoners on either side of him. In fact, he towered over everyone in the chamber, even the largest of the Nograkh. As B'Elanna watched, he turned his eye her way.

No, the lieutenant thought. Not her way, not exactly. It seemed to her he was scrutinizing the ensign beside her.

"Heads up," she whispered.

Kim looked up at her. "What?"

The alien's single eye narrowed and the striations on his neck turned a darker shade of blue. Letting his plate drop to the floor, he crossed the room. And he was headed in the ensign's direction.

"Trouble," she said, answering Kim's question.

The ensign's eyes slid to one side, but he didn't turn his head. He just frowned a little.

None of the other prisoners exercised that kind of restraint. They stopped eating and followed One-Eye's progress with great interest. And their interest heightened even more when he came to a halt in front of Kim.

One-Eye spoke in a voice surprisingly thin and reedy, as if someone had damaged his vocal cords somewhere along the line. "You," he said to the human. "Kazon-lover."

B'Elanna watched Kim's reaction. Or rather, his lack of one. The ensign didn't acknowledge the other prisoner's presence. He just scooped another dollop of gruel out of his bowl and deposited it in his mouth.

"Didn't you hear me?" asked One-Eye.

Still no response, at least from Kim. But B'Elanna could feel her pulse starting to race. The Klingon in her didn't like insults—regardless of whether they were directed at her or her friends. And when there was an implicit threat of violence in them, she liked them even less.

"I called you a Kazon-lover," One-Eye persisted.

It wasn't what he had said, really. It was the way he had said it—the taunt in his voice, so much like all the taunts B'Elanna had endured since her arrival here.

She could feel the anger rising inside her. She could feel her hands clenching into fists. But she told herself she wouldn't do anything drastic—not unless Kim was in danger.

The ensign didn't look at his tormentor. He just said, "I don't love the Kazons any more than you do. It was just a coincidence that we were captured with them. In fact—"

Suddenly, the alien reached down and grabbed the front of Kim's uniform. Almost effortlessly, he dragged the ensign to his feet, causing his plate of gruel to fall out of his hand.

"You think you can deceive me?" he rasped. "You think you can lie your way out of this? The Kazons raided my world—killed my nestlings. Who's going to pay for that, eh?"

Kim wasn't making a move to save himself. But then, maybe he didn't think he needed saving. Maybe he was hoping this would all boil over if he just kept his mouth shut from here on in.

B'Elanna disagreed. Without considering the consequences, without considering *anything* except the danger her friend was in, she got up and belted One-Eye across the mouth as hard as she could.

The alien staggered backward, releasing Kim in the process. The ensign retreated to a spot beside his benefactor.

"You shouldn't have done that," he told her. "I could have handled it."

"Like hell," she spat.

Recovering, One-Eye growled and wiped his mouth with the back of his hand. It came away red with blood.

"You will be sorry you did that," he told her, a bestial grin spreading across his face. "You will be *very* sorry."

He signaled to the clot of prisoners gathered behind him. Two of them got to their feet, large specimens in their own right. One, a being with a pinched face and horns like a ram's, rubbed his powerful hands together in anticipation of what was to come. The other, a leathery-looking bruiser with faceted yellow eyes, slammed a massive fist into his palm.

The lieutenant could feel her heart pounding. She could feel the surge of fire in her veins. *Klingon* fire.

Over the years, she had learned to deal with her battle lust—to channel it into more useful endeavors. Now, it seemed, the most useful thing she could do was tear her enemy's throat out. Anything less and he would probably do the same thing to her.

B'Elanna wished it hadn't come to this. But then, hadn't it seemed inevitable to her from the beginning? Neither she nor Kim had any friends here, only each other. And with the stigma of the Kazon on them, their status as scapegoats had been assured.

The Day of Honor was lasting a little longer this year.

"I'll take the two on the right," Kim told her. He assumed a fighting stance, no doubt one he'd learned at the Academy and hadn't used since.

The lieutenant grimaced. "Take what you can handle," she advised him, "and leave the rest to me."

Then their antagonists were on top of them, and there was no more time for strategy. There was only time for kicking and ducking and jabbing for all she was worth.

But right from the beginning, it was clear it wouldn't be enough. One-Eye wasn't just powerful, he was deadly quick. And he had help from his friend with the ram's horns.

Together, they maneuvered B'Elanna into a corner, where her own quickness wasn't as much of an asset. Then they took their shots at her, one after another, until she couldn't elude them anymore and they started landing with bone-jolting frequency.

Still, her thoughts were for her companion, who was matched up against the leathery prisoner with the yellow eyes. She tried to steal a glimpse of Kim even in the midst of her own peril, but what little she could see wasn't very encouraging.

Like her, the ensign was backed into a corner. But unlike her, he didn't have the wherewithal to deal with it. His face was bloody, his legs barely able to hold him up. Any more such punishment and he'd be a dead man.

Not that B'Elanna could do anything about it. In fact, she probably wouldn't last much longer than her friend would.

Then something happened. At first, she wasn't sure what—only that there was an uproar from the other prisoners, the ones who hadn't seen fit to participate in the slaughter. And a single shout that came through the general outcry, sounding very much like a challenge.

One-Eye didn't seem to be able to ignore it. Pausing to look back over his shoulder, he gave B'Elanna the chance she needed to slip past him.

That's when she saw what was going on. Kim was slumped in his corner, bloody but still alive. And in his place one of the Nograkh was fighting the prisoner with the leathery skin. Surprisingly, it was the killer—the one with the scar.

As the lieutenant looked on, the Nograkh blocked a roundhouse blow with one hand and launched one of his own with the other. There was a crack, and the leathery one toppled, senseless.

But no sooner had he hit the deck than One-Eye and Ram's Horns were charging his assailant. The Nograkh whirled, ready to take them both on. And for a little while, that's just what he had to do.

He didn't do badly, either. He wasn't very agile, but he was immensely strong. And what he couldn't elude, he could ward off. Of course, it was still two against one, and he couldn't have held out forever.

That's why it was so important for B'Elanna to rejoin the fray—to literally jump into it with both feet. Getting a running start, she leaped at just the right moment and plowed into the small of One-Eye's back.

Her adversary snarled with pain and sank to his knees, clutching the point of impact. In the meantime, no longer outnumbered, the Nograkh buried his fist in Ram's Horns' belly. And when Ram's Horns doubled over in pain, his adversary launched an uppercut that lifted him off the floor.

By the time he came down again, Ram's Horns was unconscious. That left only One-Eye to deal with, and he was still bent over from the blow to his back. The Nograkh crossed the floor and stood menacingly above him.

When he spoke, his voice was gravelly and his tone full of rancor. "An uneven fight," he told One-Eye, "is dishonorable. My people don't *like* dishonorable fights."

With a tilt of his head, he indicated the other Nograkh in the room. They were each as intent on One-Eye as he was. From B'Elanna's point of view, it looked like any of them would have performed the same kind of rescue—except the one with the scar had beaten them to it.

"They came in with the Kazon," One-Eye hissed. He pointed a long, gnarled finger at B'Elanna. "They deserve to die."

"I hate the Kazon as much as anyone," the Nograkh snarled. "But they aren't Kazon. As far as I can tell, the only one who deserves to *die* here is *you.*"

And he pulled his fist back for what B'Elanna feared was a deathblow.

"No!" she yelled. "Let him be!"

Without thinking, she took a couple of steps toward the Nograkh. He stopped, looked at her and then Kim.

"You'd spare his life?" he asked them.

"Yes," the lieutenant said quickly.

The ensign nodded. "Yes."

The Nograkh hesitated. Then, with a shrug, he turned and rejoined his comrades. And he didn't look back.

B'Elanna made her way to Kim's side, just in case One-Eye decided he wanted to resume hostilities. But he didn't do that. He simply returned to where he'd been sitting, grumbling and holding his injury.

"How about that?" Kim mumbled, a swollen lip getting in his way.

The lieutenant checked him to make sure he hadn't sustained any serious damage. "Yes. How about that."

She glanced at the Nograkh with the scar. He was exchanging comments with his comrades.

"Apparently," the ensign said, "we didn't give his kind enough credit. He could just as easily have watched us get hung out to dry."

"I guess," B'Elanna responded.

Despite all their belligerence, despite the cruelty that seemed part of their nature, there seemed to be a code of honor among the Nograkh. She wouldn't have thought it possible.

And yet, she'd seen it with her own eyes.

"It just goes to show you," Kim said. "Things aren't always what they appear to be."

B'Elanna glanced again at the Nograkh. This time he noticed, and glanced back at her. "Spare me the platitudes, Starfleet—at least until we find a way out of here."

Janeway stood outside Pacria's door and waited for the woman to give the captain entry to her quarters. A moment later, the door slid aside.

Pacria was sitting on a chair in front of a computer terminal much like the one Janeway had just left. The lines of her face were drawn tight. Like the gates of a citadel, the captain thought.

And she hadn't even asked a question yet.

"Captain Janeway," said Pacria, acknowledging her host.

"How are you feeling?" asked Janeway.

"Better," the alien told her.

It was a guarded remark if the captain had ever heard one.

"Don't tell me," Pacria went on. "Kes asked you to speak with me."

The captain smiled, seeing that she had inadvertently intruded on some controversy. "Actually, no. I came of my own accord."

Pacria's expression changed—became vaguely apologetic. "I'm sorry. Perhaps I jumped to the wrong conclusion." She indicated a chair on the other side of the room. "Please. Sit down."

Janeway accepted her offer. "The reason I came," she explained as succinctly as she could, "has to do with our search for a couple of our officers. They were abducted by the Kazon—"

"I've heard of the Kazon," Pacria responded, sounding a little impatient.

The captain nodded. "As I was saying, the Kazon took our people. But we came across what appears to be the wreckage of the Kazon ship—where we picked up the ion trail of another vessel entirely."

Janeway rubbed her hands together. "We've got a problem. We're hoping our friends were seized and spirited away by the destroyer, but we don't know where they were taken."

"But you said there was an ion trail," Pacria pointed out.

This time the captain was certain of the woman's impatience. Maybe Pacria hadn't gotten her strength back as much as the Doctor believed—though as far as Janeway knew, the Doctor had never been wrong before.

"That's true," the captain conceded. "But ion trails aren't always a hundred percent reliable. And they have a habit of petering out before you get to the end of them."

Pacria frowned. "What is it you wish me to do?"

"Take a look at the data," Janeway told her. "See if there's anything about it—either the ion trail or the weapons residue or anything else—that might tell you who destroyed the Kazon."

The woman looked at her for a moment. "All right," she agreed. "Give me access to it and I'll take a look. It's the least I can do, considering what your doctor did for me."

The captain smiled. "If you can tell us anything at all about our officers' whereabouts, it's *we* who'll be indebted to *you.*"

CHAPTER 10

B'ELANNA'S SECOND DAY OF WORK WAS PROBABLY NO HARDER THAN THE first—but it *felt* much harder. She knew that was due to the radiation. It sapped her strength and burned her skin and made her head ache.

When all the ore had been processed, she and the other prisoners were allowed to return to their rest chamber. In the corridor en route, she felt a hand on her shoulder. It was Kim's.

"At least we get some exercise," he gibed. He was pale, drawn, waxy-looking. "And on Friday nights, I hear there's a concert. I may be called upon to play my clarinet."

The lieutenant looked at him. "You're out of your mind, Starfleet."

The ensign grunted, touching two fingers to the cut over his eye, which had grown red and puffy. It looked like an infection had set in.

"Don't I wish," he replied. "Then I wouldn't have to put up with this torture." He lowered his voice. "B'Elanna, if the captain were on our trail, don't you think she would have—"

"I don't think anything," she told him. "I just wait and watch for a chance to get out of here. That's all either of us can do."

Kim nodded. "Right."

As they filed into the rest chamber, they passed a bunch of burly Nograkh, who had already begun to hunker down in their usual spots. One of them was the prisoner with the scar on his face—the one who had come to their aid when One-Eye and his friends attacked them.

The one who had likely saved their lives.

The lieutenant paused for a moment. Kim stopped, too.

"What is it?" he asked.

"I'd like to thank our unexpected benefactor," she told him. "It seems like the right thing to do."

The ensign glanced at the Nograkh in question. "Are you sure? I mean, I get the feeling there wasn't anything personal in what he did. He just felt . . . I don't know, *compelled* to do it."

"All the more reason to express our gratitude," B'Elanna asserted.

Kim frowned. "I'll go with you."

"Not necessary," she said. "Besides, one of us may be less threatening than two."

The ensign thought for a moment. "All right," he decided. "But I'll be right over there if you need me." He indicated a bulkhead with a jerk of his head. "I'll be the one slumped wearily against the wall."

The lieutenant smiled. "Acknowledged."

Then she walked over to the Nograkh. He saw her coming, but didn't move in response.

Taking a breath, she extended her hand to him.

He looked at it with his small silver eyes. So did the other Nograkh. But none of them seemed to understand what B'Elanna was up to.

"It's a gesture of friendship," she explained. "You grasp it."

The Nograkh looked at her and her hand for what seemed like a long time. Then he spoke.

"Why would you want to be my friend?" he asked.

B'Elanna kept her hand extended. "You came to our aid. Maybe saved our lives."

"It was an uneven contest. If it hadn't been me," he said, "it would have been one of the others."

"But it wasn't," she insisted. "It was you."

The Nograkh pondered that. Reaching out, he took her up on her offer—though he probably didn't use all his strength when he clasped her hand.

He looked at her sullenly, perhaps seeking assurance that he was performing the gesture correctly. She nodded.

Then he released her hand. And patted the deck beside him, indicating that she should sit down.

As she complied, the other Nograkh moved away a bit—though some grumbled about it. They were giving their comrade some privacy, the lieutenant realized.

"My name is B'Elanna," she told him. She smiled, though it was hard to work up much enthusiasm when she ached so much. "B'Elanna Torres."

The Nograkh grunted. "They call me Tolga." And then he added, "You are not from any world I have ever heard of."

"That's true," she said. "My people were brought here by a phenomenon we still don't quite understand. Our worlds are far away—so far, in fact, it could take a lifetime to return to them."

If one *had* a lifetime, she added inwardly. At the moment, hers looked rather inadequate. But she didn't say that. What she said was, "I want to thank you."

Tolga looked away, his face a stony mask. "It was nothing. Only what honor demanded of me."

Honor, thought the lieutenant. It was a word the Klingons used as well. And often, if her mother was any indication.

Abruptly, he turned to her again, his silver eyes catching the light. "How did you come here, anyway?"

Obviously, he was curious about her. And she had no reason to hold anything back—though she resisted an urge to mention her mother's holiday.

"We were kidnapped by the Kazon-Ogla," she explained. "Then their ship was attacked by the one that brought us here. When the Ogla were taken prisoner, so were we."

Tolga's mouth twisted as if he had a bad taste in it. "Too bad," was his only comment.

He looked down at his big, powerful-looking hands. For a while, he seemed interested in nothing else. Then he looked up and spoke again.

"You must have wondered what we Nograkh are doing here. Why we were thrown into this hole with you and the others."

"The question occurred to me," she admitted.

"Most often," Tolga told her, his mouth twisting again, "if a Nograkh is brought to a place like this, it's because he is a criminal. A thief or a murderer or a defiler of holy places. You're familiar with such people?"

The lieutenant said she was. She had met several of them when she served with the Maquis. Hell, she'd stolen a few things herself in the name of freedom from the Cardassians.

"Is that what you did?" she asked. "You took a few things that didn't belong to you?"

Tolga made a derisive sound deep in his throat. A profoundly bitter sound, B'Elanna thought.

"No. None of us here did anything like that." He paused, as if searching for words. "We were rebels. We tried to overthrow the government on our homeworld."

"I see," she said. "So . . . you're political prisoners."

He tried the notion on for size. "Yes, you could say that." A pause. "For a long time, our world was enslaved by the Zendak'aa—just like a lot of other worlds. Then we rose up against them and smashed their control over us. For those of us who had risked our lives to see the Zendak'aa gone, it was like a dream. We never expected to know oppression again."

The lieutenant saw where he was going with this. "But that wasn't the way it worked out?"

"No," he said, his eyes fixing on something she couldn't see. "It didn't work out that way at all. We had just exchanged a Zendak'aan tyrant for one who looked more familiar to us. And for some of us, like myself, the fight began all over again."

It sounded familiar. B'Elanna told him so.

"Except we fought on behalf of many different worlds—many different peoples," she said. "And our enemy," she added, unable to keep the venom out of her voice, "was a race called the Cardassians."

Tolga nodded. "Then you know what it's like. To strike and escape, then strike again. To know it's only a matter of time before you're discovered and sentenced to death."

"Actually," she said, "it was a toss-up as to what would do us in first—the Cardassians or the ships we cobbled together. But yes, I know what it's like to be on the run."

He frowned deeply, staring off into some imagined distance again. "Seven nights ago, we sabotaged a weapons factory on one of our moons. Blew it up. I suppose we didn't retreat quickly enough. We were stunned, every last one of us. The next thing we knew, we were on a ship—the one where we first saw you and your friend there." He indicated Kim with a thrust of his chin.

"No court of law?" asked the lieutenant. "No trial, no sentencing?"

His expression said she had just made a miserable excuse for a joke.

"None," he said. "When there's a need for workers on the stations, Nograkh justice can be swift."

B'Elanna understood. Klingon law could be the same way. Quick, merciless, and often irrevocable. Or so she had heard.

Tolga's nostrils flared with anger. "I wish I were free again," he said. "Just for a little while. I would have done more to weaken the tyrant." The muscles worked savagely in his temples. "I would have done a great many things."

There was silence in the wake of his comment. Then her curiosity got the better of her.

"I hope I won't offend you by asking," she said, "but that Nograkh you killed—was his death really necessary?"

Tolga nodded. "Honor demanded that as well. He was someone who had betrayed me years ago, before I joined the rebellion. There's nothing more onerous than betrayal. It can't be tolerated. That's the Nograkh way."

"Later on," she said, "there was another fight. But you didn't let that one continue."

He shrugged. "That, too, was a case of betrayal. But the combatants weren't evenly matched. The bigger one will have to find someone the size of the smaller one to fight for him."

B'Elanna absorbed the information. "I see." Silence again. "Well, it was good talking to you." She got up.

Tolga looked up at her. "You fight well," he observed. "I think you'll survive here as long as anyone."

She smiled at the dark-edged nature of his comment. Then, with the same understated irony in her voice, she said, "Thank you."

And she crossed the room again to join Kim.

Tolga intrigued her, the lieutenant acknowledged. While there was no question about his bitterness or his potential for cold-blooded violence, she couldn't help but feel there was a certain nobility about him as well—an unswerving fidelity to his own ethical code.

In fact, he'd risked his life for what he believed in. And if that wasn't nobility, she didn't know what in the universe *was*.

Kes leaned back in her chair and eyed the Doctor across his desk. "So that's the problem," she said.

"Pacria believes the cure for her disease came at the cost of her people's misery and degradation."

"Yes," she confirmed with a sigh. "And that's why she won't let us use it to save her life."

The Doctor's brow furrowed. "I don't understand. If Pacria's people hate this vaccine so much, why was it included in their ship's data base?"

The Ocampa nodded. "That's a good question. Apparently, all Emmonac vessels—including Pacria's, which was on some kind of stellar research mission—access and use scientific data gathered by the Zendak'aa. After all, in most fields of endeavor, Zendak'aan research wasn't conducted at the expense of the Emmonac."

"Only in the biological sciences," the Doctor inferred.

"Exactly," said Kes. "And where it *was* gathered at the expense of the Emmonac, it was left there anyway—for historical purposes, to remind Pacria's people of what they endured at the hands of their oppressors."

The Doctor frowned. "I see."

There was silence for a moment, as they considered the situation from their respective points of view. Kes was the first one to break that silence.

"It's insane," she concluded.

The Doctor harrumphed. "I agree. There's an old Earth expression about cutting off one's nose to spite one's face. I believe it has some relevance in this case."

"Ultimately," said the Ocampa, "research is research. Data is data. And if it can save a life, especially your own, it seems silly not to use it."

"Again," the Doctor said, "I concur wholeheartedly. But it really doesn't matter what you and I think. The only opinion that matters is Pacria's. And as far as she's concerned, the cure I offered her is tainted."

"Tainted with her people's blood. I know. But," Kes went on, "if she dies, it'll just mean more blood. More misery. At least if she lives, her people's sacrifice will have meant something. It will have had some value."

The Doctor shrugged. "Not in Pacria's estimate. And for all we know, the Emmonac who died in Varrus' clinic might have looked at this the same way she does. Since they're dead, there's really no way to know."

The Ocampa bit her lip. "There's got to be a way to help her."

"We don't have the right to decide that for her," the Doctor rejoined. "We can only help her if she *wants* to be helped. And from what I've seen so far, I wouldn't be too optimistic on that count."

Kes turned to him, her frustration flaring into uncharacteristic anger. "But you're a *physician.* How can you just sit there and watch someone die—without trying to do something about it?"

The Doctor remained calm. "In fact," he said, "I *am* going to do something about it. I'm going to seek a cure that is not based on Zendak'aan data." He sighed. "Of course, given my lack of familiarity with Pacria's disease, I'm not confident I'll find a cure in time."

"But you'll try," Kes noted. She shook her head apologetically. "I'm sorry. I didn't mean to become angry with you. None of this is your fault."

The Doctor acknowledged her remarks with a nod. "Make no mistake," he told the Ocampa. "It pains me to watch Pacria suffer. It pains me even worse to know she'll perish soon. But I'm a doctor. I can't force my patients to do what I believe is best for them. I can't make choices *for* them. I can only present a range of options and hope for the best."

"Even if the best is death?" Kes wondered.

He regarded her grimly. "Even then."

Intellectually, the Ocampa could appreciate the Doctor's position. He had been programmed to adhere to a strict code of ethics, and he couldn't diverge from that programming.

She could even see the sense in those ethics. If she were a patient, she would want the right to make decisions about her treatment. She would want to be able to decide her own fate.

But what Pacria was doing just seemed wrong to Kes. No matter what the Doctor said, she just couldn't sit still and watch the Emmonac die. There had to be a way to help Pacria despite herself.

And if there was a way, the Ocampa would find it. She promised herself that as sincerely as she'd ever promised anyone anything. But where was she to start? What was her first step?

Abruptly, it came to her. She got up from her chair. "I'll see you later," she told the Doctor and headed for the exit.

"Kes?" he called after her. "Where are you going?"

"To speak with the captain," she told him.

CHAPTER 11

Pacria had promised Captain Janeway she would go over the data they'd accumulated at the scene of the Kazon ship's destruction. And, to the best of her ability, she meant to keep that promise.

First, she looked at the ion pattern the destroyer had left behind. Though propulsion systems were hardly her specialty, the Emmonac knew enough about them to identify the technology that had created the trail.

It was Zendak'aan, of course. But that didn't tell her much of anything. Half a dozen races in this sector used Zendak'aan technology or some close variation on it.

Next, Pacria looked at the molecular decay patterns in the debris, to see what kinds of weapons had been employed. There, too, though she was not a military tactician, she detected the legacy of the Zendak'aa. But again, there were at least six or seven races currently in possession of that weapons technology—maybe more.

After that, she checked for organic debris, though surely Captain Janeway had done that as well. Pacria found only trace amounts, certainly not enough to identify the victim or victims, much less the manner in which they had perished.

Knowing how fond the Truat Nor were of ejecting memorial dust after a battle, she checked for the stuff. There was none in evidence. That ruled out the Truat Nor.

Pacria then combed the sensor data for gaps in the debris spread or indications of graviton particles. Either one would have made her suspect the Taserrat, who liked to use their tractor beams to snare trophies from the remains of their enemies.

As it happened, she found neither gaps nor gravitons. That meant the Taserrat were probably not the culprits either.

Beyond that, Pacria knew, there was little she could do. She would have liked to contact Captain Janeway and tell her she had located her colleagues. Or at least offer her some assurance they had survived the Kazon ship's destruction.

She wished she could leave these people a gift for all their kindness to her. However, it didn't appear she would get the chance.

Kes stood outside the door to Captain Janeway's ready room and waited for the computer to alert the captain to her presence. After a moment or two, the door slid open.

The captain was seated on the other side of her desk. She looked tired. Still, she managed a smile.

"Kes. What can I do for you?"

The Ocampa took a seat across the desk from Janeway. "It's about Pacria," she began.

The captain's brows knit. "Don't tell me she's suffered a setback? I just saw her in her quarters."

"Actually," Kes said, "she's recovering nicely. At least, as far as her injuries are concerned. But . . . "

"Yes?" Janeway prompted.

"She has a disease," the Ocampa explained.

The captain's eyes narrowed. "It's not contagious, is it? A danger to the crew?"

"No, nothing like that."

"Then what?" Janeway asked.

Kes described the illness in some detail. Having been trained as a scientist herself, the captain listened patiently and with great interest. Also, with great sympathy.

"Then it's fatal," she concluded.

The Ocampa nodded. "But," she added quickly, "we can help her. The doctor found a cure."

Janeway looked at her. "Then . . . what's the problem?"

Kes told her.

"What about an alternative cure?" the captain asked.

"The Doctor's working on it," the Ocampa noted. "But without success."

Taking a deep breath, Janeway settled into her chair to give the matter some thought.

"I see now," she said, "why Pacria didn't mention any of this earlier. She wanted to keep it to herself." The captain paused. "The Doctor is right, of course. You can't force Pacria to accept the cure. And it doesn't sound like any amount of arguing is going to change her mind."

Kes leaned forward, her hands clenched in her lap. "But I can't let her die. Not when we can prevent it."

Janeway smiled a sad smile. "I know how you feel. And believe me, I feel the same way. It goes against my grain to stand by and do nothing. But it's Pacria's life. It's up to her what she does with it."

Kes looked away. She had hoped the captain would be of more help—that she would come up with some fresh perspective, some brilliant insight, and therefore a way to keep Pacria alive.

Then Janeway spoke up again. "How much do you know about the Zendak'aa?" she asked.

Kes shrugged. "Only what Pacria's told me. That they were conquerors. And that they conducted hideous experiments."

"But there's information on them in our data files—correct?"

The Ocampa nodded. "All the data we downloaded from Pacria's vessel. But what does . . . " Her voice trailed off.

"But what's that got to do with your patient? And her decision to let herself die?" the captain asked. "It may have everything to do with it. If we can learn more about the Zendak'aa and the kinds of experiments they were conducting, we may obtain a better understanding of why Pacria's doing what she's doing."

The Ocampa's eyes lit up. "And maybe find a way to change her mind?"

"Yes," said Janeway, though her expression wasn't nearly as exuberant as Kes's. "At least, that's one possibility. The other is that, after coming to understand the Zendak'aa better . . . you'll come to agree with her."

The Ocampa looked at her. The captain wasn't joking. "I don't believe that will happen," Kes replied.

Janeway smiled that sad smile again. "Perhaps not. In any case, I guess you'd better get a move on. From what you've told me, our friend Pacria doesn't have much time."

"No," said Kes. "She doesn't." She got up and moved to the door, then turned around again. "Thank you," she said to the captain.

Janeway regarded her with obvious sympathy. "Don't thank me yet," she advised the Ocampa.

As Kes departed, the captain sighed. She wished she had known about Pacria's condition before she had put her to work.

She looked up at the intercom grid hidden in the ceiling. "Janeway to sick bay."

Abruptly, the holodoctor's face sprang to life on her monitor, replacing the sensor information the captain had been studying. "Yes?" he replied.

"Doctor," she said, "I just learned of Pacria's condition from Kes."

He frowned. "You would have learned of it sooner if you'd kept up with the reports I've been sending you."

"No doubt," the captain conceded. "In any case, not knowing about the disease, I gave Pacria an assignment. Nothing arduous, of course. I just asked her to look over some data for me—something that may help us find Torres and Kim. Any problem with that?"

The Doctor thought for a moment. "I don't suppose it can hurt," he decided. "Besides, she might welcome the distraction."

Janeway nodded. "Good. Keep me posted. And from now on, I'll take the time to read your reports."

The Doctor lifted his chin, only mildly pacified. "Acknowledged," he said. A moment later, he disappeared, giving way to the sensor data the captain had been studying earlier.

Propping her face on her hands, Janeway tried to concentrate on the information. She knew her work would have little value at this point, since she'd already gleaned about everything she could. If there were any other insights to be drawn from it, it would have to be Pacria who drew them.

And yet, she couldn't stop poring over the information. It was her only link to B'Elanna—and of course, to Kim. Her only way of reaching out to them. That made it hard for her to put it aside.

• • •

Pacria could no longer remain in her quarters studying the debris field data. She felt compelled to get out, to move around.

After all, she didn't have long to live. And even if *Voyager* was populated with a slew of unfamiliar faces, they were still sentient beings. They had the potential for happiness and sadness, just like her own people. Because of that, their presence was comforting to her.

As she found herself growing hungry as well, she headed for the ship's mess hall, expecting she could satisfy both her needs there—for company as well as for food. Nor was she disappointed.

As she walked in, she smelled something wonderful—so wonderful, in fact, it made her salivate. Winding her way past tables full of crewmen, she traced the smell to a cooking alcove of some sort. Inside it was a man with yellowish skin, golden eyes and a feathery tuft of hair that ran from his crown to the back of his neck.

He looked up as he saw her coming. And smiled at her, in a way no one else on the ship had done. It was an easy smile, an unassuming smile, that placed no demands on her. It simply told her she was welcome here, without limit or qualification, and always would be.

"Excuse me," she said. "I'm new here. My name is Pacria."

The man nodded. "Yes, I know. I'm Neelix. I run this place." He tilted his head to indicate a pot of stew. "Care for some?"

She didn't ask what it was. It smelled so good, it didn't matter to her. "Yes," she said. "I would. Please."

Neelix picked up a ladle that he'd hooked onto the lip of the pot and stirred the stew a bit. Then he fished up a chunky assortment of ingredients, emptied them onto a plate, and turned it over to Pacria.

"There," he said. "And if you'll wait a moment, I'll join you."

Repeating the process with obvious pleasure, Neelix prepared a second plate. Then he gathered up some implements and a couple of cloth napkins with his free hand and emerged from his alcove with them.

There was an unoccupied table just a few feet away; he took it. Pacria sat down opposite him. There were a beverage container and glasses on the table. Neelix poured some out for her, then himself.

"Thank you," she said.

"Well?" he replied, looking at her expectantly. "Dig in."

He didn't have to tell her twice. The stew was just as flavorful and satisfying as she'd anticipated. Neelix didn't start to eat right away.

"You like it?" he asked.

Pacria nodded. "Very much."

He grinned. "Good." Then he had a few mouthfuls himself. He seemed to enjoy it as well, if the look of bliss on his face was any indication.

"You know," she said, "it's very pleasant to meet a man who loves his work as much as you do."

Neelix shrugged. "What's not to like? People come to me with a need and I satisfy it. They come in frowning and leave with a smile."

"I'm not surprised," Pacria told him. "Especially if everything you make is as wonderful as this stew."

He shook his head. "I'm not talking about the food—though, of course, that fills a need as well. I'm talking about the camaraderie. The fellowship. When you're far from home, in a strange quadrant, it's important to know there's a place where you can sit down and unwind—maybe share an experience or two with someone who cares. Or failing that, with the cook."

"I see," she said, smiling at his joke. "But you *do* care. It's obvious."

Neelix became more pensive. "These people have become my family. That's why it's so hard to lose one of them. Or, in this case, two."

Pacria knew immediately whom he was referring to. "You mean the crewmen you're trying to recover."

"Yes." He sighed. "You know, I had a little tiff with one of them. But she had the decency to come in before she left and apologize. I'm glad she did, too. I would have hated to think her last thoughts of me—"

Neelix stopped himself, apparently too choked up to go on. Then he dabbed at one of his eyes, where he'd secreted some liquid.

"I shouldn't be acting this way," he said at last. "I'm the morale officer on the ship. I should be assuring you they'll be back in one piece, safe and sound. It's just that I've got this feeling. This *bad* feeling . . . "

"It's difficult to lose someone," Pacria agreed. "I know. I lost a whole ship full of colleagues. Nearly twenty of them."

Neelix's brow furrowed. "That's right. You did, didn't you? And here I am, crying over a couple of casualties that haven't even happened yet. I guess that was pretty insensitive of me."

"No, it wasn't," she insisted. She put her hand on his. "We're not talking about numbers here, Neelix. We're talking about people's lives. And every life is important."

He looked at her. "Yes," he said softly. "I suppose you're right."

Suddenly, Pacria realized what she had said. *Every life is important.* Every life.

Every life.

Even her own.

Pacria looked at her plate. In the course of the conversation, she had finished her stew. She slid her chair back.

"I ought to be going now. I told Captain Janeway I'd help her with something."

Neelix nodded. "Come by again," he told her. "As often as you like. On Monday, I'm making my famous root and tuber casserole."

Monday. Three days from now, she thought.

"We'll see," she said.

Pacria would have liked to give him an outright yes. However, as she might not be alive on Monday, it was a promise she was loath to make.

CHAPTER 12

THE SECOND NIGHT ON THE MINING STATION WAS DIFFERENT FROM THE FIRST. But it wasn't an improvement by any stretch of the imagination.

B'Elanna wasn't able to stand watch. She was too damned tired, too feverish from her prolonged exposure to the radioactive ore. Too full of pain inside and out.

Kim was no better off. He fell asleep as soon as his head touched his forearm, One-Eye or no One-Eye. But there didn't seem to be any danger of attack from One-Eye or anyone else. Like the Starfleet officers, the other prisoners were too fatigued to keep their eyes open.

Nonetheless, B'Elanna's sleep wasn't restful. It was shot through with flashes of pain, echoes of real-life aches deep in her bones.

Then she felt another kind of pain, sharper than the others. Again. And a third time. She opened her eyes and saw a Nograkh guard standing over her. He was poking at B'Elanna with his free hand. In the other one, he held a rifle pointed at the ceiling.

"You," said the guard.

"Me?" she responded.

"You," he confirmed. He jerked his thumb at the exit. "I've got an ore container that needs to be moved in the processing room."

There was another guard standing behind him, and two more at the door. They were all watching her. But all the other prisoners were asleep. Or if they weren't, they were doing a good job of faking it.

It was still lights-out on the station. A strange time for her to be lugging containers around—especially when she was the only one. Not that she had much choice in the matter.

But as she got up and started for the exit, she heard a scraping on the floor. Turning, she saw Kim scramble to his feet.

"I'll give you a hand," he said, still rubbery-limbed and bleary-eyed but obviously awake.

"No," the guard barked, raising his weapon until it was aimed at the ensign's chest. "Not you. *Her.*"

There was a look in his eye that B'Elanna didn't like. Still, she couldn't let her friend die trying to help her.

"It's all right," she told him.

Kim shook his head, never taking his eyes off the guard. "No," he whispered. "It's not all right. B'Elanna, can't you see what—"

"I said it's all *right,*" the lieutenant rasped. "That's an order."

Her companion snorted disdainfully. "Right now, that doesn't mean much. A court-martial is the least of my worries."

B'Elanna admired him for his chivalry. Quiet as he might be, Harry Kim had never been one to let down a friend. But it didn't change anything. She still couldn't let him sacrifice himself.

"Stay here," she begged him. "Please."

As she said it, she looked deep into his eyes, trying to speak to him without words. For a moment, he didn't seem to understand what she was trying to tell him. Then, finally, he got the message.

Satisfied he wouldn't make a fuss, B'Elanna crossed the room and went out into the corridor, with the guard close behind. Without speaking, they made their way to the ore-processing chamber.

Sure enough, there was a container full of ore there. But she didn't know how that could be. Hadn't Tolga and some of the others lugged all the ore containers to the storage room before they left?

No matter. It wasn't as if she could argue that this wasn't her job. She had to do whatever they told her to do. Approaching the container, she took hold of its handle. Then, following the guard's gesture, she dragged it across the floor.

Kes leaned back in her chair. Her research had given her much to think about. However, it hadn't given her a clue yet as to how she might convince Pacria to accept the Doctor's cure. Abruptly, a beeping invaded the silence. There was someone out in the corridor. "Come in," she said, swiveling around to face the door.

It slid aside, revealing Commander Chakotay. He smiled, though not with a great deal of enthusiasm. "Captain Janeway told me about your problem," he said. "Or, more to the point, Pacria's problem."

The Ocampa glanced at her monitor, which was filled with information about the Zendak'aa. "I've been trying to follow the captain's advice and find out more about the Zendak'aa. But I haven't gotten anywhere. At least, not yet." She sighed. "Would you care for a seat?"

Chakotay shook his head. "Thank you, no. I've got to get back to the bridge." He folded his arms across his chest. "Unfortunately, I don't have any special insight to share with you when it comes to the Zendak'aa. But I do have some advice."

Kes leaned forward in her chair. "I'm listening," she told him, so attentive she was almost childlike.

"When I was a teenager," he said, "my father took me on several hunting trips. At his insistence, we often hunted with bows, as in the old days on Earth. Remarkably enough, we were pretty successful.

"One time, we took my friend along on the hunt. This friend was a good shot, but not very patient. The first animal he saw was big and strong and my friend became overeager. He shot without aiming properly—without looking around to make sure it was safe."

Chakotay grimaced a little. "The shaft hit my father in the arm. I rushed to his side, intending to pluck it out—but he shooed me away. Then my uncle came over. Apparently, he'd had some experience with such things. Instead of pulling the arrow out, he pushed it in even deeper. So deeply, in fact, that it came out the other end."

By then, Kes was grimacing, too. "It must have hurt a great deal," she said. "Your father was a brave man."

Chakotay smiled, remembering. "He was very brave. And wise, too. Wise enough to know that you've often got to make something hurt more before you can make it hurt less."

The Ocampa's eyes narrowed. "You're speaking of Pacria's problem?"

"Yes," he said. "I don't know what it is you can tell her that'll make her change her mind. But I know *you,* Kes. I know how compassionate you are. How *kind* you can be. And I hope you won't let that kindness stand in the way of what you're trying to accomplish."

Kes considered what he'd told her. After a while, she nodded. "I understand. At least, I think I do."

"Good," said Chakotay. "Then I'll be going. But keep me posted, all right? And let me know if there's anything I can do."

The Ocampa assured him that she would do that.

B'Elanna gritted her teeth and strained against the weight of the metal container.

The thing was heavy enough by itself, but full of ore it was even heavier. She'd never seen one of them dragged by fewer than two workers, and sometimes it took three.

Still, she did the best she could. And slowly but certainly, she made progress. After a lot of groaning and struggling, she reached the opening that led into the corridors beyond.

On her way out, she imagined that Kim was still watching her—still worried about what she was walking into. But he'd decided to trust her when her eyes said she knew what she was doing.

And did she? B'Elanna asked herself. She sorely hoped so.

Once out in the corridor, she looked to the guard again. After all, she had never participated in the storing of the ore; she didn't know where the stuff was supposed to go.

The Nograkh pointed to her right with the emitter end of his weapon. "That way," he told her.

Once again pitting her strength against the weight of the container, she wrestled it down the corridor, its metal bottom scraping against the pocked metal deck. The guard followed her at a distance, his silver grey eyes crinkling at the corners. He seemed amused by her struggles.

That made the lieutenant angry, but she was careful not to show it. Subduing her Klingon sense of pride, she drew only on her Klingon strength. Little by little, sweat streaming down her neck until it soaked what was left of her uniform, she pulled the container along.

They passed a storage chamber, full of other containers like the one B'Elanna was dragging. But the guard signaled for her to keep going.

After what seemed like a long time, she reached another room—

another storage chamber, but smaller than the first one. And this one had a door, which slid aside at B'Elanna's approach.

Peering inside, she could see a couple of other containers full of ore. Outside of that, the place was empty.

"Inside," the guard snapped.

Light-headed from her exposure to the ore, hands chafed raw, arms cramping, B'Elanna wrestled the container into the chamber. The guard followed her in. And a moment later, the door slid closed behind him.

The Nograkh grinned savagely, his teeth gleaming in the uneven light. The lieutenant just looked at him, her chest heaving violently as she tried to catch her breath.

"The life of a slave," he growled, "is a hard one. Sometimes a deadly one. I can make it easier for you. Safer . . . if you let me."

It was just as Kim had warned her, B'Elanna told herself. It wasn't just work the guard wanted from her. It was something a lot more intimate.

And if she didn't give it to him, he would no doubt attempt to take it from her by force. After all, no one was likely to hear her calls for help in this secluded storage chamber. And even if they did, who was going to come to her rescue? One of the other guards?

"Well?" the Nograkh prodded.

B'Elanna wished she hadn't spent so much of her strength dragging the container. She wished she could lift her arms without pain, or slow the beating of her thunderous heart. But wishes weren't going to help her.

Biting her lip, she nodded. "Go ahead. Do what you want with me."

The very words were like gall in her mouth. But when one was fighting for one's life, one did what was necessary.

His grin widening, the guard propped his rifle against the wall and advanced on her. Big and powerful-looking, even for a Nograkh, he was easily a head taller than the lieutenant and twice her weight. And he hadn't been lugging around a container full of ore.

But then, strength wasn't everything. Had he been a Klingon, he would have known that.

Clenching her teeth against the acrid odor of his sweat, B'Elanna stood her ground as the guard reached out and grasped a lock of her hair. With a tug, he drew her to him, bringing her face within a couple of inches of his own. His breath stank even worse.

"Now," he grunted, "show me I've chosen well."

"Whatever you say," she breathed promisingly.

Bringing her knee up into the Nograkh's groin as hard as she could, she elicited a cry of pain and doubled him over. Then she interlocked her fingers and clubbed him over the back of his neck, drawing on the strength she'd inherited from her mother.

The guard fell to one knee, but didn't lose consciousness. It took two more blows, each louder and more vicious than the one before it, to knock the behemoth out entirely.

Without a moment's hesitation, B'Elanna scooped up the rifle he'd leaned against the bulkhead and peeked out the door. No one there. Lucky for them, she thought, and made her way out into the corridor.

She didn't really have a plan in mind. She just knew that this was a chance—maybe the only one she'd get. And she'd be damned if she wasn't going to take advantage of it.

It didn't take long to get back to the main chamber. No surprise there, she thought. It was a lot easier to run without a container full of ore dragging behind her.

It was only when she came in sight of the guards at the door that she slowed down. And even then, it was only long enough to take aim and fire her stolen rifle.

The first guard never knew what hit him. But when he went flying across the floor, it warned the second guard that something was amiss. He whirled, mouth agape with anger and surprise.

Not that it mattered. Another bolt of blue energy and he was laid out as well. Two down, she told herself, and one to go. And the best way to meet that last obstacle was the same way she'd met the first two—head-on.

Otherwise, she would let herself in for all kinds of problems. After all, the chamber was full of prisoners. It would be too easy for their Nograkh captors to use them as shields.

Without breaking stride she raced past the entrance, rifle at the ready. She could see the prisoners turning their heads as she appeared, stunned by the sudden turn of events. But no guard—at least not yet.

Then, suddenly, there he was. But he was prepared, tracking her with his weapon even as she took aim at him. They fired at the same time.

One of them cried out and was flung backwards, knocked unconscious by the force of a direct hit. Fortunately for B'Elanna, it wasn't her.

Of course, there was still a need for caution. Just because there'd been three guards there when she left didn't mean there'd be three now. But as she poked her head in past the threshold and took a quick look around, she couldn't see any other watchdogs.

She knew that could change—and quickly. Though there weren't any surveillance devices she could see, that didn't mean the Nograkh didn't have a way of detecting an uprising. Come to think of it, she mused, wasn't there a changing of the guards in the middle of the night?

Spurred on by the fear of getting caught, she darted into the chamber and found Kim. He looked just as amazed as any of the other prisoners, though he'd known what she was up to when the guard took her away.

He smiled at her with undisguised admiration. "Good going, Maquis."

B'Elanna looked around for Tolga—and found him. For a moment, their eyes met, and she imagined she'd gained some new respect in those silver orbs as well.

Then she turned back to Kim. "Let's go, Starfleet."

Together, they headed for the exit. As they ran past one of the fallen guards, the ensign helped himself to the Nograkh's rifle. Now both B'Elanna and her fellow officer were armed.

Nor were they the only ones. Tolga and the rest of the prisoners were right behind them, scooping up the remaining blasters.

Kim checked his weapon. "The odds are getting a little better, Maquis."

"Looks that way," she breathed.

But B'Elanna's optimism was tempered with a healthy respect for what they were up against. They still had a number of guards to get past—no one knew how many. And they also didn't know what internal safeguards might be used against them.

Motioning for the others to stop short of the doorway, she gritted her teeth and placed her back against the bulkhead. Then she stuck her head past it, to see if there was any sign of reinforcements.

It was almost her last act among the living. No sooner had she shown herself than the corridor was illuminated with blue energy beams. Cursing out loud, she pulled her head back.

"They're onto us," she told Kim.

"I figured that out," he replied.

"We'll rush them," said one of the Nograkh. He pounded his massive fist against the bulkhead. "They can't take down all of us."

"Yes, they can," B'Elanna barked, silencing the prisoner for the moment. "If we leave the chamber, we're as good as dead."

She could feel her anger getting the better of her as she sensed her opportunity slipping away. It was the Klingon in her, muddling her judgment, urging her to face her enemies head-on.

But she wasn't going to do that. She was going to think this through. There had to be a way out of here short of suicide.

"Wait!" snarled Tolga. "What about the ceiling?"

B'Elanna followed his gesture. The surface above them was made of individual plates, held in place by a suspended framework. If they could knock out one of the plates, they might find a crawl space beyond it. At any rate, she thought, it was worth a try.

Two of the Nograkh ran to the door, armed with rifles. They were going to give the lieutenant the time she needed to check out Tolga's suspicion.

Training her weapon on the ceiling, she blasted out a couple of the plates. Then she signaled for Tolga and one of the other Nograkh to hoist her up—which they were only too glad to do.

B'Elanna looked around. There was a crawl space, all right. And it showed her an opening that seemed to lead beyond the boundaries of their prison. She beckoned for the others to follow.

Kim came next, followed by a couple of the smaller prisoners. Lacking the luxury of waiting until everyone took to the ceiling, the lieutenant made her way toward the opening on hands and knees.

It didn't take long. Not with adrenaline pumping through her body like high-energy plasma. Not with the smell of freedom in her nostrils.

The opening turned out to be an abbreviated power conduit—though there was no evidence of the power that once ran through it. What's more, it wasn't as dark as it should have been. There was a dim, grey light up ahead.

Lucky me, thought B'Elanna. She crawled inside it.

"Harry?" she rasped, wanting to make sure he was still with her.

"Right behind you," he assured her softly, his voice nonetheless echoing in the narrow confines of the conduit.

At its far end, the conduit terminated as abruptly as it had begun—emptying into another crawl space. B'Elanna didn't know what kind of room was below it, but she didn't have time to think about it. All she could do was blast out a ceiling plate and find out.

As she approached the egress she had created, she exhaled softly. They were over one of the storage chambers for the separated ore. Giving Kim her rifle, she took hold of the metal frame that had supported the plate, swung down, and landed on the floor.

Then she looked up. One at a time, the ensign dropped their rifles to her. Then he came down after them.

Returning Kim's weapon to him, the lieutenant crossed to the door, which was wide open. Looking back, she saw several other prisoners drop down from the ceiling as well.

She didn't stop to count how many. That would depend on the Nograkh who'd volunteered to guard their retreat. Her job was to keep forging ahead.

Taking a breath, B'Elanna came closer to the door—and darted a glance out into the corridor. There weren't any guards apparent in either direction. At least, not yet.

Emerging from the storage room, she made a quick decision. A left would take them back to the air lock through which they'd entered the station—but it would also take them past the rest chamber. She opted to go right.

Heart pounding, she made her way down the corridor as quickly as she could. She didn't have any idea of what was ahead, of course. For all she knew, she was running into a dead end. But she went on in the hope she was getting closer to a way out.

That hope died as she heard the pounding of footsteps up ahead, where the corridor made a sharp turn to the right. Keeping her eyes forward, B'Elanna stopped and signaled for the others to retreat. It seemed they would have to go back past the rest chamber after all.

Then that option was taken away from them as well. Hearing a cry, then another, the lieutenant whirled and saw a flash of blue-white energy. Before her eyes, the prisoner she'd dubbed One-Eye toppled and crashed to the floor.

He wasn't stunned, either. Half his chest had been torn away by the force of the blast.

B'Elanna clenched her teeth at the sight, then turned again. The sound of footsteps was getting louder in back of her. Closer. Pinning herself against the right bulkhead, she raised her weapon and waited for the guards to show themselves.

They didn't disappoint her. They came out firing—and so did she. Except her beams bounced off an invisible shield—the kind the Nograkh had used in their takeover of the Kazon scoutship.

Great, the lieutenant thought. As if the odds hadn't been stacked against the prisoners to begin with. Clearly, they were in bad straits. Unless something went in their favor, and quickly, the escape attempt was doomed—and so were they.

As it happened, *nothing* went in their favor. Little by little, the guards whittled away at them from behind their transparent barriers. Prisoners fell all over the place, clogging up the corridor.

She didn't have time to take a head count, but she had the sense there were fewer than a dozen of them still standing. Then fewer than half a dozen. B'Elanna saw Tolga glance off a bulkhead, propelled there by a directed-energy barrage. Kim was knocked off his feet.

She did her best to blast away at the guards, but it was no use. They had the damned shields. They just grinned at her.

It couldn't end this way, she told herself. Not after all she'd been through. Not when they had come so close.

Then they cut *her* down as well.

CHAPTER 13

TUVOK WAS STUDYING HIS CONTROL CONSOLE WHEN MR. DUCHAMPS approached him. "Sir," said the junior officer, "I've got a problem."

The Vulcan nodded. "I am aware of it, Lieutenant. I have been attending to the same matter myself, after all. And if I am not mistaken, we have come to the same conclusion."

DuChamps glanced in the direction of Janeway's ready room. "I guess I should tell the captain." He seemed unenthusiastic about the prospect. Nor was it difficult to understand why.

"It is all right," Tuvok told him, letting him off the proverbial hook. "I will inform Captain Janeway myself."

The human nodded. "Whatever you say, sir." Looking grim, he returned to the station customarily occupied by Ensign Kim.

Tuvok sighed. There was no point in delaying the matter. Without another word, he rose from his seat and went to see the captain.

B'Elanna was surprised to find herself still alive. She had a nasty bruise over one eye and a soreness she attributed to incipient radiation fever, but she was still in one piece.

Quickly, she looked around. Kim was lying a few meters away, grimacing—but clearly, he had survived as well. Apparently, not all the guards they'd faced in the corridor had had their weapons set to kill.

It made sense, now that she thought about it. The Nograkh had gone to so much trouble to acquire their prisoners, why mow them all down out of spite? Why not preserve them so they could give the last of their strength to the ore-processing center?

The lieutenant heard something down the hall. The approach of footsteps—a great many of them. She crawled across the floor, grabbed Kim's arm, and roused him. His eyes blinked open.

"What's going on?" he groaned.

"I don't know," she told him. But in the back of her mind, she wondered if it had something to do with the escape attempt.

The footfalls got closer and closer. Other prisoners started to lift their heads as well, no doubt hearing the same thing. They exchanged looks but didn't say anything.

Abruptly, a squad of guards entered, walking past the pair at the threshold. At the same time, the lights came up, so brightly it made B'Elanna wince and shade her eyes. Beside her, Kim did the same.

"Up," said one of the guards. He pointed to a bulkhead with the barrel of his energy rifle. "Over there."

The lieutenant's mouth went dry. Getting to her feet, she complied with the guard's instructions. Kim moved along beside her as the prisoners formed a line against the wall.

Yes, she thought. This was *definitely* about the escape attempt. But that was all she knew, though she wished she knew more.

When the last of the prisoners was in place, the guards turned to the door. As B'Elanna watched, someone entered the room.

It was a Nograkh she hadn't seen before. Though he looked much like the others, big and ruddy and heavy-browed in his dark bodyarmor, there was an unmistakable air of authority about him.

Clearly, he was higher up in the station heirarchy than the guards were. Perhaps he was in command of the entire facility. In any case, he didn't allow the lieutenant much time to speculate.

"My name is Ordagher. I am the Overseer of this station. As such, I hold your lives in the palm of my hand."

He paused, eyeing each of the prisoners in turn. When he came to B'Elanna, he seemed to linger for a moment—but only for a moment. Then he went on.

"There was an escape attempt," Ordagher continued. "Like all escape attempts, it was a failure. Still, I cannot permit such things. They are wasteful, and waste is to be avoided at all costs." The Overseer's wide mouth twisted savagely. "I want to know who led the attempt, and I want to know it without delay."

B'Elanna's heart began to beat harder in her chest. This was it, she told herself. She shifted her eyes from one side to the other, curious as to who would finally give her away.

But no one did. In the wake of the "commander's" demand, there was silence. That is, except for the throb of heavy machinery that seemed to pervade the place at all times.

Ordagher's eyes narrowed under his overhanging brow. "I am not a patient man," he growled. "Again, I ask—who led this attempt?"

As before, his question was met with silence. B'Elanna swallowed. How could this be? She wasn't surprised that Kim would stand up for her—or maybe even Tolga, with whom she had established some kind of bond.

But the other prisoners? They didn't owe her a thing.

Nonetheless, they didn't point B'Elanna out. They didn't move at all. They just looked straight ahead in defiance of the Overseer, ignoring their instincts for survival.

What's more, Ordagher didn't get as angry as the lieutenant expected. He didn't even seem entirely surprised. But then, he was a Nograkh as well.

"You choose to be stubborn," observed the Overseer. He clasped his hands behind his back. "Very well. I know how to deal with stubbornness." He turned to one of the guards who stood behind him.

There was no order. Apparently, none was necessary. Without comment, the guard advanced to within a meter of one of the prisoners. A fellow Nograkh, as luck would have it.

Raising his energy weapon, the guard placed its business end under the prisoner's chin. Then he pushed it up a little, forcing the Nograkh's head back in response. For his part, the prisoner said nothing—did nothing. He just stood there, eyes fixed on oblivion.

Ordagher eyed the others. "Once more, and for the last time, I ask you who led the escape attempt. If I do not receive an answer, your fellow prisoner will die in the ringleader's place."

None of the Nograkh said a word. They seemed content to let their comrade perish for them. Maybe that was their way—but it wasn't B'Elanna's.

"Me," she said, loudly and clearly.

The Overseer turned to her. "You?" he replied, his brow furrowing. Obviously, there was some doubt in his mind.

"Me," the lieutenant confirmed. "I was the one who led the escape attempt." She searched inwardly for a way to back up her claim—and decided some facts might help. "One of your guards tried to rape me, and I grabbed his weapon. The rest just happened."

Ordagher shook his head. "No," he concluded.

"I swear it," she told him. She took a deep breath. "If you're going to kill someone, it should be me. No one else."

She could feel the eyes of her fellow prisoners on her. Tolga's, Kim's. And those of the guards as well. The prisoner whose chin rested on the guard's energy weapon was probably eyeing her, too.

The Overseer considered her a moment longer. Then he tossed his head back and began to laugh. It was a hideous sound, like the sucking of a great wound. Without looking, Ordagher pointed to the prisoner whose life hung in the balance.

"Kill him," he snarled.

Before B'Elanna could do anything, before she could even draw a breath, the energy weapon went off. There was a flare of blue-white light under the prisoner's chin, and a sickening snap.

Then his eyes rolled back and he fell to the floor, lifeless.

B'Elanna's hand went to her mouth. The suddenness of it, the horror and the injustice—it threatened to overwhelm her. She could feel tears taking shape in the corners of her eyes.

The Nograkh had accepted his fate impassively, unflinchingly. He hadn't said so much as a word in his defense. And all for a being he barely knew.

"Take him away," said Ordagher, with a gesture of dismissal. "And watch the rest twice as closely," he told the guards, "or the next neck that snaps will be your own." Then, glaring one last time at the other prisoners, he turned his back on them and left the chamber.

The guards took their spots at the exit. The lights dimmed. One by one, the prisoners drifted to their customary sleeping spots.

But not B'Elanna. She remained where she was, trying to get a handle on what had just happened. Trying to understand what she was supposed to do about it—what she was supposed to think.

The lieutenant felt someone's touch on her shoulder. Numbly, she turned to Kim. He looked white as candlewax.

"Are you all right?" he asked her.

She shook her head from side to side. How could she be all right? How could she just accept what had happened and go on?

Caught in the grip of unexpected anger, she looked for Tolga. Found him at the other end of the chamber, where he always took his rest. And stalked him like an animal seeking its prey.

As she approached, his back was to her. Still, the closer she got, the more he seemed to notice. Finally, he glanced at her over his powerful shoulder, his silver eyes glittering in the light from the doorway.

"You," she said, her lips pulling back from her teeth like a she-wolf's, her voice little more than a growl.

Then she made a fist of her right hand and hit him as hard as she could. Tolga's head snapped around and he staggered back a step.

She tried to hit him with her left, but the Nograkh managed to grab her wrist before she could connect. And a moment later, his hand closed on her right wrist as well. Finally, he kicked her legs out from under her and pinned her with his considerable weight.

Left with no other weapon, B'Elanna spat at him. "You could have saved him," she rasped. "You could have said something, but you just stood there and let him die for me!"

Narrow-eyed, Tolga took in the sight of her. "Should I have interfered with Manoc's sacrifice?" he asked. "Am I a barbarian, that I should have stained his honor?"

"It was me who should have died," she railed, hardly bothering to struggle. "Me! I led the escape!"

The Nograkh nodded slowly. "Yes. When circumstances allowed, you did what was in you to do. And Manoc did what was in him."

B'Elanna shook her head. "It should have been me," she moaned. "It should have been me."

Tolga didn't say anything. He just watched her expend her outrage and her sorrow. Then he got off her and let her get to her feet.

Kim had been standing nearby, ready to try to intervene if it became necessary. But it never reached that point. At no time had the Nograkh seemed willing to hurt her, even in his own defense.

Massaging her wrists, the lieutenant looked up at Tolga. "Why didn't they believe me?" she asked softly. "Why did they laugh like that?"

The Nograkh shrugged. "Ordagher didn't believe a female could lead a rebellion." He paused. "But then, he does not know you as I do."

B'Elanna nodded. Before this was over, she vowed, she would show the Overseer just how frail she really was.

Janeway was sitting behind the desk in her ready room, still poring over the debris field data, when a chiming sound told her there was someone waiting outside her door.

"Come in," she said, leaning back in her chair.

A moment later, Tuvok entered with a data padd in hand. His expression didn't give anything away, but the captain had known the Vulcan a long time. She knew when he was about to give her bad news.

"What is it?" she asked softly.

Tuvok frowned ever so slightly. "I regret to report that the ion trail has dissipated beyond our ability to recognize it. We can no longer follow it with any assurance."

Janeway bit her lip. "Can't we extrapolate a course based on the information we've accumulated so far?"

The Vulcan took his time answering. "That is not a promising strategy," he said finally. "There are any number of reasons why a vessel might diverge from its long-range course as it draws closer to its destination."

"I agree," the captain said, "it may not be promising. But unfortunately, Mr. Tuvok, it's the only strategy we've got." She leaned forward. "I would like you to create a computer model based on available data and come up with a likely course."

The Vulcan's nostrils fluttered, but he nodded. "As you wish," he replied. And without further comment, he left to fulfill that wish.

For a while, after the door closed behind Tuvok, Janeway sat and weighed the exigencies of their situation. It was something the captain had done a dozen times already since B'Elanna and Kim had disappeared.

Sighing, the captain looked to the intercom grid in the ceiling and summoned her exec.

"Commander Chakotay."

"Here," he replied.

"I would like to speak with you in my ready room," she told him.

"On my way," he said.

After all, Torres was one of the Maquis he'd commanded long before he'd even laid eyes on *Voyager.* Even if he weren't the first officer, he would have deserved to know what was going on.

CHAPTER 14

ALLOWING THE GRAY METAL DOORS TO SLIDE OPEN IN FRONT OF HER, PACRIA stopped and surveyed the place her hosts called sick bay. It seemed smaller and brighter than she remembered, even though it had been only a couple of days since she left.

The Doctor was waiting patiently for her inside. "Won't you come in?" he asked cordially.

Pacria entered. She looked around and saw that they were alone. Kes, then, was elsewhere. She found herself sorry to discover that. Despite the Ocampa's intrusiveness, Pacria had enjoyed her company.

"If you'll lie down on the bed," said the Doctor, "this will only take a few seconds. I just need to check your biolevels, perhaps take a few more esoteric readings. Of course, I can tell just from looking that you're not experiencing any setbacks with respect to tissue regeneration." His expression became a more sober one. "It's really just the virus I'm concerned about at this point."

When the Doctor had contacted her regarding this checkup, Pacria hadn't really seen the sense in it. After all, she was dying. That fact wasn't going to change, regardless of what shape her vital signs were in.

Then the scientist in her had chimed in, reminding her that knowledge had a value all its own. It was possible the Doctor's inquiries might help him refine the antigen, or at least gain a better understanding of what he was up against. And someday, that might save the life of someone less particular than Pacria about the origins of her cure.

In Pacria's estimate, that would be a good thing. She was all for saving lives. She just couldn't bear the thought of buying back her own with the coin of misery and degradation.

As the Doctor had requested, she lay down on the bed. He used a handheld device to examine her. And as he had indicated, it took only a few seconds. Then he looked up from the device.

"Thank you," he told her. "You may sit up now."

Again, Pacria complied. "I take it there are no surprises?"

"Only a small one," he told her. "It seems your exposure to so much radiation has slowed the virus down—if only marginally. Another such exposure might slow it down even more."

"How much?" she asked.

The doctor shrugged. "A couple of days, perhaps. Unfortunately, it would take almost that long to recover from the exposure."

"So nothing would be gained," Pacria concluded.

He regarded her. "Extremely little. I only wanted you to be aware of the full range of options."

Was that a note of sarcasm in his voice? Or a note of regret, because he hadn't found a way to heal her that she could accept? Either way, she decided to ignore it.

"I'm grateful," she told him.

"Think nothing of it," the Doctor replied. "Incidentally, I have something for you."

Returning to his office for a moment, he took something off his desk. Then he brought it out to her.

"I didn't know if it had any value, sentimental or otherwise," the Doctor explained. "And you weren't awake for me to ask, so I took the liberty of having it cleaned in one of our laboratories. It was coated with a considerable amount of radioactive debris, you understand."

Pacria took the object from him—and smiled. It was a flat, oblong brooch made of platinum. The raised symbol on its face was meant to represent two birds ascending in harmonious spirals.

"My badge," she said. She turned it over in her hand. "I received it less than a year ago."

Eight months later, Pacria realized she had contracted the virus. At the time, she had wondered how her crewmates would take the news of her impending death. She hadn't expected to outlive them, even in her wildest dreams.

Running her finger over the birds rendered on the badge, she made a decision—and gave it back to the Doctor. "Here," she said. "I want you to have it. For saving my life."

He looked at her askance. "I would like to say how much I appreciate the gift. However, as I've informed you, I am simply a holographic program. I have no need of possessions."

"Nor do I," Pacria reminded him. "I'll be dead soon. But your program will still exist."

The Doctor frowned and accepted the badge. "Very well, then," he said. "I will keep it . . . " He paused. "On my desk?"

She nodded her approval. "An excellent choice. That way, you won't have cleaned it for n—" Pacria stopped in midsentence, her mind churning. "Gods," she muttered. "How could I have been so stupid?"

The Doctor regarded her. "Stupid? About what?"

"I've got to get back to my quarters," she told him hurriedly, and bolted for the exit.

The doors slid aside just in time. She ran for the nearest turbolift as fast as she could, her breath coming in gasps from excitement as much as from exertion.

The captain, she thought. I've got to tell the captain.

No, another part of her—the scientist—insisted. First, she had to confirm her suspicions. *Then* she would contact the captain.

Paris was pushing some of Neelix's latest concoction around his plate when he saw Chakotay walk into the mess hall. The first officer looked as if he had lost his best friend.

Paris sighed. He knew the feeling.

As he watched, Chakotay picked up a tray and some utensils and walked past Neelix's serving area. Receiving a few hearty dollops of the same thing Paris was eating—or not eating—he proceeded to an unoccupied table.

To be alone with his thoughts? Paris wondered. Or because he didn't feel he'd be very good company right now?

The helmsman drummed his fingers on his tray as he considered joining the first officer. The risk, of course, was that he'd intrude on some private thought, some personal meditation.

But wasn't that what a person's quarters were for? If Chakotay had wanted privacy, he could've stayed in his room.

Casting discretion to the winds, Paris picked up his tray and made his way toward the first officer. What the hell, he mused, the worst he can do is convene a court-martial.

Once, the helmsman and Chakotay had been like two fighting fish in a glass bowl—ready to tear each other apart at the drop of a snide comment. It was a hostility that had its roots in their razor-edged days with the Maquis.

After all, Chakotay had left Starfleet and joined the rebel group on principle, to defend his home colony from the Cardassians. Paris, on the other hand, had screwed up as a cadet and never even made it into Starfleet.

Wandering from place to place, taking whatever jobs offered themselves, he'd steadily lost his self-esteem. He'd descended so low, in fact, he would have worked for anyone who could pay his bar tab.

In Chakotay's eyes, that made the younger man the worst kind of mercenary—someone entirely without ethics or attachments. And of course, that was no more than the truth.

Then, on the Caretaker's planet, Paris had risked his life to save Chakotay's. Though the older man had never actually acknowledged the debt, it was there nonetheless.

Perhaps because of that, their relationship had gradually become one of mutual respect—if not affection. And while Chakotay hadn't treated Paris any better than other crewmen, he also hadn't treated him any worse.

Then, one day, Janeway had called Paris into her ready room. Tuvok was standing there as well, looking even more solemn than usual. Apparently, the captain had said, there was a traitor on board. And Paris was going to go undercover to try to flush the bastard out.

The ploy was a simple one. He was going to be what everyone had believed him to be when he'd first signed on. A malcontent and a screw-up. Someone who couldn't be trusted to do his job. It had worked, too. And out of the entire crew, Chakotay had swallowed the bait the quickest.

Which was fine, at the time. It had made Paris's act that much more convincing. And in the end, they'd accomplished what they'd wanted—they'd identified the officer who was sending information to the Kazon.

For a while afterward, Chakotay was angry. After all, he hadn't been let in on the scam. It was as if the captain hadn't trusted him—though, of course, that wasn't her thinking at all. And the fact that she'd confided in Paris, of all people . . . well, that had to have hurt a little.

But to his credit, the first officer had gotten over it. Hell, he'd *more* than gotten over it. It seemed to Paris he'd found a new respect in Chakotay's eyes. In lieu of affection, it would have to do.

The helmsman stopped in front of the first officer. "Mind if I sit down?" he inquired.

Chakotay looked up suddenly, as if roused from a deep reverie. "No," he answered at last. "Of course not. Please, have a seat."

Paris sat. For a moment, neither of them said a thing. Then the helmsman broke the silence.

"So, what do you think?" he asked.

Chakotay looked at him. "About what?"

"About whether our friends are still alive."

The first officer shrugged. "I think they are."

"You don't sound very certain," Paris observed.

The other man frowned. "If you're trying to cheer me up, Lieutenant, you're not doing a very good job."

Paris smiled. "Sorry. It's hard to keep from being a little bitter about it." He paused. "You know, I felt responsible for Harry from the moment I met him. He was such an easy mark."

One that may already have met his end, the helmsman thought. But he didn't say it out loud.

"Where did you meet B'Elanna?" he asked.

Chakotay's eyes lost their focus. "Kaladan Three, not long after the Federation withdrawal from the border worlds. A group of Maquis there had gotten their hands on a load of phaser rifles. My job was to pick them up and pass them along."

Paris pushed his food around some more. "Even though the Cardassians were thick as flies there at the time?"

"Even though," the other man agreed. "As you can imagine, everything had to go like clockwork. Our people on the planet were awaiting us. I sent out the signal, dropped our shields, and gave the order to beam the rifles aboard." He chuckled. "But the rifles weren't all we beamed up. There was a humanoid in the midst of them. One you'd recognize, in fact."

"B'Elanna?" the helmsman asked—although the answer was pretty obvious already.

"In the flesh," said Chakotay. "Apparently, she felt her talents were wasted on Kaladan Three. She had some Starfleet training, so the leader of the cel there let her go. Good thing, too. We had barely taken off when a Cardassian caught sight of us."

Paris looked at him. "B'Elanna helped?"

"Did she ever. We were smaller, more maneuverable, but we couldn't match the Cardassian's speed—or his firepower. It looked like we were goners. Then B'Elanna started reprogramming our transfer conduits—funneling everything into the weapons array for one, big barrage.

"To me, it looked like suicide. Our engines were barely capable of warp eight. How were we going to generate enough force to punch through the Cardassian's shields? B'Elanna insisted there was no time to explain. I would have to trust her, she told me.

"By rights, I should have dismissed her idea and focused on evasive maneuvers. But there was something in her eyes, in her voice, that convinced me to go along with her." He grinned at the memory. "Of course, she had an ace up her sleeve. While on Kaladan Three, she'd spent her time researching and identifying Cardassian shield frequencies."

"Researching . . . ?" the helmsman asked.

"From Maquis ships' logs—what there were of them. The information had been there since the rebellion began. It was just a question of digging it up and having the ability to make some calculations."

Paris leaned forward, enthralled by the story. "But how did she know which frequency to go with?"

"She didn't," said Chakotay. "She had to pick the most popular one and keep her fingers crossed. Fortunately for us, she picked right. Our barrage pierced the Cardassian's shields as if they were never there.

"Before they knew it, they'd sustained massive damage to half a dozen systems. In the end, they were too busy trying to hold their ship together to worry much about us getting away."

The helmsman grunted. "A promising start."

Chakotay nodded. "Lucky, but promising. Unfortunately, the Cardassians eventually figured out we had their shield frequencies and changed them. But B'Elanna always seemed to stay a step ahead of them."

Again, there was silence. The first officer's lips compressed into a straight line. "I should have sniffed out the Kazons' trap in advance. I should have . . . I don't know, seen it coming somehow."

Paris looked at Chakotay disbelievingly. "You think you could have prevented this?"

The muscles worked in the other man's temples. "I'm the first officer. I'm responsible for what happens to my crew—good or bad."

The helmsman shook his head. "They're not children, Commander. You can't protect them from everything—not in space or anywhere else."

Chakotay turned to him, his dark eyes full of pain. "I understand what you're saying, Lieutenant. I understand it perfectly. But making myself believe it . . . that's another story entirely."

Yeah, thought Paris, another story. And unfortunately for Harry and B'Elanna, it doesn't look like it's going to have a happy ending.

Janeway had decided to go out onto the bridge when she heard her name called over the intercom system.

"Captain Janeway? This is Pacria."

"What is it?" the captain asked.

"I've got to speak with you," came the reply. "I may have found something in the debris data."

"I'm on my way," Janeway told her.

CHAPTER 15

A FEW MOMENTS LATER, THE DURANIUM PANEL SLID ASIDE AND REVEALED Pacria sitting at her workstation, the graphics on her monitor reflected in her eyes.

"What is it?" the captain asked, moving to the Emmonac's side.

"This," Pacria replied, pointing to the screen.

Janeway looked over her guest's shoulder and saw an analysis of the debris field—one of the dozens she had studied so intently she'd almost committed them to memory. It showed a chemical breakdown of each fragment present.

Nothing jumped out at her. The captain looked at Pacria. "I don't see it."

Pacria tapped a control padd and magnified a particular piece of debris. It filled the whole screen. At first glance, it didn't seem any different from the other fragments. The same composition, the same thickness, and so on.

Then Janeway noticed a dusting of red dots. At least, they appeared red in the graphic. "Radioactive particles," she concluded.

The Emmonac nodded. "That's right."

The captain looked at her, still not seeing the significance of it. "But couldn't the destroyer's weapons have caused that?"

Pacria shook her head. "Only one race in this part of space has that kind of weaponry—and that's my own. And we don't go around annihilating enemy vessels the way this one was annihilated."

Janeway thought for a moment. "So the radioactive particles had to come from somewhere else."

"Yes," Pacria agreed. "And if we take an even closer look at them . . . " Again, she tapped a control padd on her board. And again, the magnification jumped significantly. ". . . we see that they're made up of a particular kind of radioactive material. Orillium, to be precise."

"I've never heard of it," the captain confessed.

"It's found in only one place that I know of," Pacria told her. "An asteroid belt mined by the Zendak'aa when they were in power—perhaps a dozen light years from the coordinates of the debris field."

"Let me get this straight," said Janeway. "You're suggesting the orillium came from a mining operation? But how did it get *here?* Why wasn't it scoured off when the ship entered warp?"

"Most of the vessels in this sector were either built by the Zendak'aa or incorporate Zendak'aan design principles—and Zendak'aan shields don't fit the lines of a ship the way *Voyager*'s do. There's a considerable pocket between the deflector surface and the hull. When the shields are lowered and then raised again, debris is often trapped in that pocket."

The captain nodded. "Then a vessel could have lowered its shields in the vicinity of a mining facility, raised them, lowered them again where we discovered the debris field—and left some radioactive dust behind."

"Precisely," said Pacria.

"But it wouldn't be the Kazon," Janeway decided. "They're nomads. They wouldn't get involved in that kind of mining."

"True," the Emmonac confirmed. "At least, from what I've heard of them. But there are other races who would be only too glad to take over a Zendak'aan mining facility. The Torren'cha, for instance. Or the Nograkh."

Something else occurred to the captain. "If this dust got there the way you think it did, it means the destroyers had to lower their shields. But why would they have done that?"

Pacria shrugged. Obviously, she hadn't thought the matter through that far. "To allow a reconnaissance vessel to leave the mother ship? Perhaps to loot the vessel it had just victimized?"

"Or to take prisoners," Janeway suggested hopefully.

The Emmonac considered the possibility. "It could be." She looked up at the captain. "Then your comrades may still be alive."

"Yes," Janeway replied, trying to keep a rein on her excitement. "Pacria, can you give me the location of that mining facility?"

"Not the *exact* location," the woman said. "However, I *can* point you in the general direction. Unfortunately, my people's knowledge of that area isn't extensive."

Then she studied the screen and came up with some approximate coordinates. And added, "I wish you luck, Captain."

Janeway wanted to get up to the bridge, to tell her officers what she'd learned. She wanted to get their course corrected as soon as possible. But she restrained herself for just a moment.

Just long enough to say, "Thank you."

Pacria smiled a faint smile. "You're welcome."

Haunted by the Emmonac's expression, hoping Kes would find a way to change the woman's mind, Janeway made her way to the nearest turbolift.

As the turbolift doors slid open, Chakotay glanced at them. It was Captain Janeway, he noted. And she was clearly excited.

"What is it?" he asked as he met her at her center seat.

"A breakthrough," she told him—and explained what she meant by that.

The first officer took it all in. Before long, he was excited, too.

Unfortunately, someone had to play devil's advocate here. Someone had to question Pacria's findings and Janeway's confidence, and it looked like he was elected.

"What if that's not the only asteroid belt in the sector?" he asked.

"It's the only one Pacria knew of," the captain replied. "And her expertise is in stellar cartography."

Chakotay frowned. "But who's to say the destroyer returned to the mining station? What would it be doing there, anyway?"

Janeway considered the possibilities. "Mining stations need laborers, especially when they deal with hazardous materials. That might have been the destroyer's job—to acquire workers for their mining operation."

"Or for half a dozen other uses," the first officer commented. "As soldiers, for instance. Or to supplement the ship's crew."

"Perhaps," the captain rejoined. "But we've established that the destroyer had a link to the asteroid belt. It seems likely it would return there. At least to me, it does."

Chakotay looked at her. Janeway couldn't give him any real assurances. All she could do was guess. But in the time they'd served together, he had come to value her opinions. Her judgment.

And vice versa, apparently.

"All right," he said at last. "I'm sold."

The captain turned to Paris. "We're making a course adjustment, Lieutenant." And she gave him the coordinates.

"Aye, Captain," came the helmsman's response.

Chakotay eyed the viewscreen with its flow of stars. He desperately wanted this course correction to do the trick. But he wouldn't do any rejoicing until they had found B'Elanna and Kim.

Her clothes ragged and torn, her skin burned and blistering, Kes stood in the midst of the bustling Kazon-Ogla camp and contemplated her surroundings. They were spartan, to say the least.

The sun above her was a searing, blinding ball of fire. And though she stood in the shade of a simple tent, it offered no protection from the heat reflected up at her from the ground.

While the camp was made up largely of such tents, they weren't the only structures around. The bone-white, partially buried ruins of ancient structures were scattered about as well, bitter reminders of their mortality. And to the east, there were a half-dozen Kazon scoutships.

But that was it. No sprawling public squares, no cool blue fountains. No soaring ceilings or graceful thoroughfares or thoughtful works of art. And certainly no smiling faces.

Not in this place. Not in the desert, where the terrain outside the camp stretched as far as the eye could see in every direction, unobstructed by hills or vegetation or other camps. Only scrub plants and tiny lizards and insects lived on that barren surface, though even they could hardly be said to thrive there.

The Kazon-Ogla didn't thrive either. They were devilishly low on water, and their cracked, parched lips bore testimony to the fact. The sect only lingered to mine the ground for rare minerals, which they could then trade to other Kazon sects.

Though they told her they were her masters, they weren't dressed much better than she was. Nor were they nearly as well fed.

Kes heaved a sigh. She recalled the curiosity, the spirit of adventure that had driven her from her home underground. She remembered, too, the ferocity of the Kazon men and women who had seized her almost as soon as she'd emerged from her tunnel—then kicked her and reviled her when they realized it had somehow sealed itself after her.

Living among them had been hellish. She had served as a bearing maid, dragging about loads too heavy for her slight frame. And when she failed to pull the loads quickly enough, she had been beaten for her laziness.

The Ocampa remembered her misery here. Her shame at being treated like an animal. Her despair of ever seeing her loved ones again.

It hadn't been easy for Kes to program this holodeck recreation. Or, for that matter, to step inside it. It was so real, so visceral, she could almost imagine that her stay on *Voyager* was the dream, the illusion, and this the stark reality.

She had to keep telling herself that she was no longer a slave of the Kazon. That Neelix and the crew of *Voyager* had rescued her from her captivity. That she was safe.

In a sense, it was good that she was scared. In fact, it had been her goal to scare herself—to remind herself of the most frightening situation and the cruelest people she had ever faced. And to heighten the experience, to make it seem even more authentic, she had lifted the holodeck's built-in safeguards against user injury.

That way, she had hoped, she could empathize with Pacria. She could gain some insight into the woman's abiding hatred for the Zendak'aa. And, as Chakotay had advised, she could perhaps find the hard thing that would ease Pacria's pain.

"Ocampa dog!" bellowed someone behind her.

Kes whirled just in time to put her arms up, to protect herself from the attack. But even then, the Kazon's fist struck her a glancing blow. She tasted blood and felt herself spinning.

Abruptly, the ground came up to meet her. It slammed the wind from her chest and jarred the teeth in her mouth. Knowing her attacker was standing over her, ready to strike again, she got her hands underneath her somehow and pushed, arms trembling. But before she could prop herself up, she was seized from behind and wrenched about.

Suddenly, she found herself looking into the face of Maj Jabin, unquestioned leader of the Kazon-Ogla. It was a face twisted with anger and resentment. She should have expected this, the Ocampa told herself.

Jabin was part of the program she'd created. She'd wanted the recreation to be as painful as the memory that inspired it. And Jabin had been a big part of her pain.

"Don't you have anything better to do than lounge about?" the Kazon railed, a string of spit stretched across his mouth.

Then he struck her again, backhanded her across the mouth. Her knees buckled, but somehow she managed to keep her feet.

"Or do you think work is beneath you?" he rasped.

Grabbing her by the hair, he brought her face close to his. It hurt terribly. But she endured it.

Jabin's eyes were smoldering. "Maybe you'd rather put your feet up and watch the *Kazon* work instead?"

His lips pulled back and he struck her again. And again. And once more, until her mouth was swollen and bleeding and there was no strength left in her limbs. No strength even to plead for her life.

But the Maj didn't kill her. Why would he do that when he could take his frustrations out on her? When he could make himself feel better by making her feel worse?

No, he wouldn't kill her. But he could make her wish she were dead. Gracing her with a choice Kazon curse, he kicked some dirt on her, spat, and walked sullenly away.

Kes turned to look at him, her tears hot rivers of shame on her sunburned cheeks. She remembered it all now. The Ocampa always taught their children not to hate, but she had come closer to hatred in that moment than ever before in her young life.

By what right had Jabin held her against her will? she demanded silently. By what right had he made a burden beast of her, assaulted her body and trampled her dignity?

She would have liked to get up and tell him what she thought of him. She would have liked to wipe the savage smile from his face.

But she didn't—and not just because it would have meant an even harder beating. She held her tongue because she didn't want him to know how badly he'd hurt her. She didn't want to give him the satisfaction of—

Kes stopped herself in mid-thought. There was something there, she told herself. The kernel of an idea.

The satisfaction, she repeated inwardly.

The *satisfaction.*

Slowly, painfully, Kes got to her feet. She looked up at the sky, where the sun beat down on her mercilessly. It was also where she imagined the main controller mechanism for the holodeck to be.

The Kazon-Ogla were all staring at her. Pointing at her. Cursing her and laughing at her. And Jabin, her greatest tormentor, was laughing harder than any of them.

"End program," she instructed, though the swelling in her mouth made it difficult to speak.

Immediately, the Kazon and their camp and the surrounding desert disappeared. Mercifully, a yellow-on-black grid took its place.

The Ocampa believed she knew a way to deal with Pacria. But first, she would have to visit sick bay and ask the Doctor for some help. In this condition, she wouldn't be of much use to anyone.

CHAPTER 16

JANEWAY WENT OVER TUVOK'S LATEST UPDATE ON THEIR PROGRESS. THE news wasn't good, she reflected. Not good at all.

They had come within sensor range of the coordinates Pacria had guessed at, and there was no mining station to be detected. In fact, at this point, there appeared to be no man-made structures at all.

It seemed their hopes had been dashed yet *again.*

Given the finite nature of their supplies and the uncertainty of their mission, the commonsense approach was to abandon their search. To pull the plug, as it were . . . and live with the consequences.

And the captain was an avowed fan of the commonsense approach. She had demonstrated that over and over again to her crew.

"Janeway to Commander Chakotay," she said out loud.

"Chakotay here."

"I would like to see you, Commander. In my ready room."

Silence for a moment. "I'll be right there," he told her.

When the chimes sounded again, the captain gave him permission to enter. He looked like a man expecting the worst.

"Tuvok gave you his report," Chakotay noted.

"He did," she confirmed.

The muscles worked in the first officer's jaw. "We can't give up on them," he argued. "That's one thing we were clear about in the Maquis. No matter what, we didn't give up on anyone."

Janeway sighed and indicated the chair across her desk. "Please, Commander. Have a seat."

He sat. But it didn't diminish the determination in his posture or in his expression.

The captain swiveled her desk monitor around so Chakotay could see it. The first officer scanned the screen, saw the state of their food and water stores, then looked up.

"We're low on supplies," he said. "It doesn't change anything. At least, not for me. B'Elanna and Harry are still out there somewhere and we've got to find them."

"I don't wish to give up on our friends any more than you do," Janeway said quietly. "That's why I asked Lieutenant Tuvok to extrapolate a course when that ion trail petered out. It's also why, when he told me about the sensor scan, I didn't give the order to come about."

Chakotay's eyes narrowed. "But?"

The captain leaned forward. "I'm not giving up on them, Chakotay. You can set your mind at ease about that. I won't stop looking, supplies or no supplies."

He looked at her, surprised. Obviously, he'd expected to have a fight on his hands. "Then . . . why am I here?"

She leaned back in her seat again. "Two reasons. First, we have to impose a ration system if we're going to go on much longer. I don't think you'll get any argument from the crew on that count. There's not one of them who wouldn't rather go hungry if it means continuing the search."

"Acknowledged. And the other reason?"

Janeway frowned. "While we all hope B'Elanna and Harry are still alive, we've got to face the possibility that they're not. And both of them were important personnel on this ship."

Chakotay nodded. "In other words, we've got to plan for a transition. Just in case."

"Just in case," the captain echoed. "I'd like you to head down to engineering and lay the groundwork. So if it becomes necessary, the changeover will be as smooth as possible." She told him exactly what she wanted him to do. "I'd say we owe that much to the crew."

Her first officer smiled a little sadly. "Yes," he said, "I suppose we do." He got up. "If that's all?" he asked.

"That's all," she confirmed. "Dismissed."

The first officer started for the door, then stopped and looked back at her. "Thanks," he told her.

"For what?" Janeway asked. "They're my friends, too."

Chakotay stood there for a moment, speaking without words. Then he left the room.

Alone again, Janeway swiveled around to glance at her monitor. It didn't look any better than it had before. Common sense still dictated that they turn around and look for a Class M supply world.

And she was still a fan of the commonsense approach. But not this time. Not when two of her people were depending on her to find them.

Janeway and her crew had no one to depend on but each other. She wasn't about to forget that. And as she had told Chakotay, she wasn't going to call off the search while there was a ghost of a hope B'Elanna and Harry might still be alive.

Despite the difficulty of her shift, despite the considerable weight of her fatigue, B'Elanna couldn't sleep. Everything hurt, her throat most of all. Slowly but surely, the radiation was getting to her, drawing the strength out of her body.

She looked at Harry, who was dozing in and out of slumber just a few feet away from her. There were dark hollows under his eyes and his color was terrible. If she'd had access to a reflective surface, she was sure she wouldn't have looked any better.

Of course, they'd had their chance to escape this slow death, a better chance than any of them would have dreamed. But they had blown it sky-high. And they weren't likely to get another one.

The lieutenant saw someone stir on the other side of the rest chamber, where the Nograkh prisoners customarily congregated. It was Tolga. And he was headed her way.

She didn't say anything. She just watched him hunker down beside her, as if he had grown tired of his old sleeping place and was seeking a new one. His back was to the doorway, his eyes alive—though their sockets were beginning to look hollow.

"B'Elanna Torres," he whispered, "I need your help."

The lieutenant looked at him. "To do what?"

Tolga looked around, then whispered a little louder. "To escape this pit of a prison."

B'Elanna couldn't believe what she'd heard. Surely the Nograkh had uttered something else. "What did you say?" she asked.

He frowned and repeated himself. "To *escape.*"

The lieutenant looked at him as if he'd asked her to play dom-jot with the Kai of Bajor. That's how absurd the idea seemed to her.

"We tried that already," she reminded him. "As I recall, we didn't do so well."

"Last time," he said, "I didn't know what I know now."

B'Elanna sat up a little. "Which is?"

"That there's a secondary control location down the corridor."

"Secondary control," she murmured.

The lieutenant tried to recall seeing something of that nature as she was charging headlong through the hallways. Unfortunately, nothing came to mind.

"I spotted it before the guards stopped us," Tolga went on. He spread his hands out almost as far as they would go. "It looked like a door, this big and gray, with a couple of studs set into it. The controls are behind it. From such a location, a single warrior can shut down every hand weapon on the station." He paused. "At least, I think he can."

B'Elanna grunted. "You're not sure?"

"Until now," he said, "my experience has been limited to battle cruisers, each of which has at least two secondary control units. But what I saw here looks like the same thing. I'm willing to bet it performs the same function."

The lieutenant thought for a moment. There was a similar centralized override on Federation starships, to keep hand phasers in the possession of the overzealous from poking holes in the hull.

But this wasn't a Federation ship. It wasn't a Nograkh battle cruiser either. If Tolga was wrong about that big, gray door . . .

"If we can reach it," he told her, his whisper becoming harsher as his voice charged with excitement, "we can disable the guards' weapons. And since there are more of us than there are of them—"

"We can overwhelm them," B'Elanna noted.

"Yes. And when the next mining ship arrives, we grab it—and get out of here. No one will know there's a problem on the station for hours—maybe even days, if we're lucky." He leaned closer to her. "The Nograkh would follow *me,* but the others wouldn't. They have no love for my kind. But an outsider *like you* . . . one who has already earned their respect . . . "

She sighed. "I don't mind the idea of leading. But what if the gray door isn't what you think it is?"

Tolga shrugged. As he had pointed out, it was a gamble. And they would be wagering nothing less than their lives.

Of course, the alternative was to die by inches—and the lieutenant's confidence in the possibility of rescue was waning fast. She still believed *Voyager* would manage to track them down—but she was starting to doubt she'd be alive to see the ship arrive.

Tolga's mouth twisted. "I do not wish to rot in this place—to wither from radiation poisoning. This way, the worst that will happen is we will die fighting. For a warrior, that's not so bad . . . is it?"

B'Elanna considered the question. "No," she conceded. "It isn't."

"Then you'll lead us?" he asked.

"I'll lead you," she confirmed.

The Nograkh nodded his hairless head and moved away. That gave the lieutenant a chance to wake Kim and tell him what she had agreed to.

As Chakotay entered engineering, he looked around. Without a doubt, a change had taken place there.

It wasn't anything he could put his finger on. Certainly, everyone seemed to be going about his or her assignment with the same efficiency as before. A glance at a control console told the first officer that all systems were functioning within normal parameters.

And yet, he thought. *And yet.*

"Can I help you, sir?" said a voice.

Turning, Chakotay saw Lieutenant Carey approaching him. The redhead gave the unfortunate impression of a mother bird defending her young.

But then, in a way, Carey saw the engines as his babies and the engine room as his nest. That had been all too apparent in his brief stint as head of engineering, after the death of *Voyager*'s first chief engineer and before B'Elanna's assumption of the post.

"I need to speak with you," the first officer told him.

Chakotay ushered the man to an unpopulated corner of the engine room. Then he looked Carey in the eye and forged ahead.

"While we're continuing the search for Lieutenant Torres and Ensign Kim," he said, "we have to prepare for the possibility that we won't find them. In that event, Mr. Carey, the captain wants you to take over here as chief of engineering."

The man nodded. "I'd heard the search wasn't going well."

"That's true," Chakotay confirmed.

Carey looked down at his hands. "You know," he said, "there was a time when I might have taken this differently. Not that I ever wished anything terrible would happen to Lieutenant Torres—I wasn't *that* petty. But you'll recall we had our differences."

The first officer recalled it vividly. In one altercation, B'Elanna had even broken Carey's nose. In several places, apparently.

"At first," the engineer confessed, "I thought she was just a Maquis hothead, with no appreciation for protocols or regulations. But I found out otherwise." He looked up. "No offense, sir."

"None taken," Chakotay assured him.

Carey went on. "I've served under a good number of chief engineers, as you know from my service record. None of them was as bright or innovative . . . or as well loved as Lieutenant Torres.

The first officer swallowed. "Yes," he said. "I know. And I appreciate your saying so, Mr. Carey. But we have to carry on."

The redhead nodded. "Aye, Commander. You can depend on me."

Chakotay managed a smile. "That's what I was hoping you'd say. Keep up the good work, Lieutenant."

"I'll try," Carey said.

Taking his leave of the man, the first officer headed for the exit. He still held out the hope that his officers were still alive, and that Carey wouldn't have to take over engineering after all.

But that hope was a slim one. And, the spirit-guides help them, it was growing slimmer by the minute.

CHAPTER 17

JANEWAY WALKED OUT ONTO THE BRIDGE, NOT AT ALL LOOKING FORWARD TO what she had to do. After all, she'd been so hopeful about Pacria's hunch. They'd *all* been hopeful.

But the course they'd been pursuing hadn't been a fruitful one. They'd expended time and effort—and more important, precious resources—and they hadn't found a thing.

They had to regroup, go back to their previous plan—the one based on Tuvok's data extrapolations. Janeway didn't feel good about it, but it seemed to be their only other option.

And she was in command of this vessel. If she didn't make the hard decisions, who would?

Reaching her captain's chair, she sat. Then she turned to her helmsman. "Mister Paris?"

He turned in his seat, obviously with an inkling of what was coming. "Aye, ma'am?"

"Lay in a change of course," Janeway ordered. "Bearing two-three-four-mark-two."

"Acknowledged," said Paris, containing what had to be considerable disappointment. He turned back to his controls and made the necessary adjustments. "Coming about," he announced, in a voice that was dutiful but devoid of animation.

"Captain," said Tuvok.

Janeway glanced at him, wondering what he wanted to say to her. Surely, he wasn't having second thoughts about his advice to her.

"What is it, Lieutenant?"

The Vulcan's features remained as passive as ever. However, there was a gleam in his eye that told her he was on to something.

"I have detected something on the long-range sensor grid," Tuvok explained. "I believe it is a station of some sort."

The captain took a few steps toward him, her heart leaping in her chest. "A station?" she repeated. *The* station?

"Yes," he confirmed. "And while there is nothing to indicate that our comrades may have been taken there, it does seem to be the only fabricated body in this sector."

Janeway nodded. "Can you give me a visual, Lieutenant?"

"I will try," he replied.

A moment later, the viewscreen filled with the image of an unmoving starfield. It was only by concentrating that the captain could make out a small, gray shape in the midst of it—a man-made facility surrounded by a thick swarm of asteroids.

Asteroids. *Mining,* she thought. It was looking better and better.

The station seemed whole and in working order. And with any luck, they would find Torres and Kim there—also whole and in working order. Janeway fervently hoped so.

"Captain," said Chakotay. "We've got to check it out."

"I agree," she told him. Her eyes narrowing with determination, she turned to her helm officer. "Mister Paris? Belay that last order and resume our previous course."

The helmsman smiled at her. "I would be happy to," he responded, his fingers dancing over his console with unbridled enthusiasm.

Beside the captain, Chakotay muttered something in his Native American dialect. Though all but unintelligible to her, it was unmistakably a declaration of hope.

Janeway smiled at him. "Best speed," she added.

After all, the station was still a long way ahead of them. And truth be told, she was every bit as eager as the others were to get there.

No. *More* so.

• • •

B'Elanna woke with someone's hand on her arm. Fortunately, she had the presence of mind not to voice her surprise or lash out—at least until she saw whose hand it was.

As it turned out, the hand was Kim's. And it took the lieutenant only a moment to gather her faculties and remember why he would be waking her. Getting up on one elbow, she looked around.

Most of the prisoners were awake. And those who weren't were being prodded by those who were. There was an air of expectation in the room, like a silent predator coiling for an attack.

The trio of guards standing outside the rest chamber didn't seem to realize there was anything afoot. That was good. If the guards had suspected, her ruse wouldn't have stood a chance.

B'Elanna eyed Tolga. He noticed her scrutiny and returned it. One way or the other, he seemed to be saying, they had worked their last shift in the station's ore-processing center. One way or another, they had seen the last of this place.

That was fine with her. But the lieutenant was determined it would be *her* way. In other words, *alive.*

"It's time," Kim whispered to her.

"High time," B'Elanna agreed.

She waited until everyone seemed alert. Then she looked to Ogis, one of the Nograkh. The warrior nodded, got up and made his way to where Ram's Horns was hunkered down. Ram's Horns did his best not to make it obvious he knew what was coming.

The Nograkh mumbled something, then gave Ram's Horns a shove with the heel of his boot. Grabbing Ogis's foot, Ram's Horns toppled the Nograkh. Then Ram's Horns pounced on him.

That drew the guards' attention. They looked at each other and smiled. True to form, they came inside the rest chamber but remained aloof and apart from the fight, more entertained than concerned.

If all went as planned, thought the lieutenant, that would prove to be a mistake. A *big* mistake.

Meanwhile, Ram's Horns and the Nograkh were going at it as if they really meant it. And by then, maybe they did. Despite their dedication to a common goal, their instincts had to be crying out for them to defend themselves.

That was also fine with B'Elanna. It would only make their performances more convincing.

Finally, the guards had seen enough. While one waited by the threshold, the other two moved to break up the fight. There was a moment when B'Elanna and Kim and the other prisoners seemed to hold their collective breath. Then they boiled over into quick and brutal action.

Tolga moved first, delivering a kick to the arm of the nearest guard. As the Nograkh dropped his weapon, another prisoner grabbed it and a third tackled him at the knees.

The second guard spun around, bringing his weapon up. But someone latched onto its barrel and forced it toward the ceiling. And before he could get off a blast, he was swarming with prisoners eager to repay him for his kindnesses.

The only problem was the guard at the door. B'Elanna saw him hesitate, uncertain of whether to intervene or go for help. In the end, he decided to intervene.

Raising his energy rifle, he barked out a warning. It had no effect on the prisoners, who were still contending with the other guards. Snarling, the guard at the door got off a shot.

It hit one of the Nograkh prisoners in the back. Crying out a curse, he spun and hit the floor, a seething black hole where the energy beam had speared him. The guard fired again and laid waste to another prisoner.

By then, B'Elanna had crossed the room and was gathering momentum. The guard must have noticed her, because he whirled in her direction. But it was too late.

Hurtling across the space between them, the lieutenant reached for the Nograkh's throat. Her fingers closed on it and squeezed, cutting off his air supply. Hanging onto his weapon with one hand, he tried to tear her arms away with the other—but she held on.

Then someone else grabbed the guard from behind, and a third person ripped his weapon out of his hand, and he went down under a mountain of angry prisoners. What's more, B'Elanna couldn't find it in her heart to feel sorry for him.

Their captors had laid down the ground rules. She and the other ore-slaves were just playing by them.

Kim joined her. "Are you all right?" he asked.

"Never better," the lieutenant lied.

Tolga tossed her a weapon he'd stripped from a guard. "This way," she cried, raising the weapon like a banner.

Advancing to the entrance, B'Elanna peeked out into the corridor to make sure there weren't any guards lying in ambush. Seeing that the corridor was empty, she beckoned for the others to follow.

Then she bolted from the rest chamber in the direction of the secondary control center, with Kim and the others right behind her.

For a long time Janeway had remained in her captain's seat, regarding the image of the station up ahead of them. Gradually, almost imperceptibly, the facility and its accompanying asteroid field had loomed larger and larger, until they had nearly filled the screen.

Now they were only minutes away from their objective, and Janeway could feel butterflies in her stomach. It was one thing to search for days on end. It was quite another to face the moment of truth that would tell them if all their efforts had been in vain.

Nor was the captain the only one who had found the station of unavoidable interest. Chakotay had been intent on it as well. Tuvok, too. And Paris, who had found a family on this ship and must have hated the idea of leaving some of it behind.

Sighting the station had given them a second chance, Janeway reflected. A chance to buck the odds and bring their friends home. And it wouldn't have been possible without Pacria, who had herself been given a second chance when *Voyager* found her on her doomed research vessel.

Kindness for kindness. Measure for measure.

If the scales of Justice were in working order in the Delta Quadrant, they would find their friends Torres and Kim alive and unharmed. And the two of them would have a chance to meet the stranger who'd made the key contribution to their rescue.

The captain didn't know whether Kes would be successful in her attempts to preserve Pacria's life. She didn't know what Kes would try or how the Emmonac would react. But she hoped with all her heart that Pacria would be rewarded for all her hard work.

In whatever way she valued the most.

Janeway had barely completed her thought when she saw something new on the viewcreen. She leaned forward.

"Ships," she said out loud.

"Indeed," Tuvok confirmed. "Six of them, to be precise."

The captain studied the vessels. "They're too small to be of any tactical use," she decided. "They must be transports."

As she watched, the ships began to dock along the flanks of the larger structure. They looked like grim, gray babies trying to get nourishment from an equally grim-looking mother.

That made sense. A mining station would need raw materials brought in and pure ore taken out. And since these people had no access to transporter technology, they had only one other option.

Chakotay moved to her side. "We don't know what those ships are capable of. In the Maquis, we had transport vessels that packed quite a wallop. And they may be faster than they look as well."

Janeway glanced at him. "You're saying we should stop here and wait until they leave?"

The first officer frowned. "I guess I am. Believe me, Captain, no one wants to get to that station sooner than I do. But I can be patient if it improves our chances of getting our people back."

Janeway took that into account. "All right," she said after a moment. "We'll do it your way, Chakotay. At least for now."

She turned to her helmsman. He was already looking at her, awaiting the captain's instructions.

"All stop, Mr. Paris. We're going to give those transports some time to discharge their business and take off."

But not forever, she added silently.

B'Elanna raced through the darkened corridor ahead of the other prisoners, trusting that each step was bringing her closer to freedom and the chance to be reunited with *Voyager.*

Suddenly, a squad of Nograkh guards spilled into the corridor up ahead, blocking their path. And, judging by the looks on their faces, they weren't taking any prisoners this time.

After all, this was the second escape attempt in as many days. In Overseer Ordagher's mind, this batch of laborers had to have become more trouble than it was worth.

The guards and the prisoners fired at the same time, illuminating the corridor with their firefight. Combatants sprawled and toppled on both sides, the sounds of their dying echoing from one bulkhead to the other.

Fortunately for the prisoners, the guards didn't seem to have the personal forcefields B'Elanna had seen earlier. In their haste, they probably hadn't been able to access any. But the bastards still had a decided advantage—they were better armed and they had a narrow space to defend.

And they didn't have to advance the way the prisoners did. All they had to do was hold their ground until reinforcements arrived.

Both sides fired at will, barrage after blinding barrage. The corridor was filled with cries of rage and pain. More bodies fell. One of them was a Nograkh prisoner beside B'Elanna, wisps of smoke twisting from the bloody ruin of what had been his head.

Picking up his energy rifle and tossing it to a comrade, the lieutenant sent a vicious burst at the guards. Then she slammed herself flat against the cold, metal wall to avoid their return fire. When it missed her, she squared and fired again.

Her second shot hit a guard and sent him sprawling, leaving one of his colleagues wide open. Taking advantage of the opportunity, B'Elanna pressed the trigger and fired again. The other guard went flying as well.

Her fellow prisoners were finding their targets also. Punching holes in their enemies' ranks. Before she knew it, there were only three guards standing. Then two. Then one.

Then none.

The corridor before them was littered with bodies, but not one of them was any kind of obstacle. And, just as important, the guards' weapons were lying there for the taking.

The lieutenant looked around. Tolga was still standing. So was Kim—and he'd picked up a weapon. But nearly a dozen prisoners lay dead at their feet, having paid the ultimate price for their freedom.

If they didn't want to join them, they would have to get a move on. As before, B'Elanna led the way. The others paused only long enough to pick up energy rifles from the fallen guards.

Then, like a riptide in a dark river, the whole pack of them moved down the corridor. The secondary control center couldn't be much farther now.

CHAPTER 18

B'ELANNA HELD HER WEAPON AT THE READY AS SHE NEGOTIATED A CURVE IN the corridor—and caught sight of a big, gray door with two studs set into it. It was just as Tolga had described it to her.

Pulling up alongside her, Tolga handed his weapon to one of his fellow Nograkh and flipped the cover off one of the studs, revealing a keypadd. Without hesitation, he punched in a code.

A moment later, the door swung open. There was a small room beyond it—packed with control consoles. Gesturing for the other prisoners to stand guard, Tolga entered it.

Kim moved to the lieutenant's side. "How did he know the code?" the ensign asked her.

B'Elanna shrugged, intent on the section of corridor before her. "He served on a Nograkh warship. Maybe the code is the same all over."

Kim grunted. "Doesn't seem like much of a security measure to me."

"You're not a Nograkh," she reminded him. Obviously, they had a different way of looking at things.

Suddenly, she heard the clatter of approaching footsteps. Signaling to her fellow prisoners to brace themselves, she trained her rifle on an intersection perhaps twenty meters away.

Then a squad of guards exploded into the corridor, bristling with weaponry, silver eyes slitted with violent intent. They took aim as soon as they spotted the prisoners, meaning to obliterate them.

But B'Elanna and the others got off the first barrage, choking the corridor with a blue-white display of destruction. Then they plastered themselves against bulkheads and floors, hoping to avoid the return volley.

But there wasn't any. Not at first, at least. And much to her chagrin, the lieutenant saw why.

The Nograkh's shields—the ones she'd seen for the first time on the Kazon scoutship. They were crawling with crepuscular energy strands, though the protective surfaces themselves were still invisible.

Behind them, the guards were laughing with their wide, cruel mouths. They were still grinning as they raised their weapons and prepared to pick off the prisoners at their leisure.

And Ordagher was among them, grinning the widest of all. The prisoners had been nettlesome to him, an annoyance. But now he would see that annoyance swept away.

That was what he seemed to expect, anyway. And B'Elanna was hard-pressed to believe in any other outcome.

After all, the prisoners didn't have any shields. They were sitting ducks, as the human saying went. And they couldn't retreat—or the guards would see what Tolga was up to.

So they stood their ground and fired again, hoping to blind the guards if nothing else. But some of them fell anyway—and most of them Nograkh, because they moved forward to shield B'Elanna and the other prisoners.

Not with personal force fields, because they didn't have any. Instead, they used the flesh and bone and blood of their bodies, sacrificing themselves so the others might live.

Absorbing burst after blue-white burst. Writhing in agony as the energy consumed them, cell by cell.

It was horrible to watch. B'Elanna cried out in protest. Kim, too. But before they could stop it, the guards' attack came to a halt.

The lieutenant's eyes had been dazzled by the fire of the battle, so it took her a few seconds to see the expressions on the guards' faces. They weren't the smiles of exhilaration she'd seen there earlier. They weren't the sneers of those whose victory was assured.

Not at all. There was doubt in their expressions now. There was trepidation, even a hint of fear. Something had happened—and the guards didn't seem to understand what it was.

But B'Elanna knew. The guards' weapons, even their shields, were no longer in operation. They'd been turned off. Disarmed. Made useless by Tolga, whose observation had begun to pay off.

As she thought that, she saw Tolga emerge from the control center. His expression was cold and deadly, less triumphant than determined. As he came forward, undaunted by the presence of the guards, he reached down and relieved a fallen comrade of his rifle.

"This won't fire any longer," he grated, suffused with righteous anger. "But it will still break a few heads." And with that, he turned it over in his hands so he was grasping the barrel instead of the stock.

Ordagher couldn't have risen to the rank of Overseer without being shifty, scheming, and manipulative. But there was no guile in the guttural cry that tore from his lips. There was no deceit in the savagery with which he charged at Tolga, brandishing his energy weapon like a club.

The two of them met in the center of the corridor like rival beasts vying for supremacy, their weapons clashing with a loud, resounding clang. Then the rest of the prisoners came charging after Tolga, intent on taking down the unarmed and outnumbered guards.

To their credit, the guards didn't retreat. They withstood the charge as best they could—but their best wasn't good enough. The prisoners rolled over them like a targ trampling a colony of pincered yolok worms.

B'Elanna was in the thick of the action, uppercutting a guard with the barrel of her weapon and then—when he staggered backward—smashing him across the face. As he collapsed to his knees, however, he was still conscious—so she felled him with a blow to the back of his head.

Beside her, Kim was battling another guard, rifle to rifle, as if they were fighting with quarterstaffs. But the ensign didn't have the Nograkh's strength or his stamina. Weakened by fever and exertion, he couldn't keep his weapon from being knocked out of his hands.

For a single, sickening moment, B'Elanna saw her friend stand there helplessly, his arms his only protection as his adversary raised his rifle for a death blow.

Nor was there anything the lieutenant could do about it. She and Kim were separated by too many clawing, struggling bodies. All she could do was watch and curse.

Then Ram's Horns came out of nowhere and slammed Kim's adversary into the bulkhead. Somehow, he found the strength to wrench the guard's weapon out of his hands. And with a fury not even a Klingon could muster, Ram's Horns beat the Nograkh senseless with it.

After that, the fight seemed to go quickly. In the end, the prisoners' numbers prevailed and not a single guard was left on his feet. And when B'Elanna looked back, gasping for air after her exertions, she saw Tolga had won his contest as well.

He was standing over a beaten and bloodied Ordagher, clutching a fistful of the Overseer's tunic in one hand while he hefted his rifle-club menacingly with the other.

But there was no longer any need for it. Ordagher was dead, his skull caved in just above one eye.

Tolga allowed Ordagher to fall to the deck. Then he turned to B'Elanna, awaiting her orders.

She pointed to the weapons that lay on the floor unclaimed. "Gather the rifles," she said—not just to Tolga, but to all the surviving prisoners. "When we've got them all in hand, I'll activate them from the control center. Then we can keep the guards at bay until a transport arrives."

Abruptly, there was a flashing of red and blue lights from inside the control center. A moment later, it was followed by a ringing.

B'Elanna looked at Kim, then at Tolga. She smiled a ragged smile. "I think a transport is here."

Tolga darted into the control center, B'Elanna and Kim on his heels. The Nograkh consulted one of the instrument panels for a moment. Then he shook his head.

"Not a transport," he said. He glanced at the lieutenant. "That is, not *just* one. There are *six* of them."

Six, thought B'Elanna. "And all of them full of Nograkh who won't be pleased to see us escape."

Tolga nodded. "But they don't know what's happened here yet. If we hurry, we can catch them by surprise." And he set to work reactivating the weapons they had seized.

A couple of seconds later, the lieutenant could feel a surge of power in her rifle as its energy cell came back to life. They were armed now—at least most of them were. And, as Tolga had pointed out, the transport crew wouldn't be expecting a problem here when they docked.

But it would be too hard to take on all those transports at once. They would have to focus their efforts on one or two of them and hope they could get away before the other crews caught on.

B'Elanna said as much. Said it out loud so everyone could hear. "We'll take the first two transports that try to dock. Strike hard and fast, and we should succeed."

Tolga eyed the other prisoners from beneath his jutting brow. "I know these ships. I'll pilot the first craft. And the other . . . "

He turned to B'Elanna, but she shook her head. "Kim. He's a better pilot than I am."

Tolga regarded the man. "Kim, then," he confirmed.

The muscles worked in the ensign's temples. "I'll do what I can," he told them, his voice strong despite his pallor.

Satisfied, Tolga slammed the door of the control center and led them all in the direction of the docking ports.

Janeway was growing impatient. She and *Voyager* had been maintaining their position for nearly an hour and the transport ships were still clustered around the station.

"I'm getting antsy," she confessed to Chakotay, who was still standing by her side.

"You're not the only one," he confessed in turn.

The captain chewed the inside of her cheek. "They could remain there for hours. A day. Even several."

"And when they leave," the first officer noted, "they may take more than just ore."

Janeway looked at him. "You think they transport prisoners from place to place? Say, from this mining facility to another?"

"If casualties have been greater in the other one?" Chakotay shrugged. "Stranger things have been known to happen. And if we were to scan the station *after* B'Elanna and Kim had been taken off . . . "

"And not find them . . . " she said, picking up the thread.

"We wouldn't know whether the ships had taken them away or they'd never been there in the first place."

The captain shook her head. That way lay madness. Trying to guess where they'd gone wrong, what they might have done differently—wondering which of the transports, if any, had whisked their friends to another facility.

Of course, there was a way to avoid all that.

"I think I've changed my mind about waiting," said the first officer.

Janeway nodded. "Me, too." She raised her voice so Paris could hear. "We're going in, Lieutenant. Warp six. Drop to impulse when we get within two million kilometers of the asteroid belt."

"Aye, ma'am," came the response.

"Red alert," called the captain. "All hands to battle stations. Mister DuChamps, I'll need a tactical analysis of—"

She found herself stopping in mid-command, her mind riveted on what was going on around the station. Suddenly, a couple of the transports had begun to move—to depart. But not in the leisurely way she'd expected.

They looked like they were running *away.*

B'Elanna stood on one side of the air lock, Kim on the other. The white light on the bulkhead showed them the transport outside was in the process of docking. Or anyway, that's what Ogis had told them.

And Ogis was in a position to know. Like Tolga, he had served on a Nograkh battle cruiser.

Suddenly, the light on the bulkhead turned red. The two Starfleet officers hefted their weapons and looked to Ogis.

"How long?" asked the lieutenant.

"A minute," said the Nograkh. "Maybe less, maybe more."

Ram's Horns was with them also. He nodded. "It depends on how eager they are to off-load their cargo."

As it turned out, the Nograkh couldn't have been *more* eager. It only took ten seconds for the air lock door to open from the outside and discharge the commander of the transport. That left him a perfect target for the prisoners pressed against the bulkhead on either side.

According to plan, Ogis took out the commander with a single burst of blue-white energy fire. Then B'Elanna, Kim, and Ram's Horns, who were considerably quicker than their fellow prisoners, rushed through the air lock to take care of the transport's crew.

There were two of them in the main cabin. B'Elanna took one down. Kim blasted the other. But there were supposed to be five Nograkh aboard—again, according to Ogis.

The lieutenant and the ensign charged in to dig out the two remaining crewmembers, with Ram's Horns right behind them. B'Elanna turned right and went forward. Kim turned left and went aft.

B'Elanna found a Nograkh at the helm. He was obviously surprised to see her. Before his confusion could wear off, she stunned him with a beam to the middle of his chest.

Then she turned in time to see a flare of blue-white light in the rear compartment. There was a short, strangled cry. Kim came out with a grim semblance of a smile on his face.

"Never knew what hit him," the ensign reported.

The lieutenant grunted. "Fortunately, none of them did."

The next step was to clear out the unconscious bodies of the crew, a task they accomplished in a matter of seconds. After that, they shut the doors to the station air lock—both inner and outer—as well as the door in the hull of the transport itself.

Kim slipped into the pilot's seat. B'Elanna took her place behind him. Ram's Horns claimed the weapons station. Everyone else piled into the main cabin or the smaller rear compartment.

They were ready to roll.

"What about Tolga?" asked Ogis.

The lieutenant shook her head. "We can't wait for him—or he for us. But once we're underway, we can scan for his ship."

Something happened then that made B'Elanna's blood run cold. Something she was totally unprepared for. She heard a *voice.*

"Ebra? Are you there?"

It hadn't come from anyone in the transport. In fact, it sounded as if it had come from all around them. Cursing beneath her breath, B'Elanna looked up at the ceiling, where it was customary to conceal communications grids in Starfleet vessels.

The intership communications system had been activated accidentally. Or maybe the Nograkh she'd stunned had managed to press a padd while still conscious. Either way, they had an open—and unwanted—channel to one of the other transports.

And it wasn't the one Tolga had gone after. That was the one thing of which the lieutenant was certain.

"Answer me, Ebra!"

Ogis signed for Kim not to make a move. Then he approached the controls and made an adjustment. Finally, he looked to the ceiling and spoke.

"This is Ebra. As you can hear, we're experiencing some communications problems, some static. What is it you want?"

For a moment, there was silence on the other end. B'Elanna crossed her fingers, hoping Ebra would fall for Ogis's ruse.

Unfortunately, it didn't work out that way. They could hear someone in the other ship shouting urgent orders to his crew. Then the communications line went dead.

Clenching her teeth, the lieutenant turned to Kim. "Get us out of here, Ensign. And I mean *now.*"

Kim was staring at something through the vessel's forward observation port. B'Elanna hunkered down and saw what it was. An asteroid belt.

Abruptly, she remembered what he'd told her about Paris's holodeck program. Damn, she thought. An *asteroid* belt.

"You want me to take over?" she asked.

The ensign shook his head. "No. I can handle it."

The lieutenant bit her lip. For everyone's sake, she hoped he was telling her the truth.

CHAPTER 19

My god, Harry thought as he guided his transport forward. It figures, doesn't it?

They were surrounded by an asteroid belt, of all things. A big, dense *monster* of an asteroid belt.

Now he knew where the station got all its raw materials. They were all around it in plentiful supply. *More* than plentiful.

An asteroid belt, he repeated inwardly.

The kind in which he'd already proven his piloting skills to be woefully inadequate. The kind he'd told Paris he'd probably never encounter in a million years. And just for good measure, a bunch of enemy ships would soon be on his tail, spurring him to new heights of urgency.

Not to mention a raging fever, reflexes that had been slowed by radiation exposure and an ache in his bones he couldn't ignore. His hands were wracked with pain as they worked the controls.

Worse yet, his helm panel was different from the kind he'd learned on in Starfleet shuttles, so he couldn't operate on instinct alone. He had to watch everything he was doing or take a chance on smashing the ship into a big hunk of ore-laden rock.

One thing was the same. The monitor on the console was located on his right, just where he would have expected it in a shuttle console. And the sensor arrangement must have been similar as well, because the asteroids up ahead were represented as blips of white light.

But this wasn't a holodeck exercise. This was real life. If they cracked up, there would be no rebooting the program. They'd be dead, finis, kaput. End of the line.

As Harry studied the monitor, he shivered—and not just because of his fever. There wasn't any clear-cut path among the asteroids. Even at impulse speed, it was going to be a toss-up as to whether they'd make it out of this place alive.

He felt a hand grip his shoulder. He didn't have to look to know it was B'Elanna's. "How are we doing, Starfleet?"

"Couldn't be better," Harry said, albeit with a confidence he didn't feel. He swallowed hard. "Piece of cake."

That's when he saw a series of blue-white energy bolts strike the asteroid up ahead of him, annihilating an entire quadrant of the thing in an explosion of light and debris. What's more, the bolt had missed Harry's transport by only a few short meters.

Switching his monitor to rearview for a moment, he saw where the attack had come from. The other transports were giving pursuit. And for them, pursuit meant trying to knock the prisoners out of space.

Janeway leaned forward in her chair and followed the movements of the ships in the asteroid field with more than casual interest.

They looked for all the world as if they were trying to escape the station. No—not all of them, Janeway realized. Two of them were doing that. The others seemed to be in pursuit.

There was a flare of light. And another. The transports were firing at each other, for god's sake.

"What's going on?" asked the captain, hoping one of her bridge officers could shed some light on this.

Naturally, Tuvok was the first to answer her—though all he could do was state the obvious. "We seem to be witnessing an altercation."

It could have been a squabble among the operators of the station—one that had evolved into violence. But Janeway sensed it was something else. Something along the lines of a jailbreak.

"It's Harry!" blurted Paris.

Janeway traded glances with Chakotay and came forward. "How do you know?" she asked the helmsman.

Paris pointed to the viewscreen, where they could see the transport ships weaving their way through the asteroid belt. One of the ships seemed to be leading the way, blazing a torturous trail despite the energy beams slicing space all around it.

"Look!" he said, as if that were explanation enough. Then he added: "It's Harry, dammit! We were practicing those moves on the holodeck!"

The captain looked up and saw the conflict on the screen in a new light. It wasn't just *any* jailbreak, she told herself. Not if it was Kim on that ship—and maybe B'Elanna as well.

"Two million kilometers," Chakotay announced.

"Dropping to impulse," said Paris, knowing a cue when he heard one. His hands danced over the helm controls with practiced ease. "Heading two-three-two-mark-eight."

There were a couple more flares of light in the asteroid belt. But the escaping transport avoided them somehow.

Janeway gripped the armrests of her chair. Come on, she thought, silently urging her ship forward. She hadn't come all this way to watch her officers vanish in a barrage of energy fire.

One of Harry's pursuers seared the void with another barrage. This time, he had to pull his craft to starboard to avoid it. As before, the errant bolts smashed into a rock formation and took a chunk out of it.

"Who's at the weapons console?" B'Elanna barked, though she knew full well who it was. "Show them *we've* got some teeth, too!"

As Ram's Horns moved to comply, a deeper voice surrounded them. It was the communications system again. "This is Tolga."

"Tolga!" someone exclaimed. "He made it, then."

"For now," someone else commented.

"We'll do better if we split up," Tolga advised. "We'll meet on the other side of the belt."

"Agreed," said B'Elanna.

The other side, Harry thought, switching to forward view again. If I make it that far. If we don't run into a rock or an energy blast and become part of the scenery. If—

Suddenly, he seemed to hear a voice in his ear. Paris's voice, just as if they were back in their holodeck simulation.

"You can do it, Harry."

The ensign grunted softly and wiped sweat from his eyes. *"What makes you think this time is going to be different from the others?"* he asked in the privacy of his own mind.

Paris gave him the same answer as last time. *"I've got a feeling. Pay attention now, Harry. Those asteroids are coming up fast."*

As the first rock loomed, the ensign gritted his teeth and pulled the mining transport hard to port. Then, to avoid a second rock, hard to starboard. And again to port.

And each time he tensed a little, expecting to feel the impact of a well-placed energy beam. But nothing hit them.

Maybe the other transports were having trouble drawing a bead on him. Maybe they had their hands full just trying to keep up. Or maybe Ram's Horns was making life difficult with some well-placed shots of his own.

No matter. Harry couldn't worry about any of that. He had to stay focused on the job at hand.

A precipitous dip. A sharp turn to starboard. Another dip and a tight squeeze to port.

A rise, another dip. A torturous corkscrew maneuver to avoid a series of smaller rocks that made the deck plates shiver and groan. The next turn had to be a hairpin tack to starboard.

Harry engaged the thrusters and watched the rock ahead of them veer to port. But it didn't veer quickly enough. He had to decelerate, give the thrusters more time to work. And even then, they cleared the asteroid by only half a meter.

Harry took a breath and let it out. Squinting through the haze of his fever, he sent them hard to starboard, then to port again. Up over a big, misshapen boulder and down below another one.

A quick switch to rearview showed him the ore transports were still hot on his trail. But not all of them—just three. The fourth must have gone after Tolga's vessel.

Back to forward view. Harry estimated they'd gone through half the asteroid field. Halfway home and still unscathed.

Turn, dive, ascend, turn. Dive, ascend, twist, and dive again. Slowly but surely, they were nearing the finish line.

Harry's eyes felt hot and swollen. He blinked. Just a little farther, he promised himself. Just a little farther and they'd be out of this. Then they would be in open space and he could *really* maneuver.

He worked his controls with infinite patience, infinite attention to detail. One crag after another slid out of sight, another looming up ahead to take its place each time.

"Not bad," he heard Paris say in his head.

"I'm not out of the woods yet," Harry reminded him.

He wasn't, either. Because just as he negotiated a massive rock to starboard, he felt a jolt from behind that jerked his head back. And another, even worse than the first.

"What the *hell* is going on?" he snapped out loud.

But he knew the answer. Their pursuers had gotten a couple of clean shots at them. So far their shields were holding, but they wouldn't last long under that kind of punishment.

Harry bent over his board and got them past the asteroid to starboard, ignoring the cold spot between his shoulder blades where sweat had moistened his uniform shirt. Then he climbed sharply to avoid another rock and slid to port to dodge a third.

They were almost at the limits of the belt. As the ensign circumvented another asteroid, it erupted with a directed-energy hit. Better a rock than us, Harry thought, and got his first look at the next set of obstacles.

His jaw dropped. There were two asteroids ahead of him, almost side by side. If there were five meters between them, it was a lot.

It was just as it had been in the holodeck sequence. Well, maybe not exactly—but close enough. And the last time he'd tried this maneuver—hell, *every* time he'd tried it—he'd botched it royally. He'd blown up his ship and killed his crew.

The ensign looked around for another option, but there wasn't any. The asteroids in every other direction were too densely packed. He would have had to backtrack, weave his way in and out until he found another means of egress—and with those transports breathing down his neck, he would be blasted to bits if he even tried.

His Nograkh pursuers must have known he was headed for this—which was why they hadn't sent barrage after desperate barrage after him. No matter how deftly he piloted his craft, no matter how many asteroids he avoided, they knew they would have him cornered in the end.

Harry concentrated on the pass ahead of him again and began to rotate his craft. It wasn't rolling as quickly as the shuttle had in the holodeck.

Gritting his teeth, he tried to compensate with a few extra bursts from the thrusters as he watched the opening loom before him.

He heard Paris' voice. *"You can do it, Harry."*

But the maneuver wasn't working. Harry wasn't getting the rotation he needed.

He was going to crash into one of the asteroids, maybe both of them. And they were all going to die, he and B'Elanna and everyone else in his craft, just a few meters short of freedom.

Unless . . .

He whirled to face Ram's Horns and barked an order. "Fire forward! I need a chunk taken out of that asteroid to port!"

Ram's Horns hesitated—but only for a fraction of a second. Then he targeted the asteroid just as Harry had demanded. And with a tap of a control padd, sent a blast of blue-white fury at it.

Instantly, the asteroid's nearest quadrant blew apart, pelting the transport with a thousand tiny rock fragments. Impelled by the force of the explosion, blinded by the energy backlash, Harry felt his craft veering too far to starboard. He corrected with the thrusters, hoping it would be enough.

It *had* to be. Or else it would end here—*they* would end here—and that was an injustice too grievous for him even to contemplate.

For what seemed like a long time, he stared through the observation port, unsure of the outcome. He couldn't tell if they had cleared the asteroid or if they just hadn't hit it yet. Holding onto his armrests with all the white-knuckled strength he had left, he peered into the face of death.

Finally, he realized there wasn't going to be an impact. Their vessel wasn't going to hit a rock and explode, sending bits of flesh and bone streaming into the void.

They were going to make it.

As the glare of their energy strike dissipated, Harry could make out the void of space in front of him. No asteroids—not a single one. Just the distant sun and the even more distant stars.

The ensign had never seen such a beautiful thing in his entire life. Nor did he ever expect to, even if he lived to be two hundred.

Switching to rearview again, he tried to locate the transports behind him. It wasn't an easy task, with all the debris from the damaged asteroid cluttering his perspective. Then something happened that made his pursuers even harder to see.

Something collided with one of the asteroids and went to pieces in a ball of crimson fire. Then came a second explosion. And a third.

The other transports, the ensign thought. They didn't make it. Or anyway, the first one didn't, and that doomed the other two as well.

He felt B'Elanna grasp his shoulder. She lowered her face to his and grinned. "You did it, Starfleet."

Harry nodded, drained by his ordeal. "Yeah," he said. "I guess I did. Tom would have been proud of me."

Of course, there was still one pursuer left—the one that had gone after Tolga's vessel. But knowing the Nograkh, he'd probably blasted that one to pieces already. Still, Harry figured he'd better find out.

He switched to forward view again and maneuvered his way around the outskirts of the asteroid belt, looking for a sign of Tolga's transport. At first, there wasn't any.

Then he caught a glimpse of something moving among the asteroids, like a dark, mysterious fish swimming through the shallows of a lake. And it seemed to be moving alone, neither pursued nor pursuing.

But which transport was it—the one Tolga had commandeered or the one sent to catch him? B'Elanna must have been wondering the same thing, because she hit the communications stud on the control panel.

"Tolga!" she said. "Is that you?"

No answer. Harry swore under his breath.

"Target weapons," he called back to Ram's Horns.

Glancing back over his shoulder, he could see Ram's Horns making the necessary adjustments on his instrument board. Then the ensign turned back to his own controls, to plan an attack.

"Tolga!" cried B'Elanna. "If that's you, I need an answer!"

Abruptly, they heard a familiar voice. "It's me," their ally assured them. "Still in one piece, although—B'Elanna, watch out behind you!"

Harry reacted instantly. Switching to rearview again, he saw what Tolga was shouting about. He swallowed in his dry, feverish throat.

A huge, gray vessel filled the dimensions of the viewscreen. A battle cruiser, unless he missed his guess. Even bigger and more powerful than the ship that had destroyed the Kazon vessel and brought them to the station in the first place.

And it was headed right for them.

CHAPTER 20

B'ELANNA TOOK IN THE SIGHT OF THE VESSEL BEHIND THEM, WITH ITS bristling weapons clusters and its powerful-looking engine nacelles. It made the Kazon ships she'd seen look like excursion craft.

And it was bearing down on them with all the single-minded ferocity of a Klingon targ.

"They're powering up their weapons," Ram's Horns warned her.

But then, the lieutenant could've guessed that. The cruiser had no doubt gotten word of the prisonbreak. And it had probably scanned them with its sensors as well, just to make sure.

She turned to Kim. "Evasive maneuvers, Starfleet."

"I'll do my best," he responded.

Peeling off to port, he avoided a blast of directed energy. Of course, it might just have been a warning shot, to let them know what they were in for.

"I've got an idea," said the ensign.

"We can use one," B'Elanna replied.

Gunning the thrusters, Kim wove a circle around the top of the cruiser, where it didn't seem to have any armaments. He must have guessed right about their being safe there, because the enemy didn't attempt to fire at them.

But it did try to grab them in its version of a tractor beam.

"We've got to move," B'Elanna said.

"I'm moving," Kim assured her.

But his escape route put them back in the line of fire. And the cruiser seemed eager to take advantage of it.

Weapon-cluster after weapon-cluster lashed out at them, filling the vacuum with blue-white energy beams. Thanks to Kim, none of them found their mark—but they were getting closer with each barrage.

Tolga's vessel wasn't doing much better. It was eluding the cruiser's bursts by only the barest of margins. Then it encountered one it couldn't elude and took a hit to its starboard side.

There was no hull damage—at least none that B'Elanna could see. But Tolga's shields had to have taken a beating.

"We can't dance this dance much longer," Kim told her.

"I know," she said.

The lieutenant racked her brains for a maneuver that would put the transports in the clear. Something . . . anything.

An option came to mind. It wasn't a good one. In fact, it couldn't have been much worse. But it was also the only chance they had.

Clearly, a couple of transports couldn't go head to head with a battle cruiser. They didn't have the speed, the durability, or the arsenal. But if one of them smashed headlong into the enemy, sacrificing his or her vessel and crew in a suicide run . . .

The other transport might get away.

"Tolga," she said out loud. "This is B'Elanna."

"What is it?" he rasped in return.

The lieutenant told him what she had in mind. Her decision drew stares from Kim and the others, but no one objected. *No* one.

"It's a good idea," the Nograkh replied. "Unfortunately, I had it *first.*"

"What?" she cried.

"Go," Tolga advised her. "Get out of here as fast as you can."

Then B'Elanna saw his ship begin to loop around—to double back in the direction of the cruiser. Ice water began to trickle down her back.

"No," she said. Then a little louder: "No!"

But if Tolga still had his communications link open, he wasn't paying any attention to it. He was too busy accelerating on what seemed like a devastating collision course.

The cruiser's commander must have seen it, too, but he was nowhere near as maneuverable as the transport. After all, his ship was a lot bigger. And he didn't have to wind his way through an asteroid belt every day.

So, as Tolga's vessel sped toward him, the cruiser commander couldn't get out of the way. He could only fire at the smaller ship and hope to destroy it before it got too close.

"Tolga," the lieutenant breathed.

Then the transport plowed into the much larger vessel with an impact she could almost feel. Tolga's plasma tanks ruptured, sending out streamers of wild, undulating light. And, a heartbeat later, the viewscreen blanched as the transport exploded into flames.

They didn't last long, of course. This was airless space. But they endured long enough to show B'Elanna what was left of Tolga's vessel, which wasn't much at all.

Everything from the middle back had been destroyed in the blast. From the middle forward, it looked like the entryway into hell, an open maw full of fiery plasma that continued to eat at the cruiser's hull.

And there was no life on it at all. *None.* Because nothing living could have survived that kind of fury.

B'Elanna felt a moan deep in her throat. She stifled it. It couldn't be, she told herself. It couldn't *be.*

But another part of her, a colder and harder part, disagreed. It *could* be. It *was.* The warrior called Tolga was gone, destroyed, and the prisoners in his vessel along with him.

Not for nothing, though. All over the Nograkh cruiser, lights were going out. The nacelles were going dark as well, their propulsion coils cooling. Clearly, Tolga had known where to hit the thing.

But then, he had served on one of these monsters, hadn't he? He had told her so, back in the rest chamber.

The rest chamber . . . where he had saved Kim's life. Where the lieutenant had come to respect the warrior, even develop a certain amount of affection for him. Perhaps if she had known him better, longer, something more might have grown between them.

But not now. Tolga, she thought numbly, was dead.

Before B'Elanna could come to grips with this newfound reality, before the pain of her loss could quite sink in, she heard a beeping sound. Kim turned to her, his features confused—caught in the grip of conflicting emotions just as she must have been.

"Someone's trying to hail us," he told her.

The lieutenant glanced at the screen again and swallowed. The cruiser was almost entirely devoid of illumination now. And it was beginning to drift, the remains of Tolga's ship still protruding from its side.

"What do you think they want?" asked Ram's Horns.

The lines in Kim's forehead deepened as he worked his controls. "Hang on," he said. "I don't think it's them."

B'Elanna regarded him grimly. "It's not another cruiser, is it?" Not after Tolga had sacrificed himself for them . . .

The ensign shook his head. "No. I . . ." Suddenly, he looked up at her and smiled—with a sense of relief that seemed drastically out of place. "I think it's *Voyager*."

The lieutenant leaned over him and checked his monitor. As Kim had indicated, the frequency was one commonly used by *Voyager*. The message itself was garbled, perhaps due to the proximity of the raging plasma furnace that had once been Tolga's vessel.

But the frequency . . .

"Let's hear it," said B'Elanna.

Kim did as he was told. A moment later, they could make out the tenuous, static-ridden voice of Captain Janeway as it filled their bridge.

" . . . *Voyager*. If that's you in that . . . respond, Mister Kim. Repeat, if that's you in . . ."

The lieutenant put her hand on her comrade's shoulder and squeezed. "You're right," she said, unable to keep the excitement out of her voice. "It's *Voyager*. Can you get a visual?"

"I'm trying," he told her.

What's more, he succeeded. Like the audio portion, the video was wracked with interference. But there was no mistaking the familiar countenance of their commanding officer.

Janeway's voice continued to fill the compartment with its crackle. " . . . you, isn't . . . come in, Ensign. I need . . . "

"Captain Janeway," said B'Elanna. "This is Lieutenant Torres. Ensign Kim and I used this ship to escape the place where we were being held. We're in no danger right now, though that may change."

Janeway's brow creased as she tried to make out what B'Elanna was telling her. Obviously, the interference was affecting *Voyager*'s comm equipment as much as the transport ship's.

After a second or two, the captain turned to Tuvok, who was standing in the background, and said something B'Elanna couldn't make out. The Vulcan checked his instruments, then replied. Finally, Janeway faced forward again.

" . . . effect a transport . . . " she said. " . . . raise our shields . . . quickly so we don't leave ourselves vulnerable."

Kim glanced over his shoulder at the lieutenant. "They're going to try to beam us aboard, Maquis."

B'Elanna nodded. "I heard."

It made sense to her. Their vessel was too big to make use of *Voyager*'s shuttlebays and too small to take care of itself. The only way the captain could be sure they were safe was to bring them home.

Of course, it would take a while before *Voyager* could transport them safely. If the plasma display from Tolga's ship was wreaking havoc with communications, it would break up an annular confinement beam as well.

"*Beam* us?" echoed Ram's Horns, obviously unfamiliar with transporter technology.

That came as no surprise. *No* one in the Delta Quadrant was familiar with transporter technology—which was what had made the Kazon-Ogla so eager to get their hands on it.

"You'll see," the lieutenant told Ram's Horns.

He did, too. And in less time than she would have expected.

One moment they were on the bridge of the mining ship, looking at one another expectantly. The next, they and three of the Nograkh in the hold were standing on a transporter pad aboard *Voyager.*

Janeway had positioned herself beside the transporter operator. There was an expression on her face the lieutenant couldn't quite identify. A mixture, it seemed to her, of happiness and . . . something else.

Relief? she wondered.

"Are you all right?" the captain asked, advancing to the pad.

B'Elanna started to say she was fine, then felt a weakness in her knees. When she staggered, Janeway was there to catch her.

"Radiation," said the captain, figuring out what was wrong with her officer at a glance. She looked to Kim and her eyes narrowed. "You, too."

The lieutenant got her legs back under control. "We're not as bad as we look," she said.

Janeway frowned. "The hell you're not." She looked up at the intercom system. "Sick bay, this is the captain. Prepare some beds, Doctor. I've got some radiation cases for you."

"Bring them on," said the holophysician. "I haven't treated a case of radiation poisoning in a couple of days now. I can use the practice."

B'Elanna smiled at the ironic tone in his voice. It was good to be home, she reflected. And also to know that she and Kim had rescued half the prisoners on the mining station.

But it would have been better if they had saved the other half as well. She thought again of her friend, Tolga—of his strength and his boundless courage. And it hurt.

"What is it?" asked Janeway, tilting her head to look into the lieutenant's eyes. "Is the pain getting worse?"

B'Elanna shook her head. "It's not that, Captain."

"Then what?" Janeway prodded.

Off to the side of them, the doors to the transporter room were sliding open. No doubt to admit the security people who would escort the lieutenant and her companions to sick bay.

B'Elanna could feel a lump forming in her throat. She shrugged in response to the captain's question. "It's just that . . . a few moments ago, I saw someone die to keep me alive."

"And who was that?" asked a familiar voice.

Scarcely able to believe her ears, B'Elanna turned toward the entrance—and saw Tolga enter the room, accompanied by Tuvok and a few of the other prisoners. The lieutenant shook her head, speechless.

"What . . . ?" she finally croaked out.

Tolga's eyes narrowed. Crossing the room, he embraced her as one warrior would embrace another.

Alive, she thought, feeling the reassuring hardness of his arms around her. He was *alive.*

"How is this possible?" asked the Nograkh, releasing B'Elanna. He jerked his heavy-browed head in the Vulcan's direction. "Apparently, your people plucked us out of our vessel before we could hit the cruiser—though I am still not sure *how.*"

Tuvok looked a little discomfited as he turned to Captain Janeway. "I had intended to bring these people directly to sick bay. However, when Tolga learned he might be able to see Lieutenant Torres even sooner . . . "

Janeway nodded. "I understand. And don't worry, Mr. Tuvok—you did the right thing."

The Vulcan quirked an eyebrow. "I *never* worry, Captain. It would be illogical to do so."

B'Elanna was still at a loss. She regarded Captain Janeway. "But how did you figure out Tolga's crew was on our side?"

Now it was Janeway's turn to shrug. "Originally, we were headed for the mining station. Then we saw all those ships take off from it in a hurry—and one of them performed a maneuver Mister Paris found vaguely familiar." She glanced at Kim. "Nice flying, Ensign."

Kim managed a grin. "Thank you, Captain."

"After that," Janeway continued, "it was a little confusing as to whom your allies might be—if you even had any. But when the cruiser showed up and went after the two of you, we had a pretty good idea of what was going on."

"So you established transporter locks," B'Elanna guessed.

"Yes," said the captain. "As soon as we could." She glanced at Tolga. "It was a good thing, too. They came in handy when one of the ships surprised us with a suicide maneuver."

"Which I am told did considerable damage," Tolga commented. He was looking at B'Elanna as he spoke.

The lieutenant was still stunned—but pleasantly so. "That's true," she confirmed. "The cruiser was disabled."

"Good," said the Nograkh, his silver eyes hard and vengeful.

Clearly, he felt as if he'd accomplished something. The fact that he'd lived to tell of it seemed almost secondary.

A voice came to them over the intercom. "Captain Janeway?"

The captain responded. "Yes, Commander Chakotay?"

"We've got them all now. But they're not in the best shape."

Janeway's nostrils flared. "The Doctor's already been alerted. Get them to sick bay, Commander."

"Aye, Captain," came the response. Then he added, "How's Lieutenant Torres? And Ensign Kim?"

Janeway smiled. "Not bad," she said, "all things considered."

B'Elanna put her hand on Tolga's arm and looked up into his eyes. She could see herself in their silver gray sheen.

"I didn't think I'd ever see you again," she admitted.

His brow-ridge lowered. "That makes two of us."

Then a handful of security officers showed up and took them all to sick bay.

CHAPTER 21

PACRIA KNEW SOMETHING WAS GOING ON. SHE COULD TELL BY THE VOLUME of traffic in the corridors. She could see the crewpeople in their variously colored uniforms rushing in and out of the turbolifts.

Using the communicator badge they had given her, she contacted Captain Janeway. "What's happening?" she asked.

The captain couldn't tell her—not right away, at least. She was too preoccupied with something. Something urgent, judging by the sounds Pacria heard in the background of their brief conversation.

So she went to Neelix's mess hall, hoping to glean some information there. But to the Emmonac's surprise, Neelix wasn't around. In fact, there was no one there at all.

That meant there was only one other place she could go. One other venue on the ship where she would be known and welcomed.

Sick bay.

As she entered, she saw Kes standing in the Doctor's office. The Doctor was there, too. So was Neelix.

They turned as she entered. The Talaxian raised his arms in greeting. "We found them!" he cried. "We found Torres and Kim!"

Pacria smiled. "Really?" she asked.

"Yes," said Kes. She beckoned. "Come see."

As the Emmonac approached, the others backed off a bit so she could see the Doctor's desktop monitor. It showed her some kind of vessel, gray and spartan in design.

"That's where they are?" she asked.

"Apparently," the Doctor answered. "We have no idea as yet how they got there, but they've answered the captain's hail. It's only a matter of time now before we recover them."

Pacria spent that time standing with the others in the Doctor's office. She was there when Captain Janeway called sick bay to report the imminent arrival of Torres and Kim and their newfound allies. And she was there to see them all enter sick bay, in need of beds and treatment.

The Emmonac could have let the others attend to the flood of patients on their own. But she didn't. She helped out. After all, she was there already, wasn't she? And she sympathized with the patients, having been a victim of radiation exposure herself.

She even got a chance to meet Lieutenant Torres and Ensign Kim. They were different from the way she'd pictured them, Torres being prettier than she'd expected and Kim being quieter.

And after Neelix explained her role in their rescue, they thanked her for all she'd done. So did the Nograkh. After all, if *Voyager* hadn't found its missing officers, it wouldn't have found the other prisoners either. And in time, another cruiser would have shown up to destroy them for their audacity.

It made Pacria feel good. It made her feel as if she'd accomplished something. That was more important to her than ever before, considering how little time she had left.

Then the captain called her back. With all that was going on, Janeway almost seemed to have forgotten she had meant to speak with Pacria. In any case, the captain said, the Emmonac's efforts hadn't been in vain. Torres and Kim had been rescued.

Pacria smiled. "Yes," she said. "I know that. I'm standing here in sick bay with them." Under the circumstances, it wasn't hard to forgive the human her oversight.

As Janeway signed off, Pacria took another look at sick bay. As crowded as it was, everything seemed under control. Seeing she was no longer needed, she started for the exit.

Someone called her name. "Pacria?"

It was Kes. The Ocampa crossed sick bay to catch up with her. "Can I ask you a favor?" she inquired.

"Of course," said the Emmonac.

"Meet me on the holodeck," Kes told her. "Say, in half an hour. I ought to be done here by then."

It was an unusual request. Having learned a bit about the ship's holodeck, Pacria guessed that Kes had set up a program for her as a gift. Perhaps it was her way of saying thanks for all the Emmonac's help. Or an attempt to distract Pacria from her imminent demise.

No matter the reason, it wasn't necessary. The Emmonac said so.

"To me, it is," Kes replied.

Pacria sighed. But in the end, she agreed to meet the Ocampa in the appointed place at the appointed hour.

Kes activated her program and opened the doors to the holodeck. It was dark inside, just as she'd planned it.

Pacria looked hesitant about going inside. "I warn you, I'm not partial to surprises," she told the Ocampa.

Kes didn't say she would be partial to this one either. She just asked that the Emmonac enter—which she eventually did, despite her misgivings. When they were both inside, the Ocampa asked for illumination.

The lights went on instantly. Pacria blinked as her eyes made the adjustment. Then she looked around the holodeck—or rather, the illusion contained in it.

The room was stark, colorless—filled with metal beds, all of them empty. The Emmonac looked agitated, confused.

"What is this?" she asked.

"I think you know," Kes said gently. "It's the clinic at a Zendak'aan redistribution camp. I was able to reconstruct it using the information from your ship's logs."

Pacria looked at her, still uncomprehending. "But why? Why would you make such a terrible thing?"

The Ocampa bit her lip. She could see the pain in Pacria's face. But now that she'd begun, she couldn't turn back—not after she had promised herself she would see this through.

"Because I want you to see what you're doing," she explained.

"See?" the Emmonac echoed. "What I see is one of the places where the Zendak'aa tortured us. Where they broke and mutilated our bodies, all in the name of science."

Kes sighed heavily. That was all true, she conceded. But it wasn't the *whole* truth.

Pacria took a few tentative steps. The chamber echoed with her footfalls—like a tomb. Her eyes narrowed with dread and loathing.

She turned to the Ocampa again, a haunted look on her face. "Is this supposed to make me change my mind, Kes? Or make me more certain than ever that what I'm doing is right?"

Kes didn't answer her—not directly. Instead, she looked up at the ceiling and said: "Computer, add Doctor Arnic Varrus to the program."

A moment later, a white-robed Zendak'aan materialized in the room. He was taller than Pacria and much more slender. Where her skin was purplish and scaly, his was smooth and a very pale shade of yellow, with long slashes of black on his forehead and the backs of his hands.

But his eyes were his most noticeable characteristic. They were large and black and shiny—the eyes of someone utterly confident in his abilities, utterly secure in his preeminence.

Nonetheless, Varrus just stood there, saying nothing. That was as it should be, thought Kes. He wasn't programmed to do anything besides respond—though in a way, his air of self-assurance was a statement in itself.

The Emmonac regarded the Zendak'aan. After a while, silent tears began to trace their way down her cheeks.

"You must hate me a great deal," she whispered without looking at Kes, "to show me something so utterly disgusting."

The Ocampa swallowed. Part of her wanted to spare Pacria this misery. But it was necessary, she reminded herself. It was absolutely essential if she was going to accomplish anything in time.

"I'm sorry," she told her companion. "I don't wish to cause you any distress. Please—just bear with me."

The Emmonac took a shaky breath and let it out. "What is it you want me to do?" she asked.

Kes tilted her head to indicate the Zendak'aan. "Just talk to him. Ask him questions about his work."

Pacria grunted. "Why? So he can tell me how dedicated he was to the healing of his fellow Zendak'aa? So I can learn to forgive him for his crimes—and benefit from their results?"

Kes steeled herself. "Ask him," she said softly.

With obvious reluctance, the Emmonac eyed Doctor Varrus again. "Tell me about your research," she demanded.

"My research," Varrus replied, warming to the subject immediately, "concerned itself with certain debilitating diseases, aaniatethis in particular. Since there was an analogous virus among the Emmonac, I used a great many of them as test subjects."

"How many?" asked Pacria, her voice devoid of emotion.

Varrus shrugged. "I don't know. A thousand. More, perhaps. I would have to consult my records to give you an exact figure."

Pacria flinched. "Of course. There was no reason to keep count. They were only Emmonacs."

"Precisely," said the Zendak'aan.

"And what did you do to these . . . test subjects?" she asked.

Varrus smiled. "I exposed them to their disease. The strain that worked the quickest and did the most damage."

Pacria turned to Kes. "How much longer must I continue with this hideous charade?"

"Just a *little* longer," the Ocampa assured her.

The Emmonac swallowed and turned to Varrus again. "What happened when you exposed your test subjects to the virus?"

The Zendak'aan didn't answer right away. He seemed to be thinking. Remembering, with something akin to nostalgia.

It turned Kes's stomach to watch. She could only imagine what it was doing to Pacria.

"There were several groups, of course," he said at last. "In each one, the disease was allowed to take a firm hold before I introduced an antigen. In most cases, the subjects died right away, the antigen having no effect. In other cases, I observed a significant response—but only enough to allow the subjects to linger for a while."

"To linger," Pacria repeated, containing her shame and her anger as best she could.

Varrus didn't seem to notice the Emmonac's discomfort. "Yes," he confirmed. "To linger—and in great pain, since I wished to observe everything I could about the disease, and that would not have been possible with the administration of painkillers."

Pacria swallowed. Tears streamed down her cheeks. "I see."

"But not everyone died," Varrus was quick to add. "There were those who managed to survive, despite the suffering and the crippling effects on bone and muscle tissue. And it was this group of subjects that ultimately produced an antigen."

The Emmonac's lower lip began to tremble, but she regained control of herself. She turned to Kes. "This is pointless."

"No," said the Ocampa. "Though I understand it must seem that way."

Pacria lifted her hands up helplessly. "But what more could I possibly ask this monster?"

Varrus looked at her. "Monster?" he echoed ironically. "I think not. After all, I found a cure for aaniatethis. I saved the lives of thousands of noble Zendak'aa and spared millions more its depradations. In the eyes of my people, I am a hero."

The Emmonac cast a withering glance at the Zendak'aan. "You are a demon. An incarnation of evil. And I would not partake of your cure if my soul itself depended on it."

Clearly, she had endured all she could. Wiping a tear from her cheek, she headed for the exit.

Varrus chuckled as he watched her go. "Good," he responded.

Pacria stopped. And turned to look back over her shoulder. "What did you say?" she asked him, her face flushed with fury.

"I said it was *good,"* Varrus told her, undaunted in the face of her indignation. "Only the Zendak'aa were meant to have benefited from my research. It was for them I worked from early in the morning until late at night, studying blood samples until my eyes wouldn't focus anymore. For *them."*

He dismissed Pacria with a flick of his wrist. "The Emmonacs I dealt with were laboratory animals, nothing more and nothing less. The idea of an inferior reaping the harvest of my labors . . . " He chuckled again. "I can think of few things more loathesome."

Pacria looked at the Zendak'aan as if for the first time. "That would displease you?" she asked.

Varrus' lip curled. "It would be a knife twisting in my belly. Knowing I had helped an Emmonac to survive . . . to spawn other Emmonac . . . " He shuddered. "Fortunately, that will never come to pass—not as long as the Zendak'aan Empire endures."

Pacria smiled. "The Zendak'aan Empire has been destroyed," she said.

Varrus's eyes narrowed. "Never," he insisted.

"It has been destroyed," she repeated. "What's left of your people has been scattered across the stars. And the so-called work you did? The scientific accomplishments of the haughty Zendak'aa? They fuel the ships and ease the lives of the lowly Emmonac."

Varrus' eyes grew big and round. His face turned dark with anger as he jerked his head from side to side. "No! It cannot be!"

"It *can* be," Pacria maintained. "And it is."

"You lie!" the Zendak'aan spat through clenched teeth. "My people were the height of evolution. The Emmonac were nothing. They were *animals!"*

"They were survivors," Pacria replied. "They endured. And when the Zendak'aa grew fat and careless and lowered their guard, the Emmonac and others repaid them for the miseries they'd inflicted."

"No!" shrieked Varrus. He pointed a long, slender finger at Pacria. "You're just trying to confuse me. You want my research, don't you? But you can't have it. It wasn't meant for you. It was meant for *us,* you hear me? For *us!"*

The Emmonac laughed. It was a sound more of triumph than amusement. "I guess," she said with only a hint of sarcasm, "even the noblest of intentions can go awry."

Kes smiled. "Freeze program."

For a moment, there was silence in the holodeck. Pacria continued to consider the Zendak'aan in the white robes, his eyes wide with fury—unable to accept that his worst nightmare had overtaken him.

"I suppose you thought you were being clever," she told Kes.

"Not clever," the Ocampa corrected her. "To be honest, I was clutching at straws." She paused. "Did I clutch at the right one?"

Pacria took a long time in answering. "Yes," she said finally. "It appears you did."

Kes nodded, relieved. "In that case, I don't think we need this place anymore." Looking up, she instructed the computer to terminate the program. Instantly, Varrus and his clinic disappeared, to be replaced by a black-and-yellow grid.

The Emmonac looked around. She shook her head. "It seemed so real. *He* seemed so real."

"In a way," said Kes, "he was. He acted exactly as the real Varrus would have acted—if he were still alive."

Pacria thought about her experience a moment longer. Then she turned to the Ocampa and managed a smile.

"Come on," she said. "I have an appointment in sick bay." And she led the way out of the holodeck.

CHAPTER 22

CAPTAIN'S LOG, STARDATE 49588.4. ON LIEUTENANT TORRES' RECOMMENDATION, I have taken her friend Tolga and his fellow Nograkh to a world of their choosing. Apparently, it's one that already serves as headquarters and staging ground for the rebellion to which they've lent their support.

The non-Nograkh we rescued have chosen to make this world their destination as well. It seems a bond of mutual respect was forged in the mining station that they have no desire to break.

The location of the place would normally be a secret, of course. Based on his knowledge of Lieutenant Torres and Ensign Kim, Tolga trusted us enough to share it. Naturally I'll erase the coordinates from our files as soon as we break orbit, so we won't give anything away if Voyager's ever captured by Tolga's enemies.

Not that I anticipate that, of course. But this is the Delta Quadrant. One never knows what or whom one will encounter.

As for Pacria Ertinia, the Emmonac we took on board, things are looking up. Though I still don't know how, Kes talked her into taking the antigen for the virus she contracted. We've agreed to drop her off in Emmonac space, which—fortunately—isn't very far off our intended course.

All in all, I'd say, the last few days could have turned out a lot worse. End of log entry.

• • •

Her log entry complete, Janeway sat back in her center seat and watched the forward viewscreen. Pictured on it, Tolga's Class M hiding place spun quietly in space, unaware of the fate the rebels had picked out for it.

Unlike the planet where Torres and Kim had been captured by the Kazon, this world didn't remind the captain at all of her native Earth. Its continents were too orange, its cloud cover too dense, and there wasn't nearly enough water. But when it came to the kinds of nutrients they needed, the place was chock-full of them.

"Captain Janeway?" came a voice over her comm badge.

"Lieutenant Tuvok," she said, identifying the caller. "What kind of progress are we making?"

"Considerable," the Vulcan reported. "We are beaming up the last assortment of roots and tubers now. Mr. Neelix is quite . . . " He paused, seeking the precise word. "Excited."

"I'd be surprised if he weren't," Janeway responded. "He'll have a whole new world of tastes and textures to explore."

And to inflict on the crew, she thought, though she would never say such a thing out loud.

"I should mention," said Tuvok, "that Tolga's people were quite helpful in pointing out the most promising sites. Though they seem to have a penchant for intraspecific aggression, they can also be rather generous."

The captain smiled. "Then our little detour wasn't totally unproductive. We've not only restocked our larder, we've made some friends."

Back at his usual post with all his injuries healed, Ensign Kim nodded in agreement. "I don't think you'll get any argument from Lieutenant Torres on that count. Or," he added hastily, "from me either."

Janeway glanced at Kim, then at Lieutenant Paris, who was manning the helm. Whatever had been straining their relationship, it seemed to be gone now. But then, people tended to appreciate their friends more when they thought they had seen the last of them.

Harry Kim suppressed a yawn.

Despite the level of comfort he felt being here on the bridge, he found himself counting the minutes until his shift was over. Though he'd pretty much recovered from the beating he'd taken on the Nograkh mining station, he was still a little tired. A little out of kilter. And he would continue to feel that way for a while, according to the holodoctor.

To pass the time, he ran some diagnostic checks. On the structural integrity field and the weapons systems. On the propulsion system. On the various sensor arrays.

He would have run a test on the transporters as well, except they were still very much in use. Tolga's hideout was turning out to be a bonanza for *Voyager.* They'd be knee-deep in food for the next couple of weeks.

Finally, it was time for him to get up and let someone else man his station. In this case, it was DuChamps, who had apparently performed the function much of the time Harry was away.

The two men nodded to each other. "I went through some diagnostics," the ensign noted. "You'll see them on the screen."

"Got it," said DuChamps. "And Kim . . . welcome back."

"Thanks," Harry replied, clapping the man on the shoulder. "It's good to be back, believe me."

Glancing at Paris, he saw that his friend was yielding his post as well. Harry waited for him at the door to the turbolift. They entered together, turned and watched the doors slide closed in their wake.

Suddenly, they opened again—to admit Chakotay. "Room for one more?" he asked.

Paris smiled. "I don't see why not."

"Holodeck," said the first officer, giving the turbolift its orders. The doors closed and, almost imperceptibly, the compartment began to move.

"You know," Harry said, "that's not a bad idea, Commander. I think I'll book a little holodeck time myself—in Chez Sandrine." Chez Sandrine was Paris's holodeck recreation of a bistro he'd frequented during his days at the Academy. "Sip a little wine at the bar. Play a relaxing game of pool." He winked at Paris. "Or, the way I feel, maybe kick back and watch *Tom* play a game of pool."

"Fine with me," his friend assured him.

"No way," Chakotay remarked.

Harry looked at him. "Excuse me?"

The doors opened on the appropriate deck. The holodeck was a few meters away, just down the corridor.

The first officer gestured. "After you, Mr. Kim."

The ensign shook his head as he exited the lift. "I don't get it," he confessed.

Chakotay didn't tender an explanation—at least, not yet. Instead, he turned to Paris.

"Have a pleasant shift, Lieutenant."

Paris's expression was a puzzled one as the doors closed between him and Harry. Putting his hand on the ensign's shoulder, Chakotay guided him along the corridor.

When they reached the holodeck, the commander punched in a program. A moment later, the interlocking doors parted for them. Harry could see the inside of a Starfleet shuttle.

He stared at Chakotay, dumbfounded. "What . . . ?"

"You didn't do a *bad* job in that asteroid belt," the commander conceded. "But you could've done *better.* And we're going to keep practicing till you get it right."

Harry's jaw dropped. Then he laughed and said, "You're on."

As B'Elanna entered the turbolift, she saw Paris standing inside it. He had a bewildered expression on his face.

"Something wrong?" she asked him, as the doors closed behind her.

He thought for a moment. "I'm not sure." Then he seemed to snap out of his fog. "Hey," he noticed her, "you're back."

"So I am," B'Elanna replied.

Paris smiled. "Said your good-byes?"

"I wished them luck—Tolga and all the others. I know what it's like to take on someone big in the name of freedom."

The helmsman grunted, "Sounds exciting. You'll have to tell me about it sometime."

Now it was B'Elanna's turn to smile. And to blush a little. "Sorry. I forgot I was talking to a former Maquis."

"That's all right," he told her. "I was really in it for the challenge. The freedom part was secondary."

She looked at him. "Uh-huh. Whatever you say."

"So," said Paris, changing the subject, "it seems we're done beaming up supplies. As soon as the captain says *her* good-byes, we'll be getting underway." He regarded her for a moment. "Say, you want to do something later? When you go off duty, I mean?"

"Actually," said B'Elanna, "I'm off duty already. I requested some time off."

He seemed surprised—but only for a moment. "After what you've been through the last few days, I guess you deserve time off. Lots of it, in fact."

"Chakotay gave me all he could spare," she elaborated. "In other words, about six hours. From what he tells me, engineering can use my . . . " She cleared her throat. ". . . critical eye. That's a quote."

Paris nodded. "I believe it. Things weren't quite the same while you were gone."

B'Elanna accepted the compliment. "Anyway, I'll take whatever time I can get. And six hours will be plenty for what I have in mind."

Her colleague's eyes narrowed. "Now you've piqued my curiosity. If you don't mind my asking, just what *do* you have in mind?"

She chuckled. "I'm going to celebrate a holiday I should have celebrated days ago."

Paris's brow furrowed. "Not the Day of Honor?"

"That's the one," she confirmed.

"But I thought you *hated* the Day of Honor."

"I did," she confessed. "But I don't anymore."

"Why the change of heart?" he asked.

B'Elanna had to think for a moment before she responded. "What I hated about the Day of Honor was really what I hated about myself. The fact that I was different. I just didn't want to think of myself that way, and everyone kept insisting on it anyway."

"And that's changed?"

"Everyone is still insisting," she conceded. "That part's the same. But I think I've learned to look at it differently. I've come to see that what makes me different isn't bad. It isn't something to be ashamed of. In certain cases, certain places, it's a *good* thing."

B'Elanna sighed. "To be perfectly honest, I'm still not thrilled about my Klingon half. I don't like having to keep a leash on my emotions. I don't like the fact that my first impulse is always to lash out, to inflict damage on whoever's standing in my way.

"But I see how Klingons aren't the only ones who act that way. Tolga's people are violent, even brutal at times. And yet, there's another side to them. A noble side, you might say. There's courage and passion and a willingness to sacrifice oneself for someone else."

Paris understood. She could tell from the look on his face.

"They were willing to give their lives to save a stranger," he said. "Just as James Kirk was willing to give *his* life more than a century ago."

She folded her arms across her chest. "It's funny, isn't it? We don't expect people we've never met before to be brave or dedicated or self-sacrificing. But if Tolga hadn't shown us he was all those things—and Pacria as well—Kim and I would have been space debris by now."

"And *we* may have surprised *them,*" Paris pointed out. "It works both ways, you know." He stroked his chin. "So you want to celebrate this holiday after all."

B'Elanna pictured Tolga and the way he'd tried to bury his ship in the Nograkh battle cruiser. She pictured Kim weaving his way through that asteroid belt. And she shrugged.

"You know," she said, "I've always had bad luck on the Day of Honor. But maybe my luck has changed."

The helmsman's smile was a sincere one. "I certainly hope so."

Just then, the lift stopped and the doors opened—on the corridor where Paris had his quarters. He stepped outside.

"See you around," he told her. "And, uh . . . " He shrugged. "Happy Day of Honor."

For the first time in her life, B'elanna was pleased to hear the greeting. "Thank you," she replied. "And a brave Day of Honor to you too, Tom."

STAR TREK®

DAY OF HONOR

TREATY'S LAW

Dean Wesley Smith &
Kristine Kathryn Rusch

This one is for Jeff, Kelly, and Rich.
Thanks for all the great times.

PROLOGUE

KERDOCH MOVED WITH A STEADY, SOLID PACE ACROSS THE LARGE FAMILY room to his chair. He wore the same clothes he had worn on this day twenty cycles earlier. Frayed work clothes that still fit, even though his body had thickened with age. They were the clothes of a proud Klingon farmer, but on that special day twenty cycles ago, they had also been the uniform of a warrior.

The air was warm and still full of the smells of the huge meal prepared and eaten earlier. The tension of anticipation of a wonderful story about to be told blanketed the room, coloring everyone's sight with a special glow, as if Kahless himself were about to visit them. Kerdoch felt it. He let the sensation fill him with strength, reinforcing his tired old bones, bones worn by a lifetime of working the fields to feed the warriors of the Empire. His job was a proud one. He and his family were respected in the region.

The seventeen Klingon adults and the thirty-one Klingon children who filled the room were silent, almost not breathing. Waiting.

Kerdoch settled himself in his big chair, then looked over the group. They were his family. His *entire* family. Around his feet, his youngest grandchildren sat cross-legged, staring up at their grandfather. They too anticipated his story, and he knew it.

They all knew the story by heart. Kerdoch had repeated the story every year on the same day, and he had never tired of it. His children and grandchildren were not tired of it, either; that much was clear. A good sign for the future, in his opinion. His story was important, about a day and a fight of honor that should be remembered by all Klingons.

Kerdoch's black eyes never missed a detail, not in the fields, and not in this large room on this special day. His gaze bored through his grandchildren and his older children until it came to rest on his wife, standing near the back. He smiled, and she returned his smile. She also remembered this day twenty years earlier. It was a day on which she feared she had lost her husband, her children, and her own life. She too knew the importance of his story.

The tension in the room seemed to grow as everyone knew the story of the great fight was about to begin. The excitement of hearing it again was almost too much for the younger children to bear. Many of them squirmed and shifted their position. Kerdoch forced himself not to smile at them.

He took a deep breath, then started, letting his deep voice fill the room as he took himself and his gathered family back to that time of battle twenty cycles earlier.

To a time when he, Kerdoch, had been a warrior. And when the Klingon Empire had learned about the honor of its enemies.

CHAPTER 1

KERDOCH GRUNTED SOFTLY AS HE STOOD UPRIGHT, STRETCHING THE SORE-ness out of the tight muscles in his back. He had been a farmer for almost thirty years, and each passing year wore on his body a little more. But it was a price he was more than willing to pay.

He studied his work. The field of tIqKa SuD spread out before him like a calm ocean, blue-green stems drifting back and forth like gentle waves at the touch of an unseen wind. The health of his crops radiated from every stem.

On the horizon K'Tuj, the larger of the two yellow suns had dipped below the horizon, leaving only K'mach's faint yellow light to illuminate his work. Already the chill was returning to the air, pushing out the intense heat of the day. Kerdoch knew that within the hour the cold would settle in for the short night. Back in the farming colony the lights of the streets and in the domes would be on, the fires lit.

He and the rest of the colonists had been on this planet now for five years. They had named the planet QuI' Tu. Paradise. He loved many things about this new home, but he loved most of all the nights around the fire, letting the ale and the flame hold back the cold and soothe his tired muscles.

He turned slowly, surveying his field and his work. Not a black stalk of Qut weed could be seen above the blue-green stocks of his crop. He had again won the day's battle. The pride of a fight well fought filled him for a moment. And he let it.

Then, as the second sun touched the horizon, he focused on the tasks of tomorrow, the struggle for the approaching harvest. Feeding the Empire was a never-ending battle that must be fought every day, or the war would be lost. Kerdoch was proud of his place in the Empire. Throughout the sector he was well respected for his work and his land's output. He enjoyed that respect and had every intention of gaining more.

Moving through the plants without breaking even one stem, Kerdoch made his way to the open area between fields, then turned and headed for home down a dirt path between two shallow ditches. His family would be waiting. Dinner would be ready, the fire popping and crackling like a celebration. A celebration of a day's battle won.

Suddenly his thoughts of family and the next day's tasks were broken by the searing sound of two aircraft flashing overhead. They were low, not more than ten of his height in the air. He couldn't tell what type of craft they were. They did not look like any of the colony ships. These were flat and diamond-shaped, nothing like any Klingon ship he'd ever heard about.

The intense wind in their wake rocked him, staggering him until he caught his balance. Around him his plants whipped back and forth as if being brushed by a large unseen hand.

In his five years on this land, on this planet, he'd never seen a craft fly over his fields, even at a great height, let alone low and fast. Without doubt there would be crop damage from this foolish act. He would make sure the persons responsible would pay.

He glanced around in the dimming light to see if he could locate any damage. But it was too dark. And the night chill was settling in. His assessment would have to wait for morning.

In the faint light Kerdoch caught sight of the two craft making a high, very tight turn above the glowing orange of the sunset. They finished their turn and headed back toward him, coming in low again and very fast, two thin silver slashes in the sky.

He stopped, too startled to move.

His mind fought to make sense of what he was seeing.

The ships appeared to be making an attack run.

In his youth on the planet T'Klar he had seen such action from aircraft in the great battle of T'Klar. His mother had been killed in just such an attack led by a cowardly pilot not willing to look his prey in the eyes. Kerdoch had managed to survive and see his mother's murderer killed two years later. Revenge had tasted good that day.

Wide orange beams shot out from the noses of the two thin ships, cutting a swath of intense red and blue flame through the crops.

It *was* an attack mission!

They were heading right at him.

Instinctively Kerdoch flung himself to the right side of the path and rolled down into a shallow ditch. He trusted his heavy work shirt to protect his body. He used his arms to cover his head.

Almost instantly the two aircraft were over him and then gone past.

The concussion from their passing pressed Kerdoch into the ditch, pushing his face into the mud as an added insult. The pilots of these ships would pay for this action.

Before he could move to push himself up he felt an intense burning on his shoulder and back. He was on fire from their flame weapons.

He rolled over, rocking back and forth on his back as hard and as quickly as he could in the dirt and mud of the ditch, letting the coolness of the ground smother the flames of his clothing. Many mornings he had cursed the cold ground as his aching joints worked it. Now he thanked it.

When he was sure the flames on his back were out, he stood, ignoring his pain.

For fifty paces on either side of him, his crops were nothing more than smoking ashes illuminated by small flickering fires along the edges of the destruction. In the distance through the smoke Kerdoch could see the two aircraft as they continued their burning run through his neighbors' crops.

Who were they?

Why burn his crops? The Empire's food?

There was no sense to this action.

Behind him, from the direction of his home and the main colony center came loud explosions.

He spun around. Flames shot into the air as more strange aircraft attacked the colony.

His family, his wife, and his home were near the center of the colony. Instantly he was running, intent on saving his family.

And paying back in death whoever was doing this.

Captain James T. Kirk crossed his arms and leaned against the wall in the tiny office. The office belonged to Commander Bracker, who ran Starbase 11, one of the smallest starbases Kirk had ever been on. Small and uncomfortable. This office barely accommodated Kirk and Bracker, let alone the four other people in the room. The size of the office didn't help Kirk's mood.

He glared across the desk at the smiling face of his friend Captain Kelly Bogle of the *U.S.S. Farragut.* Bogle was standing behind Bracker, somehow making himself the center of attention in the small space. He had arrived before Kirk and taken the place Kirk would have had. The place Kirk had had when both captains arrived on the starbase.

Bogle's position was symbolic of his recent victory over Kirk. Kirk adjusted his arms, but he couldn't relieve the tension in his shoulders. He had lost. And he hated to lose, even in a friendly game of catch-the-thief. But worse, he hated to lose to Kelly Bogle, his friend and former shipmate on the *Farragut.* That galled Kirk even more.

Captain Bogle stood only three inches taller than Kirk, but to Kirk the difference had always seemed much greater. Bogle somehow carried himself with a straight-backed posture that always made him seem like the tallest man in the room, even when he wasn't. His light brown hair was never out of place. Kirk also knew that straight-backed posture and perfect hair were consistent with the way Bogle captained his ship. He did everything by the book. But in a fight, Kirk couldn't honestly think of a better ship, crew, and captain to have at his side.

He liked Kelly Bogle, partly because Bogle was one of the few people who could get the better of Kirk. Rarely, to be sure. But Bogle could do it, and he could do it by the book.

Near the door, two red-shirted *Farragut* crew members held a tiny, childlike, and extremely thin humanoid between them. The prisoner wore regulation starbase children's clothing—probably stolen—and a small duck-billed cap. He was the first member of the Liv Kirk had ever seen, but he'd heard a great deal about them over the past few years. They were reported to be a race of thieves, although Spock claimed that for an entire race to turn to theft was not logical. Logical or not, the Liv stole on every planet, every starbase, every ship they appeared on.

They were fair creatures who appeared, at first glance, to be human children. They had porcelain skin, bright blue eyes, and no body hair. The tallest member of the race most likely wouldn't have reached Kirk's chin, and this one was far from the tallest: he came up to Kirk's waist.

They were known as the "child-race," "the kids from Liv," "troublemakers," as well as by a dozen other names. They traveled in small ships of their own or stowed away on other ships. They had an uncanny ability to hide in places where hiding didn't seem possible. And they looked so sweet and childlike that unsuspecting adults of all species usually took them in, soon to be robbed blind.

"It seems," Commander Bracker said nervously, "that our situation is now resolved."

Kirk glared at Bracker, a stocky red-haired man who was clearly nervous as he sat between the two starship captains. It was obviously the last place Bracker wanted to be. But he had caused his own discomfort. He had sent a message to the *Enterprise,* which was close by at the time, asking for some quick help with robberies at the station. Kirk had felt it would be a good excuse to give his crew a few days' shore leave and had agreed to help. But just minutes before the *Enterprise* reached the starbase, the *Farragut* had arrived unexpectedly for repairs.

The contest to catch a thief had started the first night in a bar, with a friendly wager between members of the two crews. Actually, some of the *Farragut* crew had said that the *Enterprise* couldn't catch anything if they tried and a few of Kirk's crew had objected. Loudly, from what Kirk had come to understand.

The argument had grown even louder between Kirk and Bogle in the officers' mess. Then the two captains had laughed, made a friendly wager, and bought each other a drink.

When the drinks were over, both men had hurried back to their crews. Shore leave was called off until the cause of the disappearances was found.

It had taken both crews a full day of searching the small station to find the Liv, hiding in a locker in a main hallway. His loot had been stashed in a dozen places around the station.

Captain Bogle smiled at his security detail. "Escort our prisoner to the station brig."

Then Bogle turned to Kirk. "Well, Captain, I'll collect that drink in the bar anytime you are ready." Bogle did not quite manage to keep the smirk off his face, even though he was trying.

Sort of.

Kirk shook his head. The game had been all in fun, yet some pride and ship's honor had been involved. It irked him that his crew had lost.

He still wasn't sure why they had lost. He knew Bogle too well to suspect an underhanded move, but he still felt uncomfortable—and a bit responsible. He had intended to check the lockers himself, but he had been detained, talking to a yeoman in the bar.

She was worth being detained for.

She was not worth losing a bet over.

It galled him to lose, but he had no one to blame but himself. Even so, the bet had been a nice diversion from the last month, which had been filled with routine. The sector of space they were in had provided nothing new, not even an interesting debris field or an unusual moon.

He smiled at Bogle, but his smile had an edge. Bogle had won this bet, but he wouldn't win the next.

"I could use a drink right now," Kirk said. "Care to join me?" With a wide sweeping gesture he indicated the door.

Bogle laughed. "I'd be glad to."

Both nodded to the relieved-looking station commander, then turned and headed for the door side by side.

Kirk liked Bogle, and even with the ribbing for not catching the thief first, drinking with his friend would be enjoyable. Just what Dr. McCoy had ordered for him and the rest of the crew.

But before the captains had taken two steps, their communicators went off simultaneously.

Kirk had his up and open first, instantly wondering what emergency would cause both starships to call their captains at the same time. "Kirk here," he said.

Beside him Bogle turned his back on Kirk and said, "Bogle," in such a stern tone that Kirk glanced over at him.

"Captain," Spock's voice came loud and clear over the communicator. "We are receiving a distress call from the agricultural planet Signi Beta. They are under attack and asking for assistance from anyone nearby."

Signi Beta was the Federation name for the Klingon farming planet QI' tu'. Just the name Signi Beta annoyed Kirk. The Federation farmers had lost the planet to the Klingons in a fair and honest contest.

But losing to the Klingons galled Kirk more than losing to Bogle did.

The planet was not in dispute, though. Why would anyone attack it?

Behind him, he heard Bogle get the same news.

"Mr. Spock," Kirk said, "notify the crew that shore leave has been canceled. Order them back to the ship immediately. Then set a course for Signi Beta. On my mark, beam me aboard."

"Aye, Captain," Spock said.

Kirk snapped his communicator closed at almost the same moment Bogle did. The two captains turned and faced each other, all thought of the rivalry and the drinks gone. Now they were both efficient working Starfleet captains with the same problem.

"How long until you can get under way?" Kirk asked. He knew that the *Farragut* had taken a beating during a run-in with a subspace anomaly. They had to repair their warp drives as well as bring weapons and shield systems back online.

"The starbase crew told us we had to dock here for at least twenty hours," Bogle said. "But knowing my engineer, Projeff, we can get out of here in fifteen."

Kirk grinned. Projeff was one of the few engineers who could give Scotty a run for his money. "I'll keep you informed as to what we find."

"Good luck," Bogle said, his eyes intent on Kirk.

"Thanks," Kirk said, knowing that Bogle was saying much more. They ran their ships in very different manners, but the respect between the two captains was there. Kirk extended his hand, and Bogle shook it. "That drink will have to wait."

Bogle smiled. "I don't mind you owing it to me. Just make sure you stay alive to pay it off."

"Oh, I'll pay you back," Kirk said, laughing. "And then some." He flipped open his communicator. "*Enterprise.* One to beam up."

Sixty seconds later the *Enterprise* was headed at warp five for Signi Beta on the edge of the Klingon Empire.

"Dinna give me any trouble, Doctor," Chief Engineer Montgomery Scott said, clutching his right arm as he sat on the edge of the medical cot. Dr. McCoy was standing beside him, holding a tricorder and frowning. "I woulda been here sooner, but I had a project to finish."

"Do you realize how filthy this wound is, Scotty?" McCoy snapped. "If you'd waited much longer, it would have become infected. I could have treated it, but it would have taken a lot longer."

"Ah, time. That's the ticket, isn't it, Doctor?" Scotty said. "We're headin' into Klingon space and I've got parts and pieces all over her innards. I gotta get back to Engineering and put things to right before we reach that planet."

"You'll let me finish," McCoy said. "And you'll tell me how you got this mess while on shore leave at a starbase."

"Well, now, I didn't exactly get the cut on the Starbase."

"Wound," McCoy said. "This is too big to be called a cut."

Scotty shrugged but didn't look at his arm. The sleeve of his uniform was torn, and beneath it the skin had been flayed to the bone.

"So you're telling me it happened right here?" McCoy asked.

"No, not really," Scotty said.

"You aren't telling me anything. Are you afraid I'd go to the captain?"

"We weren't doin' anything wrong," Scotty said with all the dignity he could muster.

" 'We?' " McCoy asked.

"Aye, Doc," Scotty said. "Projeff 'n' I."

"Projeff?" McCoy asked. "The engineer from the *Farragut?"*

"The same," Scotty said. "We had a wee wager."

"A wager," McCoy said. "I suppose it had nothing to do with the thefts."

"Naw. That's Security's business. And the captain's." Scotty smiled his wide, impish smile, the one that had gotten them into trouble on more than one shore leave. "This was over the lassies."

"The ships? What about them?" McCoy finished cleaning and sterilizing the wound.

"Projeff claims that he found a way to use the power from hydroponics to enrich the oxygen content of the environmental controls."

"We don't need more oxygen."

"I didn't say we did. But supposin' she got herself in a fix, and we were havin' trouble with the environmental controls. We could use . . . "

Scotty launched into an explanation so technical that McCoy, who prided himself on understanding most things scientific—especially when they touched on fundamentals, like oxygen—couldn't follow a word.

"So you were testing it?"

"Lord, no," Scotty said. "We were building models. The *Farragut*'s environmental system is one of the worst I've ever seen. A pile of junkheap parts that needs to be replaced, if you ask me. 'Twouldna be fair to Projeff to attempt a modification on that scrap heap."

"So you were building computer models."

"Actually, we were using some of the base's supplies as parts for small scale models. I made some modifications to Projeff's proposal and we wanted to see who could get his model running quicker."

"I don't see why you had to take the *Enterprise* apart to do that."

"I dinna, Doctor," Scotty said. "I was merely showing Projeff some of the finer points of our environmental system so that he could improve the *Farragut*'s."

"I see," McCoy said, even though he didn't. "I still don't understand how you wounded yourself building models."

"I slid me arm up a miniature jeffries tube," Scotty said. He flushed. "To adjust the cabling. It got stuck."

"Why didn't you get help, man?"

"What, and let Projeff see me dilemma? No, sir! Montgomery Scott solves his own engineering problems, he does."

McCoy shook his head. "Next time, get one of the medical staff to help you out," he said.

"There won't be a next time," Scotty said. He glanced at his arm. There was no sign of the cut. McCoy's healing powers had worked again. "We're heading to the outskirts of Klingon space. There won't be time for models and such."

"But that won't stop you from working on them, will it, Mr. Scott?"

Scotty grinned. "If I have time ta build models," he said, "then all will be right with the world." He slid off the table and headed for Engineering before McCoy could caution him to keep the arm stable for the next few hours.

McCoy sighed and went to his desk. He doubted all would be right with the world. The captain had asked McCoy to inventory the medical supplies and order up more from storage if need be.

And Jim only did that when he was expecting trouble.

CHAPTER 2

THE ATTACKING SHIPS HAD MOVED ON BY THE TIME KERDOCH MADE IT INTO the center of the colony. Most of the dome buildings were damaged. Flames and smoke filled the air. The only newly constructed wood building in the colony, the meeting hall and tavern, had been completely destroyed. Kerdoch could see a number of bodies in the smoking piles of timbers and furniture, all of them far beyond his help.

He took a deep breath of the smoke-filled air, calming himself, as his father had taught him to do. Then he forced himself to really look at the details of what was happening around him. A battle was won in the small details, his father had said. Kerdoch had always remembered those words, both in the battle to grow crops and now.

Smoke billowed out of the house of his friend, Kehma, but Kerdoch could tell the home was in no danger of burning down. Flames also flickered on or near almost every other dome building in the colony. Yet none of the main panels of which the domes were constructed had caught fire. He knew they were designed to withstand almost anything. He was very glad now that they did just that.

Through the smoke Kerdoch could see his neighbors and friends fighting the fires or helping the wounded. He could do nothing to help any of them at the moment.

The colony was withstanding the attack fairly well so far. The domes had not been designed with combat in mind, but they had been built to hold against harsh weather and high winds on dozens of planets. There would be dead, but not too many, because of the standard colony construction he had sworn he hated so often in the past. He would never curse it again after today.

He turned and at a full run headed for his own home. It too was one of the standard-issue Klingon domes that the colonists had been using during the five-year test period. Now that the planet's future was ensured, he had been preparing to build his family a real home, outside of town on his own land. Now he would also keep the dome, if they lived through this cowardly attack.

His home showed damage from a direct hit, but it was still standing. There was no sign of his wife and five children. That fact relieved him. If they were still alive they would be inside, door blocked, ready to defend their home as best they could. He would have to be careful going in or they'd fire on him.

He tried the front door and found it securely locked. That meant someone was alive in there. The door didn't lock from the outside.

He moved around to the side, tossing burning roofing away from the walls of his home as he went. The colony living quarters had only one main door, but they were also equipped with a hidden emergency entry that could be opened from the outside.

He yanked open the small hatch and, without putting himself in front of it, shouted, "It is I, Kerdoch!"

Inside he heard sudden movement; then his wife said, "Kerdoch? Son of whom?" Her voice was full of courage, testing to make sure that no one but her husband would enter her home. She was a solid, stout woman, and Kerdoch could imagine her standing inside, weapon aimed at the emergency door.

Kerdoch smiled. "Kerdoch, son of KaDach, beloved one."

"Enter, my husband," she said.

Inside, in the dark, he hugged his wife and five children as the ground shook.

The enemy ships had returned on another attack run.

Dr. Vivian Rathbone watched as the turbolift doors slid open with a hiss. She slowly stepped through and onto the *Enterprise* bridge.

She was amazed at how nervous she felt as she smoothed her commander's uniform. This was her first time on any starship bridge, and in the six months she'd been posted to the *Enterprise,* it had never occurred to her that she would be ordered to any of the officers' areas, let alone the bridge.

She had hoped to see the bridge someday, while in space dock, perhaps, or on a tour. To suddenly be called there during an emergency was not at all what a colonial agronomist would expect. Her job was to study any planets the ship discovered for possible future colonization and food-production ability. During red alerts her most important duty was to report to her lab and stay out of the way of crew members who had important things to do.

Behind her the door hissed closed, and she stopped. Captain Kirk sat in his command chair facing the main screen, seemingly deep in thought. She had seen him from a distance when she was first assigned to the ship. Then he had seemed like any other Starfleet officer, hurrying about his business. Now, though, he seemed larger than before. A man in his element. A man who accepted his power as he accepted the design of the bridge.

A man no one should trifle with.

The stars of warp space flashed past on the screen, but nothing else was visible. The slight beeping and clicking sounds of a working bridge were the only sounds around her, but they seemed extra loud to her in her heightened nervousness.

Spock had his head pressed against a scope at his science station. She'd passed the Vulcan science officer a few times in the halls, and every time was impressed by his stern demeanor. This time was no exception.

Lieutenant Sulu and Ensign Chekov were at their stations. She had spoken to both of them before. They had seemed nice enough, but concerned with the business of the day. She'd had a sense she failed to make an impact on any of them, although she was honored just to share the same starship with them.

Lieutenant Uhura swiveled in her chair, put a hand to the device in her ear, and smiled at Vivian, who smiled back. She and the lieutenant had become occasional three-dimensional chess partners. They played when they were both off duty, which rarely happened at the same time. But they did enjoy the games they were able to play. They were evenly matched, and Uhura was cunning. Vivian appreciated cunning; it added surprise to the game.

Uhura's smile helped. At least Vivian didn't feel entirely alone on the bridge. But she did feel vulnerable.

In all of Vivian's forty-two years she couldn't remember a moment this tense. Even finishing her doctoral thesis hadn't been this draining. She smoothed her uniform again and then patted her brown hair to make sure it was in place.

Calm.

Calm. She repeated the word over and over silently. Just stay calm, damm it.

"Captain Kirk," Uhura said, nodding toward Vivian. Uhura obviously understood how nervous Vivian was. "Dr. Rathbone is here."

Sulu, Chekov, and Captain Kirk all turned to look at Vivian at the same moment. Spock kept his face to his science scope.

Vivian felt as if a dozen spotlights had been turned on her and she was under close inspection. After a short moment Captain Kirk sprang from his chair and moved toward her, smiling. The man's movements were all fluidity and grace.

And energy.

His presence was overwhelming.

"It's good to meet you, Doctor," he said.

She managed to acknowledge his greeting with a nod of her head. Somehow his smile melted her tension, and she managed to smile back. She'd been in the presence of many powerful and famous people over the years, but never one with such charm. Now she understood why there were so many stories about this young captain. Judging from this brief meeting, the stories most likely were true.

Before she could respond, Kirk motioned for her to step down beside his captain's chair.

"Spock," the captain said. "Put our destination on the main screen for Commander Rathbone."

"Aye, Captain," Spock said.

The captain sat in the command chair and indicated that Vivian remain beside him.After a moment the picture of a green and blue and orange planet flashed on the screen. Vivian stared. The planet was very familiar.

"Signi Beta," she said, shocked. She'd spent over four years of her life on Signi Beta, in the Federation farming community on the southern continent. But that community had been disbanded six months before, and she had been posted to the *Enterprise.* She had never expected to see Signi Beta again. Or really ever wanted to.

"Correct," Spock said. "Signi Beta, now the Klingon farming planet QI'tu'. Translated, the name means 'Paradise.' "

"I prefer not to remember," Vivian said, obviously not shielding the bitterness from her voice. "But that planet is far from a paradise by any definition."

Both Kirk and Spock stared at her. Spock's right eyebrow went up, giving his stoic face a questioning look.

"Your personnel file shows that you were a member of the Federation agricultural team stationed on Signi Beta," Kirk said.

Vivian took a deep breath and forced herself to look away from the damned planet framed on the main viewscreen. "I was, Captain," she said, looking into his powerful gaze. "For the first two years I was the colony's assistant chief agronomist, and for the last two years I was the chief."

"So," Captain Kirk said, his intense gaze very serious. "What happened?"

"The Klingons beat us," Vivian said. "That simple."

She could tell that Kirk didn't much like her statement or the short, curt way she said it.

"There is nothing simple about Klingons, Commander," Kirk said.

She opened her mouth, but before she could speak, Spock looked up from his scope.

"Doctor," he said, "it would aid our understanding of the situation if you supply details about the planet."

Vivian nodded and took a deep breath, forcing her feelings of anger toward what had happened on Signi Beta aside. "I'm sorry Sir," she said. "My time there . . . it's a touchy subject for me."

"So I understand," Spock said, without sounding understanding at all. "But so far you have told us little more than what our computer records."

"We were hoping," Kirk said, his voice suddenly gentle, "that you could provide us with some insight."

"Insight?" she said.

"Into Signi Beta."

Insight. How could she give them insight into years of work followed by intense frustration? How could she let them know that she—that the entire Federation colony—had underestimated the Klingons?

She took a deep breath and decided to start from some sort of beginning. "For a number of years, Signi Beta was a disputed planet between the Federation and the Klingons. Then, five years ago, a test was set up. Two colonies—one Klingon, one Federation—would work the planet to see who could manage it in the best fashion."

"Manage?" Spock said.

She nodded. "Manage. Raise crops and plan the future use of the planet's resources."

"And the Klingons won?" Chekov asked. He had spun in his chair, his eyebrows raised.

"Ensign," Kirk warned.

Vivian nodded. "They won under the terms of the Organian Treaty. Fair and square, according to the judge."

"And who judged this contest?" Kirk asked. "Certainly not the Organians."

Vivian shook her head. "Ambassador Ninties, a Sandpinian, was picked as the final judge by both sides and approved by the Organians."

"A Sandpinian?" Kirk asked, glancing at Spock.

Spock nodded. "The Sandpinians are relatively new members of the Federation. Sandpinia is covered with sand dunes, swamps, and oceans. The Sandpinians' immense agricultural talent helped the race survive there. It is my understanding that their entire culture developed around those dunes. Their transportation system, for example, is made up of small cartlike vehicles that travel on narrow paths at very slow speeds. They have developed a new branch of agriculture called—"

"All right. That's enough, Mr. Spock," Kirk said, holding up his hand to stop the information flow. He seemed to smile slightly as he did so.

"There is one other important fact, Captain," Spock said.

"Yes, Spock?"

"I believe the Sandpinians were chosen as much for their mental development as for their agricultural talents."

"Mental development, Mr. Spock?" Kirk sounded confused, which echoed the way Vivian felt.

"Humans and Klingons cause Organians mental distress."

"Ah, yes," Kirk said. "I remember that."

"Sandpinians do not."

Kirk frowned at his first officer and turned back to Vivian.

"Commander, I take it Ambassador Ninties ruled in favor of the Klingon colony?"

"Yes, sir," she said. "Unfortunately. The Federation Colonization Authority underestimated the Klingons' botanical expertise. They beat us soundly."

"I do not believe Klingons could grow a turnip, let alone farm a colony," Chekov said.

"Even Klingons have to eat, Mr. Chekov," Kirk said.

"Yes, but have you seen their menus? Live worms. Blood pies. This is not the food of a ciwilized people."

"It may not be," Vivian said, "but they can make barren land fertile in a shorter time than we can. They sustain higher yields, and they lose less to insects and weather-related causes. They succeeded partly because Klingon agriculture is better suited to Signi Beta's environment and partly because they approach agriculture as they do war—succeed or die; there is no room for failure."

"Amazing," Kirk said. "I've learned never to underestimate a Klingon, but it never crossed my mind that a warrior race could be so good at farming."

"To be honest, Captain," Vivian said, "we all felt the same way, right up until the moment Ambassador Ninties presented the plans, findings, and proof from both sides, then ruled in favor of the Klingons. In his place, I would have ruled the same way, I'm afraid."

"I can see why this is a touchy subject for you," Captain Kirk said, frowning.

"Captain," Sulu said. "We are ten minutes away from the planet."

Kirk seemed to snap to attention. "Shields up. Yellow alert," he ordered.

Vivian started to turn to go to her lab when Captain Kirk said, "Commander?"

She stopped and turned.

"Stay here on the bridge," the captain said, indicating a position beside his chair. "We might need you."

"Sir?" Vivian said, her stomach twisting even tighter than it had when she first walked onto the bridge. Why in the world would Captain Kirk need her on the bridge of the *Enterprise?* And during a yellow alert?

Captain Kirk nodded, seeming to understand her confusion. He turned back to the main viewscreen. Then he said, "The Klingon colony on Signi Beta is under attack and we're responding."

Under attack? By whom? All Commander Vivian Rathbone could do was stand near the rail, her mouth open, staring at the viewscreen as the *Enterprise* dropped out of warp near Signi Beta.

CHAPTER 3

KERDOCH LISTENED FOR A MOMENT. THE SILENCE WAS BROKEN BY THE crackle of fire, a few distant cries, and nothing else. The attack had ceased, at least for the time being.

He stepped out from behind the makeshift shield of furniture he had built to protect his family from the possibility of the dome collapsing. The dome had taken at least one direct hit but had remained standing. They were lucky, nothing more. They had survived through the night and into the morning. He imagined that was more than many of his neighbors and friends had done this night.

His wife brushed the dust from her vest as she stood and faced her husband. "Who are they?"

"Cowards" was all Kerdoch said. The anger in his voice was harsh.

He glanced around at his home. The roof still held, but everything inside was in ruins. Smoke poured from cracks in the side of the domed plating, filling the area with a thick cloud.

He turned to his wife who was helping the younger children. "Put out what fire you can. Then prepare for another attack. Use more furniture to build extra shielding."

"Understood," she said, then nodded to him. "I will see you after the fight."

She knew him all too well. They were a good team. She would defend their home. He would defend their home as well, but he would be defending their home, the planet.

It would not be easy.

The colony had four disrupter cannons in position around the perimeter, but during the fight he had heard none of them being fired. Perhaps they had been destroyed or no one had made it to them in time. It had been at least six months since the cannons had even been tested, so it would take time to get them operating. A stupid thing to have done. The colonists should have been prepared. If they survived this, they would not be caught unprepared for battle again. He would make sure of that.

He nodded to his wife, then turned and ducked out the emergency exit of the dome. Behind him his wife and two oldest children emerged and began putting out the fires on and around the structure.

The sunlight on the colony was clouded and dimmed by the smoke of a hundred fires. Women, children, and some men were emerging from the domes to fight the fires or help the wounded. Ahead Kerdoch saw two other farmers, KaHanb and Kolit, heading in the same direction he was—toward the disrupter cannons on the south side of the colony. The cowards who attacked from the sky might have gotten away with two attacks, but they would not launch a third.

He could feel his blood coursing through his veins; his heart was light, his breath steady. He felt ready, his anger turned with focus to the task at hand.

On the bridge of the *U.S.S. Farragut,* in stationary orbit above Starbase 11, Captain Bogle took three long-legged strides in one direction in front of his captain's chair.

Turn.

Three back. He knew it drove his crew crazy when he paced, but at that moment he didn't much care. The *Enterprise* had left fourteen hours before, and since then every available person had been assigned to repairs on the *Farragut.* Bogle's little voice told him Kirk was heading into a mess. Granted, James T. Kirk was one of the best captains in the Federation, especially in unusual and messy situations. But even the best needed some help at times. And being stuck at starbase wasn't the sort of help Kelly Bogle wanted to give his friend Kirk.

Richard Lee, the *Farragut*'s science officer, looked up from his scope, frowning—an unusual look on his normally smiling face. "The *Enterprise* should be arriving at Signi Beta any moment."

Bogle stopped pacing and punched the comm link on his chair. "Engineering!"

"We're ready," Chief Engineer Projeff replied, as if the announcement were just another report.

Bogle smiled. This time Projeff had beaten his own best repair-time estimate by two hours. The man was a wizard.

Status?" Bogle asked.

"Full warp drive coming online now," Projeff said. "Two hours and we'll have weapons back up. Ten hours and I could make her dance around a flagpole."

Captain Bogle dropped down into his seat, half laughing to himself. "Nice work, Projeff. Stand by for full warp speed."

"Yes, Captain," Projeff said. "Standing by."

Bogle punched off the comm link to Engineering. "Is the course for Signi Beta plotted and laid in?" he asked his navigator. He knew it was, since he'd asked the same question five hours earlier.

"Yes, Captain," Lieutenant Michael Book said, his bald head not turning away from his board.

"Warp five," Bogle said. "Now."

The *Farragut* turned away from Space Station 11 and jumped to warp in an easy, smooth movement.

"Comm," Captain Bogle said to Lieutenant Sandy at Communications, "Inform the *Enterprise* that we're under way."

"Yes, sir," the lieutenant said. "With pleasure."

Bogle sat back in his chair and took a long, deep breath for what seemed like the first time in fourteen hours.

Kirk faced the main screen as the *Enterprise* sat some distance away from the planet. Kirk had factored in the distress call, making certain the *Enterprise* had maneuvering room should she encounter a fleet of Klingon battle cruisers.

But none showed on the screen. The planet itself looked exactly like the file images: a calm-looking, blue-green Class M, vaguely Earthlike, deceptively pastoral. There were no visible signs of problems.

He clenched a fist. He didn't like the feeling he was getting.

"Are we alone up here?" he asked.

"According to our instruments, we are," Spock said. He sounded vaguely perplexed. "However, the Klingon colony shows signs of heavy damage."

"From what?" Kirk demanded.

"Unknown," Spock said. "Fields have been burned; wells and farming equipment have been destroyed. The colony itself has sustained heavy damage and casualties. It appears from the damage patterns that the colony was attacked from the air by a fairly large force."

"And that force is now gone," Kirk said.

"If the attack came from space," Spock said, "then the attacking force has left. If the attack came from the ground, I cannot say with accuracy whether or not the colony's adversaries have left."

"Spock," Kirk said, "surely you can tell me if the damage came from a starship or not."

"Not without further study," Spock said. "I can tell you that the attack was sudden. The Klingons did not even have time to mount a defense. I have never seen such damage to a Klingon colony."

"They're farmers," Rathbone said. Her voice was shaking. "They might have been Klingons, but they were farmers first. And Signi Beta was protected by a treaty. They wouldn't have expected an attack."

Kirk swiveled in his chair. Rathbone was an attractive woman who had clearly suffered a great loss when she left Signi Beta. She also seemed quite nervous to be on the bridge. But she looked straight at him when she spoke, and despite her nervousness and her visible distress at the condition of the colony, she spoke with authority.

"Why would anyone attack a farming community?" Kirk asked, thinking out loud.

Rathbone turned her attention to the screen. She shook her head. "I don't know," she said. "I honestly don't. All of us in the Federation colony were upset, angry, and bitter over the Sandpinian judgment, but not enough to do something like this. There's simply no—"

"Captain!" Chekov said. "Klingon battle cruiser!"

Suddenly the entire ship rocked as it took a first hit against the shields. Kirk nearly lost his balance. "Spock! I thought you said there was no one else up here!"

"They did not register on my equipment, Captain." Spock sounded all too calm for a man who was gripping his scope as tightly as he was.

Kirk settled in his chair as the viewscreen showed a Klingon battle cruiser opening up on the *Enterprise.* "Evasive maneuvers, Mr. Sulu."

Three more hits rocked the bridge, the sound roaring like a huge wave about to engulf them.

"Aye, sir," Sulu shouted, his fingers dancing over his board like a concert pianist's.

"It was a trap," Chekov muttered as another hit rocked the ship. "This distress call, it was a trap."

Kirk didn't think so. Such a trap, using a distress call, wasn't the Klingon way. They tended to fight in a straightforward manner, at least in his experience. And besides, it was clear that the Klingon colony had been attacked. Unless this was a rogue Klingon ship, which was always possible.

"Spock," Kirk said, "did that battle cruiser attack the colony?"

Spock glanced at the captain, then seemed to understand what Kirk was thinking. He quickly checked his scope as two more hits rocked the *Enterprise.*

"Shields at sixty percent," Sulu said.

"No, Captain," Spock said. "That ship did not attack the colony. The weapon patterns are all wrong."

"Lieutenant Uhura," Kirk said. "Hail the battle cruiser."

She pressed one long fingernail against the board, then looked at him. "There is no response, sir."

"Mr. Sulu, arm the photon torpedoes," Kirk said as the Klingon battle cruiser turned to make another run. "Full pattern."

"They're armed, sir," Sulu said.

"Fire!" Kirk shouted as the battle cruiser moved past and above the *Enterprise.*

The quick successive thumps of the torpedoes firing felt faint but reassuring to Kirk.

The *Enterprise* rocked hard and violently with the impact of two more Klingon disrupter blasts. Kirk managed to hang on and stay in his seat, but Rathbone lost her grip and was tossed against the rail. Her head smacked against the floor, and she seemed to be out cold.

Kirk couldn't spare anyone to check her. The battle cruiser was getting ready for another attack. He punched the comm button. "Dr. McCoy to the bridge. We have an emergency."

"Captain, the shields are at fifty percent," Sulu said.

Then Chekov, who had been monitoring the fighting, raised a fist. "We hit them! They are hurt!"

But the Klingon battle cruiser didn't look badly damaged to Kirk as it swung around and held position facing the *Enterprise.*

"Open a channel to that Klingon ship," Kirk said tightly. "If this was intentional, this will be the last time the Federation answers a Klingon distress signal."

"The channel is open, Captain," Uhura said.

Kirk stood and took a deep breath. "Captain of the Klingon ship, this is Captain James T. Kirk of the Federation starship *Enterprise.* Are you too much of a coward to face your enemy?"

He smiled to himself. If that didn't work, he didn't know his Klingons.

"Sir," Uhura said, "we have an incoming message."

"Put it on-screen," Kirk said, cutting off his smile.

Quickly the image of the battle cruiser was replaced by the sneering face of a very familiar Klingon. Kirk would have recognized that roundish face and those dark eyes anywhere. It was Kirk's old foe, Commander Kor.

"So, Kirk," Kor said, doing nothing to cover his sneering tone. "You attack what you cannot earn fairly."

Kirk snorted in surprise. So the Klingons were going to blame the attack on the Federation. If he hadn't trusted Spock's analysis of the damage, he would have sworn that the Klingons had set up this entire affair.

"We're not responsible for the attacks on your colony," Kirk said. "We answered a distress call."

"Lies," Kor said. "We Klingons repay the loss of a life with a life. You will pay for what you have done to our colony."

"Look, Kor," Kirk said, stepping toward the screen. "Arguing won't get us anywhere. It—"

"I do not want to hear more of your lies, Kirk."

"Then look at the proof," Kirk snapped. "Analyze the attack patterns and weapons residue on the colony. Take a look at the damage. It will become clear that we couldn't have done this."

He was gambling. Spock hadn't been that specific about the damage to the planet. And Kirk had no real way of checking before he made the claim. But he had bluffed before with Klingons, and he had won.

Kor sneered, but he made a motion with his hand that was barely visible at the bottom of the screen. So he was having an officer do the test. While he waited, he said, "You could have disguised your weapons. The Federation is known for such trickery."

"Look at the proof, Kor," Kirk said.

Someone spoke to Kor off-screen. He turned away slightly, then turned back, his small eyes narrow. "Perhaps you have a weapon we do not know about."

Stubborn pigheaded people. Kor had the evidence, but he refused to believe it. How could a man talk to people like that? Forcefully. With a firmness they cannot dispute.

"Kor," Kirk said, "if you damage my ship, I'll damage yours, and we'll keep fighting until only one of us remains. But that won't help your colony. If we're fighting each other, we won't be able to defend this planet from the real attacker, who's sitting out there laughing at us."

"We do not need the Federation's help in battle," Kor said, but he didn't sound as convinced as before. It was clear that Kirk's words were making their point to the Klingon commander.

"That may be so," Kirk said, trying not to let his frustration show. "But if we talk to the survivors we might find out who the real enemy is."

Kor nodded. "I will beam one of the colonists up to my ship. You are welcome to join in the questions, but the invitation is for you, Kirk. Alone."

Kirk glanced over his shoulder at Spock, who was staring at him. Kirk's heart was beating hard. This was the sort of challenge he loved, but he could tell that Spock didn't like the idea at all.

"We could withdraw from the area and leave you to your own devices," Kirk said, "but I am as curious as you are. I will come alone. Stand ready."

Kor nodded.

The screen went blank, then returned to the image of the Klingon battle cruiser hanging in space facing the *Enterprise.* Behind the Klingon ship the blue-green planet looked calm and peaceful, but Kirk knew better. That calm planet could prove to be the end of the Organian Peace Treaty if he didn't work this right.

Kirk took a deep breath and then turned to Spock. "I think that went well, don't you?"

Spock only raised an eyebrow.

"Forgive me, Captain, but I do not think this is wise," Chekov said. "Klingons are well known for their deception. They could—"

"They could what, Mr. Chekov? You think they staged this whole thing so that they could lure me to that battle cruiser and kill me?"

"No, sir. But—"

"You think they plan to pick off starship captains one by one and simply started with me?"

"No, sir. But—"

"But what, Mr. Chekov?"

"But I do not like this. I think it would be wise to send someone with you."

It probably would be wise. But Kirk was unwilling to do that. "I said I would go alone and I will," he said. "If something happens to me, Mr. Spock can handle the *Enterprise.* Starfleet Command will have to get involved. Any more 'advice'?"

"None," Spock said. "However, as this is a Klingon planet, and Commander Kor's vessel is here, it would be logical to allow them to handle the distress call alone, as you yourself suggested."

"It might be logical, Mr. Spock," Kirk said. "But they already suspect the attack was initiated by Starfleet. Leaving now might seem to prove their suspicions. We have a treaty to protect whether or not we like its terms."

He turned to see McCoy kneeling next to Rathbone. She was still unconscious.

"McCoy activated a scanner. "What happened to her?"

"She hit her head," responded Kirk.

Dr. McCoy studied his instrument briefly, then looked up at Kirk. "I'll say she hit her head. That's quite a bump. But she'll be fine."

"Good," Kirk said, returning to his chair.

Spock approached Kirk. "Captain," Spock said softly, "as your first officer, I must inform you that beaming alone onto a Klingon ship might not be a prudent course of action."

Kirk held up his hand for Spock to stop before he read him regulations regarding the imprudence. Beaming over to Kor's ship seemed to be the only choice they had at the moment. The *Enterprise* hadn't attacked that colony. And Kirk would have wagered anything that Kor hadn't either.

That meant another force had. And that force might return at any moment.

CHAPTER 4

KERDOCH STOOD ON THE EDGE OF THE DISRUPTER-CANNON PLATFORM TAKING a break while two of his neighbors continued to work behind him. The smell of smoke was thick in his nostrils. The colony would stink of it for days. He thought of it as an incentive to work harder and faster.

He and two others had gotten one disrupter cannon on the outskirts of the colony almost ready. Another group worked on a second cannon on the west side of the colony. The other two cannons had been destroyed in the night attacks. If the cowards returned for another run in their thin ships, they would have a fight on their hands.

Kerdoch took a deep, long drink of water from a jug. The day had turned hot under the two suns, and Kerdoch felt the sweat caked to his back and arms. In midmorning his oldest boy had brought water and food for him and his neighbors.

His son had reported that the fires were out and that his mother had completed building a shelter inside their dome. He then asked if he could stay and fight with his father on the cannon. Kerdoch ordered him to return to his mother's side, where he was needed to defend her and their home. After the boy left, Kerdoch felt proud. He had taught his children well. He hoped they all lived long enough to pass on the lesson.

He took another drink from the jug and was about to return to work when he felt the odd sensation of a transporter beam. It had been years since he felt one, but the feeling was not easily forgotten.

"Kerdoch!" his neighbor shouted, jumping toward Kerdoch as if he might hold him and pull him from the beam. A fruitless but generous gesture.

"Be prepared," he managed to say to his friends before he was gone.

Kerdoch's only thought as the transporter took him was that he wished he had a weapon in his hand. At least that way he could have died fighting.

But when the transporter released him, he found himself on a Klingon battle cruiser. He'd been on two before and instantly recognized it. But how? And why? He fought to remain calm and prepare himself for what would come.

He stepped slowly down from the pad to be greeted by a nod from the Klingon warrior running the transporter. Then through a door strode another warrior, clearly the commander of this battle cruiser. "I am Kor," the warrior said.

"Kerdoch." He hoped his shock didn't show. Kor was a famous commander, known for his fighting skills.

"Good," Kor said, nodding his respect to the farmer. "In a moment we will talk."

"I understand, Commander," Kerdoch said.

Behind Kerdoch the sound of the transporter filled the room. He turned as a human form reassembled itself on the transporter pad. Could the humans be behind this cowardly attack? That was a possibility Kerdoch had not considered. The humans in the Federation colony had been more than friendly during the years they shared QI'tu' with the Klingons.

What was a human doing on a Klingon battle cruiser?

This was very confusing. Kerdoch shook his head. After this day and last night, nothing would seem impossible ever again.

This human was puny, but then, all humans seemed puny to Kerdoch. This human also had strength; that was evident in the way he moved, the confidence with which he carried himself. He was a warrior, just as the Klingons were.

The human stepped down from the transporter pad and nodded to Kor. "Commander."

Kor nodded back. "Captain."

A Federation captain! With Kor. It was obvious to Kerdoch that these two knew each other—and didn't like each other. That he might have expected, but what was the human captain doing here? And why had they picked him, Kerdoch, off the surface? Questions. Too many questions.

"This way," Kor snapped, turning and moving out of the room without waiting for a response.

The human captain stepped in behind Kor, and Kerdoch followed the human. Fourteen hours before, he had been walking the dirt path in his field when the attack began. Now he walked the corridors of a Klingon battle cruiser with a Federation captain and one of the Empire's most famous warriors.

Someone was stabbing her in the side of the head. She was sure of it. Waves of pain kept bouncing around inside her skull, and she'd have given anything to have them stop.

"The pain'll ease in a moment, Doctor," a solid, almost harsh male voice said above her, as if reading her mind. "Just lie still."

The voice was right. The pain was slowly diminishing from stabbing to pounding.

She forced herself to try to remember what had happened. The floor under her back was hard and a little cold. She could feel the hum of something working through her shoulder blades. Around her she could hear voices, but she couldn't make out the words. Where was . . . ?

Then she remembered. She was on the bridge.

She had passed out on the bridge of the *Enterprise.* The thought was like an electric shock through her system.

Her eyes snapped open, and she tried to sit up.

"Wait a minute," the voice said. "No dancing until I say so."

No dancing? It took her a second to realize that was a joke. And as she did, she felt a hand push her back until she lay flat.

She agreed with the disembodied voice. Her vision was a blur of spinning colors. She closed her eyes, and the spinning quickly stopped. Her head was clearing, and her memory was coming back.

The *Enterprise* had been under attack by a Klingon ship above Signi Beta. They had been hit, and she'd lost her grip on the railing and hit her head on the floor. That was all she could remember.

That and the pain. She forced herself to take a deep breath, which helped wash the pain back yet another notch. This time she slowly opened her eyes without moving. After a moment the face of Dr. McCoy came into focus above her.

"You're all right," he said, his hand firm on her shoulder. "You had a nasty fall, but you'll be fine."

She'd worked with the gruff McCoy a few times on data she'd gathered from planets. He was an amazingly smart man who liked to call himself just an old country doctor. He was far from that. In her opinion, he had one of the most skilled medical minds in the Federation. Besides that, she liked him, gruffness and all. And he had seemed to like her, too.

"Thank you, Doctor," she said after a long few seconds. Her voice sounded odd to her ears, but speaking didn't cause any increase in pain.

The Doctor half snorted and gently held her arm to help her to her feet. "Go slow, now," he said. "The swelling has receded and the pain should go along with it. You tell me if it doesn't."

"Okay," she said, being very careful she didn't nod in the process. She managed to stand and hold onto the rail. The same rail she'd lost her grip on in the first place.

After a moment of making sure she wasn't going down again McCoy let go of her arm and turned to face the main screen.

Around her the bridge was functioning normally, none of the crew paying her the slightest attention. Science Officer Spock stood at his panel, face buried in his scope. Chekov and Sulu both attended their controls. Lieutenant Uhura sat facing the communication panel, intently listening to something on her earpiece. Only Captain Kirk was missing.

And on the main screen was the Klingon battle cruiser.

"What's going on?" she half whispered to McCoy.

"The captain's on that damned Klingon ship." He sounded annoyed. And slightly worried. "We're to wait here until he returns."

Slowly, keeping her head as still as possible, she turned to completely face the front screen. The Captain on a Klingon ship? What was going on?

She leaned back against the railing and forced herself to take a deep breath. The pain in her head lessened even more, but the questions remained.

Captain Kirk could not identify the type of room he found himself seated in. Federation starships had exact configurations. Captains' quarters had a different look from ensigns'. Each room was designed for a specific purpose.

This room could have been the officers' mess or an emptied crewman's quarters. It certainly didn't seem like a meeting room. The lights were dim, as they were all over the ship. Klingons seemed to prefer dark colors as well, giving the whole place the feeling of something underground, something slightly unsavory.

Something dangerous.

The small room was also hot and stuffy. Kor had placed a pitcher of fluid in the center of the table, but no cups. No one had asked for any either, and Kirk wasn't about to be the first. He wasn't even certain he should taste anything on this ship, no matter how hot and thirsty he got.

The chair, however, was surprisingly comfortable. It had arms that encircled him, and the cushion, while not soft, wasn't hard, either. It was, however, a bit larger than he was used to—and he had always thought his command chair was large.

He sat in that chair for some time, while Kerdoch told his story. It sounded like the Klingon farmer and the other colonists had had a very long night. They were more than lucky to be alive.

The farmer spoke in precise detail. His memory was astounding, his ability to recall the trivial, trying. But like a good soldier, he assumed all details might be important.

Finally, the farmer finished telling his story of the night of flames, as he called it.

"Thank you, Kerdoch," Kor said, nodding in respect as the farmer stopped talking.

The farmer nodded back and wiped the sweat from his face with his sleeve.

Kirk had been surprised during the last ten minutes at the respect Kor showed the colonist. It seemed that even in a warrior race like the Klingons, those who supplied the food and built the ships and weapons were highly regarded and respected. It was an eye-opening detail of the Klingon culture that a Federation officer would normally never get a chance to see.

Kirk had seen many other things since he'd been on the ship, things he doubted any other Federation officer had seen. Kor had tried to keep him away from the main areas of the battle cruiser, but Kirk had sneaked a look into various sections, making a mental note of their layout and size.

Kor turned to Kirk, showing no respect at all now for a Federation captain.

"Well, Kirk," he said, his voice low and mean, "was this attack from one of the Federation's mongrel races? Do you deny it?"

"Of course I deny it," Kirk said, forcing himself to keep his voice level and not play Kor's game. "If we wanted to destroy the colony, we wouldn't have used small ships to do it. And if the attackers were rogue members of the Federation, we would have had warning. I would also have recognized the type of craft used. I don't. When I return to the *Enterprise,* I'll search our database for crafts like that. But I can tell you now, I've never seen or heard of diamond shaped ships of that size and configuration."

"You would lie to protect your own," Kor said.

"No, I wouldn't," Kirk said. "If members of the Federation made this sort of cowardly attack, I'd want to catch them and punish them as much as you." Kirk kept his gaze focused on Kor's eyes.

The silence stretched until finally Kor laughed. "So you would defend a Klingon planet to keep Federation races under control?"

Kirk held his temper. "Of course not, Commander," he said, keeping his voice level and cold and staring at Kor as hard as he could. "I would defend this planet because it sent out a distress call. Commander, the Organian Treaty would mean nothing if I refused to enforce it."

"You are a strange human," Kor said, shaking his head in disgust. "I will accept your word for the moment. But do not cross me, Captain."

Both men stared at each other until finally Kerdoch said, "Commander, I would like to return to defend my family in case of another attack."

Kor slammed his fist on the table and stood. "Of course, Kerdoch. I will send men with you to help."

"So will I," Kirk said. He flipped open his communicator before Kor could say a word. "*Enterprise,* have Dr. McCoy, Dr. Rathbone, Lieutenant Sulu, and a security detail meet me in the transporter room. Stand by to beam me aboard."

"Aye, Captain." Spock's voice came back clear enough for all in the small room to hear.

Kirk turned to the farmer. "Kerdoch, if the cowards who did this return, I will be at your side to defend you and your family."

"As will I," Kor said.

Kerdoch looked first at Kirk, then at Kor. There was a puzzled, intent look in his eyes. But after a moment he nodded his agreement.

"Good," Kor said, slapping the farmer on the back.

Kirk flipped open his communicator. "*Enterprise,* one to beam aboard."

Then he turned to Kor and Kerdoch. "I will meet you at the colony."

Kor laughed, again shaking his head in mock amazement as Kirk beamed out.

But for Kirk, there was nothing to laugh about—at least not until they discovered who attacked this colony.

CHAPTER 5

For the second time in under two hours Kerdoch felt the effects of a transporter. Only this time he knew exactly where he was being beamed to: the center of the colony.

Back to his home.

Beside him stood Commander Kor and four warriors. Kerdoch had never felt so powerful before. Pride filled his heart and made his blood surge through his veins. He had been given many honors over his years as a colonist, but never one that pleased him as this did.

As the transporter released them in the open center courtyard of the colony, a shout went up from those nearby.

"Kerdoch has returned," one yelled.

"With help!" a woman's voice added.

Kerdoch stood proudly beside Kor as his neighbors and friends rushed toward them. The colony had suffered even more damage than Kerdoch had remembered. Beside him Kerdoch noticed that Kor frowned as he surveyed the remains of a once proud Klingon farming community. He must have been shocked at the destruction.

Kerdoch waited for a moment until his wife reached his side, and he hugged her. Then he held up his hands and waited for the crowd to calm.

"This is Kor," he said, "commander of the mighty battle cruiser *Klothos* of the Imperial Fleet."

At his mention of Kor's name there were several swift intakes of breath and one gasp. Suddenly everyone was again talking as the relief of having warriors and a battle cruiser here to help defend the colony grew thick in the air, and warriors led by a respected and much honored commander such as Kor.

Kerdoch's wife squeezed him, as if he were the hero responsible for bringing Kor.

Kerdoch, however, felt a distinct unease, as if the winds had shifted and things were not as right as the others might think. He looked over the smiling faces of his neighbors, but saw nothing. So he turned to Kor.

"Sir," Kerdoch said, "we must prepare."

Kor slapped Kerdoch on the back. "You are right, my friend. We must."

In front of them the air shimmered. Weapons came up and were trained on the spot as the Federation captain and several other humans appeared.

Around him Kerdoch could sense the tension returning like a thick fur blanket tossed over the crowd. Only Kor's men lowered their weapons. The colonists did not.

There were five humans with the Federation captain. One was a woman.

The human captain strode up to Kerdoch and Kor. "Do you have wounded?"

Kerdoch nodded. "Many."

"Can someone lead the doctor to them?" The human captain indicated a thin man with a bag over his shoulder who stood off to his left.

Kerdoch turned to his wife and indicated that she should help the doctor.

"This way," she said, with only a questioning glance at her husband.

The human captain turned to his people. "Commander Rathbone, you and Lieutenant Sulu scout the surrounding fields, see if you can discover what was done to the crops, with what kind of weapon, and why. Ensign Chop, Ensign Adaro, you two stay with me."

The human captain then turned to Kor. "We are here to help defend your colony. What needs to be done to get ready for another attack?"

Kor laughed at the Federation captain. "Kirk, you are still the fool. But for the moment we will gladly take advantage of your foolishness."

Kor turned to Kerdoch, who stood straight under the commander's gaze. "Do you have disrupter cannons?"

"Two are working," Kerdoch said "They are on the southwest and northeast perimeters."

"Good," Kor said. "Two are better than none. Kirk have one of your men join one of mine and one colonist at each gun."

One of the colonists put a hand on Kor's arm. "Do you think the humans can be trusted?"

Kor looked down at the offending hand. The colonist removed it quickly. "Are you questioning my judgment?"

"No, Commander," the colonist said. "It is just that when we had humans on this planet, we were instructed to keep them away from our weapons and our technology."

"That is normally a good rule," Kor said, "but I think I can handle Kirk."

The human captain rolled his eyes, but said nothing. He turned to the two humans in red shirts. "Ensign Chop, you take the southwest cannon. Ensign Adaro, take the other."

Kor turned again and faced Kerdoch. "From which direction did the ships make their attack runs?"

Kerdoch glanced around at his neighbors, who were watching.

"Most came directly from the west," Katacq said, and others around him nodded.

"Then we will set up a defensive position on the western edge of the colony," Kor said.

The human captain nodded his agreement, and without hesitation the two captains turned and moved toward the west, matching each other stride for stride.

After a moment Kerdoch realized that he and the other colonists should follow.

Dr. Vivian Rathbone forced herself to take a deep breath as she followed Lieutenant Sulu around a few of the damaged colony domes and out into the burnt fields.

Above them both suns kept the air thick and extremely hot, almost choking with the drifting smoke and black ash. The sky was the same pale blue and pink she remembered, but until now she'd forgotten how really hot it could get on Signi Beta. And how miserable. A person forgot such matters when five years of work got tossed away.

They moved a few hundred steps into the closest field and then stopped. She was having a very hard time believing she was in a landing party with Captain Kirk. And even a harder time making sense of the fact she was back on Signi Beta.

It didn't smell like Signi Beta.

The smoke filled her eyes with tears. Such destruction. And of crops. She had read about such things when she was studying history; she knew that sometimes war parties attacked supplies. But she had never seen it.

It looked as if a fire had made a selective rampage through the crops. The destruction looked all the more terrible since she knew it was deliberate.

Sulu crouched and used his scanner on the remains of the crops while she stood staring across the distant smoking fields, trying to take in what she was seeing.

She'd visited the Klingon colony twice during her years on this planet. Both times she had been struck by the beauty of the waves of blue-green crops, lush and supple even at the hottest time of day. Now those crops had been reduced to black ash. A crime.

"This is strange," Sulu said, shaking his head.

"What is?" Vivian asked, kneeling beside him. She knew why the captain had sent her and Sulu to investigate the destruction of the crops: she had lived and worked here, and Sulu was widely known for his botanical hobbies. In fact, she had hoped to someday talk to him about it. Once this mission was over, maybe she'd get the chance.

"I'm getting some strange readings here, Commander." He held up his tricorder for her to look at.

She glanced at the numbers and then smiled, impressed. "Good work, Lieutenant," she said. "It took our scientists almost two months to identify that same problem."

"You mean this is planetwide?" Sulu asked, turning to face her.

She nodded and stood slowly so as not to start her head spinning. "This planet, in its distant past, had a very different form of plant life, obviously native to these heat and soil conditions. Then something happened here about eight or nine hundred years ago that altered the planet's climate, and a second, biologically different form of plant life appeared, which slowly melded with and then overran the first."

Sulu stared at his readings, shaking his head. "Amazing."

"It is that," she said. "Now the Klingons have imported a third form of plant life that is blending with the first two. We did the same thing in our experiments on the southern continent. The Klingons were more successful than we were. That's one of the many reasons they won this planet."

Sulu stood, still studying his tricorder. "Any indication of what caused the first plant shift?"

Vivian shook her head. "Most likely it was a natural event such as a meteor strike, though some scientists think the plants were artificially introduced by a lost culture. Knowing the true story might have helped us win this planet."

Sulu nodded. "As Mr. Spock would say: Fascinating."

Vivian laughed. "That it was. And still is, I imagine, to the Klingons." Even she could hear the bitterness in her voice.

Sulu ignored her comment and moved his tricorder in a wide circle.

She watched for a moment, then bent down and used her own tricorder to study the remains of some of the plants. They had been almost flash-burned with a high-intensity heat source of some type. She picked off a stem and smelled it. "Plasma," she said.

"Exactly, Commander," Sulu said. "My guess is that this was done with a wide-focus plasma beam."

"Do you know of any ships that use wide-focus plasma beams?" she asked.

"Not a one," Sulu said. "And I can't imagine why any ship would use them unless it wanted to do this kind of damage."

Vivian looked out over the field for patterns, just as she had done when a fungus outbreak threatened the Federation crops. What she saw now was a systematic pattern of destruction that targeted only the Klingon crops.

"Look," she said to Sulu, pointing out a few distant areas. "No natural vegetation has been touched, only the Klingon fields."

Sulu frowned, focusing his tricorder on where she had pointed.

"You're right. This *is* strange." Sulu snapped his tricorder shut and turned to face her. "Let's report back to the captain. He is going to want to know this."

She nodded. "Maybe Captain Kirk can figure out what's going on here. I sure can't."

Sulu laughed. "Nothing about this seems to make sense, does it?"

"Nothing," she said. "That much I'll agree with. And I mean that in more ways than one."

Kirk turned from his work digging a bunker near the western edge of the colony to see Dr. Rathbone and Sulu approaching from the fields and Dr. McCoy coming from the center of the colony.

Kirk stopped and wiped the sweat from his forehead with the back of his arm. He'd have to make sure all of his people got enough water in this heat. Otherwise they might not survive until the next attack.

Kor and two of the colonists, including Kerdoch, were about twenty paces away, digging another bunker. They'd left him on his own and every so often laughed at him from a distance. But alone Kirk had managed to dig a fairly decent bunker that would provide some protection.

"Jim," McCoy said before he even reached Kirk, "the Klingon doctor has everyone all fixed up."

Kirk could tell that his friend was annoyed. "So that's good, isn't it?"

"Yeah, fine," McCoy said. "But the damn superior Klingon attitude is going to make me mad someday."

"Insulted your ability, did he?" Kirk asked. He managed to hide his grin from McCoy.

McCoy snorted, then said, "He can't insult my ability. He's working with patients who have constitutions like tree trunks. It would take a meteor strike to seriously damage these people."

Kirk cocked his head. "Are you saying no one was badly injured?"

"Of course not," McCoy said. "There were several serious injuries. But, dammit, Jim, the Klingon physique is built to withstand damage. I've never seen anything like it. When one part breaks down, another kicks in. Klingon doctors lack the finesse of human ones."

"Apparently they don't need finesse," Kirk said. "We are fragile creatures."

"You're telling me. This heat is reminding me with each breath."

"I thought you grew up in the heat, Doctor."

"And I live in a controlled environment for that reason, Captain," McCoy snapped. "No intelligent creature would subject himself to temperatures like this on a daily basis. And he certainly wouldn't dig ditches in this climate."

"Bunkers," Kirk said. "I'm digging a bunker."

"Well, make sure you drink enough water. The last thing I need is a captain with heat stroke."

"Yes, sir," Kirk said, smiling. "If you're worried, you can stay here and help me dig."

"Didn't I just say I didn't want to be out in the heat?"

"I don't think you have much choice, Bones." As Kirk finished the sentence, Sulu and Rathbone reached him. "I take it you two have something to report."

"The destruction," Sulu said, "was caused by a wide-focus plasma beam and focused only on the Klingon crops, leaving the natural brush and plants surrounding the Klingon fields standing."

"Wide focus?" Kirk asked.

Sulu nodded.

Kirk glanced around at the colony's domed buildings. No wonder most of them were still standing. Wide-focus plasma beams had very high heat but very little destructive power. A hand phaser could do more damage than the weapon Sulu was describing.

"It makes no sense, does it, Captain?" Sulu said.

"Not if you're trying to destroy a colony," Kirk said. "But if you just want to burn everything down without doing serious damage to the ground, it would be a good method. Right?"

"That's right," Rathbone said. "Like burning grass off a field. It clears the unwanted stubble, kills the pests, and returns most of the nutrients to the soil."

"I wouldn't let the Klingons hear you call them pests," McCoy said.

Sulu laughed, but Kirk managed to keep focused on what they were talking about. "We need some more answers." He climbed out of the bunker and strode toward Kor and Kerdoch.

"Captain," Kor said, "you seem to be lagging behind in your building. Too much work for you?"

Kirk noticed that Kerdoch didn't laugh with Kor and the other colonists.

Kirk smiled at Kor. "You might want to put a roof over your bunker," Kirk said. "Might save you a few burns in the coming attack. The weapons used the first two times were wide-focus plasma beams."

"What?" Kor said, jumping up from the bunker and facing the humans. "What fools would attack a colony with such a weapon?"

"The fools who attacked your colony," McCoy said.

"And they only targeted your crops," Kirk said. "The natural plants and brush near your fields were not harmed."

Kor shook his head, obviously puzzled. "This makes no sense."

Suddenly Kirk's communicator demanded attention. A fraction of a second later so did Kor's. Kirk wanted to laugh, but he was worried about the incoming message. Twice in twenty-four hours he and another ship's commander had been called at the same moment while away from their ships.

He flipped open his communicator. "Kirk here."

Behind him Kor said something in Klingon.

"Captain," Spock's voice came through clear and as calm as always. "Six alien ships are approaching the system at high speed. I do not recognize their type and class."

"Go to red alert," Kirk said. "We'll batten down the hatches here."

"Yes, sir," Spock said.

"And Spock," Kirk said. "Keep her in one piece."

"She would not function efficiently any other way, sir," Spock said.

"Good. Kirk out."

CHAPTER 6

KELLY BOGLE SAT IN HIS CAPTAIN'S CHAIR STARING AT THE STARS FLASHING past in warp. He'd spent the last six hours sleeping, then had a quick breakfast, and was now back on the bridge. Waiting.

He hated these times of waiting. They were the worst part of being a starship captain as far as he was concerned. Especially the times when a starship was covering an incredibly vast expanse of space to reach an emergency. Those times seemed to stretch so that every minute was an hour and every hour a day. He would never get used to it, no matter how long he sat in this chair.

Now they were rushing to be at the side of the *Enterprise.* Kirk had already had a skirmish with the Klingons, but had managed, in pure James Kirk fashion to get them to work with him. How long that would last Bogle didn't even want to venture to guess. But what worried Bogle even more was the fact that they still didn't know who had attacked the colony.

Behind him his communication officer, Lieutenant Sandy, twisted around in his chair. "Sir, a message from the *Enterprise.* They, along with the Klingon battle cruiser and the Klingon colony, are under attack by a large unknown force."

"How long until we reach scene?"

Science Officer Richard Lee said, "Six hours, ten minutes, sir."

Bogle stabbed his finger on his communication button. "Engineering? Projeff, can you get me any more speed?"

The reply came back quick and short: "Not if you want to get there safely."

"Understood," Bogle said, and clicked off the communication button. That was the third time he'd asked Projeff for higher warp. The first two times Projeff had managed to nudge their speed upward. But clearly not this time. The third time *wasn't* the charm.

Bogle turned to Sandy. "Inform the *Enterprise* of our location and time of arrival."

"Yes, sir," Sandy said.

"And, Lieutenant," Bogle said, leaning back in his chair and staring at the stars flashing past.

"Yes, sir?" Sandy said.

"Wish them luck."

Spock stood beside the captain's chair, his attention completely focused on the screen and the image of the incoming ships. All six of the approaching ships were twice the size of the *Enterprise.* They seemed to be designed in a wedge, almost winglike, thin and pointed in the front, expanding into two thick structures in the rear. A very efficient and logical design.

The Klingon battle cruiser *Klothos,* under the command of Subcommander Korath, had turned to face the incoming fleet beside the *Enterprise.* Both ships had gone to battle-ready status.

"Sir, we have had no response to our hails," Lieutenant Uhura said.

"Keep hailing them on all channels and frequencies, Lieutenant," Spock said.

"Aye, sir."

Spock moved up to his science scope and ran a quick computer check of the approaching ships. Again the computer told him what he already knew: these ships were unknown to the Federation, and—if Korath could be believed—to the Klingon Empire as well.

He stepped back down beside the captain's chair, but did not sit down. As he watched the screen, the six ships broke smoothly into three units of two. One unit turned and moved toward a high orbit over the planet while the other two units headed directly for the *Enterprise* and the Klingon battle cruiser. It would be a logical move if the two ships in high orbit intended to attack the colony on the planet again.

"Lieutenant, have we had any response to our hails?" Spock asked again.

"No, sir," Uhura said.

"Arm photon torpedoes," Spock said. "Mr. Chekov, prepare for evasive maneuver Beta Six."

"Torpedoes armed," Chekov said. "Standing by."

Spock said nothing, just stared intently at the screen. The four ships seemed to be making a standard attack formation, working to pinch the two defenders between them. Now it would be only moments before their intentions became clear.

At the moment Spock had expected, phaser beams shot out of the four approaching ships. The *Enterprise* rocked from the impact, but Spock managed to hang on to the captain's chair and keep his feet. There was now clearly no doubt of the ships' hostile intentions.

"Return fire, Mr. Chekov," Spock said. "Then break off and follow the two ships heading for planetary orbit."

Spock didn't say it, but he was concerned for the captain and the landing party. If Spock's calculations were correct, those two ships carried atmosphere-capable craft, ready for another attack on the colony on the surface.

Four photon torpedoes hit the two attacking ships as they passed by, exploding against their screens. The screens flared bright blue but withstood the force. Spock noted that the new ships were not only efficiently designed but were well armed and protected as well.

The *Enterprise* turned and moved up and to the left, working to be in a position near the two orbiting ships. The move caught the two attacking ships by surprise as they banked to turn in the wrong direction.

"Screens at eighty-five percent," Chekov said. "We hit them twice, but they sustained no damage."

Spock had already gathered as much.

The Klingon battle cruiser was taking a different approach. Korath seemed to care nothing of his Commander on the planet. He was dogfighting with the two ships that had attacked him, taking more punishment than he was handing out.

On the main screen the two orbiting ships seemed to split in half along the thick back edge as huge doors opened.

"Docking bay doors, sir, they are opening," Chekov said.

Spock had already identified the doors as part of a docking bay. He didn't need Chekov's help on that. But he did need Chekov's help conserving firepower. He was glad the ensign was a good shot.

Dozens of smaller craft emerged from each alien ship and turned toward the planet's surface.

"Fire on the smaller craft, Mr. Chekov," Spock ordered. "Ignore the larger ones."

"Aye, sir," Chekov said.

The phaser shots streaked across the blackness of space. Four shots fired in rapid succession. Apparently the mother ships had not expected the attack. The smaller ships weren't shielded.

Four of them exploded as the phaser shots found their targets.

"We got them!" Chekov cried.

"Mr. Chekov," Spock said, wishing the ensign's emotions were as well controlled as his aim. "We 'got' nothing. Continue firing."

"Mr. Spock," Chekov said. "I think we have trouble."

Spock looked at the screen as the two mother ships turned to face the *Enterprise.*

"I think we have had trouble since we arrived in this sector, Ensign," Spock said.

Two more shots destroyed two more smaller craft. But Spock noted there were still over twenty headed for the colony.

"Sir," Mr. Chekov said, "the other two ships are coming in behind us."

Mr. Spock nodded. There would be no logic in destroying the *Enterprise* in a fight of four against one. That would not save the captain or the colony below.

"Take us back toward the Klingon ship," Spock ordered as the ship rocked with direct hits from the two mother ships. "Heading 238.72. Half impulse."

"Screens at sixty percent," Chekov said as the starship turned and sped toward the battle between the Klingon battle cruiser and the two strange craft.

Again the move caught the ships pursuing the *Enterprise* by surprise. The two orbiting ships stayed in position.

One of the alien craft fighting the Klingon battle cruiser seemed to be damaged, but it was clear that at the moment the *Klothos* was taking a beating. It was also clear that Subcommander Korath would not retreat. The Klingons needed help.

"Lieutenant," Spock said, "hail Korath."

Uhura pressed a few buttons on her station, then turned to him. "On-screen, sir."

When Korath's face appeared on the screen Spock gave him no chance to speak. "On my mark focus all your firepower on the ship closest to our position."

Korath glared at Spock for a moment, then nodded. "Understood."

"Ensign Chekov," Spock said, "focus our full phaser array on that ship. Fire on my mark."

"Aye, sir," Chekov said, his fingers dancing on the board.

"Now," Spock said, both to Chekov and Korath.

The full force of weapons fire from the Klingon battle cruiser and the *Enterprise* knocked the alien ship's screens down almost instantly. In a moment the huge ship exploded in a bright flash of orange and red.

"Got him!" Chekov shouted.

Spock did not admonish him this time. There was no containing the ensign's enthusiasm.

"Take us to a position beside the battle cruiser," Spock said.

"Yes, sir."

As the *Enterprise* dropped into position, the three attacking alien ships turned away, moving back between the *Enterprise* and the planet. They took up positions near the other two, forming an effective blockade of the colony on the surface below.

"They're breaking off the attack," Chekov said, his voice excited.

Spock nodded. It was logical. They had lost a ship. They would guard their ground forces while they took time to assess the battle that had just occurred. He would have done the same thing given the chance.

Spock punched the comm button on the captain's chair. "Mr. Scott, are we within transporter range of the landing party?"

"No, Mr. Spock," Mr. Scott said.

Spock cut the connection.

"Lieutenant," Spock said. "Hail the captain."

"Aye, sir," Uhura said.

Within a moment the familiar "Kirk here" rang out on the bridge.

"Captain," Spock said, "twenty small enemy ships are entering the planet's atmosphere. We have destroyed one of their transports, but we are being held outside transporter range by five others."

"Five?" Kirk said.

"Yes, sir," Spock said.

"Is there damage to the *Enterprise,* Mr. Spock?"

"No, sir. Our shields have lost some power, but I expect to regain it shortly," Spock said. "The Klingon battle cruiser will need some repairs, but it is still functioning. The *Farragut* will arrive in six hours and two minutes."

"Understood," Kirk said. "Do not put the *Enterprise* in any undue danger, Mr. Spock. That is an order. We will hold out here until the *Farragut* arrives. Keep me informed. Kirk out."

Mr. Spock stood beside the command chair, staring at the five ships on the screen and the blue-green planet beyond. The captain's orders were logical, but as the captain had said a number of times, that did not mean there might not be a better, even more logical way. It was just up to Spock to find it.

He tapped the communications button on the arm of the captain's chair. "Mr. Scott, would you report to the bridge."

"Aye, sir," Scott's voice came back strong.

"Lieutenant," Spock said, turning to Uhura, "inform the *Farragut* of our situation. Scramble the message. Include in that message full sensor scans on the invading ships. Then tell them speed is of the essence."

"Aye, sir," Uhura said.

Spock turned back to face the five ships and the planet beyond. There should be a way to get the captain off that planet.

Or at least help him.

Kirk flipped his communicator closed. Beside him stood McCoy, Sulu, and Dr. Rathbone. All watched him with wide eyes and sweaty faces. Kor and Kerdoch had stepped a few feet away, and Kor still talked to his ship.

"Well, they're on their way," Kirk said, trying to put some hope in his voice, even though he didn't feel any. "Spock says there are twenty ships."

"How long?" Dr. Rathbone asked.

Kirk shook his head, then rubbed sweat from his eyes. "They should come through the atmosphere in about five minutes. Maybe less."

Kor snapped his communicator back onto his belt. "The attack comes," he said to Kirk.

Kirk nodded. "We need to warn the colonists to take cover."

"I will do it," Kerdoch said. He turned and, with the other colonist who had been helping him dig, headed at a full run toward the domed structures of the colony.

"I will go to the western disrupter cannon," Kor said. Without another word he also turned and moved off, striding as if it were just another normal day instead of the day he would most likely die.

Kirk glanced around at the two bunkers they had built. Shallow holes in hard dirt. Nothing more. Against plasma-beam weapons, the bunkers would be useless. They at least needed covers.

Scanning the area quickly, Kirk saw what might work. The colony domes had been constructed of prefabricated panels about four feet wide by eight feet long. If they were light enough to be carried, they might do the trick.

"Quickly," he said, gesturing for his away team to follow him.

At a run he made his way to the edge of the colony and to a mostly destroyed housing dome. The body of a Klingon man, clearly dead, was pinned inside. Kirk hoped that the man wouldn't mind them using his home to survive.

With a quick yank he pulled one prefabricated panel free and studied it. About the size of a normal door and four inches thick, it weighed no more than twenty pounds. The panels were much lighter than they looked—a nice piece of Klingon design. They would never withstand a direct hit from any major weapon, but they would serve just fine as heat shields.

He turned and handed the sheet to Rathbone. "Use this as a cover for the bunker—the one the Klingons dug."

She struggled with it for a moment, also clearly surprised at the panel's light weight. Then she picked it up, lifted it over her head, and moved off.

"Didn't know she was that strong," McCoy said, watching her go.

Kirk turned and, with Sulu's help, yanked another panel free and tossed it to the Doctor.

McCoy grabbed at it. "That explains it," he said as he easily picked it up and followed Rathbone.

Within another few seconds Kirk and Sulu had freed two more and were headed back to the bunker.

Rathbone had managed to get her panel across the top of the waist-high trench and was frantically pushing dirt over it to camouflage it.

McCoy was fitting his beside the first. Within another thirty frantic seconds they had the four panels covering the open bunker and enough dirt on top of them to make them look almost natural. The bunker was open on either end, but there wasn't enough time to do anything about that now.

Kirk took a deep breath of hot air and scanned the bright horizon. Through the heat waves, in the distance, low and just above the small foothills, he saw several bright cuts in the sky, as if someone had painted silver lines on the horizon.

Alien attack ships. They were just as Kerdoch had described.

"Take cover!" Kirk shouted.

With Dr. Rathbone and McCoy in the center and Sulu near the other open end, Kirk took his place, phaser in hand. He doubted there was much he could do with a phaser, but at the moment it felt good just holding it.

CHAPTER 7

KERDOCH HEADED INTO THE CENTER OF THE COLONY AT A FULL RUN, HIS hard steps kicking up the dust between the domed colony homes. "Take cover," he shouted every few steps. "The enemy returns."

His voice carried far ahead of his running pace and as each neighbor in turn heard his warning, they paused, then went into quick action.

Women and children scrambled for the cover of their prefabricated homes.

Husbands took up weapons and ran for the perimeter of the colony, ready to fight with anything they could find.

Kerdoch continued his mission, running and shouting his warning through the center of the colony until he reached his own home. His wife stood outside, obviously having heard his call. She now waited for him. His children were already inside, out of sight. He knew, however, that his oldest son stood guard just inside the door and would hear him.

He stopped in front of his wife and took her shoulders, looking deep into her eyes. Her muscles were firm under his grasp and for an instant he never wanted to let her go. Then he took a deep, hot breath and said, "Get yourself and the children as far under cover inside as you can. There are many ships coming."

"You go to the guns?" she asked.

"I will fight," he said. "In any fashion I can."

She nodded. "I will guard the children and our home. Fight well, my husband."

"We shall not let these cowards take our land," Kerdoch said. And inside he felt it. Deeper than he'd ever felt anything before. And with more anger and force than he had ever felt.

He still worried about his wife and his children, but he did not fear for his own life. If he died fighting on this hot afternoon, he would have died well.

He squeezed his wife's shoulders with both hands one more time, then turned and at a full run headed for the fight.

But he was too late.

The first wave of ships flashed over the colony before he'd run another hundred steps, their flat hulls gleaming like mirrors in the light of the two suns.

They were firing as they went, the same wide beams as before.

Kerdoch instinctively ducked and covered his head with his arm, but this time he didn't make it to the ground. The explosions and concussion wave from their high speed knocked him backward, picking him up and tossing him into the air like a leaf in a very hot, very strong wind.

The last thing he remembered as he was thrown into the remains of a dome was being angry that he had not reached his place on the big gun.

Very angry.

Then his head hit something hard as he crashed through the dome, and the blackness took him.

Kor could see the gleaming cuts in the sky headed his way—at least ten small ships flying in a tight wedge. Good. A tight formation was the flight of idiots. It would increase the chances of a hit from the big gun.

He stood behind a chest-high earthen wall that had been quickly erected to help protect one of the colony's large disrupter cannons. Beside him were six colonists, hand weapons aimed at the coming ships as if they might bring down a ship with one. Kor acknowledged their courage. They were true Klingons. The Federation man also stood in the bunker beside him, phaser in hand. He too had courage.

Behind Kor the cannon stood no more than a man high on a thick concrete platform. One of his men and one colonist grasped the gun. It would take both of them to track and fire at the small fast-moving ships. The disrupter cannon had been designed to defend against attacks from the air. It was not extremely accurate, but the force was powerful enough to knock almost any craft from the sky.

"At my command," Kor said to those on the gun base, as across the hot surface of the planet the ships became more distinct. Then, quicker than Kor had time to react, the ships were on and over them, a fast wave of shining metal firing wide-focus plasma beams. He had been caught by surprise before, but never like that. The ships' speed was at least ten times what he had been expecting.

The impact of the plasma beams and the shock waves of the passing ships caught Kor as he instinctively turned away, smashing him down into the dirt at the base of the big gun. In all his years he had never felt such a force, like a giant's fist pounding him square in the back.

But soon the giant stopped pounding.

Kor fought his way back to his feet. An extra sensation of heat covered his right arm and shoulder, and it took him a moment to realize his uniform jacket was on fire.

In one quick motion he stripped off the jacket and tossed it aside in disgust, leaving only his shirt on.

Beside him the colonists behind the earthen burn were shedding their shirts and jackets or rolling on the ground to smother the flames. The federation crewman lay in the bottom of the bunker, a nasty gash across his forehead.

Kor glanced around. The first wave of attack craft already beyond the colony and out of range of the big gun. He cussed at them. If they returned, he would be ready.

His officer and the colonist who had manned the gun were lying together in a burning heap about twenty feet from the gun. They had been standing in the open, and the full force of the plasma beam had caught them. Kor knew he had been lucky to be behind the earthen burn. The barrier had most likely saved his life and that of the other colonists.

He glanced quickly around. In the distance a second wave of craft dropped down out of the sky and became shimmery slits in the sky headed for the colony.

He started to stand his ground, then thought better of it. There was a time to face an enemy and a time to duck an enemy's blows. This was a time to duck, so that he could throw a blow of his own later.

"Get down!" he shouted to the colonists. "Now!"

He barely had time to drop to his stomach and cover his head as the second attack wave struck.

This time the heat and the force of the ships' passing smashed him flat into the dry ground, knocking the wind from him. But that blow just served to make him angrier.

The moment the force let up, Kor jumped back to his feet. No other wave of ships seemed to be forming, so he turned to follow the last wave as they burned more crops and then climbed into the sky, disappearing into the distance.

Slowly the intense rumble of their passing faded, leaving only the crackling of fires and the cries for help from the wounded. Behind him the colonists staggered to their feet, patting out random flames on each other's clothes.

Kor stared at the destruction throughout the colony. Everything seemed to be burning. He stepped up on the platform base to see if the big gun still functioned. A quick check showed that it was operable. But before the next attack they would need to protect it better.

Suddenly a faint rumbling sound spun him around.

Gleaming slits in the low sky filled the horizon.

"Kor!" one of the colonists shouted. "Get down!"

He dove for the protection of the bunker, but for the second time that day Kor was caught by surprise.

The impact twisted him through the air. He landed hard and rolled, pushed along by the force of the impact wave from the ships.

Part of his warrior brain said that rolling was the right thing to do. Rolling would put out the flames on his clothes. The other part of his mind said he should stand and fight.

The instant the shock wave let go of him he rolled up and onto his feet, balanced to fight.

Everything around him spun, and a sharp, biting pain cut through his chest.

"You will pay," he said to the swirling images of the departing ships.

Then the blackness swirled in from all sides, and there was nothing he could do to stop it.

Or his fall toward the ground.

Nothing.

• • •

Kirk had thought the day hot before. Now it had suddenly turned into a roaring inferno as the alien craft sped by over the covered bunker. He'd seen them as small cuts against the sky forming a wedge low on the horizon. He'd counted ten of them. If Spock's count was correct, and it usually was, that left at least ten more to form a second attack force. He wondered where they were and exactly what they were attacking.

Almost before he could get his head back under the cover the ships were over and past.

The ground shook like an earthquake, and heat washed through the open-ended bunker like a blast of fire.

McCoy shouted over the rumbling, "Cover your eyes!"

But Kirk already had his arm over his face, protecting himself. He hoped Rathbone beside him had done the same thing, because he could feel the burning against his forehead and scalp. If they survived this, they would have very strange-looking sunburns.

Then as suddenly as the intense heat and loud rumbling had hit them, it was gone, leaving somewhat cooler air swirling into their small shelter.

And quiet. Ear-ringing quiet.

Sulu and Rathbone instantly began coughing, but both indicated to McCoy that they were all right. They'd just swallowed some of the hot air, and their lungs were reacting.

"Stay under cover," Kirk said, then stuck his head out and did a quick scan of the surrounding area. The alien force was obviously using the wide-focus plasma weapons again, since just about every building was left standing, but everything that could burn was afire.

Luckily the Klingons had made the prefabricated sheets for their domes fireproof. Otherwise there would have been nothing left standing and no one left alive, including them. "If I live through this, I'll write a note of thanks to the Klingon who invented these panels," he said to himself.

He eased himself out of the bunker to check the direction the ships had gone. They were already out of sight. Kirk scanned the horizon, looking for them.

Nothing but burning buildings and fields almost as far as the eye could see. It wasn't until he'd turned back in the direction from which the first wave of ships had come that he saw the second wave dropping down toward the horizon to make a run at the colony.

"That explains where the other half of the ships went," he said to himself. "Right here.

"Cover yourself!" he shouted to the others as he dived back under the prefabricated panels that served as a cover for their bunker.

He hit the dirt, face down beside Rathbone, as the ground shook and the second blast of heat smashed into them. Kirk was amazed his clothing didn't just burst into flames. He'd felt that level of heat before, but only when opening an oven to remove a freshly roasted real turkey. And that had been years ago, back when he still had time to cook, and a kitchen to cook in.

Then, again as quickly as they had come, the ships and the intense blast of heat were past, leaving swirling dust and smoke in their wake.

Kirk sat up, his face instantly dripping wet, his clothes sticking to every inch of his skin. Beside him Rathbone also sat up and leaned back against the dirt wall. Her face was streaked black with grime and sweat, and her brown hair was plastered to her head.

"Not my kind of sauna," McCoy said, trying to pull his shirt away from his skin.

"You mean you get this hot on purpose?" Sulu said.

McCoy only snorted.

"We're going to need water, Bones," Kirk said. "How much do we have?"

"Not enough for this kind of heat," McCoy said. "But whatever you have, everyone, drink it now. Doctor's orders."

Kirk and Bones didn't have canteens, but both Sulu and Rathbone each had carried one. The four of them split the contents of the two canteens, while staying under the cover of the bunker.

As they were finishing Rathbone said, "Do you think the attack is over?"

Kirk had been wondering the same thing. It didn't make sense to end the attack with just two runs at the colony. Unless that was all the firepower the small ships could carry. But plasma weapons didn't take up that much room, so Kirk doubted that was the case. If Spock were here, he'd tell them exactly what the odds were for another attack.

Suddenly the ground around them shook, and they barely had time to cover their faces before the intense heat hit them again, this time smashing them into one another, since they weren't braced. Kirk found himself being pushed over Rathbone, his head ending up on McCoy's back.

After the attack eased, Kirk pushed himself up and away from Rathbone. "I think that was your answer. Everyone all right?"

"I was hoping for a different one," she said. She pushed some wet hair out of her face. "I'm fine, I think."

"What kind of ships were those?" McCoy asked.

"I have no idea," Sulu said. He pulled out his tricorder and assessed the area around them. "Those aren't standard plasma weapons, either. They've been modified somehow."

Kirk gazed at his crew. He was proud of them. They instantly returned to business. Rathbone looked shaken, but she was fine as well.

They had never faced anything quite like this before. No wonder the Klingons had been upset. No wonder they had tried to figure out what was happening, and no wonder they had blamed the Federation at first. These attacks were deliberately aimed at the colony, as if someone did not want the colony on the planet.

"Dr. Rathbone," Kirk said. "Signi Beta was uninhabited when the Federation planned the settlement, am I right?"

"Of course," she gasped, as if her lungs still hadn't recovered from the searing heat. "We'd never colonize a settled planet."

"I doubt the Klingons would either, Jim," McCoy said. "They might have conquered it, but they wouldn't have colonized it."

Kirk gazed up at the now empty sky. "Those attacks were meant for the colony. Who would attack farmers? And why?"

"Who knows?" McCoy said. He was checking the people around him, making certain they weren't seriously injured. "Maybe we should find out who the Klingons have angered lately and who would like to attack them," McCoy said.

"Destroying a food supply is the best way to get to the heart of a culture," Rathbone said.

Kirk looked at her. She was right. He had no data points besides this one. For all he knew, Klingon farming communities all over the sector could be under attack. He shivered despite the heat.

"Well," he said, "they gave us a small reprieve. Let's see what we can do with it."

He knew the ships would be back. They seemed to use a concentrated attack formation, and they had a scorched-earth policy—something he'd studied at the Academy, something Earth hadn't seen since the twentieth century.

Barbaric.

And dangerous.

And effective.

It destroyed the defenders' ability to mount an attack, and destroyed morale by injuring home, hearth, and kin.

Kirk wiped his hand over his brow. He was sweating profusely. He wasn't used to the heat, and neither were his companions. Their water was gone.

And the attacks weren't over.

This was going to be a very long and very hot afternoon, and if they didn't get water soon, it would be their last.

CHAPTER 8

THE ATTACK ON THE COLONY LASTED JUST UNDER TWO HOURS. TWENTY-FOUR passes of the attack fleet, never varying their direction or the intensity of their fire.

Kirk had never seen anything like it. It was as if the colony was nothing more than a spot they wanted removed from the surface of the planet, and they were going to keep wiping and wiping at it until it was gone.

After the tenth attack, Kirk had contacted Spock and asked him if he could get sensor readings on the five main ships to let him know when the smaller ships returned. Spock said he could.

Fourteen intense heat waves later, Spock informed him that the smaller craft had returned to the mother ships.

Kirk managed to drag himself out of the bunker and stand up. He was light-headed and enormously thirsty. The skin on his arms felt like leather and was very sensitive to his touch.

Dr. McCoy climbed out the other side and stood beside Sulu. "Jim," he said, his voice almost a whisper, "we need water. Quickly."

Kirk nodded, too tired and dry to talk. He helped Rathbone to stand. Then the four of them staggered toward what was left of the colony.

Kirk could barely force his legs to move one in front of the other, and from the way the others beside him were staggering, he knew he wasn't the only one having problems. If that attack had lasted much longer, they might never have climbed out of that bunker.

He had never felt so useless. The plans they had made before the attack hadn't worked. Neither he nor Kor had expected such a sustained assault. Nor had he expected to have the *Enterprise* rendered useless overhead.

The enemy they were facing was greater than he expected.

Over a third of the colony buildings were in piles of burning rubble. Not once during the attack had Kirk heard any fire from the disrupter cannons, so there was no telling what had happened to Kor and his men and to Ensigns Chop and Adaro. The chances were good that they were all dead.

They passed the bodies of two Klingons, one a woman, one a young boy, as they moved around a pile of rubble. Both bodies were burned beyond recognition. The woman's clothes and most of her flesh were gone, leaving only blackened bones and a charred black pile of what had been her interior organs. All her blood and other fluids had boiled away hours before.

"We were lucky," Sulu said.

"Very," Bones said, taking Rathbone by the arm and pulling her forward away from the bodies.

"This way," Kirk said, indicating that they should move toward the colony's center courtyard. A dozen wells were scattered through the colony, but Kirk figured the one in the center courtyard was the most protected and therefore the most likely to have survived.

He was half right. The pump and structure around the well were gone, but the pressure in the well had kept the water bubbling into a wide concrete-type pool, then running off through the dry earth toward the fields beyond. They were the first to find the well, and all four of them splashed water on their faces and arms before drinking.

Kirk couldn't remember cold water ever feeling so good. It soothed and cooled his skin like nothing he'd ever felt before.

"Drink as much as you can," McCoy said after a few large swallows of his own. "Our bodies need every bit they can get to replace what they've lost. And keep our kidneys from shutting down."

This was one doctor's order that Kirk had no trouble obeying. He let the cold water flow down his throat, almost without swallowing.

After washing as much dirt and grime as he could off his face, head, and arms, and drinking until his stomach rebelled, he straightened up and looked around.

None of the colonists had yet appeared. The ones left alive obviously thought another attack was coming. And they were probably right. But for the moment they had time to prepare for it.

"All clear," he shouted, his sour, dry throat screaming in pain at the effort.

He took another long drink of cold water, then flipped open his communicator. "Kirk to *Enterprise.*"

"*Enterprise* here, Captain," Mr. Spock's voice came back strong.

"What's your status, Mr. Spock?" He could barely croak out the words. The water had helped, but not entirely.

"All systems operational," he said. "We are standing at red alert."

"Keep an eye on those transports, Mr. Spock. Give us as much warning as you can if there's any movement toward the surface."

"Understood, Captain."

"And, Mr. Spock," Kirk said, "how long until the *Farragut* arrives?"

"Three hours, fifty-two minutes," Spock said.

"Let's hope we can last that long. Kirk out."

He flipped the communicator closed and turned to McCoy, Sulu, and Rathbone. "Enjoying landing party duty, Doctor?" Kirk asked the dirt-caked, heat-baked woman as Dr. McCoy spread burn lotion on her arms and face.

She snorted, then said, "Can't wait until my next one, sir."

Kirk studied her for a moment. He could tell she was half in shock. This experience had been doubly hard on her, since this was her first time in combat.

"Good," Kirk said, smiling at her. "We'll try to make the next one as fun."

McCoy shook his head as he turned to Sulu and began to apply the burn medication.

"We need to signal the all clear to these colonists," Kirk said, "And, Bones, don't let the Klingon doctor stop you from helping this time."

McCoy looked around. "I doubt if he's still alive. But I'll find out. Now stand still so I can apply this."

Kirk did as he was told as McCoy put cool, soothing lotion on his arms and then dabbed at his face and neck. "Rub that around," he said.

Again Kirk did as he was told, letting the lotion cut the sharp sting of the burns. Then he took another long drink and faced his landing party.

"When you hear my call, I want you heading back to the bunker at a full run. Understood? And next time we all take water with us. All right?"

Kirk waited until each nodded their agreement.

"Good," Kirk said. "Let's spread the word. Doctor, you find the Klingon doctor. Rathbone, head north, giving the all clear. Sulu, you go south. I'll see what happened to the disrupter cannons and our men. I want to figure out a way to take some action against these ships."

"And everyone keep drinking," McCoy said.

"So we can boil in our own gravy during the next attack?" Sulu asked.

"Nope," McCoy said, turning and heading off. "So you'll live long enough to see that next attack."

With that sentence hanging in the hot air, Kirk took another long drink from the bubbling well before he headed toward the cannon.

Kerdoch fought to wake from the nightmare.

Heat. Searing heat.

Fever dream.

Flames surrounding him. Trapping him.

Roaring monsters. Stamping the ground, shaking him.

Flames. Heat. Roaring monsters.

Over and over.

A nightmare. A nightmare he'd never had before.

Kerdoch knew it was a nightmare, but he couldn't awake, couldn't fight his way through the flames to get away from the deep blackness crawling at him from all sides. Cool, alluring blackness that he knew was not the right path.

He must fight to wake up. He knew there were important things to be done. He could not think of them, but the feeling of important things to finish edged him forward.

He must fight.

Fight to beat the flames.

Fight to see his family again.

He was a Klingon. Klingons never gave up. Klingons fought. He had important things to do. The blackness must not touch him.

He turned and snarled at the creeping blackness, warning it away.

Again the roaring. Again the ground shook, as if to answer his challenge.

Again the heat.

In his dream he stepped forward, stared at the flames, then ran and dived over them.

He felt as if he were flying in slow motion, his dive taking a lifetime.

He thought of his wife. His children.

He thought of the welcoming coolness of the blackness behind him. Of how easy it would be to give in to it.

But he was a Klingon. Klingons did not surrender.

He ran.

He dived.

Then he passed beyond the flames.

The rumbling of the ground stopped, the heat seemed to ease, and his eyes snapped open.

Again he was awake. And alive.

He could feel his body covered with the salt of his sweat. His throat and nose were parched from the heat, his back and arms seared by the flames.

But he was awake. The darkness had not gotten him this time.

A light weight pushed down on his body and something flat and gray hung just above his face. He moved his arms and pain shot through his shoulders as he broke the burned skin, but he ignored it, pushing himself up.

Suddenly the light of day blinded him. Two prefabricated panels had toppled over and hung above him. Around him were the remains of a colony home and a few feet away was the charred body of a colonist. It was burned so badly he couldn't tell who it was.

He shoved the life-saving panels off and pushed himself to his feet. The world spun for a moment, then slowed as he stood, taking deep, painful breaths of fresh air.

All he could remember was running for the disrupter cannons when the attacks began. He hadn't made it.

He took another deep, scratchy breath, then looked around slowly, letting the pain in his head and back sharpen his focus. The attacks were slowly leveling the colony. More buildings were down now. Clearly there would be more dead.

He was very, very lucky to be alive. He hoped his family had fared as well.

He glanced in the direction of his home, then in the direction of the cannons. His wife knew of his duty to fight. She would either be alive or dead. There would be nothing he could do there. His duty was to the fight.

He picked his way carefully out of the rubble, then staggered toward the disrupter cannon, doing his best to keep his spinning head from knocking him to his knees.

He would fight until they killed him.

McCoy had hoped his caustic statement about the Klingon doctor would turn out to be wrong. But he quickly discovered it wasn't.

The Klingon doctor's makeshift medical building was nothing more than ashes, fireproof panels, and charred bodies. The doctor had been trapped under a panel. The lower half of his body had been cooked in the plasma attacks, boiling and draining away the fluids in the upper half. It had clearly not been a pleasant death. McCoy would have wished it on no one, even an arrogant Klingon.

He did a quick check through the building, looking for survivors. He found none. A Klingon or human would have to have been in good health to survive two hours of firebombing. The injured had no chance, especially when the building came apart.

McCoy moved back into the area between the domes and took a hard look around. A surprising number of domes still stood, charred and black, with nothing left to burn off the outside. Those families inside most likely were alive if they were drinking enough fluids. He didn't know exactly the fluid needs of a Klingon compared to a human, but he doubted it was significant enough to make a difference in these conditions.

"It's all clear for now," he shouted, his voice harsh and dry.

He moved toward another dome and shouted again. Near him he could hear rustling as a Klingon colonist stuck his head out of a door. In his hand was a weapon of some sort.

"The attack has stopped for the moment," McCoy said. "Get water for yourself and your family and drink it."

The Klingon stared at him for a moment, then nodded.

McCoy turned and moved back in the direction Jim had gone. He would be needed more at the point of fighting. And he felt better keeping watch over the captain. Sometimes the captain just didn't know when to take care of himself.

On either side of the colony he could hear Sulu and Rathbone giving the all clear.

He went back to the center area and took another long drink of water. In all his years he had never remembered water simply tasting so good.

He made sure his canteen was brimming full, and then, after one more large drink, headed toward the cannon on the western corner.

On the way he met Sulu and Rathbone headed for exactly the same place.

CHAPTER 9

KIRK SHOUTED "ALL CLEAR!" AS HE PASSED TWO DOMES THAT LOOKED mostly intact, then worked his way around others that were nothing more than piles of prefabricated panels. The heat had been so intense and so long-lasting that nothing was left to burn. It was as if the attackers were trying to sterilize this area of the planet. And *if* the Klingon colony domes hadn't been fireproof, they would already have succeeded.

Kirk wondered what they were going to do next. Whatever it was, he planned on at least having something here to fight back with. Hiding in a hole just wasn't his style, even though it had saved his life and the lives of part of his land party.

Two Klingon colonists slowly climbed out of a shallow bunker near the disrupter cannon. They looked dazed and badly burned, but at least they were alive. Better than the two piles of charred bones ten paces from the guns.

The colonists watched him approach, saying nothing. Kirk doubted they could speak.

"It's clear for now," he said. "The well in the center court is working. You need water."

They nodded and shuffled in that direction. Kirk had never seen Klingons shuffle, only swagger. It was an odd sight.

Behind them Kirk saw one of Kor's men stand up from the bunker and stare down at something at his feet.

Kirk jumped up on the gun and looked down.

Kor! And sitting next to him, looking shocked, was Ensign Adaro.

"Are you all right?" Kirk asked, jumping down into the bunker beside the Klingon commander.

The warrior managed a hoarse yes.

Adaro just nodded.

It was clear to Kirk, without being a doctor, that Kor wasn't alive by much. Kirk flipped open his communication handset. "Dr. McCoy, I need you at the western disrupter cannon."

"I'm already on my way," McCoy said.

Kirk stood up and glanced around. McCoy, Sulu, and Dr. Rathbone were no more than twenty paces away. McCoy ran when he saw the captain and a moment later was kneeling beside Kor.

"The other doctor?" Kirk asked.

"Dead," McCoy said as he scanned Kor. He quickly dug into his medical kit, gave the Klingon a quick injection, then he scanned him again.

"How is he?" Kirk asked.

"Badly burned, and, like all of us, dehydrated. He's also got a number of broken bones." McCoy uncapped his canteen and forced a solid flow of water into Kor's mouth. The commander swallowed some, then choked.

McCoy shrugged and let some more water dribble into Kor's mouth.

Kirk turned to Sulu and Dr. Rathbone, who were watching from the cannon platform. "Sulu, take Ensign Adaro and this man to the well." He pointed to the warrior who still stood above Kor, looking dazed. "Force them to drink, if you have to."

Sulu nodded.

Kirk turned to Dr. Rathbone. "I need you to head for the other disrupter cannon to look for Ensign Chop."

"On my way, sir," she said, and quickly hurried off.

"Sulu," Kirk said, "after you get them to drink, I want you and Adaro to carry water back here, as much as you can. We're going to need it."

For an instant he didn't think the warrior would go with Sulu. Kirk looked him right in the eye. "I want you back here beside Kor, refreshed and ready to fight in ten minutes. Understood?"

The warrior nodded and turned to accept Sulu's helping hand. Ensign Adaro stood, his hand on the cannon platform beside him. For a moment Kirk didn't think the young man would be able to walk, but he seemed to gather his strength as he climbed from the bunker.

Behind Sulu, Kirk saw Kerdoch stagger into the open, then fall to his knees in the dirt. The man staggered to his feet and came forward some more.

"Bones, is Kor stable for the moment?" Kirk asked.

"He's as stable as I can get him," McCoy said. "Damned Klingon blood systems, anyhow."

"Then I've got another patient for you," Kirk said.

McCoy took one look at the staggering Kerdoch and grabbed his canteen. A moment later at the foot of the disrupter cannon platform, Kerdoch was drinking while McCoy applied burn cream to his arms and back.

While McCoy worked, Kirk looked around at what they were facing. From what he could tell, the disrupter cannon was still armed and ready to fire. The two piles of burned bones must have been the poor souls who tried to man the gun in the first attack. One of them must have been one of Kor's warriors.

The cannon was anchored to the top of a square concrete-type platform sitting out in the open.

"We need more protection," Kirk said to himself.

The bunker where Kor lay had been dug on the western edge of the platform. The alien craft had come on too fast to be fired upon directly and to have allowed the operator to get to safety, but the alien attack craft could have been hit while they were moving away from the colony after they'd made a run.

They needed a fireproof shelter around the cannon on three sides. Something to protect the gun operators until the craft moved past.

Kirk looked around. Somehow they had to build something out of fireproof panels that would withstand an attack.

Sulu and Ensign Adaro appeared from behind a dome carrying three pans of water each. Kirk watched as the young ensign stopped at McCoy and Kerdoch and handed the Klingon colonist a pan. Kerdoch drank almost all of the water before stopping, and McCoy patted his shoulder.

Sulu climbed up beside Kirk, set down two pans, and handed one to him without a word. Kirk drank the cold water with relish, wondering if there would ever be a time again when he wouldn't be thirsty.

"Kirk," a faint voice came from behind them.

Kirk turned as Kor tried to sit up and failed.

"Bones!" Kirk yelled and jumped down beside Kor.

"Drink this," he said, holding the water to Kor's mouth and pouring, not giving the Klingon a choice. This time Kor managed three good swallows before he choked and coughed.

"Go easy," Kirk said.

Kor only nodded as McCoy jumped down beside him and scanned him. "You shouldn't be moving," McCoy said. "You've got two shattered ribs, either one of which might puncture a lung. And in these conditions, you wouldn't last ten minutes if that happens. I've got the ribs mending, but you'll have to give them some time."

Kor nodded. "You order well, Doctor."

"Just don't cross me, Commander," McCoy said. "Or I'll give you a sedative that will make you sleep for a full month."

Kor only nodded, but Kirk could tell he was laughing at McCoy. And was glad the doctor was here.

Kerdoch and Kor's second-in-command were standing above the bunker. Kirk stood and looked at those around him. "It's time to get to work," he said. "We've got to build a cover for this bunker and a shelter for that gun. We can use those fireproof panels. Think we can do it?"

Sulu nodded.

Ensign Adaro glanced around, still looking confused.

Both Kerdoch and the warrior looked down at Kor.

Kor laughed softly. "Kirk, you are a strange one. Fighting for a planet you do not possess." Then Kor nodded to his two men. "Do as he says. His word is as mine."

Both nodded.

Kirk turned to Kerdoch. "We need more help. Round up as many men as you can find. And bring more water back with you, along with any tools that might help build a shelter out of those exterior dome panels."

Kerdoch nodded and without a word headed off.

"The rest of us need to start gathering panels from the destroyed shelters." Kirk said. "Take only whole ones. We need as many of those as we can get. We have to get this bunker covered first."

He leaned down and patted McCoy on the shoulder where he knelt above Kor. "Stay with your patient. I don't want him dying before the fight."

Kor coughed and frowned at Kirk. "I will live to the day we fight, Kirk. It will be a glorious day."

"I look forward to that," Kirk said, laughing.

And actually, at that moment he did.

Rathbone moved quickly away from the captain, heading through the burned domes of the Klingon colony. She was having a hard time grasping what was happening around her. She felt somehow detached from her burned and aching body. And the heat seemed to wrap itself around her like a blanket, smothering the sounds.

Too much had happened to her too fast and with no preparation. One moment it seemed she had been peacefully working in her lab on the *Enterprise;* the next moment she was trying to survive intense heat and seeing dead bodies everywhere. Starfleet had taught her procedures to use in emergencies and on planetary missions, but nothing could have prepared her for this.

She forced herself to slow her walk and conserve energy. But it still seemed like only a few seconds before she reached the other disrupter cannon.

There was no doubt that it would take hours or maybe even days of repair before it would fire again. It lay on its side, its barrel smashed down into the hard ground. In front of the concrete base platform were two burnt bodies, the clothes and skin completely gone, the bones blackened. All the blood and bodily fluids had long since boiled away, leaving only a red powder in the dust around the remains.

She was almost afraid to look, but hearing the captain's orders again inside her head, she moved up close to the remains.

Then she saw what she'd been afraid she'd find. Standing on end, seeming to stick out of one pile, was a charred Starfleet insignia, blackened by the heat but still recognizable. Ensign Chop, the cute brown-haired kid from Arizona.

"Oh, no," she said, holding her hand over her mouth and forcing herself to breathe deep gulps of the hot air. The water she'd drunk threatened to force its way back up her throat, but she held it down.

After two more long, deep breaths, she reached down and plucked the scrap of cloth from the pile of bones. She shuddered as she did so. How did people get used to this kind of duty? She took a deep breath of the hot, fetid air. *Calm,* she told herself. *Calm.* Then, grasping the singed insignia tightly in her hand, she turned and headed back for Captain Kirk.

Crossing the colony should have taken longer. She wondered if she blanked out as she walked. She knew that between the heat, the burns, and the stress, she wasn't thinking as clearly as she should have been.

One moment she had been standing near Ensign Chop; the next, she was beside Captain Kirk. When she saw him, she handed him the insignia.

He gazed at it a moment, then closed his fist over it. "Damn," he said softly.

And then he turned away, standing alone, facing the burned Klingon fields.

McCoy came up to her.

Nothing was said.

Nothing could be said.

Captain Bogle stood in front of his chair, facing the image of Commander Spock on the main screen. As far as possible, Bogle had his ship and his crew ready for any upcoming fight. His engineer, Projeff, said the *Farragut* hadn't been in such good shape since it left spacedock the first time. Every system had been checked and double-checked. And for the last hour Projeff had been working long-distance with the chief engineer of the *Enterprise,* Mr. Scott, on a method of strengthening the shields against the enemy weapons.

"Your estimated time of arrival, Captain?" Spock asked.

"Forty-one minutes," Bogle said.

Spock nodded, his Vulcan face unreadable. "Captain Kirk and the landing party are still trapped on the surface, along with Commander Kor and his team. Subcommander Korath reports his ship is repaired and standing by. Two more Klingon battle cruisers have been dispatched but will not arrive for twelve hours."

"All right," Bogle said as he processed the information. "Are the alien ships still holding position?"

"Yes, sir," Spock said.

"Have there been further attacks on the colony?"

"No," Spock said.

Bogle nodded. That was as he had hoped it would be. "Commander Spock, do you have a suggestion as to our course of action?"

Spock nodded. "I do, sir," he said. "When you arrive we should endeavor to find out exactly why these invaders are attacking the Klingon colony."

Bogle stared at the Vulcan for a moment, then stifled a laugh. "And how would you suggest we do that, Commander?" he asked.

Spock shook his head, his serious expression unchanged. "I do not know, sir. But logic leads us to believe that the reason for this attack is the path to the solution."

Bogle had never understood exactly how Kirk managed to function with a Vulcan at his side, even though Spock was becoming well know as the best first officer in the fleet, and most likely in line for the captain's chair. But at times like this Bogle wondered how Spock's logic didn't drive Kirk nuts. It would him.

"I would agree with you, Mr. Spock," Bogle said, "but there does not seem to be a direct course of action implied in your suggestion."

Spock nodded. "I agree. Therefore, if the situation remains the same, the course of action I would suggest is negotiation."

"Negotiation," Bogle said dryly. "Do we even know who these aliens are?"

"Clearly, we do not," Spock said in that infuriatingly calm tone. "We have no record of these ships, nor have we identified their makers. They do not answer our hails."

"Then how do you suggest we negotiate?"

"Obviously they want something from the planet," Spock said. "We must determine what that is."

"They want the colonists off it," Bogle said. "It seems fairly simple to me."

"Forgive me, Captain, but it does not seem simple to me. These ships may carry a life-form so alien that it does not recognize the life signs below."

"You'd think it'd recognize that the ships above are filled with life-forms," Bogle said.

"They did not obliterate our ships," Spock said. "They are attempting to obliterate the colony."

"Do the Klingons recognize these ships?" Bogle asked.

"They claim they do not," Spock said.

"Sounds like you don't believe them," Bogle said.

"I do not have any evidence to believe or disbelieve the Klingons, Captain. I merely report their statements. They claim they do not know."

"But you reserve the possibility that they do."

"The attack is directed at a Klingon colony," Spock said. "Perhaps there is enmity between the aliens and the Klingons. We are not the Klingons' allies. They may not believe we need to know who their enemies are."

Bogle nodded. For once, Spock's maddening logic made sense. The Klingons wouldn't want the Federation to know who their enemies were. Thought of in Klingon terms, the Federation might ally itself with the enemies to wipe out the Klingon Empire.

There was nothing more they could accomplish through such speculation. "Thank you for your insights, Mr. Spock," Bogle said. "Keep me informed if the situation changes. *Farragut* out."

The image of Commander Spock was replaced by the view of stars flashing past in warp.

Behind Bogle, Science Officer Richard Lee said, "Fascinating."

Captain Bogle could only sit and stare at the stars and wonder just what exactly he was rushing into.

Kerdoch ran at his full pace, even though his head still pounded and he felt weak. Within a few moments he was at the well in the central area of the colony. Dozens of women and men were filling pans and bottles from the bubbling pool. It was good to see that so many had survived.

He stopped at the well and allowed himself the extra few seconds to dip his face into the water and drink fully. Then he let the cool water run down over his hot arms and neck. The medication that the human doctor had spread on his burns had helped a great deal, but the water still felt wonderful.

"Attention," he said, his voice harsh and sore as he tried to force volume from it. "Commander Kor and the human captain need help defending the colony on the west side."

Around him three of the men nodded. "We will be there," Katanin said.

Kerdoch nodded. "Bring weapons and tools to work on the dome panels. Also bring water."

He turned and at a run headed deeper into the colony in the direction of his home. He had tools and water jugs there, and he had to make sure his wife and children had survived.

Relief swept over him as he discovered that his home was again one of the ones standing. His wife and eldest son were outside, doing what they could to cover a hole in the paneling with other panels.

She saw him coming, and her face lit up.

Such a look he would always remember.

Such a look would keep him fighting for his home and family until he could no longer stand or even crawl to the battle.

She hugged him, and he returned the hug. Then he slapped the back of his very excited oldest son. "Have you got water?" he asked.

"We have been to the central well twice since the all-clear signal," she said. "Will the enemy craft return?"

"Yes," he said. "And this time we will knock them from the sky."

She nodded but said nothing.

He turned to his son. "Bring me my tool belt. Quickly."

His son ducked inside their home. While he waited, Kerdoch held his wife by the shoulders, wanting to have her remain there. They had both survived the last attack. He hoped they continued to be so lucky. Many of his friends had not been.

A moment later his son appeared carrying a heavy tool belt and a canteen. Kerdoch nodded and took both. "You think clearly, son. Help your mother prepare for the next attack. Take extra panels inside and form a second line of paneling over the furniture."

The son nodded.

"He is my right hand," she said.

"You are both my heart," Kerdoch said. Then with a light squeeze of his wife's arm, he turned and jogged toward the disrupter cannon, the heavy tool belt and full canteen a comfort in his hands.

On the way he recruited three more colonists.

CHAPTER 10

Kirk, Sulu, Rathbone, Ensign Adaro, and Kahaq, Kor's officer, worked as best they could gathering the fireproof panels. Within a few minutes after Kerdoch left, three more colonists arrived with tools. Kor, from his place in the bottom of the bunker, told them to follow Kirk's orders, and within minutes Kirk had them digging Kor's bunker deeper and placing a double layer of panels over the top.

There was no way Kirk was going to let Kor get killed if he could help it. Building the bunkers big enough and deep enough for all of them to survive another attack was the first priority. The last thing he wanted was for all of them to end up as Ensign Chop had done.

Ten minutes later, Kerdoch and three more colonists returned and, also at Kor's command, set to work following Kirk's plan. Seven colonists, Sulu, Kahaq, Ensign Adaro, and Rathbone made the work go extremely fast.

Kirk could tell that Sulu and McCoy, who still sat next to the Klingon commander, didn't much care for the fact that Kor had to give his okay, but Kirk didn't care at all. As long as the bunkers got built and the protection over the gun was up and ready for the next attack, it didn't matter at all to him who gave the orders. What was important was stopping the attacks, and then maybe figuring out why they were happening.

The group, at Kirk's direction, next dug cross-bunkers on either end of the first bunker and covered them with panels. The newly dug bunkers ran up the two sides of the concrete platform for the disrupter cannon. At four places along the three bunkers an opening was left so that a person could dive from the concrete slab into the bunker for protection. As fast as the alien ships attacked, Kirk knew such an escape might be necessary.

As the group began to build the shelter over the disrupter cannon, Kirk flipped open his communicator. "Kirk to *Enterprise*."

"Spock here, Captain."

"Has the *Farragut* arrived yet?"

"It is due in twelve minutes," Spock said.

"Is there any movement from our alien friends?"

"No, Captain. We have continued to hail them and have received no response."

"Don't take them on unless you need to, Spock."

"Captain, it would not be logical to 'take on' a larger force. We shall do what we have to."

"I expect nothing more. Kirk out."

He snapped the handset shut and glanced around. The shelter over the disrupter cannon was going up quicker than he had thought. Now he just hoped Spock and Captain Bogle could figure out a way of stopping the aliens before they launched another attack on the colony.

After handing a panel to a colonist on the gun platform, Kirk watched Rathbone stop and wipe the sweat from her face. She and McCoy both looked beat. Sulu had taken off his shirt, and his body glistened with sweat. The twin suns were clearly sapping the strength out of everyone, almost as quickly as the heat from the attackers' plasma beams.

"Doctors," Kirk said. He motioned for McCoy and Rathbone to join him beside the bunker for a moment.

"Hot enough to bake a fish," McCoy muttered as he climbed up to where Kirk stood.

"I thought the saying was 'fry an egg'?" Kirk said.

"Not where I'm from," McCoy said.

"Well," Dr. Rathbone said, "I'm from the British Isles, and we don't have any saying at all for this kind of heat, because it *never* gets this hot."

McCoy only snorted, but Kirk laughed.

"I need you both, and Ensign Adaro, to go for more water," he said. "Carry as much as you can, but get back as quick as you can. I don't want you trapped outside these bunkers if another attack starts."

McCoy shook his head. "After watching you people work this hard to build them, I damn well plan to be in them."

"I'm with you, Dr. McCoy," Rathbone said.

Both of them turned to gather up the empty and half-empty water containers. Then they rounded up the ensign from his work on the shelter and headed into the colony center.

Kirk moved to the shelter that had gone up around three sides of the cannon. The colonists had actually braced the bottoms of the panels against the concrete base of the gun, and used the same dome skeleton structures to support the upper ones. Then they had added a second layer of panels.

As Kirk finished his quick inspection, the six colonists were connecting in a third overlapping layer, forming a very strong wall. Kirk had no doubt it would withstand an attack on three sides. But if the aliens broke their pattern and attacked from the opposite direction, anyone inside without protection would be baked like a potato almost instantly.

"What do you think, Captain?" Sulu asked as he fixed a panel in place near the front opening.

"I think I'll have to trust my life on it," Kirk said.

Sulu nodded. "You'll need a second on that gun."

Kirk glanced at the sweaty face of Sulu. "Yes, I will."

"I would be honored, sir," Sulu said.

"I would be honored to have your assistance, Lieutenant," Kirk said.

Suddenly the beep of his communicator he'd been fearing filled the hot air. Inside the bunker Kirk could hear the deep tone of Kor's communicator.

That was not a good sign. Not at all.

Kirk flipped his handset open. "Kirk here."

"Captain," Spock said, "the small ships are leaving the two transports. They will arrive at your location in five minutes and seven seconds."

"Where is the *Farragut,* Spock?"

"It is dropping out of warp now, Captain."

"Stop as many of those small ships as you can, Spock. And good luck."

"Luck will have nothing to do with it, Captain. *Enterprise* out."

Kirk flipped his communicator closed and glanced at Sulu's worried face. "Let's hope that's not the last time we hear those words."

"It won't be, Captain," Sulu said.

Kirk could tell Sulu was as worried as he was. But there was no time for that now. Only action.

"The ships are on their way, people," Kirk said, turning to face his work crew. The colonists had all stopped and were watching him.

He pointed to Kahaq. "Get down below with your commander and stay with him. Take any water left up here below as you go."

Kahaq nodded and jumped toward the bunker.

Kirk turned to the colonists. "The ships will be here in five minutes. Spread out through the colony and warn everyone to take cover. Then do the same yourselves. Don't come out until someone sounds the all clear."

This time the colonists didn't need Kor's permission to move. As a unit they jumped from the platform and ran toward the remaining domes, shouting the warning as they went.

Only Kerdoch held his ground. "I am here to fight," he said. "I will help you with the gun."

Kirk looked at the Klingon colonist's stern expression for a moment, then nodded. "Take some water inside the shelter."

Kerdoch jumped into action without so much as a nod.

"Mr. Sulu, ready the gun." Kirk glanced at the bare chest of his officer and remembered the coming heat. "And you might want to put a shirt on to protect your skin."

Sulu nodded and sprang into action.

Kirk grabbed another sheet of paneling. He tossed it in on the floor of the shelter near the gun. Then he did the same with two more. It wasn't much, but they might serve as one man shields in case the ships came in from another direction.

It wasn't until he jumped back up on the concrete platform and moved inside the gun shelter that it dawned on him that McCoy, Rathbone, and Adaro hadn't returned yet.

He glanced in the direction of the colony. No sign of them yet. They had less than two minutes. Surely they must have heard the warnings from the colonists.

As the seconds ticked past, Kirk's stomach twisted with the realization that his friend McCoy wasn't returning.

With one minute left, Kirk moved to the edge of the concrete platform, turned his back on the colony, and began scanning the skies on the western horizon for the ships.

McCoy was smart. He and the others would find shelter. They'd make it.

Somehow.

• • •

McCoy knew the moment he, Rathbone, and the young ensign entered the main colony square near the well that something was wrong. A large Klingon woman was sprawled on the edge of the pool, one hand dangling in the water. A boy, not more than two years old, lay with his head against her stomach. A baby in a basket moved slightly.

McCoy ran up to her, dropping the water containers and pulling the medical scanner from his belt. The woman was almost dead. It was amazing she had made it this far, she was so dehydrated.

Since the baby moved, he scanned it first. It was alive and dehydrated, but not as bad as the woman. The boy was also alive.

"Get the children water," he said to Rathbone. Then he quickly gave the woman an injection of fluids, hoping to pull her away from death enough to get water into her the natural way.

She didn't move.

"Damn," McCoy said under his breath.

"Is she going to make it?" Rathbone asked, taking the baby into her arms and patting the child's dry lips with a wet part of her uniform. Ensign Adaro put his arms around the small boy and lifted him. The child moaned. Adaro held the boy near the fountain, and he drank as though he had never had water in his life.

"I don't know if she's going to make it," McCoy said. He knew he should have studied the Federation's limited records on Klingon physiology on the way here instead of checking the medical supplies. "We need to get her out of this heat somehow, and pour water down her."

Rathbone stood with the child and looked quickly around the square. "There is no help in sight," she said, sounding perplexed.

No help in sight. He didn't like the sound of that, but he didn't have time to think about it.

He scanned the woman's vital signs. No change at all. And he didn't really know if he was doing the right thing by giving her fluids directly. For all he knew, what worked for a human might be deadly for a Klingon. It had never occurred to him to study the fluid needs of Klingons in high heat. In his worst nightmare he had never imagined he'd need to know such a detail.

Suddenly three of the colonists who had been working with the captain came running into the square. "The ships!" they shouted. "Take cover."

"Wonderful timing," McCoy said to himself. He stood and shouted at the running colonists. "We need help here!" He pointed to the woman and children.

One of the colonists veered his way while the others went on giving the warning. "My home is close," he said.

"Fine," McCoy said. "Take her anywhere. Ensign, help him."

Ensign Adaro set the small boy down and came to McCoy's side. Together he and the colonist picked up the large, unconscious woman.

"We'll follow with the children and water," McCoy said.

The Klingon who had offered his home only nodded.

McCoy quickly grabbed three pans and filled them, then took the little boy by the hand and headed after the two men. Rathbone, with full bottles of water and the baby, was right behind him.

As they ducked behind the two men inside one of the domed homes on the edge of the central courtyard, McCoy's own words about making it back to the bunker came back to him. They weren't going to be back, at least not until this attack was over.

He hoped the captain made it through the attack.

Then the woman moaned as the two men laid her on a cotlike bed, and McCoy became too busy to think about his captain.

Until the first blast shook the domed structure and the heat filled the room so fast he could hardly breathe.

"So much for deciding what to do," Captain Bogle said to himself as the *Farragut* dropped out of warp. "Battle stations everyone!"

The alarms blared and the lights dimmed slightly as his ship smoothly went to alert.

Bogle forced himself to take a deep breath and focus on the events going on in front of him. They'd been in fights before. This was just another. Even though it was five against three. And each of the five ships against them was twice the size of the *Farragut.* It was still just another fight.

On the main screen two of the five huge alien ships were opening their large rear sections. Small, thin, wedgelike craft were pouring from both ships and turning toward the planet's atmosphere, obviously heading into another attack run at the Klingon colony.

Both the *Enterprise* and the Klingon battle cruiser had turned and were moving in, firing phaser beams at the smaller ships scattered behind the larger ones. It looked as if they were firing at a swarm of large flies buzzing a cow.

"Ensign Summer, bring us in over the planet," Bogle said.

He moved up and put his hand firmly on Lieutenant Michael Book's shoulder. "Lieutenant, target any of the smaller ships you can lock on to and fire when in range."

"Yes, sir," Book said.

Bogle let go of the lieutenant's shoulder and stepped back next to his captain's chair.

The next few seconds went by slowly as the *Farragut* moved into range. Then the phaser fired three times as one of the larger alien craft turned and moved toward them, firing as it came. Two of the targeted smaller craft exploded.

"Got them," Lieutenant Book said.

"Keep firing, mister," Bogle said.

The *Enterprise* had destroyed three of the atmosphere fighters, and the battle cruiser had taken out two. But at least fifteen of the smaller craft were still dropping toward the planet's surface.

The *Farragut* rocked with the impact of phaser fire from the large alien ship.

"Shields holding," First Officer Lee said.

"Continue targeting the smaller ships!" Bogle ordered. "They'll be out of range soon."

More phaser fire shot from his ship and took out two more of the smaller craft in small balls of orange and red flame.

The larger alien ship fired its phasers again and again, all direct hits against the *Farragut*'s screens.

The *Farragut* rocked so violently Bogle was tossed to the deck.

Annoyed at himself for not being in his chair, he rolled with his fall and came up on one knee holding on to the rail.

Somehow Lieutenant Book had managed to stay in his seat, but everyone else was down on the deck, scrambling to get back to their stations.

"Arm torpedoes," Bogle yelled. "Target the large ship and fire when ready."

A moment later the *Farragut* rocked as four torpedoes were fired, all exploding in direct hits on the alien's screens.

"Evasive action," he said as Ensign Summer scrambled back to his chair.

The ship swung high and to the left of the huge alien ship, but not fast enough to avoid three more direct hits on the screens. This time Bogle remained in a kneeling position, his eyes on the screen, as the *Farragut* shook and rumbled at the impacts.

After the rocking calmed he quickly climbed back to his feet and dropped into his chair.

"Screens at forty percent," Lee said. "Damage on decks eight and ten."

"The *Enterprise?"* Bogle asked.

"Under heavy fire," Lee said, "but still returning fire. The Klingon battle cruiser is pinned between two of the big ships. One of the alien transports seems to be standing off and watching."

Bogle nodded. Lucky break there.

"The Klingons will have to take care of themselves for a moment," he said, more to himself than any of the crew. Then to Ensign Summer he said, "Take us right at the ship the *Enterprise* is firing at. Ignore the one that's after us."

The main viewscreen shifted around to show the fight between the *Enterprise* and the much larger alien ship. Even from here Bogle could see the *Enterprise* rocking with the impact of the alien phasers.

"Lieutenant Sandy, open an audio channel to the *Enterprise."*

"Open, sir," Sandy said almost instantly.

"Spock, this is Bogle." The captain didn't wait for a reply. "Target their right wing section. On my mark."

Then he turned his attention to his crew. "We're going to do the same," he said. "On the same mark. All right, Lieutenant?"

"Ready, sir," Book said.

"Now!" Bogle said to him and Spock.

The phaser beams from both starships pulsed on the alien's right wing screens for a long moment, then broke through, cutting into the skin of the ship underneath.

Then the *Farragut* rocked like a bad ride in an amusement park as the alien ship behind them hit them with a series of full, direct hits, one right after another.

Bogle managed to stay in his chair this time, but not by much.

"Aft screens failing," Lee shouted.

"Turn us around," Bogle ordered. "Return fire!"

More direct hits rocked them.

Behind them the *Enterprise* was firing over the *Farragut*'s bow, going after the ship that was attacking the *Farragut.*

"You got it, Mr. Spock," Bogle said through his teeth as his ship rocked again. "We've got a chance if we gang up on these giants."

"Shields failing," Lee shouted.

"Full fire," Bogle said. "All weapons. Now!"

If they were going to die, Bogle figured, they were at least going to put a dent in the ship that killed them, maybe give the *Enterprise* a fighting chance.

Bogle noted the *Enterprise* was also firing with all weapons at the alien ship when everything on the screen and around him suddenly exploded.

He was tossed sideways from his chair like a doll thrown by an angry child.

He cleared the handrail in the air, rolled once, and smashed shoulder and head first into the turbolift doors.

The last thing he heard was the whoosh of the lift's doors opening before the blackness took him away.

CHAPTER 11

KIRK STOOD AT THE OPENING OF THE SHELTER OVER THE DISRUPTER CANNON. He gripped the edge of the three-layer-thick material, and studied the horizon. Both suns were lower in the sky, and the light seemed to shimmer in the heat waves across the flat, blackened farmland.

Then, just at the exact time Spock had predicted, the ships appeared, thin silver lines against the sky. They were staging their run from the exact same direction as the first attacks. Whoever these aliens were, they certainly were patient, as well as creatures of habit. That fact might come in very handy in face to face meetings, if he lived long enough to get to that point.

Kirk counted seven ships in the first wave. At least three less than last run. Maybe Spock and Bogle had managed to make a dent in their numbers.

"Get ready," Kirk shouted, both to Sulu and Kerdoch behind him, and to Kor and his first officer in the bunker.

Kirk ducked back inside the shelter and took up a position near Sulu, who had the targeting controls for the cannon.

"The moment they're past us, target and fire," Kirk said. "You might have time to get two shots off before they're out of range."

Sulu nodded.

Kirk picked up a panel and slid it to Kerdoch on the other side of Sulu. Then he picked up a second. "Hold these up in front of us to slow down any heat backwash," Kirk said. "But be careful to not block Sulu's aim."

Kerdoch nodded and got the first sheet into position just as the world exploded around them.

The structure over them shook, and the heat washed over Kirk like a full-force blast furnace. The world seemed to go red, the ground trembled, wind whipped the hot air through the shelter at almost hurricane force.

Kirk barely managed to hang on to the sheet he was holding, and only then because it was braced and it had smashed back against his chest.

Kerdoch stood no chance of holding his panel. It blasted out of his hands and the shelter like it had been shot from some strange gun. It swirled in the air like a feather from a passing bird.

Somehow, the shelter the colonists had built over the gun withstood the plasma attack.

Almost instantly the ships were beyond the edge of the colony.

Sulu fired.

The report of the disrupter cannon discharging in the confined space of the shelter was more like a bomb going off inside a small room. The concussion filled the air and rocked the shelter.

Kirk's ears rang, and he hoped his eardrums hadn't been damaged.

Just beyond the edge of the colony the third alien craft from the right exploded in a ball of orange flame.

Sulu fired again.

Kirk had managed in the short instant between shots to cover his ears. The sound of the discharge still increased the ringing in his head to a painful level.

The second craft on the right exploded.

"Great shooting, Mr. Sulu," he shouted over the ringing in his head, then scrambled to the front edge of the shelter. If the alien ships stayed on the same pattern as the morning attacks, there would be almost a full sixty seconds before the next wave.

He slowly poked his head around the corner to stare through the heat waves to the west.

He was right. No ships had yet appeared for an attack run, and the remaining five ships from the first run were long out of sight.

"Get ready," Kirk said. Sulu and Kerdoch nodded as they checked over the gun.

Kirk stepped farther out on the concrete platform to get a better view of the surrounding blackened farmland. He scanned all sides once, just to make sure. Then he saw the new wave of attack ships forming in the same location.

He glanced in the other directions again. Nothing but the one wave forming in the exact same place as before. Seven ships again. If nothing else, they were consistent. That would be their downfall.

He ducked back into the shelter. "Next wave in about fifteen seconds."

"Should I try for three?" Sulu asked.

"Do you have time?"

"No way of telling exactly," Sulu said.

"His second shot," Kerdoch said, "was well within the range of this cannon."

Kirk nodded to the Klingon, then faced Sulu. "Why not? I think my ears can take it. Brace yourselves."

As the last word came from his mouth the shelter again seemed to explode in a whirlwind of heat, thundering sound, and shaking ground.

Then Sulu fired.

The concussion from the gun pounded Kirk into the side of the shelter, but he managed to keep his feet under him.

The center ship exploded.

Sulu fired again.

The next ship to the right exploded.

Sulu fired a third time.

The next ship down the line exploded.

Three down, four to go in this wave.

"Great work," Kirk shouted over the deafening ringing in his ears. He was convinced that all three of them were going to have their hearing damaged, but that was a small price to pay for staying alive.

Kerdoch laughed and slapped Sulu on the back.

Sulu patted the handholds on the gun. "We got to get us one of these," he said. "That felt good. But I might never hear again."

Kirk had to agree with his officer. Fighting back did feel good. Much better than hiding in a bunker. And he too was amazed by the ability of the Klingon disrupter cannon. A very impressive weapon.

Kirk looked around for water. Two of the pans had been knocked over by the high winds, but a large jug still looked full. He picked it up and handed it to Sulu.

"If the aliens are as consistent as I think they are," Kirk said, "we've got four minutes until the next attack."

"My ears might almost recover by then," Sulu said as he took the jug from Kirk and took a long drink. Then he handed it to Kerdoch, who did the same and passed it back over the end of the gun to Kirk.

Kirk let the warm water almost pour down his throat. Every inch of his skin was coated in sweat, and even the hot afternoon wind felt cool compared to the furnacelike temperatures caused by the enemy plasma beams.

He handed the jug back to Sulu and moved out to take his watch post. No ships in sight at all. In any direction. It would be a few minutes, if they stayed on pattern.

He moved to the end of the platform above the bunker and inspected the panels. Like the shelter, every panel had stayed in place.

"Kahaq? Kerdoch?" Kor shouted. "Are you okay?"

"We live," Kahaq's voice came back strong and defiant from inside the bunker.

"We downed five of their ships," Kirk said. "Another attack should be coming in a few minutes."

"We will join you," Kor's voice came back, much weaker than that of his officer.

"There is no more room in the shelter," Kirk said. "If we are killed, you must take our place. Until then, stay where you are. Rest and prepare for the fight."

"Kirk," Kor said, "you sometimes know us too well. We will remain here."

Suddenly Kirk's communicator beeped for attention. Kor's did not this time. The *Enterprise* still existed, but did this mean the battle cruiser did not?

Kirk flipped open his communicator. "Kirk here."

"Captain," Spock said, "nine of the small attack ships have returned. Five are unaccounted for."

"Mr. Sulu accounted for those five, Mr. Spock. How's the *Enterprise?*"

"We sustained heavy damage on seven decks. Mr. Scott has returned the screens to eighty percent. All weapons are now back on-line."

"Good," Kirk said, feeling very relieved that the *Enterprise* had made it through the fight. "The other ships?"

"The *Farragut* sustained heavy damage and casualties. Their warp, weapons systems, and screens are off-line, but Mr. Projeff, their chief engineer, informs me that the screens should be back up within two minutes. Weapons may take a little longer. Captain Bogle was injured. He is unconscious but alive."

Kirk didn't like the sound of his friend Bogle being injured, but there was nothing he could do for him at the moment. "The battle cruiser?"

"Also heavily damaged but still weapons-and warp-capable. One of the enemy ships was completely destroyed, another heavily damaged. The remaining alien ships are holding a position between the *Enterprise* and the planet, keeping us out of transporter range."

"Good work, Spock," Kirk said. "Hold your position and keep me informed. Kirk out."

Kirk flipped his communicator closed and let out a deep sigh. For the moment, at least, the attack was over. Now it was time to give the all clear.

He looked around at the blackened structures and the fields beyond. Somehow this colony still survived, holding on and fighting back.

Now it was time to see if McCoy and Rathbone had made it through the attack.

Crouched on the floor beside the Klingon cot, McCoy did his best to protect his face and the face of his unconscious patient as the second attack smashed into the colony dome, shaking it and sending waves of intense heat swirling inside.

During the first attack the dome had shaken and a blast of burning air had filled the room, twisting the interior around like a Kansas tornado had been turned loose inside the building. McCoy had felt the heat burning his face and hands and other areas of unprotected skin. He had managed to bury his face quickly against his shirtsleeve. Most likely he'd only have a sunburn level burn from this attack.

Rathbone, with the Klingon baby in her arms, had managed to protect both her face and the baby by bending over the child and pushing her face into its blanket. Between attacks the child cried, but McCoy could tell it was a healthy cry.

Ensign Adaro had managed to hide his face and arms under the blanket near the woman's feet as he sat on the floor.

The family who lived in this dome had built a protective fort of furniture near one wall, and the young boy and the family were all in there. Only McCoy, Rathbone, Ensign Adaro, the sick Klingon woman, and the baby remained in the main room.

When the second attack rocked the dome, McCoy managed to protect both his face against his shirt and the unconscious mother's face and arms with a blanket held tight over her. The last thing she needed was more heat damage.

After a few short seconds the heat eased, and McCoy quickly scanned the mother. She was still alive, still breathing, but under these attack conditions, she wouldn't be for long. Outside three explosions echoed between the colony domes.

"Let's hope that's Jim," McCoy said to Rathbone.

She nodded, then swallowed, not saying a word. Her face was red and covered with sweat. Her eyes had the look of a person nearing shock. McCoy had seen that same look a number of times in crewmen inexperienced in sudden violence. There was no doubt Dr. Rathbone had never experienced this sort of thing before. She'd have had no reason to. Considering that, combined with her finding Ensign Chop's body, she was doing better than could be expected. But now he needed to get her moving, doing something.

He glanced around. The two colonists who had carried the woman into the hut were emerging from a pile of furniture. Inside the pile McCoy could hear a child sobbing softly.

"Everyone all right in there?" McCoy asked the colonist.

"We live," he said.

"Good. Everyone needs to drink," McCoy ordered, putting as much force behind his voice as he could manage. "Now. Before the next attack. Rathbone, drink some water and then get some into that baby."

She looked at him with a blank stare for a moment, then her eyes cleared and she nodded and turned for the water.

McCoy pointed to Adaro. "Ensign, help me move this woman under this cot. We've got to keep her protected from the damn heat as much as we can."

McCoy stood, pulled out his medical scanner, and checked her again. As he was doing so, she took one large shuddering breath and died.

She just died. Before they could move her. And there wasn't a damn thing he could do to stop it.

Nothing.

"Damn, damn, damn," he said softly. He did another scan of the large woman hoping to see anything he might do to revive her. Nothing. Besides the heat, he didn't even know why she died. He didn't know enough about Klingon physiology. He knew they could die, but they were so strong that he thought it would take a lot to kill them.

She had gone through a lot, though.

In all his years he had never felt this helpless.

Adaro stood over the woman, waiting for McCoy's instructions to move her.

"Never mind," McCoy said, softly, so the children hiding in the pile of furniture wouldn't hear. "She's dead."

Ensign Adaro stared at her for a moment, then turned his back. It was clear to McCoy that the kid hadn't seen much death, either.

"Oh, no," Rathbone said. She looked down at the baby in her arms, then back up at McCoy, a questioning look on her face. What would become of the woman's children?

He didn't know what to do. It was a Klingon baby. What could he do?

The Klingon man who owned the dome came calmly around the cot and took the baby gently from Dr. Rathbone. "We will take care of the children," he said.

Without another word he took the child to the shelter of furniture and ducked inside. The other child of the dead woman was already in there.

McCoy was impressed. He'd always heard that family was very important to the Klingons, but the man's actions, as if it were expected, made McCoy feel good for the future of the woman's children. Assuming, of course, that they all survived the rest of the day.

"We need to get ready for the next attack," McCoy said. He pulled Dr. Rathbone gently by the sleeve into the area near the head of the dead woman, and they both sat down on the floor, getting ready to shelter their faces and hands at the first rumble of the coming attack.

"Ensign," McCoy ordered. "Get down and cover your head and arms."

The ensign nodded, sat down on the floor, and put his head down.

Three minutes later they heard Kerdoch outside the dome calling the all clear.

McCoy didn't even look at the woman's body as he stood and pulled Rathbone to her feet. "Come," he said to her and the ensign. "We need to get some water and then get back to the Captain."

He gently shoved her toward the door of the dome. It felt like he was pushing a zombie. They emerged into the cooler temperatures of the evening air.

Ensign Adaro followed slowly behind.

They had survived another attack.

Barely.

CHAPTER 12

BRIGHT WHITE LIGHT FLOODED THROUGH HIS CLOSED EYELIDS. CAPTAIN Bogle ached. He didn't open his eyes. The light was too bright. Where was he? He couldn't remember. He felt as if he should remember, but he couldn't. The inside of his head felt as if a dozen pins were being stuck into it at the same moment. All he could hear was a faint buzzing, and he wasn't sure if the buzzing was inside or outside his head.

Blue, orange, and red sparkling stars floated in the bright white light in front of his eyes. As they swirled around and around he began to remember: the attack on the alien ships, trying to stop the attack on the colony.

His shields failing.

The ship lurching as everything around him seemed to explode.

Maybe this was what it was like being dead.

The thought crossed his mind and he forced his eyes open.

The pain of the bright overhead light snapped them closed again. But one glimpse had been enough. Sick bay. He was in the *Farragut*'s sick bay. He could feel the relief flooding through his system.

Holding his head very still, he cleared his throat. "Is the ship still in one piece?"

Dr. Grayhawk, his chief medical officer, laughed, the sound coming from off to Bogle's right. He forced his eyes open again as the rugged face of Grayhawk blocked the light over him.

"It is," Grayhawk said in his thick, deep voice, "thanks to Commander

Lee and Commander Spock. From what I understand, after you were knocked out all our shields failed."

"As I was knocked out," Bogle said, managing to get the words out between the waves of pain surging through his head. "I remember."

Above him Grayhawk laughed again, his voice deep and full, as it always was. Grayhawk was the kind of man who could find humor in just about any situation. He always seemed to be laughing at something. Yet when shoved, the man was as hard as a desert rock and one of the best doctors in the Federation.

"Good. Either way, the shields got knocked out," Grayhawk said. "That Vulcan managed to get the *Enterprise* and her screens between the enemy craft and our ship." Grayhawk continued scanning Bogle's head as he talked, and Bogle could feel the pain ease by a degree or two. "And Commander Lee, with almost no power, somehow kept the *Farragut* in the narrow protected area behind the *Enterprise* during the last few minutes of the fight. It was an amazing show of control, if you want my opinion."

So after the rush to come help the *Enterprise,* it's Kirk's ship that ended up saving the *Farragut.* It figured it would end up that way.

"I need to get back to the bridge," Bogle said, moving to sit up.

Stupid idea.

The sharp pains in his head suddenly became major bolts of lightning, and he slumped backwards, the blackness easing in around the edges of his vision.

"You'll go back to the bridge when I say so," Grayhawk said, his voice very serious. No sign of laughter at all. "You ever heard of an aneurysm? Don't nod; just say yes or no."

"Yes," Bogle said softly, being very careful to not move his head at all. The blackness was slowly moving back away from the spinning stars and Grayhawk's face, but Bogle had no desire to test it again.

"That blow you suffered to the top of your head," Grayhawk said, again scanning Bogle's hairline, "caused a single blood vessel to explode. Basically you had a stroke. I fixed the damage, but only a few hours will tell if you'll have more problems. Even one more stroke, if it happened in the wrong place, or the wrong time, could be fatal, or so bad that I wouldn't be able to repair the cells. So no movement. Understand? Don't even nod."

"Yes, Doctor," Bogle said. "But could you do me a favor?"

"I won't call First Officer Lee down here, if that's what you want. He and Projeff are doing their best to get the ship back up and running, and they don't need to be bothered running in and out of here."

"No," Bogle said, "not that."

"Then what?" Grayhawk asked.

"Could you turn off that damn light?"

Now Grayhawk really laughed. And a moment later the light vanished, leaving Captain Bogle with pain swirling in his head along with the stars as he wondered just how much damage one stroke had caused.

He knew one thing. He didn't want a second.

Kerdoch finished giving the all clear around the colony, then checked on his wife and children. Again they had made it through the shortened attack. He made sure they had water, then told them to stay prepared and went back to the well in the center courtyard. There he drank his fill, refilled a bottle his wife had given him, and turned to head back for the disrupter cannon.

In front of him was the human doctor, the young human, and the human woman moving slowly toward the well. The doctor seemed almost to be supporting the woman.

"Your captain worried over your welfare," Kerdoch said.

McCoy nodded. "Good. I always worry about his. Help me get her some water."

McCoy steered the slowly walking woman toward the well as Kerdoch went around to her other side. He carefully grasped her arm and held her. She was walking, but she did not seem to be well. Neither did the other.

"Was she injured?" he asked.

"In a way," McCoy said, holding her on the edge of the pool and trying to lift handfuls of water to her mouth.

"Use this," Kerdoch said, handing the doctor his bottle. "I filled it a moment ago."

McCoy looked at Kerdoch as if seeing him for the first time, then nodded. "Thank you."

Kerdoch understood the look the doctor had just given him. He had always thought of the humans as enemies, but today with Kirk and Sulu he had discovered they had honor, just like Klingons. He had given Kirk the same look for the first time that McCoy had just given him. As with any day of battle, it was also a day of learning. For both Klingons and humans.

After a few long drinks of water the human woman's eyes seemed to clear. Kerdoch watched as the doctor used a scanning instrument to check her.

"Can you walk?" McCoy asked her as he snapped the instrument closed.

"I think so," she said.

McCoy nodded and gave her another drink from Kerdoch's bottle. Then he took a very long drink himself, refilled the bottle from the well, and handed it back to Kerdoch with a nod of thanks.

Kerdoch put the bottle in his belt and helped the human woman to her feet, steadying her on her left while the doctor stayed on her right.

"Ensign," the human doctor asked the younger man, "can you make it?"

"I can, sir," he said.

"Good," the human doctor said.

They all slowly started toward the disrupter cannon.

"How much light do we have?" the doctor asked after a few steps, glancing at the suns low in the sky.

"One hour," Kerdoch said. "It will get very cold then."

McCoy nodded. "I was afraid of that. We're going to need fires, but I doubt there's much left to burn."

Kerdoch agreed. Almost everything was already burned. Only the fuel stored inside the surviving domes would be usable. Kerdoch looked ahead at the shelter over the disrupter cannon.

The doctor was correct. It would be a long, cold night.

Kirk was kneeling in the dim light of the bunker beside Kor. Kahaq was on the commander's other side, and Kirk could tell he was as worried as Kirk was. Kor seemed to be sleeping, but it clearly wasn't a healthy sleep.

"Captain," Sulu called out from above the bunker.

"Stay with Kor," Kirk said softly to Kahaq. "I hope the doctor will be back shortly."

Kahaq nodded, saying nothing.

Kirk scooted quickly on his hands and knees out of the bunker and then stood. The evening air was cooler now as the suns neared the horizon. Sulu had kept his shirt on while working to secure the shelter over the gun.

Sulu pointed toward the colony's center. McCoy, Dr. Rathbone, Ensign Adaro, and Kerdoch were walking toward him. It seemed that McCoy and Kerdoch were helping Rathbone along.

He moved out to meet them. "Are you all right, Doctor?" he asked Rathbone, glancing at McCoy.

"I'm fine," she said. "Just a little weak and dizzy is all."

"She's in a mild shock," McCoy said, "but she'll be fine in a few hours."

Kirk nodded. "There's room in the bunker with Kor for her to lie down."

McCoy and Kerdoch helped Rathbone up and into the bunker as Kirk watched. Then Kerdoch turned and came back the few paces to Kirk, his firm steps kicking up small clouds of black ash and dust.

"Captain Kirk," Kerdoch said. "The night will be cold. We need to prepare."

Kirk nodded. He was afraid that might be the case in this area of the planet. Long, hot, dry days with fairly short but intensely cold nights. After all the heat punishment they had withstood today, the night would seem even colder.

"Do you have suggestions?" Kirk asked Kerdoch.

The Klingon pointed to one colony dome that still stood about fifty steps from the gun. "There is a heating unit inside with enough emergency fuel for one night, maybe two."

"Can we bring the unit out here?" Kirk asked.

"No," Kerdoch said. "It is too heavy. But the building is now empty. The owner was killed during the first attack."

Kirk stared at the dome and the distance between it and the disrupter cannon. There would be more than enough time to get back to the gun if Spock warned them, but if they only had their tricorders to warn them of a coming attack, it would be close. But close was better than freezing to death out in the open. He and Mr. Sulu could take turns standing guard on the gun just in case.

"Would you prepare the dome?" Kirk asked. "Water, heat, and any food you might be able to find. We'll move Kor and Rathbone at sunset."

"I will inform you when the dome is heated and ready," Kerdoch said.

He turned and strode off.

Kirk watched him go. This time there was no question from the Klingon that Kirk was in command. He wasn't sure what had changed, but something had.

Kirk flipped open his communicator. "Kirk to *Enterprise."*

"Spock here."

"What's going on up there, Mr. Spock?"

"Mr. Scott has the ship fully operational, Captain. The enemy ships are still holding their positions. The *Farragut* has restored full shields, phasers, and impulse power. Their engineer reports they will have full warp power within an hour."

"And the Klingons?"

"The Klingon battle cruiser is also making repairs," Spock said. "They claim to be ready to fight again."

"They'd make that claim with the ship exploding around them."

"I understand that, sir," Spock said.

"I'm sure you do," Kirk said. Then he asked the question he was afraid to hear the answer to. "And Captain Bogle?"

"Still in the *Farragut* sick bay. First Officer Lee reports he is out of immediate danger."

"Good," Kirk said. He could feel the relief easing muscles in his back and shoulders.

"Do you have any idea, Mr. Spock, as to just who we're fighting?"

"I do not, Captain," Spock said. "Or any indication as to motive. This situation is very illogical and puzzling."

"And very deadly," Kirk said, thinking about Ensign Chop. "I assume you are still hailing them without success."

"That is correct, Captain."

"Well, keep an eye on them. I want to know the moment any ships are headed this way that you and the *Farragut* can't stop."

"Understood, Captain," Spock said.

"And, Mr. Spock, you mentioned something about the Klingons sending more help."

"Two battle cruisers will arrive in twelve hours and seven minutes. There is no Federation ship within twenty-six hours of our location."

"Twelve hours, huh?" Kirk said. "Who knows how many more alien ships might arrive in that time."

"I have no way of estimating that, sir," Spock said, "since we know nothing of their origin."

"I understand, Mr. Spock. Kirk out."

Kirk looked around the burned-out Klingon colony in the fading light of the evening. The colony had withstood almost thirty hours of siege. It might not survive another twelve. But then again, it just might. If the aliens didn't change their tactics.

"But if they change . . . " Kirk said aloud to himself.

"*If* who changes, Captain?" Sulu said.

Kirk glanced at his officer. "Just talking to myself, Mr. Sulu." Then he frowned. Sometimes thinking aloud was good. "Do you think the aliens will change their attack pattern the next time?"

Sulu shrugged, glancing at the horizon where one of the two suns was just touching the top edge of the mountains. "I would have thought they would change before now. And continuing an attack with wide-focus plasma beams makes no sense at all."

"Ah, but it does," Kirk said, finally grabbing on to what was bothering him. "It does if this enemy is interested only in clearing and sterilizing the land."

"I'm not following you, sir," Sulu said.

Kirk pointed out at the burnt fields. "In the first attacks they were clearing crops and Klingons. Didn't matter which was in the way of their beams. But you and that disrupter cannon there gave them a wake-up call. Sort of like being in a garden pulling weeds and one of the weeds suddenly pulls back. Things will change now."

"That sounds likely, sir," Sulu said. "But if they do change, we need to figure out what they are going to do."

Kirk looked over the colony domes at the expanse of blackened, burned-out fields. Then he realized what would happen. They had been using a scorched earth policy. It was classic military strategy. So classic that all pre-warp cultures had used it at one time or another. "Classic military strategy," he muttered.

That was it. That was the key.

"Sir?" Sulu asked.

"Military strategy, Mr. Sulu. They'll change from a cleanup operation to a military operation. After you soften up the targets with air attacks, what comes next?"

"Ground assault," Sulu said. He quickly looked around, trying to guess where the assault would come from.

Beside him Kirk did the same thing. A ground assault was coming, most likely at sunrise. Kirk knew it. He could feel it. He would have bet his life on it.

Now the big questions: how to prepare? And what, exactly, should they prepare for?

CHAPTER 13

Scotty sat at his console. His hair was mussed and his uniform was covered with dirt, equipment casings, and small metal bits that he hadn't had time to identify. His sleeve was still ripped, even though the wound was healed. In all the confusion, he hadn't had time to change his shirt.

He was performing several difficult mathematical equations with one hand while monitoring the computer with the other. It bothered him that the alien ships could affect the shields so quickly. They were doing something—something that he hadn't been able to pinpoint.

Several of his staff were working on the shield problem. Others were maintaining the weaponry, and the rest were keeping an eye on the matter-antimatter container, making certain everything was running normally. These aliens were difficult in ways the Klingons were not: At least Scotty knew what to expect from Klingons. He didn't even know what these creatures looked like.

Then Uhura's voice echoed through engineering. "Mr. Scott, I have a communication from the engineer of the *Farragut.* Will you take it?"

"Aye, lass." He positioned himself in front of his small video screen. It flickered on. Projeff seemed to be sitting in the equivalent location aboard the *Farragut.* His dark hair was tousled, and his warm eyes had deep shadows beneath him. He looked like a man who'd been working for days with no sleep—and he probably had.

"I got a question for you," Projeff said.

"All right," Scotty said.

"Remember that experiment we were doing on Starbase Eleven?"

"I'm not likely to forget it, lad. We still haven't settled all of the technical issues. But we don't have time to play such games at the moment."

Projeff ran a hand through his hair. "I'm not interested in games. It's just that the alien ships seem to have a knack for destroying the effectiveness of our shields and—"

"Ya noticed that too, have ya? I'm doin' some calculations on it now."

"I was thinking perhaps we could work together on this."

"Laddie, you and I canna work well together," Scotty said with a grin. "We're only effective in competition with each other."

Projeff grinned. "That's really what I had in mind," he said.

"All right," Scotty said. "Let's hear what you've got."

"You first," Projeff said.

Then they both laughed with the pleasure of working with another mind so similar. They were considered the best engineers in the fleet, and were known to work miracles.

They would share, and they both knew it. And together they would come up with something.

"Here's what I have," Scotty said. "Their weapons seem to be doin' something to the shields that we're not protected against."

"Something new," Projeff said.

Scotty looked at the small screen image with fondness. "You're a young one, laddie," he said. " 'Tis something old."

"Old?" Projeff said.

"Aye. Look into your computer files. We used to have weaponry similar to this. Our new shields were designed with the new technology in mind, not the old technology."

Projeff grew excited as memory clearly kicked in. "Because the designers figured the shields would be adequate enough to handle older weapons."

"And they believed that these starships could conquer any ship with older weaponry."

"They didn't expect the older weaponry to be mixed up with alien technology," Projeff said.

"Right, lad." Scotty smiled. "Now we're gettin' somewhere."

Projeff grinned. "So it's a race then, a race to see which of us can modify the shields properly."

Scotty got suddenly serious. "I don't think a race is quite the right term, lad. I think we need to share information when we have it. We're in a serious conflict here—"

"I know that," Projeff said. "But that can't stop us from seeing who makes the right adjustment first."

"Ah, that's decided aforehand," Scotty said. "It'll be the *Enterprise.* It always is."

Then he signed off, smiling, despite the seriousness of the operation. As he had said earlier, they did better when they were competing with each other. He liked defending the honor of the *Enterprise.* But both engineers knew they were working together. The competition just helped them work faster, harder, and more effectively.

And he knew, deep down inside, that they needed all the help they could get.

Rathbone eased herself up onto one elbow and looked around at the interior of the dirt bunker. The light coming from the open ends of the bunker was getting dimmer, and for the first time in what seemed like an eternity, she felt chilled. Goose bumps covered the red, burned skin on her arms.

Dr. McCoy crouched over Kor, running a medical scanner slowly over him. After a moment McCoy sighed, sat back in the dirt, and flipped the tricorder closed, looking very upset and confused.

Kahaq, Kor's officer, glared at McCoy through the dark. "Will he live?"

McCoy sighed again, then said, "I don't really know. His broken ribs are healing fine. But Klingon burns and dehydration are not really my specialty, as I've said a half dozen times during this hellish day."

"He will live," Kahaq said, answering his own question with the answer he obviously wanted.

McCoy just shook his head in disgust at his own powerlessness and didn't move.

Rathbone was impressed at the loyalty Kor received from Kahaq. Kirk on the *Enterprise* also got that "ignore facts, follow Kirk" loyalty from his crew. And after seeing the captain in action here, she was starting to see why. And feel the same way. At this moment she trusted him totally with her life.

McCoy glanced over at her. Through the faint light she could see him smile.

"Feeling better?" he asked.

She nodded. "Much."

In reality she was. She had distant memories of the last attack, Ensign Chop's body, the intense heat, the Klingon mother dying and McCoy and Kerdoch leading her back here. But the memories felt like they had happened to someone else, as if she'd watched them on a monitor while sitting in her room.

"Good," McCoy said. He scooted over beside her on his hands and knees and pulled out his medical scanner again. After a moment he snapped it closed, smiling. "Better, but you need to keep pouring down the water."

"All right, Doctor."

"I've got to get out of this rathole," McCoy said, patting her shoulder and moving toward the open end of the bunker. "You up for a walk?"

"Yes." She followed him out and straightened up carefully, letting the cool evening air fill her lungs and calm her slightly spinning head. After a moment she followed McCoy up onto the concrete platform holding the shelter and the disrupter cannon. Kirk and Sulu were digging through the remains of a colony dome about thirty paces away. There was no one else in sight.

Beside her, McCoy took a long, deep breath. She did the same thing, looking out beyond the colony into the blackened fields. And then her gaze moved beyond the remains of the Klingon crops to the natural vegetation. The aliens had been careful not to destroy anything that was native to the planet. And something about that fact nagged at her.

"Are you all right?" McCoy asked, touching her elbow.

"I'm feeling better, Doctor," she said, then realized that he sensed her distraction. "I'm just wondering why the aliens are focusing only on the Klingon crops without touching the planet's native vegetation. That seems like such a precise attack. They must be doing that for a reason.

"I've been wondering the same thing." Kirk said.

Kirk's voice startled her, and she spun around. Kirk and Sulu had returned to the edge of the cannon platform with more fireproof panels while she'd been staring out at the fields.

"It does seem odd," McCoy said. "They must really hate the Klingons."

"Maybe there's more to it than that," Kirk said. "Nothing about this attack makes sense."

"Not much about this planet makes sense," Sulu said.

Kirk looked out at the blackened fields, then back to Rathbone. "Are you feeling well enough for a short mission?"

"Put me to work," she said. And she meant it. So far it felt as if she'd been a burden to the landing party. She wanted to carry her own weight.

"Good," Kirk said. "I want you and Mr. Sulu to make another trip into those fields, looking for anything that might give us any clues as to why they're being destroyed while the native vegetation isn't. It is just too odd an occurrence to let pass. And at this point any clues we can get might help."

"I agree. We'll find something, Captain," Sulu said. He moved forward and slipped on his tricorder.

"If something's there," Vivian said with a scientist's caution.

McCoy handed her his tricorder. "Drink some water before you go."

"Yes, Doctor," she said, smiling. She quickly moved to the edge of the shelter, retrieved a full water bottle, and took a long drink in front of the doctor. Then she passed the bottle to Sulu, and he did the same thing.

"Mr. Sulu," Kirk said, "I don't want you to go any farther from this shelter than a two-minute fast run. Is that understood?"

"Yes, sir," Sulu said.

Sulu turned and, motioning for her to follow, led her toward the edge of the burnt fields. She could feel her heart racing slightly again, but it felt good to be doing something to help.

Behind her she heard Captain Kirk say, "Bones, fill me in on Kor's condition. Can he be moved?"

Ahead of her, Sulu ducked past the edge of a ruined dome and moved out at a good pace. She increased her stride to keep up.

In front of her were the burnt fields and the dry, brown natural vegetation beyond them. Again the nagging feeling that the answer was out here overwhelmed her.

The problem was she had to find it. And do it very quickly.

Kerdoch finished lighting the dome's emergency heater, then surveyed the rest of the interior. This had been Kablanti's home. Kerdoch could feel the man's presence. His essence was with this home still. Far past the age restrictions, Kablanti had managed to get on this planet simply because he had done a favor for one of the members of the High Council. As it turned out, he had been a valued member, a good fighter, and a good singer. His presence would be missed.

Kerdoch checked the water supply. Enough. More would be needed tomorrow. Colony food supplies filled one cabinet, more than sufficient for one night.

Kerdoch finished his inspection with a quick check for weapons or anything that might be useful to the fight. Nothing. Old Kablanti had died with his weapon in his hand, outside defending his fields during the first attack. A proud death.

An honorable death.

Kerdoch picked up a stein engraved with Kablanti's family crest. He held it up in a silent toast to his dead friend. Then he said, "Thank you, Kablanti, for the use of your home to shelter our commander."

Kerdoch placed the stein on a high shelf. The dome would welcome the commander.

He ducked back out the emergency exit of the dome and started across the short distance to the disrupter cannon. Ahead, Kirk talked to the human doctor. In the field beyond the colony Sulu and the woman were walking away from the gun at a fast pace. Obviously they had a mission. Kerdoch had no idea what the human captain was thinking. Nothing existed in that direction except Kablanti's burnt fields and natural weeds.

But Kirk was a crafty one. He had a very real reason, Kerdoch would wager.

Kirk saw him coming. "Is the dome ready?" he asked. He had a clipped command style that was as close to Klingon as humans seemed to get.

"It is prepared," Kerdoch said.

"Good," Kirk said. "We need to move Kor now while we still have light."

"And before the next attack," the doctor said.

"Possibly," Kirk said. "But I doubt the next attack will come before morning."

"Why would you think that?" Kerdoch asked. "Their first attack was at dusk. They returned many times during the night with their evil fire."

Kirk looked at Kerdoch, holding his gaze. Kerdoch was amazed. This human did not back down or even look away. In the few humans that Kerdoch had met, that was not the case.

"Because," Kirk said, "I'm betting the next attack will come on the ground. They won't risk another ship to this cannon. And the logical time for a ground attack would be at sunrise. And it will come from the same direction the planes attacked from."

Kerdoch stared at the captain for a moment, then said, "If you are correct, do you have a plan as to how we will stop them?"

Kirk smiled at Kerdoch. "Not yet." He turned and headed for the bunker. "Let's get Kor moved."

The human doctor laughed and whispered to Kerdoch, "Don't worry. He always does his best work without a plan."

Kerdoch stood on the edge of the cannon platform and watched the two humans stride toward the end of the bunker. He had always thought of humans as enemies of the Empire. Yet they fought to defend a Klingon colony, and worked to save the life of a Klingon commander. If humans were enemies, this enemy had much honor.

He followed the two, wondering why all Klingons were not informed of such facts.

Kirk found it interesting that neither he nor McCoy was allowed to help carry Kor to the dome. Kerdoch and Kahaq dragged Kor out of the bunker, then picked the Commander up and supported him, as if he were actually awake and walking between them. They ended up half dragging him, half carrying him, and the toes of Kor's boots left parallel trails in the dust leading from the bunker to the dome.

McCoy protested the unusual carry position, but not loudly. He didn't know enough about Klingon physiology to be certain that the lift would harm Kor. All he knew was that it would hurt a human in Kor's condition.

The Klingons ignored him, and Kirk let them. They had customs that were based on things he did not understand. Often such customs had more than a symbolic significance. Often they were created with real physical reasons behind them.

McCoy knew that too. That was probably why his protest wasn't too loud.

McCoy paced ahead of the Klingons, and Kirk walked a few paces behind them, using his boot to smooth out the tracks Kor left. If there was a ground assault, there would be no point in leaving a direct trail from the gun to the dome for an attacker to follow. Of course, if the attackers got this far, most likely what Kirk was doing would make absolutely no difference. But he brushed out the trail anyway. It made him feel better.

After Kor was settled on the cot near a center wall of the dome, Kirk ducked back outside and stepped up on the cannon platform. The air now had a cold bite to it, and the burns on his arms and face stung. Above him the stars were starting to appear.

Sulu and Rathbone were faint figures in the fading light as the second sun dropped below the horizon. From what Kirk could tell, they were working along the edge of the burned Klingon crops and the remaining natural plants. He hoped they'd found something that would lend a clue to what was happening here. Anything at this point would help.

He turned in the direction of where the ships had attacked. Nothing but flat, burnt-out fields for a thousand or more paces. Most likely the ships would land out of range of the disrupter cannon, near the edge of those low hills. Then the ground troops would start toward the colony. They would be shielded in some fashion, but he was fairly certain they wouldn't have enough shielding to stop a disrupter cannon shot.

Kirk moved around behind the shelter over the cannon and studied it for a moment. If a ground attack did start, they'd have to find a way to turn the gun around and get it aimed at the attacking forces. Ideally in such a way that they would be able to get the shelter back in place. That might be asking too much of such a make-shift building. When Sulu returned, they'd see what they could figure out.

In the fading light he studied the perimeter of the colony. Five of the domes along the edge were destroyed. Those ruins would be a logical place to try to stand off ground troops marching across the fields, if he could get enough colonists to help.

He walked to the edge of one dome and looked out over the open, black field. He hoped it never came to an attack across this field, because if it did, they'd all die for sure.

Unless Spock could find a way to get them off this planet in time.

He flipped open his communicator. "Kirk to *Enterprise.*"

"Spock here."

"Any change, Mr. Spock?"

"None, Captain."

"Any chance you can get close enough to beam us out of here?"

"Not without attacking the alien ships directly, Captain. I've run seventeen possible scenarios and all of them end in complete failure."

"Keep working on it, Mr. Spock."

"I will, Captain."

"And Spock, I expect a ground attack on the colony at dawn. Stand ready."

"We will, sir," Spock said. "We will endeavor to stop the attack in orbit."

"And get us out of here at the same time," Kirk said.

"Of course, Captain," Spock said.

For a moment Kirk thought he heard the slightest hint in Spock's voice that his feelings were hurt by such a comment. Then Kirk realized he was just imagining it.

"Thank you, Spock. Kirk out."

He slapped the communicator closed, and headed back to the dome where Kor slept.

Inside the warm room, Kerdoch stood over the Klingon commander as if on guard. Kahaq sat beside him, and McCoy sat at a large steel table about three paces away. It looked like a deathwatch to Kirk, and he didn't want it to continue. They had too much work to do.

"Kerdoch," Kirk said, "I could use your help."

Kerdoch nodded to Kahaq and turned. "Yes, Captain."

"If our enemies attack at dawn, as I think they might, I'd like to have a line of defense set up for the colony."

Kerdoch bowed his head in acknowledgment. "What would you suggest?"

Kirk had hoped that was what the colonist would ask. He indicated that Kerdoch follow him out into the fading light.

A few steps from the dome Kirk stopped and pointed to the five destroyed domes along the perimeter of the colony. "We'll set up defensive positions in there, using the rubble for protection."

Kerdoch stared at the domes for a moment, then turned to the captain. "How many more defenders do we need?"

"As many as have guns," Kirk said. "If a ground force makes it past that line, we're all dead anyway. We might as well make our last stand there."

Kerdoch nodded. "If there are no further air attacks this night, then I will assume you are correct about the ground troops. Every colonist who can move and fire a weapon will be here."

"Have them assemble one hour before dawn," Kirk said, "so we'll have time to dig in and prepare."

"One hour," Kerdoch said.

Without a glance at Kirk, or at the door leading back to Kor, Kerdoch turned and strode off toward the center of the colony, his head high, his pace long and solid.

Kirk watched him go, glad that Kerdoch was helping. Farmers in any culture tended to be the strong, sturdy, reliable people, proud of their work and their lifestyle. It had never occurred to Kirk before that Klingon farmers would also be skilled, fearless fighters.

They were certainly not to be trifled with, as the aliens were quickly discovering. It was a lesson the Federation might want to take to heart in the future.

CHAPTER 14

IT WAS GETTING TOO DARK TO WORK, AND THE COLD WAS STARTING TO NUMB Vivian's fingers.

She slowly climbed to her feet and tried to brush the black soot off her aching knees and hands. She switched the tricorder to her left hand and put her right hand in her armpit, trying to warm it. She had no memory of ever feeling this cold, this dirty, this tired, before.

Sulu was on his knees about ten paces from her, studying readings on his tricorder in the faint light.

Neither of them really knew exactly what they were looking for. They were just hoping to find any clue to solve what was happening. Were the Klingons doing something with their crops that might cause another race to attack them? It had sounded far-fetched to her when they came out into the field, and now it seemed even more so. But both the captain and Sulu thought it likely enough to investigate, so she had tried.

Tried looking for something that didn't exist.

"Any luck?" Sulu asked, standing and moving over beside her, blowing on his hands to warm them as he came.

"I've found nothing new," she said.

"Me either," he said. "We should report to the captain, unless you think we should stay out here longer."

"What is there to report?" she asked. "Or find, for that matter."

She glanced around one last time, hoping to find anything that might help, as if it might be sitting out in the open. But there was nothing but the stubble and ashes of burned crops.

She hated failure, and this planet seemed to constantly want to hand her failure after failure. She could remember being so happy the day she got the assignment to the colony on Signi Beta. Now she wished she'd never heard of this miserable place.

"Let's go back," she said.

Quickly, through near-darkness made even blacker by the burned crops, they moved toward the colony. Once in a while a light would flash ahead of them in the colony, then disappear again.

Otherwise they were alone in the dark, under the stars. Stars she very much wished she were traveling between, instead of walking under.

It felt as if they had to go forever. Her steps seemed to merge into one another. Beside her Sulu became nothing more than a faint ghost walking silently in the dark. For a moment she thought she was having a nightmare and she would awake at any moment in her warm bed on the *Enterprise.* It would only be one of many nightmares about Signi Beta that she'd had.

Then she found herself stepping past some debris from a ruined dome and following Sulu up to a figure standing in the dark near the big Klingon gun.

"Captain?" Sulu said.

"Did you find anything?" Kirk asked, his familiar voice bringing her back to reality. This wasn't just a dream. This was very, very real. Again the image of Ensign Chop's body flashed in her mind. She focused on the captain, pushing the memory away.

"We found nothing new, sir," Sulu said.

"I was afraid of that," Kirk said.

Rathbone could tell he was tired. His voice didn't have the force it had just this morning.

"Commander?"

"I'm afraid I can only confirm what Sulu said, Captain," Vivian said, doing her best to make her voice sound firm. "All the Klingon plants I found were just their standard tIqKa SuD. It's a form of hybrid, a blend of the Klingon Doctuq and the natural grain found growing here."

"What I still find interesting," Sulu said, "is the hybrid nature of the natural plants. It's as if they'd been blended with other plants years before."

"The Federation colony botanists found the same thing interesting," she said. "We spent five years studying it and we had no more explanation for it at the end as the first day."

Kirk seemed to shift, turning to face them, most likely to see them better in the dark. "The original plants are hybrids?" he asked. "How long ago did that happen?"

"At least eight hundred years ago," Sulu said. "Maybe up to a thousand."

"The colony pinned it closer to nine hundred," she said. "And not so much as hybrids, as genetically shifted. All the records of the research are available in the Federation data banks, Captain."

She watched as he seemed to be thinking, staring off into the dark. Granted, this area was fascinating, but she had no idea how it might be important to stopping the alien attacks.

"Mr. Sulu," the Captain said. "Have Spock look over the colony records as quickly as possible. Also have him scan as best he can from his position for any previous civilizations on this planet."

"We did that, Captain," Rathbone said. "And so did the original survey team. No trace of any previous culture even visiting this planet, let alone living here."

"Except for hybrid plants," he said.

"Captain," she said, "there could be a hundred natural causes for such a genetic shifting. Asteroid collision could have caused it. So could intense solar flares. And those are only two examples. It could—"

Even in the deepening dark she could see him hold up his hand and smile. "Just checking everything. None of this makes sense. I just hate to leave anything unchecked while we have time to investigate."

Rathbone felt the heat of embarrassment crawl up her neck. "I'm sorry, Captain. I'm frustrated we didn't find more."

His smile faded. "You might have found just enough. Only time will tell." He put his hand on her shoulder and propelled her toward the shelter. "Now both of you need to get inside and get warm. I'll take the first watch near the gun. Mr. Sulu, you relieve me after you call Spock and when you get warm."

"Yes, sir," he said.

Without knowing what else to say, Vivian turned and followed Sulu through the dark to the dome and the warmth it held. Suddenly it was very clear why Captain Kirk was such a good captain. He never overlooked anything. He had the ability to step outside a situation and see it clearly.

Once again the young captain had impressed her. She wouldn't question him again.

Dr. Grayhawk, chief medical officer of the *Farragut,* huffed, then turned his back on Captain Bogle, working with something on a medical table. Bogle smiled, knowing exactly what that action meant. Grayhawk couldn't hold him in sick bay any longer even though he hated letting any patient out in anything short of perfect health.

"So," Bogle said, "am I going to live?" He reached up and gently felt the top of his head. The intense pain was gone, but the area was still very sensitive.

"You land on your head again anytime soon and I won't guarantee it," Grayhawk said. "But for now I'm returning you to duty, Captain."

Bogle eased himself down off the medical table and straightened his tunic. "Thank you, Doctor."

"Next time strap yourself into that captain's chair," Grayhawk said.

"I'll take that under consideration," Bogle said, and laughed. Both he and the doctor knew there were no seat belts on a starship.

He turned and headed for the sick bay door, moving slowly at first. As he reached the hall he was moving at a good pace again. By the time he stepped back on the bridge the dull ache in his head was forgotten as he focused on the situation at hand.

Communications Officer Sandy nodded at him and smiled. "Welcome back, sir."

"Glad to see you feeling better," Lieutenant Michael Book said from Navigation.

First Officer Lee stood at his science scope, face buried in it. Lee obviously heard and raised his head, smiling at Bogle.

"Good job, people," Bogle said as he moved to stand beside his captain's chair. It felt damn good to be back, he had to admit. And he was very proud of his crew, especially Mr. Lee, for saving the ship so that he had a bridge to return to. He would put in for commendations for his bridge crew if they survived this.

He took a deep breath, stepped down to a position beside his chair and looked forward. On the main viewscreen was an amazing sight: Five alien ships hovered in a fairly tight group over the planet. The Klingon battle cruiser was to the *Farragut*'s left, the *Enterprise* to the right—a three-against-five stand-off.

"Mr. Lee," Bogle said, "what's the ship's status?"

"Warp has been restored. Our screens are at ninety percent, and Projeff reports he'll have them back to one hundred percent in ten minutes. All weapons systems are on-line and ready."

"Good job," Bogle said. "The other ships?"

"The *Enterprise* is at one hundred percent," Lee said. "It's hard to tell with the Klingons. They took a bad beating in that last fight, just as we did, but they should be getting the repairs done by now."

"How about the enemy?"

Lee moved down and stood beside Bogle. "The transport ship farthest to the right took the most damage from us and the *Enterprise.* It's amazing it still exists. Its shields failed, and we pierced its hull in a dozen places."

"Enlarge the image of that ship," Bogle said. Almost instantly the ship filled the viewscreen. Bogle could see that it had suffered extensive damage. It floated at a slight angle that indicated it was nearly dead in space. Debris drifted close to it, indicating that no gravity fields remained on inside the hulk.

"One of the other ships used a tractor beam to get the crippled vessel to that position," Lee said. "It shows no signs of life and has no screens. It's just a hunk of useless metal."

"So that leaves four mother ships," Bogle said. He would never consider that ship again in his thinking.

The main viewscreen switched back to the scene of all the enemy ships.

"The remaining four are fully functional, from what we can tell," Lee said. "We punished one of them, but not enough to get through their screens."

"What about the *Enterprise* and Klingon landing parties?"

"Holding out," Lee said. "Kor is seriously injured, but still alive. Captain Kirk thinks the next attack on the colony will be a ground assault at sunrise, four hours from now. They're preparing for that possibility as best they can."

"Do we have help on the way?"

"Starfleet has been informed of the situation," Lee said, "but we have no starships close by. However, the Klingons have sent for reinforcements. We were told that two battle cruisers are on the way, but they won't arrive for another nine hours."

"By then, who knows how many enemy ships will be here," Bogle said.

"We're doing continuous long-range scans, sir," Book said, "watching for just that possibility."

"Good," Bogle said. He stood staring at the planet beyond the alien ships. "So if Kirk's right, it's up to us to stop the transport ships before they get to the atmosphere," Bogle said, more to himself than First Officer Lee.

"If we can," Lee said, softly.

Bogle only continued to stare at the alien ships, wondering just why they were even fighting this fight.

Kirk blew on his hands to warm them. The night had turned bitter cold, a stark contrast to the intense heat they'd survived during the day. He wondered how much of the cold he was feeling was because of that heat and the burns he'd received during the attacks. If he thought about it, he would ask Bones, just out of curiosity.

Kirk nodded to Sulu in the faint light as the lieutenant came up through the dark and relieved him of guard duty on the Klingon disrupter cannon.

Each of them had stood three shifts of guard duty. Nothing had changed. He'd checked in with Spock four times, and everything in orbit also remained unchanged. They were at a standoff, with neither side talking to the other. Actually, only the aliens refused to talk. The *Enterprise* had kept up a constant hail on all frequencies. But if the other side didn't want to talk, there was no talking.

Kirk headed back to the warmth of the dome, walking slowly to make sure he didn't trip in the extreme darkness.

Just over an hour until sunrise. It was time to start gathering the defense forces. He was convinced the next attack would be on the ground, especially since there had been no other air attacks during the last few hours. Only a ground attack made sense, if anything about this situation made sense.

Inside the dome the warm arm washed over him, taking the sharp edge off the chill. He could feel his arm and back muscles relaxing as they warmed.

Near the right wall Kahaq and McCoy watched over Commander Kor, who was stretched out on a cot. The colonist Kerdoch sat alone at a steel dining table, and Rathbone was dozing in a large chair, her head back, her mouth slightly open. Ensign Adaro had fallen asleep leaning against a wall.

He moved across the room to where McCoy sat beside Kor. Kirk could never remember McCoy looking so tired and dejected. His old friend was clearly not happy with the Klingon commander's condition and somehow blaming himself for not being able to do more.

Kirk knelt beside the Commander as McCoy shook his head slowly as a report on Kor's status. Obviously Kor remained unconscious and unchanged. Kirk very much wished his old enemy would recover. At this point the more help they all had, the better chances of surviving this.

Besides—and this was something he'd admit only in the dark of night, and only to himself—he found Kor a worthy adversary. The idea of facing the Klingon Empire without Kor simply wasn't as challenging.

Kirk patted McCoy's knee. "Stay with him, Bones."

McCoy nodded without looking up.

Kirk turned and moved over to where Kerdoch sat at the table. The Klingon colonist looked as determined and as angry as he had the first moment Kirk saw him aboard the battle cruiser.

"Time to prepare?" Kerdoch asked.

Kirk dropped down into a chair across from the colonist. "I'm afraid it is."

"What do you need?" Kerdoch asked, being as blunt as most of the Klingons Kirk knew.

"Any colonist who can fire a weapon. Most likely this fight will be our last defense, if the attackers get this far."

"They should be stopped in orbit," Kerdoch said, his tone matter-of-fact.

"I agree," Kirk said. "Kor's ship and our two Federation ships will do everything possible to stop whatever is heading our way. But they didn't manage to stop them last time, so we need to be ready, in case they fail again."

"Agreed," Kerdoch said. He put his hands flat on the table and pushed himself up, taking a deep breath, obviously preparing himself. "I will gather warriors near the cannon."

The captain watched as the Klingon farmer turned and strode out of the dome, leaving Kirk sitting alone at the table. There had to be a way to stop this fight—if they only knew the cause, or even who their attackers were.

Kirk felt as helpless as McCoy felt with Kor. He knew there must be something he could do.

But what?

CHAPTER 15

"THAT'S IT!" SCOTTY SAID, BANGING HIS FIST ON THE CONSOLE. "THAT'S IT, lads."

The engineering staff looked at him and smiled. It didn't matter that half the staff was female: when he was excited, he tended to call them all lads.

And he was excited now. He'd figured out the shield modifications, and he hadn't even looked at the figures Projeff had sent. Projeff, in the meantime, had apparently not found anything, or he would have contacted Scotty to brag—

And to share.

"It's so simple," he said to the ensign beside him. She had long black hair and the look of his mother—at least until she turned, revealing eyes a color not normally found in human beings. "We create ghost shields, harmonic echoes that— Ach, just do it." He slid the calculations to her, and the others crowded around.

Then he hit the comm button. "Mr. Scott to the bridge."

"Spock here." Spock's responses were always prompt and always dry.

"Mr. Spock, I've figured out the problem with the shields."

"I had not realized we had a problem with the shields, Mr. Scott."

Scotty blinked. Usually Spock was on top of these things. But he had a lot to think about, what with the captain on the surface and all. "You dinna notice how quickly they affected the shields' power and with such old-fashioned weapons at that?"

"Well," Spock said, "now that you mention it, I do recall thinking that the shields went down quickly, but it did not strike me as all that unusual."

"All that unusual? All that unusual! Mr. Spock, this ship can protect us against Klingon firepower, against Romulan treachery, against—"

"I take it you've solved the problem, Mr. Scott," Spock said, his voice sounding drier than usual.

"Of course I have, man. And a slight hair before young Projeff of the *Farragut.*"

"I'm sure the captain will be pleased. How long will modifications take?"

"It may be an hour or two, Mr. Spock," Scotty said.

"I would prefer a more precise estimate," Spock said.

"That is precise," Scotty said.

"I may need the shields sooner," Spock said.

"When you need them," Scotty said, "let me know. We'll be working as fast as we can."

Scotty signed off, then asked Uhura to contact Projeff.

When the visual came on the screen, Projeff was bent over his console, his hair sticking out in all directions, a smudge of dirt under one eye.

"We've found the solution, laddie," Scotty said, with more than a bit of pride, "and we're sending it to you now."

"I hope you're not talking about turning up the harmonics," Projeff said. "We've tried that and—"

"No, lad. It's an elegant solution." Scotty grinned. "Courtesy of the *Enterprise.*"

Spock noted the time.

It had been an hour since he spoke to Mr. Scott. There was still no word on the shield modifications.

If the Captain was correct that a ground attack would be launched against the colony at the colonies sunrise, adding the appropriate amount of time for a landing force to reach the surface from orbit, within the next sixty-two seconds the enemy should be deploying forces.

He pressed the comm button. "Mr. Scott, how is your work on the shields progressing?"

"We're finishing the last of it now."

"Good," Spock said. "As I believe we will need them within the next sixty seconds."

"You *believe?"*

Spock couldn't very well say that he knew. "Using the captain's calculations and my own—"

"I was merely teasing, Mr. Spock," Scotty said. "You'll have your shields. Mind you, we need to test them first—"

"We shall do so any second now," Spock said, ending the communication.

On the screen the five enemy ships remained in position. Nothing seemed to have changed, but Spock agreed with the captain. Under these circumstances, the next logical move for the attacking force would be a ground attack.

And it would happen soon.

"Red alert," Spock said as he moved down from his science station and stood beside the captain's chair, his hand gripping the back padding.

Around him the red lights snapped on, the siren filled the air of the bridge with a shrilling background sound.

"Ensign Haru, arm photon torpedoes," Spock said to the young ensign at the weapons panel.

"Yes, sir," Haru said.

Spock turned toward the screen. "Mr. Chekov, cut the distance between the *Enterprise* and the enemy ships by exactly fifty percent."

"Aye, sir," Chekov said.

"Do so slowly, Ensign," Spock said. "At one-tenth impulse."

"Aye, sir," Chekov said without looking away from his console.

On the main viewscreen the five enemy ships got gradually larger.

"The *Farragut* is hailing us, sir," Lieutenant Uhura said.

"On audio only," Spock said. "And scramble the communication, Lieutenant."

He wanted to make sure he didn't lose sight of the ships in front of him. He had worked out a possible line of attack and a point of weakness in the ships. At the moment of deployment of the ground ships, the mother ships would have their docking-bay doors open. They would be less maneuverable and more vulnerable. He planned to take advantage of that weakness, but the *Enterprise* had to be in position first.

"Spock," Captain Bogle said, his voice booming with authority, "what are you doing?"

"Preparing, sir," Spock said.

"Preparing for what?" Bogle asked. "To get us all killed?"

"To stop the coming attack on the ground colony, sir. Spock out."

On the screen a line suddenly appeared across the rear section of two of the wing-shaped enemy ships. The docking bays were opening. Captain Kirk had been correct about the timing of the attack.

"Mr. Haru," Spock said, never taking his gaze from the opening bay doors. He had studied the video from the last deployment, and he knew exactly what he was looking at. "Target the center of both those openings. Fire torpedoes."

The *Enterprise* rocked slightly as four torpedoes sped toward their targets, two at one ship, two at the other.

"Lieutenant Uhura, inform the captain of the situation."

"Yes, sir," she said.

"Continue firing on your targets, Mr. Haru," Spock said as the closest attacker opened up its weapons on the *Enterprise.*

The ship rocked slightly at the direct hits, but the stabilizers kept it level.

Spock could tell that the hits had done little damage. Obviously Mr. Scott's modifications to the screens had proved worthwhile. At least for the moment.

"Screens at ninety-six percent and holding," Chekov said.

Spock watched as the *Farragut* opened up full phaser fire on the ship attacking the *Enterprise,* distracting them for a moment, but doing little damage.

The Klingon battle cruiser jumped into the battle, running a standard attack pass above the closest alien ship, firing with full disrupters.

The two docking bays across the backs of the alien ships continued opening.

Mr. Haru fired two more torpedoes at each ship. All four torpedoes disappeared through the docking openings in the sides of the ships. Inside, the bays lit up with orange and yellow explosions.

A moment later Mr. Haru followed the first two torpedoes with two more. They also found their targets.

Both enemy ships seemed to rock in space as their docking bays were filled with bright orange and red fire.

Mr. Spock had theorized that the weakest area of the attacking ships would be inside the docking bays. It looked as if he might have been right. "Continue firing," he ordered.

The *Enterprise* rocked with direct hits against the screens. Spock gripped the back of the captain's chair and maintained his balance.

Four more torpedoes streaked from the *Enterprise* at the same moment the enemy hit with direct phaser fire.

Out of the flames and explosions of the alien docking bays two large transport ships appeared. Both were ten times larger than the small attack ships deployed before.

"Shields at sixty-percent," Chekov shouted over the rumbling sounds of phaser fire hitting the screens.

"Target the transports, Mr. Haru," Spock ordered. "Fire phasers."

Instantly phasers licked out from the *Enterprise,* making direct hits on one of the transports. Its shield instantly flared to life as an orange ball around the transport.

At that moment the *Farragut* also targeted the same transport with full phasers.

The small ship's orange shields flared to bright red, then into blue and disappeared with an explosion.

"Got him," Chekov said.

"But the other has gotten away," Spock said as the other transport quickly dropped into the atmosphere and out of range.

The *Enterprise* again rocked with the impact of more direct phaser hits. Spock managed to hang on, never taking his gaze from the screen.

"Screens at thirty percent," Chekov said.

"Return fire, Mr. Haru," Spock ordered. "Mr. Chekov, evasive maneuvers. Look for any possible course that would take us into transporter range of the captain."

"Yes, sir," Chekov said.

"Sir, we have a message from the *Farragut,"* Lieutenant Uhura said. "Their shields are almost down. They are pulling back."

Spock noted that the Klingon battle cruiser was also standing off.

"Mr. Chekov. Move to a position flanking the *Farragut* and hold there."

"But sir," Chekov said. "The captain—"

"I want you to continue looking for that course, ensign," Spock said. "Until then, move us beside the *Farragut.*"

"Aye, sir," Chekov said.

Spock moved over and stood by the captain's chair studying the alien ships re-forming into a group and standing off.

The attack had destroyed one transport and had damaged two of the larger ships. But that was not enough to change the odds in this battle. At this point the only hope the *Enterprise* and *Farragut* had of survival was to wait for the Klingon reinforcements in six hours and seven minutes.

But would the captain be able to withstand a ground assault for six hours? The odds were too long to even calculate.

"Mr. Spock," Lieutenant Uhura said, "Captain Bogle said to tell you nice work."

Spock nodded. His timing had been correct. But he had made an error: he had underestimated the defenses of the enemy ships. He would not make that mistake again.

"Lieutenant, have you informed Captain Kirk of the transport's arrival time?"

"Yes, sir," Lieutenant Uhura said.

"Good. Have Mr. Scott come to the bridge." Spock had a theory he needed to work out. And if it worked, he might be able to get within transport distance long enough to get the captain and his party off the surface.

"Mr. Spock," Chekov said. "We have company."

"Company, Mr. Chekov?" Spock asked as he looked at the screen. Three more large alien ships moved into position near the others.

"They have been on the other side of the planet," Chekov said. "It blocked our scans."

"Let's hope those Klingons can get here quickly," Sulu said.

Spock said nothing. He had just done a quick calculation of the odds of rescuing the captain now. They were odds that not even the captain would go against.

Rathbone stood in the faint morning light outside the dome, her hands tucked into her armpits trying to keep warm. Her breath formed silver crystals in front of her. She knew that in a few hours, if she lived that long, she'd be wishing for this cold again. But that thought didn't help warm her now. Just as it had seemed she'd never be cool again during the day, tonight she had felt as if she would never be warm again. If any planet was hell for her, it was this one.

Klingon colonists were starting to gather near the disrupter cannon—men, women, young adults, even children around the age of ten. All of them carried weapons of one sort or another; all ready and willing to fight for their homes.

In that respect, Klingons were just like humans and most other races she was acquainted with. They fought for their homes. But she hated to see the children carrying weapons. There seemed something very wrong with that.

Captain Kirk and Lieutenant Sulu stepped down off the disrupter cannon platform and strode toward her. Watching them come, intent purpose obviously in mind, twisted her stomach into a little knot.

She took a deep breath of the cold air and told herself to get a grip on her fear. She was an official member of a Starfleet landing party. She was trained to do what needed to be done. And she would do it.

Captain Kirk said, "Feeling better?"

"Much," she said.

"Good," he said. He glanced around at the gathering Klingons. "I'm going to send the children back to their domes. If we get overrun by the aliens, we can hope they'll spare the children."

"Good decision," she said. Inside she breathed a sigh of relief that the captain felt the same way she did.

He smiled at her. "Now I've got a job for you."

Again her stomach twisted, but she managed to say, "Anything, sir."

"If we're attacked," the captain said, "I need you and Sulu to try to get into a flanking position off to the right of the colony, dig out a little area for yourselves in a ditch or something. Some sort of cover where you'll end up behind their lines."

"Who's going to man the disrupter cannon?" Sulu asked.

Kirk smiled at him. "I was a good shot in my day. Kerdoch will help."

At that moment the captain's communicator beeped. Vivian watched as he snapped it open with practiced ease and said, "Kirk here."

"Captain," Lieutenant Uhura said, her voice coming through very clearly. "The docking bay doors of two of the alien ships are starting to open. Mr. Spock is now staging an attack on the ships, focusing on the bay doors."

Kirk nodded. "Good thinking. Keep me posted if any ships get through to the atmosphere."

He snapped his communicator closed. "The fight's going on above us. Get to positions. We need to assume Spock and Captain Bogle can't stop them."

"Yes, Captain," Sulu said. "This way, Commander."

Sulu turned and headed off in the faint light, for the second time moving toward the edge of the colony.

For a moment Rathbone couldn't get her feet to move.

"Go ahead," Kirk said. The look in his eyes was one of understanding. "I've got children to get out of the line of fire."

"Understood, Captain," she said. With her numb fingers over her phaser, she nodded to the captain and headed after Mr. Sulu.

A few moments later she once again stepped out into the blackened fields. This time it wasn't to study plants. This time she was to hide behind enemy lines to defend a planet she hated, and a colony of Klingons who had defeated her and her work.

Sometimes life was just a little too strange.

It had taken Kirk only a minute to convince Kerdoch that the children did not belong on the front lines. And that the best possible way for the young children to survive was to be in the domes, without weapons.

At first Kerdoch had argued that it was the Klingon way, but the argument had a token sound to it. After a short exchange, Kerdoch had agreed, and very shortly only adults and teenagers remained near the disrupter cannon.

Kirk stood, watching in the faint morning light as the Klingon colonists took up positions along the edge of the colony. All of them carried panels of dome-coverings in case of an air attack with plasma beams again.

Kirk blew on his hands in a vain attempt to warm them. He so much wanted to be aboard the *Enterprise,* in the middle of the fight up there. But instead he was here, with almost no weapons. And very little chance of winning.

His communicator beeped. He flipped it open. "Go ahead."

"Captain," Spock's voice came back clear and strong. At that moment

Kirk realized that he had been worried about his ship and his crew. Very worried. He was just too busy to think about them.

"Two large transport ships attempted to leave the alien craft. We destroyed one, but the other managed to get into the atmosphere. It should be on the surface in twelve minutes and ten seconds."

"Acknowledged," he said.

They were coming, as he had feared. There had to be a way to stop them.

"What's the status of the *Enterprise?"*

"The *Enterprise* and the *Farragut* came through this fight without damage, Captain. Mr. Scott is working on continuing to strengthen our shields against their weapons."

"The other ships?"

"We have had no report from the Klingon battle cruiser *Klothos.* Three more enemy craft have joined the attack force. They now have seven working ships and one hulk in orbit."

"You've pulled back, I take it," he said.

"For the moment," Spock said. "We had no choice."

Kirk knew that. Still, it was startling to hear Spock say so. "How long until the extra Klingon battle cruisers arrive?"

"Four hours, one minute, sir," Spock said.

Even then, Kirk knew it would not be an even fight. Obviously one of the alien craft at least matched the power of a starship or battle cruiser. Seven against five usually won. Not always, but more than not.

"Let me know if you come up with anything, Mr. Spock. Kirk out."

He flipped his communicator closed and started toward Kerdoch and the disrupter cannon. Unless he could think of something quickly, this was going to be a very long day. And it might be his last.

CHAPTER 16

KERDOCH STOOD ON THE DISRUPTER CANNON PLATFORM, INSIDE THE SHELTER of dome panels, staring out over the blackened fields in the orange light of sunrise. Fields that had been growing and a healthy blue and green only a few days before. Now, finally, he was about to meet, face to face, those responsible for the destruction of his crops, the death of his friends.

The enemy ship had landed just before the sun K'Tuj touched the lower edge of the sky.

Along the rims of the colony his neighbors lined up, weapons at the ready. Today they would all die defending their homes. It was an honorable way to die.

Beside him in the shelter the human Kirk stood, one hand on the disrupter cannon, also ready to fight and die for this planet, this colony. Kerdoch had spent the night wondering about such actions. Humans had always been described as cowards, butchers, animals with no honor. Yet here was a captain who had honor. He and his people could have hidden in the distant hills. He did not have to stay to defend Klingon homes. Yet he did. Without complaint. And with great courage.

This human captain had honor.

In the distance Kerdoch could see the cowards' ship standing tall and bright on the natural vegetation beyond the black crops. A line of forms had stretched out from the ship, facing the colony. Soldiers, lining up for the attack.

They stood upright on two limbs, as Klingons did.

"How many would you estimate?" the human captain asked.

"Three hundred," Kerdoch said. "They wear armor."

As Kerdoch spoke, the line started moving toward the colony.

The human captain flipped open his communicator device. "Spock, they're coming. Anything you can do?"

Kerdoch clearly heard the reply from the human ship. "No, Captain. They are holding us out of range."

"Understood. Kirk out."

The human captain flipped his communicator closed and grasped the two handles of the disrupter cannon firmly with both hands.

"The cannon fire will extend to the edge of the fields," Kerdoch told the human captain. "It was a consideration on shaping our fields."

"Good thinking," the human said. "I'll wait until they cross over the line before opening fire."

Kerdoch said nothing. He slowly drew his disrupter and checked it one more time. It was charged and ready. He would take many of the enemy with him. The cowards approaching him deserved to die for attacking his home and his family. Revenge would be sweet this day.

He glanced down the line of defenders. His wife and eldest son were tucked behind a sheet of dome paneling. Both had weapons in their hands and were staring at the coming enemy. He could feel pride filling his chest.

The line of enemy forms crossed into the blackened fields, their shining blue armor reflecting the early rays of the sun.

The human captain waited.

Kerdoch turned to him. Had he frozen from fear? No, he seemed to be studying the entire scene, his look cold and intent. This human was not one to freeze in battle.

"Okay," the human said. Then he shouted, "Now!"

With that, Kirk fired the disrupter cannon, the sound deafening inside the shelter.

Then he fired again.

And again.

And again.

Kerdoch stood, ignoring the pain in his ears as the human's first shot cut out two soldiers in the center of the line. The force of the blast also knocked others backward.

His second shot had moved to the right ten figures. Again his shot was accurate.

His third shot moved ten more to the right and did not miss.

The enemy troops continued forward.

Kirk continued firing, knocking large holes in the enemy lines to both the left and the right.

Suddenly, before the enemy soldiers could get within phaser range of the colony, the line stopped. As a unit they turned and, at the same trudging pace, moved back toward their ship.

Instantly the human captain stopped firing, even though he could have shot many of them in the back as they retreated.

Kerdoch nodded his agreement. It took no honor to shoot an enemy in the back. Humans truly did have honor in battle. It was something he would always remember.

"You fire a disrupter cannon well," Kerdoch said.

The human captain nodded as he rubbed his ears. "Thanks. But you folks really should put mufflers on these things."

"Mufflers?" Kerdoch asked. He had never heard such a term.

"Never mind," Kirk said as the line of enemy crossed back into the natural vegetation, leaving many shining armored bodies laying in the blackened fields.

Kerdoch felt the surge of revenge coursing through his blood as he stared at those bodies. It was good the enemy died in the fields they had destroyed. It felt right. Only their death at his bare hands would have felt better.

Rathbone lay face down in a deep ditch, trying her best to press her body even farther into the hard dirt.

A fine black ash covered everything in the ditch, including her. Her blackened hands held her phaser in front of her. They shook, and she tried to tell herself it was from the cold. But there was no kidding herself.

She was afraid. Very afraid.

During all the practice on the firing ranges in her youth, she had always wondered what being in a real fight would be like. It looked as if she would soon find out.

Facing her, Lieutenant Sulu also lay flat in the ditch, his tricorder tucked under his chin. He had been studying it for the last five minutes, but to her it had seemed like at least an hour.

"They're moving," Sulu whispered. "They should pass to our right in about sixty seconds."

She only nodded, far too afraid to trust her voice to speak. How the captain, Sulu, the other members of landing parties ever got used to this kind of danger was beyond her. It had her stomach clamped down into a knot and she had no idea how she was going to move if she had to fight.

She took a deep, shuddering breath and grasped the solid, reassuring feel of the phaser. Even being able to hit a pinpoint from fifty paces didn't comfort her at the moment. She had heard that some people froze in life-and-death situations while others managed to overcome their fear and fight. She hoped she was the type who overcame, but she feared even more than dying that she was the type who froze.

Now it looked as if she might find out very soon.

Suddenly the ground shook from an explosion.

She jumped, but Sulu put his hand on her arm. "Disrupter cannon fire," he said as another explosion shook the ground under her stomach, seeming much closer.

"The captain?" she whispered.

He nodded, not taking his gaze from his tricorder.

A third explosion, then a fourth, rocked the ground under her. Then more and more, one right after another.

The ground seemed to shake continuously under her, as if the explosions were linked.

Then, just as suddenly, it was silent.

Unnaturally silent.

Had the captain been killed?

Had the troops already reached the colony? She wanted to jump up and look, but she remained in the dirt, almost too afraid to breathe.

"They're retreating," Sulu whispered. He looked up at her, smiling through the black soot that covered his face. "The captain turned them with the cannon."

Suddenly she felt heavier, as if the weight of her body would punch a hole through the dirt under her.

"Thank heavens," she managed to say. Then she took the first true breath in what seemed like an eternity, let it out slowly, then took another.

It pleased her to see that Sulu was doing the exact same thing.

Kirk stood beside Kerdoch on the edge of the cannon platform, staring out at the bodies of the attackers littering the blackened fields. There must have been at least fifty of them, and he doubted that all of them were dead; many of them were probably only injured.

What would the attackers do now? Would they return for their injured? Would they attack again?

And why had they retreated? If they wanted to overrun the colony, why hadn't they simply continued forward? They were taking casualties, but nowhere near enough to prevent the success of their mission.

Yet under the type of fire he had been hitting them with, he would have pulled back too, if they had been his troops. Maybe that was the key to all this. He had guessed correctly about the ground attack. And their retreat was what he would have done. Maybe their thinking wasn't that far from human military thinking.

He flipped open his communicator. "Mr. Sulu, where are you?"

"In a ditch just to the right of where their line stopped advancing."

Kirk looked in that direction. One of his shots had knocked down four of the enemy right near Sulu's position. Maybe he could exchange their wounded for an opportunity to talk.

"Mr. Sulu, you and Rathbone check out the enemy casualties near your position. If you find a wounded soldier, bring him to me."

"Understood," Sulu said.

Kirk punched his communicator. "McCoy, I need you at the cannon at once."

"On my way," McCoy said.

Out in the blackened field two forms rose from a ditch and moved in a crouch toward a fallen enemy soldier.

"Why do you worry over the dead?" Kerdoch said. "They fell in battle. They have their honor."

"Because, like your commander in the dome there, they may not be dead."

"But they are the enemy," Kerdoch said, as if that were enough for Kirk to understand his meaning.

"Yes, they are," Kirk said. And he added silently, *So are you.*

• • •

At the captain's order, Rathbone had managed to push herself to her feet and climb out of the ditch beside Lieutenant Sulu. The second sun was starting to break above the horizon, and she could already feel the heat of the day coming, knocking back the cold that had filled her body.

Twenty paces in front of her, lying face down in the black soot, was a blue-armored soldier, the light reflecting off his armor like it was a mirror.

She glanced around. To her right were the enemy troops and the enemy ship; to her left was the colony. She felt as if she were walking naked onto a stage in front of the entire world. Even with Sulu beside her, she had never felt so exposed and vulnerable.

They both moved in a crouch, not really sneaking, but making sure they both stayed low until they reached the fallen alien who lay on his side, his back to them. Slowly, without touching the armor, they moved around in front of him.

The face inside the helmet was humanoid, with long black hair framing its face. It also had thick black eyebrows and ridges of thick hair running across its forehead. The nose lay flat against his face, giving him the look of a lion.

The soldier was also clearly dead.

Sulu picked up the enemy's rifle-looking weapon and moved to the next body. This soldier had less hair on his face, and was clearly younger. He was also very much alive, his eyes glowing green as he looked at them.

Those eyes startled her. For some reason she had not put real live creatures behind the thought of the enemy. Before now the enemy had only been fast moving ships spraying waves of deadly heat. But now the enemy had eyes and a face.

When Sulu pulled the weapon from his hand, the soldier didn't move an inch to stop him.

Then Sulu studied the alien with his tricorder. "It looks as if he's broken both legs," Sulu said to her.

She could have guessed as much. The soldier's legs were twisted underneath him at very odd angles. "Can he be moved?"

"I don't know," Sulu said. He glanced around, then leaned over the soldier. "Can you hear me?"

Behind the face plate of his helmet the alien nodded yes. His gaze darted from Sulu to Vivian, then back again.

"Are you in pain?" she asked. "Bleeding?"

He shook his head. "The medical function of my suit has stopped the bleeding, killed my pain."

She was amazed at the richness of the alien's voice. Likely it was only the suit's speakers that made it sound like that.

"Good," she said. "What race are you?"

"We are Narr," he said.

"We're going to get you help," Sulu said.

The Narr soldier shook his head. "You will not move me," he said, his voice coming through the faceplate clearly.

"Why not?" she asked. "You need medical help."

"My suit cannot be moved by you."

"Will it destruct?" Sulu asked.

Once again the alien shook his head. "It is heavy. The gravity units were damaged in the battle."

Sulu sat back, looking at the fallen soldier, nodding his head. "Your legs were broken when the antigravity units in your suit failed and the suit crushed your legs."

"That is correct," the soldier said.

She couldn't believe what she was hearing. "You mean," she said, "that these soldiers wear suits so heavy that if the suit fails they can't stand up?"

Sulu nodded. "We've seen it before."

She stared down into the green eyes of the wounded soldier, then gently touched the sleeve of his suit near his wrist. It felt solid.

Carefully she tried to pick up the arm. It was like pulling on a solid steel wall—not even a fraction of an inch of movement. "Unbelievable," she said.

"Standard for some cultures," Sulu said. "It also stops their enemies from taking prisoners."

The alien nodded behind his faceplate. "I will be rescued after the battle has been won. Until then I wait."

"Let's hope there is no more battle," Sulu said. He snapped open his communicator. "Captain?"

"Kirk here."

For some reason being reminded that the captain was so close made Vivian relax a little.

"Captain, we have a live casualty inside damaged mobile armor. It's far too heavy for us to move."

"I was afraid of that," Kirk said.

She glanced around at the open field and the other very still armored figures littering the blackness. How many of them were alive inside those heavy shells?

"Return to the colony. Kirk out."

"But what about this soldier?" she asked, shocked. How could Captain Kirk simply ignore an injured person, enemy or not?

Sulu stood. "There's nothing we can do for him at the moment. Come on." He turned and started toward the colony.

She remained beside the Narr, staring at his green eyes. Finally he smiled at her. "Follow your orders, soldier," he said. "You can do nothing to help me."

She nodded slowly.

"Rathbone," Sulu called to her.

She looked one more time into the deep green eyes of the Narr soldier. "Good luck."

"And to you," the soldier said.

Feeling as if her entire body was numb, she pushed herself to her feet and, without looking back, stumbled after Sulu toward the colony.

CHAPTER 17

SCOTTY LOOKED AT THE YOUNG ENSIGN. SHE WAS SLENDER, HER DARK HAIR falling out of its neat bun. She had been working non-stop in engineering since they left Starbase Eleven, probably the longest shift she had ever pulled.

"What I meant," she stammered, "is that I doubt we could improve them."

She was referring to the shields. Scotty's modification had worked, but not as well as he would have liked. Shield strength had still gone down, but not as rapidly as before. There was an element to the enemies' weapons that he had not yet discovered—and he had told Mr. Spock that in their brief meeting on the bridge.

"You doubt, lass?" Scotty said softly. The more established members of Engineering stepped back. They knew what was coming. They had worked with Scotty long enough to know that when he spoke softly, they had best watch out.

"Yes, sir," she said. "I have double-checked your calculations."

"You double-checked *my* calculations?" His voice got even softer.

"You asked me to, sir," she said, oblivious of his tone, "and I found nothing wrong."

"You found nothing wrong," he said.

"No," she said.

"Did you expect to, lass?"

Someone guffawed behind him. Scotty turned and, with a look, silenced the laughter.

The ensign finally got the idea that something might be wrong. She flushed. "Well, sir, you did ask me to check your figures, and I assumed that meant you thought there might be errors."

"You assumed," Scotty said.

"Yes, sir," she said.

He nodded thoughtfully. "And did you not assume that maybe I was asking you to see if you could spot a different modification?"

"Sir?"

"Did you not know, lass, that engineering is not a science of mathematics?"

She blinked those extraordinary eyes at him. "But of course it involves math," she said. "The calculations—"

"Mean nothing without creativity behind them," Scotty said, his voice rising. "Lass, the engineers on this ship are second only to the captain in their creative abilities. In fact, the ability to think on your feet and to come up with solutions not in the guidebooks is the hallmark of a chief engineer."

"But I'm not a chief engineer," she said quietly.

"Aye, you're not, and you're not likely to be, either." He picked up the small padd she had used and slammed it on the console. Then he raised his voice even more. "The *computer* can check my math. It cannot check my creative thinking, now, can it?"

"No, sir." She glanced at the others for help, but they didn't look at her. They had all been in this situation before. It was one way that Scotty trained his assistants. He had to work the rigidity out of their systems—the rigidity drilled into them by well-meaning Academy instructors. "B-b-but I'm just an ensign, sir."

"And do you think I magically became chief engineer? Do you think I was not once an ensign?" Scotty asked.

"Ah, I, ah, had not given it any thought," she said, then added, "sir."

He was about to show her how to approach the new problem when Uhura hailed him. "What is it, Lieutenant?" he snapped, forgetting for a moment that he wasn't training her.

"Projeff of the *Farragut,*" she said. "Shall I tell him you're busy?"

"No, put him through." Scotty pointed at the ensign. "Be creative," he said, handing her the padd. "And try again."

She nodded, obviously relieved to no longer be the center of attention.

Scotty looked at the screen. Projeff was grinning at him.

"Picking on children again?" Projeff asked.

" 'Tis the reason I get more work from my staff than you get from yours," Scotty said.

Projeff shook his head slightly. "The modifications worked, but not well enough, I think."

The ensign beside Scotty stiffened, obviously expecting an outburst. But Scotty knew the truth of Projeff's statement.

"I agree," Scotty said. "We're working on more improvements here, but so far we haven't found much."

"I think there's a third element to the enemy weaponry that your calculations didn't catch," Projeff said.

"And what's that?"

"Harmonics."

"You said that before, lad, but you had no evidence."

"I do now," Projeff said. "Your modifications took care of the new and the old versions of the weapons systems, but these weapons also use a harmonics sequence that is out of the range of our systems. It is, I think—"

"What makes them truly alien," Scotty said, suddenly understanding. "You're right, lad, it's worth checking out. Send me your information."

"I will," Projeff said, "and my ideas for solving the problem." Then he grinned. "Courtesy of the *Farragut.*"

Captain Bogle paced back and forth in front of his chair, his hands tucked behind his back, his gaze watching the alien ships on the main screen. Now at least the enemy had a name.

Narr.

Over the last century there had been rumors of a race called the Narr, but there was no actual record of any contact with them, and no one had any idea where their homeworld was or what they looked like. Nothing. Just rumors.

Until now.

Now seven of their wing-shaped ships formed an effective blockade of the planet below—the planet the Narr were attacking for some unknown reason.

Behind the Narr ships, on the planet's surface, Bogle knew the colony was moving into the heat of the morning. Kirk and the colonists had managed to hold off the Narr ground troops for one attack, but Bogle doubted they could do it again.

"They're moving again," Mr. Lee said.

"Red alert," Bogle said.

Around him the lights dimmed and the sirens went off.

On the main screen the two Narr ships that had released the transports were moving, shifting to a position closer to the *Enterprise* and the *Farragut.*

At the same time the three new arrivals were shifting to positions closer to the planet, more protected from the Federation ships, with their transport bays turned away.

Instantly Bogle knew what they were planning to do. More transports would be heading to the surface from the new ships any moment, reinforcements to make sure the colony didn't survive another attack.

"Arm torpedoes," he said. "Lieutenant Book, take us above the Narr ships. I want to be able to see exactly what comes out of those transport bays."

"Yes, sir," Book said.

"The *Enterprise* is moving under them, sir," Lee said. "And the two new Klingon battle cruisers are entering the system."

"Here we go, people," Bogle said as he dropped down into his captain's chair. "Stay sharp."

The two front Narr ships suddenly opened fire, their phaser beams striking out against the *Farragut* and the *Enterprise* as the two Federation ships tried to move above them, trying for a better angle on the three new ships.

The *Farragut*'s shields flared bright white and the ship rocked slightly.

"Shields holding," Lee said. "The modifications seem to be working."

Bogle nodded to himself. The changes Projeff and Engineer Scott had made on the shields were keeping the ship in much better shape than in the first encounter. And would give him more room to try to save those on the planet.

"Hold your fire until you see a transport," Bogle said.

He stared at the edges of the three Narr ships as if trying to see what was happening on the other side. He would bet money that their docking bays were opening.

Again the *Farragut* rocked from phaser impacts against the shields.

"Shields still holding," Lee said.

The two new Klingon battle cruisers dropped out of warp and instantly joined the other battle cruiser facing the Narr ships. All three opened up on the big Narr ships almost simultaneously.

The Narr shields flared from orange to red.

"Transports," Lee said at the exact moment Bogle saw the nose of one transport poking out of the docking bay of a Narr ship, then another from the second ship. All three new ships were releasing transports, just as he'd feared.

"Target transports and fire," Bogle said. "Don't let them get to the atmosphere."

Photon torpedo after photon torpedo sped from the *Farragut,* blasting the shields of the transports with direct hit after direct hit.

From the other side, the *Enterprise* was doing the same, as if Mr. Spock was mirroring Bogle's actions.

Again the *Farragut* rocked as two direct phaser hits flared against the shields.

Bogle held on.

"Shields still at ninety-six percent," Lee shouted over the rumbling noise.

"Keep firing," Bogle shouted.

On the screen the shields of one of the transports flared bright red, faded into blue, and then vanished. In the next instant a huge flash of light signaled the end of that ship.

"Target the ship that's closest to the atmosphere," Bogle said. "Fire!"

Again the *Enterprise* simultaneously mirrored his actions.

The *Farragut* sustained another direct hit, rocking Bogle almost out of his chair. He held on, his gaze never leaving the transport they were firing at.

With the full force of both Federation ships pounding it, the transport's shields flared through the spectrum and disappeared. An instant later the ship exploded like a small sun going nova.

"The third transport has already reached the atmosphere," Lee said.

"Damn," Bogle said, pounding his fist into the arm of his chair. Normally he managed to control his anger, but this failure made him angry.

He sat and watched the Narr transport, which looked like a streak of light as it cut through the upper layer of the atmosphere. It was now beyond his reach.

Again the ship rocked with more direct hits.

"Mr. Book, take us back to our previous position."

"The *Enterprise* is also withdrawing," Lee said. "And the Klingons have broken off their attack."

Bogle stared at the image of the planet on the screen. With another transport ship heading to the surface, Kirk and the colonists would have no chance of holding off a ground attack.

"Sorry, Jim," Bogle said softly to himself. "For a moment there I thought we were going to win that round."

"Excuse me, sir?" Lee said.

"Nothing, Commander," Bogle said.

Then he spoke louder to get everyone's attention. "I need ideas, people. We have to figure out a way to get Kirk and those colonists out of danger. Think, people. Think."

Bogle managed not to smile at the shocked looks he got from his crew. He almost never asked for their opinions; now he was asking for their help.

He sat back in his chair, staring at the Narr ships and the planet beyond as the silence on his bridge became almost deafening. If he had anything to say about it, his friend Jim Kirk would not die in such an awful place.

And if that meant asking for help, so be it.

Kirk flipped his communicator closed and sat down on the edge of the cannon platform. Another transport ship had made it past the *Enterprise* and the *Farragut.*

Now what? He hadn't felt this tired and discouraged in years.

Sulu, Dr. McCoy, Ensign Adaro, and Rathbone stood near him, Rathbone and McCoy both in the shade of the cannon shelter. They had all heard the news.

Kirk wiped the sweat from his forehead. Only two hours into the day and already the heat was stifling. Freezing at night, cooking during the day. What a wonderful planet to die defending.

"Dammit, Jim," McCoy said, "there's got to be something we can do. We should negotiate."

"That's hard to do, Bones, with a race that won't talk."

"That young soldier talked to us," Rathbone said. "He answered every one of our questions."

Kirk looked at her, then back out over the blackened field where the armored soldiers lay. He hoped their armor had an air supply and a cooling system. The ones out there who were still alive were going to need it.

Suddenly Dr. Rathbone's words sank in. The Narr had talked. The problem was getting them to do so.

"You have a point, Dr. Rathbone," Kirk said. "Maybe there is a way to get them to talk."

He stood. Removed the sweat-drenched shirt. He had an idea, and the only way to make it work was to show to the Narr he was no threat.

"What are you planning, Jim?" McCoy asked.

Kirk could already hear the skepticism in McCoy's voice.

"I'm going to do a little peace talking," he said.

He sat back down on the edge of the cannon platform, reached for his boots, and took them off. Then he stood again, dropped his trousers, and slipped them off, handing them to the startled doctor. Now he wore only standard Starfleet-issue shorts. The dirt-covered and burned red skin on his arms and face were a sharp contrast to the pale skin on his legs. He wagered he looked damned funny.

He slipped his boots back on quickly.

Rathbone choked back a laugh, and Kirk looked at her. Both she and Sulu had their hands over their mouths. He had been right.

"Dr. Rathbone," Kirk said, keeping his face serious while he faced her, "it doesn't do a man's ego much good to have a woman laugh at him when he takes off his clothes."

She had enough sense to blush under her dirty and sunburned skin, but her laughter didn't disappear far below the surface of her eyes.

"I'd be laughing too," McCoy said, his voice angry, "if I didn't know you were damn serious."

"That I am, Bones," Kirk said. He turned to Mr. Sulu. "Inform Mr. Spock that I'm trying to talk to the Narr. If I don't return, give them your best fight."

"Aye, Captain," Sulu said, all the laughter gone out of his eyes.

Kirk glanced at McCoy. "Bones, keep Kor alive."

"It looks at the moment as if he's going to outlive you," McCoy said.

Kirk laughed, then turned and headed out toward the blackened field and the fallen Narr. In the distance he could see the enemy transport ship. In a few minutes it would be joined by another. The time for talking was now or never.

"Jim?" McCoy called out behind him.

Kirk stopped and turned around. The three of them remained at the edge of the disrupter cannon.

"Do you know how silly you look?" McCoy asked, a grin slowly crossing his sunburned face.

"Yes, Doctor, I do," Kirk said. "I'm counting on it, in fact."

"Well," McCoy said, "for heaven's sake keep your shorts on. You don't want them laughing *too* hard when you try to talk to them."

Beside McCoy, both Rathbone and Sulu almost managed not to laugh.

"I owe you, Bones," Kirk said. Then with a smile at his old friend he turned and strode out into the blackened field, heading straight for the Narr transport ships, his hands above his head in the traditional sign of surrender.

For a moment Kerdoch could not believe his vision. The human captain, with almost no clothes on, walking directly at the Narr ships. What was he thinking? He had not seemed to be a fool in the first battles. Had the heat gotten to him?

A number of colonists stood near their shelters, pointing and laughing. It was a humorous sight, but not one that Kerdoch would laugh at until later.

Kerdoch moved quickly along the edge of the colony until he reached the other three humans near the disrupter cannon.

"Your captain," Kerdoch said. "He has gone insane?"

"It would appear that way," the human doctor said. "But he thinks he can get the Narr to talk this way. I'm not sure why he thinks that, but I gave up years ago trying to figure James Kirk out."

"Talk?" Kerdoch asked. "For what purpose?"

The human doctor looked at him. Kerdoch could tell that he was very, very angry.

"To save your stupid, ungrateful life, that's what purpose," the doctor said.

"Doctor," the one named Sulu said.

Kerdoch looked at the doctor. He felt no anger at the insult; he was only puzzled. "We are prepared to fight," he said. "It would be an honorable death to die defending our homes."

The human doctor shook his head. "Honor can be gained in more ways than fighting and dying."

"He's at the edge of the field," the human woman said.

Kerdoch turned from the doctor and watched as the human captain stopped, his hands high in the air.

Six minutes later when the other Narr transport landed beside the first, he was still standing there.

CHAPTER 18

KIRK HAD STOOD NOW FOR ONE HOUR AT THE EDGE OF THE BLACK FIELD IN the hot sun, watching the Narr transports. The sweat ran down the sides of his face and off his back. He knew if he stayed much longer he might not have the strength to stand, let alone walk back to the colony.

Every few minutes during the hour he'd lowered his arms and let the blood flow back into them. But as time went along, he was having more and more problems holding his arms above his head for even thirty seconds. Yet he kept trying.

Finally, what he hoped for happened.

Three Narr in full battle armor strode toward him from the transports. Somehow he managed to keep his hands in the air until they stopped ten paces in front of him.

"You are human," the Narr soldier in the center said.

"Yes," Kirk said, letting his arms drop to his sides. "I'm Captain James T. Kirk of the Federation Starship *Enterprise*."

The one in the center nodded slightly.

Kirk could tell no difference between the one who spoke and the others. Inside their faceplates, they all had long black hair, flat noses, and lines of hair on their foreheads. In an odd way they were almost catlike in appearance, but still very humanoid.

"Do humans have a claim on this planet?"

"No," Kirk said.

"Then why do you fight for it?"

"We fight because we were asked to help. This planet belongs to the Klingons."

"This planet is ours," the Narr soldier said. "We have kept it for years, preparing it. We want you and the ones called Klingons to leave."

"I'm afraid Klingons don't normally give up a planet they claim just by asking."

"Nor do we," the Narr said. "We will reclaim the planet at sunset."

With that all three turned their backs on him.

"Wait!" he shouted.

They stopped and slowly turned around.

"Your wounded," Kirk said, pointing to the armored soldiers lying in the field. "If you want to retrieve them, we will not fire on you."

The one in the center nodded. "We shall do so."

Again they turned their backs on him.

Kirk stood there, watching them lumber away in their heavy armor. The only thing he could think of was sunset and the coming attack. At least they had the sense not to attack during the heat of the day.

And that gave him until dusk to come up with a plan.

Dr. Rathbone stood with McCoy, Sulu, and Kerdoch at the edge of the colony, watching the captain talk to the Narr. The sun was beating down on Vivian, and she could feel the back of her uniform growing wet with sweat, but she didn't move into the shade. There was no way she was going to leave the others watching the captain. She wished she could hear what was being said, listen in to the negotiations going on at the edge of the black Klingon field.

Then suddenly the talks were over. The Narr turned and moved slowly over the natural plants in the direction of their transports.

After a moment Captain Kirk turned and started toward the colony. She could see that his skin was now bright red from the sun. He was clearly having problems. Finally, when he stumbled and fell, they all started out across the field toward him.

While Kerdoch stood watching, she sat down next to the captain and held his head.

Sulu helped him gulp down water mixed with nutrients specially prepared by McCoy.

McCoy scanned him with the medical tricorder, then grunted.

"Will I live?" Kirk asked, smiling up at McCoy.

"Another half hour and you'd have ended up beside Kor in that dome," McCoy said. "Now lie still."

As Kirk relaxed a little, his head became heavier in Vivian's hands. His hair was wet with sweat, and, like her, he was covered with black soot.

McCoy took out a medical spray and gave the captain a shot, then sprayed a fine mist over the bright red skin on his shoulders and arms. Then Vivian helped him sit up, and McCoy sprayed the captain's back and legs.

The captain started to say something, but McCoy interrupted. "Keep drinking. You're not moving until you have two of those bottles of water down you."

Kirk nodded, leaned back against her again, and drank. Then she and Sulu lifted him to his feet.

He leaned against Sulu, and with Kerdoch on his other side they slowly made their way to the shade of the cannon shelter.

The captain dropped down into a sitting position, and Sulu handed him more water.

"You are crazy, you know that?" McCoy said.

The captain started to say something, but McCoy pointed at him. "Drink."

Kirk laughed, but he obeyed. Finally, after the captain had drunk another half a bottle of water, McCoy said, "So tell us what happened."

"Kerdoch," Kirk said, his voice raspy for a moment, then clearing.

The large Klingon colonist knelt beside the seated captain.

"Tell your people not to fire on the Narr," Kirk said. "They will be unarmed and retrieving their wounded from the field very shortly."

Kerdoch nodded. "I will tell them." He stood and moved quickly away from the shelter.

McCoy watched the Klingon go, then glanced at the captain. Rathbone could tell that McCoy understood something she had missed. She wasn't sure what, but she knew that look.

"So what didn't you want to tell him?" McCoy said.

Kirk smiled and took another drink. "The Narr claim they own this planet."

"What?" she found herself asking.

"That's about all they said," the captain said. "That and that they had been preparing the planet for years."

Vivian looked at Sulu, and he glanced at her. It was clear he was thinking what she had been thinking—that it was the Narr who had modified the planet's natural plant life.

"Terraforming," she said.

Sulu nodded.

"What?" McCoy asked, glancing at her.

She took a deep breath. "Captain, remember when we told you the planet's plant life had been genetically changed at some time in the past."

"Very clearly," he said. "Now you know what I'm thinking. The Narr made the changes."

"It's possible," she said. "We've never had an explanation for that change." Her stomach told her this was the right answer. An answer to a question that had bothered her for almost five years. Everything fit. The Narr had changed the planet for their own use, just as the humans and Klingons had been doing.

"I assumed that was the problem," the captain said. "It would explain why they're so angry at the Klingons."

"And why they're destroying only Klingon crops," Sulu said.

"And why they attacked in the first place," McCoy said.

"Good point," she said, glancing at the blackened fields. "Obviously they don't like what the Klingons planted."

"Or they never bothered even to test it," Sulu said.

"So what do we do now?" McCoy asked.

Kirk took another drink of water, then glanced up at McCoy. "Doctor, if I knew that, I wouldn't still be sitting here."

"Think the Klingons will just give the planet back to them?" she asked.

The captain laughed. "Would you, if the Federation colony had won and the Narr were attacking your home?"

"Probably not," she said slowly. She hated to admit that, but it was how she felt. It was always easy to tell others to give up their homes, but she *had* been told to leave this planet, which had once been her home. She knew how it felt. She didn't like it.

The captain took another long drink, then sighed. "People, at the moment our plan is to help the Klingons defend this colony from the coming attack at sunset."

"Until a better plan comes along?" McCoy asked.

Kirk smiled. "Until a better plan comes along."

Spock stood on the bridge and listened as the captain finished relaying the conversation he'd had with the Narr to him and Captain Bogle on the *Farragut.*

"It is logical," Spock said, staring at the image of the planet on the main viewscreen.

"What's logical, Mr. Spock?" the captain asked.

"The Narr claim to this planet. They are obviously telling the truth."

"Do you have clear evidence of that, Mr. Spock?" Captain Bogle asked.

"Give me a moment, sir," Spock said. "I will run a molecular scan of the derelict Narr ship, then compare it to the data I have on the structure of the native planetary growth."

"Good idea, Spock," Kirk said. "We'll wait."

Spock moved to his science station and keyed in the commands for running a scan of the Narr ship.

"Computer," he said. "Compare molecular structure of the Narr ships with the structure of the plant samples I have selected."

"Comparison complete," the computer voice said after only a second.

Again staring at the planet and the Narr ships on the main viewscreen, Spock asked, "Is there a statistical possibility that the plant and the scanned metal came from the same planetary system?"

"Yes," the computer said.

"What is that percentage?" he asked.

"Eighty-six percent," the computer said.

"Well," Captain Kirk said, his voice filling the bridge almost as if he were there, "that settles that."

"I guess it does," Captain Bogle said.

"It would seem that way," Spock said.

"So, Mr. Spock," the captain said, "how do we convince the Klingons that they really don't own this planet?"

"How is a Klingon convinced of anything?" Bogle asked.

"By fighting," Spock said calmly.

There was a moment of silence on the bridge.

Finally Captain Kirk's voice again filled the bridge. "Mr. Spock, relay this information to the Klingon ships."

"I shall do so immediately, Captain," Spock said.

"Then, gentlemen, I hope you can find a way to get us off this oven of a planet before the fighting starts."

"We'll do our best, Jim," Bogle said.

"I know you will. Thanks. Kirk out."

Mr. Spock turned to Lieutenant Uhura. "Relay the molecular information and comparisons to the three Klingon battle cruisers. Include a transcript of what the captain said occurred in his conversation with the Narr."

"Yes, sir," Uhura said.

Spock moved back to his science station. The first half of the captain's order had been carried out. It was the second half that would pose more of a problem. Much more.

CHAPTER 19

KIRK SAT IN THE RELATIVE COOLNESS OF THE DOME, SIPPING WATER AND watching McCoy work on Kor. It had been two hours since Kirk had talked to the Narr, and he was finally starting to regain some strength. It was lucky the Narr had showed up when they did.

At the moment Sulu stood guard at the disrupter cannon, but Kirk knew it was pointless duty. The Narr would come at sundown and not one minute sooner.

Kerdoch stood near the door while Kahaq, the only surviving member of Kor's landing party sat beside his commander.

Rathbone stood at McCoy's shoulder. Her brown hair was matted back on her head, and as with all of them, her face was badly sunburned and very dirty.

Kor moaned and moved his head slightly.

Both Kerdoch and Kirk moved quickly to the Commander's side.

"Can you wake him, Bones?" Kirk asked.

Bones nodded. "I think he's finally stabilized. And his ribs are mostly healed. Damned if I know if I did anything to help anything else, but I think I can wake him up."

"Do it," Kirk said. He needed Kor awake and in command of the Klingons when the colonists were told the news about the Narr claim on the planet. There was no guarantee that Kor would react in any positive way, but at least it would be one reaction instead of six different options with the leaderless colonists.

McCoy injected Kor and then sat back as the Klingon commander moaned again, then slowly opened his eyes and looked at McCoy.

"I am having a nightmare," he said and closed his eyes again.

Kirk laughed and Bones gave him a frozen look, which made Kirk laugh even more, and after a moment Rathbone joined in.

"The next time you need sunburn spray, remember that you thought this was funny," McCoy threatened.

Kirk laughed, nudged McCoy aside, and knelt near the commander. "Kor, we need to talk."

The Klingon commander slowly opened his eyes again. "This is not a nightmare, then?"

"Oh, it's a nightmare all right," Kirk said. "But I'm afraid it's a real one."

Kor groaned and tried to sit up.

"Not yet," McCoy said.

Kirk put a hand on the Klingon's chest and held him on his back. "You were seriously injured. Give yourself a little more time to recover."

Kor looked from Kirk to McCoy. McCoy nodded to confirm Kirk's words.

"I would like water," Kor said. It was as close as a Klingon came to asking for help.

Rathbone handed the commander a bottle and he drank deeply, then sighed and seemed to relax a little.

"Are you able to talk?" Kirk asked.

Kor nodded. "What has happened?"

Kirk spent the next few minutes bringing the Klingon commander up to date on their situation, right to the moment he had talked to the Narr.

Kor took a long drink, finished the bottle Rathbone had given him, then looked Kirk in the eye. "You do not like what the Narr told you," he said. "I can tell."

Kirk nodded. "They claim to own the planet."

Kor laughed. "How can that be? The planet was awarded to the Klingon Empire by the Organians."

"I know," Kirk said. "But ask your colonists about how eight or nine hundred years ago the natural plants on this planet were biologically altered."

"Is this true?" Kor asked Kerdoch.

The colonist stepped forward. "It is true," he said. "We found no explanation for the alteration and assumed it had been caused by a natural event."

Kor nodded. "So the Narr claim they were forming the planet to their needs."

"They did not claim it exactly," Kirk said. "But they did say they had been preparing it."

"And you expect us to just give up the planet on that basis?"

Kirk shook his head. He had expected, and hoped, the conversation would get to this point.

"Kor, tests run on both the altered plants here and the materials in the Narr ships show a biological match. The natural plants on this planet were combined with Narr plants hundreds of years ago. The data has been given to your ship."

Kirk watched as Kor kept his expression blank. There was no way to tell what the commander was thinking. Finally he said, "Captain Kirk, do you have a solution to this standoff?"

Kirk did not expect that question. "I do not."

Kor nodded and closed his eyes. "How much time until the suns set?" His voice was weak and tired.

"Six hours," Kirk said.

"Then I have time to rest before I must fight," Kor said. He let out a deep sigh and seemed to fall asleep.

McCoy did a quick medical scan of Kor, then nodded to Kirk that the commander would be all right after a little rest.

"We all need the rest," Kirk said. He stood and moved back over to the table where he sat down.

No one, including Kerdoch, said a word as they settled into positions scattered around the dome. It would be a long, hot afternoon waiting to fight, and waiting, most likely, to die.

Unless Kirk could come up with some way of stopping the fight.

"Mr. Spock," Captain Bogle said to the Vulcan on the main Farragut screen in front of him, "have you gone crazy?"

"I assure you, Captain," Spock said, his expression never changing. "I am quite sane. I simply offer a possible means of rescuing Captain Kirk and the landing party."

"Have you checked with Kirk?" Bogle asked.

"I have not," Spock said.

Bogle shook his head. "Give me a moment to consider your plan."

"Certainly," Spock said and cut the transmission.

Immediately the Narr ships returned to the main screen, orbiting seemingly peacefully over the blue-green planet.

Bogle dropped down into his chair and stared at the screen, thinking about Commander Spock's plan. Actually, the idea was typically logical. There were seven working Narr ships facing two Federation and three Klingon ships. All ships on both sides seemed to be fairly matched, although with the shield modulations against Narr weapons, Bogle would now give the *Farragut* and the *Enterprise* a slight advantage. But not a two ship advantage.

Spock's idea was for the *Farragut* and the *Enterprise* to simultaneously launch unmanned shuttles in high orbits over the planet, in opposite directions. Each shuttle, logically, would draw one Narr ship into pursuit, temporarily pulling it away from the main blockade, leveling the odds. At that moment the Federation and Klingon ships would attack, with the two Federation ships working to get into a position within transporter range long enough to drop shields and get the landing party off the planet.

Bogle shook his head. It was a logical, but fool-hardy plan. It risked the lives of all the members of the *Farragut* crew, as well as all the members of the *Enterprise* crew in an attempt to save four other crew members. And that was not logical in any fashion.

Spock should know better than to use an entire crew to rescue a handful of people.

But he was Kirk's first officer, working on assumptions Kirk would make. Perhaps when Spock had his own starship, he would act differently. But now, he had to second-guess his creative captain.

He seemed to do it pretty well.

It sounded like a Kirk plan.

Bogle sighed. And because of that, it might work.

If the shields on the shuttles could be modulated to withstand the Narr phasers for at least a minute, that would be long enough.

Another idea popped into his head. The shuttles could be programmed to land near the colony if they survived long enough to get into the atmosphere; that would give the landing party yet another chance.

Then still another idea struck him: they could use Spock's same idea, only not endanger the crews of the starships.

He quickly punched his ship intercom button on the arm of his captain's chair.

"Projeff?"

"Yes, Captain," Projeff answered at once.

"Can both shuttles' shields be modified to withstand the Narr weapons long enough to get to the atmosphere?"

There was a pause, then Projeff said slowly, "They can be modified, sir. But I wouldn't wager a man's life that they would hold under full Narr attack all the way to the atmosphere."

"But is there a chance that one, or maybe both, would make it?"

"There is a chance, sir," Projeff said. "With the modifications Mr. Scott and I have come up with, it would take a full Narr attack lasting twenty-six seconds for thc shields to fail."

"Thanks, Projeff," Bogle said. "Stand by."

He clicked off the intercom, then turned to Lieutenant Sandy. "Hail the *Enterprise,* and make sure the transmission is scrambled. Then raise Captain Kirk and patch him into the conversation."

"Yes, sir," Sandy said.

Bogle stood and faced the screen as Mr. Spock's image appeared.

"Captain Bogle," the Vulcan said, nodding slightly.

"Kirk here."

At the sound of Kirk's voice Spock raised one eyebrow, but did not change his expression.

"Kirk," Bogle said, "your first officer has come up with an idea of using shuttlecraft to decoy away a few Narr ships long enough for us to get you out of there."

There was a pause, then Kirk said, "At this point I'll listen to anything."

Bogle laughed. In Kirk's situation he'd have said the same thing. He quickly explained to Kirk Mr. Spock's idea. "Did I get that right, Mr. Spock?" he asked after he finished.

"That is a correct outline of what I proposed," Spock said.

"Good," Bogle said, "because I like your idea, Mr. Spock. But I don't like endangering the entire crews of the *Enterprise* and *Farragut* to rescue four crew members. Do you agree, Captain?"

"I do," Kirk said. "The numbers would be even for only a short time, then would turn bad again as the other Narr ships returned. I'm not sure it would work."

Spock said nothing.

"Hold on a moment, Jim," Bogle said. "I think Mr. Spock's idea can be modified slightly to help the landing party escape on its own."

Again one of Mr. Spock's eyebrows lifted, but no other expression crossed his face. "That would be interesting," Spock said. "Please continue, Captain Bogle."

"You got my attention, Kelly," Kirk said.

"Instead of sending out two shuttles as decoys, then trying to fight our way into position to beam out the landing party, we send out four unmanned shuttles, in four different directions, all programmed to land at the edge of the colony."

"Do you think the Narr would chase four shuttles?" Kirk asked.

"I honestly don't know," Bogle said. "If they did, it would then be three of them against five of us, for at least a minute. We can do a lot in one minute with those odds."

"And if they don't," Kirk said, "you don't attack and we have at least one or more shuttles here to help us defend the colony, and maybe get off the planet."

"Exactly," Bogle said.

"Great idea, Kelly," Kirk said. "I think it just might work."

"Thanks," Bogle said, "but it was Mr. Spock's idea. I just modified it."

"To a much better plan, sir," Spock said.

Bogle nodded to Spock. "Thank you."

"I have two modifications of my own," Kirk said. "Kelly, Spock, I'm sending up the data from Mr. Sulu's tricorder, as well as my scans of the Narr armor. Let Scott and Mr. Projeff see if they can come up with a weapon that will slow that armor down. Or better yet short out its antigravity units."

"We'll come up with something," Bogle said. "And we'll put it and other weapons in every shuttle."

"Great," Kirk said.

"Captain," Spock said, "you said you had two modifications."

"Thank you, Mr. Spock. I was just getting to the other one." He almost sounded as if he were smiling.

"Second," Kirk said, "we need to get the Klingons involved in this. I know their battle cruisers carry at least one shuttle-sized craft. Have them launch at the same time, with weapons enclosed. That will pretty much guarantee that some of the shuttles make it down here. If you have trouble convincing them, have them talk to Kor."

"Good thinking on both counts," Bogle said. For the first time since this entire mission started, he was starting to feel there was a possibility of coming out alive.

"You gentlemen sure know how to make a fella feel wanted," Kirk said. "Let me know when you're ready to launch."

"My pleasure," Bogle said, laughing.

Spock remained expressionless as Bogle cut the connection.

"I can't do it," Scotty said. He was sitting at his console, talking to Spock, who was on the bridge. "You want me to modify the shuttle shields and come up with a weapon to short-circuit an antigravity unit I haven't even seen, all within the space of a few hours. You're asking the impossible, Mr. Spock."

"Mr. Scott," Spock said calmly. "I have heard you make this protestation before and still you have done what you call 'the impossible.' I believe this is merely a ruse to make it seem as if your talents are greater than they truly are."

"Do you, Mr. Spock?" Scotty felt heat rush to his cheeks. At times he did exaggerate, but usually it worked: he would get extra time from the captain. "A ruse, you say?"

"Yes, Mr. Scott, a ruse."

"You're a hard-nosed Vulcan, Mr. Spock. It's not logical to give a man an impossible order and then tell him that he lies when he protests."

"I simply mean, Mr. Scott, that to paraphrase your William Shakespeare, methinks you doth protest too much."

"Ah, you thinks, do you?" Scotty said.

"If you would like," Spock said with infinite calm, "I will see if I can assist you."

That offended Scotty even more. "You have your own job on the bridge, Mr. Spock. I don't need your assistance."

And then he signed off.

"Sir?" The young ensign he had upbraided stood beside him. "We could modify the shuttle's shields. I believe they're the same as the *Enterprise*'s. All we have to do is follow your instructions from the last time."

Scotty looked at her. "Is this your creative solution, lass?"

She swallowed. "Yes," she said. "None of us are as skilled at jury-rigging as you are, sir. That's why you're chief engineer."

He grinned at her. "You have a bit of the Celtic in you, lass."

"The Celtic?" she asked.

"The Irish call it blarney, but I'll take it," Scotty said. "But realize I'll be there to check your work shortly. Lives depend on your accuracy."

She swallowed again. "Aye, sir." And then she led a group from Engineering to the shuttle bays.

"Now, it's me and you," he whispered to the schematic of the various weapons on board the *Enterprise.*

At that moment, Uhura hailed him with a message from Projeff.

"All right," Scotty grumbled. "Nothing could be worse than the last few moments I've had."

Projeff appeared on the screen, grinning so wide that it looked as if his face had split in half. "I assume you heard about the modifications we were to make to the weapons," he said.

"Aye," Scotty said mournfully.

"Well, have I got a modification for you," Projeff said. "Courtesy of the *Farragut.*"

Scotty's eyes narrowed. How had Projeff solved this problem when Scotty hadn't even had a chance to work on it? The honor of the *Enterprise* had been at stake, and he hadn't even had a chance to try.

He swallowed his pride and asked, "What have you got?"

CHAPTER 20

KIRK SNAPPED HIS COMMUNICATOR CLOSED AND STOOD. EVEN IN THE HEAT OF the afternoon, finally having some sort of a plan gave him energy.

He paced back and forth, thinking. There was a great chance that at least two, if not three or four shuttles were going to be landing near the colony in about an hour. Having the firepower of the shuttles, as well as the shields and extra armament they would bring, would level the field a little. Not all the way, but enough to keep the battle from being a slaughter.

"Rathbone, would you have Lieutenant Sulu join us?"

She nodded, stood and quickly ducked out the door, letting in a hot, dry wind.

"McCoy," Kirk said, sitting down next to Kor, "can you wake your patient?"

"I am awake," Kor said. "I heard your communication with your ships."

"Good," Kirk said. "Do you think the plan will work?"

"It is a sound plan," Kor said. "It has only one drawback that I can see."

"And that is?" Kirk asked. Kor had always annoyed him in the past, and he was doing his best not to let the Klingon commander do so now.

"The Narr transports," he said.

Kirk sat back, thinking. Kor had a point.

"I have not seen the transports," Kor said. "But I assume they are considerably larger, and likely more powerful, than your tiny Federation shuttles?"

"They are," Kirk said. Kor was right and he knew it. The transports were undoubtedly armed and well shielded.

"And they will have time to launch and engage the shuttles above the colony. Correct?"

"You are very correct," Kirk said.

"Then we must have a plan," Kor said, sitting up slowly and facing Kirk, "to keep the Narr transports on the ground while our shuttles land."

Kirk nodded. "Good thinking, Commander." He turned to Kerdoch. "Can we get to that small ridge of mountains behind the transport landing sites without being seen?"

Kerdoch thought for a moment, then, with a glance at Kor, he answered Kirk's question. "It would be possible to go north into the foothills and circle west behind the Narr transports. It would take at least an hour."

Kirk turned back to Kor. "The Narr shuttles are wing-shaped, and landed standing upward."

Kor nodded. "I see what you are thinking," he said. "They might have some sort of support legs holding them in that position."

"Exactly," Kirk said. "And the transports wouldn't be shielded on the ground. All we have to do is knock a leg out from under them."

"It would certainly slow down their take-off," McCoy said.

"It would, Doctor," Kor said, dropping back on the cot and closing his eyes with a sigh. "It most certainly would."

Rathbone stood in the small sliver of shade offered by the edge of the shelter over the disrupter cannon. It was still five hours to sundown, and the heat seemed to smother her, baking every inch of her. She'd been sipping water almost continuously since sunrise, but she still felt constantly thirsty and dry. She didn't remember having the heat be this oppressive when she was here with the Federation colony. In fact, she remembered enjoying the heat and the cool evenings. Amazing how a little time could change a person's perspective.

She took another long drink of warm water from the bottle she carried. More than anything else she wanted a cool shower to take off the caked salt and black ash, followed by a long cool bath to soothe her burned skin. At this moment that would be heaven.

Just getting off this planet would be heaven.

At the front of the cannon platform Kor and Captain Kirk stood, staring out over the blackened fields at the distant Narr transports.

This was Kor's first time out in the sun, and Dr. McCoy had strenuously objected. But even McCoy's brash manner couldn't stop the Klingon commander. McCoy had managed, to the amusement of the captain, to get Kor to promise to return to the dome at once, and drink water every few minutes while out in the sun.

So far the Klingon commander was willingly complying with the doctor's orders. Kor had to be sicker than he was admitting.

"The plan should work, Commander," Kirk said, turning and finishing a conversation with Kor that Rathbone hadn't been able to fully hear from her position in the shade.

"Mr. Sulu," Kirk said. Lieutenant Sulu stepped up to face Kirk and Kor.

"Kahaq," Kor said. "Kerdoch, the colonist."

Kahaq and Kerdoch stepped up and stood near Sulu.

"You are to disable those transports in any fashion you see fit," Kirk said.

"Disrupter rifle shots to the supporting legs," Kor said. "Focus on only one spot."

"It shall be done," Kahaq said,

"And then we need you back here. Quickly. Before the sunset attack."

"Yes, sir," Sulu said.

Kerdoch and Kahaq glanced at Kor, seemingly uneasy taking too many orders from Kirk.

"At this time we fight beside our enemy against another enemy," Kor said. "It is the nature of war. At this time Captain Kirk's orders are mine."

Kerdoch and Kahaq said nothing, but Rathbone could tell they both understood.

"Okay," Kirk said. "Get moving. And good luck."

Suddenly it dawned on Vivian that Kirk wasn't planning to send her out with Sulu and the others. For some reason she had just expected him to do so, given her knowledge of this planet. She glanced at the young Ensign Adaro who stood off to one side, then back at the three who had been picked.

"Captain," she said, stepping out of her slice of shade and moving toward him, "I should be included in this mission."

Kirk's hard gaze behind the dirt-smeared face almost froze her in midstride, but she moved right up and faced him and the Klingon commander. "As a former colonist, I know the natural terrain of this planet. Also, there are two transports. There might be a need of four weapons."

Kirk nodded. "Good point. How good a shot are you?"

She glanced at Sulu, uncertain as to how to answer the captain's question. He had clearly not had the time to look at her service record before they left the ship, or he would have known.

"Captain," Sulu said, smiling, "Rathbone is a master-level marksman."

She smiled at Sulu. At least he had read her service record.

"A logical addition," Kor said, letting pass the fact that Kirk didn't know some details about his away team members.

Kirk laughed and patted her on the shoulder. "Make sure you have water."

McCoy handed her a canteenlike water carrier, which she slung over her shoulder, its solid weight a comfort against her hip. She emptied the bottle she'd been carrying with a long, warm drink and handed it to him, then slung the Klingon disrupter rifle over her right shoulder.

"Good luck," Kirk said.

"batlh Daqawlu'taH," Kor said, and nodded slightly to them all.

With that she fell in behind Kerdoch as he headed at a fast pace toward the northern edge and the hills beyond.

Spock figured that the odds were long that the Narr would attack during the hour after the transport attack mission left the colony.

And the project he had in mind could be a valuable asset to the coming attempt to stop the ground attack. So Spock left the bridge and moved straight to sickbay. Commander Scott was busy working with Projeff on a method of cutting off the antigravity units of the Narr soldiers. Therefore, if Spock's idea was to be pursued, he had to be the one to do it.

It took him only a few short minutes to modify a medical imaging device. He reversed its analytical functions and set it to emit a life-form signal where there wasn't one.

It then took him exactly nine minutes and eight seconds to alter the device enough to show ten life-forms from the same signal.

Three minutes and eight seconds more of fine-tuning and mounting the equipment in a small box and he was satisfied. Logically the device would work. But a test was necessary.

He punched the communication panel of sick bay. "Mr. Chekov, please scan sick bay and report how many life-forms are present."

"Yes, sir," Chekov said. After a pause of two seconds he said, "Eleven, sir. But ten are grouped tightly, and the signal is odd. I'm running a check to see why."

Mr. Spock expected as much. The Narr would be scanning through full screens. It would be enough to fool them. He flicked off the medical scanner he had altered.

"Sir," Chekov said, his voice suddenly agitated, "ten life-forms have vanished."

"That is correct, Mr. Chekov. Thank you." He cut the communication. He felt no need to explain his actions to Mr. Chekov at the moment.

He picked up the small box, tucked it under his arm, and left sick bay, headed for Engineering. His theory was that two such boxes on each shuttle should cause the Narr to be a little more cautious on their attack on the colony, thinking there were more soldiers defending the colony than actually existed.

It might also have the secondary function of causing them to break off their blockade and attack more of the shuttles in orbit, allowing the *Enterprise* to move into transporter range—if the captain agreed to the device being used. But Spock was sure he would. Last year in a fight the captain had noted that sometimes the best defense was nothing more than smoke and mirrors. Spock had not understood at the time, but now he was beginning to see the logical principle behind the metaphor.

The little box under his arm would substitute for the mirror in the metaphor.

Captain Kirk would have to provide the smoke, a skill at which he was very talented.

CHAPTER 21

Kerdoch set a fast, but steady pace as he crossed the blackened fields of his neighbors and moved into the rough ground of the small rolling hills. There was no shade, only small scrub brush, ankle-high blue weeds, and rocks. He continued on a northern track until the hills were the height of twenty warriors. Then he stopped.

The human woman had stayed close behind him, as had Sulu, but Kahaq had fallen behind at least fifty paces. He seemed out of breath and flushed when he finally did reach them.

Kerdoch knew the warrior could not make the full distance. The heat would fell him more surely than a phaser blast. But a colonist could not tell a warrior he would fail. So Kerdoch said nothing.

The woman took a quick drink, rinsed the water around in her mouth, then spit it out. She took another sip, which she swallowed.

Kerdoch was impressed at her actions. They showed clear thinking and practice in this climate. She would have little trouble staying with his pace.

Sulu took a quick sip of water at the same time, recapped his bottle, and seemed ready to move onward. The thin human would also be able to make the journey. That pleased him. Over the last day he had come to respect Sulu. He was a human with strength and honor, much like his captain.

"We follow this valley," Kerdoch said.

He knew the shallow valley wound its way to the east into the slightly higher hills near the Narr transports. They would have to cross over two ridges to get to the transports. But until that point the valley would give them shelter from Narr eyes on the ground. His hope was that the Narr ships in orbit were not scanning the surrounding area in close enough detail to locate them. That was a chance that both Kirk and Kor had thought worth taking.

Kerdoch turned and set his pace, moving with practiced ease through and around the natural brush.

He did not look back.

And he did not stop until he reached a point in the valley beyond the Narr transports. Above, the two suns seemed to have grown in size and energy. He was used to working the day in the sun, but after the last two days of no sleep and little water, he could feel the extreme heat.

He pulled his water bottle and let the warm water fill his mouth and throat. Then he turned around.

He was again surprised to find both the woman and Sulu stopping with him. There was no sign of Kahaq.

"Where is Kahaq?" he asked.

Sulu finished a sip of water, his face bright red and sweating. "He stopped to take a drink quite a long way back. He told me to go on."

"This heat can fell the strongest tree," Kerdoch said.

"How far to the transports?" the human woman asked. She also looked very tired and hot, but she seemed willing to continue without complaint.

Kerdoch pointed over the high ridge to his right. "We should be able to target the transports from the second ridge."

Kerdoch glanced back down the gully in the direction they had come. "We will find Kahaq on our return."

"Lead on," Sulu said.

Kerdoch took another drink, unshouldered his rifle, and began to climb toward the top of the ridge.

To his left Sulu did the same.

To his right the human woman followed.

Kirk stood alone in the slim shade offered by the shelter over the disrupter cannon. Kor, Ensign Adaro, and McCoy had returned to the protection of the dome to rest until the shuttles launched. Rathbone and Sulu were somewhere in the foothills, and the colonists were scattered along the edge of the colony facing the Narr camp. Some were digging trenches; others rested in the shade; many had gone back to their homes to check on their children.

A waiting time. Kirk hated waiting.

Beyond the blackened fields the Narr transports stood, winglike shapes pointing upward as if ready to jump back into the air. And they most likely would do just that when the shuttles were launched, unless Sulu and the others could get them grounded. Otherwise the shuttles would be sitting ducks coming in. They could be programmed to land and do basic maneuvers, but not evade or return enemy fire.

He stared out over the field where the Narr casualties had been. The Narr had used teams of four to retrieve their wounded and dead, floating them between the team members like heavy caskets in a funeral march, as they moved back to their camp. There had been over eighty Narr soldiers in the field at once, and there was no doubt that was only a small part of the force that would be coming against the colony at sunset.

There had to be a way to stop them, to end this fight. Throughout the history of Earth, wars had been fought over disputed ownership of land. Now they were fought over ownership of entire planets. He and the Federation had no real stake in the outcome of this battle, except for the fact that he and his crew were trapped in the middle of it. Somehow there had to be a way to get the two parties who had something to win or lose to talk to each other.

His communicator beeped, and he snapped it open.

"Captain," Sulu said, his voice low, almost whispered. "Kerdoch, Rathbone, and I are in position above and behind the Narr camp. The heat stopped Kahaq along the way."

"How is the camp laid out, Mr. Sulu?" Kirk asked.

"The Narr have four large tentlike structures," Sulu whispered. "Ten guards in armor are outside, posted at the doors. The others must be inside the tents and the transports."

"Can you knock down the transports?" Kirk asked.

"I don't know, Captain," Sulu said. "Like the larger Narr craft, they are wing-shaped, and have landed pointed upward, wing tips on the ground. But there are no support legs of any sort to target."

"None?" Kirk asked.

"None, sir," Sulu said.

He had been afraid that might be the case. The Narr were clearly very good with artificial gravity, and were using it to hold their ships upright.

"Stand by, Mr. Sulu. And keep your head down."

He flicked his communicator closed and at a fast walk covered the fifty paces of hot ground to the dome. Inside, Ensign Adaro sat on the cot, Kor sat at the table, a glass of water in his hand, and McCoy sat across from him. It was clear to Kirk that neither had been talking to the other.

"The team is in place above the Narr camp," Kirk said. "Kahaq is not with them. He had a problem with the heat."

Kor frowned, but said nothing.

Kirk sat down at the table next to McCoy. McCoy slid him a bottle and Kirk drank the lukewarm water gladly, filling his mouth twice. Then he gave Kor the bad news: "There are no support legs holding up the transports."

This time Kor shook his head in disgust. "Antigravity support fields."

"Most likely," Kirk said.

"So this changes the plan," Kor said.

"I know," Kirk said. "What's your idea?"

Kirk asked that way because the ideas he had come up with—finding a way to shut down the anti-gravity devices, for example—weren't possible with the small force he had.

"The shuttles must launch manned, so they can defend themselves. They must have one pilot each."

Kirk had already thought of that option as well. He didn't like it. But endangering one or two crew members to rescue four was far more acceptable than risking the entire *Enterprise*. And with the modified shields and a pilot, the shuttles would have a fighting chance against the Narr transports.

Also with the *Enterprise* and *Farragut* shuttles on the ground, the colony would have a fighting chance against the Narr troops. Kor's plan undoubtedly had a number of other advantages, but there was no way Kirk would sacrifice a pilot in a shuttle to those Narr ships in orbit. The shuttles were to be used as decoys. Nothing more.

He looked Kor directly in the eye. "I will sacrifice four unmanned Federation shuttles to this fight, but no more lives."

Kor laughed and smacked his hand down flat on the table. "Kirk, in your position, I would do the same thing. You are smarter than I gave you credit for."

Kirk sat back, staring at the Klingon commander. He had expected Kor to call him a coward. But instead he had agreed. "You surprise me, Kor."

" 'Surprise' puts it mildly," McCoy said. "The sound of my jaw hitting the table could have been heard outside, I'm sure."

Again Kor laughed. Clearly his strength was returning as his voice and laugh were increasing in volume. "Kirk, this is a Klingon planet. Our duty is to defend it. Our shuttles will be manned to engage the Narr transports. Your unmanned shuttles can be used to confuse them and draw their fire. It is a sound plan."

Kirk smiled at Kor. "The team behind the Narr camp will confuse things even more by firing on the transports."

Kor slapped the table again and stood. "Kirk, someday it will be glorious to fight you. But at the moment working together is also glorious."

Kirk stood also, facing Kor. He flipped open his communicator. "Mr. Spock, are the shuttles loaded and ready to launch?"

"Yes, Captain," Spock said.

"Stand by for my order," Kirk said. He faced Kor. "Commander, we will launch when you give the word."

Kor bowed slightly to Kirk. "It will take five minutes for my pilots to prepare," he said. "Then we shall surprise the Narr."

"That we shall," Kirk said. He sat down beside McCoy as Kor turned away to call his ship.

"Sometimes you really amaze me, Jim," McCoy said as Kirk took another long drink of water.

"How's that?"

"You're more like the Klingons than you think."

Kirk stared at his friend for a moment, then smiled. "I hope that was a compliment, Bones."

McCoy snorted, then said, "I'm afraid, in this instance, it just might have been."

Captain Bogle stood facing the main screen. For the past few hours nothing had changed. The Narr ships had remained in their blockade over the planet, facing the two Federation starships and the three Klingon battle cruisers. But Bogle knew that was about to change. He wasn't sure how, but it would change. Of that he had no doubt.

"Captain," Lieutenant Sandy said, "the *Enterprise* has signaled we should stand by."

"On their signal," Bogle said. He punched his communications button. "Projeff, status of shuttles?"

"Loaded, armed, and ready when you are, Captain," the chief engineer said. "I've patched the automatic launch controls into the bridge."

"Good work, Pro," Bogle said.

"And sir," Projeff said, "we've modified the shields even more. They should hold solidly now."

"Excellent," Bogle said and punched off the comm button.

He sat down in his chair. "Get ready, people. I suspect this is going to get somewhat wild."

Around him the bridge seemed to hum.

No one said a word, but the tension was so thick he could sense it. Licutenant Michael Book sat on the edge of his chair, his fingers tapping beside his control panel. Science Officer Lee stared into his scope, gripping it firmly with both hands.

"We are receiving a scrambled message from the *Enterprise,*" Lieutenant Sandy said, his voice slightly higher than normal.

"Put it on-screen," Bogle said. He took a deep breath and exhaled as Spock's image appeared.

"Captain," Spock said, "the Klingons will launch their manned shuttles in exactly twenty-six seconds. The *Enterprise* will launch two unmanned shuttles with them."

"Understood, Mr. Spock. We will do so also. Good luck."

Spock nodded, and his image was replaced with the familiar scene of the Narr ships and the blue-green planet beyond.

Nothing more needed to be said. All the details of the directions that the seven different shuttles would take had been worked out almost an hour before between Spock and the Klingons.

Now it was almost time to launch.

"Got the count, Lieutenant Book?" Bogle asked.

"Yes, sir," he said. "Fifteen seconds."

Bogle glanced around the bridge. Everyone was ready. "At two seconds go to red alert," he said.

"Ten seconds."

Bogle took a deep breath. "Stay put," he whispered to the Narr ships facing him. "Just stay put." He desperately hoped they would catch the Narr ships unprepared. At least enough that before they could react the shuttles would be in the atmosphere. He knew he was dreaming, but he could hope.

"Five seconds," Book said. "Four . . . three."

"Red alert!" Bogle said. Around him the lights went to a red hue and the siren blared.

"Two . . . one."

"Launch."

Lieutenant Book's fingers flew over the panel.

On the main screen Bogle could see the two *Enterprise* shuttles emerging from the shuttle bays. One turned and went along the equator of the planet to his right. The other went left.

Bogle knew the two shuttles from the *Farragut* were programmed to head for the planet's poles and drop into the atmosphere there. The three Klingon shuttles were to take courses between the Federation shuttles and, with luck, be near the colony when the Narr transports lifted to meet them.

"We have launch," Book said, his voice clearly excited.

"Captain," Lee said, "the Narr ships. Look!"

Bogle could feel his jaw drop in surprise. Of all the reactions by the Narr that he had expected, this was not it.

None of the big Narr ships moved. Not a one.

However, two of them were opening docking bays. The same two who had launched the small attack ships.

He couldn't believe it. They were going to send their attack ships after the shuttles, right on down into the atmosphere. How could they have been ready?

"Target those opening bays!" Bogle shouted. "Fire phasers!"

Bright phaser beams struck out of the *Farragut,* right on target, lighting up the insides of the Narr docking bays with intense white light.

At the same instant the *Enterprise* and Kor's ship fired, also targeting the docking bays.

A moment later the remaining two battle cruisers joined in.

Then it seemed to Bogle as if space had gone crazy.

Seven shuttles streaking away from the bigger ships, in seven different directions.

Full fire power aimed at two Narr ships from five other war ships.

Then dozens of smaller Narr attack ships suddenly filled the area from the Narr docking bays. They were like bats coming from the mouth of a cave that was on fire, pouring into space.

"How many of those things can they hold?" Book asked.

Bogle had been wondering the same thing.

"Target the Narr attack ships and take them out," Bogle shouted. "Fire at will."

"Captain," Lee said. "To the right."

Bogle had already seen what his first officer was pointing out. One of the larger Narr craft had turned, broken ranks, and was making an attack pass at the *Farragut.* Another was doing the same thing at the *Enterprise.* The other five remained in blockade position.

"Keep after any of the smaller ships," Bogle ordered. "Don't stop firing until I tell you to stop."

Around the larger Narr ships the small craft seemed to swarm. There were far more of them than during the first attacks. How in the world had the Narr had them prepared?

Unless they had planned to run attack missions at the colony before the ground troops attacked at sunset. It would be a logical tactical move. And launching the shuttles had just forced them to launch a little early.

The *Farragut* rocked as the larger Narr ship blasted it with full power.

Bogle hung on to the arms of his chair, studying the screen as the combined focus of the Federation ships blew up one small Narr attack craft after another, like small, silent firecrackers exploding in the night sky."Shields holding," Lee said.

"Ignore the big ship," Bogle ordered. "Stay on the attack craft. Knock the stupid little things out of the sky."

"Sir," Book said, "most of the smaller craft are behind the larger Narr ships, dropping toward the atmosphere."

"Take us right at them, Lieutenant," Bogle said. "Follow them to the edge of the atmosphere if you have to."

"But, sir—"

"Do it, Lieutenant!" he ordered, his voice loud and firm. He was more than aware that to follow the small attack craft they must go right through the larger Narr ships' blockade. But the Narr had been holding that blockade long enough. It was time for someone to challenge it.

The *Farragut* turned slightly and accelerated right at an opening between two of the larger Narr ships, firing constantly at the small attack ships as it went.

Then two of the larger Narr ships opened up on the *Farragut,* and the bridge seemed to explode. Sparks flew everywhere. Smoke filled the air around Bogle as something behind him caught fire. The ship rocked as the stabilizers faught to keep the ship level under the pounding it was taking. He held on to both arms of his chair, focusing on the smaller ships.

"Shields at eighty-six percent," Lee shouted.

"Keep firing at those fighters," Bogle ordered.

Another direct hit on the shields again rocked the Farragut.

Then they were past the larger Narr craft and picking off the smaller fighters like darts popping balloons.

"The *Enterprise* is following us in," Lee shouted. "Klingons are also attacking. The Narr blockade has split."

"The shuttles?" Bogle asked.

"Are all still descending through the atmosphere," Lee said. "None of them was even fired on."

"Keep firing on those fighters," Bogle ordered.

Another blast rocked the ship, sending him almost out of his chair.

Then another and another.

"Shields at sixty-five percent," Lee said. "I think we made the Narr mad."

"Good," Bogle said.

"All fighters now too far into the atmosphere to fire upon," Lieutenant Book said.

"How many got through?"

"Twenty, sir," Book said.

"Let's hope the shuttles beat them to the ground," Bogle said.

The ship rocked with another hit.

"Mr. Book," Bogle said. "Target the ship that just fired on us and return fire."

"Yes, sir," Book said.

"And hold this position. If they want to re-form the blockade, they can do so right over the top of us."

Bogle gripped the arms of his chair tightly. He wasn't about to lose this battle.

He'd had enough of the Narr.

CHAPTER 22

VIVIAN RATHBONE COULDN'T BELIEVE SHE HAD MANAGED TO KEEP UP WITH the Klingon colonist. He had walked with huge strides, seemingly never tiring. At times she had found herself almost running to stay with him through the brush and rocks. And the two short rests hadn't been near enough considering the heat. It had been everything she could do to catch her breath and drink enough water while they walked.

After the second stop, they had crawled over one ridge, hiked down through a shallow valley, and then crawled on their stomachs to the top of the second ridge. In the years of studying the natural plant life of this planet, she had never thought she would end up crawling on her stomach through it, Klingon phaser rifle in hand, desperately trying to keep her head down so she wouldn't be seen.

Sulu was to her right, Kerdoch to her left, when they stopped on the ridge.

She had found a small rock outcropping to hide behind and rest her gun on. Below her, not more than two hundred paces away, was the Narr camp. Large tentlike structures filled the flat area behind the shuttles. She wagered those "tents" were a lot harder than they looked.

The two Narr transports stood in what looked to her to be awkward positions, noses upward. They formed a perfect blockade line between the tents and the colony beyond. The nose of the closest transport was no more than fifty feet below her level. Those craft were huge and very strange looking, as if someone had buried both ends of an old boomerang in the ground.

Beside her, Sulu's communicator beeped. He had it in front of him on the ground. He flipped it open almost without moving or taking his eyes off the camp below.

"Problems," Kirk said. "The shuttles have launched, but the Narr launched their attack ships right after them."

"How many?" Sulu asked. It was the exact same question she wanted to ask.

"At least twenty made it into the atmosphere," Kirk said.

Twenty attack ships with those wide-angle plasma beams. And the three of them were out in the open with no protection. They didn't stand a chance. They'd be cooked alive in one pass.

"What are your orders, Captain?" Sulu asked.

"Is there shelter close by?"

Sulu turned to Kerdoch. "Shelter against plasma beams?"

Kerdoch seemed to think for just a moment, then nodded. "A small rock hollow down the valley behind us. It should be sufficient."

Sulu spoke into the communicator. "Captain, there is a small rock area near."

"Good," Kirk said. "Here's what I want you to do. In exactly eighty seconds, open fire on those transports."

Sulu nodded, and so did Vivian. Eighty short seconds. Her heart pounded so hard it was amazing the Narr couldn't hear it down in the camp.

"See if you can keep at least one transport on the ground. Make a thirty second attack, then run for the shelter. Don't give those transports time to fire back at you."

"Understood, Captain," Sulu said.

"Good luck. Kirk out."

Sulu snapped the communicator closed and reattached it to his belt.

She did a quick check of the Klingon phaser rifle, then made sure her Federation phaser was still on her belt. She tried to dry her sweating hands on her shirt, but only came away with dirt. If she ever got out of this heat she would never complain about cold again. Ever.

"Target the right wing of the closest craft," Sulu said. "See the vent there near the ground? Let's hope it's a thruster vent."

"A good choice," Kerdoch said.

Rathbone nodded to Sulu, then took aim over the rock at the target. It did look oddly like a closed thruster vent. If they were lucky they could blow that thruster and make it too dangerous for the transport to risk a takeoff. But they were going to have to be damn lucky.

"Ten seconds," Sulu said.

Below, a number of armored Narr were moving now, coming out of the tents like slow, lumbering ants. Picking them off would be like shooting slow targets on a training range. But she doubted that the Klingon rifle would do much damage to that heavy armor.

"Five seconds," Sulu said softly.

She took a deep breath of hot, dusty air and let it out slowly. Calm. Focus on the target. Calm.

The years of training came back to her, and her hands calmed on the stock of the rifle.

"Two," Sulu said.

She waited.

"One."

The time between seconds seemed to take forever.

"Fire!"

She pulled the trigger, and the phaser surged in her hands.

The vent area on the side of the Narr transport instantly lit up as the three beams hit it.

Quickly it turned bright red, went to white, then exploded, sending sparks and burning material out over the tents and the armored Narr.

Amazing. She wanted to stand up and cheer.

But she kept firing.

The side of the Narr hull seemed to melt away, and then, just as suddenly as it had exploded, their beams were through the outer shell and cutting into the insides the ship. She couldn't believe it.

She held the trigger down, letting the rifle beam cut into the ship like a scalding hot knife into cold butter.

Kerdoch and Kor did the same thing beside her.

Then she could hear the rumble as something inside the transport started to ignite.

"Target the same area of the other transport!" Sulu yelled over the rumbling.

She swung the rifle into position and fired. Sulu and Kerdoch were only a fraction of a second behind her.

Again the target went red, then white, then another explosion. There must have been small liquid fuel tanks of some sort right behind those vents. The heat from their fire on the surface ignited and blew away the protective outer shell, letting their phasers cut clear inside. They had gotten lucky.

Very, very lucky.

The first transport seemed to be shaking. High-pressure steam was shooting out of the hole they'd made in its side.

For what seemed like forever, they continued firing on the second shuttle until finally they were inside, cutting through the interior metal as if it didn't exist.

Suddenly the ground in front of them erupted, spraying rocks and dirt into a cloud, blocking her vision. One of the Narr soldiers must have started firing at them.

"Let's get out of here," Sulu shouted.

Instantly she had the rifle down and began scrambling on hands and knees away from the top of the ridge. Rocks and brush cut at her hands and knees, but she ignored the pain.

The rock she'd been hiding behind exploded as a shot from the camp below cut it apart.

Sulu and Kerdoch were right beside her as she gained her feet and ran. Like wild animals stampeding down the hill, they scrambled over, through, and around brush, rocks, and small shrubs.

Twice she lost her balance in loose dirt, but managed to keep her feet under her and the Klingon rifle in her hand.

At the bottom of the gully the world seemed to shake, dirt clouds lifting from the ground as on the other side of the ridge a huge explosion filled the sky with black smoke and debris.

One of the Narr transports must have exploded.

"This way," Kerdoch shouted over the rumbling. He turned toward the colony and started down the gully at a full run.

She managed to stay within ten steps of the big Klingon and keep her feet—until a second explosion shook the ground and sent her sprawling face first into a pile of sand and dirt.

Sulu tumbled beside her, rolled, and regained his feet. He grabbed her arm and yanked her up without a word.

In front of them the Klingon was scrambling up into a pile of large sun-baked boulders.

She followed, breathing hard, spitting sand out of her dry mouth.

The shelter was nothing more than a rock ledge with some loose boulders near the bottom. Large cracks ran up the side of the rock face.

She was about to say there wasn't enough shelter here against the plasma beams when Kerdoch turned sideways, stooped slightly, and slid into a dark opening at the bottom of one of the cracks.

She stopped, leaning against a rock, panting.

Huge clouds of dark smoke billowed up from just over the ridge, filling the sky with black clouds that cast huge shadows over the nearby hillside.

"Is there room?" Sulu asked.

Kerdoch's faint voice echoed out of the crack. "Yes."

Sulu glanced around, rifle at ready, then indicated she should go first.

Vivian bent down and slid inside. The crack was so narrow the stone rubbed against her chest and back. How had the larger, bulkier Kerdoch made it through?

Then after just two shuffling sideways steps, she was inside a larger area, about the size of a small cabin on the *Enterprise.*

"The children found this," Kerdoch said.

"Lucky for us," Sulu said as he came inside and stepped away from the entrance, letting the light fill the small area.

Vivian took a deep shuddering breath and tried to force her eyes to adjust to the faint natural cavelight.

The floor of the cave was the surface of a fairly flat rock. Above her was another streak of light where the cave opened up to the air. Otherwise, the narrow crack they had come through was the only opening, and the cave's only feature.

Sulu flipped open his communicator. "Captain."

"Great work, Sulu," the captain said. "You managed to blow up both transports. Are you in a safe location?"

"I'm not sure about that," Sulu said.

"Where are you? Your transmission's broken up."

"We're in a small cave just down the ravine from the Narr camp. But one direct hit on the outside of this rock pile will turn this place into an oven."

It took a moment for Kirk to respond, as if he had to decipher Sulu's words. "That's better than being in the open," Kirk said. "Stay put until I give the all clear."

"Aye, sir," Sulu said and snapped his communicator closed.

He glanced at Rathbone and shook his head while leaning his rifle up against the side of the cave.

"Looks like we're on the sidelines for the next part of this battle," she said with more relief than she cared to contemplate.

"Appearances can be wrong." Sulu said. "Stay prepared."

"I will take the watch," Kerdoch said, moving past her to the entrance and squeezing through.

She allowed herself to drop to the floor and pull out her bottle of water. Her hands were starting to shake, but she managed to get one large gulp of water into her mouth before the shaking got so bad she couldn't hold the bottle.

Spock noted what the *Farragut* was doing, jamming right through the Narr to get to the smaller attack ships trying to reach the atmosphere.

"Follow the *Farragut,"* Spock ordered. "Target any ship firing at them."

The *Enterprise* rocked as one of the Narr ships opened up at close range.

"I'm not reading any damage," Chekov reported. "The shields are holding, Mr. Spock."

Spock did not reply, but kept his attention on the *Farragut* as it fired on and destroyed fighter after fighter. Spock had never realized that Captain Bogle could be so aggressive.

Phaser fire streaked from the *Enterprise,* pounding first into the ship to the right of the *Farragut,* then next to the left.

"Continue firing," Spock ordered. He wanted to cover the *Farragut* as much as possible.

"All Narr fighters, they are out of range," Ensign Chekov said.

The *Farragut* turned and began firing on the larger Narr ships around it.

"The *Farragut* is holding her ground between the Narr ships and the atmosphere," Chekov said.

Spock said nothing. He didn't dare. It was a useless gesture by Bogle. His position was not defensible.

Suddenly it felt as if something large had rammed the *Enterprise.* The entire bridge seemed to tip up on end, then immediately right itself.

Two Narr ships had targeted the *Enterprise* at the same moment, attempting the same attack that the Federation ships had used against them.

"Shields are at eighty-five percent," Chekov said.

"Move in beside the *Farragut,*" Spock said. "Continue firing."

The ship rocked again hard left as the *Enterprise* took a position beside its sister ship. Spock managed to hold on to the captain's chair.

The three Klingon battle cruisers continued to run attack passes at the Narr craft, hitting them as they flashed past, then turning and making another run.

No ship, including the Narr, seemed to have suffered any serious damage.

"Continue targeting and firing, Mr. Chekov," Spock said.

"It looks like a standoff, Mr. Spock," Uhura said.

Spock was quite aware of the situation. Three Narr ships had the two Federation ships cornered against the atmosphere. The other four Narr ships had formed a shield against the marauding Klingon battle cruisers.

For the moment Lieutenant Uhura was correct. It was a standoff. But the Narr attacks would wear down the *Farragut* and the *Enterprise* by sheer numbers. Their position at the moment was not defensible.

The ship rocked again slightly.

"The *Farragut* is hailing us, sir," Lieutenant Uhura said.

"Audio only," Spock said.

"Spock," Captain Bogle said, "I think it's time for us to withdraw to our previous positions."

"I concur, Captain," Spock said.

"Right through the center of them again?"

"Agreed," Spock said.

"Ten seconds, on my mark. . . . Now."

"Navigator, lay in a course to our previous position, one half impulse. Mr. Chekov, continue firing at any target." Exactly ten seconds later, Spock said, "Now."

At the same moment both the *Farragut* and the *Enterprise* jumped forward, directly at the Narr ships.

Chekov continued firing beam after beam as the *Enterprise* slipped between two of the enemy ships and beyond.

Suddenly the Narr strikes against the shields stopped.

"Cease fire," Spock said.

The three Klingon battle cruisers pulled away and also took up their previous positions.

"Shields at eighty percent," Chekov said.

Spock hit the comm button. "How soon till we have full shields, Mr. Scott?"

"Ten minutes, Mr. Spock," Scotty said, sounding a bit harried.

"Thank you, Mr. Scott," Spock said, staring out at the seven Narr craft.

"It's as if nothing has changed," Chekov said.

"It only appears that way," Spock said. "The situation is very different than twelve minutes ago."

"Hold your position, Mr. Spock," Kirk said, and snapped his communicator closed. He and his team were still trapped, waiting for the coming attack. But things were changing quickly.

He and Kor stood on the edge of the disrupter cannon platform, gazing at the smoke billowing from the Narr camp. He had no idea that Sulu's mission would be so successful. From what he could tell both transports had blown up. There was no doubt that would slow the enemy down, but by how much was anyone's guess. Maybe long enough for the *Enterprise* to figure out a way to break through and get them off this planet.

If they survived the coming attack.

"Kirk," Kor said.

Kirk glanced his way, then followed his gaze up into the sky.

Four Federation shuttles were turning on final approach, all coming in for a landing, one right after the other. Kor had rounded up eight of the colonists and they were all standing by to unload the weapons from the shuttles and distribute them among the other colonists.

Since the destruction of the transports, Kirk had decided that the shuttles most likely would be an even match for the small Narr fighters headed their way, not in weapons, perhaps, but in shields. So Ensign Adaro stood in the shade to one side ready to board one.

Kirk would take a second shuttle. The other two would have to stay unmanned until Sulu and Rathbone returned.

The three manned Klingon shuttles swooped in and took up positions on three sides of the colony, hovering silently.

"It sure feels better having them there," Kirk said.

"A slight comfort," Kor said. "I agree."

As the *Galileo* touched down, Kirk stepped off the platform and headed for it. Kor turned and moved inside the disrupter cannon shelter. With the help of a colonist, he would man the weapon. Kirk just hoped he was half the shot Sulu was against the fast Narr fighters.

The other three shuttles touched down within twenty paces of the edge of the colony, one right after the other, kicking up small puffs of dust and black soot.

Behind the *Galileo* was the *Columbus,* followed by the two *Farragut* shuttles. Ensign Adaro had already reached the *Columbus* and was scrambling to open the outer lock. Two of the Klingon colonists already had the *Galileo* door open and were climbing inside.

Kirk reached the *Galileo* a second later.

He quickly helped the colonists unload the weapons, then climbed in and shut the door, slipping into the pilot's seat as if he'd been sitting in one for years.

He quickly powered up all sensors, brought up the shields, and powered up the phasers. The phasers on the shuttles were nowhere near as powerful as the *Enterprise* weapons, but they just might serve the purpose.

The Narr fighters were hovering just beyond the Narr camp, as if waiting for orders.

Kirk took the shuttle up to the same height as the hovering Klingon shuttles and held position, waiting.

Ensign Adaro did the same with the *Columbus.*

Then they waited.

Twenty minutes later they were still waiting.

CHAPTER 23

KERDOCH LEANED AGAINST ONE OF THE LARGE BOULDERS OUTSIDE THE SMALL cave. Smoke billowed from the Narr camp, filling the clear sky with a huge black cloud. Beyond the cloud he could see shiny wings hovering in formation. The Narr fighters had arrived, but were holding position.

The blood coursing through his veins during the attack had calmed, but he still breathed hard from the excitement of it all. Never had he felt so alive. The very truth of being Klingon had faced him, and he had met the challenge. He had avenged the burning of his fields, the killing of his neighbors.

If the Narr attacked again, he would avenge again.

The humans who had fought beside him had also showed great courage and honor.

Today he had learned a great lesson. Enemies have honor, also. It was a fact he had never considered before.

Sulu squeezed out of the cave mouth, followed by the human woman. He took up a position near Kerdoch while she moved to the right to find shelter behind another large boulder.

"They will wait until sunset to attack," Kerdoch said.

"I think you're right," Sulu said. He flipped open his communicator. "Captain?"

"Go ahead, Mr. Sulu," the human captain said.

"The Narr attack ships are hovering beyond the colony. Kerdoch and I believe the attack against the colony will be coming at sunset, just as the Narr told you."

"I'm starting to think you're right, Mr. Sulu. Can you make it back to camp? I don't want to risk taking a shuttle that close to their camp."

Sulu turned to the woman, who nodded. Then he looked at Kerdoch.

Kerdoch laughed softly.

"How long?" Sulu asked.

Kerdoch glanced at the woman, then at Sulu. He knew they were both tired. Two rest stops would be needed, but this valley was easier than the one they had come down one ridgeline over. However, the warrior Kahaq was in that other valley.

"We should locate Kahaq," Kerdoch said. "One hour to do so and return."

Sulu nodded, then spoke into the instrument in his hand. "Captain, we'll move over one valley to the north to search for Kahaq. We should be back in the colony in one hour."

"The first sun sets in two hours," Kirk said. "If we see any of the fighters moving, we will notify you. Then take cover. We'll be there to help. Kirk out."

Sulu snapped his communicator back on his belt.

"Your captain is a man of great common sense," Kerdoch said. "Now drink."

He lifted his own canteen and took two large swallows, letting the water fill his stomach and calm him even more.

Both Sulu and the woman opened their bottles and drank deeply with him.

When they had recapped their bottles, Kerdoch swept his rifle up over his shoulder, turned his back on the humans, and climbed up on the nearest rock, looking for a path to the top of the ridge.

Kirk set the *Galileo* down gently inside the colony, twenty paces from the disrupter cannon, and climbed out into the hot, dry air. The heat hit him like a blanket covering his body, making him stop, forcing him to take a deep breath. He'd been enjoying the controlled comfort of the shuttle cabin, but for the moment he had to talk to Kor.

Ensign Adaro remained aloft in the *Columbus,* standing guard along with the three Klingon shuttles.

Sulu, Rathbone, and Kerdoch had discovered Kahaq's body thirty minutes after they started back. Kahaq had died while lying out in the open in the heat, without water, in full Klingon warrior dress. They had left the body there and returned ten minutes before. There was now less than one hour until sunset.

Kor stepped out of the shadow of the disrupter cannon and motioned that Kirk join him in the dome.

Inside the slightly cooler interior McCoy sat at the table, his uniform drenched in sweat, a large bottle of water in front of him. Kerdoch stood near the door, his rifle still slung over his shoulder. Rathbone and Sulu were sprawled on the cot, leaning back against the dome walls. They both looked exhausted.

"Great work," Kirk said to them, then turned and indicated Kerdoch.

"I agree," Kor said to the colonist. "Your deeds this day will be remembered."

Kerdoch only nodded, but even Kirk could tell the colonist was pleased at Kor's words.

McCoy scooted a large bottle of water toward Kor. "Drink. It's actually cold. I just made three trips to the well to refill our supplies in here."

"Good thinking, Bones," Kirk said. He'd been concentrating so much on the coming fight, he'd forgotten about important basics like water and food.

"No thinking involved," McCoy said. "If we don't drink enough in this god-forsaken heat and we die. Why anyone is fighting over this planet is beyond me. If you Klingons were smart, you'd let the Narr have the place."

"Doctor," Kor said, "after one more day of this heat, I might agree with you."

"Imagine what it's doing to the Narr in those armored suits," Kirk said. He took a long, cold drink from the bottle after Kor, then passed it back to McCoy.

"We must talk," Kirk said to the Klingon commander. While sitting in the *Galileo,* he'd had time to study the situation. They had managed to level the coming fight to some degree. With Sulu and Dr. Rathbone back in camp, all four Federation shuttles could be in the fight, along with the three Klingon shuttles. They were still outnumbered, twenty fighters to seven shuttles, but with the disrupter cannon the fight might be almost even.

Mr. Scott had also sent along two specially modified sonic disrupters he thought might have a chance of canceling out the antigravity controls in the Narr suits. That, along with the new weapons brought down in the shuttle and it seemed, at least for the moment, that the ground fight might be level.

But that still meant a fight. And Kirk didn't much like that idea.

"Talk," Kor said to Kirk, sitting down in a chair at the table and placing his hands flat on the surface in front of him.

Kirk pulled out another chair and sat facing the Klingon commander.

"Kor, we must trust the Narr. We must talk with them. Now. Before the fight."

Kor slapped the tabletop with the palm of his hand, making a sharp gunshotlike noise that echoed in the small dome. "Kirk, you have gone soft. Has the heat turned you into a coward, afraid of the coming fight?"

"I'll fight," Kirk said, his voice as cold and as hard as he could make it. He stared intently into the deep blackness of Kor's eyes. "If I must."

"So why talk?" Kor asked, never letting his gaze waver from Kirk's. "Humans always want to talk before fighting. It is your worst trait."

"Because, Kor," Kirk said, "the Narr have a valid claim to this planet and you know it."

"Possession is the only right Klingons recognize."

Kirk pointed in the direction of the Narr camp. "They now have possession of one area of this planet, and they control the space above it."

"And we will take it back," Kor said.

"As they are trying to do from you," Kirk said.

"Klingons do not surrender," Kor said. "We fight."

"I am not saying you should surrender. Just give me a chance to talk to them again."

"For what reason?" Kor said.

"To stop the coming fight," Kirk said. "The Federation agreed this was to be a Klingon planet, and we left. Kerdoch and his neighbors won this planet in a fair and honorable fight, which they fought without weapons. They fought using advanced agricultural methods."

"Klingons are superior in many ways, Kirk," Kor said. "We have won this planet. And we now defend it."

"As does the Federation beside you," Kirk said.

"True," Kor said.

"We honor our agreement," Kirk said. "And the Narr may honor an agreement, given the chance to make one. If we can't make one with them, then we will fight. I will stand beside you in defending this planet. I will die beside you honoring our agreement."

"The Narr have no honor," Kor said. "They destroyed a colony of farmers."

"A colony they thought was destroying *their* planet," Kirk said. "You would have done the same thing."

Kor waved his hand at Kirk, then stood and moved toward Kerdoch, the expression on his face noncommittal. Kirk had no idea if he had gotten through to the Klingon. Arguing with Klingons had always been an annoying experience at best.

After a moment Kor turned back to Kirk. "Talk if you want," he said.

"You must come with me," Kirk said. "Kerdoch must also, to represent the colonists. The others can remain and prepare for the coming fight."

"This is stupidity," Kor said, half spitting the word onto the floor. Then he turned and headed for the door. At the entrance he stopped and turned to where Kirk still sat at the table. "Come. We will talk to the Narr. Then we will fight."

"Coming?" Kirk said to Kerdoch, who nodded.

Kirk smiled and shrugged at McCoy as he stood.

"Just make it back to shelter in enough time, Jim," McCoy said.

"Let's hope we don't need to," he said as he followed the Klingon commander out into the dry heat.

Kerdoch stood on the edge of a blackened field next to the human captain and Commander Kor, one of the most honored of all Klingon warriors. They faced the Narr camp, without weapons. Two days ago Kerdoch had stood in his own fields, working to help them grow, fighting back the weeds and the forces of nature. It had been a long two days. Much had happened.

Before him the Narr camp still poured black smoke into the air. The smoke pleased him. The Narr had burned his fields, attacked his home. He had burned their camp, destroyed their ships. It gave him a feeling of closure. For the moment the circle of revenge was complete for him.

They had stood facing the Narr camp, unarmed, for twenty minutes, letting the hot sun pound on them. Now the smallest of the two suns neared the horizon. The promised Narr attack would begin soon.

"They will kill us where we stand," Kerdoch said.

"Would you kill unarmed soldiers facing you?" the human captain said.

"No," Kor said. "It would be dishonorable."

"The Narr will act the same," the human captain said.

"You trust Narr honor?" Kerdoch asked. He did not believe the Narr were honorable. He stood in this field because he was willing to die beside Commander Kor and because he had come to trust the honor of the human captain. But he did not believe the Narr had honor.

Then he realized he had thought the same of humans just two days before. If the human enemies had honor, then the Narr might also. Enemies having honor was a difficult concept to understand.

"There," the human captain said, pointing.

Kerdoch could see five Narr in armor moving toward them through the scrub brush and rock. The human captain had been correct. The Narr did have honor.

"Keep your hands away from your sides," the human captain said. "We must show them we carry no weapons."

Kerdoch did as the human captain said because Commander Kor did also.

The Narr stopped twenty paces in front of them. Then the one in the center moved two steps closer and stopped again.

"I will talk for us," the human captain said. He took three steps forward and also stopped.

"We have discovered since we talked before," the human captain said, "that this planet does belong to you."

"Then leave this place," the Narr leader said.

"We will leave if that is what you demand, and if you give us safe passage," the human captain said.

Kerdoch could not believe what he was hearing. The human captain was surrendering for the Klingons. How could Commander Kor stand and listen?

"But," the human captain said before the Narr could respond, "first would you tell us your intended use of this planet?"

"To expand our food resources. At a time in the future we plan to grow our crops here."

"You do not seem to be farmers by nature," Kirk said.

"We are warriors," Narr said, straightening up slightly inside his armor. "We are not farmers."

"The Klingons are also warriors," the human captain said. "But they are also farmers. They work the land and grow the crops as if fighting a great war every season. They are great farmers."

Kerdoch marveled at the human captain's understanding of Klingon nature. But at the same time he was puzzled that the human captain failed to understand that Klingons never surrendered.

"The Klingons have already established a base on this planet," the human captain said. "An agreement could be struck between you and the Klingons, so that they could farm this planet. They would grow their own crops as well as yours."

The human captain was giving Kerdoch's hard work away. Kerdoch almost stepped forward at that moment, his anger was so strong, but Kor's raised hand stopped him. Kerdoch turned to question the commander.

"Let him continue, Kerdoch," Kor said, raising his hand higher, signaling Kerdoch to say nothing.

Kerdoch turned to listen to the treachery going on in front of him. At that moment he could not tell who he was most angry at. The human captain, or Kor for allowing the human captain to speak such words.

The Narr hesitated, then stepped closer to the human captain. "You suggest that the Klingons grow our crops on this planet? Is that correct?"

"Yes," the human captain said. "They would grow your crops as well as their own."

"They would grow them in exchange for the planet?"

The human captain nodded. "And I'm sure you would pay them a fair price for your crops. Details beyond that could be worked out later. But such an agreement would allow the Klingons to stay on this world, as they want. It would also allow you to expand your food base as you need, years ahead of your schedule. Both sides would win."

"I must confer," the Narr said, and turned away.

Kerdoch squeezed his fists tight. Why had Kor allowed the human captain to betray them?

The human captain turned and moved back to where Kerdoch and Kor stood. He was smiling and Kerdoch desperately wanted to smash the smile from his sickly human face.

"You are a crafty one, Kirk," Kor said. "You knew we would never surrender."

"Of course," Kirk said, laughing. "I never intended to surrender. But I had to get the Narr's attention."

"You gave away our planet," Kerdoch said, his voice almost shaking with his anger.

"You will keep the planet, Kerdoch," the human captain said. Then, facing Kor, he continued, "And the strategic advantage of its location, which is important to the Empire. Am I right, Commander?"

Kor bowed slightly, but said nothing.

Kerdoch felt his anger suddenly drain as if it were nothing more than the escaping air of a child's balloon, pricked by a needle. He looked at Commander Kor before turning back to the human.

The human captain continued. "You would also gain a strategic advantage over the Narr by controlling part of their food source in the future. And you will discover the locations of their home worlds in case a future conflict should arise."

Finally Kerdoch was starting to understand what Commander Kor had understood all along. It was why Kor was such a great warrior and he was only a farmer. His respect for the commander increased, as did his respect for the human captain, who had understood Klingons well enough to make such a deal.

"And what do you get, Kirk?" Kor asked.

"I get off this planet alive," Kirk said. "And a chance to cool down."

Kor laughed. Then he peered at Kirk. "You also get the continuation of the Organian Peace Treaty."

"That too," the human captain said, smiling.

"Human?" the Narr said.

The human captain turned to face the approaching Narr soldier.

"Do you speak for the Klingons?" the Narr asked.

"I speak for the Klingons," Commander Kor said, stepping forward beside the human captain. "I am Commander Kor of the Imperial Fleet."

The Narr soldier nodded and glanced at Kerdoch, who gave him a hard stare in return but said nothing.

The Narr soldier turned back to Commander Kor. "We will agree to talks based on the principles the human has put forth."

"You will withdraw your claim to this planet?" Kor asked.

"We will," the Narr said, "if you agree to produce a base amount of our crops on this planet each year, to be sold to us."

"It is agreed," Kor said. "We will talk."

"In twenty of this planet's days we will send a representative to this location."

"As will we," Kor said.

The Narr nodded to the commander.

Kor nodded back.

The Narr soldier turned, lumbering away in his heavy armor.

Kerdoch watched him go, not completely understanding that the fighting had been stopped that quickly.

"Come," Kor said.

Kor, the human captain, and Kerdoch all turned as one and moved back toward the colony across the blackened field. Kerdoch let his feet guide him, his mind still on what he had just heard.

After twenty paces the human captain laughed, "That armor must have been hot."

"Very hot," Kor said. "The heat must have reached his brain. He just gave away an entire planet." With that both the human captain and the commander laughed.

"Commander," Kerdoch said, still slightly confused, "what exactly occurred?"

"This human has given us a glorious victory," Kor said. "One that will be talked and written about for generations."

"And you trust the honor of the Narr?" Kerdoch said. "They will hold their side of the agreement?"

"I have learned this day," Kor said, "that my enemies may have honor. It seems humans have honor. A warrior race such as the Narr must, therefore, surely have more. Yes, I trust their word."

"I think I've just been insulted," the human captain said.

"Ah, Kirk," Kor said, clapping the human on the back. "It is the nature of our relationship for me to insult you."

At that the human captain smiled. "And for me to insult you," he said.

"On that we are agreed," Kor said.

"I'm glad to know this relationship won't change," the human captain said.

But Kerdoch knew that it had. They were laughing together, something enemies rarely did.

CHAPTER 24

VIVIAN RATHBONE SAT FOR A MOMENT AT THE CONTROLS OF THE SHUTTLE *Balboa* as the *Farragut* docking bay pressurized.

After the final sequencing was finished, she let her hands drop into her lap from the control panel. They were shaking. And she was sweating, almost as much as she had in the intense heat of the plasma attack, even though the shuttle's climate controls were working perfectly.

"Well, I did it," she said to herself. It had been almost four years since she'd piloted any form of shuttle, and she had never piloted a starship shuttle like the *Balboa.* But when Captain Kirk told her she was to fly one of the shuttles back to the *Farragut,* she hadn't objected. One thing she had learned on her first landing party was that a crew member really had no limits. You did what you were ordered to do, even if it cost you your life, as it had Ensign Chop.

But it could have been much worse than just flying a shuttle and docking it on the *Farragut.* On the way from the colony to the shuttles Ensign Adaro, who had piloted the other *Farragut* shuttle, the *De leon,* had teased her that flying back to the *Farragut* was a lot easier than flying in battle against the Narr, as they were supposed to have done.

That was the first time she had heard that Captain Kirk had planned for her to fly the *Balboa* against the Narr fighters. Ensign Adaro had been right. This flight was a lot easier than flying in combat. But the idea of the captain trusting her that much had made the flight to the *Farragut* even more nerve-racking. She didn't want to do anything wrong that would let the captain know she might not have been able to handle any assignment he would have given her.

"Ma'am?" Ensign Adaro said over the comm line. He was already standing on the hangar deck. When she looked down he waved for her.

She punched the exterior comm line. "On my way."

She stood and looked around for anything she might have left behind. Then she laughed. She hadn't taken anything to the planet and had even less coming back.

The airlock door hissed open. As she passed through it, she patted the metal side of the shuttle. "Thanks," she said to it.

Inside her head she added, "and I'm glad we didn't have to fight together."

The young ensign looked filthy and very, very sunburned standing among the *Farragut* docking bay crew. As she joined him the ten or so who made up the docking bay crew broke into cheers, standing and applauding her and Adaro.

She wasn't sure about Ensign Adaro, but she blushed. Then laughed.

Having them acknowledge that what she'd gone through and survived had been difficult, made her feel better. Made her feel as if she hadn't let Captain Kirk down quite as much as she feared she had.

"*Enterprise,*" Ensign Adaro said, "two to beam aboard."

"Stand by, Ensign."

"Thank you for coming to our rescue," she said to those still applauding.

As the transporter beam took them, both she and Ensign Adaro applauded those around them.

"By my count," Projeff was saying on the screen in front of Scotty, "it's two ideas from the *Farragut* to your one."

Scotty leaned back. He and Projeff had worked well together. Someday they might even resolve that environmental control problem they'd been discussing on Starbase Eleven. But he wasn't going to let Projeff get the last word.

"I think we're even, lad."

"How do you figure that?"

Scotty smiled. "My first idea was on how to fix the shields. It worked."

"Not well enough," Projeff said. "I had to improve it."

"Your first real idea was on how to disrupt the Narr's antigravity suits."

"I wouldn't agree with that," Projeff said. "That was my second idea."

"But your first original one, lad."

"It's still two ideas to one," Projeff said.

"Not quite," Scotty said. "You see, we dinna get a chance to test your antigravity idea."

"What?" Projeff asked. "The simulations worked fine."

"So did my shield simulations," Scotty said. "But in battle they needed modifications. I'll wager in battle your weapons would have needed modifications too.""There's no way to know that," Projeff said.

"And there's no way to know if your idea even worked," Scotty said. "So I see us as tied, one idea to one."

Projeff's eyes narrowed, but it looked as if he were using the expression to hide his amusement. "If we're tied, we need a tie-breaker."

"I agree, lad, but we're heading off to different parts of space."

"It would need to be a long term project then," Projeff said.

"That wouldn't be fair," Scotty said. "There'd be no way to know who succeeded first."

"True enough," Projeff said.

"So I challenge you, lad, to a duel of the minds the next time we share a shore leave."

Projeff grinned. "You're on, Scotty."

Scotty nodded. "It's been fun, lad."

"That it has, Mr. Scott." Projeff signed off.

Scotty sighed and leaned back in his chair. "An even score," he whispered, "courtesy of the creative mind of the *Enterprise*'s chief engineer."

The turbolift doors hissed open, and Captain Kirk strolled onto the bridge. He had showered and shaved, then reported to sick bay as Dr. McCoy had ordered. Now, feeling better than he could remember and very happy to be alive, it was time to get back to work.

"Welcome back, sir," Lieutenant Uhura said.

"Thank you, Lieutenant," he said. "It's good to be back."

Spock nodded to him as Kirk stepped down to his captain's chair.

"Good work, Mr. Spock," Kirk said. "You handled the situation very well."

"Thank you, sir," Spock said.

Mr. Sulu had already returned to his post next to Ensign Chekov. Both seemed to be busy at their stations.

On the main screen the Narr ships had moved away from their positions over the colony. According to the report he'd been given before showering, they would remain in orbit for another twenty minutes finishing up repairs and the boarding of ground troops.

The three Klingon ships were grouped in a small triangle between the two Federation ships and the Narr ships. Hanging in space to the right of the *Enterprise* was the *Farragut.* Repairs to both starships had been mostly completed.

He sat down in his chair and activated his log. He gave the stardate and then winced. He might as well get the worst duty over first. Then move on.

"Let the record show," he said, his voice solemn and low, "that Ensign Chop died doing his duty for the Federation, in a brave and noble manner."

Kirk paused for a moment.

"Mr. Spock?" he said.

"Yes, Captain?" Spock said.

"Have Ensign Chop's remains been returned to the ship?"

"No, sir," Spock said. "The ensign left instructions in his personal records that if he died on a landing party he was to be buried on the planet or in space. A detail was transported down twenty minutes ago. They buried his remains in one of the bunkers near the colony, next to other dead from the attacks. The colonists have promised to maintain the site with honor and respect."

Kirk nodded. The colonists would keep their word. He had learned that much about those people. He took a deep breath and put the ensign's death down inside him, where every death of every crew member stayed.

He could see all of their faces. He knew all of their names.

There were already far too many in there.

He let out a deep breath slowly.

"Okay," he said and reactivated the log back. "On a more pleasant subject, let the record show commendations for Lieutenant Sulu."

"Commendations also for Ensign Adaro, Vivian Rathbone, Dr. Leonard McCoy, Science Officer Spock, and Chief Engineer Scott."

He leaned back in his chair. On the screen in front of him the ships still floated above the planet. It was a place he hoped to never visit again. As far as he was concerned, the Klingons could have it.

"Lieutenant Uhura, hail the *Farragut.*"

"Aye, sir," she said. She turned her chair slightly. "I have Captain Bogle on-screen, sir."

Captain Bogle's smiling face filled the screen. "Captain," he said. "From the looks of your face, your vacation was successful."

"Nothing like a little fun in the sun," Kirk said.

Bogle laughed. "Glad it was you instead of me. I hate too much sun. Give me a nice rainy day anytime."

Kirk laughed this time. "I just might agree with you on that right now." Then Kirk got serious for a moment.

"Captain," he said, "I want to officially thank you and your crew on behalf of the crew of the *Enterprise.*"

"Accepted with pleasure, Captain," Bogle said, nodding slightly.

"And, Kelly," Kirk said, staring seriously at his friend's face, "let me convey a personal thank you as well."

"Kirk," Bogle said, "you're welcome. Just remember you still owe me a drink."

"I think it just might have to be more than one," Kirk said.

"I'll hold you to that, Kirk," Bogle said, laughing. "*Farragut* out."

The screen returned to the images of the ships orbiting the planet.

"Captain," Spock said, "the Narr ships are leaving orbit."

In a tight formation, the seven wing-like ships moved away from the planet. Between them they towed the hulk of the dead Narr ship.

Then, as one, they jumped to warp and were gone.

"Lieutenant," Kirk said, "signal Commander Kor that we are leaving."

"He's hailing us, sir."

Kirk laughed. "I thought Klingons hated to talk. Put him on-screen."

The Klingon's face filled most of the screen. "Kirk," Kor said, his voice back to the full, loud brassy sound Kirk remembered. "You have taught us much. We will remember this day for generations."

"I only honored our treaty," Kirk said. "As you would have done."

Kor bowed slightly, in what Kirk took to mean agreement.

"Kirk, someday our battle will come."

"Kor, I'm looking forward to it."

Kor laughed. "As am I, Kirk. It will be a glorious day. And a glorious fight."

With that the screen cut off. The planet on the screen looked almost empty without the Narr ships in orbit. But it was a nice empty.

"Mr. Sulu, lay in course for Starbase Eleven. This crew has some shore leave to finish."

"Yes, sir," Sulu said, smiling.

"Besides," Kirk said. "It's going to take me some time to level out this tan."

It took a moment before everyone on the bridge, except Spock, broke into laughter.

EPILOGUE

KERDOCH LET HIS GAZE TRAVEL AROUND THE LARGE ROOM FILLED WITH HIS family. The smells of the huge dinner still filled the air, even though his story had been a long one. He blinked and tried to focus on the present. When he told his story of that great battle with the Narr, he always seemed to take himself back. He relived the revenge cycle. The fear of losing his family. The hardships of battle.

Now, just from telling the story, his old bones were tired. Deep down tired. But he wasn't quite finished yet. He had to continue for just a moment longer.

All eyes were still on him. All attention was still focused on his story of that battle all those years before. Every year he held their attention with the story, and many knew it by heart. It seemed that this year he had mesmerized them again. It was not his telling. He knew that. No, it was the importance of the message of the story.

He took a deep breath and let the warmth of the room ease the tiredness in his old bones. Then he continued with the last of the story.

"Commander Kor and the Narr representative met, as they had said they would, twenty days later. Their agreement has stood for all these years."

He looked around at this family.

"But that agreement is not why we celebrate this day. Agreements come and go. But lessons remain always."

He stared down at his grandchildren, who sat at his feet. A five-year-old boy, his eyes bright with fire, stared up at him. "Young K'Ber, can you tell me the lesson?"

K'Ber sat back a moment, his eyes even brighter at the privilege of being picked by his grandfather to answer a question during the telling of the story. Kerdoch wanted to smile at his grandson, but instead kept very still.

The young boy finally said, "The enemy has honor."

"Good," Kerdoch said, smiling at the boy, who seemed to light up at the attention. "We learned that day to celebrate the honor of the enemy as well as the honor of the warrior."

Again Kerdoch looked up and caught his wife's gaze. She was smiling at him proudly, as was his oldest son. That day long ago he had been more than just a farmer, or a colonist. He had been a Klingon warrior. And the retelling brought back the pride he had felt then.

"As Klingons," Kerdoch said, "we have always given honor to those among us who fight. Dying in battle has always been our most honorable death. But it must be remembered that to our enemies, we are the enemy."

Around the room a murmur broke out as his words sank in. They were words to be remembered by them all, as he had done all these years.

He stood and held up his arms over his family gathered in the large room. "Today I tell this story to remind us all to honor those who fight and those who die in battle. Let this Day of Honor be remembered always."

Around him his family stood, cheering, all talking at once.

Again he had done his duty. For another year the story would be remembered. And so would the important lesson that went with it.

STAR TREK VOYAGER®

DAY OF HONOR

THE TELEVISION EPISODE

A Novel by Michael Jan Friedman

Based on *Day of Honor*
Written by Jeri Taylor

For Patti,
who had to leave before the second act

THEN:
NINETEEN YEARS AGO

CHAPTER 1

Five-year-old B'Elanna Torres sat in a chair in the center of her parents' great room, a Vulcan puzzle cube in her lap, and tried to make sense of the silence. It wasn't easy.

Her father, a tall, darkly handsome man with friendly brown eyes, was standing by the curved window on one side of the room, staring at something—or at nothing, maybe. B'Elanna couldn't tell.

Her mother, a Klingon with wild red hair and a spirit to match, was sitting at the kitchen table on the other side of the room, picking at a bowl of serpent worms she had prepared moments earlier. She grunted a couple of times, but she didn't seem very hungry.

That was a first. As far back as the girl could remember, her mother had *always* been hungry, even when she was sick with some human disease she didn't have antibodies for.

B'Elanna didn't like the silence, but it was better than the yelling. That had gone on for days, almost every time her parents saw each other. And it had been the worst kind of yelling, a nasty kind that made the girl feel as if she wasn't even there.

After a while, B'Elanna had begun to wonder if she might be the cause of her parents' arguments. She wasn't the ideal child, after all. She had a temper sometimes and she didn't play nicely with the other kids. And though she tried her hardest to make her mother and father proud of her, it didn't always work.

Billy Ballantine, one of the older kids in the colony, had tried to explain it to her. "It's not your fault," he had said. "Your mom's a Klingon. Klingons yell all the time. That's what my dad told me, and he knows just about everything. To a Klingon, he says, yelling is second nature."

B'Elanna was half-Klingon herself, but she hardly knew anything about her mother's people. Her mother seldom spoke of her heritage, and the girl had never met any of her Klingon relatives.

Still, she didn't think Billy Ballantine's father was right. It was only lately that her mother had been yelling. Besides, her mother wasn't the only one raising her voice. B'Elanna's father wasn't Klingon, and he had shouted just as loud as her mother a couple of times.

Anyway, they weren't yelling anymore. B'Elanna wasn't sure, just being a child and all, but she thought that was a good thing. It seemed to her that her parents were calming down, thinking about what they had said and maybe being a little embarassed about it.

Yes. The more she turned that over in her mind, the more it made sense. B'Elanna thought about how things happened sometimes that made her mad, that made her want to yell, and how she needed to be alone for a while afterward to sort it out.

But when a child felt angry about something, she could stomp into her room and close the door. B'Elanna's mother and father shared the same bedroom. It would be silly for one of them to go inside and close the door.

So maybe her parents needed to do other things to be alone. Maybe they needed to hide from each other behind a wall of silence, until they had worked out whatever was bothering them.

And maybe after they were done working things out on their own, maybe they would work things out together—and be happy again. B'Elanna smiled to herself. She would like that. She would like that a lot.

Suddenly, the girl realized she wasn't speeding things up for her parents by sitting there. If she went out and left them alone, they might start talking again a little sooner. Maybe by the time she got back, everything would be normal again, the way it used to be.

Maybe everyone would be happy.

"I'm going out," B'Elanna announced abruptly. She put the puzzle cube away on a wall-shelf meant for such things, and headed for the door.

"Be back before dinner," her mother told her, looking up momentarily from her serpent worms.

"I will," she promised.

"And do not let the Ballantine child fill your head with nonsense," her mother added.

B'Elanna looked at her for a moment. Had her mother heard Billy talking about her—about Klingons? She couldn't tell from the hooded look of her mother's eyes.

"I won't," she replied.

B'Elanna headed for the door, already thinking about what kinds of things she could do outside. But her father's voice stopped her before she could get very far.

"Hey," he said. "I need a hug, Little Bee."

For as long as she could remember, Little Bee had been her father's pet name for her. It made her tingle every time he said it.

"Oh, Daddy," B'Elanna squealed.

She ran to him as fast as she could. At the last possible moment, her father bent down and scooped the girl up in his arms, then hugged her just the way she liked it.

B'Elanna hugged him back, too. She hugged him with all her might, and she was strong for her age. Finally, she let go and he put her down.

The truth was, the girl liked her father a little better than she liked her mother. But of course she wasn't going to tell anyone that. It would only have hurt her mother's feelings.

"See you later," she said—to both of them.

Then she was out the door, running through the glare of the late afternoon sun like a wild animal. For the first time in days, she felt a weight had been lifted off her.

They'll be fine, she told herself. Just wait and see.

B'Elanna's father watched his daughter run out into the bright orange plaza, the sunlight picking highlights out of her soft, brown hair. He found he had a lump in his throat.

Little Bee, he thought sadly.

"You are a coward," his wife spat at him.

He turned to her. Every day, she seemed harder, fiercer, more determined to push him out of her life.

I should have seen it coming a long time ago, he told himself. Hell, I should never have married her in the first place.

"A coward?" he echoed.

He gazed out the window again at his little girl. His Little Bee.

"Yeah," he said. "Maybe I am."

"Hey, B'Elanna!"

The girl turned in the direction of the childish cry and saw Dougie Naismith cutting across the plaza to join her. Dougie was a tall, skinny boy with unruly yellow hair and ears that stuck out from his head.

He was also B'Elanna's best friend.

"What's up?" she asked him.

Dougie pointed to the reddish-orange hills north of the white-domed colony complex. "We found a firechute," he said. "Or really, Erva did. Come on, I'll show you."

B'Elanna looked at him, her pulse pounding all of a sudden. "A firechute? Are you sure?"

The only firechutes she knew were way on the other side of the world, where the mountains were really big. B'Elanna's father and mother, who worked as geologists for the colony, had shown them to her.

They had taken her into a crack in the earth, a deep, dark one between two towering cliffs. With her hand in her father's and her mother up ahead, lighting the way, the girl had descended along a long, twisting ledge.

At first, she had seen only a ruddy glow that chased the darkness. Then her path came out from behind an outcropping and she got a good look.

B'Elanna remembered the spiraling tongues of ruby-red flame, each as wide around as one of the colony domes and maybe five or six times as high. Of course, that was only the part she could see. According to her father, the fire had traveled a long way before it even entered the crack.

And it wasn't fire, really, though the girl could feel its immense heat on her face, pulling her skin tight across her cheekbones. It was a funny kind of energy that just looked and felt like fire—an energy trapped under the crust of the planet when the world was still forming.

At least, that was the way her father had explained it. All B'Elanna knew was that it was beautiful—so beautiful she couldn't say a word, only stop and gaze in wonder at the spectacle.

So it seemed strange that there could be a firechute in the hills so close to home. No, more than strange. Crazy.

"I'm sure," said Dougie. "Come on, I'll show you."

B'Elanna glanced over her shoulder at her family's house. Her mother hadn't told her her to stick around the colony buildings. She had just said to be back before dinner, and that was at least an hour away.

It occurred to the girl that her parents would be interested in the firechute, too. But if she told them about it, that would distract them from the patching up they needed to do.

Besides, it would be a lot more fun to see the chute for herself, first. She could always show it to her mother and father later.

"All right," she told her friend Dougie. "Let's go."

Together, they set out across the sunbaked flatlands that separated the colony from the hill country. It didn't take long to cross them, either—maybe half an hour at an easy lope. B'Elanna was so excited, she barely felt the afternoon heat.

"I don't get it," she said, as the rust-colored hills loomed in front of them. "Why didn't we ever find anything like this before?"

After all, B'Elanna and her friends had explored the hills many times already. They had found some small caves, but nothing even vaguely resembling a firechute.

"You'll see," was all Dougie would tell her.

It was another couple of minutes before they found Erva Konal. Though she was a year older than Dougie and two years older than B'Elanna, her diminutive size made her look younger than either one of them.

Erva was sitting outside one of the caves they had explored weeks earlier, her thin, delicate features hidden behind patches of sparkling, dark rock dust. Her clothing was covered with the stuff, too.

"It's about time," she said, in her high-pitched Yrommian voice. "I feel like I've been waiting forever."

"We can't all move as fast as you can," Dougie reminded her.

It was true. Despite their small stature, Yrommians had a funny, ground-eating gait, and Erva was no exception. Try as she might, B'Elanna had never been able to keep up with it.

"So where's the firechute?" B'Elanna asked.

Erva jerked her head in the direction of the cave. "In here," she said. Then she got up and went inside.

B'Elanna shook her head as she followed the Yrommian into darkness. "This isn't a joke, is it?"

"No joke," Dougie confirmed. He was right behind B'Elanna as they headed for the depths of the cavern. "I know we were in this cave before and everything, but this time we saw something in the back of it."

"Like a flash of light," Erva explained.

"We found an opening in the rock," the boy added. "It was too narrow for me to get through, but not too narrow for Erva."

"Come on," said the Yrommian. "I'll show you. Just watch your head. The ceiling gets pretty low here."

B'Elanna couldn't see well in the darkness, but she managed to keep track of Erva. Her friend got down on her hands and knees, then gestured for B'Elanna to do the same.

"I wish I could go with you," Dougie sighed.

"Maybe we'll find another chute," the Yrommian suggested. "One a little easier to get to."

"Yeah," said the boy. "Right."

B'Elanna felt Erva's hand on her arm. The Yrommian's fingers were cold, but that was normal for her people.

"It's this way," she said—and slipped forward into the darkness.

Suddenly, B'Elanna couldn't feel her friend's hand anymore. It was gone. "Erva?" she said.

She moved forward herself and extended her hand. It brushed against a rough, hard wall of stone. She moved it to the right—more stone. Then she moved it to the left.

And found an opening. The one that Erva must have gone through.

"Let's go, already," said a high-pitched voice.

With a little care, B'Elanna figured out the dimensions of the opening. It was about three feet high, but very narrow. So narrow, in fact, that she was sure she wouldn't fit through.

"What are you waiting for?" asked her friend.

"I think I may be too big," B'Elanna told her.

"Nonsense. Give it a try."

B'Elanna did as Erva told her. It was a tight fit, all right—but in the end, she *did* fit through. As she dragged her legs out of the hole, she could see the opening outlined in the faint, gray light from the cave mouth.

"You made it!" Erva cheered.

B'Elanna looked around. She couldn't see anything in the darkness ahead of her, not even the Yrommian. "Now what?" she asked.

"Now we wait," her friend told her.

But they didn't have to wait for long. The words were barely out of Erva's mouth when the place lit up with a blood-red light. And in that sudden flood of illumination, B'Elanna saw a thin lash of ruby flame emerge from a hole in the cavern floor.

It wasn't a small hole, either. It was half the size of the cavern itself, and this cavern was even bigger than the one outside.

The lash of flame died down, but not the blood-red glow. That lingered, meaning the fire hadn't subsided completely. It just wasn't visible from where they sat.

B'Elanna looked at her friend. "You weren't kidding," she said.

"Of course not," Erva told her.

Then she started to move, her shadow looming large and dancing wildly on the cavern wall behind her. It seemed to B'Elanna that her friend was inching forward, trying to get a better view of the chute.

But after a moment, she realized Erva was doing more than that. She was moving to the side as well, where a narrow ledge circumvented the pit and connected with the cavern floor on the other side.

"What are you doing?" B'Elanna asked her.

"I'm going to the other side," the Yrommian explained. "It's lower there, and there's less of a lip. I'll get a better view."

"But it's dangerous," B'Elanna protested.

"Only if the flame dies down before I get there and it becomes dark." Her friend winked at her. "And if I hurry, that won't happen."

Before B'Elanna could stop her, Erva had gotten to her feet and sidled out onto the ledge. Pressing her back into the cavern wall, the Yrommian made her way along the side of the chute.

B'Elanna watched, spellbound. The ruddy light coming up from the hole in the earth made Erva seem ruddy as well. Her hair gleamed like Klingon bloodwine, her eyes like dying suns.

"What's going on in there?" Dougie called from the next cavern. His voice echoed from one wall of the chute to the other. "I *hate* not being able to get in to see!"

You might not want to see *this,* B'Elanna thought. If Erva fell off the ledge, she would die. There was no question about it.

But the Yrommian didn't seem the least bit afraid. If anything, she seemed giddy with her nearness to the fire, all possibility of fear swept away in a tide of delight.

"Come on," said Dougie. "Somebody *talk* to me."

"Erva's going over to the other side," B'Elanna answered.

"The other side?"

"Of the chute," she added.

Dougie didn't say anything for a moment. "How?" he asked finally.

B'Elanna frowned. "She's walking."

"She can do that?"

"I guess," the girl said, trying to keep the doubt out of her voice.

Erva took a step, then slid. Another step, and slid some more. Little by little, she approached the far side of the cavern. Finally, to B'Elanna's surprise and elation, her friend came within a step or two of her goal.

Suddenly, without warning, the firechute filled with a rush of energy. The flame bounded off the ceiling and folded back on itself like a great and terrible blossom, turning the cavern a hideous red with its fury. B'Elanna closed her eyes and pressed herself as far back into the stone as she could go.

But the fire found her.

She felt its searing energy on her face, scorching her skin and superheating the air she drew into her throat, making her cry out with the pain. For a moment, she thought she had been burned beyond recognition, both inside and out.

Then the heat and the light diminished, and B'Elanna opened her eyes and felt her face with a terrible urgency. But to her surprise, her skin was still smooth, still in one piece. The burn she had sustained was no worse than the ones she got from being in the sun too long.

Swallowing, B'Elanna saw that her throat was okay too. Gathering her courage, she gazed across the chute.

She was prepared for the worst—prepared to find that Erva had fallen into the hole, or been burned to ashes by her nearness to the fire. But neither of those things had happened.

The Yrommian was on the other side of the chute, huddled against the cavern wall. She had wrapped her arms about herself and was trembling like a *naiga* spore in a strong wind, moaning in a kind of singsong rhythm.

But as far as B'Elanna could tell, her friend was all right. She hadn't been burned any worse than B'Elanna herself.

She licked her lips. "Erva?"

B'Elanna's voice echoed a bit. But it was still intelligible when it reached the Yrommian.

Erva turned away from the cavern wall and peered at B'Elanna with eyes red from crying. "I'm still here," she said with some surprise.

"For now," B'Elanna told her. "But you've got to get out of there. The next time, the fire might be worse."

It was true. Her parents had said that about firechutes. Just when you thought you had seen one at its worst, it got even fiercer.

Her friend shook her head, squeezing out tears between swollen eyelids. "I can't," she whimpered.

"You've *got* to," B'Elanna insisted.

But it was no use.

CHAPTER 2

B'ELANNA SHOOK HER HEAD. THE YROMMIAN WASN'T MAKING A MOVE TO help herself—even if it meant her death. She was just too frightened.

There was only one other possibility, the half-Klingon girl told herself. Only one other way to get her friend Erva out of her predicament—and that was to go all the way over and get her.

She took a look into the chute, where flame after twisting flame was emerging from its depths. There was no time to lose. The longer B'Elanna waited, the better the chance that the flames would shoot up again, turning both her and her friend into ashes.

Taking a ragged breath, she ventured out onto the narrow precipice. She took a sideways step. Then another. And another.

With each one, she got a little closer to Erva. She focused on that, forgetting about everything else. All she had to do was get one step closer each time and she would be all right.

"I'm coming," she said, to steady her own nerves as much as her friend's. "I'll be there before you know it."

As if in response, a tongue of flame rose high enough to lick at B'Elanna's feet. Clenching her jaw shut, she waited until it subsided, then continued along the ledge.

She had come halfway, she estimated. It was a milestone, something she could build a hope on. If she could come halfway, she could make it all the way across.

And if she could make it across one way, she could get back.

It sounded good, B'Elanna told herself. But even as she thought it, she knew there were no guarantees. This time, there weren't any adults around to help her out. If everything came out all right, it would be because of her and no one else.

She smiled at the idea. Her parents would be proud of her then. They couldn't be anything else. And they would love her so much, they would forget about their quarreling.

B'Elanna slid her right foot sideways, then followed with the left. Right, then left. Right, left . . . always certain to test her footing before she put any weight down.

Things would be good again, she told herself. She pictured herself as a baby in her parents' embrace, just the way she had seen it in the family holos. As she brought her right foot forward, she imagined the feel of her parents' arms around her, firm and reassuring.

Left foot now, B'Elanna thought. But as she moved it, she could feel it slip off what she had believed was solid rock.

And keep going.

For a long, terrible second, she thought she felt herself falling, dropping dizzily into the searing embrace of the flames. Then she threw herself back into the cavern wall as hard as she could.

The impact jarred B'Elanna to the roots of her teeth, but it kept her from going over. And before she could topple again, she found purchase with her left foot and lifted herself up.

Her heart was pounding so hard it was difficult to breathe, much less to continue along the ledge. So she waited a moment, taking long, deep breaths, until she was calm enough to go on.

Strangely enough, the going was much easier after that. It was as if B'Elanna had confronted the worst that could happen, and after that nothing seemed quite so scary anymore.

Finally, she reached the other side of the cavern floor, where her friend Erva was staring at her wide-eyed. It wasn't as if she wasn't glad to see B'Elanna. In fact, she was very glad.

But she knew that, having reached her, B'Elanna would want to take her back. And Erva was still about as afraid of that as she could be.

"It's all right," B'Elanna told her friend. She knelt beside Erva and put her hand on the Yrommian's shoulder. "You got here, right? That means you can get back."

Erva shook her head. "No, it doesn't. I'm too scared, B'Elanna, too scared even to *move.*"

B'Elanna glanced into the pit, where the tongues of crimson flame seemed to be lengthening each time they shot up. "If you don't move," she explained, "you'll die here, Erva."

"Then I'll die!" the Yrommian screamed.

"And I'll die *with* you!" B'Elanna shouted back. "Because I'm not leaving you here. Either we both go back or neither of us does."

She didn't know what made her say that. She sure hadn't had that in mind when she set out to rescue Erva. But as soon as the words came out, she was glad they had—because they made a change in her friend.

It was one thing for Erva to sacrifice her own life because she was afraid. But to sacrifice B'Elanna's life as well—that was something else again.

The muscles worked in the Yrommian's little jaw. A light showed in her eyes. "All right," she said. "We'll do it."

B'Elanna nodded. "Together."

And they did.

They made their way back along the entire ledge, Erva's hand clasping B'Elanna's in a white-knuckled grip. They didn't slip, either. They didn't even come close to slipping. The two of them just took their time and managed to ignore the fire raging in the pit in front of them.

When they reached the other side, they fell to their knees, thankful and relieved that they had made it. As they pulled themselves up again to make their way out of the cavern, B'Elanna took a last look back. Then Erva slipped through the crack in the wall and her friend wriggled after her.

It was just in time, too. Because a moment later, the crimson geyser of energy erupted again—this time, with an intensity B'Elanna hadn't imagined possible. Even from the next cavern, she could see its brilliance and feel the heat of it blistering her skin.

If she and Erva had remained in the chute-cavern any longer, they would have been burned to cinders. But they had escaped.

"Wow!" said Dougie. "That was something!"

Erva nodded. "Something," she echoed.

B'Elanna smiled wearily. Her friend was safe and sound, and so was she. No one had gotten hurt.

And as a bonus, she had a tale of bravery to tell her parents.

• • •

B'Elanna's mother stood beside her bed, in the bedroom she and her husband shared, and considered the jewel-encrusted object in her hand. It was a *jinaq* amulet, worn by Klingon maidens from the day they came of age—a signal that they were ripe for conquest.

She hadn't worn it since her wedding day, when she had vowed to honor and cherish her human husband. Those vows seemed hollow now, the words of a fool. But no matter what happened, she wouldn't wear the amulet again.

She was no maiden, after all. And she never intended to leave herself open again for conquest.

Suddenly, she heard the front door swing open. Her first thought was that her husband had come back. Then she realized it was her daughter, and she steeled herself for what was ahead.

B'Elanna's voice was shrill with enthusiasm as she called from the next room. "Mama? Daddy? You'll never guess what happened!"

"In here," said her mother, her throat as dry as the ground outside the colony buildings.

A moment later, the girl burst into the room, her face flushed beneath a layer of rock dust. "Mama," B'Elanna cried, "you're not going to believe it! I saved Erva's life! She and Dougie were exploring the caverns out north by the mines and they found a firechute! Then Erva got stuck in the cavern with the chute and—"

It was then that her daughter seemed to realize something was wrong. B'Elanna met her mother's gaze and seemed to see the anger that the woman held clenched within her. The anger—and the shame.

"Mama?" she said tentatively. "Is something wrong?"

Her mother didn't answer. She had called her husband a coward not so long ago, but now she discovered the same cowardice in herself.

B'Elanna came over and embraced her. "There *is* something the matter, isn't there? Tell me, Mama. What is it?"

Her mother looked past her, nostrils flaring. She was a Klingon. It was her duty to say what there was to say, good or bad. Still, she found it difficult to speak, and it irked her that it should be so.

You've been living among humans too long, she thought bitterly. They've made you weak and sentimental.

Suddenly, B'Elanna knew without being told. Her mother could see it in her eyes. "It's Daddy," the girl whispered.

There, her mother thought. Your duty has been done for you, *p'tahk.* "Your father is leaving us," she said. "In some ways, he is already gone."

B'Elanna didn't understand. "Where is he, Mama?" Her little girl's voice was little more than a whimper.

Her mother jerked her head in the direction of the front door. "Making arrangements at the administration office. There is a ship coming by in a few days. He will be on it when it departs."

"But why?" asked B'Elanna, still numb, still disbelieving. "Why would Daddy want to go somewhere else?"

Her mother shook her head, her long red tresses sweeping her shoulders. When she spoke, her words were like knives, cutting them both.

"You will have to ask him that yourself, child."

It can't be, B'Elanna thought.

She ran across the plaza in the direction of the administration building, her breath rasping in her throat, her heart pounding from more than her exertion.

It can't be, the girl repeated. It's not fair.

She had thought she was going to make her father proud of her. She had imagined he would listen to her story and tell her how brave she was, and want to stay with her forever and ever. But now her father was going to leave anyway, no matter *how* brave she had been.

It hurt to think that. It hurt worse than the energy in the chute. B'Elanna wanted to cry, but she couldn't. Other people cried, but not Klingons or even half-Klingons. She had learned that early on.

Suddenly, she caught sight of him. Her father was coming out of the administration dome, his eyes downcast. Then some sixth sense told him to look up and he saw her.

He tried to smile, but he didn't get very far. His eyes stayed sad, no matter what the rest of his face did.

"Oh, Daddy," B'Elanna said, and leaped into his arms.

"Little Bee," he whispered in her ear, clasping her to him. "How did you get so dirty?"

"You can't leave," she told him. "You can't. Not after I was so brave. Not after I saved Erva in the cavern."

He held her away from him. "What?"

B'Elanna told him all about it, barely taking a breath. The whole story spilled out in a matter of moments.

"So you *can't* leave," she insisted. "Not after I've been so good. And I can be good like that *all* the time."

Her father shook his head, tears welling in his eyes. "I wish it was that simple," he said. "I really do."

"But it *can* be that simple," B'Elanna argued. "All you have to do is tell the administrator you've changed your mind—or made a mistake or something. You want to stay home with me and Mama."

Her father swallowed. She could see his Adam's apple move up and down in his throat. "Come on," he said softly. "We can go home for now, at least, Little Bee."

B'Elanna looked into his eyes. They were still sad, still wet with human tears. "But not for good," she said. "Right?"

He didn't answer for a moment. It seemed to her it hurt him too much to answer. But eventually, he found the words.

"Not for good," he sighed at last.

For a moment, the girl got angry. She didn't want her father to go away—and she was his daughter, wasn't she? Why couldn't he just stay and do what made her happy?

As if he had read her mind, he said, "You'll get over it, Little Bee. You'll be happy again. And so will your mother. Just remember that and it'll happen before you know it."

"But how can I be happy," she asked, "without you?"

Even before she could get all the words out, she was overcome by the need to hug him again. She hugged her Daddy long and hard, harder than she had ever hugged him before. And when she was done, he took her hand and they walked back to their dome.

A couple of days later, he was gone, just the way her mother said he would be. And B'Elanna and her mother were all alone.

THEN:
ONE YEAR AGO

AGRON LUMAS WALKED OUT ONTO HIS BALCONY AND SURVEYED THE TAWNY hills of the Konoshin river valley. The rays of the late afternoon sun slanted across the tableau, making white-hot points of the pollen clusters rising from the *treybaga* trees lining each slope.

It was a sight few on his world could afford. But then, Lumas was successful at his profession. He had earned his perquisites in life.

Smiling at the notion, he breathed in and then out. It was the growing season. The air was sweet. And for the first time in what seemed like a long time, he had a few minutes all to himself.

After all, Lumas's workday was over, and the stringed-instrument concert up the mountain wasn't slated to begin for half a decacycle. His wife and two daughters, who would normally have been buzzing about the great room like insects, were still downstairs selecting clothes for the occasion.

Lumas chuckled to himself. His elder daughter, Finaea, meant to impress a young man who would be playing the chinharp. He knew this because she had told him so. Hence, the fuss over which outfit to wear.

Of course, Lumas's wife outwardly disapproved of Finaea's obession with the lad. That was only proper. But it didn't stop her from reveling in the opportunity to dress her daughter up.

Suddenly, something occurred to Lumas. He could stand on his balcony any time he wished. But with the great room empty, he had a rare chance to try out the new realizor his wife had purchased.

Yes, he thought. This is the perfect time to try it out.

Re-entering the great room, with its strategically positioned works of two-dimensional art, Lumas brushed his fingers against the sensor on his western wall. Instantly, the portals in the room irised down to nothing. A brush of an adjacent sensor and the overhead lights dimmed, leaving the vast chamber dark and deliciously expectant.

Next, Lumas approached the stand in the corner of the room, where the realizor band sat in its simple metal cradle. Picking up the device, he admired its sleek, black lines. Then he placed it over his head.

The realizor was so light, he barely knew it was there. But then, this was a state-of-the-art unit, and its physical attributes were only the smallest part of the advantages it offered.

Lumas touched his finger to one of the studs on the side of the band, activating its creator function. A tap on a second stud notified the mechanism that he wasn't seeking anything permanent.

Only a moment's diversion—it was all Lumas had time for. But even that might turn out to be immensely satisfying, if all he had heard about this realizor was true.

Closing his eyes, he pictured a sculpture garden he had visited in Changor Province a year or so before. He recalled the way the willowy pieces of molded metal had glinted in the light of the twin moons, swaying and turning under the influence of an insistent sea breeze.

Beautiful, he thought. Unutterably beautiful.

Then Lumas opened his eyes and saw that the sculptures had invaded his great room. The place was filled with them. And though there were neither moons nor sea breezes present, the sculptures rolled and undulated just as they had that evening in Changor.

Lumas heard a sound: laughter, he thought, childlike and uninhibited. Then, with a thrill of surprise, he realized it was coming from his own throat—and laughed some more.

But then, who wouldn't have laughed? Who wouldn't have been delighted by such an experience? Lumas had recreated the sculpture garden with impeccable verisimilitude and vivid detail. It was even more than he had hoped for.

He reminded himself to congratulate his wife on her purchase. This was worth every gem note she had paid for it.

"Father?" said a voice, high and thin.

"Agron?" said another—that of an adult.

Lumas turned and saw that his family had entered the great room. They were standing at the other end of the chamber, their eyes wide with wonder at what he had made.

"Why," said Finaea, "it's wonderful." She turned to Lumas. "Did you make this yourself, Father?"

He nodded, pleased that his daughter should approve. It had been a long time since any of his works had made her smile. But then, that was only normal when it came to budding adults.

Lumas's wife ran her fingers along a delicate limb of one of the sculptures. She smiled. "I didn't know this place had had such a profound effect on you. But I see now how beautiful it must have seemed."

More so to him than to her, he realized now. Strange that that should be so, after they had been mates for so long. Yet there it was.

"Can I add something?" asked Lumas's younger daughter, Anyelot. "A stream, maybe? Or a walkway?"

He grinned. Anyelot would be an architect some day. There was no doubt of that. He reached out to touch her brow with his fingertips.

Then something happened—something he found alarming. Suddenly, Lumas and his loved ones weren't alone in the swaying sculpture garden.

Suddenly, there were three other figures.

Their skin was pasty-pale, their bodies encased in hard black harnesses. Instead of hands, they displayed mechanical appendages. Tubes sprouting from their chests ended in connections to their hairless skulls.

The strangers' faces were even more disturbing—that is, the part that could be seen. Half of each visage was concealed behind a mysterious black prosthetic. The other half was cold, expressionless, yet for all that driven by some arcane purpose.

Lumas didn't understand. He hadn't asked the realizor to create these beings. To his knowledge, he had never even seen anything like them.

Yet there they were. And if they were chilling to him, he could only imagine what his wife and daughters were feeling.

"Father . . . ?" Anyelot whimpered, her voice climbing in pitch. "What *are* these things? Make them go away!"

"Don't worry," Lumas told her, his voice sounding strange to him with the band on his head. "They'll be gone in a moment, little one."

All it would take was an effort of will. Lumas stared at the strangers and wished them into oblivion.

But nothing happened. The creatures remained. One of them even went so far as to grab his wife's wrist—and since the realizor's creations had substance, she couldn't pull it back again.

"Help me!" she cried, with genuine panic in her voice.

Lumas didn't know what to do. He had never heard of anything like this happening before. A realizor was supposed to be attuned to its wearer's whims, completely and utterly. It wasn't supposed to *defy* him.

Chilled to his core, Lumas reached up and tore the band off his head. As he threw it to the floor, the sculpture garden wavered and vanished. But the nightmare beings remained.

Only then did Lumas get a glimpse of the truth. The invaders had nothing to do with the realizor. They weren't products of his imagination. They existed on their own, just like him and his wife and his daughters.

In short, they were *real.*

As Lumas watched, one of them pulled Finaea to him and embraced her—but not as the youth who played the chinharp would have embraced her. The invader's grip was powerful, stifling—unyielding.

"No!" Lumas shouted.

But it didn't come out as the bellow of rage he had intended. It emerged as little more than a murmur, a sigh.

Lumas lunged at the invader, intending to rip his arm off if need be—anything to free his baby, his treasure. But he barely shuffled forward. His legs felt leaden, useless, his hands little more than lumps of flesh at the ends of his arms.

Of course, Lumas thought, in a still-rational part of his mind. It was an aftereffect of the realizor. It always took several seconds for the wearer to regain full use of his faculties.

"Agron!" his wife cried. "Please, it's hurting me!"

He tried to move again, but he was still too weighted down. As he looked on, horrified beyond measure, Anyelot flung herself at the intruder who had grabbed her mother—but she couldn't pry open that viselike grip.

Then Anyelot, too, was seized—in her case, by the back of the neck. The deathly pale stranger raised her off her feet, choking her, seemingly oblivious to the croaking sounds coming from her throat or the frantic kicking of her legs.

"Leave me alone!" Anyelot bawled. "Leave me alone!"

It didn't help. It was as if her tormentor hadn't even heard her.

Lumas felt hot tears streaming down his face. A second time, he attempted to push himself forward, but couldn't move his feet quickly enough. So instead of lunging, he simply fell.

He lay there on the floor as his wife screamed for him. As Finaea screamed for him. As little Anyelot screamed for him, twisting desperately in the grasp of her silent captor.

How could this be? Lumas asked himself. How? Was it his fault? Had he somehow *inflicted* this fate on them?

"Agron!" his wife shrieked—and reached out for him.

Lumas had accomplished one thing with his fall—he was closer to her now. Close enough, perhaps, to grasp her hand. Lifting his own, he fought his paralysis and stretched it to within inches of her fingers.

Their eyes met. Lumas saw something dark and hideous in hers, something more than terror and loathing. It was as if the intruder had somehow begun to infect her with his darkness.

Feeling control flooding back into his limbs, he reached still further—and grasped his wife's hand. But as he did this, her fingers went limp, and the light left her eyes altogether.

Still he held on, unwilling to give her up, unwilling to surrender. That was when her captor pulled her away from him and raised a mechanical appendage. Lumas tried to roll out of the way, but it was too late.

The appendage came down across his head with a force he couldn't have imagined. He felt himself falling into a deep, dark emptiness—though it wasn't nearly as great as the emptiness of loss inside him.

When he woke, some time later, his world was in flames.

NOW

CHAPTER 1

B'ELANNA TORRES, CHIEF ENGINEER OF THE STARSHIP *VOYAGER,* FOUND HERself standing in the center of a large, redstone plaza, the sky above her dark and dusky and vibrating with desert heat.

A hot, gritty wind caressed her face as she looked around. The circle of arches surrounding the plaza looked as if they had been carved from solid rock. But for all their majesty, they were no more impressive than the tall, rough-hewn structure that rose beside her, a flat, metal gong in the shape of a hexagon hanging from its only protrusion.

As B'Elanna watched, a tongue of pale flame leaped from the structure's goblet-shaped top. Turning to smoke, it twisted on the wind and vanished.

Suddenly, she saw movement. A powerful, bare-chested figure appeared on either side of the plaza. Each one was armed with a *lirpa*—an ancient weapon with a curved blade on one end and a heavy bludgeon on the other.

The wind blew again, leaching moisture from B'Elanna's every pore. She had only been here a few seconds and she was already beginning to sweat.

She knew this place—or rather, not the place itself, but its type. It was the sort of age-old temple one might find on Vulcan, where the indigenous race's once-tumultuous nature had been tamped down under centuries of severe mental discipline.

But here, in this primitive place of worship, surrounded by ocher-colored wastes and the vague black shapes of far-off mountains, the prospect of violence was still very much alive. B'Elanna glanced again at the figures holding the *lirpas.* A half-Klingon by birth, she had never before appreciated how much Vulcans and her mother's people had in common.

Still, she hadn't come to this setting of her own free will. When B'Elanna arrived at the holodeck a couple of minutes earlier, she had called up a new program she had been building from the inside out. Or anyway, she *thought* she had called it up.

But her new program involved cool, dank caves and chill mists—not a hot, arid desert that looked for all the world like an open wound. And it certainly didn't contain Vulcans.

No matter, she told herself. Anybody can make a mistake. She simply called for the half-finished cave program again. Then she closed her eyes and inhaled, anticipating a breath of subterranean cold.

What she got was another torrid wind playing over her face, with a familiarity she was beginning not to like. B'Elanna opened her eyes and saw that nothing had changed. She was still standing in the middle of the Vulcan temple, heat waves rising off the stone all around her.

There was only one explanation. The holodeck was malfunctioning. This wasn't good news, considering how much *Voyager*'s crew depended on the ship's holodecks.

Sighing, she said, "Computer, terminate program."

Abruptly, the temple and the Vulcan desert around it vanished. They were replaced by an intricate network of electromagnetic field emitters and omnidirectional holodiodes—the devices that enabled the holodeck to create and sustain its illusions.

"Well," B'Elanna breathed, "at least *that* command still works."

As she walked toward the exit, a pair of interlocking doors automatically slid away from each other. The engineer could see the corridor beyond them, where the holodeck controls lurked beyond the bulkhead.

B'Elanna knew she didn't have the time to do a thorough repair job. Eventually, she would have to turn it over to someone else. Nonetheless, she pulled away the appropriate bulkhead panel and started diagnosing the problem.

After all, on a ship like *Voyager,* there was always too much to do and not enough time in which to do it. If she didn't tackle each difficulty as it came up, she would soon be deluged.

Worse, B'Elanna would have to explain that deluge to the captain—and that was *not* her idea of a good time.

Tom Paris found the object of his search in the corridor outside the ship's holodeck: she had taken a bulkhead plate off and was tinkering with the controls located behind it.

"Morning," he said.

Paris had learned not to approach B'Elanna without giving her sufficient warning. The one time he had done that, he had gotten a couple of bruised ribs for his trouble.

The engineer glanced at him. "Morning," she replied. Then she went back to her work.

Stopping alongside her, he propped his hand against the bulkhead. Then he peered over her shoulder at the holodeck's control mechanisms.

"Mm," Paris said judiciously. "That doesn't look good."

"It's *not* good," B'Elanna agreed, without sparing him another glance. Suddenly, she straightened, causing him to straighten, too. "Unfortunately, I don't have the time to devote to it right now."

"Oh?" said Paris.

"I've got an emergency shutdown drill in engineering a few minutes from now." Picking up the bulkhead plate, she put it back in its place. "So someone else will have to fix this—when they can find the time."

"Too bad," he commented. "I was hoping to use the holodeck this evening."

"For what?" B'Elanna asked.

"Dinner," said Paris. "For two."

She gave him her trademark look—a half-scowl, half-smile that never failed to fascinate the hell out of him. "Dinner," she echoed.

He nodded. "With you."

The engineer rolled her eyes. "I'm too busy, Tom." She started down the corridor, all business.

He caught up to her, then created an imaginary vista with a sweep of his hand. "Picture it, B'Elanna. A table for two, on a plateau high above the Yrommian rain forest. The setting sun dissolving in a rising sea of mists. A cool breeze caressing your bare shoulders . . . "

She waved away the suggestion. "One doesn't bare one's shoulders near an Yrommian rain forest, Tom. Not unless one wants to be a meal for a horde of *gorada* flies."

He shrugged. "I've never had any problems with them."

"You're not half-Klingon," B'Elanna reminded him. "Those gorada flies like *hot*-blooded species."

"And you think your blood's hotter than mine?" Paris asked frankly.

She met his gaze. "I'd say that's a conversation for another time, wouldn't you?" Coming to a turbolift, she stepped inside.

He followed her. "Okay. Forget about our blood temperatures. Let's go back to the dinner discussion."

"That was a discussion?" B'Elanna asked, as the lift doors closed behind them. "Don't you think that's a bit of an exaggeration?"

"There you go again," Paris told her.

The engineer's eyes narrowed. "There I go what?"

"There you go folding your arms," he said. "That's body language for 'I'm scared stiff of you.' "

B'Elanna looked down and saw her arms woven tightly across her chest. She unwove them immediately. Then she made a point of staring into Paris's eyes almost belligerently.

"You're out of your mind," she told him. "I'm not frightened of you or anyone else." She rubbed her arm with one of her hands. "For your information, I'm a little chilly, that's all."

He grinned at her. "A nice warm mudbath could take care of that. When the holodeck is fixed, of course."

"And I suppose you'd be willing to share it with me," B'Elanna surmised.

"Well," said Paris, "I could be persuaded."

"You never give up, do you?"

"Never," he confirmed.

She sighed. "Look, tonight's not a possibility. But how about tomorrow night? That is, if nothing ridiculous comes up."

Paris spread his hands expansively. "Tomorrow it is." Suddenly, he remembered. "Hey, isn't tomorrow the Day—"

"—of Honor. Yes, it is." B'Elanna glanced at him. "In fact, I've been working on a holodeck program to celebrate it."

"My," he said, "we *have* come a long way. Last year, you wanted to run and hide on the Day of Honor."

"Well," she replied, "last year's Day of Honor was a little better than all the others. Hence, the program. Actually, I was going to shape it up a little, but then I discovered the holodeck was on the blink."

That gave Paris an idea. "Listen, you're so busy and all—why don't I shape up the program for you? That is, when the holodeck's fixed."

B'Elanna looked skeptical. "You?"

"Why not? I probably know as much about Klingons as you do. And what I don't know, I could look up."

"I don't know," she said.

"Hey," Paris declared, "what have you got to lose?"

Just then, the doors opened. As B'Elanna exited the lift, he accompanied her. After all, he wasn't due on the bridge for another couple of hours.

"So what do you say?" Paris asked. "It'll give us a chance to do something creative together. And you'll enjoy the program more if there's an element of surprise . . . right?"

She stopped in the middle of the corridor, exasperated. "Fine, Tom. Complete the program." As she looked at him, her gaze softened. "I mean, I appreciate the sentiment and everything. Just don't do anything I wouldn't do, all right?"

"No problem," he assured her.

Then Paris watched her walk the rest of the way to engineering. The doors slid open as B'Elanna approached, and then closed behind her, depriving him of her company.

The flight controller sighed. He'd had trouble with a lot of things in life, but the opposite sex wasn't one of them. He had always had a knack for attracting women and keeping them attracted.

What's more, he wasn't sure B'Elanna was any exception. But if she *was* attracted to him, she sure had a funny way of showing it. Even arranging a dinner date was like pulling teeth.

Of course, he mused, that only made her more desirable to him.

Ensign Harry Kim stopped in front of his friend's quarters and waited for the door sensors to register his presence. A moment later, he heard Paris's voice: "Come on in."

As the door slid aside, Kim entered. He found the flight controller sitting at the computer terminal in his living room, staring at the monitor.

"What's so interesting?" Kim asked.

He peered over Paris's shoulder to get a look at the screen. It displayed a line drawing of a monstrous being with Klingon features.

"Fek'lhr?" he said, reading the name underneath the illustration.

His friend frowned. "A mythical beast, the guardian of *Gre'thor*—which is about as close as Klingons get to hell and the devil."

Kim nodded. "Interesting." But, now that he thought about it, not really Paris's cup of tea. He said so.

"True," said Paris, leaning back in his chair. "That is, until today. Suddenly, I have a burning desire to know more about Klingon culture."

Kim smiled. "And why is that?"

Paris looked at him apologetically. "It's kind of confidential. At least, I think it is."

"But it has something to do with B'Elanna," Kim guessed.

"What makes you say that?"

"Oh, I don't know," Kim said. "Maybe the fact that she's the only one in the entire quadrant with a Klingon heritage. Or the fact that you have a poorly disguised interest in her. Or the fact that, as I recall, tomorrow is that holiday she used to hate."

Paris grunted. "The Day of Honor."

"Yeah, that one."

The flight controller regarded him. "Harry, my man, you've become quite the detective. You know that?"

"So that *is* what this is about," Kim deduced.

Paris held his ground. "Can't say. It's confidential. And besides, B'Elanna would kill me if she knew I'd told anyone about this."

Swiveling his monitor around, he tapped out a new command on his keyboard. The image on the screen changed. Now *Fek'lhr* was a fully fleshed-out figure placed in a cavern setting.

"Very nice," Kim said. "What is it?"

"You're the detective," his friend answered. "You tell me."

The ensign shrugged. "The basis of a holodeck program?"

Paris's eyes widened. "You're better than I thought."

Kim stroked his chin. "A holodeck program . . . to commemorate the Day of Honor. That's it, right?"

The flight controller put his arm behind him and pretended someone was twisting it. "You forced it out of me," he rasped.

The ensign nodded. "And it's a surprise?"

"Not really. B'Elanna started it. I'm just adding some finishing touches for her. You think she'll like *Fek'lhr?"*

Kim winced. "You might want to tone him down a little."

Paris swiveled the monitor back and took another look. "I think you may be onto something." He tapped out another command on the keyboard. "There we go. A little less *Fek'lhr*ish."

"Anyway," said Kim, "I came here to ask you something."

His friend was squinting as he considered his creation. "Fire away, Harry. What's on your mind?"

The ensign told him. "Actually," he explained, "it was Bandiero's idea. But it sounds like fun."

"That it does," Paris agreed. "Count me in. Just let me know when."

"Will do," said Kim, his mission accomplished. He patted the flight controller on the shoulder. "Good luck with *Fek'lsh."*

"Fek'lhr," Paris said, correcting him.

The ensign chuckled. "Whatever."

Then, leaving his friend to his Klingon enterprise, Kim turned down the corridor and headed for Neelix's quarters.

Paris arrived at the holodeck just as Lt. Carey was completing his repairs. The engineer seemed amused.

"You know," he said, "most people aren't as eager as you are. You must have really missed this thing."

"With all my heart and soul," Paris told him.

Carey snorted. "Right." Then he replaced the panel on the bulkhead. "All yours, Lieutenant."

"Thanks. I'm forever in your debt."

"Goes without saying," the engineer replied good-naturedly. Then he gathered his tools and walked away.

Paris approached the interlocking holodeck doors and said, "Institute program Torres Alpha Omicron."

The doors opened, revealing a dank, fog-laden cavern. Torches were stuffed into crevices at intervals, creating enough light for him to see where he was going. But the place needed something more.

"Let's see," Paris said. "How about some candles—the long, twisted kind? And a little more of a breeze?"

At his command, the place filled with clusters of twisted candles. Their flames wavered and smoked in the mildew-ridden breeze.

"Better," he decided.

Paris looked around. What else? The sound of *krad'dak* drums? *Abin'do* pipes? A chorus singing Klingon war songs?

That might be a little *too* much, he told himself.

But certainly, there had to be an interrogator. Visualizing the figure he had come up with—not *Fek'lhr,* in the end, but merely a large and imposing warrior—the flight controller described the character to the computer.

A moment later, the interrogator appeared. He was big, all right, and meaner looking than Paris had envisioned. But that was all right. B'Elanna wouldn't think much of him if he wasn't mean-looking.

"And give him some assistants," Paris said.

Instantly, a half-dozen warriors appeared behind the interrogator. Somehow, that seemed like too many.

"Make it just two of them," he ordered.

The computer was quick to respond. All the assistants except two disappeared.

It went on like that for some time. Little by little, Paris added to the program, drawing on his research into Klingon traditions to devise the interrogator's behavior and speech patterns.

Finally, he was done. Looking around the cavern, he nodded. "Pretty good," he announced, "even if I do say so myself."

But the real test would come when B'Elanna arrived.

CHAPTER 2

PARIS MADE SURE HE WAS WAITING OUTSIDE ENGINEERING A COUPLE OF MINutes before B'Elanna's shift was over. He just couldn't wait to show her what he'd come up with.

As the doors to engineering parted and she emerged into the corridor, she was surprised to see him. Pleasantly, the flight controller hoped, though he couldn't be entirely sure. After all, B'Elanna had that enigmatic half-frown, half-smile on her face.

"Fancy meeting you here," he said.

"Yes," B'Elanna replied, "fancy that."

"You'll never guess where I've been all day."

She looked at him. "I give up."

"In my quarters," Paris told her. "And then in the holodeck. But I think you'll agree that it was worth it."

B'Elanna sighed. "Don't tell me you were working on the Day of Honor program."

"I was working on the Day of Honor program." He held up his hand before she could respond. "Sorry. You asked me not to tell you that."

But his flip remark just covered his disappointment. Paris had come to know B'Elanna pretty well, and he could tell by her expression that she was having second thoughts about the program.

After he had worked so hard on it, too. But then, maybe he was reading too much into the look on her face.

"I'm having second thoughts about the program," B'Elanna told him.

Then again, maybe not.

"Why's that?" Paris asked.

The engineer shrugged. "I don't know. In retrospect, it seems a little . . . silly or something."

"Silly?" he echoed. "You wouldn't say that if you'd seen what I've done with it. There's nothing that's not downright solemn about this program—and I mean *nothing.*"

She considered him for a moment. "Tell you what, Tom. Let me sleep on it, okay?"

It wasn't as if Paris had a choice in the matter. "Sure. Whatever you say. I mean, it's up to you."

B'Elanna smiled. "Thanks." She patted him on the shoulder. "See you tomorrow."

Once again, he found himself standing there in a corridor as she made her getaway. Someday, he told himself, I'm going to find a way to make that woman a captive audience.

Yeah, right, he added—the day *targs* learn how to fly.

Kim picked up the three playing cards lying face down on the table and added them to the two already in his hand. Then he fanned the cards out in front of him, so he could see all five of them at a glance.

The two cards on the right were the jacks he had been dealt originally. Now, they had been joined by a deuce, a ten . . . and another jack. That gave Harry three of a kind—a pretty potent poker hand.

"All right," said Bandiero, the dark-haired man sitting across from him in *Voyager*'s echoing mess hall. He spoke without looking up from his cards. "Read 'em and weep."

Harry scanned the faces around the table. Bandiero, a lieutenant in astrophysics, was the one who had proposed the poker game in the first place. He, at least, might be a formidable opponent.

Ardan Trayl, a long-necked, green-skinned Mastikaan and a former Maquis, was new to the game. So were Neelix, the ship's Talaxian cook and unofficial morale officer, and Tuvok, its Vulcan security officer.

Or so they said.

Harry didn't expect much competition from Trayl or Neelix, at least until they learned how to play. But Tuvok was another question entirely. With his mastery of Vulcan logic, he had proven himself capable of some pretty amazing intellectual feats.

Of course, Tuvok wouldn't have a whole lot to go on, considering that all the cards in this game were dealt facedown. Theoretically, the only cards the Vulcan had seen were the eight that had passed through his hand.

Still, Harry wasn't about to underestimate Tuvok. He had seen people make that mistake in other situations and live to regret it.

Neelix, who was sitting next to the Vulcan, nudged Tuvok with his elbow. "Don't go reading my mind now, Mister Vulcan."

"You need not be concerned," Tuvok assured him, his voice free of resentment. "I cannot probe your thoughts unless I am in physical contact with you, Mr. Neelix. And even then, I would not do so without your permission."

"Kim bets," said Bandiero.

The ensign didn't want to chase anyone away. The idea was to reel the other players in slowly, getting them to increase their commitment each time, until, finally, they were too committed to turn back.

"Two replicator rations," he said. Removing two red chips from the stack in front of him, he added them to the pile in the center of the table.

Deep in contemplation of his cards, Neelix tapped his fingers on the table. Then he tapped them some more. And kept tapping them, much to the annoyance of everyone present.

"Neelix," Kim said at last.

The Talaxian looked up at him. "Yes?"

"We're waiting," the ensign reminded him.

"Ah," Neelix replied. "Sorry. I didn't mean to take so much time." Then he tapped his fingers some more.

"Neelix," said the astrophycisist.

"Hmmm?"

"We're not getting any younger."

The Talaxian glanced at him. "I'm just not sure what to do." His eyes narrowing, he picked up ten chips, one after the other. Then he jiggled them in his hand.

"That's ten chips," Harry observed. "The maximum bet is five."

Neelix looked at him. "Is that true?"

"It is what we decided at the beginning of the game," Tuvok confirmed, skillfully containing whatever impatience he may have been experiencing.

The Talaxian took a breath, then slowly let it out. "I'm going to fold," he announced finally, then slapped his cards facedown on the table.

"You fold?" Bandiero echoed incredulously.

Neelix smiled at him. "It was either that or make a bet I didn't feel right about—if you know what I mean."

Bandiero shook his head. "No, as a matter of fact, I don't." He sighed and looked at Kim.

"Obviously," the ensign told Neelix, "you haven't quite mastered that part of the game. But we'll work on it. *Later.*" After all, Harry had three jacks and he was determined to make the most of them.

Bandiero turned to Tuvok. "It's up to you, sir."

The Vulcan frowned ever so slightly. "I, too, will fold. Of all the possible combinations of five playing cards, nearly fifty-two percent of them would be superior to the hand I hold. Therefore, it would be imprudent to place additional chips at risk."

"Now that," said Neelix, "is an interesting insight."

Tuvok glanced at him almost disdainfully. "I am glad you approve."

Harry bit his lip. There were only two other players left. Please, he thought, let *somebody* take the bait.

"It's my bet?" asked Trayl, his large black eyes turning in Bandiero's direction.

"That it is," Bandiero told him.

"Very well," said the Mastikaan. "I bet five chips." Separating them from his other chips with his long, slender fingers, he pushed five chips into the pot at the center of the table.

Inwardly, Harry smiled. Things were finally beginning to go his way.

Bandiero eyed Trayl the way a fisherman eyes a prize fish. "Tell you what. I'll see your five and raise you five."

Harry took another look at the astrophysicist's expression. It was completely deadpan—as emotionless as Tuvok's. There was no way of telling whether the man had a good hand or was bluffing.

Still, the ensign had the courage of his convictions. He didn't know what his opponents had, but he doubted they could beat three jacks.

"I'll see that bet," he said, taking chips out of his pile, "and bump it five more." He moved the chips into the center, then turned to the Mastikaan. "That's ten to you."

Trayl didn't so much as flinch. He simply moved the requisite number of chips into the pot.

Bandiero chuckled and tossed his cards on the table. "So much for my bluff. I'll let you two guys fight it out."

The Mastikaan regarded Harry with his big black orbs. "I believe I've beaten you." He placed his cards on the table, face up. "I have two pair—queens and fives. And all you have is three jacks."

"Two pair doesn't beat three jacks," said the ensign. Suddenly, he realized something. "Wait a minute. I haven't shown you my cards yet. How did you know I had three jacks?"

Trayl blinked. "Simple," he replied. "I could see your cards reflected in your eyes."

Harry stared at the Mastikaan. "Ardan, you're not supposed to do that." He gestured to Tuvok. "That would be as bad as reading someone's mind."

The Mastikaan looked at him. "I wasn't cheating, Harry. Bandiero should have been more explicit when he explained the rules."

"I *was* explicit," Bandiero insisted. "Everybody knows you're not supposed to look at other people's cards. If you were, we would have played them all faceup."

Trayl frowned. "Obviously, not *everybody* knows it."

And before anyone could respond to his statement, he got up and left the mess hall. There was a moment of silence in his wake.

"Well," said the astrophysicist, "that went well."

Tuvok looked at him. "That leaves four of us, Mr. Bandiero. I believe it was you who said poker is most enjoyable with a minimum of five participants."

Bandiero shrugged. "Four can work, too."

"Listen," said Harry, "we can get someone else." He looked around the all-but-empty mess hall and tried to think of someone.

Tom had wanted to sit in. Unfortunately, he was on duty at the moment. So were the half-dozen others whose names occurred to the ensign on short notice.

He shook his head. He had heard of other ships with regularly scheduled poker games. Sometimes, several of them. Maybe it just took a while to get something like that started.

"I'm drawing a blank, too," Bandiero confessed. By then, he had begun gathering up the cards.

"How about Chell?" Neelix suggested. "He seems to be the gaming sort."

"Sure," said Harry, "when the game is *norr'tan,* or something else Bolians play. Chell already told us he wasn't interested."

Just then, the doors to the mess hall opened and two figures walked in. One was the Doctor—also known as the ship's Emergency Medical Hologram. The other was Seven of Nine.

Seven of Nine was a Borg.

Like everyone else on the ship, Harry knew she had once been a human. She had laughed, cried—done all the things humans do. But since her assimilation into the Borg collective as a child, she hadn't done any of those things.

It was creepy having her on *Voyager,* watching her walk the corridors, looking into those dead, cold eyes of hers. Still, the ensign reminded himself, there was something still alive in Seven of Nine. With a little luck, it could be brought to the surface again.

The Doctor seemed surprised to see Harry and the others sitting there. "Excuse me," he said. "I didn't think this facility would be in use."

"We are merely engaged in a game of poker," Tuvok explained. "If you require the use of the mess hall for something more important—"

"Not at all," the Doctor replied. "I was just showing Seven of Nine where the crew congregates to ingest foodstuffs. Pretty soon, she'll be doing the same thing."

"Oh?" said Bandiero, shuffling the cards in his hands.

"Yes," the Doctor replied. "I'm slowly weaning her off the energies she obtains from her cubicle and restoring her digestive system to full function. Mind you, it isn't a simple procedure—but if anyone can do it, I can."

Humility wasn't one of the Doctor's strongest qualities, Harry mused. But then, he didn't have a lot to be humble about. As an amalgam of the most gifted physicians in the Federation, he was the master of every medical technique and discipline known to man—and then some.

Suddenly, Harry had an idea. It was a little unorthodox, but he didn't want the poker game to die before it ever got started. Besides, he would be taking a step toward making an outsider an integral part of the crew.

"Say," the ensign said, "how'd you like to sit in? We could use another poker player."

The Doctor waved away the suggestion. "I'm no poker player, Mr. Kim. It's simply not part of my programming."

Harry smiled. "I could have guessed that, Doc. Actually, I was talking to Seven of Nine."

The Borg looked at him, evincing surprise—or anyway, a glitch in her otherwise detached behavior. "You wish me to take part in this . . ." She glanced at the deck of cards in Bandiero's hands. "What did you call it?"

"Poker," said the ensign. "It's a game of chance."

Seven of Nine tilted her head slightly. "And what is its purpose?"

Bandiero leaned closer to Harry. "You're barking up the wrong tree," he said. "Borg don't *play* cards. They *assimilate* them."

The ensign frowned at him. "That wasn't called for."

Bandiero didn't apologize. He just went back to shuffling the cards.

Harry turned to Seven of Nine again. "The purpose of poker—or any game—is to provide enjoyment. To take one's mind off one's work."

The Borg regarded him. "I have no work, Mr. Kim. And I do not believe I am capable of enjoyment."

"You see?" said Bandiero. "I told you you were wasting your time."

But the ensign wasn't ready to throw in the towel just yet. "You *might* be capable of enjoyment," he told Seven of Nine. "How do you know for sure until you've tried?"

"I know," said the Borg. And with that, she turned to the Doctor. "I believe you were going to show me the food preparation facilities."

The Doctor nodded. "Yes. Of course. Right this way," he said, gesturing to the cooking area.

Without waiting for him, Seven of Nine crossed the mess hall. In her wake, the Doctor turned back to Harry and shrugged. He seemed to be saying, "Even *my* manners are less reprehensible."

It was true, too. Compared to Seven of Nine, the Doctor had the social skills of a Federation ambassador.

Bandiero began doling out the cards. "The name of the game is seven-card stud. Nothing's wild." He glanced at Harry. "Except some people's imaginations. I mean . . . a Borg rubbing elbows with real, live people? What's next? Tea with the Breen?"

Harry glared at him. "Shut up, Bandiero."

He glanced at Seven of Nine as she scrutinized Neelix's cooking equipment. She showed more interest in the pots and pans than she had in Kim or his fellow poker players.

"Just shut up," he added, for good measure.

As the Doctor escorted Seven of Nine out of the mess hall, he asked her if she had any questions. He expected that, if she did, they would concern the acquisition and digestion of foodstuffs.

For once, he was wrong.

"Ensign Kim mentioned work," she said.

The Doctor looked at her. "Yes, I believe he did."

"What work does he do?" the Borg asked.

The Doctor shrugged. "Mostly, he mans the ops station on the bridge. On occasion, however, he'll help out with some project. Why?"

"As members of the collective," said Seven of Nine, "we all had specific functions. After we performed them, there was a sense of accomplishment."

"I see," the Doctor responded. "And you would like to feel that sense of accomplishment again?"

The Borg blinked. "I would, yes."

"Well," said the Doctor, "I don't see why that couldn't be arranged. I mean, there always seems to be lots to do on the ship, and too few people to do it. I'm sure another set of hands would be quite welcome."

Seven of Nine turned to him. "Where would I work?"

"I don't know," the Doctor responded. "Where would you *like* to work?"

She didn't answer. However, the Doctor could tell she was giving the matter considerable thought.

"I'll tell you what," he said, realizing this was starting to fall outside the bounds of his expertise. "Why don't I take you to Commander Chakotay?"

"Why him?" the Borg asked.

"As first officer, he takes care of the duty assignments on the ship. You can discuss with him what type of thing you're looking for, and then he can tell you what's available."

Seven of Nine thought about it. Finally, she nodded. "Yes," she said. "That would be a good idea."

CHAPTER 3

As the door ahead of him irised open with a creaky complaint, Temmis Rahmin came out onto the bridge of his people's ship. The place was stark and dreary, the only light coming from the monitors that hung above a dozen consoles along the periphery.

Still, it was functional. He was grateful for that, at least.

Nodding to the technicians standing at the consoles, Rahmin assumed his customary position in the center of the bridge. In the process, he did his best to ignore the hunger gnawing at his insides like a cruel, infinitely patient predator. After all, his comrades were just as hungry as he was, and they weren't complaining.

Fortunately, Rahmin had gotten rather good at ignoring his discomforts in the last year or so. At this point, only his memories had the power to cause him any pain.

He raised his eyes to the hexagonal viewscreen that loomed in front of him. The image on the screen flickered and jumped and fell victim to waves of static, which had gotten worse over the last several months. But in between these inconveniences, the screen gave Rahmin an adequate picture of the stars flowing by his vessel.

In his younger days, when he was part of his people's great, forward-looking push to explore the universe, he had seen the stars flow by faster. But that was a different time, before those same stars rained doom on them—a doom from which they were still struggling to recover.

Yes, Rahmin thought, a *very* different time—when they could be proud of their creations, when they could depend on them.

The maximum velocity of *this* vessel was only ten times the speed of light. Rahmin sighed. At such a speed, interstellar travel took forever. He and his crew had left their home system behind an entire year ago, and since then they had encountered only one other system.

It had afforded them little in the way of supplies. They were hoping the next one would serve them better—that it would have planets similar enough to that of their birth to provide them with food and perhaps even medicinal herbs. But by their cartographer's estimate, it would be another month before they got there.

In a month, more of them would falter. And having faltered, some would die. It was a hard fact of the life they had been forced to adopt.

Rahmin shook his head ruefully. If only their power sources hadn't diminished so quickly. If only they had had the materials and the expertise to keep their engines in good repair.

If, if, and if again. He was sick to death of *ifs.*

"Rahmin!" someone called out.

He turned and saw one of his technicians beckoning to him. Curious, Rahmin crossed the bridge to stand by the man's side.

"What is it?" he asked.

The technician, a fellow named Aruun, pointed to his monitor, which hung from the bulkhead at eye level. Following the gesture, Rahmin inspected the monitor's blue-on-black grid.

"I don't see—" he began.

Then he *did* see. In the corner of the screen, there was a tiny red blip—so tiny, in fact, he would have missed it if he hadn't been looking for it.

"A ship," he breathed.

"A ship," Aruun confirmed. "And it is not one of ours."

It was the first alien vessel they had spotted since they left the world of their birth. Rahmin swallowed. This was an important occasion—and it would require him to make an equally important decision.

He turned to Aruun. "Have you been able to gauge their speed?"

The man nodded. "They're traveling at twenty times the speed of light. If we were behind them, we would have no chance of catching up. However, our courses seem to be converging."

"So we can intercept them," Rahmin concluded.

"We can indeed," Aruun assured him.

Rahmin considered the information. By then, a crowd of technicians had begun to gather about them. Only those in charge of the piloting mechanism and life support had remained at their posts.

"Did I hear correctly?" asked a woman named Yshaarta. "Have we sighted an alien ship?"

"Yes," said Aruun. "And we can make contact with it." He turned to Rahmin, containing his excitement in deference to his superior. "That is, if Rahmin thinks it's a good idea."

Everyone looked at Rahmin. He frowned under their scrutiny. He had never expressed a desire for this kind of responsibility. But then, that was not the only burden he hadn't asked for.

"So?" asked a man named Tarrig. "What *do* you think, Rahmin?"

Rahmin took a breath, then let it out. If they established contact with the aliens, one of three things would happen. They would benefit from the association, emerge from it much as they were now . . . or be damaged, perhaps even destroyed.

On the other hand, he thought, their situation was a bad one—and it was getting worse each day. If there was ever a time to take a chance, this appeared to be that time.

Rahmin turned to their pilot, who like everyone else was looking at him. "Set a course to intercept," he commanded.

The pilot smiled and obeyed. And Rahmin hoped to heaven that his choice had been the right one.

B'Elanna was dreaming. In her dream, she was in a lecture hall at Starfleet Academy. But none of her classmates were there—only B'Elanna herself and her warp-physics instructor, Benton Horvath.

Horvath was tops in his field. B'Elanna respected him for that. Time and again, she had done her best to impress the man. But somehow, despite all her preparation, all her love for the subject, she had fallen short.

The professor's back was to her as he made some calculations on a data padd. His bald spot caught the light. Suddenly, he spoke up.

"I asked you a question, cadet."

B'Elanna knew he could only mean her. But she hadn't heard any question. Or, at least, she didn't *remember* hearing one.

"I'm sorry," she said. "Could you repeat it?"

Horvath cast a glance at her over his shoulder. A *withering* glance.

"All right, Mr. Torres. Once again, and this time I'll try to make it a bit more memorable." He cleared his throat. "Is that all right?"

B'Elanna nodded. "Yes, fine. I mean, thank you."

Horvath turned back to his padd. "All right. You're proceeding at warp 1. No remarkable engine inefficiencies, no unusual subspace hindrances. All is going according to plan. Got it?"

"Yes," said B'Elanna.

"Well, don't pat yourself on the back just yet, Mr. Torres. Back on this ship of ours, a problem arises. Something rips off one of our two nacelles. I don't care what it is, frankly—a subspace anomaly or what-have-you. The point is, the damnable thing is wrenched away. Still with me?"

"So far," she assured him.

"The question," said Horvath, "is what do you do?"

B'Elanna looked at him—or rather, at his back. "Do?" she echoed. "I mean . . . what can I *possibly* do?"

The instructor turned to her. "I asked you first. Come on, Mr. Torres. This isn't so difficult."

She shook her head. "If a nacelle falls off, different parts of the vessel end up travelling at different speeds. The ship is torn apart. There's nothing *anyone* can do about it."

Horvath smiled a wicked smile. "Isn't there? Think, Mr. Torres."

B'Elanna found her mouth was dry all of a sudden. She licked her lips. "I . . . I don't know," she whispered.

The instructor looked disgusted. "Come on," he said, his voice like a lash. "People are depending on you, Mr. Torres. Your captain is depending on you. If you can't help them, they'll all die."

The cadet grabbed her head with both hands. It was insane. Snippets of warp-field engineering lore flitted crazily through her brain, as elusive as black butterflies on Kessik IV, where she grew up.

Field formation is controllable in a fore-to-aft direction. The cumulative field-layer forces reduce the apparent mass of the vehicle and impart the required velocities. During saucer separation . . .

"The interactive warp-field controller software," B'Elanna blurted. "It alters the field geometry—"

"No!" Horvath barked. "It doesn't react quickly enough." He shook his head disdainfully. "The deckplates are shivering, Mr. Torres. The stress is unimaginable. Do something! Do it now!"

"It's impossible!" she growled. "There's nothing a person can do!"

His eyes narrowed. "You're telling me it's impossible?"

"Yes," B'Elanna grated between clenched teeth. "Impossible!"

Horvath's mouth twisted. "You'll never be an engineer in *this* fleet with an attitude like that! You're a quitter, Mr. Torres! A quitter!"

"No!" she screamed. "No! N—"

Suddenly, B'Elanna found herself in her bedroom. She was sitting upright in the darkness, covered in cold sweat, her heart banging against her ribs so hard it hurt.

It was a dream. Only a dream, for godsakes. And, she told herself, you were absolutely right. There's nothing you can do if a nacelle tears off—except try to make your last thought a happy one.

Benton Horvath was a bastard, but he would never have asked her a question like that. Not in real life. Only in an irritating, soul-scouring gut-wrencher of a dream.

B'Elanna took a breath and let it out. Suddenly, a strange feeling crept up on her—a feeling that she had forgotten something important.

"Computer," she asked, "what time is it?"

"It's seven forty-five a.m.," the computer told her.

B'Elanna cursed beneath her breath. Seven forty-five? She was due to conduct a fuel-cell overhaul in engineering in fifteen minutes. How would it look if the chief engineer was late for something like that?

Somehow, she realized, she had forgotten to give the computer a wake-up command. But how? She *always* gave the computer a wake-up command. Of all nights to slip up, she thought.

Then B'Elanna remembered. It was the Day of Honor.

No, she thought. Don't say it. Don't even think it. You've shaken your Day of Honor luck.

From now on, she reminded herself, only *good* things are going to happen on this day. You'll see, she insisted. Only good things.

Except, apparently, bad dreams. And forgotten wake-up calls.

Putting both those things out of her mind, B'Elanna tossed her covers aside, swung her legs out of bed, and padded into the bathroom, where she manipulated the controls on the side of the sonic shower stall. When she heard the emitter heads begin to hum, she stepped inside.

If she hurried, B'Elanna told herself, she could still make the cell overhaul. A minute in the shower, another minute to pull on her uniform, and maybe three more minutes for breakfast. That would leave her as many as ten minutes to reach engineering.

It could happen. It *would* happen.

B'Elanna had built up her resolve to a fever pitch when she heard the emitter heads sputter. Huh, she thought. That's strange. Suddenly, they let out a shriek so loud and so grating she thought her eardrums would burst.

"Damn!" she yelped, leaping out of the shower stall.

The emitter heads continued to shriek, undaunted by the glare B'Elanna was leveling at them. All over the galaxy, she imagined, animals were hearing the sound and going nuts.

So was she—but for an entirely different reason. After all, she was standing in the middle of the bathroom without her clothes, no cleaner than she had been a minute ago.

Worse, B'Elanna couldn't let the shower keep screeching like that. Aside from the discomfort it would cause her neighbors, the mechanism could build up a feedback loop. Then every EPS relay in the corridor would have to be reset—or, if luck went against them, replaced.

The Klingon in her wanted to rip the shower out of the wall. Fortunately, that Klingon had human company.

Still naked, teeth grating against the noise, B'Elanna knelt and removed the cover from the relay next to the shower. It wasn't a difficult task, but it *was* one that couldn't be rushed.

Then, without benefit of the tools one usually used for something like this, she cut off power to the shower unit. As suddenly as it had begun, the shrieking stopped.

It was quiet in the bathroom. Unnaturally quiet—except for the ringing in B'Elanna's ears.

Unfortunately, she had used up not only her shower time, but her breakfast time as well. And unless she got a move on, she wouldn't have time to get dressed either. Muttering beneath her breath, she went back into her bedroom and opened the door to her closet.

Picking out one of the uniforms she found hanging there, she pulled it on as quickly as she could. Then she bolted for the door, unnerved, unshowered, and unfed.

And even with all that, there was no guarantee she would make it to engineering in time.

CHAPTER 4

CHAKOTAY FOUND SEVEN OF NINE STANDING IN HER BORG CUBICLE. IT chilled him a little every time he saw the thing, in that it was a remnant of the ship's transformation.

As the first officer approached the cubicle, Seven of Nine noticed him and stepped down. "Commander Chakotay," she said.

"I understand you wanted to see me."

"I am told you are the officer in charge of personnel," said the Borg. "That you prepare the 'duty assignments.' Is that the correct phrase?"

"That's right," he replied.

But inside, he was wondering why Seven of Nine was suddenly interested in duty assignments. Unless . . .

The Borg blinked. "I'm finding it difficult to spend so much time alone," she said. "I'm unaccustomed to it. The hours don't pass quickly."

Chakotay couldn't help but sympathize. He knew how great a loss it had been for Seven of Nine when she was disconnected from the Borg collective.

"Also," she said, "I had a sense of accomplishment among the Borg. I wish to experience that sense again."

"I can understand that," Chakotay said. "How can we help?"

But even before the Borg opened her mouth, he had an idea what her answer would be.

"I have been considering the matter carefully," Seven of Nine told him. "I would like to request a duty assignment."

It was just what the first officer had expected. He mulled over the ramifications before he spoke again.

"Did you have something specific in mind?" he asked.

The Borg blinked. "Yes."

Then she told Chakotay what it was.

He sighed. Why couldn't she have asked to help Neelix in the mess hall? Or to take a shift in astrophysics?

"I'll see what I can do," he told Seven of Nine.

The corridor outside the turbolift was empty except for B'Elanna. Abandoning any pretense of decorum, she sprinted down the hall as if the devil and all his demons were after her.

That is, she thought wildly, the devil of my father's people. Klingons didn't really have such a thing.

As B'Elanna approached the doors to engineering, she had to decelerate to give the metal panels time to slide aside for her. Naturally, they did this with the most agonizing slowness. Then, with what she estimated as seconds to spare, the lieutenant burst into engineering.

As she stood there, illuminated by the brightly pulsating warp core, she wondered where everyone was. Instead of the four engineers she had expected to see, only two were present—Carey and Vorik. Both of them were sitting at consoles, performing diagnostics in accordance with standing orders.

Carey looked up at her. "Ah. Morning, Lieutenant." After a moment, his brow furrowed. "Say . . . are you all right?"

"Fine." B'Elanna breathed. "Why?"

The redheaded man shrugged. "You seem to be perspiring. I thought it might be a symptom."

She returned his stare. "A symptom of what, Mr. Carey?"

He shrugged again. "You know, the thing that's got Nicoletti and Chafin under the weather." Suddenly, understanding dawned. "Wait a minute. You don't know about Nicoletti and Chafin, do you?"

B'Elanna shook her head. "No."

"They are ill," Vorik interjected. He swiveled his chair around to face his superior. "The Doctor informed us a moment ago."

Annoyed, B'Elanna tapped her commbadge. "Torres to sickbay. Are you there, Doctor?"

"Indeed," came the response from the ship's "physician"—actually, a holographic manifestation of the Emergency Medical Program. "If you're concerned about Nicoletti and Chafin, don't be. They have a simple virus, for which I possess a simple cure. In four or five hours, they should be as good as new."

"In four or five hours," B'Elanna echoed.

"That's correct," said the Doctor. "Now, if there's nothing else, Lieutenant, I'll finish up with my patients."

"Go ahead," said the chief engineer. She turned to Vorik, then Carey, and realized she'd acted like a complete madwoman for nothing. "I suppose it's silly to overhaul the fuel cells when half the shift is absent."

"It would seem so," Vorik agreed.

B'Elanna sighed. "Let's do it tomorrow, then. I'll notify Nicoletti and Chafin. And while I'm at it, I'll remind them that I'm to be notified *personally* whenever they're sick."

"Whatever you say," Carey told her.

Abruptly, a throaty yet eminently feminine voice cut into their conversation. "Janeway to Lieutenant Torres."

B'Elanna looked up at the intercom grid hidden in the ceiling. "Torres here. What can I do for you, Captain?"

"Harry's having some trouble with his console," Janeway told her. "Can you send someone up here to take a look at it?"

"Right away," the chief engineer replied.

"Thanks," said the captain. "Janeway out."

"I've fixed that console before," Carey noted. "I think I know what might be wrong with it."

B'Elanna nodded. "Go to it."

In one motion, Carey got up and headed for the exit. A moment later, he was gone, on his way to the bridge.

She turned to Vorik. "How are the diagnostics going?"

"I have not detected any problems or anomalies," the Vulcan responded. "All systems appear to be functioning within acceptable parameters."

B'Elanna nodded. "Good." Maybe this day would turn out to be a decent one after all, despite its hectic start.

She had barely completed the thought when she heard something pop. Before she could turn to find the origin of the sound, she heard another one—a high-pitched hissing.

Then B'Elanna saw the reason for it. A conduit was leaking plasma coolant. The gas was coming out in a sizzling, white jet.

She glanced at Vorik. The Vulcan was working at his console, trying to determine what had happened.

"Now what?" B'Elanna asked.

Vorik turned to her, chagrined. "It seems there has been a rupture in the coolant injector."

"I can see that," she told him. "Why haven't you sealed it off?"

"I am attempting to do so," he replied.

But he wasn't having much luck. B'Elanna darted to the nearest workstation to see why.

In the second or two it took her to get there, the problem got worse—a lot worse. By the time she brought up the coolant system on her screen, the tiny stream of gas had turned into a geyser.

So much for diagnostics, B'Elanna thought bitterly.

If this went on, engineering would become uninhabitable. Worse, a whole range of operating systems would be compromised.

Ergo, it *couldn't* go on. B'Elanna held on to that thought as she worked furiously at her console. Unfortunately, though she had pinpointed the leak, she couldn't seem to stop it any better than the Vulcan could.

Then she realized why. There was a point farther up the line where coolant pressure had built past the breaking point. If she was going to stop the leak, she would have to take care of the pressure problem first.

"I am having difficulty identifying the cause of the leak," Vorik reported. He was bent over his monitor, eyes narrowed with concentration.

"So am I," she told him.

Suddenly, B'Elanna's workstation seized up. As she had feared, the leak was starting to affect other systems in the vicinity.

Cursing beneath her breath, she tried another workstation—and got the same results. In other words, nothing. And though she tried not to breathe in the coolant, it was already starting to make her head throb.

B'Elanna checked out a third workstation and a fourth before she found one that was still functioning. This time, she didn't try to locate the problem—she just reacted to it. If she cut off every possible source of the gas, she would eventually stem the tide.

At least, that was her strategy. Desperately, she ran her strong, slender fingers over her padd, shutting down access point after access point. All around engineering, conduits were closing up, containing the gas that flowed through them.

But it didn't seem to be working. The leak wasn't abating—and B'Elanna was swiftly running out of possibilities.

She bit her lip. Think, she told herself. Where else can this damned gas be coming from?

The EPS manifold? It seemed unlikely, but . . .

"Try shutting off the EPS manifold," she called over the hiss of the escaping coolant. "Maybe that'll help."

Vorik did as she suggested. It didn't diminish the stream of coolant one iota. "The EPS manifold is not the problem," the Vulcan told her.

"I don't get it," B'Elanna rasped.

Vorik looked at her, his brow wrinkling ever so slightly. "Is it possible the pressure is coming from . . . the field coils?"

She considered the possibility. "No," she decided finally. "But let's give it a try anyway."

Vorik tapped out a command on his console—then shook his head. Obviously, thought B'Elanna, the thing had stopped working.

She tried the same thing at her own station. Nothing happened. Pounding on it savagely, she watched the Vulcan dart across engineering and plant himself at another station.

Let this one work, B'Elanna pleaded inwardly.

It *did.*

Vorik worked with a sense of urgency B'Elanna had seldom seen in a being of any species. A moment later, the stream of plasma coolant began to decrease noticeably in volume.

"That's better," B'Elanna cried out. "Close it down completely."

Vorik worked some more. The jet of escaping gas diminished by degrees, until it stopped altogether. Silence reigned in engineering, punctuated only by the subtle throbbing of the warp core.

B'Elanna took a deep breath. Another crisis averted, she thought. She glanced at Vorik, who was still standing over his console.

"Good work, Ensign."

The Vulcan met her gaze. "Perhaps it would be advisable to reconfigure the coolant assembly. That would give us greater control over pressure valve emissions in the future."

B'Elanna felt herself sagging a little. "Vorik," she said, "you're probably right. And tomorrow we can do it first thing. But not today."

The Vulcan looked puzzled. She didn't blame him.

"I do not understand," he said. "Why wait until tomorrow when it would be to our advantage to start—"

"Not today," B'Elanna barked, surprising even herself with the ferocity in her voice.

Vorik lifted an eyebrow at her vehemence. But wisely, he didn't question her judgment.

"As you wish," he replied.

Then he turned and moved toward a more distant workstation. B'Elanna watched him go, more than a little angry with herself. Vorik had deserved better from his superior officer—especially after he'd come through for her in the clutch.

But before she could go after the Vulcan, she saw Tom enter engineering. He had a padd in his hands. And he was more cheerful than usual, though the reason for it wasn't readily apparent.

"Good morning," he said. "Here's the conn evaluation you wanted."

B'Elanna regarded him. "Thanks."

Tom took note of her sullen mood. Sensing something was awry, he looked around and noted the hole in the coolant conduit. Then he sniffed the ozone in the air. His nose wrinkled.

"Something happen in here?" he inquired.

"Don't ask," she told him.

Tom chuckled. "But—"

"I said don't ask."

The flight controller regarded her for a moment. When he spoke again, it was with a bit more care. "We still on for dinner tonight?"

B'Elanna frowned and looked away. "I don't know. I may have to work." She shrugged. "I'll let you know."

Tom nodded. "Okay . . . " He hesitated, obviously not sure whether to raise the next subject or not. "And have you decided if you're, uh, going through with it? The Day of Honor program, I mean?"

She turned on him. "I have—and I'm not. This has started out to be a lousy day and the last thing I need is to get involved with some obscure Klingon ritual. Okay?"

He held his hand up as if in self-defense. "Hey, it's all the same to me. You were the one who suggested it."

"I know," the engineer said. "And for one sentimental minute, I thought I might go through with it. But not anymore."

Tom cracked a smile. "Of course not. Wouldn't want to get too sentimental, would we?"

B'Elanna realized that she was being unfair with him—just as she had been unfair with Vorik a moment earlier.

"Look, she said, "it hasn't exactly been the most pleasant morning of my life. First, I overslept because I forgot to tell the computer to wake me. Then the acoustic inverter in my sonic shower blew out."

Tom cringed. "That'll make your hair stand on end."

"So I didn't have time for breakfast," B'Elanna went on. "And when I got here, two people were out sick and I had to cancel the fuel-cell overhaul, and then an injector burst for no reason at all and started spewing plasma coolant over everything."

Tom grunted. "That's a run of bad luck, all right."

"So I'm in a bad mood," she told him. "And I know I'm being a little testy, and I apologize in advance . . . but I'm not very good company right now."

He didn't try to talk her out of her mood. He just smiled affably and headed for the door.

"It's okay," Tom said. "Think about that dinner . . ."

But he looked back at her for a moment. And when he did, their eyes locked, and B'Elanna found herself grateful for his understanding.

"Thanks," she said.

"It's okay," Tom assured her. "I've had bad days, too."

With that, he left her. But as he walked out of engineering, Commander Chakotay walked in.

"Morning, Commander," said Tom.

Chakotay nodded to him. "Lieutenant."

Then, in a voice just loud enough for B'Elanna to hear, the flight controller said, "Be careful."

The first officer glanced at him as he passed.

Crossing engineering, Chakotay approached B'Elanna.

Abruptly, the first officer's nose scrunched up. He looked around—and his gaze fell on the damaged conduit. Then he turned back to B'Elanna.

"Something happen in here?"

"It's under control," she told him.

Chakotay's eyes went hard for a moment. When he asked a question, he liked it answered—accurately and completely. B'Elanna knew that. After all, she was serving under him before either of them had heard of *Voyager.*

But over the years, the first officer had gotten used to B'Elanna's flares of temper. He had come to understand her. And at that moment, he obviously realized all was not well with her.

Instead of taking umbrage at her response, he smiled. "That's good," he said. "I'm glad."

B'Elanna sighed. "You came here for a reason, I imagine."

Chakotay shrugged. "What makes you think I haven't stopped by just to say hello?"

The engineer was in no mood for games. She was about to say so, but thought better of it. Instead, she bent over a workstation and checked to see if it was functional again.

Another executive officer might have interpreted that as insubordination. Chakotay knew her better than that.

"Actually," he conceded, "you're right. I came to tell you that something interesting just happened."

"And what's that?" the engineer asked absently.

"Seven of Nine requested a duty assignment."

"Fascinating," B'Elanna responded.

"You don't know the half of it," the commander told her. "She wants to work in engineering."

B'Elanna whirled to face the first officer. In her fury, "What?" was all she could get out.

"As you know," he said reasonably, "the Borg use transwarp conduits to travel through space faster than warp speed. If we could create one of these conduits for our *own* use—"

"We don't know anything about transwarp technology," B'Elanna snapped. "Playing around with it could be dangerous."

"That's where Seven of Nine comes in," Chakotay countered. "She's offered to work with you. To make sure nothing goes wrong."

"And you *believe* her?" the engineer asked. "She's a Borg. Who knows what her real motives might be?"

"As a matter of fact," the commander said, "I *do* believe her. She's having a tough time making the transition from the collective. She wants something to occupy her mind. Something to make her feel useful."

B'Elanna flashed him a scornful look. "I never thought of you as naive, Chakotay. The Delta Quadrant has turned you soft." She bit her lip. "The bottom line is I don't want her working here in engineering."

The commander's expression hardened again. His eyes became chips of obsidian. "The bottom line," he told her, "is I'm giving you an order and you're going to follow it . . . *Lieutenant.*"

They glared at each other for a moment, neither of them eager to give ground. B'Elanna wanted to rage at Chakotay, but she held her emotions in check—because, patient as he was, even *he* had his limits.

Finally, she replied, "Whatever you say, sir."

The commander didn't seem altogether satisfied with that response—but he accepted it. Turning, he left engineering.

B'Elanna looked after him, angry and resentful. She had been in a bad mood before Chakotay arrived. Now, it was positively foul.

Returning her attention to her workstation, she assessed the damage to operating protocols caused by the coolant leak. Then, her jaw clenched, she set about repairing it.

CHAPTER 5

JANEWAY WAS SITTING BEHIND THE DESK IN HER READY ROOM, GOING OVER supply reports, when she heard a chime.

"Come in," she said.

As the doors slid aside, they revealed her first officer. Chakotay wasn't smiling as he entered.

Not a good sign, the captain thought. But then, she hadn't expected Chakotay to come back from engineering with a grin on his face. Pushing back her chair and getting to her feet, she gestured to the window seat in front of her observation port.

Her exec accepted the seat. A moment later, Janeway came around her desk and sat beside him.

"Not the easiest thing you've ever had to tell her?" the captain asked.

Chakotay grunted softly. "B'Elanna wasn't happy about the idea."

"But she'll get over it," the captain suggested.

He nodded. "Yes, she will."

Janeway stood again, stretching out the kinks in her neck. "Unfortunately, B'Elanna isn't the only member of the crew who's uncomfortable with the idea of a Borg on the ship."

Chakotay frowned. "I'm afraid Seven of Nine doesn't help her own case. She tends to put people off because she's so direct. So—"

"Honest," said the captain.

The commander nodded again. "That's one word for it."

Janeway smiled sympathetically. "I know. That's what I like about her. Her directness. Her honesty."

"But," Chakotay pointed out, "she still doesn't have any real perspective on what it is to be human."

"And that's the challenge," the captain replied, warming to the subject. "To help ease her back into humanity."

Chakotay smiled. "To make her comfortable among us."

"Exactly. That's the only way she'll be able to rejoin the world she was born into. The human world. I think it's a good sign that she wants a duty assignment. She's taking a step toward us."

Her exec grunted. "No argument there."

Janeway thought for a moment. "I need to speak with Seven of Nine. Give her the lay of the land, as it were. After all, in the collective, no one person was in charge. She's never encountered a chain of command before."

"I'll tell her you want to speak with her," said Chakotay.

The captain nodded. "Please do."

Tuvok glanced at his tactical board, where one of the monitors showed that there had been a release of plasma coolant in engineering. Since neither Captain Janeway nor Commander Chakotay was on the bridge, the Vulcan contacted the individual in charge of that section directly.

"Tuvok to Lieutenant Torres. Please respond."

There was silence for a moment. Then Torres said, "I'm here, Tuvok. And if you're going to ask me about the coolant release . . . *don't.* It's over, all right? Let's leave it at that."

With that, she terminated the intraship communication. The Vulcan cocked an eyebrow. Such a reply was unusual, even for such a volatile personality as the chief engineer's.

What was *not* unusual was the incident Torres had described as "over." As *Voyager*'s tactical officer, Tuvok had gotten used to the occurrence of minor systems dysfunctions. In fact, he had come to expect them.

After all, *Voyager* wasn't like other starships. She wasn't able to put into drydock for an overhaul every so often, the nearest starbase being decades away at high warp.

As a result, the ship and her crew were forced to face each problem as it arose, and handle it as best they could. In most cases, that meant a considerable amount of improvisation.

It was a tribute to the ingenuity and dedication of Captain Janeway and her operations staff that they had met each new challenge and surmounted it. In fact, it stirred a certain amount of pride in Tuvok to be associated with such capable people.

Not that he would ever tell them that to their faces. He was a Vulcan, and his species didn't indulge in displays of emotion.

Returning his attention to his monitors, Tuvok initiated a long-range scan. After all, it was the lieutenant's job to scan for external occurrences as well as internal ones.

As Seven of Nine entered the captain's ready room, Janeway turned away from her observation port. "Thank you for coming," she said.

The Borg didn't answer. She just stood there in the center of the room, awaiting the captain's next remark.

"I understand you want to work in engineering," Janeway noted.

"That's correct," Seven of Nine replied.

"Engineering is a sensitive area."

The Borg looked at her. "Sensitive?"

"Important," the captain explained, "in the sense that a . . . mistake there could cause a great deal of damage."

Seven of Nine blinked. "I can see how that would be so."

Janeway decided to quit beating around the bush. "You told me you wouldn't make any more attempts to contact the Borg . . . and, of course, I want to believe that's true."

"I assure you it is," said Seven of Nine.

The captain regarded her. Janeway's instincts told her the Borg was on the level, and her instincts were usually right.

"I've decided not to post a security detail while you're in engineering, Seven of Nine. But you have to realize, there are rules. You'll be expected to follow our protocols."

The Borg nodded. "I will do so."

Janeway believed she would, too. "You'll report directly to Lieutenant Torres and obey any order she gives you."

"I understand," said Seven of Nine.

The captain shifted gears. "One more thing. Your 'designation'—Seven of Nine. It's a little cumbersome. Wouldn't you prefer to be called by your given name, Annika?"

The Borg seemed vaguely troubled by the prospect—as if she felt things were moving a little too fast. "I have been Seven of Nine for as long as I can remember," she responded.

Mindful that too much change could be threatening, Janeway looked for a compromise. "All right. But maybe we could streamline it a little. How would you feel about . . . Seven?"

The Borg considered it. "Imprecise," she decided. "But acceptable."

Abruptly, a familiar voice filled the room. "Tuvok to Captain Janeway."

"I'm here," the captain answered.

"Please come to the bridge," the Vulcan requested in his clipped, efficient tone. "A ship is approaching."

Janeway looked at Seven of Nine. The Borg looked back.

Curious, the captain led the way out onto *Voyager's* small but efficient bridge, where Chakotay was waiting for her. Janeway's eyes were drawn instinctively to the forward viewscreen.

She saw the image of a small alien ship there. Clearly, the vessel had seen better days. Its exterior hull looked worn in spots, and some of the devices that projected from it were slightly bent.

The captain turned to Tuvok, seeking whatever information he could provide. "Report," she said.

"The vessel is damaged but still functional," the Vulcan informed her, intent on his readouts. "Energy emissions are so low it probably isn't capable of warp speed. However, sensors show several dozen lifesigns aboard." He paused. "We're being hailed, Captain."

"Open a channel," she told him.

Tuvok complied. A moment later, the face of a wizened, thin, and sickly being appeared on the screen.

The being's skin was a pale green, his eyes a deeper shade of the same color—though they lacked luster. His only other remarkable feature was the hard-looking ridge that ran back from the bridge of his nose through the middle of his scalp.

His ship's interior seemed stark, devoid of any and all amenities. Energy seemed to be in short supply as well, if the lights flickering behind him were any indication.

Janeway lifted her chin. "I'm Captain Kathryn Janeway of the Federation starship *Voyager.*"

The being on the viewscreen nodded. "I am Rahmin. My people are the Caatati." He glanced at his surroundings. "I apologize for our appearance, and for the condition of our ship. We were assimilated by the Borg over a year ago. We lost . . . everything."

Everything, the captain thought. There was a world of pain in the word. It seemed the devastation created by the Borg was everywhere.

Reminded of Seven of Nine, she glanced over her shoulder. The Borg was standing off to the side, where Rahmin couldn't see her. Just as well, Janeway thought, as she turned back to the Caatati.

"How many of you escaped?" she asked.

Rahmin sighed. "A few thousand, on thirty ships. All that's left from a planet of millions."

Chakotay winced. The captain, too, felt a pang of empathy for these people. "I'm sorry," she said earnestly.

Rahmin seemed uncomfortable with the response. He shifted his weight from one foot to the other.

"Captain," he replied, "I want to assure you of something. My people were once proud and accomplished. Before the Borg came, we had enjoyed peace for centuries. We pursued scientific inquiry . . . produced art and literature." He shook his head. "We weren't always in such reduced circumstances."

Janeway nodded. "I understand."

"It pains me to have to ask this," Rahmin said. "But I have eighty-eight people to care for on this vessel. If we are to survive much longer, we need food . . . medicines. Is there any way you could help us?"

Clearly, Rahmin was a proud man, and it was difficult for him to make the request. Janeway didn't want to make it any harder on him.

"Of course," she told the alien. "Send us a list of your needs and we'll see what we can do."

Rahmin smiled at the captain, though his expression was only a faint echo of her own. "I'm deeply grateful," he said. "If it's not too much to ask . . . is there any way you might also spare a small quantity of thorium isotopes? Without it, our systems can't function."

"I think we can arrange that," Janeway responded. "I'll speak to my chief engineer, B'Elanna Torres."

Rahmin looked as if a weight had been lifted from him. "You can't imagine what this means to us, Captain. Thank you."

And with that, his image blinked out, giving way to that of his vessel.

Janeway looked to the intercom grid in the ceiling. "Bridge to engineering," she said.

B'Elanna was working at a console in engineering, making sure there were no further pressure buildups in the coolant lines, when she noticed a flashing symbol in the corner of her screen. It was a sign that sensor information or other important data was being relayed to her by a bridge officer.

Tapping her keyboard, she accepted the data. An image showed up on her monitor—that of a thin, sickly-looking alien in a dim, almost featureless environment. He was in the middle of a sentence.

" . . . assimilated by the Borg over a year ago," the alien related, his voice taut with pain. "We lost everything."

B'Elanna heard the captain ask for details, and she heard the alien supply them. But she was no longer looking at her monitor—not really. The engineer was thinking about Seven of Nine.

After all, that Borg may have been on the vessel that attacked the alien's people. She may have aided in the devastation of the alien's homeworld. And if she hadn't, she had no doubt done the same thing elsewhere.

Seven of Nine was a Borg, a cold-blooded killer. How was it so easy for people to forget that?

Focusing on her monitor again, B'Elanna followed the rest of the captain's conversation with the alien. She learned what kind of race the Borg had assimilated and nearly destroyed—a proud and accomplished one.

"It pains me to have to ask this," the alien said, "but I have eighty-eight people to care for. If we are to survive much longer, we need food . . . medicines. Is there any way you could help us?"

Janeway assured him that she would do so. Then the alien made another request—this time, for thorium isotopes. The captain said she would have to speak to her chief engineer first.

The alien thanked her. A moment later, his image vanished, replaced by a view of his ship. B'Elanna shuddered at the sight of it. It was a wonder it still functioned.

Then, as she had expected, she received a call from Janeway on the intercom. "Bridge to engineering."

B'Elanna looked up at the ceiling. "Torres here." And to save time: "I'm aware of what's going on, Captain."

"Good," said Janeway. "Then you know I'd like to help the Caatati in any way we can. Can you and your people come up with the isotopes Rahmin requested?"

B'Elanna thought for a moment. "It might take us a while to modify the intermix ratio to produce thorium, but we should be able to work it out."

"Keep me informed," the captain told her.

B'Elanna assured her that she would do that. Then, glad for the chance to do something productive before the day was over, she got to work.

CHAPTER 6

JANEWAY SAT AT THE HEAD OF THE TABLE IN *VOYAGER'S* BRIEFING ROOM AND watched Rahmin stare at the unblinking stars. The Caatati's expression was a decidedly wistful one.

"They seem so much friendlier here," he remarked.

"The stars?" she asked.

Rahmin nodded, his eyes glinting with reflections of their light. "I'd forgotten how beautiful they can be. The last year or so, they've been my enemies—always dancing out of my reach, reminding me how far I must go to bring comfort to my people."

"This may surprise you," said the captain, "but I thought of them that way, too, for a little while."

He turned to her. "You did?"

"Yes. You see, my crew and I are more than seventy thousand light-years from our home galaxy."

He looked at her, barely able to wrap his mind around such a distance. "How did you come to stray so far?"

"It's a long story," she told him. "Suffice it to say we didn't come here of our own free will. And when we realized how long it would take us to get back, we were daunted—to say the least."

Rahmin grunted softly. "I'm not surprised."

"But in time," Janeway said, "we realized an opportunity had been set before us. We were in a part of the universe that had never been explored by our people. We had a chance to see phenomena, life-forms and civilizations that none of our people had ever seen before."

The Caatati smiled. "A chance to explore."

"That's right," she said. "And that's when the stars stopped looking like our enemies."

Rahmin glanced again at the points of light in the darkness. "Perhaps that will happen some day for the Caatati as well. It would be a pleasant change, I assure you."

"Captain?" came a voice over the intercom.

"Janeway here. What is it, B'Elanna?"

"A small problem," the engineer reported. "One of the impulse engines has developed a variance in its driver-coil assembly. I'm going to have to shut it down until I can make adjustments."

Janeway frowned. That was a two-man job, and only B'Elanna and Lt. Carey had the expertise to do it quickly.

"So there'll be a delay in the thorium project," the captain concluded.

"I'm afraid so. I'll put Vorik on it, but as you know, he's had no experience with isotope generation."

"Acknowledged," Janeway told her. "We'll sit tight."

Rahmin's face was a silent question. Obviously, he was concerned about the delay, perhaps even to the point of wondering if the isotopes would be generated at all.

"Don't worry," the captain told him. "We'll produce those isotopes for you. It's just a matter of time."

The Caatati seemed to accept that. But then, Janeway remarked inwardly, it wasn't as if he was likely to find a *better* offer.

B'Elanna headed back to engineering with a certain amount of impatience. Her companion seemed to notice it.

"Eager to get back?" Carey asked.

"Damned right," she told him.

After all, B'Elanna had promised the captain that thorium for the Caatati. Having to deal with the variance in the driver coil had been an annoyance she could have lived without.

Fortunately, the driver-coil problem had turned out to be less complicated than B'Elanna expected. She and Carey had finished the job in a little under an hour.

Now, she thought, she could devote her full attention to the thorium project—unless something else went wrong. And considering what day it was, she wasn't ruling anything out.

A moment later, B'Elanna walked into engineering. As she looked around, she noticed Seven of Nine standing off to the side. Though she might have been standing there for a while, the Borg looked unperturbed.

Something stiffened in the lieutenant. After all, this was *her* place, and had been for the last few years. She didn't appreciate intruders in engineering—especially the kind that had murdered and assimilated their way through the galaxy.

Since Chakotay had pulled rank on her, B'Elanna had no choice but to let Seven of Nine work there. But she didn't have to like it.

If the Borg had any idea of how her superior felt about her, she didn't show it. Approaching the lieutenant, she said, "I am reporting for duty." Her face was a mask of equanimity.

How lovely for you, B'Elanna thought. But what she said was, "Commander Chakotay told me to expect you."

"Where may I work?" asked Seven of Nine.

Somewhere out of my sight, B'Elanna mused. But she didn't say *that* out loud either. Besides, engineering wasn't big enough for the Borg to conceal herself very well.

B'Elanna jerked a thumb at one of the consoles on the other side of the room—as far from her own console as possible. "That'll be your workstation," she told Seven of Nine. "You can conduct your computations there to your heart's content."

The Borg hesitated a moment, obviously unfamiliar with the expression. Still, she must have gotten the gist of it, because she didn't ask any more questions. She simply made her way to the workstation.

As B'Elanna watched, Seven of Nine inspected the console. Then she tapped out a few commands on its keypadd. Her eyes moved in tandem with the data scrolling across the screen.

At least she's obedient, B'Elanna mused. She may be sabotaging the ship, but she's doing it politely.

Suddenly, the Borg looked up and saw the engineer staring at her. "This will be satisfactory," she said.

"Good," said B'Elanna. "If you're happy, I'm happy."

Her sarcasm was apparently lost on Seven of Nine. The Borg had no reaction that the lieutenant could discern. She just turned back to her screen and began to make her calculations.

The engineer shook her head. Then, forgetting about the Borg for the moment, she approached Vorik. He was working at his usual console.

"How are those thorium isotopes coming?" she asked.

The Vulcan stopped to look at her. He didn't look happy. "I will admit I am having trouble, Lieutenant."

"What sort of trouble?"

"Controlling the neutron absorption," he said.

B'Elanna pondered the problem. "Try increasing the temperature of the plasma above the neutron-activation threshold. That ought to help."

Vorik's brow creased as he considered his superior's approach. "Yes. I can see how it would."

She smiled. "Let's get that thorium to the captain as soon as it's ready."

The Vulcan nodded. "I will do that."

Leaving him to his labors, B'Elanna moved to the next workstation and then the one after that, seeing if there were any other difficulties that had arisen in her absence. There weren't.

Finally, she approached Seven of Nine. After all, the Borg was engaged in a project of particular interest to the captain. If she was approaching some aspect of the problem the wrong way, B'Elanna couldn't just let her flounder. She would have to set her on the right path again, just as she would do with anyone else in her section.

"How's it going?" she asked Seven of Nine, trying to keep the rancor out of her voice.

The Borg looked at her with that empty expression of hers. "I am doing well," she responded.

Her tone was matter-of-fact, almost devoid of inflection. There was something about it that grated badly on B'Elanna's nerves—something that made her want to wring some emotion out of Seven of Nine.

"I'm glad to hear it," the engineer replied. She sized the Borg up. "Tell me something, Seven of Nine."

"Of course."

B'Elanna knew she shouldn't be asking the question. She asked it anyway. "When you hear about people like the Caatati, a race that was all but destroyed by the Borg . . . do you have any feelings of remorse? Do you regret what you did to them?"

Seven of Nine's eyes seemed to lose their focus for a moment. She seemed to be searching for the appropriate response.

Finally, she came up with one. "No."

B'Elanna eyed her. She wasn't sure what kind of answer she had expected, but that wasn't it. "That's it? Just . . . 'no'?"

Seven of Nine regarded her with that cold, distant gaze of hers. "What further answer do you require?"

The engineer stared at the Borg. "Oh, maybe some kind of acknowledgment of the billions of lives you've helped to destroy . . . a justification for what you did." She shook her head. "Maybe a little sense of guilt . . . "

"Guilt is irrelevant," Seven of Nine told her.

B'Elanna frowned. "Heartwarming."

The Borg regarded her. "An animal in the wild doesn't feel remorse for slaughtering its kill."

B'Elanna could feel the vitriol rising within her. "That's about what I'd expect from an unfeeling machine."

Seven of Nine was neither hurt nor offended . . . nor anything else. Completely unmoved, she gestured to indicate her console. "I have set up the parameters for the tachyon burst we'll need to create a transwarp conduit."

The lieutenant grunted. The Borg was fast, she'd give her that.

Seven of Nine went on. "It will be several hours before the main deflector can be modified accordingly. I think it would be best if I waited in my alcove in the meantime."

B'Elanna nodded. That was the best idea she'd heard yet. "I think you're right," she told the Borg.

Seven of Nine turned and headed for the exit. The sliding doors parted and then closed behind her, leaving B'Elanna alone with her feelings.

The most immediate one was regret. After all, the captain had taken Seven of Nine under her wing. She had tried to make the Borg feel comfortable on *Voyager,* tried to help her remember what it was like to be human.

Not that B'Elanna agreed with any of that. As far as she was concerned, a Borg was a Borg was a Borg. But it wasn't her place to try to goad Seven of Nine into a confrontation.

What the hell was I thinking? the lieutenant asked herself. I'm not a brat with a chip on her shoulder any longer. I'm a professional. I should be able to control my emotions.

Next time, she promised herself, she would do a damned sight better—even if she had to have herself gagged and bound to the warp core to do it.

As Neelix directed the packaging and deployment of the various foodstuffs he'd set aside for the Caatati, he saw Captain Janeway walk in with Rahmin at her side. The alien seemed amazed at the size of the cargo hold where all this was taking place.

Obviously, Janeway had discounted Tuvok's concerns about Rahmin coming aboard the ship. And rightly so, Neelix thought. He'd seen his share of strangers in his day, and none of them seemed half as much in need of help as the Caatati.

Turning to Ensign Parke, who was shoving half a bale of *m'binda* grass into a container, the Talaxian said, "I'll be right back."

Parke nodded patiently. "Take your time," she said, her blue eyes sparkling beneath brown hair. "I've got plenty to do until you get back."

Neelix took a look at the other bale of *m'binda* grass in the ensign's vicinity, as well as the piles of *maqnorra* leaves and *snorrla* bark. "Yes," he said, "I guess you do."

Then he made his way across the hold to join the captain and the Caatati. They seemed pleased to see him—especially Rahmin.

"Things seem to be going well," the alien noted.

"They are," Neelix agreed. "Of course, it's a lot of work, but fortunately, we've got a lot of willing hands to help with it."

"And as I've just told Rahmin," Janeway added, "we're generating lots of thorium for him in engineering."

"Ah, yes," said the Talaxian. He had an idea. "Say, wouldn't our guest be interested to see how Lieutenant Torres—"

The captain gave him a funny look.

"—is generating those isotopes?" he finished.

"Actually," Janeway replied, "it's a rather mundane procedure. Besides, Lieutenant Torres's time is better spent producing thorium than conducting tours of engineering."

Neelix wondered at the tone of her voice. "But—"

"No buts about it," the captain told him. "Especially when I think Rahmin would be a great deal *more* intrigued by our airponics bay."

Obviously, the Talaxian concluded, something was going on. He didn't know what it was, but it seemed best to play along with it.

"I imagine that's true," he answered. "The airponics bay is something you have to see to believe."

"And the Caatati can use all the growing techniques they can get their hands on," Janeway pointed out.

Rahmin nodded. "We certainly can."

"Then we'll make that our next stop," the captain decided. She turned to the Talaxian. "Keep up the good work, Mr. Neelix."

He shrugged. "I'll do my best."

A moment later, Janeway and the Caatati had departed. Neelix stood there, scratching his head. "I don't get it," he muttered.

"Don't get what?" asked Ensign Parke, who had come up beside him.

"Why the captain wouldn't want our friend Rahmin to see engineering," he replied. "After all, it's one of the most interesting parts of the ship. And it *is* where the isotopes are being produced."

Parke chuckled. "Are you serious?"

The Talaxian looked at her. "What do you mean?"

"The Borg were the ones who almost destroyed the Caatati—right?"

He nodded. "Right."

"And Seven of Nine is a Borg."

Neelix smacked his forehead with the heel of his hand. "Of course—Seven of Nine is working in engineering now. What kind of idiot am I not to have thought of that?"

Parke regarded him sympathetically. "As far as I can tell, a very well-meaning idiot." She pointed across the hold at the containers she'd been working on. "So, I've got the *m'binda* grass, the *maqnorra* leaves and the *snorrla* bark packed away. What's next?"

The Talaxian stroked his chin judiciously. "How about the *granik* roots?"

The ensign smiled again. "Your wish is my command."

And she left Neelix to think about the horrific faux pas he'd almost made. Imagine Rahmin bumping into Seven of Nine, he thought. What a disaster *that* would have been.

CHAPTER 7

THE CAPTAIN STOOD BETWEEN NEELIX AND TUVOK AND WATCHED RAHMIN take his place on the transporter grid. As the Caatati did so, he smiled at her.

Janeway had seldom seen anyone as happy or as grateful as Rahmin was at that moment. Of course, as he had told her again and again, the captain and crew of *Voyager* had given his people more than supplies. They had given the Caatati new hope—and it was hard to place a value on that.

"I cannot thank you enough," Rahmin said.

"You already have," Janeway assured him. "Many times over, I assure you. Good luck, my friend. I hope you find what you're looking for."

Neelix nodded. "Me, too."

Tuvok raised his hand in the splay-fingered Vulcan salute. "Live long and prosper," he told the Caatati.

Rahmin inclined his head. "With the help of people like you," he said, "I will endeavor to do just that."

The captain turned to the transporter operator, a blond woman named Burleson. "Energize." After all, Janeway added silently, there's only so much gratitude a person can take.

"Aye, Captain," said Burleson. Her fingers moved over her control board with practiced precision.

A moment later, a corruscating pattern of light enveloped Rahmin. Then both he and the light pattern vanished.

Janeway tapped her commbadge. "Commander Chakotay?"

"Chakotay here, Captain."

"I'm on my way back to the bridge. The Caatati should be going their own way any moment now."

"Acknowledged," said the first officer.

"So," Neelix remarked, "the Caatati were everything they claimed they were—refugees in need of assistance." He turned to Tuvok. "You see, Mr. Vulcan? Your fears were unfounded."

Tuvok's brow furrowed ever so slightly. "As security officer, I'm required to take precautions against all potential threats," he explained. "Despite their apparent neediness, the Caatati were unknown to us. Thus, they, too, had the potential to become a threat."

"But they didn't," the Talaxian pointed out.

"But they *could* have," the Vulcan countered.

"Gentlemen," said Janeway, "the Caatati are water under the bridge. If you don't mind, I'd like to move on."

Tuvok thrust his chin out. "Of course."

"Fine with me," Neelix replied cheerfully.

Chuckling to herself, Janeway led the way out of the transporter room. Tuvok and Neelix were such opposites. She wondered if any other captain had ever had to put up with a bickering pair like that.

Agron Lumas sat on the edge of his bed, in the cramped, Spartan quarters that were the best his ship had to offer, and considered the realizor he had salvaged from the wreck of his world.

The device no longer looked new. Its band had been bent, its sleek, dark metal tarnished in places. But it still worked.

The question was . . . did he want to use it? Sometimes Lumas regretted that he'd taken it with him. All it ever brought him was pain and guilt, after all. But if pain and guilt were all he had . . .

With trembling fingers, he lifted the thing to the level of his head. Then he put it on and closed his eyes.

Lumas thought of a picnic on the shore of the Aranatoc Sea. His wife was there—not as he had seen her last, but with a smile on her face. Finaea was there as well, just a few days shy of her tenth birthday. And sweet little Anyelot was only six, her thin shoulders browned by the sun.

He felt a lump in his throat, but he swallowed it away. After all, his wife and daughters would be concerned if they saw sadness in his eyes, and Lumas desperately didn't want to ruin their picnic.

Opening his eyes, he saw his memories had come to life, there in the confines of his cabin. His loved ones were as warm and tangible as he was—and a good deal healthier looking. If nothing else, they had been spared the miseries their world's survivors had been forced to endure.

At least, Lumas thought, there was *that* very small consolation.

"Father?" said Finaea, her face full of innocence.

He smiled at her. "Yes, child?"

"You've barely touched your *ranghia.*"

Lumas looked down at the bowl that had appeared in his hands. It was full of an aromatic orange puree—one that made his stomach growl as loudly as if the food were real.

"No," he said, "I haven't, have I?" He held the bowl out to his daughter, just as he had done that day at the shore. "Would you like some of it?"

Finaea's face lit up—then dimmed again. "I don't want to take it if you want it, Father."

But Lumas knew that she *did* want it. Even at that age, she was too considerate to say so.

"It's all right," he told her. "I'm not very hungry right now."

At the time, he hadn't been lying. He had eaten too much the night before. Now, it took a great deal of willpower to hand Finaea the bowl of *ranghia,* even if it *wasn't* real.

But hand it over he did. It was the least he could do for his daughter, now that she had become . . . whatever it was she had become. Again, he felt the lump in his throat, and this time it was much harder to make it go away.

"Agron," said his wife, "are you all right?"

It was one of the most wondrous things about the realizor—that it could ascertain the mood of the user and make it manifest to his or her creations. Lumas shook his head and held his hand out to his wife.

"I'm fine," he said. "It's just the seamotes. You know how they tickle my nose this time of year."

Looking at his wife, Lumas wanted to say more. He wanted to tell her how much he missed her. He wanted to say how badly he felt that he hadn't done more to keep her safe.

Instead, he added, "Where's that libation we packed? I'm in the mood for a good celebration. In fact—"

Suddenly, Lumas realized the door was open. Sedrek, his second-in-command, was standing at the threshold.

"Excuse me," he said, "but we're in communications range."

Immediately, Lumas wrenched the realizor from his head, making his family blink out of existence. For a moment, he stared at the places his wife and children had occupied, feeling once again the terrible, heartwrenching pain of losing them.

Then he gathered himself and turned back to Sedrek. The man made no mention of the realizor-generated apparitions.

"Let's go," said Lumas.

He got up, his limbs heavy but far from useless. Fortunately, the realizor's debilitating afteraffects diminished with frequent use. And in the time since the Borg attack, he imagined he must have employed the device a hundred times.

Still, Lumas was glad the bridge was just down the corridor. Making his way to the bridge with Sedrek a step behind him, he entered the room and turned expectantly to the viewscreen.

Rahmin looked back at Lumas. "Ah," he said. "There you are."

There was no love lost between Lumas and Rahmin. Though their paths had crossed several times since they left the Caatati homeworld, they seldom agreed on a course long enough to remain in contact.

To Lumas's way of thinking, survival was survival. One did whatever it took to go on and enable his followers to do the same. One didn't stand on principle when lives hung in the balance.

Rahmin, on the other hand, believed in dealing fairly and openly. To him, it was more important to be honest than to endure.

But then, Rahmin had been a teacher on their world. A gentle, unassuming soul with no appetite for conflict.

Once, as a young man, Rahmin had served as technician on a far-reaching Caatati spaceflight. It was that fact that evidently had earned him command of his survivor vessel.

But since his youth, Rahmin had merely helped *train* technicians. His practical knowledge was actually quite limited—and his leadership abilities, in Lumas's view, were virtually nonexistent.

Lumas, by contrast, had been a man of accomplishment, a builder. He was better suited to solving complex and difficult problems—sometimes in ways the squeamish did not approve of.

"So," he said, eyeing the image of Rahmin on the screen. "We meet again, my friend. And, as I understand it, none too soon."

The other man's eyes narrowed. "What do you mean?"

Lumas shrugged. "I've heard you had dealings with a ship called *Voyager.* And that you profited by the experience."

"Who told you that?" asked Rahmin.

"Traders," said Lumas. "They had offered to take one of our ships off our hands, in exchange for a quantity of food. When I declined their offer and suggested something more equitable, they remarked that the Caatati were not nearly as desperate as they had heard. Why, a ship commanded by someone named Rahmin had actually spurned them altogether."

He tapped his chin with a forefinger, pretending to give the matter some thought. "Now, how could a Caatati vessel reject a trader out of hand? Especially when that trader might have food and medicine, which it would be willing to exchange for spare engine parts?"

Lumas acted as if he had suddenly been struck with an idea. "Unless, of course, that same Caatati vessel had all the food and medicine it needed. And perhaps a supply of thorium isotopes as well."

Rahmin's eyes grew wide with trepidation. "You'll not get our thorium," he declared. "Even if there *are* three of you to our one."

Lumas shook his head. "Generosity was never one of your best qualities, my friend. But don't worry. You need not part with your newfound wealth. All you have to do is tell me where to find this treasure-laden *Voyager.*"

Rahmin hesitated. "They treated us well. Too well to send the likes of *you* after them, Lumas."

Lumas flushed with indignation. "The likes of *me?"* he raged. "Have you forgotten where you come from, Rahmin? Or that I came from the same place? Does the same blood not run in *both* our veins?" He gestured to his bridge technicians. "And theirs as well?"

The Caatati on the viewscreen looked pained by the accusation—just as Lumas had intended. Now was the time to press his case.

"We're all Caatati," Lumas said in a softer voice. "All victims of the same devastation. If we can't help each other, Rahmin, do we still deserve to survive at all?"

Rahmin swallowed. "Perhaps you're right," he replied contritely. He looked down. "Forgive me, Lumas. We've been wandering so long, living hand to mouth, I've forgotten what common decency is."

Lumas smiled. "Then you'll help us?"

The other Caatati nodded. "Yes. Of course. As you so aptly put it, the same blood runs through all of us. May you have as much luck with Captain Janeway as I did."

Turning to one of his own technicians, Rahmin said, "Transmit the coordinates where we encountered *Voyager.* And also her heading at the point when we left her." He turned back to Lumas. "That's the best we can do."

Lumas inclined his head. "Then it will have to be enough."

And it *would* be, he thought. He and his fellow survivors would find this *Voyager.* And when they did, they would be as well off as Rahmin's bunch.

Maybe better.

CHAPTER 8

B'ELANNA SAT IN A FUNK AT A TABLE IN VOYAGER'S MESS HALL, PICKING AT her lunch in a desultory fashion. Nothing was going her way.

And the day was still young. Who knew what horrors awaited her before it was over?

Out of the corner of her eye, she saw Neelix coming her way. The engineer sighed. The Talaxian was no doubt bent on cheering her up. Little did he know what he was up against.

"My, my," said Neelix. "If ever I saw a job for the morale officer, it's sitting right here."

Some time ago, the captain had given him that honorary position on the ship. The Talaxian took it seriously, too—almost always to good effect. But not this time, B'Elanna thought.

She tried to smile, but it didn't come out right. "I don't think you've ever faced a greater challenge, Neelix."

"I *enjoy* a challenge," the Talaxian told her.

Then Neelix brought something out from behind his back—something he had been holding there without her realizing it. It was a small bowl full of something noxious-looking. B'Elanna wrinkled her nose.

"Is that supposed to make me feel better?" she asked.

"Blood pie," the Talaxian said—as if any explanation was necessary. "In honor of the Day of Honor."

Neelix was acting as if this were the first time they had ever discussed the Klingon holiday. It wasn't, of course.

The year before, he had tried to commemorate the Day of Honor by serving her a surprise assortment of Klingon dishes—*rokeg* blood pie, serpent worms, heart of *targ,* and the like. And she had stalked out of the mess hall, not caring to be reminded of the holiday.

So why was Neelix standing there with a smile on his face, proudly holding out the bowl of *rokeg* blood pie?

She narrowed her eyes. "Has Tom been talking to you?"

"Not at all," said Neelix. "I am nothing if not persistent."

"Are you really?" the engineer asked.

"Yes," he said, setting down the bowl. "And if I'm correct, many Klingon families traditionally serve *rokeg* blood pie on the Day of Honor."

"How interesting," she replied, smiling. "I appreciate the gesture, Neelix—but I've decided to ignore the Day of Honor."

The Talaxian was surprised. "Oh? But what about the ritual you prepared in the holodeck?"

B'Elanna stared at him, amazed. "You know about that?"

He shrugged.

She shook her head. "I'm going to kill Tom when I see him."

"Actually," said Neelix, "it was Ensign Kim who told me."

The lieutenant made a sound deep in her throat. "Look," she said, "I thought I had shaken the bad luck that used to dog me every year on the Day of Honor. Now, I see I was mistaken. My bad luck is back—with a vengeance.

"So no *rokeg* blood pie," B'Elanna said. "No examining my behavior over the last year to see if I measure up to Klingon standards of honor. Let's just forget the Day of Honor ever existed, all right?"

She was serious. She hoped her look told him so.

Neelix swept the bowl of *rokeg* blood pie off the table. "Understood," he responded cheerfully.

The Talaxian started away from the table, then stopped himself. He turned back to her. "Lieutenant," he said, "without prying into the cause of the, er, black cloud that's hanging over you, may I suggest something—based on my observations of you over the months we've served on *Voyager* together?"

"Go right ahead," B'Elanna told him.

Neelix pulled out a chair and sat down with her. "It seems to me," he said, "you have a bit of a temper . . . that you try to keep reined in, but sometimes all those feelings build up in you until you explode at someone."

She frowned. "I'd say that about sums it up."

"Well," the Talaxian went on, "I'm offering to be a pressure valve."

B'Elanna tilted her head. "A what?"

"A pressure valve," he repeated. "You may use me to blow off steam. When you're angry or feeling stressed, come see me. Call me names. Insult me."

"Neelix," she said. "I—"

"Even question my parentage," he told her. "Give me a tongue-lashing like you've never given anyone before. I promise I won't take it personally. And," he said, leaning closer to her, "you won't have to keep things bottled up inside anymore."

The engineer regarded him fondly. Then she reached out and covered his hand with hers.

"That's probably the nicest offer I've gotten in a long time. Thank you, Neelix. You're awfully sweet. But I'm not sure I could do that to you."

He looked back at her with what was obviously genuine affection. "Well," he said, "I'm here if you need me. Remember that."

Rising from his chair, he started off. B'Elanna watched him go, touched by his concern for her.

"Neelix?" she said.

He stopped and turned back to her. "Yes?"

"About this Day of Honor program," the engineer said. "Do you think I should go through with it?"

The Talaxian returned to her table. "I've always thought traditions were good things. That is, worth preserving."

B'Elanna sighed. "I've been thinking a lot about the rituals my mother taught me, and they don't seem so hateful as they did when I was a child. Maybe being so far away from anything Klingon has changed me."

"It certainly can't hurt to go through with the ceremony," he told her.

She looked at him. "I don't know what effect it'll have on me. That's what's so frightening."

Neelix gave her a smile of encouragement and put his hand over hers. He didn't say anything more—but then, he didn't have to.

"All right," said B'Elanna. "Bring on the *rokeg* blood pie. I can do this."

The Talaxian winked at her. Returning the bowl, he stood there and watched her dig in.

The Caves of Kahless were filled with thousands of long, guttering candles and a collection of twisted torches. As B'Elanna negotiated a path among them, a tendril of fog wrapped around her like a giant snake.

She breathed in the cool, dank air. It carried a metallic scent. Like a *bat'leth.* Or blood.

It hardly mattered to the engineer that this was a holodeck program. It seemed real. And the farther she delved into the earth, the more real it became for her.

Tom did a good job on this, she thought. He must really have put his heart and soul into it. It made her even more certain that she had done the right thing by trying out the program.

B'Elanna wound her way from one cave to the other. Each one contained the same torches, the same candles, the same sinuous drifts of fog. But to Tom's credit, no two caves were exactly alike.

Finally, she reached the cavern she was seeking. Three tall, muscular Klingons awaited her inside, their bare shoulders festooned with braids of their smoky, dark hair. B'Elanna approached them tentatively, not really knowing much about the ritual that would follow.

After all, she had only had a small part in the program's design. Tom had done the rest, drawing on authentic Klingon traditions.

"*Qapla'!* I am Moklor the Interrogator," said the tallest of the Klingons, his very tone an invitation to combat. "What warrior goes there?"

"My name's B'Elanna," she answered.

Moklor's grey eyes narrowed beneath his brow ridge. "Have you come to have your honor challenged?"

She shrugged. "I guess so, yes."

"Are you willing to see the ceremony through to the end?"

"That's the idea, isn't it? What do I do?" B'Elanna asked.

"It will be a lengthy ordeal," the interrogator told her. "First, you must eat from the heart of a sanctified *targ.*"

He gestured and one of the other Klingons brought forth a platter. There were several lumps of raw, lavender-colored meat on it. The Klingon presented the platter to B'Elanna.

"Pak lohr!" bellowed Moklor.

The engineer had never been a fan of Klingon food, and *rokeg* blood pie was tame compared to heart of *targ*. Steeling herself, she picked up one of the lumps of meat and put it in her mouth. Then, with an effort, she chewed.

The interrogator nodded approvingly. "The heart of a *targ* brings courage to the one who eats it. Next," he said, "you will drink *mot'loch* from the grail of Kahless."

He gestured, and the warrior who held the platter of *targ* meat backed away into shadow. At the same time, another Klingon stepped forward into the light. He was carrying a large metal cup.

As he handed it to B'Elanna, she sniffed it. It didn't smell pleasant by anyone's standards.

Moklor's eyes opened wide. "Drink to the glory of Kahless, the greatest warrior of all time."

B'Elanna took the cup and swallowed back her nausea. Then she forced herself to drink the noxious concoction.

The interrogator grinned as she handed the grail back to his helper. Obviously, the engineer thought, he was getting quite a kick out of this. It was nice to see someone enjoy his job so much.

"Kahless defeated his enemies on the field of battle," Moklor intoned, "and built a mighty empire." He regarded B'Elanna. "How have *you* proven yourself worthy of the name Klingon?"

She considered the question. Not being particularly devoted to her Klingon heritage, she had never asked herself anything like it before.

"Well," B'Elanna said at last, "I haven't built any empires lately—or at all, in fact. But not so long ago, I forced an entire culture to admit it had committed genocide."

Moklor looked puzzled. "In what way was that a Klingon deed?"

"I didn't let them sweep millions of deaths under a rug," she explained. "I made them acknowledge what they had done."

Moklor still didn't seem to get it. "But . . . what battles have you fought? How many enemies have you defeated?"

"I can't say I've *personally* defeated any," B'Elanna responded—a little lamely, she thought. "But the crew of my ship was able to dispel an army of warriors from another dimension."

Moklor scowled. Obviously, he was still unimpressed.

"You have to realize," the engineer went on, "I'm not living among warriors. That limits my opportunities a bit."

The interrogator spat. "Then how do you expect to distinguish yourself as a Klingon warrior?"

A good question, she thought. At least, from Moklor's point of view. "I don't really know. I guess I'm doing the best I can."

"What of your enemies?" the interrogator asked. "Have they been more worthy of a warrior's attention?"

B'Elanna frowned. "Worthy?"

"Strong," Moklor elaborated. "And honorable."

She chuckled grimly. "Frankly, I haven't seen a whole lot of honor in my enemies. Take the Borg, for instance—a race of unfeeling, machine-like monsters. They assimilate one species after another, destroy whole worlds full of innocents. Oh, they're strong, all right. They're absolutely deadly. But from where I stand, I'd say they don't rack up many honor points."

Moklor pondered her answer, his eyes gleaming in the firelight. "Those acts alone are not dishonorable," he concluded.

Frustrated, B'Elanna shook her head. She had never comprehended Klingon ways, and apparently she never would.

"Well, then," she said, "maybe I don't understand the notion of honor. Maybe I don't *want* to understand it. Maybe this is all . . . I don't know . . . just meaningless gibberish."

Moklor shook his head reproachfully. "A pitiful reply."

The engineer did her best to control her annoyance. "You think so?"

The interrogator nodded slowly. "Let us proceed."

B'Elanna didn't say anything. She just waited for whatever came next.

Moklor lifted his bearded chin. "A warrior must endure great hardship. To test your mettle, you will undergo the Ritual of Twenty Painstiks. After that, you will engage in combat with a master of the *bat'leth.* Finally, you will traverse the sulfurous lagoons of Gorath . . . "

B'Elanna held a hand up. "You know," she said, "I don't think so. I mean, I didn't want to do any of this stuff *before* you described it. I certainly don't want to do it now."

She inclined her head. "Have a good day, Interrogator. I'm leaving."

B'Elanna started to go around him, but Moklor barred her way. His eyes bulged and turned red with fury as he answered her.

"Not until you have completed the ceremony, *p'tahk.*"

Then he grabbed her shoulders, to make good on his threat. Surprised, B'Elanna cursed and tried to break Moklor's grip on her. But before she could get very far, two of his lackeys came out of the shadows with painstiks.

The devices were aptly named. The charge they sent through her made her feel as though she were being seared from within.

Howling with agony, B'Elanna shoved Moklor as hard as she could. He staggered backward, releasing her. Then she dropped into a crouch, ready to fight the other Klingons in the cave.

One of them assumed a *Mok'bara* stance, showing himself to be a practitioner of the Klingon martial art. He approached B'Elanna with his hands held out in front of him, moving in a rhythmic pattern.

Before she knew it, he had gotten hold of her and flipped her on her back. The impact against the hard stone took her breath away for a moment. Looking up, B'Elanna saw her adversary aiming a blow at her face.

She rolled just in time to avoid it. The Klingon hit the cavern floor instead of her, causing him to cry out in pain. As he grasped his injured hand, B'Elanna scrambled to her feet and straightened him up with a two-fisted punch. A second punch laid the warrior out cold.

Her lips drawn back, B'Elanna confronted Moklor's other helper. He seemed less eager to tackle her than the first one.

The engineer glared at Moklor. "Thanks so much," she told him. "It's been lovely. But we won't be doing it again some time."

The interrogator's mouth twisted with anger. He pointed a long, gnarled finger at her. "You cannot leave! You have yet to complete the ceremony!"

But B'Elanna stalked out of the place. She'd had dumb ideas before, she told herself, but this was by far the dumbest.

CHAPTER 9

B'ELANNA WAS LYING IN A FETAL POSITION ON THE COUCH IN HER QUARTERS when she heard the door chime. Go away, she thought.

But what she said was, "Come in."

The door slid aside, revealing her visitor. It was Tom.

He looked at her lying there. "Are you all right?" he asked.

With an effort, B'Elanna sat up. "I'm fine."

"I tried to find you before," Tom explained. "But you were in the holodeck."

"That's right."

Tom frowned. "I gathered as much. You know you left it running? There was a Klingon in there who didn't look too happy."

B'Elanna grunted. "Really."

"Yeah," said Tom. "He was nursing a whale of a black eye. Looks like he had a run-in with someone who's having a bad day."

She frowned at him. "Very funny."

Tom didn't say anything more for a while. It seemed to B'Elanna that he was waiting for her to talk about the program. Of course, that was the *last* thing she wanted to talk about.

"So," he said finally, "how did it go?"

"It didn't," the engineer replied, unable to keep the pique out of her voice. "Do you mind if we talk about something else?"

Tom regarded her—first with surprise, then with a certain resolve. "As a matter of fact," he told her, "I do. You've been spitting like a cobra all day. And frankly, it's getting boring."

"Is it?" B'Elanna muttered, looking away.

"It sure as hell *is.* We designed that holodeck program together, if you recall, and I think you owe me the courtesy of telling me what happened."

She looked up at him. "It was ridiculous—a lot of meaningless posturing. Honor, dishonor . . . what does it matter, anyway?"

Tom's eyes narrowed. "It matters because it's part of who you are. You've been running away from that all your life."

Anger flared in her, sudden and white-hot. "Who are *you* to tell me that?" B'Elanna wondered.

"I care about you," the flight controller told her bluntly. "I care what happens to you. But if you keep pushing me away, there's not much point in my sticking around—is there?"

She shrugged. "Fine. Leave me alone, then." Purely out of spite, she gestured toward the door.

Tom darkened with rage. "Don't worry," he said. "If this is the way you treat people who try to be your friend, you'll be alone, all right. You'll be *all* alone."

Then, with a hard look, he turned and left her quarters. The door whispered closed in his wake.

Suddenly, B'Elanna realized what a child she had been. She let her head sink into her hands.

Good going, she thought. There's only one living being on the ship who has an outside chance of understanding what you're going through—and you just sent him away.

Maybe Moklor had been right. Maybe she *was* a *p'tahk.*

Lt. Carey put his tools away and massaged his shoulder where a muscle had tightened up on him. Then he replaced the bulkhead plate that covered the replicator circuitry.

For the last time, he thought. At least, I *hope* it's for the last time.

Tapping his commbadge, he said, "Carey to Lt. Torres."

"Torres here," came the response.

"Listen," he said, "Lt. Paris mentioned that his replicator wasn't working. I could've waited until it turned up on the assignment list—"

"But you didn't," said Torres. "You just fixed it. Even though you're supposed to be off-duty."

"Basically, yes. I figured that's what you would have done."

"You figured right," she assured him. "Good work, Carey. Just don't rest on your laurels."

"I never do," he reminded her.

And that was that. Carey smiled and shook his head.

Before *Voyager* left Earth orbit a few years earlier, he was second-in-command in the engineering section. Then the ship got shunted into the Delta Quadrant, and his chief was killed in the process.

For a while, Carey figured he was the only one capable of being in charge of engineering. Then Torres moved in, with her take-no-prisoners approach. Naturally, they banged heads.

He was just standing up for what he thought was best—not only for himself, but for everyone on the ship. Unfortunately for him, Torres wasn't buying any of it. Finally, she brought the matter to a boil.

She broke his nose in three places.

Naturally, Carey thought the captain would stand by him. After all, his Starfleet record was impeccable. But Janeway had her own problems to contend with. *Voyager* was no longer purely a Starfleet ship—not with a contingent of Maquis aboard. When he heard the captain was even considering Torres for the engineering post, he nearly ruptured a blood vessel—and not in his nose. After all, she was an ex-Maquis—someone who had attended the Academy for a while but couldn't cut it. Or so he had heard.

In the end, the captain didn't give in to pressure from anyone. She picked the best person for the job—and that person was B'Elanna Torres. Eventually, even Carey agreed with the choice.

Since that time, Torres had distinguished herself over and over again. And Carey, as her first assistant, had served her as loyally as he had ever served any Starfleet lifer.

He had also gotten to know her as a friend as well as a colleague—and he knew when one of his friends was having a monster of a bad day. That's why he didn't mind fixing the replicator, even if he was supposed to be resting his weary bones.

"Day of Honor," he said out loud. "More like Day of Horror."

Only Klingons would put each other through such torture, he thought, as he picked up his tool case and headed for his quarters.

• • •

When the Doctor had the ship's computer place him in the holodeck, he believed he was visiting the Talaxian resort environment that had become so popular over the last few months—not only with himself, but with a majority of the crew.

As it turned out, he was wrong.

He found himself in a cave full of torches and twisted, tapering candles that struggled against wisps of fog. The Doctor looked around and saw that the cave connected with other caves, both in front and behind him. The other caves were full of candles and fog as well.

The Doctor harrumphed. "Either someone's been tinkering with the resort program," he observed sardonically, "or the holodeck is malfunctioning again." No doubt it was the latter.

Still, he mused, this milieu intrigued him. The Doctor wondered who had devised it and why. Unfortunately, there was no one present to provide answers to his questions. There were only the guttering candles, and they made no sound at all.

Then the Doctor heard what sounded like voices. Deep, gruff voices, speaking in some kind of rhythm. No doubt, the owners of those voices could shed some light on the situation.

"Well," he declared, "I'm not much of a spelunker. However, my curiosity has been aroused."

With that, he made his way in the direction of the voices. As it turned out, their source was closer than he had imagined. By the time he had traversed his third cavern, he caught sight of three tall, swarthy figures. They glared at him from beneath bony brow ridges.

"Klingons," the Doctor concluded. "How charming."

His direct experience with the species had been limited to his interactions with Lieutenant Torres. Those interactions had been positive ones, for the most part.

However, the Doctor's program included a great many references to Klingon culture and psychology. It didn't require any mental gymnastics for him to realize he might have placed himself in a sticky situation.

Of course, this was only a holodeck program. He could stop it any time he liked. With that assurance in mind, he approached the Klingons and inclined his head.

"Greetings," said the Doctor. He flashed a smile. "If I may ask, what exactly is your function here?"

The largest of them stepped forward. *"Qapla'!* I am Moklor the Interrogator. What warrior goes there?"

"I'm not a warrior," the Doctor answered. "I'm a physician."

Moklor looked at him askance. "What is your name?" he insisted.

The Doctor sighed. "I haven't selected a name yet. In the meantime, you may refer to me as the Emergency Medical Hologram."

The Klingon didn't seem pleased with that option. He cast glances left and right at his underlings.

"Or," the hologram suggested, "you may call me the Doctor."

Moklor didn't seem thrilled with that option either. However, he appeared to accept it. "Have you come to have your honor challenged?" he asked, his eyes narrowing.

"My . . . honor?" the Doctor repeated.

"Your honor!" the interrogator thundered. The word echoed throughout the cave as if it had been shouted by a chorus.

"Er . . . yes," said the Doctor, seeing no harm in agreement. "Of course I have. Why not?"

"Are you willing to see the ceremony through to the end?" Moklor asked.

"That all depends."

"On what does it depend?" the interrogator asked him.

"On how long it takes. I've alotted myself an hour for recreation—no more than that. Anything beyond an hour and I'll have to take a rain check."

Moklor's brow furrowed. "A rayn'chek?"

"In other words," the Doctor explained, "I'll have to continue the ceremony another time. Now, then . . . what's involved, exactly?"

Moklor's lip curled. "It will be a lengthy ordeal. First, you must eat from the heart of a sanctified *targ.*"

He gestured and one of his lackeys placed a platter in front of the Doctor. It held several lumps of bloody meat. As far as the Doctor was concerned, the sanctified *targ* could have had them back—with his compliments.

Still, he was inclined to be polite. "Mmm," he said. "They look delectable. My compliments to the chef."

"Pak lohr!" roared the interrogator.

"Er . . . whatever you say," the Doctor replied.

Picking up one of the bloody lumps, he ingested it. Actually, it wasn't as bad as it looked.

Moklor nodded as his underling withdrew with the platter. "The heart of a *targ* brings courage to the one who eats it. Next, you will drink *mot'loch* from the grail of Kahless."

A moment later, the interrogator's other helper came forward and produced a large metal cup. The Doctor took it from him and peered at the goopy brown liquid within it.

The Doctor had heard of a number of favorite Klingon beverages. *Mot'loch* was not one of them—and now he knew why. The smell of it alone was enough to make one retch.

Moklor raised his fist for emphasis. "Drink to the glory of Kahless, the greatest warrior of all time."

The Doctor sighed. He wasn't looking forward to this. However, he was rather curious as to how it all would turn out.

Steeling himself, he drank. Then he returned the cup to the interrogator, who passed it on to his lackey and grinned.

"Kahless defeated his enemies on the field of battle and built a mighty empire," he cried. Moklor eyed the Doctor. "How have *you* proven yourself worthy of the name Klingon?"

"Actually," the Doctor answered, "I'm not sure I *am* worthy—that is, of that particular name. Of course, I am no doubt worthy of a host of *other* titles and honorifics."

"It is only your worthiness as a Klingon that concerns me." As if to reinforce his point, the interrogator pounded his chest with his fist.

"Have it your way," said the Doctor. "But I'm still not sure how to respond to your inquiry."

Moklor considered him. "In what ways have you demonstrated your devotion to honor this last year?"

The Doctor chuckled. "My devotion to honor? Surely, you jest. It may interest you to know that I am an amalgam of the finest medical minds and personalities the Federation has ever known. It is absolutely impossible for me to do anything that is *less* than honorable."

Moklor looked unsatisfied. "But what have you *done?*"

The Doctor frowned. "I see. You require a list." He looked at the cavern's ceiling and gathered his thoughts. "All right. One year ago to the day, I stabilized and attended an Emmonite with severe burns over most of her body. Several days later, I treated Lieutenant Torres, Ensign Kim, and several other individuals, all of whom were suffering from radiation sickness. Later on that same week, I discovered a virus which—"

"No!" bellowed Moklor, his eyes blazing red with anger. "Speak of the battles you fought! Tell me the names of those you defeated!"

The Doctor harrumphed. "I believe I mentioned that I'm a physician. It's my job to preserve life, not to destroy it."

"You mock me?" said the Klingon, his hands turning into fists.

"Not at all," the Doctor told him warily.

Moklor regarded him with suspicion. "What of your enemies?" he asked. "Have they been worthy of a warrior's attention?"

The Doctor frowned. "No offense, but I don't think you've been listening very closely. I'm a physician. I heal people when they're sick. I have no enemies . . . unless, of course, you're speaking of the diseases I fight. But even then, it would be less than accurate to say—"

"You fight diseases?" the interrogator asked.

The Doctor paused. "That's one of my functions, yes."

"*Deadly* diseases?"

Once again, the Doctor could answer only one way. "Yes. Deadly ones."

"And you destroy them?"

The Doctor saw where Moklor was going with this. "As a matter of fact, I do. But I don't use a weapon."

The interrogator shrugged. "Weapons come in many forms. The important thing is that you confront your enemies and kill them. Now, how many of these diseases have you destroyed?"

The Doctor considered the question. "I don't know. Dozens? Hundreds?"

"Hundreds?" Moklor echoed. "And all by your hand?" He grinned. "Now *that* is a tale of honor worth the telling."

The Doctor had always thought so. And here, apparently, was someone willing to listen to it. In fact, it seemed to be the interrogator's job to listen to such accounts.

The Doctor was tempted to describe his victories over all manner of malady and bodily injury in protracted detail. However, it occurred to him that he still didn't know what this program was about.

"If you don't mind my asking," he told Moklor, "just what are we doing here? What's the function of an interrogator?"

The Klingon snorted. "An interrogator determines a warrior's worthiness on the Day of Honor."

"Ah," said the Doctor. *Now* he understood.

He had heard about the Day of Honor. It was a Klingon holiday established a century earlier, when a Starfleet captain by the name of Kirk helped rescue a planet full of Klingons.

Until then, Klingons had recognized honor only in one another. From that point on, they made it their business to celebrate honor in other species as well—even if those species were their enemies.

It brought up an interesting question. Since the first time the Doctor materialized on *Voyager,* he had been experimenting with the various traits and trappings of humanity, trying to find a combination that would define and even enhance his personality.

However, he had overlooked the value of embracing a holiday—or perhaps several of them. And yet, holidays seemed to have a valued place in the lives of the crew. Perhaps they might enrich his existence as well.

The more the Doctor thought about it, the more inclined he was to adopt a ritual celebration. The question was . . . which one?

The Day of Honor? He didn't think so. As interesting as his dialogue with Moklor had been, he didn't feel particularly moved by it. Then again, that was understandable. Klingon virtues were an acquired taste.

Some other holiday, then. The Bajoran Gratitude Festival, for instance. Or Cinco de Mayo, which Ensign Andujar had described in great detail. Or perhaps the Bolian Feast of Nineteen Sublime Pleasures.

There were so many. Clearly, in order to make an intelligent choice, he would have to embark on a rigorous schedule of experimentation. Only then could he find the celebration best suited to him.

Luckily, the Doctor boasted the expertise of the Federation's greatest scientists. No one could be better equipped to assess each holiday on its respective merits.

"Let us proceed," said Moklor. His gaze hardened. "A warrior must endure great hardship. To test your mettle, you will undergo the Ritual of Twenty Painstiks. After that, you will engage in combat with a master of the *bat'leth.* Finally, you will traverse the sulphurous lagoons of Gorath . . ."

"Perhaps some other time," the Doctor told him. He looked up at the stalactite-studded ceiling of the cavern. "Computer, terminate this program and return me to sickbay."

Abruptly, the Doctor found himself outside his office. Negotiating a path to his desk, he sat down at his terminal and brought up the information he needed. After a while, he smiled to himself.

"Now *that,*" he said, "sounds intriguing."

CHAPTER 10

It wasn't Susan Nicoletti's idea to spend her day in sickbay. But when she woke up shivering and saw the green blotches under her jawline, she hadn't had much choice but to see the Doctor.

Then she saw that Lt. Chafin had come down with the same virus. Something new to Federation science—and the biofilter as well, apparently.

The Doctor didn't have a name for it. He referred to it by a medical designation—delta nine-nine. His guess was that Nicoletti and Chafin had picked it up a week or so earlier, on one of the seedier space stations *Voyager* had run into.

A less versatile physician might have been thrown by the virus. Fortunately, the Doctor was as versatile as they came. In a matter of minutes, he had identified it, classified it, and come up with something to kill it.

The only problem was that the treatment was going to take four or five hours. But as the Doctor reminded Nicoletti and Chafin more than once, they were lucky to have a cure at all.

With no other option except to remain on her biobed, Nicoletti had eventually dozed off. When she woke up, the Doctor was standing beside her, a bemused expression on his face. Chafin, she noticed, was already gone.

"Is everything all right?" she asked, a little alarmed.

He nodded. "Everything is fine."

Nicoletti relaxed. "That's good."

The Doctor looked at her. "Lieutenant Nicoletti . . . are you a virgin?"

She felt her cheeks flushing. "I beg your pardon?"

"A virgin," he repeated. "Someone who has yet to—"

"I know what it *means,*" she told him. "I just don't know what it has to do with my virus."

"Oh," the Doctor said, "it has nothing to do with it. In fact, there's no longer any trace of the virus in your system."

"In that case, it's none of your business, Doctor" said Nicoletti, swinging her legs out of bed, "and I think I'll report to engineering."

"You don't understand," the Doctor protested. "This is not a matter of simple curiosity."

"It's still none of your business," she muttered. Then she made her way out of sickbay by the quickest route possible.

The Doctor approached the holodeck, still a little embarassed by his exchange with Lieutenant Nicoletti. His function on *Voyager* was to heal people, not send them flying out of sickbay.

Still, his intentions had been honorable. In the course of his survey of various holidays, one on the planet Tiraccus III had caught his eye. In ancient times, it had involved the ritual sacrifice of a virgin on a slab of newly cut obsidian.

In modern times, a virgin was still required, but his or her sacrifice was only conducted on a symbolic level. One might say many things about the Tiraccans, but at least they hadn't let the march of progress pass them by.

In any case, the Doctor's experience with the lieutenant had led him to consider another holiday.

"Computer," said the Doctor. "Initiate Wedding of Rixx program, complete with recent modifications."

A moment later, the interlocking doors slid away and revealed the fruits of the Doctor's labors. He stepped inside the holodeck and looked around.

Very nice, he thought. Very nice indeed. And as anyone who knew him could attest, he was notoriously difficult to please.

The room in which he found himself was expansive, with a high vaulted ceiling and a columnlike structure in each corner. It was lit in a way that gave the walls a mellow, golden glow.

The wall hangings were free-form, comprised of burnished metals in a great variety of pleasing shapes and sizes. The furniture was made up of velvet divans and satin love seats presented in a half-dozen pastel hues, the floor an intriguing pattern of light and dark tiles.

"Stately," the Doctor said out loud. "Even regal." But then, as a guest of the Fifth House of Betazed, he had expected no less.

He looked out his window at the elaborate white marble stair that connected the sprawling lower lawn with the even more sprawling upper lawn. The rails on either side of it, also cut from white marble, were festooned with garlands of dark blue and blood-red uttaberry blossoms.

Beyond the stair, between two towering trees with silver leaves, a white canopy shot through with thread-of-latinum had been elevated on yellow-and-white striped poles. The sun filtered through the canopy, glinting off the ancient silver chalice that graced a marble stand within.

The Sacred Chalice of Rixx, the Doctor noted with some satisfaction.

It was one of the most valuable artifacts on Betazed, and had been for the last seven hundred years. The chalice was brought out only once a year, in recognition of the emperor Rixx's mythical marriage to the goddess Niiope.

In the twenty-fourth century, Betazoids no longer worshipped gods and goddesses, of course. However, they were still eager to celebrate the holidays associated with said gods and goddesses—particularly *this* one.

The Wedding of Rixx, he thought excitedly, was the most important celebration on the entire planet, observed by young and old alike. Indeed, it was one of the most festive occasions anywhere in the galaxy.

Never having set foot on any planet in the Alpha Quadrant, where Betazed happened to be located, the Doctor couldn't know this from personal experience. However, *Voyager*'s computer had given a wealth of information on the subject. In fact, he had perused only a fraction of it, preferring to be surprised and delighted by the experience.

Just then, he heard the strident tinkling of Betazoid cymbals. Their purpose was to alert all and sundry that the ceremony would begin in five minutes. The Doctor smiled with anticipation.

Now, he thought, all I need are some appropriate garments. However, he couldn't see anything even vaguely resembling a closet in the room. His first impulse was to ask the computer for an explanation—but in the end, he decided against it.

When on Betazed, he mused, do as the Betazoids do. Spotting what looked like a set of wind chimes near a particularly elegant divan, he crossed the room and tapped them with his finger.

Surprisingly, the sounds that came from them were nearly as strident as those made by the cymbals a moment earlier. However, they had an almost immediate effect, as the Doctor heard footfalls approaching from outside the room. Before long, there was a knock on the door.

"Come in," he said.

The door opened and a female attendant entered the room. She had long red hair and a rather pleasing appearance.

"How may I assist you?" she asked the Doctor.

"I need some clothing appropriate for the celebration," he told her. He indicated his black-and-blue Starfleet uniform. "Obviously, I can't attend in this old thing."

The Betazoid looked at him as if he had suggested she lay an egg in the center of the room. Then she smiled. "You're joking, aren't you?"

The Doctor returned her gaze. "That wasn't my intention. Just what is it about my request you find humorous?"

The attendant didn't answer right away. She seemed to be searching for the right words. But before she could find any, the Doctor saw something attract her attention.

Something seen through the window, he thought. Frowning, he turned and took a look in the same direction.

Suddenly, no explanation was necessary. The Doctor approached the window and leaned on the sill, his gaze fixed on the procession of thoroughly *naked* Betazoids marching across the lower lawn.

Naked, he repeated silently for emphasis.

No clothes.

None at all.

As he watched, the procession reached the stair and ascended it, then headed for the wedding canopy. The Betazoids chatted and laughed and clasped their hands with joy. None of them seemed to feel the least bit self-conscious about their nakedness.

The Doctor tried to picture himself in the midst of the celebrants—and shuddered. As a physician, he had been trained to view the humanoid form dispassionately, even clinically—but not when that form was his own.

Perhaps it was a glitch in his programming, or an idiosyncrasy derived from one of the physician-personalities he was modeled after. The Doctor didn't really know where his sense of modesty came from.

He was certain of only one thing—he very much did *not* wish to traipse around without clothes in public. Ergo, he would have to forgo any participation in the Wedding of Rixx.

Sighing, the Doctor turned away from the window—and realized that his attendant was still present. She smiled at him again.

"That's a very nice shade of red," she told him.

His hand flew to his face. "I do *not* turn red," he insisted.

"Er . . . of course not," the Betazoid replied.

"You may go," the Doctor told her.

She started to leave, then stopped and turned to look at him. "If you hurry," she said, "you can still make the ceremony."

"Thank you," he said, "but I don't think I'll be attending this year." He looked up at the ceiling. "Computer, end program."

A moment later, the Doctor was standing in an empty holodeck. Glancing over his shoulder, he saw that the naked Betazoids were gone—and with them, any possibility of his becoming naked and joining them.

Oh well, he thought, pulling down his uniform front with a sense of propriety. Back to the proverbial drawing board.

As Janeway emerged from the turbolift onto *Voyager*'s bridge, she took in the image on the forward viewscreen. It was just as Chakotay had described it to her.

Three ships were hanging motionless in space. With the exception of a minor detail here and there, they were almost identical to one another. They also bore a strong resemblance to the Caatati vessel *Voyager* had encountered days earlier.

"They're in bad shape," Chakotay told her, joining her as she took up a position by her center seat.

"How bad?" the captain asked.

"As bad as Rahmin's ship," the first officer told her. "Maybe worse."

Janeway glanced at Tuvok, then Ensign Kim. Their grim expressions only confirmed Chakotay's report.

"The vessel in the center continues to hail us," the Vulcan noted for the captain's benefit.

"Open a channel," Janeway told him. "On screen."

A somber visage appeared on the viewer. As the captain had expected, he was a Caatati. And he was every bit as pale and emaciated and hollow-eyed as Rahmin had been. No, Janeway thought—even *more* so.

She suppressed a sigh and identified herself. "I'm Captain Kathryn Janeway of the Federation starship *Voyager*."

"Yes," said the Caatati, "I know. My name is Lumas. I'm in charge of my vessel as well as the two that accompany it."

"You've spoken recently with Rahmin," the captain deduced.

"I have been in contact with him," Lumas admitted. "While we Caatati don't usually travel as a group, we still communicate from time to time." He paused, as if seeking a way to phrase his thoughts. "Rahmin told us of your great generosity."

"He needed help," Janeway responded succinctly. "We did whatever we could for him."

Lumas looked like a hungry man forced to watch as someone else ate. "Captain," he ventured, "would it be possible for me to have a word with you? In private, perhaps?"

Janeway glanced at Chakotay. He shrugged, indicating he had no objection to the idea. Tuvok was another matter.

"Captain," he said, "I must advise you—"

"I know," she replied. "And thank you, Lieutenant."

Despite the Vulcan's warning, she wasn't particularly wary of Lumas and his ships. After all, Rahmin's Caatati had been just what they claimed to be—refugees from a Borg attack. According to *Voyager*'s sensor scans, Lumas's group was in much the same straits.

Of course, the captain had an inkling of how her conversation with Lumas might go. But that didn't deter her in the least.

"If you lower your shields," she told the Caatati, "I'll have my transporter operator bring you aboard."

Lumas's brow wrinkled. "Transporter . . . ?" he asked.

Janeway smiled a sober smile. "Trust me. It'll be easier to explain once you're here."

The Caatati smiled back as best he could. Then he turned to some off-screen technican and gave an order. A moment later, Lumas returned his attention to the captain.

"Our shields are down," he said. "That is, what's left of them."

Janeway nodded. "Transporter room one. Lock on to the coordinates of the Cataati with whom I've been speaking and beam him aboard."

"Aye, Captain," came the response from the transporter room.

Janeway glanced at Tuvok. "See to it our friend Lumas is escorted to the briefing room. And ask Mr. Neelix to join us there as well. He knows our food supplies better than anyone."

"Acknowledged," said the Vulcan.

The captain turned to the viewscreen again. After a moment or two, Lumas was surrounded by the shimmering aura of the transporter effect. Then he vanished from the screen altogether.

Janeway heaved a sigh. This wasn't going to be easy. She could cope with subspace anomalies and hostile life-forms. But a people who needed more help than she could give?

That was a different story entirely.

CHAPTER 11

THE DOCTOR STOOD IN A DRY RIVERBED IN THE MIDDLE OF THE PHAELONIAN Wasteland and gazed at the native Phaelonians amassed all around him.

Tall, graceful beings with golden eyes and scaly, purple skin, they wore black breeches, shirts, and headbands to commemorate their holiday, the Vernal Processional. Having had his fill of costuming traditions after his Betazoid experience, the Doctor wore his uniform instead.

Thanks to some tinkering he had done with the program, no one noticed that he was dressed any differently. For that matter, no one noticed that he was a human instead of a Phaelonian. That was one of the advantages of a holographic simulation—one could diverge from the norm and get away with it.

Most of the Doctor's fellow observers were gazing upriver, the direction from which the processional was to arrive. They seemed excited by the prospect, despite the oppressive waves of heat that rose from the riverbed.

The Doctor admitted that he was excited, too. The thought of a parade appealed to him. No doubt, it would have its share of well-dressed Phaelonians and festively decorated carriages. Maybe even a juggler.

After all, this event was an important one to the Phaelonians. In ancient times, it was considered an inducement for the gods to flood the riverbed with snowmelt from nearby mountains—and, in the process, make fertile the land all around it.

As with so many other holidays, it had outlived its original intent.

However, one couldn't deny its prominence in Phaelonian arts and culture. There were, for instance, some seventy-two metaphors in the local tongue that focused on the processional, though the Doctor had bothered to read only a couple of them.

In fact, he had done in this case pretty much what he had done in his study of the Wedding of Rixx. In other words, very little—even though, in the Betazoid program, the Doctor's minimal scholarship had proven his undoing.

But how could he judge the full value of a celebration if he knew in advance everything that would happen? How could he be spontaneous? Indeed, how could he have a good time?

Turning to a Phaelonian who seemed even more eager than the others, the Doctor said, "It should be a good one this year."

It was an innocuous enough remark, he thought. And yet, it was calculated to initiate a conversation.

The Phaelonian smiled. "It depends on the *abendaar.*"

Ah yes, thought the Doctor. The *abendaar*—a Phaelonian beast of burden. He had learned that much, at least.

Long ago, *abendaar* had pulled the Phaelonians' carts and carriages. It was only logical that they would figure prominently in a ceremonial march.

"I take it you've done this before?" the Doctor asked.

"Once," the Phaelonian told him. "My sibling did it three times."

"Oh?" said the Doctor. "Is he here?"

The Phaelonian's enthusiasm seemed to dim a bit. "No, though I wish he were. No one enjoyed the processional as much as he did."

"Too bad," the Doctor remarked sympathetically. "Maybe he'll be able to make it next year."

The Phaelonian looked at him, but didn't answer. And a moment later, he moved away.

An odd response, the Doctor mused. Perhaps I *should* have studied local customs a bit more thoroughly.

Looking about, he noticed a change in his companions' behavior. Many of them were bending over, stretching their limbs this way and that. A few even went so far as to help each other.

Rather than appear iconoclastic, the Doctor began to stretch as well. Still, he felt a little foolish. After all, how limber did one have to be to appreciate a parade?

Then the Phaelonians stopped stretching. But they seemed edgy, the Doctor thought, taut with anticipation. His curiosity got the better of him.

"Why is everyone so jumpy?" he asked one of them.

The Phaelonian laughed grimly. "As if you didn't know."

"In fact," he said, "I don't know."

But that Phaelonian didn't seem to believe him. No doubt the Doctor's native appearance had something to do with that.

Then the Doctor heard it. It started as a subtle rhythm in the ground beneath his feet. Then it got stronger, more insistent.

The Doctor looked around. "What is that?"

The Phaelonians on every side of him were still looking upriver. But now, one by one, they seemed to be bracing themselves in the manner of sprinters preparing for a race.

"Won't somebody tell me what's going on?" the Doctor entreated.

By then, the rhythm in the ground had become forceful enough to make his bones shudder. And soon it was more than a rhythm—it was a sound.

A sound of thunder.

As the Doctor watched, spellbound, a cloud of dust rose from somewhere upriver. Something was stirring it up, he concluded. He couldn't imagine what that something might be.

Or for that matter, how it would effect the processional.

"There!" yelled a Phaelonian, pointing to the cloud.

No, the Doctor realized. Not the cloud itself, but the mass of muscular black flesh and ruby-red eyes that was emerging from it.

The *abendaar* were coming, all right. But not in a neat parade, drawing well-dressed Phaelonians in festively decorated coaches. They were coming in a wild and untamed horde.

And they were advancing on the Doctor and his companions with the speed of summer lightning.

Suddenly, he understood. The Phaelonians hadn't gathered in the river bed to act as spectators. They had come here to race the *abendaar* from some prearranged point to some other point, presumably one of safety.

But in the process, they would be risking their lives against what amounted to a prodigiously powerful force of nature.

It was insane. It went against the entire complex of instincts that had enabled the Phaelonians to survive their evolution into sentient beings.

And yet, in some ways, it was a classic sacrifice, offering up existing life in the hope the land would make new life possible.

Of course, the Doctor was tempted to put an end to the program then and there. He had no desire to suffer the indignity of being trampled by large, smelly beasts—or to watch his fellow celebrants become smears on the granular surface of the riverbed.

But he reminded himself of why he had initiated the program in the first place. He was seeking a particular kind of experience—and here it was, in all its primal splendor.

If he shut it down, he would never know what he had missed. So against his better judgment, he hunkered down like all the other Phaelonians and waited while the *abendaar* bore down on them.

The sound in the ground grew louder and louder still, loud enough to rattle the Doctor's holographic bones. But no one else was moving, so he didn't either. He just watched the darting eyes and tensing muscles of the Phaelonians and braced himself for the race's start.

In the event, there was no signal the Doctor could discern—no cry of encouragement, no starting gun. The Phaelonians didn't seem to need one. They simply surged forward as one.

The Doctor started forward, too. But right from the beginning, he was a step behind them. With their natural grace and long strides, the Phaelonians soon widened that gap from one step to two and then three.

The *abendaar,* meanwhile, were flooding the dry channel like a dark and malevolent riptide, tossing their triangular, tufted heads and beating the sand with their rock-hard hooves. The Doctor spared only a glance at them, but the sight wasn't encouraging.

He ran as hard as he could, his arms pumping, his feet digging into the riverbed with all the rapidity he could muster. But as fast as the Doctor raced, as hard as he pushed himself, it was clearly not fast enough. The beasts behind him were gaining on him at an alarming rate, while the Phaelonians were gradually leaving him behind.

Come on, the Doctor urged himself. Accelerate. Get a move on, you laggard.

But he couldn't. In fact, it became more and more difficult merely to maintain the same pace. His physical limitations, never an issue before, were suddenly and shockingly brought to the fore.

This was a new experience for him, and not a very pleasant one. The

Doctor would have stopped altogether but for his determination to complete the holiday experience.

The snorting and pounding behind him was increasingly audible. Wretched animals, he thought. Didn't they have anything better to do with their time than run down the premiere physician in the quadrant?

Gradually, the Doctor felt himself faltering. Slowing down, despite his desire to the contrary.

The *abendaar,* however, showed no signs of sympathy. If anything, their eyes seemed to get wilder, their chomping more furious, the roar of their progress ever more deafening.

The heat, meanwhile, was intense, almost tangible. It attacked him from within and without, seeming to rob him of energy.

As he plumbed himself for some reserve he hadn't yet tapped, he made a mental note to add more stamina to his program.

Thinking this, distracted by it, the Doctor stumbled—and nearly pitched forward in the riverbed. But somehow, he caught himself and kept on.

How much longer could this go on? he wondered. How much longer could he push his holographic form to its limits?

Then the Doctor saw them. Up ahead, in the distance. Two crowds of Phaelonians, one on each side of the riverbed.

Unlike the runners, these people were dressed all in white. And some of them were kneeling along the banks, as if they wished to get as intimate with the action as possible.

By then, the Doctor was nine or ten strides behind even the slowest of the Phaelonian sprinters, and as many as fifteen behind the quickest. But he could see the leaders splitting off to one side of the riverbed or the other.

As they approached the crowds, those who were kneeling knelt even lower. Then they stretched their arms out toward the runners.

Abruptly, the Doctor figured out their intent. The white-garbed Phaelonians were going to lift their black-garbed brethren out of harm's way.

That is, he added, if they made it there in time.

At the moment, it looked as if every one of the native racers would do that. The lone exception was the Doctor himself.

Once more, he allowed himself a glance at the beasts pursuing him. Immediately, he wished he hadn't. They were even closer than he had imagined—fifty meters at best—and they were getting closer with each thunderous beat of their hooves.

Facing forward again, he set his sights on his potential saviors. As the first of the runners reached them, he was swept up out of the riverbed and embraced by the crowd. On the other side, another runner was pulled out of harm's way. And another.

The sprinters seemed exhilarated—intoxicated with their triumph. The Doctor longed to feel the same thrill, but he had a long way to go.

The *abendaar* behind him grunted and whined in their attempts to overtake him. He could smell their musky odor. He could even feel their hot breath on his neck.

Up ahead, most of the other runners had finished their race, and the crowds on the banks were plucking more of them out of the channel every second. Only a handful of stragglers remained.

And even *they* had a lead on the Doctor.

He lifted his chin and thrust out his chest. Then he poured everything he had into one last, magnificent effort.

It wasn't enough. Fewer than thirty meters from salvation, the Doctor felt something hit him from behind. Sprawling forward, he cried out in instinctive panic. "Computer—terminate program!"

The next thing he knew, he was standing in an empty holodeck. The *abendaar* were gone. So were the Phaelonians.

He had failed to finish the program, he noted with regret. Or, perhaps more accurately, the program had succeeded in finishing him. And yet, he had been so close . . .

Disgruntled, disappointed, the Doctor exited the holodeck. Yet another holiday experience had proven troublesome for him. Clearly, he told himself as he emerged into the corridor, he would have to rethink his approach.

CHAPTER 12

JANEWAY SAT ACROSS THE BRIEFING ROOM TABLE FROM LUMAS, FLANKED BY Neelix and Tuvok. All she could think of was that the Caatati looked worse in person than on *Voyager*'s viewscreen.

"Your transporter technology is amazing," Lumas told her.

"Only if you've never seen it before," the captain assured him. "But then," she said gently, "you didn't ask to see me to discuss technology."

The Caatati smiled a wan smile. "No," he agreed. "I didn't." He lowered his eyes, as if he had suddenly found some interesting detail in the surface of the table. "It is not easy for me to speak of this, Captain Janeway."

"Which is why you wished to speak in private," said the captain. "I understand."

Lumas took a breath and let it out. "There are over two hundred people on our three ships alone," he began. "Every one of them suffers from malnourishment, to one degree or another."

"It must be difficult," Neelix observed.

"It is," said the Caatati. "But it's been hardest on the children. Every parent sacrifices for his or her child, but even so, there's not enough food. If you could hear the crying of the babies . . . " He shook his head. "You would have as much trouble sleeping at night as I do."

"Have you considered relocation to a planet?" asked Tuvok. "One, perhaps, where you could grow your own food?"

Lumas gave him a withering look. "You speak as though such planets are easily found, Lieutenant. Believe me, they're not. And those that exist have already been claimed."

"Perhaps their occupants would be willing to share their resources with you," the Vulcan suggested reasonably. "In the same way that we shared our resources with Rahmin."

"You'd be surprised," said Lumas, "to find how unwelcome people can be when they've fallen on hard times. Because we have nothing of value, we're treated like vagrants . . . even criminals."

"We're not unsympathetic," Janeway told him. "But *Voyager* isn't an entire planet—it's just a ship. We have limited supplies. We can't possibly provide enough for all your people."

Lumas looked around at the briefing room. He ran his fingers over the flawless surface of the table.

"Forgive me," he said, "but from my perspective, Captain, you live in the midst of luxury. You don't suffer from debilitating diseases. You have many energy sources, not to mention transporters and replicators. And your crew is well fed." The Caatati leaned forward. "Apparently, keeping your bellies full is more important to you than helping those less fortunate."

Suddenly, his tone had become bitter. His mild-mannered request had become an accusation. Janeway found she didn't care for the transformation.

"Wait just a second," Neelix interjected. "That's decidedly unfair. Captain Janeway is the most generous person you could ever hope to meet." He held his hands out in an appeal for reason. "But if we were to give supplies to everyone who asked . . . we wouldn't have anything left."

Lumas's anger seemed to drain away. He shook his head in despair. "Of course not," he agreed. "It was unfair of me to suggest otherwise. You're just trying to survive . . . as we are."

Janeway frowned. Then she turned to her chief cook and morale officer. "Neelix, how much food can we spare?"

The Talaxian shrugged. "We could provide each ship with several hundred kilograms. It would alleviate their problem for a while, at least."

"Arrange for transport," the captain ordered. "And check with the doctor to see if he can spare any medical supplies."

Neelix nodded. "Aye, Captain."

Lumas laid his ridged forehead against the briefing room table. He seemed overwhelmed with gratitude.

"Thank you," he told Janeway. He lifted his head again. "May the gods smile on you and your crew. Tonight, our starving children will go to sleep without hunger. When they ask, I will tell them it is because of the generosity of the captain of *Voyager*."

Janeway wished she could feel good about Lumas's gratitude. Unfortunately, she didn't. In fact, if she didn't know better, she would have felt she was being used.

After all, Tuvok had had a point. As the captain's father had often pointed out to her, Providence helped those who helped themselves.

"I urge you to keep looking for a homeworld," she told the Cataati. "One that might support you and your people. We want all those children to grow up strong and healthy."

"Perhaps now they will," Lumas replied.

Janeway turned to her tactical officer. "Tuvok, please escort our guest back to the transporter room."

Lumas got up and approached the captain. Taking her hand, he squeezed it in a final gesture of gratitude. Then he followed the Vulcan out of the room.

Janeway sat back in her seat and looked at Neelix. The Talaxian didn't seem any more gratified than she did.

"Well," he said, "I guess I'll see about those supplies."

But he didn't go anywhere. Obviously, there was something on his mind.

"What is it?" the captain asked.

Neelix's brow furrowed. "Rahmin said there were nearly *thirty* of these ships. What happens when we run into the next bunch? And the next? What do we tell *them?*"

The captain didn't have an answer—because there wasn't one. She put her hand on the Talaxian's shoulder. "I guess we'll just have to cross that bridge when we come to it."

The Doctor glanced around the table and smiled at each of the seven people seated about it.

The children, Naomi, Benjamin, and Aaron, smiled back at him. So did Lt. Rabinowitz and his sister and brother-in-law, Carla and David Sokolov. Only the elderly Aunt Pearl gave him less than a hearty acknowledgment.

Lt. Rabinowitz, who was seated on the Doctor's left, leaned closer to him. "It's not you," he said. "It's her gall bladder. It always acts up this time of year."

The Doctor nodded politely. "I see," he responded, though he was at a loss as to why such an ailment might manifest itself on a seasonal basis. He was still considering the problem when David picked up his padd and cleared his throat.

"Shall we begin?" he asked.

"Isn't that why we're here?" Aunt Pearl answered drily.

David smiled at her. "So it is."

With one hand, he indicated the glass of wine set before him. In fact, all the people present had glasses of something set before them—wine in the case of the adults, grape juice in the case of the children.

With the other hand, David held up his padd. "Baruch attah adonai, elohainu melech haolahm, borai p'ree hagahfen. Blessed art Thou, O Eternal, our God, King of the Universe, Creator of the fruit of the vine."

"You needn't translate for my benefit," the Doctor assured him. "I'm quite conversant in a variety of Terran languages and dialects."

David glanced at him. "Thank you for sharing that, but we always say the prayers in both Hebrew and English. It's sort of a tradition in our family, going back some four hundred years."

"Ah," the Doctor replied. "I see. In that case, please proceed."

His host did just that—almost as if he were the real David Sokolov and not a holographic recreation of the lieutenant's brother-in-law. "Baruch attah adonai, elohainu melech haolahm, shehecheyanu v'keeyamanu v'heegeeyanu lazmahn hazeh. Blessed art Thou, O Eternal, our God, King of the Universe, who has preserved us, sustained us, and allowed us to enjoy this season."

With that, David picked up his glass and drank from it. Looking around, the Doctor saw that everyone else was following suit. Lifting his own glass, he inhaled its bouquet for a moment, then sipped at it.

"Chateau Picard '64," he noted. "An excellent year."

Carla darted a glance at her husband. "I'm glad *someone* around here appreciates fine wine."

Lt. Rabinowitz chuckled. "An old debate. I'm sorry you stumbled on it, Doctor."

The Doctor looked around the table. "Well, it *is* a fine wine."

"*Thank* you," Carla said pointedly.

David shot them both a look of forced tolerance, then returned his attention to his padd. "I will now wash my hands."

"Always a good idea," the Doctor remarked. "As they say, cleanliness is next to godliness."

"Who says that?" asked Aaron, the youngest child. He eyed the Doctor with undisguised skepticism.

"Never mind," his mother told him. "Just pay attention."

Ignoring the exchange, David cleansed his hands in a small bowl apparently reserved for the purpose. Then he said another prayer—this one over a small bundle of parsley, which he dipped in a second bowl and distributed to everyone at the table.

Seeing Lt. Rabinowitz munch on his sprig of parsley, the Doctor did likewise. He found it salty, and since parsley was not salty in and of itself, he gathered that the water in the bowl had contained salt.

"It represents the tears of the Israelites," Lt. Rabinowitz pointed out to him. "Because of the oppression they suffered in Egypt."

The Doctor nodded. "Thank you. You're being very helpful."

"No problem," said Rabinowitz.

The Doctor congratulated himself on his strategy. With the lieutenant as a guide, he would no doubt avoid the problems he had encountered in his previous holiday scenarios—while preserving the potential for surprise and spontaneity.

As it happened, Rabinowitz had been eager to relive this holiday meal—a celebration of the ancient Jewish feast of Passover. He had even offered to set up the program parameters, obviating the need for the Doctor to conduct any further research.

After all, the lieutenant had been exploring the Delta Quadrant for the last few years, along with the rest of *Voyager*'s crew. He hadn't seen his sister and her family in quite some time—and unless the captain found a way to accelerate their journey home, he would never see them again.

Except *this* way, of course. In a holodeck setting, where Rabinowitz could make his most poignant memories manifest.

"It's too hot in here," Aunt Pearl said suddenly. "Somebody open a window or something."

"It's too soon for Elijah," Benjamin piped up.

The Doctor looked to his "guide" for an explanation. Rabinowitz chuckled and mussed Benjamin's hair.

"Elijah was a prophet," he told the Doctor. "He represents the needy—the stranger. Later on, after we finish eating, we open the door for him so he can come in and share our food."

"Of course," said the Doctor. "Much as the Caatati have been given a portion of *Voyager*'s resources."

"Actually," the lieutenant told him, "that's not a bad analogy."

As David opened a window for Aunt Pearl, Carla was doing something with a stack of crumbly-looking flatbreads on a plate near the center of the table. The Doctor craned his neck in order to watch.

"Matzoth," explained Rabinowitz. "Pieces of unleavened bread—like those baked in a hurry by the Israelites as they left Egypt. Carla's breaking the middle piece in half for a kids' game that'll happen later."

David sat down again. Then the lieutenant's sister elevated the plate of matzoth and read from her own padd.

"This is the bread of affliction which our ancestors ate in the land of Egypt. Let all those who are hungry come in and eat. Let all those who are in distress come in and celebrate the Passover. This year, we celebrate here, but next year we hope to celebrate in the land of Israel. This year, we are slaves; next year, may we be free men."

The Doctor didn't understand everything Carla had said. He turned to Rabinowitz for an explanation—and was surprised to see tears standing in the lieutenant's eyes.

"Sorry," said Rabinowitz. He smiled. "It's just that I've been away for a long time and I miss them."

The Doctor nodded. "As you should. You have a fine family." He gave the lieutenant a moment to compose himself. "If you don't mind, I have a question."

"Ask away," Rabinowitz told him. "Answering questions is what the seder is all about."

"I heard your sister speak of the bread of affliction—clearly, a reference to the matzoth she was holding up."

"That's right," said the lieutenant.

"And she expressed the ethic of charity which you mentioned in connection with the prophet Elijah."

"Right again."

"But," the Doctor noted, "she spoke of a wish to be in the land of Israel, though—as you told me—she and her family live in North America. Also, she referred to herself as a slave . . . ?"

"When she appears to enjoy the same freedoms as any other Federation citizen."

The Doctor nodded. "Exactly."

Rabinowitz picked up the padd in front of him and tapped in a command. Then he read out loud.

"In every generation, each individual is bound to regard himself as if he himself had gone out of Egypt. As it is said, 'And thou shalt relate to thy son this very day, this is what the Lord did for me when I left Egypt.' Thus, it was not our ancestors alone who were redeemed, but us as well."

"Hey, Unk—no skipping ahead," Naomi insisted.

"Sorry," said the lieutenant, feigning contrition. Then he turned to the Doctor. "You see? In a sense, we *are* slaves, just like our ancestors. And just like them, we yearn to leave Egypt and be free."

The Doctor looked at him. "So . . . you're asserting a bond of kinship with those who came before you."

"Actually," Rabinowitz told him, "it's more than that. We're saying, in a literal way, that we are the people the Pharaohs enslaved in Egypt—and that those people are us."

The Doctor thought about that for a moment. Obviously, this was a rather considerable leap of faith.

"What if one doesn't feel that way?" he asked. "What if one merely sees the liberation from Egypt as an intriguing historical event?"

Rabinowitz looked at him with a touch of sadness in his eyes. "One would still be welcome at the seder, Doctor."

The Doctor felt as if he had lost something important. "Thank you," he told the lieutenant.

"Glad to be of service," said Rabinowitz.

CHAPTER 13

PARIS TRIED TO IGNORE THE STARES HE AND HIS COMPANION WERE GETTING AS they negotiated one of *Voyager*'s corridors. Apparently, people still weren't used to the idea of a Borg with the run of the ship.

"I've never navigated a transwarp conduit," he told Seven of Nine. "Any problems I should be aware of?"

She gave him an imperious glance. "You'll have no idea what you're doing. If we attempt to enter a transwarp conduit, I will have to take conn control. Any other course would be foolish."

Paris shrugged good-naturedly. "I *am* a quick study."

But the Borg was persistent. "There will be a number of gravimetric instabilities in the conduit. If they're not handled in precisely the right manner, the ship will be torn apart."

Paris chuckled. I can be persistent, too, he thought.

"Just out of curiosity, I'd like to take a look at the field displacement parameters. Could you set them for me?"

Seven of Nine glanced at him. "They will be of no use to you."

"Even so," he said, turning on the charm.

The Borg frowned ever so slightly. "All right."

There, the helmsman thought. We're having a conversation. A *productive* conversation. This isn't nearly as difficult as I thought it might be.

Of course, from the moment Seven of Nine had been disconnected from the Borg collective, Paris had had less trouble accepting her than some of his crewmates. He had been inclined to treat her as a person, not someone who might try to assimilate him at the drop of a nanite probe.

There was a corner up ahead. As they approached it, Paris tried to think of what other data he might need from Seven of Nine.

The flight controller was still thinking when he and the Borg made their turn—and saw two people walking in the opposite direction. One was Lieutenant Tuvok. The other was a Caatati.

Paris wasn't surprised to see the visitor. He hadn't been present on the bridge when *Voyager* encountered the Caatati ships, but word spread quickly on a starship.

Then Paris remembered who was with him. Seven of Nine, whose collective had assimilated most of the Caatati and all but destroyed their civilization. This could be trouble, he told himself.

For a moment, the alien didn't seem to realize what he was looking at. Then he stopped in the middle of his sentence and stared at the Borg with increasing intensity.

"What species is that?" he asked Tuvok.

By then, the Vulcan must have known there was no way to defuse the situation. But to his credit, he still tried.

"Her name is Seven of Nine," he replied reluctantly. "She is a human who lived as a Borg."

Suddenly, the alien's expression changed. His face twisted with hatred and loathing. Stopping dead in his tracks, he raised a bony hand and pointed a spindly finger at Seven of Nine.

"Borg!" he grated.

Seven of Nine returned the alien's scrutiny, but she said nothing.

"Do not be alarmed," Tuvok advised his companion. "She is disconnected from the Borg collective. She won't harm you."

But the Caatati seemed to have other problems with the Borg's presence. "Where's my wife?" he demanded raggedly, advancing on Seven of Nine. "Where are my children?" His voice became shrill and tremulous. "What did you do with them after you took them?"

Without warning, the alien lunged at Seven of Nine. By then, he was shrieking like a banshee, filling the corridor with his cries.

"What have you done with my family, you vicious predator? Give them back, do you hear? I want them back!"

Tuvok grabbed the Caatati by the waist and pulled him back. At the same time, Paris stepped protectively in front of Seven of Nine.

He doubted that the Borg was in any real danger. She seemed more than capable of taking care of herself, especially against someone as feeble as the alien. But Seven of Nine was a guest on *Voyager,* and he wasn't going to allow her to be manhandled by another guest.

"Mr. Paris," said the Vulcan, "please proceed." Then he ushered the Cataati down the corridor.

"You don't have to tell me twice," Paris muttered.

Taking the Borg's arm, he guided her in the opposite direction and didn't look back. It was a while before the echoes of the alien's venom faded with distance.

The flight controller turned to Seven of Nine. "Sorry about that."

"About what?" she asked.

"Well," said Paris, "the way he reacted to you."

The Borg seemed puzzled. The concern he was showing was obviously beyond her range of understanding.

"He didn't injure me," she pointed out.

He nodded. "Good."

For a moment, they walked in silence, Paris glancing at Seven of Nine only once or twice. Then she spoke up again.

"There are many on this ship who have similar feelings toward me," she observed, "though I will admit I don't fully understand the reasons for their resentment." She turned to him, as if for affirmation.

He sighed, reluctant to lie to her. "I'm afraid you're right. I guess some people are having a harder time than others adjusting to the idea of a Borg on the ship. They see you and they think of destruction and assimilation."

Seven of Nine tilted her head slightly. "Hence, the resentment."

"That's right." Paris studied her features. "Does that bother you? The way they feel, I mean?"

The Borg went silent again for a moment. "No," she said at last. "It doesn't."

He continued to study her. "I just want you to know I'm not one of those people—the ones who resent you. I mean, we all have a past we're not proud of." The flight controller rethought the sentiment. "Well, maybe not all of us, but *I* certainly do."

Seven of Nine didn't ask what he had done. Still, Paris had the feeling she wanted to know.

"A while back," he said, "I accidentally caused the death of a colleague. Worse, I lied about it. In the end, I disgraced my family and myself. I became a mercenary, a dead-ender without principles—willing to fight for anyone who would pay my bar bills."

He looked into the Borg's eyes. "But none of that matters anymore—not what I did, not what you did. What matters is what we say and do *now.*"

Seven of Nine tilted her head slightly. "I am uncertain of what you're attempting to say."

Paris tried to explain. "That . . . if there's any way I can help you adjust to life on *Voyager* . . . please ask me."

The Borg cast a sidelong look at him. She seemed cautious, even wary. But then, she barely knew him—barely knew anyone on *Voyager.* In her place, in a strange environment, he would have been uncertain about the motives of everyone around him.

But Paris was sincere in his desire to help her. He hoped Seven of Nine knew that.

"I will remember your offer," she told him.

A moment later, they reached engineering.

Tuvok guided Lumas along the corridor as gently as he could. The Caatati seemed stunned by his encounter with Seven of Nine, as if he had been dealt an actual, physical blow.

"She's a Borg," Lumas spat, and not for the first time. "A Borg . . . "

When they entered the transporter room, Janeway was waiting for them with Burleson, the transporter operator. It didn't take the captain more than a glance to see that something was wrong.

The Caatati glowered at her. "How could you?" he gasped.

"How could I *what?*" asked Janeway.

"We encountered Seven of Nine in the corridor," the Vulcan explained, regretting the incident with an intensity no human would understand. "Our guest did not react positively to her presence."

Janeway nodded. "I see."

Lumas's mouth twisted with hatred. "She's a killer, Captain Janeway. She must be destroyed."

Janeway frowned. "She's not a killer anymore. She's been cut off from the Borg collective."

"No!" the Caatati insisted, his eyes blazing in their deep, shadowed sockets. "She'll betray you first chance she gets!"

"I'll take that into account," the captain said. Then she glanced at Tuvok. "If you please?"

The Vulcan took hold of Lumas's arm and escorted him to the transporter grid. The Caatati struggled for a moment, but soon realized he had no chance against Tuvok's great strength.

"Don't be a fool!" Lumas rasped, remaining on the grid as the Vulcan stepped back. "Don't you know what the Borg are capable of? Kill her while you still can!"

Janeway didn't comment. Instead, she turned to the transporter operator. "Energize, Lieutenant."

Burleson did as she was told. The glittering transporter effect began to appear around the Caatati.

"Kill her!" Lumas insisted, his hands clenching into fists. "Make her pay for what she did! Make her—"

He was gone before he could get the rest out.

Tuvok looked at the captain. "I take full responsibility for what happened. I should have made certain of Seven of Nine's whereabouts before I escorted Lumas to the transporter room."

Janeway returned his gaze. "You're not perfect, Tuvok. No one is."

"I am the security officer on this ship," he pointed out. "Some oversights are inexcusable."

She sighed. "You'll do better next time."

"Indeed," said the Vulcan. "You may rely on that."

Changing the subject, the captain turned to the empty transporter grid. "You know," she remarked, "I liked it better when we were saying goodbye to Rahmin. He, at least, remembered to say thank you."

It was an unfortunate way to end their dealings with the Caatati, she mused. She just hoped it wouldn't come back to bite them in the end.

CHAPTER 14

When Janeway returned to her ready room, she found the Doctor waiting for her there.

"I hope you don't mind," he said. "I took the liberty of transferring my program to this location."

The captain frowned. "To be honest, Doctor, I'd prefer you didn't make a habit of it. A captain's ready room is her refuge. Her sanctum sanctorum, if you will. It's unsettling to come back to such a place and find someone else already there."

The Doctor nodded. "I understand. It won't happen again."

Janeway crossed the room and sat at her desk. "Thank you. But since you're here already, what can I do for you?"

"Are you . . . er, busy?" he asked.

"No more than unusual. What's on your mind?"

"I wish to . . . vent my frustrations," he said. "I was hoping you wouldn't mind if I did it here. With you."

"Go ahead," she replied, though she had a feeling she might regret it.

The Doctor began to pace. "As you know, I've been sampling various holidays in an effort to find one to my liking."

"Yes," said the captain. "I know. Lieutenant Nicoletti is still wondering what you were up to."

The Doctor sighed. "An unfortunate incident. I made every attempt to explain my motivation to the lieutenant later on."

"I'm sure you did," Janeway told him, trying not to crack a smile. "In any case, you say you've been sampling various holidays . . . "

"But none of them appear to suit me. The Day of Honor ritual seemed barbaric and, frankly, a little disgusting as well. The Phaelonian holiday seemed unnecessarily rigorous. Also, I tend to shy away from leisure activities in which my life is at stake."

"Understandably," the captain noted.

"There was also the Betazoid holiday, which . . . " The Doctor glanced at her. "Which was inappropriate for other reasons."

"Didn't you attend a ceremony with Lt. Rabinowitz?"

"I did indeed," said the Doctor. "And, I must say, the lieutenant couldn't have been more helpful. However, I ultimately found that it. . . . did not relate to my personal experience."

"So you haven't had much luck," Janeway observed.

"That," said the Doctor, "would be putting it mildly. Fortunately, I believe I see the problem now. In fact, it's something I probably should have seen a long time ago."

"And what's that?" Janeway asked him.

"One can't just embrace a holiday at random. A holiday is a cultural milestone—an event with which its celebrants have an intimate and long-standing relationship. And since I have no culture of my own, no heritage, it's impossible for me to ever feel part of such an event."

"I don't believe that," the captain responded. "Difficult, yes—but not impossible." She leaned forward. "Your problem, Doctor, is that you've been looking at the other man's grass."

He looked at her askance. "I beg your pardon?"

Janeway smiled. "The other man's grass. You know—the stuff that's always greener? In the old saw?"

"Ah," he said. "You mean I've valued other belief systems above my own."

"That's what I mean, all right."

"But," the Doctor complained, "I *have* no belief system. I only deal in those things that can be proven empirically."

"Not true," the captain insisted. "You believe in the value of friendship and family. You believe in courage and self-sacrifice—"

"The benefits of which are self-evident," he argued. "They can all be reduced to causes and effects. I mean a belief in something that *can't* be demonstrated or dissected—something that has no obvious benefits in the material world."

He was talking about a leap of faith. She said so.

The Doctor nodded. "A leap of faith."

Janeway regarded him. This wasn't going to be easy. On the other hand, she desperately didn't want to let the Doctor down.

After all, he had helped or comforted almost everyone who served on *Voyager* over the course of the last few years. The least she could do was provide *him* with some help and comfort.

And then it hit her.

"You know," the captain said, "you're right."

"About what? My having no belief system?" the Doctor asked.

"About a holiday being an event with which its celebrants have an intimate relationship—and a long-standing one. But you're *wrong* when you say you have no culture and no heritage. And you're even *more* wrong when you say you have no belief system."

He looked at her skeptically. "How so?"

"What do you do?" Janeway asked him.

The Doctor shrugged. "I'm a physician."

"A healer," she suggested.

"Yes . . . "

"And why do you do that? Because you have to? Because you're programmed to do so?"

The Doctor pondered the question. "I am programmed with certain knowledge—certain skills. But I act of my own volition. It would be inaccurate to say I heal people simply because my program calls for it."

"So you could choose *not* to heal them?"

He shrugged. "I suppose so, yes. But the context would have to be a rather bizarre one."

"Because life is sacred to you," Janeway suggested.

"One could say that, yes."

"And why is that?" she asked.

The Doctor grunted. "Surely you're joking."

"I'm not," the captain told him. "Why is life so sacred?"

He held his hands out. "Without life, the universe has no meaning."

"And what does the universe need with meaning, Doctor? Indeed," she pressed, "what difference does it make to the universe if any or all of your patients live or die?"

The Doctor looked about the room as if he thought he could find the answer floating in midair. After a while, he turned to her again, a bewildered expression on his face.

"Now that you mention it," he said, "it probably makes no difference at all."

Janeway smiled. "No difference. So life isn't so sacred after all?"

The Doctor did his best to understand the problem. "But it is. It *is* sacred."

"Despite all logic to the contrary? Despite the empirical evidence?"

"Despite that," he agreed.

The captain stood. "Then I suggest, Doctor, that you have made a leap of faith. What's more, you do it every day, without fail—just like every healer in the history of the universe, from the time of Hippocrates and even earlier."

He considered the possibility. "You're suggesting I'm part of some larger community after all. A community of physicians."

"That's right. And you don't wait for a holiday to celebrate your faith. You do it all the time, morning, noon, and night."

The Doctor didn't speak for a long time. Then he said, "Perhaps you're right."

"You *know* I am," Janeway told him.

B'Elanna looked up from her console and saw Tom enter engineering with Seven of Nine. Deep inside, she felt a twinge. She was surprised to find that seeing the two of them together annoyed her.

Vorik, Carey, and the other engineers acknowledged Tom's presence with a nod. B'Elanna just turned back to her monitor.

Still, she couldn't help asking the question. "What brings you here, Tom?"

Paris glanced at her coolly. Obviously, he hadn't forgotten what they had said to each other in her quarters.

"I'm going to look at the field displacement parameters of the transwarp conduits. Seven's offered to establish them for me."

"How thoughtful," B'Elanna said.

He smiled a chilly smile. "I'm glad you approve."

"Actually," B'Elanna said, "I think we're ready to try opening one of the transwarp conduits—just as a test, of course."

"Great," Tom replied. "Let's give it a try."

By then, Seven of Nine had taken her place at her assigned workstation. "All systems are ready," she said flatly—even though no one had asked her for her assessment.

B'Elanna looked around. "All right. For now, we're only going to take a peek. We'll open a conduit, get as much sensor data as we can, and then close it up again. I want to take this one step at a time—understood?"

Everyone nodded. Everyone except the Borg, of course, but she didn't seem to have any objection either.

Vorik spoke up. "I've set up a temporary tachyon matrix within the main deflector. It's on-line."

B'Elanna hit her commbadge. "Engineering to the bridge."

"Janeway here," came the response.

"We're ready to start, Captain."

"Go ahead, Lieutenant. We'll monitor your progress from here."

"Captain," said B'Elanna, "we'll have to be traveling at warp speed to create a large enough subspace field. I'd like permission to reroute conn control to engineering."

"Agreed," Janeway responded.

Turning to Tom, B'Elanna nodded. The flight controller went to a console and made the necessary adjustments. Seven of Nine watched him like a hawk the whole time. Eventually, Tom seemed to notice.

"Just for the purposes of this test," he assured the Borg.

Seven of Nine didn't answer. She just turned back to her own console.

B'Elanna didn't know what Tom was referring to, and right now she didn't care. She just wanted to get this over with.

"Mr. Paris?" she said.

Tom looked at her. "Yes, Lieutenant?" That chilly tone again.

"Take us—"

"Past warp 2," he said. "I know."

He worked at his controls. B'Elanna could feel the subtle surge in power as the ship accelerated.

"We're at warp 2.3," Tom reported.

B'Elanna turned to Vorik. "Start emitting the tachyons."

"Energizing the matrix," the Vulcan responded.

"Power is building," Carey announced.

B'Elanna checked her monitor. It didn't seem to her that anything was happening.

"There's no indication of a subspace field," Seven of Nine observed. "I'd recommend switching to a higher energy band."

The lieutenant hated the idea of taking advice from the Borg. Still, Seven of Nine was the expert in this field.

B'Elanna nodded to Vorik. "Do it."

"Yes, Lieutenant."

He switched to the higher band. B'Elanna checked her monitor again. She could see a subspace response.

"That did something," Tom sang out, unable to keep the excitement out of his voice.

"The subspace field is forming," said Seven of Nine.

"Continuing to emit tachyon pulses," B'Elanna noted.

"The field is enlarging," said Seven of Nine.

By then, even the engineer was beginning to enjoy their success. For the moment, all thoughts of the Borg were submerged.

We're going to do it, B'Elanna cheered inwardly. We're going to open that conduit, damn it.

Suddenly, a siren sounded, freezing everyone in engineering. B'Elanna cursed beneath her breath.

"What's that?" asked Seven of Nine.

"An overload alarm," said Vorik.

A moment later, the computer initiated a red alert. The entire section was bathed in a lurid red light.

B'Elanna switched consoles, then keyed the controls. Immediately, she saw what the problem was. She described it for the others.

"There's a power surge in the emitter matrix. Tachyon particles are leaking into the propulsion system."

Tom shouted at Vorik. "Shut down the deflector!"

The Vulcan complied with the order. "Done," he said. His brow creased. "But the leak is continuing unabated."

B'Elanna heard an explosion behind her. Whirling, she saw one of the consoles erupt in a shower of sparks. Her engineers rushed about, attempting to contain the damage.

But it was too late. B'Elanna knew that in a flash, even before *Voyager* began to shudder. This wasn't a broken coolant conduit or something else confined to engineering. This had the makings of a shipwide disaster.

Vorik looked up from his console. "Impulse engines are out."

"Tachyons are flooding the warp core," B'Elanna groaned. "Emissions are increasing exponentially."

Suddenly, Janeway's voice cut through the turmoil. "Bridge to engineering. What's going on down there?"

B'Elanna took a breath. "We've got a power surge in the emitter matrix. Tachyons are flooding the warp core."

"What are the radiometric levels?" asked the captain.

"Fifty rems and climbing," B'Elanna told her.

She imagined Janeway rifling through her options—and rejecting all but one. When the captain spoke, she sounded calm, but there was an undeniable undercurrent of urgency in her voice.

"Listen to me, Lieutenant. If you can't get the core stabilized immediately, evacuate engineering."

B'Elanna didn't like the idea. Unfortunately, she had little choice in the matter. "Aye, Captain. I'll get back to you."

Vorik appeared at her side. "I've cut all power relays, but tachyon levels are still rising."

B'Elanna turned to the other engineers. "Everybody out. Now!"

Her colleagues headed for the door. Vorik went as well. But Tom and Seven of Nine hadn't moved.

"That means you two as well," she told them.

"But I could be of help to you," the Borg noted.

"Get out!" B'Elanna snapped. "That's an order!"

Seven of Nine hesitated a moment, then backed away and left engineering. But Tom stayed where he was, working feverishly at a console.

"You can't order me," he reminded her. "I outrank you, remember?"

B'Elanna didn't argue with him. It wouldn't have gotten her anywhere anyway. "We've got to neutralize the core," she said.

He nodded. "I'll try decoupling the dilithium matrix."

But an ominous whine was beginning to build. Plasma coolant began escaping, just as it had before.

"No effect," B'Elanna growled. "Try it again."

Tom did as she asked. A few seconds later, he shook his head. "It's not working, B'Elanna. The core's going to breach."

She bit her lip. "Let me try one more thing."

Tom grabbed her arm. "B'Elanna, there's no time. We have to get out of here. *Now.*"

The engineer hesitated—but only for a fraction of a second. After all, she knew he was right.

"Computer," she said, "prepare to eject the warp core. Authorization Torres omega-phi-9-3."

The computer responded instantly. "Core-ejection system enabled."

That done, B'Elanna pushed Tom in the direction of the exit and hurried out after him. Once they reached the corridor, she saw the other engineers waiting for them.

First, B'Elanna tapped the control that closed the doors to engineering. Then she steeled herself.

"Computer," she cried out, "eject the warp core."

She couldn't see the core blow out from beneath the ship and tumble away into the void—but, unfortunately, she could imagine it. She couldn't feel *Voyager* listing drunkenly to one side, thanks to the inertial dampers—but she could imagine that, too.

B'Elanna felt as if her own core had been ripped from her. She looked up at the intercom grid.

"Torres to Janeway. We've dumped the core," she reported, feeling a twinge as she said it. After all, it was the last thing a chief engineer wanted to have to say.

"Acknowledged," said Janeway, her voice devoid of emotion. "I'm on my way down, Lieutenant."

B'Elanna looked around at her small, dispirited clutch of engineers. They looked back at her, not knowing what to say.

She saved them the trouble. "Welcome to the worst day of my life."

CHAPTER 15

B'ELANNA STARED AT THE DARK, EMPTY SPACE OCCUPIED BY THE WARP CORE until just a little while ago. Engineering looked naked to her without the core, like a solar system suddenly deprived of its sun.

Of course, without a sun, the planets in a system would freeze over. Engineering hadn't done that. In fact, the place was busier than ever, with all kinds of personnel assisting in the repair efforts.

Neelix was among them. So was Tom. But not Seven of Nine. B'Elanna had dismissed Tom's new friend. The chief engineer had plenty to worry about without having to keep an eye on a potentially treacherous Borg.

For instance, there was the little matter of getting a propulsion system back on-line. That alone could take hours.

Out of the corner of her eye, B'Elanna saw Captain Janeway walk into engineering and look around. The lieutenant frowned. Before she got involved in an extended conversation with the captain, she wanted to make sure her key officers had their assignments laid out for them.

"Vorik!" she called. "Carey! Rabinowitz!"

All three of them stopped what they were doing and came over. "How may I be of assistance?" asked the Vulcan.

B'Elanna told him. "We have to get the impulse engines on-line. You and Nicoletti check the driver coils."

Vorik nodded as he retreated. "Yes, Lieutenant."

The chief engineer turned to Rabinowitz, a man with light brown hair and a baby face. "We've got a problem with the microfusion initiators. See if you can trace it to its source."

"Done," the man assured her.

"And while you're at it," B'Elanna told him, "see to the command coordinator. It's a mess."

"On my way," he said.

"And me?" asked Carey.

"Go over the plasma injectors. If they're damaged, they could decide to fire on their own."

"Got it." Carey started to move away.

"When you're done," B'Elanna added, "take a look at the structural integrity field. Blowing out the core could have created some weak spots."

"No problem," Carey assured her, hastening to take care of it—and almost bumping into the captain in the process.

The engineer girded herself. More than anything, she hated the idea of letting Janeway down. After all, the captain had demonstrated faith in B'Elanna from the beginning.

"Report," said Janeway, obviously in no mood for niceties.

"We're stopped cold," B'Elanna told her. "The warp core is millions of kilometers away by now, and the impulse engines are seriously damaged. I can give you a few thrusters . . ."

"But that's it," the captain finished for her.

"That's it," the engineer confirmed.

Janeway frowned. "How long before I can have impulse power?"

B'Elanna shrugged. "I can't give you an estimate. We're still assessing the damage." She sighed. "So much for opening a transwarp conduit. I never thought it was a good idea in the first place."

"No sense in rehashing the past," the captain said pointedly. "What's done is done, Lieutenant."

The engineer nodded. "I sent the Borg back to her alcove. We won't be needing her in here anymore."

Janeway declined to comment on that subject. Instead, she looked around—and stopped when she found what she was looking for.

"Mr. Paris," she called.

Tom raised his head from his console. "Yes, Ma'am?"

"We have to retrieve the warp core," the captain said. "Take a shuttle and find it. See if you can tractor it back to *Voyager*."

"Yes, Ma'am," said the helmsman. He tapped out a few last commands at his console and started for the door.

"It's going to be damaged," B'Elanna interjected, getting the captain's attention. "And unstable. It should be repaired before Tom tries to put a tractor beam on it."

Janeway considered the problem for a moment. "All right," she remarked at last. "Then go with him, Lieutenant. Do whatever you have to, just get it back here in one piece."

B'Elanna didn't like the idea of leaving her staff to muddle through without her. But they were capable enough. They would be all right.

"Right away, Captain," she replied.

Then she and Tom headed for the exit.

Lumas stood on his bridge, still dumbfounded by what he had seen. His pilot and his technicians worked all around him, propelling his vessel through space as they took stock of *Voyager*'s largesse.

A Borg, he told himself. A living, breathing Borg, walking the corridors of *Voyager* as if she were just another crew member.

The memory chilled the Caatati to his bones. It left him weak and unnerved. But it also brought with it hot flashes of anger and spite.

If only there were some way to strike at the Borg, Lumas thought. If only he and his ships could seize *Voyager* and remove the devil from their midst. Then she would know what pain was.

And maybe, in the process of exacting his revenge, he would free himself from his *own* pain. Maybe he would achieve some kind of peace by tearing the Borg limb from limb. He tried to picture it . . .

No. He was dreaming if he thought he could capture the Borg. Janeway's vessel was too quick, too well-armed, too powerful for the Caatati. They would gain nothing by converging on *Voyager* except their own annihilation.

"Lumas?" said his second-in-command.

He turned to look at Sedrek. "What is it?"

"We have food for a month, maybe more. And the isotopes they gave us will keep us going even longer than that."

Lumas dismissed the information with a gesture. "They gave us the smallest part of what they had. So what?"

Sedrek shrugged. "I thought you would want to know. You did well."

Lumas glared at him. "If I had done well," he said, "I would have brought you the head of their Borg."

The other man looked at him disbelievingly. "Their Borg? What are you talking about, Lumas?"

"A Borg walked their ship. I swear it. Had I not—"

"Lumas! Come quickly!" called one of his technicians.

Lumas frowned and joined the man at his console. His curiosity aroused, Sedrek came along as well.

"Is something wrong?" Lumas asked. He gazed at the monitor hanging from the bulkhead.

"Not wrong at all," the technician replied. "In fact, it may be something very *right.*" And he pointed to a spot on the monitor.

Lumas took a closer look and saw a red dot tumbling across the screen. "What am I looking at?" he asked.

"I'm not sure," the technician told him. "But it contains some kind of energy—a great *deal* of energy."

Lumas wanted to know more. "Put it on the forward viewscreen."

Then he turned to the hexagonal screen, where the even flow of stars was suddenly displaced by another sight entirely—that of a glowing cylinder plunging end over end through space.

Lumas took a step forward and tilted his head. He had never seen anything like it. "What's its purpose?" he asked.

"It's a power source," the technician responded. "That much is clear. But I can't tell you what it powered."

"*I* can," said another voice.

Lumas glanced over his shoulder at Grommir, another of his technicians. The man was studying the monitor above his console with great intensity.

"It's the energy core from *Voyager*'s main propulsion system," Grommir announced. "Or if it's not, it's an exact duplicate of it."

"How do you know?" asked Lumas.

The technician turned to him. "I scanned *Voyager* and all her systems while the supplies were in transit to us. The signature of this object is a perfect match for *Voyager*'s energy core."

Lumas turned to the viewscreen again. The cylinder was still twirling its way through the void, a treasure beyond description.

"But what is it doing out here?" he wondered.

"That," said Grommir, "I can't tell you."

"Then tell me this," said Lumas, keeping his eyes on the power source. "Can we adapt it to our own needs? Can we make it give us the power we need to survive?"

The technician thought about it. "I suppose so, yes."

Lumas grinned. "Then get a beam on it. I don't care who it belonged to before. It's *ours* now."

Voyager's crew had believed its captain generous, he recalled. It seemed she was more generous than she had intended.

CHAPTER 16

As B'Elanna followed Tom into the shuttlebay, she saw a crew member repairing a burned-out EPS link in one of the bulkheads. Still, the place was a study in decorum compared to engineering.

Tom headed right for the *Cochrane*—his favorite among the ship's several shuttles, though the engineer had forgotten why. He said a few words to Browning, the officer on duty. Then they boarded the craft.

Tom took the controls. After all, he was the hotshot pilot. Besides, B'Elanna was too disgusted with recent events to concentrate.

The bay doors opened and the shuttle slipped easily into space. But she wasn't leaving her troubles behind—far from it.

Crossing her arms over her chest, B'Elanna slouched in her seat. "What else can go wrong today?" she asked out loud.

She hadn't meant to do that. It had just slipped out. Still, it had a positive effect in that it got a smile out of Tom. Not a grin, not a smile that said he enjoyed her company, but a smile nonetheless.

"You know," he said, "you really know how to hurt a guy."

"Yes," B'Elanna answered. "I know." She glanced at him with mock seriousness. "You mean the Klingon in the holodeck, right?"

Her companion glanced back at her, just as mock-serious. "Of course. Who did you think?"

"Just wanted to make sure we understood each other," she told him.

Suddenly, the shuttle vibrated. B'Elanna sat up and looked at her controls. "We're getting close to some random ion turbulence."

Tom nodded. "I'll change course to avoid it."

The crisis past, B'Elanna sank back in her seat. "If we get this core back, I'm going right to bed and sleep straight through until tomorrow. I mean . . . " She heaved a sigh. "I just want to get this day over with."

"Look at it this way," Tom suggested. "How much worse could it get? Having to dump the warp core has to be the low point of *any* day."

She didn't answer—at least, not at first. She just watched the stars fly by at warp 1. At that rate, it would only be a matter of minutes before they found what they were looking for.

"Maybe it's me," B'Elanna speculated. "Maybe I'm asking for all this trouble somehow."

"Or," he said, "maybe it's just a string of bad luck."

She shook her head ruefully. "I never should have gone through that Day of Honor ceremony. It was ridiculous. No . . . worse than ridiculous."

B'Elanna recalled the sensation of being flat on her back, looking up into the face of her Klingon adversary. She saw his fist, raised and ready to pound her into the cavern floor. I must have been crazy, she thought. Warrior rituals and B'Elanna Torres don't mix.

She attended to some rudimentary tasks on her control console. Still, it didn't take her mind off her misfortunes.

"I shouldn't have gotten *near* anything Klingon," she breathed. "By now, I should know better."

Tom gave her a sidelong glance—but he didn't challenge her, not this time. He looked at his controls instead.

Good, she thought. Because I'm too tired to withstand a challenge. Too tired and too beat up.

Abruptly, Tom's eyes lit up. "Sensors have picked up a polymetallic object. It could be the core."

B'Elanna straightened and worked at her own console. Her findings confirmed her companion's. "That's the warp signature, all right. But there's something else out there. . . . "

"Something else?" he echoed.

She worked at her controls some more. "It's a ship."

It was an ominous thought. Tom looked out the observation port.

"I don't see anything yet," he said.

"We're not in visual range," the engineer advised him. "It'll be a minute or two more."

In the meantime, she did her best to get some information about the ship. She didn't want to confront it without knowing what they were dealing with. But the more data B'Elanna obtained, the less she liked it.

She turned to Tom. "According to our sensors, the ship has the same energy signature as the Caatati."

He met her gaze. "I'm getting a bad feeling about this."

She nodded. "Me, too."

Tom's brow wrinkled. "Maybe they're guarding it for us," he suggested only half-seriously.

B'Elanna frowned at him. "Right. And the Cardassians are really teddy bears in disguise."

A moment later, they came into visual range. "I see it," said Tom.

She followed his gaze, craning her neck to see out the window. "What do they think they're *doing?"* she asked.

There was a narrow shaft of yellow-white energy extending from the Caatati vessel to *Voyager*'s warp core. The shaft wasn't holding together well, either—it kept breaking up.

"They're trying to put a tractor beam on it," she snapped. "If they're not careful, they'll rip it apart!"

Tom cursed beneath his breath and opened a communications channel. "This is the shuttle *Cochrane* to the Caatati ship. Please respond."

The Caatati didn't hesitate to respond on audio. "Don't come any closer, *Cochrane*. We're performing a salvage operation."

"What a coincidence," said Tom. "So are we."

"That warp core was ejected from our ship," B'Elanna pointed out. "We've come to retrieve it."

"I'm afraid we got here first," said the Caatati. "Don't interfere with our operation or we'll open fire."

B'Elanna couldn't hold herself back any longer. Arrogance was one thing; stupidity was another.

"Don't you realize that core is highly unstable?" she demanded. "If you try to tractor it like that, you could cause an antimatter explosion."

There was no reply. Tom worked at his console. Then he cursed again, this time more volubly. "They aren't answering."

"Idiots!" B'Elanna snarled.

Tom nodded. "We have to keep them from destroying the core."

B'Elanna thought quickly. Then she got up and went to another control panel at the aft end of the cabin.

"What are you doing?" the helmsman asked.

"I'm going to try to disrupt their tractor beam. Then we can initiate one of our own."

As she manipulated her controls, the shuttle sent out a particle beam. As it met the Caatati beam, the two sizzled and sparked.

Tom checked his sensors. "It's working. Their tractor is breaking down. Pretty soon—"

He was interrupted by a loud thump. Then the shuttle pitched sharply to port and the red-alert lights came on.

B'Elanna felt ice water trickle down her spine. Righting herself in her seat, she checked her monitors again.

"What was that?" Tom asked.

B'Elanna bit back her frustration. "They sent an antimatter pulse back through our particle beam."

"Shut off the beam," he told her.

"It shut *itself* off," she snapped.

The shuttle began shaking. "Warning," said the onboard computer. "The structural integrity field has been compromised."

"Great," said Tom.

"Structural integrity now at fifty-three percent and falling," the computer continued. "Hull breach in one minute, twenty seconds."

B'Elanna worked at her controls. "We've got to reroute power from the propulsion and weapons systems."

"Warning," said the computer. "Hull breach in one minute, ten seconds."

"Do it!" she snapped.

"I'm doing it!" Tom snapped back. "It's having no effect!"

"Warning," the computer declared. "The structural integrity field has collapsed. Hull breach in sixty seconds."

Tom got up and pulled B'Elanna away from her console. "We've got to get out of here!"

She tore away from him. "Where do you suggest we go?"

There was only one place they *could* go, B'Elanna realized. Tom seemed to have come to the same conclusion.

Together, they looked to the rear of the cabin, where the environmental suits were stored. Then they looked at each other again.

"Hull breach in fifty seconds," the computer reminded them.

"Come on," Tom said. "We don't have much time."

Before B'Elanna knew it, he was opening the suit locker and pulling out a suit. Then another. Tom handed her one of them.

The engineer took it with no great enthusiasm. As she began to pull it on over her uniform, she caught a glimpse of her console.

The monitors showed the Caatati ship making off with *Voyager*'s warp core. And there was nothing she or Tom could do to stop it. In fact, they would be lucky to escape with their lives.

"Computer," said Tom, as he pulled on his own suit, "send a distress call to *Voyager,* giving Captain Janeway our coordinates."

Suddenly, a bulkhead panel blew out, releasing a cloud of gas. Then another panel blew, and another. Sparks flew in every direction, blinding B'Elanna with their brilliance.

And the computer wasn't answering Tom's command.

"Computer," he demanded, "respond!"

B'Elanna shook her head as she fastened the last clasp on her suit. "The comm system must be down."

Tom made his way to a console. "Fortunately," he reported, "transporters are still on line."

The shuttle began to shudder, then jerk like a dying beast. The two of them were thrown against a bulkhead.

"Stand by to energize!" Tom yelled over the clamor. Then he reached out and tapped out a command on his control panel.

A moment later, B'Elanna found herself floating in the void of space, her suit protecting her from the harsh realities of the vacuum. She turned and confirmed that Tom was with her.

Then, before she could say or do anything else, a flash of white light caught her eye.

It was the shuttle, she realized. It had been vaporized in the explosion of its destablizing warp core. If she and Tom had waited another second, they would have been vaporized as well.

Of course, their prospects weren't exactly cheery as it was. They were hanging in space, two tiny specks against the infinite—together, of course, but still very much alone.

CHAPTER 17

ONE MOMENT, LUMAS'S VIEWSCREEN SHOWED HIM *VOYAGER*'S SHUTTLE-craft amid the customary flickers and lines of static. The next moment, there was a blinding white flash.

Then the screen showed him nothing at all—except stars and static.

He turned to his technicians. "Where did it go?" he demanded. "Where are the people from *Voyager?"*

Grommir was the first to speak. "They're gone."

Lumas stared at him disbelievingly. "Gone?"

"Their ship exploded," the technician explained. "I think it was a result of the antimatter pulse we sent out."

Lumas turned back to the screen. He was so used to aberrations in the thing's performance, he had assumed the shuttle's disappearance was just another technical problem.

But Grommir had indicated otherwise. "Gone," Lumas repeated. He liked the sound of it. He liked it a lot.

That meant the energy core was his—completely and indisputably. If he could beat away one shuttle, he could beat away another one. And without its core, *Voyager* herself didn't scare him much either.

"Wait," said Grommir.

Lumas looked back over his shoulder. "What is it?"

The technician's brow puckered. "For a moment . . ."

"Yes?" Lumas pressed.

Grommir shook his head. "Nothing. I thought something had registered on the sensor grid. It was probably just bits of debris."

Lumas smiled, enjoying his victory. Then he turned to Sedrek. "How is the tractor beam holding up?"

His second-in-command looked up from his console, the glare of his instruments turning his face a lurid red. "It seems to be stable for the moment, Lumas, but we shouldn't use it any longer than we have to. It's a considerable drain on our thorium stores."

His superior made a sound of disgust. "You think too small, Sedrek. With *Voyager's* energy core in our possession, we'll soon have no need for thorium. We'll have something better."

Then something occurred to him. Maybe Sedrek wasn't the only one guilty of thinking too small. He glanced at Grommir again.

"How long would it take to contact the other Caatati?" he asked.

"Which vessel?" the technician inquired.

Lumas grinned. "All of them."

Grommir looked puzzled. "For what purpose?"

Under normal circumstances, Lumas wouldn't have tendered an explanation. After all, it was *he* who commanded this ship. However, he found himself in an uncommonly generous mood.

"We may have *Voyager's* core," he pointed out, "but she still has a great many other possessions we could benefit from. Food, for instance. Medical supplies. And other things . . ."

He thought again of the Borg he had seen in *Voyager's* corridor. He would never forget how she had looked at him. Coldly. Disdainfully.

Entirely without remorse.

"Yes," he said. "A great *many* other things."

B'Elanna stared at the part of space where the shuttle had been. "The captain's going to kill us," she said.

"She's got to find us first," Tom reminded her.

"Which she will, of course. I mean, who *couldn't* find two fully grown people in a place as small as the entire universe?"

Tom quirked a smile. "I'm glad you haven't lost your sparkling sense of humor, Lieutenant."

"No," said B'Elanna, "I guess I haven't. And it's a good thing, because there are few experiences I find more hilarious than watching my warp core ride into the sunset."

He nodded. "Yeah, I kind of enjoyed that myself."

The banter was good, she thought. It helped them adjust to their circumstances—which were grim at best.

Gazing at Tom through her faceplate, B'Elanna reached out and touched his hand. Looking back at her, he closed his fingers over hers.

It made her feel better. Less isolated, less alone—for all the good it did either one of them.

"As entertaining as this is," Tom said, "it'd be selfish to stay here by ourselves." He pressed a comm pad on his suit. "Paris to *Voyager.* Do you read us? Respond, please. Paris to *Voyager* . . . "

"It's no use," she told him. "The comm system in these suits isn't strong enough to carry that far."

He tried again anyway. "Paris to *Voyager* . . . "

Still nothing.

Tom frowned. "When they get the impulse engines repaired, they'll come looking for us."

"I guess we can't do anything but wait and hope." He managed a smile. "Heard any good jokes?"

She looked at him, wanting very much not to give into pessimism. But despite herself, she sighed.

"What?" he asked.

"You said it couldn't get any worse," B'Elanna reminded him. "You said that dumping the core was about as low as it could go." She looked around them at the vastness of space. "Never figured on this, did you?"

Tom's smile faded. "I will admit that this particular possibility didn't loom large in my mind."

"Still think it couldn't get worse?" she asked him.

"Actually," he said, "the thought that we might run out of oxygen . . . or spring a leak in one of these suits *is* looming large. I guess one of those things would be a little worse."

B'Elanna grunted. "Well, I don't plan on just drifting through space, hoping somebody will come along and rescue us. There must be something we can do to help ourselves."

Tom nodded. "Agreed."

He went silent for a moment. She hoped that meant he was thinking. B'Elanna made an effort to do the same.

"You know," Tom said at last, "if we could interplex the comm systems in both suits, we might be able to create a phased carrier wave. *Voyager* would read the signal and know it's from us."

"Good idea," she told him. In fact, it was a *very* good idea. "Let me access your controls."

He grinned. "I thought you'd never ask."

The two of them pulled closer together until they could grab each other with both hands. Then, in a somewhat more stable position, B'Elanna began fiddling with the controls on Tom's sleeve.

"This would be a lot easier if I had a hyperspanner," she observed.

"It'd be even easier without these gloves," he remarked.

"Hold still . . . "

"I'm trying," he assured her. "Careful we don't lose contact and start drifting apart."

B'Elanna looked at him. Were they still talking about not getting separated in space . . . or something else?

"Right," she replied.

She wrapped one arm around Tom's shoulder to keep him from drifting away as she worked. Then, since that didn't feel secure enough, she hooked her right leg around his left one.

Suddenly, B'Elanna was overwhelmed by the ludicrousness of their situation. Despite the circumstances, she laughed out loud. "I hope no one has us on a viewscreen," she chuckled.

Tom's voice softened. "Tell me, Lieutenant. Why is it we have to get beamed into space, dressed in thick environmental suits . . . before I can initiate first contact procedures?"

The engineer shot him a discouraging look. "Why is it if we're alone for more than thirty seconds, you start thinking about 'contact'?"

He wagged a finger at her. "Not fair, B'Elanna. Not fair at all. The other day in engineering, I must have gone four or five minutes before I started thinking about it."

She scowled at him. Then, with dogged determination, she completed her work. "Okay," she said at last. "I think I've got our comm systems interplexed. I'm going to initiate the carrier wave."

B'Elanna tapped the appropriate controls. Suddenly, there was an earsplitting whine. She could see Tom react in openmouthed shock as the sound filled his helmet.

"Sorry!" she said.

She fiddled with the controls some more. Finally, the whine subsided.

"Better?" she asked.

"Yeah. Was that what your shower sounded like?"

"No," B'Elanna told him. "The shower was worse."

He shook his head. "Let's hope the signal is still that strong by the time it gets to *Voyager*."

B'Elanna looked around them. "Let's hope," she echoed.

CHAPTER 18

The Captain was sitting at the desk in her ready room, reviewing a long list of damage reports. After all, the ejection of the ship's warp core had had any number of cascade effects—a disturbing percentage of them critical to *Voyager*'s operation.

Hearing a chime, Captain Janeway looked up from her monitor. She had no doubt as to who was on the other side of the door.

"Come in," she said.

The door slid aside and Seven of Nine walked in. As before, the Borg didn't say anything. She just stood there.

The captain got to her feet. "Would you like a cup of coffee?" she asked. "Perhaps some tea?"

"I have no need to ingest liquids," the Borg informed her. "I still receive energy from the Borg alcove."

Janeway nodded. Yes, she thought. Of course you do.

"But my understanding is that you're almost ready to begin eating food like everyone else."

Seven of Nine's expression didn't change one iota. Her only response was, "That is what the Doctor says."

"Well, he should know," said Janeway.

Seven of Nine blinked. "Why have you asked me here?"

The captain indicated the informal seating area off to her right, by the observation port. "Please," she said.

The Borg seemed to understand what she meant. As she sat down, Janeway crossed the room and took a seat beside Seven of Nine. Then the captain gathered her thoughts, wanting to be as precise and inoffensive as possible.

"Whenever there's an accident on the ship," she began, "even a minor one, we investigate it. Rather thoroughly, sometimes. That way, we minimize the chances of its happening again."

"A prudent course of action," the Borg remarked.

"I didn't have a chance to talk to Lieutenant Torres before she left the ship," the captain continued. "So I wanted to ask you some questions about what happened in engineering."

Seven of Nine looked unflinchingly at Janeway. "Go right ahead."

The captain didn't hurry. "Sensor logs indicate that tachyons were leaking into the warp core. Do you have any idea how it started?"

"No," said the Borg. "We had reconfigured the deflector shield to emit tachyon bursts, in order to open the transwarp conduits. The procedure must have triggered the leak."

"I see," Janeway said. "And who was controlling the tachyon bursts?"

Seven of Nine didn't hesitate. "Ensign Vorik."

"What were *you* doing?"

"Monitoring the transwarp frequencies."

"And did you at any time access deflector control?"

"No," said the Borg.

"Or maybe disengage the magnetic constrictors?"

Seven of Nine was silent for a moment. "You believe I'm responsible for the accident. That I deliberately sabotaged the ship."

Janeway shook her head. "That isn't what I meant at—"

"But it is," the Borg insisted. "You are like all the others on this ship. You see me as a threat."

The captain's first impulse was to deny the accusation. Then she thought better of it.

"I won't lie to you," she told Seven of Nine. "Part of me is suspicious. We've dealt with tachyon fields before on *Voyager* and never had this problem. And it wasn't so long ago that you made a serious attempt to send a signal to a Borg ship."

"That is true," Seven of Nine conceded.

"But," Janeway went on, "I suspect that if you really wanted to disable this ship, you would have found a much more clever way to do it."

The Borg absorbed the comment. Then she spoke.

"Captain, I am unaccustomed to deception. Among the Borg, it was impossible. There were no lies, no secrets in the collective. I do not think that I am capable of fabrication. And I assure you, I had nothing to do with the accident in engineering."

The ball was in Janeway's court. She could slam it back at Seven of Nine or keep the volley going. She chose the latter.

"Thank you," she told the Borg. "I believe you."

Seven of Nine took on a distant look. "I am finding it a difficult challenge to integrate into this group."

The captain nodded. "That's understandable."

"It is full of complex social structures that are unfamiliar to me. Earlier today, I witnessed something called a poker game."

Janeway smiled. "Ah, yes. I'd heard Ensign Kim was trying to start one up. On some ships, it's a tradition."

"A tradition," the Borg echoed.

"Yes. A ritual. Something that gives us comfort over time."

Seven of Nine shook her head. "The Borg have no rituals. No moment is different from any other."

The captain shrugged. "We look at life as more than a series of moments. We try to place them in context, so we can understand them. So we can celebrate them, each in his or her own way."

"That, too, is new to me," said the Borg. "The idea that, in a given situation, in a uniform set of circumstances, each person may act differently."

"It's what makes us individuals," Janeway explained.

The muscles worked in Seven of Nine's jaw. "Compared with the Borg collective, this crew is inefficient and contentious. It lacks discipline and uniformity of purpose."

Janeway sensed that Seven of Nine hadn't completed her thought. "But?" she said softly.

The Borg's brow creased as she considered the matter. "But it is also capable of surprising acts of compassion."

The captain was pleased that Seven of Nine could detect such behavior. "Unexpected acts of kindness are common among our group. That's one of the ways in which we define ourselves."

The Borg seemed to absorb the information. "It is all so different," she breathed. She looked at Janeway. "Is there anything more?"

"There is," the captain told her. "We still have to figure out what caused the tachyon leak." She reached for a padd lying nearby. "Tell me what you remember about the power fluctuations in the propulsion system."

Together, she and the Borg bent to their work.

Paris had forgotten how much he liked floating free in space.

It was invigorating to sit at the conn of a starship and skim through the void, breasting a sea of stars at warp 6. But there was no substitute for swimming that sea on one's own, unfettered and unencumbered, at one with all of creation.

Nor was the universe the immense thing he had once expected it to be. Somehow, when one was drifting through it, one's mind reduced it to a personal space—almost an *intimate* space.

So while someone else might have been frightened by the circumstances in which the flight controller found himself, Paris himself wasn't frightened at all. If he felt anything, it was curiosity.

He turned to B'Elanna, wondering if she felt the same way. Gazing at her faceplate, he could see her eyes darting this way and that, as if she were trying to figure something out.

"How are you doing?" Paris asked.

"This isn't anything like the simulations we had at the academy. I remember them feeling peaceful—"

"Like floating in the womb."

"Yes."

She was getting a queasy look on her face. Clearly, he thought, she wasn't enjoying this as much as he was. He would have to distract her.

"Harry once told me he could remember being in his mother's womb."

No reaction.

"But then," Paris added, "he also told me Susan Nicoletti had a crush on him."

That got B'Elanna's attention. "Why do you say that as though it's ridiculous?"

Paris shrugged. "Well . . . I mean Harry's a great-looking young man and all, or so I've heard . . . but . . . "

"But what?" asked B'Elanna, her nausea apparently forgotten, driven off by indignation. "He's no Tom Paris?"

"It was a long time ago," Paris explained patiently. "But yes, I'd been pursuing Susan rather vigorously, and she wouldn't so much as have a cup of coffee with me."

"And it was *impossible* that she might have taken a liking to Harry instead. Is that what you're saying?"

He frowned. "You're making this sound like something it isn't. I'm not putting Harry down. But at that point, he was naive. Inexperienced. Green, I'd guess you'd say."

"And at that point," B'Elanna noted, "I remember *you—"*

She stopped suddenly. Her queasiness seemed to be coming back.

"I think I'm feeling a little sick to my stomach," she said.

Paris darted to the rescue. "That's because you dropped out of the academy too soon. In the third year there's a six-week program of actual space walks—so you can get used to them."

B'Elanna grunted. "I never would have lasted to the third year. If I hadn't dropped out, they would have asked me to leave."

He chuckled. "I can't believe you were as bad as you say you were."

She scowled. "I was *worse.* Always getting into trouble, arguing . . . fighting. I don't know why they put up with me as long as they did."

"Big, bad B'Elanna. I wish I'd known you then."

She gave him a sidelong glance. "You'd have hated me."

Paris shook his head. "I can't imagine a time when I wouldn't have found you fascinating."

B'Elanna turned to him, not knowing what to say. Obviously, she was unaccustomed to fielding compliments.

Before she could respond, he heard a sound like comm static. A curtain of light seemed to ripple around them for a moment.

"What the hell was *that?"* Paris wondered.

B'Elanna checked the sensors on her padd. "More ion turbulence," she told him.

Suddenly, he heard something else—a series of shrill alarm beeps. Paris checked his padd and felt a chill climb his spine.

Looking at his companion, he said, "My oxygen supply is leaking."

He'd barely gotten the words out when a computer voice confirmed them. "Warning. Oxygen level at one hundred fourteen millibars and falling."

Paris started pushing controls on his sleeve, but nothing he did seemed to help. "I can't stop it," he groaned.

The computer spoke up again. "Warning. Oxygen level at ninety-three millibars and falling."

B'Elanna looked at him, her face a mirror for his dismay. Then her eyes hardened with resolve. "We'll have to share *my* oxygen."

"Yours?" Paris asked.

"Mine," she confirmed. "It's the only chance you've got."

Before he could protest, B'Elanna pulled him close again. Then she worked at her neck to open a small compartment.

"Warning," the computer voice in the flight controller's suit announced. "Oxygen level at seventy-nine millibars."

Paris could feel his air thinning quickly. He had to draw painfully deep breaths to get what he needed from it.

B'Elanna pulled out an air hose from the vicinity of her neck. Then she attached it to a like compartment in Paris's suit.

"Are you getting air now?" she asked him.

At first, he wasn't. Despite his efforts to remain calm, to breathe evenly, he felt himself gasping, on the edge of panic.

Then, as his lungs filled, he was able to control his breathing better. He was able to relax, at least a little.

"Yeah," Paris rasped. "Much better. Thanks."

"Don't mention it."

B'Elanna turned to the controls on her sleeve—and did a double take. Even through their faceplates, Tom could see the consternation on her face. The *fear.*

"What's wrong?" he asked.

"That turbulence damaged my suit, too," she said. "I should still have at least twenty-four hours' worth of oxygen . . . "

"But?" he prodded.

B'Elanna's face was as devoid of color as he had ever seen it. "But there's only about a half hour left."

Paris cursed beneath his breath. This wasn't good, he thought. This wasn't good at all.

Janeway and Seven of Nine had been at it for over an hour.

They had been sitting side by side in the captain's ready room, making computations on their padds and comparing them, trying to figure out what could have gone wrong with *Voyager*'s attempt to open a transwarp conduit.

To that point, they hadn't found a thing.

Janeway was completing a calculation when Vorik's voice interrupted her. "Engineering to Captain Janeway."

"Yes, Ensign?" the captain responded.

"I'm pleased to inform you that we are making excellent progress. Impulse power should be restored within the hour."

"Good news," said Janeway. "*Very* good news. Let me know as soon as the engines are on-line again."

"Yes, ma'am."

Just then, Seven of Nine raised her head. "Captain . . . "

Janeway looked into the Borg's eyes and saw a flicker of discovery there. "What is it?" she asked eagerly.

Seven of Nine handed the captain her padd. Janeway took it and studied the figures on it with interest.

"I believe I've found the cause of the accident," said the Borg. "Erratic fluctuations in the ship's warp power output."

"Fluctuations . . . " Janeway muttered.

She saw them now in the midst of all the other information. Unfortunately, they had been within established tolerances, so they hadn't set off an alarm or otherwise called attention to themselves.

"When the tachyon levels rose to a resonant frequency," Seven of Nine explained, "core pressure increased—"

"Exponentially," the captain said. "And the magnetic flow field constricted at the same rate."

The Borg nodded. "Yes."

"Then it *was* an accident," Janeway concluded triumphantly.

She slumped in her seat, relieved. She hadn't wanted to believe Seven of Nine was responsible for the incident—and now, with the answer in hand, she didn't have to.

Her door chimed, drawing her attention. "Come in," she said.

The door slid aside, revealing Janeway's first officer. He looked worried about something.

"Captain, we just picked up a carrier wave with a Starfleet signature. I'd guess it's Tom and B'Elanna . . . but they're not answering our hails."

Janeway nodded. "They may be in trouble. As soon as we get impulse power back, we'll—"

She never finished her sentence. It was interrupted by Tuvok's intercom voice. "Tuvok to the captain. Can you come to the bridge?"

Janeway exchanged looks with Chakotay, and then with Seven of Nine. "On my way," she replied.

The three of them filed out onto the bridge. Kim, who was manning the ops station, was as serious as Janeway had ever seen him.

Tuvok barked out his report. "We're being approached by an armada of Caatati ships. I count twenty-seven of them."

"They're hailing us," Kim announced.

Janeway turned to the forward viewscreen, wondering what this could be about. "On screen, Mr. Kim."

Abruptly, the Caatati named Lumas appeared on the screen. "Hello, Captain," he said. "We meet again."

"You've brought some friends," she pointed out.

Lumas smiled a hollow smile. "Needy friends, I fear. We're hoping you will offer us more supplies."

Janeway gathered herself. She could see where this was going. "I made it clear last time that we couldn't possibly provide enough for all your ships. Our resources are limited."

"And I had to accept that, because your ship was more powerful than mine," Lumas told her. "But the situation has changed, hasn't it? You're at a disadvantage now. We have your warp core."

Janeway glanced at Tuvok. He confirmed the boast with a subtle nod. Cursing silently, the captain turned to Lumas again.

"So we both know you can't escape," the Caatati told her. "I'm hoping that will make you . . . shall we say, more generous?"

"I'm afraid you're wrong," the captain told him. "We've given you everything we can spare. Return the core and we'll be on our way."

The Caatati's expression hardened. "We don't really care if you can 'spare' it or not. Prepare to hand over your food, your weapons, and your thorium supply."

"And if we don't?" Janeway asked.

"One of our ships might not seem threatening to you," Lumas noted. "But I assure you, twenty-seven can inflict real damage. And as you've seen, we are desperate. We have very little to lose."

The Caatati let his threat soak in for a moment. The captain didn't take it lightly, either.

"One thing more," he said. "That Borg you're protecting—we want her, too. There are many of us who'd enjoy a chance to repay one of them for what they did to us."

Janeway glanced at Seven of Nine. On the surface, the Borg seemed unmoved. But deep down, where a human still existed in her, she had to be more than a little concerned.

Certainly, the captain was.

CHAPTER 19

B'ELANNA KNEW HOW BAD THE SITUATION WAS. AFTER ALL, IT DIDN'T TAKE an engineer to figure it out.

Half an hour's worth of oxygen had sounded bad. Now she and Tom had even less. Soon, they would have less than that.

Then nothing.

Silence. Fade to black. End of story.

Tom knew what was going on, too. That's why he had been so quiet the last few minutes. Knowing him, he wanted to encourage her, wanted to give her hope—but, obviously, he couldn't find anything to say.

B'Elanna was quiet, too. But then, she had a lot to think about. A lot to deal with. After a while, it seemed like a maze.

Abruptly, Tom pressed the controls on his sleeve. "I'm cutting the oxygen ratio," he said. "That should give us a few more minutes."

B'Elanna realized she was dozing off. "I'm feeling kind of groggy," she told Tom.

He nodded knowingly. "Oxygen deprivation."

"And you're lowering it?" she asked him.

Tom smiled wanly at her. "Have to try to make it last as long as possible, you know?"

Normally, she would have argued with him. But by then, all the fight had gone out of her.

More silence. They drifted through space, tethered neck-to-neck by B'Elanna's oxygen hose. She ran through the maze some more.

Then something occurred to her, something she felt compelled to share. "It's ironic, isn't it?"

"What is?"

"Today," she said. "The Day of Honor . . . is the day I'm going to die. If only my mother knew."

Tom shook his head emphatically. "We're not going to die, B'Elanna. Stop talking like that."

She grunted. "Just what do you think is going to happen?"

He shrugged. "Anything can happen. Anything at all. And stop arguing—it wastes oxygen."

B'Elanna shot Tom a look, but did as he asked. After all, arguing *would* be a drain on their oxygen supply.

But she couldn't keep silent. Not anymore. "We have to face up to it, Tom. We're going to die."

He frowned. "I don't want to talk about that." Then he glanced in her direction. "There's something I've been wanting to ask you."

"I guess now would be the time."

"When we first met," Tom recalled, "you didn't have a very high opinion of me. Right?"

B'Elanna chuckled. "That's putting it mildly. I thought you were an arrogant, self-absorbed pig."

He smiled. "Flattery won't get you any more oxygen. So . . . now what do you think? Have I changed?"

"A lot," she told him. "Now you're a stubborn, domineering pig."

Tom looked at her, surprised.

"Just kidding," B'Elanna assured him.

Then she realized what she had done. It hit her with the impact of a phaser blast in the stomach.

"There I go again," B'Elanna said, her annoyance evident in her voice. "I'm pushing you away, any way I can. You're right about me, Tom. That's what I do—I push people away."

"Well," he replied, "I'll give you one thing—it's a surefire way of not getting hurt."

She nodded. "You're right." And then, "I'm such a coward."

"No, you're not."

"I am," she insisted.

Tom wrapped his arm around her. "Shhh. Save your air."

But she couldn't stop talking, couldn't stop facing things she hadn't wanted to face before. "Funny. Now I wish I'd finished the Day of Honor ritual, even though I wasn't faring too well. At least if I'd seen it through, maybe I'd feel . . . I don't know. Complete."

"Complete?" he echoed.

She was having trouble putting the right words together. It was the lack of oxygen—she knew that. Still, it was frustrating.

"I don't know what I'm trying to say," she told Tom. "All my life, this has all been so confusing—this Klingon business. My mother, my father. It's always been easier just to ignore it."

"Until I dredged it up," he interjected.

B'Elanna nodded. "Until you dredged it up." She looked at Tom. "No, that's not fair. Not fair at all. I've spent my life running from who I am. All you've done is help me stop and turn around. And now that I have . . ."

Suddenly, she was overcome with emotion.

"And now that you have?" he prodded.

B'Elanna heaved a sigh. "It's too late."

Anger flared in Tom's eyes. "Stop that."

She shook her head. "We have to look at it, Tom. We have to stop kidding ourselves. If I'm going to die, I want to acknowledge it. Maybe there are things that . . . that should be said."

He gave her a long, searching look. "Maybe so," he agreed.

"Don't you have any regrets?" B'Elanna asked. "Things you'd like to get off your chest?"

Tom laughed softly. "Too many to list."

She held his gaze with her own. "Why not start?"

The flight controller hesitated. The conversation had unexpectedly turned back on him, and he was clearly no more comfortable talking about himself than B'Elanna was.

"I wish my parents could know me now," he said. "My father especially. I wish he could see me wearing a Starfleet uniform again. I guess that's my main regret." He looked at her. "How about you?"

B'Elanna pondered the question. "I wish . . . I wish I knew my father better. I was only five when he left us. One day I came home and he was making arrangements to ship out—just like that."

Tom looked sympathetic. "Sometimes those things just happen."

Silence again. All B'Elanna could hear was the sound of her breathing, harsh and labored.

"Feel better?" asked Tom.

"You?" she countered.

He thought for a moment. "I guess so."

B'Elanna nodded. "Me, too."

Janeway glared at the viewscreen. Lumas's image had disappeared, leaving her and her officers with a view of the nearly thirty Caatati vessels amassed against them.

She wondered if Rahmin's ship was among them. She wanted to think that it wasn't, but she couldn't know for certain.

"Our weapons are a lot more powerful than theirs," Chakotay pointed out. "I say we put up a fight."

Tuvok frowned. "Perhaps they will settle for less than they demanded. It is a common bargaining strategy."

Kim agreed. "Maybe if we give them *something,* it'll appease them."

Janeway shook her head. "Given the mood the Caatati are in now, I can't imagine what would satisfy them—short of all we have."

"I will go," said the Borg, who had been silent to that point.

All heads turned. Seven of Nine met their gazes evenly.

"They asked for me," she pointed out. "If I surrender myself, perhaps they will let you leave."

Janeway stared at her. It was the first altruistic gesture she had ever heard from a Borg. In that sense, it was as remarkable as any cosmic phenomenon she had ever been fortunate enough to witness.

"Seven," the captain said, "that's very generous of you. And very courageous. But I will *not* turn you over to them."

The Borg tried to absorb Janeway's remark. "I was only offering to do what would be best for this group," she explained.

The captain smiled. "You're *part* of this group now. And we're going to protect you, one way or the other."

Seven of Nine's brow puckered. Clearly, she was struggling to understand this ethic.

"You . . . want to protect me?"

Janeway nodded. Then she turned to the others.

"It's time to stop talking about this," she said. "Tom and B'Elanna are in trouble and we have to find them. Tuvok?"

"Yes, Captain."

"What's the status of our weapons array?"

The Vulcan's answer was quick and to the point. "Weapons are at the ready. However, our shield strength is extremely low."

Janeway considered that. "We can shut down nonessential systems. Reroute power to the shields." She looked around the bridge at her officers. "We're going to fight."

"That might not be necessary," declared Seven of Nine.

She seemed excited—or perhaps agitated. It was difficult for the captain to tell which.

In any case, Janeway dismissed the suggestion. "I've already said that giving you up is not an option."

"I am referring to another strategy," the Borg told her.

"In that case," said Janeway, "let's hear it."

"Caatati technology," said Seven of Nine, "depends on thorium isotopes. That is what drives their ships. It is what powers their systems. If they had enough thorium, they could become self-sustaining."

"But we don't have that much thorium to give them," Kim reminded her. "In fact, we have very little."

Seven of Nine had an answer for him. "When we assimilated the Caatati, the survivors lost their ability to replicate the isotopes. But I have retained that knowledge. I could design an energy matrix which would produce thorium in large quantities."

Janeway realized her mouth was open. She closed it.

"Seven," Chakotay asked, "if you had this knowledge all along, why didn't you say something?"

The Borg hesitated. She seemed almost annoyed. "I am not accustomed to thinking that way. Borg do not consider giving technology away. They only think of assimilating it."

When the captain spoke, it was in her gentlest tone. "And what do you suppose made you consider it now?"

Seven of Nine turned to her, clearly at a loss. "I am not certain."

"Maybe," the captain suggested with a certain satisfaction, "it was just an unexpected act of kindness."

The Borg pondered that possibility. "Maybe," she allowed at last.

Clearly, Seven of Nine had a long road to travel before she could call herself human again. However, in Janeway's eyes, she had taken a big step along that road.

Progress, the captain thought. It was nice to see.

"Let's go," she said to all and sundry. "Seven, you work with Vorik to build the energy matrix, while I convince the Caatati there's a better way out of this than bloodshed."

As Janeway watched the Borg head for the turbolift, she was already choosing the words she would use to pitch the deal to Lumas.

CHAPTER 20

JANEWAY WATCHED LUMAS'S REACTION ON THE VIEWSCREEN. OBVIOUSLY, HE hadn't expected a counteroffer.

"A limitless supply of thorium isotopes?"

"That's what I said," the captain told him. "Imagine, never having to beg for them again. Imagine never having to beg for *anything*."

The Caatati made a derisive sound. "It's impossible."

"What if it's not?" she rejoined.

Lumas's eyes narrowed. "You're trying to deceive me."

"If that were the case," Janeway declared, "would I have picked such an outlandish premise?"

Actually, she thought, I might have. But he doesn't know me well enough to realize that.

The Caatati still wasn't buying it. "How is it you never mentioned an energy matrix before?"

"I didn't know there was such a thing," the captain replied honestly. "It was suggested to me only a few minutes ago."

Lumas looked at her askance. "Then how do you know it will work?"

"Actually," said Janeway, "I don't. But if I were you, I'd be willing to exercise a little patience to find out. Then, if it turns out we can't come up with the matrix after all, you haven't lost a thing. You can still use your greater numbers to try to pound us into submission."

Though I'd still put my credits on *Voyager*, the captain mused. But she kept her sentiment to herself.

The Caatati considered her proposition. "How long do you need to create the matrix?" he asked at last.

"An hour," she told him.

He chuckled dryly, thinking Janeway was joking. "That's all?"

The captain smiled. "That's what *I* said."

Lumas watched Janeway's image vanish from his viewscreen. Once again, he found himself looking at *Voyager*'s predicament—that of a single starship surrounded by a swarm of Caatati vessels.

Sedrek approached him. "Captain Janeway says she can give us all the thorium we need."

"That's what she says," Lumas agreed.

"Can we believe her?" Sedrek asked.

Clearly, he hoped that they could. It showed in his eyes and in the way the muscles rippled in his temples.

Lumas shrugged. "Perhaps. But even then . . . "

His second-in-command looked at him. "Yes?"

"I need some time alone in my quarters," said Lumas. "I have a great deal to think about."

Sedrek seemed to understand. "And in the meantime?"

"If *Voyager* makes a move," Lumas told him, "let me know. Otherwise, simply maintain our position."

The other man nodded. "Understood."

Lumas clapped him on the shoulder. Then he left the bridge and retired to his cabin. After all, he *did* have a great deal to think about.

As the door to his cabin irised open and Lumas looked inside, he was struck by how small his quarters looked. How cramped and confined.

But then, his perspective had changed. Lumas was seeing the place with eyes that Janeway had opened to new vistas—new possibilities. And not just for him, but for his long-suffering people.

Certainly, the prospect of being able to generate thorium isotopes whenever necessary was an attractive one. It would mean an end to poverty, an end to sickness and hunger. It would mean the Caatati could again devote their lives to something besides survival.

But Lumas had yet to see proof of Janeway's claims. He had yet to see her miracle machine with his own eyes.

And if she showed it to him? he asked himself. If she demonstrated it could do everything she had said it could?

Then what?

Was he to embrace it without reservation—and in doing so, embrace the insidious deal the human had set before him? Was he to forget all the misery and devastation his people had endured and let the Borg witch go free?

Lumas shook his head. He couldn't do it. He couldn't forget what the Borg had done to him. Even if it meant the death of his people, even if it meant the extinction of the entire Caatati race, he couldn't let a chance for revenge slip through his fingers.

He would tell Janeway that he rejected her proposition. And if she remained steadfast in her refusal to turn over the Borg, he would carry out his threat. He would set his ships on her like a pack of sharp-toothed *g'daggen* on a fat-laden *quarril.*

Either way, the Borg would have occasion to regret what her race had done. Either way, she would—

"Father?" came a voice.

Astounded, Lumas turned to look back over his shoulder. He saw his daughter Finaea standing there. She looked concerned.

"You're unhappy, father. Do you want to talk about it?"

For a moment or two, he didn't understand. Then his fingers climbed to the crown of his head and felt the cool, slender form of the realizor there.

"I don't remember—"

"Remember what?" asked Finaea, smiling gently at her father's confusion.

I don't remember putting on the realizor, he mused, finishing the thought. But he didn't tell his daughter that, because it would also have meant telling her she wasn't real—and she had endured enough pain.

Lumas smiled back at her. "I didn't remember seeing you come in. That's all." He reached for her hand and held it. "Where are your mother and your sister? At the marketplace?"

Finaea seemed to look more deeply into his eyes than ever before. "They didn't come because . . . because they couldn't," she explained.

"Couldn't?" he echoed.

Lumas didn't understand. After all, his wife and daughters *always* came together, except on those rare occasions when he preferred the company of only one or two of them.

Finaea paused, as if searching for words. "You needed to talk," she said finally. "With me. *Just* with me."

He felt a chill climb the rungs of his spine. "How would you know that?" he asked softly.

She shrugged. "I'm part of you, Father. I always have been. And right now, I'm the part you need the most."

Lumas looked at her with dread in his heart. The way Finaea was speaking to him, it was almost as if she knew . . .

No, he insisted. That was impossible. She wasn't real. She had no awareness except for his awareness, no reality except that which—

—that which he *gave* her.

Suddenly, Lumas figured out what must have happened. As he sat there pondering Janeway's offer, he had unknowingly taken hold of the realizor and placed it on his head—and entirely without meaning to, he had conjured up the image of his daughter Finaea.

Yes, he thought. That was it.

And because she had come from his subconscious mind, she wasn't the Finaea that he knew and loved. Or rather, not *just* that Finaea. This one was aware of herself as a construct. She knew that she was there for a reason.

And that reason was . . . to assure him he had made the right decision? Or to argue against it? There was only one way to find out, he supposed.

"You know of the human captain's proposal," Lumas said.

It felt strange speaking to his daughter of such things—so strange, in fact, he thought about replacing her with the Finaea he remembered. But in the end, he didn't.

"I know of it," she confirmed.

"Then you also know I've decided to reject it."

Finaea regarded him. "You'll destroy *Voyager?"*

"Only if necessary," he told her. "More than likely, Janeway will give up the Borg first. And even if she doesn't, there's no reason to annihilate the ship—not when we can strip it for its resources."

"I see," said his daughter. "And this is just. After all, the Borg destroyed our homeworld, through no fault of our own."

"Exactly," Lumas replied.

"And you'll take no joy in battering and stripping *Voyager,*" Finaea went on. "It's not as if you mean the captain and her crew any harm. You're just doing what you have to in order to survive."

"That's right," he responded, relieved that Finaea had the sense to see things his way.

She nodded. "Just like the Borg."

Lumas felt as if he had been dealt a physical blow. He shook his head from side to side. "No," he said. "Not at all like the Borg. I'm not a cold-hearted murderer, Finaea. You know me better than that."

"But you would sooner kill innocent people than let a Borg go free."

"I'm doing it for you!" he told her. "For you! The Borg took my family away and made monsters out of them! If I have a chance to strike back at them, how can I ignore it?"

His daughter looked at him as lovingly as she had ever looked at him in life. "You can ignore it," she said, "because you're *not* like them. When the Borg took me and mother and Anyelot, they turned us each into one of them. But it'll be a greater tragedy if they turned *you* into one of them, too."

Lumas's throat hurt. He swallowed hard and fell to his knees at Finaea's feet. Tears streamed down his cheeks—just as they had his last day on the Caatati homeworld.

"They took you away from me," he moaned. "They took you all. And there was nothing I could do about it."

Lumas felt a hand on his shoulder. Looking up, he saw that his daughter was smiling down at him. "It's all right," she said. "I forgive you, Father." And then again: "I forgive you."

They embraced. And they stayed that way for a long, long time.

CHAPTER 21

As Lumas took his place on the bridge of his ship, every technician there turned to look at him. Sedrek was no exception.

After all, they knew what kind of decision he had to make. What's more, they knew how important it could be to them—and to all Caatati.

On the viewscreen, nothing had changed. *Voyager* was still surrounded by the force Lumas had assembled.

"Contact Janeway," he said.

One of his technicians worked at his controls for a moment. "I've established a communications link," the man reported.

Lumas nodded. "On screen."

A moment later, Janeway's face appeared. "Hello again. I take it you've had enough time to consider our offer?"

"I have," he confirmed.

The human regarded him. "And?"

"I want to see this matrix of yours. Is it ready?"

"It is," Janeway told him. "And I'll be glad to show it to you." She gave an order to someone offscreen, then looked to the Caatati again. "If you lower your shields, we'll beam you over."

Then her image vanished and was replaced by that of her vessel. Sedrek came to stand by Lumas.

"Are you sure about this?" he asked. "What if they open fire once our shields are down? Or try to make a hostage out of you?"

Lumas shook his head. "They won't try either—not with so many Caatati ships surrounding them."

"All the more reason to destroy us—or take you hostage," his second-in-command argued. "They know you're the one who brought the Caatati together. With you out of the way . . . "

Lumas dismissed the idea with a gesture. "You flatter me," he said. "I am no more important than anyone else, Sedrek. There are any number of commanders here who can lead an assault as well as I can."

The Caatati didn't believe that, of course. It just seemed like the right thing to say.

He turned to Grommir. "Lower shields."

Reluctantly, the technician did as he was told.

Lumas took a breath, then let it out. Before he had finished exhaling, his surroundings had changed. He found himself standing in a large room full of complex equipment.

He wasn't alone, either. Janeway was there.

And so was the Borg.

Janeway watched Lumas's face as he materialized in engineering.

The Caatati noticed her first. Then he turned and saw that Seven of Nine was present as well, and his eyes widened.

"The Borg . . . " he said.

"Her name is Seven of Nine," the captain told him. "And she's the one who designed the energy matrix for you."

She indicated the device, a globe with a flat surface at each of its poles. It was rather small, considering the magnitude of its importance to the Caatati. Lumas tore his eyes away from the Borg and studied it.

But he was still thinking about Seven of Nine. Janeway could see it in his expression, in the way the muscles in his temples fluttered. He was thinking about what the Borg had done to his people.

Allowing Seven of Nine to present the matrix was a calculated risk. The captain had known that at the outset. However, she wanted Lumas to see that the Borg wasn't the monster he imagined her to be.

Not anymore. Now she was simply another member of *Voyager's* crew. And without Seven of Nine—without her knowledge and experience—Janeway could never have offered the Caatati the hope of prosperity.

"This matrix," said the Borg, "will produce nine hundred and forty-four grams of thorium per day."

Lumas took a closer look at the energy device. He gave the impression that he was qualified to understand its workings, though Janeway wasn't at all sure that was the case.

"Now you can power all your systems," the captain told him, "and begin to rebuild your replication technology. You can feed all those children you spoke of." She let that tantalizing prospect hang in the air for a moment.

The Caatati looked up—not at Janeway, but at Seven of Nine. "You think this makes up for what you've done?"

"It can't," said the captain. "Nothing can. But as you can see, this woman is no longer part of the Borg collective. She has changed. And if she can do it, perhaps you can, too."

Lumas eyed her. "It's easy for you to say that. It wasn't your family her people killed."

Janeway sighed. "I haven't lost family to the Borg—but I've lost friends and colleagues. My people have experienced their share of misery at the hands of the collective."

The Caatati seemed surprised by that. "And you don't hate them?" He glanced at Seven of Nine. "You don't hate *her?"*

"I hate what they've *done,"* said the captain. "But I can't hate *them* any more than I can hate a planet for orbiting its sun. Remember—every Borg was a victim before he became an aggressor. Every one of them was plucked from the heart of a civilization he loved. And in that regard, Seven of Nine is no exception."

And neither, Janeway thought, was any loved one Lumas had lost to the Borg invasion. She hadn't come out and said that, hoping the Caatati could make that leap of logic for himself.

"Will you call off your armada and allow us to leave?" she asked.

Lumas frowned. "One device isn't enough for all our ships."

"True," said Seven of Nine. "But using this matrix as a template, you can construct as many matrices as you like. We can provide you with all the necessary components and specifications."

Lumas stared at her. Somewhere inside him, a struggle was taking place. The captain imagined she understood part of that struggle, but not all of it.

After all, she knew so little about the Caatati, and even less about Lumas himself. She could only hope her words had made some sense to him.

Because if they hadn't, the future looked bleak indeed. But not for the Caatati—for Janeway and her crew.

Lumas picked up the matrix and hefted it in his hands. Then he turned to the captain, his expression a difficult one to read.

"You're free to go," he told her. "And . . . thank you."

The captain smiled. She was about to respond to Lumas's expression of gratitude when the Borg did it for her.

"You're . . . welcome," said Seven of Nine.

The Caatati looked at her. Obviously, he hadn't expected that.

Neither had Janeway. She regarded the Borg in a new and more hopeful light. Progress, she thought. And just in the nick of time.

B'Elanna sighed in the confines of her mask.

She wanted to see her father one last time. She wanted to ask him what he had been doing with his life the last twenty years or so.

She wondered if he was happy—if he was glad that he had gone his own way. If he ever missed his Little Bee.

After all, she hadn't heard from him since that day he left the colony. Not even once. He had promised her he would visit all the time, and keep in touch via subspace packet. But he hadn't.

And when B'Elanna pleaded with her mother for an explanation, her mother told her that was how humans were. *Some* humans, anyway.

Her father was alive and well, her mother said—she knew that for a fact. But if he didn't care enough about his daughter to stay in touch, he was to be forgotten—treated as if he were dead.

Of course, her mother was a Klingon, the offspring of a prominent house. To such a woman, pride was everything. Pride and that stiff-necked sense of honor she was famous for.

As a child, B'Elanna had always hated those qualities in her mother. She had always blamed them for driving her father away.

And maybe they had.

But looking back now, she saw that they were part of her mother—part of what made her what she was. And part of her mother's half-Klingon daughter, too, no matter how hard she tried to deny it.

What a mess I am, B'Elanna thought. On one hand, looking for love—and on the other, pushing it away as hard as I can. On one hand, seeking approval—and on the other, resisting it.

Maybe her mother had had the right idea. Maybe she had been more courageous than . . . courageous than . . .

"Warning," said a voice.

B'Elanna started at the sound. It was only then that she realized she had begun to doze off.

"Oxygen level at one hundred four millibars and falling," said the computer in Tom's suit.

B'Elanna shook him. Tom's eyelids fluttered, but didn't open. Apparently, his slumber had been deeper than hers.

"Tom," she said, her voice thick and a little slurred. It was getting harder and harder to speak, much less make herself understood.

"Mmmm," was his only response.

"Tom," she said again, this time with more urgency.

"Leave me alone," he replied, like a child telling his mother he was too tired to go to school that morning.

"Come on," she insisted. "Open your eyes."

He squinted at her. "I was having a dream. A really nice dream. We were home. There were lots of people cheering and pinning medals on us." He smiled happily. "Don't be afraid, B'Elanna. It's not going to be hard. It's going to be really . . . peaceful."

"Warning," said the computer in Tom's suit. "Oxygen level at eighty-seven millibars and falling."

B'Elanna believed what Tom had told her. In the end, it would be peaceful. But she couldn't face the end. Not just yet.

"Tom, there's something I have to say . . . "

"Me, too," he said. "I'm glad the last thing I'll see . . . is you. . . . "

B'Elanna found herself pulling Tom closer, environmental suit and all. He was pulling her closer as well. And it wasn't just the fact that neither of them wanted to die alone.

"No," she told him. "Something else . . . "

"What?" Tom asked softly.

It was hard for B'Elanna to remain focused. She was so light-headed, the words seemed to dissipate and drift off into oblivion. But her determination won out.

"I've been a coward," she confessed. "About everything. Everything that really matters."

"You're being a little hard on yourself," he said dreamily.

"No," B'Elanna declared. "I'm going to die—without a shred of honor. And for the first time in my life, that bothers me. So I have to tell you something. I have to—"

"Warning," Tom's computer interrupted. "Oxygen level at seventy-one millibars and falling."

Tom's eyes were closing.

"Tom," B'Elanna said.

He came awake with a start. "I'm here," he told her. "It's okay. It won't be long now."

"I have to tell you the truth," B'Elanna said. "Maybe then I can die with a little honor after all."

"Truth about . . . about what?" he asked.

"Something I haven't said before," she sighed. "So at least, I won't pile up any more regrets."

B'Elanna swallowed. It was harder than she'd thought it would be.

"If I . . . if I didn't know we were dying . . . I could never say this." She smiled. "Silly, isn't it?"

"Warning," said Tom's suit computer—like the knell of doom. "Oxygen level at six-two millibars and falling."

"Better say it now," Tom told her. "We don't have much longer . . ."

"Okay," B'Elanna said. "Okay." She looked into his heavy-lidded eyes. "It was all for you, Tom."

He seemed puzzled. "For me?"

"All for you," she repeated. "The Klingon rituals, the Day of Honor. I just wanted you to be proud of me."

Tom shook his head. "You didn't have to . . . to do anything to make me proud, B'Elanna. I was proud . . . of you already. . . ."

It was so *frustrating.* Why couldn't she just come out and say it? "No, you don't understand . . . what I'm trying to say . . . " She took a deep, ragged breath and got it out.

Finally.

"I love you, Tom."

He didn't answer. He just looked at her, stunned by her admission and losing consciousness from lack of oxygen.

"Well," B'Elanna said at last, "say something."

Tom gave her a weak smile. "You picked a great time to tell me . . ." Then his eyelids began to flutter dangerously. "To tell me . . . "

As his eyes closed, a peaceful look came over him. B'Elanna's secret revealed, she felt a great burden fall away from her. Maybe it was time to let her eyes close as well, she thought.

And they did.

But not before she hugged Tom as hard as she could. And somehow, even though he was all but unconscious, he hugged her back.

B'Elanna's last thought was that Tom was right. It *was* peaceful dying this way. And their being together made it even more so.

But something wouldn't let her go. At first, she didn't know what it was, but it kept tugging at her, insisting that she pay heed to it.

She opened her eyes.

"My god," B'Elanna whispered.

There was something in the distance. Something bright and shiny. It was too far away for her to make out its shape, but it hadn't been there before. And unless she was completely crazy, it was getting larger.

Suddenly, another voice came to her. Not the computer voice they'd been listening to, measuring the time left to them. No, this was a different voice. A more welcome voice.

"*Voyager* to Tom Paris. This is the captain, Tom . . . do you read me? Respond. *Voyager* to B'Elanna Torres. This is the captain . . ."

Tom's eyes came open again. He looked around, dazed. Then he licked his lips and spoke in a voice so low, B'Elanna could barely hear it. "We're here . . . Captain . . . we're here . . . "

Janeway's voice soared with joy. "We were beginning to get worried about you. Prepare to beam aboard."

B'Elanna smiled. Then she turned to Tom. She looked at him, searching his face for whatever emotion she might find there.

Tom looked back at her, doing the same thing. But even she didn't know what he saw.

B'Elanna knew only one thing for certain—nothing would ever again be the same between them. She was still holding on to that thought as the familiar confines of the transporter room appeared around them . . .

Nothing would ever again be the same.

EPILOGUE

The Doctor was in his office, thinking about all that had happened to him in the last several hours, when he received a communication over the ship's intercom system.

"Doctor, this is Commander Chakotay. I have a couple of patients for you."

"I see," said the Doctor. "And who might these patients be?"

"Lieutenants Paris and Torres. We've just recovered them. Seems they were a bit low on oxygen."

"Bring them in," the Doctor advised him. "At the very least, someone should take a look at them."

"They're on their way," said Chakotay.

The Doctor approached the nearest biobed and waited patiently for Torres and Paris to arrive. Another day, he thought, another holiday.

He couldn't wait to celebrate.

DAY OF HONOR

HONOR BOUND

Diana G. Gallagher

Interior Illustrations by Gordon Purcell

With respect and affection
for Ray Sehgal,
a brilliant young scientist
and my youngest Trek advisor

With special thanks to
L.A. Graf
for providing invaluable information
from "Armageddon Sky"
in the interest of consistency
concerning the Day of Honor rites and rules

STARFLEET TIMELINE

2264

The launch of Captain James T. Kirk's five-year mission, U.S.S. Enterprise, NCC-1701.

2292

Alliance between the Klingon Empire and the Romulan Star Empire collapses.

2293

Colonel Worf, grandfather of Worf Rozhenko, defends Captain Kirk and Doctor McCoy at their trial for the murder of Klingon chancellor Gorkon.

Khitomer Peace Conference, Klingon Empire/Federation (Star Trek VI).

2323

Jean-Luc Picard enters Starfleet Academy's standard four-year program.

2328

The Cardassian Empire annexes the Bajoran homeworld.

2346

Romulan massacre of Klingon outpost on Khitomer.

2351

In orbit around Bajor, the Cardassians construct a space station that they will later abandon.

2353

Kathryn Janeway enters Starfleet Academy.

2355

Kathryn Janeway meets Admiral Paris and begins a lifelong association with the esteemed scientist.

2363

Captain Jean-Luc Picard assumes command of U.S.S. Enterprise, NCC-1701-D

2367

Wesley Crusher enters Starfleet Academy.

An uneasy truce is signed between the Cardassians and the Federation.

Borg attack at Wolf 359; First Officer Lieutenant Commander Benjamin Sisko and his son, Jake, are among the survivors.

U.S.S. Enterprise-D defeats the Borg vessel in orbit around Earth.

2369

Commander Benjamin Sisko assumes command of Deep Space Nine in orbit over Bajor.

2371

U.S.S. Enterprise, NCC-1701-D, destroyed on Veridian III.

Former Enterprise captain James T. Kirk emerges from a temporal nexus, but dies helping Picard save the Veridian system.

U.S.S. Voyager, under the command of Captain Kathryn Janeway, is accidentally transported to the Delta Quadrant. The crew begins a 70-year journey back to Federation space.

2372

The Klingon Empire's attempted invasion of Cardassia Prime results in the dissolution of the Khitomer peace treaty between the Federation and the Klingon Empire.

Source: Star Trek® Chronology / Michael Okuda and Denise Okuda and Star Trek® Voyager™ Mosaic/Jeri Taylor

CHAPTER 1

ALEXANDER ROZHENKO WAS ONE-QUARTER HUMAN, THREE-QUARTERS Klingon and totally furious!

Sitting between his human grandparents in the shuttle terminal at Earth Station Bobruisk, Alexander stubbornly refused to look them in the eye. He didn't want to relax or listen to reason. He didn't want to see the troubled patience in Sergey Rozhenko's eyes or the disappointment his grandmother hid behind a stoical smile. But he especially didn't want to see his father, Worf.

"I don't understand this hostility toward your father, Alexander," Sergey said gently.

"Nor do I." Helena sighed with deep sorrow. "Worf is taking special leave from his duties on *Deep Space Nine* just to come see you. So you can celebrate the Klingon Day of Honor together. You were so upset when he canceled his vacation plans to visit Earth, we thought you'd be happy."

Alexander's upper lip curled in a snarl, a low, guttural expression of displeasure that was distinctly and uncomfortably Klingon. It was the kind of Klingon trait he usually struggled to suppress. Now, he didn't bother to try. He resented his grandparents' patronizing attitude toward him.

"He is taking *emergency* leave, and it's not because he wants to celebrate his sacred Klingon holiday with me!" Eyes flashing, Alexander snapped his gaze from his grandfather to his grandmother, then focused straight ahead. "My father is taking time away from his duty because *you* asked him to come."

Catching the worried glance that passed between the elderly couple, Alexander choked back the hurtful words he was about to add. It wasn't fair to take his anger out on his grandparents. That made about as much sense as blaming the Romulans who had attacked the Khitomer Outpost in 2346. If they had killed his father instead of leaving him alive at the age of six, Sergey and Helena Rozhenko wouldn't have adopted the orphaned Klingon and they wouldn't be saddled with a problem they couldn't handle now—him—their mostly Klingon grandson. Desperate, the Rozhenkos had turned to the one person in the Federation who might be able to help: Lieutenant Commander Worf, Strategic Operations Officer on *Deep Space Nine* and the only Klingon in Starfleet.

Sergey glanced at the time. "Worf's shuttle should be landing in a few minutes."

Alexander stiffened when the old man gripped his shoulder.

"At least try to be civil, Alexander." Removing his hand, Sergey spoke sternly. "Regardless of your misguided feelings right now, Worf is your father and you *will* treat him with respect."

Bristling, Alexander clenched his fists and concentrated on the steady movement of air in and out of his lungs. His grandfather rarely used that commanding tone of voice with him. In the past, Alexander would have felt ashamed and sorry for whatever he had done to deserve it. This time, it took every ounce of his willpower not to attack the old man.

In. Out. In. Out.

Alexander breathed, calming the explosive urge, but not the emotional torment he felt. His mother, K'Ehleyr, had been half-human and the Federation ambassador to the K'mpec government in the Klingon Empire before she was murdered by Duras. Like her, Alexander had embraced human behavior and customs with all his heart and soul. Now his cherished human value system and code-of-conduct was being threatened by a passion for violence that surged through his veins like a virus.

Alexander didn't know why, but he had suddenly become prone to enraged fits of temper that were getting harder to control. He was terrified that one day he wouldn't be able to stop himself and someone would get hurt. What he feared most was that the victim of his fury would be his beloved grandfather or grandmother.

And for that reason alone, Alexander was glad his father had agreed to visit Earth. He would rather die than bring harm to the kindly couple that

had given him a loving home as they had his father before him. His disruptive behavior had already caused his grandparents more heartache and worry than he cared to admit. The Rozhenkos did not have much to say about Worf's adolescent years, either, which made him suspect that his own faults were a lot worse than his father's had been.

Worf must have been a model child compared to him.

And that thought caused another spasm of intense anger to rise within him.

"It's here." Helena stood up. Anxious and excited, she gazed at the door where the disembarking passengers from the shuttlecraft *von Braun* would soon enter.

Nudging his sullen grandson to his feet, Sergey smiled tightly. "There is one thing you must never forget, Alexander. Worf loves you very much and nothing you do or say can change that."

Alexander nodded curtly, still avoiding his grandfather's gaze. He was certain of his father's feelings, too, but with a twist that Sergey didn't understand. Worf was Klingon and Klingons valued honor above all. His father had made *that* perfectly clear when he had gone back to the *Enterprise* to live after spending a year on Earth following his mother's death.

Alexander thought back to the traumatic and uncertain beginnings of his relationship with Worf. Even then, he had become too much of a discipline problem for the aging Rozhenkos to handle. Deanna Troi, the counselor aboard the starship, had recognized that his disgraceful lies and disruptive behavior were expressions of his feelings of loss and insecurity. Worf had understood and had decided not to send him to a Klingon school as he had planned. Being forgiven and accepted by his father had given him the stability he needed to resolve his emotional problems and explore his mixed heritage.

But I'm not a scared little kid anymore, Alexander thought dismally, and I don't have an acceptable excuse this time. Dragged away from his post on *Deep Space Nine* to deal with his unruly son, Worf would feel angry, betrayed and dishonored. Love didn't matter.

Bracing himself, Alexander watched the door as a stream of human and alien travelers walked through. Most of them were civilians and families returning from business trips or vacations on other worlds. An occasional flash of Starfleet red, blue or yellow caused the breath to catch in his throat before the silver sheen of the Klingon sash his father wore caught his eye.

Alexander couldn't help but feel a sense of awe as the imposing Klingon moved into view. Tall and muscular with an expression that always seemed grim, Worf paused in the doorway to scan the crowded waiting area. The human family ahead of him fumbled with bundles of souvenirs and carry-on baggage. He did not seem to notice the nervous glances the man and woman cast over their shoulders at him as they frantically tried to get out of his way. In fact, Alexander realized, everyone in the waiting area was giving him a wide berth and watching him suspiciously.

Which was no surpise to Alexander.

Hostilities had broken out between the Federation and the Klingon Empire after decades of peace. The tenuous alliance had dissolved when Gowron led a Klingon attack against the Cardassian Empire, believing it had been infiltrated by the Dominion. Starfleet had defended the Cardassians, an insult and breach of faith the Klingon Empire could not ignore even though Gowron had started the conflict because he was afraid and misinformed.

Worf, a Starfleet officer, had fought against the Klingons, but the uniform he wore with such fierce pride, evidence of his loyalty to the Federation, might as well have been invisible now. A mere piece of black and red cloth could not negate Worf's genetic heritage.

Or mine, Alexander thought dismally.

The boy wondered if his father was aware of the hostile shunning he would experience on Earth because he was a Klingon. Since the beginning of the break between the Empire and the Federation, Alexander's life at school and in the neighborhood had become a nightmare. His uncontrollable temper had flared up about the same time. He assumed the tantrums were provoked by the cruel and unjust actions and attitudes of his peers.

"Worf!" Helena waved and called to her adopted son. "Over here!"

Alexander tensed as his father greeted them with a slight nod. There was no warmth in the hard eyes that met his son's equally hard stare. As the boy expected, the reunion was not going to be pleasant. He had not even realized he was harboring a faint hope that Worf would be glad to see him. The unspoken rejection made his blood burn with a feverish fury.

"My boy!" Grinning, Sergey rushed forward, accidently brushing against the human man scurrying out of Worf's path. "Excuse me. I'm—"

"Watch where you're going!" The man's son, a large, husky boy about Alexander's age, shoved Sergey aside. "Klingon lover!"

Helena gasped and steadied Sergey as he stumbled into her.

"Howard!" The boy's father snapped, then paled.

The boy glared at the Rozhenkos.

Worf's eyes flashed and his lip quivered in a silent snarl. Every muscle in his powerful body tightened, poised to strike the boy who had pushed Sergey, but he did not attack.

In the fraction of a second Worf paused to calm himself, and everyone else in the area became frozen in shocked fear, Alexander reacted with pure Klingon rage.

Roaring, Alexander sprang toward Howard with his clawed hands aimed at the fragile human throat. The fury coursing through his young body blinded him to everything except the need to destroy the arrogant, offensive boy. Howard had insulted and shoved one of the few people in the galaxy Alexander loved.

"Alexander! No!"

Alexander barely heard his grandmother's scream as he tackled the stunned boy, knocking him to the ground. A strong hand gripped his arm, pulling him off the shrieking human before his fingers closed around tender flesh.

"That is enough!" Worf barked.

"Get him away!" Howard squealed as he scooted backward, then scrambled to his feet. "Get him away!"

Infused with strength as the savagery locked in his Klingon genes erupted, Alexander ripped free of the hand that held him.

Screeching with terror, Howard ran.

"Alexander!"

As Alexander gave chase, Worf's demanding voice was lost in the thunder of his own blood pounding in his ears. He was only vaguely aware of the alien-dotted, human sea parting before him or the shouts of those pursuing him. He was totally focused on the panicked boy fleeing through the terminal.

Leaping luggage and darting between supporting pillars and rows of seats, Alexander quickly closed the distance between himself and his prey. The stench of human fear flooded his nostrils, feeding the hunter frenzy that drove him. A terminal security guard jumped into the aisle ahead. Dodging to the right, Alexander shoved the man and ran past.

Howard looked back as the guard thudded against the wall. Eyes widening in fear, he stumbled over his own feet and sprawled on the tiled floor.

The cry of victory rising in Alexander's throat as he lunged toward the boy was abruptly silenced. A hand with a grip like iron clamped around his arm, stopping him dead in his tracks. He fought against the hold, but this time he could not break free.

"Alexander."

The calm, commanding sound of his father's voice broke through the fury. Pulse racing, Alexander blinked and tried to still his rapid breathing. Through a slowly clearing fog he saw Howard's parents help him up and draw him into the comfort of their arms. Then his grandmother's arms were around him, holding him close as she murmured soothing sounds into his ear. He buried his face against her chest and began to shake.

If he had caught Howard, he might have killed him.

A strong, but gentle hand gripped his shoulder. Alexander looked up, expecting his father to be furious, but there was no anger in the warm brown eyes that gazed down on him. Worf's face softened with relief and worry and a tight-lipped smile of reassurance.

Stunned, Alexander did not immediately realize that the deep, unfamiliar voice he heard next was addressing him.

"You're under arrest."

CHAPTER 2

IT'LL BE ALL RIGHT, ALEXANDER," HELENA WHISPERED. "YOU'LL SEE."

Alexander nodded and managed a wan smile to please his grandmother, but he was sure nothing would ever be all right again. He sat on one side of the Terminal Security Office with the Rozhenkos. Howard Chupek and his mother sat on the other side. Mr. Chupek and Worf stood stiffly before the chief of security's desk.

Like two Starfleet Academy cadets on report, Alexander thought glumly. Any chance there had been of closing the emotional gap between himself and his father was gone now. Worf would never forgive him for this embarrassment. Just as the sins of the father brought dishonor to the child in Klingon society, the sins of the child dishonored the father.

"I see no reason why this unfortunate situation cannot be settled rationally." Worf's deep base voice resounded through the small room even though he spoke with calm reserve.

"Rationally?" Mr. Chupek blustered. "That Klingon spitfire of yours would have ripped Howard apart if you hadn't stopped him, Mr. Worf!"

Howard glanced at Alexander with a triumphant smirk. The smug smile disappeared when Alexander countered with a menacing stare.

"My *son* was defending his grandfather," Worf argued quietly. "I do not condone Alexander's methods, Mr. Chupek. However, we would not be here now if your son had not insulted and pushed my father to begin with."

Security Chief Clausen flicked an anxious gaze between the two fathers. He seemed concerned that they might pick up the fight where the boys had left off.

"Your father?" The man frowned uncertainly.

"That is correct." Shifting his attention back to Chief Clausen, Worf used Mr. Chupek's confused silence to press the advantage. "My son is going through a phase that is difficult for a young Klingon under ordinary circumstances."

What does he mean by "phase"? Alexander shifted uncomfortably, losing all interest in Howard. He didn't think of himself as a Klingon. The idea that he might not be able to stop acting like one was very disturbing.

"And your point, Lieutenant Commander Worf?" Chief Clausen prodded cautiously.

"Present hostilities between the Federation and the Empire are compounding the..." Worf hesitated, groping for an acceptable word. "...problem. Howard Chupek's insulting actions are a perfect example of why this is so."

"My son may have exercised poor judgment," Mr. Chupek said hotly, "but an insult hardly justifies your son's violent behavior!"

Alexander tensed and clenched his teeth. His grandmother's hand closed over his wrist, an alarming reminder that the rage could escape if he let down his guard for even an instant.

"The boy was provoked." A glint of warning flared in Worf's eyes, but he remained in total control.

"Mr. Chupek," Chief Clausen said sternly. "I would prefer to resolve this incident without causing irreparable harm to either boy. I'd appreciate it if you'd allow Mr. Worf to finish without further interruption."

Mr. Chupek nodded, but his cheeks flamed red.

"Thank you, Chief Clausen," Worf said. "I have come to Earth for the sole purpose of helping Alexander adjust to certain changes in his life. If you will release him into my custody, I give you my word as a Starfleet officer that he will cause no further trouble."

"Not if I have anything to say about it!" Mr. Chupek bellowed. Placing his hands on the desk, he glared at the security chief. "I'm pressing charges against that alien delinquent for assault with intent to do bodily harm! You can't just release him on this—this Klingon's word!"

Alexander inhaled sharply, expecting his father to lash out at the human who dared question his given word. It wasn't because he was a Starfleet officer, either. It was a matter of Klingon honor.

A Klingon's word is his bond. Without it he is nothing.

Worf would rather die than break an oath. Alexander didn't understand why his father clung so fervently to this as well as other rigid Klingon traditions, but he did. In Klingon society, Mr. Chupek's reckless accusation—that Worf would not do as he promised—would have triggered an attack that might have cost the imprudent man his life. But the only evidence of his father's intense indignation was a squaring of the shoulders and a narrowed, penetrating stare.

Chief Clausen was not easily intimidated, either.

"You are quite wrong in that regard, Mr. Chupek." Rising, the security man's scowl faded as he turned to Worf. "Since no one was injured, no property was damaged and both boys were instrumental in causing the incident, I'll let Alexander go with a warning this time. Take your son home, Mr. Worf."

Mr. Chupek sputtered, too angry to speak.

Sergey nodded in approval.

Helena squeezed Alexander's arm and smiled. "See? I told you it would work out."

Alexander just stared in disbelief. The security chief's leniency surprised him almost as much as his father's defense and request on his behalf. He had been positive that Worf would insist he take responsibility for his outrageous conduct and pay whatever penalty the law required.

Then again, Alexander thought, as Worf executed a stiff bow and turned away from Chief Clausen to face him. *Maybe he preferred to make me pay in some horrible Klingon ritual that was far worse than anything Federation law would demand.* He had seen that frustrated frown on his father's face too often when they had lived together on the *Enterprise.*

Worf gestured toward the door and waited for the Rozhenkos and Alexander to go first.

Getting to his feet, Alexander gladly turned his back on his father to leave. Worf's dark, unblinking eyes were as cold as the ridged Klingon face was impassive. The troubles he had blindly plunged into when he had rushed to his grandfather's defense were far from over. They were just beginning.

Flanked by his grandparents and with his father watching every move from behind, Alexander felt like a condemned prisoner being marched through the terminal. No one spoke, which only added to his anxiety. By the time they had picked up his father's duffel bag and arrived at the local shuttle stand, his nerves were dangerously on edge. Slipping into the front seat of the vehicle, he sat in brooding silence while his father programmed the Rozhenkos' residential coordinates into the automated navigation system.

Helena leaned forward as the shuttle lifted off the ground. "I'm making your favorite dinner tonight, Worf."

Worf glanced back. "*Rokeg* blood pie?"

"What else?" Sergey shuddered with disgust. "I still haven't acquired a taste for it. Never will, either."

"I'm making a pot roast, too, Sergey," Helena said, patting her husband's knee. "You can tell your stomach to relax."

Laughing, Worf settled back to watch the green hills and valleys of the Russian landscape skim by below.

The family small talk and ensuing quiet strained Alexander's nerves even further. His grandparents were chattering about Klingon glop for dinner as though his father had just dropped by for a casual visit instead of coming halfway across the galaxy to deal with him. His life was falling apart and everyone was acting like nothing was wrong.

As the shuttle began its descent over Mirnee Doleena, Alexander squirmed in his seat. Staring down at the small town where he lived and went to school stoked the fires. Mirnee Doleena translated as Peaceful Valley and the community had been exactly that when he had come to live with his grandparents on Earth again. But the town was not a welcoming, tranquil haven anymore. Between the Federation's renewed conflict with the Klingon Empire and his own uncontrollable temper, the local population had reason to despise him. Consequently, he had to cope with the vicious prejudice of strangers he met on the street as well as intolerant classmates who had once been his friends.

Alexander didn't blame them, but it was impossible to ignore the unfair and painful torment. He didn't have anything to do with the troubles between the Federation and the Empire and he had *chosen* to embrace his humanity in spite of his predominantly Klingon heritage. The rages were as much his enemy as anyone's.

Except for him, there was nowhere to run to escape them.

Like now.

He could feel his temper racing toward critical mass. He had to get away from his father and grandparents long enough to calm down—or until the rage ran its course.

Struggling to contain the anger, Alexander slammed his hand against the door latch when the shuttle touched down on the drive leading up to the Rozhenkos' modest house. As the door *whooshed* open, he sprang out and started to run toward the tall trees bordering the front lawn.

"Alexander!"

Worf yelled as Alexander leaped over his grandmother's carefully tended bed of brilliantly colored rosebushes. He reacted instinctively to his father's sharp command and whirled as he landed.

"Alexander, wait." Rushing around the front of the shuttle, Worf paused, then slowly advanced.

"It's all right, Alexander," Sergey pleaded as he stepped down from the rear compartment. "We're not angry with you."

But Alexander *was* angry and the rage deafened him to the concerned words. Feeling cornered and pushed to the limit, he gave in to the overwhelming fury.

A fury that was getting more violent and powerful with each outburst.

A fury that had to have an outlet.

Alexander attacked the only thing within reach. Screeching, he pulled Helena's prized hybrid rosebush out of the ground by the roots and tore it apart. Delicate yellow petals and green leaves rained on the grass around him. Sharp thorns dug into his skin, drawing blood. He did not even notice the pain until he tightened his grip on the main stem. A large thorn drove into his palm, piercing the enraged daze as effectively as it had pierced his tender flesh. His mind cleared in an agonizing instant.

Alexander stared at the demolished remains of the rosebush in shock. Limp roots dangled from the trunk he still held in his hand. Looking up, he saw his grandparents and his father staring back.

Worf's jaw flexed.

Sergey's gentle eyes filled with stunned pain.

Helena's hand covered her mouth and her face was ghostly pale. The glorious Butter Beauty Rose she had cultivated, pruned and raised with such pride and loving care was dead.

And he had killed it.

Dropping the thorned trunk, Alexander ran. This time, his father's booming voice could not call him back.

CHAPTER 3

ALTHOUGH THE ROZHENKOS' HOUSE WAS WITHIN WALKING DISTANCE OF THE small town, it was nestled on the edge of an expansive forest. Alexander sped across the lawn and darted into the cover of the thick woods. His worst fear had been realized. Destroying his grandmother's favorite rosebush was almost as bad as attacking Helena herself.

Avoiding the deer trails he and his grandfather used on their morning and evening strolls, Alexander drove deeper into the forest. The sound of Worf and Sergey's calling voices became muffled by the dense foliage, then faded completely into the quiet of the wilderness. Ashamed and confused, he kept running. Not because he was afraid of being yelled at or punished. He simply couldn't face the hurt and disappointment in his grandmother's eyes or his father's Klingon judgment.

Dry leaves crackled under Alexander's pounding feet. Brambles and broken branches scratched his skin and ripped his jumpsuit as he crashed through overgrown tangles of brush. Jumping from one moss-covered rock to another to cross a wide stream, he slipped and fell. Snarling with frustration as he scrambled to his feet, he plunged through the rushing water and clawed his way up the far bank. Mud and leaves clung to his wet hands, clothes and hair, but he ignored the discomfort. The thunder of water cascading over rocks in the woods upstream called to the savage essence of his Klingon blood, and he ran toward it.

Heart thudding against his ribs and breathless, Alexander finally stopped when his sleeve snagged on a young tree. Freeing himself, he sank to his knees a short distance from the high, roaring waterfall and focused on the spindly tree that was struggling to survive in the dim light. The canopy of leaves crowning its towering parent blocked the sun. His rage and energy spent, Alexander was suddenly consumed by a sorrowful empathy with the frail sapling.

Sighing with despair, Alexander sat and dropped his head into his folded arms. When he sensed his father moving through the forest and heard him call, he did not look up or try to flee.

"Alexander." Worf strode through the trees to stand before him. "We must talk."

"Just go away and leave me alone."

Worf stood his ground. "You are not to blame for what happened today. I am."

Alexander looked up sharply. "No, you're not! I'm the one who chased Howard Chupek through the terminal and tore up Grandma's rosebush!"

Nodding, Worf eased his bulk down onto a nearby log. "Do you know why?"

"Yeah! Because I'm a Klingon and Klingons are always mad and want to fight all the time!" Tears stung Alexander's eyes.

"That is not true," Worf said. "A race that was always mad and fought *all* the time wouldn't survive."

"What's happening to me isn't funny!" In the past, his father's attempt at humor would have both surprised and amused Alexander. Now, it was a dangerous annoyance that poked and prodded the anger.

"I was not trying to be funny," Worf said calmly. "Even the Klingon Empire needs farmers and craftsmen. If everyone fought constantly, nothing would get done. We would still be prowling the forests with wooden spears."

"So Klingon farmers don't get mad?" Alexander asked sarcastically.

"I did not say that." Worf paused to eye Alexander with thoughtful concern. "We are a highly aggressive race. It is in our blood, the core of what we are—of who you are. But it is not the end of the world. Every problem has a solution and this one is no different."

"Oh, yeah! How would you know?" Jumping to his feet, Alexander glared at his father. Worf was talking to him with the calm understanding he had always wanted when they were together on the *Enterprise.* Why was he suddenly so furious with him? Bewildered and frustrated, Alexander started to pace.

"I know because I am a Klingon, too."

Alexander kept walking, too intent on fighting his mounting agitation to respond.

"Your body is going through some intense physical changes because you are growing up," Worf explained. "And those changes are causing these violent outbursts."

"So *that's* what you meant by 'phase' in Chief Clausen's office."

"Yes." Worf's face clouded slightly, as though he had momentarily drifted off to another place. "Every young Klingon experiences difficulty controlling the impulses that make them great warriors."

"So I'm *stuck* with being like this?" This was something he had suspected since the violent tantrums had begun a few weeks ago, but having his father confirm the awful truth out loud was a shock anyway. There was one thing he had always been sure of, something he had told his father when they had first started getting to know each other. He didn't *want* to be a warrior!

The emotional impact unlocked still more of Alexander's innate Klingon traits. His blood burned hotter, enhancing his senses. Every leaf and twig came into sharp focus and every nuance of sound rang crystal clear in his ears. The tang of decaying leaves and pungent fungi teased his nose, making him keenly aware of every subtle scent rising on the still air.

Worf started slightly. "You are *stuck* with your Klingon genes—"

His father's voice blended with the forest sounds, unheard as Alexander's attention was drawn to an enticing aroma.

Warm muscle and fur.

Prey.

A rabbit crouched in the thicket to the left, still except for the twitching nose and the quiet heaving of its life's breath.

"—but that does not mean you can not conquer the impulses they generate."

The scent of fear was irresistible. With every muscle tensed and primed, Alexander savored the anticipation coursing through his hunter veins for a moment before he sprang. With a quickness and agility he did not know he had, he snatched the cowering rabbit from the brush. His own chest heaving with exhilaration, he clutched the fear-frozen animal by the throat and whirled to face his father.

"Your skills are excellent, Alexander. If we were on a ritual hunt, I would be very proud of your prowess." Rising slowly, Worf stepped forward. "Are you hungry?"

The blunt question disrupted Alexander's feeling of triumph but did not dampen the instinct to hunt and kill. His pulse raced and his hand tightened around the prey's fragile neck. It would be so easy to squeeze the life out of the dangling body, but his mind rebelled against causing a senseless death.

"No—" Alexander's voice was a harsh rasp. "I'm not hungry."

"Then why are you holding that rabbit in a death grip?"

Because I want to kill it! Alexander trembled as reason battled the genetic instincts within him. *But I don't want to kill it!*

"We are not on a ritual hunt designed to test your skills," Worf continued evenly. "There is no feast being planned to make use of the kill and you are not hungry."

Alexander focused on his father's voice.

"There is no honor in taking a life without purpose. Killing to vent anger or frustration is meaningless. Do you understand?"

Desperate, Alexander nodded, but he did not release the rabbit. His hand wanted to choke the terrified animal. His mind wanted to see it go free. He stood frozen with indecision, trapped between his primitive impulses and his civilized values, with the hapless rabbit's life hanging in the balance.

"Do you want to let the rabbit go?"

Again Alexander just nodded. He was afraid to move because his Klingon blood might overwhelm his desire. The rabbit could die in his hand in an instant and death could not be undone. There would be no second chances.

"Concentrate on your hand, Alexander. It is merely an extension of you. A tool that does your bidding, nothing more." Speaking in a soothing monotone, Worf held Alexander's frightened gaze. "You command the tool, Alexander. Open your hand."

Shaking with the effort, Alexander loosened his grip. The rabbit stirred slightly. The movement tempted the hunter and the hand flexed to close again. Beads of sweat broke out on his ridged forehead as he concentrated, forcing himself to squat down, to keep his killing hold in check.

"Remove your hand, Alexander. You control it and it will do as you command."

Lowering the captive rabbit to the ground, Alexander stared at his father while he focused his will on his hand. His fingers snapped open. Stunned and limp with fear, the animal did not immediately dash for safety. It just lay there in his open hand, taunting the hunter and testing his rational will.

And then it was gone.

Gasping, Alexander collapsed as the rabbit darted into the brush and fled.

Worf dropped to one knee on the ground beside him. "There is a solution and you have just taken the first step. By letting the rabbit go, you have proven that *you* are the master of your actions and your destiny. Your Klingon blood cannot control you."

Pulling himself up into a sitting position, Alexander sighed wearily. "It almost did. You don't know how hard it was not to strangle that rabbit."

"Yes, I do," Worf said sympathetically. "It will not be an easy fight, but it *is* a fight you can win."

I sure hope so, Alexander thought. The rabbit's escape was too narrow for comfort and a sickening sensation churned in his stomach. The Klingon warrior impulses were more powerful than he had imagined and they were getting steadily stronger.

What if he couldn't learn to control it without fail?

There had been too many times in the past few weeks he had wanted to silence Jeremy Sullivan's taunting insults by strangling him.

CHAPTER 4

THE NEXT MORNING AT BREAKFAST, ALEXANDER WAS ALL TOO AWARE THAT his grandparents were trying extra hard not to do anything to upset him.

And that upset him.

If he was a human kid and not mostly Klingon, they wouldn't be afraid that he might take offense at some innocent remark or minor incident and go berserk.

"Be careful, Alexander," Helena said as she set a plate of freshly baked biscuits on the table. "I just took them out of the oven and they're still hot."

Nodding, Alexander stared at the biscuits his grandmother still made the old-fashioned way. They had a replicator, but she preferred to measure and mix all the ingredients herself. Famished, he couldn't wait for the steaming biscuits to cool. He picked one up, inhaled with a hiss and dropped it on his plate.

Sergey tensed with a fork full of fried potatoes poised before his open mouth, staring at him as though he might fly into a rage and demolish the kitchen.

Helena smiled tightly. "Do you want some ice for the burn?"

Alexander shook his head and gritted his teeth to quell an angry outburst. He was not angry because he had been stupid enough to burn himself. Or at the Rozhenkos because they expected him to react violently. He was furious with the Klingon genes that triggered the tantrums and gave his grandparents good reason to worry.

And because there was nothing he could do about it.

"You didn't make any plans for today, did you?" Slipping the potatoes into his mouth, Sergey chewed and glanced at Alexander.

"Of course he didn't." Gently cuffing Sergey's shoulder, Helena sat down. "He knew his father was coming."

Alexander sighed. Not long ago deciding between spending the time with Worf or with his friends would have been a problem. However, it had been ages since he had gone to see the latest holoflick or participated in a casual game of soccer or just sat around the Galactic Cafe in town stuffing himself. Hanging out alone wasn't fun and none of his old friends were talking to him.

"No, I don't have any plans." Picking up the dropped biscuit, Alexander buttered it. "Why?"

"Well—" Sergey swallowed. "Worf thought you might like to join him for his *Mok'bara* workout today."

"I have your things ready." Helena gestured toward a neatly folded stack of white clothes on the counter. "Just in case."

"He's waiting for you outside." Sergey reached for a biscuit. "If you want to, of course."

Alexander hesitated, frowning. "Why didn't Father ask me himself last night?"

Sighing sadly, Helena shrugged. "Perhaps he didn't want you to feel pressured. Or maybe he just didn't want to be around if you refused."

Alexander nodded. He had made a habit of rejecting most of Worf's attempts to teach him anything Klingon, but not this time. Knowing how rigorous his father's exercise routines could be, he'd probably be too tired to throw a temper tantrum for days.

Wearing a belted, white tunic and matching pants, Alexander joined his father on the lawn behind the house. Perhaps sensing that he was nervous, Worf instructed him in some basic loosening up exercises before launching into the intensive *Mok'bara* ritual.

"What happened to the green lamp that used to stand in the front foyer?" Worf asked casually as he rolled his head back and then from side to side. "Did your grandmother finally decide to get rid of it?"

"No." Alexander parroted his father's movements. "I finally broke it."

Worf did not even blink. "That was inevitable, I suppose."

"That's what Grandma said." Flexing his shoulders, Alexander tried not to smile. When Helena had found the smashed remains of the old lamp he had accidently knocked off the hall table, she had laughed. As a child, Worf had repeatedly bashed into and knocked it over, too. He just hadn't bashed into it so hard that it literally hurled itself to certain destruction on the floor.

"What did she say?" There was just a hint of anxiety in Worf's deep voice.

"That it was a miracle the lamp had survived one Klingon. Expecting it to survive two had been foolish."

Laughing, Worf straightened. "Your grandmother is a very wise woman."

Yes, she is, Alexander thought soberly. Knowing her adopted son and grandson better than they knew themselves, she had reunited them a second time. The dread he had felt before Worf disembarked at the shuttle terminal had been unfounded. There had been no punishment for the incident with Howard Chupek, only understanding. Maybe the gap separating him and his father wasn't as big as he had thought.

Finishing his warm-up, Worf suddenly grew serious. "The *Mok'bara* is one of the most effective disciplines young Klingons use to control the violence of adolescence. *If* they want to control it."

Alexander frowned suspiciously. "Meaning a lot of Klingons would rather fight?"

"It is in our nature and difficult to resist."

"That's *not* what you said yesterday," Alexander countered hotly. "You said—"

"I remember what I said." Worf sharply cut him off. "When I was at the Boreth Monastery after the *Enterprise* was destroyed at Veridian Three, Master Lourn tried to convince me that our violent Klingon nature could not be conquered, that Klingons will deliberately create conflict when there is none because of our innate aggressive tendencies. I *know* that is not true. Klingons can rise above their instincts—if they want to."

Alexander crossed his arms and cocked his head, challenging the statement. "For sure?"

"I did, eventually." Worf frowned slightly, but the fleeting shadow of pain in his eyes quickly vanished. "Discovering the *Mok'bara* helped. If I had sent you to a Klingon school when you first came to the *Enterprise,* you would have learned these techniques years ago."

"Maybe, but I'm glad I stayed with you instead." Alexander shrugged. He had never been interested in learning the martial arts discipline of *Mok'bara* before. It was so . . . Klingon. Now, he was desperate enough to try anything. He didn't quite believe that a ritual designed to hone combat skills could help him *control* the urge to fight, but Worf was so certain that he decided to give it a shot.

"I am glad you stayed, too. But it appears I did not teach you many of the things you need to know. For instance, there is no honor in attacking those weaker than yourself because you can not leash your anger."

"Howard Chupek insulted your father!" Seething, Alexander gritted his teeth.

"But there were other ways to handle the situation," Worf said patiently. "Fighting to settle grievances is acceptable in Klingon society. It is not acceptable here. I should have anticipated your current problem and taken measures to prepare you to cope with it."

"You tried," Alexander said honestly, relieved as the surge of anger subsided. "I wouldn't cooperate."

"That was then. This is now." Moving in front of the boy, Worf assumed a pose with his body bent slightly forward and his feet spaced wide apart. "Watch me and remember. When I stop, execute the movements as best you can."

Alexander anxiously studied his father's controlled stance and memorized the slow, deliberate motions of his hands and arms. When Worf paused, he tried to duplicate the exercise. His movements felt awkward and clumsy compared to the powerful grace his father displayed. Performing the Klingon ritual in the Rozhenkos' backyard on a bright, sunny morning only added to his sense of being totally out of place in his adopted world. The colorful flower gardens, fruit-laden trees, stone birdbaths and wooden climbing toys were hardly an appropriate setting for the intensive *Mok'bara.* For once, he was glad there were no close neighbors to spy on them.

"The form clears the mind," Worf said. He moved his hands forward, then brought them to an abrupt halt with a sharp intake of breath. "As the movements become ingrained, connecting your mind and body in a natural flow, you will feel more in control."

"I feel silly." Alexander instantly regretted the words and hastened to qualify the remark. "I mean, I used to pretend I was a Cossack fighting off European invaders in this yard. Don't Klingons do these ritual things in ancient caves with torches and stuff?"

Freezing in position, Worf slowly turned his head. "No. Obviously, I have neglected your Klingon education to a greater degree than I thought. However, we will address that at a later time. As far as the *Mok'bara* is concerned, it is a discipline of mind and body. Location is irrelevant."

"Oh. Sorry." Alexander watched attentively as his father resumed the exercise. If nothing else, Alexander told himself as he self-consciously executed an intricate pattern of quick thrusts and turns, maybe he'd learn to fight better. And that couldn't hurt. He was the only Klingon attending his school—one against three hundred.

After half an hour of grueling concentration, Worf relaxed and gestured toward a stone bench under a large shady tree. "That's enough for now."

Alexander nodded. He felt both drained and invigorated by the constant mental and physical tension inherent in the *Mok'bara* exercises. His own fitness routine utilized more energetic activities that strengthened muscles, agility and endurance without making such rigid demands on the mind. Still, he was in superb physical condition and the weariness surprised him. Rejecting it, he suddenly sprinted across the lawn toward the jungle gym his grandfather had built out of logs. Executing a high vault in a layout position with a half twist, he landed solidly without a misstep and raised his arms.

Worf roared with Klingon approval and shook his fist in the air.

Grinning, Alexander ran over and flopped down on the bench. Pouring two glasses of lemonade from the pitcher Helena had left on the side table, he handed one to his father.

"I did not know you had such a talent for gymnastics," Worf said. "Are you on the team at school?"

"No." Alexander frowned and shook his head. The question instantly darkened his mood as surely as a sudden storm cloud would have blotted out the sun.

"I am surprised the gymnastics coach has not insisted." Worf scowled. "An athlete with your abilities would ensure victory for the school's team."

"The coach doesn't know," Alexander mumbled. Besides, Jeremy Sullivan and Kim Ho *were* on the gymnastics team. They would not welcome a Klingon, no matter how well he performed.

Worf raised a more surprised eyebrow. "How can he not know? Do you not participate in gymnastics in physical education?"

"Yes. It's required." Alexander evaded the whole truth and shifted uncomfortably.

"But you do not perform as well as you could."

Alexander blinked, then nodded. His father's insight was astounding. It had been hard enough being the only one of his kind at school before the new Klingon-Federation conflict had started. Even then, he had quickly learned that showing off his superior prowess in sports was not the way to make friends. Flaunting his abilities now would just cause more trouble with his hostile classmates—and he already had more than he could handle. Jeremy Sullivan, Kim Ho and Bernard Umbaya were making sure of that.

"I often wish I had had the strength of character to overcome my competitive nature when I was your age. If I had been secure enough to hide my abilities . . ." Worf paused with a faraway look in his eyes.

"Huh?" Alexander squinted, totally puzzled. During their times together, Worf was always saying or doing something that caught him off guard. But his father had never paid him this ultimate compliment before. To his shame, his father's assumption was false. "I don't hold back because I have strength of character. I don't let anyone see what I can do because I'm a coward."

"You are many things, Alexander, but you are not a coward."

"Yes, I am." The confession hurt Alexander to the very core of his human-Klingon soul, but he had made a vow long ago never to lie to his father again. "I'm afraid all the kids will gang up on me."

"I see." Worf sighed. "Would you fight back to defend yourself?"

"Of course!" Alexander sat back indignantly. "But I'd probably lose."

"There are far more dishonorable things than losing an unfair fight."

"Like what?"

Worf sighed. "Like being so positive you are better at something than everyone else, you cause a friend to die needlessly."

Alexander gasped. "You didn't do that. You couldn't have!"

"Not deliberately, no." Worf's eyes filled with sadness. "Your grandparents and I lived on the farm world of Gault for several years before coming here. I was captain of the school soccer team when I was thirteen. Because the score was tied in a game I desperately wanted to win, I pushed a teammate to intercept a play that was rightfully his. I shoved Michail so hard, he broke his neck and died the next day."

Speechless, Alexander just stared at his father's face. The intense pain was only evident in Worf's eyes.

Worf gripped Alexander's knee tightly. "That was when I realized that because I was bigger and stronger, I had to learn how to harness my aggressive nature. It is a lesson I do not want *you* to learn the hard way."

"Me neither," Alexander whispered, recalling how he had felt in the terminal. If his father hadn't stopped him, Howard Chupek would be in the hospital—or dead. "I'll learn control. I have to."

Worf nodded. "It will be a difficult task, especially if your friends are provoking you like Howard Chupek did."

"I can do it." Alexander eyed his father with grim determination. "And I promise I won't start another fight or break anything in a fit of temper ever again."

"That is not a promise you should make lightly, Alexander. I know how easy it is for the anger to take over." Another almost-smile played at the corner of Worf's mouth. "I remember one glass table on the *Enterprise* that was a particularly spectacular victim because I was frustrated and lost control. That was not the first time I failed to contain it and it may not be the last."

"My word of *honor!*" Alexander's eyes flashed. The oath was a bond stronger than any restraint or potential punishment and it was absolutely necessary to protect himself and those around him. Like his father and all Klingons, he would rather die than break his given word.

"For a week," Worf said gravely. "That is a reasonable goal and one you can achieve. You can renew your vow in seven days when we celebrate the Day of Honor."

"Okay. One week for starters."

"So be it." Rising, Worf set his glass down. "We have today and tomorrow before you return to school. I strongly suggest we accelerate your training with the *Mok'bara.* Then I will teach you some ancient meditations that have helped me."

Alexander followed his father back into the center of the lawn stricken with a deep sense of irony. Having denied his Klingon heritage for most of his young life, it was unsettling to find out that he *had* to acknowledge and accept his genetic inclinations in order to reject them. Without knowledge of his nature and proper training in Klingon methods, he would be fighting blind and unarmed with no way to win.

And sooner or later someone would get hurt—or worse.

CHAPTER 5

OUT OF MY WAY, LUMPHEAD!" SHOVING ALEXANDER ASIDE, BERNARD Umbaya laughed and kept walking down the crowded school hallway.

As Alexander stumbled backward against his locker, his PADD slipped out of his hand. When he leaned over to pick up the compact computer, a foot stomped down on it.

A Tellarite exchange student walking by snorted with jeering disgust. Two girls heading in the opposite direction giggled.

"Get off it!" Alexander snapped, then looked up into Jeremy Sullivan's scowling face.

Somehow, he had managed to avoid a direct confrontation with Jeremy and his friends during the previous two days. Using the *Mok'bara* mental skills his father had taught him, he had also managed to appear unaffected and in control when the other kids had shunned or insulted him. A lot of them had given up trying to provoke him. His faked indifference took the fun out of it. Jeremy was not so easily put off.

"Your PADD doesn't belong on the floor, Klingon!" Blue eyes gleaming with arrogance, Jeremy lifted his foot, then kicked the PADD away when Alexander reached for it. The personal access display device shot across the corridor and banged against the far wall.

Alexander froze, silently counting to ten as he tried to confine the rage. His pulse and breathing quickened as he locked gazes with the red-haired boy. He kept counting, desperately wishing Jeremy would just move on before the rage won. But Jeremy didn't move and Kim Ho suddenly appeared beside him. Surrounded with his back against the wall, Alexander rose into a defensive posture, fists clenched at his sides.

"You don't scare me, Alexander." Jeremy leaned toward him, his voice low and intimidating. "Starfleet officers aren't afraid of Klingon dogs like you."

"We're not Starfleet officers, yet," Kim said with an uneasy glance at Alexander.

"But we will be." Jeremy's jaw flexed as his hateful gaze bore into Alexander.

Alexander stared back, his hard nails biting into the skin of his palms as he tightened his fists. One more word and Jeremy Sullivan would be heading toward the nurse's office with a broken jaw.

"Come on." Kim tugged on Jeremy's sleeve. "We're gonna be late."

Jeremy's cold gaze remained fastened on Alexander as Kim pulled him into the stream of students on their way to class. "Watch yourself, Klingon."

Feeling the rage begin to slip past his defenses, Alexander whirled and slammed his fist into the locker. Hearing a startled cry, he snapped his head around and gasped.

Brown eyes wide with anxious uncertainty, Suzanne Milton stood beside him clutching his PADD. She shoved it toward him. "You dropped this."

Swallowing hard, Alexander self-consciously took the PADD. Suzanne sat behind him in fundamental physics and he had become uncomfortably aware of her recently. She had long, flowing brown hair and freckles and he had often caught her watching him with guarded curiosity. Convinced that she would refuse any friendly overtures, he had not had the courage to start a conversation. Now that she was here, talking and being nice, he felt totally tongue-tied.

"Jeremy can be such a jerk." Suzanne smiled shyly.

"Thanks." Alexander smiled back and was appalled when the smile turned into a guttural snarl.

Drawing back with surprised indignation, Suzanne turned and walked away.

"I'm sorry. I..." Slumping against his locker, Alexander watched as she disappeared into a classroom. The bright, pretty girl was the only person in school who had been friendly toward him in weeks! He was sure she wouldn't make *that* mistake again. He had snarled in her face! No wonder humans despised Klingons.

Keying in his lock code, Alexander opened his locker and took out a data bar. He had had library authorization coded into the pass earlier. Although he could access any information he needed for his paper on thermal dynamics with his PADD, he preferred working in the library to being in regular study hall. The rows of computers and long, tall stacks of old-fashioned bound books provided a seclusion that wasn't possible in an open classroom.

As he trudged up the stairs to the second floor, Alexander was only vaguely aware of the sneers and whispered comments of the other students he passed. His anger at himself for growling at Suzanne was potentially more explosive than an anger directed at someone else. He imagined he was climbing a treacherous mountain, a mental exercise that kept his mind focused on his feet instead of on the disturbing incident with Suzanne.

"Hello, Alexander." The librarian, Ms. Marconi, smiled tightly as he handed her the pass. "How are you today?"

"Fine," Alexander mumbled. Before his Klingon temper had emerged to totally disrupt his life, he had liked the attractive librarian. Slim with shoulder-length blond hair and laughing green eyes, Ms. Marconi had always treated him with respect and kindness. But she wasn't fooling him with her pleasant attitude now. Last week he had almost smashed a computer screen when it failed to respond to a simple voice command. He had roared and kicked the sturdy desk instead. No permanent damage had been done, but the outburst had brought him dangerously close to being banned from the library for the rest of the semester. Ms. Marconi wasn't worried about him. She was worried about the safety of the library, its contents and the students in her charge.

"So. What's on your agenda this time?" Ms. Marconi ran the pass through a scanner to check the authorization, then gave it back.

"Physics." Jamming the data bar into his pocket, Alexander nodded toward the towering shelves of bound books. "I want to look up a few things in the original texts."

"Oh." Ms. Marconi smiled, looking both relieved that he wouldn't be using the computers and nervous because he would be using the precious leather-bound books with paper pages. "Let me know if you have trouble finding anything."

"Okay." Alexander hurried away from the front desk and quickly found a table in a far corner. No one else was in sight. Grabbing a physics reference book off the shelf just in case Ms. Marconi came by to check on him, Alexander eased into the corner chair.

Concealed by high shelves lined with books of different sizes and colors, he settled down to work, hoping the hour would pass without interruption. He had only two classes after this. With luck, he'd get through another day without starting a fight or breaking something. There were only two more days to go until the *Batlh Jaj,* the Day of Honor, and his vow to his father remained unbroken.

Alexander was surprised at how much that meant to him. Thinking about it in the quiet solitude of the library, he realized that the significance of the *Batlh Jaj* went far beyond a holiday that celebrated the Klingons' unwavering dedication to honor. It was the oath itself. The belief that a person was only as trustworthy and strong as his given word was the one Klingon tradition he agreed with without reservation. It was the first lesson Worf had taught him on the *Enterprise.* More importantly, swearing to abide by it had been the first solid thread binding them together as father and son.

Honor bound.

He *would* rather suffer a horrible punishment than disgrace himself and his father by breaking his promise.

"I'm not kidding," a boy's voice insisted. "It's a first edition of Zefram Cochrane's *The Potential of Warp Propulsion* and it has a type error in it."

"They called that a typo." Kim corrected Bernard as they walked around the end of the long bookcase forming an aisle that ran along the back wall.

Sitting at the far end of the row, Alexander held his breath as Jeremy followed, looking bored.

"So what?" Jeremy asked.

"So he corrected and initialed it." Bernard scanned the upper shelves, looking for the volume.

"No, he didn't," Jeremy scoffed. "Some joker with a replicated pen initialed it so fools like you would *think* Zefram Cochrane did."

Kim noticed Alexander and tapped Jeremy on the shoulder.

Alexander stiffened, sensing that his oath was about to be tested. He reinforced the heavy, metal door imprisoning the imaginary lion in his mind with a huge padlock and several duranium bars. As long as the symbolic beast didn't get out, his very real rage wouldn't escape, either.

"Well, well. Look who's here." Jeremy sauntered down the aisle with Bernard and Kim close behind. They stationed themselves around the table, blocking Alexander's only way out. "What's a Klingon doing in a library?"

"My homework," Alexander said evenly.

"On what?" Bernard grinned and nudged Kim. "The only thing Klingons are any good at is hunting and killing."

"Like the savages you are," Kim added. He wasn't smiling. "My uncle was killed in a Klingon raid near the Cardassian border."

"I'm sorry." Tense with the effort of caging his temper, Alexander knew he didn't sound as sincere as he felt. "But I didn't have anything to do with that."

"You're a Klingon, aren't you?" Eyes narrowed, Kim lunged toward the table with his fist raised. Jeremy, the undisputed leader of the trio, put a staying hand on Kim's chest. Bristling, Kim stepped back.

"I'm surprised Ms. Marconi let you back in after the fit you threw last week." Thumbing through the physics reference book on the table by Alexander's PADD, Jeremy frowned. "This is a Starfleet reference!"

Alexander didn't respond. The rage was gaining strength. The imaginary lion repeatedly threw itself at the metal door in his mind. The door boomed and bowed, snapping one of the duranium bars and cracking another. Closing his eyes, he mentally replaced the broken bar with a newer, stronger one. It broke almost instantly when Jeremy grabbed the front of his shirt.

"Are you spying for the Empire?"

"I am a Federation citizen." Alexander's lip curled in a snarl, revealing sharp canine teeth. His gaze was like a steel rod boring into Jeremy's eyes. "My father is a Starfleet officer."

"Right. And my father's an Orion pirate!" Jeremy talked tough and released his hold with a flourish, but Alexander didn't miss the flash of uncertainty on his face.

Lowering his gaze to stare at the edge of the table, Alexander hoped Jeremy would take it as a sign of defeat and leave. What he really needed was to focus on something nonthreatening while he willed the fury into submission. Every muscle strained in the struggle to subdue an enemy far more dangerous than Jeremy Sullivan.

Falling for the ploy, Jeremy backed off.

Alexander continued to stare at the table, afraid to look up before the rage was completely gone.

"Ready?" Jeremy's quiet voice pierced Alexander's concentration. "One. Two…"

Too late Alexander realized that his tormentors had not left, but had only retreated to execute a more damaging plan. His gaze snapped up.

Standing behind the end section of the aisle bookcases, Jeremy, Bernard and Kim pushed the stack over on the count of three. The shelving unit wasn't tall enough to reach and crush their Klingon target, but it would hit the table, trapping him behind it.

A combination of fear and fury broke through all of Alexander's mental defenses. Shrieking, he vaulted over the table as the bookcase toppled and the three boys darted for cover. He was only a split-second short of jumping clear when the unit crashed, spilling books all over the floor. The top corner edge landed on his sleeve, pinning his shirt to the top of the table.

Snarling with frustration, Alexander yanked his arm and tore his shirt. The sound of ripping fabric calmed the rage, but that wouldn't help him now.

Ms. Marconi and several curious students rushed up to the fallen bookcase to stare at the mess and him. Jeremy, Bernard and Kim had disappeared. The librarian looked like she was on the verge of tears in spite of her troubled frown, but Alexander didn't harbor any illusions about why she was upset. Her grief was for the dumped and battered books, not for the Klingon boy who was so obviously guilty of the crime. She showed no mercy.

"The principal's office, Alexander," Ms. Marconi said in a flat voice. She pointed toward the door. "Now."

CHAPTER 6

ALEXANDER SAT RAMROD STRAIGHT AND AS UNMOVING AS STONE, HIS EYES riveted on the bulletin board hanging on the wall across from him. He had not shifted position since arriving at the school office over an hour before. His grandmother had not been able to contact his father immediately after Mrs. Miyashi called, but Worf was on his way now. Alexander focused on the hard bench, welcoming the discomfort. It helped him imprison the fury aroused because he had been falsely and unjustly accused. It also distracted him from his anxiety over the impending and unavoidable conflict with his father.

The bell for the last period of the day rang.

Alexander watched the wall, bearing the disgusted sighs of the office personnel and the cloaked glances of students in stoical silence. There was nothing he could do to alter their distorted perceptions of him. No human understood the degree to which a Klingon valued his honor.

And in this, Alexander realized, he was truly Klingon.

He would not break his silence just as he had not broken his oath.

His only regret was that his father would not know the truth.

All eyes turned toward the door as Worf strode through it. Everyone but Alexander held their breath. Even dressed in a casual shirt, loose pants and boots with his long hair clipped at the base of his neck, his father was an imposing and impressive sight.

Resolved not to shame himself further in his father's eyes, Alexander kept his expression blank when Worf paused before him. Neither one said a word as he stood up and they approached the counter.

"You must be Alexander's father." Mrs. Miyashi's voice singsonged with a nervous lilt.

"Yes."

The single word spoken in a deep, commanding bass set the office clerk fluttering to the end of the counter. "I'm sure Mr. Houseman will see you immediately."

"That would be appreciated."

"Yes, of course. Right this way." Nodding vigorously, Mrs. Miyashi rushed to the principal's office to announce their arrival.

If he hadn't been in so much trouble, Alexander would have smiled. Aside from the fear all Klingons evoked because of their appearance and reputation, his father had a way of sounding intimidating even when that wasn't his intention. Few outside himself had ever experienced the unique sensitivity his father hid so well.

But I don't think I'm going to see that side of him today, Alexander thought as he followed Worf into Mr. Houseman's office.

Tall, muscular and a commanding personality himself, Mr. Houseman motioned for Alexander and Worf to sit in the chairs in front of his desk. "Thank you for coming so promptly, Lieutenant Commander. I regret having to call you in, but Alexander's unruly behavior seems to be getting worse."

"So I have heard."

Worf did not even glance in his direction and Alexander cringed inwardly, but like his father, his face revealed none of the emotions churning within. He was determined to conduct himself with dignity. Fixing his gaze directly ahead, he listened without fidgeting as the principal explained what had happened in the library.

"There was a similar, although less destructive incident last week," Mr. Houseman finished. "We did give him a warning."

Worf turned to address Alexander. "Is that true?"

"Yes," Alexander said, still staring at the wall. His father asked the question in a way that allowed him to answer honestly. "I kicked a desk and I was warned."

Worf nodded, eyeing him thoughtfully. "I find it very difficult to believe you would deliberately destroy a bookcase after you gave me your word."

Alexander didn't respond. It wasn't a question.

Hoping to head off a dispute, Mr. Houseman interjected. "No one else was in the vincinity, Mr. Worf."

Worf's brow furrowed for a long moment before he pressed Alexander. "Do you have anything to say?"

"No, sir." Alexander could not defend or clear himself without snitching on Jeremy, Bernard and Kim. And that was something he simply couldn't afford to do. They would launch a campaign of unbridled revenge and he did not trust his ability to cage the fury. It was growing too powerful and at a much faster rate than his progress with the *Mok'bara.*

The three arrogant and unsuspecting boys could not possibly survive an encounter with him.

He wouldn't survive the oppressive guilt, especially if he ignored a way to avoid a fatal confrontation to save himself. His father had killed someone accidently. Yet, as strong and confident as Worf was, even he couldn't exorcise the guilt that haunted him.

The bitter alternative was to let his father believe he had lost his temper in the library, toppled the bookcase and broken his promise.

Alexander swallowed a sigh. Suffering Worf's disappointment would hurt, but no one would die from it. Besides, his father would be returning to *Deep Space Nine* in a few more days. He had to live with Jeremy Sullivan.

And himself.

Growing anxious in the prolonged silence, Mr. Houseman cleared his throat. "I am not unsympathetic to the fact that things have become rather difficult for Alexander, given the recent hostilities and a general lack of understanding between our two cultures."

Giving no indication of his inner feelings, Worf turned back to the principal. "Unfortunately, that is quite true. However, Alexander's loyalties do not lie with the Klingon Empire."

"No, of course not." Mr. Houseman shifted uncomfortably, weighing his options. "But I can't let his actions go unpunished. A week of detention, beginning tomorrow. Since his last class has already started, you may as well take Alexander home now."

"Is that acceptable to you, Alexander?"

For the first time since entering the office, Alexander looked at his father. It seemed like an odd question, but nothing in Worf's eyes or expression gave him a clue as to why he had asked it. In the overall scope of things, that hardly seemed important. "Yes, sir."

"Then the matter is settled." Worf stood up.

"Not quite," Mr. Houseman added quickly. "If anything like this happens again, I'll have no choice but to expel Alexander from this school."

"Understood. Good day, Mr. Houseman." Worf deftly dismissed the principal and motioned Alexander out the door.

Even through his daze of despair, Alexander heard Mr. Houseman sigh with relief as they left his office.

When Worf pointed him toward the nearest exit, Alexander stopped. "I have to put my data bar in my locker. We're not allowed to take them out of the building."

"Very well."

As Alexander led the way through the deserted corridors, his anxiety increased. His father's unemotional calm was worse than the flustered displays of annoyance he had exhibited on the *Enterprise.* Worf had been completely out of his element when he first accepted the responsibility of fatherhood. In his confused and frightened innocence, Alexander had been able to reduce the noble Klingon to a state of sputtering, bewildered frustration when not even the High Council's decree of discommendation two years before had caused a ripple in Worf's veneer of proud poise. He knew because Counselor Deanna Troi had found his unusual effect on his father both fascinating and amusing.

Alexander wasn't fascinated or amused now. Worf's apparent unconcern was making him more nervous and upset than the furious lectures ever had. Why wasn't his father fuming with anger? The boy choked back a gasp of alarm. Maybe Worf didn't care enough about him anymore to *be* devastated and disappointed by his misbehavior!

"Here it is." Alexander paused in front of the locker, and froze, his worry about his father's feelings suspended for a moment.

Suzanne Milton was walking briskly toward them with her own data bar clutched in her hand. As she passed, she raised her chin and tossed her long hair over her shoulder. The deliberate snub hit Alexander like a bucket of ice water.

Worf frowned. "Is this how everyone treats you?"

"Mostly." Sighing, Alexander keyed in his lock code. Since it didn't seem possible to make his situation worse, he decided to confess all.

"But Suzanne has a *real* reason. She was being nice and I *snarled* at her."

Stunned, Worf blinked, then leaned closer. "Snarled at her?"

"I didn't mean to insult her. It just happened. I still can't believe it." Shaking his head, Alexander pulled the data bar out of his pocket. He was prepared to accept whatever punishment his father had in store for him when they got home, but he wasn't prepared for what he saw when he looked back around. Worf was headed down the hall toward Suzanne.

Aghast, Alexander sagged against his locker and watched helplessly. If the girl's view of the hall hadn't been blocked by her open locker door, she probably would have run screaming in terror. However, Worf took her by surprise with a smile. She's probably too shocked to scream, Alexander thought miserably, wondering and yet not really wanting to know what his father was up to.

When Worf finished speaking, Suzanne nodded, then dashed to the side exit.

Closing the locker door, Alexander confronted his father when he returned. "Why did Suzanne run out of the building? What did you say to her!"

"She was excused early because she has a rehearsal for a dance recital," Worf said.

"Oh."

"And I explained that when a Klingon boy snarls at a girl, it is a compliment, an expression of—affection."

"What?" Alexander's mouth fell open. He couldn't deny that he liked Suzanne and wanted to be friends. But even if that happened, which didn't seem likely now, it was foolish to think a friendship could ever develop into something more when they got older. "But she's a girl! I mean, she's pretty and smart and—human."

"She seemed pleased."

"She did?" Alexander frowned uncertainly. He wasn't sure which was more confounding: Suzanne's attitude toward a complimentary Klingon snarl or his father's efforts to rectify the unintended misunderstanding.

Worf urged him toward the door. "Human females are unpredictable, almost without exception. And many of them are not as fragile as they look."

Human females aren't the only ones who are unpredictable, Alexander thought. His father was doing a pretty good job of throwing him completely off-guard, too.

CHAPTER 7

LATE THE NEXT AFTERNOON, ALEXANDER WATCHED THE SECONDS FLASH BY on the detention hall clock, but he wasn't watching the time. He was lost in puzzled thought. After returning home the day before, Worf's attitude of unruffled acceptance had not wavered. He had neither dictated a punishment nor said another word about the library incident. Even his grandmother had seemed perplexed.

Alexander was pretty sure the startling change in his father's attitude was not because he didn't care. If that were the case, Worf wouldn't have tried to correct the problem with Suzanne. It was also safe to assume that the Starfleet officer with the Klingon soul would not accept a dishonorable act in patient, unaffected silence.

Which, Alexander finally had to conclude, could only mean that somehow Worf *knew* he had not pushed over the bookcase, that his honor-bound promise not to break anything in a fit of temper was intact.

Alexander smiled as the significance of that sank in. Worf's belief, based solely on faith without supporting evidence, was a demonstration of the absolute trust he had always hoped to earn, but never honestly thought he could.

The only question that remained was why his father hadn't challenged Ms. Marconi's and Mr. Houseman's assumption that he was guilty, especially since Worf obviously thought he was innocent.

"That's all for today. You're free to go."

Alexander shook himself out of his reverie as Mr. Cunningham dismissed him, the only student in the classroom. He didn't care. Discovering how much his father trusted him was worth spending a whole semester in detention. However, it was only five days.

One down and four to go.

He didn't even mind having to stay late at school tomorrow on the *Batlh Jaj,* Alexander realized as he grabbed his PADD and ran for the door.

"Walk!" Mr. Cunningham smiled as Alexander skidded to a halt. "Please, Mr. Rozhenko."

"Yes, sir." Grinning, Alexander made a show of walking as fast as he could without breaking into a jog—until he burst through the doors to the outside. Leaping into the air, he laughed aloud. For the first time in a long time, he had actually had a good day.

Jeremy, Bernard and Kim had left him alone. Since they hadn't been hauled into the principal's office, they must have figured out that he hadn't accused them. Maybe that had made them reevaluate their unfair attitudes and tactics. More likely, they were just afraid he'd change his mind and tell if they continued to torment him. Either way, their absence had made it much easier for him to control the persistent rage. The twinges of annoyance he had felt during the day had quickly been suppressed.

On the other hand, *he* had avoided Suzanne. In spite of his father's impression, he wasn't at all sure her reaction to his unwitting display of Klingon affection had been positive. Maybe she had run out of the building because the very idea made her sick to her stomach. If so, he didn't want that terrible truth confirmed. It was enough to know that she knew he had not deliberately been rude.

Yep, Alexander thought happily. All things considered, it had been an extremely good day.

And it wasn't over yet.

Anxious to get home, Alexander walked toward the soccer field to take the shortcut through the woods on the far side. As part of their Day of Honor celebration tomorrow evening, he and his father were going to stage an Honor Combat for his grandparents. When one Klingon challenged the honor of another, they fought the *Suv'batlh* to decide whose honor would be preserved. It was similar to the medieval practice of trial by combat between knights in that a warrior's character and courage were thought to determine victory as much as his skill. Wielding *bat'leths* and wearing full Klingon armor, he and his father would battle it out in the backyard, hopefully to the delighted horror of the elderly Rozhenkos. Although Worf wouldn't admit it, he had never quite outgrown his own mischievous delight in trying to shake his adopted parents' unruffled acceptance of his "brutal" Klingon nature.

Eager to practice with his *bat'leth,* the traditional curved sword of honor, Alexander started to run. He didn't want to waste what was left of the warm, sunny afternoon. Halfway across the playing field, he realized he had made a gross tactical error.

Jeremy Sullivan darted from the edge of the forest onto the field in front of him. Bernard Umbaya and Kim Ho jumped out from behind the goals and raced toward him from the base lines.

Alexander's near-perfect day turned as sour as a bunch of rotting Argelian grapes.

The boys were launching an attack even though he had protected them—from the principal, detention and himself.

His initial dismay was instantly dragged under a rising tide of outrage. Even he had his limits, and it wouldn't take much to push him over the edge of reason into a ferocious, fighting madness.

Keeping a tight rein on the aggressive impulses, Alexander stood his ground as the boys slowed and stopped about five feet away.

"So what's the deal, Klingon?" Jeremy asked, regarding him warily.

"No deal," Alexander said shortly. He was only guessing that Jeremy was referring to his silence, but asking a question, even for clarification, would imply that he was uncertain and intimidated. He was neither.

"You don't expect us to believe you're going to take the blame for smashing that bookcase without trying to get back at us, are you?" Kim's eyes narrowed in a dark scowl.

"Believe what you want," Alexander countered.

"Don't play dumb with us, Alexander," Bernard snapped. "No self-respecting Klingon would let us off the hook."

"That's right. Don't you Klingons have this thing about defending your *ho-nor.*"

Bernard put a ridiculing emphasis on the word that made Alexander bristle. Still, he held his temper even as the tension in his muscles mounted and the impatient fury sparked. "You don't know anything about honor, Bernard."

"Maybe you don't, either." Jeremy took a daring step forward. "Maybe you didn't snitch because you knew *we'd* do something about it."

"I had reasons you don't understand." Gritting his teeth, Alexander fought the terrible, burning desire to rip the smug, challenging sneer off Jeremy's face.

"Because you're a coward!" Kim's chest heaved. "My uncle was killed by a bunch of no-good, rotten, Klingon cowards!" The angry boy charged.

Alexander staggered backward with the momentum as the smaller boy's body smashed into him. The power of unleashed Klingon adrenaline surged through him. Staying on his feet, he grabbed Kim's arm and easily freed himself from the boy's tackling grasp. Every cell in his Klingon body screamed for blood, urging him to yank the frail arm out of its socket. He tossed Kim aside instead.

Landing on his back with a thud and a *whooshing* grunt as the impact forced the air from his lungs, Kim lay without moving.

Time came to a screeching halt for Alexander. He stared at Kim, stricken as he recalled the soccer player who had died because Worf had been careless with his superior strength. That image was one hundred percent more effective than trying to cage an imaginary lion and the heat of Alexander's anger turned cold with dread.

Get up!

Moaning softly, Kim struggled into a sitting position and drew a long, deep breath.

Relieved and focused on the stunned boy, Alexander didn't see Jeremy and Bernard lunge at him until the last second. His reflexes engaged before the attack registered in his mind. Jumping back and to the side, he deflected the force of Jeremy's fist against his jaw and eluded Bernard's clumsy grasp.

The Klingon rage exploded from the depths of every gene, demanding its innate right to fight. Alexander mentally shoved the urge back as efficiently as he evaded Jeremy's second attempt to smash his face. He ducked the punch, then whipped around, freeing his leg from the arms Bernard wrapped around it.

Howling in frustration, Bernard rose into a crouch with his fists raised before him. Jeremy circled, trying to flank him.

Getting a second wind, Kim stood up and advanced with Jeremy and Bernard.

Sweat glistened on Alexander's brow from the dual exertion of controlling the rage within and fending off the boys' assault without seriously hurting anyone. Realistically, he knew he couldn't keep the fury blocked indefinitely. And even though it was three against one, if the Klingon fury got out, the fury would win.

But the price of his assured victory would be too high.

Retreat was not a maneuver any Klingon considered except as a last resort. And even though a fleeing Bird-of-Prey survived to fight again, many Klingon commanders preferred to die. For Alexander, retreat was the only option. He could bear being branded a coward. He could not bear inflicting a crippling injury or causing a death.

Hoping the implied threat would keep his attackers at bay, Alexander raised his hands in a defensive *Mok'bara* position and slowly moved back.

"Come on!" Jeremy screamed. "Fight! Fight!"

"Chicken!" Bernard ran forward, swinging wildly.

Kim didn't say anything. He just charged.

Still moving backward toward the school, Alexander deftly warded off the blows. He instantly recognized an opportunity to flip Bernard, but didn't take it. He had not been practicing the offensive aspects of the art long enough to guarantee precision control. One wrong move and Bernard could snap his neck.

Coming in from behind, Jeremy slammed himself into the back of Alexander's knees. Unprepared, Alexander went down. All three boys fell on him with fists flying.

While Jeremy, Bernard and Kim battered muscle and bruised bone, the denied rage stormed a Klingon-human mind that would not and did not surrender.

A fist clobbered him in the eye and another blow split his lip. The salty taste of his own blood amplified the rage, but Alexander did not fight back.

The pounding stopped suddenly as new voices mingled with the boys' shouted curses and insults.

"Stop this!" A man demanded. "Stop this now!"

"Enough, Bernard!" An authoritative female snapped. "Kim! Alexander!"

Breathing hard, Alexander watched as Mr. Cunningham pulled Jeremy away. Ms. Marconi stepped between him and Bernard, saving him from one last punch. Kim backed off on his own.

"You know," Mr. Cunningham said crossly as Alexander struggled to his feet. "I was really looking forward to getting home, but thanks to the four of you, we'll all be spending the rest of this beautiful day with Mr. Houseman."

"And I don't think *he's* going to be too happy about being stuck here, either." Standing with her hands on her hips, Ms. Marconi glared at all four boys.

"He started it!" Bernard pointed to Alexander. Jeremy and Kim, looking suitably ashamed, nodded in agreement.

The librarian's incensed gaze shifted to fix on Alexander's dirt-streaked face. "How could you? Especially after Mr. Houseman gave you another chance."

"I did not start it." Alexander said, wondering if the slight narrowing of Ms. Marconi's eyes indicated disgust or uncertainty.

"Everything was fine when you left detention, Alexander." Either disregarding or not hearing Alexander's denial, the science teacher threw up his hands in exasperation. "What could these three possibly have done that was worth starting a fight and getting thrown out of school?"

I was ambushed, Alexander thought. He would have said so if he thought anyone would listen. He seriously doubted anyone would. Sighing he fell into step beside Jeremy as Mr. Cunningham marched them back to the building and the principal's office.

"Gotcha, Klingon," Jeremy whispered. "You're out of here."

Alexander didn't give the gloating boy the satisfaction of a response. The disgrace of being expelled would pass someday, but if he couldn't convince his father he had not started the fight, the breach of faith between them might never be healed.

Who would Worf believe?

A rebellious son who had challenged his ideals and brought him more trouble than joy over the years?

Or everyone else?

CHAPTER 8

SITTING ON THE HARD BENCH IN THE SCHOOL OFFICE, ALEXANDER STARED AT the three boys perched on chairs across from him. With an expression of inscrutable indifference frozen on his face, he did not blink, twitch, or in any way react to their whispered discussion. The cut on his lip stung and his blossoming black eye throbbed. He ignored those irritations, too.

Behind the counter, Mrs. Miyashi watched all of them like a hawk, ready to sound the alarm at the first hint of trouble. Mr. Houseman was still in his office. Jeremy's father and Bernard and Kim's mothers had already arrived and were waiting in the conference room with Mr. Cunningham and Ms. Marconi. Alexander didn't know when his father would show. Worf had gone to Starfleet Headquarters to attend a research and development briefing about new security technologies. Alexander was sure he would not leave before the presentation was finished.

A buzzer sounded on Mrs. Miyashi's desk. Rising, she headed for the principal's office and paused at the door to glance at her charges. "Nobody moves. Do I make myself clear?"

The human boys nodded.

"Yes." Alexander answered without moving anything except his mouth. The instant Mrs. Miyashi closed the door behind her, the boys fastened their intent, triumphant eyes on him.

"Defeat is as bitter as they say, isn't it, Alexander?" Jeremy smiled.

"And victory is sweet." Bernard nodded emphatically. "We'll probably get a month of detention, but you know? It's worth it to get rid of you."

Kim just stared back.

Remembering how devastated he had been when his mother died, Alexander sympathized. But unlike Kim, who had targeted the entire Klingon race because he did not know the face or the fate of his uncle's killer, he knew a certain, painful peace. Duras would never kill again. His father had risked his Starfleet career to claim the right of revenge under Klingon law and had killed the murdering traitor. Kim had no such comfort and Alexander sincerely wished there was some way he could diffuse the emotional time bomb the boy was carrying around.

"We won our war against you, Alexander." Jeremy leaned forward to drive his point home. "And Starfleet will win against the Klingon Empire, too."

"But," Worf's deep voice boomed from the doorway. "It would be more beneficial for all concerned if our differences could be settled peacefully."

As though operating as a single unit, all three boys gasped. Eyes widened and jaws fell open as Lieutenant Commander Worf, wearing his red and black Starfleet uniform and a silver Klingon sash, stepped into the room.

"You really are a Starfleet officer!" Jeremy stated the obvious in a hushed rasp. "How can that be?"

"I graduated from Starfleet Academy." Worf spoke without a hint of humor and dismissed the stunned boy by simply looking away.

Alexander tried not to smile. It was a struggle easily won when he saw the hard gleam in his father's gaze when their eyes met.

Mrs. Miyashi's hand clamped to her chest as she left Mr. Houseman's office and spotted the towering Klingon standing by the counter. "We've been waiting for you to arrive, Mr. Worf. If you'll just have a seat in the conference room with the other parents—"

"You and they will have to wait a while longer," Worf said bluntly. He was not asking permission.

"Oh, uh… really?" Mrs. Miyashi swallowed hard.

"I will discuss this matter with my son first. In private."

Alexander's heart lurched.

Jeremy and Bernard couldn't stop staring.

Kim frowned.

Stricken mute, Mrs. Miyashi pointed to the door leading into the guidance counselor's office.

With a curt nod, Worf turned toward the indicated door. "Come with me, Alexander."

Breathing in deeply, but keeping his own impassive expression fixed, Alexander stood up and followed his father. He did not acknowledge the four pairs of eyes that followed him.

"Sit down." Motioning toward one of two chairs by an uncluttered desk, Worf closed the office door.

Alexander sat, bracing himself for the worst as Worf sank into the other chair.

"Have you been falsely accused again, Alexander?"

Alexander had expected his father to be direct, but he had not anticipated the question asked. He answered in stammering awe. "Uh… yes."

"I see." Worf lapsed into thoughtful silence a moment before continuing. "Did these same boys push over the bookcase in the library yesterday?"

Alexander could only nod, astounded yet again by his father's blind belief that he had kept his given word. The questions Worf asked did not challenge his honesty, but merely sought additional information.

"Why did you not say so when we were in Mr. Houseman's office?"

Shrugging, Alexander explained. "Everyone was so sure I did it, I didn't think anyone would believe me."

Worf frowned. "That is not sufficient reason to take the blame and accept punishment for something you did not do."

"No." Alexander paused, but he didn't even consider trying to hide the truth. "I thought that if I told, Jeremy and Bernard and Kim would try to get back at me. I wasn't afraid of a fight," he added quickly. "I just wasn't sure I'd be able to… control myself if I got into one."

"You did not want to risk hurting or… killing anyone."

Alexander shook his head. "No."

"But they attacked you anyway."

"Yeah. They wanted to get me before I got them, except I wasn't even *thinking* about getting revenge."

Nodding, Worf gently touched the dried blood on Alexander's lip, then glanced at the closed door. "They do not appear to have any broken bones, bruises or black eyes."

"I could have torn them apart with my bare hands!" Alexander's eyes flashed with Klingon fire, then he exhaled in self-disgust. "But I didn't

fight back. I *am* a rotten Klingon just like Kim said. Just not for the reasons he thinks."

"I was not aware that you *wanted* to be Klingon." Worf blinked, unable to hide his surprise.

"I don't. Not exactly." Alexander shifted position and averted his gaze. "I want to be like you."

Worf just stared at him.

Misinterpreting the long silence that followed, Alexander tried to cover the admission he had not intended to voice. "I wanted to make you proud, not ashamed."

"Ashamed?" Worf started. "I am *not* ashamed of you and *you* are not a . . . rotten Klingon. Your ability to control your temper under such trying circumstances is impressive. And there is no dishonor in not fighting back when the decision is made in the interest of a greater good."

"There isn't?" Alexander looked up with a puzzled frown.

"No. After I avenged K'Ehleyr by killing Duras, I made a decision *not* to challenge the High Council to clear our family's name for the good of the Empire."

"But Duras's father betrayed Khitomer to the Romulans, not Mogh!"

Worf sighed. "That is true, but the entire High Council had supported the lie and shared the dishonor that went with it. To expose them would have thrown the Empire into chaos."

Alexander raised an eyebrow. "But that happened anyway."

"Yes." Worf sighed. "When the Duras family challenged Gowron's right to lead the High Council, the result was civil war. My silence only delayed the inevitable."

"Yeah." Alexander nodded. "Now I wish I had defended myself about the bookcase, too. But it's too late now."

Worf sat back with a frown. "My decision bought Gowron valuable time. Taking the blame for the bookcase to avoid a potentially dangerous confrontation was a wise decision as well."

"Except it didn't work!" The heat of anger warmed Alexander's blood, but the heat quickly dissipated in the cold of bitter despair. "There was still a fight and everyone thinks I started it. Just like everyone thinks I dumped that bookcase. Even if I told the truth, no one would believe me now."

"Truth does not stay buried forever," Worf said. "The Duras lie was exposed and our honor *was* restored by Gowron when he emerged victorious in the civil war."

"Yeah, but then Gowron kicked us out of the Empire again."

"Yes." Worf's jaw flexed with tension. "He wanted me to join him when the Empire broke the alliance with the Federation. I chose to remain in Starfleet. He did not understand that being truly Klingon, my oath of allegiance to the Federation was just as binding as if I had sworn to be loyal to him."

Alexander couldn't help but notice the fleeting sadness that clouded his father's eyes. Gowron had robbed them of their place on the High Council, their lands and their titles and evicted them from the Klingon Empire. Worf had even lost his brother, whose memories had been erased and replaced with a new identity to save him. Not only did Kurn no longer remember Worf as his brother, he despised and reviled him.

Now, Alexander realized with a profound sadness he had not felt before, all they had left of their Klingon heritage was each other and their honor—which Worf had never compromised.

"However, that is beside the point," Worf continued. "Gowron *had* to set aside my discommendation because his honor would not allow him to ignore the truth about Mogh's loyalty to the Empire at Khitomer. And I believe that someday he will pay highly for dismissing my oath to the Federation as irrelevant. Honor does prevail."

"When you're dealing with Klingons," Alexander pointed out. "My word doesn't mean anything here because these people don't understand the importance of a Klingon's oath. None of what's happened is my fault, but I'm going to be expelled anyway."

Worf bristled. "I will not allow them to expel you for something you did not do."

Alexander appreciated that, but his father's perspective had been distorted by his years in Starfleet. Because Starfleet incorporated so many different races and species, tolerance and understanding of alien cultures was imperative. With the exception of himself and an occasional exchange student from another world, the school's teachers and students had never had to take critical cultural differences into consideration.

"I don't think you can stop them," Alexander said honestly. "It's my word against the word of three humans who lie."

Worf's eyes narrowed thoughtfully. "By lying, those boys have challenged your honor. Consequently, they may also have provided us with the means to solve both your problems."

"Both problems?"

"This school's lack of knowledge about Klingon culture and the false accusation. There is a way, but you must trust me without question."

How? Alexander wondered, his mind racing with a dozen more questions. He did not ask them.

"You have my word," Alexander said solemnly.

CHAPTER 9

As Alexander took his place back on the bench, Worf looked at all four boys in turn, then addressed Mrs. Miyashi. "They will remain here until called. I must speak to their teachers and parents alone."

"Uh, well. If it's all right with Mr. Houseman, I suppose—"

"If what's all right?" Mr. Houseman frowned as he stepped out of his office.

"I will explain in the conference room, Mr. Houseman." Without giving the principal a chance to reply or argue, Worf opened the conference room door and strode inside. He stopped at the near end of the long table. All five humans seated around it reacted to his entrance with varying degrees of alarm and curiosity.

Mr. Houseman followed, remaining calm and collected as he walked past Worf and sat down at the head of the table. "Please, Mr. Worf. Have a seat."

"Thank you. I will stand."

"You're not on trial here, Mr. Worf," the principal assured him kindly.

"No, but Alexander is and I am convinced he has been falsely accused—for the second time in two days." Worf had never understood the human tendency to "beat around the bush" and chose to get directly to the point. It was more efficient and gave him an immediate insight into the attitudes of the other people in the room.

He noted that the two women and one man seated to his left took exception to his statement. The dark-skinned woman frowned, but with consideration for his blunt declaration. The guarded stares of the woman of Asian descent and the man transformed into hostile glares. They were, he surmised, the other boys' parents. The pretty, blond woman on his right looked startled, then deeply troubled, suggesting she might agree. The man to her right appeared to be thoughtfully reserving judgment.

Mr. Houseman quickly introduced everyone. Nods were exchanged instead of handshakes, providing Worf with more helpful information. Mrs. Umbaya, the librarian and the science teacher greeted him with tight, hesitant smiles, indicating they were willing to listen. Mr. Sullivan and Mrs. Ho would be difficult to convince.

"The matter of the library bookcase is closed, Mr. Worf," Mr. Houseman said evenly. "We're here today because Alexander, Jeremy, Bernard and Kim were caught fighting on school property."

"Today's fight is a direct result of Alexander's silence concerning the bookcase." Worf also kept his voice even. "He did not defend himself yesterday because he mistakenly thought that taking the blame would *prevent* a confrontation. He did not start the fight."

"Are you saying that our kids did?" Mr. Sullivan demanded hotly.

"But why would they?" Mrs. Umbaya asked, genuinely puzzled.

Mrs. Ho shifted uncomfortably, but didn't speak.

Worf was not unsympathetic to their distress. He had not forgotten how embarrassed he had been when Ms. Kyle, Alexander's first teacher on the *Enterprise,* had informed him of his son's disturbing behavior in class. However, although he was determined to clear Alexander, he was more concerned with correcting the circumstances that had prompted the incidents than he was with seeing the other boys punished.

"As concerned and responsible parents, the question we must address is not who did what, but why—as Mrs. Umbaya asked a moment ago."

Mrs. Umbaya nodded, pleased with Worf's recognition.

"We are all aware that Klingons are savagely aggressive," Mr. Sullivan huffed. "Obviously, Mr. Worf's son must have done *something* to antagonize the others."

"Obviously?" Ms. Marconi glared at Jeremy's father. "Are all people of Irish descent alcoholics and terrorists?"

"Of course not!" Mr. Sullivan snapped, then blinked. A flush of humiliation crept up his neck as he cleared his throat. "Although, a few hundred years ago there were a lot of people who thought so. My deepest apologies for my prejudicial remark, Lieutenant Commander."

Worf accepted with a gracious nod.

"Prejudice." Mr. Cunningham sighed. "Humans have lived together without caring about our differences for so long, I didn't recogize the ugly beast when it was staring me in the face. Prejudice is the problem, isn't it, Mr. Worf?"

"I believe so." Worf scanned the troubled faces before him, noting that everyone but Mrs. Ho now seemed open to discussion. "In spite of the long alliance between the Federation and the Empire, Earth knows very little about our culture and values. Ignorance breeds misunderstanding."

"That doesn't change the fact that your son went berserk in the library yesterday!" An anger completely out of proportion to the circumstances twisted Mrs. Ho's face and flared in her eyes. *"That* was no misunderstanding. Kim told me that Ms. Marconi caught Alexander red-handed."

"Actually—" The librarian sheepishly glanced at Mr. Houseman and then at Worf. "I didn't *see* Alexander push the case. His sleeve was caught between the bookcase and the table and he was the only one there when I arrived. But..."

"Yes?" Worf prodded.

Ms. Marconi sighed deeply. "Jeremy, Bernard and Kim were in the library at the time, too."

Mr. Houseman started. "And you think it's possible they did it?"

Ms. Marconi shrugged. "Possible, yes. But I can't prove it. Not unless they confess."

"The same is true of the fight today," Mr. Cunningham added. "Bernard *said* Alexander started it and the other two agreed, but we don't know that for a fact."

Appalled, Mrs. Umbaya gasped. "I can't believe Bernard would lie or do any of these terrible things just because Alexander is a Klingon."

"Kim would." Tears flowed freely down Mrs. Ho's cheeks. "My brother was killed by Klingons."

No one spoke for several seconds.

"I hate to admit it," Mr. Sullivan said softly, breaking the anguished silence, "but Jeremy could be guilty, too. He's been set on a Starfleet career since he was six years old. According to him, Bernard and Kim share his dream. Perhaps, in their youthful enthusiasm, they've forgotten

that the primary function of Starfleet is exploration. The dispute with the Empire *has* put an unusual emphasis on combat."

"And Alexander is the face of the enemy." Exhaling, Mrs. Umbaya lowered her gaze.

"I'm at a loss how to proceed," the principal admitted, running his hand through his hair. "Without proof or confessions, we may never know what really happened in the library. However, I'm no longer *convinced* Alexander is guilty. Even so, they were all caught fighting on school grounds. I don't see any option but to punish all of them."

"I have a better idea." When everyone turned to regard him attentively, Worf plunged ahead. "The boys are the only ones who know the truth. It cannot be forced out of them, but must be offered willingly, as a matter of honor. Honor is not a concept unique to Klingons. It has been valued as a measure of an individual human's worth throughout your history. It is absolutely essential in Starfleet officers."

"Go on, Mr. Worf," Mr. Sullivan urged with a smile.

Alexander stood with Jeremy, Bernard and Kim at the edge of the table. The adults sitting around it watched them with expressions so grim and foreboding, he wondered if his father had been giving them lessons. He aimed his own gaze straight ahead, but he was aware of Worf standing off to the side. His father's narrowed, piercing stare and proud stance were unmistakeable signs that he had shifted into pure Klingon-mode.

"Alexander!" Worf barked sharply.

Jeremy, Bernard and Kim flinched.

"Yes, sir." Swallowing hard, Alexander tried to bear in mind that his father had a plan. No matter what happened, he had to trust him—blindly and without question.

"Did you knock over the bookcase in the library?"

"No, sir. I did not."

"Do you know who did?"

"Yes."

Arms crossed over his massive chest, Worf strode forward and stopped before him. "Name them."

Alexander felt Jeremy tense beside him and hesitated. He wasn't sure what response his father expected. An honest and honorable one, he realized. "No."

Worf paused, tightening the tension with his silence. "That is your right. However, Bernard Umbaya *has* accused you of starting the fight on the soccer field."

Bernard sucked in his breath with a soft cry of alarm.

Mrs. Umbaya's hand quickly covered her mouth, but Alexander couldn't tell if she was hiding a smile or a gasp of horror.

Worf's attention remained riveted on him. "Did you?"

"No, sir."

Still speaking to Alexander, but moving so he faced Bernard, Worf spoke in a low, threatening tone. "Then *he* has insulted your honor."

"Yes."

"And tomorrow is the *Batlh Jaj!*"

Turning pale, Bernard jumped and looked imploringly at his mother. "Mom?"

Her only response was an unsympathetic scowl.

"*Batlh Jaj,*" Worf repeated slowly.

Alexander frowned. Was he supposed to say something?

"The Klingon Day of Honor," Worf said with a prodding look at Alexander. "The only day non-Klingons are allowed to participate in—"

"The *Suv'batlh!*" Shouting the word, Alexander suddenly realized what his father was trying to set up. Donning his most ferocious Klingon face, he turned to confront Bernard and snarled softly. "Because you've accused me with a lie, I challenge you to fight the Honor Combat."

"Combat?" Bernard squeaked.

Worf moved back, allowing Alexander to look each boy in the eye as he moved from one to the next. Normally, the *Suv'batlh* was fought three on three. Alexander had no companions to stand by him and decided to even up the odds.

"Three on one."

"Uh..." Desperate, Bernard looked at Jeremy, then Kim.

"We accept." Kim's eyes filled with his poisonous hatred.

"We do?" Bernard blinked uncertainly, then shrugged. "Right. We do."

"Gladly." Jeremy smiled with smug confidence.

Moving in again, Worf addressed Bernard. "Although the *Suv'batlh* traditionally takes place in the territory of the one whose honor has been challenged, this battle will be held on neutral ground. The school gym. Tomorrow morning. *Qapla!*"

Turning abruptly, Worf strode boldly out the door.

Alexander hesitated, then caught Ms. Marconi waving under the table for him to go, too. Holding his head up, he marched boldly after his father.

Worf did not alter the speed or cadence of his pace until they were outside and striding across the soccer field. Even then, Alexander had to jog to keep up.

"How did you get Mr. Houseman and the other parents to agree to a *Suv'batlh?"*

"Honor is just as important to most humans as it is to Klingons," Worf explained, deliberately slowing so Alexander didn't have to run. "They just do not advertise it as loudly or constantly as Klingons do."

"Oh." Alexander walked, feeling as darkly troubled as the twilight sky. "There's just one thing that bothers me about this whole thing, though."

"And that is?"

"Jeremy, Bernard and Kim don't know the first thing about using a *bat'leth* and I've been practicing for years. Fighting an Honor Combat with such an overwhelming advantage just doesn't seem fair."

Worf nodded. "An honorable observation. However, I assure you, tomorrow's *Suv'batlh* will be fairer to your opponents than they have been to you."

Bursting with curiosity, Alexander had to ask. "How can you be so sure?"

"Because…" Worf paused on the edge of the forest to look down on him. "The choice of weapons is yours."

CHAPTER 10

STANDING BY A FOLD-OUT SCREEN POSITIONED CENTER STAGE JUST OFF THE back wall, Alexander watched as the school gym was transformed for the Day of Honor assembly. If this had been a large school in a metropolitan area, the setting and props could have been programmed into the hologym, but the small Mirnee Doleena school was not equipped with that technological luxury. Worf, Ms. Petrovna and Mr. Santiago, the physical education teachers who had volunteered to help, were setting up the Klingon props his father and grandmother had taken out of storage or replicated the night before.

The gymnastics equipment had been relocated in the far half of the gym to make room for the *Batlh Jaj* presentation. The bleachers along both sides had been lowered to accommodate the students and teachers and chairs had been set in front of the tiers for Mr. Houseman, nonteaching personnel, his three opponents and their parents.

Ms. Petrovna and Mr. Santiago came into view pushing two metal *bat'leth* racks. After placing the racks a few feet to each side of the screen, they hurried out again.

Bustling with energy, Helena and Sergey Rozhenko attached a large Klingon banner to the front of the screen.

"What do you think, Alexander?" his grandmother asked, her eyes bright with enthusiasm. "I made it for your father a long time ago."

Alexander cocked his head, studying the red banner with the symbol of the Empire emblazoned in gold at the center. "It looks great. Very… Klingon."

"So do you!" Sergey beamed as he gave Alexander an appreciative once-over. "You look quite… terrifying."

"Just like a warrior," Helena declared with proud delight.

Alexander rolled his eyes, but the intended compliments pleased him. Although the fitted black pants and knee-high boots were comfortable, the belted, plated-metal armor he wore over a black shirt felt awkward. The buckled, metal-studded leather combat gloves itched. He fought the urge to brush back his long hair, which had been teased into a wild disarray that cascaded over his shoulders. Still, he was glad to know his appearance was intimidating. However, he doubted that he looked nearly as fierce as his father.

"Your *bat'leth,* Alexander." Also dressed in the armor of a Klingon warrior, Worf strode toward the small group. Placing the ancient family *bat'leth* on the taller rack, Worf handed another traditional sword to his son. Alexander carefully put it on the shorter metal rack. "Where are Ms. Marconi and Mr. Cunningham?"

"Right here!" Wearing a long Klingon robe made of large blue, silver and brown patches over a black shirt and pants secured with a wide, silver belt, the science teacher hurried across the gym floor. Ms. Marconi moved at a more sedate pace, looking regal in a similar robe of patched greens and golds worn over a long black dress belted in gold. Both of their faces shone with an eager excitement.

"So!" Mr. Cunningham clapped his hands together, obviously thrilled to be actively participating in the *Batlh Jaj* ceremony. "What do you want us to do?"

Waving Mr. Santiago over, Worf took a tall standard from the gym teacher's hands. The pole was fitted with metal balls alternated with curved and spiked, metal Klingon symbols. Then he pointed to one side of the screen. "You will stand here."

The teacher obediently stepped into the spot Worf indicated.

"Ordinarily," Worf said, "there are specific moments during the ritual when the standard bearer makes the staff sing." Small metal plates attached to chains hanging from the curved pieces jangled as Worf gently shook the pole. "However, since we do not have time for instruction, you may jangle at your discretion." He handed the standard to the teacher and turned away.

The science teacher hesitated, then shook the pole.

The plates jingled, drawing Worf's attention back.

Mr. Cunningham shrugged with a mischievous twinkle in his eye. "Just practicing."

Alexander smiled as his father left to get the remaining props. He was pretty sure the Klingon Empire would not approve of including non-Klingons quite so liberally in the ceremonial proceedings. His father's willingness to deviate from acceptable Klingon tradition was encouraging, though. If Worf could be this flexible, maybe their human audience would be, too.

"What about me?" Ms. Marconi looked at Worf expectantly when he returned.

"You will light the torches." Worf handed her a small, tech-torch. The tip would burst into flame when she pressed a button on the long shaft.

Ms. Petrovna and Mr. Santiago came back on stage pushing two more racks, each mounted with three unlit torches made of wood and pitch.

Worf caught Alexander's questioning glance as the gym teachers rolled the racks into position behind the *bat'leth* stands. "Under the circumstances, torches seemed… appropriate."

Alexander held up his hands, indicating he wasn't going to argue the point.

"It's almost time, Mr. Worf," Mr. Santiago said. "I just hope I don't miss my cues."

"The lighting is only for dramatic effect," Worf assured him with another glance at Alexander. "Part of the *stuff* so many people seem to associate with Klingon rituals. We are, after all, striving to make a symbolic point."

"I think everyone will be impressed." Giving Worf a thumbs-up, Ms. Petrovna followed Mr. Santiago to the far side of the gym.

After giving Alexander a supportive pat on the back, his grandmother went to join his grandfather on the chairs in front of the bleachers. Clasping the tech-torch in both hands, Ms. Marconi moved to center stage between the *bat'leth* racks. Taking a deep breath, Alexander followed Worf to wait behind the screen.

Seated behind the technical control board, Mr. Santiago opaqued the windows, throwing the gym into total darkness. A minute later, leaving the *Batlh Jaj* stage darkened, he raised the lights in the rest of the gym to a dim, twilight glow.

Alexander listened to the faint whisper of his father's breath and the muffled sounds of students and teachers filing in and finding seats. He could almost hear the pounding of his own anxious heart as it throbbed against his ribs. Heat flowed from the pulsing muscles into his blood in anticipation of the battle soon to be waged and the honor soon to be avenged. It coursed through major arteries, spreading to smaller ones, infusing every muscle and nerve with the raw power of being Klingon.

Alexander trembled as the intensity of the moment triggered a memory buried in the depths of his mind. The image of a familiar, aging Klingon face suddenly appeared.

K'mtar.

The trusted family advisor had arrived to prevent Worf's assassination at a *Kot'baval* festival on a remote Klingon outpost not long before the *Enterprise* had been destroyed. K'mtar had tried to force him into becoming a warrior with as much, if not more, fervent determination than his father. He had resisted, just as stubbornly as he had always rejected Worf's attempts. Then, without even saying good-bye, K'mtar had vanished from his life—and his thoughts.

Remembering now, Alexander was once again reminded of the irony inherent in his present circumstances. He had not consciously realized that Worf had stopped pressuring him to learn Klingon ways following K'mtar's departure. Their time together had been too short afterward. The destruction of the *Enterprise* had brought him back to Earth and sent his father to serve on *Deep Space Nine.* But even on his return, knowing his son's ignorance of Klingon control methods was partially responsible for his fits of violent temper, Worf had not pressed him. His father had only suggested. And finally, left to decide for himself, Alexander had agreed to explore the power of the Klingon self he had always denied.

But, Alexander realized in amazement, that power did not have a will of its own. Focusing his thoughts, he kept the fire from running wild, banked it to be called upon and used when and as he directed. Or so he hoped. He would not know if he was still a slave to the savage in his genes or if he had tamed it until the *Suv'batlh* began.

The lights dimmed to near darkness and Worf tensed beside him.

The hiss and crackle of Ms. Marconi's tech-torch bursting into flame and the audience's collected gasp of hushed awe touched Alexander's ears. He watched his father as the librarian lit the wooden torches on their right and left. When Worf turned to signal him that it was time to begin, their gazes locked for a long moment. He could sense the tension mounting in the crowd waiting for whatever happened next. His own nerves were taut with excitement. Then, returning Worf's nod, he moved around the right end of the screen as his father moved to the left.

Matching his father's movements, Alexander paused before the rack of burning torches on his side of the stage. Ms. Marconi stood in front of the Klingon banner, still clutching her torch. A subtle scowl of Klingon contempt was fixed on her pretty face. Mr. Cunningham waited on his right, holding the standard steady and silent, looking impressively superior and composed. Which, Alexander reflected, wasn't all that difficult for a teacher.

Their dramatic appearance had the desired effect, though. More gasps and anxious whispers rippled through the assembly. The audience's undivided attention had been captured as surely as a shuttle snagged in a starship's tractor beam.

"Batlh Jaj!" Worf's booming voice roared. A spotlight suddenly illuminated his head and upper body, augmenting the flickering light from the torches.

"The Day of Honor!" Alexander translated loudly as a flash of light enveloped him, too.

Mr. Cunningham jangled.

Perfect! Tensing, Alexander listened as his father recited a brief explanation of the holiday's origin in sharp, staccato Klingon.

"Jatlh ta' tlhIngan Du yuQ! Nob'ta Wo' che—"

Mesmerized by the power of Worf's commanding voice, no one stirred in the darkness even though they didn't understand a word. Alexander wouldn't have understood, either, except that he had memorized the recitation in English and rehearsed it endlessly the night before.

When his father paused, Alexander translated the passage with a clipped, emphatic rhythm. "Declared on the Klingon Farm World Soch! A planet awarded to the Empire under the terms of the Organian Treaty of 2267. Where enemies with wounds still raw from war united to repel the invading Narr."

Catching his breath while Worf continued in Klingon, Alexander launched into the next passage feeling empowered by the passionate words.

"To honor Captain James T. Kirk, who fought for a world he was *not* sworn to defend."

Worf's powerful Klingon words echoed off the rafters.

"To honor Commander Kor," Alexander repeated the phrase in English. "Who recognized honor in an enemy and had the courage to risk his own for victory!"

"Batlh hoch yIn vI'tak je pol qaHegh 'Ip!"

Alexander's eyes narrowed and his own voice became harsh with menace as he delivered the final passage. "To honor *all* who live by truth and uphold to the *death* their given word!"

With the exception of Mr. Cunningham's jingling standard, absolute silence greeted the closing remark. Alexander suspected everyone was either too shocked by the reference to death or too intimidated by his father to risk offending him with applause. Or maybe they were just stunned to learn that the Federation's most notorious and honored starship captain, James T. Kirk, was responsible for the Klingon Empire's most respected holiday, too. Whatever the reason, their reaction would work to his advantage in the end.

The spotlights followed as Worf and Alexander moved to retrieve their *bat'leths.* The lights over the audience remained dark, but brightened over the stage area as father and son gripped the curved weapons with both hands and raised them above their heads.

"The *Suv'batlh* is fought when a warrior's honor is challenged by another." Worf's gaze scanned the darkened faces before him.

Alexander saw his opponents out of the corner of his eye. Sitting in chairs and visible in the dim light coming from the stage, Jeremy, Bernard and Kim stared at him with expressions ranging from cautious curiosity to wide-eyed terror to open hostility. Alexander smothered a smile and braced himself as his father went on.

"The ancient Honor Combat tests the courage of a warrior's heart as well as his skill!"

The metal standard sang as the science teacher shook the pole.

Taking the cue and moving in unison with his father, Alexander lowered his sword. He kept his eye on Worf's face as they both began to circle each other, swinging and dipping the deadly, pointed ends of the curved *bat'leths* in front of them. A rush of thrilled and anxious sound escaped the audience as Alexander suddenly spun, drew back and swung his blade overhand. Worf instantly raised his own blade to block the downward strike.

Alexander froze, holding his position.

Worf turned only his head to address the audience. "A Klingon warrior never resorts to deception when fighting the *Suv'batlh.* To evade by any devious means or trick would be dishonorable."

Instantly, Alexander pulled back and parried his father's series of side-to-side strikes. Metal clashed against metal until he stopped Worf's sword with a vertical block and froze once again.

"The *Suv'batlh* is *never* conceded." Worf snarled, causing the crowd to inhale with alarm. "It is *always* fought to the finish."

As lightning strikes—in a flash and without warning—Alexander leaped into action for the final, climactic sequence. Pushing his father's blade away, he circled and flipped the meter-long sword, then blocked Worf's overhand strike. Spinning around, he came out of the turn whipping his blade to the side. Worf blocked. Alexander swung to the other side. Worf blocked, then drew back to land a resounding overhand strike against Alexander's defending blade. Then, as planned, Alexander lunged slightly, throwing his father "off balance." With a last, overhand swing of the *bat'leth,* he struck the "killing" blow to Worf's chest. As Worf fell, Mr. Santiago doused the lights.

Silence reigned as Worf got to his feet and raised his sword over his head to match Alexander's victorious stance. The hushed quiet erupted into cheers, whistles and thunderous applause when the lights came on again, revealing father and son in all their majestic Klingon glory.

Alexander noted that Mr. Houseman and his grandparents were applauding and grinning along with everyone else. His opponents' parents sat quietly, their expressions rigid and cold. Jeremy, Bernard and Kim seemed to be the only other spectators who hadn't thoroughly enjoyed the demonstration.

The hush that followed when the applause died down was one of tense anticipation rather than anxiety.

Cradling his sword in the curve of his arm, Alexander moved forward, then stood at attention as Worf placed his *bat'leth* back on the rack. He kept his eyes trained straight ahead when his father addressed the audience again.

"On his word of honor, Alexander Rozhenko has denied destroying the library bookcase."

Teachers and students frowned and a whisper of disturbed discussion swept the room.

"He refuses to name the persons who *are* guilty. Why?" Worf demanded, whirling to confront his son.

Alexander flinched even though he had expected the question, but quickly recovered. "A heart without honor is hollow. To live without honor is to forsake self. To die without honor is to be forever reviled." He paused to let those words sink in before he concluded. "It would not be honorable to deny anyone their right to do the honorable thing and confess."

Alexander saw all three boys frown. Jeremy's expression was still hostile, Bernard's one of fear. Kim looked thoughtfully troubled.

Worf went on. "Alexander Rozhenko has been openly accused of starting a fight on school grounds. This he has also denied on his word of honor. Therefore, because his honor has been insulted, he has issued a challenge and the challenge has been accepted." Scowling ominously, Worf turned and pointed at the three boys. "*You* will come forward now and face the challenger!"

Behind him, Alexander heard the intense jangling of Mr. Cunningham's metal standard.

Murmurs of nervous surprise and fright rippled through the audience as Jeremy, Bernard and Kim stood up and slowly approached. Alexander did not meet their eyes as they paused before him, but he could tell that they were all scared. Even Jeremy's protective crust of smug confidence had crumbled.

"Honor will be restored to the victor and any request he makes will be granted." Worf looked at Alexander, then barked as he backed off. "Challenger! Choose your weapons and let the *Suv'batlh* begin!"

Alexander's eyes flashed as he instantly shifted his gaze to his opponents. Pressing the *bat'leth* over his head, he shouted and shook the sword. *"Batlh Daqawlu'jlH!"*

Bernard trembled. Jeremy tensed and Kim set his jaw. All three boys turned white as the blood drained from their faces.

"Qab jlH nagil!" Alexander snarled. "I will be remembered with honor! Face me if you dare!" With a flourish, he whipped the sword up above his shoulder, intending to stay the blade.

The rage blindsided him as it burst free.

CHAPTER 11

ALEXANDER'S ARMS TREMBLED AND HIS HANDS FLEXED ON COLD METAL AS he fought the savage command urging him to swing.

Jeremy and Kim cringed. Bernard ducked, throwing his arms over his head.

Gasps and cries of alarm rose from the assembly. Students jumped up in horrified disbelief and teachers glanced at each other uncertainly. Mr. Houseman, the office personnel and parents perched on the edge of their seats.

Filled with the power surging through his veins, Alexander felt the overwhelming desire of the Klingon predator to draw blood. He rebelled, calling on a stronger passion and a different strength. This was not a hunt and he was not a mindless beast. Clenching his teeth, he swung the sword and deftly pulled the swing, bringing the *bat'leth* to an abrupt halt in front of his chest. He stood perfectly still as he withdrew into himself and used the *Mok'bara* to calm the rage. Exhaling slowly, he turned, flipped the cutting edge toward him and offered the sword to Worf.

"The *Suv'batlh,"* Alexander said, turning back to face the boys, "must be fought fairly if honor is to be served. These are the weapons I chose." As he pointed toward the far side of the gym, spotlights suddenly illuminated the pommel horse, the high-bar and the vault.

The boys blinked in dazed confusion.

Jeremy recovered first and asked warily. "You're challenging us to a gymnastics meet?"

Alexander shrugged. "Well, if you'd rather settle this with *bat'leths*—"

His dark face shining with relief, Bernard emphatically shook his head. "Not me!"

Jeremy held up his hands. "I wouldn't mind learning how to use one, but right now—I'll pass."

Kim just smiled.

The crowd, suddenly realizing what had just happened, roared with approval as Alexander removed his wrist gauntlets and slipped out of the plated-metal chest armor. Then, motioning for the other three boys to go first, he followed them onto the gym floor where Ms. Petrovna directed them to halt and face the principal.

"In the interest of fairness," Mr. Houseman began, "we have invited three gymnastics coaches from other schools to judge the *Suv'batlh.*"

Enthusiastic applause met the woman and two men who entered through a side door and seated themselves at a table. Their presence left no doubt that Alexander's choice of "weapons" had been planned and came as no surprise to the adults in charge.

Alexander glanced back at his father, who was watching intently with the *bat'leth* comfortably settled in his arm. He nodded slightly with a not-quite smile that warmed Alexander to the core. For Worf, it was the same as an ear-to-ear grin.

Smiling as she walked over to stand by Worf, Ms. Marconi gave him a thumbs-up. Mr. Cunningham winked and gently shook the bangled staff.

"Alexander will compete against a different one of his opponents in each event. Their scores will not be revealed until the match is finished. The highest total score wins." Mr. Houseman looked at the three other boys. "You may decide among yourselves who will compete in each event. However, you will all go first."

The boys conferred as Ms. Petrovna marched to the vault. When she blew her whistle, Bernard removed his shoes and socks and darted to the starting line.

In keeping with the spirit of human sports events, the crowd applauded and screamed encouragement.

Kicking off his own boots and socks, Alexander shook his arms and legs to limber up. The vault was the easiest of the three events. Although Bernard was athletic and fast, gymnastics was not his sport. Jeremy and Kim, however, were on the school gymnastics team. They were used to performing under pressure and both competed on the high-bar and pommel horse, the most difficult apparatus.

Silence fell as Bernard paused to take several deep breaths. Then he was off and running. He jumped, hit the leather vault with both hands and executed a single somersault. Taking a step to keep from falling on landing, he threw his arms in the air.

The spectators whistled and cheered even though Bernard had not attempted a difficult vault or performed perfectly. His father applauded wildly and his mom jumped up and down with excitement. With a broad grin, Bernard bowed and shook his fist in the air. He had met the Klingon challenge and survived.

Alexander returned Bernard's nod as they passed each other on his way to the vault. It was a small gesture, but it signified a measure of acceptance. Perhaps, Alexander thought as he paused on the line, his war against prejudice had already been won. If so, there would be no losers in the *Suv'batlh* being waged on the gym floor.

Focusing on the leather vault, Alexander drew a deep breath and took off at a run. With a flying leap, he hit the vault with his hands and pushed off into a perfect layout body turn and a solid landing. Straightening, Alexander punched the sky with his fists.

A silence even more absolute than the one after the Day of Honor origin recitation fell over the crowd. He held his pose, knowing his vault had been spectacular and his landing perfect. Still, maybe he had been right all along. Demonstrating his superior agility and strength would not ingratiate him to his human peers.

Then someone whooped and whistled from the bleachers. Within a split second, the gym filled with the thunder of clapping hands, shouts and whistles of enthusiastic appreciation. Worf roared with unabashed Klingon pride.

A shudder of emotion swept through Alexander and tears of joyous relief swelled in his eyes. Clamping down on the decidedly non-Klingon reaction and blinking back the mist, he smiled as he bowed and jogged back toward the others.

"That was perfect!" Bernard laughed.

"Very close anyway," Jeremy agreed, shaking his head in wonder. "Looks like we've got some *real* competition."

Kim nodded, then looked up as Ms. Petrovna moved to the high-bar and blew her whistle. With a curt salute that Alexander was sure included him, the slim boy ran to the mat.

"Go, Kim!" Alexander shouted.

Grinning, Jeremy and Bernard hooted encouragement.

Everyone lapsed into respectful silence again as Kim leaped to grab the bar. Swinging forward, then back to pick up momentum, he completed two rotations of the bar in exquisite form, then executed a handstand. On his downward swing, he released his hold, turned his body in the air and caught the bar again. As he swung over the top, he dismounted with a single somersault and nailed the landing.

As Alexander approached the bar, he couldn't help but be impressed with Kim's flawless routine. Scoring higher wouldn't be easy.

"The bar feels a little slippery," Kim said as he stepped off the mat. "Be careful."

"I will," Alexander said, his voice choked with shock. It was the first time Kim had ever spoken to him as a person and not an enemy. "Thanks."

"Sure." Smiling, Kim jogged away.

Dipping into the chalk bucket, Alexander dusted the excess carbonate of magnesium off his hands, then paused to breathe in deeply. He jumped, caught the bar and swung instantly into three rotations topped off with a handstand. As his body fell forward, he bent his legs into a pike position and slipped them through his arms, released and turned to catch the bar again. His left hand slipped. He managed to hang on, but the fluidity of his movement had been interrupted, which would cost him with the judges. Swinging his body up again, he released into a single somersault dismount and landed squarely on the mat.

No one seemed to care about Alexander's small mistake. Whether releasing their tension after the intensity of the Klingon segment of the program or just thoroughly enjoying a thrilling gymnastics competition, the crowd went wild.

"Too bad about that slip," Jeremy said when Alexander joined the group. "But I gotta warn you, the horse is my best event. I'm gonna try like crazy to beat you."

"Great. It wouldn't be any fun otherwise."

"Exactly." Responding to Ms. Petrovna's whistle, Jeremy dashed to the pommel horse in the center of the floor.

Jeremy paused to compose himself, then jumped and grabbed both pommels. With quick, sure releases of his hands as he moved, he swung his extended body to the left, then back to the center, then to the right, traveling the length of the horse. With both hands on the pommels again, he drew up into a handstand. Then, spreading his legs, he slowly lowered them until they extended in front of his body on either side of his arms. Swinging smoothly back into a handstand, he pushed off and nailed the landing. After saluting the audience with raised hands, Jeremy bowed then jumped with delight.

Alexander sighed, then headed across the gym. Jeremy had executed the difficult routine without a single glitch. There was only one way to beat him—if he dared.

"I think that's the best I've ever done, Alexander." Standing with his hands on his hips, Jeremy gasped for breath. "If you beat it, I'll—"

What? Alexander stiffened automatically.

"—buy your ticket to a holoflick in town tomorrow. That new Ferengi comedy just started and Bernard and Kim are bustin' to see it."

"You're on!" Alexander beamed. Jeremy's proposal wasn't a dare or a gamble. It was just the boy's way of apologizing and opening the door to friendship. "And if I don't beat it, I'll buy for all three of you."

"Good luck." Cuffing Alexander's arm, Jeremy waved to a cheering audience as he left.

Recognizing an edge of nervousness that might distract him, Alexander paused and closed his eyes before starting. Using the *Mok'bara* discipline, he cleared his mind of everything except the pommel horse beside him. For a brief few moments, nothing else existed in his universe.

Grabbing the pommels, Alexander extended his legs and traveled the horse, demonstrating the same basic movements Jeremy had. Still following Jeremy's routine, he drew into a handstand, then scissored his legs. He followed through by slowly lowering his legs and holding position with them in front of his body. However, instead of finishing, he suddenly flashed into a difficult and complex movement known as the Thomas Flare since it had first been executed in a late twentieth-century Olympic Games. Whipping his scissored legs from one side to the other, he released and grabbed the pommels with lightning quickness. Then, with a burst of energy, he pushed off and dismounted with a half twist.

Alexander didn't need to hear the tumultuous roar of the crowd or see his father shaking the *bat'leth* in the air to know that his routine had been

dazzling. If he had had any doubts, they would have been instantly vanquished as Jeremy, Bernard and Kim rushed up to surround him.

"I've never seen anyone do that before!" Bernard was breathless with excitement.

"Not in real life." Kim qualified the other boy's observation. "Only in *major* competitions."

"I'm so flabbergasted, I don't know what to say." Jeremy shrugged, then extended his hand.

Alexander shook it, making sure not to squeeze with the full power of his Klingon grip. Breaking Jeremy's hand at this point might end a wonderful friendship before it ever got started.

"Attention!" Mr. Houseman shouted, moving his arms in a downward motion as he tried to quiet the audience. "Please! May I have your attention!"

Ms. Petrovna blew her whistle and Mr. Santiago flashed the lights. Order returned within a minute.

"The results, if you will." Mr. Houseman glanced at the judges. The woman keyed a panel on the table. Each boy's total score flashed on the board attached high on the end wall.

Alexander's point total was higher by a wide margin.

With the *bat'leth* ceremoniously cradled in his arm, Worf, followed by Ms. Marconi with her light tech-torch and Mr. Cunningham with his jangling standard, came forward.

"The *Suv'batlh* has been fought and won!" Worf announced. "Alexander Rozhenko's honor has been avenged and restored."

Cheers and applause rose and quickly died when Worf frowned.

Alexander struggled to keep a straight face.

"Any request you make will be granted! *Yay'lIj!* Victory is yours!"

Alexander started uncertainly as all eyes focused on him. He hadn't really thought about the request part of the *Suv'batlh.* He already had everything he wanted—his honor and the respect of his father and peers. Still, one thing suddenly came to mind.

"I would like to try out for the gymnastics team."

Mr. Santiago jumped to his feet. "You've got it, Alexander! See me right after school."

"Uh…" Alexander's cheeks flushed slightly. "I can't. I've got detention."

Silence.

"No!" Glancing at Kim and Bernard, Jeremy stepped forward. "We tipped over that bookcase, not Alexander."

"And we started the fight!" Kim added.

"We're the ones who should be punished," Bernard concluded.

Alexander stared. The *Batlh Jaj* ceremony had apparently been far more impressive than he had imagined.

Mr. Houseman rubbed his chin, then looked up with a smile. "In keeping with Klingon tradition, the *Suv'batlh* has settled these matters. We'll just call it even. As long as—" He scowled pointedly at all three boys. "—you promise not to do anything like this again."

"Word of honor!" The boys swore in unison, raising their right hands as was the human custom.

"Dismissed." Mr. Houseman grinned.

And Mr. Cunningham jangled the standard one last time.

As the students and teachers began to file out to return to class, the boys' parents and the Rozhenkos hurried over to congratulate the contestants.

"You were magnificent, Alexander!" Sergey beamed.

Mr. Sullivan clasped Jeremy by the arms. "I'm proud of you, son. You may have the makings of a good Starfleet officer after all."

"Thanks, Dad."

"Alexander is thinking about going to Starfleet Academy, too." Helena smiled, her eyes twinkling.

Alexander gasped. He had never, ever told anyone he wanted to join Starfleet. The idea had never entered his mind. "Who told you that?"

"Your father!" Helena said brightly. "He told me that you said you wanted to be just like him. He's so proud."

"But did he say Starfleet specifically?" Alexander pressed. It hadn't been that long since Worf had stopped trying to push him into a Klingon way of life. He didn't think he could stand it if his father suddenly started pushing him toward Starfleet.

Helena frowned. "Specifically? No, I don't believe he did."

Alexander sagged in relief. For a long time he had thought he wanted to be a diplomat like his mother, K'Ehleyr. They shared the mixed human and Klingon heritage that had allowed her to be so effective in trying to bridge the gap between the Federation and the Empire. Recently, though, he had come to realize that his interest in that career path had been greatly influenced by his father's stubborn determination to turn him into a Klingon warrior. In truth, he knew that K'Ehleyr wouldn't want him to become a diplomat for her sake any more than she had wanted him to become a warrior to please Worf. To make his mother truly proud, he would have to find his own path—whatever it was. He had plenty of time to decide whether he wanted to be a diplomat or a Klingon warrior or a Starfleet officer or something else entirely. Right now, he just wanted to be a kid.

A mostly Klingon kid living in a human world, he realized soberly. He would never be free of the savage rage that lurked in his Klingon blood. For the rest of his life he would have to guard and struggle against his natural tendency to fight first and think later. However, now he knew he *could* conquer those powerful, warrior impulses just as his father had.

Feeling better about himself than he had in a long time, Alexander looked at the students leaving the gym. He inhaled softly when he caught Suzanne Milton staring at him.

Alexander snarled, then smiled.

Suzanne flushed, waved shyly and smiled back.

Glancing over his shoulder, Alexander watched as his father demonstrated how to use a *bat'leth* for Ms. Marconi. However, the librarian's rapt attention was on Worf and not the sword.

Starfleet officer and Klingon warrior.

Alexander frowned thoughtfully. He had to admit there were advantages to being both.